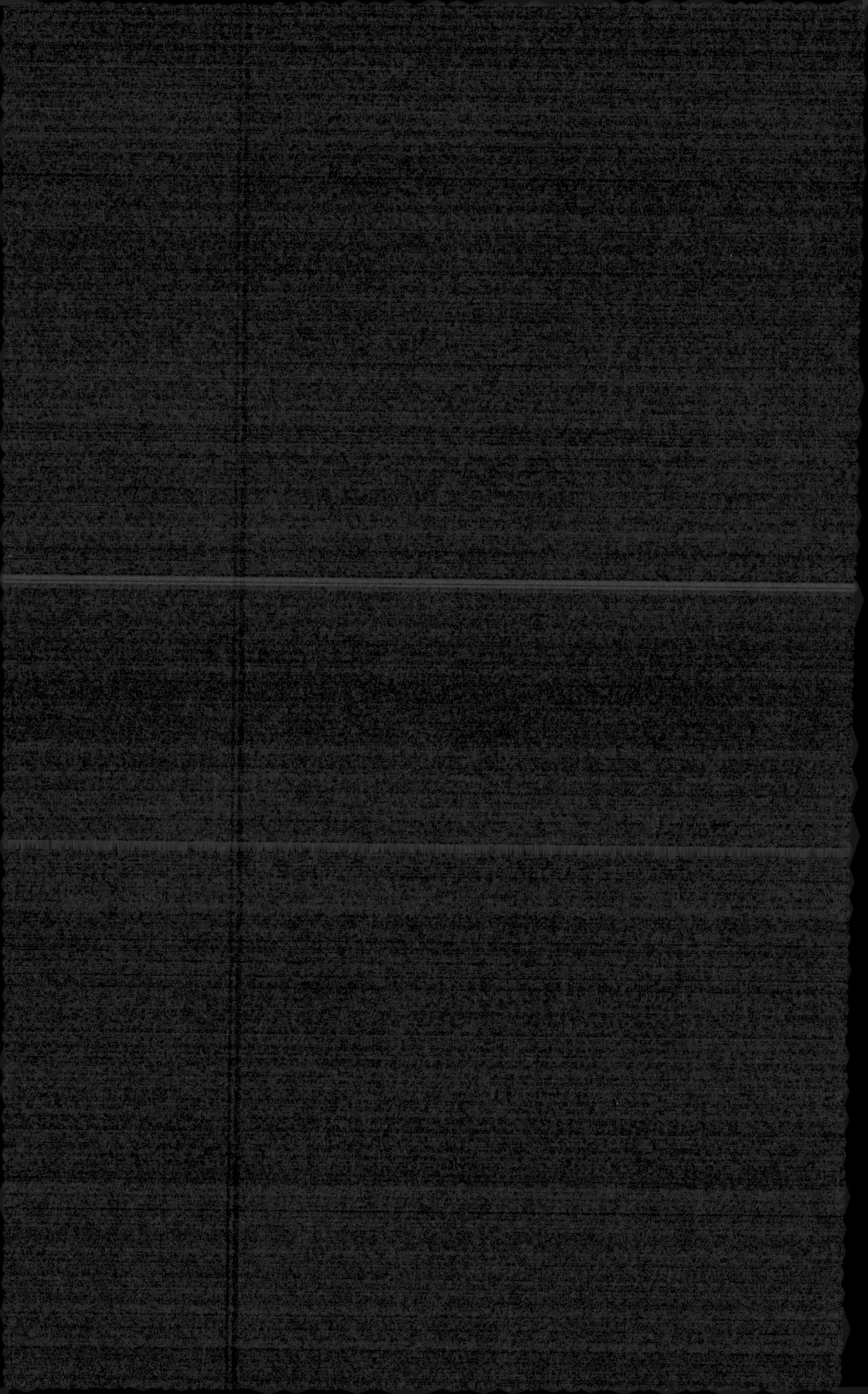

THE COLLECTED PROSE OF
SYLVIA PLATH

By Sylvia Plath

poetry
ARIEL
THE COLOSSUS
CROSSING THE WATER
WINTER TREES
COLLECTED POEMS
(edited by Ted Hughes)
SELECTED POEMS
(edited by Ted Hughes)
ARIEL: THE RESTORED EDITION
(Foreword by Frieda Hughes)
POEMS
(chosen by Carol Ann Duffy)

fiction
THE BELL JAR
JOHNNY PANIC AND THE BIBLE OF DREAMS
MARY VENTURA AND THE NINTH KINGDOM

non-fiction
THE LETTERS OF SYLVIA PLATH
Volume I: 1940–1956
(edited by Peter K. Steinberg & Karen V. Kukil)
THE LETTERS OF SYLVIA PLATH
Volume II: 1956–1963
(edited by Peter K. Steinberg & Karen V. Kukil)
LETTERS HOME: CORRESPONDENCE 1950–1963
(edited by Aurelia Schober Plath)
THE JOURNALS OF SYLVIA PLATH
(edited by Karen V. Kukil)
SYLVIA PLATH: DRAWINGS
(edited by Frieda Hughes)

for children
THE BED BOOK
(illustrated by Quentin Blake)
THE IT-DOESN'T-MATTER SUIT
(illustrated by Rotraut Susanne Berner)
COLLECTED CHILDREN'S STORIES
(illustrated by David Roberts)

THE COLLECTED PROSE OF
SYLVIA PLATH

Edited by
PETER K. STEINBERG

faber

First published in 2024
by Faber & Faber Limited
The Bindery, 51 Hatton Garden
London EC1N 8HN

Typeset by Sam Matthews
Printed in the UK by TJ Books Ltd, Padstow, Cornwall

All rights reserved

© The Estate of Sylvia Plath, 2024
Introduction and editorial matter © Peter K. Steinberg 2024

The right of Peter K. Steinberg to be identified as editor of this work has been asserted in accordance with Section 77 of the Copyright, Designs and Patents Act 1988

A CIP record for this book
is available from the British Library

ISBN 978-0-571-37764-0

Printed and bound in the UK on FSC® certified paper in line with our continuing commitment to ethical business practices, sustainability and the environment.
For further information see faber.co.uk/environmental-policy

2 4 6 8 10 9 7 5 3 1

Contents

Illustrations — xii
Acknowledgements — xv
Preface — xvii
Chronology — xxi

PART I: FICTION

1940–1	Winter and Magic	3
1942	Trixie and the Balloon	3
1943	Aunt Rennie and the Elves	4
1944	The Bookland Carpet	5
1946	Spring Song	6
	The Pond in Spring	6
	The Mummy's Tomb	7
	On the Penthouse Roof	10
	A May Morning	14
	Victory	15
	Mary Jane's Passport	17
	A Morning in the Agora	19
	From the Memoirs of a Babysitter	20
1947	The Miraculous End of Miss Minton	22
	The Thrilling Journeys of a Penny	23
1948	The Attic View	27
	Sarah	31
	The Visitor	34
	The Island: A Radio Play	38
	Gramercy Park	43
	Heat	46
	The Brink	48
	In This Field We Wander Through	51

1949	Among the Shadow Throngs	58
	The Dark River	63
	East Wind	66
	Place: A Bedroom, Saturday Night, in June	70
	Place: A City Street Corner, in the Rain	72
	Place: Inside a Bus on a Rainy Night	74
	And Summer Will Not Come Again	75
	A Day in June	79
	The Green Rock	82
1950	First Date	88
	The New Girl	90
	The English Bike	94
	Den of Lions	98
1947–50	Watch My Line!	103
1951	Room in the World	105
	The Perfect Setup	113
	Mary Ventura	119
1952	The Latvian	128
	'Though Dynasties Pass'	133
	Sunday at the Mintons'	137
	Marie	146
	The New Day	150
	Initiation	158
1953	Dialogue	166
	Mary Ventura and the Ninth Kingdom	178
	Among the Bumblebees	191
	I Lied for Love	197
1954	Superman and Paula Brown's New Snowsuit	228
1955	Home Is Where the Heart Is	234
	Tomorrow Begins Today	240
	The Day Mr. Prescott Died	245
	Tongues of Stone	252
	Platinum Summer	258
	The Christmas Heart	274
1956	That Widow Mangada	289
	All the Dead Dears	306
	The Wishing Box	312
1957	The Smoky Blue Piano	318

1958	Change-About in Mrs. Cherry's Kitchen	329
	Stone Boy with Dolphin	335
	Johnny Panic and the Bible of Dreams	356
	The Fifteen-Dollar Eagle	370
	The Shadow	382
1959	Sweetie Pie and the Gutter Men	389
	Above the Oxbow	399
	The Daughters of Blossom Street	404
	The It-Doesn't-Matter Suit	419
	The Fifty-ninth Bear	426
1960	The Lucky Stone	436
1961	Day of Success	446
	Shadow Girl	457
	A Winter's Tale	466
1961–2	Mothers	477

PART II: NON-FICTION

1943	Hike to Lovell River	489
1944	Girl Scout News: Troop 5 Valentine Party	489
	Seventh-grade Girls	490
1946	Assembly Lineup: January 30	490
	Cove Unit Report	490
	Junior High Briefs	492
	Club Doings: Book Lovers and Recreational Reading Club	494
1947	Club Doings: Book Lovers	494
	Introducin'	495
1948	The Atomic Threat	495
1949	Who Are They???	497
	High School Highlights	498
	When I'm a Parent	498
1949–50	*Bradford* Editors Attend Boston Tea Party!!	499
1950	Youth's Plea for World Peace	500
	The International Flavor	502
	Rewards of a New England Summer	504
1951	In Retrospect: A Plea for Moderation	505
	As a Babysitter Sees It	508

	Suburban Nocturne	511
	Somebody and We	515
1952	TV or Not TV	519
	Be Mine—For Now	520
1953	The Ideal Summer	521
	Smith Review Revived	525
	We Hitch Our Wagons: Elizabeth Bowen and Sylvia	527
	Poets on Campus	528
	MLLE's Last Word on College	530
1954	The Neilson Professor	530
	Articles for *Vogue*'s Prix de Paris Competition	532
1955	Social Life Without Sororities: A Profile of Smith College	540
	The Arts in America: 1954: Collage by a Collegian	545
	Tea With Olive Higgins Prouty	554
1956	Cambridge Vistas	559
	Fulbright Scholar Sylvia Plath Describes Her Impressions As . . . An American in Paris	563
	Smith College in Retrospect	566
	B. and K. at the Claridge	568
	Cambridge Letter	573
	Sylvia Plath Tours the Stores and Forecasts May Week Fashions	575
	Sketchbook of a Spanish Summer	577
	Poppy Day at Cambridge	580
1958	Beach Plum Season on Cape Cod	586
1959	Kitchen of the Fig Tree	588
	A Walk to Withens	591
	Watching the Water-Voles	595
	Mosaics—An Afternoon of Discovery	598
	Explorations Lead to Interesting Discoveries	599
1961	Introduction (*American Poetry Now*)	601
	'Context'	601
1962	A Comparison	603
1963	The All-Round Image	605
	Snow Blitz	608
	Landscape of Childhood	616

PART III: SMITH COLLEGE PRESS BOARD

1951	Says Capitalism May Save Asia	625
	Can Benefit by the Writing of the Satirists	626
	Smith Girls to Take Exams in Civil Service	626
	'True Health' Lecture Topic at the College	627
1952	Says Music Can Illustrate Cultural Life of a Nation	628
	Universal Faith Has the Answer, Dr. Niebuhr Says	629
	'Crisis' Is Topic of Dr. Niebuhr in Northampton	630
	Smith Students Have Service of Koffee Klatch	631
	Dr. A. Gesell Gives Lecture for Day School PTA	632
	'Heresy Hunts' Menace Liberty; Struik Claims	633
	Life University Second Program Slated Sunday	634
	Rev. Mr. Roberts Will Be Vespers Speaker	634
	Misery of Man Is Due to His Defects	635
	Marxism Seeks to Replace God, Lecturer Says	636
	Smith Hears Frost in Muse and Views	637
	Frost Presents Poetry Readings	637
	Smith College	638
	Ogden Nash's Rhyming Knack Makes Up for His Talent Lack	639
	Ogden Nash Is Speaker	640
	Smith Library Displaying 'Fanny Fern Collection'	641
	15 Area Girls to Graduate from Smith College June 9	642
	Smith Freshman Given Welcome	644
	Freshmen at Smith Will Meet Local Ministers	645
	Can Rent Reproductions	645
	Smith Events	646
	Faith Groups Open Center	646
	Smith Outing Club Will Bike to Hatfield	647
	Varied Religious and Cultural Program Planned for Smith College Students	648
	First Recital at Smith College Is Sunday at 8:30	649
	Smith College Holds Clinic	650
	Cheers, Jeers Promised for Smith Game	650
	Week-End Dance	651
	Smith Provides Writing Clinic	652

	More Than a Hundred Varieties Of Chrysanthemums	
	Will Be Seen at Lyman Plant House	653
	Mrs. L. Diem of Cologne Visiting Smith	654
	Newly Revised Edition of *Smith Review* Has Articles	
	by Students	655
	College Group Will Debate on February 11	656
1953	Drive For Hymnals at Smith College	657
	Passover Will Be Marked Monday at Smith College	657
	Fencing Techniques to be Demonstrated	658
	Shale that Is 400 Million Years Old at Smith Lab	659
	John Mason Brown Lectures on Writer's Responsibility	660
	Literary Speakers Mark Symposium at Smith College	661
	Laughton Holds Audience Spellbound with Readings	662
	Smith Christian Group Points to Achievements	663
	Smith College Field Events Saturday Afternoon, Night	665
	Smith College Play Delights 'Hamp Audience	666
	Austrian-Born Junior Enlists in Women's Marine Corps,	
	'Can't wait to get there'	667
	Many Area Students Are Among the 464 Who Will Get	
	Smith Degrees on June 8	670
1954	14 Colleges to Take Part in Poetry Reading Festival	672

PART IV: BOOK REVIEWS

1948	Miss Palmer's Treasures	677
1957	Review of *The Stones of Troy* by C. A. Trypanis	677
1961	General Jodpur's Conversion	685
1962	Pair of Queens	687
	Oblongs	688
	Oregonian Original	690
	Suffering Angel	693
1963	Sylvia Plath on *Contemporary American Poetry*	696

APPENDIX I: STORY FRAGMENTS

1946–7	Stardust	703
c.1948–50	'About a year ago I was babysitting . . .'	719

	'A few armchairs and a table . . .'	721
	'The music wailed out from the radio . . .'	721
after June 1949	Story Ideas	722
c.1949–50	Irene	723
	Sally	724
	The Garden Party	725
	An Evening at the Hoftizers	725
c. summer 1950	'The New Zealand spinach was good that morning . . .'	726
c. January–May 1952	'The Skaters'	730
1952	My Studio Romance	734
c.1955–6	'Sassoon was coming . . .'	736
1956	The Matisse Chapel	739
	Side-Hall Girl	741
	The Black Bull	742
	Remember the Stick Man	745
	Afternoon in Hardcastle Crags	746
	The Invisible Man	747
1957	Venus in the Seventh	754
	Hill of Leopards	773
	Operation Valentine	775
	The Laundromat Affair	778
1957–8	Mrs. McFague and the Corn Vase Girl	782
1958	Runaway	784
	DAR Park	786
1958–9	Two Fat Girls on Beacon Hill	788
1959	A Prospect of Cornucopia	789
	The Mummy	795
c.1960–2	'Alison'	796

APPENDIX II

1955	Teenagers Can Shape the Future	798
	Bibliography of Published Prose	799
	Permissions	805
	Index of Titles	807

Illustrations

   1 'The Fifteen Dollar Eagle', typescript page 1. Reproduced by courtesy of the Lilly Library, Indiana University, Bloomington, Indiana.

   6 Drawing of an eye. Diary, 14 May 1946. Reproduced by courtesy of the Lilly Library, Indiana University, Bloomington, Indiana.

 22 Drawing of an opened book. Diary, 10 February 1947. Reproduced by courtesy of the Lilly Library, Indiana University, Bloomington, Indiana.

487 'Poppy Day in Cambridge', typescript page 1. Reproduced by courtesy of the Lilly Library, Indiana University, Bloomington, Indiana.

623 Press Board notebook, Dr Arnold Gesell lecture. Reproduced by courtesy of the Lilly Library, Indiana University, Bloomington, Indiana.

675 Review of *Lord Byron's Wife*, typescript page 1. Reproduced by courtesy of the Mortimer Rare Book Collection, Smith College.

719 Drawing of a young girl's head. 'About a year ago I was babysitting . . .' Reproduced by courtesy of the Mortimer Rare Book Collection, Smith College.

721 Drawing of a room with 'desk' and 'fireplace' labelled, 'A few armchairs and a table . . .' Reproduced from Sotheby's Auction.

723 Drawing of a face and drawing of an eye. 'Party Girl' ['Story Ideas']. Reproduced by courtesy of the Mortimer Rare Book Collection, Smith College.

All illustrations © the Estate of Sylvia Plath.

Write to recreate a mood, an incident. If this is done with color and feeling, it becomes a story.

Sylvia Plath, journal entry,
4 October 1959

Acknowledgements

I began compiling the works contained in this volume in 1998. But only during the editing of *The Letters of Sylvia Plath* in the mid-2010s did it began to take shape. My sincere gratitude goes to Frieda Hughes for allowing me to obtain photocopies of Plath's prose (and poetry) as well as other documents during the *Letters* project. These enabled me not only to annotate Plath's correspondence, but also to begin to assemble this present edition with intention. Thank you also to Matthew Hollis, Lavinia Singer, Jane Feaver, Anne Owen, Sarah Fish and Rali Chorbadzhiyska at Faber. I am grateful to Sam Matthews for her careful and conscientious copyedits to the manuscript.

I am immensely indebted to the archivists and librarians who oversee the Sylvia Plath archives wherever they may rest, the three largest being Indiana University at Bloomington, Smith College and Emory University. Additional material was found at the British Library, Middlebury College, New York Public Library, University of Cambridge, University of Manchester, University of Victoria and Wellesley High School. Sarah McElroy Mitchell at Indiana University and Helen Melody at the British Library were particularly beneficent. I utilised microfilm versions of historical Massachusetts newspapers at the Boston Public Library to locate the press releases Plath wrote while a student at Smith. Personal collections were used as well, notably Judith Raymo's copy of 'Mary Ventura and the Ninth Kingdom' – first published by Faber in 2019.

My most sincere thanks to David Trinidad, Julie Goodspeed-Chadwick, Paul Alexander, Peter Fydler, Karen V. Kukil and Amanda Golden, who has made many significant contributions to this volume. Their friendship, words of support, and counsel sustained me in fathomless ways. I am incalculably grateful to Luke Ferretter, whose pioneering work in *Sylvia Plath's Fiction: A Critical Study* (Edinburgh University Press, 2010) was instrumental in organising Plath's short stories. Additionally, I would be remiss if I did not also acknowledge the love and support of my family, biological and otherwise: thank you Courtney, Mom, Dad, Jennifer, David, Jon, Jack, Andrew, Janis, Steve and so on.

Preface

In Sylvia Plath's journals and letters, the writer documents the creation, submission, acceptance and rejection of scores of prose works. While most of these pieces reside in archives now, only the most ardent of researchers have an understanding of how her efforts in this style fit into her entire body of work. The first edition of the prose collection *Johnny Panic and the Bible of Dreams* (1977) printed what was deemed at the time to be the best of Plath's prose work in three genres: short fiction, 'essays' and journals. While it contained many previously printed works, it did not include everything Plath saw to print. Stories like 'And Summer Will Not Come Again', 'Den of Lions' and 'The Perfect Setup', which earned Plath a national audience, acclaim, prizes and money in her first years at Smith College, were left out. It excludes, as well, the last story Plath published in her lifetime, 'The Perfect Place' (titled 'The Lucky Stone' in typescript by Plath, and presented in Part I). Following the publication of Plath's adult journals[*] and the two volumes of her letters,[†] in which she mentions many of the works in this volume, the need for a fuller edition of her prose has never been greater.

Throughout her writing life, Plath endeavoured to be proficient and successful at authoring prose works. The earliest stories show an active imagination that reflects the reality of her environment in suburbs of the metropolitan region of Boston during the Second World War and just after. The characters she created and the situations she imagined have concerns with material wealth, poverty, depression, loneliness and magic, to name a few themes. As Plath honed her skill, the stories steadily grew longer and fuller. Through her study of periodicals such as *Seventeen*, *Mademoiselle*, the *New Yorker* and *Ladies' Home Journal*, she gained an awareness of what her target magazines would print. As a student of Smith College, she succeeded in placing stories in *Seventeen* and *Mademoiselle*. Later when at Newnham College and as an adult, full-time writer, her works appeared in university publications such as

---

[*] *The Journals of Sylvia Plath, 1950–1962*, ed. Karen V. Kukil (London: Faber, 2000).
[†] *The Letters of Sylvia Plath, Volume 1: 1940–1956* and *Volume 2: 1956–1963*, ed. Peter K. Steinberg and Karen V. Kukil (London: Faber, 2017, 2018, rev. 2019).

Granta and *Gemini* and literary periodicals like the *London Magazine* and *Sewanee Review*.

Plath periodically attempted to shelve poetry in favour of prose. In January 1956, she wrote in a letter to her ex-boyfriend Gordon Lameyer, 'Am much more desirous of writing prose, good short stories, now, than poetry, which isn't wide enough for all the people and places I am beginning to have at my fingertips' (*Letters, Volume 1*: 1088). The following summer, she was honest concerning the tug-of-war between writing prose versus poetry: 'Prose is not so easy to come into maturity as the poetry which, by its smallness & my practise with form, can look complete. The main problem is breaking open rich, real subjects to myself & forgetting there is any audience . . .' (*Journals*: 293). A few months later, on 14 January 1958, the pendulum had swung back: 'Poems are out: too depressing. If they're bad, they're bad. Prose is never quite hopeless' (312).

Following her Fulbright fellowship and a year of teaching at her alma mater, Plath left academia to try her hand as a full-time writer. In her year in Boston (1958–9), Plath completed several dozen poems and at least seven short stories, including a trilogy – 'Johnny Panic and the Bible of Dreams', 'The Fifteen-Dollar Eagle' and 'The Daughters of Blossom Street' – set in her birth city, as well as some works no longer extant or existing in fragments only.

But Plath was never content with short fiction. Eager for writing projects and to have her work out for consideration, Plath consistently experimented with various forms of non-fiction: writing reports as a summer camper and covering events at her junior high school, through to relating the harrowing experience of living through the infamous Big Freeze of 1963 in the last weeks of her life. She found most success with writing about her travel and work experiences, primarily for the *Christian Science Monitor*, during her years of study at Smith and Newnham, and then later, in 1959.

Among the many values of these writings is the way they relate to the lives Plath leads and which she records in her other works: her letters, her journals and even her poetry. She admitted as much to her mother in a letter, 'When I say I *must* write, I don't mean I *must* publish. There is a great difference. The important thing is the aesthetic form given to my chaotic experience' (*Letters, Volume 1*: 1090). She mined her life and work, exchanging themes and images across all forms of her writing. The result is that the works in this volume exhibit a richness of intertextuality when read in concert with her autobiographical writing and poems. To borrow from poet and Plath scholar David Trinidad, reading Plath's works together creates a 'movie of her life'. She shows, ultimately, a determination to write in any genre, to never stop the act of writing, no matter what. This is Sylvia Plath's achievement.

This edition of Sylvia Plath's prose collects all the known works she published in her lifetime as well as unpublished pieces held in archives. It demonstrates Plath to be a prodigious writer in the genres of fiction and non-fiction; though it does not include school papers, her thesis 'The Magic Mirror: A Study of the Double in Two of Dostoevsky's Novels' or *The Bell Jar*. Her short stories and two works for children in Part I comprise the largest section of the book. The non-fiction sections are sub-divided into the following categories: non-fiction (Part II), Smith College Press Board (Part III) and book reviews (Part IV). While there are a few exceptions, Plath's non-fiction journalism in Part II primarily contains texts about her lived experiences: be it a school assembly, the joys and throes of babysitting, walking to Top Withens near Haworth in Yorkshire, or recalling the land and seascape of her childhood. The Smith College Press Board articles are separate from Plath's other non-fiction writing because in style, content and purpose, they represent a distinctive unit from those works appearing, sometimes concurrently, in Part II. Plath worked for the Press Board in her second and third years as an undergraduate. The majority of the pieces – only two published pieces are attributed to her – were identified by reading Plath's letters, calendars and notebooks and then searching microfilm for the *Daily Hampshire Gazette*, the *Springfield Daily News* and the *Springfield Union*. On occasion, two articles ran in two different newspapers and so there are some instances where both appear as the content varies, giving, potentially, a fuller flavour of Plath's reporting. These pieces were possibly heavily revised by the newspaper editors for space considerations. The Smith College Archives holds some original typescripts with Plath credited as 'Correspondent'. In these instances, the typescript is the source for the text and full bibliographic citations for the printed articles appear in the footnotes. Plath's book reviews show her to be a close and careful reader. The flurry of reviews from 1961 to 1963 show Plath to be on the cusp of a new aspect of her career, particularly in the case of her BBC review, which aired on 10 January 1963.

Two appendices follow the book reviews in Part IV. Appendix I prints fragments of works – some quite well known, others more obscure – that are incomplete portions of both finished and abandoned works and story ideas Plath jotted down. Appendix II is an introduction to 'Marcia Ventura and the Ninth Kingdom' – a revision of the story 'Mary Ventura and the Ninth Kingdom' – which Plath adapted in late 1954 and early 1955 when she was considering submitting the story to the Christopher Awards, an annual contest for creative works that 'affirm the highest values of the human spirit'.

Though there are some exceptions, the following are the general principles informing editorial decisions. If the work was published during Plath's lifetime, then the publication copy is used, correcting obvious typographical errors. If a piece is in manuscript or typescript, then the copy deemed the most final is the copy text. For compositions printed after Plath's death, I revert to the final typescript. I exercised some light editing of texts to modernise and to make consistent the spelling and forms of words. For example, 'extra-curricular' becomes 'extracurricular'; 'kleenex' is 'Kleenex'. Punctuation, spelling and forms of words vary depending on the location of writing. Works written in the USA appear with US style. Those written in England and Spain have UK formatting. The aim here is to showcase Plath's transatlanticism.

Text that falls within angle brackets are editorial interventions; square brackets indicate Plath's own interjections. Words or phrases that Plath underlined in her diaries, journals and letters, as above and primarily in notes, appear in italics. However, misspellings, when they occur in quoted diaries and letters, have not been corrected, following standard practice in the unabridged editions of Plath's writings.

Peter K. Steinberg, 7 July 2023

Chronology

1932
27 October — Sylvia Plath born in Boston, Massachusetts, to Otto Emil and Aurelia Schober Plath; the family lives at 24 Prince Street, Jamaica Plain, a neighbourhood in Boston.

1935
27 April — Warren Joseph Plath born.

1936
Autumn — The Plaths move to 92 Johnson Avenue in Winthrop, Massachusetts.

1938
September — Enters Annie F. Warren Grammar School, Winthrop. Hurricane, dubbed the 'Long Island Express', hits New England.

1940
September — Enters E. B. Newton School, Winthrop.
October — Otto Plath admitted to the New England Deaconess Hospital, Boston; his left, gangrenous leg amputated.
5 November — Otto Plath dies from an embolus in his lung.

1941
10 August — 'Poem' appears in the *Boston Herald*, her first publication.

1942
October — Family moves to 26 Elmwood Road, Wellesley, Massachusetts. Enters the Marshall Perrin Grammar School.

1943/4
Summers — Attends Camp Weetamoe in Center Ossipee, New Hampshire. Serves as reporter for campus newsletter.

1944
January — Begins writing in a journal.
September — Enters Alice L. Phillips Junior High School, publishes journalism and creative writing in school paper, *The Phillipian*.

1945/6
Summers — Attends Camp Helen Storrow in Plymouth, Massachusetts.

1947/8
Summers — Attends Vineyard Sailing Camp at Oak Bluffs, Martha's Vineyard.
September — Enters Gamaliel Bradford Senior High School, Wellesley. Actively publishes in school newspaper, *The Bradford*.

1948
April — Publishes article on the atomic bomb.

1949
June — Named co-editor of *The Bradford*.
Summer — Attends Unitarian conference at Star Island, New Hampshire.

1950
March — Publishes co-written article 'Youth's Plea for World Peace' in the *Christian Science Monitor*.
May — Accepted into Class of 1954 at Smith College, Northampton, Massachusetts. Receives Olive Higgins Prouty scholarship.
Summer — Works at Lookout Farm with Warren Plath in Natick, Massachusetts.
August — Publishes short story 'And Summer Will Not Come Again' in *Seventeen*.
Autumn — Enters Smith College, resides at Haven House.
December — Meets Prouty.

1951
January — Story 'Den of Lions' wins Third Prize in *Seventeen*'s short-story contest.
February — Begins dating Richard Norton, a senior at Yale University.

Summer	Works as nanny in Swampscott, Massachusetts. Her friend Marcia Brown nannies nearby.
Autumn	Writes articles for local newspapers as Press Board correspondent for Smith College.

1952

Summer	Waitresses at the Belmont Hotel in West Harwich, Massachusetts. 'Sunday at the Mintons'' wins *Mademoiselle* short fiction contest. Later works as nanny in Chatham, Massachusetts.
September	Moves to Lawrence House, a co-operative house, at Smith College.
Autumn	Continues writing for Press Board. Norton treated for exposure to tuberculosis in the Adirondacks.
October	Story 'Initiation' wins Second Prize in *Seventeen*'s short-story contest.
December	Breaks leg in skiing accident at Mount Pisgah, New York.

1953

February	Dates Gordon Lameyer, a senior at Amherst College.
April–May	*Harper's* accepts three poems; wins position as a Guest Editor for *Mademoiselle* in New York City.
June	Lives at Barbizon Hotel in New York; works at *Mademoiselle*.
July–August	Treated for insomnia and exhaustion; counselled by psychiatrist; given poorly administered outpatient electro-convulsive shock treatments.
24 August	Attempts suicide by taking an overdose of sleeping pills.
26 August	Found in a basement crawl space in her house; admitted to Newton-Wellesley Hospital.
September	Transfers first to Massachusetts General Hospital, Boston, then to McLean Hospital, Belmont, Massachusetts. Begins treatment with Dr Ruth Beuscher.

1954

January	Re-enters Smith College; repeats second semester of her junior year.
April	Meets Richard Sassoon, a junior at Yale University.

Summer	Attends Harvard Summer School and lives in Cambridge, Massachusetts.
Autumn	Senior year at Smith College on full scholarship; writes thesis on Dostoevsky.

1955
February	Accepted by Newnham College, University of Cambridge.
April	Competes in Glascock Poetry Contest, Mount Holyoke College, Hadley, Massachusetts.
May	Wins Fulbright fellowship to University of Cambridge.
6 June	Graduates Smith College, *summa cum laude*.
September	Sails on the *Queen Elizabeth* to UK.
October	Begins courses at Newnham College. Acts for Amateur Dramatics Club.
Winter	Travels to Paris and the south of France with Sassoon; visits Matisse Chapel.

1956
25 February	Attends party at Falcon Yard, meets Edward 'Ted' James Hughes.
March–April	Travels through France, Germany and Italy with Gordon Lameyer.
Spring	Writes for *Varsity*, the Cambridge student newspaper.
16 June	Marries Ted Hughes at St George the Martyr, Queen Square, London.
Summer	Honeymoons in Paris, France, and Alicante and Benidorm, Spain. Returns to the Hughes home, the Beacon, in Heptonstall, Yorkshire.
Autumn	Begins second year at Newnham College.
December	Moves to 55 Eltisley Avenue, Cambridge, UK.

1957
12 March	Smith College offers Plath teaching position on English faculty.
June	Finishes programme at Newnham, earning her second BA in English. Sails on *Queen Elizabeth* to New York.
Summer	Vacations in Eastham, Massachusetts.
September	Moves to 337 Elm Street, Northampton, Massachusetts; begins teaching at Smith College.

1958

June	Leaves position at Smith College. Records poems for Woodberry Poetry Room, Harvard. Receives first *New Yorker* poetry acceptances for 'Mussel Hunter at Rock Harbor' and 'Nocturne' ('Hardcastle Crags').
9 August	'Mussel Hunter at Rock Harbor' appears in the *New Yorker*.
Autumn	Moves to 9 Willow Street, Beacon Hill, Boston, and works at Massachusetts General Hospital as a secretary for the Psychiatric Clinic in the Out-Patient department.
10 December	Resumes seeing Dr Beuscher, records details in her journals.

1959

February	Records more poems for Woodberry Poetry Room. Attends Robert Lowell's poetry course at Boston University, meets Anne Sexton.
8 March	Visits father's grave in Winthrop.
May–December	Regularly publishes prose and poetry in *Christian Science Monitor*.
July–August	Travels across North America and Canada; becomes pregnant.
Autumn	Spends two months at Yaddo, an artist's colony located in Saratoga Springs, New York.
December	Sails on the *United States* to UK.

1960

January	Rents flat at 3 Chalcot Square, Primrose Hill, London.
10 February	Signs contract with Heinemann in London to publish her first collection of poetry, *The Colossus and Other Poems*.
1 April	Daughter, Frieda Rebecca Hughes, born.
May	First story appears in *London Magazine*.
31 October	*The Colossus* published in Britain.

1961

Spring	Begins writing *The Bell Jar*.
June–July	Records poems for BBC series *The Living Poet*. Aurelia Plath visits England from mid-June to early August. Travels to France.

August	Purchases Court Green in North Tawton, Devonshire.
1 September	Moves to Court Green.
October	Signs contract with Heinemann for *The Bell Jar*. 'The Perfect Place' published in *My Weekly*.
November	Wins Eugene F. Saxton Memorial Trust grant to write a novel. Begins to publish book reviews in *New Statesman*.

1962

17 January	Son, Nicholas Farrar Hughes, born.
September	Visits Irish poet Richard Murphy in Cleggan, Ireland.
October	Writes twenty-five poems; records poems for British Council/Woodberry Poetry Room. After months of marital trouble, Ted Hughes leaves family.
November	Rents flat at 23 Fitzroy Road, London, formerly a residence of W. B. Yeats. Commissioned by BBC to write 'Landscape of Childhood'.
10 December	Moves with Frieda and Nicholas into Fitzroy Road flat.

1963

January	London experiences its coldest winter of the century, dubbed the 'Big Freeze of 1963'.
10 January	Reviews Donald Hall's *Contemporary American Poetry* for BBC.
14 January	Heinemann publishes *The Bell Jar* under the pseudonym Victoria Lucas.
11 February	Protects children then dies by suicide.
18 February	Laid to rest in Heptonstall.

PART I
FICTION

Published in Sewanee Review

Sylvia Plath
Suite 61
9 Willow Street
Boston 8, Massachusetts

THE FIFTEEN DOLLAR EAGLE
~~(Conversation Piece At Carmey's)~~

There are other tattoo shops in Madigan Square, but none of them a patch on Carmey's place. He's a real poet with the needle-and-dye, an artist with a heart. Kids, dock bums, the out-of-town couples in for a beer ~~(and a view of Lady Lou with the rattlesnake G-string and the rhinestone navel)~~ put on the brakes in front of Carmey's, nose-to-the-window, one and all. You got a dream, Carmey says, without saying a word, you got a rose on the heart, an eagle in the muscle, you got the sweet Jesus himself, so come in to me. Wear your heart on your skin in this life, I'm the man can give you a deal. Dogs, wolves, horses and lions for the animal lover. For the ladies, butterflies, birds of paradise, baby heads smiling or in tears, take your choice. Roses, all sorts, large, small, bud and full bloom, roses with name scrolls, roses with thorns, roses with dresden-doll heads sticking up in dead center, pink petal, green leaf, set off smart by a lead-black line. Snakes and dragons for Frankenstein. Not to mention cowgirls, hula girls, mermaids and movie queens, ruby-nippled and bare as you please. If you've got a back to spare, there's Christ on the cross, a thief at either elbow and angels overhead to right and left holding up a scroll with "Mount Calvary" on it in Old English script, close as yellow can get to gold.

Winter and Magic

Ms, *c.*1940–1,[*] New York Public Library

The snow was sifting upon little towns. It was night on Christmas Eve. Everybody in the town was having a feast, all but one house in which the blinds were torn; there was no smoke coming out of the chimney. Inside there were four children and a poor mother, dividing a crust of bread, with a candle in the middle of the table.

Next to the poor family in a great house, there was one child, a mother and father, and plenty of guests, and all the food you can imagine. The child was proud and vain, she had the richest of clothes. When they had finished the feast, the whole town went to sleep. Christmas morning as the poor family awoke they saw a loaf of bread on the table. When they got over their joy, they took a bite of the bread they found to their surprise and delight that another crust appeared in its place! So that way their cupboard was always full. As for the rich I do not know what became of them but I am sure they are very disagreeable to live with.

Trixie and the Balloon

Ts, 1942, New York Public Library

Trixie was Warren's little yellow teddy bear, and a very important member of his family.

One night she thought she would take a walk as the spring air was very fragrant and cool. As she walked along a little path leading to the woodland she saw a glint of red among the trees.

Walking over to investigate she saw a little basket with a red balloon at each handle tugging at a piece of vine that was holding it to the ground.

Amazed at what she saw, she stood still and gazed at it. Then said to herself, "One of the fairy's airships, I think I will take a ride." Hopping in she untied the vine and off she went.

---

[*] Signed at bottom: 'By Sylvia Plath / 8 years old.'

The balloon was blown playfully around by a little breeze. All of a sudden she looked down. "My," she gasped, "I'm falling, the air is slowly going out of my balloon and there is a big puddle underneath me. Is this the end, shall I drown?"

As you know, teddy bears hate water and Trixie was among them. Although she did not know it she was right above Warren's front yard. It had rained the night before so there was a puddle in his yard.

Just then she sighted Puck, one of her best fairy friends, sailing around in a boat made from a bird's nest.

"Help, Puck," she called. "Save me."

"Jump in my boat. I'll save you," he yelled back.

Trixie jumped and landed safely, just in time for a minute later the airship sank beneath the surface to stay there for ever more.

"O," sighed Trixie cuddling up to Puck, "I am never going up in a balloon again."

Aunt Rennie and the Elves

Ts,[*] *c.*1943, Middlebury College

Once there lived a poor little boy who had a cruel stepfather. They lived in a little hut on the edge of a deep dark and dense forest.

One day the stepfather bade the boy goodbye and said: "You may play in the woods until I get back." And then he walked toward the village to get some food.

Unknown to the little boy, his stepfather thought he was a bother and really wanted to get rid of him.

As far as the stepfather knew there was no path in the dark wood. The boy did as he was told not suspecting a thing.

All of a sudden he realized he was lost, he stepped forward and hunted for a path or landmark, then he started to cry as he found it to no avail.

A few hours later he chanced upon a beautiful path surrounded by flowers with a rippling brook running amongst them. Trying his luck he followed the lovely path. Soon he came upon a little house with a cheery light streaming out

---

[*] Offered for sale via Bloomsbury Auctions in 2008. Illustrated with two coloured cut-outs by Vernon Grant pasted on to the page. The larger image captioned: '"I go all over the world turning tears into happy smiles" . . . says Aunt Rennie.' The slogan was copyrighted on 29 January 1943, for Junket Rennet Powder for rennet-custard desserts. Signed in pencil 'By Sylvia' at end.

from one of the windows as it was near nightfall. He went up the steps and rapped on the door, it was opened by a tiny lady no more than a foot high.

She curtsied politely and said, "Welcome to Aunt Rennie's house, the dwelling place of the elves!" The little boy was invited in and given goodies of all sorts including ice cream. While he was eating Aunt Rennie told him that she goes all over the world turning tears into happy smiles. Then she asked him if he would like to live with her. He replied that he would enjoy it very much, for he had forgotten about the cruel stepfather and was looking forward to a happy life with the elves.

Meanwhile the stepfather had come home and had just gone into his house when a terrific gale came up and blew the house with the man in it far out of sight and no one has seen him since. While the little boy is leading a happy life with the elves.

The Bookland Carpet

Ms, *c.*2 December 1944,* Lilly Library

It was Christmas Eve and Jimmy and Joyce, the Johnson twins, were so excited that they were sure they could not go to sleep.

Outside their open window they heard a clear voice crying, "All aboard the Bookland Carpet." The twins jumped out of bed, pulled on their bathrobes, and rushed to the window. Wonder of wonders! There floated a magic carpet; however, there was no one on it, not even the owner of the beautiful voice. Jimmy stepped on the carpet, dragging Joyce with him.

Off they sailed, higher and higher, among the frosty stars. The twins did not feel cold as they looked down on the passing world. This was really seeing different lands and not just reading about them. Snow-covered villages and towns passed by, also lighted stores and houses. Church bells were ringing; carolers were heard faintly; all was peace. Although each foreign land celebrated Christmas differently, each had the same idea of peace and happiness. The twins grew sleepy as they sailed through the deep-blue night sky lit by millions of twinkling stars. Carols from all over the world drifted upward,

---

* In her 1944 diary, SP mentions working on a 'Christmas Booklet' as an English class assignment in November and December. On 2 December 1944, SP wrote, 'After lunch I finished writing up my Christmas story.'

blending in one great song, praising the Lord for His blessings. The stars and planets echoed in harmony, rejoicing, rejoicing. From afar angels caroled the same wonderful song, echoing o'er all the world.

Spring Song

Written: *c*.28 March 1946[*]
Published: *The Phillipian* (April 1946): 13

The sun hung low in the heavens; a rosy glow flooded the earth. A sweet breeze wafted through the tranquil shadows of the woods; the air was cool. The silence was broken only by the scream of a blue jay as it flashed through the brush. The trees were just putting forth their experimental pale green buds. Stalwart pines were reflected in a deep, dark pool. Thick moss carpeted the woodland floor. Everything seemed to be waiting . . . waiting. Lingering rays of sun reached pale fingers of light through the yet bare tree branches. Soon a blanket of gray twilight enveloped all. Then, through the night, came the shrill sweet piping of the peepers which heralded the spring.

The world relaxed. The soft music of the songsters rose about the pit-pat, pit-pat of spring rain.

The Pond in Spring

Written: *c*.14 May 1946[†]
Published: *The Phillipian* (June 1946): 26

The pond was smooth as glass, ruffled only by an occasional breeze whispering past or by the thin, curving trail of a waterbug, skimming over the surface. Deep shadows were dappled by flecks of sunlight. Upon the mud floor of the pond, long, jellylike strings of frog eggs lay among the pebbles. Close to them baby tadpoles could be seen, lying motionless, like tiny black commas.

---

[*] In her diary on 28 March 1946, SP wrote, 'After school I sent a short description into The Phillippian.' The *Phillippian* was the student newspaper of Alice L. Phillips Junior High School.
[†] In her diary on 14 May 1946, SP wrote, 'Today nothing of terribly great moment happened except that (I) came right home after school. I am writing down an entry I'm turning into The Phillippian titled: *The Pond In Spring*'.

The trees sighed and the pond shivered as an evening breeze passed by in a wave of coolness.

The Mummy's Tomb

Ts,* 17–18 May 1946, Lilly Library

I had come to the museum to do some research work on Egypt for my history notebook. I went through the large archway into the first of the five rooms that made up the Egyptian exhibit. The high-ceilinged walls were dank and cheerless. The restful gray light of a rainy day was all that illumined the room. Deep shadows lurked behind the cases and statues, and crouched in the corners. A musty odor pervaded the chill atmosphere which penetrated my very bones. I was alone in this memorial of ancient days.

The only bright spots were some dull tapestries. In the cases was some tarnished jewelry of the Egyptian period. Against one wall were some huge stone edifices, carved with grotesque figures. I made some notations about the type of material at the time in the Egyptian era, and then went quickly on to the next room.

It was entirely devoted to pottery. My eyes traveled over the accumulation of traditional work—the vases were mainly colored Indian-red, aqua, and black. The figures on them were painted in contrasting colors. They were familiar from my elementary school days—faces and legs side view, body and eyes front view.

The third room contained only a boring variety of tools and implements that the Egyptians used. I listed some of these, and went on to the fourth room.

In here was some imitation furniture. Only a few genuine pieces graced the walls.

The fifth room, however, fascinated me. The walls were lined with old mummy cases, and a row of glassed-in showcases ran through the center of this

---

* Though the typescript is dated 17 May 1946 by SP, her diary includes the following written on 18 May 1946: 'After lunch we both wrote stories. I started a frightful murder-mystery (Morbid-Dribble is recalled to mind) titled "The Mummy's Tomb". After supper we put the children in bed and then went to Margot's room and we finished our respective stories and caught up in our diaries.' SP wrote on a similar theme to this story in a letter to Margot Loungway Drekmeier on 17 November 1945, published in *The Letters of Sylvia Plath, Volume 1*. A holograph copy of 'The Mummy's Tomb' sold via Bonhams on 11 November 2015. Peter Harrington Rare Books in London offered the same copy for sale in March 2023.

mysterious place. I saved my enthusiasm for the mummies, and walked to the row of tables. My casual gaze was suddenly arrested by something shining among the pendants. It flashed through my thoughts that it was an eye. A *human* eye! I usually congratulate myself for the fact that I have a very calm, though inquisitive, nature, but at this moment I began to shake inwardly and outwardly. My clothes clung to me, damp with perspiration, while an icy cold shiver traveled slowly up my spine. As I was gathering up the tangled shreds of what I like to call my composure, I read the sign beneath the eye. It was only made of agate! However, under my frenzied gaze the eye was jellylike, and the pupil seemed to dilate as it stared at me.

I gladly left the case and hurried to look at the six mummy tombs. The first five were interesting—bits of the paint had chipped off, and this gave them a pleasant sense of antiquity. The flat, unsmiling faces drawn on the outside of the cases stared straight up in the air, as if they were trying to see beyond the heavy ceiling and get a glimpse of the sunny skies that they had not seen for so many years. At the sixth case I paused in amazement. From it there arose the strong smell of decaying flesh!

"Distinctly," I thought, "there can be no ancient mummy in here."

Suddenly a gruesome thought dawned—but it was too unfathomable, too horrible for the human mind to conceive. As I was thus occupied in thought, I heard a stealthy footstep behind me. I whirled about.

In my imagination I saw all kinds of bloody specters. However, I was somewhat reassured by a harsh cackle of laughter coming from the wizened old man next to me as he saw my surprise. He then spoke:

"I was watching you from behind that pillar over there; I saw you admiring the eyeball in the case. Looks real, doesn't it?"

Here the old man cackled again in his peculiar way, and drew me back to the case once more. I felt as though I was being propelled by some unseen, unheard of spell; the way it happens in dreams when you are being chased and cannot move a muscle. Powerless, I watched the white-haired man draw from his pocket a tiny magnifying glass and hold it over the eye. To my terror, the eye rolled about and looked pitifully at me as the man moved the glass around over the horrible organ. I tiptoed out after casting a furtive glance at the hunched figure, still happily engrossed in his queer game.

All night long terrible thoughts haunted me. I could not sleep because frightful visions of liquid eyes and living mummies paraded before me. I tried to convince myself that the fact that the eye was real was only a figment of the old man's imagination, but to no avail.

When the first streaks of dawn showed on the horizon it was still raining. I awoke and dressed. I then began to reason with myself about the best course to follow. This was no time for foolhardy moves. At five-thirty in the afternoon the museum closed, I could not escape the Electric Eye. I then had a notion—if only it would work! By this time it was eight-thirty, I had breakfast with the landlady of the boardinghouse and then went to the First National around the corner and purchased a loaf of bread and a jar of peanut butter. When I got back to my room, I made four peanut butter sandwiches and wrapped them in waxed paper before putting them in a paper bag. I then provided myself with a slouch hat and an umbrella. At four o'clock I took my sandwiches and umbrella, pulled down the hat and pulled up my coat collar and took the 4:10 bus to the museum.

Fifteen minutes later, as I walked up the marble steps, I saw that the museum was empty save for a few guards. No one was about as I passed through the Electric Eye. I then took my umbrella and passed it through the Electric Eye as if someone were making an exit. I lifted up the handy umbrella and walked down the long, unlighted corridors of the museum. No one could see me in the inky blackness, but (I gasped) I could see no one either. I had no flashlight! I had forgotten perhaps the most important thing. I then made my cautious way along the hall that led to the Egyptian room. I found a bench in one dark corner of the hallway. There I lay down, trembling with excitement. Hungrily I devoured my sandwiches and promptly went to sleep.

I know not how long I tossed in troubled slumber or what woke me, but I sat upright and then was startled by a frail gleam of light cutting the black night like a knife. It was coming from the Egyptian room, from the direction of the mummy's tomb! Again the sharp odor of decaying flesh reached my nostrils. I slipped unseen into the room. What I saw there left me standing motionless in horror. My body was numbed, and I could only watch helplessly the almost inconceivable actions being accomplished by an inhuman monster, devoid of sanity.

The light of the burning candle on the tomb flickered as gusts of drafty wind swept by, causing fearful shadows to spring about on the wall. In the candlelight I could dimly see the wild features of the white-haired janitor of my previous acquaintance—yesterday. He was carrying a *living* body, swathed in white wrappings, open only at the eyes and nose. The figure uttered muffled groans and writhed about. The janitor then opened the fifth mummy case, next to the one from whence came the peculiar odor. To my horror I saw that the top half opened like the cover of a box and was inlaid with long sharp spikes—no doubt to torture the imprisoned victim! The janitor then laid the human thing into the case but did not close it. I crept closer, hugging the shadows on the wall. The janitor then took a sharp spoon and was leaning down to scoop out the eyes of the terrified victim, when he saw me step into the light. Recognition!!

"Ha!" he leered. "You got away yesterday, but you won't now. I'll muffle your screams of anguish and let you die from loss of blood and in terrible pain. You must meet the Egyptian gods. I will slowly cut out your eyes and harden them for the showcase display!"

As he lurched forward I struck him with my umbrella, and he fell senseless to the floor with a hollow thud. Too many years in this silent horror chamber had weakened his heart and crazed his senses. I unbound the young girl, who had fainted from fright, and tied up the janitor with the liberal roll of gauze and tape. Then I traveled the now-familiar corridors to the office in the museum, where I called for the police to tell them that I had found the missing girl, whose picture had been published in all the papers, as well as the crazed kidnapper and would-be murderer. When I went back to the fateful room to soothe the reviving girl, the shriek of the police sirens already shattered the air.

The next morning I awoke at the ringing of my telephone at about ten o'clock and answered it sleepily, for I was still lame and had a splitting headache. The caller was the chief of police, who said that the janitor had confessed to one murder and one attempted murder before dropping dead with another heart attack. The chief also told me that the girl's father was going to give me a big reward. I smiled as I remembered her and told the chief to thank her father for me but to tell him to keep the intended reward. After I hung up, I jumped back into bed, falling asleep immediately into an untroubled slumber, free from dreams.

On the Penthouse Roof

Ms,[*] 18–19 May 1946, Sotheby's

According to Carol Stanley, Friday night was the most wonderful night she had ever experienced. She was a lovely girl, very popular—just the kind of person

---

[*] Though the manuscript is dated 18 May 1946 by SP, she wrote in her diary on 19 May 1946: 'This morning Margot and I did not go to church. We were alone in the house with Susan and Duncan. After completing our tasks we sat in the warm kitchen for a few hours composing our stories (new). Margot's was titled "Feathers" and mine was "On the Penthouse Roof," a smuggler's story.' Included as part of a lot in a Sotheby's auction of an archive of SP's papers on 2 December 2014 by Sotheby's. The lot did not sell and later portions of the archive appeared in piecemeal fashion via Bonhams.

every other girl longs to be like. She was a wealthy heiress, and had important parents, both in the business and social world. Among her many artistic talents, she played the violin like a master. She would entertain her family for hours by playing original melodies. She would stand erect, her blonde hair framing her thoughtful face in an aurora of shimmering gold, and lift her mellow instrument. A hush would fall on the group as liquid notes would pour from under her flying fingers, as they plashed quickly over the strings. Sometimes the song would be gay and would fill the air with laughter and smiles. Other times the violin would draw out sad, mournful tones. Carol's friends all admired this blue-eyed girl with her changing moods. All her luxuries did not spoil her, even at eighteen. Carol's parents were looking for a suitable match for her. When she met the dashing, handsome and wealthy Lawrence Worthington, they were delighted. She met him at the nightclub dance on Friday evening. The sweet strains of the "Blue Danube" waltz floated through the air as Carol, in a froth of creamy satin and foamy lace which brought out the flush of the roses in her hair and the rosy blush on her cheeks, was cut in on by the dark-haired Lawrence. He claimed her for almost all of the dances after that, and while they were dancing to the "Missouri Waltz," he led her out on the cool terrace. It was a pleasant change from the crowded dance floor. The trees shaded the dewy lawns and the silvery moonlight gleamed on the deep, dark waters of the pool. They sat down on a stone bench and told each other about their homes. Lawrence, it seemed, was left alone in America because his mother was a victim of cancer, and his father had taken her on a tour to Europe to cheer her last days.

The next week enveloped Carol in a whirlwind of plans. Her parents were overjoyed at the frequent dinner-engagements that Carol had with Lawrence. Two weeks later he invited her to come to his penthouse for the evening and dinner. Carol was ready in a cool blue dinner dress when Lawrence drove up in a sleek black sedan. They sped through the glare of street lights and signs, through the noise of honking car horns, until they reached the building overlooking the waterfront. The elevator sped up until it reached the next to the top floor. Carol alighted and climbed the last flight of stairs with Lawrence. She gasped in appreciation as they walked out in the open air. From way, way down below arose the muffled sound of traffic. She forgot all noise as she gazed on the modern white house, flanked on both sides with shrubs. Flame-red roses on a trellis permeated the air with a dewy fragrance. Lawrence gently drew Carol inside. They had a dinner served by the hotel below and then sat outside in the cool evening to talk. The night sky was a deep blue-black and was spangled with stars. Their reflections made wavering lines on the water, a few rods away.

A cool breeze arose and gently whispered through Carol's hair. She had only known Lawrence for over two weeks. He was nice. Yet there was something about him that made her feel uncomfortable. She frowned when he said, "I love you Carol."

"No," she replied, "please don't spoil this beautiful night."

Lawrence then went in the house. He soon reappeared with a small white box. Opening it, he clasped around Carol's slender throat a gleaming necklace of pearls. Her hands reached up to take them off but he pleaded, "Keep them, if only in memory of me."

Carol hesitated. He was in earnest. She relented, unsmiling. Then she murmured that she must be going for it was almost eleven o'clock. Refusing his offers to drive her home she writhed out of his grasp and rushed down the long flight of steps into the night. She took a taxi home and realized too late that her gold bracelet set with diamonds had fallen off in her hurry to get away. She resolved to return for it the next evening when he would probably not be home.

Following suit, she took the elevator up the fateful building once more the next evening. She could see no signs of life about the house. She looked all about outside but could find no trace of the bracelet. "Maybe Lawrence found it and brought it in the house," she thought, as she tried the door, which opened; she did not think for a moment of how wrong it was. She stopped, involuntarily, as she saw a shaft of light streaming from a half-opened door and heard three voices rise in conflict. One voice she recognized with a start, it was that of Lawrence. The others rose, harsh and unfamiliar . . .

"Forget her and make a getaway. The bracelet isn't worth the pearls, but our lives are. We scram tonight."

"Yeah. But her father will probably hear about my disappearance and try to find me in hope that I'll marry Carol and combine our fortunes. That's all I wanted anyway, not her looks, but her money."

Carol had heard enough. So his "love" for her had just been a farce! She tiptoed out silently and went downstairs to a phone and called the police. She hurriedly tumbled out the incoherent story and rushed back to the house. If only she could stall them! She would pretend to be unsuspicious. She walked in and knocked on the door of the room, now closed. She heard a chair scrape on the floor and a muffled voice say, "Who could that be?" The door opened a crack and a strange, yet familiar bloodshot face peered out. It was decidedly not Lawrence's. Carol forced a laugh as she said with attempted gaiety, "Is Lawrence home?" The man stifled some hot words and roughly shoved her past him. She pretended to be accustomed to seeing half-drunk men draining beer bottles. Lawrence was sitting at the table, quite sober. She rushed past the other two men and stammered, "Oh! Lawrence d-darling! I just remembered I left my little old bracelet here last night, so I just dropped by to take it home."

Lawrence seemed pleased, but the other man at the table said gruffly, "Aw, cut the mush before she gets wise."

Carol pretended not to notice. She was startled when the short man with the beady eyes who had opened the door said, "She's probably already called the police." Carol murmured something about, "What on earth for?" But Lawrence said, "He's right. We can't take any chances at this stage of the game. You're coming with us."

Carol rushed to the door, but too late. The man put out his foot, and she tripped and fell. Carol struggled and cried out, but they gagged her with a handkerchief and bound her hands to her ankles behind her; this left her in an uncomfortable sitting position. The handkerchief was stuffed part way down her throat. Dryly she choked, and one man laughed harshly. Lawrence lifted Carol up and carried her down a flight of back steps that she had never noticed before. He took her in the front of the sedan with him and the two strange men got in back. Just as the car started off with a whir, the sirens of the police cars broke the night air. Lawrence muttered a curse under his breath, as he careened around corners, and increased his speed. Soon they reached a seemingly vacant boathouse. Lawrence drove in a gaping hole that served as a part-garage and turned off the ignition. Before Lawrence dragged her out, Carol cast a quick glance about her. One man had turned on a light which cast a bright glare over the shabby boards. The weather-beaten house was a silver-gray and the opaque windows regarded Carol with a vacant stare. Below the boards on one side was a steep drop. Carol saw that it was full of water which lapped hungrily against the edge of the boards. She saw that this water was a part of the ocean and a dark hollow showed the exit for the yacht. This she saw dimly outlined against the entrance. Her observances were rudely interrupted by Lawrence, who pulled her out of the sedan and tossed her into the yacht. Her head struck the seat, and she was stunned. A warm trickle of blood flowed from her temple. She was aware of the hum of the motor and of the presence of a pile of boxes beside her. One corner jabbed into her arm. She was somewhat revived by the salt night air, as the boat set a straight course, and headed for the open sea. The brine flicked Carol's face in a fine spray as Lawrence deftly turned to avoid a reef, protruding jagged and forbidding above the waves. Carol caught her breath and listened. Yes! She heard the hum of a speedboat—the police—if only they had followed her! Lawrence evidently had the same idea. One man took the wheel as he came toward her. The noise of the speedboat was becoming louder. "Hurry! Hurry!" the motor seemed to say. Lawrence told her briefly that the load of the yacht must be lightened. She could not be found as his captive. To Carol his features were almost unrecognizable—distorted with passion; unrelenting. She knew she could expect no mercy from this fugitive of justice. To her horror he took a heavy rope from the bottom of the boat and bound her tightly to one of the boxes beside her. He then heaved her overboard. How hard the shock was as she struck the water. Icy fingers reached to drag her down, down into the icy depths. The box was dragging her down. The ropes were sawing at her skin. The water was pounding in her ears, pushing at all sides: she was drowning, drowning . . .

She felt only vague sensations—she was spinning on a record, the momentum was going to throw her off. She must cling on—but she could not, it was flat surface—she was flying in space. Now she was running. Running away from a horrible monster, hidden by fog. But she couldn't move. She couldn't get anywhere! A humming was in her ears. It grew louder, louder, unbearably louder and then broke . . .

"She's coming out of it now."

The glare was blinding, the sunlight was reflecting dazzling whiteness on the bed. Someone was bending over her. A salt tear fell on her face. Carol knew now. In his hurry Lawrence had crashed. The police had found her floating a week ago, almost dead. Somehow she was glad that she did not see Lawrence meet his defeat. She would never disgrace him further by revealing his secret of the smuggling gang. They were all done for. No one would know that it was Lawrence who had almost killed her. Carol knew that *she*, however, would never forget her terrible discovery on the penthouse roof.

A May Morning

Ts, 23 May 1946, Lilly Library

Carol awoke when the first pale streaks of dawn were showing in the horizon. Outside the early spring morning was beckoning her. Unable to resist, she dressed quickly and silently tiptoed out of the house.

The day was yet cool. Gentle breezes wafted through her hair and whispered in her ears. The gnarled branches of the apple tree lifted up their frail fingers, holding their bouquet of fragile pink and white blossoms high up to the azure sky. A few petals drifted down slowly like stray snowflakes.

Walking leisurely across the lawn, Carol could smell the new-mown grass, still damp from last night's rain. Crystal dewdrops were caught on every blade, and the long rays of morning sunlight made myriads of rainbows dance among them.

As Carol wandered through the backyard and under the slender groups of graceful white birches, she saw that they were just getting their shiny new yellow-green leaves. The birch catkins hung down in straight lines like green rain.

"How I love those trees," Carol thought, "they seem to be almost human."

She looked proudly at her own woodland garden. The violets were deep purple, and hid shyly among their heart-shaped leaves. The pure lilies-of-the-valley were thriving in the shade of the stiff blue-green pines, that held their new sprouts aloft like tiny candles. The stately iris held erect their haughty heads among pointed leaves.

From the tall, friendly maples lining the walk came the mingled morning songs of the birds as they twittered about in the protecting screen of leaves.

Carol then stopped, entranced, for in one of the birch trees she saw the brilliant orange and black plumage of a Baltimore oriole. From its slender throat poured liquid tones. If only her mother could hear! She turned toward the house and saw the smiling face of her mother framed in the window. The oriole continued to warble as if to please them. The magic spell was broken when the beautiful bird flew off in a flash of color and a torrent of melody.

Carol sniffed delightedly as the tantalizing smell of bacon and eggs reached her nostrils. Rushing into the kitchen, she gave her mother a loving hug; she cried happily.

"Oh mums! Isn't this a wonderful morning!"

Victory

Written: 12 November 1946[*]
Published: *The Phillipian* (April 1947): 6

An impenetrable blanket of heavy fog veiled the night and added to its forbidding atmosphere. The wind blew the rain in little gusts, while the dim gleam

---

[*] In her diary on 12 November 1946, SP wrote, 'After school I finished writing my short story titled "Victory" before taking out the Boonisar baby for which I earned thirty (30) cents! I typed up my story.' The Lilly Library holds a typescript, written for English 7 at Alice L. Phillips Junior High School, dated 15 November 1946, with her teacher's comments.

of the street light seemed to flicker as the trees bowed down under the fury of the storm. The air was chill; and a sharp, cold blast sent the shadows of the bare trees dancing grotesquely on the slippery pavement of the long, solitary country road.

"Only a short way to go now," Judith sighed, as she bent her head against the onslaught of the wind and rain and pushed on into the storm. Ah! There was the faint light of the farmer's cottage around the bend of the road. She strained her eyes to see farther into the black void ahead, but it was no use. The tap-tap of her shoes echoed in the lonely night as she hurried on to her destination.

The telephone lines were down, and a great part of the farmlands was already submerged by the flood. The strong stone foundations of the dam that held the irrigation supply for the farms had, by some singular means, become undermined. Already the water was relentlessly seeping down into the valley. Being a telephone operator, Judith had been informed of the imminent danger of the flood and told to warn the few families in the outer districts to move to higher land with their livestock. She had mired her car about a mile back when she had driven over a road partially washed out by a rain-swollen river. This was the last house. She must reach it before it became too late!

Along with the purposeful thought that urged her on, many questions flocked to her mind.

"What will happen if I don't make it? Will I be a failure forever? Who began all this strange business anyway?"

Then Judith started with fear. Footsteps resounded in quick tempo behind her, while a deep voice shouted, "Hey, there! Stop!" Judith turned in her tracks and saw a dark figure looming up behind her. Someone evidently did not want her to reach the farmhouse. The girl stood paralyzed with fright as she heard the labored breathing of her pursuer. He loomed tall beside her. The next moment she felt his fingers close about her neck, choking the cry of terror that had risen to her throat.

With a sigh of relief, Judith sank to the floor. As if by magic the rain stopped and lights flashed on. The director was approaching her with a happy smile, and her pursuer turned to her with a grin.

A song rose in Judith's heart. The hardest scene was over! Her first movie was going to be a success!

Mary Jane's Passport

Ts,[*] 23 November 1946, Lilly Library

"I don't see what can be the matter with her," said Mary Jane to her best friend, Cathy, as they walked home from school. "Imagine refusing to stop in the drugstore for a coke with the gang! I thought Judy seemed to be a nice girl. She could at least have been civil and given me a reason for not coming."

"Well," replied Cathy slowly, "I don't think I'd bother chasing after that new girl. She's too snobbish, and she doesn't come from the best part of town, either."

"I s'pose so," sighed Mary Jane, as she said goodbye to Cathy and started down her own street.

As she walked along, Mary Jane thought about Judy. Having done some private investigating on her own, she had found that Judy was living with Mrs. Rogers, that young widow who had three little children to support and all she could do to manage the sweetshop down in the market district. In fact, Mary Jane had caught a glimpse of Judy wheeling Mrs. Rogers' youngest baby around a corner of the park only a few days ago.

When Mary Jane opened the door of her home and walked into the hall, her mother called down from the top of the carpeted stairway, "Have you been out yet this afternoon, dear?"

Mary Jane groaned inwardly as she tossed her books on the table and thought of all the time she had to spend outside each day. Didn't the doctor know that the gang just never went on hikes or walks or anything like that? Why, they either went to the movies after school, or hung around the ice cream parlor, or held informal meetings at Cathy's house or danced at Jack's house, or—or did anything but take silly old walks. Why, they were too old to play outside. Yet the doctor had said in so many words that if she wanted to keep healthy and go to high school at all, she had to get plenty of fresh air.

"I know that it must be boring for you to take walks all alone," said Mary Jane's mother, smiling as she came downstairs. "It's too bad that Cathy won't accompany you, but I have a plan. Why don't you take Aunt Jo's little girl,

---

[*] Typed with holograph corrections in SP's hand. Written for English 7 at Alice L. Phillips Junior High School. On 23 November 1946, SP wrote in her diary, 'For the life of me I couldn't get an inspiration. However, mother planted some ideas after long minutes of thought, and accordingly I began to write a story after mother went over to the Ortons. I produced a story twice as long as my other one, and mother titled it "Mary Jane's Passport." It is more or less a character story.'

Susie, and wheel her around the park? That way you could earn a little extra money, and I know that Aunt Jo will be glad to have a few hours free every afternoon."

Mary Jane hesitated with a frown; then her face brightened as she thought of a plan, and she said, "Yes, I believe I will take Susie out. I'll begin wheeling her tomorrow."

The next afternoon Mary Jane was hopefully wheeling the cooing baby around the park. Perhaps, she thought, she might meet Judy wheeling Mrs. Rogers' baby. And Judy might be more inclined to be friendly if she saw Mary Jane pushing a baby, too. The park was in the glorious stage of spring, and the breezes were soft and fragrant with the smell of growing things. The earth felt good beneath Mary Jane's feet. There were purple crocuses and yellow daffodils blooming everywhere in the sunny meadows, and the trees were uncurling their pale green buds. Mary Jane looked about happily and wondered that the park could have changed so.

Little children were playing gaily under the watchful eye of mothers or nurses, and a few grown-ups were strolling here and there. Everyone who passed Mary Jane nodded a friendly greeting or smiled at her. Perhaps it was little Susie, so contented in her carriage, or perhaps it was just the effect of the clear spring air that Mary Jane's spirit seemed lighter.

That afternoon Mary Jane did not see Judy, but when she took Susie out the next day, she saw a girl sitting on one of the benches. It was Judy, bent over something in her lap. It must be her day off, Mary Jane decided, as she wheeled Susie over and peered curiously over Judy's shoulder.

Judy was sketching the fountain under the willow tree and making the picture seem almost real as her pencil flew over the paper. Seeming to sense someone's presence, Judy turned around, and seeing Mary Jane, she said quickly, "I think you're downright mean to come and spy on me. Why don't you stay with your own gang?"

"B-but," Mary Jane stammered, as she realized for the first time that even though Judy was a poor orphan, she had some pride, too. And then Judy saw Susie. Miraculously her face softened, and she leaned over the carriage and lovingly touched the baby's soft curls as she said, "I didn't know that you took care of a baby, too."

"You see," said Mary Jane hurriedly, "I want to be friends with you so much that I brought Susie out to the park, and I did hope to meet you with Mrs. Rogers' baby. We can take walks and talk together and—and," here Mary Jane stopped breathlessly. "Say," she continued as she saw a warm smile light up

Judy's face, "the gang has been looking for someone like you to draw posters for the class elections. You could do them in your school art classes and on your days off, couldn't you?"

"Why, I'd love to," Judy replied gratefully. "I thought that you were only teasing me the other day, and I guess I've been pretty unfriendly, too. I didn't think you'd want a working girl like me for a friend."

The conversation was interrupted by a loud wail from Susie.

"Why, what is the matter with her?" Mary Jane exclaimed worriedly. "She seemed all right a minute ago!"

Judy laughed happily as she stood up, put the sketch pad into the carriage and said, "Susie just wants to be wheeled some more. Come on, let's push together!"

A Morning in the Agora

Written: 30 November 1946[*]
Published: *The Phillipian* (February 1947): 5

Lavinia awoke just as the first rays of early-morning sun were streaming in through the open window of her room. She stretched luxuriously and was just about to turn over in her soft bed and go back to sleep when she remembered with a start that this was the day that she was going to the agora with her nurse, Chloe. In fact, at this very moment Chloe's dusky, smiling face was peeping around the doorway. Seeing that her young Greek mistress was awake, Chloe walked into the room, her sandals slapping softly on the woven grass of the floor mats. The two exchanged a cheerful greeting, and the maid began to make Lavinia ready for the morning's excursion. By the time Lavinia and Chloe were ready to begin the walk to the marketplace, the sun had risen in the heavens, and the day had grown much warmer.

Lavinia walked along with a spring in her step, conversing gaily with Chloe, who was carrying two small jars filled with pure olive oil. These were to be sold at one of the little booths in the agora. Lavinia herself held the flower wreaths and the sweets that she would place at the foot of Athena's shrine. The carts and wagons passing by came closer together now, and Lavinia knew that they must be at the outskirts of the agora.

---

[*] The Lilly Library holds a typescript dated 30 November 1946; written for SP's Ancient History course.

Sure enough! There were the colonnaded porches surrounding the marketplace. The graceful white shafts gleamed in the sun and stood out against the fresh green leaves of the poplar and plane trees growing nearby. Chloe and Lavinia drew closer to the market square and rested for a short while in the cool shade of the trees and watched the colorful pageant going on around them.

The merchants were seated in small booths crying their wares to the people milling about. They were selling brilliant silk robes, graceful pottery jars and vases, wines, gay jewelry, oils, sugar candies, and offerings that could be placed in the shrines of the many gods and goddesses. Some of the buyers were resplendent in purple, blue, and gold robes; others were more simply clad in white robes with crimson borders; and then there were the dark glistening skins of the African slaves, who wore only short tunics as they followed their masters.

The grassy hills sloped away from this noisy scene of busy life, and the terrace walls were wide and strong. Around the marketplace were the important civic buildings—the library, the general's residence, the basilica where the court sat, the treasury, and the council hall.

Chloe put the two jars in the care of a friendly merchant who promised to sell them as soon as possible. She then took Lavinia on a tour of the agora, and the two spent hours admiring the various displays. They paid Athena tribute, and by the time they arrived back at the merchant's stall, the jars had been sold, and the money was ready for them.

Now the full heat of the noonday was upon them, and the sun beat down mercilessly on the dusty pavement. The two companions took refuge, as the others did, in the large colonnaded porches about the marketplace. Quenching their thirst by drinking a dipper of cold water from the pail of a passing vendor, Lavinia and Chloe waited until the coolness of the afternoon descended before making their way home after an enchanting morning in the agora.

From the Memoirs of a Babysitter

Ts,[*] 2 December 1946, Lilly Library

In my opinion, little children are bothersome beings that have to be waited on hand and foot, who are generally around when not wanted, and who are, all in all, a nuisance. My ideas on this subject have become considerably hardened. It

---

[*] Written for English 7 at Alice L. Phillips Junior High School.

is all a result of my experiences as a "babysitter," which have altered my ideas about angelic children noticeably. I will tell you how this all began.

It was my first experience of real babysitting! This time I didn't have to push a gurgling little infant about in a baby carriage; instead, I was going to take care of two little boys from three to seven o'clock on Sunday afternoon while their mother and father were attending a tea. I walked over to Mrs. Snow's home in an excited state of anticipation. Why, it would be simple to amuse those little fellows—all I needed to do was to turn on *The Shadow* on the radio, or something equally interesting, to hold the kiddies' interest and sit down and read all the magazines that were in the house.

With this cheerful thought in mind, I walked up the front steps of the house and bravely poked the doorbell. A pretty, smiling young woman greeted me and showed me into the living room, gave me a few hurried instructions, then dashed out the door and was gone! Where, oh *where* were the children? Then I heard a giggle, and two impish faces peered at me from behind the sofa. These rosy countenances were soon followed by the rest of the two sweetest little boys I had ever seen. The mother had said, "The five-year-old is Donnie, and the three-year-old we call 'Cookie'."

"Well, boys," I suggested brightly, "how would you like to listen to the radio?"

"Read to us," they chorused. "We don't like the radio."

I had not reckoned on such a strong will from the younger generation, and, thinking it best to humor them, I read. I read until my throat ached; I read until I was on the point of collapse; I read everything from *The Grasshopper Man* to *Betty Grable and Her Life History*; and still they brought more and more books. Finally, when they wanted me to sing a songbook from beginning to end, I put my foot down.

"*Now* we will have supper," I remarked firmly. Donnie obligingly set six places at the table; and then he took Cookie by the hand, and together they stood gravely in the center of the kitchen watching my every move. I took out a saucepan in which to cook the soup.

"No," Donnie yelled in a horrified tone, "*that's* what mamma cooks our *cereal* in!" Before I could stop him, he pulled the pile of pots and pans to the floor and triumphantly produced "the pot to cook soup in."

I struggled for a full fifteen minutes before I discovered how to make a stubborn can opener open cans. While the boys were peacefully slurping up the rather cold soup in the dining room, I undertook the task of popping the popcorn. I shuffled the popper back and forth over the stove for just ages, when I heard a loud crack and a fluffy white object appeared. The corn was popping!

To me, the uninitiated, this seemed like the eighth wonder of the world. Anxious to have every last grain of corn popped, I kept shuffling the popper over the flame. Then, by some terrible trick of fate, or call it science, the popper of popcorn burst into flame. Billows of smoke filled the kitchen as I rushed to the sink with the popcorn burning up merrily before my eyes. At last the water extinguished the blaze, and I sadly gazed at the black ashes—all that remained of my lovely, fluffy popcorn. My one remaining sensation, however, was one of gratitude that those two little Sherlock Holmeses had remained completely oblivious of the near-catastrophe and were still stuffing themselves with bread and butter in the dining room.

Later, when Cookie was trying helpfully to put away the unpopped corn, he took the package by the wrong end, and little grains of corn bounced all over the kitchen floor. While I was hurriedly sweeping these out the back door, Donnie announced that he wouldn't finish his noodle soup and overturned the soup plate in the middle of the kitchen. Fate was still kind, however, for the mother of these two dear children did *not* arrive at this opportune moment. Oh, no! She waited until I was lying on the floor, red-faced and panting, with the two small boys climbing gaily over me, playing a game they called "Kill the Bear," before she calmly walked in the front door.

Do you—now tell me truly—do you blame me for having become somewhat of a cynic in regard to the loudly acclaimed, endearing charms of little children?

The Miraculous End of Miss Minton

Ms,[*] 10 February 1947, Lilly Library

Miss Minton walked with precise steps about her apartment living room, dusting each bit of antique furniture with meticulous care. It was spring! Against her will, Miss Minton had opened wide her front window to give her apartment its annual airing. She felt

---

[*] Story written out in full in SP's diary. The text on 10 February 1947 preceding it reads:
 'Darn it! I had to miss school to day, and all because of a cemented head cold. I altered my first chapter of "Stardust" and began my third. By some trick of fate I wrote a few silly paragraphs about someone I thought of. The idea came whole out of thin air, so I just put it down on paper. I have decided to copy it down in here, and then destroy the original paper.
 'Listen now to the story of . . .'

an odd softening in her heart, as ice must feel before a thaw. Rather uncomfortable, she thought. Suddenly Miss Minton felt a strange pang of loneliness. Odd that she, one who had always done her duty (no matter how hard), odd that *she* should feel lonely.

A soft breeze whispered through the open window and stirred the starched white curtains. It seemed to say something, Miss Minton thought guiltily, seemed to say that something was going to—to . . .

The breeze grew a little stronger, and rustled the stiff coverings on Miss Minton's treasured furniture. In fact the little breeze began to rush about in the once tidy room in a veritable gale. It knocked over pictures, lamps, vases, tables, and chairs. Miss Minton stood paralyzed with horror—unable to cry out. The very rug beneath her feet was being lifted from the varnished floor by the raging wind! Miss Minton felt one terrible moment of being swept into the air like a bubble and spinning about upside down, nothing solid beneath her feet. Before she could regain her balance, she felt herself being blown outside, lifted right out the open window—feather duster and all, into the warm spring air. She fell down, down, down—all topsy-turvy inside like you feel in dreams, only this wasn't a dream—oh, no! Miss Minton flew so fast that no human eye could follow her; no human ear could hear her last breathless gasp of terror. There was one last moment of bright April sunshine and then total darkness. The earth had opened, and had closed over the head of the terrible Miss Minton forever!

Since this day the name of Miss Minton has never been heard again. But since we should never forget this awful lesson, this tale was sent to me by some unseen power to tell to you.

The Thrilling Journeys of a Penny

Ms,[*] *c.*26 February 1947, Smith College

My first glimpse of this world was in the dark, black recesses of a huge metal box. I was surrounded by my comrades who were talking in thin, shrill voices

---

[*] SP wrote in her diary on 26 February 1947: 'Finished my story about the penny and continued chap. III of "Stardust".' Some of the paper on which the story is written is torn away and is identified by <damaged> in the text. Composed in a small memorandum notepad with 'O. E. Plath' embossed on front cover. Includes a holograph draft of Chapter I of 'Stardust', as well as poems and phrases.

among themselves. One accosted me in a seemingly friendly manner. "Say," he squeaked, "you're new here, ain't you?"

"I guess so," I replied in a quavering voice. "I don't remember being anywhere before this."

"Aw," he replied, "you're probably the last of the second batch they sent into the furnace."

"Furnace!" I gasped.

"Yeah," drawled my comrade, "we're just those that have cooled off, and we've been waiting to be sent out."

"My gracious! How *do* you know so much?" I questioned.

"Wal, I just picked up a few words here-n-there from those things they call people outside. They dropped me by accident and I had time to hear a lot before they found me and put me in this box," my friend remarked rather smugly.

Before I had a chance to ask more, I felt a terrible jolt, and I was tumbling around the box in confusion among all of my trembling comrades.

"Here we go," shrieked one high voice.

My companion was parted from me in the noise and motion of the rest, but I got along pretty well by myself. The jogging motion in that awful box continued for seeming ages. Suddenly it stopped with a jerk and a click. The box lid flew open and I was blinded by a sharp, bright light. Gradually I grew accustomed to the glare and looked about me. I was still in the open box. I could see my companions gleaming reddishly beside me. I then heard a murmur of human voices, and a gigantic hand came down and picked up about twenty-five of my frightened comrades. Soon I was singled out by this same hand and I was lifted high into the air and put down on a marble counter. While another hand picked me up, I heard the voices more clearly.

"Here's your change, Mr. Moneybag! Happy New Year to you!"

"Goodbye, sir," answered my new owner, as he dropped me deep into his back pocket. I fell with a clink among many other coins much grander than I. They immediately started to squawk.

"Some new urchin," remarked a shiny quarter staring at me loftily.

"Well, I should say! Do not even bother to *talk* to those common pennies. That's *my* advice," snapped a saucy dime. "I'm worth ten of them any day."

I was rudely elbowed aside, feeling mighty lonely, mind you. Some of my beautiful shine had been chipped off by those—those—

"Don't mind them, young feller," whispered an old nickel to me, "you'll get used to their high-and-mighty ways."

I was glad to have found a new friend that condescended to speak with me, and we chatted for some time. I learned a lot from this old nickel, indeed. We were both the property of a wealthy old bachelor, and probably would not have to part for a long time. Sooner than we expected, however, we were both taken up by Mr. Moneybag and exchanged, along with a few other coins, for a can of tobacco. The young cashier opened a box where the drawers shot out and separated us into our respective compartments. I went into a drawer full of pennies. Here, at least, I hoped to find a favorable reception, but—

"Will ya look at de swell," shrieked a ragged neighbor of mine as he gave me an experimental kick in the shins.

"We'll fix him up fine!" cried a whole bunch of rude pennies falling upon me. I stood their anger and jealousy for a while, but was relieved when I was handed to a young woman as change. I slipped blissfully between the folds of an over-perfumed handkerchief in her pocketbook and fell into a deep sleep. The next thing I knew, I was flying through the air. I hit the sidewalk of a busy street with a painful jar to my ribs. The woman had hurriedly removed her handkerchief, and I fell to the ground unnoticed. It was a dark, wet day, and soon it began to rain. The sand on the sidewalk gritted into my back, and each time a raindrop hit me I gasped for breath, hoping I wouldn't drown. However, pennies are made for a hard life, and many hurrying feet passed carelessly over me before I was finally picked up by a tattered little newsboy, who had seen me shining in a puddle, and stopped long enough in the rain to pick me up. We two soon became great friends, and Tim, for that was the newsboy's name, vowed solemnly to keep me forever-n-ever as a good luck penny. Just so he wouldn't lose me, he hammered a fine hole in my stomach with a hot nail, and strung me about his neck. By this time I was used to rough handling, and, well, I'd do anything for a friend, so I submitted to the ordeal willingly. But the promise of saving, and having money in the future, does not shine so brightly in young minds as the promise of spending and having candy *now*, so, on one sad day I was removed from the string and held for a moment in Tim's grubby hand before being spent for a gaily striped red-and-white peppermint stick.

Now, as I look back on my rather hard life, I am glad that I had a chance to be out in the world. My gay experiences were over all too soon. My goals have been high. Well do I recall the day when I first fell in love. It was with a young lady nickel from the South. She had many beaus around her all the time, and she never cast so much as a look at me. I was then an overconfident young chap, and quite conceited, I must admit. I had acquired a new shine from a little girl who begged her parents to polish me, and I did not bother to think that Rosie, the secret name I gave to my lovely sweetheart, that Rosie was far above me. Rosie's rather jealous girlfriends were crowded in the background of the box that we all occupied. We had been donated to a church mission drive, and the nickels and pennies were put together. Rosie's popularity was due mostly to the fact that she was regarded as a movie star. She had once been dropped on the floor of a theater and had sat there through a double feature before being picked up. This set her somewhat above most of the common coins who had never seen anything vaguely resembling a movie. I remember with some embarrassment how I first acquired sweet Rosie's attention. I started to sing "That's What I Like About the South" in my special tenor voice that I had picked up while going around in the hat of an organ grinder's monkey. Lo and behold! Illustrious Rosie turned her blue-eyed gaze on me and flashed me a southern smile to the chagrin of the young nickels flocking around her.

"Why, ef'n it ain't mah favorite song from the sout! Quiet yo'all!" she drawled in her thick accent and waved her lilywhite hands for silence. When I had finished singing I waited hopefully. But— "Thank yo' kindly, little man," was all she said as she turned and began to talk once more with her bright, silvery friends.

That was the last I saw of Rosie for some time. I was not a little hurt that she thought I was so young, for I had seen by her date that she was born at the same time I was. That very day we were collected and spent in a grocery store for food for the poor. This time I had no trouble in my compartment in the cashier register.

I was born just before New Year's and this was around the Christmas approaching my third year, so I was regarded with respect for the most part. I exchanged hands too many times to keep track of during the Christmas rush, and I ended up by being cleaned until I shone by some poor people and then stuck in a kid's stocking. That was one of my happiest experiences. The little girl who found me played happily with me by the hour. She took me out to play on the sidewalk. Suddenly she dropped me down a chink in the pavement by the curbstone. You should have heard the poor little dear cry! It would have broken your heart. She tried to get me up with a stick, but I was gone down too far. She only succeeded in knocking dirt and snow on top of me. I would never be found again, I thought sadly; no eyes would spot me stuck in such a deep, narrow crack. It was true. The February thaws seeped down and I began to rust or disintegrate, or something equally sad. The summer suns beat down and cracked the pavement with their heat. Fall winds blew dry leaves lightly <damaged> my head. A painful <damaged> led by. On one <damaged> ay I sniffed the <damaged> air. If only I could <damaged> out of my miserable little hole! I was much weaker and thinner—if this kept on—

My thoughts were interrupted by a clinking noise. A battered coin fell to my side. I would not wish my fate of slow-wasting away on my worst enemy, but here was company for the long trial ahead. We sat side by side talking softly to each other. Our cares were forgotten in the joy of friendship forever. The coin was Rosie!

♥

The Attic View

Ts, 21 February 1948, Lilly Library

The rusty iron bedstead had been pushed next to the dingy attic window so that she could look down at the passing crowds. She would sit up and lean against the flat, lumpy pillow until she became too weak to hold herself erect any longer. Then she would slip down under the ragged blanket, shiver a bit as she clutched its grimy folds about her shoulders with cold, thin fingers, and gaze at the square of pale sky that stretched above the rooftops.

She had no visitors. No relatives came to sympathize with her. No friends came to chat about unimportant daily trifles. She sat alone by the window, watching the changing scene below her, preoccupied with her own thoughts. The attic room overlooked a bustling backstreet in the shabby section of town. Small stores and insignificant shops crowded close to the gutter in a jumbled confusion of sordid brick walls, smoke-stained glass, and yellowed signs. A warehouse spread its awkward bulk over part of the block and was separated from the shopping district by a short alleyway. She liked to look down this cobblestoned by-street to the harbor beyond, and never tired of seeing the ocean waves foam about the remains of an old pier standing close to the shore.

She had never had much time for reflection before, but now there was such a considerable amount of this commodity that she was quite overwhelmed. When she had rented her room a few months ago she had been down on her luck. Breathing heavily from exertion, the proprietress of the boardinghouse had led the girl up the three steep flights of warped wooden steps to the garret. The sharply sloping roof left space for but a small room under the eaves. The dusky chamber was lighted by one window, and the relentless chill of winter penetrated its thin walls.

"You're just lucky to get any room at all," the landlady had observed complacently. "All the apartments in town are filled up to the brim. 'Course there isn't any electricity or much heat, but—ah—there's a lot of light coming from the window and you can see almost across the bay in clear weather."

The girl had begun her routine existence once more, and the days dragged into weeks—the weeks into tedious months. She would leave for work after the early boardinghouse breakfast of watery coffee, dry toast, and pallid oatmeal, buy her lunch at a cheap, out-of-the-way restaurant, and arrive "home" barely in time for supper.

Then, unexpectedly, one of the girls at the office had told her about a free secretarial night course for working girls. This sudden possibility of a future—of advancement—was like a glittering rainbow in her dismal world. A hasty supper—sometimes none at all—and she would attend night classes, desperately eager to learn.

Then there had been that heavy blizzard a few days ago. She had come out of school into the cool white hush of falling snow and gotten chilled and damp while hurrying back to her room. The next morning, try as she might, she could not get up. Her bones ached, she had a racking cough, and tears of pain sprang to her eyes when she tried to swallow.

No one noticed her absence at the breakfast table save a shy young artist. When he asked the landlady, somewhat bashfully to be sure, if the girl in the attic room had left, she cut short his question and remarked tartly that if the girl were too lazy to come down for breakfast she, for one, wouldn't bother about her, and she advised him not to either.

"'Tis none of my affair when my boarders come and go," said she by way of concluding the matter.

They say that the winter was cold that year—so cold that the lake in the city park froze solid and didn't melt till spring. They say the snow fell deep that year, and men groaned laughingly as they told their friends how many times they had had to shovel out their driveways.

The world continued to pass by beneath her window, and she viewed it from the solitude of the bleak attic room. She was an outsider watching a cross-section of humanity limited by the confining boundary of her window frame. None of the passersby noticed the pale, wan face of the girl looking down.

How could the world go on without her, she wondered. It would be strangely impersonal, as it was now, below, for if she were gone there would be no center of interest for life to revolve about. She experienced a curious longing to fling open the casement and cry out, "Here I am! Look, up here!" to the ever-changing crowds below. She could visualize the white blur of startled faces, upturned for but a brief moment before passing out of the range of her view. They would all carry a sharp mental impression of her presence with them. In this way, at least, she would live a little beyond her life. How much better that would be than dying totally unremembered!

In a sudden fever of excitement she leapt out of bed and gave a tremendous push to the window. It didn't budge! It was swollen shut by ice and snow. Coughing fiercely, she fell back on the pillow, gripping the coverings closer about her with trembling fingers. That night her room was colder than ever before, or so it seemed. Lingering between ghastly dreams and total oblivion, she drifted into a fevered sleep.

The next morning she felt tired and listless, but the fever had left her, and it was good to lie in the silence of her secluded room with no one to disturb her. The cold atmosphere did not bother her any longer, and the view from her bed was so lovely.

The window glass was etched with frost around the edges, and the calm, early sunrise over the harbor was framed with a lacy white tapestry of spangled flowers and graceful crystal trees. The ocean shimmered dusty apple-green in the daylight, and occasionally one could see the chalky whiteness of ice cakes bobbing past. The ancient warehouse across the street had always blotted out part of the harbor scene, but today, in the chill of morning, she could clearly see the waves sloshing against the tarry black piles of the lonely wharf. For a brief, breathless moment the sun tinged the shingled rooftops of the city with a ruddy flush of color, and the rays shone through her frosty windowpane, making rosy sparks on the icy glass.

Closing her eyes with a sigh of contentment, she slipped into a tranquil slumber. It was late afternoon when she woke. The sun had disappeared behind a bank of heavy storm clouds, and it was difficult to see beyond the steamy wetness of the rain-spattered window. The colors of the neon store signs ran together in the rivulets of water tumbling down the pane and made a blurred jumble of shifting crimsons, emerald greens, and lemon yellows. Beyond the warehouse, the sea was a disturbed mass of darkness, and the dullness of the melting snow showed a bleached white against the wet, sooty, twilit streets. She stared at the window unseeingly, thinking about nothing in particular, and filled with a sudden peace and serenity. She was completely detached from the world—nothing in it affected her any longer. She was *so* sleepy. As her eyelids closed slowly once more, her mind was filled with one burning question. She fumbled mentally for the answer. She knew, but she could not remember.

What was it like in the hereafter? What was it like—what was—what was—? Her thoughts trailed down into darkness. She was sliding uncertainly into flowing black space when there was a sudden blinding flash. Warm light enveloped her and shot glinting golden arrows about her. Beyond the radiant blaze she saw a vision of silvered palm trees swaying in a perfumed breeze. Then all dissolved into blank nothingness.

The landlady trudged up the creaking attic steps, the flickering light of the candle in her hand making grotesque shadows leap upon the walls. The elderly woman walked toward the girl's bed and spoke, "I've come to collect the rent."

Receiving no answer, she leaned over and shook the motionless form. Then she uttered a startled exclamation, lingered a moment, turned, and descended the stairs once more.

The sound of her footsteps echoed hollowly in the passageway, and the room was left in shadowed silence. Darkness filled the garret, and rain rattled on the slanting roof. The streetlight cast its beams on the drenched window, making sad little stars twinkle in the limpid drops sliding down the pane.

Early the next morning, a slim, ebony-colored box was carried out of the boardinghouse and off into the rainy gray dawn. A sign advertising "Room for Rent" appeared in a first-floor window.

Two of the landlady's closest friends sat in the stiff formality of the front parlor, sipping tea from cracked china cups and clucking their tongues sympathetically as she explained, in detail, just how she had been done out of a month's rent.

The attic room was left in tranquil loneliness for a long while. Dust motes hung motionless in the rays of light slanting through the window, and time was at a standstill. Winter softened almost imperceptibly into spring, and on one sunny day, when the trees were putting forth their first fragile tapestry of green against the sky, and the caressing zephyrs were wafting damp, delicious earthy smells into the air, the musty hush of the garret was disturbed by footsteps ascending the stairs. Light footsteps tapped nearer and nearer, followed by the heavy, halting tread of the proprietress. The attic door creaked open on rusty hinges to admit the elderly woman and a young girl. The latter stood silent in the center of the room, her gaze swiftly encompassing all the surroundings, resting with disappointment on the sagging bed, the dingy wash-stand, the cobwebbed rafters, and the muddy-colored dresser.

The landlady, noticing the girl's crestfallen glance, hastened to say almost apologetically, "It *is* a little small, but a bit o' scrubbin' an' polishin' can make a world o' difference, I allus say."

"Of course," the girl replied quickly, as she walked over to the bedstead and leaned to look out of the window. Her face flushed with pleasure as she exclaimed, "My! What a perfectly lovely view. I had no idea that you could see the ocean from here!"

"Yes," replied the older woman with no little pride, "the room *does* overlook the harbor, more or less. Well. I guess I'll leave you to get settled." Her voice floated back as she lumbered down the stairs.

With much tugging and coaxing, the girl opened the window and sat on the bed in the sunshine, sniffing the salty breeze delightedly. The beams cast a coppery gleam on her hair as she daydreamed in the refulgence of the spring afternoon and discovered that she could see romantic vistas of ocean, land, and sky from her attic window.

Sarah

Ts,[*] 7 March 1948, Lilly Library

The rhythmic thud of shelled peas falling into the copper saucepan filled the sunny kitchen with a pleasant, almost musical, sound. Through the half-open kitchen door the drowsy summer landscape showed broad fields and green patches of woodland hemstitched together by a thin line of dusty white road that wound down through the valley and then lost itself in the dim blue haze of far-off hills.

The woman rocking back and forth in the sturdy wicker chair was a product of a harsh, barren winter countryside, and her stiff, reserved posture seemed out of place in the midst of the mellow summer afternoon. The rigid angle of her back did not conform to the comfortable curves of the cushioned rocker. As she moved to and fro, her gnarled, gaunt hands traveled from the pile of pods on the table beside her to the pan in her lap with perfect economy of motion. Straight wisps of steel-gray hair were drawn back relentlessly from her face to a tight, gray bun at the nape of her lean, wrinkled neck; and Age, with its unflinching crayon, had penciled deep wrinkles that spread in a network from her keen blue eyes to her thin, taut mouth.

---

[*] Typescript with holograph corrections and additions by SP.

A noisy little clock on the shelf above the stove proclaimed the passage of minutes with loud, self-important ticks.

"Sary, Sary!" The plaintive voice rose and trembled querulously in the warm summer air. With a serene, unruffled countenance, Sarah rose, deposited her unfinished task on the checkered cloth of the kitchen table, and proceeded with firm steps to the inner recesses of the house from whence issued the complaining cry. The rocking chair, left empty, gradually slowed its tempo and came to a standstill.

Sarah returned after a while, bearing a tray of dirty dishes. She placed them in the sink, ran water into the tub, and began to wash them. The chore was so simple and familiar that it required no concentration on her part, and while she went through the motions automatically, bits of scenes and scattered thoughts flashed unbidden to her mind. As she gazed out of the window before her, her musings were accompanied by the companionable clatter of sudsy chinaware and occasional tinkling crescendos of sound as glasses and silver collided blindly in the depths of the dishpan.

"Aunt Jane always takes a nap after lunch . . . Poor thing. Must be tiresome to be caged up in the same room week and week, month after month . . . Never would let us get her a wheel chair . . . Mother can't help around the house like she used to before Dad died . . . two winters ago . . . It seems longer'n that, somehow . . . She got a lot of her strength from Dad, I guess. Her resolve sort of fell away when he was gone . . . She's no better than a child without him . . . Must get Mandy to go down the pasture to get some berries . . . Preserves are almost gone, and Jane does like them so. Mandy . . . that girl! Always off somewhere when I want her . . . Couldn't manage without her runnin' errands and cookin' meals when I go callin' . . . Gracious, but it's hot today . . . Don't the garden smell nice, though! . . . How long have I kept it up now?"

She fumbled mentally into the past.

A young girl about ten years old came running up the road to the freshly painted farmhouse that blinked complacently in the morning sunshine. Banging the screen door heedlessly behind her, she danced inside.

"Mother! Mother!" she shouted jubilantly as she raced from room to room, searching. The figure of a woman detached itself from the shadows in the hall and glided toward the child.

"Hush, hush!" she said petulantly. "Can't a body have a moment's peace without you rushing about the banging doors?" Then, more kindly, "Now, what is it, Sary-girl?"

The child looked down at the braided rug on the floor and replied in a subdued tone, "Daddy's going to show me how to plant a real garden in the yard." Then, in a second wave of enthusiasm, she burst out, "And I'm going to grow everything—even pansies!"

Yes, Sarah sighed briefly as she dried the last glass, the flower garden *had* been a comfort when all else failed. It had grown dear to her heart with the passing of years. The freshness of the larkspur, sweet william, hollyhocks and the rest reminded her of her vivacious, young niece, Mandy. Almost sixteen she was now. Sixteen!

Sitting down in the rocker again, Sarah took up the saucepan, and the kitchen was once more lulled by the soft thud of peas falling into the copper saucepan.

The road to the old farmhouse was bathed in moonlight, and occasionally an arched yellow line in the heavens marked the path of a shooting star. The creaking tune of crickets sounded in the dew-drenched grass as a slim young girl slipped up the front walk, smiling a secret smile to herself in the twilight. She was met at the door by her mother, older now, and prematurely stooped. At once the elderly woman greeted the girl with a tearful, "It's your father, Sary."

Fear clutched at the girl's heart. "Wh-what's happened, Mother? What's wrong?"

"He was j-just chopping wood . . . The axe slipped and . . . and cut his leg." Here the woman's shoulders shook with dry sobs. "I don't know when he'll walk again," she whimpered. "I'll need you, Sary."

The girl stared at her mother in stunned bewilderment and disbelief.

"But, Mother! Just when Tom wants to marry me and . . . and be a minister . . . and go out West!"

"You just can't leave me now, Sary," whined the older woman. And Sarah was never to forget her mother's pleading, accusing eyes.

The clock wheezed on. The soft patter of shelled peas marking time unevenly. Somehow I never did leave, thought Sarah. Somehow there was always something.

The rosy light of late afternoon shone through the window and fell in a faint square on the linoleum floor. A burst of song filled the air, and Sarah saw Mandy walking up the back steps with her usual buoyant tread. She carried a bouquet of flowers, and she seemed to radiate life and warmth as she pushed the kitchen door open wide and turned toward the stairs.

"Oh, Aunt Sarah!" she exclaimed breathlessly, unable to hold back her enthusiasm, "Louisa's brother drove us down to the bay and took us sailing. We had the most wonderful picnic . . ." Here she trailed off, gazed at her aunt moving primly about the stove in preparation for supper and wondered pityingly if this withered woman had ever been young.

"We had *such* fun," she announced, and then, commiseratingly, "But you wouldn't understand." Mandy smoothed down her wind-blown hair and disappeared upstairs. "I'll be right back and help get supper," she called.

Sarah turned to hide a bitter little smile. "You wouldn't understand . . ." The universal echo of youth . . .

She stood by the table and gazed out through the doorway into the gathering dusk. The red disc of sun sank still lower in the west. A sudden gust of evening breeze started up and, with a sound that reverberated through the quiet house, the kitchen door blew shut.

The Visitor

Ts,[*] 27–8 March 1948, Lilly Library

She's been here for five days, now, and I'm almost sorry that she's going to leave this afternoon. Of course, I felt entirely different about her before yesterday's episode with Susan and the dog.

As I write, the faint light of dawn is rosy behind the mountains, and an early-morning fog veils the valley. The summer heat has not yet descended, and the long fringe of grass around the porch is still frosted with the night dews. A locust is droning in the elm tree, and the drowsy voice of a cricket accompanies him. The atmosphere is so calm and cool that it's hard to believe the events of yesterday are more than a distant dream. The whole affair would have never occurred if Esther Holbrook had not come to spend a few days with us.

She arrived almost a week ago in a confusion of suitcases, boxes, and leather leashes for her pampered cocker spaniel, Rusty. Mother had told me about Esther after we received her telegram. She was traveling up in our part of the state and wanted to visit us for a few days before leaving for her work

---

[*] Typescript with holograph corrections by SP and comments by her English teacher, Wilbury Crockett. Written for English 21 at Wellesley High School, which she completed in 1947–8. Only SP's corrections are reflected in the text.

in New York. Esther and Mother had gone to Art School together, and both had planned careers in fashion designing. However, Mother had married after graduation, and Esther had been the one who succeeded in her ambition. She and Mother had somehow been too busy to see each other for many years—Esther with her annual trips from New York to Paris and Mother with four children to take care of—but they had maintained a faithful written correspondence. Now, at last, the two friends were going to meet again.

Mother and I arranged the house and made sure that everything was spotless before we drove to the station with Susan. I don't know exactly how I had pictured Miss Holbrook, but I was surprised to see a slim, blonde woman with a poised, self-assured smile step gracefully down to the railroad platform, a cocker spaniel tugging impatiently at the leash wrapped firmly about her wrist. Esther Holbrook glanced about, saw Mother, hesitated a moment, then rushed toward us, arms outstretched. Even in the first confused moments of greeting, I could not help but notice that Esther Holbrook had a fascinating air about her. There was no definable thing in her apparel, from her low straw sandals to her frothy flowered hat, that in itself suggested an unusual character, but, nevertheless, a delightful cosmopolitan atmosphere was there. Little Susan was intrigued by the dog, for the playful puppy jumped around in the car, trying to lap everyone's face at once. We made the long journey up the mountain road to the farm in a seemingly brief time. Daddy was at the gate to greet us, Duncan in his arms and John standing somewhat beside him.

Esther was delighted with the entire farm and seemed charmed with Father's customary explanation that in the summer he was "just a farmer," although he served the community as a minister during the rest of the year. One could see that she and Father liked each other immediately, and when they discovered that they had been to many of the same spots in Europe, Mother told them to sit down and chat while she prepared supper.

The evening passed quickly. When Mother and I left Esther to her room, she was amazed at its neat pine-paneled walls, the dainty, ruffled curtains and bedspread. Evidently she had not expected to find such a cozy place in the "wilds of Maine."

It was a change to have such a totally different person become a temporary part of our household, and Esther's presence certainly cast an influence over us all. Daddy was at once chivalrous and entertaining. Mother went about her work quietly and serenely, listening when she could to the charming little stories that Esther told about her experiences abroad. John would frequently linger in the background, awed, and yet somewhat unwilling to be found listening to women's conversation. Little Susan displayed her best behavior, as she had been immediately attracted by the pretty woman who paid so much attention to her; and baby Duncan was his usual smiling self.

On the first morning after Esther Holbrook's arrival, we had all eaten breakfast and begun the morning chores before she came lightly downstairs and into the kitchen, looking young and rested. Suddenly I was aware of the contrast between Esther and Mother. It just didn't seem fair! Esther's life had been so thrilling and carefree, it's no wonder that she looked years younger than Mother. Yet, at that moment, I didn't like Esther at all—she was just too beautiful and flawless.

The days slipped by unobtrusively. Up on the mountain in the warm summer sunlight and pure air, time seems to be nonexistent, and eternity is marked only by the succession of dark, star-spattered nights and lazy, sun-mellowed days. In the evening, Esther, Mother, and Dad would sit outside on the porch after the two youngest were in bed and talk of old times. While they watched the shooting stars, Esther would describe an experience in Paris or an amusing incident that occurred in London, always managing to suggest the slight superiority of the career woman over the woman who had forfeited ambition and settled down in marriage.

Yesterday, at dawn, I awoke with the realization that it was only one more day before Esther would depart on the train for New York and points abroad. I hoped for Mother's sake that everything would continue smoothly to the very end—that the children's unusually co-operative behavior would last that long.

The last of the luncheon dishes had been put away, and Dad and John were chopping wood behind the barn while Mother and Esther reminisced together in the backyard. Duncan was taking his afternoon nap, and Susan was frolicking with Rusty on the lawn, playfully pulling his ears every now and then. Suddenly Rusty gave an agonized growl and Susan emitted a piercing scream as a furious bundle of fur hurled itself at her face.

Esther cried out, "He's bitten her!" and Mother dashed over and picked up Susan, who was choking with sobs. Blood spurted from a deep claw mark between her eye and the bridge of her nose. For a dreadful moment we thought that her eye had been injured. After bathing the cut with cold water and partially stopping the bleeding, Mother called Dad to get the car, and the trio vanished down the hill in a cloud of dust, bound for the village doctor.

John, who had arrived in time to see Susan carried off, asked if she would be all right, and then, unwilling to display any emotion before Esther, went resolutely back to chopping wood.

Esther Holbrook was badly shaken by the incident, especially as Susan had been attacked by her dog. She collapsed weakly in the deck chair and managed, amid nervous sobs, to ask me pleadingly how soon we'd know if Susan was all right. Repeatedly she murmured that Rusty had never hurt anyone before, that she just didn't know what had come over him, and that she felt so guilty about the whole affair. As accidents were almost commonplace occurrences in our family, it seemed strange that an adult should be so overwrought. I attempted to calm her by explaining that evidently Susan had pulled the puppy's whiskers and, blinded by pain, the little dog had clawed her face. Of course, I could well understand Miss Holbrook's feeling of responsibility and, as she gradually quieted down, I persuaded her to tell me more about herself.

"You know, Margot," she said, "I never realized how empty my life has been without a family until I saw your mother and father together. They form a unit—one incomplete without the other. I always used to pity women who married right after finishing school, because I never realized what a full life they can experience. Your mother, for instance, is one of the happiest women I know. I admire her and, I think, envy her just a little."

Somehow, after she had admitted that her life had not brought her the completeness which she desired, Esther Holbrook didn't appear so flawless and invulnerable any longer. Strangely enough, I liked her very much better from then on, and I was delighted when she told me that she wanted me to spend a week with her in New York next winter.

When Mother and Dad came home at dusk with a subdued Susan, we were infinitely relieved to find that the child's injury was not as serious as we had feared at first. After the children were in bed, I went upstairs to finish a story I was writing. As I sat by my open window, I could hear the voices of the three grown-ups rising and falling companionably as they sat on the porch together.

This afternoon, Mother, Dad, and I drove with Esther down the mountain to the railroad station in the valley. We helped her up the steep train steps with her suitcases and waited on the platform until her face appeared at the window. Even though Esther was as attractive as always, there were shadows beneath her eyes and a general attitude of weariness. As the hoarse shriek of the train whistle rent the air, the smiling face of Esther Holbrook moved past us with increasing momentum. Just before the train curved out of sight around the bend, I glimpsed the gay wave of a bright silk handkerchief.

Dad turned to Mother with a whimsical smile. "It's been pretty hard for her," he said sympathetically.

The Island: A Radio Play

Ts,* *c.*13 May 1948, Lilly Library

Sound of water on shore: Shhh . . . Shhhhhh . . . Shhhhhhhh.

MAN'S VOICE: (*Calling faintly from distance*) Hel . . . ennnnn . . . Hel . . . ennnn . . . Hel . . . ennnnnn . . .

HELEN: (*Meditatively*) The island. I had never noticed it until that day—that day when they found his boat drifting empty, alone, near the shore. The sea was calm by then—calm as a cat after it has devoured a struggling bird. Almost a year ago it was—a year ago when the village fishermen brought in his boat. They had come up from the beach and stood before my cottage door, obviously ill-at-ease, muttering among themselves. I opened the door. They stood silently, looking at me. As I remember, Horace Cooper moistened his lips and spoke first . . .

Music fades in and out slowly.

HORACE: (*Brokenly*) We saw . . . we saw your husband's boat . . . drifting near the reef . . . the storm . . . last night . . . he must have . . . must have been . . .

Sound of water again.

HELEN: (*Continuing narrative*) For days and nights after that I sat waiting . . . waiting. Although his boat was moored empty off shore I could not believe that he was gone forever. I listened for his footsteps above the ceaseless sounding of the breakers on the beach. At times I fancied I could hear them—the steps—approaching the house as they used to every evening. I would listen eagerly, then rush to the door, fling it open, and peer out into the darkness. (*Brokenly*) Nothing. Nothing but the waves washing, always washing in the pebbles. (*Pause, then, more bravely*) Gradually I became

---

* Co-authored by Mary Ventura and written for broadcast as part of Wilbury Crockett's English 21 at Wellesley High School, which SP completed in 1947–8; with holograph corrections and additions in an unknown hand, probably by Ventura. Typescript dated 1949 by SP; however, an article published in the Wellesley *Townsman* on 13 May 1948 reads, 'Two members of the class, Sylvia Plath and Mary Ventura, have collaborated in the writing of an original radio play, *The Island*, which will bring to a close the Sophomore series.'

accustomed to living alone—accustomed to the continual waiting—for I still hoped that he might be found somehow—found alive. The days slipped by, one after the other, monotonous, lonely, marked only by the arrival of the grocery boy each week. He would stop a while and chat with me—I know not why. (*Bitterly*) Why should he have bothered to talk to a lonely woman like me, who lived by herself, away from the sociable circle of the villagers—who did nothing but braid rugs and weave mats for the crowd of tourists that came and went each summer?! Yes, this was my only livelihood. Once in a while I would take out the rowboat and row along the shore, but that was not often. Well, as I was saying, the grocer's boy came each week, and I grew to look forward to his visits . . .

Sound of knocking.

Sound of groceries banging on table.

HELEN: (*Coming in*) Oh, Andrew! Put everything on the table.

ANDREW: (*Cheerfully*) OK. Nice weather we've been having. (*Pause*) But it looks like a storm's coming up.

HELEN: (*Dully*) Yes. (*Pause, then, more brightly*) I suppose you still have a long way ahead of you. Doesn't it get tiresome after a while?

ANDREW: Oh, no! I only have to stop at the Coopers' before I'm through for the day. Well, I guess I'll be going.

Door bangs shut.

HELEN: Yes . . . I knew there'd be a storm tonight. That feeling of dread always comes over me before a storm, for still I remember . . .

Music fades in strongly, then out.

MRS. COOPER: (*Sugary*) He*l*loo, Andrew!

ANDREW: H'lo there, Mrs. Cooper! (*Bangs groceries down.*)

MRS. COOPER: (*Inquisitively*) Had a hard day today? It's too bad you have to make such a long trip out to Helen Thomas' house. The poor lonely woman. How has she been lately?

ANDREW: Oh, she seems to be all right—just a little lonesome, I guess.

MRS. COOPER: (*With eager curiosity*) I wonder what she does with herself all day! I think she's carrying it a little too far—living like a hermit when we'd be just as glad to have her move to the village. What with all our clubs and societies we could help her forget her . . . grief. It's a wonder she doesn't become a bit . . . queer, seeing she's just by herself all this time.

ANDREW: Well, I don't know, she seems to keep herself busy, and her house is as neat as any others I've seen.

MRS. COOPER: (*Indignantly surprised*) Well! I suppose that's only natural since she's indoors *all day*!

ANDREW: (*Defending Helen*) Oh, she goes out sometimes in her boat.

MRS. COOPER: Well! I never!

Pause.

Music fades in slowly, then out.

Clinking of china, silver, sound of tea pouring.

MRS. COOPER: More tea, Horace?

HORACE: Yes, just a cup.

MRS. COOPER: You know, Horace, I was talking with Andrew today about Helen Thomas, and what do you suppose he told me? (*Dramatic pause*) He said she actually goes out rowing every day! (*Very indignant*) What woman in her right mind would do that?!!

HORACE: (*Wryly*) I'm sure *you* never would, dear.

MRS. COOPER: (*Ignoring him*) Well, all the same, I think it's perfectly horrid that she should live all by herself without any normal activities . . . no company or anything.

HORACE: Well, *you* might go to see her once in a while.

MRS. COOPER: (*Shocked*) Me? See *her*?! (*Meditatively*) See her? You know, I actually think I will.

Music fades in

HELEN: Yes, she came to see me one afternoon, as if I didn't know why. The minute she stepped into the room, she looked around curiously and then started to ask questions. She thought she was doing me a favor, trying to get me to tell her all about my husband and my life after his disappearance. But, pry as she might, she could never find out my one secret—the island. I had seen its shape looming in the fog that night they brought in his boat. A few times since then I saw it again—usually it appeared at dusk, in the fog, or sometimes even at night when the moonlight shone on the water, I could see its dark shadow. Although I could never see the island in the daytime, the thought of it was ever present in my mind—elusive, yet inviting. One night I could resist the island's beckoning no longer. I was determined to explore it, for somehow it appeared to be the missing link between me and my husband. I arose in the foggy darkness before dawn and headed the rowboat for the island. As I left the shore, the outlines of the island became clearer. Suddenly an uncanny sensation overcame me and I shivered. In the dense, chill, cold air, I had an odd feeling of nearness to something—someone familiar. The feeling increased its magnetic power of attraction as I approached the island. I was on the brink of some discovery. Then, as the clear pink light of dawn touched the sky, the mist began to melt away, and even as I watched, the island faded and was gone. Incredulous, I looked around me . . . The sun shone on an empty sea!

Music fades in.

Door bangs.

Pause.

ANDREW: Here I am again with your groceries, Mrs. Thomas. Sorry I'm so late. It's already getting dark.

HELEN: Oh, hello, Andrew. (*Aside, in a softer tone*) Now I shall ask him if he can see the island, too. I *can't* be wrong. It must be there . . . I can see it in the dusk. (*Casually to Andrew*) How's fishing been lately?

ANDREW: It's been pretty good.

HELEN: (*Casually*) Have you ever tried fishing by the island out there?

ANDREW: (*Innocently*) What island?

HELEN: (*Mumbling*) Oh, nothing . . .

ANDREW: (*Ill-at-ease*) Well . . . guess I'll be going.

Door bangs.

HELEN: (*Confusedly*) He asked me "what island," but it's right there in the bay. I can see it. If I can see the island, why can't he?

Music fades in.

Clinking of china and glasses.

HORACE: What's the matter dear? You look sort of disturbed tonight.

MRS. COOPER: (*Exclaiming*) Oh, it's no wonder! I heard the most awful thing today! (*In a gossiping tone*) You know, Andrew, the grocer's boy, told me only this morning that that Thomas woman thinks there's an island out in the bay. I told you there was something odd about that woman, and . . . mark my words . . . someday she'll do something dangerous.

Music fades in.

HELEN: I have tried to forget about the island, but I cannot. I must force myself to concentrate on my work. I *will* not . . . I *will* not look out of the window. (*Pause*) But wait! . . . I hear it now! . . . His voice—calling my name. (*Like an amazed child*) And out of the window! . . . It is there! . . . The island!!!! Etched in the moonlight . . . (*Tenderly*) And his voice . . . his voice drifts to my ears even over the sound of the waves. And it is coming from (*dramatic pause*) the island! (*Brokenly*) It's no use. I can't stay in this little room while he is out there . . . calling. I am stumbling down the beach . . . starting out in the rowboat . . . approaching the island. The voice grows louder, louder. (*Triumphantly*) But this time . . . this time the island remains! It *is* real, after all! Ah! The keel is grating on the shore. I see a dark shape—a human shape—off in the shadows. (*Joyously*) At last my longing is to be satisfied! (*Slowly . . . carefully*) I must step out of the boat. (*A splash.*) It is icy cold (*Faintly gurgling* [*if possible*]) . . . I'm sinking down . . . down . . . Oh, but I know . . . I *know* . . . *he* is . . . *waiting* . . .

MAN'S VOICE: (*Growing louder, gurgling* [*if possible*]) HEL . . . ENNNNNNN . . . HEL . . . ENNN . . . HEL . . . EN.

Sound of waves drowns it out.

Music comes in triumphantly.

THE END.

Gramercy Park

Ts,* 1948, Lilly Library

Spring is always a rather difficult time for an old lady like me because it's a kind of opposite mood. I mean, everything in the world is growing young and fresh, while only I seem to be growing old. Spring has always been a little hard for me to take. This year, however, it was different. This year I met Alison.

The winter lasted so long that I thought I'd never see the earth again, so deep was the snow. But spring did come at last, and with none of the usual hovering between warm and cold weather. One day it was winter, with ice on the ground, and the next it was April, with soft, earthy-smelling breezes blowing in the streets. I had a second-floor room right across from Gramercy Park, and I could look on a level with the treetops over a sea of dancing green leaves that moved to and fro in little waves at the slightest puff of wind.

In preference to all other city places, Spring chooses to make the parks bloom first. While the undersized maple trees by the sidewalks are yet gray and bare, the trees in the park are putting forth a tapestry of leaves against the sky. But although the neat green lawns and the mathematically arranged tulip beds offer some relief from the sooty streets and the geometric rows of buildings, there should be one corner where trees, shrubs, and flowers are planted in profusion and allowed to grow wild. Such a place may be found in my corner of Gramercy Park, and it was here that I like to go each afternoon. While I sat on a bench in the metallic spring sunlight, I would watch the people passing by and amuse myself by trying to guess what they were thinking and where they were going. Gradually, since I came often, I began to recognize a few of the people who frequented this corner as I did.

There was a young girl, about eight or nine years old, who came alone each day. I can remember her plainly. Even now I can see her skipping rope gracefully over the winding gravel paths, the sunlight gleaming on her long, yellow hair. She always wore a ruffled white dress, and her shiny black patent-leather shoes twinkled in the sunshine as her feet jumped swiftly over the flying rope. She was, at times, essentially a child, yet she had such a wise old look in her eyes that I began to wonder just who she was. Anyway, she seemed to belong

---

* SP included a print of *Gramercy Park* (1920) by American realist painter George Bellows with the story.

to everybody. She would stop to talk to people along the path as if they were familiar friends, and I never did discover her secret of conversation. She used to sit seriously on a bench, her jump rope dragging on the ground, and talk to a white-haired man in a rusty black suit just as if she were another grown-up. I didn't know what she said, but after she had walked away, the old man would smile to himself as he listened to the robins singing in the trees.

Among the other strollers in the park was a plump, motherly nursemaid, wheeling a baby carriage and carefully watching her two other charges—a small boy on a wooden tricycle and a little girl that ran along beside him. The nurse sat in the shade by a lilac bush, rocking the carriage back and forth while the other children played nearby. The boy and girl took turns riding, but once they both wanted the tricycle at the same time. The boy was on the bike, and the girl stood in front of him, trying to pull his hands off the handlebars.

"It's my turn," she cried.

"It's my bike," the boy returned smugly.

"It is not! It's mine," she shrieked unreasonably.

"Why you naughty children," said the girl with the jump rope, coming over, "you can both ride together, sillies."

And she showed the little girl how to stand on the back of the bike while the boy pedaled.

"What's your name?" they asked her as a kind of children's password. She hesitated a moment.

"Alison," she said at last.

"How many times can you jump without stopping?" the girl asked shyly.

"Oh, hundreds," replied Alison with airy superiority. "Watch."

She started to jump in the same spot, counting. The rope flew faster and faster, while her flashing feet hardly touched the ground. The two children watched in mute admiration.

"Ninety-eight—ninety-nine—a hundred. There! See!" gasped Alison breathlessly. "I could get up to five hundred if I really wanted to."

Each afternoon a tall young man escorted a slim young woman and her dog to a bench in the sunlight. The couple sat and talked until the air grew chill and twilight drew near. Evidently the two were good friends, for they seemed so happy with each other. They came from work, I guess, because they both arrived through different entrances. As I said, these two came regularly, and I only noticed them because they appeared so gay and youthful.

The spring days passed as swiftly as the raveled white clouds overhead, torn by the wind and swept away down the sky. One afternoon, when I was feeling especially lonely, I found Alison seated on my bench, waiting, as it turned out, for me. I greeted her in a friendly manner, and somehow we got to talking. She gossiped in her frank, childish way about the people in the park, and I realized that this companionable chatter was what I had been longing for.

"That man," she said, nodding toward the young couple, "is a reporter, and she works in a store. They meet here every afternoon."

She rambled on, telling about the old man who was a violinist out of a job and about the nursemaid and the three children.

"The girl is the boy's cousin, but they've been brought up as brother and sister. Have you noticed how nicely they've played with each other lately? They have to make the most of every minute together."

"And why is that?" I queried.

Alison looked hard at me for the moment and then answered nonchalantly, "Oh, the girl is going away soon, I guess."

The following day I noticed the young woman sitting on the bench alone for the first time. She waited until dusk, but her companion didn't come that day, nor the one after that, nor the one after that. Alison stopped at the woman's bench once or twice, patting the furry dog and talking. The woman's thin face brightened at something the girl told her, and the very next day, a Sunday it was, a tall figure entered the iron gates and hurried over to the place where she was sitting alone. After a few words of greeting, they started talking earnestly.

"He's been given a promotion," explained Alison, who was resting beside me, as she saw where I was looking. "He couldn't meet her at the usual time, because his office hours were changed, and he didn't know how to get in touch with her. She thought he didn't want to see her anymore and, well—I knew that he could come on Sunday afternoon, so I persuaded her to come here every day for a week. Everything's all right now."

After Alison had finished her rather lengthy story, I saw the nursemaid walking past us, pushing the carriage. The little boy was the only other child with her, and he lagged behind, scuffing the gravel with his shoes. He was dressed in a somber black suit.

"I wonder where his playmate is," I mused aloud.

"Why, I've told you," said Alison, surprised. "She has gone away."

The next morning I awoke to the sound of rain splashing in the gutters and the low rumble of summer thunder. Sleepily I shuffled into my slippers and got up to close the window, for the rain had blown in and made a little puddle on the sill. Across the street, in the deserted corner of the park, I saw a white-gowned figure skipping lightly down the paths.

"In all that rain," I said to myself. "How careless of her mother to let her go out in that thin dress."

Her golden hair clinging damply about her face, Alison knelt down by the tulip bed and touched a white blossom gently with one finger. Already, I noticed, the tulip season was gone, and most of the blossoms had faded. Then, before she passed out of sight down the sodden gravel walk, she turned and waved to someone I couldn't see.

The summer heat descended to stay after that rainstorm, and it was good to sit quietly in the cool, leafy shade of Gramercy Park. Children played on the lawns, and the old man in the rusty black suit walked by often, carrying his violin case. The young couple came with their dog, and I could see the sparkle of a ring on the woman's left hand as she held the leash. They nodded happily in my direction as they passed, and I realized that they had come together.

Nowhere did I see Alison. The last time I had seen her was on that drizzling morning of the thunderstorm. As I remembered her parting wave, I wondered if she had moved away.

Heat

Ts,[*] 1948, Lilly Library

There was no escape. The heat was everywhere. It penetrated the apartments and the air-conditioned offices. It permeated steel, brick, and stone. It rested like a palpable blanket over the city.

Judith Anders let the door of the office clang shut behind her. As she stepped out into the street, the heat from the pavement struck her with an almost physical impact. She braced herself against it and began to walk toward the corner. Mechanically she boarded the waiting bus and sank into a green plush sheet.

The only way to exist in such weather was to let one's mind slip easily into a semi-conscious state. She was dimly aware of the blood throbbing rhythmically against her temples. Her thoughts were brief, fragmentary, and they ran through idle channels.

Strange. Where did that sound come from? It was as if drums were beating softly in the distance. As she listened, they became louder, still louder. Then, suddenly, she heard a voice intoning solemnly, "Think, Judith, think. Think,

---

[*] Typescript has holograph and typewritten corrections and additions by SP.

Judith, think." The words were repeated over and over again, in perfect time with the drum.

"I'm thinking," she said to the voice inside of her. "I'm thinking."

She waited, concentrating.

"Why are you out in all this heat, Judith? Why?" The question hammered at her brain.

"I don't know, I don't know," the girl whispered, "but it's so hot, so hot."

"Ask yourself, Judith. Why are you here? Think."

She pressed a moist, sticky hand against her forehead. Then she rallied.

"Now, that's a silly question," she retorted somewhat defiantly. "Why is anybody here?"

"Exactly," remarked the voice. "Observe the man by your side. Mark his glazed stare—his limp form. See how he attempts to read that newspaper. The words, the numbers, flit without meaning though his brain. His world is completely impersonal. He can't think. He *won't* think." The voice continued in a kinder tone, "How many years have *you* lived here, worked here, Judith?"

"Five years, six years, how do I know?" she answered dazedly.

"Is it really so painful to reflect, to remember, Judith?" the voice asked gently.

"Oh yes, yes," the girl sighed wearily. "The same work, day in, day out." She went on bitterly, "Filing letters, pounding typewriters. So dull, so dull."

"Ah, but Judith," the tones were rich and vibrant, "you can get away if you try. You're young yet. There's still time." The voice grew urgent. "Break the pattern, Judith. Find yourself."

"Find myself," Judith repeated stupidly. "How? I'm already settled."

"Never say that," the voice interrupted sharply. "You have other interests, haven't you? You like to draw, to write, to play piano! Any job, any job that you're interested in, any job that's alive and vital do. Opportunity waits everywhere, once you are aware of it."

Judith rose automatically as the bus paused at her stop, but the voice followed her as she crossed the street to her boardinghouse.

"You can do it if you try, Judith."

Mrs. Smith was rocking her huge bulk back and forth in the chair on the porch. She fanned herself vigorously.

"Hello, Miss Anders," she greeted her fellow-boarder. "Hot enough for you?" She chortled at her witticism. Judith managed a small, artificial smile.

She opened the door and moved across the shabby front parlor to the staircase, where she encountered the landlady.

"Hot enough for you?" the older woman questioned sympathetically.

The girl trudged up the two flights to her room. She opened the door. The place was stifling.

"Doors, doors, always opening and shutting doors, Judith," mocked the voice. "But there's one you haven't opened yet. One more door, Judith."

"Where? Where?" the girl cried piteously.

The voice was silent for a moment. It did not answer.

Judith lay down on the bed. The heat panted outside the window like a live thing.

"Stay awake, Judith," the voice commanded sternly.

"It's too hot," she whimpered. Her eyelids closed heavily, and she began to breathe more slowly. Almost immediately she was lost in the depths of sleep.

Suddenly the telephone rang.

"Judith, Judith," the voice prodded frantically. The girl lay motionless.

"Your chance, Judith, your chance to open the door! Answer before it's too late! A new life, Judith! Answer, before they call someone else!"

She slept on.

"Wake up, Judith, before it's . . ." the voice faded, "too late . . ."

The phone stopped ringing. The voice ceased.

Only the sound of Judith's even breathing broke the heavy silence.

The heat penetrated everywhere. It enveloped all, conquered all. There was no escape.

The Brink

Ts,* 1948, Lilly Library

Janet sat motionless on the green plush seat of the bus, staring vacantly out of the window. She was conscious of nothing but the ever-changing view. Her whole being concentrated itself in her large brown eyes. She seemed to possess no body. Tentatively, without moving, she sent thought waves down to her hands. Yes, they were resting on her lap as usual, and she could feel the crumpled thinness of the bus transfer between her fingers. A numbing lassitude flooded through her veins, and she was conscious only of the scenery once more. She gazed steadily

---

* Typed in top-right corner: 'Sylvia Plath, Age 15 / 26 Elmwood Road / Wellesley 81, Mass.' An additional typescript of the story indicates it was submitted for English 21 at Wellesley High School, which she completed in 1947–8. Submitted to *Seventeen* in 1950 with 'A Day in June', 'Among the Shadow Throngs' and 'And Summer Will Not Come Again'.

at the passing landscape. It didn't look real. The bus window framed something artificial—something prepared solely for her amusement. The people were mere puppets going about trivial tasks. For what purpose? She almost smiled. With an impersonal curiosity, she watched the women scurrying from store to store. Their motions appeared frenzied, aimless.

Janet let trifling thoughts play across her mind. How distorted her reflection was on the side of that car! Her features blended, ran into each other, and finally vanished as the car sped past. Another auto took its place and kept pace beside the bus for a short while. The driver, a woman with a fat, pallid face, stared ahead at the road with glassy eyes, her fingers clutching the steering wheel. Janet watched her casually until the car dropped behind. As soon as the woman passed out of the range of her vision, Janet promptly forgot her.

All the while, the bus rolled on, on. At each turn of the wheels, the perspective of Janet's view shifted. Her eyes scanned the continuous rows of houses and city buildings. Already it seemed that she had passed too many of them. Why were there so many buildings—so many people? It was quite annoying that there be a superfluous quantity of such puppets—such absurd little lives.

On a nearby railroad track, a riveter was repairing a dented tie. His machine sent an arc of glowing copper sparks into the air. All about him were men—rushing back and forth with tools and wire. The picture held Janet's attention for a moment, but then was replaced quickly by a new one.

A young girl stood by a drugstore, talking to a friend, not heeding the cries of the little child in the carriage beside her. These, and a thousand other images, came and went with each turn of the wheels. What did they signify? Nothing. Janet could have seen all the people lying dead in the gutters and not felt one twinge of emotion. These people, these things she saw, had no identity. She was utterly remote from them, feeling complacent, almost happy that nothing mattered. Once more she was conscious only of the thoughts eddying through her mind as they accompanied the shifting window pictures. The thoughts, too, were odd, detached. She rejoiced in the ruthless, forward motion of the bus.

She had sat thus for a long time, when somewhere at the bottom of the deep pool that was her mind, she felt a curious stirring. The curious feeling grew and started upward in tiny bubbles that broke when they reached the pool's surface.

Across the street there was forsythia blooming on the riverbank. She could see the winding river between those two tall buildings. There was another bus over there, too, only it was headed in the opposite direction from Janet's. She could see the faces at the window, smiling, nodding, but they did not see her.

The cold, impersonal waters of her mind closed over the bubbles. Why should she arouse herself about forsythia or people on a bus? They were inconsequential, as was everything else.

But the bubbles rose again. Insistently they burst against the surface of her mind.

There was something familiar in the lines of that marble building across the street. The familiarity tugged painfully at her heart. She began to hope that the bus would stop for a traffic light so that she could look at the window-picture more carefully. If she wanted to look at that building, to walk over its grassy lawns, why couldn't she? Why not?

The bubbles hurtled upward, breaking loudly against the surface.

When had she started her journey? She had been on the bus for ages, but she remembered nothing before that. There had been houses, people, and cars, but no beginning—nothing before her bus ride. Her memories suddenly trailed down into darkness. The motion of the bus was ironic now. The turning wheels mocked her. They gulped up the miles and mocked her for not remembering. Darkness, she recalled. A dark tunnel! That was it! She had come out of a dark tunnel on the bus. Still, there was something, something more.

The icy waters tried to close over the bubbles, but she would not let them.

The forsythia waved gently in the breeze. The buildings beckoned her to stop and loiter in the streets. The bus had stopped for a traffic light, and the picture remained—tantalizing, but somehow unattainable. She had to get off the bus. Get off!

The bubbles rose together and burst with a tremendous impact.

Janet struggled to her feet and stumbled down the narrow aisle. She stood beside the bus driver. A nervous sensation passed over her. Why was he staring at the road like that? She tried to get his attention, shaking him by the shoulder.

"I want to get off. Open the door! Let me out!" Her voice was urgent, trembling.

At last the driver turned to her with a deep stare. His eyes were thrown into shadow under the visor of his black cap, but she could feel them regarding her contemptuously.

"You don't understand," she cried desperately. "I'm on the wrong bus. I've got to get off."

She forced the crumbled transfer into his cold white hand. Still his eyes looked out at her. Then he spoke slowly in a stern, hollow voice. "No one gets off my bus till the end of the line. This is an express."

Janet regarded him with horror. As he saw her terrified countenance, a slight softening passed over his hitherto inflexible features. He pressed a switch, and the door beside her creaked open with a reluctant sound. She bounded lightly, swiftly over the step; and a blast of fresh, salty air struck her face as she reached the street. The door closed behind her, shutting her out, irretrievably. Warm relief overwhelmed her. Unaccountably she felt as if she had escaped something deadly—escaped after a difficult struggle. The wind whipped her coat about her legs and blew her long hair into her eyes. The air was raw and cold, but she didn't care. Across the street the forsythia and friendly buildings beckoned. The something that had eluded her on the bus would be waiting across the street. Her heart took up the lilting refrain—across the street, across the street—it sang inside her.

The light changed to green, and the bus moved past her with gathering speed. It was headed for a dark tunnel just a little further on. As the bus rolled by, she glanced up. It was only then that she noticed the pale, cadaverous faces of the other passengers staring down at her. Their gaze was remote—curious—impersonal.

In This Field We Wander Through

Ts,[*] 1948, Lilly Library

As the bell rang to end the last period, Joyce picked up her books mechanically and started down to her locker. The chatter of gay voices rose on all sides, but she walked through the eddies of conversation calm, unscathed. Beneath her mask-like smile confused thoughts whirled. She attempted to arrange them in their customary neat patterns.

(Math done . . . science . . . English . . . Latin . . . history . . . No homework over vacation . . .)

She shoved her books into her locker and slammed the door with a reckless bang.

(Going to forget I ever heard of school for a whole week . . . I don't have to worry . . . Got all As again this term . . . Darn!)

"Hey, Joyce! Wait a sec!"

The voice affected her like the sound of a dentist's drill. She gritted her teeth as Tracy, her supposedly best friend, came running down the stairs, hastening with surprising agility through the slow-moving crowd.

---

[*] Typescript with holograph corrections by SP.

"Going home?" Tracy questioned breathlessly, glancing up at Joyce with the confident look of one who asks a question that has only one inevitable answer. Joyce moaned inwardly.

(Why can't I ever get away from her . . . the old pest . . .)

"Guess so," she replied.

"What are you planning to do this vacation," Tracy queried brightly as they came out of the school into the faded winter afternoon. The sharp, cold air filled Joyce with a sense of freedom.

"Oh . . . I'm going out tonight," she remarked airily.

"Where to?"

"Just dancing." With hidden malice Joyce watched Tracy give a gasp as if she had been slapped in the face.

"With who?" Tracy's voice was taut with jealousy.

(She's jealous . . . Well, I'll show her . . . just cause *she's* never had a boyfriend . . .)

"Oh, Tommy . . . you know, Tommy Grayson."

Tracy's envy overcame her. She gave a forced laugh.

"That drip! You poor kid. You should see how dumb he is in Latin."

(That little cat . . . just cause *she's* never had anyone . . .)

"Mee-yow," returned Joyce, laughing. She purred inside with a contented smugness.

(No one can hurt me anymore . . . nothing can go wrong . . . I have a date . . . nothing else matters . . .)

Joyce shut her ears to Tracy, who was babbling endlessly about her Christmas plans.

(Poor kid . . . nothing to compensate . . . just books . . . books and violin lessons . . . I'll get free from her somehow . . . it was different before . . . now she's dull . . . How I hate her talk . . . always about herself . . . me, me, me all day long . . .)

Joyce sniffed the cool, moist air.

(Damp pine needles . . . wood smoke . . . wet snow . . . Christmas smells . . .)

There was an expectant pause in Tracy's chatter. She repeated her question, pleasantly oblivious of Joyce's inattentiveness.

"Can you come to my recital?"

(Recital? . . . Recital . . . oh, yes . . . Saturday . . . Before I'd go and hear her play that violin . . .)

"Gee, I'd love to, Tracy, but I'll be dead after tonight. You know how I sleep in the mornings."

Tracy maintained a hurt silence for a brief second, but then continued proudly:

"My violin teacher says I might be able to go to the international music festival in France if I keep practicing. Mother and Dad are going to give me my passport as a graduation present the year after next."

Joyce felt sudden pain and sickening in her stomach.

(Huh! . . . Just cause her family's got money . . . she *can* play the violin though . . . but I can do a lot more . . . I'm going on a date and she isn't . . . She's not even pretty and I am . . . well, almost . . .)

Fierce triumph overcame her, and she began to listen to Tracy, who was describing the dress she was going to wear to the recital.

"It's red with black velvet for a collar," Tracy was saying. "Red is always becoming to people who are pale, like me."

(She's so darn sure everything she says is right . . . she's so darn positive . . . I'd like to see anything become *her* . . .)

"I can imagine how nice you'll look," said Joyce.

Joyce looked at the trees made feathery, cold, and white by the snow, and she felt a sudden affection for them.

(I love the world . . . I love everyone . . . almost Tracy, even . . . poor Tracy . . .)

She gazed with grudging pity at the girl who walked beside her.

(She can't see beyond herself . . . everywhere she turns she'll stand in her own way . . . and she'll never know . . . never, unless someone tells her . . .)

"Well, Trace, here's where I turn off. Hope you have a good recital," she added with a burst of generosity, as she arrived at her street.

Tracy's blue eyes clouded with momentary indecision, and then she replied knowingly, "Oh, don't worry. I will." Before Joyce could think up anything to say, Tracy had disappeared around the bend.

(That infernal smugness . . . I'm so tired of going around with her . . . she thinks she can manage *me* . . . well, I'll show *her*.)

Joyce scuffed up the snow in a glittering white cloud. The wind blew a flurry back to her, and the flakes touched her uplifted face with a chill, damp caress. She paused beside her driveway and watched her younger brother shoveling snow into a huge pile.

"What are you doing, Davy?" she asked, although she knew.

He straightened and looked at her.

"I'm building a snow hut," he said proudly. His round little face was rosy with enthusiasm, and his jacket was powdered with snow.

"Just a sec and I'll be out to help you."

She ran into the house and soon returned bearing another shovel.

As she came down the front walk, she saw two boys from high school approaching.

(If they ever saw me digging a snow hut! . . . Bill Jennings and Mart Moore . . . both of them are nice-looking . . . They're stuck-up, though . . . I wish I could go out with one of *them* . . .)

The boys avoided looking in her direction with studied indifference and stared ahead until they passed. With blind anger Joyce dug her shovel into the snow.

(Darn them! . . . They don't even notice me . . . Well I'll show them . . . wait till they find out I've gone on a date with Tommy Grayson . . .)

Davy was still digging his snow hut, uncomprehending. His sister's moods were beyond him. They did not affect his for the most part, and they soon passed over harmlessly, like the shadows of clouds.

Tommy called for Joyce precisely at eight. When she made her descent down the stairs, her black hair lay in soft waves on her shoulders and her wine-colored skirt made a swishing sound. She forgot the dragging moments of anxiety she had spent upstairs, waiting for a doorbell to ring.

"Hi, Tommy," Joyce said.

"Gee, Joyce," Tommy said.

Tommy helped Joyce put on her coat rather awkwardly, and she called, "Well . . . bye, Mother," as they went out the door.

(I'm scared . . . what if I can't follow his dancing . . . what if he doesn't like me . . . what if he tells everyone I'm a drip . . . what if . . .)

There was another couple in the back seat of the car—a friend of Tom's and a girl from high.

(I'll bet she's surprised to see me . . . she hardly speaks to me in school . . .)

"Hi, Jim; hi, Ginny," Joyce said.

"Hi," said Jim.

"Hi," said Ginny in a friendly tone.

As the car sped along the highway, the headlights carved out a path in the darkness ahead of them. Joyce began to feel happy and bubbly inside.

(I never thought Tommy could drive that well . . .)

She listened to Ginny, who was telling about a night ride she had taken with her brother.

"We got lost about here," she was saying, "and Bob drove around till we hit a familiar place."

"What was it . . . a tree?" Joyce asked innocently.

Everybody laughed, and she settled back comfortably. The conversation flowed gaily from there on.

(It's funny how easy it is, once you begin . . .)

The evening went by unbelievably fast. Joyce found herself dancing easily in Tommy's arms.

(I'm dancing . . . dancing at the nicest place in town . . . and he *does* like me . . . I don't care what Tracy says . . .)

When Joyce said goodnight to Tommy it was almost midnight. She stood in the frosty air and waved to the dark as the car raced off into the night. With a sigh, she opened the door and stepped into the black, velvety warmth of the quiet house. As she tiptoed upstairs, she remembered the bright, tireless hours they had spent dancing to lilting music under colored lights.

But when Joyce took off her shoes, she realized that her feet ached, and when she surveyed her pale, white face under the merciless glare of the bedroom lamp, she was glad that the colored lights had been so dim and soft.

She went to bed, too tired to put her hair up on its customary curlers.

First Joyce experienced the sensation of shooting up through deep waters, cold to the point of numbness. Then, just as her lungs felt ready to burst, she broke the surface and was almost blinded by the sudden sunlight.

She stretched slowly, deliberately savoring every moment between sleep and complete consciousness. Gradually, with her awakening, fragments of thoughts and recollections flooded to her mind.

(Wonder what time it is . . . boy, I sure had fun last night. Tommy likes me . . . wait'll Tracy hears about it . . . Wonder how long I slept . . . ye gods! It's ten-thirty . . .)

Rubbing her cold nose gingerly with one hand, Joyce took a resolute breath and kicked off the covers. She slipped quickly into her navy slacks and cherry-red sweater and started downstairs to get her breakfast.

The sunlight poured in through the windows, and as Joyce glanced out in the yard, she saw Davy industriously building a snowman under the snow-laden birches.

About an hour later she took him coasting. The frosty air was so sharp that it almost hurt to breathe. Joyce was filled with a reckless joy as she and Davy stood alone on top of the glittering, snow-packed hill. The sky was a dazzling blue, and the woods were green with pine trees. The wind cracked past her ears, and her eyes blurred with tears as they shot down the hill together. Davy held her tightly.

(I love the world . . . I wish this ride would never stop . . . why can't life *always* be so uncomplicated . . .)

Christmas came and went swiftly. Joyce lay in the bed the night afterwards and thought over the events of the day.

(That ballerina skirt is my favorite present . . . and I love that reindeer sweater . . . somehow I always have a letdown feeling after Christmas though . . . I always feel so overstuffed . . . I like the waiting and the wrapping presents most, and the peaceful expectancy of Christmas Eve . . .)

"Oh, darn!" said Joyce as she put down the telephone receiver. "Tracy wants me to go to the movies with her on New Year's Eve."

"That's nice," remarked Joyce's mother, and then added with twinkling understanding, "or is there something else you'd rather do?"

"It's not that," said Joyce with a thoughtful frown. "It's just that you don't go out with a *girl* on New Year's Eve. I'd rather stay home than have people think I'm a social flop or something."

The phone rang again while Joyce was upstairs, and her mother called to her, "For you, Joyce," adding *sotto voce*, "It's a male."

Joyce clattered eagerly down, seized the phone and managed a nonchalant, "Hello?"

Tommy's voice filled her with relief and hope.

"I just wanted to know if you'd like to go to the New Year's Dance at the Country Club."

Joyce gulped, "I'd love to."

"See you around eight, then. Bye, now."

Joyce hung up starry-eyed. "*Mum*! I'm going to the Country Club dance! I never even *dreamed* of going *there*!"

"Well, you'd better let Tracy know," came the reply.

"All right."

(She'll understand . . . she'll just have to . . .)

Joyce laughed happily as she dialed Tracy's number.

"Hello?" came Tracy's voice.

"Hi, Tracy, this is Joyce again. Tommy just called up and asked me to go to the Country Club dance. Will you mind awfully much if I do?"

"Heavens no, go right ahead. I won't mind in the least."

"Okay, and thanks, Trace."

(Slightly rude of her . . . practically said she didn't want me in the first place . . . Oh, well, what can you expect . . .)

This night Joyce felt more at ease. Getting used to social life, she told herself.

As she and Tommy entered the ballroom, she cast an appraising glance at the elaborate decorations and couples dancing effortlessly about the floor.

(Only a few kids I know from high . . . none of my special friends . . . not that I have many . . .)

The evening progressed without event for Joyce until Ginny danced by with Jim. Jim flashed her a friendly grin over Ginny's shoulder, and, with sudden realization, Joyce saw how handsome he was—tall, blonde, and clean-cut.

(Oh, if only I could go out with *him* . . . I'd be the luckiest girl in the world . . . I'd give anything to have him like me . . . if only . . .)

Joyce turned back to Tommy.

(Tommy likes me . . . why, oh why can't I be satisfied with what I've got . . . It's because I'm sure of Tommy . . . that's why I don't care about him anymore . . . that's the reason . . .)

When the horns blew at midnight, she held her hands to her ears and laughed as Tommy clowned, anxious for her approval. But all the while she watched Jim across the room with longing eyes.

(If only he were talking to *me* . . . I don't see why he likes *Ginny* so much . . . I should think he'd be tired of her by *now* . . .)

Later, at her doorstep, Joyce said absently to Tommy, "Thanks for a super time," and bade him a preoccupied "Goodnight."

That night she smiled in her sleep, for her dreams were full of Jims. Jims with wonderful, flashing grins. Jims who said tenderly, "You know, Joyce, I've always liked you a lot."

"Oh," groaned Joyce a few mornings later. "I simply can't get up. I'm *so* sleepy."

"It's past seven," said her mother, continuing to pull up the blinds and let the wintry gray light of dawn into the room.

Somehow Joyce was almost eager to get back to school. She gulped down her oatmeal hurriedly.

(Things'll be different, now that I've gone out . . . Wonder how Tracy'll take it . . . Wonder if that snobby crowd of Ginny's will ask me to go around with them . . .)

Walking to school through the snow with Tracy that morning, Joyce felt a little relieved to start back in the old routine.

(It's always comfortable to settle back in the old rut . . . Got to review that Latin vocabulary before school . . .)

". . . and everyone came up afterwards and wanted to know how long I'd been taking lessons," Tracy was saying.

(Still harping on the old recital . . .)

"How nice," Joyce replied mechanically, her thoughts far away.

She left Tracy downstairs and started up to her own homeroom. There was a carry-over of holiday gaiety in the laughter and chatter of the boys and girls clustered in small groups along the hall, but no one stopped Joyce, or called knowingly, "I hear you went out with Tommy the other night."

She walked down to her locker in angry disappointment.

(I should have known it wouldn't be any different . . . I should have known . . . They just take dates for granted . . . They've gone out a million times to my two . . . Well, someday they'll see . . . someday . . .)

Just as she was arranging the books in her arms, she was halted by a girl's voice calling, "Hey, Joyce! Wait up!"

A wave of hope surged up inside her.

(*Ginny* knows . . . *Ginny* wants to be friends . . .)

She smiled.

"Oh, Joyce," Ginny began in a wheedling tone, "could I just see your history chart for a minute. I haven't had a speck of time all vacation, and . . ."

The smile froze like a mask on Joyce's face.

(So *that's* all she wants me for . . . a slave . . .)

"Sorry," Joyce lied coolly, "I haven't finished it yet."

"Oh, darn!" And Ginny turned away.

The Latin teacher said, "Joyce, give the principal parts of the word meaning 'to bear' or 'to carry.'"

"Ferō, ferre, tulī, lātus," Joyce rattled off, and then settled back comfortably in her seat.

This, at least, was something she was sure of. This, at least, was a world she knew.

Among the Shadow Throngs

Ts,[*] 1949, Lilly Library

Long rays from the afternoon sun shafted through the grimy bedroom window and made a faint square of light on the threadbare blue rug. The white paint

---

[*] Handwritten at top right: 'Sylvia Plath (Age 16) / Wellesley, Mass.' Typescript with holograph corrections by SP. Submitted to *Seventeen*. SP quotes from Nathaniel Hawthorne's *The House of Seven Gables*, which she read for English 21 in 1947–8.

was peeling off the iron bedstead and the lumpy mattress was covered by a gaudy patterned quilt. Inserted in one corner of the spotty mirror on the wall was a scrap of pink letter paper. A curious observer, leaning close to scan its mimeographed contents, might have read as follows:

Dear Miss Lane:

We sincerely regret that we are unable to accept your manuscript.

Although your contribution was carefully considered, it did not quite meet our needs.

Very truly yours,
Youth Publications

The owner of the room, Miss Lane, otherwise known as Terry, was reclining on the bed, meditatively chewing a yellow pencil and staring dreamily in the general direction of the ceiling. Her brown pageboy was bleached blonde across the top by the sun, and her clear brown eyes were the color of maple syrup, flecked with amber.

Her best friend, Louise Thurber, sat hunched over the desk, running nervous fingers through her short black hair and scribbling something in a notebook. She paused suddenly. She flung her pen down on the desk.

"Terry!"

"Uh-huh?" Terry murmured absently, peeling the nail polish off one fingernail.

"Why can't we get one little thing published . . . just one?"

Terry sighed. For a year now, she and Louise had been sending stories and poems in to youth magazines, and with disappointing regularity the big manuscript envelopes found their way home again.

"I got my best story back yesterday. If that didn't get published, nothing will."

Louise looked despondently out into the watery afternoon sunlight. "What do they *want* anyhow?"

"I've got a lot I want to say," Terry mourned, "but it never comes out right. Sometimes I have lots of queer thoughts I'd like to write about, but if I told them to anybody else, they'd think I was crazy."

Louise brightened. "I know just what you mean. Like this room. Think of all the conditions that make it possible for you and me to be here now. What if we hadn't moved to the same town . . . what if one of my parents had married someone else? Would you still be you and I be I?"

Terry concentrated, rolling up one cuff of her faded blue dungarees. "If only we could trace back all the little threads of coincidence that made this room, we could find out about the people who were involved in making the house and everything in it . . . the ones who cut the trees to make the wood and got the sand for the glass. We'd cover the whole world, maybe. And always after we'd met the people, we'd be back in the forests, back on the beaches at the beginning of time."

The sun came through the blinds and filled the room with translucent orange light, honey-colored. Dust motes floated in the drowsy summer quiet.

"Do you ever have that feeling," Louise began slowly, "that you'd like to subject yourself to every sort of situation and then write about it? I'd like to do that . . . to be someone else for a while, just long enough to know how it felt . . . to know all the feelings of a cripple, or of someone about to die, and yet be able to come back to myself again and write down my thoughts and emotions. I never want to be trapped in one personality . . . I want to be everyone, and still myself, too."

"Oh, I don't know. It sounds so confusing when I try to explain."

"It does not," Terry retorted. "It's wonderful to have *one* friend who I can really talk to. I can tell you anything . . . and you understand."

"If we could only travel together around the world . . . or to New York, even!"

"New York!" Terry breathed the magic words. Her eyes shone. "If ever we could go *there* we could really write about life . . . all the slums and the nightclubs and the people . . . millions of people."

She was carried away on a wave of longing. "I'd like to go around all the streets and lift up the roof of every house and look inside . . . to listen to the people talking and know what they're thinking and oh . . . everything!"

"I know." Louise looked fondly at Terry. "You want to get beneath the surfaces . . . inside the buildings . . . inside the people."

A silence hushed the room. Each girl saw herself walking down the streets of the great city. People paused to stare, whispering to each other in discreet admiration, "See that girl over there . . . the one in the Hattie Carnegie suit? Well, she's that brilliant young writer . . ."

"But gosh, Terry." Louise broke the spell. "We're just outnumbered. Thousands of kids like us want to write. What makes us any different? I feel so hollow, somehow, like an echo . . . like the ghost of somebody else."

Terry looked intently at her friend's dark, thoughtful face. She felt a sudden flood of warmth for this girl, so much like herself.

"We'll get something published someday if we keep hacking. Look at all the writers who had to wait twenty years for the first check. You're supposed to write about something you know, something you're familiar with . . . or so they tell us."

Louise smiled lazily and stretched, arching her slim back and yawning like a cat. "You inspire me. You know, you're awfully encouraging."

"If you get anything printed, I'll be just as glad as if it were me."

"Same here." Louise glanced at her watch. "Gosh. Five-thirty. I've got to go!" She rose abruptly and her chair clattered back on the floor.

Terry accompanied her to the door and then went back to her desk. She sat down, chin propped in her hands. Visions swam before her in a rosy mist: A letter of acceptance from a leading magazine (even *Youth Publications* would do) . . . recognition at last . . . an invitation to the editor's office in New York . . . she could see the reviews already . . . the title of her forthcoming novel . . . her name in firm black letters: Terry Lane.

Her writing, she resolved, would be life as she saw it: realistic, bitter, but wonderful, too. "Marble and mud," she remembered from somewhere. The dream hung in her mind, perfect and shining.

Outside, the afternoon beckoned. The wind ran laughing through the leaves . . . the sunlight was warm and yellow, thickly spread like butter on the grass. Never again would there be such a cloudless afternoon. Terry pushed the thought of her novel into a dusty corner of her mind where it lay, nebulous and vaguely comforting. There would be time for that later . . . there would be time.

She wandered out into the garden . . .

The Saturday mail rattled through the slot onto the floor. Terry yawned and leaned down to pick it up. She pulled her worn maroon bathrobe tighter about her and riffled through the letters. When she reached *Youth Publications*, she paused and turned automatically to the section of the original contributions from the readers.

She stiffened suddenly. She stood frozen. The name leaped out at her . . . the letters struck like icy knives into her brain. It couldn't be! Not Louise Thurber! But the malicious words remained before her eyes, and nothing she could do would erase them. Nothing could tear those words from the page. Mingled feelings surged through her. "How could she! . . . not telling me! . . . but it's good . . . it's good . . . and I'm jealous . . . for all I said, I'm jealous."

Terry read the lines of the poem carefully, deliberately. "Portrait," it was called. Portrait of whom, she wondered absently. There was something oddly familiar about the last stanza. Was it something Louise had said? . . .

> Among the shadow throngs
> I pass:
> An idle whisper
> Through the grass.*

She tortured herself, reading the lines over and over. A dagger turned in her stomach, hot and nauseating. A chilly lump prickled at the base of her neck. She went to the phone and dialed.

"Louise?" Her voice was dazed, mechanical. "I've only got a minute, but congratulations . . . the poem . . . it's wonderful."

The voice at the other end of the wire was tremulous with joy. "Oh, Terry . . . I'm so happy . . . I got the letter of acceptance with the magazine . . . I mailed the poem after that day I was at your house . . . I might never have written it otherwise."

"I'm so glad for you," Terry's voice was taut. "See you later." She let the

---

* SP quotes the final stanza of her poem, 'Portrait' (1948; typescript held by Lilly Library).

> The storm is breaking,
> and the savage rain
> dashes headlong in blind anger
> against the pane.
>
> The roof is strong,
> the walls are stout,
> but can they keep
> the deluge out?
>
> The bell tolls loud,
> and I arise
> to answer it
> with empty eyes . . .
>
> I start to speak:
> each word, alas,
> is but an echo,
> meaningless . . .
>
> By reflections on the water
> I am caught;
> I revolve in narrow rings
> of surface thought . . .
>
> Among the shadow throngs
> I pass,
> an idle whisper
> through the grass.

receiver drop from numb fingers and stared despondently out the window. So much for Louise, she thought, but what about me?

The sunlight twinkled on the leaves, and the warm air teased her, beckoning, beckoning. Terry rose and stood wavering. At last she turned and trudged up to her room. She sat down at the typewriter. Fragments of thoughts hammered at her brain. "Write something you know . . . something familiar . . ."

She smiled grimly and started to punch the keys. The story flowed out easily . . . Like a pent-up emotion it ran from her fingertips:

"Long rays from the afternoon sun shafted through the grimy bedroom window and made a faint square of light on the threadbare blue rug. The white paint was peeling off the iron bedstead . . ."

The Dark River

Ts,* 1949, Lilly Library

The woman who sat beside me on the park bench stared into the moving waters of the river flowing past the grassy bank. There was a dreaminess about her which fascinated me. Although her hair was white, there was a fluid youthfulness in her features and a strange, radiant light in her eyes.

All about us was the misty green of spring, and the winding paths were bordered by a golden flutter of daffodils. Children were chattering at play, but in our corner of the park there was a little island of silence.

At last, as if she sensed my curious gaze upon her, the woman stirred, as though awakening from a hypnotic sleep, and turned to look at me. The wild, exuberant brightness of her face was at once frightening and compelling. I think I lost myself in the depths of her eyes.

"You were wondering about me," she said simply. Her frankness took me off guard.

"Yes," I admitted.

"I have had the words inside me for a long time," she began, "but they were not ready until today. You will be the first to know my story and that of the dark river." Her voice flowed musically, like the murmur of a quiet fountain.

"As I recall my childhood," she went on, "I can see shapes move before me, clear, as if seen through glass, but their motions are as mechanical, their

---

* Typescript has some holograph corrections in SP's hand.

reactions as inevitable as those of figures in a dream.

"The park fades away, but the sound of the river is constant, and it forms the background of my reverie."

Lulled by the languid voice of the woman, a scene, strange and yet familiar, materialized before me.

There was a huge mansion on a hilltop, and there was desolation in its bleak metallic windows and its ivy-covered walls. The old-fashioned garden to the rear of the ancient house was bordered by a lilac hedge, and these leafy bushes leaned aslant over their reflections in a river.

At first I did not see the child sitting motionless at the river's edge, so still she was and lost in dreams. She was an elfin creature, thin and graceful, with a long tangle of yellow hair. A storybook lay open in her lap.

The voice went on, narrating as the picture came to life.

"You see, I was not a lonely child. Although I had no companions my own age, I was content to spend pleasant afternoons beside the river. The river was near me even then, but I did not understand its significance until a much later time.

"Deep within me there was rooted a love for the lilacs with their delicate fragrance, for the dark, singing waters, and for the friendly sky. I lived in a world of fancy—but do not all children live so?

"There was a cool, green place among the reeds where I liked to sit and watch the cloud patterns mirrored in the glassy black surface of the water. Sometimes the cloud reflections seemed to assume distorted human forms, but these images would quickly blend and change.

"The opposite bank of the river was always shrouded with a heavy mist, and I often longed to cross over to see for myself what mysteries were concealed in that never-lifting fog. But there was no bridge, no boat, and the calm waters were at the same time forbidding and perilous.

"In a way I was glad the mist was there. I felt sure that, veiled in the dense haze, all my unfinished thoughts and dreams lay waiting for an awakening . . .

"I feel a wave of sadness for that child. She is no longer I, but a solitary creature without a place in time, doomed forever to wander through the lonely hallways of my mind."

The picture faded slowly, and another took its place.

This time it was the city, and it was the spring of another year. The snows were melting, and the winds were damp and warm. The door of an apartment house opened, and a young girl came walking lightly toward us. I recognized in her the child that I had seen before.

The voice continued, "That spring I met Colin. He was a part of the rain, a part of the breathless life unfolding everywhere. Sometimes I think he lived only in my mind. He emerged from the April gardens and the mists of morning, and suddenly he was beside me; and there was a full, complete feeling in my heart.

"His face was lean and sensitive, I remember. We did not talk much, for there was mutual awareness between us that required no feeble, inadequate words.

"There were long walks together down the avenues of spring, and we were one with the world around us. The lilacs were in bloom on the green ribbon of lawn before the tall, dusty buildings; the park was fragrant and inviting. There was a lightness about our companionship that lasted . . . for a while.

"I do not know when I sensed the first heaviness, or when the dream world began to fade, but it came increasingly awkward to talk with Colin. I felt, with sudden horror, that he was drifting away from me. I tried to find an answer in his eyes, but they were dark and evasive. I longed to cry out to him, but the words were destined never to leave my lips.

"One afternoon when Colin called for me at my house, I ran quickly down the creaking wooden stairs to meet him. As I glanced at his face, I felt a sudden chill as if an icy wind had struck my heart with an odd sense of impending doom. And I knew that this was the last time I would ever see Colin again.

"The old, familiar walks in the park were almost deserted; it was very quiet. A haze arose from the humid earth; the sky was low with clouds. On either side stretched the lawns, the tulip gardens, and the daffodils. A moist, earthy fragrance hung in the air; and there was the waiting, windless calm that comes before a rain.

"As we walked hand in hand, I felt nearer to Colin than I had for a long while. My fears began to vanish, one by one. The spring had passed its first perfection, I noticed reluctantly, for already a few petals lay crumpled on the ground. The early golden tints were gone, and the deeper green of summer was approaching.

"Suddenly I saw that Colin was watching me strangely. We had stopped walking and stood facing each other on the gravel path. There was a desperate pleading in Colin's eyes for me to understand something that he could not tell me. The chill breath of foreboding touched me again, and then I heard it . . . the sound of a river rushing, rushing between us, dark and invisible, but more powerful than either of us. Why had I never noticed it before? Why had I never understood its meaning?

"The memories of my childhood flooded back, and with awful clarity I realized that the mysterious black river of my youth would be with me forever, always withholding from me a complete communication with those I wished to love.

"Colin read my eyes and the terror mirrored there.

"'So you hear it, too,' he said.

"Wordless, I nodded."

Here the voice trailed off, but I no longer needed the woman to explain the picture or the words which now issued from Colin's lips.

"You know why I've brought you here?" he questioned softly.

The rain poured down, and the girl's hair clung about her face in moist ringlets. Her white dress hung limp and wilted. She knew. She knew. She avoided his eyes, because she could not meet that look of gentle pity.

"Goodbye, goodbye!" she cried out into the rain, then turned and ran, leaving him standing there alone.

It was good to run. As her feet thudded over the gravel path, the blood pounded in her ears and drowned out the sound of the river, which still echoed in her brain. Something pent-up inside her broke, free and wild. Her hair flew out behind her as she ran, and her eyes were blinded by the warm, compassionate rain.

She only glanced back once. He was still standing there, faintly outlined against the liquid green of the park; but even as she looked, the rain beat down harder and he seemed to dissolve, to melt away like a phantom into the spring mists.

There was no one to see her running down the deserted streets, no one to see her dash up the steps of the old apartment house and slam the front door behind her. The crash reechoed through the empty hall as she flung herself on the bed in her room.

A low growl of summer thunder sounded in the distance; the spring was gone, and Colin, but the river was with her forever. Even with her eyes closed she could see the dark relentless waters flowing, flowing.

The form of the young girl faded, and I found myself staring at the cloud patterns reflected in the river. Suddenly I recalled the woman beside me, but even as I looked up I knew that she, too, would be gone; for she was part of the river, and the radiance in her eyes had only been the sunlight dancing on the surface of the water.

East Wind

Ts,[*] 1949, Lilly Library

Miss Minton shrank back into a doorway as a fresh blast of wind rushed past her down the street. She watched the soiled newspapers and candy wrappers careen

---

[*] Handwritten in top-right corner: 'Sylvia Plath / 26 Elmwood Road / Wellesley, Mass.' Typescript with holograph corrections by SP. Submitted to *Mademoiselle*.

along the gutter in the wake of the gale, whirling frantically for a moment, but then, inevitably, faltering, scraping on the sidewalk, drifting aimlessly to lie in some quiet, cobwebbed corner or to rot in the rain between the grimy apartment houses. The cabs sped by with shrill horns and shrieking brakes, but high above all the city noises rose the voice of the wind, wild and triumphant.

Shivering and gritting her teeth, Miss Minton started forth once more. She hated the fierce gusts that tore by her, slapping her face like huge ghostly hands, pushing her back, slowing her steps. There was an untamed note in the damp, icy blast, as if some strange insane creature were singing off-key and loud. Sometimes, when there was a lull, the roar would soften so that it sounded almost like husky laughter . . . or muffled sobbing.

Miss Minton found something disturbing in the persistent rush of wind music in her ears. A vague, uncomfortable foreboding nagged at her brain as if something unpleasant were about to be revealed . . . as if she were going to discover some disagreeable secret.

If only she had known how late it was, and how the wind whistled around the bleak buildings . . . if only she had known, she would never have started out so near to dusk.

When she had left the bakery, it was already twilight, and she had been reluctant to depart from the buttery golden warmth . . . the cozy room that smelled of dry flour and fresh bread dough. Clutching the parcel of rolls closer, she savored the heat that reached her fingers through the stiff brown paper.

She must not stop, for the dark was engulfing and the wind was ever at her side. The mad shrieking filled her ears. Why must it scream so, she wondered irritably, as a strong breeze almost tore the bag of rolls from her grasp. Suddenly there was another momentary lull. Miss Minton halted to get a better grip on her package. It was then that she noticed the child.

He was standing barefoot in the gutter . . . a wild, elfin creature with tangled hair and a tattered coat about his scrawny shoulders. Miss Minton saw that his hands were quite blue with the cold. For a moment the two stared at each other, and as they did so, the woman felt an inexplicable stirring of compassion.

The child gave her a queer look and then was off with a bound. He disappeared down an alley, kicking up a cloud of dust and sooty scraps behind him. A shrill peal of laughter floated back on the wind.

The icy blasts descended in sudden fury. They stung Miss Minton's cheeks and brought tears to her eyes. Then, unexpectedly, she had the revelation. It came into sharp focus, springing at her abruptly, as when one twists a telescope and the hazy distance all at once stands out with breathtaking clarity. Everything seemed so neat and simple! She was overcome with one driving determination. She did not care about her apartment anymore. No, not the apartment with its patched brown rugs, the worn brown table, and the ugly brown clock that ticked away seconds, hours, years, in monotonous similarity. Not those rooms, loud with heavy silence, but rather an escape from them. That was it. She almost laughed, it was so easy. But why hadn't she known sooner? It was the apartment she hated. All along it had been the apartment, and she had never known. Never till now, in the east wind that pushed her back, pushed her back the other way.

She had to stop . . . stop and go where she could think. Groping blindly, she pulled open the nearest door and stepped into a small restaurant. As she sank to a seat by an empty table, she fancied she heard someone outside give a cry of disappointment.

After the incessant rush of air, it was a relief to hear the musical clink of china and the low murmur of conversation. The warmth overcame her with a languid drowsiness, and the urgency which had driven her into the shop blurred and dimmed.

A graceful black-clad waitress glided toward Miss Minton and stood poised, waiting. A cool voice asked, "And what did you have in mind?"

What was it? She had wanted something. She had come for something. What was it?

"In mind? . . . Oh, just a pot of tea."

Miss Minton toyed with the glass at her place, and sipped the water to cover her embarrassment. When the tea came, she could almost sense the waitress' disdain, and she was ashamed of her small order. The tea was good, though, and the heat crept into her veins, relaxing her and smoothing away the ugly, disturbing edges of her thoughts. She drained the last drop and put her cup back in the saucer with a sigh.

A couple had just come in and were looking about the crowded room for a table. The waitress left her check and was hovering expectantly.

"All right, all right, I'm going," Miss Minton muttered to herself as she started toward the cash register. She felt deflated, beaten somehow. A chill passed over her as she thought of the inevitable apartment. It would be quite dark now, and cold. She would need the patchwork quilt on the bed to keep warm. As she waited for her change, she glanced out the restaurant window. A child's face was pressed up against the pane. She started as she recognized him. However had he known she was there?

The door slammed behind her. She was out again in the night with the cold like a knife, and he was waiting. She stared ahead, her lips pressed together in a thin determined line. Only another block now. Her heels clicked briskly on the cement walk. But all the time she could hear the bare feet pattering softly along beside her. The boy was there, scampering to keep up with her long strides. His eyes gleamed fathomless and deep as he danced down the pavement. At last Miss Minton could stand it no longer.

"Well, what do you *want*?" she asked nervously.

Her voice sounded odd, she reflected. There was a lowness, an unaccustomed softness. The child did not reply, however, but he tugged playfully at her sleeve and then ran off a little way, shrieking with delight. Laughing impishly, he skipped back and forth, playing a weird sort of game. And all the while he watched her with those strange eyes. There was something there . . . was it teasing? No . . . it was more like pity, like pleading, almost.

She only had to cross the bridge over the river, and there would be the apartment house . . . a bulky, brown, familiar shape looming out of the bitter night.

Miss Minton shivered. There it was again, that clearness. The apartment. No, not the apartment, please . . . no, she begged silently. There was a strange humming in her ears, shrill and piercing.

All at once a freakish gust lifted her hat off her head and sent it spinning crazily beyond her. With the wind buffeting her all the way, Miss Minton broke into a run, chasing her hat. All that mattered was her hat. She must stop that hat, somersaulting wildly over the bridge. She almost had it . . . not quite. The black shape flapped suddenly to the side. She reached out over the railing, and there was the water down below. Way, way down the dark surface of the river leered up at her. If she leaned a little farther, just a little . . . there would be no more apartment, no more ugly brown clock, no more . . . The wind would bear her up. She would be floating on the wind; light as feather she would be caught and tossed up, up. For one breathless exultant moment she leaned out, her eyes shining. She laughed giddily. She was going to . . .

The humming stopped. The wind veered. Silence. Miss Minton drew back from the railing slowly, furtively. A few more steps and she was at her own front door. There, lying at her feet, was a lifeless black shape. She stooped, her legs creaking beneath her, and picked up the hat. With numb, gloved fingers, she turned the key in the lock and went in, shutting the door behind her. For a moment she stood in the hallway, and then, feeling unaccountably old, she turned slowly and started wearily up the stairs. As she pulled the beaded chain of the lamp, she steeled herself to the familiar sight. The cold, frosty windowpanes, the white iron bedstead, the terrible varnished bureau. She laid down the paper bag and took out the rolls. They were greasy and unappetizing now. She put them back with distaste and got into her gray flannel nightgown. As she slipped between the icy sheets, she shuddered. I won't open the window, she thought. It's cold enough without that. She turned out the light.

The clock ticked through the dark, and memories crowded in upon her like an album of pictures. She turned them over in her mind: gay fantastic pictures, faded and blurred with age. Where had they all gone, she wondered. Miss Minton closed her eyes against the night and determined not to think of the future, the tomorrow. Forget, forget . . .

But from somewhere outside the window there came the sound of a child sobbing, and there was nothing she could do to shut out the thin, lonely weeping.

Place: A Bedroom, Saturday Night, in June

Ts,[*] June 1949, Lilly Library

The light is on over your bed, and you sit propped up against the pillows reading and listening to music on the radio. The windows are open, and the breeze blows the curtains against the screen. Across the cool dark comes the complaining sound of crickets chirping. The words on the page begin to swim in front of your eyes, so you put the book down and let the music fill the big, empty places inside you. The sound of the trumpets, low and melancholy, twists inside you, and the saxophones drop mellow, nostalgic notes, round, golden notes. You sigh, and it hurts. There's a hard place in you, a tight, sobbing loneliness that makes you want to cry. The music comes in, and you relax, letting the tones fill you to the brim. You think of all the boys and girls dancing together tonight, lilting, twirling to waltz tunes, always laughing. The music comes singing out into the night, outside the colored lights, the music comes rippling, fading. The moon, misty and pale, seen through tears, sails to the music, and the clouds trail silver in time to the music. You nod your head in time to the music. And all the while, the songs go round and round inside you, aching, weeping inside

---

[*] Typescript has holograph corrections by SP. Each of the three 'Place' pieces appears to be connected and may even be considered one narrative with subdivisions. SP met Roland 'Robin' Homet, Jr, Carlton Knight and 'Cookie' (possibly William Cooke, Jr) at the Spring Promenade dance held on 13 May 1949 at Phillips Andover Academy, Andover, Massachusetts. See SP's High School Scrapbook, page 15, where 'Cookie' is called 'Twinkle-Toe Cookie' in a caption.

you. You wonder where that boy of yours is now, the tall one with the dark hair and the red cheeks, the one who nibbled your ear when you danced . . . the one who kissed you while you danced. You wonder where Robin is, and Carl, the lean, light-haired one with the gentle eyes. You remember the feeling of his strong hard cheek against yours, and there's a shiver that comes over you when you remember how it was. And Todd, and Cookie, with the sharp, knife-dark eyes and the twinkling, magic, dancing feet. The music comes over the radio . . . the same songs they played such a little while ago. And you wonder where all the boys are who danced with you . . . who held you tight against the warmth of their bodies, who danced with you . . . cheek to cheek with you. A sad little trill, and the waltz rhythm carries you off on a wave of tears. The vocalist hums, husky, mournful, and a shiver comes over you, shut in your room with the book fallen on your lap. Each word of the song was meant for you, and the melody is slow and haunting . . . "Some enchanted evening . . . you may see a stranger . . . you will hear him call you . . . across a crowded room . . ." How can music make one feel so queer, you wonder . . . sad, yet with a reflection of happiness from the Japanese lanterns at the summer dance . . . a little while ago. You ache to be held again in some boy's arms . . . You long to be kissed again while you're dancing, and then the music will flood the skies and overflow along the hills, and the whole evening will sing with the strange, high voices of the violins, the throaty sobbing of the bass, and the laughing, crystal tinkling of the piano. How can the singer build up the words so . . . those hollow words? . . . A huskiness, a plaintive regret, a sustained note, and the song spirals upward, a perfect golden cone of love and tears. The song spirals up, twisting like a thin spear inside you, and you echo the words, brimming with portent . . . "Some enchanted evening . . ."

The program is over, and the announcer's voice intrudes on the last, long note. A harsh shock, a crude sharp voice. You turn off the radio; you turn off the light, and you lie there for a long time, staring with dry, sleepless eyes into the dark . . .

All right. Now I've got to begin. I've been sitting here half the night, trying to fool myself into thinking I wasn't wasting time, when every minute the blood was pounding in my ears and the hours were going fast. First I wanted to sit here, in this quiet house and write the things that have been on my mind for a long while, but the ideas were too perfect. So I didn't want to spoil them, no. I sat and kept my eyes reading those printed magazines. You could do that all night, you know, read magazines and shut yourself away from everything around you. It's only too easy to kid yourself and slide into escaping. Sure, I could read all night. The magazines, with their flashy pictures, lie on the other end of the couch. I look at them. Trash. Cheap stories. I look at the paper in front of me. Blank. Too clean. So I reach over to a magazine. Just to see the setup. Nothing more. Just to see how much better I could write if I really tried. If I ever got around to trying. I open to a page and the words catch hold. Just see how this guy develops his ending. Then it's another story. And then I'm lost. So it's about time I stop letting the minutes go by. It's about time I work things so I won't kick myself for a fool after it's too late. I've got ideas, sure, and I'll spoil a lot of them, writing. But it's no good to keep putting them off. Letting that vague, comfortable feeling of "Someday . . ." stay inside, and never doing anything about it. So now I've got to begin . . .

Place: A City Street Corner, in the Rain

Ts,[*] 1949, Lilly Library

There was a long time of standing shivering in the rain, in the city, watching the way the buildings jutted up against the gray sky. It was about five, and the lights were coming on early. It's funny . . . the way the lights get inside you . . . all the flashy neons down the street . . . pink, blue, and lemon yellow, winking through the rain and reflecting in the slippery road like spilt watercolors. Maybe it's the rain that makes you feel so queer inside, like crying, almost. Anyhow, you lean back in the doorway and watch the people going by, all bent down against the wind, hunching behind their umbrellas like the Roman soldiers with their shields. Only there's nothing heroic about these. They pass like dark shadows in front of the store windows, and the water shines on their umbrellas. The shops, now, in the twilight, are little wedges of glowing golden light. The people in apartment houses forget to pull down the blinds, so you can look into all the different rooms and watch them moving around and talking to each other in pantomime. Then you think: all over the city people are forgetting to pull down blinds, and all over the city people are moving around like puppets in their tiny furnished rooms. So you stand there, crying almost, when by chance you see yourself in the glass of the display case, with the greeting cards and notebooks showing through. For a minute you feel like the ghost of somebody else. But you're back inside yourself again, feeling invincible, all of

---

[*] Typescript has holograph corrections by SP. Handwritten in pencil at top left, by SP: 'Please – send this back.' At top right, in pen, 'S. Plath'.

a sudden. You could walk right out into the street, into the slithering sound of the car tires on wet pavement, you could walk right out, with the headlights coming at you like animal eyes in the dark, and not be killed or hurt, or anything. You pity those two vulnerable girls going into the restaurant, with their shrill, artificial laughter. As the door closes behind them, you smell the heavy, sensual odor of food, and you feel at once sick, defeated, humiliated. You feel a pang in your stomach, and despise yourself for the gnawing of hunger just beginning. (After all, in spite of the skyscrapers and the plastic surgeons and the automobiles, in spite of these, the smell of food calls louder, stronger.) For all the sniveling sentimentality, for all the spirit-worshippers, for all the devout and pious ones, for all these, the call of the flesh is stronger. The heat of the body, the network of throbbing veins, the animal longings: these conquer. And then the descent. Sure, sure, we keep the grass mowed in the cemeteries and the neat white crosses on the deserted battlefield, and the flowers at the altar, but underneath these is the decay, the decomposed flesh, the stench of death. You've seen the pictures. The dead soldiers upon the beaches. You've seen the dark stain spilled out on the ground, the mottled faces and the foolish, gaping mouths; the awkward sprawl of stiffened legs and arms. And all the time the busy ants beginning; and all the time the worms beginning. You've seen the pictures, all right. And all the while, under the neat white crosses, the vermin gorging; and all the while, beneath the pretty poppies, the flesh putrescent and the bones rotting into the earth. The garbage, the carrion of the back alleys. The taint forever present. In the squalid tenements and the blowsy women with the rouged cheeks; the skinny kids with the big eyes; the paunchy, meateating men. The nauseating smell of cabbage forever on Saturday nights. The comic strips always on Sunday morning, and the deadly job Monday, Tuesday, Wednesday . . . beginning, never-ending. The beery smell of bars and the fatal hypnosis of television. The plushy movie house and the stale cigarette smoke and the nicotine-stained fingernails. The tinny jazz of the juke joint on the corner, and the nervous, giggling girls in the booth; the platinum-tinted hair and the cheap, strong perfume. The gaudy lights and the gilt letters. Oh, see them! See them and be sick. For beneath all this, in the cool, deep caverns below the city, in the maze of sewers under the city, blind things grope and writhe in the dank scum, in the fetid pools of pollution and decay. Blind pallid things squirm ceaselessly, never at rest. For the brief interlude is but a passing; eternity waits serenely in the winding tunnels beneath the city.

    You stand there, with the streets reflecting the sky, and the lights twisting inside you. The people pass always; and if it would help, you'd scream. And if it would help, you'd cry. But no. You stand there and listen. Above the auto horns, above the voices, you hear the wind, moaning in the rooftops. So you stand there and listen . . .

Place: Inside a Bus on a Rainy Night

Ts,[*] 1949, Lilly Library

After a while, the bus comes, so you get on and walk up to a seat in the back. The floor rocks back and forth, so you're glad to sit down. The rain streams over the window in wet drops, shutting out the streets going past, and the lights outside twinkle and blur in the water always running down the pane. It's quiet inside. The click-click of the windshield wiper sounds loud in the moist silence, and it is punctuated by the occasional hoarse wheeze of the air-brakes as the bus plunges to a halt. No one talks. No one moves in the gray tranquility of the rainy twilight. You look at the faces around you. No one notices you staring. The woman next to you gazes constantly out of the window. Her face has the dry, wrinkled pallor of bread dough, and her features are coarse and mottled. Her stringy hair is drawn back into a knot at the nape of her neck, and her form is vague and bulky under the cloth coat. It is as if someone had started to model a figure out of clay and then tired of his work and left the form in a lumpy, half-finished state. But it's the hands that get your attention. They lie restless in her lap, rubbing each other with a dry, sandpapery sound. They are strange hands, always moving, clasping and unclasping, as though she were continually washing them. Where is the woman coming from? Where is she going . . . this woman with the expressionless face and the nervous, twisting hands? You sit there, the two of you, side by side for an hour, and you can only wonder what her thoughts are, what her life is. You can only wonder, and you can never know.

Then, there's the man across the aisle. You can just see his profile, so you trace with your eyes the heavy features: the strong nose, the keen forehead, and the full, curved lips. He's the one with the golden skin and the oily black hair. His eyes are big and liquid and dark. He's the one that smiled at you when you got on. He stares ahead now, not seeing the bus at all, but something beyond . . . some pleasant fancy, for he is still smiling. You feel warm inside, like smiling

[*] Typescript has holograph corrections by SP.

back. You'd like to lean over and say, "Please, tell me your dream." But you don't. You don't do that sort of thing on buses. There's the old man on the other side of you, coming home from work. It's odd, you think, but all old men look alike. Their heads are strangely reminiscent of flesh-colored prunes. There are fat puffy ones and skinny withered ones. This was the withered variety. But the lines gave his face depth, slanting into wrinkles of laughter around his eyes. His skin was pink and raw, as if it had been shaved too much, and his eyes were blue and watery behind his glasses. His neck muscles hung loose, like those of a plucked chicken. His legs dangled limp, so that the shoes on his feet were sprawled awkwardly, like those thrown carelessly in a closet. He was motionless, too. Where do people go on buses? Their bodies are still and lifeless. Their unseeing eyes are glassy. Are they unconscious, or in a kind of coma, or do they create scenes in their minds where they live for a while? You sit there amid the silent forms, amid the unspoken secrets. You feel a compassion for the woman with the nervous hands; a love for the man with the golden skin. You are in the presence of myriad mysteries, never to be revealed. You will never be together with these same people again. The old man may die tomorrow; the woman may find a peace to still her restless hands, and you will never know. You will never know. A thousand chances have drawn your lives together, and already the connection is thinning, spinning out finer and finer. Already your stop is approaching. Already you can feel the nearness to home throbbing in your blood. So you get up and walk down the aisle, and the bus swings to a stop. So you go down the steps out into the rain, and the bus moves on with gathering speed, a lighted little world. The bus moves out of sight into the obscurity of the falling rain.

And Summer Will Not Come Again

Written: *c.* August 1949
Published: *Seventeen* (August 1950): 191, 275–6[*]

The rain started at four o'clock that afternoon. Celia saw it begin from the porch where she sat curled up in the chintz-covered armchair, trying to read.

---

[*] Printed with a photograph of SP and a biographical sketch: 'Sylvia Plath loves being seventeen. "It's the *best* age." She lives in Wellesley, Massachusetts. Life is filled with senior activities, helping to edit her high school newspaper, working on the yearbook art staff, college weekends. She plays a lot of basketball and tennis and she pounds the piano "strictly for my own enjoyment". Jazz makes her melt inside, Debussy and Chopin suit her dreamier moods.'

Aimlessly she let the book fall into her lap and stared at the big drops making dark, wet polka-dots on the gray pavement.

Perspiration stood out on her upper lip and trickled in a little stream down her back. Her face was shiny, and she had tied back her limp brown hair with a wilted blue bow. From outside there came the strong smell of melted tar and the sweet, sickening odor of damp grass. A fly buzzed frantically against the screen.

The whole day had been hateful from the morning on. With the rest of the family away for the afternoon, the house was left quiet. The silence was like an expectant vacuum. It's like that when you're waiting for the phone to ring, Celia thought. There's an empty, unfilled place in the atmosphere just waiting to receive the sound. But when it does come, it's not for you, and you know that never, never . . .

She wondered how that would sound out loud. "Never, never again," she addressed the flowerpot firmly. Her voice was flat, final. The words hung there in the moist, spongy air. Never, never again.

Here she was. It was late August, and it was raining hard now, relentless drops spattering the sidewalk. She was like any other girl, she tried to tell herself. But it didn't work. She was special. She was Celia. The rain beat out a tattoo on the streets. Never . . . never . . . never again.

Just how do you go about forgetting a guy, anyway? A freckle-faced guy named Bruce, tall, with knife-blue eyes that can see right into you and tell you what you're thinking.

It had all started ordinarily enough down at the tennis courts at the beginning of summer. But it wasn't ordinary. This had happened to *her*. She was banging a ball up against the green wooden backboard, missing more often than she hit, when unexpectedly a boy's voice drawled behind her, "How about a set?"

Celia whirled. She surveyed the newcomer with a quick, appraising glance. Gosh, but he was nice-looking. "I-I'm just learning," she stammered confusedly. "I mean I really can't play." Something like this would happen. Why hadn't she started practicing sooner?

"No excuses," he laughed. "You've got to begin someday. I'll yell when you do anything wrong. By the way, I'm Bruce."

Standing opposite him, Celia wished for some miracle that would make her play well all of a sudden. This was worse than a nightmare. Frozen, she watched his arm come up, sending the ball in an easy loop over the net. She just had to hit it. Rushing forward, she swung desperately. The racket whished through empty air.

Now maybe he'll see I can't play and leave me alone, she thought frantically. But he called over to her, "Keep your eye on the ball and just swing easy . . ."

This time, when the ball came, she waited, watching it sail toward her. She swung again. There was a reassuring twang and the ball flew back over the net. For a whole hour she stood there, trying to hit back his easy serves and listening to his constant coaching. By the end of the afternoon she had made a few good returns.

As Bruce strolled over to her, she thought, Well, that's that. He was nice to stick out the afternoon. And she smiled up at him, "Shouldn't I shake your hand or leap over the net?"

His blue eyes teased her. "Let's settle for a drink after all that strenuous exercise."

She wasn't sure what he meant. "There's a water fountain over there . . ."

"Oh, let's get something with flavor in it."

Sitting together in the cool dimness of the ice cream parlor, they sipped ginger ale and got acquainted. Bruce liked to do the same things Celia did. He even wrote for his college magazine.

"Don't tell a soul," Celia confided, laughing, "but I've got a collection of rejection slips a mile high."

As they parted at the door, Bruce grinned a grin that made her all watery inside, "See you around," he said.

The next day, as she approached the courts, she felt an odd stirring as she recognized a pair of blue shorts. When she came near, Bruce turned and smiled. "I've been waiting for you," was all he said. He knew, then, that she would be there. She felt like singing all of a sudden. He knew and he had come to meet her.

After that he would always be at the courts waiting for her. Celia often wondered if he thought of her as a kid sister . . . he was nice and yet so casual. (Nineteen wasn't so much older than sixteen.) Once, though, while he was walking her home, she had glanced up suddenly and caught him looking at her intently, his blue eyes serious. As soon as she met his gaze, however, there was the accustomed veil of merriment again.

"Know something," he said one day, "your hair smells just like pine needles."

"As long as it doesn't look that way," she laughed. But something about his look puzzled her.

Then for a week she didn't see him and Celia was miserable. Late one afternoon, the phone rang. It was Bruce, "Look," he sounded sheepish, "how about going canoeing tonight?"

A date! He'd never asked her out before. Celia gulped, "I'd love to!"

Out on the lake it was dark and very quiet. Celia leaned back on the cushions and watched Bruce silhouetted against the star-filled sky. The canoe glided through the whispering lily pads, through the deep velvet shadows alongshore. There was something about the liquid silence that made them talk in low voices. Celia was so relieved to see Bruce again that she accepted his sudden reappearance without question. She stopped worrying that he had another girl.

But still there was a vague, nagging doubt. She had to know something . . .

As they said goodnight she said, "You're not mad at me then? You still like me? I know I'm an awful tennis player, but . . ."

"You little fool," Bruce replied softly. Slowly he pulled her toward him, tilting her chin up with one hand, and kissed her.

The next day, biking down to the courts, Celia hummed to herself as her lean, tanned legs pedaled rhythmically. The sun was warm on her skin and her hair blew back in the wind.

Suddenly Celia's eyes flew wide open. Her stomach tensed. It couldn't be, but there was Bruce coming out of the ice cream parlor, talking and laughing with an adorable blonde girl. Celia felt sick. There was a hard, taut pain below her ribs. "You dope," she told herself dully, "getting churned up over a mere boy. He never belonged to you in the first place." Celia noticed carefully, deliberately, how nice that other girl looked in her white shorts and aqua jersey. She pedaled so hard her legs ached. As she went by, the blonde looked up candidly and Bruce called out airily, "Hi, there." He didn't even look guilty, Celia thought, furious.

Oh, oh, she muttered between her teeth as she banged the ball viciously against the backboard. How could he? She was concentrating so hard on whamming the ball that she barely heard the familiar voice drawl behind her. "May I have the pleasure of a set?"

Celia turned. He had come back alone after seeing that blonde girl home. If he thought she would just take him back meekly . . . Her eyes narrowed. She let out a torrent of angry phrases . . . mean, cutting things she had stored up inside her. "Why, won't your girlfriend play with you anymore? . . . I should have known gentlemen prefer blondes . . ." But her sarcastic voice trailed off breathlessly as she saw Bruce's friendly grin vanish. A strange alien look masked his eyes as he waited for her to finish. Too late she stopped the flood of words, frightened at the silence hanging between them. At last he said quietly, "All right, Celia. I won't bother you anymore. I hadn't figured you were like this. My mistake."

He turned and walked away. Celia stood, congealed with horror. There was something so final in the way he left, not looking back. Suddenly the sun was unbearably bright. It beat down mercilessly on the flat, rectangular courts.

That was yesterday. Miles and miles ago, if you could measure time by miles. Maybe he'd already had a date with that girl. She would never know. She had turned him away and that was what hurt. The rain spattered against the screen and a cool, wet breeze caressed her skin. All at once she remembered a few lines from Sara Teasdale:

On the long wind I hear the winter coming,
The window panes are cold and blind with rain;
With my own will I turned the summer from me
And summer will not come to me again.

She realized she was crying. The tears fell, hot between her fingers. There would be other summers, she knew, but this one would not come again.

The rain slowed its tempo, keeping time with her tears. Never . . . never . . . never again.

A Day in June

Ts,[*] *c.*1949, Lilly Library

There is one day you can never forget, no matter how hard you try. You always remember when the summer comes again, and it's warm enough to go canoeing. When the first blue June day comes, there is the memory, vivid, crystal, as if seen through tears . . .

You and Linda are going canoeing on the lake for the first time this season. You walk down to the boathouse . . . to the wharf of rotting planks that slants into the water . . . to the empty canoes along the dock, waiting, like shallow green peapods afloat. You step shakily into the bow of one while Linda takes the stern, and all the time the light boat prances and bounces beneath you, impatient to be off. It's one of those perfect days in June you try to describe but never quite can. Take the smell of fresh washed linen; of sweet grass drying after a rain; take the checkered twinkle of sunlight in a meadow; the taste of

---

[*] Typescript with holograph corrections by SP. Typed at top right: 'Sylvia Plath / Wellesley, Mass.' Submitted to *Seventeen*.

mint leaves cool on the tongue; the clear-cut brightness of tulips in a garden; green shadows, thinning to yellow, thickening to blue . . . the dazzle . . . the hot touch of sun on your skin . . . blinding arrows of sunlight glancing off the deep glassed blue of the water . . . the exhilaration . . . bubbles rising, bursting . . . the gliding motion . . . the liquid singing of water past the bow . . . shifting specks of color dancing: all this to love, to cherish. Never again such a day!!

You paddle to a cove . . . you drift . . . you lie back and close your eyes against the sunlight, hot upon the lids . . . you squint into the sunlight and there are webs of rainbows on your lashes. Lulled by the rhythmic lapping of waves against the prow, the rocking . . . the gliding . . . you drift near the shore.

Suddenly you hear voices . . . unmistakable . . . boys' voices. There is a tremor of excitement in your veins, a sudden tenseness. You and Linda are at once alert. Adventure is in the offing. You smooth your hair and look slyly about. Sure enough . . . another canoe is skirting the shore behind you . . . two boys . . . How to delay? How to pause accidentally? The steep bank toward which you are drifting is covered with rhododendrons . . . tempting clusters of scarlet and white blossoms hang over the lake and cast dark reflections on the water. Linda says in a tremulous voice, "Let's pick some flowers." That's all . . . four words . . . and you two understand each other completely. You stand up in the canoe, teetering perilously and laughing as you reach out and tear the blossoms off . . . snapping the stems recklessly . . . all the time you laugh . . . a little too excitedly perhaps, but you laugh, picking the flowers and aching to look over your shoulder, but not quite daring. All the time there is a delicious excitement tingling inside you. The voices grow louder. You hear one say, "Let's go over and see the girls . . ." You pick the rhododendrons more carefully now, with a conscious attempt at grace and nonchalance. "Hello there!" exclaims a warm masculine voice behind you. You both turn abruptly with feigned surprise. "Oh, hello . . ." you manage breathlessly, nearly tipping over the canoe as you sit down. And the rest? You wonder nervously what happens now? But the rest comes along of its own accord. You look at Linda, giggling with nervous gaiety and tossing her blonde hair back from her eyes. You look at the two boys . . . not so handsome close to . . . but nice. The two canoes bob side by side and you exchange a steady stream of meaningless patter. You think back and can't quite remember what you've said. But you laugh . . . knowing that they think you're cute . . . knowing that they think you're nice. You tease the boys . . . which one can paddle faster? They look at each other, laughing. Let's race, you suggest. Oh, no, that wouldn't be fair. One of them will paddle you. You protest gaily. They insist. You hope secretly that the dark-haired fellow will come with you . . . He steps easily into your canoe and takes the stern. Buck, his name is. The other boy, Don, lets out a mock groan. "I can't paddle alone." He looks at Linda. Flattered, she pretends to hesitate and says, "Should I?" But she steps over, too, and everything is perfect. You lean back on the pillows, facing the boys, and you and Linda exchange secret looks of satisfied pride. Nothing like this has ever happened to you before. None of the boys at school have ever been this nice to you. You concentrate on Buck. He is thin and pale, with dark eyes and stringy black hair, but you don't notice his uncombed hair, his pallor; you look always at his eyes. Here is a boy . . . paddling you in a canoe . . . he likes you. Immediately Buck is enveloped in a dreamy haze. Minute by minute he grows more appealing. You push aside the nagging thought, "Whatever would people say?" You laugh always, being mysterious, and, you think, coquettish.

    The sun's rays are getting cooler now. You can't push back the twilight. The boathouse looms in the distance. The unspoken question rises between all four of you simultaneously . . . how to pay? You have an uncomfortable notion that you should trade canoes again and go in alone, but an absurd perverse part of you rebels. Why not prove your power? Why not? "How much'll your canoe cost you?" Buck asks laconically. Again you and Linda exchange glances and understand. "Cost?" you falter innocently. "Do you have to pay?" It takes a while to persuade the boys that you have no money, but you conceal your wallets in your pockets and play the game. Buck paddles ahead and asks you, his eyes hard and burning, "Just what were you planning to do if we hadn't come along?" You look at him, churning inside, heat pounding at your temples. This is getting a bit too uncomfortable. Tears of embarrassed anger blur your eyes, hot and wet, stinging with salt. Miraculously his face softens. "Aw, heck, don't cry. I'll pay for us. I just don't want them to know I've got money." You feel queer inside, very small and mean in the face of such generosity. You want to say, "I'm sorry, it's all a lie," but the words just won't come out. He trusts you now. His face is friendly and you can't . . . you won't . . . change that by telling him the truth. "Oh, Buck," you stammer, choked by emotion. "Help me out when we get there, like you were an old friend, so the man will think we've known each other all along."

    "Sure, sure," he says. The canoe glides into the dock, and the man is there waiting. You can't look at him. Head averted you get out on the dock, hardly realizing that Buck has helped you up, has paid the man. You start away, ashamed, hating yourself. He calls to you. Linda and Don have just come up together. You walk beside her and the boys follow along the wooded road in the green shade and the long cool shadows. You talk in low tones. What can you do now, you wonder. How to make up for being so mean? You walk faster. "Don't try to get away," Buck says quietly behind you. Your legs wobble with unreasoning panic. "I'm going to tell them," Linda whispers to you.

"No," you hiss back vehemently. How can you explain to her how things are . . . how Buck trusts you? Everything will be spoiled . . . ruined. But Linda has turned to them. You all stop. The afternoon is heavy with waiting. You want to scream, to drown out her repentant voice as she says to Buck and Don, "We were only kidding. We had the money all along, but just to prove we're not mean clear through we'll pay you now." The silence is sickening. There's no looking at Buck now, no telling Linda what she has done. How can she go on? But she does. "If we give you the money will you leave us alone?" Buck's voice is dangerously even. He says to you, to you alone, "So that was all an act in the canoe then?" Your eyes stare down at the road. There is a strange high singing in your ears. You nod, wordless. The afternoon shatters around you into a million glassy fragments. Malicious, dancing slivers of green and blue and yellow light rise and whirl about you . . . suffocating, smothering flakes of color. You are aware that the boys have taken the money, have turned and are getting smaller down the road. You and Linda stand there a while, watching. There is something so final about someone disappearing down a road, not turning, not looking back. Linda sighs with satisfaction. She has done that which was necessary, and she dismisses the incident accordingly. But you, you walk slowly beside her, not talking. How can you ever explain how it was? How can you ever explain that you betrayed with more than just money? There's something so desolate, so final about an empty road. You walk on, not talking.

The Green Rock

Ts,* winter 1949, Lilly Library

The yellow bus rattled and bounced over the cobbled streets, and the suitcase banged against David's legs.

"Are you sure you know the right stop?" he asked Susan anxiously.

---

* Typescript with holograph corrections by SP. Typed at top left: 'Sylvia Plath / 26 Elmwood Road / Wellesley 81, Massachusetts.' Her mother added a note: 'Winter 1949 / Atlantic Monthly Award 1950.' Submitted to *Seventeen*.

"Of course," Susan replied, and then, forgetting her attitude of cool superiority toward her younger brother, she burst out, "I can smell the salt in the air. Look, between the houses!" She pointed through the mud-spattered window, and David's eyes followed her gaze.

Sure enough! There was a gleam of blue between the crowded city tenements. The dingy buildings with their identical fronts were like stage scenery, but behind them the ocean sparkled in the warm June sunlight, and that brief glimpse was a promise—a preview of what was to come.

For David and Susan were traveling back to their childhood. This would be their first visit to their home town since they moved away five years ago.

David wrinkled his sunburnt nose enthusiastically. Along with the fresh salt breeze, memories came crowding back.

He laughed. "Remember the time we dug to China?"

Susan's eyes misted. Remember? Of course she did.

There was a grassy backyard with a flower bed where they used to play together. And there were the long mornings they had spent, digging in a corner of the garden with a small spade and shovel. She recalled the feeling of moist earth on her hands, drying and clinging.

Some grown-up had come by and asked, "Where are you digging to? China?" and then had laughed and gone away.

"We could if we digged hard enough, you know," David had observed wisely.

"No, not unless we did for ever and ever so long," replied Susan.

"Let's see how far down we can get before lunch, then."

"They'd be upside down," Susan mused aloud. The prospect of digging through to another land intrigued her.

"*Something* will be there if we dig," David said confidently. He tossed up a shovelful of earth. "See, the dirt's turning yellow."

After Susan had scooped up a great deal of sand, she exclaimed, "Wait a minute, I've hit something!" She scratched away the earth with her fingers and triumphantly produced a white, six-sided tile.

"Let *me* see," David cried. "Why, it's just like the ones in our bathroom floor. It's part of some old house."

"If we dig deeper we might come up into the cellar."

But in a little while the shovels began to move more slowly. Susan squatted back on her heels, and her eyes grew dreamy. David listened to her words as reverently as if she were an oracle.

"Perhaps . . ." she began slowly, "perhaps if we could find a white rabbit hole we wouldn't have to dig anymore, and we could just fall . . . and fall . . . and fall."

David understood. It would be just like *Alice in Wonderland*, only Susan would be Alice and he . . . well, he would still be David.

Susan heaved a sudden sigh. "We couldn't dig far enough anyway," she said, standing up and wiping her soiled hands on her yellow pinafore.

"I s'pose not," David agreed resignedly, his dream shattered. He rose, too. "Let's go out front," he said.

The two children raced over the side lawn into the front yard. The street was lazy with the drugged quiet of the summer afternoon, and the heat rose in waves from the pavement.

"I bet I can walk just touching the lines," Susan challenged her brother. She began to step carefully, treading only upon the cracks in the sidewalk.

"So can I." David tried to imitate her, but his legs were not long enough to span the large, flat cement squares, so he gave up and concentrated on something else. A small bug ran across the stones.

"I squashed an ant," David chanted proudly, moving his foot to reveal the tiny insect mutilated on the walk.

Susan would not praise him. "That's mean," she reproached. "How would *you* like to be stepped on? Poor little ant," she murmured to the spot on the path.

David said nothing.

"Poor little ant," Susan crooned sadly.

David's lower lip began to quiver. "I'm sorry," he said. "I won't ever do it again."

Susan's heart softened. "It's all right," she said magnanimously. Then her face lighted. "I know! Let's go down to the beach!"

There was a lonely little cove at the end of the street, too small for public bathing. It was here that the children liked to play in the summertime. Susan ran along with David close behind. Their bare feet thudded on the pavement, and their long, thin legs moved with a swift grace. The road dipped to the beach, and the sand had drifted up over the tarred surface.

It was good to dig your toes down in the warm sand to the cooler layer beneath, Susan thought. Something within her soared at the sight of the cloudless sky and the waves washing on the shore with a scalloped fringe of foam. The land behind her was a ledge, a narrow shelf from which she could fling herself into the vast blue space.

The children were silent as they moved down the beach, searching for shells in the line of the last high tide. The sound of the water rushing in and then withdrawing with a sigh filled their ears.

"Ouch!" David exclaimed suddenly.

"What's the matter?" questioned Susan.

"Something bit me." He lifted one foot in both hands to examine his toe. A dry piece of brittle seaweed still clung to his skin.

"That's all it was! Just seaweed!" She brushed it off scornfully.

"It *might* have been a crab," David retorted, wishing that it had been.

Picking up a piece of water-smooth glass, Susan squinted through it into the sun. "Look," she held it out to David. "Everything's so much nicer all blue."

"I wish I lived inside a glass bottle like the old woman in the story," he said. "We could have a little ladder up the side."

Susan giggled.

The sun shone down on the two figures wandering along the water's edge. Susan thoughtfully chewed the end of one pigtail; she gazed across the stony beach to where the tide was beginning to go out, revealing the oozing slime of the mud flats. Near the shore, the retreating waves foamed about a large, flat rock. As she stared at the noisy receding waters, a delightful idea came to her.

"Let's go over by the green rock," she said.

David followed her, ankle-deep through the cold, sloshing waves. The mud was soft and cool between his toes, but he walked gingerly, hoping there weren't any jagged clam shells beneath the surface. Susan climbed up on the slippery rock and stood triumphant, her pinafore flapping about her bare legs, her hair blowing in the wind that sang across the bay.

"Come on!" she shouted above the roar of the tide. David grabbed her firm, outstretched hand and sprang up beside her. They stood there, motionless, like two sturdy figureheads, until the rock was left dry by the ebb tide.

It was a large boulder, deeply imbedded in the sand so that only the upper part was visible. Above the slimy black stones, it raised a smooth green surface, like the shell of some giant turtle. There was a flat place on top where one could sit, and a few graded planes on one side formed a row of shallow steps. Indeed, the rock was like some docile animal, lost in sleep.

The children loved to climb up the friendly, irregular surface and play all sorts of magic games. Sometimes the rock would be a sailboat in stormy seas, and sometimes it became a lofty mountain. But today it was a castle.

"You dig a moat so no one can cross," commanded Susan, "and I'll sweep out the rooms."

She began to brush off all the sand while David dug a little trench around the rock itself.

There were bits of colored glass to arrange for windows, and all the periwinkles that clung to the moist side of the rock had to be flicked from their comfortable habitat on to the sharp pebbles.

David and Susan were giants in a world of minute miracles. They laid out broken shells for plates and fancied themselves a part of the miniature universe. The faintest stir of spotted crab or mud-colored sea worm could not escape their quick eyes. But they saw even more than this, for they beheld the golden turrets of the castle rising above their heads.

The sun was sinking when they stopped their play. Susan had been resting on the rock while David was searching for more colored glass. Her feet were cold and sore, but she had curled them under the skirt of her pinafore, which rested like a soft caress on her skin. As she stared out at the ocean, she wondered if she could ever explain to anyone how she felt about the sea. It was part of her, and she wanted to reach out, out, until she encompassed the horizon within the circle of her arms.

When David returned, Susan arose to meet him. She felt the mud, wet and clammy beneath her feet, and a disagreeable consciousness of the late hour passed over her. Brushing back her sticky, salt-caked hair with one hand, she said, "C'mon, Davy. Time for supper."

"Aw, just a little longer," her brother pleaded. Yet he knew it was no use, so he followed his sister's retreating back up the beach, limping a bit as he bruised his tender feet on the sharp stones.

In her mind's eye Susan saw the two small figures moving out of sight up the beach. David nudged her, and the picture faded. Slowly she returned to the present.

"We're almost there," she said, the excitement rising like tingling bubbles of ginger ale through her veins. David sat beside her, erect and proud, very conscious of his new polished brown shoes. His eyes shone.

"Let's go down to the beach when we get there," he suggested. "Maybe we can see our old house."

Susan felt a twinge of sadness. It would be hard to go past the familiar lawns and not stop to play as they had before. It would be hard to remember the places where they had had such good times . . . and pass them by. But there was the beach. Nothing could change that. There they could pretend they were little again, and no one would see.

She smiled at her reflection in the window and adjusted her wide-brimmed straw hat. Ever since she had cut her hair short, she had looked more grown-up. She might even pass for fourteen . . . well, almost.

David pointed. "There's the roof of our old school! See, between the trees." Susan saw.

The houses became more familiar, and she felt a warmth in her heart. The streets came faster now, and the children could recall old landmarks.

"That's where the carnival was."

"We used to coast down that street."

"Remember the oak tree we used to climb!"

It was as if they were riding an immense wave of recollection, rushing swiftly backward toward the past, toward their early childhood. They would not have been surprised to find themselves shrinking back into the David and Susan that used to be.

"Quick!" hissed Susan. "Pull the buzzer!"

David obliged, and the bus swung to a stop. Suitcase in hand, Susan bounded eagerly down the steps, forgetting her resolution to be prim and ladylike. David followed her out on to the sidewalk. They stood still for a moment, sniffing the salty air. The familiarity of the street tugged painfully at their hearts. They started walking. The sea twinkled blue far ahead of them.

"There's the Johnsons' house, and Andersons'," Susan announced as they progressed.

"I see Aunt Jane's," David exclaimed.

As they mounted the creaking wooden steps to the shady porch, Susan recalled the countless rainy afternoons that she and David had played on this very same front piazza while Mother visited their elderly aunt.

The door opened suddenly, and the beaming face of Aunt Jane confronted them. After the preliminary greetings were over and their suitcase had been tucked into the old-fashioned guest room, which smelled of lavender, Aunt Jane proposed, "Why don't you take a little walk before dinner? You might like to visit your old house. It looks so nice with all the new paint."

Welcoming her suggestion, Susan and David ran eagerly to the end of the street, turned the corner, and there, gleaming with a fresh coat of paint, stood the house. Susan stopped abruptly, and David tightened his grip on her hand. A hurt resentment filled them both. The new curtains in the windows, the fresh paint, the strange, shiny car in the driveway—all these things were an affront.

"I liked it a lot better without the paint," said Susan bitterly.

"Me too," agreed David.

Soberly they walked on toward the beach. There, at least, things would be the same—the ocean, the sand, and the green rock.

"Come on!" Susan rallied.

She raced David down to the shore. Her hair blew back in the wind, and the salt tasted good on her lips. The tide was out, and the smell of the seaweed was strong in the sun. The two children halted a moment, bewildered.

The beach looked smaller than they had remembered it, and there was something strange and alien concealed beneath the smooth sand and the calm, unruffled surface of the water. There was an emptiness that rose to meet them and a queer silence above the lapping of the waves. It was like entering a familiar room after a long absence and finding it vacant, desolate.

Susan made a last attempt. "Let's go down to the green rock," she said to David. It had to work, she thought. The magic must still remain by the green rock.

The boulder, too, seemed to have diminished in size. It lay among the pebbles, a heavy, inert shape; a green rock . . . nothing more. Where were the castles, the sailboats, the mountains that once had been? Only the rock remained, stark and bare.

The two children stood there for a while, mute, uncomprehending. At last Susan said wearily, "Come on, David, let's go back." They sadly turned and trudged slowly up the beach, out of sight.

The tide came in gradually, creeping up over the slimy black stones; the wind died down and whispered idly through the sand. Inward, inward rolled the waves until they closed at last over the summit of the green rock. Only a thin line of foam remained above the spot where the rock lay, silent, dark, sleeping beneath the oncoming tide.

First Date

Ts,[*] 1950, Lilly Library

It's early in July; the rain is falling outside in the afternoon twilight. And because it's falling so quietly, you have to look hard to see the thin lines of it against the trees. Only then can you be sure the rain is coming down.

(A boy in a yellow convertible is coming to call for me in fifteen minutes.)

The clock on the bureau ticks faintly; a wet breeze lifts the limp white curtains against the screen. Without looking I can hear the rain now, beating louder. The streets are slippery with it.

(I can almost fancy that no one is coming for me after all. If only the sick

---

[*] Submitted to the *Christian Science Monitor*.

feeling in my stomach would go away. If only it were tomorrow or even yesterday. But it's ten minutes of three. Today. He said he'd come at three.

Oh, I don't want to see him. Not at all.)

Car tires slither along the pavement out front, slow down, pass by.

(I will tell them downstairs that I am ill, and he will have to go home. I'll hear his footsteps retreating down the walk. The car door will slam; the engine will shudder into motion and fade away in the distance.)

My nose is shiny and my blouse is starched too much. It prickles the back of my neck when I move.

(Once I get downstairs I'll have to leave with him. Mother will be there. Mother will smile and say: How nice, dear; do have a good time, dear; and, dear, don't forget to wear your raincoat.)

That was lightning just then, flickering yellow across the sky. The rain is coming down in sheets now, splashing on the windowsill. Two drops have fallen on my arm.

(I can't go out in such a storm. I'll come to the door and say: I'm terribly sorry, but I simply can't go anywhere in this weather. Some other day, perhaps.

And I'll smile politely. Goodbye, I'll say, closing the door oh, very politely.)

It's three. The minute hand and the hour hand clip off a quarter of the clock between them. If I look long enough I'll see the minute hand move forward with a little jerk.

(I know exactly how it will be. The bell will ring metallically, echoing through the whole house. There'll be a moment's silence, just long enough to seem natural, and then she'll hurry to the door.

Why, do come in, she'll say. How wet it is outside. Please sit down. I'll call Julia.

JOO-LIA! The words would come spiraling up the staircase.

I won't answer. I might not have heard. I might have fainted. But then Mother would come up the stairs with a firm, resolute tread. The door would burst open noisily.

Julia! Mother would hiss sharply. Why aren't you ready? Why don't you come down?

I can't, Mother.

Of course you can. Don't be silly. Hurry up, now. He's waiting.)

Another car, coming slowly. This must be the one. This must be it.

But no.

(Why didn't it stop? He said he'd be here at three. Maybe he's sorry he asked me. Maybe he really didn't want to come. He may even call up and say: Julia,

I'm awfully sorry, but I got a flat tire on the way over. Guess I won't be able to make it. Some other day perhaps.

Goodbye, Julia, he'll say politely, hanging up the receiver with a final little click.)

It's after three, and the second hand keeps whirring, whirring.

(Oh, Lord, why doesn't he come. He *said* he'd be here at three. Why . . .

I know. Yes. That's it. He's going to stand me up. Why didn't I think of that before? He's probably laughing somewhere right now. He's most likely telling his friends: Sure, I called her up for a date. But who'd go out with her? It was only for a joke. That's all it was.

Yes, he's going to stand me up. But what will I tell them downstairs? I'll say casually: Our date? Oh, we decided to postpone it. The rain, you know.)

I think I am going to be sick. This time I really am.

"JOO-LIA!" Mother's voice called from downstairs.

Julia pattered down softly, swiftly in her ballerinas. Miraculously he stood here in the hallway, smiling shyly.

"I-I hope I didn't keep you waiting," he said.

"Keep me waiting?" She laughed almost hysterically. "Waiting? Why, no. Not at all."

And as he helped her into her raincoat she smiled up at him, her eyes twinkling.

"Oh, no!" she said again. "Not at all."

The New Girl

Ts,[*] 1950, Lilly Library

Judy Jordan. Even the name was too perfect, thought Clara Williams as she turned automatically in to English. Her thin red mouth tightened into its customary artificial smile. She sat down stiffly.

All the kids were clustered around Judy's chair as usual, but Clara opened her book, pretending not to see. Even Mr. Arnold was smiling benignly on the little group from his desk at the front of the room. The bell rang for class to begin with a harsh metallic clangor. Clara gritted her teeth. Today was the day. All week she had been dreading it.

---

[*] Typescript has holograph corrections and additions by SP.

Mr. Arnold stepped forward. Loose ends of conversation softened, melted into silence. Smiling enigmatically, cherishing the feathery, expectant hush which awaited his words, he spoke slowly.

"As you know, the winner of the short-story contest is to be announced this period. No doubt you are all a bit curious to know the outcome of the judging and to hear the story itself. But first there are several business matters to discuss." And his voice lapsed into a dry monotone, rising and falling like a rowboat moored on a calm sea.

Clara slouched down in her seat. With a strange fascination she stared at the perfect being next to her, while Judy Jordan, oblivious of this minute inspection, continued to gaze in the direction of Mr. Arnold's voice. Her black hair was cut short and fluffy, just the right length. She was small and neatly made. Fair skin. Black eyes. Her red sweater and navy blue pleated skirt were unbearably bright. Even the silver sparkle of her identification bracelet seemed to assert smugly: "I belong to Judy Jordan."

Clara was forced to admit her grudging admiration, however. She was almost tempted to do a furtive pencil sketch of this terrible and lovely creature, but she didn't dare. Mr. Arnold was strict about inattention in class. He would make one of his sarcastic remarks, and she would be laughed at, embarrassed.

In a big high school like this, she mused, you'd think one new girl wouldn't make much difference. But ever since Judy had arrived, Clara had had that cold sick feeling at the pit of her stomach, that uneasy chill at the nape of her neck. She thought back.

It had all begun one morning about two weeks ago. Just before the last bell rang, Susie Lane had dashed into homeroom, her pale eyes gleaming, her chubby pink cheeks shining with perspiration and importance. She breezed to her seat, banged her books on the desk dramatically, and announced in a breathless voice to everyone in general, "Guess what! Judy Jordan is coming back!"

Clara had raised her eyes from her Latin book for a moment. Judy Jordan. The name meant nothing to her. Ignoring the excited buzz of chatter which had arisen, she went back to her scansion of Virgil. A new girl was nothing to get excited about. If it had been a boy . . . well, that was something else again.

Clara sat at her desk, a serene island of self-sufficiency in a green wool dress. Around her flowed waves of the latest morning gossip. She was very tall, very slender, with long brown hair curled about a face some people would have considered extremely attractive. But Clara was smart—a "brain," and she had decided long ago that the accepted version of popularity didn't come hand in hand with an all "A" report card. A leader in all subjects, particularly English and Art, she didn't seem to mind when other girls whispered endlessly about their dates last weekend or about a coming dance. She had a secure position at the head of the class, and there was Allan.

Allan was smart, too, and he was trying for a scholarship to college, so he didn't have much time for weekend dating. He liked a girl with original ideas, so he took Clara to the school dances each month. All the girls thought Allan was awfully good-looking (a bit too diligent about his studying perhaps, but how could one find fault with his crest of blonde hair and his easy, melting grin?)

So Clara had prestige. She was accepted, if not applauded, as she was secure in her position. Every time she walked into class she had a warm solid feeling of belonging—yet she remained somewhat aloof, never quite conforming to the teenage standard of feminine cuteness. Oh yes, it was all fine—until Susie had come up to her that day before English and said, not maliciously exactly, but sort of gloating, "You know, Clara, you better watch out. Judy will be here in a week, and she's already got one of her stories published in a regular magazine."

That period Mr. Arnold had read one of Clara's themes and praised it in the roundabout way he had of paying a compliment. Ordinarily that would have made her glow with pride, but that casual teasing remark of Susie's had stuck a cold needle of foreboding under Clara's left rib.

As she went to Math she smiled a wooden smile. She felt it slipping jerkily. She frowned. Oh, she could handle those cute little fluffs who stammered wrong answers in French, or dashed off a term paper in one study period. These girls were no threat to her, but this Judy Jordan . . . Maybe she was fat, Clara thought hopefully. Maybe she was even homely. But it was no use to reason that way. She had to know.

Susie was supposedly Judy's best friend, so when the Math teacher had turned his back, Clara had leaned over to Susie's desk and hissed, "Hey, Sue, what's Judy like, anyhow? I'll bet she's terrific." The words had hurt her a little, but she managed them carelessly enough.

Susie had scribbled a hasty note, tossed it to Clara with a practiced hand. "You'll see for yourself in a day or two," it read. "She's real intelligent and pretty, and popular with the boys."

The blood had begun to pound hotly in Clara's forehead. She could hear the dull rhythmic thud of her heart knocking against her ribs. This wasn't happening. Not to her. Susie and the rest of them were just fooling, just trying to make her miserable.

But the next few days had confirmed Clara's fears. Already the newspaper staff was planning to ask Judy to join, and so was that exclusive sorority. The boys hung around Susie who, giggling with plump satisfaction, was enjoying her position as reporter.

"She's five feet three with dark eyes and black hair," she was telling the track captain.

Clara's imagination went to work. She pictured a glamorous petite girl saying to her, "Why yes, I've almost finished my novel. You only got an A minus in the French test? Me? Oh, A plus, naturally. And I can't make up my mind which boy to go to the sorority dance with." Clara thought Judy must be insufferably proud.

At last the fateful day had come, and Clara walked into homeroom with her monotonous Mona Lisa smile. Her books were wet where her fingers gripped them.

There she was. Judy Jordan. Solid. Three-dimensional. And real. She was all Clara had imagined, only instead of bragging, she was asking eager questions of the group of boys and girls crowding around her.

Clara went to her seat feeling left out. No one noticed her. Everybody was too busy laughing and explaining the intricacies of the lunch shift to Judy. Clara was being slighted, and Judy was to blame.

The next two weeks were a nightmare. The initial excitement had died down of course, but each day saw that lively laughing girl more firmly entrenched in the school pattern. If only she were *just* smart or *just* pretty or *just* popular, Clara agonized. But not all three at once. And the boys and girls liked her even if she was smart. Nobody called her a brain, either.

Then there came the short-story contest. All through the week while writing her story, Clara had wondered what Judy was writing. It was no use. No matter what it was, Judy was sure to win. And she, Clara, had wanted so much to receive the prize and Mr. Arnold's rare praise. It would have meant so much more to her who had nothing, while Judy had all she ever could want. The new girl took on the proportions of a hateful monster, bent on taking all of Clara's honors away from her.

And now the winner was to be announced. It was decided, but only Mr. Arnold and the judges knew. Clara was in anguish. Of course it would be Judy, and yet, and yet . . .

Mr. Arnold's voice had risen to the pitch reserved for very special statements. A few preliminary remarks, and then:

"Although the decision was difficult, the judges have agreed to award the first prize to . . ." Oh, unbearable uncertainty, dripping thick and moist, prickling down Clara's back.

"The first prize goes to Clara Williams."

Something broke. Sunlight shattered into a million glassy fragments; desks and faces blurred, seen through tears. Somewhere far off, indefinite music rose, shrill and triumphant. And there, miraculously, was Judy Jordan across the aisle. "I'm so glad, Clara . . ." she was saying, warmly, her black eyes shining with admiration. The music soared in a crescendo of song.

Mr. Arnold read the story. He read it as he alone could read. But Clara only half heard the familiar words, for over and over she was repeating to herself, incredulous, "Why, I do believe she's actually glad. I can see why they like her. She actually is glad for me. Actually glad."

Suddenly she realized that she didn't hate Judy after all. The distorted image had vanished, and Clara's ears were red with shame. It was *she* who had been the hateful one, the malicious one. When class was ended she went up to Judy, smiling her first real smile for weeks. A bit shyly, she ventured, "Judy—how about coming over my house after school tomorrow afternoon? You could bring some of your stories and . . ."

"I'd love to. I thought your story was just wonderful," Judy answered quickly. And she added with something like relief, " You know, I've been wanting to get to know you for weeks."

So they went walking down the hall together. One new girl beside another.

The English Bike

Ts,* summer 1950, Lilly Library

It was already dark when she started to bike home from the farm; her cotton shirt was wet through from the thin rain which had begun to fall. The bicycle tires, slim and patrician, made a slithering sound as they cleft neatly through the inky pools of water on the street. It was past suppertime.

---

* The typescript has holograph corrections and additions in SP's hand. Accompanied by an earlier start to the story which was identified as 'The English Bike' by Aurelia Schober Plath, and consisting of one typed paragraph: 'It was cold for May, and the rain that had been threatening all morning was coming (beginning to) down thin and wet. The girl bicycling behind the red-haired boy, bent low over the handlebars of her English bike, her hair loose and straight about her face, her sweatshirt damp and steaming. They had been going steadily for two hours now, and there was no thinking of turning back, not with Perry in the lead, his back lean and uncompromising in the plaid lumber shirt which stretched tautly over his shoulders, sticking wetly to his skin. The tires of her bike cleft neatly through the inky pools of water on the tarred street with a slithering sound.'

For over an hour she had been pedaling along the wooded road when all at once the lights of a house spilled out across the dusk and shone in her eyes. It was the Saunders' place. As she approached, she could see through the window. The family was gathered about the table in a mellow, honey-colored square of light. Dinner was about to be served.

She slowed her pace, squeezing gently on the handbrakes. Home was still far off, and she was hungry. She would stop at the Saunders' even though Bob was away for the weekend. Gravel crunched under the wheels of her bike as she turned sharply into the driveway.

Mrs. Saunders was pleased to see her and set an extra place at the table.

"I'm starved," the girl laughed apologetically, sitting down. The warmth, the gleaming white linen, were a comfort to her.

"Potatoes," she said. "I like them awfully." She ate six small ones, hot with butter and salt. That, at least, would hold her till she got home.

After the meal the family sat and talked for a while preliminary to clearing away the dishes. Mrs. Saunders was extremely attentive to her guest, exchanging conversation about family affairs. When the question came, the girl was taken unawares.

"And do you remember your mother's friend, Mrs. Eaton?" The silence was all interrogation, smooth and poised. But there was something underneath. The ominous suggestion of an ambush somewhere.

The girl was naturally uneasy; she was conscious of being watched intently by everyone in the room. Mrs. Saunders' lips were parted in a smile, waiting.

Mrs. Eaton. No, there was nothing there. Merely a harmless query. Really, she was being absurd.

"Why of course, Mrs. Eaton," the girl burst out in a rush of words which tumbled after one another gaily, a bit frantically.

"Of course I remember. A comfortable fat sort of woman. And there was Laurence. Oh, he was lovely, and he played the violin."

Was she being too intimate, too confiding?

"Mother was quite taken with him when she was a girl."

She stopped. There was nothing more to say. The silence was worse now because of all the tumbled little words. It was like sweeping dust under a rug; the rug was still there, more aloof, more formidable than ever because of the dust.

She had said something wrong. It had been a trap after all. She could tell by the way Mrs. Saunders' eyes caught the light as a cat's do, absorbing it quickly, becoming deceptively blank. She could tell by all the secret, amused little smiles that flickered around the table.

Unnerved, she got up hurriedly. She would go home and tell Mother. Mother would know what she had done wrong.

Mrs. Saunders moved her large soft bulk with a sigh. Her smile was frightfully kind; it was curved with pity.

"Must you go so soon, dear?" she asked.

"Y-yes. Mother is expecting me."

"But just a moment. Please. Here comes Peter. You must say hello to Peter before you go."

The front door had opened and a small boy stood there. Bob's brother. His lumber shirt was silver with mist and he brought the smell of rain in with him. He gave the girl an obedient grin, reserved for company; his freckled nose crinkled up.

The girl stared at him in silent horror. There was a plant growing from his face. A spidery sort of green weed.

They were all waiting to see what she would do. It was a deliberate trick, a carefully planned pitfall. The front door was open over there, but she must not scream, she must not run. What then?

No one moved; the small boy still grinned vacantly up at her. It was terribly important that she did not make another mistake.

With a deprecating little laugh she stepped forward and plucked the vegetable growth from the boy's face as nonchalantly as one would remove a thread from a friend's lapel.

"Why," she said, "I thought it was growing from your mouth. But it was really from your cheek."

That did it. They were momentarily baffled by her calm approach. She left them there and walked out of the door, across the grass to where her bike was waiting for her in the rain, the bike that Mother had given her for a graduation present, shiny and black, with the gear lines like an insect's antennae, sensitive and down-curving.

She kicked up the stand, mounted. As she began to pedal home, the headlight flickered, grew brighter, and then burned steadily, carving a luminous tunnel out of the darkness ahead.

Mother was lying on the porch when the girl came in. Mother had been crying; her face was pale and her eyes were full of unshed tears.

The girl knew that she was to blame for the tears. She sat down soberly on the green chair. The metal was dull and cold against the back of her thighs.

"Mother," she began. But she knew that it wasn't right. The words came out so queerly when she attempted to explain. She tried to speak calmly; it was no use. The tears would come, hot and wet, drowning the confused pathetic little words. From somewhere inside her, laughter welled up, giddy and uncontrollable.

This had to stop. They'd think she was hysterical. But it was so awful; it was so funny. Mother was still looking at her sorrowfully. Mother wasn't even trying to understand. And the girl knew it was all wrong. She swallowed her tears and became silent save for an occasional gulping sob, a spasmodic gasp of laughter. She listened.

Mother spoke sadly, as if to someone else, someone far off, someone who really couldn't hear her.

"They read Bob's letters."

Bob's letters. The girl visualized the countless thin crackly white envelopes bordered with airmail red and blue. Those witty, inimitable letters she had sent him all summer while he was out west. He had liked them. It had been like writing a diary full of all the incoherent unconventional little thoughts she could never have told to anyone else.

They had read Bob's letters. But how? Somewhere she had been betrayed. Someone she trusted had betrayed her.

The metal chair was dull and frigid under her. Sickened, she gazed morosely outside through the porch screen at the rain, which was still falling in a chill mist.

The bike stood there, arrogantly erect on the lawn. Black, shiny, accusing, it glittered viciously under the hazy nimbus of the street light. A thousand cold little eyes stared at her from the polished surface. And hate froze in her heart like a rod of steel.

The bed was soft under her, and the furniture was indistinct, hazy with before-dawn grayness. In an adjoining room a voice croaked, hoarse and broken, "Mama, Mama, Mama."

She wondered idly who was calling.

"Mama, Mama, Mama."

Slippered footsteps approached in little sandpapery rushes across the floor. Warm, sympathetic arms encircled her; flesh comforted flesh.

Mother was saying, "It's all right, baby. It's all right."

The girl began to weep silently, weakly. But Mother kept on rocking her back and forth in her arms repeating, "It's all over, baby. It's all over."

Den of Lions

Written: *c.* September 1950
Published: *Seventeen* (May 1951): 127, 144–5[*]

Marcia had put her thumb to her mouth and was clenching the tip of it between her teeth. Emile, next to her on the blue leather couch, removed her thumb gently and shot an amused glance at Alby. Seated lumpishly on the chair, his heavy frame slouched, his hands dangling loosely from his coat sleeves, Alby appeared to be steeped in lethargy, lost in a sluggish torpor. But he had caught Emile's gesture, and his keen, gluttonous eyes crackled back a signal of electric mirth.

There were eight of them around the little table. Marcia flicked her gaze from face to face. Peter, Alby, Gordon, Emile. Beverly, Natalie, Lucy. The names rolled around in her mind, rich and rhythmic as a biblical chant.

Peter was leaning forward, his face blurred in a bland, buttery smile. He was telling another one of his stories. Lucy nudged Marcia.

"Sit front. You can't hear otherwise."

Lucy's voice was delightfully fluid; the words swam about like slippery fish, undulating, blending into one another.

Obediently Marcia sat front, attempting to reproduce Lucy's attitude of gay, attentive nonchalance.

The drinks were on the table, and the glasses had marked wet rings on the polished surface. Marcia liked the different shades of amber. Her ginger ale, white-gold, looked quite dashing with the cherry in it. The beer was several shades deeper, golden brown. And the rest; she wasn't sure what the rest were made of. In the glass ashtray there was a heap of cigarette butts now—papery white grubs with ashen entrails strewn in a fine gray dust across the table.

Peter had finished the story. It was one of his worst, and the boys grinned

---

[*] Winner of third prize in *Seventeen*'s short-story contest. Printed with a photograph of SP and a biographical sketch: 'Sylvia Plath who wrote "Den of Lions" is a Wellesley, Mass., native. Now 18 and a freshman at Smith College (she received a full scholarship), this marks Sylvia's fourth appearance as an author in *Seventeen*. Not bad, we say, for someone who plans to study creative writing next year.' SP's previous appearances were an anonymously printed response to a question posed by the magazine, 'When I'm a Parent', *Seventeen* (November 1949): 77; 'And Summer Will Not Come Again', *Seventeen* (August 1950): 191, 275–6; and her poem 'Ode to a Bitten Plum', *Seventeen* (November 1950): 104. Accompanied by an illustration by Floyd Johnson, eighteen, from Topeka, Kansas, captioned, 'The waitress seemed like a hangman ready to execute her.'

appreciatively. Marcia had not been listening; still, some reaction was expected of her. She tried a little laugh, but the timing was wrong and it tinkled like broken glass onto the table where everyone could stare at the pathetic, splintered pieces.

As if her laughter had been a signal, the tide of attention turned. The telescope spun, focused on her. Peter was staring at the red poppy in her hair.

"Is that a real flower, Marcia?" he asked with a suave, oily smile that said: Watch this, kids.

He had her cornered. No matter what she thought to say, it would be meat for the sacrifice.

"Yes," she said slowly, deliberately. "It's real; it's basic." She was ready, the spark of amusement in her eyes. They could laugh, but she was there first, wrapped in the transparent, crinkled cellophane of mirth.

Basic. The word had been what they wanted. Toss a slab of raw meat to the lions. Let them nose it, paw it, gulp it down, and maybe you'll have a chance to climb a tree out of their reach in the meantime.

Basic. The laughter needled in and out.

"That's Pete's expression," Gordon said.

"Oh, could we squelch someone now," chortled Alby.

The words kept coming, whirling lower and lower. Marcia could hardly understand them. Miserable, white-hot embarrassment flared through her, licking at her cheeks, her neck, her ears. If she smoked, she would have taken a long drag and leisurely exhaled an insolent little cloud to cover her panic. As it was, she reached for the reassuring three-dimensional solidity of her ginger ale glass. They pounced on that, too.

"Ginger ale . . ." Natalie's voice was seared with scorn.

"Not really," someone derided.

"Too much kick for me," laughed someone else.

The fire was getting heavy. Marcia shrank inward, hearing the shells burst closer.

Peter was about to begin another story, but first he slanted a mocking look in her direction and said in a taunting, baby voice, "I'd tell the Swiss one, only Marcia's here."

Her voice astringent as vinegar, Marcia stabbed back, "Oh, I'll crawl under the table."

"I will, too." Miraculously Lucy was there, leaning over the boundary line, the fifty-four forty mark. She drawled liquidly, very low, "He's not always this way, honey. Don't let it throw you."

Throw me, Marcia thought bleakly. Is it as obvious as all that? You'd think that in seventeen years I could have learned to be calm and self-possessed in a situation like this. You'd think I could have learned to laugh it off. But no, I sit here like a wooden duck at the circus. Two free cigars and a toy dog, ladies and gentlemen, if you hit the target. I suppose it amuses them; they must get quite a satisfaction out of tearing me methodically into little pieces.

Lucy, at least, means well. Very likely her room is wallpapered with good intentions. Still, that remark of hers eased the pressure.

Marcia turned toward Emile and smiled. His impudent one-sided grin flashed back. Was he with her? Anything to keep him there, in the balance. Lean a little this way, her eyes pleaded.

Emile's pupils widened, questioning. In that critical moment she had to score a victory.

"Think the rain'll hurt the rhubarb?"

It was an absurd cliché she had heard somewhere. If he didn't understand, everything would be all right. His eyes clouded. Baffled, he said, "Tomorrow? . . . I don't get it."

He had gone under. She wasn't on the bottom of the deck anymore. As if to preserve her small moment of triumph, the music flooded in from the dance floor and broke in waves of sound at her feet.

"Come on." Emile's hand was warm and comforting on hers. Marcia got up with him and they left the room together. She didn't look at the other six, sitting there in a smug little haze of smoke, but she tossed her long, brown hair proudly as she went past.

On the dance floor the music took them in, lapping about them, an intimate, golden sea of pulsing rhythm. Marcia felt the shattered fragments of her composure growing back together again.

"You know," Marcia smiled lazily up at Emile, "I understand how the Christians felt in the arena before the second pack of lions was brought in."

"*What?*"

Perhaps she had gone too far. After all, how could he be expected to see what she meant?

"Oh, nothing worth repeating." Her smile was apologetic and appealing. The question in his eyes dissolved, and he nuzzled his face in her hair, his lips wet and gentle on her cheek.

All right, her body yielded to his, dipping and swaying in time to the music. We'll call it off for now. We won't think about it. From now on we're together. They were unfair weapons, those remarks of mine, but I'd gone under twice; I was drowning. I had to be sure you were on my side, Emile.

Emile. The name reached out and caught at her thoughts like a jagged nail. This was the first time he had asked her out; no doubt it would be the last. He was an integral part of that crowd in there. Like them he was poised and polished on the outside, moving blithely from one cocktail party to another, from one pretty girl to the next.

Strange that he should have made the mistake of asking her out. Under the circumstances he was behaving admirably. He had even asked if she minded his drinking, which was laughable, since the only ones who had minded anything at all were the others. Yes, Emile had been considerate. In fact, he was not only considerate, but he was also quite handsome. In fact, Marcia admitted, she liked him rather well.

Enough. She made an effort and turned her thoughts away from him, switching to another topic. Take Lucy, now. She was something more than the other girls there tonight. She was the symbol of what Marcia might be someday . . . lovely, sleek, and vivacious; the sort of girl one could invite on fraternity weekends . . .

Marcia's attention spiraled back to the dance floor. They were playing the last number now, a waltz. This dance, she told herself, is the reprieve, the white flag, the pause that refreshes. Eat of it; drink of it; be merry in it. For tomorrow . . .

At last the set was over and Emile was steering her back across the floor to the room where they had left the others. She could feel the tension mounting again, taut as a violin string being tightened to pitch. As she went by the great hall mirror, the silver surface tossed her reflection back at her.

I shouldn't have worn the brown cotton, she thought. It's too homespun. Taffeta, something arrogant, something that would retaliate with a rustle, with a swish; that would have been better. The gold is good, though. The gold ballet shoes, the gold bracelet, the encircling gold belt. They fight back for me with barbed arrows, tiny gold needles of light.

The group was still there when Marcia and Emile returned. Marcia sat down. The waitress was there taking orders, a nondescript, commonplace woman.

"Last call," she said, "before twelve."

The impartial hangman, Marcia smiled to herself. She doesn't know the noose is around my neck. I simply will not hear her repeat ginger ale after him again.

"Not a thing, thanks," she murmured to Emile in a plump, fed voice.

At five minutes to twelve the waitress returned to collect bottles and glasses hurriedly.

Pete gave a throaty sigh. "Nothing I hate more than rushing beer."

The counter was swept clean. Voices and footfalls were muted into softness by the tufted rug. As the peaceful sabbath silence descended, the others prepared to leave.

Lucy and Gordon were driving home with Alby and Natalie. That left Marcia and Emile to go home with Beverly and Pete.

Once in the car, Marcia let the tension trickle out of her pores. The center of resistance faded, circling outward. The opposition was dissolved. Emile had closed his eyes and was leaning back, relaxed, his hand on hers.

Through half-shut eyes Marcia watched the windshield. It had begun to rain, and the heavy summer evening flowed about her like thick molasses. She let the night come at her, with the lights blurred and fluid against the window glass. Raindrops on the pane threw phantom shadows, fleeting polka dots, across Emile's face.

The two in the front seat were on another planet, while Marcia swung in her orbit alone, spinning in vast space. Thoughts whirled in a dizzy carnival through her brain. And then, suddenly, the realization came to her. It came swift and frozen, as the second when a roller coaster balances on top of the highest loop before flinging itself down the steep incline. It sprang into sharp focus, as when one twists the lens of binoculars and the hazy distance leaps out all at once with breathtaking clarity.

In that crystallized moment, Marcia knew that no matter how much she liked Emile, no matter how much she envied Lucy, she would never pay the price. For the cost of admission into that brilliant tinsel world was high. You had to sacrifice part of your identity; you had to compromise things that were intangible, yet terribly important.

Still, it was hard to choose. It was like putting away a Christmas ornament. You held the lovely, lacquered globe a bit before laying it aside. It was patterned with red and blue and trimmed with spangles, so you held it tenderly a little while, knowing that inside there was nothing, only loneliness enclosed in a fragile gift shell.

Emile was quiet, his eyes still shut. She gazed at him with something like affection. When you knew that this was the last time, the goodbye, it hit you harder. She looked at his eyelashes, long and shadowy on his lean cheeks; his dark hair, and his slender jaw white, chalky, in the strange light. She looked at his mouth, sensuous and lovely. This was Emile. Layer after layer, and then this, the core, the heart.

He opened his eyes, and the moment retreated slowly, reluctantly as a wave sucking back into the sea. There was a brief sheen on the sand, a glassed blue reflection of the sky. And it was gone.

Emile watched Marcia for a moment, his eyes catching the light, absorbing it. Then his hands slid down the cool bareness of her arms and his mouth was sweet on hers. The car slowed its plush cradle-rocking and glided up before her drive.

At the door Emile said, "Come here, I want to whisper something." He put his lips to her ear, and the breath of his words fluttered her hair.

"I like you a lot," he said, "but not too much. I don't want to like anyone too much."

It was a challenge; the cards were on the table, and she could bid or pass.

She drew back, her smile a bright flag of hurt.

"You know, Emile . . ." It was hard. She had not known it would be so hard. "You know, Emile," she said, "I'm not going to see you anymore."

Amused acceptance flickered in his black eyes. He had known somehow that it would end like this.

Being a girl, being vulnerable and very young, she needed something to cling to. Even words would help.

"I came close, didn't I?" she said.

"A lot closer than anyone for a long time," he told her.

Her face had crumpled like newspaper in the rain; she was crying softly.

"Stop it," he commanded. He held her at arm's length, his fingers digging into her flesh. The words came out harshly, bitten off between his teeth: "You lucky kid. You don't know how lucky you are."

And he turned away down the walk with his jaunty, independent stride. No last, long look. Nothing.

Watch My Line!

Ts,[*] *c.*1947–50, Lilly Library

You know, Jim, every now and then the little woman gets ideas about improving the house. Starts hankering after some fancy gadget to make chores a bit easier. Like that combination apple-corer-and-peeler, cherry-pitter, and fluted-cucumber-slicer Mabel bought last week. Worked like a breeze and cost me a

---

[*] Typed in top-right corner: 'Sylvia Plath / 26 Elmwood Road / Wellesley, Massachusetts.'

pretty penny. She doesn't use it anymore, though. Seems it took longer to clean the doodad than it did to polish off the job herself. Like I say, live and learn.

Well, sir, this week Mabel started to hit me pretty regular for an extension phone upstairs. Now we've already got one phone, a perfectly dandy little black model in the kitchen. But anyway, the little woman began getting after me to have this extension phone installed upstairs right in the bedroom. Can't say I'm not fair. Heard all her pros and then came up with the cons. Didn't go out for debate at good old State U. for nothing, eh, Jim?

First of all, she says, an extension phone means extra privacy. For example, when that nosey Mrs. Doogle comes over to chat, if Mabel is on the phone upstairs, Mrs. Doogle will just have to wait downstairs, until Mabel is finished talking, without hearing a word. Instead of Mrs. Doogle standing outside the back door and listening in for Lord knows how long before she rings the bell. Sure, I know it sounds funny, Jim, but you know these women. Give them an inch.

What did I say? "Well, Mabel," I says, "knowing Mrs. Doogle, she'll just pick up that downstairs phone real quiet-like and listen in on every word you say upstairs." That stopped Mabel for a minute. But you know the little woman once she gets an idea. Nothing if not persistent. Went right on about the extra convenience angle. Seems the phone always rings when she's upstairs cleaning. An extension would eventually save thousands of steps and for only a few cents a day.

"Okay, okay," I say, calm as a hard-boiled egg. "But you know yourself how convenient it is to have the phone muffled down in the kitchen so you can't hear it when you're upstairs in the shower. This way you never have to bother running around through the house dribbling soapsuds. And another thing, shut the bedroom door upstairs and weekend mornings you can sleep right through the ringing without feeling guilty."

Well, Jim, she admits this too. But there's one more ace up the sleeve. The extra protection line. When I'm away on a sales trip, Mabel says, looking very unprotected and pathetic, wouldn't I like to know she was safe and sound and had a phone right by the bed in case there was a burglar or anything?

"Sure, sure," I say, "But ever heard about the brutal murder of that hoity-toity society lady, Flora Finkel? No? Well, it seems this burglar sneaked in merely to snitch a few diamond bracelets and heard the Finkel dame lift up her bedside phone to call the police. Made him so angry he upped and killed her. Yup, strangled her with the old extension cord."

Like I say, Jim, you got to nip these fancy female notions in the bud.

Room in the World

Ts,* 7 March 1951, Lilly Library

Characters
  AB, a factory worker out of a job
  PAULINE, his wife
  FRANCES
  JAPPY

SCENE—*A tenement house in any city.*
The curtain is lowered in the middle of the act to note the passing of two hours.

SCENE—*The kitchen of a tenement house. On the left wall there is a door leading to the bedroom. Downstage left there is an old bureau with a mirror over it. A greasy black stove stands a few yards out from the rear wall on the left. Near the stove is a market basket partially covered with a soiled baby blanket. On the right wall are a sink, under which is a tin pail and some paper bags, and an ice chest. Downstage right is a kitchen table covered with pea-green oilcloth. On the rear wall is a door leading down the back stairs, and to the right of it are two small dingy windows, curtained with cheap yellow chintz. A clock is on the shelf above the sink and it ticks loudly.*
It is late afternoon, and the wan spring sunlight comes in through the fly-speckled windows, making squares of light on the stained hardwood floor.
  PAULINE *is sitting at the kitchen table, sewing, her mending basket on the floor beside her. She is past forty, plump, with a tired yet patient face. Her hair is graying, and her housedress is faded to a gray. In fact, she is in perfect harmony with the kitchen which, except for the gaudy tablecloth and curtains, is a subtle study in varying tones of gray and brown. Footsteps are heard ascending the back stairs, and* PAULINE *rises to close the door to the bedroom.*
  AB *enters. He is dressed in workman's dungarees and shirt. He carries a worn leather jacket and the day's paper.* AB *stands in the doorway, staring sullenly at* PAULINE, *who jabs her needle nervously into the material. After a moment of silence she masters herself and speaks.*

---

* Written for English 11b at Smith College, assignment 7. Misdated 1950 by SP. Typescript has holograph corrections and additions by SP and comments by her teacher.

PAULINE (*in a studied conversational tone*): Either the clock is fast, or Frances must have been kept in. (AB *still stares at her from under lowered brows.*) She's done her homework, I know.

(*She turns her mending over and examines it with careful scrutiny.*)

AB (*between his teeth*): I tried every God-damned one of them. I seen all their chippy secretaries. They're all too God-damned busy to see me. I'm only working there *nine* years. Maybe that ain't long enough.

PAULINE: No one can say you ain't tried.

AB: Tried? I done everything but crawl along the corridors on my belly. It's "see the super. It's up to the super." Nuts!

(AB *smacks the paper viciously on the kitchen table and slumps down into a chair opposite* PAULINE.)

PAULINE (*sympathetically*): Them real-estate people are over the super.

AB: They won't even see me. You seen what they written me.

PAULINE: It was a sin the old super had to die.

AB (*ominously*): The new one will take me back. I ain't saying how but I'm gonta get back on the job.

(*A child's footsteps are heard on the stairs.* PAULINE *hurries to open the door.* FRANCES *skips excitedly into the room. She is a pale thin girl of eight, dressed in a worn yellow sweater and brown skirt which serve to emphasize her sallow complexion. She carries a brown jacket over one arm and a spelling book in her hand.*)

AB (*ignoring* FRANCES, *bangs a hand on the kitchen table, crying out angrily*): I ain't going back crawling to them, neither, to get it!

PAULINE (*glancing anxiously at the baby basket to see if the sleeping child has been wakened by the noise*): Maybe . . .

AB (*interrupting*): Maybe, nothing! I'll be back on the job, wait and see.

FRANCES (*who has been tugging on* PAULINE's *sleeve to get attention*): Ma! I been telling you.

(AB *glares at* FRANCES.)

106

PAULINE (*quickly*): We're talking now, Pa and me.

FRANCES (*breathless with excitement*): Only, Ma, let me tell you about the new little girl, she came today. She's got curls just like Shirley Temple.

AB (*impatiently*): Shut up!

FRANCES: The new little girl, she looks just like Shirley Temple.

PAULINE (*pinching* FRANCES' *cheek gently*): Play in the other room. Jappy's asleep in yours and his.

FRANCES: No, I don't wanta. I wanta tell you about the new little girl, Ma, she's got red paint on her fingernails. Can't I have . . .

PAULINE (*interrupting*): You're getting your Pa worked up, not minding. (*She crosses to the sink and reaches for a tin pail which she hands to* FRANCES.) Go on down and get me five cents' worth of milk, hear me. Tell him your Ma said she'd stop in and pay up tomorrow.

(FRANCES *leaves the room.* AB *heaves a heavy sigh.* PAULINE *has sat down and taken up her sewing again.*)

PAULINE (*without looking up*): She's only eight.

AB (*grumpily*): I'm trying to think out what to do and she comes in babbling till she gets me all mixed up.

PAULINE: Try to think what you was thinking before.

AB: What do you think I'm trying to do?

(*There is one of those silences pregnant with unspoken words. The clock can be heard ticking with monotonous persistence.* PAULINE *keeps her head bent over her work till* AB *speaks.*)

AB (*meditatively*): You know how they do when a lot of them go out on strike.

PAULINE: Well?

AB: Like I read once in a newspaper, see, a fellow and his whole family, they go out with signs, asking for his job back.

PAULINE: Like them pickets is what you mean.

AB: Yeah, I guess that's it.

PAULINE (*stopping her sewing and looking at* AB): I couldn't leave Frances take care of the baby.

AB: No, she'd let it smother or something. (*He looks down at his hands for a while.*) I could take the kids, see, all of us wearing signs asking for my job back.

PAULINE: I could make the signs OK, if we had some kind of stiff paper. You wouldn't walk Jappy too long, would you, Ab? He don't stand much walking.

AB (*standing up, face aglow*): That would get them, all right, you bet. Maybe them newspaper guys will come around and take our pictures. (*He takes a pencil from his pocket and rummages under the sink for some paper bags. He finds one and takes it to the table, smoothing out the wrinkles.*)

PAULINE: Maybe down at the corner, they'd give you some stiff paper.

AB (*excitedly leaning over the table, wetting the pencil on his tongue*): Now we'll say . . . (*He wets the pencil again.*) What'll we say?

PAULINE: If the sign's for the kids it had oughta say something about "My pa" and so on.

AB (*admiringly*): You got brains, Pauline. "Please get my pa back his job." How's that?

PAULINE: OK.

AB: We'll make Jappy's and Frances' alike. Now mine. (*He wets the pencil.*) What would you say?

PAULINE: "Get me back my job at the Stark Building," how about that?

AB: No. (*He starts to print.*) How's this? "Fired for no reason after nine years being watchman at the Stark Building."

PAULINE: That's OK.

AB (*gleefully*): OK? It's the nuts? Wait till I see the faces of them birds who think they ain't gonta take me back.

(PAULINE *looks at the clock, and starts toward the bedroom to wake* JAPPY. FRANCES *comes in the back door with the pail of milk, puts it down on the ice chest, and comes to lean over* AB's *shoulder, watching curiously as he letters the three signs on brown paper.*)

FRANCES: Pa?

AB: Yeah?

FRANCES: Pa, what are them paper bags for?

AB (*surveying his handiwork with pride*): Signs, Franny. (*He turns toward her.*) Say, kid, how'd you like to help your pa get back his job? Look.

(AB *starts to pin one sign on* FRANCES. PAULINE *comes into the room with* JAPPY, *who is a pale skinny little boy about four. Evidently she has told him a little about the plan, for he goose-steps around the table.*)

JAPPY (*chanting*): I'm a picket, I'm a picket, I'm a picket.

(PAULINE *pins a sign on him while* FRANCES *tries to see how hers looks in the little mirror over the dresser.*)

AB (*shouting*): Let's go to town. Come on, you kids.

 (*Almost simultaneously.*)

JAPPY: I'm a picket, I'm a picket, I'm a picket.

PAULINE: Them signs are going to blow all around on them.

AB: Don't worry about the signs. (*Shouting*) Come on, you kids.

JAPPY (*putting his forefinger into the top of his cap and whirling around wildly*): I'm a picket.

PAULINE (*calling out to him*): You'll get dizzy. Stop it!

FRANCES (*running to her mother*): I can't see what I look like, Ma.

 (JAPPY *falls down. He doesn't know whether to cry or smile.* AB *picks him up;* JAPPY *decides to smile.*)

AB (*crossly*): See, you bent the sign.

PAULINE (*going to sewing basket and threading a needle*): It'll only take a minute to sew it down. (*To* FRANCES.) I'll sew yours on too.

FRANCES: Lift me up, Pa, by the mirror, so's I can see.

 (AB *lifts her up as* PAULINE *finishes sewing on* JAPPY's *sign.* JAPPY *still is singing his refrain.*)

PAULINE (*to* JAPPY *in exasperation*): Keep still, will you!

JAPPY: I'm gonta be a picket. I'm gonta go up to them dopes . . .

PAULINE (*biting off thread*): Where did you learn that?

JAPPY: I'm gonta be a dope, I'm gonta be a picket.

FRANCES (*sulkily*): I can't read what it says in the mirror.

AB: You know what it says. (*To* PAULINE.) I told her.

JAPPY: What's mine say?

FRANCES (*holding still while* PAULINE *sews the bottom corners of her sign onto her jacket*): It says "Give my pa back his job."

JAPPY (*starting to goose-step again*): Give my pa back his job.

AB (*grabbing* JAPPY's *hand*): Come on, I ain't gonta wait another minute.

   (PAULINE *follows them to the door. As soon as she closes it she hears the sound of bawling outside. She opens the door.*)

PAULINE (*calling*): Now what's the matter?

AB (*off*): He wantsta take his Popeye doll along with him. He ain't gonta.

   (JAPPY, *off stage, cries more loudly.*)

PAULINE: Aw, let him. It won't do no harm. I'll get it. (*She goes into the bedroom and comes back with an old wooden doll.*) Might do them good seeing a little kid with a doll.

   (JAPPY *is at the door with* FRANCES *just behind.*)

JAPPY (*smirking*): Popeye the Sailor's gonta be a picket.

AB (*off*): Hurry up!

JAPPY: Popeye wants a sign. (*He holds the doll up to his mother.*) Make him a sign.

PAULINE (*snatching a scrap of paper from the table and scribbling on it*): Oh, all right. (*She pins the paper on the doll and gives both children little pushes to the door.*) Hurry!

(JAPPY *and* FRANCES *go out.* PAULINE *stands at the door, listening to them talk as they go down the stairs.*)

JAPPY (*off*): Popeye's sign says "Give my pa back his job."

FRANCES (*off*): It don't say nothing. It's only scribble.

JAPPY (*off*): It do too.

(*Their voices becomes fainter.* PAULINE *sighs and goes back to her sewing . . . The curtain slowly falls.*)

SCENE—*The same. A lapse of two hours.* PAULINE *is mixing something in a bowl on the kitchen table. Occasionally she stops and listens for something. It is nearing suppertime, and the light in the room is grayer and dimmer. Footsteps are at last heard coming up the stairs.* AB, FRANCES, *and* JAPPY *come in the back door.* AB *looks grimly satisfied.* JAPPY *yawns sleepily.* FRANCES, *however, looks close to tears.*

PAULINE (*looking questioningly at them*): Well?

AB: You shoulda seen the new super's face. I guess we showed him.

(PAULINE *has knelt down to rip the stitches off* JAPPY's *sign.* FRANCES *stands off to one side, head lowered, lips trembling.*)

PAULINE (*looking over to* FRANCES): Why, what's the matter, honey?

(FRANCES *tries to speak, but before she can say a word, she bursts into tears. She stands in the doorway, a thin, desolate figure, sobbing like a baby.* JAPPY *has curled near the stove and gone to sleep.*)

PAULINE (*to* AB): What happened to her?

AB (*gloomily*): I don't know.

PAULINE (*putting her arms around* FRANCES): Tell Ma.

FRANCES (*choking between sobs, tears streaming down her screwed-up face*): The . . . the new little girl seen me.

PAULINE (*trying to keep her voice steady*): A lot of people seen you. That don't make no difference.

FRANCES (*breaking out of her mother's arms and running to the bedroom and slamming the door*): The new little girl seen me.

AB (*heavily*): I try to get back my job, and that's the thanks I get.

PAULINE (*looking around and seeing* JAPPY *asleep on the floor, speaks carefully*): She got a crush on some little girl at school she says looks like Shirley Temple.

AB (*bending over the table where his sign and* JAPPY's *lie*): That ain't gonta get my job back.

(FRANCES' *sobs are heard through the closed door.*)

PAULINE (*swallowing*): Other people seeing her don't make no difference, on account of she's at the age, see what I mean?

AB (*in a lowered voice, curiously strained*): No.

PAULINE: She's high-strung, Ab. To some other kid it mightn't mean nothing, only with her it might set her back, you know how kids are.

(PAULINE *waits for* AB *to reply, watching him make marks on the back of the sign with his pencil.* FRANCES' *weeping in the next room subsides gradually into long sighs and occasional hiccoughs.*)

AB (*without looking up*): I shouldn't oughta take her tomorrow.

PAULINE (*hopefully*): Jappy likes it.

AB (*making more marks on the sign*): We could change the words tomorrow. (*He pushes the lettering towards* PAULINE, *avoiding her eyes.*)

PAULINE (*frowning as she reads the crooked printing aloud*): "Ain't there . . . room . . . ain't there room in the world for us?"

(*There is a moment of heavy silence as* PAULINE *struggles within herself to master the lump that rises in her throat. Finally she speaks in the casual conversational tone she has lately learned to use.*)

PAULINE: It don't seem like "ain't" is the right word there.

(*The curtain descends slowly.*)

The Perfect Setup

Written: September–October 1951
Published: *Seventeen* (October 1952): 76, 100, 102–4[*]

Gray fog was raveling thin along the beach and small waves folded over on each other in a lather of dirty white foam. The whole shoreline was bleached out in a soapy haze. Over the noise of the tide came the screams of children playing down by the water.

After a while the sun began to burn through the layers of fog, blinding and stinging the eyes like bright spurts of lemon juice. Light glittered fresh and creamy on the sand, where striped umbrellas made round smudges of shade.

A boy in wrinkled khaki pants and a T-shirt was spearing up dried snarls of seaweed with a pitchfork. He moved slowly along down the beach, picking up the litter left by the last high tide.

I was feeling very comfortable, very lazy, just lying back on my beach towel and keeping an eye on Janey, who was digging in the sand a few feet away with a little playmate of hers. Now that the sun was out, I felt like going in for a swim. So I turned to Ruth Jacobs, who was lying on a towel beside me, and said, "I know what."

"What?" she said, grinning up at me, her teeth showing white against her tanned face.

"How about you watching Janey and Esther while I go in for a swim, and then take over afterward so you can cool off too?"

"Great idea."

I got up and put on my bathing cap, pushed my hair up under the edge and snapped the strap under my chin. The water was ice cold, so it took me a few minutes to get ducked. Air bubbles prickled around me like ginger ale when I started to swim, and I turned over till I was floating on my back, kicking a great spout of foam up into the sun. It was like looking at a bright light through broken glass, I guess, with all the sparks of sun pricking and

---

[*] Printed with a photograph of SP and a biographical sketch: 'Sylvia Plath, nineteen, a junior at Smith College, Massachusetts, spends summers at odd jobs in search of background material for her writing—also for the money; one result being "The Perfect Setup" which won an honorable-mention in *Seventeen*'s last Short Story Contest. Edith Sitwell and Dylan Thomas are Sylvia's cup-of-tea in poetry. A roommate "took responsibility for introducing me to New York." Playgoing is its greatest attraction to her.'

hurting my eyes . . . but it made me feel really good inside.

Ruth was laughing at me when I finally came running up out of the water, the salt drying on my skin in the warm wind.

"Go on in," I said, grabbing a towel and drying my hair which had gotten wet even under the cap. "It's perfect."

I sat there in the warm morning air, and inside me there was the same comfortable glow that the sun made on the sand and rocks. You know how sometimes you get a flash of understanding and you think all of a sudden that you know what everything in the world is all about? Well, that's the way it was then. I was positive that if I closed my eyes and lay back on the sand I would melt right into the beach, and my feet would grow roots, and I would become part of the wind and the sun and the blue water.

Sitting there and watching Janey and Esther playing their endless children's games in the sand, I knew that I could tell Ruth the way I felt, and she would understand. Because she felt the same way, too.

That was all part of the perfect setup I had that summer. It was the first time I had ever lived away from home, but I loved my job babysitting for the Bradleys. For one thing, I had a big airy room of my own with two windows looking right out over the ocean. And Janey was an adorable two-year-old.

After I did the dishes and beds and laundry every morning, I could take Janey down to the beach and stay out till lunchtime. We used to go down in the afternoon, too, if it was nice. For this I got board and room, plus a tidy sum per week. All the friends I wrote to said what a perfect setup I had.

"Wake up," said Ruth, coming back. "If you could see the expression on your face! You look like a sun worshiper."

"Sun worshiper," I grinned. "And how did you get that shade of cocoa brown yourself, may I ask?"

She laughed. "What time is it?"

"Almost twelve," I said. "Time for lunch."

"Wait a few minutes more. Mrs. Altman won't want Esther and me back for a little while yet."

"Mrs. Altman sounds nice," I said.

"You know how it is," Ruth explained. "When you live in the house where you work, everything depends on the people you live with."

"I know. You can be part of the family or just the hired help."

"I'm so glad we both get along with our families. It would be awfully hard if we didn't. You can't just stow your job away at five in the evening till nine the next morning and forget about it. You've got to live under the same roof all the time.

Even at night, if they go out a lot, you're still working, if you know what I mean. But when you figure, it's really pretty wonderful the way we get to stay down here at the beach almost all day. Imagine working in a stuffy office in the city!"

"I can't see that," I said.

"Me either."

We started picking up the towels, shaking the sand out, and getting all the toys together.

"Come on, Janey," I said.

Ruth carried Esther and we walked up the beach together.

On the way, I saw the Bradleys' next-door neighbor, Mrs. Avery, sitting on the sand with her two little girls, Nicki and Alice.

"Hello, Lisa," she said as I went by.

"Hello, Mrs. Avery," I said. I was feeling very good. I guess that's why I didn't pay much attention to the funny look she gave Ruth and me.

"Don't forget to come over tonight after work," I said to Ruth as she turned down her street.

"You're later than usual today," Mrs. Bradley said, as we finally sat down to eat.

"I know. I didn't mean to be. Ruth and I got talking, and the time went by before we knew it."

"Ruth?" Mrs. Bradley's eyebrows arched in questioning. I hadn't told her about Ruth yet.

"Yes, Ruth Jacobs. She's the nicest girl. I met her down the beach about a week ago. She takes care of a baby, too, and I think she's coming over tonight after work, if that's all right with you."

"Why, of course. Any time you want friends over, do feel free. Mr. Bradley and I are going over to the Averys for dinner tonight, so it'll be nice for you to have company."

That afternoon Janey played with the two little Avery girls, and Mrs. Bradley went over to help Mrs. Avery fix up the things for the dinner party that night.

I was in the kitchen getting supper for Janey when Mrs. Bradley walked in the way she always did before she went out anywhere.

"We'll be over at the Averys all evening," she said. She paused a minute and twirled a glass on the kitchen counter absent-mindedly. Then she asked very casually, "Oh, by the way, who did you say your friend worked for?"

"You mean Ruth?" I hadn't said anything about whom she worked for, but I explained now.

"The Altmans? But they don't live around here. At least, I never heard of anyone by that name. They must be summer people."

"I guess they are," I said. "They live over on Ocean Avenue."

"Oh," Mrs. Bradley said. A queer look came over her face. "Oh, I see," she said again. And then she left for the Averys.

Ruth and I had a wonderful time that night. We read together in the living room and pretended that the house was our own and all. We decided that every night Ruth was free she would come over and we'd talk or read or play the piano softly after the children were asleep.

"You see how nice Mrs. Bradley is," I said at about ten o'clock as we raided the icebox for part of a chocolate pie left there especially for us.

"You sure do have a perfect setup here," Ruth agreed, pouring out milk into the two glasses on the kitchen table.

"I'm so glad you're going to be coming over," I said. "It gets sort of lonesome after a while, with the baby asleep upstairs, and everybody out, and no one to talk to."

"I know. I feel the same way," Ruth said. After we had washed up the dirty dishes, she left, and I read for a while before I went to bed.

The next morning I was just going into Janey's room to get a dry bathing suit for her, when I happened to run into Mrs. Bradley. I was standing there in the doorway when she came up to me and said it. I knew something was wrong because she had a very odd smile on her face, the sort of smile that you practice in front of a mirror first.

"Oh, Lisa," she said.

"Yes, Mrs. Bradley." Something was the matter with my smile, too.

"I see the Averys are going down to the beach now," she said.

There was a little pause. I think I said "Yes," or "Why, sure." Something like that.

"The Averys are such nice children," she said. "I like Janey to play with them."

I was being very dense. I merely stood there with the same easy, open smile pasted on my face. For all I know, I said, "Why, yes. Of course," again. I kept saying the same thing every time she stopped for breath. I don't know why I didn't let her spill the whole speech out by herself. Maybe I didn't want to make it any harder for her. She was embarrassed enough as it was. I'll say that much.

"What I mean is," she began. The words came out fast, and they were big and ugly and ashamed of themselves. You could tell, the way they sneaked out, trying to hide behind that very odd smile.

"What I mean is, I like Janey to play with her own kind. I know it seems silly to segregate children so young. Not that we're intolerant or anything, you understand, but the whole street across the way is just full of those people in the summertime. It's fine here in the winter, but every summer they all come down to the beach, you know . . . Of course, I don't mean to say you can't have Ruth come over, or anything like that. Just so that Janey plays . . . well, the Averys are such nice children . . . You do understand, don't you?"

"Of course. Why, yes, Mrs. Bradley, of course I understand." I made the words very sympathetic and intense. I don't know why I tried to look so understanding, because I didn't agree with her. Not at all.

Somewhere a mistake had been made. Somehow a little unspoken code had gotten mislaid, and now that it had been found again, everybody was very happy, very effusive and apologetic about the rather unpleasant business of mentioning it at all. Tomorrow, no one would remember; once again, everybody would smile quite naturally.

They say if you do something often enough, it becomes a habit. If you learn to skate when you're five, you may be a Sonja Henie when you get to be fifteen. It's that way with thinking, too, I guess. When you start an idea growing in somebody's mind, you can pretty safely leave it alone after a while. You can let it grow by itself, and you don't have to worry, because it's always there, rooted deep inside.

I was thinking these things while I pushed Janey down to the beach in the wicker stroller. The tide was going out and there was a big stretch of flat wet sand left, very good for digging.

There were children, all sizes, running up and down with sandy faces and tin pails and shovels. A lot of them were getting excited about the baby waves, and some were crying, maybe because another kid had just stepped on a very special sand castle or something. Anyway, they all looked the same to me; and to Janey, too, I guess, because she reached out her fat baby arms and laughed.

The Averys were down there, all right. Nicki and Alice and Mrs. Avery in a neat, tight little group. I spread out my towel a few yards away from Mrs. Avery. It was just the right amount of distance—near enough to let the children play together, far enough to get out of any polite conversation.

Mrs. Avery looked up when I sat down.

"Hello, Lisa," she called over.

"Hello," I said. You don't have to be stingy about words, so I got really sociable. "Nice day, isn't it?"

"Yes, isn't it?" She glanced away then, and her face had a bored expression.

I couldn't stop thinking about what Mrs. Bradley had said, though, and wanting to throw stones at something, or yell about what fools people were right out loud in front of everybody. You know how it is. You get some crazy ideals about how people ought to act, liking each other just for themselves and not fixing up all those silly signs saying, "No Trespassing." It might just so happen that you could be best friends with someone on the other side of the fence.

It was a perfect setup, all right, just so long as people knew which side of the fence they belonged on. I hadn't been sure where *I* belonged, though, even when I had stood in front of Mrs. Bradley saying, "Why, yes, of course, I understand." I hadn't understood at all. I had been wondering: Who am I. Who is this girl I hear talking?

It was a house of cards, a chain reaction. But I wasn't going to be the card that didn't collapse with the rest, or the strong link that didn't break. No, I wasn't going to be noble, the way I used to think I would be, and leave the Bradleys just because I didn't agree with some of their ideas about things. I'd just go on living the way I always had, the easy way, being very quiet, very blameless, staying safely in the middle of the road.

Yet all the while, inside me, it was very hot and uncomfortable.

Ruth was right beside me before I saw her. It was her day off and she was alone.

"Hi, Lisa," she said, dropping her towel on the sand and sitting down to take off her sneakers. Her black hair was very crisp and curly, cropped close around her head. Her smile made me feel that, out of all the people on the beach, I was the one she had specially hoped to see there.

"Been swimming?" she asked.

"No," I said. I must have sounded as cheerful as a death sentence, because she was on guard right away.

"Say, what's the matter? Something wrong back at the house?"

"Sort of."

"Tell me."

I told her. It made me sick to do it, but I told her. I knew she'd see it wasn't my fault, but that didn't help much.

When I got all through talking, she was staring hard at a stick or something in the sand.

"Well, I guess we don't sit down here together anymore," she said.

I didn't answer right away. Finally I said, "I don't want you to stop coming over the house after work the way we planned. Please."

"Of course not," she said, getting up. But I knew she wouldn't come. She tried very hard and came through with one of her old smiles. "I'm going in for a swim. I don't care how cold it is."

"Good," I said, and sat there watching her run down into the waves until she was knee-deep and throw herself headlong into the water with a great splash.

You know how sometimes you could slap yourself for a stupid remark you made or a big chance you missed to do the best you could? Well, right then I wanted to worm my way down into that sand until I was covered all over and couldn't see the line of foam Ruth was making out there in the water. I just sat there with the whole summer turning sour in my mouth.

Mary Ventura

Ts,* 13 December 1951, Lilly Library

It had been a year since I last saw Mary Ventura, and now, suddenly, she was walking toward me down the street, half smiling as she approached. She

---

* Typescript has holograph corrections and additions by SP as well as annotations by her instructor. Written for English 220a, Practice in Various Forms of Writing. A note in SP's 1951 calendar indicates she had lunch with 'Mary', probably her high school classmate Mary Ventura, at 12:30 on 14 September 1951. SP typed the following note about the story:

This is a diffuse attempt to reveal the change of character of the Italian girl, Mary. She is sensitive, musical and quite intelligent. But she has been born into a poor family, coarse, crude, and animal-like. She is persecuted by her parents who sense vaguely that she is dissatisfied with the life they have offered her. She wishes to escape, to rise above them, to develop her musical abilities. The seeds of her destruction, however, are in her environment and in her own nature. Her emotional sensitivity which makes her interpretation of music meaningful is her undoing as far as her love affairs are concerned. Her dreamy laziness prevents her from either transcending her environment or becoming a success in it (her hatred of the routine store work). She is in the pathetic position of being unlike her relatives and fellow workers, and therefore misunderstood by them, and also unable to rise above the circumstances of life which are destined to crush her, the way her mother has been crushed.

The technical devices I used to try to get my point across are:

Dialogue: (I would like to be able to reveal character through conversation rather than relying on narrative to explain what's going on.) Here I tried to contrast Mary's changing view of life with the static view of the narrator.

Description: To reveal the sensuous, emotional side of Mary.

Illustrative incident: To reveal the character of Mary's parents and the poverty of her environment which will victimize her in the end.

Symbols: Which reveal Mary's emotions & situation. For example, the burning of the picture, the agitated flutter of her mother's hand, the desire to escape on one of the trains always going by.

(As usual, I am dissatisfied with the result.)

s.p.

came at me out of the crowd of people that pushed and jostled in front of the shop windows, and her stride was lithe and pliant, thighs moving rhythmically under the dark cotton folds of her skirt, breasts firm and full beneath her shirt.

"Hello," she said. Her voice was low and husky, the way it always had been.

"Hello, Mary," I grinned back, glad to see her.

"Well, how are you?" she asked.

"Me? Oh, I'm fine. It's been so long, Mary."

"I know. What have you been doing with yourself? How's college?"

"Great. Just great." The words came out flat, dead. They shouldn't have. But it had been a year, and in a year I had forgotten how easily we had once talked together.

"Mary," I said, "I want to see you. I want to have a real talk and find out all about what's happened to you since I've been away."

"Oh, nothing much. I've been working at Filene's for a couple of months now."

"You're still keeping up with your piano lessons, though, aren't you?"

Mary smiled, avoiding my eyes. Her bright lipsticked mouth trembled a little. "Oh, I quit," she said carelessly. "I really don't have time anymore."

"Not really! But that's a shame. Look, I've *got* to talk to you. When do you have time?"

"Do you honestly want to see me?" she said. "Don't feel you have to or anything."

"Of course I want to see you. Don't be silly."

"Well, all right, then. How about tomorrow, when I've got my lunch hour. You can meet me at the store, and we'll eat out in the park somewhere. Under the trees, maybe."

"Wonderful. Why don't I bring a picnic?"

"That would be neat," she said softly, her smile relaxed and curved now, as it used to be. "I've got to go back to work."

"Goodbye, then," I said. "See you tomorrow."

I watched her walk away down the street, her skirt brushing and swaying against the calves of her bare legs, her black hair shining in the bright noon sunlight. Unique she was; I had never known anybody quite like her.

I had met Mary in my art class back at high school and started using her for a model. There was something about the full rounded lines of her body, the way she could sit relaxed, with a certain feline grace, that made every position of hers become an intriguing pose. She had the Italian's infinite capacity to vary in mood, and at will she could become angry, sullen, lazy, passionate, or tender. Her rich, vibrant appeal was a refreshing change from the thin, fair-skinned, often superficial prettiness of most of the girls in the high school crowd.

One day in the spring of our Senior year, I visited Mary for the first time. She lived on the second floor of an apartment house across the railroad tracks from school. As we walked into the dark front hall I could smell the mingled, musty odors of furniture polish, sour milk, and stale tobacco. We had just started to climb the narrow staircase when a voice called querulously from above, "That you, Mary?"

"It's me, Mother," Mary called back.

From out of a back room there came the sound of footsteps shuffling toward the head of the stairs. A plain, drab little woman came into view. When she saw me, she stopped with a suspicious, unfriendly stare.

"You got company, Mary," she said accusingly. "I didn't know you was bringing anybody home."

Mary ignored the hostile reception. "We're going to be in my room," she told her mother. "We won't be bothering anybody."

"You remember your father, now. He don't like noise, and you know that."

"Sure, sure, Mother, I know," Mary said.

Without saying another word, Mrs. Ventura turned her back on us and went into her room again, shutting the door behind her with a peevish click.

In spite of the uncivil attitude of Mary's parents, we spent many afternoons together, playing tennis sometimes, reading aloud, or just sitting and talking on her front steps, watching the trains go by.

All day long the trains shuttled past, roaring out of the distance and away again, making the windows rattle, and the very house shudder on its foundations.

That summer we used to sit out until it got dark, and the lights came on. Then the passenger cars glowed into life as they sped by, dark long shapes, with row after row of lighted windows. We could see the people inside the cars, moving slowly, talking leisurely in their small brilliant boxes. Unreal figures, they were, cradled in comfort, cutting through the summer night with the speed of a thousand pistons and revolving wheels. Calmly oblivious of their precarious motion, they habitually read the evening paper or stared blindly out of the windows into the dark.

"Someday," Mary said one time, "we will be on a train like that. We will ride and ride to the end of the earth. And we will look out of the window as we go whizzing by all the people in the world sitting on their front doorsteps. We will feel very sorry for them, sitting there in their narrow front yards like so many puppets taking an airing.

"Sometimes we will stop and talk to them. They will tell us their grotesque little dreams and deformed little fancies, and we will take notes and go away, not knowing whether to smile or cry. You will paint a great picture about them, maybe, and I will write a big piece of music. We will make them worth something after all."

It was a wide, soft summer night, and Mary's voice had dropped to a low, cadenced rhythm that went on and on. The wind had blown a warm yellow moon up over the trees, and it took root in the sky and grew there like a tulip, raining down on us winking white petals of light. The world was ours to make or break, and we were quite drunk with the new power inside us. Right there, on Mary's front steps, we resolved never to let ourselves become stagnant, victims of custom or of circumstance.

"If only I could get away," Mary sighed at last. "Away from this town and this house and these people. You don't know how trapped I feel sometimes."

"You will get away, Mary," I said firmly. "Someday we both will."

The door opened behind us, then, and a dark, stocky figure stepped out onto the veranda. It was Mr. Ventura. He didn't speak as he passed us, but went over to sit on the porch railing, his shirt making a strange whitish patch of light against the darkness beyond. He sat there silently, staring morosely into the distance, not moving, his heavy arms hanging loosely by his side, his head jutting sullenly forward on the thick column of his neck.

I wondered how Mary could stand living with him, or with her mother too, for that matter. They were such a moody, bitter pair. I had never seen either of them laugh. Mrs. Ventura took in laundry, and often, when I walked into the kitchen with Mary, she would be standing over the wash machine, the sleeves of her faded cotton dress rolled up over her elbows, plunging load after load of soiled clothes into the tubs of steaming water. She would say hello to me sometimes, or, with a quick glance, acknowledge my presence, but always her face maintained the same implacable expression. She looked as if she had been hurt once, beaten until she learned the art of being withdrawn and silent in her brooding. There was no light in her eyes. They did not smolder with excitement, the way Mary's did, or turn soft and liquid with reverie. Mrs. Ventura's stare was bleak, and her eyes were the color of burned-out ashes, dull and vanquished.

Mr. Ventura never kept a job because he had spasmodic epileptic spells. Usually he was somewhere around the house whenever I came, sitting in a chair outside, or slouched deep into the old couch in the living room, listening to a ball game on the radio, or just staring aimlessly at nothing, oblivious, apparently, to all that went on around him. A coarse growth of short wiry black hair covered his muscular arms, and his skin was rough and sallow. His occasional outbursts of temper were often violent, always unreasonable.

"Mary!" he would yell suddenly, his voice hoarse and pained. "Mary, get me something to eat. I'm hungry."

And Mary would get up, her face at once blank of expression, like her mother's, and go into the kitchen, coming back with a plate of cold meat, perhaps, the pieces coated with a white film of congealed fat.

Mr. Ventura would take the plate from her and eat with his fingers, loudly sucking his tongue between his teeth to dislodge the remaining particles of food, or running a thick stubby finger around inside his gums. With a guttural sigh of content, then, he would sink back onto the couch, often lapsing into a noisy slumber, snoring or wheezing as he slept.

Mary was the only child of this Italian couple, and although they did not seem to understand her, or her desire to rise above them, they were grudgingly proud that she took music lessons, even if nothing would bring them to admit it. Mary earned the money herself by working a few days a week after school, yet even then her parents complained that she was a burden to them and should have been supporting herself long ago.

But when she would sit down at the rickety piano that was in their apartment and begin to play, low, rich, sultry melodies, Mrs. Ventura would always find some excuse to come into the living room. Usually she would sit down with her sewing, and although she bent her head stiffly over her work, it was evident that she was softened by the music, that it touched some vague responsive chord in her, for the corners of her mouth relaxed, and her dull cheeks grew flushed. Her husband would come, too, and stand in the doorway, leaning heavily against the woodwork, with only the slow sound of his breathing to reveal his presence.

The notes of the music would blend, one into the other, and the harmonies would die away sadly, regretfully, into the depths of the piano, fading with a plaintive twang along the inner strings.

I could not say how many afternoons we spent sitting in the living room, listening to Mary's capable fingers draw melody after melody from the cracked yellow keys of the piano. She would stop at last, and the hypnotic fusion of four spirits would be broken, each withdrawing quickly into itself, as if afraid, embarrassed at having displayed a kind of weakness or vulnerability.

Mr. Ventura would grunt, or grumble something unintelligible to himself and lumber off to his room. Mrs. Ventura would gather up her spools of thread and swatches of material. Then, inexplicably, she would become resentful, and would usually turn her peevishness on Mary.

"Suppertime, Mary," she would snap. "I need you to help me in the kitchen. You laze around all day long and never do a lick of work unless I get after you."

Whereupon she would leave the room in anger. I wondered if she had always been this way, morose and petulant, as if some small animal were always biting her, plaguing her continually.

The answer to these questions came one day shortly before I left for college. I stopped to see if Mary was home because I wanted to give her a picture I had finished. I had painted her standing on a street corner, leaning against the edge of a building and staring deeply from under dark brows. There were no other people in the picture, just the barren streets under the queer green light of a small unripe moon. Everywhere there were dark, ominous shadows leaning toward her, but she stood firm, a small, solid figure in the cold, indestructible light. Proud and enigmatic in the midst of desolation.

I had been working on the picture for a week or more, and I had promised to give it to Mary before I went away. It was a tribute of sorts, the way I wanted to remember her, victorious over the environment that reached out to confine her.

I didn't have to worry about myself anymore, for I was going away. Ever since the scholarship had come, I had felt that I was free to escape, to rise above my home town and see the world as we had always planned to do. But I would have to leave Mary. I made her promise to keep on with her music lessons, no matter what. Someday, then, she would be good enough to get a scholarship to music school, even if she had to work for a few years beforehand. So I had painted her, with the lovely sensuous lines of her body sheathed in a purple dress, standing triumphant, inviolate, in the midst of the greedy, flowing shadows.

There was the painting, then, and Mrs. Ventura was opening the door, peering at me with half-closed eyes from the darkness of the narrow hill.

"What do you want?" she demanded sulkily. "Mary's not home. She's gone to town."

"When will she be back? I just wanted to give her this."

"I'll give it to her." Mrs. Ventura accepted the picture unwillingly, almost as if she hated to touch it. She held it by her side without glancing down. Then she looked around as if to see if anyone was within hearing distance. There was no one. Her eyes narrowed, and she leaned forward, glaring at me.

"Listen," she hissed between her teeth, "I tell you something. If you know what's good, you leave Mary alone."

I just stood there in amazement, saying nothing. Never before had I seen her display such emotion. The closest she had come to revealing any sensitivity at all was when, now and then, she had listened to Mary play the piano.

"Listen," she went on, "you're not good for my girl. You make her want things she can't have. Things she can't ever have. You make her unhappy. You turn her against us. I know. I know what you're doing, being so nice to her. Oh, so nice." Her voice was harsh with grief.

"Once I was like Mary, too, a young pretty girl. But I had no money, nothing. Nothing. And look at me now, working myself to the bone for her. She has to work too. No more school. She can't go away like you. She can't be lazy, do nothing all day, just talk, talk, talk. Daydreaming all the time."

Mrs. Ventura's tirade stopped as abruptly as it had begun, and the blaze died out of her eyes. Her face once more resumed its implacable stony expression. She smoothed the front of her dress with one agitated hand, breathing quickly. Once again she was the dull sour-faced woman, lumpish and insensible. The only trace of her sudden outburst was the hand that plucked fretfully at the collar of her dress.

"I'll tell Mary you left her this," she said at last, quietly, her voice still resonant with emotion.

I walked away slowly. Mrs. Ventura didn't turn to go in, but stood in the doorway, staring after me, the tremulous hand still darting, smoothing, quivering, a pale birdlike shape against her dark formless breasts.

That was a year ago, and now it was summer again. I met Mary at the store, and we headed off for the park to eat the lunch I brought. It was good to sit in the dim green shade of the big maple trees, with the grass cool and soft under us. I opened the paper bag and handed Mary a cheese sandwich.

"Thanks," she said, taking a bite, her lipstick leaving a faint red smudge on the white bread. "Well, tell me, now, all about what you've been doing."

"No, first I want to hear about you," I said through a mouthful of bread and cheese. "I don't just want polite talk, either. You know what I mean."

Mary laughed. "I know. But there's nothing to tell, really."

"There must be. How about your job. Tell me what it's like."

Mary's underlip pouted out, glistening and pink-lined beneath the scarlet of her lipstick. Her black eyes clouded. "Well, if you really want to know, I hate it."

"Why, though? Tell me."

"Oh, if you only knew," her voice dropped to a low disgusted whisper. "If you only knew how dull it is. Every little sale has to be filed on all these charts, and if you make a mistake or anything, the woman who's head of the department comes over and gives you a lecture.

"You have no idea how awful it is to wake up every morning and face the same routine. I hate to go to bed at night because it means waking up in the morning all over again. And all the other girls, they have such little minds. You wouldn't believe it. They don't talk about anything except sales slips, or customers, or the latest movie at the playhouse. They don't know anything exists besides their own puny little world."

"But Mary, can't you get another sort of job? Something that would really be vital?"

She laughed shortly, and she looked at me with a queer smile, almost compassionate. "You're funny, you know. You're so intelligent about some things, and still I can't expect you to understand. It was different when we were in school together, because we were talking about the same things, in the same language. But now it's harder. I know you're going on the way you said you would; you always will. You say you want to do something and you do it. Me, I'm different."

"No, you aren't different," I wanted to shake her. "Don't even say things like that. I want us always to be able to talk, really talk, and be friends. Nothing's different, nothing's changed."

Mary stared musingly at the grass, where her hand was absently pulling up little green tufts by the roots. "Someday you'll find out," she said softly, "how the world really works."

"What do you mean?"

"I'm going to tell you something," she said. "It might be good for you to know. It might hurt you, I don't know. Maybe I just need to tell somebody."

"Go ahead, then."

"You know that music teacher I went to in Boston? The one I could always talk to when I felt depressed or anything about life?"

"Sure," I said. "His name was George, wasn't it?"

"Yes," she said, still staring at the ground, "George."

"Well, what about him?"

"Well, what do you think?" Her eyelids quivered, and her voice rocked uncertainly between laughter and tears.

"You mean . . ."

"Sure, I mean." She began talking quickly in dry clipped sentences. "He said he never loved his wife. He said he felt sorry for her, that's all, and had to be nice to her. He said he wanted me more than anybody."

"Mary . . ."

"What?"

"Tell me, what was it like? Was it worth it?"

"Worth it? I don't know. I just went into the studio a couple of times a week for a while, that's all. And now I've quit taking lessons. For good."

"There wasn't anybody else, then?"

"Only two," she said. "Only two others." Her voice was cold and detached, her face impassive. But at last her defense melted. She looked up at me pitiably, asking me something silently, pleadingly. Her eyes brimmed with tears. "Say something. Tell me you think I'm awful."

"I don't think anything of the kind." I was angry. "You should know me better than that. I won't ever change the way I feel about you. Ever."

"I guess I knew you'd say that," she said. "That's why I told you. The girls at the store talk behind my back all the time, and someone even called up Mother and told her some awful things. She cried and cried. It hurt her terribly. She says she hates me, but she doesn't. Not really, you know."

"But what about you?" I asked. "What are you going to do, Mary? Whatever are you going to do?"

"Do? I'll just go on working, that's all. What else is there? Don't worry about me. You'll be going off to college again, and it will be easy to forget. I know you get mad when I say things like that, but that's all there is to it. There's nothing I can do, nothing you can do, so let's forget it, huh?"

"I won't forget. I'll write you, and I'll see you whenever I come home."

"All right, all right," Mary got up and brushed away the grass that was clinging to her skirt. She pulled her yellow-green blouse down tighter over her firm breasts and tucked it in at the waist. "I've got to get back to work, now," she said. "They'll give me heck if I'm late."

Her features were composed again, but even the taut expression of her mouth could not stop the slight, nervous trembling of her lips.

"Oh," she said, "I forgot to tell you. You know that picture you left with me before you went off to school last year?"

"Yes," I said. "I remember."

"Well Dad found it one day when he was in one of his moods. It got burned. I'm awfully sorry. It was a great picture."

"Yes," I said. "It was, wasn't it?"

Mary was walking away down the crowded street, then. Her hips swung rhythmically under her skirt, and the lift of her head was proud, defiant still, as she lost herself in the crowd, moving away into darkness, into the narrow shadow of the buildings.

The Latvian

Ts,[*] 29 February 1952, Lilly Library

The July sun stood high over the field of New Zealand spinach, and across the slope of the next hill Lisa could see the dust rising in a faint smudge behind the truck Bernie was driving back to the washroom. There was no other sound on the thick summer air but that of the flies which buzzed, paused, and stung. Lisa swatted at one that was setting on her arm and turned to the older girl who was picking beside her.

"I've got to get some water, Mary," she said. "I'm thirsty again."

Mary looked up from where she squatted in the dry dirt, a red kerchief around her black hair, her face brown and sweat-streaked.

"There's a pailful down the end of the row under some paper," she said. "Bernie left it." She turned back to picking.

Lisa bent to finish filling her bushel basket. A week of work at the farm had taught her to pick fast, breaking off the tops of the spinach in clean quick handfuls and bunching them in solid tiers. She packed the top layer tightly and tested the weight, lifting the basket with both hands. It was about right. Slinging it on one hip, she walked barefoot down to the end of the field to leave it and get another.

The pail of water was there by the baskets, covered with a sheet of yellow wrapping paper to keep it shaded from the sun. But already the ice floating in it was almost all melted. Lisa tilted the pail and drank deep. The water had a queer metallic taste, yet it was good. Wiping her wet mouth with the back of her hand, she covered the pail again and put it down in the tall grass by the roadside.

As she was lifting an empty basket from the pile she noticed that a young man was coming down the road from the orchard, whistling to himself. A blonde young man of medium height, browned deeply by the sun. A khaki

---

[*] Typescript has holograph corrections by SP and instructor's comments. Written for English 220b, Practice in Various Forms of Writing. SP wrote an earlier version entitled 'The Estonian' the previous semester on 30 October 1951.

128

shirt was knotted about his waist. When he saw Mary, his tan face crinkled up in laughter and he called out with a guttural accent, "Hullo, Mary."

"Hello, Ilo," Mary shouted back from where she was picking out in the field.

"Hot today, ya?" He grinned at Lisa as he went by. His eyes teased her, and she felt the blood rise hotly from her bare throat and burn in her cheeks. She picked up her basket and walked back slowly.

"Who was that?" she asked Mary.

"That's Ilo," Mary said. "Funny you haven't seen him around before. He came over from Latvia, some place like that. Been living in the barn since spring."

"In the barn? How come you know him?"

"Oh, I've been working with him a couple of months or so," Mary said, settling back on her heels and squinting against the sun. Once she had started talking she slowed her picking, reaching mechanically now and then for the leafy spinach heads. "Anyhow, this spring we were on tomatoes in the greenhouse. You know how the windows get all steamed over so you can write on them? Well, I was trying to do a horse with my finger on the glass, and he just came up and drew a man on that horse as quick as anything. It was good, too."

"Really," Lisa demanded. "Can he really draw?"

"Well, he wants to be an artist," Mary said. "Wants to save up enough so he can go to New York City and be a regular artist."

An approaching cloud of dust and the sound of rattling fenders and creaking springs heralded the truck that came to collect the baskets. It was lunchtime, and Kenny and Freddy, two of the boys from the washroom, leapt out to load up. Usually they teased Mary, who had worked with them long enough to be on familiar terms, but today Kenny called over to Lisa, "Angel face, come here a minute."

"Don't tease her, Kenny," Mary begged.

"I'm not," Kenny told her. "I just wanted to tell her what Ilo said. He said she's a pretty girl."

Lisa bent over the basket of spinach she was bringing up, trying to hide a pleased smile.

That same afternoon Mary and Lisa went to set strawberry runners with Mr. Tompkins, the head of crews, and Ilo. On the truck going out Lisa listened to Ilo and Mary joke together, and she felt shy, thinking of what Kenny had said in the morning. Ilo's eyes sought her face and she looked away, her cheeks beginning to burn again.

Setting strawberry runners was slow business, because the stems of every plant had to be stretched out along the ground in star formation and weighed to the soil in several places with small clods of earth. Ilo had chosen a row next to Lisa's and was keeping pace with her, while Mary was up ahead talking with Mr. Tompkins as they set the runners side by side.

After a while, Ilo cleared his throat. He grinned at Lisa and said with his marked accent, "You go to college?"

"No," Lisa said. "Not till next year."

"What are you liking best at school?" he said then.

"Oh, I guess I like art best," she said and waited.

"Art? You like art?" The skin around Ilo's blue eyes crinkled with delight. "I study art in Munich. For four years I go to art school there."

"Really?" Lisa exclaimed. "I would so like to see something you've drawn."

"I draw you a picture someday, you wait," Ilo laughed at her. "Now I am doing a picture of John. You know the John I mean."

John was the father of the colored children, Lisa remembered.

Later on, Lisa told Mary about her conversation with Ilo. "Mary," she confided, "you know what? Ilo said someday he'd give me a picture he drew."

Mary looked carefully at Lisa. "I know," she remarked dryly. "Last spring he asked me to come up to the barn and sit for a picture, but I wouldn't. Not up there, anyway."

Lisa didn't see Ilo for about a week after that, because he was working in the squash fields with the other men. It wasn't until she was walking back from the bean field in her slicker one raw, rainy afternoon that Ilo called to her. He was coming up from the orchard, heading toward the barn.

"Lisa," he said. "I finished the picture of John yesterday. You want to see it?"

"Yes," said Lisa. "Why don't you bring it over tomorrow. I'll probably be working out in the bean field again."

"Today it has to be," Ilo told her. "Tomorrow you do not work. It is Sunday. Besides, tomorrow I go away."

"Go away!" Lisa had not meant to sound so surprised.

"Yes. To New York, finally. Come and see the picture. It's only a little walk."

"Well, all right," Lisa said.

On the way to the barn they passed Mary who was walking home.

"Hullo, Mary," Ilo said jovially, with a magnanimous and brilliant smile. There was laughter lurking in the accents of his voice.

"Hello, Ilo," Mary said coldly. She stared hard at Lisa. Uneasily, Lisa avoided Mary's accusing black eyes. She wanted to turn back, but it would be impossible for her to stop now. Ilo was grinning and walking very fast. She lengthened her stride to keep up with him.

The barn was a great, gray, wooden building, and in the rain it seemed to offer shelter and warmth. Inside, the big high-ceilinged room was dim, smelling of hay and the steamy breathing of the horses in the stalls. The sound of the horses' soft occasional whickering mingled with the garbled voices of the Negro children playing on a pile of hay. Far, far at the other end of the barn, beyond the avenues of stalls, there was a gray square marking an open door. Lisa thought she saw the figure of another person there, but she wasn't sure.

Ilo said nothing. He began to climb a flight of narrow wooden stairs leading to the loft rooms of the barn. Lisa knew she would follow him. Already her feet were mounting the lower steps.

"You live up there? All these little stairs?" Her voice came from somewhere far off.

Ilo still did not say anything. He kept walking up, and Lisa followed, hesitating at the top. He opened a door and motioned her across the threshold with a gracious sweep of his arm.

"Come in, come in," he said, all hospitality, all charming apology for the smallness of his quarters. Lisa walked into the center of the room. It was a narrow place, with two windows giving a watery gray light, overlooking the sodden bean fields. There was a table spread with pencils, drawing papers and unfinished sketches, and a cot covered with a dark blanket. Oranges and a bottle of milk were set out on a stand that held a battered radio.

"The picture," Lisa said at last. There was a loud humming of wind or of swarms of bees in her ears.

"Oh, yes," Ilo said. "Here." He went over to the table and picked up a piece of paper, handing it to Lisa. It was a pencil sketch of John's head that followed the broad flat planes of his face with firm sure lines.

"Why, how do you do it?" Lisa asked. She stood there in the center of the room, holding the picture. Her hand was unsteady, and the drawing quivered in her grasp. Without lifting her eyes, she knew that Ilo had shut the door, closing them in. He turned on the radio, then, and the music came out, filling the room.

"I really must go," she said faintly. "I really must go. The picture is just lovely."

Ilo was smiling between Lisa and the door. He was standing in front of her so that when she made a move to get past she found his blue eyes confronting her, suddenly too close. She could feel his breath stir her hair.

"Please . . ." she began, but Ilo grinned and pulled her young body to him. Warm and strong his mouth moved over hers, silencing the words on her lips. Lisa fought against the unyielding circle of his arms, but he only tightened his hold until her breasts ached against the hardness of his ribs.

At last Ilo let her go and stepped back. Lisa stood there, her hand against her mouth, warm and bruised from his kiss. She was crying softly.

"Why, why," Ilo made gentle placating noises when he saw that she was shaken. "Why," he said, "I get you some water."

He poured some water from a white pitcher on the table into a glass. Lisa took the glass and drank a few swallows, but her mouth was quivering, and the salt from her tears mixed with the water, making it taste bitter. She handed back the glass and tried to speak, but the words wouldn't come. Still holding the back of her hand to her mouth, she walked past Ilo who stood aside and watched her go back down the steps with a smile of kind and quizzical amusement.

Downstairs, the little colored children called her name in their queer dialect. She stumbled blindly past them out into the rain. A truck was going by, coming from behind the barn. She broke into a run, thinking maybe she could get a ride back to the washroom. Bernie was driving, and as he came by he slowed down. She jumped up on the running board and opened the door, sliding onto the frayed leather seat beside him.

Bernie's eyes glittered with malicious delight, and his wide mouth stretched into an ugly grin. Lisa remembered that figure half seen in the doorway at the other end of the barn and felt sick.

"What's the matter?" Bernie said with his cruel smile. "You're crying."

"I am not," Lisa said stubbornly.

Bernie let her off at the gasoline pump by the washroom. She watched him go inside, thinking of what he would tell the boys working at the long tables, bunching and crating carrots, or grading tomatoes.

Mr. Tompkins came up to the pump to watch Kenny and Freddy run the old stock car. His ruddy face and blonde hair were friendly under the slouched cloth hat he wore. He was nice, but he knew. They all must know.

"There's cutie pie," Freddy said.

"Cutie pie and angel face," Kenny said.

Lisa stood there a minute before going over to get her bicycle that was leaning up against the side of the washroom. She stared into the whirring engine, smiling as though nothing had happened, her arms folded across her young breasts as if to protect something inside her from the cold onslaught of the rain.

'Though Dynasties Pass'

Ts,* 14 March 1952, Lilly Library

The New York train was about an hour outside of Providence when the veteran came back from the bar and sat down beside the girl again. He swung himself into his seat with a low grunt and stood the crutches up against the seat in front of him. Reaching into the pocket of his khaki jacket he pulled out a crumpled pack of cigarettes and a book of matches. He fumbled with them for a moment. Then, hesitantly, he held the cigarettes out to the girl.

"Have one?" he asked.

The girl looked up from her reading. "No thanks." She smiled. He withdrew the pack slowly. She turned back to her book.

The veteran bent forward and lit his cigarette. The light flared for a second, and the orange color flickered on his face, deepening the lines into shadows. Exhaling a cloud of smoke, he stared past the girl out of the window with expressionless eyes.

Beyond the glass there was only the dark of winter, broken now and then by the quick moving of single lights on the snow flats or by the distant winking crest of a town springing up suddenly far from the tracks and dwindling off against the horizon.

The cigarette burned down to a stub. He lit a fresh one from it and crushed the old one out under his right heel. The floor of the car around him was littered with dirty butts now, like gray worms with ashy guts strewn out across the surface.

The girl was reading her book still. Her head was bent and her hair was brown and soft with the light of the car on it. The veteran glanced down at the book. It was full of little paintings and write-ups.

"Say," he leaned over with an engaging grin and tried again, "would you mind telling me what that's all about? I never could catch on to that stuff."

The girl smiled up at him. Her gray jersey dress fitted softly over her breasts and her red mouth curved very sweetly. A nice kid. In the light her hair was almost yellow. Damn, the beer was making him sentimental again. He blinked fast.

---

* Typescript has holograph changes by SP. Written for English 220b, Practice in Various Forms of Writing. SP wrote an earlier version in February 1952 entitled 'Brief Encounter' which she submitted to *Seventeen*. The title comes from Thomas Hardy's poem 'In Time of "The Breaking of Nations".'

"Why," she was explaining in a low voice, "it's really awfully simple. It's only a different way of saying things."

"Like how?" he asked.

"Well, take apples just for instance. You could draw apples just the way everybody sees them, round and red and shiny. But these guys, they don't want to paint apples in the same old way, so that's why they use all these little blobs of color . . . to make people get excited and see things fresh and all . . ."

The girl broke off with a sudden embarrassed laugh. "You see what I mean?" she said then.

"Sure, I see," he said. "That's good, the way you make it sound so simple. Where'd you pick up the book? New York?"

"Yes, in the Museum of Modern Art. I'm just heading back to Boston for the vacation." The book had fallen shut in her lap and she was sitting forward now, half facing him.

"Your family live there?"

"In the suburbs. You know," she was getting conversational, "Christmas is a funny time. Everybody going home and all. I mean don't you wonder about the places the people on this train are going? Just imagine the hundreds of relatives in the hundreds of towns getting ready for them, waiting for train time, driving down to the station. It's almost frightening, don't you think?"

"Yeah," said the veteran reflectively. His new left leg was beginning to ache again. Reaching down, he lifted the leg from under the thigh with both hands and moved it to a more comfortable position.

"I'm going home, too," he said. "To my sister's in Providence."

"That's nice."

"It's funny," he went on. "Seeing the old place again, you know. I haven't been back for two years."

"You've been over there?" the girl asked vaguely, casually.

"Yeah," he said. "Korea."

"What's it like? I've always wondered."

"Oh, not much different. Flatter and muddier, that's all."

He glanced beyond her out the window then, his face all at once eager and boyish, as if he were going to recognize the lights any time now. As if there would be a familiar combination of street lamps that said home to him somewhere out there in the dark.

"You know something?" she said.

"What?" He turned to her with the new expression still in his eyes.

"You look good when you get excited."

"Heck," he said, pleased.

"No, really, I mean it."

"Well, I haven't been back for so long and all. You know," he confided, "my sister got married last year, and I haven't even seen her husband yet. She doesn't even know I'm coming home now."

"You mean you didn't tell her you were coming?"

"No."

"Well, why on earth? She'd probably be just dying to have you back for the holidays."

"Well," the veteran explained sheepishly, "it's like this, see. I didn't want to bother her. I didn't want to make her fuss or anything. I feel kind of queer about butting in on her . . . them. Not having met him even."

"Why, that's awful. Of course she'd love to have you. Her own brother."

"I know, I know, but I feel kind of funny about it still."

The girl was suddenly suspicious. "Where are you going tonight after you get off in Providence?"

"Well," the veteran was turning his cap around in his hands slowly, staring down intently at the rim, "I sort of thought I'd get a room in a hotel for the night and head over there the first thing in the morning maybe."

"You know what you're going to do?" The girl leaned forward, her brown eyes narrowed.

"What am I going to do?" He laughed, pleased at her anger.

"You're going to lie awake all night worrying. I can see you now, lying awake in that hotel room all night, wondering what you're going to say in the morning."

"Yeah, I guess maybe you're right," he agreed with a little smile.

"You shouldn't do that, putting it off, you know."

"I know. But I can't help it."

"You can too," she said. "Maybe it's none of my business, but you can too help it."

"Maybe," he said. "I'm only out of the hospital for seven days. My first leave since I got in the place."

"Well, you go see her right away, then. She'll be mad as anything, I bet, if you waste a night away from home."

"OK. OK." He grinned at her, and she sat back and began to laugh at herself for getting so mad. Her throat was long and white, and her fingers, lying in her lap, were relaxed and loosely interlaced. They would be cool to touch, he thought.

"I think I want to tell you about something," he said then.

"What?" she asked softly, her laughter trailing off.

"Oh, about something that made me mad today. A woman on the subway got up to give me her seat. I said I wouldn't take it though. I said: thanks anyway, lady, but I can stand just as well on one leg as you can on two."

The girl said quietly, "You know what to do with people like that."

"I could stand anything," the boy beside her went on, "if the old women wouldn't get up and say, sit down fella, or if my sister, when she came to visit, wouldn't cry the way she always does."

"You know what to do with people like that," the girl repeated in an even tone. "You tell them to go to hell, that's all. If they're going to be damn fools they can just go to hell, that's all."

The boy grinned at her. "Yeah," he said. "Yeah, I guess so."

The train was swinging into lights, now. Neons lurched past, and the dark buildings crowded up at them. People were getting suitcases down off the racks, putting on coats. The door of the car clicked open and the conductor came rocking down the aisle.

"Next stop Pro-vi-dence. Tickets-please-have-your-tickets-ready-tickets-please."

The veteran stretched and sighed. He handed his ticket stub to the conductor and pulled himself to his feet. Adjusting the crutches under his arms, he crammed his cap down on his head with one hand. The train slowed, cradling gently into the station.

"Well," the veteran said, looking down at the girl. The people began to push past him to the door.

"Well," she said, looking up. "Well," she said very softly, "say hello to your sister for me."

"You bet." He swung off down the aisle.

The girl sat motionless, staring out at the dark forms hurrying beneath along the platform. Her book had long since fallen to the floor.

All at once there was a banging, a thumping of someone's fist on the window. She leaned her face against the cold glass, looking down at the man below.

It was the veteran, and he was waving goodbye, standing and swaying on his crutches with the light from the window on his face. But even his pale grin could not hide the scared nakedness of his eyes as he stood there alone, still waving as the train began to pull away.

New people were crowding through the car now. A fat woman sank into the seat beside her. The smell of damp wool, the placid, comfortable settling of the masses of flesh was somehow obscene.

The girl kept her face turned to the window. The pane was wet and cold against her burning cheek.

"Something the matter, kid?" the woman beside her asked sympathetically.

The girl did not answer. She kept her face turned to the window and pretended to be asleep.

Sunday at the Mintons'

Written: 25 March–8 April 1952
Published: *Mademoiselle* (August 1952): 255, 371–8[*]

If Henry were only, sighed Elizabeth Minton as she straightened a map on the wall of her brother's study, not so fastidious. So supremely fastidious. She leaned dreamily aslant his mahogany desk for a moment, her withered, blue-veined fingers spread whitely against the dark, glossy wood.

The late morning sunlight lay in pale squares along the floor, and the dust motes went drifting, sinking in the luminous air. Through the window she could see the flat sheen of the green September ocean that curved far beyond the blurred horizon line.

On a fine day, if the windows were open, she could hear the waves fall. One would crash and go slipping back, and then another and another. On some nights, when she was lingering half-awake about to be engulfed in sleep, she would hear the waves, and then the wind would begin in the trees until she could not tell one sound from the other, so that, for all she knew, the water might be washing in the leaves, or the leaves falling hushed, drifting down into the sea.

---

[*] Written for English 220b, Practice in Various Forms of Writing. Winner of *Mademoiselle's* 1952 college short fiction contest. Printed with a photograph of SP and a biographical sketch: 'Sylvia Plath was scrubbing furniture at a Cape Cod hotel when our award wire arrived. A soph. Eng. major at Smith, she's working her way through with a scholarship, newspaper work, summer jobs that have netted her an amazing variety of characters "who manage to turn up, dismembered or otherwise, in stories".' Reprinted in *Smith Review* (Fall 1952), with following contributor note: 'Sylvia Plath, 1954, had three stories and four poems published in *Seventeen*, as well as winning one of two five hundred dollar prizes in the short story competition sponsored by *Mademoiselle* for her story, "Sunday at the Mintons'" reprinted in the fall *Smith Review* from *Mademoiselle's* August issue. Sylvia is also a member of Press Board, the student branch of the Smith College News Office and is on the Editorial Board of *Smith Review*.'

"Elizabeth," Henry's voice echoed deep and ominous down the cavernous hallway.

"Yes, Henry?" Elizabeth answered her older brother meekly. Now that they were back together in the old house again, now that she was looking after Henry's wants once more, she could at times fancy herself a little girl, obedient and yielding, as she had been long ago.

"Have you finished tidying the study?" Henry was coming down the hall. His slow, ponderous footstep sounded outside the door. Nervously Elizabeth lifted her slender hand to her throat, fingering, as if for security, her mother's amethyst brooch, which she always wore pinned to the collar of her dress. She glanced about the dim room. Yes, she had thought to dust the lamp shades. Henry could not tolerate the dust.

She peered at Henry, who was now standing in the doorway. In the vague light she could not see his features clearly, and his face loomed round and somber, his substantial shadow blending with the darkness of the hall behind. Squinting at the indistinct form of her brother, Elizabeth felt an odd pleasure in observing him without her glasses. He was invariably so clear, so precise, and now for once he was quite thoroughly obscured.

"Daydreaming again, Elizabeth?" Henry chided sadly, seeing a characteristic far-off look in her eyes. It had always been that way with the two of them, Henry coming out to find her reading in the garden under the rose arbor or building castles in the sand by the sea wall, Henry telling her that Mother needed help in the kitchen or that the silver needed polishing.

"No, Henry," Elizabeth drew herself up to her fragile height. "No, Henry, not at all. I was just about to put the chicken in the oven." She brushed past her brother with the merest suggestion of an indignant flounce.

Henry stared after his sister as her heels tapped lightly down to the kitchen, her lavender skirts balancing and swaying about her shins with an alarming hint of impertinence. She had never been a practical girl, Elizabeth, but she had at least been docile. And now this . . . this almost defiant attitude of hers, recurring so often of late. Ever since she had come to live with him in his retirement, in fact. Henry shook his head.

Out in the pantry Elizabeth was rattling china plates and silverware, setting out the dishes for the Sunday meal, piling the grapes and apples high in the cut-glass dish for the table centerpiece, pouring ice water into the tall, pale green goblets.

In the dimness of the austere dining room she moved, a soft violet figure in the half-light of the drawn portieres. It was thus that her mother had moved years ago . . . when was it? How long? Elizabeth had lost track of the time. But Henry could tell her. Henry would remember the exact day, the very hour of Mother's death. Scrupulously exact Henry was about such things.

Seated at the head of the table at dinner, Henry bowed his head and said grace in his deep voice, letting the words come rolling rich and rhythmic as a biblical chant. But just as Henry reached the amen, Elizabeth sniffed something burning. Uncomfortably she thought of the potatoes.

"The potatoes, Henry!" She jerked up out of her chair and hurried to the kitchen, where the potatoes were slowly blackening in the oven. Turning off the flame, she lifted them out on the counter, dropping one on the floor first as it scalded her thin, sensitive fingers.

"It's just the skins, Henry. They'll be all right," she called into the dining room. She heard an annoyed snort. Henry *did* always look forward so to his buttered potato skins.

"You haven't changed in all these years, I see, Elizabeth," Henry moralized as she returned to the dining room bearing a dish containing the burned potatoes. Elizabeth sat down, shutting her ears against Henry's rebuke. She could tell that he was about to begin a long, reproachful oration. His voice oozed sanctimoniousness like plump golden drops of butter.

"I sometimes wonder at you, Elizabeth," Henry went on, cutting laboriously into a particularly stubborn piece of chicken. "I wonder how you managed to fend for yourself all these years you've worked alone at the library in town, what with your daydreaming and such."

Elizabeth bent her head over her plate quietly. It was easier to think of something else while Henry was lecturing. When she was small she always used to block her ears to shut out the sound of his voice as he marshaled her to duty, carrying out Mother's directions with such perseverance. But now she found it quite simple to escape Henry's censure unobtrusively by drifting off into a private world of her own, dreaming, musing on anything that chanced into her thoughts. She remembered now about how the horizon blurred pleasantly into the blue sky so that, for all she knew, the water might be thinning into air or the air thickening, settling, becoming water.

They ate on in silence, Elizabeth moving now and then to clear away some dishes, to refill Henry's glass of water, to bring in the dessert bowls of blackberries and cream from the kitchen. As she went about, her full lavender skirts brushing and rustling against the stiff, polished furniture, she felt oddly that she was merging into someone else, her mother perhaps. Someone who was capable and industrious about household tasks. Strange that she, after all these years of independence, strange that she should again be back with Henry, circumscribed once more by domestic duties.

She gazed then at her brother, who was bent over his dessert, ladling spoonful after spoonful of berries and cream into his cavernous mouth. He blended, she thought, with the dim, translucent gloom of the shaded dining room, and she liked to see him sitting so, in the artificial twilight, when she knew that beyond the drawn blinds the sun shone, exact and brilliant.

Elizabeth lingered over washing the lunch dishes while Henry went to pore over some of the maps in his study. There was nothing he liked better than making charts and calculations, Elizabeth thought, her hands fumbling in the warm soapsuds as she stared out of the kitchen window to the blinking flashes of blue water beyond. Always when they were small Henry would be making charts and maps, copying from his geography book, reducing things to scale, while she would dream over the pictures of the mountains and rivers with the queer foreign names.

In the depths of the dishpan the silver collided blindly with the glassware in little tinkling crescendos of sound. Elizabeth put a few last plates into the pan of soapy water and watched them tilt and sink to the bottom. After she was through she would join Henry in the parlor, where they would read together for a while, or perhaps go for a walk. Henry thought the fresh air was so healthful.

Somewhat resentfully Elizabeth remembered all the long days she had spent in bed when she was small. She had been a sallow, sickly child, and Henry had always come in to see her with his round, ruddy face aglow, beaming with vigor.

There would come a time, Elizabeth thought, as she had thought so many times before, when she would confront Henry and say something to him. She did not know quite what, but it would be something rather shattering and dreadful. Something, she was sure of it, extremely disrespectful and frivolous. And then she would see Henry for once nonplussed, Henry faltering, wavering helplessly, without words.

Smiling to herself, her face rapt with inner enjoyment, Elizabeth joined Henry, who was looking at a book of maps in the parlor.

"Come here, Elizabeth," Henry directed, patting the seat on the sofa beside him. "I have found a most interesting map of the New England states I want you to see."

Obediently Elizabeth went to sit beside her brother. The two of them sat on the couch for a while, holding the encyclopedia between them and perusing the shiny pages with the pale pink and blue and yellow maps of States and counties. All at once Elizabeth glimpsed a familiar name in the middle of Massachusetts.

"Wait a minute," she exclaimed. "Let me look at all the places I have been.

Here," she traced a line with her finger up over the surface of the page west from Boston to Springfield, "and up here," her finger swung to the corner of the state to North Adams, "and then just over the borderline into Vermont when I went to visit Cousin Ruth . . . when was it? Last spring . . ."

"The week of April sixth," Henry prompted.

"Yes, of course. You know, I never thought," she said, "of what direction I was going in on the map . . . up, down or across."

Henry looked at his sister with something like dismay.

"You never have!" he breathed incredulously. "You mean you never figure whether you're going north or south or east or west?"

"No," flashed Elizabeth, "I never do. I never saw the point."

She thought of his study, then, the walls hung with the great maps, carefully diagramed, meticulously annotated. In her mind's eye she could see the black contour lines painstakingly drawn and the faint blue wash of color about the shore of continents. There were symbols too, she recalled. Stylized clumps of grass to indicate the swamps and green patches for the parks.

She imagined herself wandering, small and diminutive, up the finely drawn contour lines and down again, wading through the shallow blue ovals of lakes and shouldering her way among stiff symmetrical clumps of swamp grass.

Then she pictured herself with a round, white-faced compass in her hand. The compass needle spun, quivered, quieted, pointing always north, no matter where she turned. The relentless exactness of the mechanism irritated her.

Henry was looking at her still with something akin to shock. She noted that his eyes were very cold and very blue, rather like the waters of the Atlantic on the encyclopedia map. Fine black lines rayed out from the pupil. She saw the short black fringe of lashes drawn suddenly distinct and clear. Henry would know where north was, she thought desperately. He would know precisely where north was.

"Really, I don't think direction matters so much. It's the place you're going to that's important," she announced petulantly. "I mean do you truly think about the direction you're going in all the time?"

The very room seemed to take offense at this open insolence. Elizabeth was sure she saw the rigid andirons stiffen, and the blue tapestry above the mantel had paled perceptibly. The grandfather clock was gaping at her, speechless before the next reproving tick.

"Of course I think where I'm going on the map," Henry declared stanchly, a ruddy color rising to his cheeks. "I always trace out my route beforehand, and then I take a map with me to follow as I travel."

Elizabeth could see him now, standing brightly in the morning on the flat surface of a map, watching expectantly for the sun to come up from the east. (He would know exactly where east was.) Not only that, he would know from which direction the wind was blowing. By some infallible magic he could tell from which slant of the compass the wind veered.

She visualized Henry in the center of the map, which was quartered like an apple pie under the blue dome of a bowl. Feet planted firmly, he stood with pencil and paper making calculations, checking to see that the world revolved on schedule. At night he would watch the constellations go ticking by like luminous clocks, and he would call them cheerily by name, as if greeting punctual relatives. She could almost hear him bellowing heartily: "What ho, Orion, old man!" Oh, it was thoroughly unbearable.

"I suppose telling direction is something anyone can learn," Elizabeth murmured at last.

"Of course," Henry told her, beaming at her humility. "I would even lend you a map to use for practice."

Elizabeth sat quite still while Henry turned the pages of the encyclopedia, studying maps that he found of special interest. Elizabeth was cherishing the way she would a dear, slandered friend, the vague, imprecise world in which she lived.

Hers was a twilight world, where the moon floated up over the trees at night like a tremulous balloon of silver light and the bluish rays wavered through the leaves outside her window, quivering in fluid patterns on the wallpaper of her room. The very air was milkily opaque, and forms wavered and blended one with the other. The wind blew in gentle, capricious gusts, now here, now there, coming from the sea or from the rose garden (she could tell by the scent of water or of flowers).

She winced under the benevolent brightness of Henry's patronizing smile. She wanted to say something brave and impudent, then, something that would disturb the awful serenity of his features.

Once, she remembered, she had ventured to say something spontaneous and fanciful . . . what was it? About wanting to lift up the tops of people's heads like teapot lids and peer inside to find out what they were thinking. Henry had stiffened at that, had cleared his throat and said with a sigh, as if speaking to an irresponsible child, something like "And what would you expect to find inside? Not cogs and wheels, certainly, nor thoughts stacked about like sheaves of paper, labeled and tied up with ribbon!" And he had smiled at his ponderous wit.

No, of course not, Elizabeth had told him, deflated. She thought now of how it would be in her mind, a dark, warm room, with colored lights swinging and wavering, like so many lanterns reflecting on the water, and pictures coming and going on the misty walls, soft and blurred like impressionist paintings. The colors would be broken down in small tinted fragments, and the pink of the ladies' flesh would be the pink of the roses, and the lavender of the dresses would mingle with the lilacs. And there would be, from somewhere sweetly coming, the sound of violins and bells.

Henry's mind, she was certain, would be flat and level, laid out with measured instruments in the broad, even sunlight. There would be geometric concrete walks and square, substantial buildings with clocks on them, everywhere perfectly in time, perfectly synchronized.

The air would be thick with their accurate ticking.

There was a sudden brightening outside, and the room seemed to expand in the fresh light. "Come, it will be a fine afternoon for a walk," Henry said, rising from the couch, smiling, and holding out a square, substantial hand to her.

Every Sunday afternoon after dinner it was his habit to take her for a stroll along the boulevard by the ocean. The brisk salt air, he said, would be a bracing tonic for her. She was always a bit sallow, a bit pinched about the cheeks.

In the blowing air Elizabeth's gray hair would loosen and flutter about her face in a wispy halo, damp and moist. But in spite of the healthful breeze she knew that Henry disliked to see her hair untidy and was glad to have her smooth it back in the accustomed bun and secure it with a long metal hairpin.

Today the air was clear, yet warm for early September, and Elizabeth stepped out on the front porch with a sudden gaiety, her gray cloth coat open loosely over her lavender dress. In the distance she could see a small pile of dark clouds that might be a storm rising slowly on the far horizon. Like tiny grape clusters the purple clouds were, with the gulls wheeling in cream white flakes against them.

Down against the stone foundations of the boardwalk the waves were breaking powerfully, the great green crests hanging suspended in a curve of cold glass, veined bluish, and then, after a moment of immobility, toppling in a white surge of foam, the layers of water flaring up the beach in thin sheets of mirrored crystal.

Her hand resting securely on Henry's arm, Elizabeth felt tethered, like a balloon, safely in the wind. Breathing in the drafts of fresh air made her feel peculiarly light, almost inflated, as if at a slightly stronger puff of wind she would go lifting, tilting out over the water.

Far, far out on the horizon the grape clusters were swelling, dilating, and the wind was queerly warm and pushing. The September sunlight seemed suddenly diluted, weakened.

"Henry, I think there's going to be a storm."

Henry scoffed at the distant looming clouds. "Nonsense," he said resolutely. "It will blow off. The wind is wrong."

The wind was wrong. Blowing in impulsive, freakish gusts, the wind teased Elizabeth. It flickered at the edge of her petticoat. Playfully it blew a strand of hair in her eye. She felt strangely mischievous and elated, secretly pleased that the wind was wrong.

Henry was stopping by the sea wall. He was taking his massive gold watch from his waistcoat pocket. The tide, he said, should be high in fifteen minutes now. At seven minutes past four exactly. They would watch it from the old pier that jutted out over the rocks.

Elizabeth felt a mounting exhilaration as they walked out on the boards of the pier, which creaked and complained beneath them. Between the cracks she could see the deep green water winking up at her. The seething waves seemed to be whispering something mysterious to her, something that was unintelligible, lost in the loudness of the wind. Giddily she felt the moss-covered piles of the pier sway and squeak beneath them in the strong pull of the tide.

"Out here," said Henry, leaning over the railing at the end of the pier, his conservative blue pin-stripe suit rippling in the skittish wind, which lifted the carefully combed hairs from the crown of his head until they vibrated, upstanding in the air, like the antennae of an insect.

Elizabeth bent over the railing beside her brother, staring down into the waves churning up on the rocks below. Her lavender skirt kept billowing and flapping about her legs, and although she tried to hold it down with her thin, frail fingers it would still blow about rebelliously.

Something was pricking her throat. Absently she lifted one hand only to feel her amethyst brooch loosen, slip through her fingers and fall, raying purple flashes as it spun down to lie on the rocks below, sparkling spitefully.

"Henry," she cried, clinging to him. "Henry, Mother's brooch! Whatever shall I do?" Henry's gaze followed her pointing hand, her angular, trembling index finger, down to where the brooch lay glinting. "Henry," she cried, half-sobbing, "you must get it for me. The waves will take it!"

Henry, handing her his black bowler hat, was suddenly responsible and protecting. He leaned over the railing to see what was the best possible footing. "Never fear," he said bravely, and the words were flung back at him by the derisive wind, "never fear, there is a ladder of sorts. I will get your brooch for you."

Carefully, expertly, Henry began his descent. He placed his feet, one after the other, precisely in the angles of the wooden crosspieces, letting himself down at last onto the dry, mossy top of the rocks, where he stood in triumph. The waves crashed a little below him, rhythmically rising and falling, making ominous knocking sounds in the caverns and crevices among the great rocks. Steadying himself with one hand on the lowest rung of his improvised ladder, Henry leaned bulkily to pick up the brooch. He bent slowly, majestically, puffing a little from his heavy dinner.

Elizabeth realized that the wave must have been coming for quite some time, but she had not noticed that it was so much taller than the rest. There it was, though, a great bulk of green water moving slowly, majestically inward, rolling inexorably on, governed by some infallible natural law, toward Henry, who was just straightening, about to smile up at her, the brooch in his hand.

"Henry," she whispered in an ecstasy of horror as she leaned forward to watch the wave engulf the rock, spilling an enormous flood of water over the very spot on which Henry stood, surging up around his ankles, circling in two whirlpools about his knees. For a long moment Henry balanced valiantly, a colossus astride the roaring sea, an expression of unusual and pained surprise growing on his white, uplifted face.

Henry's arms revolved in the air like two frantic plane propellers as he felt the moss go sliding, slipping away under his submerged, well-polished shoes, and with a last helpless look, faltering, fumbling, without words, he toppled back into the depth of the next black wave. With a growing peace Elizabeth watched the flailing arms rise, sink, and rise again. Finally the dark form quieted, sinking slowly down through level after green level of obscurity into the sea. The tide was turning.

Musingly Elizabeth leaned on the railing, her pointed chin cupped in her blue-veined hands. She envisioned a green, aquatic Henry dropping through layers of clouded water like a porpoise. There would be seaweed in his hair and water in his pockets. Weighted by the round gold watch, by the white-faced compass, he would sink down to the ocean floor.

The water would ooze inside his shoes and seep into the workings of his watch until the ticking stopped. Then no amount of irritated shaking and knocking would be able to jar the works into motion again. Even the mysterious and exact cogs of the compass would rust, and Henry could shake and prod them, but the fine quivering needle would stick stubbornly and north would be everywhere he turned. She pictured him taking his afternoon stroll alone on Sundays, walking briskly below in the dilute green light, prodding curiously at the sea anemones with his cane.

And then she thought of his study with all the maps and the sea serpents drawn decoratively in the middle of the Atlantic Ocean; of Neptune sitting regally on a wave with his trident in his hand and the crown on his blown white hair. Even as she meditated, the features of Neptune's kingly visage blurred, puffed, rounded, and there, turned to look at her, was the startled face of a much altered Henry. Shivering without his waistcoat, without his pin-stripe suit, he sat huddled on the crest of the wave, teeth chattering. And as she looked she heard a minute and pathetic sneeze.

Poor Henry. Her heart went out to him in pity. For who would look after him down there among all those slippery, indolent sea creatures? Who would listen to him talk about the way the moon controlled the tides or about the density of atmospheric pressure? She thought sympathetically of Henry and how he never could digest shellfish.

The wind was rising again, and Elizabeth's skirts lifted in a fresh gust, billowing, belling up, filled with air. She tilted dangerously, letting go of the railing, trying to smooth down her petticoats. Her feet rose from the planking, settled, rose again, until she was bobbing upward, floating like a pale lavender milkweed seed along the wind, over the waves and out to sea.

And that was the last anyone saw of Elizabeth Minton, who was enjoying herself thoroughly, blowing upward, now to this side, now to that, her lavender dress blending with the purple of the distant clouds. Her high-pitched, triumphant, feminine giggle mingled with the deep, gurgling chuckle of Henry, borne along beneath her on the outgoing tide.

The afternoon was shading into twilight. There was a sudden tug at Elizabeth's arm.

"Come along home, Elizabeth," Henry said. "It's getting late."

Elizabeth gave a sigh of submission. "I'm coming," she said.

Marie

Ts,[*] c.4 May 1952, Lilly Library

It was nine o'clock when the girl walked into the kitchen. She was wearing light blue flannel pajamas, and her dark hair was up in rag curlers. For a

---

[*] Typescript has holograph corrections and additions by SP as well as comments from her instructor. Written for English 220b, Practice in Various Forms of Writing.

minute she stood in the doorway, looking at the table where the cooks left the milk and dessert before bedtime. There was a white enamel pitcher put out, and a bowl of half-melted ice cream. The girl sniffed disappointedly.

Walking over to the great black stove, she stood on tiptoe and peered into a copper tin on the shelf above. Stale bread crusts rattled against the sides of the container. The girl took out a piece of dry toast and perched on the table. Her teeth bit through the crust with a grating crunch. She was staring reflectively at her left leg, which dangled aimlessly over the counter, when the head cook walked in.

Marie didn't really walk, she shuffled. Her skimpy black dressing gown was splashed with a gaudy pattern of pink and yellow flowers, and her long gray hair fell down over her thin bent shoulders. Under her squinting, black eyes hung two pockets of flesh that wobbled when she talked, and the sag of her wrinkled skin was like the rutted contour of melted candle wax.

"Hello, Marie," the girl said politely.

"Allo," Marie croaked. Her high, nasal voice quavered in an unpleasant piercing tone. She shuffled over to the icebox, opened it, and took out a small dish of strong-smelling salmon, also a little bowl of tartar sauce, curdled thick and yellow.

"Want some?" Marie asked plaintively. She pulled up a stool and sat down at the table opposite the girl, spreading the salmon and sauce thickly on a piece of bread. When she chewed, her whole long jaw rotated rhythmically, masticating the mass of food with obvious relish.

"No, thanks," the girl said. "I'm really not hungry. I'm on a diet."

"You?" Marie snorted. "Where you fat?"

"It's my seat," the girl explained. "It gets fat when I eat a lot. Otherwise I'm thin."

Marie looked very old and very wise. Her ugly long nose quivered with importance as she leaned forward, waving a piece of bread forebodingly.

"You know what you got?" Marie intoned solemnly. The girl shook her head. "You got natural fat. You remember Miss Shake last year?"

There had been no Miss Shake as far as the girl was concerned, but she nodded vaguely.

"Well, Miss Shake had natural fat. She had a bee-youtiful face, but she had natural fat. So she went on a diet. She used to come out into the kitchen and say, 'Marie, give me some meat,' so I give her the meat, and she sit down on the back stairs eating it. That's all she ate. Meat. All right, Miss Shake got thin. But look what happened to her face. You remember how nice she look when she smile before? Well, her face get all little wrinkles, and the skin get folds like an old woman when she smile."

The girl said, "How awful." An expression of worry and concern grew upon her face.

Marie noticed this expression and felt sorry. "I tell you what to do," she said. "You eat all the things you like, but in little pieces. You eat those things they call . . ." Here she stopped in confusion, moving her hands helplessly in front of her as if trying to pull the word she wanted out of the salmon bowl. "Those things they call . . . I don't speak English so very good, you know . . . those things they call carrots . . ."

"Carrots?" the girl frowned questioningly.

"Yes, carrots. They eat them in little pieces, and you can eat all the things you like, only . . ."

"Oh, *calories*," the girl exclaimed, laughing. "You mean *calories*."

"I come from Monreal," Marie said. "I don't speak English very good. I'm not educated like you girls." Marie bent over her plate, and took a large mouthful of bread and salmon. "Have some," she mumbled thickly.

"Well, all right, just a little." The girl reached over and took a piece of salmon from the bowl and spread it out on another dry square of toast.

"Someday, Marie," she said, then, musingly, "you know what I'd like? I'd like the recipe for your chocolate pie. I just love your chocolate pie."

Marie bridled. "Aw," she depreciated in a pleased drawl, "the way you talk, you'd think we could cook around here."

"You sure can," the girl insisted. "Everybody says so. Everybody says we get the best food on campus.

"I remember last year," the girl went on. "I used to try to get a table where everybody was on a diet, so I could get all the extra pieces of chocolate pie. I don't see how you make it. I bet you work awfully hard."

"Hard!" Marie cried out, flinging her arms in the air. "I get up sometimes at five in the morning. You remember last year how I got sick and in the hospital?"

"Sure," the girl said. "We all missed you."

"Yeah," said Marie, very softly. "I know, you all sent me flowers. Bee-youtiful flowers. I was so glad."

"What happened then," the girl prodded, "about the hospital?"

"The hospital. Well, you know that other cook last year? Gladys? Well, she put it over on me when I'm sick. She slow. She stay upstairs before dinner, no help. She always doing something like that."

"Oh, no!" the girl exclaimed.

"Yes." Marie warmed to her subject. She leaned back perilously on the tall stool, flinging her arms out again, exclaiming dramatically in her cracked, wailing voice, "Work! I work my fingers to the bone, and no good help. When I go back to Monreal last summer, my family say, 'Marie, Marie, what's the matter with you? You aren't the same.' 'Matter,' I say. 'Matter? I'm wore out to the core, that's what I am.'"

The girl shook her head sadly. "You like to cook?" she asked then. She had taken another piece of salmon and was squeezing the oil out with her fingers.

"Cook? That's my life," Marie's voice flared with proud fire, and then dropped to a whine, "But I'm lonely. I don't know anyone here. All my family is in Canada. I don't know what I'd do if you girls hadn't been all so nice to me. Believe me, I been here so long that I seen all girls, bee-youtiful girls and girls just rotten." Marie spat out the last word in a guttural hiss of scorn.

"Rotten?" the girl asked. "What were they like?"

"Ach, they wouldn't lift a finger. They wouldn't come out even in the kitchen. They think they are too good, too much ladies to do work."

"I think that's just terrible." The girl drew herself up in indignation at her less perfect fellows.

"You know something?" Marie leaned forward, breathing in a low, confidential undertone. "You know something? I'm not educated. I ain't never had the chances you girls had. But you know what I bet?"

"What?" the girl leaned forward, intent to catch the husky whisper.

"You know Mrs. Johnson?"

"Of course." Mrs. Johnson was the housemother.

"Well, she walk in here every day, proud and pretty as a baby. I bet, I bet if I had the education she had and you girls had . . . I bet I could do her job and do it better!"

There was a silence. Marie sat, leaning forward, her lined face contorted with a deep conviction, breathing hard. She didn't move, but sat hunched over the table like some ancient seeress prophesying a glory that might have been.

The girl didn't say anything. Finally she got down from the table. "Guess I'll be going to bed," she said. She walked out of the kitchen, leaving Marie sitting there, a silent figure, shrouded in a black-flowered dressing gown.

The New Day

Ts,* 3–5 June 1952, Lilly Library

"I don't believe you've ever met Mark," Mrs. Vernon had said to Lisa when she drove up to the house shortly after seven o'clock that August morning. No, Lisa had thought, smiling at the tall boy in the front seat of her car, she had never met Mrs. Vernon's son before. But ever since she had seen the oil portrait of Mark that his mother had hanging up in her studio, she had hoped someday to have the chance to meet the dark-haired boy with the clear, laughing blue eyes and the strong cleft chin.

Mark had never been around when Lisa went to Mrs. Vernon's house for her painting lessons that summer, so she guessed that maybe he was away working somewhere. Mrs. Vernon didn't talk much about her son, but when she received word that Mark was coming home at the end of the summer she told Lisa, "He likes to draw, too. Someday, when you and I go on a painting trip, I'll let him come along."

And now, in the luminous morning air, the three of them were driving up to Rockport for a day of picnicking, swimming, and watercoloring. Sitting as she was, in the back seat of the car, amid the big glass water jars that jangled and clinked together on the floor and the fresh white oblong sheets of watercolor paper tacked taut to the painting boards, Lisa felt excitement rise in her. It was a new day, hardly soiled—fresh as the sheets of watercolor paper and just as challenging.

Even though it was yet early morning, the August sun was hot, and already the black macadam road was giving off the strong, pungent smell of melted tar. Lulled by the speed of the car, Lisa leaned back, idly watching the telephone poles spring up along the roadside, dwindling again into the distance along thin lines of streaming black wire. Sunlight flared like yellow fire on the grasslands and lay warm and brilliant on the red flanks of substantial barns.

"How goes it back there?" Mrs. Vernon glanced over her shoulder at Lisa.

"Fine," Lisa said, "just fine."

She was thinking of how she would mix her palette. Earth, freshly turned, was burnt sienna, umber, and rich black. Shadows along the barns were warm,

---

* In the scene set at the fruit store, 'strawberries' was changed to 'raspberries' in the typescript in an unknown hand, possibly Aurelia Schober Plath's. Submitted to *Seventeen*.

tinged with orange like the smoky sky that paled above the horizon line. Dark caverns in pine groves were a rich Prussian blue with a touch of alizarin crimson. She was eager to begin painting, to squeeze out little pools of crimson, blue, and yellow from silver tubes.

Lapsed into thoughtfulness, Lisa did not notice that Mark had been silent for about an hour now, nor did she think it strange. There would be time enough to talk with him when they arrived in Rockport. Then, seated at last by the blue of the bay, she would think of some question or other to ask him—something to do with painting or with the way he felt about the sea.

The old black Plymouth was swinging into narrow streets now, and the shingled houses stood closer together on their green plots of lawn, shaded by tall elms and maples. There were angular white picket fences and verandas covered with interlacing vines. Between the trees, Lisa saw a ragged flag of blue that was the ocean, and her spirits lifted with the promise of the day ahead.

Mrs. Vernon slowed the car as she turned a corner and pulled into a parking space on the right-hand side of the street beside a row of stores.

"Well, this is it," she said, turning off the ignition and setting the emergency brake. "But before we go down to the waterfront I want to buy some fruit for our picnic."

Mark got out of the car and opened the rear door for Lisa.

"Thanks," she said, glancing up at him. He must be in his late twenties, she guessed, for his face was heavier, a bit squarer than in the portrait in the Vernons' living room. And there was a light of some kind in the painting that was missing here. As he looked down at her, he smiled, but his eyes did not smile. They remained a flat, bleak shade of blue.

When Lisa stepped up on the sidewalk, a blast of heat reached her from the pavement, along with the sweet, pleasant smell of cut grass. Striped red and tan awnings shaded the street, and from the fruit store came the odor of ripe strawberries and bruised plums, stickily cool and fragrant.

"I like watermelon," Mark said to Lisa. "How about you?"

"Oh, so do I," Lisa exclaimed.

"Watermelon it shall be, then," laughed Mrs. Vernon, pushing a strand of gray hair back under her blue denim cap and smiling at the two of them. She looked relieved about something, Lisa thought.

Mark and Lisa followed Mrs. Vernon into the store. The screen door slammed loudly behind them as they entered, and from a back room, smelling of damp sawdust, a short heavy man bustled forward, rubbing his fat hands on his white apron.

"Yess, yess," he said, with a thick guttural accent, coming up to them. "Some fruit? Blueberries, maybe, or cherries? We got some fine cherries."

"No," said Mrs. Vernon, "I think we'll take half a watermelon."

The man shuffled over to get a melon, and lifted the dark green fruit to the chopping board on the counter. He raised a long knife and brought it down heavily. The watermelon rind split with a crack, revealing the bright red of the flesh inside, peppered with dark seeds.

"Mmm," Mark grinned. "Watermelon. I can't wait."

Why, Lisa thought, he is as appreciative about the watermelon as a small child would be.

The little man stretched his mouth in a smile, and the flushed, greasy skin of his face crinkled up about the eyes and mouth as he bent down behind the counter for a brown paper bag. "You gotta good buy there," he said.

Lisa was almost sorry to leave the cool interior of the fruit store with the ripe, heavy smell of berry juice and melons and the languorous hum of the flies that circled slowly around a curl of yellow flypaper hanging down from the ceiling.

"One more thing," Mrs. Vernon said, "before we go down to the beach. I've got to leave a watercolor at the Art Center for an exhibit they're having. It's just across the street."

She asked Mark to unlock the trunk of the car and carry the painting up for her.

The Art Center was a large white-shingled house with green shutters and a sign over the door that proclaimed EXHIBIT: OPEN TO THE PUBLIC. The noon sun was hot along the street, Lisa noticed, as they stood on the doorstep after ringing the bell. The light lay creamy on the colored housefronts, dusty pink and lemon yellow.

The woman who answered the door smiled at Mrs. Vernon. "Come over to the desk," she said, taking the painting from Mark, "and I'll register this for the exhibit."

"Lisa, why don't you and Mark go in and look at the exhibit while I settle this business?" Mrs. Vernon said. "I'll come and get you when I'm through. Mark, you show Lisa where to go, won't you?"

Obediently, Mark took Lisa's arm. There was something strange about his touch, Lisa thought. It was rather mechanical, almost lifeless. "Through this way," he said, guiding her down a hall into the exhibition rooms where large windows let in the light, and dust motes went drifting, sinking in the luminous air.

The walls were covered with paintings by artists from all over New England. Most of them were watercolors, bright and vivid, of country scenes, waterfronts, and people. Mark stood silent before a large painting of a boatyard. Sunlight sparkled on the curving hulls that bent in clean arcs against the background of a Technicolor blue sea.

"You like that?" Lisa ventured, standing beside him.

"I don't see how they do it," Mark murmured.

"Do what?" Lisa asked, curious.

"Paint with all those colors," he said gravely. "I mean, mixing them all. It's so confusing that way."

"But how would you do it, then?" Lisa queried, taken aback.

"Oh, I'd only use one color in a painting. It'd do it all in red, or yellow, maybe blue. Much simpler, you know."

"Of course." Lisa felt a faint chill at the base of her spine.

"I like to travel better than anything, you know," Mark was saying, still looking at the boats.

"Me too," Lisa said, "only I've never been outside of the New England states, even."

"Oh, I don't mean traveling that way," Mark said softly. "I mean I read magazines and all. *National Geographic*, for one. It's really better than actually *going* places. No bother about packing or anything."

"I can imagine," Lisa replied faintly, thinking: Why doesn't Mrs. Vernon come back? Why did she take me, anyway? Did she think I wouldn't notice about Mark? That I wouldn't be able to see?

And then Mrs. Vernon did come into the room, smiling, her blue eyes clear and happy, as if there were nothing the matter, nothing wrong with the world at all.

"Come on, people," she called gaily. "The painting is all registered, labeled and such. To the beach!"

Relieved, Lisa followed Mrs. Vernon back to the car, and Mark walked along beside them, saying nothing and humming softly to himself.

Down by the waterfront, weather-beaten lobster shacks clustered close along the shoreline, and there were wildflowers springing up tall and lanky from the cracks in the boardwalks. Everywhere there were groups of tourists, sunburnt and casually clad in pastel cotton dresses or white trousers and shirts, chattering as they strolled in and out of the little antique shops. Fishermen's dinghies were moored in the inlets, and there was the good dry smell of salt, warm grass, and sun on silvered wood. And beyond, Lisa exulted, there was the blue, the unbelievable blue of the open sea.

The three of them carried their picnic to a shaded spot where the water washed up among great gray boulders and there was a good view of the harbor. Mrs. Vernon did most of the talking during lunch, reminiscing about the times she had brought Mark up to Rockport when he was small, and chattering about various favorite places where artists like to paint.

The watermelon was very good, Lisa thought, biting into the cold pink flesh and tasting the sweet juice that flooded into her mouth as she swallowed the succulent pulp. But even in the shade it was terribly hot. She could feel beads of perspiration breaking out on her forehead, her upper lip, and trickling down the small of her back where her cotton dress was stickily damp and clinging. The water lapped at her feet, clear and inviting.

"Is there any place," she asked Mrs. Vernon, "where we could go swimming around here?"

"Surely," Mrs. Vernon smiled. "Why don't you and Mark change in the bathhouse down the street, and then go in for a short dip before we start painting? I'll sit here and wait in the shade."

Mark walked back to the car with Lisa, and they picked up their bathing suits. Walking down the street to the bathhouse, Lisa cast a side glance at Mark. He was really extremely attractive, broad-shouldered, with long legs, neatly muscular and firm. Already he was getting tan.

But there was still something about him that troubled her. His preoccupied stare, perhaps. As if, she shivered, she were not there at all. Or as if he were seeing beyond her, through her, to something quite absorbing and rather sobering, something invisible to all but himself.

He met her outside the bathhouse after they had changed into their suits, and they walked slowly down the beach to the water's edge. The shouts of children rose shrilly in the air, and the waves were breaking powerfully alongshore, the great green crests hanging suspended in a curve of cold glass, veined bluish, and then, after a moment of immobility, toppling in a white surge of foam. Clear, thin sheets of water flared up over the sand like layers of crystal, momentarily reflecting the sky. The whole bay was spread out before them in the sun like a large plate of blue water, and the sunlight lay flat and brilliant on the land and buildings.

We shouldn't be walking this way, Lisa thought. So silently, so gravely, as if we were marching to a death of some kind in the sea. We should be running. I want to run and feel my hair blow back in the wind, and the water splash coldly around my legs.

"Race you into the water, Mark," she yelled, her voice taut in her throat, attempting gaiety. She threw down her red striped towel like a challenge on the sand and started for the water with long swift strides. And as she ran, she felt suddenly released and free, as if she were leaving something behind her, some intangible fear.

She could hear Mark breathing hard as he ran along at her heels. He beat her, too, plunging with a dash of speed into the surf a moment before she did, and coming up sputtering, shaking the water out of his curly black hair. Lisa floated on her back, kicking up a jet of foam into the sun so that the water drops broke and fell in blinding slivers of light. It was good to fan her arms in the cool green waves and see the silver bubbles rising about her legs that looked so strangely pale and wavering and unsubstantial, as if they had begun to wither and bleach in the cold sea.

The remaining tension inside her melted at the sight of Mark cleaving through the water with a strong crawl, obviously enjoying himself. She had probably been imagining things back there at the art exhibit, she told herself. There was nothing wrong after all. Mark had been teasing, perhaps, trying to shatter her composure. And now he was swimming up beside her, spouting a jet of water from his mouth like a playful whale.

"I could stay in here all day," Lisa said breathlessly, treading water.

"I'm glad I'm with you," he said. "You need somebody to protect you."

"You really think so?" Lisa felt strangely touched.

"Yes. You never can tell about kidnappers these days. Did you see those two men up there beside the breakwater? Looking at us that funny way? You could tell they were up to something." Mark looked at Lisa seriously.

"I guess you're right," Lisa said slowly. The bright glare of the sun struck her with sudden horror. Even in broad daylight, she felt a cold unreasoning fear begin in her brain. The glittering sea was all at once ominous, treacherous. A wave fell loudly, and the crash made her start nervously.

"Where did you go to school?" she asked suddenly, desperately, realizing even as she said the words that she had foolishly fallen back on the old cliché one used in high school when introduced to a stranger.

"I went to a special school," Mark told her. "The teacher was very nice and very fat, I remember." He laughed, then, an odd, flat laugh that held no suggestions of mirth. "She used to read us *Pinocchio*. It was my favorite story."

"Really?" To her surprise, Lisa found herself continuing, "My favorite story was *Alice in Wonderland*. *Pinocchio* always scared me a little. Especially the part about his nose growing and the birds pecking at it. I felt so sorry for him."

Mark was looking at her now with something like interest, and Lisa found herself grinning back at him companionably. She felt a surge of strength flood into her, beating proudly in her veins at the sight of Mark listening to her.

What was it, she wondered, treading water there, talking naturally to Mark, what was it that marked the growing up, the changing from childhood to adulthood? There were days when she felt the weight of the ages, the questions of centuries on her shoulders, and yet, now, here with Mark, she was a little girl again, splashing in the water and laughing as if she had never grown up at all.

"You know," Mark was telling her. "I'm glad you read him. Even if you like Alice better, at least you know who he is. So few people do."

His face was serious, trusting, and Lisa felt that at last she was beginning to understand. There was, just then, she was sure of it, a sudden brightening of the sky and sea, a freshening of color, almost as if a new day were beginning. She turned away lest Mark see that she was trying not to cry.

Mrs. Vernon was still sitting in the shade when they came back, refreshed and laughing. "I envy you two," she exclaimed gaily. "You look so energetic, so cool."

They went down to the waterfront, then, to paint. Lisa waited a bit before she began to sketch in the outlines of the sun-gray wharf and the colored slices of the boats against it. In her mind she visualized the scene before her, transposed on the paper the way she wanted it, bright, vivid, with the lines slanting, balancing in a subtle counterpoise, yet firm and unyielding, as if riveted to each other.

"Between the idea and the reality," she quoted silently to herself, "falls the shadow,"* and she began dipping her brush into the paint, sketching a line here, there, on the paper. And even as she mixed a shade of blue, a shade of green, the hollows of the waves mocked her, moving always, rising, falling, swelling, never the same from moment to moment.

What is life, after all, Lisa thought, stroking on the color with her brush, squinting, first at the scene, then at her paper. What is life but a moving and a changing, a growing and an altering, lighted occasionally by a sharp awareness that lets you see things clearly and accept them for what they are. An awareness that comes like a new day where, with the dawn, you look around as if it were the first day of the world.

When Mrs. Vernon had painted Mark that time, long ago, with the light in

---

* T. S. Eliot, 'The Hollow Men'. <SP's footnote.>

his keen eyes and the laughter on his lips, she had been right in her way. That was what Mark might have been, and to her, then, it was the painting, not this Mark, that was the reality. So we persist in making our own little realities, Lisa thought, just as now I am painting my particular wharf, my own boats—and my finished painting will be like no other.

On the ride home, Mark sat in back, and Lisa sat up front and talked with Mrs. Vernon. While they drove, Mark hummed and whistled to himself in his flat, tuneless voice. It was dark when Mrs. Vernon let Lisa off at her house.

"Mark, please help carry Lisa's things up to the door."

"Sure, Mother." Mark got out of the car obediently. He has been well trained, Lisa thought. She said goodbye to him at the door, softly.

"I'm glad you came," he said politely.

"So am I," Lisa smiled, turning to go into the house, lifting the latch and stepping up into the warmth and security that still was home, but no longer quite the protective, sheltering cocoon it had been.

For she felt as if she had been away a long while, as if the rooms of the house had become smaller, stuffier, somehow, and all the furniture shrunken. She felt that she had expanded and grown tall. And yet, when her mother came to meet her, she knew that the change inside her didn't show, that behind the tan, the snub nose, the wind-blown brown hair, the alteration in her was not visible.

"Did you have a nice time?" her mother asked.

"Yes," Lisa replied, wondering how you told someone so close to you that you were different, that you had walked into another world and back again in the space of a few hours.

"I wanted to tell you, before you left, about the Vernon boy," Lisa's mother said. "But I thought it best to let you work it out for yourself. Did Mrs. Vernon explain to you during the trip?"

"She didn't have to," Lisa answered. Why must you say anything about it, she wanted to ask her mother. It was all fine; I got along fine by myself.

"Let's see what you painted," Lisa's mother bent over the watercolor, still tacked to its board. "Why, Lisa, it's good! You really got the light in wonderfully."

And as Lisa looked at her painting again, she smiled. For she had made the light like dawn. Like the breaking of a new day.

Initiation

Written: 16–18 July 1952
Published: *Seventeen* (January 1953): 65, 92–4[*]

The basement room was dark and warm, like the inside of a sealed jar, Millicent thought, her eyes getting used to the strange dimness. The silence was soft with cobwebs, and from the small, rectangular window set high in the stone wall there sifted a faint bluish light that must be coming from the full October moon. She could see now that what she was sitting on was a woodpile next to the furnace.

Millicent brushed back a strand of hair. It was stiff and sticky from the egg that they had broken on her head as she knelt blindfolded at the sorority altar a short while before. There had been a silence, a slight crunching sound, and then she had felt the cold, slimy egg-white flattening and spreading on her head and sliding down her neck. She had heard someone smothering a laugh. It was all part of the ceremony.

Then the girls had led her here, blindfolded still, through the corridors of Betsy Johnson's house and shut her in the cellar. It would be an hour before they came to get her, but then Rat Court would be all over and she would say what she had to say and go home.

For tonight was the grand finale, the trial by fire. There really was no doubt now that she would get in. She could not think of anyone who had ever been invited into the high school sorority and failed to get through initiation time. But even so, her case would be quite different. She would see to that. She could not exactly say what had decided her revolt, but it definitely had something to do with Tracy and something to do with the heather birds.

What girl at Lansing High would not want to be in her place now? Millicent thought, amused. What girl would not want to be one of the elect, no matter if it did mean five days of initiation before and after school, ending in the climax of Rat Court on Friday night when they made the new girls members? Even

---

[*] Winner of second prize in *Seventeen*'s 1952 short-story contest. Printed with by line 'Sylvia Plath, Age 19, Wellesley, Massachusetts' as well as with a photograph of SP and a biographical sketch: 'SYLVIA PLATH, reviewing her long friendship with us, says ". . . at fifteen and sixteen, I got rejection slips! Then, my first acceptance at the appropriate age of seventeen. Now the swan song in the form of a second prize!" A moral here, we think, for all contributors.' Accompanied by an illustration by Marjory Carolyn Clark.

Tracy had been wistful when she heard that Millicent had been one of the five girls to receive an invitation.

"It won't be any different with us, Tracy," Millicent had told her. "We'll still go around together like we always have, and next year you'll surely get in."

"I know, but even so," Tracy had said quietly, "you'll change, whether you think you will or not. Nothing ever stays the same."

And nothing does, Millicent had thought. How horrible it would be if one never changed . . . if she were condemned to be the plain, shy Millicent of a few years back for the rest of her life. Fortunately there was always the changing, the growing, the going on.

It would come to Tracy, too. She would tell Tracy the silly things the girls had said, and Tracy would change also, entering eventually into the magic circle. She would grow to know the special ritual as Millicent had started to last week.

"First of all," Betsy Johnson, the vivacious blonde secretary of the sorority, had told the five new candidates over sandwiches in the school cafeteria last Monday, "first of all, each of you has a big sister. She's the one who bosses you around, and you just do what she tells you."

"Remember the part about talking back and smiling," Louise Fullerton had put in, laughing. She was another celebrity in high school, pretty and dark and Vice President of the Student Council. "You can't say anything unless your big sister asks you something or tells you to talk to someone. And you can't smile, no matter how you're dying to." The girls had laughed a little nervously, and then the bell had rung for the beginning of afternoon classes.

It would be rather fun for a change, Millicent mused, getting her books out of her locker in the hall, rather exciting to be part of a closely knit group, the exclusive set at Lansing High. Of course, it wasn't a school organization. In fact, the principal, Mr. Cranton, wanted to do away with initiation week altogether, because he thought it was undemocratic and disturbed the routine of school work. But there wasn't really anything he could do about it. Sure, the girls had to come to school for five days without any lipstick on and without curling their hair, and of course everybody noticed them, but what could the teachers do?

Millicent sat down at her desk in the big study hall. Tomorrow she would come to school, proudly, laughingly, without lipstick, with her brown hair straight and shoulder-length, and then everybody would know, even the boys would know, that she was one of the elect. Teachers would smile helplessly, thinking perhaps: So now they've picked Millicent Arnold. I never would have guessed it.

A year or two ago, not many people would have guessed it. Millicent had waited a long time for acceptance, longer than most. It was as if she had been sitting for years in a pavilion outside a dance floor, looking in through the windows at the golden interior, with the lights clear and the air like honey, wistfully watching the gay couples waltzing to the never-ending music, laughing in pairs and groups together, no one alone.

But now at last, amid a week of fanfare and merriment, she would answer her invitation to enter the ballroom through the main entrance marked "Initiation." She would gather up her velvet skirts, her silken train, or whatever the disinherited princesses wore in the storybooks, and come into her rightful kingdom . . . The bell rang to end study hall.

"Millicent, wait up!" It was Louise Fullerton behind her, Louise who had always before been very nice, very polite, friendlier than the rest, even long ago, before the invitation had come.

"Listen," Louise walked down the hall with her to Latin, their next class, "are you busy right after school today? Because I'd like to talk to you about tomorrow."

"Sure. I've got lots of time."

"Well, meet me in the hall after homeroom then, and we'll go down to the drugstore or something."

Walking beside Louise on the way to the drugstore, Millicent felt a surge of pride. For all anyone could see, she and Louise were the best of friends.

"You know, I was so glad when they voted you in," Louise said.

Millicent smiled. "I was really thrilled to get the invitation," she said frankly, "but kind of sorry that Tracy didn't get in, too."

Tracy, she thought. If there is such a thing as a best friend, Tracy has been just that this last year.

"Yes, Tracy," Louise was saying, "she's a nice girl, and they put her up on the slate, but . . . well, she had three blackballs against her."

"Blackballs? What are they?"

"Well, we're not supposed to tell anybody outside the club, but seeing as you'll be in at the end of week I don't suppose it hurts." They were at the drugstore now.

"You see," Louise began explaining in a low voice after they were seated in the privacy of the booth, "once a year the sorority puts up all the likely girls that are suggested for membership . . ."

Millicent sipped her cold, sweet drink slowly, saving the ice cream to spoon up last. She listened carefully to Louise who was going on, ". . . and then there's a big meeting, and all the girls' names are read off and each girl is discussed."

"Oh?" Millicent asked mechanically, her voice sounding strange.

"Oh, I know what you're thinking," Louise laughed. "But it's really not as bad as all that. They keep it down to a minimum of catting. They just talk over each girl and why or why not they think she'd be good for the club. And then they vote. Three blackballs eliminate a girl."

"Do you mind if I ask you what happened to Tracy?" Millicent said.

Louise laughed a little uneasily. "Well, you know how girls are. They notice little things. I mean, some of them thought Tracy was just a bit *too* different. Maybe you could suggest a few things to her."

"Like what?"

"Oh, like maybe not wearing knee socks to school, or carrying that old bookbag. I know it doesn't sound like much, but well, it's things like that which set someone apart. I mean, you know that no girl at Lansing would be seen dead wearing knee socks, no matter how cold it gets, and it's kiddish and kind of green to carry a bookbag."

"I guess so," Millicent said.

"About tomorrow," Louise went on. "You've drawn Beverly Mitchell for a big sister. I wanted to warn you that she's the toughest, but if you get through all right it'll be all the more credit for you."

"Thanks, Lou," Millicent said gratefully, thinking, This is beginning to sound serious. Worse than a loyalty test, this grilling over the coals. What's it supposed to prove anyway? That I can take orders without flinching? Or does it just make them feel good to see us run around at their beck and call?

"All you have to do really," Louise said, spooning up the last of her sundae, "is be very meek and obedient when you're with Bev and do just what she tells you. Don't laugh or talk back or try to be funny, or she'll just make it harder for you, and believe me, she's a great one for doing that. Be at her house at seven-thirty."

And she was. She rang the bell and sat down on the steps to wait for Bev. After a few minutes the front door opened and Bev was standing there, her face serious.

"Get up, gopher," Bev ordered.

There was something about her tone that annoyed Millicent. It was almost malicious. And there was an unpleasant anonymity about the label "gopher," even if that was what they always called the girls being initiated. It was degrading, like being given a number. It was a denial of individuality.

Rebellion flooded through her.

"I said get up. Are you deaf?"

Millicent got up, standing there.

"Into the house, gopher. There's a bed to be made and a room to be cleaned at the top of the stairs."

Millicent went up the stairs mutely. She found Bev's room and started making the bed. Smiling to herself, she was thinking: How absurdly funny, me taking orders from this girl like a servant.

Bev was suddenly there in the doorway. "Wipe that smile off your face," she commanded.

There seemed something about this relationship that was not all fun. In Bev's eyes, Millicent was sure of it, there was a hard, bright spark of exultation.

On the way to school, Millicent had to walk behind Bev at a distance of ten paces, carrying her books. They came up to the drugstore where there already was a crowd of boys and girls from Lansing High waiting for the show.

The other girls being initiated were there, so Millicent felt relieved. It would not be so bad now, being part of the group.

"What'll we have them do?" Betsy Johnson asked Bev. That morning Betsy had made her "gopher" carry an old colored parasol through the square and sing "I'm Always Chasing Rainbows."

"I know," Herb Dalton, the good-looking basketball captain, said.

A remarkable change came over Bev. She was all at once very soft and coquettish.

"You can't tell them what to do," Bev said sweetly. "Men have nothing to say about this little deal."

"All right, all right," Herb laughed, stepping back and pretending to fend off a blow.

"It's getting late." Louise had come up. "Almost eight-thirty. We'd better get them marching on to school."

The "gophers" had to do a Charleston step all the way to school, and each one had her own song to sing, trying to drown out the other four. During school, of course, you couldn't fool around, but even then, there was a rule that you mustn't talk to boys outside of class or at lunchtime . . . or any time at all after school. So the sorority girls would get the most popular boys to go up to the "gophers" and ask them out, or try to start them talking, and sometimes a "gopher" was taken by surprise and began to say something before she could catch herself. And then the boy reported her and she got a black mark.

Herb Dalton approached Millicent as she was getting an ice cream at the lunch counter that noon. She saw him coming before he spoke to her, and looked down quickly, thinking: He is too princely, too dark and smiling. And I am much too vulnerable. Why must he be the one I have to be careful of?

I won't say anything, she thought, I'll just smile very sweetly.

She smiled up at Herb very sweetly and mutely. His return grin was rather miraculous. It was surely more than was called for in the line of duty.

"I know you can't talk to me," he said, very low. "But you're doing fine, the girls say. I even like your hair straight and all."

Bev was coming toward them, then, her red mouth set in a bright, calculating smile. She ignored Millicent and sailed up to Herb.

"Why waste your time with gophers?" she caroled gaily. "Their tongues are tied, but completely."

Herb managed a parting shot. "But that one keeps *such* an attractive silence."

Millicent smiled as she ate her sundae at the counter with Tracy. Generally, the girls who were outsiders now, as Millicent had been, scoffed at the initiation antics as childish and absurd to hide their secret envy. But Tracy was understanding, as ever.

"Tonight's the worst, I guess, Tracy," Millicent told her. "I hear that the girls are taking us on a bus over to Lewiston and going to have us performing in the square."

"Just keep a poker face outside," Tracy advised. "But keep laughing like mad inside."

Millicent and Bev took a bus ahead of the rest of the girls; they had to stand up on the way to Lewiston Square. Bev seemed very cross about something. Finally she said, "You were talking with Herb Dalton at lunch today."

"No," said Millicent honestly.

"Well, I *saw* you smile at him. That's practically as bad as talking. Remember not to do it again."

Millicent kept silent.

"It's fifteen minutes before the bus gets into town," Bev was saying then. "I want you to go up and down the bus asking people what they eat for breakfast. Remember, you can't tell them you're being initiated."

Millicent looked down the aisle of the crowded bus and felt suddenly quite sick. She thought: How will I ever do it, going up to all those stony-faced people who are staring coldly out the window . . .

"You heard me, gopher."

"Excuse me, madam," Millicent said politely to the lady in the first seat of the bus, "but I'm taking a survey. Could you please tell me what you eat for breakfast?"

"Why . . . er . . . just orange juice, toast and coffee," she said.

"Thank you very much." Millicent went on to the next person, a young businessman. He ate eggs sunny side up, toast and coffee.

By the time Millicent got to the back of the bus, most of the people were smiling at her. They obviously know, she thought, that I'm being initiated into something.

Finally, there was only one man left in the corner of the back seat. He was small and jolly, with a ruddy, wrinkled face that spread into a beaming smile as Millicent approached. In his brown suit with the forest-green tie he looked something like a gnome or a cheerful leprechaun.

"Excuse me, sir," Millicent smiled, "but I'm taking a survey. What do you eat for breakfast?"

"Heather birds' eyebrows on toast," the little man rattled off.

"*What?*" Millicent exclaimed.

"Heather birds' eyebrows," the little man explained. "Heather birds live on the mythological moors and fly about all day long, singing wild and sweet in the sun. They're bright purple and have *very* tasty eyebrows."

Millicent broke out into spontaneous laughter. Why, this was wonderful, the way she felt a sudden comradeship with a stranger.

"Are you mythological, too?"

"Not exactly," he replied, "but I certainly hope to be someday. Being mythological does wonders for one's ego."

The bus was swinging into the station now; Millicent hated to leave the little man. She wanted to ask him more about the birds.

And from that time on, initiations didn't bother Millicent at all. She went gaily about Lewiston Square from store to store asking for broken crackers and mangoes, and she just laughed inside when people stared and then brightened, answering her crazy questions as if she were quite serious and really a person of consequence. So many people were shut up tight inside themselves like boxes, yet they would open up, unfolding quite wonderfully, if only you were interested in them. And really, you didn't have to belong to a club to feel related to other human beings.

One afternoon Millicent had started talking with Liane Morris, another of the girls being initiated, about what it would be like when they were finally in the sorority.

"Oh, I know pretty much what it'll be like," Liane had said. "My sister belonged before she graduated from high two years ago."

"Well, just what *do* they do as a club?" Millicent wanted to know.

"Why, they have a meeting once a week . . . each girl takes turns entertaining at her house . . ."

"You mean it's just a sort of exclusive social group . . ."

"I guess so . . . though that's a funny way of putting it. But it sure gives a girl prestige value. My sister started going steady with the captain of the football team after she got in. Not bad, I say."

No, it wasn't bad, Millicent had thought, lying in bed on the morning of Rat Court and listening to the sparrows chirping in the gutters. She thought of Herb. Would he ever have been so friendly if she were without the sorority label? Would he ask her out (if he ever did) just for herself, no strings attached?

Then there was another thing that bothered her. Leaving Tracy on the outskirts. Because that was the way it would be; Millicent had seen it happen before.

Outside, the sparrows were still chirping, and as she lay in bed Millicent visualized them, pale gray-brown birds in a flock, one like the other, all exactly alike.

And then, for some reason, Millicent thought of the heather birds. Swooping carefree over the moors, they would go singing and crying out across the great spaces of air, dipping and darting, strong and proud in their freedom and their sometime loneliness. It was then that she made her decision.

Seated now on the woodpile in Betsy Johnson's cellar, Millicent knew that she had come triumphant through the trial of fire, the searing period of the ego which could end in two kinds of victory for her. The easiest of which would be her coronation as a princess, labeling her conclusively as one of the select flock.

The other victory would be much harder, but she knew that it was what she wanted. It was not that she was being noble or anything. It was just that she had learned there were other ways of getting into the great hall, blazing with lights, of people and of life.

It would be hard to explain to the girls tonight, of course, but she could tell Louise later just how it was. How she had proved something to herself by going through everything, even Rat Court, and then deciding not to join the sorority after all. And how she could still be friends with everybody. Sisters with everybody. Tracy, too.

The door behind her opened and a ray of light sliced across the soft gloom of the basement room.

"Hey, Millicent, come on out now. This is it." There were some of the girls outside.

"I'm coming," she said, getting up and moving out of the soft darkness into the glare of light, thinking: This is it, all right. The worst part, the hardest part, the part of initiation that I figured out myself.

But just then, from somewhere far off, Millicent was sure of it, there came a melodic fluting, quite wild and sweet, and she knew that it must be the song of the heather birds as they went wheeling and gliding against wide blue horizons through vast spaces of air, their wings flashing quick and purple in the bright sun.

Within Millicent another melody soared, strong and exuberant, a triumphant answer to the music of the darting heather birds that sang so clear and lilting over the far lands. And she knew that her own private initiation had just begun.

Dialogue

Ts,* 17–19 January 1953, Lilly Library

It is seven o'clock on Saturday night in the college dormitory. A girl named Alison sits on the bed in her single room. A girl named Marcia sits in a chair opposite. She has been trying to persuade Alison to come to the movies with her. The light in the room is on, and the blinds are not drawn. Outside is the dark of winter. The door to the room is shut, and they are alone. Marcia is talking.

M: You never do any crazy things with girls. I mean just going off and doing something silly, like drinking beer or seeing a couple of movies.

A: I can't see it, that's all. Doing things with girls.

M: But you've got to give sometime. I can't ever tempt you. You won't eat candy, you never want to spend money on the movies . . .

A: I don't have money to spend like that.

M: I know, but . . .

A: And besides, I figure why spend money myself when I can get a guy to treat me. I like it better that way.

M: You mean like that taxi driver? He sure treated you for a while.

A: You know I don't mean like that. I was bored, that's all. You get just so

---

* Typescript has holograph corrections by SP, instructor comments, and is dated 19 January 1953. Written for English 347a, Style and Form. SP's 1953 calendar indicates she started 'Dialogue' on 17 January and completed it the following day. SP quotes from *The Rubaiyat of Omar Khayyam*.

fed up eating with a hundred girls every meal. Living all the time with a hundred girls. Oh, God, I don't see how you never get fed up with it.

M: Well, sure I do. Everybody does. But a couple of cocktails downtown or a break for a movie is a sure cure for that.

A: With the girls, though. Always with the girls.

M: And what's wrong with that? It's better than going alone, isn't it?

A: That depends.

M: What do you mean, depends?

A: On what you're trying to get away from.

M: Yourself, isn't it? That's your trouble, and you won't let anybody help you. You won't try anything anybody says. You're always pounding your head on a brick wall and getting hurt.

A: Oh, cut it. You make me sound like a martyr. So maybe I am running away, but not from myself. That's what you've got wrong. I'm looking for something, and it's not the sort of thing you find downtown with ten screaming potted girls.

M: Maybe you find it with a potted taxi driver, huh?

A: Listen, you don't understand the first thing about that. I could tell you, oh, I could tell you, but you just wouldn't get it. Talk about being conventional. Why, you've got so many rotten layers of middle-class morality wrapped around you . . .

M: All right, all right, you don't have to get bitter; you don't have to get nasty.

A: . . . you might as well be living in a shroud. A nice, permanent, ready-made shroud.

M: Well, granted, there are some things you do I wouldn't be seen dead doing. Everybody talked for weeks and you didn't give a damn.

A: First my head is bloody, and now I've got a thick hide. I can stand everything but your being inconsistent. All the time inconsistent. You start arguing about one thing and keep dragging stinking fish over the trail. One fish after another. Why don't you stick to the point?

M: Point? You don't have to have a point when you talk to somebody. What do you think conversation is, anyway? A damn debating society? Why don't you go find a lawyer. You'd get along fine, arguing out case histories, one, two, three. Very neat, like that.

A: That's not it. You know that's not it. All I want to do is get things talked out, right down to the bottom. Just for once.

M: That's the trouble. You can't do that with people all the time. They don't like it. You've got to accept that. You've got to live on the surface and like it. Most of the time, anyway.

A: No you don't. Not me, anyhow. I'm sick of the damn desiccated ritual: "Hello. How are you? How is he? Oh no. Oh really. Oh divine." I'm sick to death of it.

M: So what are you going to do? Invent a new language? You're going to burn yourself out if you keep it up this way. Relax for a change. Get philosophical.

A: Sure, I know your kind of philosophy. You get numb. You blunt the edges of things. Then nothing hurts. Fine, oh, very fine.

M: Look, I don't mean get insensible, and you know it. I mean just take it easy. In ten years from now you'll never know the difference.

A: But that's just it. I want to know the difference. I want very badly to know the difference.

M: About important things, all right. But not about little things. Not about every little thing. The trouble with you is the little things. You let yourself get broken up at the drop of a hat. You'd think it was a brick. You'd think everybody was throwing bricks at you the way you act sometimes.

A: Listen, lay off, will you. You've got no right to complain over something you don't know the half of. I don't notice you going around shedding joy all over the place like merry sunshine. You're a great one to talk.

M: You need a talking to. You've been needing someone to talk to you about a few things all year now. So I stick my neck out and this is what I get.

A: So say your piece and leave me be, will you. I don't feel like talking to anybody. I don't care.

M: Talk about being inconsistent. You pretend you don't care. It was the same way about the taxi driver. But really you do care. You know it and I know it.

A: You always have been just that much smarter than the rest, haven't you? I knew that the minute I saw you. Nosy. Not quite like the other girls, not like the string of pretty paper dolls. What do you want to bother with me for?

M: Nosy. That's not a nice word. You might at least be euphemistic. You might at least say intellectual curiosity.

A: Euphemisms. That's it, too. That's what I can't stand either. Why not use the good vile words. Damn. Dung. Hell. God, they sound great. Scrawl them on the sidewalks and fences and shock the ladies and the gentlemen.

M: That's better. That's what you need. Get mad, go ahead. Soapbox stumping they call it on Boston Common.

A: Oh, God, listen. I'm sorry. Honestly I am. I don't mean to be like this. Really I don't.

M: I know.

A: But sometimes I get so fed up I think I'll crack open. So full of words I could choke. Honestly, some nights I can feel the words piling up and piling up inside my ribs, tighter and tighter, and then into my throat in a great horrid lump I can't swallow.

M: I know. Really I do.

A: Oh, how can you know? How can anybody really know? You think you can. But it's impossible. You interpret everything in relation to yourself. How can you ever really know how someone feels?

M: Maybe you can't know exactly. Maybe you can only guess. But sometimes it helps to talk it out to somebody. Somebody you don't know very well. It's easier when you don't know them very well.

A: Why is that? Why is it that you can talk to a perfect stranger on a bus and tell them all, and have them tell you all, and go away quite clean inside and never see them again. While here we live in boxes, in airtight cells strung out in rows, piled sky high. Above you someone is bawling for a dead love. Below someone is gone hysterical, packed to the gills with misery. Across the street they fornicate. And we don't know. We don't know anything but: "Hello. How are you?"

M: It's all part of the machinery that makes life easy. You know that as well as I do. The automatic handshake, the tilt of the hat, the dry kiss on the cheek of the maiden aunt. You've got to have something convenient to cover awkward situations. What would you substitute? Nothing? Silence?

A: Maybe that would be better. More honest, anyway, to make no noise at all. At the table sometimes, at dinner, I could go quite mad listening to the voices. Did you ever let your ears blur the sound of voices, the way your eyes, forgetful, can blur the print on the page? The voices fall apart, senseless, like the inane clucking of birds. Saying nothing in another language.

M: Do you think you are the only one in the world who is an alien? The only one who has seen the daily comfortable routine disintegrate and fall away, and thinks that the center doesn't hold. And thinks that there isn't any center.

A: There *is* a center, though. That is the horrible part. Your center is you. My center is me. That is what is so hard to find.

M: Is that it, then? Is that what you are looking for?

A: Oh, partly. Whatever you want to call it. The center, the purpose. Whatever lost magic it is that puts together the pieces of the Chinese puzzle. The only trouble is, everybody has got a different kind of puzzle, so everybody needs a different kind of magic.

M: I don't get it. You mean once you figure out what your own purpose is, and catch on about fitting together the pieces, it's all right with you. But everybody else keeps struggling.

A: What I mean is: there isn't any universal purpose. None at all. Oh, sure, there are a lot of conceited little systems that claim to have the sole rights to the secret of life, but they don't. Arrogant jabbering little doctrines, that's all they are. Good for a few people, maybe, but not more than a few. Never more than a few.

M: All right, so there isn't any universal purpose. So what is there then? So what do you put up for a roof after you knock down the sky? You've got to have some insulation from the black vacuum, don't you?

A: Sure, sure. That's just it. People make up their own little dream realities. Like that paper grab-bag game we played when we were kids. You know, everybody gets a paper bag with a whole lot of crazy unrelated items, and you put them together to make a costume or a story. You integrate the chaotic jumble into something reasonable. And that last word is in quotes. Big red quotes.

M: But the world isn't a chaotic jumble. You imply it is. Look at the order, the logic. You've got planets running around the sun like clocks, and the circle of the seasons, and babies getting born by the millions with two arms, two eyes, two legs. The freaks are rare. That's why we hear so much about them. There must be a reason, and a big one, and I am not using quotes.

A: All right, I admit there is an orderly universal force, but I still claim it's blind and neutral. You take a fact of nature, an absolute fact, say a rainstorm. It's a neutral, natural phenomenon, fine. Until you get people to interpret it in a moral framework. Is the rainstorm good or bad? Well, if it waters the fields after a dry spell, it's great. They make prayers to the rain god, or the rain makers in the airplanes today. But if the storm lays the wheat fields flat with hail, it's bad. Evil spirits, that sort of thing. Everything's interpreted subjectively. Our ancestors were pragmatists from way back.

M: But if everything's relative, how can you ever be sure of anything ever at all? How can you ever believe in anything? You say: If something doesn't exist in your own mind, it's not real. That's a hell of a way to look at the world.

A: Well, to all practical purposes it's not real, from your own point of view. Oh, you can extrapolate, and generalize beyond your own immediate experience. You can work like a dog at making more of the world come real for you. You can accept someone else's word for a lot of the realities. But what I want to say is that you have to work out your own solution. That's just the way I happen to see things.

M: So I can disagree and you won't call me a fool?

A: Well, of course I won't. You take your grab-bag and make up your own story. Variety is the spice, you know.

M: But doesn't it ever make you afraid? The horrible responsibility of making up your own world? It's a ghastly job.

A: A lot of people think so. Look at all the different brands of opium the genius man has invented: absolute churches that slit your throat if you don't believe in their brand of truth, god-guarded nations that blast other god-guarded nations, fire water that helps you make up your own feeble escape dreams, movies, television. God, anything to get rid of the agony of free will, the responsibility of deciding how you will spend the thirty million minutes of your life.

M: That sounds pretty bad. What do you think we are, anyway, a race of escapists?

A: No, of course not. I just mean that everywhere you look people are trying to reconcile themselves to the contradictions and the hypocrisies they find in the man-made world. And a lot of them don't want to bother figuring it out for themselves, so they worship autocratic institutions that tell them what to do. And a lot of others don't give a damn anyway, so they dope themselves into a stupor and walk the plank blind.

M: You make it sound as if the world was always this way, man-made. "In the beginning there was Columbus, and darkness was on the face of the deep." That sort of thing.

A: That's good. You could add a benediction: "And God make his face to shine upon you in neon lights, and bless you, and keep you safe in his bullet-proof kingdom forevermore."

M: Seriously, though, where do you think the world is running to anyway? Granted it swings in ellipses actually, but socially, historically, or whatever adverb you want to use there, don't we progress? Don't we move in a line from a beginning to an end? The only alternative I can see to that kind of progress is continual repetition, like a trapped Victrola record. Turning in circles, over and over, going nowhere.

A: No, that doesn't sound encouraging, does it? I like better the idea of the spiral. You know, the gyre, the staircase in the tower, the dialectic. But what I object to really is that any one person or one institution, in a splurge of clairvoyance, can see what the ultimate end is for everyone in general.

M: You have your own theory of the end, though, I take it.

A: Well, all right, but you must admit that I haven't tried to convert you to belief in my grand finale.

M: Not a trumpet-toppling doomsday, I trust.

A: No, I'm afraid not. And no intricate bookkeeping of sins either. No righteous hellfire or eternal contemplation of an egocentric Perfection. Just a quiet decomposition.

M: How can you live with a brick-walled dead end ahead like that? And a puddle of rotting sludge. So it's all physical after all, is it?

A: Not just the way you mean physical. I admit, there isn't much consolation in that philosophy as far as the individual ego is concerned. Don't you think I would like to consider my personality important enough to be saved for singing on a cloud in the empyrean, or what have you? Sure, I don't like to think that someday the world is going to blink out for me like a candle. No more subjective reality, no nothing. It hurts, don't let me kid you.

M: But what do you get out of the private little theory of ashes to ashes, dust to dust? No comfort, certainly. If every reality is completely subjective as you say, you might as well build a snug little world that makes you happy. You might even conjure up a heaven after death like a DeMille extravaganza, and spend a safe life in pleased anticipation.

A: You're getting sarcastic, now. You know I couldn't do that. It's dishonest. At least it is as far as I'm concerned. I can't honestly believe in anything beyond the proved physical deterioration, the stopping of the blood, the freezing of the mind, and all the rolls of picture film inside it. I've seen cadavers on the dissecting table like so much cold, blackened turkey. I've held a dried-out human brain in my hand. Not pleasant to think that's the final distillation of the thirty million minutes, but there are compensations.

M: Like what?

A: Oh, like becoming part of the great blind forces that move the world. You know, Omar's vegetable immortality: "Ah, lean upon it lightly." And there is a peculiar comfort in the idea of losing the identity, the ego. The crippling ego that makes me the center of my distorted little world and you the center of yours.

M: We're back to the center of things again. The prickly pear.

A: The eternal prickly pear. Know thyself, the man said. It's a neat trick if you can do it.

M: You call the ego crippled. Psychologically, then, we are all grotesques.

A: Distortion has its uses. Artistic effect, you know. Grotesques aren't so bad. They're even lovable, if you have that turn of mind.

M: Sure, and garbage is the most euphonic word in the English language. But you still haven't explained why you're so glad to get rid of the individual ego in the great impersonal dispose-all of the graveyard.

A: Well, it's like this, see. I figure, in very simple terms, not complicating it at all, that there is the fact of the world. Houses, trees, people. You know what I mean. And in order to experience the world, you get born into it.

M: You made a slip there. "In order to." That phrase smacks of purpose. Who or what intends us to experience the world? Aren't you getting a bit personal? We denied the kind father in the sky by implication a while back.

A: Sorry, I let the sentence out wrong. Take the accomplished fact first: we get born into the world. Then we experience it. We see it, feel it, smell it, taste it, listen to it. Later we start to think about it.

M: Elemental. All right so far. We have now a beginning and an end. A birth, for why no one knows, or at least you don't claim to. And a delicate disintegration. A charming and fortunate equilibrium, when you look at the life insurance charts.

A: Don't get cute, please. I am trying to explain about the ego.

M: All right again. This I want to hear.

A: Well, I can put my hunch very simply. The fact of birth, the crossing of the natural doorway, cripples you right from the start. You've got potentialities, latent abilities, sure. But you've also got the incipient boundary lines too. The limitations beyond which there is no passing.

M: You mean time and space. Heredity and environment?

A: Those are pretty nebulous words, but that's about it. You have your thirty million minutes dealt you, and you can only run through the hand once. Think of all the countless combinations and permutations of incident and action possible. And then think that of all the hundreds of ways you could play each minute you have to choose one.

M: There's your agony of responsibility again. No wonder people invent varieties of opium. You make it sound so grim.

A: I know. The horror of choices. Like a tree of thorns and flowers. You start climbing to the top. You can't see ahead to the top, but you climb anyway.

M: Maybe there's a lion at the roots, huh? Or a clever enormous beaver.

A: Maybe the Devil. Anyway, you climb, and every branch you choose at a forking in the tree precludes your choosing any other of the branches at that particular subdivision. So you keep on choosing, and you keep on climbing. Sometimes you think you are choosing the easy way, and then the thorns begin to rip at your guts. You see ahead in flashes, but never very far. Never to the top.

M: But when you get to the top, what then? Who are you?

A: You are, first of all, in the same tree you started out in. In other words, you had a certain range of possibilities to begin with. You were born into, *ipso facto*, assigned to your own tree, if you want to carry the analogy to the point of absurdity.

M: Heredity and environment, yes. But who are you?

A: You are one of the multitude of potential yous that branched out ahead of you when you began. The number of possibilities narrowed down each time you made a choice. And you ended up with one twig. And looking back, you don't see how you ever could have come up any other way. The whole trip seems pretty inevitable when you look back on it.

M: Don't some of the thorn scratches still sting a little? Don't you wish maybe you'd been smart enough to pick a few more of the flowers on the way up?

A: Sure, I suppose so. But you can always say, along with the psychiatrist in *The Cocktail Party*: "the best of a bad job is all any of us make of it."

M: And if you haven't even made the best of it?

A: That's tough, too. You can blame fate, or destiny, if you want to. It's easier that way. Me, I merely want to smile and say: it was a good fight, kid. That's all. That's all, and yet it's everything.

M: You mean after you've done the best you could with your limited ego you trade it in philosophically for a berth in the great blind unconscious?

A: How exquisitely you put it! Seriously, though, I like to think of life as a series of tensions and relaxations. Birth is the first great tension. And death is the final colossal relaxation . . .

M: But I still don't see how you can be satisfied with your blind impersonal force. You say it isn't purposeful. You imply that every man is responsible for making his own purpose in life. Would you call your force logical?

A: Logical? What do you mean by logical? Who are we to foist our limited inconsistent schemes of logic on the force that holds the world together? I call it arrogance to claim we comprehend the logic of the universe. I call it conceited to assume the great mind is a hyper-swollen version of our own. A personal and righteous god growing out of our own ignorance. It's ridiculous.

M: That's a pretty distorted picture of belief. Why not look at the other side. You admit the wonder of nature and the material world. Why couldn't all that be taken as an obvious manifestation of a beneficent creator?

A: I challenge the word "beneficent" there. As far as I can see, if you presuppose a creator who intended all this world, you are also admitting that the creator is sadistic and egoistic, like the old biblical jealous and wrathful Jehovah.

M: How come? The misery and mess and the wars are man's fault, not God's. Why blame God and call him a sadist?

A: I don't call him a sadist. I just say that it's not fair to make it a one-way proposition, giving God all the credit of everything good and man all the blame for everything bad. If this hypothetical god created everything, if he created a perfect Eden and put man in it to test him, God created the potential for evil right there. God gave man the ability to deny him. If he planted the pitfalls, as Omar said, it's not fair to call our weakness sin. That's the danger of a personal righteous god, you can call him downright malicious.

M: But why egocentric?

A: Oh, that's obvious. Supposedly God is the great ultimate eternal perfection. According to certain theologies, at least. And man is made to mirror that perfection and to love it. What happens if man turns away from idolizing the one true light? He gets pitched into Dante's inferno, or an orthodox hell, unless he says he's sorry. Rather a totalitarian dictatorship, don't you think? Anybody who can listen to the screams of the tortured in hell and be happy in heaven isn't human. Maybe "just," in the hardest sense of the word, but not human.

M: You don't believe in heaven and hell, then, I take it.

A: Not the traditional after-death kind. On earth, yes. You know: "I myself am heaven and hell." Again, I consider it a subjective state of mind.

M: Just what do you label yourself anyway? A humanitarian?

A: Depends on your definition. If you mean the idea that man's obligations are limited to and dependent solely on other men, on human relations, maybe that approaches it. But mainly I think man is responsible for the good and bad at the same time. He should get both the credit and the blame for what he makes out of the impersonal fact of existence in the world.

M: So now, according to you, we have no personal god, but a neutral force, unknowable. And we have no afterlife, but rather a subjective heaven and hell in this one. Why, may I ask, do you think life is worth living? In other words, what's your own particular individual subjective purpose?

A: That's a rough one. Sometimes I'm not sure, I admit it.

M: Your system has got a flaw, then. It's not consistent. It wavers.

A: Sure it does, what do you think I'm pretending to be anyway? Infallible?

M: No, but at least pretty sure of yourself. Surer than you seem to be.

A: All right, so I have doubts. This thing is growing, this idea of mine. The more I live, the more I experience, the more it grows. It's a kinetic theory. Take the dialectic, again, only this time relate it to your personal experience in the realm of ideas. The thesis is the easy time, the happy time. The antithesis threatens annihilation. The synthesis is the consummate problem. I have a tough time with it. Maybe I always will. But that's just a consequence of a system that isn't static.

M: It would be ironic if, after this, you died and woke up in someone else's hell.

A: That *would* be a fluke, wouldn't it? I've often thought it would be poetic justice if everyone died and woke up in their own conception of the afterlife. Think of all the pious bored dowagers singing Alleluia on pink clouds. Delightful to contemplate, what?

M: You, at least, wouldn't know the difference, rotting peacefully away and becoming part of the eternal cycle of decomposition.

A: All right. But seeing I know I've just got so many years roughly, I'm most concerned with the affirmation of life here and now. No mere contemplating my navel, no nirvana, or what have you.

M: Sounds noble. And just how do you go about affirming life?

A: Trying to figure the most creative way I can spend those thirty million minutes, that's all. No opium, even if the hurt is bad.

M: "Creative" meaning just the development of your own potentialities, or do you include altruism and helping others?

A: Of course I do. My way may look strange to you. But for me it's the honest solution. Conditionally, that is: for me, at the present time, in the present place. You may think I look like a blind girl playing with a slide ruler of values. That's your privilege.

M: Don't get me wrong. I don't mean to sound like I'm needling you. I just want to find out what you believe in. What you think is most important.

A: Well, I've generalized a lot, but you can see what I mean, can't you? You could say religion is the core of belief you choose to orient your life around, and God is the integrating center. That makes just about everybody religious, doesn't it?

M: Sure, communists and materialists. It's all a matter of definition.

A: That's it. And, according to my theories, I can still be fallible, and lacerate myself with thorns. The main thing is my reaction to the wounds. Do I sit and cry? Do I take opium? Or do I keep climbing?

M: That's what I wonder about. Do you keep climbing?

A: I try. I really do. Only I'm guilty of breaking faith with myself and my theoretical convictions now and then, sure. So many decisions are just between the lesser of two evils. Case history: the taxi driver.

M: The taxi driver. Was he the lesser?

A: I'm not sure. I don't know. It was good for a while, but now I'm wondering if maybe I wasn't just rationalizing and inventing another kind of avenue to numbness. I didn't think so then. I really believed in myself. Maybe I was obnoxious about it.

M: No, not that. Just defiant, that's all. And everybody gets defiant. Especially when they aren't quite sure of something.

A: Oh, I guess I thought it was daring . . . and unconventional. Finding yourself in the simple dregs of existence, you know. He was honest. That was what I wanted very badly.

M: To find someone honest?

A: Well, someone I could be honest with.

M: Don't you feel honest? Didn't you feel honest then?

A: I do now, but not then. I felt hollow. I felt that the outside of me was just a shell, an artificial shell. Do you mind if I try to tell you how I felt? I think I would like to, now. Will I bore you?

M: Of course not, idiot.

A: Well, I felt like I was decayed inside. As if some queer disease had eaten me all away inside and I wasn't anybody at all. And I began to get afraid that all at once maybe my eyes would break open like soap bubbles and everybody would see there wasn't anything there, just a vile mess. And I was afraid that maybe the rot inside me would break out in sores and warts, screaming, "Traitor, sinner, impostor."

M: God, and you didn't tell anyone. Why didn't you tell anyone?

A: I didn't think I could. I was afraid. I was afraid that maybe they would look at me, into my eyes, and say: "Why, I do believe you are right. There is nothing there. Nothing there at all."

M: You mean this was real to you, and you were afraid to have it become real to anybody else.

A: I guess that's about it. And the taxi driver happened along then. It was so easy, so natural. I was trying to prove something to myself, though I wasn't sure what. I guess I was trying to prove I was creative, and human and positive, and not the frozen hard numb core I felt inside me.

M: But now. How is it with you now?

A: Better. I can't tell you how much better. But I know it is.

M: I am glad. I think I will go now. I think I will let you go to bed.

A: Thank you.
M: For what?
A: For talking. For listening.
M: We will do it again. Talking like this.
A: Yes, I think we will.

The girl named Marcia goes. The girl named Alison sits for a while staring out of the dormitory window into the winter dark, where the light of the street lamp is lanced across by the thorny network of black tree branches.

Mary Ventura and the Ninth Kingdom

Ts,[*] c. January 1953, Smith College

Red neon lights blinked automatically, and a voice grated from the loudspeaker. "Train leaving, on track three . . . train leaving for . . . train leaving . . ."

"I know that must be your train," Mary Ventura's mother said. "I'm sure it is, dear. Hurry. Do hurry now. Have you your ticket?"

"Yes, Mother, I do. But do I have to go right away? So soon?"

"You know how trains are," Mary's father said. He looked anonymous in his gray felt hat, as if he were traveling incognito. "You know how trains are. They don't wait."

"Yes, Father, I know."

The long black hand of the clock on the wall clipped off another minute. Everywhere there were people running to catch trains. Above them, the vault of the railroad station lifted like the dome of a huge cathedral.

"Train leaving on track three . . . train leaving for . . . train leaving . . ."

"Hurry, dear." Mrs. Ventura took Mary by the arm and propelled her through the glittering marble halls of the railroad terminal. Mary's father followed with her suitcase. Other people were hurrying to the train gate marked

---

[*] Typescript with holograph corrections made probably by Aurelia Schober Plath. Written originally for English 347a, Style and Form, and submitted on 12 December 1952. SP made revisions in early 1953 and asked her mother to re-type the story and submit it to *Mademoiselle* later that month. *Mademoiselle* returned it, rejected, on 11 March 1953. The copy text here is from this returned story which sold via Bonhams on 15 June 2016. At top right is 'Sylvia Plath / Lawrence House / Smith College / Northampton, Mass.' SP revised the story in December 1954 and considered submitting it to the Christopher Awards. This shorter version she called 'Marcia Ventura and the Ninth Kingdom' and wrote an introduction for it entitled 'Teenagers Can Shape the Future'; see Appendix II.

three. A conductor in a black uniform, his face shaded by the visor of his cap, herded the crowd in through the intricate black grillwork of the iron gate to the platform beyond.

"Mother," Mary said, halting, hearing the colossal hissing of the engine on the sunken track. "Mother, I can't go today. I simply can't. I'm not ready to take the trip yet."

"Nonsense, Mary," her father cut her short jovially. "You're just getting jittery. The trip north won't be an ordeal. You just get on the train and don't worry about another thing until you get to the end of the line. The conductor will tell you where to go then."

"Come, now, there's a good girl." Mary's mother tucked a strand of gilt blonde hair up under her black velvet hat. "It will be an easy trip. Everyone has to leave home sometime. Everyone has to go away sooner or later."

Mary weakened. "Oh, well, all right." She let herself be led through the wrought-iron gates, down the incline of the cement platform, where the air was thick with steam.

"Extra, extra." Newsboys were crying out headlines, selling papers at the doors of the train. "Extra . . . ten thousand people sentenced . . . ten thousand more people . . ."

"There is nothing," Mary's mother crooned, "absolutely nothing for you to worry about." She pushed through the chaotic jostling crowds, and Mary followed in her wake, on to the next to the last car of the train. There was a long row of red plush seats, the color of wine in the bright light from the ceiling, and the seams of the car were riveted with brass nails.

"How about this seat, here in the middle?" Mr. Ventura didn't wait for an answer, but swung Mary's suitcase up on the rack. He stood back. Mrs. Ventura touched a handkerchief to her painted red mouth, started to say something, stopped. There was, after all, nothing left to say.

"Goodbye," Mary said with automatic fondness.

"Goodbye, dear. Have a good time, now." Mrs. Ventura leaned to give Mary a vague, preoccupied kiss.

Mr. and Mrs. Ventura turned and began moving away, then, starting back down the aisle and retreating through the open doorway. Mary waved, but already they were gone and did not see. She took the seat by the window, slipping out of her red coat first and hanging it on the brass hook next to the window frame. The rest of the passengers were almost all settled, now, but a few were still coming down the aisle, searching for seats. A lady in a blue jacket, carrying a baby wrapped in a soiled white blanket, paused at Mary's seat for a minute, but then continued to the back of the car where there was more room.

"Is this seat taken?" The woman had come lurching down the aisle, puffing and red-faced, an earth-colored brown satchel in her hand. Her blue eyes crinkled up in a mass of wrinkles and her large, generous mouth stretched into a smile.

"No, no one's sitting here," Mary could not help smiling back. She moved closer to the window and watched the woman take off her battered brown hat and her brown cloth coat.

"Oof," sighed the woman, sinking heavily into the red plush seat. "I almost thought I wouldn't make it this trip. Train's just about to start up."

The engine gave a snort, shuddered, and paused. "Board . . . all 'board!" a voice yelled from outside. The door to the car slammed shut with a final click, closing them all in.

"This is it," the woman said. "The departure." Steam rose up beyond the windowpane as the train slowly chugged down the track, and they could not see beyond the clouds of smoke and cinders.

The woman reached into her satchel and pulled out some knitting, the beginnings of a soft fabric of leaf-green wool.

"Oh," Mary exclaimed. "How pretty. What's it going to be?"

"A dress, eventually." The woman appraised Mary with half-shut eyes. "For a girl just about your size, too."

"I'm sure she'll just love it."

The woman looked at Mary with an amused smile. "I hope so," she said, and fell silent.

The train was still hurtling through the black tunnel when the squabble started on the seat in front of them. Two little boys were sitting there, across the aisle from their mother who was reading a magazine. They were playing with tin soldiers.

"Give me that," the bigger boy with the black eyes said to his brother. "That's my soldier. You took my soldier."

"I did not," the pale tow-headed fellow said. "I did not take it."

"You did too. I saw you." The older boy picked up a tin soldier and struck his brother on the forehead. "There! Serves you right."

Blood oozed from a purpling bruise. The younger boy began to whimper. "I hate you," he whined. "I hate you."

The mother kept on reading her magazine.

"Here, here, that's enough," said the woman beside Mary, leaning forward over the back of the seat. She reached out to dab gently at the blood on the young boy's forehead with the hem of her white linen handkerchief. "You boys ought to be ashamed of yourselves, making all that fuss for no reason at all. Over a couple of silly tin soldiers."

The little boys pouted sullenly at the interference and began to play quietly again.

The woman leaned back. "I don't know what's the trouble with children these days. They seem to get worse and worse." She sighed, and took up her knitting again. Outside there was a sudden increase of light.

"Look," said Mary. "We've come out of the tunnel."

The train had shot into the somber gray afternoon, and the bleak autumn fields stretched away on either side of the tracks beyond the cinder beds. In the sky hung a flat orange disc that was the sun.

"The air is so thick and smoky!" Mary exclaimed. "I've never seen the sun that strange color before."

"It's the forest fires," the woman replied. "The smoke always blows down from the north this time of year. We'll be getting into more of it later on."

A wooden shack with boarded windows sprang up beside the tracks and dwindled off into the distance.

"What is that house doing out here so far away from everything?" Mary asked.

"That wasn't a house. It used to be the first station on the line, but now they don't use it much anymore, so it is all shut up. This trip has gotten to be pretty much of an express."

Lulled by the clicking rhythm of the train wheels, Mary stared out of the window. In one of the cornfields a scarecrow caught her eye, crossed staves propped aslant, and the corn husks rotting under it. The dark ragged coat wavered in the wind, empty, without substance. And below the ridiculous figure black crows were strutting to and fro, pecking for grains in the dry ground.

The train sped on. "I think I will get a cup of coffee in the dining car," the woman was saying to Mary, then. "Want to come?"

"Sure," Mary said. "Sure, I'd like to stretch my legs."

The two of them got up and walked down the aisle to the car ahead. It was the smoker, and the thick air stung Mary's eyes. Card tables were set up by the windows, and most of the men were playing poker. Waiters in white coats glided up and down with trays, serving drinks. There was the sound of loud laughter, and the clinking of ice cubes in glasses.

"Next car is the diner," the woman tossed back over her shoulder. She pushed through the door, across the swaying platform, and into the car ahead with Mary close behind.

On red plush lounges the diners reclined, eating apples and plums and hothouse grapes from the bowls of fruit on the polished wooden tables. Languid dinner music drifted from a loudspeaker concealed somewhere in the wall.

The woman stopped at a table for two and signaled Mary to sit down.

"May I take your order?" queried the black waiter in the white tailored suit, the pencil poised in his hand above a tablet of paper. Mary had not even seen him approach. He had brought ice water for each of them.

"I think I would like a glass of ginger ale," Mary said.

"I'll have the usual," the woman smiled at him.

"Sure thing . . . coffee, cream, and sugar." The black waiter flashed the woman a grin and scribbled hieroglyphics on his paper tablet.

The order came, the coffee steaming in a glazed green pottery cup, and the ginger ale, shot through with small silver bubbles, in a tall glass with a red cherry at the bottom.

"How delicious!" Mary cried. "I've never eaten in a dining car before. It's so luxurious."

"Yes," the woman agreed, warming her hands about the cup of steaming brown liquid. "Yes, they do their best to make the ride as pleasant as possible."

Mary relaxed in the soft ease, sipping her ginger ale. In the subtle indirect light, the cushioned seats were a warm red color, and the music came lilting continually from the hidden loudspeaker. Mary sucked up the last of her ginger ale and tipped the glass so that the cherry rolled down into her hand. She popped it into her mouth and bit into the sweet fruit.

Outside the picture window the orange sun was sinking in the gray west. It seemed smaller than when Mary had last looked at it, and the orange color was deepening into red.

"Goodness, it's getting late fast," Mary remarked, gazing out at the barren, darkening landscape.

"One hardly notices the time go by on this trip," the woman nodded. "It is so comfortable here inside the train. But we have just passed the fifth stop along the way and that means we'll be going into the long tunnel soon. Shall we go back to the car?"

"Yes, let's. Do we pay now?"

"No," the woman told her. "They will just add the amount on to your bill at the end of the trip." She rose and started back to the car, planting her feet firmly, one after the other, on the swaying aisle of the speeding train.

Back in their seats, the woman took up her knitting again, and Mary idly watched the sterile farmlands going past. At the end of the car, the baby began to cry, spoiled and petulant. Three businessmen came down the aisle from the cocktail bar, lurching with the motion of the train and laughing. The lights in the ceiling were hard glaring stars.

"Damn brat," one man said.

"Yeah, you're not kidding," said the second man. And under their gray felt hats all three men were exactly alike. Blundering, lurching, they shouldered through the car, and the baby kept on crying as if it would cry forever.

The train shot into another subway tunnel, then. Dark rocks bulked silent and swift past the window, and the wheels clicked away like the cogs of a gigantic clock.

A vendor opened the door at the front of the car and came swinging slowly along the aisle, crying "Can-dy, pop-corn, cash-you nuts . . . get your can-dy, pop-corn, cash-you nuts . . ."

"Here," said the woman, opening her brown satchel and taking out a worn purse, "I'll get us both a chocolate bar . . ."

"Oh, no," Mary protested. "Please, I'll pay for it."

"Nonsense, dear," the woman said. "This is my treat. The chocolate will be good for your sweet tooth. Besides, you'll have enough to pay for by the end of the trip."

The vendor stopped at their seat and pushed his red cap back on his forehead, sticking his thumbs in his red-and-white-striped silk vest.

"What'll it be?" he began in a routine, bored voice, "We have . . ." He paused, looked closely at the woman, then, and burst out into raucous laughter.

"You making this trip again?" His voice dropped to a low, confidential tone. "There's nothing for you in this load, you know. The whole deal is signed, sealed, and delivered. Signed, sealed, and delivered."

"Don't be too sure, Bert," the woman smiled amiably. "Even bookkeepers can go wrong, now and then."

"Bookkeepers, maybe, but not the boss," Bert jingled his black change purse with a sly grin. "The boss has got his all sewed up. Personally, this time, personally."

The woman broke into rich laughter. "Yes, I should think so, after the mistake he made on the last trip, getting the trains crossed on the higher level. Why, he couldn't get those people out of the flower gardens now if he tried. They took to the gardens like children, happy as larks. You think they'd obey him and go back on the lower subway where they belong? Not on your life."

Bert screwed his face up like a monkey. "Yeah," he said, subdued. "Yeah, I suppose you gotta get some percentage some of the time."

"That's why I'm here," the woman said. "I'll take a chocolate bar."

"Large or small?"

"Large," the woman said, and handed him a quarter.

"Well, bye now," Bert said, touching his cap. "Happy hunting," and he swung off down the aisle, calling in a bored singsong, "Can-dy, pop-corn, cash-you nuts . . ."

"Poor Bert," the woman remarked to Mary, unwrapping the chocolate bar without tearing the fragile silver foil. "He gets so lonely for someone to talk to on this run. It's such a long trip that hardly anybody makes it twice." She broke a section from the chocolate bar and handed a large piece of the flat brown candy to Mary. The smell of the chocolate rose rich and fragrant.

"Mmm," said Mary. "It smells good." She took a bite and let the candy dissolve on her tongue, sucking at the sweetness and letting the syrup run down her throat.

"You seem to know a lot about this trip," Mary said to the woman. "Do you travel a great deal?"

"Goodness, yes. I've been traveling here and there as long as I can remember. But I make this trip most often."

"I shouldn't wonder. It *is* a comfortable ride, really. They do so many nice extra little things, like the refreshments every hour, and the drinks in the card room, and the lounges in the dining car. It's almost as good as a hotel."

The woman flashed her a sharp look. "Yes, my dear," she said dryly, "but remember you pay for it. You pay for it all in the end. It's their business to make the trip attractive. The train company has more than a pure friendly interest in the passengers."

"I suppose you're right," Mary admitted with a laugh. "I hadn't thought about it that way. But tell me, what will it be like when we get off the train? I can't imagine. The travel folders don't say anything about the climate, or the people in the north country. Nothing at all."

The woman bent over her knitting, suddenly intent. There was a knot in the thread. Swiftly, she straightened out the wool and went on stitching.

"You're going to the end of the line, I take it," she said.

"That's right, the end of the line. Mother said I didn't have to worry about connections or anything, and that the conductor would tell me where to go from there."

"The last station," the woman murmured. "Are you sure?"

"Yes. At least that's what it says on my ticket. It is such a strange ticket that I remembered the number, red on black. The ninth kingdom, it said. That's a funny way to label railroad stations."

"One gets used to it after a while," the woman said, as if talking to herself. "And to all the absurd little divisions and subdivisions and classifications. Arbitrary, that's what it is. Arbitrary. But nobody seems to realize that nowadays. One little motion, one positive gesture, and the whole structure would collapse, fall quite apart."

"I don't quite see what you mean," said Mary.

"Of course not, of course not, my dear. I quite forgot myself. I was talking in circles. But tell me, have you noticed, just as you sit here, anything at all unusual about the people on this train?"

"Why no," Mary said slowly, looking around. "Why no," she repeated, puzzled. "They look all right to me."

The woman sighed. "I guess I'm just overly sensitive," she said.

Red neon blinked outside the window, and the train slowed shuddering into the station of the sixth kingdom. The car door swung open, and the tread of the conductor came down the aisle to the blonde woman up ahead with the red painted mouth, who paled, drew her furs about her, and shrank back.

"Not yet," she said. "Please, not yet. This is not my stop. Give me a little longer."

"Let me see your ticket," the conductor said, and the woman wet her lips, the color of blood.

"I mislaid it. I can't find it," she said.

"It is in the second finger of your right glove," the conductor said tonelessly, "where you hid it as I came in."

Angrily the woman jerked the glove off her right hand, scooped out the stub of red cardboard and thrust it at the conductor. With his punch he clipped the ticket, tore it across and handed her the smaller half.

"Your transfer for the river crossing," he said. "I think you had better leave now."

The woman did not move to go. The conductor put out his hand and gripped her arm. "I am sorry," he said, "but you must go now. We can't have any dallying around on this train. We have a schedule to keep. We have a quota of passengers."

"I'm coming," the woman pouted sullenly. "But let go my arm. It hurts. It burns."

She got up and walked down the aisle, her crimson wool skirt balancing and swaying about her legs, her head held proud and defiant. Outside the door of the car, on the platform, there were two station guards waiting for her. In the red glare of neon light that fell full upon them, they took the woman away, one on either side of her, through the barred exit gate.

The conductor came back down the car, wiping his forehead with a large red silk handkerchief. He paused at Mary's seat and grinned at the woman. His eyes were black, bottomless, but flecked now with cold spots of laughter.

"We don't usually have that much trouble with the passengers when their stop comes," he said to the woman.

She smiled back at him, but her voice was tender, regretful. "No, they generally don't protest at all. They just accept it when the time comes."

"Accept what?" Mary stared curiously at the two of them, remembering the frightened face of the blonde woman, her mouth wet, the bright color of blood.

The conductor winked at the woman and walked away down the aisle, with lights burning in the sockets of the walls like candles and the metal vault of the car arching overhead. The red light of the station slanted through the car windows and briefly stained the faces of the passengers scarlet. Then the train started up again.

"Accept what?" Mary pursued. She gave an involuntary shiver as if struck by a sudden chill draft of air.

"Are you cold, dear?"

"No," said Mary. "Accept what?"

"The destination," the woman replied, picking up the knitting from her lap and beginning again to add to the mesh of leaf-green wool. Expertly she jabbed the needle into the growing fabric, caught a loop of thread, and slipped it off on the needle. Mary stared at the competent, deft-moving hands. "The passengers buy their tickets," the woman went on, counting silently the stitches on the needle. "They buy their tickets, and they are responsible for getting off at the proper station . . . They choose the train, and the track, and travel to their destination."

"I know. But that woman. She looked so frightened."

"Yes, sometimes the passengers are like that. Last-minute jitters, you know. The awareness strikes them too late, and they regret buying the ticket. Regret doesn't help, though. They should have thought about taking the trip beforehand."

"I still don't see why she couldn't have changed her mind and not gotten off. She could have paid more at the end of the ride."

"The railroad company doesn't allow that on this trip," the woman said. "It would create confusion."

Mary sighed. "Well, at least the rest of the passengers seem content enough."

"Yes, don't they. That is the horror of it."

"Horror?" Mary's voice rose, "What do you mean, horror? You make everything sound so mysterious."

"It's really quite simple. The passengers are so blasé, so apathetic that they don't even care about where they are going. They won't care until the time comes, in the ninth kingdom."

"But what *is* the ninth kingdom?" Mary cried petulantly, her face anguished, as if she were about to burst into tears. "What is so awful about the ninth kingdom?"

"There, there," the woman comforted, "have some more of my chocolate bar. I can't finish it all by myself." Mary took a piece and put it in her mouth, but the taste was bitter on her tongue.

"You will be happier if you do not know," the woman said gently. "It is really not too bad, once you get there. The trip is long down the tunnel, and the climate changes gradually. The hurt is not intense when one is hardened to the cold. Look out the window. Ice has begun to form on the subway walls, and no one has even noticed or complained."

Mary stared out of the window at the black walls hurtling past. There were gray streams of ice between the cracks in the stones. The frozen surface caught the light from the car and glittered as if full of cold silver needles.

Mary shuddered. "I would never have come if I had known. I won't stay. I won't," she exclaimed. "I will get the next train back home."

"There are no return trips on this line," the woman said softly. "Once you get to the ninth kingdom, there is no going back. It is the kingdom of negation, of the frozen will. It has many names."

"I don't care. I will get off at the next stop. I won't stay on the train with these horrid people. Don't they know, don't they care where they are going?"

"They are blind," the woman said, looking steadily at Mary. "They are all quite blind."

"And you," Mary cried, turning on the woman angrily, "I suppose you are blind, too!" Her voice spiraled high and shrill, but no one paid any attention. No one turned to look at her.

"No," the woman said, suddenly tender, "not blind. Nor deaf. But I do happen to know that the train will make no more stops. No more stops are scheduled until we arrive at the ninth kingdom."

"But you don't understand," Mary's face crumpled and she began to cry. Tears dropped wet and scalding through her fingers. "You don't understand. It's not my fault I took this train. It was my parents. They wanted me to go."

"You let them buy the ticket for you, though," the woman persisted. "You let them put you on the train, didn't you? You accepted and did not rebel."

"It's still not my fault," Mary exclaimed vehemently, but the woman's eyes were upon her, level after blue level of reproach, and Mary felt herself sinking, drowned in shame. The shuttle of the train wheels struck doom into her brain. Guilt, the train wheels clucked like round black birds, and guilt, and guilt, and guilt.

Guilt, said the click of the knitting needles. "You don't understand," Mary began again. "Please, let me explain. I tried to stay at home. I didn't want to come really at all. Even in the station I wanted to go back."

"But you didn't go back," the woman said, and as she caught and looped the green wool, her eyes were sad. "You chose not to go back, and now there is nothing you can do about it."

Mary sat suddenly upright, glaring through her tears. "Oh, yes there is!" she said defiantly. "There *is* still something I can do. I am going to get off anyway, while there is still time. I am going to pull the emergency cord."

The woman flashed Mary a sudden radiant smile, and her eyes lit with admiration. "Ah," she whispered, "good. You are a spunky one. You have hit upon it. That is the one trick left. The one assertion of the will remaining. I thought that, too, was frozen. There is a chance now."

"What do you mean?" Mary drew back suspiciously. "What do you mean, a chance?"

"A chance to escape. Listen, we are nearing the seventh station, I know this trip well. There is time yet. I will tell you the best moment to pull the cord, and then you must run. The platform of the station will be deserted. They were expecting no incoming or outgoing passengers on this trip."

"How do you know? How can I believe you?"

"Ah, faithless child," the woman's voice was rich with tenderness. "I have been on your side all along. But I could not tell you. I could not help you until you had made the first positive decision. That is one of the rules."

"Rules, what rules?"

"The rules in the book of the train company. Every organization has to have bylaws, you know. Certain commandments to make things run smoothly."

The woman continued, "We are approaching the station of the seventh kingdom. You must walk down the aisle to the back of the car. No one will be watching. Pull the cord from there, and don't hesitate, no matter what. Just run."

"But you," Mary said. "Aren't you coming, too?"

"I? I cannot come with you. You must make the break yourself, but be certain, I will see you soon."

"But how? I don't see how. You said there is no return trip. You said no one ever leaves the ninth kingdom."

"There are exceptions," the woman said smiling. "I do not need to obey all the laws. Only the natural ones. But you must hurry. The station approaches, and it is time."

"Wait, just a minute, I must get my suitcase. I have all my things in it."

"Leave your suitcase," the woman instructed. "You will not need it. It would only hinder you. But remember, run, run like the wind." Her voice dropped. "There will be a brightly lighted gateway. Do not take that. Go up the stairs, even if they look black, even if there are lizards. Trust me, and take the stairway."

"Yes," said Mary, standing up, sliding across in front of the woman and out into the aisle. "Yes."

She began to walk slowly, casually to the back of the car. There was no one watching her. At the end of the aisle, she reached over and pulled the cord labeled "Emergency" that was nailed along the length of the wall.

At once the terrible siren began to shriek through the train, splitting the silence apart. Mary flung the door open and slipped out onto the swaying platform between the two cars. There was a grinding of gears, a screech of metal careening upon metal, and the train lurched to a stop.

It was the platform of the seventh kingdom, and it was deserted. Mary cleared the three steps of the train in one leap, and the cement floor struck up with a shot of pain under the soles of her feet. There were shouts, now, of the conductors on the train.

"Hey, Ron, what's the matter?" The voice was hoarse. Red lanterns flared through the cars.

"Matter, Al? I thought it was you."

Ahead was a gateway, studded with brilliant red neon lights, and there was jazz coming syncopated from the distance, beckoning. No, not the gate. To the right an unlighted stairway rose, menacing and narrow. Mary turned and ran toward it, the echo ricocheting back from the stone walls. Under her ribs the breath was caught, tight and hurting. The shouts were louder now.

"Look! It's a girl. She's getting away!"

"Catch her, quick!" Red light spilled after her, flooding closer.

"The boss'll fire us if we lose a soul this trip!"

Mary paused a second at the bottom of the flight of stairs and glanced back. The windows of the train were gilt squares, and the faces staring out were bored, cadaverous, impersonal. Only the conductors were running down the steps of the train after her, their faces red in the glare of neon from the gateway, their fiery lanterns swinging, smoking.

A scream caught at her throat. She turned to run up the stairs, dark, steep stairs that twisted upward. A cobweb stung her cheek, but she ran on, stumbling, scratching her fingers against the rough stone walls. Small and swift, a snake darted from a chink in one of the steps. She felt it coil icily about her ankle, but she kept on running.

The cries of the conductors stopped at last, growing weak in the distance, and then she heard the train start up once more, rumbling away into the frozen core of the earth with a sound like sunken thunder. Only then did she stop running.

Leaning aslant the soot-stained wall for a moment, panting like a hunted animal, she tried to swallow the slick taste of brass in her mouth. She was free.

She began again to trudge up the dark stairs, and as she climbed, the steps became broader, smoother, and the air thinned, growing lighter. Gradually the passage widened, and there came the sound, from somewhere beyond, of bells chiming in a clock tower, clear and musical. Like a link of metal, the small snake fell from her ankle and glided away into the wall.

As she rounded the next bend of the stair, the natural sunlight broke upon her in full brilliance, and she smelled the forgotten fragrance of sweet air, earth, and fresh-cut grass. Ahead was a vaulted doorway, opening out into a city park.

Mary emerged at the top of the stairs, blinking at the fertile gold webs of sunlight. White and blue pigeons rose from the pavement and circled about her head, and she heard the laughter of children playing among the leaves of the bushes. Everywhere about the park the pinnacles of the city rose in tall white granite spires, their glass windows flashing in the sun.

Like one awakening from a sleep of death, she walked along the gravel path that twinkled with the mica of the little pebbles. It was the spring of the year, and there was a woman selling flowers on the street corner, singing to herself. Mary could see the full boxes of white roses and daffodils, looped with green leaves, and the woman in a brown coat bending maternally over the display.

As Mary approached, the woman lifted her head and met Mary's eyes with a blue gaze of triumphant love. "I have been waiting for you, dear," she said.

Among the Bumblebees

Ts, spring 1953,[*] Lilly Library

In the beginning there was Alice Denway's father, tossing her up in the air until the breath caught in her throat, and catching her and holding her in a huge bear hug. With her ear against his chest, young Alice could hear the thunder of his heart and the pulse of blood in his veins, like the sound of wild horses galloping.

For Alice Denway's father had been a giant of a man. In the blue blaze of his eyes was concentrated the color of the whole overhead dome of sky, and when he laughed, it sounded as if all the waves of the ocean were breaking and roaring up the beach together. Alice worshipped her father because he was so powerful, and everybody did what he commanded because he knew best and never gave mistaken judgment.

Alice Denway was her father's pet. Ever since Alice was very little, people had told her that she favored her father's side of the family and that he was very proud of her. Her baby brother Warren favored Mother's side of the family, and he was blonde and gentle and always sickly. Alice liked to tease Warren, because it made her feel strong and superior when he began to fuss and cry. Warren cried a lot, but he never tattled on her.

There had been that spring evening at the supper table when Alice was sitting across from her brother Warren, who was eating his chocolate pudding. Chocolate pudding was Warren's favorite dessert, and he ate it very quietly, scooping it up carefully with his little silver spoon. Alice did not like Warren that night because he had been good as gold all day, and Mother had said so to Father when he came home from town. Warren's hair was gold and soft too, the color of dandelions, and his skin was the color of his glass of milk.

Alice glanced to the head of the table to see if her father was watching her, but he was bent over his pudding, spooning it up, dripping with cream, into his mouth. Alice slid down in her chair a little, staring innocently at her plate, and

---

[*] Submitted, along with several poems, for the third assignment in *Mademoiselle*'s College Board Contest. Contains holograph corrections to pagination by SP and additions by Aurelia Schober Plath and also in an unknown hand. First published in *Bananas* (Autumn 1978): 14–15. The story links thematically with SP's villanelle 'Lament' written on 5 February 1955, as well as with 'The Disquieting Muses' written in March 1958. A typescript photocopy of an earlier version of this story, titled 'The Two Gods of Alice Denway', and written for English 347a, with comments by her teacher Robert Gorham Davis, is held by Smith College. My thanks to Amanda Golden for the identification.

stretched her leg out under the table. Drawing her leg back, she straightened it in a sharp, swift kick. The toe of her shoe struck one of Warren's frail shins.

Alice watched him carefully from under her lowered lashes, concealing her fascination. The spoonful of pudding halfway to his lips dropped out of his hand, tumbling streakily down his bib to the floor, and a look of surprise sprouted in his eyes. His face crumpled into a mask of woe and he began to whine. He did not say anything, but sat there meekly, tears oozing out of the corners of his shut eyes, and blubbered wetly into his chocolate pudding.

"Good Lord, doesn't he do anything but cry?" Alice's father scowled, lifting his head, and making a scornful mouth. Alice glared at Warren in safe contempt.

"He is tired," her mother said, with a hurt, reproving look at Alice. Bending over the table, she stroked Warren's yellow hair. "He hasn't been well, poor baby. You know that."

Her mother's face was tender and soft like the Madonna pictures in Sunday school, and she got up and gathered Warren into the circle of her arms where he lay curled, warm and secure, sniffling, his face turned away from Alice and their father. The light made a luminous halo of his soft hair. Mother murmured little crooning noises to quiet him and said: "There, there, angel, it is all right now. It is all right."

Alice felt the lump of pudding stop in the back of her throat as she was about to swallow, and she almost gagged. Working hard with her mouth, she finally got it down. Then she felt the steady encouraging level of her father's gaze upon her, and she brightened. Looking up into his keen blue eyes, she gave a clear triumphant laugh.

"Who's my girl?" he asked her fondly, tweaking at a pigtail.

"Alice is!" she cried out, bouncing in her chair.

Mother was taking Warren upstairs to bed. Alice was aware of the retreating back, of the measured clicking of her mother's heels going away up the stairs, sounding faintly on the floor above. There came the sound of water running. Warren was going to have a bath, and Mother would tell him a made-to-order story. Mother told Warren a story every night before she tucked him in bed because he was good as gold all day.

"Can I watch you correct tonight?" Alice asked her father.

"*May*," said her father. "Yes, you may, if you are very quiet." He wiped his lips on his napkin, folded it, and tossed it on the table, pushing back his chair.

Alice followed her father into the den and went to sit in one of the big, slippery leather chairs near his desk. She liked to watch him correcting the papers he brought home from town in his briefcase, fixing up all the mistakes that people had made during the day. He would go reading along, and then all at once stop, pick up his colored pencil and make little red gashes here and there where the words were wrong.

"Do you know," her father had said once, looking up suddenly from his work, "what will happen tomorrow when I hand these papers back in class?"

"No," said Alice, shivering a little. "What?"

"There will be," her father intoned in mock severity, with a black frown, "a weeping and a wailing and a gnashing of teeth."

Alice had thought, then, of the great hall at college where her father stood, high upon a platform. She had been there once with Mother, and there had been hundreds of people who came to listen to her father talk and tell them wonderful strange things about how the world was made.

She had pictured him standing up there, handing down papers to the people, calling them by name, each one. He would look the way he did when he scolded Mother sometimes, strong and proud, and his voice would be hard, with a sharp edge to it. From up there, like a king, high on a throne, he would call out the names in his thundering voice, and the people would come, trembling and frightened, to take their papers. And then, rising mournfully, there would be the sound of weeping, of wailing, and gnashing of teeth. Alice hoped that she would be there someday when the people were gnashing their teeth; she was sure that it would make a terrible and awe-inspiring noise.

Tonight, she sat and watched her father correct papers until it was time for her to go to bed. The light of the study lamp circled his head with a crown of brightness, and the vicious little red marks he made on the papers were the color of the blood that oozed out in a thin line the day she cut her finger with the bread knife.

Every day, that year, when her father came home just before supper, he would bring her surprises from town in his briefcase. He would come in the front door, take off his hat and his heavy rough coat with the cold silk lining, and set the briefcase down on a chair. First he would unbuckle the straps, and then he would take out the newspaper that came all folded and smelling of ink. Then there would be the sheaves of papers he had to correct for the next day. And at the very bottom there would be something especially for her, Alice.

It might be apples, yellow and red, or walnuts wrapped in colored cellophane. Sometimes there would be tangerines, and he would peel off the pockmarked orange skin for her and the spongy white threads that laced over the fruit. She would eat the sections one by one, the juice spurting sweet and sharp into her mouth.

In the summertime, when it was very nice out, her father did not go to town at all. He would take her to the beach when Mother had to stay at home with Warren, who always coughed and fretted because he had asthma and couldn't breathe without the steam kettle beside his bed.

First Father would go for a swim himself, leaving her on the shore, with the small waves collapsing at her feet and the wet sand sliding up cool between her toes. Alice would stand ankle-deep, watching him admiringly from the edge of the breakers, shielding her eyes against the blinding glare of summer sun that struck silent and brilliant on the surface of the water.

After a while she would call to him, and he would turn and begin swimming shoreward, carving a line of foam behind him with his legs and cleaving the water ahead with the powerful propellors of his arms. He would come to her and lift her onto his back, where she clung, her arms locked about his neck, and go swimming out again. In an ecstasy of terror, she would hold to him, her soft cheek prickling where she laid her face against the back of his neck, her legs and slender body trailing out behind her, floating, moving effortlessly along in her father's energetic wake.

And gradually, there on her father's back, Alice's fear would leave her, and the water, black and deep beneath her, would seem calm and friendly, obeying the skillful mastery of her father's rhythmic stroke and supporting both of them upon the level waves. The sun, too, fell warm and cordial upon her thin arms, where the skin was stippled with gooseflesh. The summer sun did not burn her skin raw and red, the way it did Warren's, but turned her a lovely brown shade, the color of cinnamon toast.

After swimming, her father would take her for a brisk run up and down the beach to make her dry again, and as she raced him along the flat hard packed sand at the water's edge, laughing into the teeth of the wind, she would try to match her steps to the easy piston-powered pace of his swift stride. Then it seemed to Alice, as she felt the growing strength and sureness of her young limbs, that someday she, too, would be able to ride the waves in safe dominion, and that the sunlight would always bend deferentially to her, docile and generous with its creative warmth.

Alice's father feared nothing. Power was good because it was power, and when the summer storms came, with the crackling blue sheet lightning and the ear-splitting thunderclaps, like the sound of a city toppling block by block, Alice's father would roar with laughter as Warren scurried to hide in the broom closet, his fingers in his ears and his pale face grave with terror. Alice learned to sing the thunder song with her father: "Thor is angry. Thor is angry. Boom, boom, boom! Boom, boom, boom! We don't care. We don't care. Boom, boom, boom!" And above the resonant resounding baritone of her father's voice, the thunder rumbled harmless as a tame lion.

Sitting on her father's lap in the den, watching the waves at the end of the street whipped to a ragged froth of foam and blown spray against the sea wall, Alice learned to laugh at the destructive grandeur of the elements. The swollen purple and black clouds broke open with blinding flashes of light, and the thunderclaps made the house shudder to the root of its foundations. But with her father's strong arms around her and the steady reassuring beat of his heart in her ears, Alice believed that he was somehow connected with the miracle of fury beyond the windows, and that through him, she could face the doomsday of the world in perfect safety.

When it was the right time of year, her father took her into the garden and showed her how he could catch bumblebees. That was something no one else's father could do. Her father caught a special kind of bumblebee that he recognized by its shape and held it in his closed fist, putting his hand to her ear. Alice liked to hear the angry, stifled buzzing of the bee, captured in the dark trap of her father's hand, but not stinging, not daring to sting. Then, with a laugh, her father would spread his fingers wide, and the bee would fly out, free, up into the air and away.

One summer, then, Alice's father did not take her out to catch bees. He lay inside the house on the couch and Mother brought him trays with orange juice in tall glasses, and grapes, and plums to eat. He drank a lot of water, for he was very thirsty all the time. Alice would go often into the kitchen for him and get a pitcher of water with ice cubes to make it cold, and she would bring him a glass, frosted with water drops.

It went on like that for a long while, and Father would not talk much to anyone who came into the house. At night, after Alice was in bed, she could hear Mother speaking to Father in the next room, and her voice would go along very soft and low for a while, until Father would get cross and raise his voice like thunder, and sometimes he would even wake up Warren, who began to cry.

One day, after a night like this, the doctor came to see Father. He brought a black briefcase and silver tools, and after he had left, Father began to stay in bed. It was the doctor's orders. There was whispering, always now, upstairs instead of talking, and the doctor wanted the blinds in Father's room kept down because the sunlight was too bright and hurt Father's eyes.

Alice could only go to see Father once in a while now because they kept the door shut most of the time. Once when she was sitting on a chair by the bed, talking to him softly about how the violet seeds were ready to collect in their dry brown pods in the garden, the doctor came. Alice could hear the front door open downstairs and Mother asking him in. Mother and the doctor stood together for a while in the downstairs hall, the low murmur of their voices sounding solemn and indistinct.

Then the doctor came upstairs with Mother, bringing his black bag and smiling a foolish bright smile. He pulled playfully at Alice's pigtail, but she switched it away from him with a pout and a toss of her head. Father winked at her, but Mother shook her head.

"Be nice, Alice," she begged. "The doctor's here to help Father."

This was not true. Father did not need any help. The doctor was making him stay in bed; he shut out the sun and that was making Father unhappy. Father could tell the plump silly doctor to go out of the house, if he wanted to. Father could slam the door after him and order him never to come back again. But instead, Father let the doctor take a big silver needle out of the black bag and swab a sterile place on Father's arm and stab the needle in.

"You should not look," Mother told Alice gently.

But Alice was determined to look. Father did not wince at all. He let the needle go in and looked at her with his strong blue eyes, silently telling her that really he did not care, really he was only humoring Mother and the absurd fat little doctor, two harmless conspirators. Alice felt her eyes fill up with tears of pride. But she blinked back the tears and did not cry. Father did not like anyone to cry.

The next day Alice went to visit her father again. From the hall she glimpsed him lying in bed in the shaded room, his head on the pillow, and the light, pale and dusty orange, filtering through the drawn blinds.

She tiptoed into the room, which smelled sweet and strange with alcohol. Father was asleep, lying motionless on the bed except for the rhythmic rising and falling of the blankets over his chest and the sound of his breathing. In the muted light, his face was the sallow color of candle wax, and the flesh was lean and taut about his mouth.

Alice stood looking down at her father's gaunt face, clenching and unclenching her thin hands by her side and listening to the slow thread of his breathing. Then she leaned over the bed and put her head down on the bedclothes above his chest. From somewhere, very faint and far off, she could hear the weak pulsing of his heart, like the fading throb of a distant drum.

"Father," she said in a small pleading voice. "Father." But he did not hear, withdrawn as he was into the core of himself, insulated against the sound of her supplicant voice. Lost and betrayed, she slowly turned away and left the room.

That was the last time that Alice Denway saw her father. She did not know then that in all the rest of her life there would be no one to walk with her, like him, proud and arrogant among the bumblebees.

I Lied for Love

Ts,[*] 4–7 April 1953, Lilly Library

I'm pretty sure you've heard people smile and give out with the old saying that "the grass is always greener in the other fellow's yard." Well, there was a time when I blinded myself into envying the nice green grass in someone else's yard until I got to thinking I could carve myself a good sizeable slice of it. There was a time when I forgot how important your own lot was, the place you lived, and your own folks, no matter how poor or how simple they happened to be.

And that's what I want to tell you about. Me, Jenny Martin, the farmer's daughter who got big-time ideas, so big that they blotted out everything else but the glitter and the gold for a while, and even the people that loved me best.

I want to tell you my story because maybe you, right now, are faced with some of the decisions that I had to make. And maybe, if I can talk to you in time and show you how foolish I was, how I went wrong, you can keep from making the same mistakes I did.

I am going to tell you how I met Phil Forester, and fell in love with him, and bore his child out of wedlock. But I am also going to tell you how I fell in love with more than Phil. How I fell in love with the big city, and the lights, and the blue convertible, and all the lovely things that Phil's money could buy.

This is the story of me, Jenny Martin, and how I made vanity and pride and ambition part of my love, because I thought that love could buy me the things I wanted. Things I wanted so much that I would lie and deceive those who cared for me most just so I could get what I selfishly desired.

But first I want to tell you about how it was before I met Phil, when I was still satisfied with the old life because I didn't know or care about anything

---

[*] Typed at top right: 'Sylvia Plath / 26 Elmwood Road / Wellesley, Massachusetts.' Under the title, SP wrote '(13,500 words)'. Typescript has holograph and typewritten corrections. Written for *True Story* 'confessions' magazine.

beyond Dad and the farm. You know how that feeling hits you sometimes about home? Sure you do!

It can come from the simplest things, like the smell of a rich meat stew cooking on the stove, or the sound of your dad whistling gaily in the shower, or the sight of geraniums blooming red in the window box. It can be any one of these little things that hits you, and you suddenly feel a glow all over and think: home, there's no place like it!

I only wish I'd known then what it really meant to love your home and folks, to trust them and confide in them, no matter what. I only wish that I'd kept on feeling that warm glow without a change for the rest of my life. But that wasn't the way it turned out for me. It took a long hard struggle to make me finally realize that home is where the heart is. It took a lot of pain and heartbreak to make me see how I'd sinned against my dad and his love for me.

My dad, "Pop" Martin, the farmhands called him, was just about the best father a girl could have. He ran a vegetable truck farm two miles outside Turnerville, and ever since I could remember, he'd been in love with the farmland and the work about the fields and greenhouses. He always sang or whistled when he worked, and was ready and glad to answer the questions of the little girl that followed him around adoringly.

The little girl was me, Jenny. Dad had brought me up ever since I was a baby, because Mother had died when I was born. Dad never talked about Mother to me. Only when I asked about her would he say anything. Like the time I wanted to know what she died of, and he told me of the snowstorm when I was born, and how the town doctor couldn't come in time to save Mother because the roads weren't plowed.

I figured Dad had been really broken up about Mother's death and all, and that was why he didn't want to talk about her. Because her absence had left a sore place in his heart that hurt when anyone touched it. But I never realized how strongly Dad felt about recalling Mother's memory until one rainy Saturday when I was about thirteen.

Dad was out in his slicker in the washroom in the big barn, helping load the trucks, and I'd wandered up into the big farm attic to explore. It was there that I happened to discover a trunk of Mother's old dresses, all packed away carefully in newspapers and still smelling faintly of sweet spicy perfume.

The dress that caught my fancy was made of a soft, silky yellow material, with flounces of lace on the skirt and a black velvet sash around the waist. All the rest of the dresses were plain and sensible cottons and calicos. The yellow dress was like something a princess would wear in a storybook.

I dug down deeper into the trunk, and then, at the very bottom, I felt something square and flat. I picked it up, and there was a colored picture, in a gold frame, of the most beautiful woman I'd ever seen.

She had a cap of yellow curls, and the biggest dark brown eyes you could imagine. She laughed out of the picture at me so that I could almost imagine her in the same room. And on the picture was written: "To George. All my love, always, Marianne."

George was the name of my father, and Marianne, I knew from Dad's telling me, was Mother's name. It was then that I got the idea to dress up in Mother's yellow gown and surprise Dad. If I dressed up I might even look like her, because I had yellow hair, too, only I'd always worn it in long pigtails, and my eyes were brown, just like hers.

How can I explain the strange excitement that filled me as I slipped out of my faded blue dungarees and white sweatshirt and pulled the yellow silk dress on over my head! I was a skinny kid for my age, still undeveloped, always looking like a tomboy around the farm. But something queer happened to me as I felt the scented folds of the lacy dress fall into place about my body, clinging and soft.

I tiptoed downstairs to my room, flushed with pleasure, and looked at my reflection in the cracked mirror above my dresser. There I was, Jenny Martin, impish and feminine, almost like Marianne in the picture.

Except there was one thing wrong. My hair. It hung down on either side of my face in two blonde pigtails and made me look like a kid still. Dad liked my hair long, and used to call me "Jenny-with-the-long-blonde-hair" just for fun.

Without thinking, I unbraided my hair quickly and picked up a pair of scissors lying on my dresser. I snipped, and a big soft piece of hair fell to the floor. I guess I got scared, then, because I cut the rest off fast before I lost my courage. And there I was, blonde curls clustered short around my head. The spitting image of Marianne!! Wait till Dad sees me, I thought.

I'll never forget that day as long as I live. Dad came home from the barn all dripping and wet in his yellow slicker, and he called, the way he always did, "Where's my best girl!"

I slipped downstairs and stood in the hallway in the yellow dress.

"Here I am, Dad," I said very softly, being a bit scared all of a sudden of what he'd say.

Dad turned then, and looked at me. He gave a hoarse ragged gasp. "Marianne!" His face turned an ugly gray color and he lifted a shaking hand to wipe his forehead.

"You, Jenny!" he said then, moving heavily toward me. "You've cut your hair!" I stood there, too frightened to run away. This wasn't my dad. This wasn't any man I'd ever seen before. A purple vein pulsed on his forehead, and his dark eyes were narrowed in an angry frown.

"I'll teach you," he said slowly, his voice thick with disgust. "I'll teach you to put on fancy airs."

He lifted his hand then, and brought it down hard across my face. The room reeled and rocked. "Dad," I screamed. The blackness closed in.

I guess my cry must have brought him to his senses, because when I came to I was lying on the living-room couch, and he was bending over me tenderly, bathing my face with cool water and saying brokenly over and over again, "Jenny, Jenny baby. I'm sorry. I didn't mean to hurt you. Forgive me, Jenny."

Everything was all right once more. This was my dear loving dad again. I'd been thoughtless and hurt him by bringing back Mother's memory fresh and sharp. It must have cut him to the quick to see me standing there in Mother's dress.

Dad went on, trying to explain. "For a minute I thought it was Marianne, your mother, come back again. And then I saw it was you, my precious baby. I couldn't bear it."

"I understand, Dad," I said, wanting to make it easy for him. "I understand."

I ran upstairs and put the dress back in the attic and came down to get supper for Dad and me. And just to show him there were no hard feelings, I baked a batch of his favorite chocolate cookies for our dessert. As the years went by, the incident faded away in my memory, and I never dreamed of what would happen to bring it back vivid and clear later on.

I turned sixteen the summer before I started at the consolidated Turnerville High School down in the village two miles away. And that was where I met Phil, and my life started to change. I was pretty excited at the prospect of going to a real big high school after the local country grammar and junior high nearby.

All that summer I worked as a crew boss on the truck farm for Dad and got regular pay for it to help buy the dress material and books I would need for school.

That summer was different from the other summers I'd worked on the farm. I was getting to be a big girl, now, and even when I wore my dungarees and plaid cotton shirts I was conscious that the older farmhands followed me with their eyes when I went by.

I'd always been great pals with them, but now they began to tease me in a different way from the old comradely joking I was used to.

It was like when Jake Nelson, who worked harrowing the fields, called out one day, "Say there, angel face, you're old enough to have a boyfriend now, aren't you?"

I laughed, the way I always did when the farmhands joked with me, but I couldn't help blushing to the roots of my hair at the way Jake looked me over. It wasn't the usual friendly glance. It was a keen look that traveled up and down me, and a knowing smile that made me feel queer and kind of naked.

I kept away from Jake as much as I could from that day on. But still, every time I went by him he'd look at me with a sort of slick, secret smile that made my cheeks burn.

Other than that, days on the farm went on peacefully, and I got a golden-brown tan from being out in the fields picking vegetables or weeding all day. It was late August when Ivan Kazanov came to work for Dad, and if it hadn't been for him, I might have gotten into serious trouble.

Ivan was a tall, lean blonde refugee from Estonia who'd come to live with the Gulacks down the road a way, and Dad hired him on the spot to work on the farm. Ivan was only a couple of years older than I was, but he had a bayonet scar on his chest from fighting overseas in the war.

I could see that Dad admired Ivan right away, because Ivan really was one of the best workers on the farm after he got into the swing of things. Somehow, he made any kind of work, no matter how grubby, seem like a lot of fun, like playing a game almost.

But when you needed help of anything, Ivan was right there, always ready to do what was necessary. Ivan's good-hearted strength was brought home to me the time I had the run-in with Jake in the old barn at the end of the cornfield.

It was a mellow twilight when I walked out on the dirt road to the old barn where I'd left my jacket that afternoon. Ivan was coming over that evening to talk with Dad, and I didn't want to miss any of his visit, so I was in a hurry.

The barn was dark inside, and smelled sweet of hay. I saw my jacket in a little white pile, just where I'd left it. I was just bending down to pick it up when I heard footsteps and the sound of someone breathing behind me.

I turned. "Jake!" I could barely make out his features in the dark, but I could see that his teeth were bared in a nasty smile.

"Well, if it isn't angel face!" he said, and his voice was blurred with drink. He lurched a step closer to me and reached out to grip my arm. I could smell the whisky on his breath, and I was scared to move. A scream stuck in my throat. I was too far away for anyone to hear.

"You've had this coming to you for a long time, sweetie," Jake said, jerking me toward him.

Nobody had ever kissed me or touched me before. And I'd always thought kissing was meant to be sweet and tender and loving, like in the movies or in stories. But this was different. This was cruel.

Before I could get breath enough to cry out, Jake had pulled me into the viselike embrace of his arms and pushed his mouth down hard on mine. I could feel his teeth on my soft lips, and I tried to jerk myself away, but he was too strong for me.

His hands began to move hungrily over my body, pressing me close to him. His fingers found where my shirtwaist was tucked in, and slid up eagerly along my bare flesh.

I was frantically struggling against the muscular heat of his body when he pushed me down onto the hay, his mouth still moving insistently on mine, his hands seeking out the curves of my body. I fought against him with all my fury, but this was no man anymore. This was a beast. A selfish, savage beast.

The next thing I knew, someone was pulling Jake from me, striking him, and Jake, with an angry frustrated grunt, let me drop and turned to fight whoever was attacking him.

It was too dark for me to see anything more than the battling forms in the dimness. I just lay there panting on the hay, whimpering quietly and thanking God that Jake had been stopped in time.

There was a sudden sharp crack, like the sound of a plank of wood splitting, and one of the forms crumpled to the floor of the barn with a thud. Please God, I prayed silently, let it be Jake!

I lay there, not daring to move. "Jenny, Jenny, are you all right?" The voice sounded hoarse and worried. It was Ivan.

"Oh, Ivan," I said, and I began to cry. "I'm all right . . . but I . . . I thought no one would ever come . . ."

Ivan picked me up tenderly, as if I were a child, and rocked me gently in his arms. "There, there, Jenny. Everything's OK now. I'll take you up to the house, and we'll tell your dad about Jake."

We left Jake lying there in the barn, still unconscious. Ivan carried me up to the house in his strong arms, as I was still too shaken to walk. On the way back he explained to me how Dad had said I'd gone out to the old barn to pick up something I'd left there. And so Ivan had strolled out to meet me.

Dad took one look at my bruised, tear-stained face and torn shirtwaist and said gravely, "I was afraid something like this might happen if one of those guys got more than his share of corn likker . . . Take her upstairs, Ivan, and then come down. I want to talk to you."

Ivan carried me upstairs and gently laid me down on the bed in my room. "It'll be all right, Jenny, I promise," he whispered in my ear. I smiled shakily to show that I believed him. And only then did he go downstairs.

I don't know just what Ivan told Dad, but Jake never came back to work on the farm. He'd been one of the best hands, but Dad fired him point blank, and Ivan began to work in his place.

Dad took me aside the next day and told me to keep away from boys on the farm. Boys anywhere, for that matter, he said. For regardless of how nice a guy was, regardless of how he'd sweet-talk a girl, all he wanted in the long run was his own way. And that was to do a girl dirt.

I knew from the look in Dad's eye that he would never put up with me, his only child, dallying around with any boy. And after my shattering experience with Jake, I thought Dad was right. That is, I thought he was right until I met Phil.

Nobody ever said anything more about the incident after that, and I tried as best I could to forget it, but every now and then I'd wake up in the middle of the night in a cold sweat out of a nightmare where Jake came leering at me from the dark, and not even Ivan could hear my frantic cries.

I was glad when it came time for me to take the bus to high school that fall, because I got so caught up in meeting new people and making new friends that I forgot the trouble with Jake in the barn for the time being. I even didn't see Ivan much anymore, because after supper I'd go upstairs to do my homework, and I didn't have time to sit around and talk.

I don't know if I can explain how the new life at high school affected me. But maybe you can see how after years of going to a small country school with farm kids I'd known all my life, it was really a treat to dress up in pretty plaid cottons I'd made myself out of material from my farm job money, and take the bus that traveled two miles to Turnerville High.

And maybe you can see how excited I was when I met Phil Forester, the senior captain of the basketball team at high, and how thrilled I was when he asked me to go out for my first date!

Phil Forester was my passport to approval in the social circles of Turnerville High. Or so I thought for a long while. He sat next to me in study hall, but where I first really *met* him was when I started working after school at the jewelry counter in the New Modes dress shop. And I don't think I would have ever taken an after-school job in town if it hadn't been for a snatch of conversation I'd overheard in the girls' powder room.

You see, there were a lot of different cliques at Turnerville High, and when

I first started going there I didn't seem to fit into any of them. The only kids I knew were the ones who'd gone to classes with me back at the small farm county school. I wasn't used to seeing the girls who came from the best side of town. Girls whose fathers were successful businessmen and had the money to buy all the fine cars and clothes and good times they wanted.

These girls went together in a little group headed by a tall, attractive dark-haired girl named Alison Greenwood. As far as I was concerned, Alison Greenwood had everything in the world a girl could want. Beautiful dresses, wealthy parents, and a big white house in the Turner Estates, the very best part of town. On top of that, she was more friendly than most of the other girls in her crowd. Girls like Meg Prescott and Nancy Lynch, who had to be stuck-up to prove that they were better than anyone else.

At first I didn't realize there was any reason why I couldn't be friends with these girls just as with anyone else in Turnerville High. I began to understand why, though, after one day that winter when I went into the powder room to comb my hair after lunch in the cafeteria. That was the day I accidentally happened to overhear the middle of a conversation going on between Meg Prescott and Nancy Lynch.

I'd come in quietly, and there was a lot of noise and chatter going on, but I just happened to be standing behind Meg and Nancy. Nancy was preening in front of the mirror and pulling her cashmere sweater down tighter to show off her well-developed figure, and Meg was telling her something awfully funny that made both of them giggle in a nasty way.

"It's that bookbag she carries," Meg was saying. "It makes her look like an old farmhand the way she carries it over her shoulder to school."

"And she always *brings* her lunch. Wrapped up in a greasy brown paper bag," Nancy tittered.

"Well, you know, she *is* a farm girl . . ." Meg glimpsed me, then, and broke off in confusion. And it was only then that I was smart enough to realize that the poor dope they were talking about was *me*!

I turned about as red as a radish, and the tears sprang to my eyes as if I'd been slapped. I stood there and fumbled in my pocketbook for a comb to hide the naked hurt in my eyes.

"We're sorry," Meg mumbled, turning to go. "We didn't realize . . ."

No, they didn't realize. They didn't realize that I was more than a dumb clod who lived in an old farmhouse away from the parties and date life of their tight little crowd. But I wasn't going to sit back and take their insults. Not me, Jenny Martin. I'd show them.

And I guess that's where it started, my determination to prove that I was as good as those snobby girls were, that I could know how to act, that I could belong to their kind of crowd and have the same expensive possessions they took so for granted.

Right from there on my whole outlook changed. I began to be more critical of my homelife. I noticed how Dad made noise eating his soup, and I thought with shame that Alison Greenwood's father would never eat like that, or pick his teeth after meals. And I cried secretly at night because I didn't have a pretty mother to help me with my clothes, and invite friends in and make the house all festive and special the way Turner Estates mothers were sure to do.

Yes, I got to feeling sorry for myself all right. I even got sick of seeing Ivan sitting on the steps waiting for me when I came home from school in his old faded dungarees and dirt-caked shoes. I thought he looked crude, like a mere farmhand. And that was funny, because his clothes had never bothered me before.

Finally, after moping around for a few weeks, I decided that I'd get a job after school downtown in one of the dress shops. I'd tell Dad that I wanted to earn money so's I could buy my lunches at school instead of carrying them, and I'd maybe be able to get a few dresses at a discount. That was the beginning.

Everything worked out OK at first, and I started my job at the New Modes dress shop a week later right after school instead of going home by bus the way I always did. Best of all, that was how I first met Phil Forester.

I was working at the jewelry counter one Tuesday afternoon in late March when I noticed a tall, dark good-looking guy had come in the door and was looking over the bracelets. It was Phil Forester! My heart caught in my throat. He was so casual and so handsome!

"H-hello . . ." I said, trembling inside and trying to be businesslike. "May I help you?"

Phil looked up with the friendliest, most engaging grin. My heart did a flip-flop right then, and I thought to myself: Jenny Martin, this is the boy for you! But I didn't say anything. I just waited.

"Hello yourself," Phil said, as friendly as you please. "I'm shopping for a very special bracelet for a very special girl. It's her birthday," he explained with another grin. "And I'd like it engraved with her name. Alison."

My heart sank as I showed him the shiny gold and silver bracelets that were our specialty. Never in my life had a boy ever given *me* a present. I felt a surge of envy for Alison Greenwood. She didn't have to worry about anything. She was just born in the midst of wealth and position and she'd probably never had to lift a lily-white hand to work in her life.

"Here," Phil said, picking up an expensive silver bracelet studded with blue stones. "I think I'll get this one. Do you approve?"

He was asking my opinion! I tossed my head merrily then, and laughed and said, "Sure, provided those blue stones *exactly* match her eyes!"

Phil laughed, and went up to the cash register to pay for the bracelet. But instead of leaving the store from there, he came over to me again and said, "Say, don't you sit next to me in study hall?"

I blushed. He had noticed me. He had remembered. "Yes," I said. "Yes, I guess I do."

"Phil Forester is the name." He bowed low, grinning at me all the while. "And yours?"

"Jenny," I stammered. "Jenny Martin."

"See you around, Jenny," he said, and he was gone.

That was the beginning of it all. I went home and dreamed about Phil Forester. The next day in study hall he passed me a note across the desk. With shaking fingers I opened it.

"Hello again," it said. "Are you busy this Saturday night? If so, why so? If not, how about a movie date down at the Palace?"

I couldn't believe it. Me, Jenny Martin, being asked out by Phil Forester! But it was with misgivings that I wrote, "I'd love to," and tossed the note back. What would Dad say!

I'd never been out on a date before, and I knew that he wouldn't want me to go with any of the town fellows. Ever since last August, with Jake and all, he'd been terribly strict about letting me be around any of the farm guys, and I just knew that he'd never let me go out with Phil.

That night, Phil walked me to the bus stop and carried my books, as it was my afternoon off from the shop.

"Where do you live, Jenny?" he asked me with the nicest smile.

How could I tell him? How could I tell him that I lived on "Pop" Martin's farm two miles out of town? But I had to explain. I couldn't keep him in the dark. It would be better for me to tell him the truth than for one of Alison Greenwood's crowd to give him the scoop. If he didn't want to go out with a farm girl he could always back out now.

"I live on Martin's farm out along the Post Road," I told him, watching his face for a sign of surprise, of change. Nothing happened. He just kept on smiling and said, "Fine, Jenny, I'll be around about seven thirty."

"Oh . . . oh, Phil," I stammered, not knowing how to tell him. "Could you pick me up about a quarter of a mile down the road, at the crossing with Old

County Lane? Because Dad doesn't like the idea of my going out with boys. I'll just tell him I'm going to take the bus to the movies with a girl friend and he won't mind."

"Sure, Jenny," Phil said quietly. "Sure, if that's the way you want it."

That was the beginning of my mistake. Thinking I could deceive Dad and get away with it. Thinking I could break faith with the person who loved me more than anyone in the world just to prove that I could date a society boy. That I, Jenny Martin, was just as good as any other girl in the Turner Estates crowd. But at that time I didn't care. I was too caught up thinking about myself and how I wanted to be Phil's girl and share his rich, fast life.

Phil picked me up in his light blue convertible that night at the crossroads, and I was all dressed in my best red sweater and black velvet skirt. I'd just washed my hair that afternoon and I knew I looked pretty special with my blonde curls clustered over my head, and my new black winter coat that I'd bought on sale at the dress shop.

When Phil saw me, he whistled appreciatively, and we started off on what was to be the beginning of a series of wonderful weekend dates. Phil was easygoing and friendly right from that first night. A lot of kids from high school were at the Palace show with their dates, and being as I was with Phil Forester, they all treated me like a queen, even though some of them must have been pretty surprised at first.

That night Phil Forester told me I was the prettiest girl he knew, and said that he went for blonde hair and dark eyes in a big way. And when he asked to meet me again the next Saturday night, I could have skipped for joy. The Turner Estates girls would be simply green with envy when they found out!

I don't know when I admitted to myself that I was falling in love with Phil Forester, but it came over me all of a sudden one Saturday morning in early spring when I woke up with a song on my lips. That night I was going to Turner City to go dancing with Phil. "Jenny Martin," I said to myself, laughing, "you are in love with that boy!"

I'd gotten it all fixed up with my closest girl friend in Turnerville, Mary Jackson, that I'd stay over at her house that night so Dad wouldn't notice my coming in late, because tonight was no small movie date. It was a very special occasion!

I packed my overnight case, put on my red velvet suit dress, and kissed Dad goodbye, telling him not to worry about me. He looked at me suspiciously as I turned to go.

"Seems to me as you're all dressed up to kill," he drawled, puffing on his pipe. "Awful dressed up for movies with a girl friend."

A cold hand of fear clutched at my heart. What if Dad had guessed about my secret trysts with Phil! What if he wouldn't let me go tonight. This special night that we were celebrating dating each other for exactly one month!

But I fought down my uneasiness and managed a laugh. "Why, Dad," I said, "a girl's got to get dressed up now and then. It's not every night that I'm company at Mary Jackson's!"

That seemed to pacify him, and he went back to reading his newspaper. I hurried down the road, hoping that I hadn't kept Phil waiting.

Sure enough, his blue convertible was parked in Old County Lane, and as I came running up, Phil opened the door for me.

"Hi, cutie," he said. "Hop in."

It was a long drive to Turner City, and I felt a forbidden excitement rise in me as we left the residential district behind and came into the busy streets with the gay red, blue, and yellow neon lights dancing off and on like at a carnival. I'd never been to Turner City at night before, only in the daytime with Dad that summer when he'd driven in now and then to sell vegetables at the market in his old farm truck.

"Happy?" Phil reached over to hold my hand with a smile.

"Happy as the day is long," I told him. And I meant every word of it. Ever since I'd met Phil, my whole life at school had changed. Alison Greenwood, who was dating Greg Parker, the president of Student Council, said hello when I passed her in the hall, and even Meg and Nancy smiled at me now because they knew I was dating Phil Forester.

I wasn't Jenny Martin, farm girl, anymore. I was Jenny Martin, Phil Forester's girl, and that was all I cared about in the world. Because dates with Phil Forester were a wonderful bridge that spanned the gap between the girl I used to be, in dungarees and old shirts and pigtails, to the girl I wanted to be, Jennifer Martin, pretty, well-dressed, and sophisticated. Phil Forester was my ticket to a new life, and I was going to cash in on it!

That night Phil took me to the Blue Champagne Club, a pine-paneled night spot in the heart of Turner City which had a staggering cover charge, low lights, and slow, potent music for dancing. Phil had been there before, but as this was my first introduction to city nightlife, I drank in every minute of it with eagerness and excitement, as if I could never get enough.

Phil led the way to the table he'd reserved for us near the dance floor. At the table, I slipped off the jacket to the strapless dress, and I saw Phil glance at my bare shoulders and low-cut neckline with smiling approval. I'd bought the dress with one whole week's pay at the shop, and gotten rhinestone earrings and a necklace to go with it. But it was more than worth it to see the admiration in Phil's eyes.

He leaned across the table, reaching for my hands. "You know, Jenny," he murmured huskily, "you're the prettiest girl in the world!"

I laughed in the new carefree way I'd learned since dating Phil and tossed my blonde curls gaily. "You'll have me believing you if you're not careful," I teased.

He grinned, and we got up to dance. On the dance floor, Phil pulled me close to him, so that his cheek rested against my forehead, and our two bodies moved as one in time to the low pulsing beat of the blues music.

We'd never danced together before, and I was nearly floating with joy. Phil held me tightly in the circle of his arms, and once he leaned down to kiss my cheek. I was so thrilled I almost cried. This was the way love should be, sweet and thoughtful. Oh, I loved Phil! I knew it now. I never wanted to date another boy as long as I lived!

Phil was quieter than usual that evening, and very gentle to me, as if I was somebody special he wanted to take care of. And while we were sipping drinks back at the table he pulled a small gold-wrapped package out of his pocket and handed it to me saying, "I had a hard time finding something as sweet as you are!"

It was a lovely small globed bottle of fragrant, expensive perfume! My first real gift from a boy! Pleased at my delight, he leaned across the table and kissed the tip of my nose.

When we left the Blue Champagne Club it was still early, and Phil headed out to Lakeside Drive. I knew about Lakeside Drive, even if I'd never been out there. It was the parking place for the kids at high, and every night the cars were lined up in the moonlight, and the couples sat and necked together.

I felt suddenly very queer inside. I loved Phil dearly, but somehow I didn't want to spoil it. In the back of my mind, I remembered Jake, and I felt sort of sick. Why couldn't things stay beautiful and tender, the way they were?

"Phil," I said, very low, as he pulled the car over by the side of the wooded road. "Phil, please don't stop here."

"Why, Jenny," Phil said softly, "don't you understand? I don't want to hurt you. I love you, Jenny. I just want to show you how terribly much I love you."

I could hardly believe my ears. Phil Forester loved me! It didn't matter to him where I came from. It didn't matter that my dad was just a farmer. Suddenly everything came back into proportion again, and my memories of Jake faded for a moment.

"Oh, Phil," was all I could say. The world was all silver with spring moonlight, and I could hear lyrical music sing in my heart. "Oh, Phil, I love you too!"

And then I was in his arms, and he was holding me to him as if he would never let me go, and kissing me. For a minute another picture came up before my eyes, the picture of Jake, forcing me to him in the barn. For a minute I almost cried out and pulled away.

But Phil's mouth was gentle and loving on mine, and when his hands began to touch my body they were tender and fond, not hard and cruelly searching. So I gave myself to the sweet warm embraces of Phil's love.

It was Phil who let me go first, and I became conscious of the real world again. The world of time, and place, and me, Jenny Martin, who had gone parking on Lakeside Drive when her father thought she was safely at the Jacksons' house after an early movie.

In spite of myself, I felt a wave of shame flash over me. How long could we go on this way, without my father finding out? And how could I ever be happy living without dating Phil? More than anything I wanted to keep Phil. I couldn't bear the thought of losing him, of being forever doomed to drudging on the farm year after year. I wanted a chance at the gay whirl of life the Turner Estates girls would lead . . . even after they were married.

Married! It was then I realized I wanted to marry Phil Forester! Marry him and go away with him and live his kind of life, and leave the farm behind me.

And leave your dad? a nagging voice in my mind asked. I ruthlessly pushed the uncomfortable thought away. I loved Phil more than anybody. Phil understood me, thought I was pretty, and gave me expensive presents. Why should I grub on a farm all my life?

And then I thought of that pert attractive face laughing out of the photograph at me. Mother! She never let herself get old and dowdy. She was pretty and young till the day she died. But it was the farm that killed her, really. That decided me. I would get Phil Forester to marry me somehow and learn to live in his carefree, easygoing style!

Mary Jackson was waiting for me at the door of her house when Phil drove up about one o'clock that morning. He kissed me goodnight and whispered huskily, "Next Saturday, angel?"

"Next Saturday," I agreed, and slipped into the Jacksons' house.

"Shh," Mary said, "the family's all asleep. I told them you'd gone to a late movie with the girls so they don't suspect a thing."

Getting ready for bed in Mary's room, I told her, in a rosy haze, about my love for Phil, and how I hoped someday I'd marry him.

"Marry him?" Mary said soberly. "Honey, do you think his family will let you marry their only son? His father's got him in line to take over his printing business. Everybody knows that. And his parents will want him to pick a society girl of their own class, like Alison Greenwood. For your own good, Jenny, get any pipe dreams of marriage out of your head!"

Mary was my best friend at high school. Her folks raised chickens just outside of town and had been friendly with Dad and me for a long time now. But still her words, kind as she meant them to be, stabbed like knives into my heart. The knives of my conscience!

Because deep down I knew that Phil had never taken me home to meet his family any more than I'd taken him home to meet Dad. The kids at school knew we dated, but that was all. As far as our families went, we couldn't be farther apart. But still I didn't want to admit it to myself.

"Phil can get along without his family," I maintained proudly. "He doesn't need to depend on them for a living. He can get a good job himself, if that's all that matters."

"Well, what about your dad, then?" Mary persisted. "You know how he feels about the idea of your dating out. You've told me yourself. He'd have a fit if you got married and left the farm. You're all he has. You know that."

I knew that, all right, but I didn't want to think about it then. Then or any other time either! I just wanted Phil, and that was all. Let Mary practice what she preached and settle down with Ned Potter, the skinny town guy who helped her family raise chickens. She could raise chickens all the rest of her life and have a dozen children to scrimp and save for, as far as I was concerned. But not me. I was going to be smart. I wasn't going to have to spend my life slaving for a big family with no money!

"Ease up, Mary!" I tried to toss the matter off lightly. "I'm sleepy. Let's turn in now."

If I'd only realized what was waiting for me when I got home, I wouldn't have been half so lighthearted and gay. I wouldn't have reacted to Mary's thoughtful advice so selfishly!

Dad wasn't out on the lawn when I walked up the drive the way he usually was Sunday afternoon, pottering around in the flower beds. The house was strangely quiet.

"Dad, Dad!" I called, entering the front door. Ivan met me at the door to Dad's bedroom, motioning me to be quiet. His handsome face was unusually serious. He took me out to the kitchen where we wouldn't be overheard.

"Whatever is the matter, Ivan?" I begged, frightened, a catch in my throat. If anything had happened to Dad while I was gone . . . "Is Dad . . . ?"

"Your dad's all right now," Ivan said. "He had a heart attack yesterday, that's all. But the doctor came and said he'll be fine if he takes it easy and doesn't have anything more to upset him."

Ivan told me the story of how Dad was loading heavy crates on the truck and had felt a sudden pain spread down his left arm. He'd slipped backwards and fallen, knocking himself unconscious on the corner of the washtub. Ivan was right there, and carried Dad to the house and took care of him all during the night.

I felt a wave of self-incrimination. Where had I been when Dad needed me? Out with Phil Forester, parking on Lakeside Drive. No matter how I loved Phil, no matter how much I wanted to marry him, I had no right to neglect the man who'd brought me up, who'd loved me as much as any father could love his daughter! Ivan's eyes were full of reproach, too. I blushed. I couldn't help it.

The first part of that week I stayed out of school to take care of Dad who was still pretty weak and dazed. He was a strong man at heart still, though, and so he was on the mend well enough by the end of the week that I could leave him to Ivan's care and start back to classes and my job again.

I really meant to cut going out with Phil for a while. I really meant to stay around home. But when I saw him sitting next to me in study hall, when I remembered, with a flush of warmth, the way his lips had moved over mine, thrilling me to the depths of my soul, I couldn't be any different. I smiled at him, and inwardly I could hardly wait until Saturday night.

It was a beautiful spring evening Saturday, and I told Dad that I was going to Turnerville to the movies again with Mary and that I'd stay at Mary's overnight because the buses didn't run after ten o'clock.

By now the familiar lie came so easily that I didn't have to think about it even. I didn't even feel the old shame that I had to hide my wonderful love for Phil because my father didn't want me to date boys. I didn't even trouble to explain to Dad the way it was. I knew he'd forbid me to date Phil, to date any boy. And I wasn't going to stop having fun just because Dad was old-fashioned, just because Jake Nelson had made trouble for me once.

Phil and I went to the Blue Champagne Club in Turner City again, because Phil knew how I loved the bright lights, the crowds of gay people, and the dancing. At intermission we were standing out in the hall under the big glittering chandelier on the thick plush carpet, when suddenly I felt a coarse hand on my bare shoulder.

"Well," a thick voice drawled, "if it isn't little angel face out on a toot in the big city. Wonder how your pa'd like that if he knew about it!"

I whirled with a sick pang of horror. I knew that voice! I knew that touch! I turned to stare straight into the mocking, bloodshot eyes of Jake Nelson. He was wearing a cheap, sleazy blue suit, and he'd been drinking. Phil tugged at my arm. His face had gone stiff and white.

"Come on out of here, Jenny," he said to me. "We haven't time to talk with drunks."

Jake doubled his fists and growled, "Why you stinking son of a . . ." For a minute I was scared he was going to knock Phil in the face right there. But I guess he remembered the beating he'd gotten the last time he'd tried to fight Ivan, and he just stood there, swaying and leering at me.

"All dressed up sexy in your black dress, angel face," he taunted me. "I bet you let your rich Prince Charming have his way with you. Like you never did me . . ."

I wanted to cover my ears, to drag Phil away from Jake's filthy words. What would Phil think of me, knowing such vile farmhands as Jake! Thank God Jake didn't work for Dad anymore. Thank God Dad would never know!

"Phil," I murmured, "I want to go home."

Without a word, Phil led me away to the door, picked up our coats, and we started back to the car. I was so heartsick I couldn't say a word. So ashamed I couldn't look Phil in the face. What if he never wanted to see me again? I would die. I would just die!

He let me off at Mary's without so much as a kiss. Before I went in, he touched my arm and said soberly, "Are you ashamed to have me meet your father, Jenny? Is that why you've been acting this way, having me meet you on the corner, like a pick-up?"

Like a pick-up! The words were a slap in the face. Is that what Phil thought of me? A cheap pick-up! Was it true, then, that he'd never be serious about me, the way Mary had said? Oh, why did Jake Nelson have to turn up at the Blue Champagne Club that night! If I'd only been honest. If I'd only told Dad, introduced him to Phil, then everything would have been all right. I could have met Jake's accusations with a proud, uplifted head, with a certainty that I, at least, had played fair with Dad and Phil, the two people who said they loved me!

Tears were streaming down my face as I said to Phil, "Please, darling, let me explain. Let me make you understand! I'll introduce you to Dad. I'll find a way to make him approve of my going out somehow. Jake isn't working for us anymore. He . . ."

And standing there, I told Phil about what had happened to me last summer. A change came over his face. "You poor kid!" he exclaimed. "If only I'd known! I thought that maybe you'd gone out with him, that maybe once . . ."

And then he took me in his arms and kissed me, and everything looked all right again. I'd tell Dad, and try to make him understand somehow, and then I could date Phil without worrying if anybody Dad knew saw us. I didn't see how Dad could object if I told him how nice Phil was, and what a good family he came from.

Mary was waiting up for me again when I came in. "I have a surprise for you," she whispered excitedly the minute I stepped in the door, and from the happy look on her face, I could guess what the surprise was.

"Ned proposed tonight," Mary said. "He's saved up enough money to buy the Petersons' little cottage across the way, and Dad's giving him a sort of partnership in the chicken business. It's coming along real well."

I hugged her and said how happy I was, really. And I honestly was glad that she was so much in love and all. But I couldn't help feel a twinge as I remembered what she'd said about Phil and me. It was fine for her to be so pleased at getting married, but I still was a long way from having Phil propose to me. He was a senior, now, and his father was just waiting for him to take over the printing business. Somehow I just had to make Phil realize that he wanted me, that he needed me very badly.

I was pretty tense when I went home the next day. But, I told myself, I didn't have anything to worry about, really. I figured on telling Dad about Phil, and explaining how things were. He might fuss and complain a bit, but I was old enough now to hold my own. And Dad might even take a shine to Phil, once he met him.

I walked into the kitchen, and there was Dad, sitting moodily over the kitchen table, drinking coffee he'd made in the old china pot. He had a black scowl on his face, the same mean look I'd seen him give a farmhand who tried to get away with taking boxes of berries home, or ears of corn, on the sly. I went over to him and said softly, "Hey, Pop, what's the trouble?"

"So it's you," he growled at me sullenly. "It's about time you came back!"

I stood motionless, stricken with fear. Had someone told him already about Phil and me? A cold tremor rose up my spine and his next words confirmed my worst fears.

"Saw Jake Nelson slinking around the barn this morning. Asked him what his business was, snooping around like that. Gave me a nasty smile and said he'd seen you at that low city dive, the Blue Champagne Club, last night. What've you got to say for yourself?"

My mouth dropped open, but no words came. Dad went on. "Ivan was with me, and he gave Jake another belt in the jaw for spitting out filthy lies. Well, say something! Don't just stare at me!"

His voice rose to a high, jagged pitch. I shuddered, sick at heart. I couldn't lie. I couldn't lie this time, even if they might believe my word over Jake's. How could I ever explain about Phil now? How could I ever make Dad understand? If only I'd told him the truth sooner!

I stammered, "D-Dad, I've . . . I've been meaning to tell you . . . I did go, but . . ."

"So, it *is* true!" Dad rose heavily from his chair, his face purple with rage. "My own daughter, playing around fast and loose with those rich fellows. Lying to me! After the way I brought her up! Oh, I'll teach you, you little cheat . . ."

And as he moved in toward me, I remembered in a flash that time I'd dressed up in Mother's gown and he'd come at me and struck me. I stood there, powerless to move, my whole world collapsing about my ears.

Dad raised his arm to strike, then, and I instinctively braced myself for the blow. But something happened. He dropped his hand, clutched at his side, and stood there, swaying unsteadily, his face gray with agony.

"My . . . my heart . . ." he groaned, and with that, he slumped to the floor.

I rushed to him, overcome with remorse. I'd been the cause of this, of my father having another heart attack. He might even die, all because of me.

I dragged Dad up onto his bed and called the doctor to come right away. My voice shook as I described what had happened to Dad. I just said he'd had a shock, but I didn't say whose fault the shock was. I didn't say that it was all my fault.

It seemed years before the doctor came, and I was alone in my anguish and self-torment. I dropped to my knees by Dad's bed and gave thanks to God when the doctor told me Dad was going to be all right again. Never the same, never able to do the heavy work he was used to. But he would live.

That night as I sat up and watched over Dad, lying there on the bed, breathing feebly, I vowed to tell him as soon as he was well enough that I was in love with Phil Forester, that I even wanted to marry him if he ever saw fit to ask me.

I never realized then that the Foresters might cause more trouble for Phil when they found out about his love for me than I'd caused Dad by my lying. I never realized that when people like the Foresters are rich and well-off and proud, they won't see their son marry a poor farm girl, no matter now pretty he thinks she is, no matter how he says he loves her!

But for the time being, I was satisfied with my choice, with my determination to persuade Dad how good and right my love for Phil Forester was.

All during spring vacation from high I stayed around the house and nursed Dad. He had orders to stay in bed for about a month, and to go easy on anything strenuous from that time on. I don't know what we would have done if Ivan hadn't been around to take things over and manage the farm for us.

I could do a lot of the farm chores, but it was Ivan who took over the heavy man's work and directed the other farmhands the way Dad had done. I never realized how much Dad had been getting to depend on Ivan until one day I walked into Dad's bedroom with some hot beef broth for him.

Ever since I'd admitted to the truth of Jake's story, Dad hadn't really talked to me, or given me a chance to explain myself. Every time I'd bring up the subject of Phil he'd wave all my talk aside with one sweep of his hand and say wearily, "Some other time, Jenny. I don't want to hear about anything now. Some other time."

What could I do? Phil had gone away with his family to spend the two weeks of our spring vacation in Bermuda, and I knew the Greenwoods were going to Bermuda for vacation, too. The Foresters and the Greenwoods were very close friends. They lived in the same part of town, and belonged to the same country club, and played golf together. How could Phil help but be influenced by his parents?

I was sick with fear that he might never come back to me. That these two weeks away might decide him that he'd be a fool to risk spoiling the wonderful easy kind of living he'd known all his life for me, a girl who had nothing to her name but a few acres of farm soil.

Matters began to come to a head when I walked into Dad's room that day with the beef soup. Ivan was standing there in his farm overalls, deeply tanned, even in early May, from working in the greenhouses. He and Dad were in serious discussion, but they broke off as soon as I came in the door. I had an uneasy feeling that they were talking about me, the way they stopped in the middle of what they were saying and looked sort of sheepish. The same feeling had hit me a long while before, back in the girl's powder room at Turnerville High.

Ivan was the first to speak. "Mr. Martin," he said, "I really think we ought to talk this over with Jenny before we do anything about it. After all, she should have the right to say what she feels inside."

Dad sighed. "You tell her, Ivan. I haven't got the strength." He lay back on the pillow, and suddenly I noticed with a shock how pale and withered Dad's face looked, and how his eyes, that once twinkled with such spirit, were dulled and faded. The change in him hit me all at once, and I wanted to run and throw my arms around him and beg his forgiveness for all the hurt I'd given him. Oh, if only I'd obeyed my impulse then, how different everything might have been! Why is it that we realize how proud and selfish we are only when it is too late!

But I didn't move. I just stood there, silent. If there was one thing Jenny Martin had learned at Turnerville High, that was pride. Here was one girl who wouldn't take sympathy and pity . . . or give it.

Ivan looked at me and twisted his visor cap in his hands.

"It's like this, Jenny," he said very low. "Your dad has been getting to think as how he isn't as strong as he used to be, and how he needs a sort of partner about the farm, and . . . and he's offered the job to me."

I began, "Why, I think that's wonderful, Ivan! You've been such a help around here for so long! I can't think of anyone who deserves a partnership more . . ."

But Ivan went on, moistening his lips. "That isn't all, Jenny. Your father wants to leave the farm to me in his will. He'd kind of figured that someday you'd . . . you'd marry, maybe, and sort of settle down and pick up where he left off . . . but he thinks now you maybe haven't got the feeling for the land he'd hoped you would."

Ivan tried to soften the blow as much as he could, and inwardly I was desperately grateful to him for it. But every word struck into my brain like a poisoned arrow. Me, leave the farm! That's what it amounted to in the end. Jenny Martin, "Pop" Martin's daughter, leaving the farm! Backing out of something that had been part of the family for generations now. All the shame I'd had for Dad's manners, and Ivan's simple good-heartedness, all the hatred I'd built up for my background dissolved right then.

But even as I stood there, a clear, mean little voice inside me spoke up selfishly and said: Jenny Martin, isn't this just what you've been waiting for? A way out? Think of Phil, and the pretty clothes you can buy at the shops in town, and the music, and the dancing, and the laughing crowds in the city. Think of your pretty mother who died in childbirth on the farm in winter, just because no doctor could get to her in the blizzard. You owe it to her to have a wonderful life. You owe it to yourself!

"If you feel any different, Jenny," Ivan was saying, "if you really would like to help keep the Martin farm running, just say so. Just say so right now, and everything will be all right with us."

I took a deep breath. On my choice hung so many things. The possibility of a happy future with Phil, Dad's peace of mind in old age. And strangely enough, something in Ivan's eyes said he'd be deeply affected by my decision too.

"Could I have some time?" I asked. "About a week or two to think it over, to decide?"

Dad spoke up for the first time. "Let her have two weeks, Ivan. Two weeks from today."

In my head a plan was beginning. I'd see Phil when he came back. I'd find out if he was really serious about me, serious enough to get married. And if he wasn't . . . well, I wouldn't think about that yet.

School started up again, and during the day I left Dad in the care of Ivan, confident that he was in safe hands. I started back that first day feeling that I had the weight of the world on my shoulders.

It was in study hall that I first saw Phil. He was tan from his vacation in Bermuda, and handsomer than I'd ever remembered him. My heart caught in my throat. Was everything the same? Did he still love me? I was worried.

Because Alison Greenwood had a beautiful tan after her vacation. And she looked radiant and glowing and very happy. I was in a cold sweat of nervousness until Phil grinned at me the way he always had, across his books, and signaled me to wait for him after class.

"You're looking pale, honey," he said. "Anything wrong?"

Wrong! How could I tell him that everything was wrong, everything was uncertain. I tried to make light of his remark.

"If I'd had a vacation in Bermuda, maybe I wouldn't look so anemic!"

"The same old Jenny," Phil laughed as we walked down the hall to my next class. His face grew serious, then. "Say, Jen, I've got a couple of important things I want to talk over with you when we've got a big stretch of time together. How about this Saturday? How about coming over to my house for dinner?"

I gasped. Phil had never before asked me to come to his house, any more than I'd asked him to come to mine. We'd had a sort of unspoken agreement that there was no sense of bringing our families into this, because it would only cause trouble.

And now he was asking me to dinner! I'd meet his parents! Could it be that Phil wanted to marry me after all? Was this why he had invited me to his home? Was this what he wanted to talk over with me?

The excitement was unbearable. "Yes, Phil," I exclaimed. "Yes, I'd love to. Pick me up at my house, Phil. At my house."

His eyes met mine in a smile of understanding. "You're sure it's all right with your dad?"

"I'll make it all right," I promised happily.

And that very afternoon when I went home after working in the dress shop I went in to see Dad, who was sitting up now, and shuffling around the house in his slippers a bit whenever he felt up to it.

"Dad," I said, "Phil Forester, the boy I've been going out with, is coming to call for me this Saturday. I'm going over to his family's for dinner. I want you to meet Phil, Dad. I think you'll like him."

Dad slanted me a hard look. "So we're not good enough for you," he grumbled.

"Of course you are, Dad. It's just . . . it's just . . ."

"I know," he finished for me. "It's just that you're sick of the farm, and all caught up with the stuff big money can buy . . ."

"That's not fair, Dad," I cried hotly. "That's not fair! I love Phil. Money has nothing to do with it."

But even as I spoke those words, I knew that deep down inside I didn't quite believe myself. You know the old saying, "The lady doth protest too much"? Well, that's what I was doing. Protesting how much I loved Phil for himself alone, and not for his money. It was just, I reasoned to myself, that his money would help make life together more enjoyable. That was all. Or at least I was determined then to think that was all.

Well, Saturday came at last, and I got dressed up in my best navy blue silk dress and white topper that I'd bought down at the shop. Just about all my pay went for clothes, now, because I could get really ritzy things at a big discount, and I felt I had to keep getting new expensive dresses to please Phil, to prove that I could live up to the Turner Estates crowd.

Phil pulled up in the drive, and it looked funny to see the shiny light blue convertible there, instead of the old black farm truck that Ivan always drove. Dad shook Phil's hand and grunted something, and went back to his paper. It started the evening off on a strained note, but I felt it was a beginning, anyway. Better than me walking down to the crossing as if I were ashamed of my home, and of my dad.

On the way over to his house, Phil told me his news. His draft papers were waiting for him when he came back from Bermuda, and he was being shipped across the States to a training camp in California as soon as he got his things together.

The thought of Turnerville without Phil made me sick with loneliness. I couldn't let him go away, I couldn't let him go without me. If he really loved me, he'd marry me before he left. This was the test I'd been waiting for . . . and deathly afraid of.

That evening at the Foresters', instead of being the homey companionable little gathering I expected, was really an ordeal. A butler met us at the door, after we'd parked in the long, curved gravel drive, and for an awful minute I made the mistake of thinking he was Phil's father. With that for a beginning, I entered the living room with shaking knees, in spite of the fact I knew I looked my best.

Mrs. Forester sailed up to meet me in a full-length gold lace dinner gown and a corsage of orchids. She was tall, white-haired, and very stylish. But her greeting was as chilly and forbidding as an iceberg.

"So this is little Jenny Martin from the farm," she caroled, lingering too long on the last word. "I'm so pleased to meet you." But what her look said was: You cheap little farm girl. I wouldn't have you in the house if Phil hadn't begged me to invite you.

I managed a shaky smile, and stammered, "Pleased to meet you, Mrs. Forester."

A maid in a green uniform announced dinner then, and we went into the dining room. The table was set with candles, and a gorgeous centerpiece of red hothouse roses was arranged in the middle of the shining white linen cloth. I was awestruck by everything in the Foresters' mansion, the high ceilings, the spiral staircase, the chandeliers, and the way Mrs. Forester managed her servants with just a nod or a motion of her little finger.

But I could see right from the start that she meant to make the evening as unpleasant for me as possible. "You'll have to excuse Mr. Forester for not being here," she explained over the steaming bouillon. "But he's at a banquet of the trustees of the Turner City College. One of the jobs Phil will probably have someday." And she smiled proudly at her son.

I tried to say something, but the words just stuck in my throat, and every time I did manage to comment on anything, like the beautiful flowers, Mrs. Forester would twist my remarks to make me either sound like a stupid country girl or a cheap little gold-digger.

"Yes, I suppose you're not used to much but daisies and dandelions out on the farm," she said, giving a crystal laugh at her own cruel little joke.

I could see Phil was disturbed by his mother and her snide innuendoes, because he hardly talked all through the meal, but his jaw grew tense, and his mouth set hard. Right after supper we went into the living room to have after-dinner coffee, and Mrs. Forester brought up the subject about Phil's being drafted.

"Phil will probably have to serve in the army for a while, and both Mr. Forester and I want him to be free to come back and take over Mr. Forester's printing firm, and more or less carry on our place in the Turner Estates."

The words were innocent enough, but the way she twisted them and with the firm, supercilious expression on her face, I could see that she meant every word for Phil's benefit, as well as mine. In other words, she didn't want Phil getting attached to anybody who would hinder his rise in their social world. And anybody meant very especially me, Jenny Martin, the farm girl from the wrong side of town.

I wanted to cry out to spite her. I wanted to tell her that someday I'd have a house and a car and clothes just as fine as hers. But I controlled myself, and bit my tongue to keep from answering back.

Right about then, Phil had enough. He got up and said, "Excuse us, Mother, but Jenny and I are going to a show in town, and we have to leave now if we don't want to be late."

I was never so glad to get away from anywhere as I was from the Foresters' house, and all the luxury they took so for granted.

Sitting beside Phil in the car, I couldn't bring myself to say anything, my face still burned so from Mrs. Forester's taunting double-edged remarks. I felt anger and pride rising in me. I'd show her! I'd show her that I could make Phil happy!

As if by unspoken agreement, Phil headed out to Lakeside Drive. He took a lonely road into the woods then, to a turnoff where hardly anybody ever went, and stopped the car.

"Jenny," he said, turning to me, "I'm real sorry about the way Mother acted tonight. She had no right. She and Dad know how fond I am of you, how much I've been seeing you lately, and they'll do anything to keep us apart."

"Oh, Phil," I said miserably, "I love you so!"

"I love you, too, darling. More than I can say." And then he took me in his arms, as if to shut me away safe from all the meanness and cruelty in the world, and we clung together in hungry kisses that spoke tenderly of our love.

How can I explain what happened to me in the next minutes? I felt so lonely, so bereft at the thought of Phil's being drafted, of his having to leave school, that I wanted to die. And after that agonizing evening, I felt that the only way I could win out against the Foresters was to give Phil my love, all my love.

"I need you so, darling," Phil whispered passionately in my ear, straining me to him, tight against his body. I began to thrill with a desire I'd never experienced before. Desire to know Phil's body, to give myself to him in complete love.

His strong hands, moving surely over the curves of my young flesh, awoke in me flames of longing. Insistently, huskily, he murmured, "Jenny, dear! Please, please, love me while we have time. Before I have to go away and leave you. Oh, my darling! I need you so desperately!"

Something in my heart answered Phil's broken plea. This was the man I loved, and he was going to be taken from me. If I did not love him now, I might never see him again. Responding to Phil's urgent kisses, I let all thoughts of Dad, of the farm, of the problems that lay in wait for both of us on the morrow, fade away as if they never were.

All that was left was the warm spring darkness, the comforting circle of Phil's arms, and the desire of our mutual love.

"Phil, darling, I need you too. I need you terribly!" I breathed my answer lovingly into his ear, and he gave a hoarse little cry that tore at my heart and drew me to him.

His long deep kisses made me arch my back up against the driving strength of his body in a frenzy of inflamed longing. The fierce power of his love made me melt beneath his touch in a heated yearning for fulfilment. The June darkness enfolded the moving passion of our union, and in the sweetness of love, our hearts pulsed at last as one.

Phil left for California the next week. He did not marry me. You see, Mr. and Mrs. Forester made it plain that they would disinherit Phil and see that I had a hard time of it while he was away if he so much as thought of crossing them.

And Phil explained to me that when he came back from the service he'd have saved enough pay for us to get married comfortably on, and by then, his family might have come around. If he married me now, we'd both be left without a cent.

Phil's arguments seemed sensible enough. Almost too sensible. He evidently hadn't thought of the one solution to our troubles that seemed possible. I put it to him the last night we were together.

"Phil, couldn't I come with you? Couldn't we face the world together in California, and get a fresh start? I could get a job and wait there for you while you were overseas."

Phil didn't answer for a minute, and then he said. "Darling, you've never been away from home before. I couldn't bear to leave you in a strange town in California all alone. What if something happened to me? What if I never came back . . . ?"

"Phil!" I cried, stricken with horror at his voicing the thought that had haunted me so often lately. "Phil, don't talk that way! Of course you'll come back!"

"To the sweetest little girl this side of the ocean," he said tenderly, taking me in his arms. And in the final farewell that followed, we dropped the subject of my going with him. I would stay at home, safe on the farm, until Phil Forester returned to make me his rightful bride.

That last night was the most beautiful memory of our love that I had. The familiar tenderness of Phil's hands on my body, the growing passion of his kisses, awaked the answering response in me that thrilled to the depths of my soul. We were lost in the wonderful union of two people hopelessly in love. Two people about to be separated for heaven knew how long.

That night I cried myself to sleep, wanting to remember always the burning warmth of Phil's lips upon the softness of my body, wanting to conserve in me forever the beautiful afterglow of his love.

After Phil was gone, I didn't have much heart for anything. School, or work in the shop, or my old friends. I didn't have anything to look forward to anymore but Phil's letters.

Dad knew now that I would stay on the farm only till Phil returned from the army. He knew that I would never consent to give up the life that Phil had offered me, and so Ivan was put down in Dad's will as the next owner of the farm.

Phil wrote the dearest, most loving letters from camp every day. I would read them over and over, hardly able to wait till I got home from work to see if I'd gotten any mail. In his letters he told me how much he missed me, and needed me, and how he hoped someday soon to come back and give me his name as well as his love.

The year ripened into summer, and I decided I might as well work on the farm again as crew boss, because Ivan and Dad could use somebody who knew the ropes, and I actually liked being out in the sun, working in the fields again for some strange reason. It gave me a kind of peace at heart, I guess, in place of the quick-paced work indoors at the shop in town.

One week, then, there were no letters from Phil, and after that only a brief note to say that he was through with training and being shipped suddenly to Korea.

From then on I waited day by day in agony for some word, some news that my loved one was still safe and well. But I heard nothing. Nothing until I read in the *Turnerville Sentinel* that Philip Forester, beloved son of Mr. and Mrs. Forester, was killed in action on a mud slope in Korea.

The news came at the same time that I found out I was going to have Phil's baby. Plunged in an emotional whirlpool, torn between shattered grief at Phil's death and a blind horror at the knowledge I was going to become an unwed mother, I retreated to my room, too sick to eat.

Lying there on my bed, ravaged with tears, I heard the words go on over and over again in my head like a phonograph record: "Why didn't you marry him, why didn't you marry him?"

If only I'd begged, pleaded with Phil to marry me, I wouldn't be in the trouble I was in now. I would be able to bear his child proudly, to salvage this part of Phil and his love, and to devote to the baby the adoration I had lavished on Phil.

But even in the midst of my pain and anguish, I realized deep down that Phil could have married me if he'd really wanted to, no matter what his family said. We'd have gotten along somehow if we'd kept our love strong and alive. How many couples before us had faced the same problems . . . and solved them? But Phil had chosen to keep the prestige and backing of his family, even if in the long run it meant hurting me.

Salt tears of self-pity ran down my cheeks as I buried my face in the pillow and cried as if my heart would break. I'd wanted Phil's love, and all the things Phil's world could offer. I gave him my love, my mind and body, and what did I end up with? An illegitimate child!

Oh, if Phil had known, if he had imagined what would happen to me, I know he would have married me! But the fact remained, cold and heartless: Phil was dead. Nothing would ever be the same again.

And then something in me woke up. Something that had been neglected for a long time: my sense of honesty, of fairness. Mercilessly I faced myself for what I was the first time in months: a selfish, proud girl with ambitions too big for her to manage. A girl who hurt her dad to the quick, lied to him, cheated him, for the secret, passionate embraces of a rich boy, a boy who could not understand what it meant to live on a farm, to love the land. A boy who would never be able to understand.

I decided then that I would begin facing up to myself and stop trying to run away, to escape the consequences of my wrong actions. I would have the baby on the farm, and bring it up, and face the shame and scandal, if necessary. Or if Dad disowned me, sent me away in disgrace, I would get a job in Turner City so I could support my child and give it the love that was its due in the eyes of God, if not in the laws of man!

Right away I went downstairs to find Dad. He was out behind the farmhouse, puttering around in the garden.

"Well, daughter?" he asked when he saw I wanted to talk to him. Then he noticed the tear-stains on my face and asked what was wrong.

"Dad," I said, struggling to hold back the tears, "Dad, Phil Forester is dead . . . killed . . . over in Korea . . ."

Dad straightened his back and looked at me long and hard. "It's a bitter blow for you, Jenny, I'll warrant. But truth to tell, I'm a darn sight happier for you that you won't have to bear the brunt of living under the shadow of those high and mighty Foresters. They'd have made life a sore trouble for you, Jenny girl."

Even though I knew the truth of Dad's words, and of his deep love for me through all the struggles and disappointments he'd had, I could hardly bear to tell him what I had to say. But he'd find out sooner or later, and it was best for me to be the one to break the news to him. I knew that now.

"But Dad," I whispered faintly, "you don't understand. I'm . . . I'm going to have Phil's baby."

Dad's face blanched white and the gardening trowel fell from his hand. In a stroke of horror I remembered what the doctor had said about his heart, about how any deep surprise or shock might be fatal. In my grief and shame, I hadn't realized what my news would do to Dad.

"Help me, Jenny," he gasped. "Help me into the house."

I tried to lift Dad from the ground, but he was too heavy for me alone. Frantically I ran to the greenhouse and called for the one person who would be able to help and understand. Ivan.

Ivan came running, pulling off his gardening gloves, and between the two of us, we got Dad into bed. The doctor came, but this time his face was grave. There was nothing he could do, he said. Dad's heart was fast giving out. This final blow had been too much for him.

But before Dad died, he managed to tell me the one secret he'd kept from me all my life. The horrible truth he'd tried to protect me from all during my childhood. Mother hadn't died in childbirth the way he'd always said. She'd run away with a rich actor from Turner City a few months after I'd been born.

Mother had been a pretty girl like me, Dad said, eager for parties, and novelty in life. The farm had been fun for her for a while when the experience was still fresh, but after a bit, she'd gotten bored with the daily routine, and she'd hated the idea of being pregnant and having a baby because it spoiled her slim, attractive figure.

So she'd taken up with an actor in traveling stock whom she'd met on a shopping spree in the city. And one night, when Dad was away getting some new farm equipment, she packed her bags and went off in the actor's convertible.

Only the two of them never got very far. They'd both been drinking, and the car was speeding along the causeway outside Turner City when it swerved into a ditch, and both Mother and her lover had been thrown out. Mother died instantly, her neck broken, and the actor remained unconscious and died in the hospital the next day.

The scandal had been spread in all the papers, but Dad had brought me up in the sheltered farmhouse, away from the mainstream of life, and gradually the sensational story was forgotten, fading into oblivion after the first splash it made in the headlines. And Dad had lavished on me all the love he had wanted to give to Mother, and protected me from the shame her escapade had caused him.

In the hour before Dad's death, I told him I would help Ivan and stay with the farm, if Dad would let me. Because along with my heritage of Mother's looks, I'd inherited Dad's deep love of the land. I knew that now.

And Dad died with a faint smile on his lips. His last words were a blessing upon me and my unborn child and a whisper, "The land will heal you, daughter. The land will heal you."

Heartbroken, I bent in tears over Dad's body, after the last breath of life had gone, and I cursed myself for causing such hurt and hardship to the person who loved me most in the world.

As I sat there sobbing by Dad's bed, I was aware of another presence in the room. Ivan had remained nearby in case he was needed. In the lean power of his muscular frame, I sensed a comfort and security that I clung to spiritually.

"Oh, Ivan," I sobbed brokenly. "What shall I do? Whatever shall I do? It's my fault! It's all my fault Dad died. I was so selfish, so thoughtless!"

In answer, Ivan came over to me, saying the same words he'd said so long ago when he had found me shaken and afraid. "It'll be all right, Jenny." Awkwardly, with his big, strong hands, he kindly stroked my hair. "It'll be all right, I promise you."

"But how can you bear me, Ivan?" I cried out in a frenzy of self-torment. "How can you stand to be so nice to me when you know what I've done? Lied to the most wonderful dad a girl ever had! Gotten . . . gotten pregnant . . ." The word choked me.

"You want to know?" Ivan said slowly. "You really want to know?"

Something in his voice compelled me to stop crying and listen to him.

"It's like this, Jenny," Ivan began. "I love you. I've loved you for a long time, now. And someday, if ever you could learn to love me, I'd like to marry you. I'd like to give you and . . . and the baby my name."

I could not speak for humbleness at Ivan's revelation of his love. He went on.

"Your dad's been like a father to me, Jenny, ever since I've been here. And ever since I began working on the farm, I've wanted to carry on his work, and to marry you. That is, if ever you'd consent to have me."

It came to me then, in a flash of clearness, how blind I'd been. For it had always been Ivan who was there to comfort me and sustain me in a crisis. To give me safety, support. And I had always taken his blonde good looks and gentle manner for granted, the way I had taken Dad's love for granted. I had used it when I needed it, and never given anything in return.

"Oh, Ivan!" I cried out. "How can I ever deserve your love?"

"You would make me happy for the rest of my life, Jenny, if you would be my wife," Ivan said.

"But Ivan . . . the baby . . . can you forgive me? Can you ever forgive me?"

"I love you, Jenny," Ivan said simply. "One cannot be heartless and unforgiving when one loves."

I waited for a while before I gave Ivan my answer. I had to be sure, I had to know this time that I could come to him with honesty and love in return for the faith he had in me.

And after I truthfully searched my heart, I gave him my answer. Ivan and I were married soon in a quiet simple ceremony, with just Mary and Ned Potter for witnesses. And in the months that followed, I bore Phil's child, a little son.

We still live on the farm, Ivan and I, and Ivan has shown himself to be the most wonderful husband and father a woman could wish. It has been from Ivan that I learned how rich and satisfying unselfish, faithful love could be.

There is a little girl, now, Ivan's child, to play with my son, and Ivan looks on both of them with equal love. The farm flourishes too, these days, prospering under our watchful care, growing well, as all things grow under the sunshine of true love.

The lesson I learned in my struggles and my torment was a hard one. And even now there are times when I recall the grievous wrongs I committed and wonder how I deserve the unbounded joy of sharing Ivan's love.

But from Ivan I found that no matter how black one's sins are, there is grace and forgiveness in honest love and faith. It was when I first began to be honest with myself that I realized home is truly where the heart is.

For neither Phil nor I could have been completely happy if we had always been haunted by the sorrows of our parents, pulled apart by conflicting tensions. I see now that deep love and good living far outweigh the flashy tinsel excitements of big spending and secret, shameful passion.

As Ivan and I sit out on the farm porch, looking at our two beautiful children playing together happily in the fresh air and sunshine, we both give thanks to God for letting life work out so joyously for both of us. And in the light of the warm sun, the grass of our own fields is far greener and brighter than the grass in anybody else's yard.

Superman and Paula Brown's New Snowsuit

Written: 6–7 November 1954
Published: *Smith Review* (Spring 1955): 19–21[*]

The year the war began I was in the fifth grade at the Annie F. Warren Grammar School in Winthrop, and that was the winter I won the prize for drawing the best Civil Defense signs. That was also the winter of Paula Brown's new snowsuit, and even now, thirteen years later, I can recall the changing colors of those days, clear and definite as patterns seen through a kaleidoscope.

---

[*] Printed with a biographical sketch of SP: 'Sylvia Plath, '55, has been a long and faithful contributor to the *Review*. The story on Page 19 and the poem on Page 12 <'Danse Macabre'> mark her last appearances in this magazine. She has been published before in *Harper's* and *Mademoiselle*.' Reprinted in *Harper's and Queen* (October 1977): 222–8.

Probably written for English 347a, Short Story Writing. SP took 347a twice at Smith College, in autumn 1952 as 'Style and Form' under the tutelage of Robert Gorham Davis and in 1954–5 as 'Short Story Writing' during the autumn of her senior year with Alfred Kazin. During the term in Kazin's course, SP produced several stories; however, it is unclear which of the following she turned in as assignments: 'Broken Glass', 'Christmas Encounter', 'Coincidentally Yours', 'The Day Mr. Prescott Died', 'In the Mountains' (later rewritten as 'The Christmas Heart'), 'The Smoky Blue Piano', 'Superman and Paula Brown's New Snowsuit' and 'Tongues of Stone'. Three stories, 'Christmas Encounter', 'Coincidentally Yours' and 'Broken Glass' do not appear to be extant. Three stories composed in late 1954 and early 1955, 'Home Is Where the Heart Is', 'Marcia Ventura and the Ninth Kingdom' and 'Tomorrow Begins Today' were written for the Christopher Awards.

I lived on the bay side of town, on Johnson Avenue, opposite the Logan Airport, and before I went to bed each night, I used to kneel by the west window of my room and look over to the lights of Boston that blazed and blinked far off across the darkening water. The sunset flaunted its pink flag above the airport, and the sound of waves was lost in the perpetual droning of the planes. I marveled at the moving beacons on the runway and watched, until it grew completely dark, the flashing red and green lights that rose and set in the sky like shooting stars. The airport was my Mecca, my Jerusalem. All night I dreamed of flying.

Those were the days of my Technicolor dreams. Mother believed that I should have an enormous amount of sleep, and so I was never really tired when I went to bed. This was the best time of the day, when I could lie in the vague twilight, drifting off to sleep, making up dreams inside my head the way they should go. My flying dreams were believable as a landscape by Dalí, so real that I would awake with a sudden shock, a breathless sense of having tumbled like Icarus from the sky and caught myself on the soft bed just in time.

These nightly adventures in space began when Superman started invading my dreams and teaching me how to fly. He used to come roaring by in his shining blue suit with his cape whistling in the wind, looking remarkably like my Uncle Frank, who was living with Mother and me. In the magic whirring of his cape I could hear the wings of a hundred seagulls, the motors of a thousand planes.

I was not the only worshipper of Superman in our block. David Sterling, a pale, bookish boy who lived down the street, shared my love for the sheer poetry of flight. Before supper every night, we listened to *Superman* together on the radio, and during the day we made up our own adventures on the way to school.

The Annie F. Warren Grammar School was a redbrick building, set back from the main highway on a black tar street, surrounded by barren gravel playgrounds. Out by the parking lot David and I found a perfect alcove for our Superman dramas. The dingy back entrance to the school was deep set in a long passageway which was an excellent place for surprise captures and sudden rescues.

During recess, David and I came into our own. We ignored the boys playing baseball on the gravel court and the girls giggling at dodgeball in the dell. Our Superman games made us outlaws, yet gave us a sense of windy superiority. We even found a stand-in for a villain in Sheldon Fein, the sallow mamma's boy on our block who was left out of the boys' games because he cried whenever anybody tagged him and always managed to fall down and skin his fat knees.

At first, we had to prompt Sheldon in his part, but after a while he became an expert on inventing tortures and even carried them out in private, beyond the game. He used to pull the wings from flies and the legs off grasshoppers, and keep the broken insects captive in a jar hidden under his bed where he could take them out in secret and watch them struggling. David and I never played with Sheldon except at recess. After school we left him to his mamma, his bonbons, and his helpless insects.

At this time my Uncle Frank was living with us while waiting to be drafted, and I was sure that he bore an extraordinary resemblance to Superman incognito. David couldn't see his likeness as clearly as I did, but he admitted that Uncle Frank was the strongest man he had ever known, and could do lots of tricks like making caramels disappear under napkins and walking on his hands.

That same winter, war was declared, and I remember sitting by the radio with Mother and Uncle Frank and feeling a queer foreboding in the air. Their voices were low and serious, and their talk was of planes and German bombs. Uncle Frank said something about Germans in America being put in prison for the duration, and Mother kept saying over and over again about Daddy: "I'm only glad Otto didn't live to see this; I'm only glad Otto didn't live to see it come to this."

In school we began to draw Civil Defense signs, and that was when I beat Jimmy Lane in our block for the fifth-grade prize. Every now and then we would practice an air raid. The fire bell would ring and we would take up our coats and pencils and file down the creaking stairs to the basement where we sat in special corners according to our color tags, and put the pencils between our teeth so the bombs wouldn't make us bite our tongues by mistake. Some of the little children in the lower grades would cry because it was dark in the cellar, with only the bare ceiling lights on the cold black stone.

The threat of war was seeping in everywhere. At recess, Sheldon became a Nazi and borrowed a goose-step from the movies, but his Uncle Macy was really over in Germany, and Mrs. Fein began to grow thin and pale because she heard that Macy was a prisoner and then nothing more.

The winter dragged on, with a wet east wind coming always from the ocean, and the snow melting before there was enough for coasting. One Friday afternoon, just before Christmas, Paula Brown gave her annual birthday party, and I was invited because it was for all the children on our block. Paula lived across from Jimmy Lane on Somerset Terrace, and nobody on our block really liked her, because she was bossy and stuck-up, with pale skin and long red pigtails and watery blue eyes.

She met us at the door of her house in a white organdy dress, her red hair tied up in sausage curls with a satin bow. Before we could sit down at the table for birthday cake and ice cream, she had to show us all her presents. There were a great many because it was both her birthday and Christmastime too.

Paula's favorite present was a new snowsuit, and she tried it on for us. The snowsuit was powder blue and came in a silver box from Sweden, she said. The front of the jacket was all embroidered with pink and white roses and bluebirds, and the leggings had embroidered straps. She even had a little white angora beret and angora mittens to go with it.

After dessert we were all driven to the movies by Jimmy Lane's father to see the late afternoon show as a special treat. Mother had found out that the main feature was *Snow White* before she would let me go, but she hadn't realized that there was a war picture playing with it.

The movie was about Japanese prisoners who were being tortured by having no food or water. Our war games and the radio programs were all made up, but this was real, this really happened. I blocked my ears to shut out the groans of the thirsty, starving men, but I could not tear my eyes away from the screen.

Finally, the prisoners pulled down a heavy log from the low rafters and jammed it through the clay wall so they could reach the fountain in the court, but just as the first man got to the water, the Japanese began shooting the prisoners dead, and stamping on them, and laughing. I was sitting on the aisle, and I stood up then in a hurry and ran out to the girls' room where I knelt over a toilet bowl and vomited up the cake and ice cream.

After I went to bed that night, as soon as I closed my eyes, the prison camp sprang to life in my mind, and again the groaning men broke through the walls, and again they were shot down as they reached the trickling fountain. No matter how hard I thought of Superman before I went to sleep, no crusading blue figure came roaring down in heavenly anger to smash the yellow men who invaded my dreams. When I woke up in the morning, my sheets were damp with sweat.

Saturday was bitterly cold, and the skies were gray and blurred with the threat of snow. I was dallying home from the store that afternoon, curling up my chilled fingers in my mittens, when I saw a couple of kids playing Chinese tag out in front of Paula Brown's house.

Paula stopped in the middle of the game to eye me coldly. "We need someone else," she said. "Want to play?" She tagged me on the ankle then, and I hopped around and finally caught Sheldon Fein as he was bending down to fasten one of his fur-lined overshoes. An early thaw had melted away the snow in the street, and the tarred pavement was gritted with sand left from the snow trucks. In front of Paula's house somebody's car had left a glittering black stain of oil slick.

We went running about in the street, retreating to the hard, brown lawns when the one who was "It" came too close. Jimmy Lane came out of his house and stood watching us for a short while, and then joined in. Every time he was "It," he chased Paula in her powder blue snowsuit, and she screamed shrilly, and looked around at him with her wide, watery eyes, and he always managed to catch her.

Only one time she forgot to look where she was going, and as Jimmy reached out to tag her, she slid into the oil slick. We all froze when she went down on her side as if we were playing statues. No one said a word, and for a minute there was only the sound of the planes across the bay. The dull, green light of late afternoon came closing down on us, cold and final as a window blind.

Paula's snowsuit was smeared wet and black with oil along the side. Her angora mittens were dripping like black cat's fur. Slowly, she sat up and looked at us standing around her, as if searching for something. Then, suddenly, her eyes fixed on me.

"You," she said deliberately, pointing at me, "you pushed me."

There was another second of silence, and then Jimmy Lane turned on me. "You did it," he taunted. "You did it."

Sheldon and Paula and Jimmy and the rest of them faced me with a strange joy flickering in the back of their eyes. "You did it, you pushed her," they said.

And even when I shouted, "I did not!" they were all moving in on me, chanting in a chorus, "Yes, you did, yes, you did, we saw you." In the well of faces moving toward me I saw no help, and I began to wonder if Jimmy had pushed Paula, or if she had fallen by herself, and I was not sure. I wasn't sure at all.

I started walking past them, walking home, determined not to run, but when I had left them behind me, I felt the sharp thud of a snowball on my left shoulder, and another. I picked up a faster stride and rounded the corner by Kelly's. There was my dark brown shingled house ahead of me, and inside, Mother and Uncle Frank, home on furlough. I began to run in the cold, raw evening toward the bright squares of light in the windows that were home.

Uncle Frank met me at the door. "How's my favorite trooper?" he asked, and he swung me so high in the air that my head grazed the ceiling. There was a big love in his voice that drowned out the shouting which still echoed in my ears.

"I'm fine," I lied, and he taught me some jujitsu in the living room until Mother called us for supper.

Candles were set on the white linen tablecloth, and miniature flames flickered in the silver and the glasses. I could see another room reflected beyond the dark dining-room window where three people laughed and talked in a secure web of light, held together by its indestructible brilliance.

All at once the doorbell rang, and Mother rose to answer it. I could hear David Sterling's high, clear voice in the hall. There was a cold draft from the open doorway, but he and Mother kept on talking, and he did not come in. When Mother came back to the table, her face was sad.

"Why didn't you tell me?" she said, "why didn't you tell me that you pushed Paula in the mud and spoiled her new snowsuit?"

A mouthful of chocolate pudding blocked my throat, thick and bitter. I had to wash it down with milk. Finally I said, "I didn't do it."

But the words came out like hard, dry little seeds, hollow and insincere. I tried again. "I didn't do it. Jimmy Lane did it."

"Of course we'll believe you," Mother said slowly, "but the whole neighborhood is talking about it. Mrs. Sterling heard the story from Mrs. Fein and sent David over to say we should buy Paula a new snowsuit. I can't understand it."

"I didn't do it," I repeated, and the blood beat in my ears like a slack drum. I pushed my chair away from the table, not looking at Uncle Frank or Mother sitting there, solemn and sorrowful in the candlelight.

The staircase to the second floor was dark, but I went down the long hall to my room without turning on the light switch and shut the door. A small, unripe moon was shafting squares of greenish light along the floor and the windowpanes were fringed with frost.

I threw myself fiercely down on my bed and lay there, dry-eyed and burning. After a while I heard Uncle Frank coming up the stairs and knocking on my door. When I didn't answer, he walked in and sat down on my bed. I could see his strong shoulders bulk against the moonlight, but in the shadows, his face was featureless.

"Tell me, honey," he said very softly, "tell me. You don't have to be afraid. We'll understand. Only tell me what really happened. You have never had to hide anything from me, you know that. Only tell me how it really happened."

"I told you," I said. "I told you what happened, and I can't make it any different. Not even for you I can't make it any different."

He sighed then and got up to go away. "Okay, honey," he said at the door. "Okay, but we'll pay for another snowsuit anyway just to make everybody happy, and ten years from now no one will ever know the difference."

The door shut behind him and I could hear his footsteps growing fainter as he walked off down the hall. I lay there alone in bed, feeling the black shadow creeping up the underside of the world like a flood tide. Nothing held, nothing was left. The silver airplanes and the blue capes all dissolved and vanished, wiped away like the crude drawings of a child in colored chalk from the colossal blackboard of the dark. That was the year the war began, and the real world, and the difference.

Home Is Where the Heart Is

Ts,[*] 27 January 1955, Lilly Library

"I really wish, Susan," Mrs. Arnold said to her eldest daughter with a sigh, "that you'd come home right after school just this once to take care of Ann. I need to do some shopping for the week, and then I'd like to drop in to see old Mrs. Cooper who just got back from the hospital yesterday, and it's simply impossible with the baby toddling around . . ."

"But Mother," Susan said tossing her pigtails with irritation, "I *told* you, Louise and Karen are going to the Dairy Bar again after school, and the whole gang will be there. I don't see why *I* have to be the only one who doesn't go . . ."

"All right, all right, Susan," Mr. Arnold said, looking up impatiently from his newspaper, "that's enough. I don't see why you couldn't help your mother just once in a while, Susan. It's not asking too much for you to come home . . ."

"Oh, never mind, Michael," Mrs. Arnold told her husband. "Susan wants to be with her friends, of course. It's important to belong at this stage . . . I can get the Cummings woman to come over again if I have to . . ."

The Arnold family of five was sitting around the table in the sunny breakfast nook. Warren Arnold, a good-looking dark-haired boy of sixteen, was

---

[*] Typescript with significant holograph and typewritten corrections and additions by SP. Written for the Christopher Awards. On versos are typed the following poems: 'Ennui', 'Bluebeard', 'Terminal' (two copies), 'To the Boy Inscrutable as God', 'Eve Describes Her Birthday Party', 'March 15 Muse', 'Sonnet: Van Winkle's Village' and 'The Complex Couch'.

finishing his cereal while Susan and her father were busy with their fried eggs. Baby Ann banged her spoon loudly against the high chair, and made several contented gurgling noises.

Mrs. Arnold rose to get more bread from the toaster, paused by Ann to wipe up a puddle of spilled orange juice from the highchair with a dishtowel, and then took a pot of steaming coffee from the stove. It was a Monday morning, like any other morning in the Arnold household.

A pile of dirty laundry lay in the corner of the kitchen by the basement door, and the sink was already full of pots and pans. Mrs. Arnold, a pretty, cheerful woman in her late thirties, gulped down the last of her coffee and got up to clear away the dirty dishes. Susan pushed back her chair in a hurry. "Scuse me, have to meet Karen at the corner. Bye, Mom, bye, Dad." And she was gone.

Warren had finished his breakfast and was sitting toying with his empty milk glass. His face was pensive. "Say, Dad," he said tentatively, "do you suppose I could have the car tonight?"

"Tonight?" Mr. Arnold looked up from his paper in surprise. "Why Monday night? You know I'll be needing it, I've got an important dinner engagement with a client."

"Oh, forget it," Warren said, sulkily, "it was just the basketball game tonight, that's all. I just thought I might possibly drive June over to Fairfax to watch me play, that's all."

"You can take June on the bus, can't you Warren?" Mrs. Arnold asked gently, running hot water into the dishpan. "I know it's not as glamorous, but why not save your car-night for the weekend? We only have one car, you know, and Dad does need it tonight. I'm sure June will understand."

"Oh, never mind." Warren shoved his chair back from the table and went to get his schoolbooks. The front door slammed behind him. At this point Ann began banging loudly on her highchair with her spoon again.

"Honestly," Mr. Arnold sighed to his wife, folding up the morning paper, "never a quiet minute. Have to go out for a little peace. Sometimes I wonder how you do it, darling. Managing to keep this three-ring circus running."

Mrs. Arnold managed a slightly tired smile. "I do manage, dear, and that's what counts. But what about this client tonight? Wouldn't you like to bring him home for dinner? He'll probably appreciate a home-cooked meal after that long trip east."

Mr. Arnold hesitated. "Oh, I wouldn't want to put you to any trouble, darling. He's really an important chap, head of the law firm in San Francisco. Wants to look our place over. I was the lucky one picked to explain the setup here to him. Thought I'd show him the town. You know, without distractions . . ."

Mrs. Arnold bent over the dishpan, biting her lip. "Yes, darling," was all she said. "Yes, I . . . know."

Mr. Arnold went to get his briefcase then, and came back in coat and hat to kiss his wife goodbye. "Keep the home fires burning, darling," he said, and was gone.

Mrs. Arnold sighed deeply as the door shut behind him and went to turn the radio on the kitchen counter to a program of morning music. Baby Ann began to cry. Drying her hands, wet from the dishpan, Mrs. Arnold picked up the baby to change her, putting her in the playpen in the corner of the kitchen. Then she started to dry the dishes, staring reflectively out of the kitchen window into the small, sunny backyard with its few birch trees and a patch of flower garden. The music on the radio gave place to an announcer's persuasive voice:

"Ladies, are you tired of the daily routine, worn out by the same old household chores? Do you wonder where those glamorous days of your youth have gone . . . ?"

Mrs. Arnold listened with an amused smile growing on her face. She went to the cupboard to get out her electric eggbeater and a battered recipe book.

"We are offering the opportunity of a lifetime for you ladies," the announcer went on. "Just write a simple statement in twenty-five words or less about why you use our product, and the winner will get . . ."

Mrs. Arnold turned on the eggbeater, and through the faint static the announcer's voice continued.

". . . two glorious weeks in Paris, a complete new wardrobe prepared by fashion stylists, and a beauty consultation by a famous New York . . .

Baby Ann began to throw her toys out of the pen onto the kitchen floor with sudden energy, laughing at each noisy bang. Radio music played softly in the background, and on the stove a pot of water steamed and began to boil over.

Mrs. Arnold rushed to the stove to turn down the gas. Then she went back to mixing up her cake, thinking a bit wistfully of the radio advertisement, of her own skimpy wardrobe which she'd pieced out with January sales, with her mother's ancient sewing machine. But a young lawyer had it hard those first long years, until he got established, made a name for himself . . . and living with Michael, loving Michael, made up for all those difficult mornings, like this one, when the jobs to be done seemed to stretch before her endlessly . . . mountains of laundry, perpetual meals . . . and what was it all coming to?

Here she was, Betty Arnold . . . who had been one of the smartest girls in her college, editor of the college paper . . . mixing up a cake that any illiterate could whip together. People at the magazine office had said she would go places . . . that her future articles would win her an editorial job . . . and she *was* just about to really go places when she met Michael, fresh out of law school.

Setting the timer on the stove, Mrs. Arnold remembered, smiling, the fiery idealistic talks she and Michael used to have during the days of their courtship. He would become an international lawyer, and she would follow him around the world, writing feature articles about the exotic places they'd been. But then Warren came along, and Susan, and they'd thought themselves lucky to settle down in Clinton in a little white house instead of an apartment, to save for a car and a new refrigerator instead of a trip to Paris, or Africa, or Bali.

The back doorbell rang, and Mrs. Arnold went to let the milkman in. "Morning, Miz Arnold," he said, setting out eight clinking bottles on the kitchen counter. "Happy Monday to you."

"Same to you, Eric," Mrs. Arnold smiled, and then, half-jokingly, "What would you say, Eric, if I won a contest and took a trip to Paris?"

"Paris?" Eric paused in the doorway. "That place with the radio tower and all the little archways? What's *there* to go traipsing around the world for?"

"Oh . . ." Mrs. Arnold face lighted dreamily. "People and lights, and champagne and dancing, I guess. I've never been out of the USA, so I can just tell from what I've read . . ."

"Well, if you'll pardon my saying so, Miz Arnold," Eric grinned, "I've got people and lights in my own little place, and as for the champagne and dancing, I'm satisfied with enough of that at a wedding or two a year. Kids would miss you, you know. Husband too."

"Sometimes I wonder," Mrs. Arnold laughed as Eric left. After the door had shut behind him, she paused a minute, thinking hard. Then, resolutely, went to get a portable typewriter from the living-room desk, and put it on the kitchen table. She had just rolled in a piece of paper, and typed: "Why I use Lyric Soapsuds" on it when the phone rang interrupting her. It was Mr. Arnold calling from the office.

As Mrs. Arnold listened to him, her face lighted, and she spoke with growing enthusiasm. "Why yes, darling, of course I'll make a nice dinner . . . so the big man would like a home-cooked meal after all? . . . Well, I'll run down for some canned shrimp and toss together that casserole you like . . . and you know what? I guess it was intuition, but I've got the most magnificent chocolate cake in the oven! . . . Don't worry, darling, I'll manage. See you at seven!"

Humming gaily to herself, Mrs. Arnold began to write out a shopping list with fresh energy, a happy smile playing about her lips. Glancing at the kitchen clock, she realized that it was almost time for lunch, and that the children would be coming home from school any minute. Taking the typewriter, she moved it into the living room, leaving it on the desk, and was just in time to take the cake from the oven when the timer rang.

Susan came home from school first, and sat down to the soup-and-salad lunch waiting for her in the sunny dining room.

"Susan," Mrs. Arnold said, picking baby Ann out of the highchair where she had just finished her noon meal, "I've been thinking about this afternoon. I have a proposition for you."

"What?" Susan asked curiously.

"How about having a make-your-own snack party over here for the girls this afternoon instead of going to the Dairy Bar? I've got everything from peanut butter to pickles in the cupboard, and you could bring a quart of ice cream home after school for sundaes. That way I could get some extra things at the store and visit Mrs. Cooper and not worry about the baby."

Susan pondered this. "You know," she said slowly, as the idea took hold, "that wouldn't be half bad. We could put on some of the records I got for my birthday, and kind of take over the kitchen while you're gone. I promised to teach Karen how to Charleston sometime, anyway."

"Home isn't so hard to take really, Susan," Mrs. Arnold laughed, "if you go about it in the right spirit."

Just then, Warren came in through the back door and dropped his books on the counter. "I'm starved, Mom," he said, sitting down at the table. "That game is going to be a real fight tonight."

"Heck," Susan said, "if you make as many baskets as you always do, they're licked to begin with."

Warren grinned sheepishly. "Say, Mom," he said. "I talked with June about that bus deal, and she said it was perfectly okay with her. What I wondered was, would you mind looking over this article she's got written for the school paper? It's a sort of a feature on three of the professors, and I told her you used to do that sort of stuff in college . . ."

Mrs. Arnold smiled with pleasure. "I don't guarantee I'm not rusty, Warren, but I'd love to see June's article. When did she want to bring it over?"

"Well, we thought tonight after the game, if it's okay with you . . ."

"Dad is having some important company for dinner," Mrs. Arnold said, "but he'll be gone early in the evening, I'm sure. So why don't you and June come over after the game. We'll celebrate your victory, and I can run through

June's paper. I'm sure it will be excellent, if I know June."

"Do we have walnuts?" Susan asked suddenly. "For the sundaes, I mean?"

"Yes," Mrs. Arnold said. "I've a whole jar chopped in the left-hand kitchen cupboard."

That afternoon, Mrs. Arnold took the bus downtown, leaving the house to a group of young enthusiastic girls who somehow seemed to find the novelty of creating sundaes in the kitchen a challenge to their creative, if bizarre, imaginations. Baby Ann was dressed for company, and showing off in a most amiable fashion before the interested strangers.

On her return, later in the afternoon, Mrs. Arnold found Susan making block houses with Ann. The kitchen was spotless. Not a trace of ice cream or cookie crumbs was visible. "It was fun," Susan said simply. "We decided we're having a club, and going to a different person's house for a snack every week."

By the time Warren came home from basketball practice, a shrimp casserole was in the oven, and Mrs. Arnold had bathed and dressed for dinner in a blue frock that made her appear slim and youthful. Perhaps the key to her charm was the radiant, contented smile that played about her lips. The dining-room table was set with a lace cloth and candles, and she had made a centerpiece of roses from the bush in the garden. It looked, she told herself, fit for Napoleon.

At seven, Mr. Arnold arrived with a tall, distinguished gray-haired man named Mr. Kirkland. Mr. Kirkland shook hands with Susan and Warren and gazed around the living room with pleasure. "Nice place you have here, Arnold," he said. "A relief from those impersonal hotel rooms, let me tell you."

"We like it," Mr. Arnold said with a quick smile at his wife, who was bringing in drinks and hors d'oeuvres on a tray. Susan had made herself at home by Mr. Kirkland's elbow and was asking him in her best ladylike manner about the natives in California.

"Excuse me a minute, Mr. Kirkland," Mr. Arnold said, turning to follow his wife to the kitchen.

"Certainly," Mr. Kirkland smiled. "I feel quite at home in the company of your charming daughter."

In the privacy of the kitchen, Mr. Arnold exclaimed enthusiastically to his wife, "Darling, this is it! The whole day's been grand, and I think I'll be the man for the position of law consultant in his eastern firm! Do you know what that means! It means we can pay off the mortgage! It means we can really relax. I know how you've always wanted to travel, darling," Mr. Arnold told her, "and write, and see the world . . . perhaps now . . ."

"Whoa," laughed Mrs. Arnold, putting her finger to her husband's lips. "I'm terribly thrilled, darling, but I'm happy just the way things are, you know."

She took out a piece of paper from her pocket and began tearing it up in small pieces into the wastebasket.

"What are you doing?" her husband asked, fondly.

"Tearing up a radio tower and a lot of little archways," Mrs. Arnold smiled. "I've just changed my mind about something. I somehow really knew things would work out for us all along. Sue's growing up to responsibilities, Warren is learning that the important things in life is companionship, not cars. And Ann—Ann is the most adorable baby in the world. We have lights and people right here, darling, and that's what counts."

"That's true, Betty," Mr. Arnold smiled tenderly down at her. "You don't know how happy I am to hear you put into words what I've know in my heart for a long time."

"Now I know what I was really meant for, Michael," Mrs. Arnold said. "That Arch of Triumph they talk about . . . coming up the walk this afternoon, I knew deep down inside that all the while it was really our own front door!"

Tomorrow Begins Today

Ts,[*] 28 January 1955, Lilly Library

It was three o'clock in the morning, and the hospital waiting room was deserted except for a tall, haggard young boy of seventeen. Pete Gregory had been waiting to see Marcia Vale for almost two hours now, but every minute seemed an eternity of question and self-torment. Glancing at the clock, with its slowly revolving second hand, Pete lit another cigarette with trembling fingers.

An attractive white-clad nurse came into the room on soft-soled shoes. "It will be a little while longer, Mr. Gregory," she said. "She's just come out of the anesthetic now."

Pete looked up, his face ravaged by the internal conflict that had been raging in him ever since the car had missed the turn in the rain a few hours before. "Is she—will she be all right?" he asked in a voice husky with emotion.

"Fractured arm, a few forehead stitches," the nurse said, adding a bit more sympathetically, "She's coming fine." And she was gone.

---

[*] Typescript has holograph and typewritten corrections and additions by SP. Written for the Christopher Awards. Copies of SP's poem 'Bluebeard' are typed on the verso of pages 1 and 2.

Pete buried his head in his hands and the crucial scene leapt to life again in his mind. He'd been wanting to ask Marcia Vale for a date ever since she'd transferred to the senior class at Clinton High, ever since she'd walked into study hall that first day in late September, tall, with long brown hair . . . the loveliest girl he'd seen in his life. But somehow she wasn't like the other pretty, popular girls at Clinton, although they all admired her, flocked around her, and had talked among themselves of asking her into the secret sorority that fall.

Marcia Vale was different, that's all there was to it. She'd showed them that from the beginning. Not only was she intelligent, but she was popular. She had been chosen editor of the *Clinton Weekly* newspaper, and was obviously the best editor they'd had since the old days when Clinton had won the state competition for high school papers. And Clinton was a cinch to win this year, with Marcia running things.

But, Pete remembered ruefully, he wasn't having any of Marcia those first weeks. She was too good. Now, he realized, deep inside he'd been afraid Marcia wouldn't care for him, that she'd humiliate him before the gang by refusing him a date, and so he hadn't asked. He'd just gone on, hanging around the corridors and watching, wondering during every hockey practice he blazed through at the arena whether Marcia Vale was somewhere in the cheering high school crowds watching him slam through to goal after goal. Secretly, he had hoped she was there. Or that she would hear about his exploits from her friends at Clinton High.

Then there was that winter afternoon she'd come to him at lunch hour and asked if she could interview him for the paper. They were doing a series of personalities plus, she said, and he'd been chosen as Clinton hockey star. He'd been gruff at the time, tossing off his feats with a casual shrug of the shoulder, but in his heart he'd really looked forward to their after-school interview. In fact he'd thought about nothing else that whole afternoon.

In the soda shop he'd sat at a booth with Marcia Vale and told her about his likes and dislikes, his home background, his first encounter with a hockey stick, and somehow he found himself talking more freely than he ever had before to the attractive, radiant girl opposite him. More amazing still, he didn't have to brag, to swagger or show off the way he was tempted to do with the gang of guys, of which he was the accepted leader. He was just himself now, and it was a marvelous new feeling.

Then he had asked her a question that had been on the lips of most of the boys and girls at Clinton High ever since the sorority initiations in October.

"Say, Marcia," Pete had said curiously, "do you mind telling me why you went through all those fantastic silly initiations for the sorority and then got up that night and told them you refused to join? Louise Acker, the former president, mentioned something about it to me, and I've always wondered how you had the guts to do it."

Marcia smiled and stirred her soda with a straw. "Oh, Pete," she said gently, "it wasn't so hard to do. I knew I had to do it all along. The girls are wonderful, really, but when I saw all the hurt feelings that sorority made, and the little divisions between girls who'd otherwise be best friends, I just knew I couldn't belong."

"Okay," Pete had said, "it was a snobbish little clique, but why did you go through with the initiations then?"

"Well, you know, Pete," Marcia said seriously, "when you haven't been asked into a group and then throw darts at it, people call it a 'sour grapes' attitude. I didn't want that to happen, I wanted them to realize that I would find out all I could about the sorority before refusing to join. And I didn't like what I found out."

"Secrets?" Pete asked, laughing.

"Not even that," Marcia said. "They didn't *do* anything at their weekly meetings but sit around and gossip about who'd been out with whom the last weekend, or which girls committed the social crime of wearing knee socks to school . . . Oh, you know, it was all so petty . . . and they could have spent their time and energy so much better with just as much fun."

"Like the way they're doing now," Pete said with an earnestness that had surprised him, "at the teenage canteen they made out of the old lumber shack down by the lakefront. Never saw such eager beavers, scraping and painting . . ."

"You put in a few strokes with the paintbrush, too, if I remember rightly," Marcia told him, with a smile.

Pete grinned sheepishly. "Yes, I guess I thought the sorority was foolish too, in a way. Anyhow, I was glad to see it break up and something like this come out of it."

"Well," said Marcia, "I've wanted to thank you for some time now for getting the boys to pitch in. They wouldn't have done it if you hadn't come . . . You know, they think a good deal of your opinion . . ."

"Heck," said Pete, pleased in spite of himself, "I just know how to talk tough when I have to."

"It's important," Marcia agreed, "to have the courage to do that. It's hardest when you have to talk alone, but very wonderful when you find people really listening."

"You must feel that way about the paper here," Pete said. "Everybody reads those editorials. They're really great. You know," he went off on a tangent, "I've always wanted to write an article about the way it feels to fight with the team through to a goal. There's nothing like it."

Marcia was suddenly very earnest. "Would you, Pete?" she asked. "We could run a series of first-person articles that way, sort of giving everyone the thrill of experience that comes actually only to a few experts . . ."

"Oh." Pete suddenly came to himself. "I couldn't do that. It's okay for girls to write and all, but I'd feel a fool, blowing my own horn . . ."

"That's where you're wrong, Pete," Marcia had cut in. "It's not 'blowing your own horn' when you share your ideas and experiences with others . . . it's giving them a part in something that's more than personal . . . something, well, universal! Oh, I know what you mean, but being talented doesn't mean you have to show off . . ."

She had broken off then, realizing no doubt that she had cut rather deep. For Pete was a noted show-off, and the gang of boys around him applauded his daredevil acts . . . the racing of jalopies along the river drive after school, the perilous teetering on the highbars . . . but there was a difference between beneficial skill and tempting fate. Pete knew that only too well now.

The ex-sorority, now the Clinton High social club, open to all who wished to join, was putting on a benefit dance in a few weeks at the social center. The proceeds would go to the neediest families in Clinton City, distributed by the Social Service unit there. Pete knew this was the first big performance of the club, and that its success would stand or fall on the support it received from the high school students. Already the boys were debating about whether they should go or not, and Pete knew intuitively when Mal Kramer asked him if he had a date yet, that the general verdict would be decided by his opinion.

Remembering Marcia's words at the soda shop, her own personal attempt to break up a group of needless, even harmful, prejudices, he had replied to Mal, "Sure I'm going. I'm going to ask Marcia Vale." And he had. More wonderful, she'd accepted.

In the hospital waiting room, Pete Gregory ground out his cigarette in the ashtray. Would they never let him see her? It was his fault, all of this. And just because he'd wanted to impress her after the big dance to which all Clinton High had turned out enthusiastically. It had been raining when they came out of the canteen that night, a cold freezing February rain.

Heading back to Marcia's house along the deserted river drive, Pete had become suddenly overwhelmed by the marvel of this girl Marcia, this girl who was amazingly enough sitting beside him in his favorite jalopy, this girl who had changed the orientation of a whole high school by simply being herself, by living up to her convictions. Somehow he had to show her that he was strong too, that he could dare the heights.

"Look, Marcia," he'd said impetuously, "watch this pickup. Watch me catch up with that car ahead there . . ."

"Pete . . ." Marcia had begun anxiously, but already it was too late. The drive that overcame him when he smashed through to a goal on the ice rink rose up in him, and his foot went down on the accelerator. The headlights cut through the rain, the curve came at him, and the car went spinning crazily out of control on the thin, invisible glare of ice. The last thing he remembered was throwing his arm out frantically to protect Marcia . . .

"Mr. Gregory . . . Mr. Gregory." Pete looked up, startled at the interruption to his thoughts. The nurse was touching his shoulder. "Mr. Gregory, you can go in now. But remember, no scenes. She mustn't be upset in any way."

Mutely Pete let himself be led down the shining antiseptic corridors. A door opened, and he was facing Marcia. She was propped up on the pillows, her face pale, her arm in a sling, but she was beautiful and she was smiling.

"Marcia . . ." Pete said, and his voice broke with emotion.

"It's all right, Pete," she said gently. "You don't get over wanting to prove yourself that way in just one day. But you've begun, and that's what counts."

"Prove myself!" Pete burst out. "Prove what a fool I've been! Tell me, Marcia, is there anything . . . anything I can do to make up some of this . . ."

Marcia reflected a minute and then said, "Yes, Pete, there *is* something I've been worried about. You might be able to help there . . ."

"What?" he asked eagerly. "What can I do? Just tell me."

Marcia smiled again. "It's not spectacular in the way you think, Pete, but it can be, inside you. I . . . I don't think I'll be typing for some little while again, or writing either, with this arm. What I was wondering was . . . would you sort of take over the paper while my arm's in this cast?"

Pete gasped, "Who, me?" It was incredible. Such a small thing, and yet so enormous, so important.

"Yes," Marcia told him, and her eyes said how she believed he would come through this, too, like the hockey goals. "Yes, you can be a wonderful reporter, I think. Not just tomorrow, today. And when people ask you in ten years how you began your career, you can say it was all because of a broken arm . . ."

"Arm, nothing," Pete told her tenderly, a new strength rising in him, "all because of a girl named Marcia Vale. All because she lives the way she does . . ."

The early dawn light was breaking through the window, and the two turned to look. "It's not tomorrow anymore," Pete said to her, "it's today."

Marcia smiled gently at him. "Good morning, Peter," she said.

The Day Mr. Prescott Died

Written: January 1955
Published: *Granta* (20 October 1956): 20-3[*]

It was a bright day, a hot day, the day old Mr. Prescott died. Mama and I sat on the side seat of the rickety green bus from the subway station to Devonshire Terrace and jogged and jogged. The sweat was trickling down my back, I could feel it, and my black linen was stuck solid against the seat. Every time I moved it would come loose with a tearing sound, and I gave Mama an angry "so there" look, just like it was her fault, which it wasn't. But she only sat with her hands folded in her lap, jouncing up and down, and didn't say anything. Just looked resigned to fate is all.

"I say, Mama," I'd told her after Mrs. Mayfair called that morning, "I can see going to the funeral even though I don't believe in funerals, only what do you mean we have to sit up and watch with them?"

"It is what you do when somebody close dies," Mama said, very reasonable. "You go over and sit with them. It is a bad time."

"So it is a bad time," I argued. "So what can I do, not seeing Liz and Ben Prescott since I was a kid except once a year at Christmastime for giving presents at Mrs. Mayfair's. I am supposed to sit around and hold handkerchiefs, maybe?"

With that remark, Mama up and slapped me across the mouth, the way she hadn't done since I was a little kid and very fresh. "You are coming with me," she said in her dignified tone that means definitely no more fooling.

---

[*] The text here is from *Granta*, but the story was republished in *Spare Rib* (June 1973): 36-8, with the following biographical sketch: 'Between 1950-52 Sylvia Plath wrote prolifically for American women's magazines, in a romantic style unlike her later writing. In "The Day Mr Prescott Died", written in 1952 when she was 20, she shows glimmerings of her later writing and her pre-occupation with death. Shortly after, she had her first nervous breakdown. Her second breakdown precipitated her third and finally successful suicide attempt in 1963.' It should be clarified that the story was based on events from June 1954, drafted later that year, and finalized in January 1955. Also, SP is known to have made only two attempts at suicide.

So that is how I happened to be sitting in this bus on the hottest day of the year. I wasn't sure how you dressed for waiting up with people, but I figured as long as it was black it was all right. So I had on this real smart black linen suit and a little veil hat, like I wear to the office when I go out to dinner nights, and I felt ready for anything.

Well, the bus chugged along and we went through the real bad parts of East Boston I hadn't seen since I was a kid. Ever since we moved to the country with Aunt Myra, I hadn't come back to my home town. The only thing I really missed after we moved was the ocean. Even today on this bus I caught myself waiting for that first stretch of blue.

"Look, Mama, there's the old beach," I said, pointing.

Mama looked and smiled. "Yes." Then she turned around to me and her thin face got very serious. "I want you to make me proud of you today. When you talk, talk. But talk nice. None of this fancy business about burning people up like roast pigs. It isn't decent."

"Oh, Mama," I said, very tired. I was always explaining. "Don't you know I've got better sense. Just because old Mr. Prescott had it coming. Just because nobody's sorry, don't think I won't be nice and proper."

I knew that would get Mama. "What do you mean nobody's sorry?" she hissed at me, first making sure people weren't near enough to listen. "What do you mean, talking so nasty?"

"Now, Mama," I said, "you know Mr. Prescott was twenty years older than Mrs. Prescott and she was just waiting for him to die so she could have some fun. Just waiting. He was a grumpy old man even as far back as I remember. A cross word for everybody, and he kept getting that skin disease on his hands."

"That was a pity the poor man couldn't help," Mama said piously. "He had a right to be crotchety over his hands itching all the time, rubbing them the way he did."

"Remember the time he came to Christmas Eve supper last year?" I went on stubbornly. "He sat at the table and kept rubbing his hands so loud you couldn't hear anything else, only the skin like sandpaper flaking off in little pieces. How would you like to live with *that* every day?"

I had her there. No doubt about it, Mr. Prescott's going was no sorrow for anybody. It was the best thing that could have happened all around.

"Well," Mama breathed, "we can at least be glad he went so quick and easy. I only hope I go like that when my time comes."

Then the streets were crowding up together all of a sudden, and there we were by old Devonshire Terrace and Mama was pulling the buzzer. The bus dived to a stop, and I grabbed hold of the chipped chromium pole behind the driver just before I would have shot out the front window. "Thanks, mister," I said in my best icy tone, and minced down from the bus.

"Remember," Mama said as we walked down the sidewalk, going single file where there was a hydrant, it was so narrow, "remember, we stay as long as they need us. And no complaining. Just wash dishes, or talk to Liz, or whatever."

"But Mama," I complained, "how can I say I'm sorry about Mr. Prescott when I'm really not sorry at all? When I really think it's a good thing?"

"You can say it is the mercy of the Lord he went so peaceful," Mama said sternly. "Then you will be telling the honest truth."

I got nervous only when we turned up the little gravel drive by the old yellow house the Prescotts owned on Devonshire Terrace. I didn't feel even the least bit sad. The orange-and-green awning was out over the porch, just like I remembered, and after ten years it didn't look any different, only smaller. And the two poplar trees on each side of the door had shrunk, but that was all.

As I helped Mama up the stone steps onto the porch, I could hear a creaking and sure enough, there was Ben Prescott sitting and swinging on the porch hammock like it was any other day in the world but the one his Pop died. He just sat there, lanky and tall as life. What really surprised me was he had his favorite guitar in the hammock beside him. Like he'd just finished playing "The Big Rock Candy Mountain," or something.

"Hello, Ben," Mama said mournfully. "I'm so sorry."

Ben looked embarrassed. "Heck, that's all right," he said. "The folks are all in the living room."

I followed Mama in through the screen door, giving Ben a little smile. I didn't know whether it was all right to smile because Ben was a nice guy, or whether I shouldn't, out of respect for his Pop.

Inside the house, it was like I remembered too, very dark so you could hardly see, and the green window blinds didn't help. They were all pulled down. Because of the heat or the funeral, I couldn't tell. Mama felt her way to the living room and drew back the portieres. "Lydia?" she called.

"Agnes?" There was this little stir in the dark of the living room and Mrs. Prescott came out to meet us. I had never seen her looking so well, even though the powder on her face was all streaked from crying.

I only stood there while the two of them hugged and kissed and made sympathetic little noises to each other. Then Mrs. Prescott turned to me and gave me her cheek to kiss. I tried to look sad again, but it just wouldn't come, so I said, "You don't know how surprised we were to hear about Mr. Prescott." Really, though, nobody was at all surprised, because the old man only needed one more heart attack and that would be that. But it was the right thing to say.

"Ah, yes," Mrs. Prescott sighed. "I hadn't thought to see this day for many a long year yet." And she led us into the living room.

After I got used to the dim light, I could make out the people sitting around. There was Mrs. Mayfair, who was Mrs. Prescott's sister-in-law and the most enormous woman I've ever seen. She was in the corner by the piano. Then there was Liz, who barely said hello to me. She was in shorts and an old shirt, smoking one drag after the other. For a girl who had seen her father die that morning, she was real casual, only a little pale is all.

Well, when we were all settled, no one said anything for a minute, as if waiting for a cue, like before a show begins. Only Mrs. Mayfair, sitting there in her layers of fat, was wiping away at her eyes with a handkerchief, and I was reasonably sure it was sweat running down and not tears by a long shot.

"It's a shame," Mama began then, very low. "It's a shame, Lydia, that it had to happen like this. I was so quick in coming I didn't hear tell who found him even."

Mama pronounced "him" like it should have a capital H, but I guessed it was safe now that old Mr. Prescott wouldn't be bothering anybody again, with that mean temper and those raspy hands. Anyhow, it was just the lead that Mrs. Prescott was waiting for.

"Oh, Agnes," she began, with a peculiar shining light to her face, "I wasn't even here. It was Liz found him, poor child."

"Poor child," sniffed Mrs. Mayfair into her handkerchief. Her huge red face wrinkled up like a cracked watermelon. "He dropped dead right in her arms, he did."

Liz didn't say anything, but just ground out one cigarette only half smoked and lit another. Her hands weren't even shaking. And believe me, I looked real carefully.

"I was at the rabbi's," Mrs. Prescott took up. She is a great one for these new religions. All the time it is some new minister or preacher having dinner at her house. So now it's a rabbi, yet. "I was at the rabbi's, and Liz was home getting dinner when Pop came home from swimming. You know the way he always loved to swim, Agnes."

Mama said yes, she knew the way Mr. Prescott always loved to swim.

"Well," Mrs. Prescott went on, calm as this guy on the *Dragnet* program, "it wasn't more than eleven-thirty. Pop always liked a morning dip, even when the water was like ice, and he came up and was in the yard drying off, talking to our next-door neighbor over the hollyhock fence."

"He just put up that very fence a year ago," Mrs. Mayfair interrupted, like it was an important clue.

"And Mr. Gove, this nice man next door, thought Pop looked funny, blue, he said, and Pop all at once didn't answer him but just stood there staring with a silly smile on his face."

Liz was looking out of the front window where there was still the sound of the hammock creaking on the front porch. She was blowing smoke rings. Not a word the whole time. Smoke rings only.

"So Mr. Gove yells to Liz and she comes running out, and Pop falls like a tree right to the ground, and Mr. Gove runs to get some brandy in the house while Liz holds Pop in her arms . . ."

"What happened then?" I couldn't help asking, just the way I used to when I was a kid and Mama was telling burglar stories.

"Then," Mrs. Prescott told us, "Pop just . . . passed away, right there in Liz's arms. Before he could even finish the brandy."

"Oh, Lydia," Mama cried. "What you have been through!"

Mrs. Prescott didn't look as if she had been through much of anything. Mrs. Mayfair began sobbing in her handkerchief and invoking the name of the Lord. She must have had it in for the old guy, because she kept praying, "Oh, forgive us our sins," like she had up and killed him herself.

"We will go on," Mrs. Prescott said, smiling bravely. "Pop would have wanted us to go on."

"That is all the best of us can do," Mama sighed.

"I only hope I go as peacefully," Mrs. Prescott said.

"Forgive us our sins," Mrs. Mayfair sobbed to no one in particular.

At this point, the creaking of the hammock stopped outside and Ben Prescott stood in the doorway, blinking his eyes behind the thick glasses and trying to see where we all were in the dark. "I'm hungry," he said.

"I think we all should eat now," Mrs. Prescott smiled on us. "The neighbors have brought over enough to last a week."

"Turkey and ham, soup and salad," Liz remarked in a bored tone, like she was a waitress reading off a menu. "I just didn't know where to put it all."

"Oh, Lydia," Mama exclaimed, "let *us* get it ready. Let *us* help. I hope it isn't too much trouble . . ."

"Trouble, no," Mrs. Prescott smiled her new radiant smile. "We'll let the young folks get it."

Mama turned to me with one of her purposeful nods and I jumped up like I had an electric shock. "Show me where the things are, Liz," I said, "and we'll get this set up in no time."

Ben tailed us out to the kitchen, where the black old gas stove was, and the sink, full of dirty dishes. First thing I did was pick up a big heavy glass soaking in the sink and run myself a long drink of water.

"My, I'm thirsty," I said and gulped it down. Liz and Ben were staring at me like they were hypnotized. Then I noticed the water had a funny taste, as if I hadn't washed out the glass well enough and there were drops of some strong drink left in the bottom to mix with the water.

"That," said Liz after a drag on her cigarette, "is the last glass Pop drank out of. But never mind."

"Oh Lordy, I'm sorry," I said, putting it down fast. All at once I felt very much like being sick because I had a picture of old Mr. Prescott, drinking his last from the glass and turning blue. "I really am sorry."

Ben grinned. "Somebody's got to drink out of it someday." I liked Ben. He was always a practical guy when he wanted to be.

Liz went upstairs to change then, after showing me what to get ready for supper.

"Mind if I bring in my guitar?" Ben asked, while I was starting to fix up the potato salad.

"Sure, it's okay by me," I said. "Only won't folks talk? Guitars being mostly for parties and all?"

"So let them talk. I've got a yen to strum."

I made tracks around the kitchen and Ben didn't say much, only sat and played these hillbilly songs very soft, that made you want to laugh and sometimes cry.

"You know, Ben," I said, cutting up a plate of cold turkey, "I wonder, are you really sorry?"

Ben grinned, that way he has. "Not really sorry, now, but I could have been nicer. Could have been nicer, that's all."

I thought of Mama, and suddenly all the sad part I hadn't been able to find during the day came up in my throat. "We'll go on better than before," I said. And then I quoted Mama like I never thought I would: "It's all the best of us can do." And I went to take the hot pea soup off the stove.

"Queer, isn't it," Ben said. "How you think something is dead and you're free, and then you find it sitting in your own guts laughing at you. Like I don't feel Pop has really died. He's down there somewhere inside of me, looking at what's going on. And grinning away."

"That can be the good part," I said, suddenly knowing that it really could. "The part you don't have to run from. You know you take it with you, and then when you go any place, it's not running away. It's just growing up."

Ben smiled at me, and I went to call the folks in. Supper was kind of a quiet meal, with lots of good cold ham and turkey. We talked about my job at the insurance office, and I even made Mrs. Mayfair laugh, telling about my boss Mr. Murray and his trick cigars. Liz was almost engaged, Mrs. Prescott said, and she wasn't half herself unless Barry was around. Not a mention of old Mr. Prescott.

Mrs. Mayfair gorged herself on three desserts and kept saying, "Just a sliver, that's all. Just a sliver!" when the chocolate cake went round.

"Poor Henrietta," Mrs. Prescott said, watching her enormous sister-in-law spooning down ice cream. "It's that psychosomatic hunger they're always talking about. Makes her eat so."

After coffee, which Liz made on the grinder, so you could smell how good it was, there an awkward little silence. Mama kept picking up her cup and sipping from it, although I could tell she was really all through. Liz was smoking again, so there was a small cloud of haze around her. Ben was making an airplane glider out of his paper napkin.

"Well," Mrs. Prescott cleared her throat, "I guess I'll go over to the parlor now with Henrietta. Understand, Agnes, I'm not old-fashioned about this. It said definitely no flowers and no one needs to come. It's only a few of Pop's business associates kind of expect it."

"I'll come," said Mama staunchly.

"The children aren't going," Mrs. Prescott said. "They've had enough already."

"Barry's coming over later," Liz said. "I have to wash up."

"I will do the dishes," I volunteered, not looking at Mama. "Ben will help me."

"Well, that takes care of everybody, I guess." Mrs. Prescott helped Mrs. Mayfair to her feet, and Mama took her other arm. The last I saw of them, they were holding Mrs. Mayfair while she backed down the front steps, huffing and puffing. It was the only way she could go down safe, without falling, she said.

Tongues of Stone

Ts,* January 1955,† Emory University

The simple morning sun shone through the green leaves of the plants in the little sunroom making a clean look and the patterned flowers on the chintz-covered couch were naïve and pink in the early light. The girl sat on the sofa with the ragged red square of knitting in her hands and began to cry because the knitting was all wrong. There were holes, and the small blonde woman in the silky white uniform who had said that anyone could learn to knit was in the sewing room helping Debby make a black blouse with lavender fish printed on it.

Mrs. Sneider was the only other one in the sunroom where the girl sat on the sofa with the tears crawling like slow insects down her cheeks, falling wet and scalding on her hands. Mrs. Sneider was at the wooden table by the window making a fat woman out of clay. She sat hunched over her clay, glaring angrily at the girl every now and then. Finally the girl got up and went over to Mrs. Sneider to look at the swollen clay woman.

"You make very nice clay things," the girl said.

Mrs. Sneider sneered and began to take the woman apart, tearing off the arms and head and hiding the pieces under the newspaper she was working on.

"You really didn't need to do that, you know," the girl said. "It was a very good woman."

"I know you," Mrs. Sneider hissed, squashing the body of the fat woman back into a shapeless lump of clay. "I know you, always snooping and spying!"

"But I only wanted to look," the girl was trying to explain when the silky white woman came back and sat down on the creaking couch asking, "Let me see your knitting."

---

* Typescript has holograph corrections and additions by SP. Typed at top right: 'Sylvia Plath, Age 22 / Lawrence House / Smith College (Class: 1955) / Northampton, Massachusetts // 26 Elmwood Road / Wellesley, Massachusetts.' Scenes and imagery in the story appear in other works by SP including 'Miss Drake Proceeds to Supper', 'Lady Lazarus' and *The Bell Jar*, to name a few.

† According to SP's calendar, she wrote a story called 'Broken Glass' for her short-story writing course with Alfred Kazin on 30 October 1954. It is possible that was the first draft of what became 'Tongues of Stone'. On 28 January 1955, SP wrote in her calendar: 'Polished "Mr. Prescott" & rewrote "Tongues of Stone" with new ending for Mlle story contest w. letter for CA.' CA was Cyrilly Abels, then managing editor of *Mademoiselle*. See *The Letters of Sylvia Plath, Volume 1*: 880.

"It's all holes," the girl said dully. "I can't remember how you told me. My fingers won't do it."

"Why it's perfectly fine," the woman countered brightly, getting up to go. "I'd like to see you work on it some more."

The girl took up the red square of knitting and slowly wound the thread over her finger, stabbing at a loop with the slippery blue needle. She had caught the loop but her finger was stiff and far away and would not make the yarn go over the needle. Her hands felt like clay, and she let the knitting fall in her lap and began to cry again. Once she began to cry there was no stopping.

For two months she had neither cried nor slept, and now she still did not sleep, but the crying came more and more, all day long. Through her tears she stared out of the window at the blur the sunlight made on the leaves which were turning bright red. It was sometime in October, she had long ago lost track of all the days and it really didn't matter because one was like another and there were no nights to separate them because she never slept anymore.

There was nothing to her now but the body, a dull puppet of skin and bone that had to be washed and fed day after day after day. And her body would live on for sixty-odd years or more. After a while they would get tired of waiting and hoping and telling her that there was a God or that someday she would look back on this as if it were a bad dream.

Then she would drag out her nights and days chained to a wall in a dark solitary cell with dirt and spiders. They were safe outside the dream so they could jargon away. But she was caught in the nightmare of the body, without a mind, without anything, only the soulless flesh that got fatter with the insulin and yellower with the fading tan.

That afternoon as always she went out alone into the walled yard behind the ward, carrying a book of short stories which she did not read because the words were nothing but dead black hieroglyphics that she could not translate to colored pictures anymore.

She brought the warm white woolen blanket which she somehow liked to wrap around her and went to lie on a ledge of rock under the pine trees. Hardly anyone came out here. Only the little black-clad ancient women from the third-floor ward used to walk out in the sun now and then and sit stiff against the flat board fence, facing shut-eyed into the light like dried-up black beetles until the student nurses came to call them in for supper.

While she lay in the grass, black flies hovered around her, buzzing monotonously in the sun, and she stared at them as if by concentrating she could shrink herself into the compass of a fly's body and become an organic part of the natural world. She envied even the green grasshoppers that sprang about in the long grass at her feet and once caught a shiny black cricket, holding it in her hand and hating the small insect because it seemed to have a creative place in the sun while she had none, but lay there like a parasitic gall on the face of the earth.

She hated the sun too because it was treacherous. Yet it was only the sun that talked to her still, for all the people had tongues of stone. Only the sun consoled her a little, and the apples which she picked in the orchard. She hid the apples under her pillow so that when the nurses came to lock up her closet and drawers during the insulin treatment she could still go into the bathroom with an apple in her pocket and shut the door to eat in large, ravenous bites.

If only the sun would stop at the height of its strength and crucify the world, devour it for once and for all with her lying there on her back. But the sun tilted, weakened, and betrayed her and slid down the sky until she felt again the everlasting rising of the night.

Now that she was on insulin the nurses made her come in early so that they could ask her every fifteen minutes how she felt and lay their cool hands on her forehead. All that was a farce, so she said only each time they wanted to know: "I feel the same. The same." And it was true.

One day she asked a nurse why she couldn't stay out till the sun went down because she wouldn't move and was just lying there, and the nurse had said it was dangerous because she might have a reaction. Only she never had a reaction. She just sat there and stared or sometimes embroidered on the brown chicken she was making on a yellow apron and refused to talk.

There was no purpose in changing her clothes, because every day she sweated in the sun and got her plaid cotton shirt wet, and every day her long black hair got oilier. Daily she grew more oppressed by the suffocating sense of her body aging in time.

She felt the subtle slow inevitable corruption of her flesh that yellowed and softened hour by hour. She imagined the waste piling up in her, swelling her full of poisons that showed in the blank darkness of her eyes when she stared into the mirror, hating the dead face that greeted her, the mindless face with the ugly purple scar on the left cheek that marked her like a scarlet letter.

A small scab began to form at each corner of her mouth. She was sure that this was a sign of her coming desiccation and that the scabs would never heal but would spread over her body, that the backwaters of her mind would break out on her body in a slow, consuming leprosy.

Before supper the smiling young student nurse came with a tray of orange juice thick with sugar for the girl to drink to terminate the treatment. Then the dinner bell rang, and she walked wordless into the small dining room with the five round white linen-covered tables. She sat rigidly opposite a big bony woman who had graduated from Vassar and was always doing Double-Crostics. The woman tried to get the girl to talk, but she just answered in monosyllables and kept eating.

Debby came into supper late, rosy and breathless from walking because she had ground privileges. Debby seemed to be sympathetic, but she smiled in a sly way and was in league with all the rest and wouldn't tell the girl: You are a cretin and there is no hope for you.

If someone would once say that, the girl would believe them because she had known for months that this was true. She had gone on circling at the brink of the whirlpool, pretending to be clever and gay, and all the while these poisons were gathering in her body, ready to break out behind the bright, false bubbles of her eyes at any moment crying: Idiot! Impostor!

Then came the crisis, and now she sat trapped for sixty years inside her decaying body, feeling her dead brain folded up like a gray, paralyzed bat in the dark cavern of her living skull.

A new woman in a purple dress was on the ward tonight. She was sallow as a mouse and smiled secretly to herself as she walked precisely down the hall to the dining room, stepping with one foot after the other along a crack between the floorboards. When she came to the doorway she turned sideways, keeping her eyes demurely on the floor, and lifted first her right foot, then her left, over the crack as if stepping over an invisible little stile.

Ellen, the fat, laughing Irish maid, kept bringing dishes out from the kitchen. When Debby asked for fruit for dessert instead of pumpkin pie, Ellen brought her an apple and two oranges and right there at the table Debby began to peel them and cut them up in pieces into a cereal dish. Clara, the girl from Maine with the blonde Dutch bob, was arguing with tall, heavy Amanda who lisped like a little child and complained continually that there was a smell of coal gas in her room.

The others were all together, warm, active, and noisy. Only the girl sat frozen, withdrawn inside herself like a hard shriveled seed that nothing could awaken. She clutched her milk glass in one hand, asking for another piece of pie so she could postpone for a little longer the beginning of the sleepless night that would speed in the same accelerating way, without stopping, into the next day. The sun ran faster and faster around the world, and she knew that her grandparents would soon die, and that her mother would die, and that there would finally be left no familiar name to invoke against the dark.

During those last nights before her blackout the girl had lain awake listening to the thin thread of her mother's breathing, wanting to get up and twist the life out of the fragile throat, to end at once the process of slow disintegration which grinned at her like a death's head everywhere she turned.

She had crawled into bed with her mother and felt with growing terror the weakness of the sleeping form. There was no more sanctuary in the world. Creeping back to her own bed then, she had lifted up the mattress, wedging herself in the crevice between mattress and bedsprings, longing to be crushed beneath the heavy slab.

She had fought back to darkness and lost. They had jolted her back into the hell of her dead body. They had raised her like Lazarus from the mindless dead, corrupt already with the breath of the grave, sallow-skinned, with purple bruises swelling on her arms and thighs and a raw open scar on her cheek that distorted the left side of her face into a mass of browning scabs and yellow ooze so that she could not open her left eye.

At first they thought she would be blind in that eye. She had lain awake the night of her second birth into the world of flesh, talking to a nurse who was sitting up with her, turning her sightless face toward the gentle voice and saying over and over again, "But I can't see, I can't see."

The nurse, who had also believed that she was blind, tried to comfort her, saying, "There are a lot of other blind people in the world. You'll meet a nice blind man and marry him someday."

And then the full realization of her doom began to come back to the girl from the final dark where she had sought to lose herself. It was no use to worry about her eyes when she could not think or read. It would make no difference if her eyes were blank, blind windows now, because she could neither read nor think.

Nothing in the world could touch her. Even the sun shone far off in a shell of silence. The sky and leaves and people receded, and she had nothing to do with them because she was dead inside, and neither all their laughter nor all their love could reach her anymore. As from a distant moon, extinct and cold, she saw their supplicant, sorrowful faces, their hands stretching out to her, frozen in attitudes of love.

There was nowhere to hide. She became more and more aware of dark corners and the promise of secret places. She thought longingly of drawers and closets and the black open gullets of toilets and bathtub drains. On walks with the fat, freckled recreational therapist she yearned toward flat pools of standing water, toward the seductive shadow under wheels of passing cars.

At night she sat up in bed with the blanket wrapped around her, making her eyes go over and over the words of the short stories in the tattered magazines she carried about until the night nurse came in with her flashlight and turned out the reading lamp. Then the girl would lie curled up rigidly under her blanket and wait open-eyed until the morning.

One night she hid the pink cotton scarf from her raincoat in the pillowcase when the nurse came around to lock up her drawers and closet for the night. In the dark she had made a loop and tried to pull it tight around her throat. But always just as the air stopped coming and she felt the rushing grow louder in her ears, her hands would slacken and let go, and she would lie there panting for breath, cursing the dumb instinct in her body that fought to go on living.

Tonight at supper when the rest had gone, the girl took her milk glass down to her room while Ellen was busy stacking dishes in the kitchen. There was no one in the corridor. A slow lust spread through her like the rise of a flood tide.

She went to her bureau and, taking a towel from the bottom drawer, she wrapped up the empty glass and put it on the floor of her closet. Then with a strange heavy passion, as if caught in the compulsion of a dream, she stamped on the towel again and again.

There was no sound, but she could feel the voluptuous sensation of the glass crushing underneath the thicknesses of the towel. Bending down, she unwrapped the broken pieces. Amid the glitter of small fragments lay several long shards. She selected the two sharpest of these and hid them under the inner sole of her sneaker, folding the rest of the bits back in the towel.

In the bathroom she shook the towel out over the toilet bowl and watched the glass strike the water, sinking slowly, turning, catching the light, descending into the dark funneled hole. The lethal twinkle of the falling fragments reflected in the dark of her mind, tracing a curve of sparks that consumed themselves even as they fell.

At seven the nurse came in to give the evening insulin shot. "What side?" she asked, as the girl bent mechanically over the bed and bared her flank.

"It doesn't matter," the girl said. "I can't feel them anymore."

The nurse gave an expert jab. "My, you certainly *are* black and blue," she said.

Lying on the bed, wound round with the heavy wool blanket, the girl drifted out on a flood of languor. In the blackness that was stupor, that was sleep, a voice spoke to her, sprouting like a green plant in the dark.

"Mrs. *Patterson*, Mrs. *Patterson*, Mrs. *Patterson*!" the voice said more and more loudly, rising, shouting. Light broke on seas of blindness. Air thinned.

The nurse Mrs. Patterson came running out from behind the girl's eyes.

"Fine," she was saying, "fine, let me just take off your watch so you won't bang it on the bed."

"Mrs. Patterson," the girl heard herself say.

"Drink another glass of juice." Mrs. Patterson was holding a white celluloid cup of orange juice to the girl's lips.

"Another?"

"You've already had one."

The girl remembered nothing of the first cup of juice. The dark air had thinned and now it lived. There had been the knocking at the gate, the banging on the bed, and now she was saying to Mrs. Patterson words that could begin a world: "I feel different. I feel quite different."

"We have been waiting for this a long time," Mrs. Patterson said, leaning over the bed to take the cup, and her words were warm and round, like apples in the sun. "Will you have some hot milk? I think you'll sleep tonight."

And in the dark the girl lay listening to the voice of dawn and felt flare through every fiber of her mind and body the everlasting rising of the sun.

Platinum Summer

Ts,[*] July–August 1955, Lilly Library and Emory University

Sweating drivers along Route 6 craned their necks in interest as the canary-yellow convertible careened past at 70 mph. Swerving ahead on the banked left lane, the car sliced through the sultry afternoon heat until the platinum blonde hair of the girl at the wheel showed like a daub of melted butter in the distance.

"Am I," Lynn Hunter asked Ira Kamirloff, son of Kamirloff Pictures, Inc., "driving too fast for you?"

Her bronze face was neatly boned and her white bathing suit revealed the classic lines of a purebred winner. Ira sighed. A lean, dark young man with Slavic cheekbones and no sense whatever of material limitations, he seldom had anything but dishonorable intentions.

---

[*] The text here combines the Lilly typescript draft and the Emory typescript fragments. Lilly typescript has significant holograph corrections by SP. Emory typescript contains only pages 6, 7, 12 and 19 with one deletion by SP, and appears to be from a later or final version. Footnotes indicate where the shift in source text appears. Ted Hughes's 'New Athene, Daughter of Zeus, Descended', 'The Odyssey' and 'Theology' on verso of Emory typescript pages.

In answer to Lynn's question, he jammed his foot down over hers on the accelerator. The yellow car leapt forward like a sprinter straining for the tape.

"Stop!" Lynn screamed in an ecstasy of horror. "We'll be pulverized!"

"Do you realize," Ira smiled possessively at her as he let up on the accelerator, "there isn't one guy who hasn't leered at you as we passed?"

"I suppose," Lynn said dryly, "that's why you wanted us to pass them all. To test my box office rating again."

Ira had a notorious talent for capitalizing on the sensational. Every summer this talent induced him to break Oceanview Hotel rules by picking a college-girl waitress, never a guest, and giving her a whirl on the Kamirloff merry-go-round. These extravagant social gyrations left a girl with stars in her eyes, champagne on her lips, and occasionally a devastating snapshot of Ira in her heart which took several months to erase after the party was over.

Intuitively, Lynn knew this. But she had a Douglas Fairbanks streak when it came to opening Pandora's Box. With that natural tendency which makes every woman consider herself an exception to rules, particularly those concerning men, Lynn was dating Ira purely for kicks.

Besides, her heart was perfectly safe, being already very much involved in other matters. Other matters consisted solely of a certain enigmatic pre-med student at State U. by the name of Eric Wunderlich who seemed to prefer *Gray's Anatomy* to Lynn's.

Now Eric was a busboy at the Oceanview Hotel and Lynn was a waitress. The difference being that ever since Lynn had startled herself by becoming platinum blonde, her social life had picked up with the speed of a roller coaster. Picked up, that is, everything but Eric Wunderlich.

Nothing, Lynn rapidly discovered, was more morale-building for an intelligent young woman working her way through college than being appreciated properly by a man. Particularly if he happened to be a reputedly dangerous man, like Ira Kamirloff. Ira had the agreeable habit of looking at Lynn as if she were stock in some very promising private gold mine.

"You better take over the wheel," Lynn said now, "before we get back to the elegant acres of the Oceanview Hotel. My services do not include chauffeuring." She switched to the right lane and pulled up at the next turnoff.

Ira got out and came around to Lynn's side of the car. He walked, she admitted to herself, like a California panther, not wasting the ripple of a single muscle. As he slid in under the wheel, she moved over against the opposite door.

"You don't have to rub it in," he said, slamming the car into gear and swinging it back out on the highway.

"Rub in what?" Lynn asked innocently, knowing very well what.

"You know what Papa Leo says."

Lynn laughed in spite of herself. "Underprivileged waitresses," she adlibbed from the hotel rules book, "should under no circumstances fraternize with the Oceanview guests."

"Ergo, you sit several light years away."

"You were lucky Papa Leo let me go swimming with you, even if it wasn't at the hotel beach. He is very strict with us girls."

"It was," Ira assured her, "very much to his own advantage. There's another rule in that little handbook, too, remember: 'When a guest asks for anything, make that request the most important thing in your life till it's done.' Leo's a smart manager."

Ira angled a side look at Lynn. She was blushing furiously under her tan and her exquisite chin had a dangerous tilt. Ira enjoyed the challenge of courting brilliant women, particularly if, like Lynn, they never went to the movies except for rare esoteric films in foreign languages. And especially if they obviously never considered the yearly box office receipts of Kamirloff Pictures, Inc. Ira was a connoisseur when it came to working against odds.

"Easy, baby, easy," he said as they turned into the white gravel drive of the expensive Oceanview grounds. "This is just your Uncle Ira talking. Nothing in mind but your welfare."

"And your ego!" Lynn blazed as they came to a halt behind the waitresses' dorm. She snatched up her beach bag from the seat like a hot potato and banged the car door behind her. Turning haughtily, she stalked up the front steps of the dorm.

"See you at dinner," Ira called after her. "Temper of a redhead," he sighed happily to himself as he raced his convertible up to the hotel garage, tipped the boy, and strode jauntily across the veranda of Oceanview.

With cheeks burning, Lynn ran down the hall to her room. Happy O'Connor, her attractive snub-nosed roommate, was sitting in a yoga position on the floor, painting her toenails tangerine.

"Hello, blondie," Happy greeted fondly. "I hear you've made a fortune in the platinum mines."

"Don't remind me," Lynn said, sinking down on her bed and burying her head in her hands. "I wish I'd never seen that bottle. Then this . . . this . . ."

"Mickey Jelke," Happy supplied helpfully.

". . . would never have seen *me*! Oh, the insults, the humiliations!"

"Who would fardels bear?" Happy quoted, wiggling her toes to dry them. "You know, I always wondered what a fardel was. Probably some antique kind of Elizabethan dinner-tray. Seriously, Lynn, what did King Farouk say today?"

"Only," Lynn muttered, "that he practically *bribed* Papa Leo so he could take me swimming. I'm sick of feeling like some hush-hush kitchen dish that can't be printed on the main dining-room menu. I'm sure most of the guests know Ira's been taking me out anyway. Why, that Smith-Biddeford girl would stab me with an oyster fork if her blueblood mother wasn't looking."

"We must endure," Happy said stoically, "but a few short weeks till Labor Day. Meanwhile, you should be getting a commission for extra social duties."

"But that's just it! Ira *isn't* an extra social duty. I am dating him simply for fun, remember?"

"Ah, yes," Happy sighed, remembering. "I'll never forget that bright June day at State when we were roasting together on the sundeck plotting how to earn next year's expenses. You'd just finished passing your finals with straight As. Happy, you said to me, I want to become a New Woman this summer."

"It was partly your fault," Lynn retorted. "You *made* me leave all my T. S. Eliot books home. Be a Woman for a change, you said, not a walking library stack. Have fun, you said. So I come with you to work at this . . . this . . ."

"Harem," Happy finished placidly. "But I didn't think you'd actually go through with the blonde hair deal. That did it. Looks completely natural, too. I might just write my psych thesis about it next fall: Scientific Case Studies in Why Gentlemen Prefer . . ."

"Listen, Adler," Lynn broke in ominously.

"Polly or the psychiatrist?" Happy had finished drying her toenails and was now doing hip-rolling exercises on the floor. "You know, Lynn, ever since that historic day you decided 'brown' was synonymous with 'mouse,' something very subtle has been happening to your character."

"You and your analyzing!" Lynn said. "You claimed that nothing attracts a difficult man to a woman more than flocks of other men around said woman. What happens when I try it? Enter flocks, exit difficult man. Why don't you analyze Eric Wunderlich and show me how I can make something subtle happen to *his* character."

"I might just try that," Happy meditated. "Another possible thesis topic there: Why Intellectual Males Are Prey To Phobias About Platinum Blondes. A bit involved, maybe, but not bad. Alliterative, too."

Lynn sighed. It was hopeless to argue with Happy, who spoke with the double authority of an engaged girl and a psych major. With half an hour left before they had to change into their dinner uniforms, Lynn lay back on her bed, eyes shut, while Happy went on with her hip-rolling.

Regularly now, Lynn saw recurrent visions of that fatal fashion article which had led her to the most daring and uncharacteristic action of her life: turning from a quiet, studious brunette into that contradiction in terms: a quiet, studious blonde.

BE A NEW WOMAN! the feature had pleaded. EMPHASIZE SOME ONE FEATURE. MAKE IT A TRADEMARK. Lynn had thumbed idly past the suggestions for frosty green eyeshadow and ignored exercises for losing the extra flabby pounds she most emphatically did not have. The arresting photograph of a glossy blonde stopped her cold.

IS YOUR HAIR DRAB? the caption had accused Lynn suggestively. Pulling a strand of her pageboy forward for inspection, she decided that brown was definitely drab. WERE YOU A BLONDE BABY?* the blurb went on, trying to be helpful. Lynn had once, she remembered wistfully, been a blonde baby.

The rest was simple. A mere matter of bringing out the hidden natural highlights in her hair gradually by applying a guaranteed lotion every night. She had timed the change very carefully, just after classes were out for the summer, so none of her professors would become apoplectic. Reliable students working their way through college simply did not bring out platinum blonde highlights in their hair. Lynn did.

The highlights, however, were of rather more vivid voltage than Lynn remembered from her childhood. Not only that. Some of the brightening lotion seemed to have filtered into her system. She began to walk as if she were wearing the crown jewels. She felt phosphorescent all over. It was catching, too. By the end of her first month at Oceanview she had more prospects lined up than Princess Margaret.

Men approached thinking Lynn was the worldly platinum blonde type of woman only to find out she was something quite different. They were enchanted. They were mystified. They came back for more. Mystification was good for men, Happy maintained. Even for pre-med students who didn't believe in Peter Pan.

"Happy," Lynn said thoughtfully now as they donned their lettuce-green uniforms, "did it ever occur to you that Eric might be one of those rare guys who doesn't react to competitive psychology?"

"That," exclaimed Happy with all the satisfaction of Freud diagnosing a dream trauma, "is precisely what I think. The time has come to be actively

---

* The Emory typescript begins here with 'the blurb went on . . .'

strategic with Eric. Subtly make him feel indispensable."

"If it were the rivalry of another woman," Lynn sighed, "it would be so simple. But what chance have I against those laboratory skeletons?"

"Since when have cadavers," Happy scoffed, "felt more than a passing need for a doctor?"

"I fail to follow your drift, Frankenstein."

"It's easy. Everyone needs to be needed. Especially emotionally shy pre-med students with defense mechanisms. Only a stone is self-sufficient."

"I often wonder if that isn't just what Eric has in his ribcage," Lynn said as they started to the waitresses' dining room.

That evening at dinner it was the old story. Lynn watched Eric carry her tray, loaded with three fruit cups, one shrimp cocktail and four orders of vichyssoise. He possessed that unbeatable combination of rumpled reddish hair and tall coordinated lankiness which Lynn invariably associated with rough tweeds, briar pipes, and well-stocked bookcases. More specifically, with her own future front living room. Sacrificing her pride like a kamikaze pilot, she plunged.

"Eric," she said resolutely as they stood together by the salad cage.

Eric looked down at her as if she were a rather special variety of abnormal cell tissue. "What?" he asked with interest.

"Would you," Lynn blurted out, "care to go swimming with me tomorrow. For your health, you know. That sort of thing."

Eric answered with a grin that beat Eisenhower's. "There is nothing," he said with enthusiasm, "that I would like better. I'll meet you down the beach at two thirty, after I finish up in the kitchen." Shouldering her tray full of mixed greens with all the mastery of Atlas hefting the world globe, he followed her into the dining room.

Lynn served her party of eight with the benevolence of Perle Mesta. Psychology was all very well. But so was woman's intuition. Ask and it miraculously shall be granted unto you, she thought, growing exuberant as the Song of Solomon.

Utterly unaware of this significant change in climate, Ira was showering for dinner in his luxurious room. After dressing, he went down on the cocktail terrace where a few people still lingered at the gaily painted tables.[*]

---

[*] Emory's typescript page 7 ends here; the following is from the Lilly Library typescript.

As always, the Smith-Biddeford woman was on the lookout for him like a neurotic hen with a golden egg up for market. The golden egg being Miss Constance Smith-Biddeford, an angular young lady with all the charm of Lucrezia Borgia.

Papa Leo was throwing his weight around behind scenes in the kitchen per usual, roaring at the head waitress, blasting the busboys. But when he saw Ira coming, his round face broke into an aurora borealis of smiles. He knew only too well which side of his melba the caviar was on.

Young Kamirloff brought in a good part of Oceanview's posh clientele. Wealthy dowagers with film-struck daughters, debutantes on the make, or even, when the season was at its height, a foreign princess and perhaps a countess or two.

"My boy, my boy!" Papa Leo waddled up, talking expertly around the cigar stub wedged in the corner of his mouth. "How is it with you today?"

"Fine, Papa Leo, just fine." Ira turned on his most winsome multi-millionaire smile. "There's a bit of business I'd like to talk to you about, though."

Papa Leo's face fell. Knowing Ira, it would be about the Hunter girl again. Papa led Ira to his desk where they would not be overheard. "Business," he said sadly, "is business. Only I beg of you," he spread his hands expressively, "nothing like last summer, when you make the public announcement at the final dinner."

Ira looked puzzled for a second. "Oh," he laughed, remembering, "about the screen test."

"Yes, the screen test," Papa Leo said reproachfully. "To the Evans girl it was given. A chambermaid."

"But that raven hair," Ira said dreamily, his memory switching into sharper focus, "those lapis lazuli eyes, those . . ."

"I know, I know," Papa Leo interrupted. "I pick these girls, from thousands. With great care. They are beautiful, college-educated . . . but . . . but . . ." he stammered, at a loss for delicacy.

"But," Ira picked up, patting Papa's shoulder kindly, "the lady guests go bilious with envy. Still, they come back, don't they?"

"Ah, they come back all right," Papa Leo sighed.

Ira tossed his handsome dark head and laughed. "Tomorrow, afternoon, Papa Leo, I'm hiring a yacht and taking Miss Hunter for a brief cruise."

Papa Leo groaned.

"Don't worry," Ira reassured him, "she'll be back in time to wait on dinner. Saturday night," he continued airily, "I think I just might ask her to the Pavilion Dance."

Papa Leo sputtered like Vesuvius. "But my boy," he glowed red with emotion, "there is, after all, a limit."

Ira passed Lynn on the way to his private table overlooking the ocean. She was clearing off her station and smiling like the Mona Lisa. Simply shining with character.

Ira paused beside her, pleasantly aware of several covetous pairs of female eyes trained upon him from behind menus and spoonfuls of Lobster Newburg.

"Tomorrow," he said between his teeth, making like Peter Lorre, "I have hired a small ocean liner. For an afternoon cruise."

"I'm sorry," Lynn beamed at him. "But I won't be able to make it. I already have a date."

Women very definitely did not already have dates when Ira Kamirloff asked them out. "And with whom," he asked grammatically, "might this date be?"

"With Eric," Lynn said. "Eric Wunderlich."

"Ah! The busboy!" Ira made a mental note to speak with Papa Leo once more.

"Yes."

"Well, in case he disappears, I will find you to ask again."

"I'm afraid it won't do any good. Eric is very punctual."

And he really used to be punctual, Lynn reflected as she glanced at her watch the next afternoon at three o'clock. He hadn't missed one of their platonic coffee shop appointments at State by a minute, and here it was half an hour and no sign of him whatever.

From her prone position beside Happy on a large striped beach towel, Lynn watched the other waitresses swimming and making merry with the season's crop of bellhops and busboys. The help's beach differed from the guests' only in location. There was the same invigorating green water, the same bright white sand. Only this afternoon it all seemed flat as stale beer.

Lynn turned over on her stomach and closed her eyes to shut out the empty tar road down which Eric should have walked long ago. Face it, Madame Pompadour, she told herself dully. He's not coming. He's thought it over and he's not coming. That damn cadaver-lover.

"I hate," Happy prodded Lynn gently in the ribs, "to squelch your belief in Santa Claus. But look who is chauffeuring Miss Constance Smith-Biddeford down the ocean drive toward town."

Lynn raised her head in time to see a white Jaguar disappear around the bend of the road skirting the beach. In the Jaguar she noticed the regal profile of Miss Smith-Biddeford and, prominently displayed at the wheel, the lanky frame of one Eric Wunderlich.

"That settles it," Lynn sat up, brushing sand from her legs. "This hotel is going anarchist. I might just hand in my resignation and try for a last-minute job at Howard Johnson's."

"A cat," said Happy obscurely, "may look at a king."

"That may well be, but when it comes to sharing the same Jaguar with him, I put my foot down. I am going to take a swim. To cool off."

Resolutely, Lynn raced for the surf line. Diving into a wave crest, she came up a few yards beyond the breakers. Then out by the string of small sandy islands in the bay, she noticed what was apparently a large black pirate ship heading toward Oceanview.

Lynn was treading water and curiously watching the ship make its way through the green waves, when all at once she heard the approaching whir of a small motorboat behind her. The motor cut off.

"Care for a brief cruise?" Ira asked pleasantly. "Just passing by. Thought you might enjoy a ride. Take your mind off lesser things."

Lynn looked up at Ira's confident tanned figure in the white Riviera trunks. Then she looked at the schooner, beautifully idle in the middle of the bay. "Is that," she asked, treading water furiously, "your small ocean liner?"

Ira shrugged in apology. "Ninety feet, complete with crew and chef," he said. "Awfully hard to come up with something small and intimate these days. But it's got a dandy cocktail deck and shipshape galley."

So okay, Lynn thought, hoisting herself aboard the motorboat. So I am destined to endure a life of ninety-foot yachts and filet mignon instead of stethoscopes and economical casseroles for two.

"Sail on," she said tragically to Ira, seating herself in the bow. Ira raced the motor, and the little boat cut boldly out toward the yacht.

"Why so pensive?" Ira asked later as they sat side by side on the cocktail deck in comfortable lounging chairs. The kitchen boy had brought up a tray of daiquiris and exotic hors d'oeuvres from the hold. Lynn bit absently into a lobster puff.

"Do you always," she carefully avoided his question, "conjure up ninety-foot yachts when the mood strikes you?"

Ira gave a satanic smile and poured himself another daiquiri. "Only," he said, "when I wish to conquer Annapurna for a certain young lady. It is then I say abracadabra." His eloquent black eyes left no doubt as to the identity of the certain young lady.

"Machiavelli," Lynn muttered into her daiquiri.

"Perhaps." Ira did not bother to deny this. Again, he shrugged. "Timing," he remarked succinctly, "is of the essence. Another daiquiri?"

Lynn looked at the lowering sun and shivered. "It must be getting late. I should go back. Timing," she mocked him, "is of the essence."[*]

"As you wish," Ira rose and went up onto the main deck to speak with the captain. When he returned, he found Lynn leaning against the railing, staring with great melancholy into the green depths of water slicing past.

Nonchalantly, Ira tilted her chin with his hand, turning her face to his. Then, capitalizing upon the moment, he ran his fingers through her damp hair. "Up to now, blonde one," he said, "it has been your welfare. Now," he took her expertly in his arms, "it is mine."

At the first kiss, Lynn stiffened. During the second, she thought emphatically: T. S. Eliot was never like this. And with the third, she was participating with considerable enthusiasm.

By the time they left the yacht to sail back beyond the blue horizon from whence it came, Lynn had agreed to be Ira's partner at the Pavilion Dance.

Let it be said here in all fairness that Lynn had not forgotten Eric. She remembered him only too well, and when he approached her eagerly before dinner, his face full of explanations, Lynn's glacial reception outdid the polar ice cap.

"Do I," she asked him coldly as she loaded her tray with salad plates, "have galloping leprosy? Or perhaps von Recklinghausen's disease?"

"Listen, Lynn," Eric began, "I can explain everything . . ."

"So could Casanova!" Seizing the dramatic potential of the instant, Lynn lifted the heavy tray herself and turned on her heel to go into the dining room.

This was Lynn's last act as an independent woman. Her foot slipped on a grease spot by the coffee vats. As if caught in the slow horror of a Dalí dream, she felt her tray waver, tilt, and spill as she crashed to the floor. A stiletto of pain knifed through her ankle.

"Oh, oh," she moaned from a welter of hearts-of-lettuce and Russian dressing. "My leg. It's broken."

With the speed of light, Eric was kneeling beside her. "Where does it hurt?" he asked with infinitely more than professional concern, putting an arm around her shoulder to steady her.[†]

---

[*] The Emory typescript begins here with '"As you wish," . . .'
[†] Emory's typescript page 12 ends here; the following is from the Lilly Library typescript.

FICTION | 267

"Oh, there, there . . ." Lynn gestured vaguely, feeling suddenly in vast need of masculine protection. "I think it's broken. I heard something snap . . ."

"That was probably just the plates breaking," Eric said reassuringly as Papa Leo hurried up.

"Scat! Scat!" Papa Leo waved off the curious waitresses and busboys. "Back to work! It is not Rome that has fallen."

The bystanders dispersed and Papa Leo bent over Lynn's horizontal form. "A doctor must see this girl."

"I'm pre-med," Eric told him, "and I know Doctor Lewis, the bone specialist in town. He's got an X-ray machine. I think it's only a sprain, but just in case."

"Take her then, take her, boy," Papa Leo ordered with great magnanimity. "Take the hotel station wagon. Drive like an ambulance!"

As Eric lifted Lynn up in his arms, she stiffened, remembering through her pain the vision of Constance Smith-Biddeford and the white Jaguar.

"I don't think you should try to walk," Eric said sternly tightening his hold about her. "Please put your arms around my neck. Easier to carry you that way."

Lynn obeyed with obvious reluctance and Eric carried her out through the back door of the kitchen toward the hotel garage.

"It is about time," he said as he settled her in the front seat of the beach wagon, "that you began to take care of yourself."

"Care of myself!" Lynn flamed. "Who, may I ask, are you to tell me how I should manage my life!"

Eric backed the beach wagon out of the big garage before he answered her.

"It seems," Eric said at last as they headed for town, "that I am the only one who is going to be frank and tell you to stop flinging yourself at life with such a vengeance. You collect danger signs like the little boy in the Charles Addams cartoon. But even *you* can't lead a charmed life all the time. Someday you'll really break a leg or get chained to the mast of a yacht for life by a morbid Dane."

"And you," Lynn retorted with a fine sense of poetic justice, "may accidentally drive off a cliff in a white Jaguar."

Eric silenced her with a look. "Papa Leo," he said as if he were teaching her the alphabet, "*ordered* me to drive Miss Smith-Biddeford to town for an afternoon of shopping immediately after lunch. It happened to be her chauffer's day off and someone had evidently recommended me very strongly for the job. So strongly, in fact, that I had to choose between a refusal and my rather lucrative position here."

Lynn was abnormally quiet.

"Miss Smith-Biddeford," Eric went on firmly, "bought red rope sandals, three bathing suits, and a miniature toy penguin for her parakeet. I found Happy down the beach when I got back and learned that you were last seen on a black yacht heading in the general direction of Spain."

Eric allowed ample time for this to sink in.

"Have you any idea," Lynn asked at last in a subdued tone, "why Papa Leo insisted on *you* for this errand?"

"None whatever. Have you?"

"Yes," said Lynn in a very small voice. "I think so." In her mind, as on the Road to Mandalay, dawn had a way of coming up like thunder. "Timing," she said thoughtfully, "is of the essence."

Doctor Lewis, a plump jovial man, was just finishing supper when Eric and Lynn arrived. After developing the X-ray of Lynn's right leg in his office, he confirmed Eric's diagnosis of a sprained ankle.

He bound the swollen foot, pulled a large wool sock over it, and handed Lynn a pair of crutches. With all the cheerfulness of a professional endomorph, he ordered her to keep off her ankle for a week or two.

"I feel as if I had elephantiasis," Lynn sighed on the way back. "But either time will cure me, or I'll get used to it."

"And since when have you become so philosophical?"

"Since," Lynn said, "very suddenly."

"Well then, perhaps you'd feel in the mood to answer a philosophic question I've been trying to figure out."

"Ask away."

"Why," Eric said abruptly, "did you turn your hair blonde?"

Taken off guard, Lynn was silent for a minute. She had grown so accustomed to her shining platinum blonde self that she could hardly recall those quiet days when a rather pleasant but undistinguished brown-haired girl looked back at her from the bedroom mirror. The blonde hair was almost symbolic now, an audacious banner which had given her courage to assert her full identity.

"I think," Lynn said, "I felt like a blonde inside all along. You know, sort of sparkling and gay. So I guess subconsciously I decided if I stopped *looking* merely brown-haired and industrious my platinum personality would have a chance to come out in public, too."

"I thought that might be it," Eric grinned at her. "So I waited."

"Waited?"

"Waited until you'd had enough time to feel at home in public with the platinum side of your personality before proposing a switch back."

"Switch back?" Lynn realized she was beginning to sound like an echo chamber.

"Yes. A mere exterior switch back to your own very attractive chestnut-brown locks. Look," Eric pulled up the beach wagon in a rest area, "I want to try an experiment."

Reaching into the glove compartment, he took out a clean square of dark cloth. He leaned over and made it into a kerchief to cover Lynn's hair.

"Now," he said, "look in the mirror and imagine your hair is brown again. How do you feel?"

Lynn obediently did as she was told. Except for a rather more syncopated heartbeat, she felt the way she always did when Eric was around: as if there was a magnum of champagne sparkling through her veins.

"The same," she said. "Only better."

"You see!" Eric grinned at her triumphantly. "It's still there! It'll always be there! You're definitely an effervescent platinum blonde type inside and, what's more, you can feel it without the stage props."

Lynn pondered briefly on the vagaries of cause and effect. Eric wanted her to be her natural self now. But it had taken several jolts, such as dyeing her hair blonde, to make him realize just how much he wanted this. Men, when it came right down to it, could only be handled properly by something as illogical as woman's intuition.

"Would you be aesthetically happier," Lynn asked, "if I went back to nature again?"

It was a rhetorical question. Eric would be more than happy. He would be delighted.

"I simply can't wait six months for it to grow out," Lynn mused aloud. "It would look so peculiar."

"Can't you have it dyed back to its natural color?"

"I suppose so." Lynn felt a slight tremor of misgiving at this decisive proposition. There was an off-chance, after all, that Eric might just feel she didn't need his continued vigilance once she looked like her safe natural self again.

"I'll make an appointment at the beauty parlor for tomorrow morning and have them dye it back," she declared in a surge of daring. Daring, she realized with pleasure, had become a habit with her.

"And I," Eric told her, "will drive you to town in case you get last-minute jitters."

Eric, Lynn saw with a gratifying flash of intuition, would from this day forward never be quite sure how safe her natural self was.

Lynn hobbled down to her room at the waitresses' dorm with amazing rapidity, considering that she had never navigated on crutches before. Nearing the door, she heard peculiar thumps and mutterings, as if Happy were wrestling with a large collection of human heads.

Lynn stopped astounded in the doorway. "What in the name of Luther Burbank," she demanded, "has been happening here!"

The small room was simply engulfed by an extravagant tidal wave of roses. Happy was literally up to her waist in attempting to wedge armfuls of them into several ill-assorted vases which she had evidently stolen from the kitchen.

"The road to excess," Happy declared, thumping a vase on the floor in a vain effort to thrust in more roses, "leads to perdition. For you," she thrust out a card, covered with a large affluent scrawl, "from the Black Prince. How, by the way, is your leg?"

Card in hand, Lynn sank to her bed, pushing aside a leafy heap of roses. The card read: For my beautiful fallen blonde. See you tomorrow afternoon. With love, Ira.

"Fine," said Lynn, tearing the card slowly into small pieces and dropping them into the tangle of roses on the floor. "Only get rid of these roses. I have suddenly become allergic to roses."

Happy stared at her roommate in disbelief. "There are," she intoned with the precision of a census taker, "at least twelve dozen roses in this room. Such a fact no girl can afford to be allergic to. You are rapidly becoming legendary in this hotel. Like Camille."

"Unlike Camille, I merely happen to have a sprained ankle."

"You also," Happy regarded Lynn more intently, "merely happen to look incandescent. Surely it can't be because Papa Leo is giving you a week off with pay to get your leg in shape again."

"Is he?" Lynn asked with interest. "No, that's nice, but not it. I simply feel like a New Woman."

Happy groaned in mock despair. "This is getting to be seasonal. What color this time? Strawberry?"

"No," Lynn said calmly. "Brown."

"Brown?" Happy looked skeptical. "Somehow that just doesn't fit you anymore."

"I know, but it's my own color and Eric seems to prefer it . . ."

"Aha! I figured there must be some drastic motive for this casual casting away of twelve dozen perfectly good roses."

"There is." Lynn's smile was enchanting to behold.

FICTION | 271

"Not that I want to pry, but what happens to our perennial Lothario? Mind you, the worst will be less than he is worth, but the shock might prove fatal. They say he's never gone above six dozen roses before. This could be serious."

"I have a feeling the problem will take care of itself. When he sees how pedestrian brown hair looks with brown eyes he may well begin betting on a more colorful filly."

"Papa Leo," Happy informed Lynn as she crammed the roses callously into a carton, "has hired a new redhead to take your place until your leg recovers. She has what the exotic love stories call violet eyes. Looks precisely like the type to go gaga over a roomful of hothouse roses."

"Let her," Lynn waved her hand generously. "Meanwhile, throw this particular roomful of roses into the ocean. I am going to have symbolic Freudian dreams tonight. About stethoscopes and economical casseroles for two."

The Saturday of the Pavilion Dance dawned clear and cool, with a brandy nip of autumn in the air. The ocean was sparkling like tons of blue champagne and the rolling hotel lawns were the color of crisp dollar bills.

"A day and a half," Eric grinned at Lynn as they drove back from town at noon.

"A multi-million-dollar day," Lynn expanded, happily tucking back a wisp of her chestnut-brown pageboy. It had taken a whole tedious morning at Anthony's Beauty Parlor, but it was well worth it. Anthony himself had attended to Lynn's unique request and guaranteed that when her hair grew out it would be a perfect match.

But as Lynn swung over to the waitresses' dorm on her crutches with Eric beside her, she felt her first slight chill of foreboding. Two strikingly familiar figures were waiting in the wicker chairs on the front porch.

Happy was rocking and knitting an argyle with all the grim satisfaction of Madame Defarge. Ira was staring at Lynn's head as if she were carrying it in her hands.[*]

"Hello, old chap." Ira nodded at Eric. "You look," he turned morosely to Lynn, "different."

"I told him," Happy said, "but he wouldn't believe me."

"It's brown," Ira accused in a hollow voice as if just deprived of the Koh-i-noor diamond.

"Yes," Lynn was merciless. "My hair is quite brown. It has been brown, off and on, for twenty years."

---

[*] The Emory typescript begins here with '"Hello, old chap," . . .'

"Well," Ira sighed with the philosophic attitude of Socrates accepting the cup of hemlock, "I guess you won't be able to go to the dance with me tonight after all."

"As a matter of fact, old chap," Eric put in, "she wasn't really planning to. It's a devilish bother to waltz with a sprained ankle, you know. Old chap."

"Ah yes, the ankle," Ira said absently, still gazing at Lynn's brown hair. "I suppose you won't mind, then," he rose with a cavalier shrug, "if necessity forces me to find another partner at the last minute."

"Not in the least," Lynn smiled sweetly. "Necessity has a way of doing that."

"It so happens," Ira brightened visibly, "that I noticed a new young lady waitressing at your table during breakfast. Remarkable eyes, that girl. The color of . . ."

"Concord grapes," Happy supplied dryly.

"No," Ira corrected, "I should say a rather more subtle mauve than Concord grapes. Well," he started away bravely down the steps with the air of Columbus, forever in search of the Indies, "I must be off."

"Timing," Lynn remarked when Ira was out of earshot, "is of the essence."

"Poor guy," Eric said. "What happens when he runs through the whole color wheel?"

"By that time," Happy gathered up her knitting, "Pygmalion may have managed to cook up a woman to change color with his whims like a kaleidoscope."

"*I* like your hair brown," Eric told Lynn with masculine simplicity after Happy had gone in. "It reminds me of autumn* leaves and the smell of pine needles. I always wanted a girl who reminded me of the smell of pine needles."

"That sounds terribly unscientific," Lynn said, her heart beginning to syncopate again.

"Did you ever," Eric asked with significance, "really think that doctors want wives who remind them of scalpels and dissecting tables?"

In all honesty, Lynn had never really thought this.

"Will you ever," she returned, "want me to act like a kaleidoscope?"

"You already do," Eric grinned down at her. "That's what worries me. With that impulsive streak of yours, you'll always need someone masterful around to keep you from going quite wild."

"Someone like a lion tamer?"

---

* Emory's typescript page 19 ends here; the following is from the Lilly Library typescript.

"Someone," Eric illustrated by kissing her masterfully on the mouth, "exactly like me."

And to Lynn's amazement, right there on the front porch with her brown hair and sprained ankle, she felt as if she were wearing the crown jewels. Absolutely anybody could see she was phosphorescent all over.

The Christmas Heart

Ts,[*] 22–5 August 1955, Lilly Library

Rocketing up through the Adirondacks in the bus with the December day graying to blackness, they came into snow spitting dry against the windows. Outside, beyond the cold glass panes, rose the mountains and behind them more mountains, higher than Sheila had ever seen, crowding tall against the low skies.

"I can feel the land folding away," Michael told her confidently as the bus climbed, "and I can feel the way the rivers lie, and how they come down making valleys."

Sheila did not say anything. She kept looking past him out of the window. On all sides the mountains shot up into the evening sky and their black stone slopes were chalked with snow. The mountains were remote and self-sufficient, she thought, like Michael.

"You know what I mean, don't you," Michael persisted with that strange, new intensity he'd acquired since living at the tuberculosis sanatorium. "You know what I mean, don't you, about the contours of the land?"

Sheila avoided his eyes. "Yes," she replied. "Yes, I know."

But it was not true. She no longer felt the old desperate passion to identify with Michael, to leap through the flaming hoops he set up for her until she reached the summit where he sat, calling the stars by name and clocking her

---

[*] Typescript with holograph corrections and additions by SP; with a rejection note from *Woman's Day*. Typed at top right: 'Sylvia Plath / 26 Elmwood Road / Wellesley, Mass.' This is a substantial re-writing of her earlier story 'In the Mountains' (written: *c.* autumn 1954; published: *Smith Review* (Fall 1954): 2–5 and in *Johnny Panic and the Bible of Dreams*). See *The Letters of Sylvia Plath, Volume 1*: 879 and 1143–4, and Luke Ferretter, *Sylvia Plath's Fiction: A Critical Study* (Edinburgh University Press, 2010). SP later used some of the scenes from this story in *The Bell Jar* and cites here, as in the novel, Cole Porter's 'Wunderbar'. Late in the story, SP references T. S. Eliot's 'East Coker', which starts: 'In my beginning is my end.' SP submitted 'Operation Valentine', 'The Christmas Heart' and 'The Launderette <Laundromat> Affair' to *Woman's Own* on 24 October 1960.

heartbeats with his watch. That time was gone, Sheila knew now, and before she left the sanatorium tomorrow afternoon Michael must know too.

Then Michael put his arm about her shoulder and Sheila felt, as from the distance of another planet, that something was missing there between them. For the first time she did not need to justify herself on the narrow tightrope of his approval.

The old man at the far end of the long back seat was looking at them and his eyes were kind. Sheila smiled at him and he smiled back. He was a nice old man, and she was not tense anymore the way she used to be when Michael put his arm around her in public with that half-proud, half-condescending air of ownership.

"I've been thinking a long time about how good it would be to have you up and all," Michael was saying. "For the first time, seeing this place. It's been three months now, hasn't it?"

"Just about. You left medical school early in October."

"I can forget those three months, being with you again this way," he grinned down at her. Still strong, she thought, and sure of himself. Even now, although everything was changed for her, she felt a touch of the old hurting fear, just remembering the way it had been.

His arm lay warm and possessive across her shoulders, and through her tweed coat she could feel the warmth of him against her. But even his fingers, now twining gently in her hair, did not make her want to go to him.

"It is a long time since the fall," she said, "and it has been a long trip up to the san."

"But you made it. The subway connections and the crosstown taxi and all. You always hated traveling alone. You always were so sure you would get lost."

She laughed. "I manage. After all, I've had to learn with you away. But you. Aren't you tired from the trip down and now back, all in one day?"

"You know I don't get tired! Why do you think they let me go down to the city to meet you? I feel fine."

"You look fine, too," she said to pacify him and then fell silent.

In Albany he had been waiting at the bus terminal when her taxi skidded to the curb, and he had looked just the way she remembered him, his blonde hair cropped short and close to his handsome, aristocratically boned head and his face pink with the cold. No change there.

Living with a bomb in your lung, he had written her from medical school after they told him, is no different from living any other way. You can't see it.

You don't feel it. But you believe it because they tell you and they know.

It had seemed incredible to Sheila then that anything could ever go wrong with Michael. He had never so much as caught cold in his life and always treated her frequent sinus infections like a rather unnecessary feminine indulgence.

In all his letters from the sanatorium he never actually mentioned his illness, but talked at great length about his strictly disciplined schedule of reading and research. His reports of fellow patients sounded like sociological case studies.

In the beginning, Sheila had almost envied his profitable leisure. Her days were barren without him. Michael had always planned their weekends together with the precision of a Cook's tour. It was only slowly that Sheila began to participate in college activities on her own, first as a means of filling up the emptiness in her heart, later, as a genuine creative satisfaction.

Gradually, however, her acute sense of loss diminished. She started writing lecture covers and interviews with visiting speakers and felt a new pride when stories appeared with her byline in the town paper. If Michael had been around, she would have found it necessary to rationalize her writing. Now she realized she was simply doing it for herself, because it was fun.

It was fun, too, going out occasionally to plays and concerts with Adam Shapiro, her roommate's brilliant, witty brother who worked in a publishing house in New York City and now and then managed to get up for a weekend.

Once, out of habit, Sheila asked Adam gravely, "What shall I plan to wear next week? What are we doing?"

Adam had laughed at her earnestness. "Wait and see," he teased, "how the spirit moves us!"

With Adam, life was casual and spontaneous, and Sheila relaxed accordingly. For the first time she didn't feel it was a matter of life and death if she accidentally picked up the wrong fork when they were eating out or quoted a line of Dylan Thomas when she swung impromptu into a poetic mood.

Sheila's new sense of identity grew richer with the passing weeks, yet she felt the ultimate test of her independence would not come until she was alone with Michael again. In the past, her repeated resolutions to assert herself always crumbled under Michael's eloquent analysis of her faults, and the faults of people in general.

Now, with a bittersweet mingling of regret and joy, Sheila understood that Michael had never really needed her, or desired her as a whole person. He had wanted only to master her, to cut out her tender softness like a cancer spot, until she saw life as he did: a stimulating scientific experiment where people were the guinea pigs.

And he had almost, Sheila shivered, almost convinced her that he was right, that the world ticked on in the light of logic alone. The chill diamond-faceted brilliance of his mind had almost blinded her to the warmer, softer radiance that spoke from her own heart.

From somewhere in the front of the bus there was a cold draft of air coming. It blew back, freezing and cutting. Three seats ahead a man had opened a window.

"It's so cold!" Sheila exclaimed aloud, pulling her Black Watch plaid scarf closer about her throat. The old man at the other end of the back seat heard her and smiled, saying, "Yes, it's the open window. I wish he would shut it. I wish someone would ask him to shut it."

"Shut it for him," Sheila whispered to Michael. "Shut it for the old man."

Michael looked down at her keenly. "Do *you* want it shut?" he asked.

"I don't care, really. I like fresh air. But the old man, he wants it shut."

"I will shut it for *you*, but I won't shut it for him. Do you want it shut?"

"Shh, not so loud," Sheila said, fearing that the old man would hear. Michael's jaw was tight and his mouth shut firm. He got angry like cold steel, beyond reach of words, of compromise.

"All right, I want it shut then," she sighed. Her acquiescence was merely a surface token, instead of the deep commitment it had once been. It served.

Michael got up and went forward three seats and asked the man to please shut the window. Coming back to her, he smiled. "I did that for you. No one else."

"That's too bad," she said. "What have you against the old man?"

"Did you see him? Did you see the way he looked at me? He was perfectly able to go up and shut the window himself. And he wanted me to do it."

"I wanted you to do it too."

"That's different. That's altogether different."

Sheila kept quiet then, feeling sorry for the old man and hoping he hadn't heard. Michael had always scorned people who were helpless, who needed others. He could not understand her desire to give of love because he had never wanted to accept anything from anyone.

The rhythmic jolting of the bus and the warmth of the heater under the seat was making her drowsy. Her eyelids dropped, lifted, and dropped again. Leaning her head back on Michael's arm, she let herself be lulled by the rocking of the bus.

Then, at last, he was saying in her ear, "We're coming to the stop."

Slowly Sheila opened her eyes and let the lights and the people and the old man come back. She straightened up, yawning hugely. The back of her neck was stiff from leaning her head against the arm Michael still kept around her shoulders.

"But I don't see anything," she said, rubbing a dark clear spot on the steamed window glass and peering out. "I don't see anything at all."

"In just a minute," Michael promised. "You'll see. We're almost there. I'll go and tell the bus driver when it's time to stop."

He stood up and began edging his way down the narrow aisle. The passengers turned their heads to look as he walked by. Everywhere he went, people always turned to look.

Sheila glanced again through the window. Out of the dark sprouted sudden rectangles of light. Windows of a low-eaved house in a pine grove.

Michael was beckoning her to come to the door. Already he had taken her suitcase from the rack. Rising, she went to him, rocking unsteadily down the aisle with the motion of the bus.

Abruptly, the bus swung to a stop and the door folded back into itself with an accordion wheeze. Michael leapt down the high step into the snow and reached up his arms to help her. After the warm damp air inside the bus, the coldness struck her dry and keen as the blade of a knife.

"Oh, all the snow! I've never seen so much snow!" she exclaimed in wonder, stepping down beside him.

The bus driver heard her and laughed, closing the door from inside and starting to drive away. Sheila watched the lighted window squares move by, misted with steam, until the face of the old man looked out at them from the back. Impulsively, she lifted her arm and waved to him. His return wave was like a salute.

"Why did you do that?" Michael asked, curious.

"I don't know," she laughed up at him, triumphant. "I just felt like it. I just felt like it, that's all." Numb from sitting still so long, she stretched and stamped her feet in the soft powder of snow. Michael stared carefully at her a moment before he spoke.

"Doc Allen's place is just over there. That's where you're staying." He pointed to the blazing windows of the low-eaved house. "And the san is only a little farther along the road, around the bend."

Picking up the suitcase, Michael took her arm and they started walking between the tall banks of snow along the driveway to the house. Overhead the stars blinked cold and distant. As they tramped up the front walk, the door of the house opened and a shaft of light sliced out across the snow.

"Hello there!" With languid blue eyes and blonde hair curling about her heart-shaped face, Emmy Allen met them at the doorway. She wore black toreador pants and a pale blue plaid lumbershirt.

"I've been waiting for you all," she drawled, and her Southern voice had the slow clear quality of honey. "Here, let me take your things."

"Why, she's lovely!" Sheila whispered to Michael while Emmy Allen was hanging their coats in the hall closet.

"That's a doctor's wife for you!" Michael said. And it was only when she noticed his admiring expression that Sheila realized he was not joking. For Emmy was a soft woman, her kind of woman. A woman who would need to love.

Emmy came back to them, smiling drowsily. "Doc Allen is on night duty," she explained. "You two go in the living room and take it easy awhile. I'm going upstairs and read in bed a little. If there's anything you want, just call."

"My room . . ." Sheila began.

"At the head of the stairs. I'll take your suitcase up. Just lock the front door after Michael goes, will you?" Emmy turned and padded catlike over the rug in her moccasins to the stairs.

Blue-patterned wallpaper in the hall widened to a long living room with a log fire dying in the grate. Crossing to the couch, Sheila sank into the depths of the cushions and Michael came to sit beside her.

There was a small, awkward silence. "Will they let me see you most of the time?" Sheila asked finally, wondering how discreet she should be in asking about rules. Michael had never approved of any schedules but his own.

"Most. Except after lunch at rest hour. But Doc Allen is getting me passes while you're here. You're staying at his house, so it's legal."

"What's legal?"

"Don't say it like that," he laughed. "My visiting you, that's all. Just so long as I'm back in bed by nine o'clock."

"I can't understand the rules they have. They keep you strictly on drugs and make you go to bed at nine o'clock, and yet they let you come down to the city. It doesn't follow."

"Well, every place has a different system. Up here they let us have an ice-skating rink and they're pretty lax about most things. Except walk hours."

"What do they say about walk hours?"

"Separate walk hours for the separate sexes. Never coincide."

"But why not?"

Michael hesitated. "They figure the love affairs up here are quick enough without that."

"Oh, really?" she said, conscious of the calm center within her where three months ago there would have been a cyclone of anxiety.

"But I can't see that sort of thing. No point to it."

"Oh?"

"No," he said seriously. "There's no future in that sort of thing up here. Gets too complicated. Every now and then, though, something turns out well enough. Take what happened to Joey, for instance."

"You mean Joey, the punchy fighter you wrote me about?"

"That's the one. Fell for a Greek girl up here. Well, he married her over the Thanksgiving holidays. Back here now with her, she being twenty-seven, he twenty."

"But why did he marry her?" For some reason Michael's answer was suddenly important to her.

"Says he loves her, that's all," Michael said simply, with no trace of his old scorn. Matrimony, he had claimed scathingly once long ago, was a social convenience by which two weak links could join together and support the world.

"Affairs are one thing," Sheila said, "but signing your life away merely because you're lonely or because you're afraid of being lonely, that's something else again. It's dangerous. It's weakening."

Michael gave her a quick look. "That sounds strange, coming from you."

"Maybe," she said. "But that's the way I figure it now. It takes two strong people to build a creative marriage, not just one."

Michael was looking at her so curiously that she broke the tension with a little laugh and, lifting her hand, patted his cheek. Aloof, staccato pats, but she saw that somehow her spontaneous gesture had made him happy. His arm tightened about her shoulder in response.

"I have a surprise for you." He changed the subject.

"What is it?" Michael had always thought surprises were childish.

"Remember when you wrote me about wanting to learn how to ski?"

"Yes." Sheila recalled how intensely she had once wanted to master a sport, any sport, to match Michael in at least part of his active athletic life. There was no trace of that frantic competitive spirit left now, though. Only the thought that it would be marvelous fun to swoop birdlike down snow-covered slopes.

"Well, I've arranged for you to borrow Emmy Allen's skis and boots tomorrow and I'll take the Allens' car and drive you over to Mount Pisgah and start teaching you."

The words had a familiar ring. Michael liked nothing better than the role of teacher. Confident, didactic, he had always made her feel inept in her wild attempts to follow his directions. But it would be different now. Paradoxically, now that she had resolved to end it once and for all, she felt a freedom and happiness with him that she had never known before.

"I'd love to go," she smiled. "But you? Will they let you ski too?"

Michael flushed. "No," he said briefly, "that's one of the few things I can't do yet. But I can stand on the bottom of the slope and tell you what to do from there."

"Of course," Sheila rose, yawning. "But it's almost nine. It's time for you to go." Tomorrow would be time enough to tell him. To face him and say: it has been good, Michael. Some of it has been very good. But not good enough.

"Sheila . . ." he said hesitantly at the door.

"Yes."

"I . . . I can't kiss you, you know."

"I know." Something almost humble in his expression made her want to cry. Only for a flash, and then it vanished. Impulsively, she stood on tiptoe and kissed him on the forehead.

"There," she said. "Until tomorrow."

He was gone. Slowly she locked the door behind him.

"I do hope you'll stay here over Christmas tomorrow," Emmy Allen said to Sheila as they finished their breakfast alone together. "We'd love to have you and it would make Christmas for Michael."

Sheila was taken aback. "Oh, but I've promised to be with my own family. I'm never home except on vacations and Michael's parents are driving up here for the day."

"That's not the same," Emmy smiled. "Michael's missed you so. Ever since you wrote you were finally coming up for a visit Jack and I have heard about nothing but."

"Nothing but what?" Sheila asked, incredulous.

"Nothing but you. About your writing. And about how pretty and sympathetic you are. Don't blush, it's quite true. Michael, you know, is very much in love with you."

"But it's . . . it's a mistake!" Sheila exclaimed. "It's only being shut up here so long, away from medical school, that makes him talk this way. When he comes home, it will all be the same again. He'll want to go and be a general practitioner in the backwoods, up night and day, with no time for anything but his work."

"A general practitioner. That's what my husband Jack wanted to be," Emmy said gently. "Until he came down with tuberculosis."

"I'm sorry. I didn't know."

"You see," Emmy said, "Jack was very much of a perfectionist when I first knew him. Getting tuberculosis was a terrible shock to him, almost an insult. Men are strange that way. Sickness becomes a challenge to their whole concept of strength, not just a physical thing."

Emmy got up to pour them fresh coffee. "But in a way," she went on, "it was the best thing that could have happened to Jack, to both of us. He's reached an understanding of his patients, a warmth and sympathy for their needs, which he would never have otherwise."

"But why couldn't he be a general practitioner?" Sheila asked. "Wasn't he cured?"

"Oh, the scars healed all right. But Jack still has to take naps in the afternoon. He could never swing the strenuous, demanding life of a general practitioner. He'll always have to be more careful than most people."

"But Michael! It would kill him to give up his career."

"It won't necessarily mean giving it up. It *will* mean compromising."

"Michael never compromises."

"He'll need help," Emmy looked intently at Sheila. "Perhaps he is not yet quite aware of how much help he will need."

"It isn't weakness," Sheila said to Emmy, half pleading, "to need someone."

"On the contrary, it's a kind of weakness to think we *don't* need each other. There are so many kinds of need, healthy and unhealthy. But there is a mutual need born of love, a need for each to give and for each to receive. Sometimes it is almost harder to admit the need to receive."

Sheila was thoughtfully wiping the dishes for Emmy when the doorbell rang and Michael came to take her skiing.

During the drive to Mount Pisgah, Sheila found it difficult to reconcile Emmy's words with Michael's cheerful, confident conversation. Was it a cover-up for a new and troubling uncertainty or had he really changed at all? She had to know.

The new snow was blindingly white in the morning sun, and the ski slope, dotted with brightly clad figures, looked colorful and primitive as a painting by Grandma Moses.

"I want you to try that little slope first," Michael instructed, as he knelt to fasten her bindings. "Just walk up making a herringbone, and push off."

The slope was a gentle incline at the foot of the rope tow, and Sheila obediently plodded up, breathing in great gulps of the dry, cold air which went to her head like brandy. It seemed wonderfully simple, just to push off with her ski poles and glide down the gradual little incline to where Michael was standing watching her.

"You're doing fine," he said at last, after she had made the descent several times. "Now why don't you try the rope tow. It's easier than walking."

Sheila looked up at the tall slope, crowded with vacation skiers. Suddenly, unexpected and destructive as a saboteur, the old fear was with her again.

"I don't think that would be a very good idea," she said. "I can't steer yet. I can just come straight down, and they all go in zigzags."

"Oh, the turns. You'll do all right. Just get off the rope tow at the halfway mark. Then you won't pick up too much speed coming down."

There was the ancient challenge, the white glove. It was the final game, and she could bid or pass. Michael was looking at her with a strange expression, and all at once in his eyes she recognized his enormous need. His need to be strong as she was now. His need to feel that she was not indifferent to him.

Sheila turned toward the beginning of the rope tow. "All right," she said, "I'll try it."

For a moment she stood beside the running rope. The young boy before her in line reached out, let the rope slide through his mittened hands at first, and then suddenly he was being swept up the mountainside. People were waiting behind her.

Sheila grabbed the rope too abruptly and was yanked forward. Balancing with luck, she managed not to fall. The young boy was far ahead of her, and the rope was heavy. Once, as she went up over a ridge, she thought her hands would be crushed where the rope almost touched the ground. Faster and faster she went, realizing with sudden shock that she had no idea how to get off the tow. She would have to stay on until the top.

The landscape dropped away behind her, and the gay music from the lodge loudspeaker seemed a lilting mockery. She watched the boy above let go of the rope and glide to a stop at the top of the hill. Desperately, she imitated him and found herself on a level place at the summit. Already the boy was plummeting down the slope, now to this side, now to that, with the insolent poise born of long practice.

Sheila looked down past the interweaving crowds on the slope to the bottom of the hill where there was a small, khaki-colored spot. Michael. Now *she* stood on the summit and he below. In the distance, snow glittered on the powerful bulk of the mountain range. The sun blazed high up in a Technicolor-blue sky.

There were two ways she could return to Michael, for it was to Michael that she would aim. She could go down taut with terror like the old Sheila, to seek protection in his arms. Or she could swallow the strength of the shining mountains and descend to meet him with the daring of an equal in the only way she knew, as the crow flies. It was this way, and this way alone, that they could grow together.

The music from the lodge waltzed along her veins: "Gazing down on the Jungfrau . . . From our secret chalet for two . . . " Seeing a cleared space between her and the minute khaki figure below, Sheila thrust off. She had made her choice. Would Michael be strong enough to accept it?

Whistling wind stung tears to her eyes as she gained speed. Hurtling straight down, she exulted in the bend of her knees, the control of her thighs. This she had learned, and learned well. This, but no more.

Through a blur of snow and tears, Sheila saw Michael's pale uplifted face. I'm coming, every fiber of her body rejoiced, I'm coming. But the laugh of triumph froze on her lips.

Ahead on the slope a man had stopped, turning to talk to a friend. Instinctively, Sheila knew he was in her path. His ski extended only a few inches in her way, but she could not steer aside. Someone shouted. It was too late. Already the tip of her ski had caught and the force sent her spinning headlong.

Sheila felt the hard-packed slope rise and knock the breath out of her. Cartwheeling, she slid to a stop. Snow gritted wet between her teeth, and the scene jumped back into focus. Michael was running toward her.

She managed a shaky laugh. "How was that for a fall?"

"Are you all right?" His face was peculiarly white. "Can you get up?"

"Of course." Trying to hoist herself up, she found her legs tangled hopelessly under her. "Maybe if you took my skis off it would help."

Michael knelt to undo the bindings.

"You know," she said, "I wasn't half bad, was I? What happened to the man I blasted?"

"He's all right. Barely lost his balance."

"Now, old chap, just give me a hand."

Sheila rose gingerly. Her feet felt as if they were asleep, but they moved under her, bound firmly by the ski boots.

"Anything broken?" Michael asked.

"Me! Break anything! Not on your life!" Sheila started to limp toward the parking lot. Her right leg had begun to ache a little. "I'll take up where I left off tomorrow, only you can teach me how to do snowplow turns first."

Michael followed her to the car in silent concern, carrying the poles and skis. "Let's see your ankles." He bent over and unfastened her boots. Pulling them off with care, he removed the thick white ski socks.

Sheila's right ankle was swelling rapidly. "It doesn't really hurt much," she said, "but what a revolting shade of purple!"

"I think it may be broken." Michael moved her ankle slightly.

"Ouch!" The pain startled her.

"We'll have Doc Allen X-ray it before lunch."

"But Michael," Sheila objected, "I'm sure it's all right. I couldn't have walked if it were broken."

"You could, but you shouldn't have. I wish I'd made you walk back down that hill!"

Sheila smiled. She felt as if she and Michael had changed scripts halfway through a play. Could it be that even as she had grown toward strength, he had grown toward tenderness?

"But I don't believe it." Sheila protested later to Doctor Jack Allen as she lay on the X-ray table. "It can't be broken!"

Grinning, Jack showed her the cloudy black-and-white X-ray with the unmistakable dark line slanting across the fibula.

"We'll put it in a cast," he said, "and in ten years from now you'll never know the difference."

"Is that how long it will take to mend? Ten years?"

"A month. Maybe a little more. Depends." Jack Allen was exasperatingly laconic.

"A month!" Sheila bit her lip as she remembered Michael had been under the rest cure for three months and it was just beginning. "Why, that's nothing," she added, subdued.

"Why not rest up here a few days?" Jack Allen puffed casually on his pipe. "Over Christmas, for instance."

Sheila avoided his eyes. "I'll see," she said briskly. "I'll think about it." Sheila thought about it while they were binding on her cast that afternoon and she thought about it during the delicious supper of Southern fried chicken Emmy made for the four of them that Christmas Eve. Her plans had been settled before she came up. She was going to tell Michael goodbye and leave that afternoon, the day before Christmas. For good.

But while it took strength to make a final decision, it sometimes took more strength to change it when conditions changed. Sheila had acted in accordance with the alterations in herself. She had not allowed for alterations in Michael.

Behind Michael's brave, gay manner she sensed new depths she had not yet fully sounded. Emmy's talk that morning had been a guide, but she had to drop the final plumb line herself. She decided to telegram her family and stay with Michael through Christmas.

"We're going to a Christmas Eve skit at the san tonight," Jack Allen said after dessert. "You folks care to come?"

Michael glanced at Sheila and she read reluctance in his eyes. "I think I'd rather get used to my brand-new white leg first," she said. "Let us do the dishes, why not."

"Quick, Emmy!" Jack grabbed his wife's hand. "Let's get out of here before the girl comes to her senses!"

Emmy followed him to the coat closet. "Oh, I almost forgot . . . " She turned back with a grin. "Coffee's hot on the stove in the kitchen." And, calling goodbye, they were gone.

"Will you have coffee?" Michael asked with a sudden touch of formality.

"Yes," Sheila said. "Yes, I think I need something hot to drink."

He came back bringing two steaming cups and Sheila hobbled after him on her crutches into the living room.

"You too?" she said, surprised. "You never used to like coffee."

"I have learned to drink it," he told her, smiling. "Black, the way you do, without cream and sugar."

She bent her head quickly so that he could not see into her eyes. It shocked her to see him acquiesce even in this small way. He who had been so proud, so unyielding. Lifting her cup, she drank the hot black liquid in slow sips, saying nothing.

"I am reading a book," he had written in one of his latest letters, "where the man is a soldier and the girl he is in love with dies, and oh, I began thinking that you were the girl and I was the man and I could not stop thinking about how terrible it was for days."

Sheila had wondered a long time about that, about Michael alone in his room reading, day after day worrying about the imaginary man and the dying girl. It was not like him. Before, always, he used to say how silly she was to feel sorry for people in books because they were not real. It was not like him to worry about the girl dying in the book.

Together they finished the coffee, tilting the cups and draining the last warm drops. In the fireplace one thin blue flame flared, small and clear, and went out. Under the white ash of the gutted log, coals still showed red, fading.

Michael reached for her hand and she let him interlace his fingers with hers.

"I have been thinking," Michael said to her then, slowly. "All this long time I have been away I have been thinking about us. We have been through a lot together, you know."

"Yes," Sheila said guardedly, "I know."

"Remember that Friday night we stayed in town so late we missed the last bus out, and the crazy boys we thumbed a ride back home with?"

"Yes," she said, remembering how it was all so lovely and hurting then. How everything he said had hurt her.

"That crazy guy," he persisted, "in the back seat. Remember him? The one who kept tearing up the dollar bill in little pieces and letting them fly out the open window?"

"I'll never forget that."

"That was the night we saw the baby born. Your first time at the hospital, and you had your hair all wound up under a white cap, and a white coat on, and your eyes were all dark and excited over the mask."

"I was afraid someone would find out I wasn't a medical student."

"You dug your nails into my hand while they tried to get the kid to breathe," he went on. "You didn't say anything, but your nails left little red crescents in the palm of my hand."

"That was half a year ago. I'd know better now."

"I don't mean that. I liked it, the red marks. It was a good hurt. I liked it."

"You didn't say so then." Her heart was playing tricks on her, syncopating every once in a while.

"I didn't say a lot of things then. But I have been thinking up here of all the things I never told you. All the time up here while I am lying in bed, I remember the way it was with us."

"It is because you have been away so long that you remember all the time," she said, trying to convince him. "When you get back to med school and the old fast life again you will not need to think like this. It is not good to be so introspective all the time."

"That is where you are wrong. I didn't want to admit it for a long time, but I think I needed this. Getting away and thinking. I am beginning to learn who I am."

Sheila looked down into her empty coffee cup, stirring dry circles with her spoon. In my end, she remembered from a poem by Eliot, is my beginning. From how many ashen ends would love rise, phoenix-like, to flame again?

"Tell me then," she said softly. "Who are you?"

"You already know. You already know better than anyone."

"What are you trying to tell me?"

"Can't you see," he said simply. "I mean you have taken me always the way I am, no matter what. I've needed that. Like the time I told you about Carol and you cried and turned away. I thought for sure that was the end then, with you sitting and crying on the other side of the car, looking out at the river and not talking."

"I remember that," she said. "It was going to be the end."

"But then you let me kiss you. After all that you let me kiss you, and your mouth tasted wet and salt from the tears. You let me kiss you and it was all right again."

"That was a long time ago. It is different now. It is not so simple now."

"I know it is different now because I never want to make you cry again. Do you believe that? Do you know what I am trying to say?"

Sometimes, Emmy Allen had said, it is harder to admit the need to receive.

"I think so," Sheila said. "But you have never before talked to me like this, you know. You always let me guess at what you meant."

"That is all over now," Michael said. "And my getting out of here won't make it any different. I will get out of here and we will begin again. A year is not a very long time. I do not think it will take me more than a year, and then I will come back."

"I have to know something. I have to ask it of you in words to make sure."

"Do you need words now?"

"I have to know. Tell me, why did you ask me to come?"

They sat there together, suspended in the balance between end and beginning, between dark and dawn. Michael looked at Sheila and his eyes reflected her wonder.

"I needed you," he confessed, quite low. "I needed you very badly."

"Is that so very terrible to you, Michael?"

"No, not anymore." He hesitated, then said quietly, "It is unfortunate that I can't kiss you. I need to love you now. I always will."

He put his face into the hollow between her neck and shoulder, blinding himself with her hair, and she could feel the sudden wet scalding of his tears.

Stricken with love, she did not move. The patterned blue walls of the room melted away, and outside the snow-scarred mountains stood strong against the dark. The dawn-star of a thousand ages shone down on Sheila and Michael, sharers of the Christmas heart. There was no wind at all and it was hushed and still.

That Widow Mangada

Ts,[*] August–September 1956, Lilly Library

It was a blazing hot Spanish morning when they met her. The bus from Alicante to Villaviento, packed with jabbering Spaniards, jolted along the narrow road raising a cloud of red dust. Sitting beside her husband Mark, Sally tried to keep the heavy green watermelon from bouncing off her lap. Mark's rucksack and their antique black-cased portable typewriter jounced in the rack above their heads. They were house-hunting again.

'Now that's the sort of place.' Mark pointed through the window at a square white pueblo set on the barren hillside. 'Quiet. Simple. Nobody rolling oil-cans down the street and ringing bells all night the way they did in Alicante.'

'Not so fast,' Sally countered. Experience was beginning to make even Sally cautious. 'It's so far out there's probably no electricity. Or drinking water. Besides, how would I ever get to a market?'

The bus lumbered on through arid reddish hills terraced with groves of olive trees, their dark leaves blanched by dust. They'd been on the road for almost an hour when, caroming around a curve, the bus began plummeting down toward a small village bordering a peacock-blue bay. Its white pueblos shone like salt crystals in the sun.

Sally was leaning over the seat in front of her, exclaiming at the brilliance of the sea, when, all at once, the little black-haired woman in the seat ahead turned around. She was heavily made-up and wore a pair of dark sunglasses.

'You understand Spanish?' she asked Sally. Slightly taken aback, Sally answered, 'A little.' She could understand Spanish well enough, but spoke haltingly as yet. Mark's Spanish was fluent; he was translating some modern Spanish poetry that summer for an anthology.

'It is very beautiful here, isn't it?' The woman quickly picked up the drift of Sally's last sentences. She tossed a nod toward the bay. 'I myself have a house

---

[*] Typescript with holograph corrections by SP. Typed at top right: 'Sylvia Plath / Whitstead / 4 Barton Road / Cambridge, England.' According to SP's calendar, she sent 'That Widow Mangada', 'The Black Bull' and 'Afternoon in Hardcastle Crags' to *Mademoiselle* on 17 September 1956. See Appendix I for extant pages of 'The Black Bull' and 'Afternoon in Hardcastle Crags'. SP's letters and journals mention the original of Widow Mangada, Enriqueta Lohoz Ortiz, from whom they rented rooms in Benidorm on their honeymoon in July 1956. A Spanish newspaper article from 1962 refers to Ortiz as 'viuda de Mangada'.

in Villaviento,' she ran on. 'A lovely house, with a garden and a kitchen. Right on the sea . . .'

'How nice,' Sally said. Vaguely she wondered if this were at last a fairy godmother in disguise, about to offer her palatial villa to them for the summer. Sally had never quite gotten over her childhood conviction that there were still whimsical magic agents operating in the workaday world.

'I rent rooms in the summer,' the woman pursued, waving her expensively manicured hand on which several rings winked and shone. 'Beautiful. Comfortable. Kitchen rights. Garden rights. Balcony rights . . .'

Sally relinquished her dream of free castles in Spain. 'Is it really near the ocean?' she asked eagerly. Already weary of the dry Spanish landscape, she could not conquer her nostalgia for the great honest blue sea pounding along Nauset Beach at home.

'Of course! I'll show you everything. Everything!' the dark little woman promised. Carried along by the momentum of her own rapid speech, she seemed unable to stop, but went rattling on in staccato phrases, dotted with abrupt, dramatic gestures. 'I'm Señora Mangada. They know me here. Just ask anybody: who's Widow Mangada? They'll tell you. Of course,' she shrugged eloquently, as if Mark and Sally might not, after all, be wise enough to appreciate the privilege she was offering them, 'of course, you can decide for yourselves. It's up to you . . .'

The bus was pulling up in the centre of Villaviento. One large dusty palm tree sprouted in the middle of the little square, surrounded by simple white shop fronts and private houses, their slatted wooden shutters tightly drawn.

'Villaviento!' Widow Mangada proclaimed, with a proprietary flaunt of her red-nailed hand. She bustled out from her seat then, and preceded them down the aisle, short and lumpy as a plum pudding. Her stylish white lace dress revealed a black slip underneath; her blue-black hair was elegantly marcelled in a broth of little waves and curls.

Mark's eyes followed her meditatively as she flounced down the steps into the street with an important air.

'You might think,' he mused, 'that a row of photographers was lying in wait for her.'

A motley crew of tanned native boys battled among themselves to carry the Widow's luggage. She scurried about, at last electing a young boy with a cart to load on her bulging canvas suitcase and an immense knobbly burlap bag.

Then she was back, with the boy and laden cart in tow, chattering and gesticulating as if she'd never left off. Mark hoisted the rucksack on his shoulder and Sally balanced typewriter and watermelon.

'This way,' the Widow said, sliding her hand under Sally's arm in an intimate, friendly fashion and trotting along beside them in her stumpy openwork pumps.

Modern hotels lined the main *avenida*, with bright red, yellow and green balconies, gaudy as if coloured at random from a child's paint box.

'Hotels!' The Widow clucked disapprovingly and hurried them on. 'Terrible! Expensive! A hundred pesetas a night, for one person only. And then all the little extra charges. Cigarettes. Telephone.' She shook her frizzed black curls.

Mark slanted Sally a warning look over Widow Mangada's head. The Widow was already launched on an enthusiastic sales talk.

'Look!' She threw out her arm triumphantly as they turned the corner to walk along the ocean boulevard. The bay lay before them, vivid, blue, rimmed by a crest of orange hills. 'And here we are.' Widow Mangada was unlocking the gate of a creamy beige stucco villa.

Sally stood, mouth open. 'Talk about dreams,' she said to Mark. The house, with a vine-grown second-floor terrace, was set deep in a grove of palm trees. Beds of red geraniums and white daisies blazed like bonfires in the garden; spined cacti bordered the flagstone path.

Chattering on about natural beauty, the Widow led them around back to point out her grape arbour, her fig tree thick with green fruit, and the splendid view of purple hills in the background, suspended in a scrim of mist.

Within, the stone-tiled house was cool and dark as a well. The Widow flew about, throwing open shutters and indicating the shining rows of aluminium pans in the kitchen with its blackened one-ring petrol stove, the stacks of plates and wine glasses amassed in the dining room. She yanked out drawers, rummaged in cupboards. Sally, already delighted with the housekeeping possibilities, was won completely by the tiny bedroom upstairs. It opened, together with one of the larger rooms, onto the balcony terrace and a view of the blue Mediterranean framed in palm fronds.

'Oh, Mark,' Sally pleaded. 'Let's stay.'

The Widow's black beady eyes darted from one to the other. 'Nothing like it. Perfect.' Her words rippled over themselves, smooth as oil. 'I'll show you the town. The market. Everything. We'll be friends. Not impersonal as they are in the hotels . . .'

'How much,' Mark asked matter-of-factly, 'does it cost?'

The Widow paused, hesitating, as if he had brought up something just a touch indelicate. 'One hundred pesetas a night,' she said at last. She hurried on then: 'For both of you. Plus the service. You'll have all the comfort . . .'

'Service?' Mark stopped her. 'How much does that make it?'

'A hundred and ten.'

Mark exchanged a look with Sally. 'That's more than we can spend for two months,' he said simply.

Wistfully, Sally recalled the wire whisks and soup ladles lining the kitchen. 'But I'll cook,' she volunteered, although as yet rather dismayed by the stubborn look of the unfamiliar petrol stove. 'We'll go to the peasant market, and that will bring the cost of living way down.'

'We're writers.' Mark turned to the Widow. 'All we want is a quiet place where we can write for the summer. We can't afford one hundred and ten pesetas a night.'

'Ah! You are writers!' Widow Mangada grew effusive. 'I, too, am a writer. Stories. Poems. Many poems.' The Widow subsided then, dropping her blue-shadowed lids. 'For you,' she said, stressing her words, 'I will not charge service. But you understand,' she glanced up quickly, 'you must not tell anyone. The Others will pay service. The government demands it. But you and I, we will be friends.' She gave them a blinding smile, displaying a row of large, protruding yellow teeth. 'I will treat you like my own son and daughter.'

Mark shifted uneasily from one foot to the other, glancing at Sally's eager face. He sighed. 'All right, then,' he said at last. 'We'll take it.'

Shortly after three o'clock that afternoon, Mark and Sally were lying on the deserted beach in front of the Widow's house, drying off after a swim in the mild green surf. They had spent the rest of the morning at the outdoor peasant market shopping for food supplies.

Sally glanced up at the balcony across the street and giggled. 'The Widow's mincing around in our room now, putting those embroidered sheets and valuable bedspreads on the beds. "Especially for us."'

Mark grunted sceptically from where he lay stretched face down on their beach towel. 'I still think there's something queer about her being a landlady after all the talk of noble birth and university degrees and her brilliant dead doctor husband she gave us over lunch.'

'I wonder what her poems are like,' Sally mused, gazing out at the barren island in the middle of the bay. An elaborate white schooner was slowly crossing along the horizon line, like the fabulous relic of an old legend. 'She told me she's written an exquisite description of moonlight on the water at Villaviento. "A lustre of pearls," she called it.'

'Don't let that fancy tinsel fool you,' Mark cautioned. 'She probably writes torrid Spanish love stories for the pulp magazines.'

That evening, Sally struggled to light the smoking petrol stove while Mark lay upstairs, burned raw from the afternoon sun, radiating heat like a Sunday roast. She was just warming up the frying pan of olive oil when Widow Mangada materialised in the doorway. In a flash, the Widow was at the range, turning down the wick of the petrol stove.

'Not so high,' she chided Sally. 'Or it wastes the wick. What are you making?' She peered curiously at the heap of sliced potatoes and onions Sally was planning to fry.

'Ah!' the Widow exclaimed. 'I'll show you how we do things!'

Sally lounged patiently against the big black range while the Widow got the pan of oil steaming and tossed in the potatoes and onions, prattling rapidly all the while about how Sally must order milk to be delivered daily, go early to market for fresh fish, and take care to watch the scales and not get cheated; those tricky peasants weren't above using rocks instead of proper weights and measures.

When the potatoes and onions were browning, the Widow whipped up two eggs in a cup and poured them into the pan. 'Somebody came to look at the front room while you and your husband were at the beach this afternoon,' she said gaily, poking at the pan, as if thinking of nothing but the welfare of the onions and potatoes. 'They asked about the balcony going off the big front room and I told them, of course: the balcony is for the use of everybody.'

Sally felt a queer catch in her stomach, as if knifed unexpectedly from behind. She thought fast. The only windows to their tiny bedroom, which wasn't even big enough for a writing table, were in the French doors opening onto the balcony. If other people sat out there, she and Mark would have absolutely no privacy.

'Why,' Sally covered her incredulity with a calm, reasonable tone, 'that would really be impossible.' The Widow seemed deeply absorbed in sliding the tortilla out onto a plate. As Sally spoke, she flipped the plate expertly upside down, dropping the tortilla back in the pan to brown on the other side.

'The other tourists can sun on the beach or in the garden,' Sally went on, 'but we can't write in public. We can only write where it's quiet, on our balcony. Being a writer, as you are,' Sally picked up the Widow's words, amazed at her own sudden turn for flattery, 'I am sure you understand that absolute peace is essential for work.'

The Widow flashed Sally a grin, which sheathed an intent side glance. Then, almost immediately, she broke into a rich, deep chuckle, as if laughing at a joke on both of them. 'But of course. Of course I understand,' she said soothingly. 'To the next person who asks about the balcony, I'll say: why, I've rented that to two American writers. It is just for them.'

In triumph, Sally bore the savoury tortilla upstairs together with a bottle of wine. She felt she had somehow outfinessed the Widow at a game yet new to her.

As she shut the bedroom door behind her, Mark groaned, 'Listen!'

'What's the matter?' Sally asked, concerned. She went out on the balcony to set the tray on the table. It was already twilight, and a bright white moon was rising out of the sea. From below their balcony, along the ocean boulevard, came a loud murmur as of gathering multitudes before some large mob scene.

Sally stared. Crowds of lavishly dressed summer tourists were strolling below, glancing up in curiosity at the balcony. Along the low wall bordering the beach, white-uniformed Spanish maids sat tending squalling children. A donkey was pulling a hand organ past. Vendors pushed by carts of coconuts and ice cream.

'It's the town's evening sport,' Mark lamented. 'The idle rich. Gabbing and gawping. They siesta all afternoon. No wonder the beach was so magnificently empty today.'

'Well, if it's just in the evening,' Sally consoled, 'we'll get up and start work at dawn.' But she, too, felt a bit self-conscious pouring wine, trying to avoid the inquisitive eyes below. The Widow had put up a 'Rooms for Rent' sign on the balcony that afternoon.

'I feel like a living illustrated ad of Balcony Dwellers in Villaviento,' Mark grumbled.

'Oh, it's only for an hour or so,' Sally said, watching Mark take his first bite of the tortilla. He murmured approval. 'Wait till you hear about the *coup d'état* I've just managed,' she went on proudly, and told him that the balcony was now exclusively theirs.

'I was beginning to worry about the balcony,' Mark said. 'She's a subtle lady, that one.'

Sally woke early the next morning to hear the seethe and rush of waves on the beach. Slipping carefully out of bed so as not to wake Mark, still sleeping, shrimp-red, in a tangle of sheets, she crossed the hall to the bathroom to wash up. No water came from the single cold-water tap. Dimly she remembered that yesterday, in the flurry of instructions and useful information, the Widow had switched on the lever of a strange, blue-painted box in the kitchen, claiming that the motor made water.

Sally tiptoed downstairs in the still house. The kitchen was darkly shuttered. Opening the shutters, Sally regarded the blue box mistrustfully, with its odd blue spigots and frayed wires. She had a blind respect for electricity. Bracing herself, she pulled the lever. A flash of blue sparks shot from the box, and a thin column of acrid smoke began twisting out from the heart of the machine.

Guiltily, Sally switched back the lever. The smoke stopped. She knocked on the Widow's door, next to the kitchen. There was no answer. She called, softly, then louder. Still no answer. This is ridiculous, Sally thought, shifting from one cold bare foot to the other: no water, no Widow. No coffee, either, she added to the list of grievances. For a moment she had the absurd conviction that the Widow had sneaked away overnight, leaving them with an unmanageable elephant of a house. She went upstairs to wake Mark.

'There's no water,' Sally announced in tragic tones. Mark squinted up at her from swollen pink eyelids. 'And the Widow has disappeared.'

Sleepily, Mark pulled on his bathing trunks and accompanied Sally downstairs to the kitchen. He turned the lever of the water-making machine. No response. He tried the light switch. No electricity. 'Something's fused,' he said. 'The whole house is probably a web of defective wiring.'

'*You* knock on the Widow's door and call her,' Sally said. 'Your voice is louder. If she's renting us the house, the least she can do is keep the water running.'

Mark knocked on the door. He called the Widow. The house was deathly still except for the grandfather clock in the hall, ticking like a coffined heart.

'Maybe she's dead in there,' Sally said. 'I have the strangest feeling there's nobody breathing behind that door.'

'Maybe she went out early.' Mark yawned. 'I miss my coffee.'

At last they decided to go back to bed and wait for the Widow. Just as Sally was closing her eyes, she heard the screak of the front gate hinges, and brisk staccato footsteps tripping up the walk. Jumping into her bathrobe, she padded downstairs to meet the Widow, fresh and lacy as a daisy in her white dress, coming in the door with a bundle of parcels.

'Ah,' the Widow crowed merrily on seeing Sally. 'Have you slept well?' Sally, looking at the Widow with a more jaundiced eye than on the previous day, wondered if there wasn't an ironic note veiled in her honey tones.

'There's no water,' Sally stated bleakly. 'No water for washing. Or coffee.'

The Widow laughed brightly, as if Sally were a charming but rather maladroit child. 'Why of course there's water,' she said, dropping her parcels on a chair and making a little rush into the kitchen. 'So simple!'

Following her, Sally felt grimly positive that the machine was primed so it would work only for the Widow. With a certain satisfaction, she watched the Widow turn on the lever. There were no results.

'I tried that, too,' Sally told her, lounging casually against the door jamb. 'And nothing happened.'

The Widow tried the light switch. 'No light!' she exclaimed triumphantly and gave another one of her deep, confidential laughs with a long shrewd look at Sally hidden in the middle of it.

'It is so in all the village,' the Widow said then. 'No light, no machine.'

'Then this is usual in the morning?' Sally queried coolly.

The Widow appeared, for the first time, to realise that Sally was annoyed. 'Ah, you mustn't take things so serious,' she shook her dark head reprovingly. 'There is always water here. Plenty of water.'

Sally waited, with what she trusted was a sceptical, challenging expression.

With the lofty air of a woman far above mere worldly emergencies, the Widow glided over to the sink, lifted from the counter a wooden lid which Sally had used as a chopping board the night before, and revealed a bottomless black hole. Whisking a pail and long rope from one of her myriad cupboards, the Widow dropped the pail down the hole. There was an echoing splash. The Widow gave the rope a series of short, energetic tugs, and hauled up a sloshing bucketful of sparkling water.

'You see,' she moralised to Sally. 'Plenty of water. All the time.' She began filling three pitchers of various sizes. 'Marvellous water. Beneficial for the stomach.' She motioned at the cold water tap in the sink, wrinkling her nose up in a grimace of disgust and shaking her head: 'That water's bad,' she told Sally. 'Non potable.'

Sally gasped. Fortunately she and Mark had drunk wine the previous evening. The tap water was no doubt slow poison. Had the Widow forgotten to mention it before? Or hadn't she wanted to bring up any disadvantages until they were well settled in her house? Sally wondered, then, with increasing unease, whether the Widow *ever* would have told them about her secret store of drinkable, health-giving water if the machine hadn't broken down that morning.

With a new reserve, Sally took a pitcher of water from the cheerfully voluble Widow and went upstairs to wash. In a few minutes, the Widow trilled up that the lights were on and water was coming everywhere.

'She's probably been prancing around the yard with a divining rod,' Mark said grumpily. He went down to heat a kettle of water on the petrol stove for shaving.

As they sat on the balcony, shaded by a slatted bamboo awning, sipping their steaming mugs of coffee, Sally rambled on about the quirks of Spanish housekeeping. 'Imagine,' she told Mark, 'the Widow doesn't have any soap and washes her dishes in cold water with little tangles of straw. She was sermonising at me just now about how neat I have to be when the Others come. Well, you should see her own cupboard – all higgledy-piggledy, with scraps of cold beans and dead fish and a pack of ants carrying away her sugar grain by grain. It'll be gone by tomorrow.'

Mark broke into a laugh. 'I'd give anything to know what the townspeople of Villaviento think about her. We've probably got in with the village witch.'

Sally typed some letters home on the balcony that morning, while Mark propped himself up on pillows in the bedroom, nursing his burn and writing an animal fable. From the street below came the cry of the bread woman, strolling by with a basket of fried rolls over her arm; the milk boy biked past with a gallon can in his basket. As Sally lazed, her fingers lagging over the keys, the sound of voices drifted up to her.

Widow Mangada was showing a young Spanish couple about the garden, gesturing grandiloquently at the geraniums, the view of the sea. Sally peered down at them through the vine leaves. She half hoped the Widow would have no other customers, it was so quiet and pleasant in the dark house with just Mark and herself.

Preparing lunch that noon, Sally put a pan of string beans on to boil and began cutting up some cold sausage. After ten minutes, she checked the beans. They were as hard as ever, and the water wasn't even warm. Sally turned the wick higher, hoping to make more heat come out of the stove. An unhealthy flame flared up, thin, smoking green.

At that moment, as if beckoned by some occult signal, Widow Mangada appeared in the doorway, took one look at the smoke funnelling out of the stove, and rushed bleating in horror to the range. Whipping off the pan of beans and the chimney of the petrol stove, she revealed, with a flourish, the criminal evidence of over an inch of frayed, charred wick.

'No petrol!' she announced with all the drama of a doctor diagnosing cancer. She scuttled over to her cupboard, pulled out a bottle of transparent liquid, and poured it into the tank of the stove. Then she fussed about with the wick, snipping off the charred ends with her fingers, raising the wick higher on the shaft. She lit the wick again and replaced the beans. Not satisfied with this, she tasted a bean and shook her head sadly at Sally.

'You wait a minute,' she said, and went running out of the room. She returned with a handful of powder which she tossed into the beans, just now beginning to boil. The water fizzed and foamed.

'What's that?' Sally asked, suspicious.

The Widow gave her a coy little look and shook her finger as at a naughty child. 'It's just something,' she smiled evasively. 'I've been cooking a lot longer than you and know a few small tricks.'

Then, as if in chance afterthought, the Widow went on: 'Oh, by the way, a doctor has rented the room upstairs for a few days.' She hung poised in the doorway like a white gull ready for flight. 'He's coming in about an hour.'

'Oh, just *one* man,' Sally remarked in prosaic tones. She was beginning to enjoy playing dense and making the Widow detail her manoeuvres at a slower rate.

'No,' the Widow said, obviously a bit nettled. 'He has a wife. And two friends.' She hesitated. 'And the other couple has a baby.'

'Oh,' Sally said eloquently, bending over the steaming beans.

The Widow, about to retreat, thought better of it and advanced again to the stove. 'You understand,' her playful tone with Sally changed, barbed now with an odd emotional intensity, 'I do not care how many people are in the house as long as it is always full. You must learn to share. The cupboards, the stove, they are not just for you. They are also for the Others.' She put on her glittering yellow-toothed smile then, as if to outshine her bluntness.

'Why of course!' Sally said to the Widow in bland astonishment. But something else was evidently bothering the Widow's conscience, too.

'The Spaniards, Señora,' she told Sally gravely, 'are very different from you Americans.' Her tone made no secret of which side her sympathies were on. 'They sing all the time. They turn radios loud. They leave things here and there.' Carried away by her own speech, the Widow began to sway her plump little body to and fro dramatically, acting it all out in a sort of pantomime. 'They come in late at night. And their children cry. It is very natural.'

Sally couldn't restrain a smile as she envisioned a bevy of Spaniards bellowing arias in the cold shower and executing flamenco dances around the petrol stove. 'I understand perfectly,' she assured the Widow.

'Perhaps,' the Widow brightened, as if struck by a new and marvellously advantageous scheme for Sally, 'you would like to move your cooking things out of the cupboard, over here. Then the cupboard would not bother you, helter-skelter with Spanish dishes.' Sally's look followed the Widow's cavalier gesture. She was pointing to an open shelf over the garbage can.

So that was it. Sally's intuitions were quickening; she felt stripped for action. 'Why, I am perfectly delighted where I am,' she told the Widow in demure, but firm tones. 'I wouldn't dream of being bothered.'

The Widow disappeared from the kitchen with a dazzling, false grin, which Sally felt lingering on as she finished preparing the meal, disquieting as the smile of the Cheshire Cat.

While Mark and Sally were eating lunch on the balcony, a car drew up in front of the house. The Spanish couple Sally had seen that morning got out, with another couple and a little girl, frilled as a peony in her starched petticoats.

The Widow ran out to greet them, swinging the gate wide as if it were crusted with gold and costly gems, almost curtsying as the four Spaniards walked in, carrying the child.

At three, Mark and Sally left their room to go for a swim. Mark disliked the crowds of fat, swarthy women and oiled dandies thronging the beach at midday, and during siesta time, from three to five, they had the beach completely to themselves. In the upstairs hall, all the window shutters were closed and the other rooms were hushed and darkened as in a hospital. Sally shut the door behind them. The sound echoed sepulchrally.

'Ssst!' With a venomous hiss, Widow Mangada was at the foot of the stairs. In a tirade of exaggerated wavings and whispers, she announced that the Spaniards were all sleeping and ordered Mark and Sally to be more considerate.

'Whew!' Mark exclaimed as they were safe on the beach. 'What a change of tone.'

It developed that the Spaniards were going to eat at one of the town hotels. Sally stood over the petrol stove that night, stirring tuna in a thick cream sauce and listening warily for the light, almost inaudible tread of the Widow. She had grown to dread those footsteps. Outside of their bedroom, now, she felt vulnerable as a sniping target in enemy territory.

After she had turned off the petrol stove, she heard the fire still burning in the chimney. Leaning down, she blew to extinguish it. With a loud pouf, a long leaping tongue of flame forked up at her. Startled, Sally jumped back. Aiming for my eyes, she thought uneasily as she rubbed away the tears from the stinging smoke.

While she was letting the water run freely over her cooking dishes, the Widow darted in, crossed to the sink, and put the cork in to stop the drain.

'You mustn't waste water here,' she lectured Sally. 'It is very precious.'

Sally waited until the Widow was out of the kitchen, removed the plug, and turned the water on full force with a rich sense of illicit extravagance.

The next morning, Sally woke to hear the Widow's voice in the hall. From her unusually flustered, apologetic tones, Sally gathered something was wrong. Curious, she tiptoed to the door. As if developing symptoms of the Widow's tactics like a contagious disease, she stooped to peer out from the keyhole. Giggling, then, she poked Mark awake.

'Guess what,' she informed him. 'The five of them are all queued up around the bathroom and the Widow's in her bathrobe, lugging up great pitchers of water. The doctor's in there shaving now.'

The water machine had broken down completely. 'From overwork,' Mark hazarded. 'Her whole fancy house is probably tottering over a pit of quicksand.'

When Sally went downstairs to draw water from the well for their coffee, she found the Widow in the hall, swathed in a soiled yellow satin wrapper, wet-mopping the stone tiles. In the frank morning light, her face appeared haggard and slightly green; her eyebrows were not yet pencilled on, and her mouth hung loose and froggish without lipstick.

'Ah!' the Widow sputtered, leaning on her mop and speaking in hoarse, fretful tones. 'This morning I go to town to look for a maid. I am not used to this. At home in Alicante I had three maids . . .'

Sally murmured sympathetically. With dignity, the Widow stretched to her full height, her chin not reaching far above the mop handle. 'When I go out to town,' her look blurred beyond Sally, lost in some luminous far vision, 'I am a grande dame. I do not work when the front door is open, for the people to see. You understand? But,' the Widow fixed Sally with a stern, proud glare, 'when the door is shut,' she shrugged her shoulders and spread her hands comprehensively, 'I do everything. Everything.'

The Widow sailed home from town that morning with a black-clad maid in her wake. She supervised imperiously for an hour, while the maid swept, scrubbed, and dusted. Then the maid returned to town.

'It is very difficult,' the Widow confided to Sally, with the air of a born duchess fallen upon hard times, 'to find a maid in Villaviento. They are so expensive in the summer. They get paid too much by the hotels. If you have a maid nowadays, you must be very careful of her feelings.'

The Widow rallied enough to mimic the tender treatment a maid must have. She nodded, minced about, grinned sugarily. 'If she breaks your priceless crystal vase, you must laugh and say: "Ah, do not trouble yourself over it, mademoiselle."'

Sally smiled. The Widow was always complaining about expense; how much of her moaning was an act, Sally couldn't truly tell.

That morning, from the balcony, Sally and Mark watched Widow Mangada fussing about with repairmen, a gardener, and three native workers with a donkey cart who began to remove all the stones and rubble choking her unused driveway.

'I suppose it's a sign of aristocracy here,' Mark said, 'having a team of men constantly slaving for you. And a donkey or two.'

'She's so desperate about keeping up her royal front in Villaviento,' Sally said.

'Royal front,' Mark snorted. 'It's rank humbug. She may have taught Spanish to the governor's wife in Gibraltar but I haven't been able to corner her for one of her promised lessons yet.'

'Wait till she gets the house settled down,' Sally soothed. 'She still hasn't found anyone to rent the front room, and it's probably bothering her.'

'I'm sure she can't rent it because of the balcony being shut off. No doubt she's furious with herself for letting us win her best selling point.'

'She knows she would have lost us if she didn't give in,' Sally reminded.

Mark shook his head. 'She'll try to fox us yet.'

'I don't see how,' Sally said. 'If we just keep to ourselves.'

As Sally was dreamily peeling the potatoes for lunch, Widow Mangada entered the kitchen. She pounced on the potato in Sally's hand and took up the knife. 'Now *this* is the way you should peel a potato!' she instructed Sally patronisingly, making the brown skin fly off in one continuous corkscrew strip. Sally sighed. More and more she resented the Widow's little meddling forays into the kitchen. The Widow even rearranged her cupboard on the sly, mixing the onions in the egg dish to free another bowl for her own sodden dabs of cold, fishy pottage which she left lying about on her shelves for days.

As the Widow plucked up another potato, Sally realised she was using even more flowery oratory than usual. '. . . Every other summer, of course,' the Widow was saying, 'I've rented the house out to one family. Complete. For twenty, thirty thousand pesetas. But,' the knife flew, stripping the potato bare, 'this summer for the first time I stay here to rent rooms. Only it proves impossible.'

Sally felt a chill of foreboding. She waited. 'The government . . .' Widow Mangada smiled up ingratiatingly with a helpless shrug at Sally, all the while continuing to skin the potato by some deft sleight-of-hand, 'the government forces us to fill every room. And today the Alcalde, the Mayor of Villaviento, tells me I must rent the house entire since I cannot fill all the rooms.'

Sally caught her breath and took her first clear look at the Widow. The ornate painted mask cracked in a wolfish grin. Eyes exposed a black, bottomless pool into which a stone had vanished, ring after surface ring rippling outward.

Leaving the Widow holding the scraped white potato, open-mouthed, in the middle of a sentence, Sally turned and ran. Her breath caught tight in her chest, she burst in on Mark.

'Oh, stop her,' she cried, throwing herself on the bed. There was the sound of quick, tapping footsteps following her up the stairs. 'Stop that woman,' Sally begged, almost hysterical now. 'She's going to evict us.'

'Señora,' the Widow was calling in dulcet tones outside the door. Sally heard the cockroach rustle in the cupboard, the spider knitting hexes across the well.

Mark opened the door a crack and looked down at Widow Mangada. 'Well?' he said.

Widow Mangada practised her charms. With beseeching eyes, she gazed up at Mark, crooning: 'Ah, Señor. The Señora is so excitable. She does not even listen to what I am going to say. Men are . . .' she fumbled prettily, '. . . so much more practical than young girls about such things.'

Mark beckoned to Sally, who was eyeing them broodingly from the bed. 'Come on back to the kitchen and finish getting lunch,' he said. 'We'll talk about it there.'

In the kitchen, the Widow spoke beguilingly to Mark while Sally tended the fried potatoes, still shaken, ashamed of letting her defences down in front of the Widow.

'Now of course,' the Widow was assuring Mark in mellifluous tones, 'I do not want you and the Señora to go. I do not look for anybody to rent the whole house. But,' she shrugged with wheedling philosophy, 'if the Alcalde sends someone, what am I to do?'

'Ask her how much notice she'll give us,' Sally said to Mark sulkily in English. She refused to speak Spanish to the Widow now, retreating as if for protection to the language the Widow did not understand and putting Mark between them as interpreter.

'How much notice?' Mark asked the Widow. She looked surprised at Mark for bringing up such apparently trifling concerns. 'Ah, two days, three days . . .' she drawled finally, as if conceding a great favour.

Sally was aghast. 'And where do we go then?' she stormed at Mark. 'Into the streets?' She felt sick at the thought of packing up and moving again, furious at the Widow's sly weathercock shifts.

'We'll talk about it later.' Mark closed the subject. Silenced for the time being, the Widow retreated.

'If she thinks,' Sally raged over lunch, 'that we're going to live here at her convenience, paying her until she finds someone else, so she won't lose a peseta . . . And using the government as an excuse for her own sweet whims . . .'

'Take it easy,' Mark placated. 'She's crooked as a crab, that's all. Face up to it.'

They decided to go house-hunting around Villaviento early that evening without telling the Widow until they were actually moving out.

That night, over supper on the balcony, Sally exulted: 'We've bought a house. A whole house. I'll have my own kitchen. And my own snarls of straw for the dishes.'

'Oh, our new landlady's probably having a fiesta right now at the way we let her jump the rent.' Mark was characteristically reserved, but even he couldn't hide his pleasure. They were paying almost a thousand pesetas less for a quiet house in the native quarter than they were spending for Widow Mangada's cramped, noisy room. And they were moving in the next morning.

Mark and Sally lingered over the wine, toasting their success, relaxing easily and fully for the first time since they had arrived at Widow Mangada's.

Sally laughed happily as they finished the bottle of wine. 'It's like being freed from a jinx,' she said.

While Mark was helping Sally wash up the dishes, the Widow tripped blithely into the kitchen. 'Ah,' she chirruped with a bright new-minted smile, 'and did you have a nice walk? I do hope,' she raced on, 'you won't trouble yourselves over what the Alcalde said.' She gave them a cajoling look. 'We'll have such a nice summer. Probably no one will even ask about the house. Now, if you were Spanish . . .' she tossed Mark an arch glance, 'you wouldn't dream of being so serious about such a little thing . . .'

'I think we should tell you,' Mark said without preamble, overriding Sally's motions to silence, 'that we've found a new place. With a summer contract. And we're moving out tomorrow.'

Sally forgave Mark for springing the surprise a day early. Widow Mangada's jaw dropped. Her face flushed an ugly purple.

'What?' her voice shrilled up a scale, incredulous. She began trembling, as if shaken in the teeth of a high wind. 'After all I've done for you! After I gave you the balcony . . .' Her voice frayed to a coarse squawk.

'Our room's too small to live in without the balcony, and you know it,' Sally inserted truthfully.

Widow Mangada flew at her like a maddened wasp, brandishing a furious finger in Sally's face. 'It's you, you!' she accused spitefully, shedding all pretence of decorum. 'Always complaining. The room's too small! This and that! Your husband never complains . . .'

The Widow veered in a last desperate bid to flatter Mark.

'I ask my wife to manage household affairs,' he cut the Widow off firmly. 'I'm ready to stand behind everything she's said.'

'Well!' the Widow fumed, outraged. 'After all my consideration, my generosity, my frankness . . .' She paused, breathless.

Then, her flair for rhetoric returning, she began to gather up the ragged shreds of ceremony. 'As you wish,' she managed at last with a wobbly smile; the yellow teeth gleamed. 'You say you leave tomorrow?' she asked, the metallic light of the adding machine already back in her eye. She turned on her heel. The front door slammed behind her.

Late that night, the front gate screaked open. Mark and Sally could hear the Widow muttering from the lower hall. She began to mount the stairs, grumbling loudly and incoherently all the while. Sally drew the sheet up over her head, fully believing some immediate judgement was at hand. Savagely, the Widow stamped across the upstairs hall, through the vast, empty front room and onto the balcony, spitting out curses and unintelligible snarls. Sally could see her squat, lumpish shape silhouetted in the moonlight, busy about the balcony railing.

'She's ripping down the rental sign,' Mark whispered.

Bearing the sign as if it were a severed human head, the Widow stormed downstairs.

The next morning, as Sally boiled mounds of potatoes and eggs for a picnic lunch to take to their new home, pleasantly conscious she was using up much of the Widow's petrol, Widow Mangada appeared in the kitchen. Her mood of the night before had altered completely. She was bland as butter.

'I met the woman who owns the place you're moving to last night,' she informed Sally. 'She told me exactly what you're paying for the summer.' The Widow pronounced the sum with something akin to reverence. 'Is that correct?'

'Yes,' Sally said a bit shortly. She resented Widow Mangada's finding out such details. Yet she was aware that the Widow could not accuse them of being cheated: she herself was charging them more for so much less.

'It's a beautiful big house,' Sally could not resist adding. She lifted the hard-boiled eggs from the steaming kettle.

The Widow made a wry face. 'I wouldn't know. I never walk up to that part of town. So far from the beach and all.' The house was a mere ten minutes from the sea.

'Mark and I love to walk,' Sally replied sweetly.

'I told the woman,' the Widow went on, fiddling with the lace collar of her dress, 'that you and your husband were very nice. I said of course you would have stayed on with me for the summer if I hadn't been forced suddenly by the Alcalde to rent the house as a whole to one family.'

Sally was silent, letting the fib hang fire in empty air.

'We will still be good friends,' the Widow proclaimed then, with a magnanimous smile. 'Anything you need, you just come over and ask me. Haven't I taught you all about Spanish cooking?' She teetered on tiptoe and peered almost pleadingly into Sally's face.

Before they left, the Widow had enthusiastically made an appointment for an English lesson from Mark at her home the following afternoon.

'I want to know everything. Everything!' she repeated, accompanying them to the door, her black saucer-eyes brimming with a thirst for scholarship.

Mark and Sally woke the next morning in their spacious new house to hear a thin jangle of bells as a herd of black goats went stepping delicately up the street on their way to pasture. A strong, freakish wind was blowing out of the low hills. At market, the old banana vendor claimed Villaviento hadn't seen a wind like that for eighty years.

The day grew bleak, curded over with clouds. Sally tried to read in the unhealthy yellow light, waiting for Mark to return from his afternoon English lesson with Widow Mangada.

The wind howled about the house, raising eddies of dust and rattling the window frames. Scraps of paper and torn grape leaves swatted against the panes. Some storm was brewing.

Mark was back twenty minutes after he'd left. 'She's vanished,' he said, tramping in and brushing the dust off his jacket. 'There's a German family living there now. She must have skipped back to Alicante the minute we left yesterday morning.'

Rain began to splatter down in large drops on the dusty pavement outside.

'Do you suppose she honestly had all those university degrees?' Sally asked. 'And a brilliant doctor husband?'

'Maybe,' Mark said. 'Or maybe she's just a clever quack.'

'Or a weird sister.'

'Who's to tell?'

The wind screeched around the corners of the house, whirling this way and that, blinding the windowpanes with rain out of the labyrinth of those dark, malignant hills.

All the Dead Dears

Written: September–October 1956
Published: *Gemini* (Summer 1957): 53–9

'I don't care what Herbert says,' declared Mrs Nellie Meehan, dumping two spoonfuls of sugar in her tea, 'I saw an angel once. It was my sister Minnie, the night Lucas died.'

The four of them were sitting late around the red coal fire that November evening in the Meehans' new-bought house: Nellie Meehan and her husband Clifford, Nellie's Cousin Herbert, lodger with the Meehans since his red-headed wife left him at haymaking time some twenty-seven years before, and Dora Sutcliffe, who had dropped over for a pot of tea on the way back home up Caxton Slack after visiting her friend Ellen, just out of hospital, recovering from a cataract operation.

The dying fire still glowed warm, the battered aluminium tea kettle steamed on the hearth, and Nellie Meehan had gotten out her hand-embroidered linen tablecloth, all wreathed with violets and crimson poppies, in honour of Dora's coming. A snowdrift of currant cakes and buttered scones banked the blue-willow platter and a little cut-glass bowl held generous dollops of Nellie Meehan's homemade gooseberry jam. Outside, in the clear, windy night, the moon shone high and full; a blue, luminous mist was rising from the bottom of the valley where the mountain stream flowed black and deep over those foaming falls in which Dora's brother-in-law had chosen to drown himself a week ago come Monday. The Meehans' house (bought early that autumn from spinster Katherine Edwards after her mother Maisie died at the doughty age of eighty-six) clung halfway up the steep hill of red-berried ash and bracken which flattened out at the top, stretching away into wild and barren moorland, twigged with heather and prowled by the black-faced moor sheep, with their curling horns and mad, staring yellow eyes.

Already, during the long evening, they had discussed the days of the Great War, and the various ends of those who thrived and those who died, Clifford Meehan creaking to his feet at the appropriate point in the course of conversation, as was his habit, and taking out of the bottom drawer in the polished mahogany china cabinet the cardboard box of souvenirs – medals, ribbons, and the shattered paybook providentially in his breast pocket when the bullet struck (bits of shrapnel still lodged in its faded pages) – to show Dora Sutcliffe the blurred ochre daguerreotype snapped in hospital the Christmas before Armistice, with the faces of five young men smiling out, lit by the wan winter sun that rose and set some forty years back. 'That's me,' Clifford had said, and, as if naming the fates of characters in some well-known play, jutted his thumb at the other faces, one by one: 'He's got his leg off. He was killed. He's dead, and he's dead.'

And so they gossiped gently on, calling up the names of the quick and the dead, reliving each past event as if it had no beginning and no end, but existed, vivid and irrevocable, from the beginning of time, and would continue to exist long after their own voices were stilled.

'What,' Dora Sutcliffe asked Nellie Meehan now in hushed, church-going tones, 'was Minnie wearing?'

Nellie Meehan's eyes grew dreamy. 'A white Empire smock,' she said. 'All gathered about the waist, it was, with hundreds and hundreds of little pleats. I remember just as clear. And wings, great feathery white wings coming down over the bare tips of her toes. Clifford and I didn't get word about Lucas till the next morning, but that was the night I had the pain and heard the knocking. The night Minnie came. Wasn't it, Clifford?'

Clifford Meehan puffed meditatively on his pipe, his hair silvery in the firelight, his trousers and sweater bayberry grey; except for his vivid, purple-veined nose, he seemed on the verge of becoming translucent, as if the chimney mantel, hung with its gleaming horse brasses, might at any moment begin to show faintly through his thin, greyed frame. 'Aye,' he said finally. 'That was the night.' His wife's undeniable flashes of second sight had always awed and somewhat chastened him.

Cousin Herbert sat dour and sceptical, his huge, awkward hands, cracked with wrinkles, hanging loose at his sides. Herbert's mind had long ago riveted itself on that distant sunny day, the first fair weather after a week's downpour, when his wife Rhoda's folks, up visiting to help with the haymaking, jaunted off to Manchester with Rhoda, leaving Herbert alone with the hay. On returning at dusk, they'd found their luggage packed, hurled into the far corner of the cow field; Rhoda had left him then, indignant, with her parents. Stubborn and proud, Herbert had never asked her back; and, stubborn and proud as he, she had never come.

'I woke up . . .' Nellie Meehan's eyes blurred, as if in some visionary trance, and her voice grew rhythmic. Outside, the wind blasted away at the house which creaked and shuddered to its foundations under those powerful assaults of air. 'I woke up that night with a terrible pain in my left shoulder, hearing this loud knocking all around, and there was Minnie, standing at the foot of the bed, right pale and sweet-faced – I was about seven, the winter she took pneumonia; we slept in the same bed then. Well, as I looked, she kept fading and fading, until she went fading clear away into nothing. I got up real careful so as not to wake Clifford, and went downstairs to make myself a pot of tea. My shoulder was hurting something terrible, and all the time I heard this knock knock knock . . .'

'What *was* it?' Dora Sutcliffe begged, her watery blue eyes wide. She had heard the story of Lucas' hanging countless times, at second and third hand, but with every fresh telling the previous tales blurred, merging into one, and each time, at this juncture, she asked, eager, curious, as if part of some perpetually enquiring chorus: 'What was knocking?'

'First I thought it was the carpenter next door,' Nellie Meehan said, 'because he was often up till all hours hammering away in his workshop in the garage, but when I looked out the kitchen window it was pitch dark. And still I kept hearing this knock knock knock, and all the time the pain throbbing so in my shoulder. I sat up in the living room, then, trying to read, and I must have fallen asleep, because that's where Clifford found me when he came down to go to work in the morning. When I woke up it was dead quiet. The pain in my shoulder was gone, and the mailman came with the letter about Lucas, all bordered in black.'

'It wasn't a letter,' Clifford Meehan contradicted. Without fail, at some point in her story, Nellie was carried away by inaccuracy of this sort, improvising whatever details eluded her memory at the moment. 'It was a telegram. They couldn't have had a letter in the post and you getting it the same morning.'

'A telegram, then,' Nellie Meehan acquiesced. 'Saying: Come, Lucas dead.'

'It must be one of your uncles, I told her,' Clifford Meehan put in. 'I said it couldn't be Lucas, him so young, a real fine master joiner he was.'

'But it was Lucas,' Nellie Meehan said. 'He'd hung himself that night. His daughter Daphne found him in the attic. Imagine.'

'Just imagine,' Dora Sutcliffe breathed. Her hand, as if independent of her motionless, attentive body, reached for a buttered scone.

'It was the war,' Cousin Herbert announced suddenly in sepulchral tones, his very voice gone rusty from disuse. 'No lumber to be had for love nor money.'

'Well, however it might be, there was Lucas,' Clifford Meehan knocked his pipe against the grate and took out his tobacco pouch. 'Just made partner of his joining firm. Only a few days before he went and hung himself, he'd stood out where the new apartments were going up and said to his old boss, Dick Greenwood: "I wonder, will these apartments ever get built." Folks spoke to him the night he did it, and noticed nothing wrong.'

'It was his wife, Agnes,' Nellie Meehan maintained, shaking her head sadly as she recalled the fate of her departed brother, her brown eyes gentle as a cow's. 'Agnes killed him sure as if she'd poisoned him; never a kind word had Agnes. She just let him worry, worry, worry to his death. Sold his clothes at an auction, too, straight off, and bought a sweetshop with the money she took in, that and what he'd left her.'

'Fancy!' Dora Sutcliffe sniffed. 'I always said there was something mean about Agnes. She kept handkerchiefs over her scales, and everything in her shop was just that many coppers dearer than anywhere else. I bought a Christmas cake off Agnes only two years back and priced one exactly like it in Halifax the next week. Half a crown more, Agnes' cake was.'

Clifford Meehan tamped the fresh tobacco down in his pipe. 'Lucas went driving about the pubs with his daughter Daphne on the very night,' he said slowly; he, too, had told his part of the story so many times, and each time it seemed to him as though he were pausing here, expectant, waiting for some clear light to spring out of his own words, to illumine and explain the bleak, threadbare facts of the going of Lucas. 'Lucas went upstairs after dinner, and when Daphne called him down to drive out, it was a couple of minutes before he came – his face was puffed funny, Daphne said afterwards, and his lips kind of purple. Well, they stopped for a few bitters at the Black Bull, as was Lucas' habit of a Thursday night, and when he came back home, after sitting about downstairs with Daphne and Agnes a bit, he put his hands down on the arms of his chair and heaved himself up – I remember him getting up like that a hundred times – and said "I guess I'll go get ready." Daphne went up a little later and called to Agnes: "Pa's not upstairs." Then Daphne started up the attic steps; it was the only other place he could have been. And there she found him, hanging from the rafter, stone dead.'

'There was a hole bored in the middle rafter,' Nellie Meehan said. 'Lucas had fixed a swing up there for Daphne when she was just a young thing, and he strung the rope he hung himself with through that very hole.'

'They found scuff marks on the floor,' Clifford Meehan reported, coldly factual as the account in the yellowed newspaper dated nine years back preserved in Nellie's family album, 'where Lucas tried to hang himself the first time, just before he went out, only the rope was too long. But when he came back he cut it short enough.'

'I wonder Lucas could do it,' Dora Sutcliffe sighed. 'Like I wonder about my brother-in-law Gerald.'

'Aye, Gerald was a fine man,' Nellie Meehan sympathised. 'Stout and red-faced, husky as you could wish. What'll Myra do with the farm, now he's gone?'

'Ee, Lord knows,' Dora Sutcliffe said. 'It was in and out of hospital with Gerald this past winter. On account of his kidneys. Myra said the doctor'd just told him he'd have to go back again, they still weren't right. And Myra all alone now. Her daughter Beatrice married the one who's experimenting with cows down in South Africa.'

'I wonder your brother Jake's kept on so chipper, like he has these thirty years, Nellie,' Clifford Meehan mused, taking up that fugue of family phantoms, his voice melancholy as a man's might be whose two stalwart sons had left him in his old age, the one for Australia and the sheep farms, the other for Canada and a flighty secretary named Janeen. 'With that witch of a wife Esther and his one surviving daughter Cora twenty-eight and numb as a tree. I remember Jake coming to our place, before he married Esther . . .'

'Those days absolutely shone with bright and funny conversation,' Nellie Meehan interrupted, her own smile pale and wistful, as if already frozen in some dated family photograph.

'. . . coming to our place and throwing himself down on the sofa and saying: "Don't know as I ought to marry Esther; she's in weak health, always talking about ailments and hospital." Sure enough, one week after they were married, Esther's in hospital having an operation that cost Jake a hundred pound; she'd been saving it up till he'd married her and would have to pay for the whole do.'

'Slaved all his life for his woollen mill, my brother Jake did.' Nellie Meehan stirred the cold dregs of her tea. 'And now he's a fortune and ready to see the world, and Esther won't stir a step out of the house; just sits and nags at that poor silly Cora; wouldn't even let her be put in a home where she'd be among her own kind. Always taking herbs and potions, Esther is. When

Gabriel was on the way, the only good one of the lot, right in his senses, after that queer Albert was born with his tongue in wrong, Jake came right out and told Esther: "If you ruin this one, I'll kill you." And then pneumonia took the two boys, good and bad, not seven years after.'

Nellie Meehan turned her tender eyes on the red embers in the grate as if the hearts of all those dead glowed there. 'But they're waiting.' Her voice dropped, low and reassuring as a lullaby. 'They come back.' Clifford Meehan puffed slowly on his pipe. Cousin Herbert sat stone-still; the fading fire carved his brooding features in stark light and shadow, as if out of rock. 'I know,' Nellie Meehan whispered, almost to herself. 'I've seen them.'

'You mean,' Dora Sutcliffe shivered in the thin, chill draught sifting through the window frame at her back, 'you've seen *ghosts*, Nellie?' Dora Sutcliffe's question was rhetorical; she never tired of Nellie Meehan's accounts of her spasmodic commerce with the spirit world.

'Not ghosts, exactly, Dora,' Nellie Meehan said quietly, modest and reserved as always about her strange gift, 'but *presences*. I've come into a room and I've felt somebody standing there, big as life. And it's often I've said to myself: "If you could just see that bit *harder*, Nellie Meehan, you'd see them plain as day."'

'Dreams!' Cousin Herbert's voice rasped harsh. 'Stuff!'

As if Cousin Herbert were not in the room, as if his words met deaf ears, the three others spoke and gestured. Dora Sutcliffe rose to leave. 'Clifford'll walk you up Slack way,' Nellie Meehan said.

Cousin Herbert got up, without another word, his shoulders hunched, as if labouring under some great, private, unspeakable pain. He turned his back on the group about the fire and stalked to bed, his footsteps hollow and heavy on the stairs.

Nellie Meehan saw her husband and Dora Sutcliffe to the door and waved them off into the gusts of wind and drifting moon-haze. For a minute she stood in the doorway, gazing after those two figures vanished in the dark, feeling a cold more deadly than any knife strike to the marrow of her bones. Then she closed the door and went back toward the parlour to clear away the tea things. As she entered the parlour, she stopped, stunned. There, in front of the flowered upholstered sofa, hung, a few inches above the floor, a column of dazzle – not so much a light bodied on the air, but a blur superimposed upon the familiar background, a misting across the sofa, and the mahogany china cabinet behind it, and the sprigged rose and forget-me-not wallpaper. As Nellie Meehan watched, the blur began to shape itself into a vaguely familiar form, its features pale, solidifying like ice on the vaporous air until it bulked real as Nellie Meehan herself. Nellie Meehan stood, unblinking, and with her steady eyes fixed the bright apparition. 'I know you, Maisie Edwards,' she said in soft, placating tones. 'You're looking for your Katherine. Well you won't find her here any more. She's living away now, away down in Todmorden.'

And then, almost apologetically, Nellie Meehan turned her back on the glimmering form, which still hung in the air, to stack and wash the tea service before Clifford returned. It was with a queer new lightness in her head that she noticed the plump, tiny little woman propped stiff, mouth open, eyes staring, stock-still in the rocking chair next to the tea table. As Nellie Meehan gaped, she felt the encroaching cold take the last sanctum of her heart; with a sigh that was a slow, released breath, she saw the delicate blue-willow pattern of the saucer showing clear through the translucence of her own hand and heard, as if echoing down a vaulted corridor sibilant with expectant, gossiping shadows, the voice at her back greeting her like a glad hostess who has waited long for a tardy guest: 'Well,' said Maisie Edwards, 'it's about time, Nellie.'

The Wishing Box

Written: 8–11 October 1956
Published: *Granta* (26 January 1957): 3–5[*]

Agnes Higgins realised only too well the cause of her husband Harold's beatific, absent-minded expression over his morning orange juice and scrambled eggs.

'Well,' Agnes sniffed, smearing beach-plum jelly on her toast with vindictive strokes of the butter-knife, 'what did you dream *last* night?'

'I was just remembering,' Harold said, still staring with a blissful, blurred look right through the very attractive and tangible form of his wife (pink-cheeked and fluffily blonde as always that early September morning, in her

---

[*] Reprinted in *Granta* (15 February 1964): 4–6; and *The Atlantic* (October 1964): 86–9, with the biographical sketch: 'Sylvia Plath, who died last year, grew up in Wellesley, Massachusetts, and graduated from Smith College in 1955, where she studied under Alfred Kazin. She won a fellowship to Cambridge, and there she met and married the poet Ted Hughes. This story was written during her Cambridge years and originally appeared in *Granta*.' SP later used some of the themes from this story in *The Bell Jar*. SP cites Gertrude Stein's poem 'Sacred Emily'. Submitted to *London Magazine* in autumn 1959.

rose-sprigged peignoir), 'those manuscripts I was discussing with William Blake.'

'But,' Agnes objected, trying with difficulty to conceal her irritation, 'how did you *know* it was William Blake?'

Harold seemed surprised. 'Why, from his pictures, of course.'

And what could Agnes say to that? She smouldered in silence over her coffee, wrestling with the strange jealousy which had been growing on her like some dark, malignant cancer ever since their wedding night only three months before when she had discovered about Harold's dreams. On that first night of their honeymoon, in the small hours of the morning, Harold startled Agnes out of a sound, dreamless sleep by a violent, convulsive twitch of his whole right arm.

Momentarily frightened, Agnes had shaken Harold awake to ask in tender, maternal tones what the matter was; she thought he might be struggling in the throes of a nightmare. Not Harold.

'I was just beginning to play the "Emperor" Concerto,' he explained sleepily. 'I must have been lifting my arm for the first chord when you woke me up.'

Now at the outset of their marriage, Harold's vivid dreams amused Agnes. Every morning she asked Harold what he had dreamed during the night, and, quite seriously, he told her in as rich detail as if he were describing some significant, actual event.

'I was being introduced to a gathering of American poets in the Library of Congress,' he would report with relish. 'William Carlos Williams was there in a great, rough coat, and that one who writes about Nantucket, and Robinson Jeffers looking like an American Indian the way he does in the anthology photograph; and then Robert Frost came driving up in a saloon car and said something witty that made me laugh.' Or: 'I saw a beautiful desert, all reds and purples, with each grain of sand like a ruby or sapphire shooting light. A white leopard with gold spots was standing over this bright blue stream, its hind legs on one bank, its forelegs on the other, and a little trail of red ants was crossing the stream over the leopard, up its tail, along its back, between its eyes and down on the other side.'

Harold's dreams were nothing if not meticulous works of art. Undeniably, for a certified accountant with pronounced literary leanings (he read E. T. A. Hoffmann, Kafka, and the astrological monthlies instead of the daily paper on the commuter's special), Harold possessed an astonishingly quick, colourful imagination. But, gradually, Harold's peculiar habit of accepting his dreams as if they were really an integral part of his waking experience began to infuriate

Agnes. She felt left out. It was as if Harold were spending one third of his life in an exhilarating world among celebrities and fabulous legendary creatures from which Agnes found herself perpetually exiled, except by hearsay.

As the weeks passed, Agnes began to brood. Although she refused to mention it to Harold, her own dreams, when she had them (and that, alas, was infrequently enough), appalled her: dark, glowering landscapes, peopled with ominous unrecognisable figures. She never could remember these nightmares in detail, but lost their shapes even as she struggled to awaken, retaining only the keen sense of their stifling, storm-charged atmosphere which would haunt her, oppressive, throughout the following day. Agnes felt ashamed to mention these fragmentary scenes of horror to Harold for fear they reflected too unflatteringly upon her own powers of imagination. Her dreams – far and few between, as they were – sounded so prosaic, so tedious, in comparison with the royal baroque splendour of Harold's. How could she tell him simply, for example: 'I was falling'? Or: 'Mother died and I was so sad'? Or: 'Something was chasing me and I couldn't run'? The plain truth was, Agnes realised, with a pang of envy, that her dream-life would cause the most assiduous psychoanalyst to repress a yawn.

Where, Agnes mused wistfully, were those fertile childhood days when she believed in fairies? Then, at least, her sleep had never been dreamless, nor her dreams dull and ugly. She had, in her seventh year, she recalled wistfully, dreamed of a wishing-box land above the clouds where wishing boxes grew on trees, looking very much like coffee-grinders; you picked a box, turned the handle around nine times while whispering your wish in this little hole in the side, and the wish came true. Another time, she had dreamed of finding three magic grass-blades growing by the mailbox at the end of her street: the grass-blades shone like tinsel Christmas ribbon: one red, one blue and one silver. In yet another dream, she and her younger brother Michael stood in front of Dody Nelson's white-shingled house in winter snowsuits; knotty maple tree roots snaked across the hard, brown ground; she was wearing red-and-white striped wool mittens and, all at once, as she held out one cupped hand, it began to snow turquoise-blue sulfa gum. But that was just about the extent of the dreams Agnes remembered from her infinitely more creative childhood days. At what age had those benevolent painted dream-worlds ousted her? And for what cause?

Meanwhile, indefatigably, Harold continued to recount his dreams over breakfast. Once, at a depressing and badly aspected time of Harold's life, before he met Agnes, Harold dreamed that a red fox ran through his kitchen, grievously burnt, its fur charred black, bleeding from several wounds. Later, Harold confided, at a more auspicious time shortly after his marriage to Agnes, the red fox had appeared again, miraculously healed, with flourishing fur, to present Harold with a bottle of permanent black Quink. Harold was particularly fond of his fox dreams; they recurred often. So, notably, did his dream of the giant pike. 'There was this pond,' Harold informed Agnes one sultry August morning, 'where my cousin Albert and I used to fish; it was chock full of pike. Well, last night I was fishing there, and I caught the most enormous pike you could imagine – it must have been the great-great-grandfather of all the rest; I pulled and pulled and pulled, and still he kept coming out of that pond.'

'Once,' Agnes countered, morosely stirring sugar into her black coffee, 'when I was little, I had a dream about Superman, all in Technicolor. He was dressed in blue with a red cape and black hair, handsome as a prince, and I went flying right along with him through the air – I could feel the wind whistling, and the tears blowing out of my eyes. We flew over Alabama; I could tell it was Alabama, because the land looked like a map, with "Alabama" lettered in script across these big, green mountains.'

Harold was visibly impressed. 'What,' he asked Agnes then, 'did you dream last night?' Harold's tone was almost contrite; to tell the truth, his own dream-life preoccupied him so much that he'd honestly never thought of playing listener and investigating his wife's. He looked at her pretty, troubled countenance with new interest; Agnes was, Harold paused to observe for perhaps the first time since their early married days, an extraordinarily attractive sight across the breakfast table.

For the moment, Agnes was confounded by Harold's well-meant question; she had long ago passed the stage where she seriously considered hiding a copy of Freud's writings on dreams in her closet and fortifying herself with a vicarious dream-tale by which to hold Harold's interest each morning. Now, throwing reticence to the wind, she decided, in desperation, to confess her problem.

'I don't dream anything,' Agnes admitted in low, tragic tones. 'Not any more.'

Harold was obviously concerned. 'Perhaps,' he consoled her, 'you just don't use your powers of imagination enough. You should practise. Try shutting your eyes.'

Agnes shut her eyes.

'Now,' Harold asked hopefully, 'what do you see?'

Agnes panicked. She saw nothing. 'Nothing,' she quavered. 'Nothing except a sort of blur.'

'Well,' said Harold briskly, adopting the manner of a doctor dealing with a malady that was, although distressing, not necessarily fatal, 'imagine a goblet.'

'What *kind* of a goblet?' Agnes pleaded.

'That's up to *you*,' Harold said. '*You* describe it to *me*.'

Eyes still shut, Agnes dragged wildly into the depths of her head. She managed, with great effort, to conjure up a vague, shimmery silver goblet that hovered somewhere in the nebulous regions of the back of her mind flickering as if at any moment it might black out like a candle.

'It's silver,' she said, almost defiantly. 'And it's got two handles.'

'Fine. Now imagine a scene engraved on it.'

Agnes forced a reindeer on to the goblet, scrolled about by grape leaves, scratched in bare outlines on the silver. 'It's a reindeer in a wreath of grape leaves.'

'What colour is the scene?' Harold was, Agnes thought, merciless.

'Green,' Agnes lied as she hastily enamelled the grape leaves. 'The grape leaves are green. And the sky is black—' She was almost proud of this original stroke. 'And the reindeer's russet flecked with white.'

'All right. Now polish the goblet all over into a high gloss.'

Agnes polished the imaginary goblet, feeling like a fraud. 'But it's in the *back* of my head,' she said dubiously, opening her eyes. 'I see everything somewhere way in the back of my head. Is that were you see *your* dreams?'

'Why no,' Harold said, puzzled. 'I see my dreams on the front of my eyelids, like on a movie screen. They just come; I don't have anything to do with them. Like right now,' he closed his eyes, 'I can see these shiny crowns coming and going, hung in this big willow tree.'

Agnes fell grimly silent.

'You'll be all right.' Harold tried, jocosely, to buck her up. 'Every day, just practise imagining different things like I've taught you.'

Agnes let the subject drop. While Harold was away at work, she began, suddenly, to read a great deal; reading kept her mind full of pictures. Seized by a kind of ravenous hysteria, she raced through novels, women's magazines, newspapers and even the anecdotes in her *Joy of Cooking*; she read travel brochures, home appliance circulars; the *Sears, Roebuck Catalogue*, the instructions on soap-flake boxes, the blurbs on the back of record-jackets – all from beginning to end; anything to keep from facing the gaping void in her own head of which Harold had made her so painfully conscious. But as soon as she lifted her eyes from the printed matter at hand, it was as if a protecting world extinguished.

The utter self-sufficient, unchanging reality of the *things* surrounding her began to depress Agnes. With a jealous awe, her frightened, almost paralysed stare took in the Oriental rug, the Williamsburg-blue wallpaper, the gilded dragons on the Chinese vase on the mantel, the blue-and-gold medallion design of the upholstered sofa on which she was sitting. She felt choked, smothered by these objects whose bulky pragmatic existence somehow threatened the deepest, most secret roots of her own ephemeral being. Harold, she knew only too well, would tolerate no such vainglorious nonsense from tables and chairs; if he didn't like the scene at hand, if it bored him, he would change it to suit his fancy. If, Agnes mourned, in some sweet hallucination, an octopus came slithering towards her across the floor, paisley-patterned in purple and orange, she would bless it. Anything to prove that her shaping imaginative powers were not irretrievably lost; that her eye was not merely an open camera lens which recorded surrounding phenomena and left it at that. 'A rose,' she found herself repeating hollowly, like a funeral dirge, 'is a rose is a rose . . .'

One morning, when Agnes was reading a novel, she suddenly realised, to her terror, that her eyes had scanned five pages without taking in the meaning of a single word. She tried again, but the letters separated, writhing like malevolent little black snakes across the page in a kind of hissing, untranslatable jargon. It was then that Agnes began attending the cinema round the corner regularly each afternoon. It did not matter if she had seen the feature several times previously: the fluid kaleidoscope of forms before her eyes lulled her into a rhythmic trance; the voices, speaking some soothing, unintelligible code, exorcised the dead silence in her head. Eventually, by dint of much cajolery, Agnes persuaded Harold to buy a television set on the instalment plan. That was much better than the movies; she could drink sherry while watching TV during the long afternoons. These latter days, when Agnes greeted Harold on his return home each evening, she found, with a certain malicious satisfaction, that his face blurred before her gaze, so she could change his features at will. Sometimes she gave him a pea-green complexion, sometimes lavender; sometimes a Grecian nose, sometimes an eagle-beak.

'But I *like* sherry,' Agnes told Harold stubbornly when, her afternoons of private drinking becoming apparent even to his indulgent eyes, he begged her to cut down. 'It relaxes me.'

The sherry, however, didn't relax Agnes enough to put her to sleep. Cruelly sober, the visionary sherry-haze worn off, she would lie stiff, twisting her fingers like nervous talons in the sheets, long after Harold was breathing peacefully, evenly, in the midst of some rare, wonderful adventure. With an icy, increasing panic, Agnes lay stark awake night after night. Worse, she didn't get tired any more. Finally, a bleak, clear awareness of what was happening broke upon her: the curtains of sleep, of refreshing, forgetful darkness dividing each day from the day before it and the day after it, were lifted for Agnes eternally, irrevocably. She saw an intolerable prospect of wakeful, visionless days and nights stretching unbroken ahead of her, her mind condemned to perfect vacancy, without a single image of its own to ward off the crushing assault of smug, autonomous tables and chairs. She might, Agnes reflected sickly, live to be a hundred: the women in her family were all long-lived.

Dr Marcus, the Higgins' family physician, attempted, in his jovial way, to reassure Agnes about her complaints of insomnia: 'Just a bit of nervous strain, that's all. Take one of these capsules a night for a while and see how you sleep.'

Agnes did not ask Dr Marcus if the pills would give her dreams; she put the box of fifty pills in her handbag and took the bus home.

Two days later, on the last Friday of September, when Harold returned from work (he had shut his eyes all during the hour's train trip home, counterfeiting sleep, but, in reality, voyaging on a cerise-sailed dhow up a luminous river where white elephants bulked and rambled across the crystal surface of the water in the shadow of Moorish turrets fabricated completely of multicoloured glass), he found Agnes lying on the sofa in the living room, dressed in her favourite princess-styled emerald taffeta evening gown, pale and lovely as a blown lily, eyes shut, an empty pillbox and an overturned water tumbler on the rug at her side. Her tranquil features were set in a slight, secret smile of triumph, as if, in some far country unattainable to mortal men, she were, at last, waltzing with the dark, red-caped prince of her early dreams.

The Smoky Blue Piano

Ts,[*] *c.* May 1957, Smith College

It is amazing how easily one slips into criminal habits. I don't mean anything enormous, like murder or grand larceny, but illegal little quirks, such as

---

[*] Typed at top right: 'Sylvia Plath / 55 Eltisley Avenue / Cambridge, England.' Typescript has holograph corrections and additions by SP as well as a cover sheet listing periodicals, editor's names and addresses. Submitted to either *Everywoman's* or *Woman's Day* magazine on 12 August 1955. Additional typescripts held by Indiana University and Emory University (one of which has a note in Ted Hughes's hand on bullfrogs). In a letter to her brother, Warren Plath, on 7 May 1957, SP wrote that she modified the original story to a London setting.

housebreaking to play on a smoky blue piano. Which I found myself doing one fine summer afternoon. This particular situation came about simply because of an argument I had with my roommate, Jill, at breakfast.

'Honestly,' she insisted, 'I really did see this dark, devastating man coming out of the flat next door to us.'

'That,' I said sternly, 'is impossible. It was merely an hallucination. From too much wishful thinking. You didn't actually see him coming out of the door, did you?'

'Well,' Jill admitted, 'I only *heard* the door open, and then some footsteps going away down the hall, and I was curious. So I went to the kitchen window to look through the slats in the venetian blind, you know, where we can see all the people coming and going out the main entrance, and . . .'

'And you saw a sweet little old lady with a parrot.'

'No,' Jill said, still stubborn. 'There was this man. I could see him very clearly through the leaves of the ivy plant.'

'It remains to be seen,' I said, 'whether he really lives there or was just visiting a sweet old lady who happens to be his great aunt twice removed.'

'*You* look then,' Jill instructed. 'You look today and see for yourself. And if he really *does* live next door, we will start with strategy tonight.'

All this sounded very ominous and military, but I was somehow curious too, especially about the mysterious part. Since I got home from my office earlier than Jill did from the Hat-And-Glove shop, I said all right, I'd watch for this fellow while I made dinner. Because it was no trouble at all to look out every couple of minutes and see who was going by.

At five-thirty that afternoon, I saw him for the first time. I spotted him right away, because he was a good head taller than anybody else in the rush-hour crowd coming in the main entrance. He had black, close-cropped hair and the most amazing *bone* structure. I don't mean the way he was built, but his *face*. There was a lean slant to his cheekbones that made him look, I don't know, sort of sardonic.

Now I'm kind of obsessed about bone structure in people's faces, probably because I haven't got any to speak of myself, but mainly because I think it's bone structure that reveals character. Not that I don't have *character*, but my features are just so vague to begin with. That's where Jill is lucky, because of her beautiful bone structure. That, and the green tiger-cat eyes.

Anyway, Jill and I began our first attack that same evening and knocked on his door. I don't think I would have gone if I hadn't had some of the cooking sherry while I was making the chicken casserole, but the way I felt was, I wanted to be in on whatever happened. And Jill was certainly set on meeting this fellow.

For some reason, *I* was the one who was shaking, even though I knew Jill had the tactics all figured out and would really impress him no matter how sardonic he was. Well, we knocked, and there was no answer.

'Oh, he's probably entertaining Kim Novak or somebody,' Jill said at last. She sounded very disappointed.

'No,' I said, 'I saw him come in alone.'

So we knocked again very loudly, and almost immediately heard footsteps coming toward the door. The door opened a crack, and this fellow peered out, his face all white and foamy with shaving lather and his eyes black and really *inscrutable*.

I couldn't say a word, I just looked at him. But Jill began to talk smoothly the way she does about how we were new here in town and wanted to know a few domestic details about the flat. Like where you could get a reliable cleaning lady and a good milk company, and how we'd just decided to run over to our neighbour and find out, only we hadn't known who lived there and were sorry to bother him at such an inconvenient time.

I had to smile the way Jill carried it off, especially the part about the cleaning lady, because we are living on the grandiose sum of next to nothing a day apiece for food and could afford a cleaning lady about as well as seven butlers and a tame panther. But by the time she was through explaining, I was almost convinced we *hadn't* known who would open the door when we knocked.

So what could this fellow do, with Jill standing there in her caramel sheath dress and with that faultless bone structure? He gave us both one very measured look which made my heart contract like a slide ruler.

'Do come in,' he said, with a smiling twist of the mouth under all that lather. 'Please,' he went on, with a gracious gesture toward the fireplace, 'sit down. I shall be with you in a minute.' And he went off to finish shaving.

Well, we sat on the edge of the black-textured divan and stared. Jill just said: 'Good heavens, will you look at this!'

The room was right. It was so right that we didn't see how anyone could possibly *live* in it. It was very modern, all black and white, with red and yellow pillows shaped like triangles and moons thrown about here and there with calculated abandon. In the dining alcove there was a piano painted a light smoky blue to match the colour of the walls. It was the piano that attracted Jill.

She was dallying over a few chords from 'Stardust' on the smoky blue piano, and I was examining a large wrought-iron pineapple and wondering if it could be used as an umbrella stand when this fellow came back.

'My name is Chris,' he said, with a flickering smile that made me think about how Mephistopheles always had his own private motives for everything. 'I'm sorry because I'm going out to dinner tonight, but since you're already here, won't you join me for a glass of wine beforehand anyway?'

It was a rhetorical question, and we found ourselves talking over three elegant glasses of ruby-red wine. Somehow the question of a reliable cleaning lady got lost in the shuffle like a low trump card. In answer to Jill's subtle questions, Chris admitted that he was assistant director on a TV programme, getting practice before starting to direct on his own.

During the course of conversation, Jill mentioned casually that she was working in a little shop on Oxford Street waiting for a chance at modelling. She also said that my ambition was to write sonnets on some sunny little island off the coast of Italy. I forget the name of the island now, but it all sounded highly probable at the time.

Finally I noticed how Chris was twirling his empty wine glass as if he was wanting to leave, so I gulped down the last of my drink and murmured, 'My chicken casserole is in the oven and I am afraid the sherry sauce will evaporate if we don't get back.'

'Ah,' said Chris at the door, 'I am terribly fond of chicken casseroles with sherry sauce.'

All Jill talked about at supper was Chris. I don't mean obviously, because she is not obvious, only she would every now and then casually break in with some remark about him.

'Did you notice how brilliant and intuitive he was,' she asked, 'when I was talking about women having modelling careers?'

'Yes,' I said, reaching for another piece of bread.

'And the simply fluid way he moved around pouring those drinks?'

'Yes,' I said, wishing for a fleeting instant that I too had a faultless bone structure.

I could see while doing dishes that Chris wasn't going to be inscrutable for long. There hasn't been a man yet that Jill couldn't handle when she really wanted to, only they all end up eventually wanting to marry her, which is too bad for them.

Like this fellow Robin whom Jill almost goes steady with. He is a shaggy but very intelligent young journalist, and the only man Jill has ever met who is more intelligent than she is. He thinks he would be the best thing in world history for her. But Jill is having none of this. Not yet, anyway. She will talk and *reason* with Robin but there is nothing she can *do* after all, because of being so determined to be a career girl. And, as she says, she can't sacrifice herself to her emotions at this early stage of life.

Well, it was only a little over a week after our beachhead when Chris came to dinner at our flat. Jill very logically planned to have some friend from her shop to supper that night, but somehow at the last minute this girl couldn't make it. So what could we do with an intimate meal for three hot in the oven and with candles in the two Chianti bottles left over from our spaghetti dinner with Robin last Saturday, but run over next door to see if Chris would oblige and have supper with us.

'After all,' Jill argued, 'he treated us to wine and the least we can do is give him the chance to refuse.'

But after one look at Jill in her black skirt with the apricot-coloured blouse and the utterly useless frilled white apron, I figured Chris didn't even have a *chance*. Jill went, naturally, and sure enough, she came running back to the kitchen while I was taking the veal-and-mushroom casserole out of the oven.

'He's coming,' she said simply, like Cleopatra reciting a telegram from Antony. But even though she was more triumphant than I'd ever seen her, she managed to treat Chris lightly, as a matter of course, sort of served up impromptu with the hors d'oeuvres. Chris made himself at home at the head of the table, looking unbelievably suave in a tan summer jacket.

'My,' he said amiably, 'I am terribly fond of veal-and-mushroom casserole.'

He even said he liked the grape-and-melon compote, especially the way we served it in the champagne glasses the previous tenants had left us with the flat. And he had a second helping of the casserole. We were just beginning the butterscotch parfait I'd made that afternoon when the doorbell rang. I knew it would be Robin, coming over to see Jill, and I could tell from her look that she knew it too and wasn't going to let a small trifle like Robin interfere with her plans.

'Tell him I'm not here,' she said to me, and went to hide in the broom closet.

So I buzzed for Robin to come down, feeling sort of apologetic that Chris would see what a shaggy type of man sometimes came to visit us, this one being stoop-shouldered and near-sighted from bending too long over a typewriter in the news office. In spite of his shagginess, Robin has a peculiarly affectionate sense of humour, and the first thing he did when he came in was say, 'Hello, darling,' and bend to kiss my fingertips, continental style.

Chris got up to shake Robin's hand with an expression that can only be described as chilly.

'Why Robin,' I said gaily, 'how surprised we are to see *you* here, of all people. Chris and I were just dining together. It's really unfortunate, but Jill is not in at the moment.' I mentally added, 'Not in the dining room, but in the broom closet,' because I do not like to fib, even to people such as Robin.

Robin blinked obligingly and left. After he had gone, Jill emerged from the broom closet with all the poise of Venus from her cockleshell.

'This sort of thing happens rather frequently,' she told Chris. 'I cannot bear being dishonest.'

Chris nodded sagely and said, 'I see.' And then he got up to go, explaining that he had a late rehearsal to watch that night.

Afterwards, over the dishes, Jill said sarcastically that she wondered just who he was going to watch, but I could see she was really glad that he had come, because after all it was the first step. She went to bed early, humming 'Almost Like Being In Love' while I sat up in the living room to quiet myself with the latest Simenon thriller.

A week went by before I decided that things simply could not go on the way they were going on. I was losing face just watching. It was all very strange. Nothing had happened since our dinner with Chris. Nothing except seven phone calls for Jill from Robin and a jolly note from the Electric Company saying how they hated to deprive us of an essential thing like electricity, but it seemed that the previous tenants had neglected to pay their last bill. Jill had taken up chain smoking and was living stoically on coffee, Wheat Thins and such wine and song as Robin provided.

The final straw fell one night as I walked back down the hall after going out to mail a letter. I could hear the phone in Chris's flat ringing and ringing through the door. I figured he must be out because the phone just went on ringing.

But then, as I eased open the door of our flat, I saw Jill sitting by our phone with the receiver in her hand, just staring at it. When she heard me come in she hung up fast with a guilty look and asked if I had gotten her some postage stamps in a very tight voice. This girl has had it, I said to myself. And I really don't blame her. If I had a bone structure and a brain like hers, Chris wouldn't be a bachelor long. But some things there is absolutely no point in thinking about.

Anyhow, I couldn't let her go on this way, so I said very sternly, trying to shame her out of it, 'He isn't home, is he?'

'No,' she said, and wouldn't look at me.

'Look,' I said, trying for the light touch, 'this fellow is obviously conceited and no doubt a bigamist, or worse. He makes a living by leading innocent young girls astray and partaking of veal casseroles while he probably has several wives and innumerable children in Australia.'

But none of that did any good. So I sat up until two o'clock in the morning to find out who strangled Lady Montague in the bath and all this time there was the low, melancholy sound of a very smoky blue piano coming from the next flat.

The day after that, it rained enough to discourage Noah. The phone rang during a dismal dinner, and Jill jumped like she's been doing lately whenever there's a noise, but caught herself up and then walked in a bored way to answer. This time, though, it was Chris.

Jill was fine until she hung up, and then she went wild. I've never seen anything like it. First she ran to make sure the front door was locked so he couldn't hear, and then she rushed to hug me and called me a dear old thing just as if I had arranged all this.

'He's coming over in half an hour to take me out,' she said. 'Do you think the peacock-green cocktail dress will be dramatic enough?'

I thought it certainly would. So I sat up that night too, reading about a homicidal butler with a split personality, while waiting for Jill to come home. For some reason, I was in an extremely nostalgic mood, as if I could hear this smoky blue piano playing 'These Foolish Things' over and over again in the back of my head.

Well, around one o'clock I heard footsteps, lots of them, coming down the hall, stopping outside our door. There was a murmur of conversation for a minute, and then our door opened and Jill sailed in, slamming it behind her. There was a little laughter outside, and then I heard Chris's door open and a few people go in.

Jill threw herself down on the red leather chair, breathing hard. She looked furious.

I just said: 'What's the matter?'

'Matter! The whole evening was a farce, a silly farce. Chris behaved despicably!'

'Well,' I said, 'any man will make passes.'

'Passes!' she blazed. 'Ridiculous! He spoke to me just once the whole time and that was to ask what I'd have to drink at this little bar we went to with some terrible, sarcastic friends of his. They all acted as if they'd *planned* it that way, just to ignore me completely.'

'So no man deserves your time, being a callous beast,' I said with a sudden strange relief flooding up inside me.

'Robin, at least,' she went on, not paying any attention, 'is a gentleman. Robin would never treat a woman this way.'

'You know Chris isn't worth it if he's like that,' I said very reasonably, wondering in passing what it took to get a sadist out of a girl's system. Especially a sadist with cheekbones like Chris's.

'But no, you don't understand,' she said impatiently. 'It isn't so simple. He wasn't like that. I mean, he was so devilishly clever that he didn't *seem* cruel. In fact, outwardly he acted perfectly polite, but he implied things. He talked on several levels all at once. And if you read between the lines, he was actually very insulting – as if . . . as if I *bored* him, or something.'

The several levels intrigued me. 'Well, why didn't you go back to the flat with him for a nightcap and straighten things out, then?' Sometimes I am very practical.

Jill positively glared at me. 'You don't think I was going to sit around and listen to him talk to his *friends* all night, do you?'

But she wouldn't go to bed. I tried persuading, but there was nothing I could do, short of beating her over her beautiful stubborn head, so I gave up and when I turned in, she was still sitting in the living room, listening to the little bursts of laughter from Chris's flat. With a tragic expression.

Something had to be done. And I decided then and there that if I knew the world like I knew my whodunits, I was going to be the one to do it!

So the next day I worked out this ingenious plan. It was all very clever, if I do say so. I decided I would find out what was hindering Chris very subtly, without Jill knowing anything about it. She is proud concerning such matters and would not like to think I had helped her solve her problems with other men.

When Jill said she was going out for frog legs and wine with Robin that night at this little French café to improve her morale, I went immediately to the landlady and told her I had lost the key to our flat and my roommate was out so I needed another key temporarily. Just the way I hoped, the landlady loaned me the skeleton key to the whole building.

It was late afternoon. I had had a hard day at the office and I felt like blowing off steam. So I made this exotic chocolate cake with mocha frosting and walnuts and cut out two very large, generous pieces. In case Chris was having company for dinner. Subconsciously, I guess, I remembered the old saying about the way to a man's heart. I would say Jill baked the cake. The only thing I wasn't quite sure of was if Chris *had* a heart. From the way things had gone so far, I was worried.

Arming myself with the plate of cake, I opened the door of our flat very quietly and slipped out. No one was in the hall. Feeling like a bank robber, I let myself into Chris's apartment with the skeleton key. The door shut behind me as if the hinges were made out of velvet, and for a minute I was scared.

Don't be silly, I said to myself sternly the way I always do when I am being silly. I rationalised about how I would be sitting in the apartment very calmly when Chris got home from his TV rehearsals. I would be playing the smoky blue piano, something classical, like 'Clair de lune', and the chocolate cake would be prominently displayed.

'I have several bones to pick with you,' I would say, and then would proceed to tell him how brilliant and beautiful Jill was. I would also ask him what he meant by pretending to be a cad. You see, all the time I knew he really wasn't. Don't ask me how. I just knew.

I sat down at the piano and began to thumb through the stacks of music piled up on the rack. I had a lot of time before beginning 'Clair de lune' and so I started with 'September Song'.

I got carried away by my dreams. Dreams about Chris with his magnificent cheekbones going steady with Jill and her tiger-cat eyes. I began to feel noble and tragic. I would be maid-of-honour at the wedding and wear a smoky blue dress. Smoky blue is flattering for someone with vague features.

I was in the middle of 'These Foolish Things' on the smoky blue piano when I heard a key in the lock. I looked up. Chris was leaning against the doorjamb with a strange, satisfied smile on his face. He didn't look angry. He didn't even look inscrutable.

'Hello,' he said pleasantly, 'have a piece of chocolate cake.'

All at once my hands began to tremble and I forgot about how I was going to pretend Jill made the cake. 'Thanks,' I managed, 'only I've already eaten once today. I'm sorry, but I didn't have time to begin "Clair de lune".'

'There are a few things,' said Chris, 'that need to be explained. How you got into this flat, for instance. They arrest people for such indiscreet acts, you know. Housebreaking it's called in lower circles.'

'I came to have a talk with you,' I retorted, regaining my sense of purpose.

Chris grinned down at me with an expression one generally reserves for someone who has a faultless bone structure.

'Come on over to the couch,' he said, taking me firmly by the hand. 'And I don't guarantee I'll believe a word you say.'

I sat down beside him on the sofa. It would have been much easier if he looked sardonic. Or like a cad. But somehow he just looked very happy.

'I never thought I'd be seeing you here,' he said. 'But I was going to call you up anyway.'

'Call *me* up?' I didn't even have time to think about my tone of voice. This was obviously no time to think about tones of voice.

'Yes,' Chris said, playing with a piece of polished driftwood on the glass coffee table. 'You see,' he smiled ruefully, 'my plans didn't work out quite the way I'd planned. Plans have a way of doing that.'

This was something I knew about. 'Look, Chris,' I said in a big sister tone of voice, 'so you don't know how to treat the Brigitte Bardot type when she also has the brains of Marie Curie. So I am here to tell you. I am your fairy godmother, in person. Complete with chocolate cake.'

Chris looked as if he really believed the fairy godmother part, so I forged on.

'You see, Chris,' I began reasonably, as if I were selling an expensive insurance policy I sincerely believed in, 'there is this magnificent unusual girl who is very much in love with you, only she is too proud to tell you so unless you beat her over the head with your affection. She is like that.'

'Oh she is, is she,' Chris said. 'Well, then, life suddenly becomes extremely simple.'

And right then and there Chris took me capably in his arms and kissed me on the mouth. I must give myself credit. I fought away, while a hundred smoky blue pianos reeled around, spangled with red triangles and yellow moons. At last he stopped and held me at arm's length.

'I never was any good,' Chris said, 'at beating a girl over the head. Will that do?'

'Do!' I gasped, hunting frantically for my original purpose and finding only a million little songs having a New Year's party in my heart. 'This is a clear case of mistaken identity,' I said then, severely, trying for equilibrium. 'You do not practise for Brigitte Bardot on a girl with vague features. You find a skeleton with bone structure. A skeleton does not get susceptible to delusions of grandeur.'

'You are,' Chris said sadly, 'again talking Greek.'

'Me!' I exclaimed, injured in more than dignity. 'I tell you honestly as your own Aunt Olive about how there is this prize next door to you whom you do not know how to treat according to Emily Post. And you . . . you . . .'

Chris interrupted me again. Only this time I knew how his mouth went. And I began to wish I was an unscrupulous and wicked woman. But I wasn't.

'Look,' I said desperately, 'Jill is very unhappy. Jill is my best friend. I am born to self-sacrifice. You both will be awfully jolly once you realise you can hit the same wavelength at the same time.'

I thought of Jill having frog legs and wine with Robin and wondered how much self-sacrifice one girl could bear.

Chris was gazing at me with horror. 'You,' he said accusingly, 'are going to marry that Robin character. That newspaper hack who embraced you positively indecently that time I was over for dinner. He didn't want to go out with Jill, he wanted to go out with *you*. I could see it in his eyes.'

Now it was my turn, 'But I can't bear Robin,' I said, utterly bewildered, 'for more than two minutes. He is so . . .'

'Vague,' finished Chris. 'Did it ever occur to you,' he said with fearful calm, 'that two people with vague features simply do not go together?'

It had never occurred to me.

'Did it ever occur to you,' Chris pursued, 'that I cannot *bear* fibbing girls with bone structure?'

I was very quiet.

'Oh, I've tried, all right,' he went on. 'Only it just didn't work. My heart wasn't in it.'

Suddenly everything became beautifully scrutable. 'You,' I said at last, 'you took Jill out because . . .'

'Because,' Chris was exquisitely angry, 'I wanted to take *you* out. The old story. Make a girl interested by dating her roommate. Roommate says guy is delightful. Wins difficult girl over. Only with Jill I somehow didn't feel like being so delightful.'

'So,' I said, as if I had just invented the rainbow, 'so *I* am the difficult girl? And you expect me to believe this?'

Chris obviously expected me to believe this.

'My eyes,' I said diffidently, 'are not tiger-cat green.'

'Did you ever,' Chris demanded, 'hide in a broom closet?'

'No,' I said.

'Did you ever want to write sonnets on an Italian island?'

'No,' I said, 'but it sounded impressive at the time, didn't it?'

Chris ignored that one. 'Would you ever say no when a real nice fellow with a promising future asked you to dinner?'

'No,' I began, thinking as how no really nice fellow with a promising future had ever asked me.

'Well, then,' Chris said triumphantly, 'we are now on the same wavelength. For a while you had me worried.'

'But what about Jill?' I asked half-heartedly, thinking about Robin being morale-building over a red-and-white-checked tablecloth.

'Jill,' Chris explained, 'is going to grow up for a long time. When she grows up I predict she will marry some chap who is shaggy but very brilliant, probably a footloose newspaper reporter.'

'Robin!' I exclaimed, struck with admiration at Chris's amazing insight. And this time I knew I was not wicked or unscrupulous. I was simply a very happy girl with vague features.

'Dinner for two?' Chris said at last.

I had a lovely vision of Jill preceding me down the aisle in a peacock-green dress while somebody played the chorus from *Lohengrin* on a smoky blue piano. Green goes beautifully with tiger-cat eyes.

'Yes,' I said, suddenly feeling as if I had just solved the biggest mystery of them all. 'Oh, yes!'

Change-About in Mrs. Cherry's Kitchen

Ts,* 24 January 1958, Lilly Library

Mrs. Myrtle May Cherry had the spickest, spannest, shiniest, merriest kitchen in all Appleton Lane. Everybody said so, and they say so still. From Mrs. Cherry's kitchen floated the most delicious smells. Fried chicken and blueberry cupcakes one day, crackling pork roast and gingerbread the next. No wonder Mrs. Cherry grew round and rosy, and Mr. Cherry too!

Now on one certain Monday morning, sun came streaming in through Mrs. Cherry's kitchen windows and made a square of light, yellow as butter, on the sparkling linoleum floor.

The smell of savory bacon and hot coffee perfumed the air. In fact, on the surface, this Monday morning looked just like every other morning in Mrs. Cherry's kitchen and not one bit special. Even Mrs. Cherry didn't know it was to be the day of her amazing kitchen change-about.

"Pong!" said Toaster, and up popped two slices of golden toast. One for Mrs. Cherry and one for Mr. Cherry. Mrs. Cherry put strawberry jam on her toast, and Mr. Cherry spread clover-blossom honey on his.

"Mmm!" murmured Mr. Cherry dreamily. "I *do* enjoy crisp toast in the morning."

"Thanks to our fine, shiny toaster," Mrs. Cherry said with becoming modesty.

---

* Typescript has typewritten and holograph additions and corrections by SP. Typed at top right: 'Sylvia Plath / 26 Elmwood Road / Wellesley, Massachusetts.' SP wrote in her journal on Sunday, 26 January 1958, 'NB: A postscript. Wrote, all day Friday, through versions & versions to finished version of "Change-About in Mrs. Cherry's Kitchen" – mailed in hope & fatalistic despair, to *Jack & Jill*', a US children's magazine.

She always gave praise where it was due. "It's made us golden-brown toast each day without fail all these years." And at these words, Toaster fairly glistened with pride.

"Blrip. Blrip," gurgled Coffee Percolator, not to be outdone, and winked on his red eye.

Mrs. Cherry poured out steaming coffee in two blue-bordered cups. "You know," she smiled at her husband, "this coffee percolator makes such uncommonly good coffee that I sometimes think it must be magic!"

Mrs. Cherry didn't know how true her words were. Even as she spoke, the kitchen pixies poked each other and giggled behind the sugar tin. Now way back in Mrs. Cherry's great-grandmother's day, there were special kitchen pixies to turn the churned milk into butter and to see that bread rose light and crusty in the old-fashioned ovens. Sometimes, when these pixies felt mischievous, they'd curdle the cream or unsettle the laying hens. But mostly they were good, reliable pixies. And often, at night, wise housewives set out saucers of porridge on the doorstep for them, with honey and raisins in it.

Mrs. Cherry had no idea that two descendants of these pixies lived right in her kitchen. These two pixies had long, unpronounceable names, handed down from father to son and from mother to daughter. But they called themselves Salt and Pepper for short. One pixie wore a white suit and slept in Mrs. Cherry's silver salt-shaker, while the other pixie wore a speckled brown suit and slept in Mrs. Cherry's silver pepper-shaker. It was their job to see that all the kitchen folk did their daily work and lived in harmony and content.

After Mr. Cherry had located his tortoiseshell-rimmed spectacles which he claimed some imp hid away every morning just for fun, he kissed Mrs. Cherry goodbye.

"I'll probably have to eat lunch in town today," Mr. Cherry said. "I have a lot of work to do."

Mrs. Cherry waved to Mr. Cherry from the kitchen window until he passed out of sight behind the Dimblebys' hedge down Appleton Lane. Then she turned to her morning tasks. Behind her back, Salt and Pepper kept the kitchen running smooth as silk.

Mrs. Cherry hummed to herself, sitting at the sunny kitchen table and paring carrots for Mr. Cherry's favorite supper of beef stew. She flashed a bright, happy look around her kitchen: at the washing machine washing, and at the oven baking, and at the icebox rumbling gently as it kept the vanilla ice cream cold for Mr. Cherry's dessert.

"What a fortunate woman I am!" Mrs. Cherry said aloud to no one in particular.

"Fortunate is right," murmured Icebox.

"To be sure," whispered Oven.

"Brumm," Washing Machine cleared her throat. "Exactly so."

But Mrs. Cherry couldn't understand their language, and so she didn't answer. Salt poked a slender white finger between Pepper's ribs and the two pixies almost slid off the slippery top of the round kitchen clock in a burst of laughter. But they caught themselves just in time. For if they fell, they would fall right into Mrs. Cherry's bowl of diced carrots before her very eyes. And then what would they have to say for themselves?

Now on this particular morning, the pixies received some complaints from the kitchen folk for the first time. Not that they were unhappy, no indeed. Mrs. Cherry praised them to the skies in front of all her neighbors and relatives, and this made them very pleased. For nobody likes to be taken for granted. But so much praise had begun to make the kitchen folk a bit conceited. Each one felt he could do his own work well enough, but each one of them cast longing looks at the jobs the other kitchen folk did.

"It's not that I don't *like* whipping eggs," explained Egg-Beater. "It's just that Iron turns out such frilly white ruffled blouses for Mrs. Cherry. I'm sure *I* could make lovely white ruffles on Mrs. Cherry's blouses too, if I were given the chance. Just look how beautiful and frothy my whipped cream is! I'd like a change of chores for a day."

"Ssss. So would I!" sighed Iron. "I'd like to take over Cousin Waffle-Iron's work. Mr. Cherry smacks his lips over those waffly waffles. But I could make even better dents with my shiny tip. Do let me try!"

And believe it or not, every electric appliance in Mrs. Cherry's kitchen had a similar request! Washing Machine wanted to bake a sponge cake. Oven wanted to iron Mr. Cherry's shirts crisp as pie-crusts. Coffee Percolator longed to taste ice cream.

"I'm sure I could be cold as Icebox," Coffee Percolator boasted, "if I just put my mind to it."

"And I," bragged Toaster, "could pop out better-shaped ice cubes at the drop of a hat!"

All this while Mrs. Cherry was merrily cutting up potatoes and onions to toss into Mr. Cherry's stew without an inkling of the problem facing Salt and Pepper.

"If we don't satisfy the kitchen folk," Salt whispered to Pepper, who was skating thoughtfully from cube to cube on the ice cube tray, "they may go on strike and stop work altogether. And then where would Mrs. Cherry be!"

"Do you suppose," Pepper said, "we should let them try it?"

"Try it!" Salt's eyes widened big as the big blue buttons on Mrs. Cherry's best company dress. "Why think of the mess they'd make!"

"It *would* mean a lot of extra work for us, of course," Pepper admitted. "But it's our job to keep the kitchen folk happy. Once they see how much better off they are, doing their own tasks, we'll never hear another complaint again."

Salt considered, chewing a leaf of parsley. "As Mr. Cherry remarks so often," Salt said at last, "experience is the best teacher."

Pepper nodded. "Once the kitchen folk *experience* how impossible it is to do each other's work, they'll be twice as happy tending to their own. But we mustn't let on that we doubt their talent."

"No," Salt agreed. "Let them find out for themselves."

So the pixies shook hands on their secret behind a leafy head of lettuce which towered over them like a great green bush. "Done!" And they went out to calm the kitchen folk.

"We say okay," Pepper sang, "to each one."

"Choose your day," sang Salt, "and have fun."

All the kitchen folk hummed and whirred and clicked with delight.

"Let's do it this very day!" Egg-Beater cried. And everybody joined in. "Let's make today the day for Operation Change-About!" They decided to wait for a moment when Mrs. Cherry's back was turned: when she was talking on the telephone, or visiting a neighbor's, and then! Icebox purred with dreams of cooking an honest-to-goodness plum tart instead of merely keeping the milk and butter cold. Iron glided sizzling over damp sheets, picturing acres of artistically dented waffles. Even Mrs. Cherry, setting the pot of stew to simmer on the gas range, felt her kitchen was in an especially good mood.

All the kitchen folk waited eagerly for Mrs. Cherry to leave them alone. Just for five minutes! Then they could show her how versatile they were. But Mrs. Cherry spent that whole Monday morning scouring and scurrying around the kitchen, whisking away invisible dust, polishing silver that gleamed to begin with, washing, mixing cake batter, ironing her best dirndl skirt with the daisies on it. She didn't turn her back for a minute. The kitchen folk hummed and whirred and sizzled in impatience. When would they have a chance for their wonderful Change-About! When would Mrs. Cherry turn her back so the pixies could get to work?

But just before lunchtime, as they were all ready to give up their marvelous plan in despair, Sunny and Bunny, the Dimbleby twins, chorused from Mrs. Cherry's back porch:

"Oh, Mrs. Cherry! Come and see our new kittens! Fudge Ripple has *five* new kittens!" Fudge Ripple was half Sunny's cat, and half Bunny's cat. She was mostly white, with long ripply black marks, and reminded the twins of their favorite ice cream.

"Whew!" breathed Icebox.

"Ah," rejoiced Oven. "Here we go now!"

Sure enough, Mrs. Cherry was brushing the flour from her hands and untying her apron strings. Then she followed Sunny and Bunny down the back steps. Through the kitchen window, Coffee Percolator saw the three of them turning into the Dimblebys' gate next door with his bright red eye.

"Quick," Salt cried, hopping out of the soup ladle in the silver drawer.

"Ready!" sneezed Pepper, skipping from behind an onion on the chopping board.

And Whizz! Whirr! Bang! Clang! Doors opened and shut. Lids jumped off and on. All the kitchen folk rattled their cords in excitement as Salt and Pepper answered their wishes and changed their jobs about. Mr. Cherry's shirts rose from Washing Machine and flew over into Oven. Doughy unbaked plum tarts skimmed from Oven to Icebox. Coffee Percolator gulped down cold ice cream. Finally they were all set. Wouldn't Mrs. Cherry be surprised when she came back! How she would praise their talent!

But what the kitchen folk didn't know was that they were going to be surprised themselves sooner than they thought. Mr. Cherry's work finished earlier than he planned, and even now he was whistling home down Appleton Lane to surprise Mrs. Cherry in time for lunch. What would he say when he saw how Mrs. Cherry's kitchen was behaving!

"Blrip! Blrip!" exclaimed Coffee Percolator, trying to keep the ice cream cold. But try as he would, the ice cream melted and grew hotter and hotter, bubbling up under his lid and foaming out onto the table.

"Oh dearr, dearrr!" whirred Egg-Beater. "I beat and beat, but Mrs. Cherry's blouses only tie into knots with no frills at all. Look what knots I've got them into! Oh, dear!"

"Bump! Bump!" Iron hopped up and down on the ironing board, plunging his silver point into the waffle batter Mrs. Cherry had mixed up for her lunch. "Bump!" But the waffle batter only stood in a sticky puddle and every time Iron made a dent, the batter splattered onto his shiny face and all over the kitchen wall.

"Brumm! Brummm! Brummmm!" Washing Machine's cake dough went whirling round and round in a soggy slush, no nearer to being an airy yellow sponge cake than it had been five minutes ago.

Toaster wept tears and steamed instead of popping out beautifully shaped ice cubes.

"Oh dear! Oh dear!" the kitchen folk chorused. "This is hard work! This is worse than we bargained for!"

From their ringside seat in the kitchen matchbox, Salt and Pepper exchanged knowing winks.

But then, right in the midst of these wails and groans, who should stalk into the kitchen but Mr. Cherry, looking for his round, rosy-cheeked wife! Mr. Cherry blinked. Mr. Cherry gaped. A smell of roasting shirts rose from the oven. The coffee percolator burbled and foamed strangely. Waffle batter polka-dotted the walls. Mr. Cherry staggered to the icebox and opened the door for a quietening snack of cheese and pickles and found a dozen doughy frost-bitten plum tarts staring him in the face.

Salt and Pepper clutched each other in dismay, crouching down behind Mrs. Cherry's sweet-scented box of cloves. What an expression on Mr. Cherry's face! How would they ever clean up the terrible clutter the kitchen folk had made before Mrs. Cherry came back?

"Myrtle! Myrtle!" Mr. Cherry cried, running out onto the back porch waving his hands. At that same moment, Coffee Percolator's red eye spotted Mrs. Cherry coming up the back walk with Sunny and Bunny.

"Quick!" coughed Coffee Percolator. "Fill me up with my fragrant black coffee again!"

"Please," begged Oven. "Give me back my sponge cake. And my plum tarts. These shirts taste terrible!"

And from every corner Salt and Pepper heard the same cry: "Oh, let me do my own work once again!"

Quicker than a wink and a blink, they jumped to work. Whizz! Whirr! Bang! Clang! Doors opened and shut. Lids jumped off and on. Cords rattled. Salt and Pepper huffed and puffed, and scrimbled and scrambled, and rubbed and scrubbed. And in the nick of time, too.

"J-just look!" Mr. Cherry's trembling voice was saying outside the kitchen door. "Just see what's happened to your kitchen, Myrtle!"

Mrs. Cherry sailed into the kitchen, followed by Sunny and Bunny, each twin holding a tiny furred kitten. Sunny's kitten was all white, Bunny's all black. Mr. Cherry came in last, spectacles in his hand, huffing on them and polishing them with his best pocket handkerchief. He seemed very upset.

"Why, what's the matter?" Mrs. Cherry asked. "Did you smell something burning?" Whisk! Mrs. Cherry opened the oven door and took out a feathery gold sponge cake and a tray of hot plum tarts.

"Mmmm!" chorused the Dimbleby twins.

Mr. Cherry was too surprised for words.

Whoops! Up came Washing Machine's lid. Mrs. Cherry lifted out a pile of damp snow-white shirts to lay beside the frilly blouses Iron had finished. Click! Icebox produced a chunk of vanilla ice cream which Mrs. Cherry ladled into two blue saucers, one for Sunny, one for Bunny, to celebrate Fudge Ripple's five new kittens.

"Waffles for lunch!" Mrs. Cherry announced, lifting the top of Waffle-Iron to show two crisp brown waffly waffles.

"Mmm!" Mr. Cherry said, blinking behind his spectacles. "I must have been seeing things!"

When Sunny and Bunny had gone home, Sunny holding a hot plum tart and a white kitten, Bunny holding a hot plum tart and a black kitten, Mr. and Mrs. Cherry sat down to lunch.

"Yum," Mr. Cherry said when he got to the plum tart. "What a fine lunch!"

"It *is* good," admitted Mrs. Cherry. "Thanks to my oven."

Salt and Pepper didn't say anything except: Zzzz! Zzzz!! They had fallen sound asleep side by side in the flour tin after Mrs. Cherry's kitchen change-about and change-back-again!

Stone Boy with Dolphin

Ts,* *c.* March 1958, Lilly Library

Because Bamber banged into her bike in Market Hill, spilling oranges, figs, and a paper packet of pink-frosted cakes, and gave her the invitation to make up for it all, Dody Ventura decided to go to the party. Under the striped canvas awnings of the fruit stall she balanced her rust-encrusted Raleigh and let Bamber scramble for the oranges. He wore his monkish red beard barbed and

---

* Typescript with holograph corrections and additions by SP. Typed at top right: 'Sylvia Plath / Apartment 3 rear / 337 Elm Street / Northampton, Mass.' SP cites her poem 'Conversation Among the Ruins' and 'Greensleeves', a favourite song of hers, in the story.

scraggy. Summer sandals buckled over his cotton socks although the February air burned blue and cold.

"You're coming, aren't you?" Albino eyes fixed hers. Pale, bony hands rolled the bright tang-skinned oranges into her wicker bike-basket. "Unfortunately," Bamber restored the packet of cakes, "a bit mashed."

Dody glanced, evasive, down Great St. Mary's Passage, lined with its parked bikes, wheels upon wheels. The stone façade of King's and the pinnacles of the chapel stood elaborate, frosty, against a thin watercolor-blue sky. On such hinges fate turned.

"Who'll be there?" Dody parried. She felt her fingers crisped, empty in the cold. Fallen into disuse, into desuetude, I freeze.

Bamber spread his big hands into chalk webs covering the peopled universe. "Everybody. All the literary boys. You know them?"

"No." But Dody read them. Mick. Leonard. Especially Leonard. She didn't know him, but she knew him by heart. With him, when he was up from London, with Larson and the boys, Adele lunched. Only two American girls at Cambridge and Adele would have to nip Leonard in the bud. Hardly bud: bloom it was, full-bloom and mid-career. Not room for the two of us, Dody had told Adele the day Adele returned the books she had borrowed, all newly underlined and noted in the margins. "But *you* underline," Adele justified sweetly, her face guileless in its cup of sheened blonde hair. "I beat my own brats," Dody said, "you wipe your handmarks off." For some reason, at the game of queening, Adele won: adorably, all innocent surprise. Dody retreated with a taste of lemons into her green sanctum at Arden with her stone facsimile of Verrocchio's boy. To dust, to worship: vocation enough.

"I'll come," Dody suddenly said.

"With whom?"

"Send Hamish along."

Bamber sighed. "He'll be there."

Dody pedaled off toward Bene't Street, red plaid scarf and black gown whipping back in the wind. Hamish: safe, slow. Like traveling by mule, minus mule-kicks. Dody chose with care, with care and a curtsey to the stone figure in her garden. As long as it was someone who didn't matter, it didn't matter. Ever since the start of Lent term she had taken to brushing snow from the face of the winged, dolphin-carrying boy centered in the snow-filled college garden. Leaving the long tables of black-gowned girls chattering and clinking glasses of water over the sodden dinners of spaghetti, turnips and slick fried eggs, with purple raspberry fool for dessert, Dody would push back her chair, gliding, eyes lowered, obsequious, a false demure face on, past high table where Victorian-vintage dons dined on apples, chunks of cheese and dietetic biscuits. Out of the scrolled, white-painted hall with its gilt-framed portraits of principals in high-necked gowns leaning altruistic and radiant from the walls, far from the drawn, wan blue-and-gold ferned draperies, she walked. Bare halls echoed to her heels.

In the vacant college garden, dark-needled pines made their sharp assaults of scent on her nostrils and the stone boy poised on one foot, wings of stone balancing like feathered fans on the wind, holding his waterless dolphin through the rude, clamorous weathers of an alien climate. Nightly after snows, with bare fingers, Dody scraped the caked snow from his stone-lidded eyes, and from his plump stone cherub foot. If not I, who then?

Tracking across the snow-sheeted tennis courts back to Arden, the foreign students' house with its small, elect group of South Africans, Indians, and Americans, she begged, wordless, of the orange bonfire-glow of the town showing faint over the bare treetops, and of the distant jewel-pricks of the stars: let something happen. Let something happen. Something terrible, something bloody. Something to end this endless flaking snowdrift of airmail letters, of blank pages turning in library books. How we go waste, how we go squandering ourselves on air. Let me walk into *Phèdre* and put on that red cloak of doom. Let me leave my mark.

But the days dawned and set, neatly, nicely, toward an Honors BA, and Mrs. Guinea came round, regular as clockwork, every Saturday night, arms laden with freshly laundered sheets and pillowcases, a testimony to the resolute and eternally renewable whiteness of the world. Mrs. Guinea, the Scottish housekeeper, for whom beer and men were ugly words. When Mr. Guinea died his memory had been folded up forever like a scrapbook newspaper, labeled and stored, and Mrs. Guinea bloomed scentless, virgin again after all these years, resurrected somehow in miraculous maidenhood.

This Friday night, waiting for Hamish, Dody wore a black jersey and a black-and-white-checked wool skirt, clipped to her waist by a wide red belt. I will bear pain, she testified to the air, painting her fingernails Applecart Red. A paper on the imagery in *Phèdre*, half done, stuck up its seventh white sheet in her typewriter. Through suffering, wisdom. In her third-floor attic room she listened, catching the pitch of last shrieks; listened: to witches on the rack, to Joan of Arc crackling at the stake, to anonymous ladies flaring like torches in the rending metal of Riviera roadsters, to Zelda enlightened, burning behind the bars of her madness. What visions were to be had came under thumbscrews, not in the mortal comfort of a hot-water-bottle-cozy cot. Unwincing, in her mind's eye, she bared her flesh. Here. Strike home.

A knock beat on the blank white door. Dody finished lacquering the nail of her left little finger, capped the bottle of blood-bright enamel, holding Hamish off. And then, waving her hand to dry the polish, gingerly she opened the door.

Bland pink face and thin lips set ready for a wiseguy smile, Hamish wore the immaculate navy blue blazer with brass buttons which made him resemble a prep school boy, or an off-duty yachtsman.

"Hello," Dody said.

"How," Hamish walked in without her asking him, "are you?"

"I've got sinus." She sniffed thickly. Her throat clotted, obliging, with an ugly frogging sound.

"Look," Hamish laved her with water-blue eyes, "I figure you and I should quit giving each other such a hard time."

"Sure." Dody handed him her red wool coat and bunched up her academic gown into a black, funereal bundle. "Sure thing." She slipped her arms into the red coat as Hamish held it flared. "Carry my gown, will you?"

She flicked off the light as they left the room and closed the cream-painted door behind them. Ahead of Hamish down the two flights of stairs, step by step, she descended. The lower hall stood empty, walled with numbered doors and dark wainscoting. No sound, except for the hollow ticking of the grandfather clock in the stairwell.

"I'll just sign out."

"No, you won't," said Hamish. "You'll be late tonight. And you've got a key."

"How do you know?"

"All the girls in this house have keys."

"But," Dody whispered protest as he swung the front door open, "Miss Minchell has such sharp ears."

"Minchell?"

"Our college secretary. She sleeps with us, she keeps us." Miss Minchell presided, tight-lipped and grim, over the Arden breakfast table. She'd stopped speaking, it was rumored, when the American girls started wearing pajamas to breakfast under their bathrobes. All British girls in the college came down fully dressed and starched for their morning hot tea, kippers and white bread. The Americans at Arden were fortunate beyond thought, Miss Minchell sniffed pointedly, in having a toaster. Ample quarter-pounds of butter were allotted each girl on Sunday morning to last through the week. Only gluttons bought extra butter at the Home and Colonial Stores and slathered it double-thick on toast while Miss Minchell dipped her dry toast with disapproval into her second cup of tea, indulging her nerves.

A black taxicab loomed in the ring of light from the porch lamp where moths beat their wings to powder on spring nights. No moths now, only the winter air like the great pinions of an arctic bird, fanning shivers up Dody's spine. The rear door of the cab, open on its black hinges, showed a bare interior, a roomy cracked-leather seat. Hamish handed her in and followed her up. He slammed the door shut, and, as at a signal, the taxi spun off down the drive, gravel spurting away under the wheels.

Sodium vapor lights from the Fen Causeway wove their weird orange glare among the leafless poplars on Sheep's Green and the houses and storefronts of Newnham Village reflected the sallow glow as the cab bounced along the narrow pot-holed road, turning with a lurch up Silver Street.

Hamish hadn't said a word to the driver. Dody laughed. "You've got it all set, haven't you?"

"I always do." In the sulfur light from the street lamps Hamish's features assumed an oddly Oriental cast, his pale eyes like vacant slits above high cheekbones. Dody knew him for dead, a beer-sodden Canadian, his wax-mask escorting her, for her own convenience, to the party of teatime poets and petty university D. H. Lawrences. Only Leonard's words cut through the witty rot. She didn't know him, but that she knew, that shaped her sword. Let what come, come.

"I always plan ahead," Hamish said. "Like I've planned for us to drink for an hour. And then the party. Nobody'll be there this early. Later they might even have a few dons."

"Will Mick and Leonard be there?"

"You know them?"

"No. Just read them."

"Oh, they'll be there. If anybody is. But keep away from them."

"Why? Why should I?" Worth keeping from is worth going to. Did she will such meetings, or did the stars dictate her days, Orion dragging her, shackled, at his spurred heel?

"Because they're phonies. They are also the biggest seducers in Cambridge."

"I can take care of myself." Because when I give, I never really give at all. Always some shrewd miser Dody sits back, hugging the last, the most valuable crown jewel. Always safe, nun-tending her statue. Her winged stone statue with nobody's face.

"Sure," said Hamish. "Sure."

The cab pulled up opposite the pinnacled stone façade of King's, starched lace in the lamplight, masquerading as stone. Black-gowned boys strode in twos and threes out of the gate by the porter's lodge.

"Don't worry." Hamish handed her down to the sidewalk, stopping to count his coppers into the palm of the featureless cab driver. "It's all arranged."

From the polished wooden bar of Miller's, Dody looked to the far end of the carpeted room at the couples going up and down the plush-covered stair to the dining room: hungry going up, stuffed coming down. Greasy lip-prints on the goblet edge, partridge fat congealing, ruby-set with semi-precious chunks of currant jelly. The whisky was starting to burn her sinus trouble away, but her voice was going along with it, as it always did. Very low and sawdusty.

"Hamish." She tried it.

"Where have you been?" His warm hand under her elbow felt good as anybody's warm hand. People swam past, undulant, with no feet, no faces. Outside the window, bordered with green-leaved rubber plants, face-shapes bloomed toward the glass from the dark outside sea and drifted away again, wan underwater planets at the fringe of vision.

"Ready?"

"Ready. Have you got my gown?" Hamish showed the black patch of cloth draped over his arm, and started to shoulder a path through the crowds around the bar toward the swinging glass door. Dody walked after him with fastidious care, focusing her eyes on his broad navy blue back, and, as he opened the door, ushering her ahead of him onto the sidewalk, she took his arm. Steady as he was, she felt safe, tethered like a balloon, giddy, dangerously buoyant, but still quite safe in the boisterous air. Step on a crack, break your mother's back. With care, she square-walked.

"You'd better put your gown on," Hamish said after they'd been walking a bit. "I don't want any proctors to nab us. Especially tonight."

"Why especially?"

"They'll be looking for me tonight. Bulldogs and all."

So at Peas Hill, under the green-lit marquee of the Arts Theatre, Hamish helped her to slip her arms into the two holes of the black gown. "It's ripped here on the shoulder."

"I know. It always makes me feel as if I'm in a straitjacket. Keeps slipping down and pinning my arms to my sides."

"They're throwing gowns away now, if they catch you in a ripped one. They just come over and ask for it and tear it up on the spot."

"I'd sew it up," Dody said. Mend. Mend the torn, the tattered. Salvage the raveled sleeve. "With black embroidery thread. So it wouldn't show."

"They'd love that."

Through the cobbled open square of Market Hill they walked hand in hand. Stars showed faint above the blackened flank of Great St. Mary's Church which had housed, last week, penitent hordes hearing Billy Graham. Past the wooden posts of the empty market stalls. Then up Petty Cury, past the wine merchant's with his windows of Chilean burgundy and South African sherry, past the shuttered butcher shops, and the leaded panes of Heffers where the books on display spoke their words over and over in a silent litany on the eyeless air. The street stretched bare to the baroque turrets of Lloyd's, deserted except for a few students hurrying to late dinners or theater parties, black gowns flapping out behind them like rooks' wings on the chill wind.

Dody gulped cold air. A last benison. In the dark, crooked alleyway of Falcon Yard, light spilled out of upper-story windows, bursts of laughter came, dovetailing with the low, syncopated strut of a piano. A doorway opened its slat of light to them. Halfway up the glaring steepness of the stair, Dody felt the building waver, rocking under the railing her hand held, her hand slimed chill with sweat. Snail-tracks, fever-tracks. But the fever would make everything flow right, burning its brand into her cheeks, blotting out the brown scar on her left cheek in a rose of red. Like the time she went to the circus when she was nine, with a fever, after putting ice under her tongue so the thermometer wouldn't register, and her cold had vanished when the sword-swallower sauntered into the ring and she fell for him on the spot.

Leonard would be upstairs. In the room at the top of the stairs she and Hamish were now ascending, according to the clocked stations of the stars.

"You're doing fine." Hamish, just behind her shoulder, his hand firm under her elbow, lifted her upward. Step. And then, step.

"I'm not drunk."

"Of course not."

The doorframe hung suspended in a maze of stairs, walls lowering, rising, shutting off all the other rooms, all the other exits but this one. Obedient angels in pink gauze trolleyed away on invisible wires the surplus scenery. In the middle of the doorway Dody poised. Life is a tree with many limbs. Choosing this limb, I crawl out for my bunch of apples. I gather unto me my winesaps, my Coxes, my Bramleys, my Jonathans. Such as I choose. Or do I choose?

"Dody's here."

"Where?" Larson, beaming, his open American face hearty, faintly shiny, as always, with an unsquelchable easy pride, came up, glass in hand. Hamish did away with Dody's coat and gown and she laid her scarred brown leather pocketbook on the nearest windowsill. Mark that.

"I've drunk a lot," Larson observed, amiable, shining with that ridiculous pride, as if he had just successfully delivered quadruplets in a nearby maternity ward. "So don't mind what I say." He, waiting for Adele, stored niceness spilled honey-prodigal, with Adele's lily head in mind. Dody knew him only by hellos and goodbyes, with Adele ever in attendance. "Mick's gone already." Larson jutted his thumb into the seethe and flux of dancers, sweat smells and the Friday night stew of pungent warring perfumes.

Through the loose twining rhythms of the piano, through the blue heron-hover of smoke, Dody picked out the boy who was Mick, sideburns dark and hair rumpled, doing a slow wide brand of British jive with a girl in sweater and skirt of hunter's green close-cloven as frog skin.

"His hair's standing up like devil's horns," Dody said. They would all be girled then, Larson, Leonard. Leonard up from London to celebrate the launching of the new magazine. Straight-faced, she had taken in Adele's rumors, questioning, casual, spying from her battlement until Leonard loomed like the one statue-breaker in her mind's eye, knowing no statues of his own. "Is that Mick's artist girl?"

Larson beamed. "That's the ballet dancer. We're taking ballet now." A deep knee-bend, sloshing his glass, spilled half. "You know, Mick is satanic. Like you say. You know what he did when we were kids in Tennessee?"

No. Dody's eyes scanned the peopled room, flicking over faces, checking accounts for the unknown plus. "What did he do?"

There. In the far corner, by the wooden table, bare of glasses now, the punch bowl holding only a slush of lemon peel and orange rind, a tall one. Back to her, shoulders hunched in a thick black sweater with a rolled-up collar, elbows of his green twill shirt stuck through the sweater holes. His hands shot up, out, and scissored air to shape his unheard talk. The girl. Of course, the girl. Pale, freckled, with no mouth but a pink dim distant rosebud, willowed reedy, wide-eyed to the streaming of his words. It would be what's-her-name. Delores. Or Cheryl. Or Iris. Wordless and pallid companion of Dody's classical tragedy hours. She. Silent, fawn-eyed. Clever. Sending her corpse for a stand-in at supervisions. To read about the problem of Prometheus in a rustling, dust-under-the-bed voice. While shut miles away, sanctuaried safe, she knelt in her sheet before the pedestaled marble. A statue-worshiper. She, too. So.

"Who," Dody asked, sure now, "is that?"

But nobody answered.

"About wild dogs," Larson said. "And Mick was king of the wild dogs and made us fetch and carry . . ."

"Drink?" Hamish emerged at her elbow with two glasses. The music stopped. Applause spattered. Ragged scum on the surge of voices. Mick came, finning the crowd apart with his elbows.

"Dance?"

"Sure." Mick held Leonard's hours in his navy-man's hand. Dody lifted her glass and the drink rose up to meet her mouth. The ceiling wavered and walls buckled. Windows melted, belling inward.

"Oh, Dody," Larson grinned. "You've spilled."

Wet drops watered the back of Dody's hand, a dark stain extended, spreading on her skirt. Marked already. "I want to meet some of these writers."

Larson craned his thick neck. "Here's Brian. The editor himself. Will he do?"

"Hello." Dody looked down at Brian who looked up at her, dark-haired, impeccable, a dandy little package of a man. Her limbs began to mammoth, arm up the chimney, leg through the window. All because of those revolting little cakes. So she grew, crowding the room. "You wrote that one about the jewels. The emerald's lettuce-light. The diamond's eye. I thought it was . . ."

Beside the polished black hearse of the piano Milton Chubb lifted his saxophone, his great body sweating dark crescents under the arms. Dilys, shy, fuzzy chick of a thing that she was, nestled under his arm, blinking her lashless lids. He would crush her. He must be four times her size. Already, at college, a private fund had been raised among the girls to send Dilys to London to rid herself and her small rounding belly of Milton's burgeoning and unwanted heir. A whine. A thump thump.

Mick's fingers gripped for Dody's. His hand, lean, rope-hard, palm calloused, swung her off the hook of her thought and she kept going out, out of gravity's clutch. Planets sparked in the far reaches of her head. M. Vem. Jaysun Pa. Mercury. Venus. Earth. Mars. I'll get there. Jupiter. Saturn. Turning strange. Uranus? Neptune, tridented, green-haired. Far. Mongoloid-lidded Pluto, then. And asteroids innumerable, a buzz of gilded bees. Out, out. Bumping against someone, rebounding gently, and moving back to Mick again. To the here, to the now.

"I can't dance at all."

But Mick turned a deaf ear, whorls waxed against siren-calls. Grinning at her from far, from farther away, he receded. Over the river and into the woods. His Cheshire Cat grin hung luminous. Couldn't hear a word in his canary-feathered heaven.

"You wrote those poems," Dody shouted over the roar of the music which swelled loud, louder, like the continuous roar of airplanes taking off from the runway across Boston Harbor. She taxied in for a close-up, the room blinking on, seen through the wrong end of a telescope. A red-headed boy bent over the piano, fingers cake-walking, invisible. Chubb, sweating and flushed, lifted the horn and wailed, and Bamber, there too, flicked his bony chalk hand over and over the guitar.

"Those words. You made them." But Mick, wrinkled and gone in his baggy checked pants, swung her out, and back, and caught her up again, with Leonard nowhere. Nowhere at all. All the hours wasting. She, squandering hours like salt-shaker grains on the salt sea in her hunt. That one hunt.

Hamish's face kindled before her like a sudden candle from the ring of faces that spun away, features blurred and smeared as warming wax. Hamish, watchful, guardian angeling, waited in attendance, coming no nearer. But the man in the black sweater had come near. His shoulders, hunching, closed out the room piece by piece by piece. Pink, luminous and ineffectual, the face of Hamish winked out behind the blackness of the worn, torn sweater.

"Hello." His square chin was green and rough. "I'm out at the elbows." It was a beard of moss on his chin. Room and voices hushed in the first faint twirl of a rising wind. Air sallowed, the storm to come. Air sultry now. Leaves turning up white-bellied sides in the queer sulfur light. Flags of havoc. His poem said.

"Patch the havoc." But the four winds rose, unbuckled, from the stone cave of the revolving world. Come thou, North. Come thou, South. East. West. And blow.

"Not all their ceremony can patch the havoc."

"You like that?"

Wind smacked and bellowed in the steel girders of the world's house. Perilous scaffold. If she walked very carefully. Knees gone jelly-weak. The room of the party hung in her eye like a death's-door camera shot: Mick beginning again to dance with the girl in green, Larson's smile widening great as the grin on Humpty's head. Knitting up the sleeve of circumstance. She moved. And moved into the small new room.

A door banged shut. People's coats slumped in piles on the tables, cast-off sheaths and shells. Ghosts gone gallivanting. I chose this limb, this room.

"Leonard."

"Brandy?" Leonard plucked a fogged glass from the yellowing sink. Raw reddish liquid sloshed out of the bottle into the glass. Dody reached. Her hands came away drenched. Full of nothing.

"Try again."

Again. The glass rose and flew, executing first a perfect arc, an exquisite death-leap, onto the flat umber-ugly wall. A flower of winking sparks made sudden music, unpetaling then in a crystalline glissade. Leonard pushed back the wall with his left arm and set her in the space between his left arm and his face. Dody pitched her voice above the rising of the winds, but they rose higher in her ears. Then, bridging the gap, she stamped. Shut those four winds up in their goatskin bags. Stamp. The floor resounded.

"You're all there," Leonard said. "Aren't you?"

"Listen. I've got this statue." Stone-lidded eyes crinkled above a smile. The smile millstoned around her neck. "I've got this statue to break."

"So?"

"So there's this stone angel. Only I'm not sure it's an angel. This stone gargoyle maybe. A nasty thing with its tongue stuck out." Under floorboards tornadoes rumbled and muttered. "I'm crazy maybe." They stopped their circus to listen. "Can you do it?"

For answer, Leonard stamped. Stamped out the floor. Stamp, the walls went. Stamp, the ceiling flew to kingdom come. Stripping her red hairband off, he put it in his pocket. Green shadow, moss shadow, raked her mouth. And in the center of the maze, in the sanctum of the garden, a stone boy cracked, splintered, million-pieced.

"When can I see you again?" Fever-cured, she stood, foot set victorious on a dimpled stone arm. Mark that, my fallen gargoyle, my prince of pebbles.

"I work in London."

"When?"

"I've got obligations." The walls closed in, wood grains, glass grains, all in place. "In the next room." The four winds sounded retreat, defeat, hooting off down their tunnel in the world's sea-girdled girth. O hollow, hollow. Hollow in the chambered stone.

Leonard bent to his last supper. She waited. Waited, sighting the whiteness of his cheek with its verdigris stain, moving by her mouth.

Teeth gouged. And held. Salt, warm salt, laving the tastebuds of her tongue. Teeth dug to meet. An ache started far off at their bone-root. Mark that, mark that. But he shook. Shook her bang against the solid-grained substance of the wall. Teeth shut on thin air. No word, but a black back turned, diminished, diminishing, through a sudden sprung-up doorway. Grains of wood molding, level floorboard grains, righted the world. The wrong world. Air flowed, filling the hollow his shape left. But nothing at all filled the hollow in her eye.

The half-open door thronged with snickers, with whispers. On the smoke-burdened air of the party that fissured through the crack Hamish came, intent, behind a glistening pink rubber mask.

"Are you all right?"

"Of course I'm all right."

"I'll get your coat. We're going now." Hamish went away again. A small boy wearing glasses and a drab mustard-colored suit scuttled from a hole in the wall on his way to the lavatory. He ogled her, propped against the wall as she was, and she felt her hand, held to her mouth, jerking sudden like a spastic's.

"Can I get you anything?" A queer light flickered in his eye, the light people have when the blood of a street accident gathers, puddling prodigal on the pavement. How they came to stare. Curious arenas of eyes.

"My pocketbook," Dody steadily said. "I left it behind the curtain on the first windowsill."

The boy went out. Hamish appeared with her red coat, black gown dangling its rag of crepe. She shoved her arms in, obedient. But her face burned, unskinned, undone.

"Is there a mirror?"

Hamish pointed. A blurred, cracked oblong of glass hung over the once-white sink that was yellowed with a hundred years of vomit and liquor stains. She leaned to the mirror and a worn, known face with vacant brown eyes and a seamed brown scar on the left cheek came swimming at her through the mist. There was no mouth on the face: the mouth-place was the same sallow color as the rest of the skin, defining its shape as a badly botched piece of sculpture defines its shape, by shadows under the raised and swollen parts.

The boy stood beside her holding up a pocketbook of scratched brown leather. Dody took it. With a cartridge of red lipstick she followed the mouth-shape and made the color come back. Thank you, she smiled at the boy with her bright new red mouth.

"Take care of me now," she told Hamish. "I have been rather lousy."

"You're all right." But that was not what the others would say.

Hamish pushed the door open. Out into the room. No one stared: a ring of turned backs, averted faces. The piano notes still sauntered underneath the talk. The people were laughing very much now. Beside the piano Leonard hunched, holding a white handkerchief to his left cheek. Tall, pale, Delores-Cheryl-Iris with the tiger-lily freckles willowed up to help him blot the blood. I did that, Dody informed the deaf air. But the obligation got in the way, smirking. Obligations. Soap-and-water would not wash off that ring of holes for a good week. Dody Ventura. Mark me, mark that.

Because of Hamish, protecting, not angry at all, she got to the doorway of the room with no stone thrown, not wanting to go, but going. Starting down the narrow angled stair, with Adele's face, cupped by the shining blonde hair, coming up at her, open and frank and inviolable as a waterlily, that white-blondeness, all pure, all folding purely within itself. Multi-manned, yet virginal, her mere appearance shaped a reprimand like the hushed presence of a nun. Oswald backed her up, and behind him marched the tall, gawky, and depressive Atherton. Oswald, his receding Neanderthal head brushed straight across with slicked hair to hide the shiny retreating slope, peered at Dody through his tortoiseshell glasses.

"Tell us something about bone structure, Dody." She saw, clear in the yet unbreached light of minutes to come, the three of them, together, walking into the room brimming with her act, with versions and variations on the theme of her act which would have marked her by tomorrow like the browned scar on her cheek among all the colleges and all the town. Mothers would stop in Market Hill, pointing to their children: "There's the girl who bit the boy. He died a day after." Hark, hark, the dogs do bark.

"That was last week." Dody's voice rasped hollow, as from the bottom of a weed-grown well. Adele kept smiling her sublime, altruistic smile. Because she knew already what she would find in the room: no grab-bag of star-sent circumstance, but her chosen friends, and Larson, her special friend. Who would tell her everything, and keep the story on the tongues, changing, switching its colors, like a chameleon over smeared and lurid territory.

Back to the wall, Dody let Adele, Oswald, and Atherton move past her up the stair to the room she was leaving and to the red circle of teeth marks and Leonard's obligation. Cold air struck, scything her shins. But no faces came to recognize Dody, nor fingers, censorious, to point her out. Blind storefronts and eyeless alley walls said: comfort ye, comfort ye. Black sky spaces spoke of the hugeness, the indifference of the universe. Greening pricks of stars told her how little they cared.

Every time Dody wanted to say Leonard to a lamppost she would say Hamish, because Hamish was taking the lead, leading her away, safely, though damaged and with interior lesions, but safe, now, through the nameless streets.

Somewhere, from the dark sanctuarial belly of Great St. Mary's, or from deep, deeper within the town, a clock bonged out. Bong.

Black streets, except for the thin string of lights at the main corners. Townfolks all abed. A game began, a game of hide-and-go-seek with nobody. Nobody. Hamish stationed her behind a car, advancing, alone, peering around corners, then returning to lead her after him. Then, before the next corner, Dody ducking again behind a car, feeling the metal fender like dry ice, magnet-gripping her skin. Hamish leaving her, again, walking off to look, again, and then coming back and saying it was safe so far.

"The proctors," he said, "will be out after me."

A damp mist rose and spired about their knees, blurring patches of the buildings and the bare trees, a mist blued to phosphor by the high, clear moon, dropping over a maple tree, a garden shed, here, there, its theatrical scrim of furred blue haze. After back alleys, after crossing the corner of Trumpington Street under the blackened scabrous walls of Pembroke College, a graveyard on the right, askew with stones, snow drifted white in patches and patches of dark where ground showed, they came to Silver Street. Boldly now they walked past the woodwork frame of the butcher shop with its surgical white venetian blind drawn on all the hanging heel-hooked pigs and the counters full of freckled pork sausages and red-purple kidneys. At the gate of Queens', locked for the night, five boys in black gowns were milling under the moon. One began to sing:

A-las, my love, you do me wrong

"Wait." Hamish placed Dody in a corner outside the spiked gates. "Wait, and I'll find a good place to get you over."

To cast me off discourteously.

The five boys surrounded Dody. They had no features at all, only pale, translucent moons for face-shapes, so she would never know them again. And her face, too, felt to be a featureless moon. They could never recognize her in the light of day.

"What are you doing here?"

"Are you all right?"

The voices whispered, batlike, about her face, her hands.

"My, you smell nice."

"That perfume."

"May we kiss you."

Their voices, gentle and light as paper streamers, fell, gently, touching her, like leaves, like wings. Voices web-winged.

"What are you doing here?"

Backed up against the barbed fence, staring at the white snowfield beyond the crescent of dark Queens' buildings and at the blued fen fog floating waist-high over the snow, Dody stood her ground. And the boys dropped back, because Hamish had come up. The boys began to climb, one by one, over the spiked fence. Dody counted. Three. Four. Five. Sheep-counting sleepward. Holding onto the metal railing, they went swinging themselves over the pointed black spikes into the grounds of Queens', deft and drunken, reeling pussyfooted on the crusted snow.

"Who are they?"

"Just some late guys going into the court." The boys were all over now, and they went away across the arched wooden bridge over the narrow green river, the bridge that Newton had once put together without bolts.

"We're going over the wall," Hamish said. "They've found a good place. Only you mustn't talk until we're in."

"I can't go over. Not with this tight skirt. I'll get spikes through my hands."

"I'll help you."

"But I'll fall." Still, Dody pulled her tweed skirt up to her thighs, to the top of her nylon stockings, and put one foot up on the wall. Game, oh, game. She lifted her left leg over the spikes where they were lowest, but the black tips caught and pierced through her skirt. Hamish was helping, but she stuck there, one leg over the spikes, teetering. Would it hurt? Would she bleed at all? Because the spikes were going through her hands, and her hands were so cold she couldn't feel them. And then Hamish was all at once on the inside of the fence, cupping his hands into a stirrup for her to step in, and without arguing it out or thinking, she simply stepped, pivoting herself over with her hands, and the spikes looked to be going right through them.

"My hands," she began, "they'll bleed . . ."

"Shh!" Hamish put his hand over her mouth. He was looking around the inside of the crescent toward a dark doorway. The night stood still and the moon, far off and cold in its coat of borrowed light, made a round O mouth at her, Dody Ventura, coming into Queens' court at three in the morning because there was nowhere else to go, because it was a station on the way. A place to get warm in, for she felt very cold. Wasted, wasting, her blood gone to redden the circle of teeth marks on Leonard's cheek, and she, a bloodless husk, left drifting in limbo. Here with Hamish.

Dody followed Hamish down the side of the building, tracing her fingers along the rough-textured brick until they were at the doorway, with Hamish being furtive and quiet for no reason, because there was no sound, only the great snow silence and the silence of the moon and the hundreds of Queens' men breathing silent in their deep early-morning sleep before the dawn. The first stair on the landing creaked, even though they had taken their shoes off. The next was quiet. And so the next.

A room all by itself. Hamish shut the ponderous oaken door behind them, and then the thin inner door, and lit a match. The big room jumped into Dody's view, with its dark, shiny cracked-leather couch and thick rugs and a wall-full of books.

"Made it. I'm in a good entry."

From behind the paneled wainscoting, a bed creaked. There sounded a stifled sigh.

"What's that? Rats?"

"No rats. My roommate. He's all right . . ." Hamish vanished, and the room with him. Another match scritched, and the room came back. Hamish, squatting, turned on the gas jet for the fire. The hissing sound lighted with a soft whoosh, a blue flare, and the gas flames in their neat row behind the white asbestos lattice started shadows flickering behind the great couch and the heavy chairs.

"I'm so cold." Dody sat on the rug, before the fire which made Hamish's face yellowish, instead of pink, and his pale eyes dark. She rubbed her feet, putting her red shoes, which looked black, into the grate before the fire. The shoes were all wet inside, she could feel the dampness with her finger, but she could not feel the cold, only the numb hurt of her toes as she rubbed them, rubbing the blood back into them.

Then Hamish pushed her back on the rug, so her hair fell away from her face and wound among the tufts of the rug, for it was a deep rug, thick-piled, with the smell of shoe leather about it, and ancient tobacco. What I do, I do not do. In limbo one does not really burn. Hamish began kissing her mouth, and she felt him kiss her. Nothing stirred. Inert, she lay staring toward the high ceiling crossed by the dark wood beams, hearing the worms of the ages moving in them, riddling them with countless passages and little worm-size labyrinths, and Hamish let his weight down on top of her, so it was warm. Fallen into disuse, into desuetude, I shall not be.

And then at last Hamish just lay there with his face in her neck, and she could feel his breathing quiet.

"Please scold me." Dody heard her voice, strange and constricted in her chest, from lying on her back on the floor, from the sinus, from the whisky. I am sick of labeled statues. In a gray world no fires burn. Faces wear no names. No Leonards can be for no Leonards live: Leonard is no name.

"What for?" Hamish's mouth moved against her neck, and she felt now again how unnaturally long her neck was, so that her head nodded far from her body, on a long stem, like the picture of Alice after eating the mushroom, with her head on its serpent neck above the leaves of the treetops. A pigeon flew up, scolding. Serpents, serpents. How to keep the eggs safe?

"I am a bitch," Dody heard her voice announce from out of the doll-box in her chest, and she listened to it, wondering what absurd thing it would say next. "I am a slut," it said with no conviction.

"No you're not." Hamish made a kiss-shape with his mouth on her neck. "But you should have learned your lesson. I told you about them, and you should have learned your lesson."

"I've learned it," the small voice lied. But Dody hadn't learned her lesson, unless it was the lesson of this limbo where no one got hurt because no one took a name to tie the hurt to like a battered can. Nameless I rise. Nameless and undefiled.

One more lap of her journey loomed ahead: the safe getting in the door at Arden, and then up to her room with no stairs creaking. With no simmering Miss Minchell bursting out of her room on the landing between the first and second stair, raging in her red flannel bathrobe, her hair undone for the night from the bun and hanging in a straight black braid down her back, with the gray strands braided into it, down to her buttocks, and no one to see. No one to know that Miss Minchell's hair, when undone, reached her buttocks. Someday, some year hence, it would be a braid of battleship gray, probably, by that time, reaching down to her knees. And by the time it grew to touch the floor, it would be turned pure white. White, and wasting its whiteness on the blank air.

"I am going now."

Hamish heaved himself up, and Dody lay indifferent, feeling the warm place where he had been, and the warm sweat drying and cooling on the cool air through her sweater. "You do just what I tell you," Hamish said. "Or we'll never get out."

Dody put on her ribboned shoes, grown so hot from the fire that they seared her footsoles.

"Do you want to climb over the spikes again? Or try the brook?"

"The brook?" Dody looked up at Hamish, standing over her, solid and warm, like a horse, breathing hay in its stable. "Is it deep?" It might have been Larson, or Oswald, or even Atherton standing there, standing in with the pleasant warmth common to horses. Immortal horses, for one replaced another. And so all was well in an eternity of horses.

"Deep? It's frozen over. I'd test it first, anyway."

"The brook, then."

Hamish stationed Dody by the doorway. First he opened the inside door, and then, after peering out the crack, the outside door. "You wait here." He wedged her against the doorjamb. "When I signal, come."

Stairs chirked faintly under his weight, and then, after a pause, a match flared, lighting the entrance, showing the grain of wood, worn to a satin patina by the hands of ghosts. Dody began to descend. How we pass and repass ourselves, never fusing, never solidifying into the perfect stances of our dreams. Tiptoeing down, her right hand sliding along the rail, Dody felt all Queens' crescent list and recover, and list again, a ship rolling on heavy seas. Then a splinter entered her index finger, but she kept her hand sliding down along the rail, right on into it. Unwincing. Here. Strike home. The splinter broke off, imbedded in her finger with a small nagging twinge. Hamish stationed her in the dark niche of the entry, a dressmaker's dummy.

"Wait," he whispered, and the whisper ran up the stairs, twining around the banisters, and there might be someone on the next landing, wary, listening, with flashlights and an official badge. "I'll beckon if it's all clear, and you run like hell. Even if anyone starts coming after, you run, and we'll get over the brook and across the road before they can catch us up."

"What if they arrest you?"

"They won't do any more than send me down." Hamish dropped the match to the ground. He crushed it under his foot. The small yellow world went out and the courtyard flowered, large, luminous, blue in the light of the moon. Hamish stepped out into the courtyard, his dark shape cut itself clear against the snow, a pasteboard silhouette, moving, diminishing, blending into the darkness of the bushes bordering the brook.

Dody watched, hearing her own breathing, a cardboard stranger's, until a dark figure detached itself from the shrubbery. It made a motion. She ran out. Her shoes crunched loud, breaking through the crust of the snow, each step crackling, as if someone were crumpling up newspapers, one after the other. Her heart beat, and the blood beat up in her face, and still the snow crusts broke and broke under her feet. She could feel the soft snow dropping like powder into her shoes, in the space between the arch of her foot and the instep of the shoe, dry, and then melting cold. No sudden searchlight, no shouts.

Hamish reached for her as she stumbled up and they stood for a moment by the hedge. Then Hamish began shouldering through the rough-thicketed bush, making a path for her, and she followed him, setting her feet down, tramping the lower branches, scratching and scraping her legs on the brittle twigs. They were through, at the bank of the brook, and the hedge closed behind them its gate of briars, dark, unbroken.

Hamish slid down the bank, ankle-deep in snow, and held out his hand, so Dody would not fall coming down. Snow-covered ice bore them up, but before they had reached the other shore, the ice began to boom and crack in its depths. They jumped clear onto the opposite bank and started to crawl up the steep, slippery side, losing their footing, reaching for the top of the bank with their hands, their hands full of snow, their fingers stinging.

Crossing the snow field toward the bare expanse of Queen's Road, stilled now, muted and relieved of the daily thunder of lorries and market vans, they walked hand in hand, not saying a word. A clock struck clear out of the dead quiet. Bong. Bong. And bong. Newnham Village slumbered behind glazed windows, a toy town constructed of pale orange taffy. They met no one.

Porch light and all the house lights out, Arden stood dark in the weak blue wash of the setting moon. Wordless, Dody put her key in the lock, turned it, and pressed the door handle down. The door clicked open on the black hall, thick with the ticking of the coffin-shaped clock and hushed with the unheard breathing of sleeping girls. Hamish leaned and put his mouth to her mouth. A kiss that savored of stale hay through the imperfect clothwork of their faces.

The door shut him away. A mule that didn't kick. She went to the pantry closet just outside Mrs. Guinea's quarters and opened the door. The smell of bread and cold bacon rose to meet her nostrils, but she was not hungry. She reached down until her hand met the cool glass shape of a milk bottle. Taking off her shoes again, and her black gown and her coat, she started up the back stairs with the milk bottle, weary, yet preparing, from a great distance, the lies that would say, if necessary, how she had been in Adele's room, talking with Adele until late, and had just come up. But she remembered with lucid calm that she had not looked in the signing-out book to see if Adele had checked herself back yet. Probably Adele had not signed out either, so there was no knowing, unless she tried Adele's door, whether Adele really was back. But Adele's room was on the first floor, and it was too late now. And then she remembered why she did not want to see Adele at all anyway.

When Dody flicked on the light switch, her room leapt to greet her, bright, welcoming, with its grass-green carpet and the two great bookcases full of books she had bought on her book-allowance and might never read, not until she had a year of nothing to do but sit, with a locked door, and food hoisted up by pulleys, and then she might read through them. Nothing, the room affirmed, has happened at all. I, Dody Ventura, am the same coming in as I was going out. Dody dropped her coat on the floor, and her torn gown. The gown lay in a black patch, like a hole, a black doorway into nowhere.

Carefully Dody put her shoes on the armchair so she would not wake Miss Minchell, who slept directly below, coiled up for the night in her braid of hair. The gas ring on the hearth, black and greasy, was stuck with combings of hair, speckled with face powder fallen from past makeup jobs in front of the mirror on the mantel over the fireplace. Taking a Kleenex, she wiped the gas ring clean and threw the stained tissue into the wicker wastepaper basket. The room always got musty over the weekend and only really cleared on Tuesdays when Mrs. Guinea came in with the vacuum cleaner and her bouquet of brushes and feather dusters.

Dody took one match from the box with the swan on it which she kept on the floor by the gray gas meter with all its myriad round dial-faces and numbers stenciled black on white. She lit the gas fire and then the gas ring, its circle of flames flaring up blue to her retreating hand, leaping to scorch. For a minute she squatted there, absorbed, to remove the splinter from her right hand where it had dug itself into a little pocket of flesh, showing dark under the transparent covering of skin. With thumb and forefinger of her left hand she pinched the skin together and the head of the splinter came out, black, and she took the thin sliver between her fingernails, slowly drawing it out until it came clear. Then she put the small, battered aluminum pot on the gas ring, poured the pint of milk into it, and sat on the floor, cross-legged. But her stockings cut tight into her thighs, so she got up and ripped down her girdle like the peel of a fruit, and pulled the stockings off, still gartered to it, because they were shredded past saving from the twigs of the bushes outside Queens'. And she sat down again in her slip, rocking back and forth gently, her mind blank and still, her arms around her knees and her knees hugged against her breasts, until the milk began to show bubbles around the brim of the pan. She sat then in the green-covered chair, sipping the milk from the Dutch pottery cup she had picked up in New Compton Street that first week in London.

The milk seared her tongue, but she drank it down. And knew that tomorrow the milk would not pass, all of it, out of her system, extricable as a splinter, but that it would stay to become part of herself, inextricable, Dody. Dody Ventura. And then, slowly, upon this thought, all the linked causes and consequences of her words and acts began to gather in her mind, slowly, like slow-running sores. The circle of teeth marks hung out its ring of bloodied roses for Dody Ventura to claim. And the invariable minutes with Hamish would not be spat out like thistles, but clung, clung fast. No limbo's nameless lamb, she. But stained, deep-grained with all the words and acts of all the Dodys from birth-cry on.Ced Ventura. She saw. Who to tell it to? Dody Ventura I am.

The top floor of Arden did not respond, but remained dead still in the black dawn. Nothing outside hurt enough to equal the inside mark, a Siamese-twin circle of teeth marks, fit emblem of loss. I lived: that once. And must shoulder the bundle, the burden of my dead selves until I, again, live.

Barefoot, Dody stripped off her white nylon slip, and her bra and pants. Electricity crackled as the warmed silk tore clear of her skin. She flicked out the light and moved from the wall of flame, and from the ring of flame, toward the black oblong of the window. Rubbing a clear round porthole in the misted pane, she peered out at the morning, caught now in a queer no-man's-land light between moonset and sunrise. No place. No place yet. But someplace, someplace in Falcon Yard, the panes of the diamond-paned windows were falling in jagged shards to the street below, catching the light from the single lamp as they fell. Crash. Bang. Jing-jangle. Booted feet kicked the venerable panes through before dawning.

Dody undid the catch on the window and flung it open. The frame screaked on its hinges, banging back to thud against the gable. Kneeling naked on the two-seated couch in the window-niche, she leaned out far over the dead dried garden. Over the marrowless stems marking iris roots, bulbs of narcissus and daffodil. Over the bud-nubbed branches of the cherry tree and the intricate arbor of laburnum boughs. Over the great waste of earth and under the greater waste of sky. Orion stood above the peaked roof of Arden, his gold imperishable joints polished in the cold air, speaking, the way he always spoke, his bright-minted words out of the vast wastage of space: space where, he testified, space where the Miss Minchells, the Hamishes, all the extra Athertons and the unwanted Oswalds of the world went round and round, like rockets, squandering the smoky fuse of their lives in the limbo of unlove. Patching the great gap in the cosmos with four o'clock teas and crumpets and a sticky-sweet paste of lemon curd and marzipan.

The cold took her body like a death. No fist through glass, no torn hair, strewn ash and bloody fingers. Only the lone, lame gesture for the unbreakable stone boy in the garden, ironic, with Leonard's look, poised on that sculpted foot, holding fast to his dolphin, stone-lidded eyes fixed on a world beyond the clipped privet hedge, beyond the box borders and the raked gravel of the cramped and formal garden paths. A world of no waste, but of savings and cherishings: a world love-kindled, love-championed. As Orion went treading riveted on his track toward the rim of that unseen country, his glitter paling in the blue undersea light, the first cock crew.

Stars doused their burning wicks against the coming of the sun.

Dody slept the sleep of the drowned.

Nor saw yet, or fathomed how now, downstairs in the back kitchen, Mrs. Guinea began another day. Saver, cherisher. No waster, she. Splitting the bony kippers into the black iron frying pan, crisping the fat-soaked toast in the oven, she creakily hummed. Grease jumped and spat. Sun bloomed virginal in the steel-rimmed rounds of her eyeglasses and clear light fountained from her widowed bosom, giving back the day its purity.

To her potted hyacinths, budding on the windowsill in their rare ethereal soil of mother-of-pearl shells, Mrs. Guinea affirmed, and would forever affirm, winter aside, what a fine, lovely day it was after all.

Johnny Panic and the Bible of Dreams

Ts, 16 December 1958,[*] Smith College

Every day from nine to five I sit at my desk facing the door of the office and type up other people's dreams. Not just dreams. That wouldn't be practical enough for my bosses. I type up also people's daytime complaints: trouble with mother, trouble with father, trouble with the bottle, the bed, the headache that bangs home and blacks out the sweet world for no known reason. Nobody comes to our office unless they have troubles. Troubles that can't be pinpointed by Wassermanns or Wechsler–Bellevues alone.

---

[*] Typescript with holograph corrections and additions by SP. SP finished the first version of the story in December 1958 and sent it to a number of periodicals including the *Atlantic Monthly*, *London Magazine*, *Sewanee Review*, *Chelsea Review* and *New World Writing*. The Smith typescript features her Chalcot Square address typed in the top-right corner which was updated, by SP's hand, to her Fitzroy Road, London address. First published posthumously in *The Atlantic* (September 1968): 54–60, with the following biographical sketch: 'The beginnings of a cult were gathering about the Massachusetts-born poet Sylvia Plath, even before her suicide, at the age of thirty, in London in 1963. This story was among the works she left behind.' SP used some of the scenes from this story in *The Bell Jar*. SP made 'Hospital Notes' when she worked part-time as a secretary in the adult psychiatric clinic at the Massachusetts General Hospital in autumn 1958. See Appendix 14 of *The Journals of Sylvia Plath*: 624–9.

Maybe a mouse gets to thinking pretty early on how the whole world is run by these enormous feet. Well, from where I sit, I figure the world is run by one thing and this one thing only. Panic with a dog-face, devil-face, hag-face, whore-face, panic in capital letters with no face at all—it's the same Johnny Panic, awake or asleep.

When people ask me where I work, I tell them I'm Assistant to the Secretary in one of the Out-Patient Departments of the Clinics Building of the City Hospital. This sounds so be-all end-all they seldom get around to asking me more than what I do, and what I do is mainly type up records. On my own hook, though, and completely undercover, I am pursuing a vocation that would set these doctors on their ears. In the privacy of my one-room apartment I call myself secretary to none other than Johnny Panic himself.

Dream by dream I am educating myself to become that rare character, rarer, in truth, than any member of the Psychoanalytic Institute, a dream connoisseur. Not a dream-stopper, a dream-explainer, an exploiter of dreams for the crass practical ends of health and happiness, but an unsordid collector of dreams for themselves alone. A lover of dreams for Johnny Panic's sake, the Maker of them all.

There isn't a dream I've typed up in our record books that I don't know by heart. There isn't a dream I haven't copied out at home into Johnny Panic's Bible of Dreams.

This is my real calling.

Some nights I take the elevator up to the roof of my apartment building. Some nights, about three a.m. over the trees at the far side of the park the United Fund torch flare flattens and recovers under some witchy invisible push and here and there in the hunks of stone and brick I see a light. Most of all, though, I feel the city sleeping. Sleeping from the river on the west to the ocean on the east, like some rootless island rockabying itself on nothing at all.

I can be tight and nervy as the top string on a violin, and yet by the time the sky begins to blue I'm ready for sleep. It's the thought of all those dreamers and what they're dreaming wears me down till I sleep the sleep of fever. Monday to Friday what do I do but type up those same dreams. Sure, I don't touch a fraction of them the city over, but page by page, dream by dream, my Intake books fatten and weigh down the bookshelves of the cabinet in the narrow passage running parallel to the main hall, off which passage the doors to all the doctors' little interviewing cubicles open.

I've got a funny habit of identifying the people who come in by their dreams.

As far as I'm concerned, the dreams single them out more than any Christian name. This one guy, for example, who works for a ball bearing company in town, dreams every night how he's lying on his back with a grain of sand on his chest. Bit by bit this grain of sand grows bigger and bigger till it's big as a fair-sized house and he can't draw breath. Another fellow I know of has had a certain dream ever since they gave him ether and cut out his tonsils and adenoids when he was a kid. In this dream he's caught in the rollers of a cotton mill, fighting for his life. Oh, he's not alone, although he thinks he is. A lot of people these days dream they're being run over or eaten by machines. They're the cagey ones who won't go on the subway or the elevators. Coming back from my lunch hour in the hospital cafeteria I often pass them, puffing up the unswept stone stairs to our office on the fourth floor. I wonder, now and then, what dreams people had before ball bearings and cotton mills were invented.

I've a dream of my own. My one dream. A dream of dreams.

In this dream there's a great half-transparent lake stretching away in every direction, too big for me to see the shores of it, if there are any shores, and I'm hanging over it looking down from the glass belly of some helicopter. At the bottom of the lake—so deep I can only guess at the dark masses moving and heaving—are the real dragons. The ones that were around before men started living in caves and cooking meat over fires and figuring out the wheel and the alphabet. Enormous isn't the word for them; they've got more wrinkles than Johnny Panic himself. Dream about these long enough and your feet and hands shrivel away when you look at them too closely. The sun shrinks to the size of an orange, only chillier, and you've been living in Roxbury since the last ice age. No place for you but a room padded soft as the first room you knew of, where you can dream and float, float and dream, till at last you actually are back among those great originals and there's no point in any dreams at all.

It's into this lake people's minds run at night, brooks and gutter-trickles to one borderless common reservoir. It bears no resemblance to those pure sparkling-blue sources of drinking water the suburbs guard more jealously than the Hope diamond in the middle of pine woods and barbed fences.

It's the sewage farm of the ages, transparence aside.

Now the water in this lake naturally stinks and smokes from what dreams have been left sogging around in it over the centuries. When you think how much room one night of dream props would take up for one person in one city, and that city a mere pinprick on a map of the world, and when you start multiplying this space by the population of the world, and that space by the number of nights there have been since the apes took to chipping axes out of stone and losing their hair, you have some idea what I mean. I'm not the mathematical type: my head starts splitting when I get only as far as the number of dreams going on during one night in the State of Massachusetts.

By this time, I already see the surface of the lake swarming with snakes, dead bodies puffed as blowfish, human embryos bobbing around in laboratory bottles like so many unfinished messages from the great I Am. I see whole storehouses of hardware: knives, paper cutters, pistons and cogs and nutcrackers; the shiny fronts of cars looming up, glass-eyed and evil-toothed. Then there's the spider man and the webfooted man from Mars, and the simple, lugubrious vision of a human face turning aside forever, in spite of rings and vows, to the last lover of all.

One of the most frequent shapes in this backwash is so commonplace it seems silly to mention it. It's a grain of dirt. The water is thick with these grains. They seep in among everything else and revolve under some queer power of their own, opaque, ubiquitous. Call the water what you will, Lake Nightmare, Bog of Madness, it's here the sleeping people lie and toss together among the props of their worst dreams, one great brotherhood, though each of them, waking, thinks himself singular, utterly apart.

This is my dream. You won't find it written up in any casebook.

Now the routine in our office is very different from the routine in Skin Clinic, for example, or in Tumor. The other Clinics have strong similarities to each other; none are like ours. In our Clinic, treatment doesn't get prescribed. It is invisible. It goes right on in those little cubicles, each with its desk, its two chairs, its window and its door with the opaque glass rectangle set in the wood. There is a certain spiritual purity about this kind of doctoring. I can't help feeling the special privilege of my position as Assistant Secretary in the Adult Psychiatric Clinic. My sense of pride is borne out by the rude invasions of other Clinics into our cubicles on certain days of the week for lack of space elsewhere: our building is a very old one, and the facilities have not expanded with the expanding needs of the time. On these days of overlap the contrast between us and the other Clinics is marked.

On Tuesdays and Thursdays, for instance, we have lumbar punctures in one of our offices in the morning. If the practical nurse chances to leave the door of the cubicle open, as she usually does, I can glimpse the end of the white cot and the dirty yellow-soled bare feet of the patient sticking out from under the sheet. In spite of my distaste at this sight, I can't keep my eyes away from the bare feet, and I find myself glancing back from my typing every few minutes to see if they are still there, if they have changed their position at all. You can understand what a distraction this is in the middle of my work. I often have to reread what I have typed several times, under the pretense of careful proofreading, in order to memorize the dreams I have copied down from the doctor's voice over the Audograph.

Nerve Clinic next door, which tends to the grosser, more unimaginative end of our business, also disturbs us in the mornings. We use their offices for therapy in the afternoon, as they are only a morning Clinic, but to have their people crying, or singing, or chattering loudly in Italian or Chinese, as they often do, without break for four hours at a stretch every morning, is distracting to say the least.

In spite of such interruptions by other Clinics, my own work is advancing at a great rate. By now I am far beyond copying only what comes after the patient's saying: "I have this dream, doctor." I am at the point of recreating dreams that are not even written down at all. Dreams that shadow themselves forth in the vaguest way, but are themselves hid, like a statue under red velvet before the grand unveiling.

To illustrate. This woman came in with her tongue swollen and stuck out so far she had to leave a party she was giving for twenty friends of her French-Canadian mother-in-law and be rushed to our Emergency Ward. She thought she didn't want her tongue to stick out and, to tell the truth, it was an exceedingly embarrassing affair for her, but she hated that French-Canadian mother-in-law worse than pigs, and her tongue was true to her opinion, even if the rest of her wasn't. Now she didn't lay claim to any dreams. I have only the bare facts above to begin with, yet behind them I detect the bulge and promise of a dream.

So I set myself to uprooting this dream from its comfortable purchase under her tongue.

Whatever the dream I unearth, by work, taxing work, and even by a kind of prayer, I am sure to find a thumbprint in the corner, a malicious detail to the right of center, a bodiless midair Cheshire Cat grin, which shows the whole work to be gotten up by the genius of Johnny Panic, and him alone. He's sly, he's subtle, he's sudden as thunder, but he gives himself away only too often. He simply can't resist melodrama. Melodrama of the oldest, most obvious variety.

I remember one guy, a stocky fellow in a nail-studded black leather jacket, running straight in to us from a boxing match at Mechanics Hall, Johnny Panic hot at his heels. This guy, good Catholic though he was, young and upright and all, had one mean fear of death. He was actually scared blue he'd go to hell. He was a piece-worker at a fluorescent light plant. I remember this detail because I thought it funny he should work there, him being so afraid of the dark as it turned out. Johnny Panic injects a poetic element in this business you don't often find elsewhere. And for that he has my eternal gratitude.

I also remember quite clearly the scenario of the dream I had worked out for this guy: a gothic interior in some monastery cellar, going on and on as far as you could see, one of those endless perspectives between two mirrors, and the pillars and walls were made of nothing but human skulls and bones, and in every niche there was a body laid out, and it was the Hall of Time, with the bodies in the foreground still warm, discoloring and starting to rot in the middle distance, and the bones emerging, clean as a whistle, in a kind of white futuristic glow at the end of the line. As I recall, I had the whole scene lighted, for the sake of accuracy, not with candles, but with the ice-bright fluorescence that makes skin look green and all the pink and red flushes dead black-purple.

You ask, how do I know this was the dream of the guy in the black leather jacket. I don't know. I only believe this was his dream, and I work at belief with more energy and tears and entreaties than I work at recreating the dream itself.

My office, of course, has its limitations. The lady with her tongue stuck out, the guy from Mechanics Hall—these are our wildest ones. The people who have really gone floating down toward the bottom of that boggy lake come in only once, and are then referred to a place more permanent than our office which receives the public from nine to five, five days a week only. Even those people who are barely able to walk about the streets and keep working, who aren't yet halfway down in the lake, get sent to the Out-Patient Department at another hospital specializing in severer cases. Or they may stay a month or so in our own Observation Ward in the central hospital which I've never seen.

I've seen the secretary of that Ward, though. Something about her merely smoking and drinking her coffee in the cafeteria at the ten o'clock break put me off so I never went to sit next to her again. She has a funny name I don't ever quite remember correctly, something really odd, like Miss Milleravage. One of those names that seem more like a pun mixing up Milltown and Ravage than anything in the city phone directory. But not so odd a name, after all, if you've ever read through the phone directory, with its Hyman Diddlebockers and Sasparilla Greenleafs. I read through the phone book once, never mind when, and it satisfied a deep need in me to realize how many people aren't called Smith.

Anyhow, this Miss Milleravage is a large woman, not fat, but all sturdy muscle and tall on top of it. She wears a gray suit over her hard bulk that reminds me vaguely of some kind of uniform, without the details of cut having anything strikingly military about them. Her face, hefty as a bullock's, is covered with a remarkable number of tiny macula, as if she'd been lying underwater for some time and little algae had latched on to her skin, smutching it over with tobacco-browns and greens. These moles are noticeable mainly because the skin around them is so pallid. I sometimes wonder if Miss Milleravage has ever seen the wholesome light of day. I wouldn't be a bit surprised if she'd been brought up from the cradle with the sole benefit of artificial lighting.

Byrna, the secretary in Alcoholic Clinic just across the hall from us, introduced me to Miss Milleravage with the gambit that I'd "been in England too."

Miss Milleravage, it turned out, had spent the best years of her life in London hospitals.

"Had a friend," she boomed in her queer, doggish basso, not favoring me with a direct look, "a nurse at Bart's. Tried to get in touch with her after the war, but the head of the nurses had changed, everybody'd changed, nobody'd heard of her. She must've gone down with the old head nurse, rubbish and all, in the bombings." She followed this with a large grin.

Now I've seen medical students cutting up cadavers, four stiffs to a classroom, about as recognizably human as Moby Dick, and the students playing catch with the dead men's livers. I've heard guys joke about sewing a woman up wrong after a delivery at the charity ward of the Lying-In. But I wouldn't want to see what Miss Milleravage would write off as the biggest laugh of all time. No thanks and then some. You could scratch her eyes with a pin and swear you'd struck solid quartz.

My boss has a sense of humor too, only it's gentle. Generous as Santa on Christmas Eve.

I work for a middle-aged lady named Miss Taylor who is the Head Secretary of the Clinic and has been since the Clinic started thirty-three years ago—the year of my birth, oddly enough. Miss Taylor knows every doctor, every patient, every outmoded appointment slip, referral slip, and billing procedure the hospital has ever used or thought of using. She plans to stick with the Clinic until she's farmed out in the green pastures of Social Security checks. A woman more dedicated to her work I never saw. She's the same way about statistics as I am about dreams: if the building caught fire she would throw every last one of those books of statistics to the firemen below at the serious risk of her own skin.

I get along extremely well with Miss Taylor. The one thing I never let her catch me doing is reading the old record books. I have actually very little time for this. Our office is busier than the stock exchange with the staff of twenty-five doctors in and out, medical students in training, patients, patients' relatives, and visiting officials from other Clinics referring patients to us, so even when I'm covering the office alone, during Miss Taylor's coffee break and lunch hour, I seldom get to dash down more than a note or two.

This kind of catch-as-catch-can is nerve-wracking, to say the least. A lot of the best dreamers are in the old books, the dreamers that come in to us only once or twice for evaluation before they're sent elsewhere. For copying out these dreams I need time, a lot of time. My circumstances are hardly ideal for the unhurried pursuit of my art. There is, of course, a certain derring-do in working under such hazards, but I long for the rich leisure of the true connoisseur who indulges his nostrils above the brandy snifter for an hour before his tongue reaches out for the first taste.

I find myself all too often lately imagining what a relief it would be to bring a briefcase into work, big enough to hold one of those thick, blue, cloth-bound record books full of dreams. At Miss Taylor's lunchtime, in the lull before the doctors and students crowd in to take their afternoon patients, I could simply slip one of the books, dated ten or fifteen years back, into my briefcase and leave the briefcase under my desk till five o'clock struck. Of course, odd-looking bundles are inspected by the doorman of the Clinics Building and the hospital has its own staff of police to check up on the multiple varieties of thievery that go on, but for heaven's sake, I'm not thinking of making off with typewriters or heroin. I'd only borrow the book overnight and slip it back on the shelf first thing the next day before anybody else came in. Still, being caught taking a book out of the hospital would probably mean losing my job and all my source material with it.

This idea of mulling over a record book in the privacy and comfort of my own apartment, even if I have to stay up night after night for this purpose, attracts me so much I become more and more impatient with my usual method of snatching minutes to look up dreams in Miss Taylor's half-hours out of the office.

The trouble is, I can never tell exactly when Miss Taylor will come back to the office. She is so conscientious about her job she'd be likely to cut her half-hour at lunch short and her twenty minutes at coffee shorter, if it weren't for her lame left leg. The distinct sound of this lame leg in the corridor warns me of her approach in time for me to whip the record book I'm reading into my drawer out of sight and pretend to be putting down the final flourishes on a phone message or some such alibi. The only catch, as far as my nerves are concerned, is that Amputee Clinic is around the corner from us in the opposite direction from Nerve Clinic and I've gotten really jumpy due to a lot of false alarms where I've mistaken some pegleg's hitching step for the step of Miss Taylor herself returning early to the office.

On the blackest days when I've scarcely time to squeeze one dream out of the old books and my copywork is nothing but weepy college sophomores who can't get a lead in *Camino Real*, I feel Johnny Panic turn his back, stony as Everest, higher than Orion, and the motto of the great Bible of Dreams, "Perfect fear casteth out all else," is ash and lemon water on my lips. I'm a wormy hermit in a country of prize pigs so corn-happy they can't see the slaughterhouse at the end of the track. I'm Jeremiah vision-bitten in the Land of Cockaigne.

What's worse: day by day I see these psyche-doctors studying to win Johnny Panic's converts from him by hook, crook, and talk, talk, talk. Those deep-eyed, bush-bearded dream collectors who preceded me in history, and their contemporary inheritors with their white jackets and knotty pine paneled offices and leather couches, practiced and still practice their dream-gathering for worldly ends: health and money, money and health. To be a true member of Johnny Panic's congregation one must forget the dreamer and remember the dream: the dreamer is merely a flimsy vehicle for the great Dream-Maker himself. This they will not do. Johnny Panic is gold in the bowels, and they try to root him out by spiritual stomach pumps.

Take what happened to Harry Bilbo. Mr. Bilbo came into our office with the hand of Johnny Panic heavy as a lead coffin on his shoulder. He had an interesting notion about the filth in this world. I figured him for a prominent part in Johnny Panic's Bible of Dreams, Third Book of Fear, Chapter Nine on Dirt, Disease, and General Decay. A friend of Harry's blew a trumpet in the Boy Scout band when they were kids. Harry Bilbo'd also blown on this friend's trumpet. Years later the friend got cancer and died. Then, one day not so long ago, a cancer doctor came into Harry's house, sat down in a chair, passed the top of the morning with Harry's mother and, on leaving, shook her hand and opened the door for himself. Suddenly Harry Bilbo wouldn't blow trumpets or sit down on chairs or shake hands if all the cardinals of Rome took to blessing him twenty-four hours around the clock for fear of catching cancer. His mother had to go turning the TV knobs and water faucets on and off and opening doors for him. Pretty soon Harry stopped going to work because of the spit and dog turds in the street. First that stuff gets on your shoes and then when you take your shoes off it gets on your hands and then at dinner it's a quick trip into your mouth and not a hundred Hail Marys can keep you from the chain reaction.

The last straw was, Harry quit weight lifting at the public gym when he saw this cripple exercising with the dumbbells. You can never tell what germs cripples carry behind their ears and under their fingernails. Day and night Harry Bilbo lived in holy worship of Johnny Panic, devout as any priest among censers and sacraments. He had a beauty all his own.

Well, these white-coated tinkerers managed, the lot of them, to talk Harry into turning on the TV himself, and the water faucets, and to opening closet doors, front doors, bar doors. Before they were through with him, he was sitting down on movie house chairs, and benches all over the Public Garden, and weight lifting every day of the week at the gym in spite of the fact another cripple took to using the rowing machine. At the end of his treatment he came in to shake hands with the Clinic Director. In Harry Bilbo's own words, he was "a changed man." The pure Panic-light had left his face. He went out of the office doomed to the crass fate these doctors call health and happiness.

About the time of Harry Bilbo's cure a new idea starts nudging at the bottom of my brain. I find it hard to ignore as those bare feet sticking out of the lumbar puncture room. If I don't want to risk carrying a record book out of the hospital in case I get discovered and fired and have to end my research forever, I can really speed up work by staying in the Clinics Building overnight. I am nowhere near exhausting the Clinic's resources and the piddling amount of cases I am able to read in Miss Taylor's brief absences during the day are nothing to what I could get through in a few nights of steady copying. I need to accelerate my work if only to counteract those doctors.

Before I know it, I am putting on my coat at five and saying goodnight to Miss Taylor, who usually stays a few minutes overtime to clear up the day's statistics and sneaking around the corner into the Ladies' Room. It is empty. I slip into the patients' john, lock the door from the inside, and wait. For all I know, one of the Clinic cleaning ladies may try to knock the door down, thinking some patient's passed out on the seat. My fingers are crossed. About twenty minutes later the door of the lavatory opens and someone limps over the threshold like a chicken favoring a bad leg. It is Miss Taylor, I can tell by the resigned sigh as she meets the jaundiced eye of the lavatory mirror. I hear the click-cluck of various touch-up equipment on the bowl, water sloshing, the scritch of a comb in frizzed hair, and then the door is closing with a slow-hinged wheeze behind her.

I am lucky. When I come out of the Ladies' Room at six o'clock the corridor lights are off and the fourth-floor hall is as empty as church on Monday. I have my own key to our office; I come in first every morning, so that's no trouble. The typewriters are folded back into the desks, the locks are on the dial phones, all's right with the world.

Outside the window the last of the winter light is fading. Yet I do not forget myself and turn on the overhead bulb. I don't want to be spotted by any hawk-eyed doctor or janitor in the hospital buildings across the little courtyard. The cabinet with the record books is in the windowless passage opening onto the doctors' cubicles, which have windows overlooking the courtyard. I make sure the doors to all the cubicles are shut. Then I switch on the passage light, a sallow twenty-five watt affair blackening at the top. Better than an altarful of candles to me at this point, though. I didn't think to bring a sandwich. There is an apple in my desk drawer left over from lunch, so I reserve that for whatever pangs I may feel about one o'clock in the morning, and get out my pocket notebook. At home every evening it is my habit to tear out the notebook pages I've written on at the office during the day and pile them up to be copied in my manuscript. In this way I cover my tracks so no one idly picking up my notebook at the office could ever guess the type or scope of my work.

I begin systematically by opening the oldest book on the bottom shelf. The once-blue cover is no-color now, the pages are thumbed and blurry carbons, but I'm humming from foot to topknot: this dream book was spanking new the day I was born. When I really get organized I'll have hot soup in a thermos for the dead-of-winter nights, turkey pies and chocolate eclairs. I'll bring hair-curlers and four changes of blouse to work in my biggest handbag on Monday mornings so no one will notice me going downhill in looks and start suspecting unhappy love affairs or pink affiliations or my working on dream books in the Clinic four nights a week.

Eleven hours later. I am down to apple core and seeds and in the month of May, nineteen thirty-one, with a private nurse who has just opened a laundry bag in her patient's closet and found five severed heads in it, including her mother's.

A chill air touches the nape of my neck. From where I am sitting cross-legged on the floor in front of the cabinet, the record book heavy on my lap, I notice out of the corner of my eye that the door of the cubicle beside me is letting in a little crack of blue light. Not only along the floor, but up the side of the door, too. This is odd since I made sure from the first that all the doors were shut tight. The crack of blue light is widening and my eyes are fastened to two motionless shoes in the doorway, toes pointing toward me.

They are brown leather shoes of a foreign make, with thick elevator soles. Above the shoes are black silk socks through which shows a pallor of flesh. I get as far as the gray pinstriped trouser cuffs.

"Tch, tch," chides an infinitely gentle voice from the cloudy regions above my head. "Such an uncomfortable position! Your legs must be asleep by now. Let me help you up. The sun will be rising shortly."

Two hands slip under my arms from behind and I am raised, wobbly as an unset custard, to my feet, which I cannot feel because my legs are, in fact, asleep. The record book slumps to the floor, pages splayed.

"Stand still a minute." The Clinic Director's voice fans the lobe of my right ear. "Then the circulation will revive."

The blood in my not-there legs starts pinging under a million sewing-machine needles and a vision of the Clinic Director acid-etches itself on my brain. I don't even need to look around: fat potbelly buttoned into his gray pinstriped waistcoat, woodchuck teeth yellow and buck, every-color eyes behind the thick-lensed glasses quick as minnows.

I clutch my notebook. The last floating timber of the *Titanic*.

What does he know, what does he know?

Everything.

"I know where there is a nice hot bowl of chicken noodle soup." His voice rustles, dust under the bed, mice in straw. His hand welds onto my left upper arm in fatherly love. The record book of all the dreams going on in the city of my birth at my first yawp in this world's air he nudges under the bookcase with a polished toe.

We meet nobody in the dawn-dark hall. Nobody on the chill stone stair down to the basement corridors where Billy the Record Room Boy cracked his head skipping steps one night on a rush errand.

I begin to double-quickstep so he won't think it's me he's hustling. "You can't fire me," I say calmly. "I quit."

The Clinic Director's laugh wheezes up from his accordion-pleated bottom gut. "We mustn't lose you so soon." His whisper snakes off down the white-washed basement passages, echoing among the elbow pipes, the wheelchairs and stretchers beached for the night along the steam-stained walls. "Why, we need you more than you know."

We wind and double and my legs keep time with his until we come, somewhere in those barren rat tunnels, to an all-night elevator run by a one-armed Negro. We get on, and the door grinds shut like the door on a cattle car, and we go up and up. It is a freight elevator, crude and clanky, a far cry from the plush passenger lifts I am used to in the Clinics Building.

We get off at an indeterminate floor. The Clinic Director leads me down a bare corridor lit at intervals by socketed bulbs in little wire cages on the ceiling. Locked doors set with screened windows line the hall on either hand. I plan to part company with the Clinic Director at the first red Exit sign, but on our journey there are none. I am in alien territory, coat on the hanger in the office, handbag and money in my top desk drawer, notebook in my hand, and only Johnny Panic to warm me against the ice age outside.

Ahead a light gathers, brightens. The Clinic Director, puffing slightly at the walk, brisk and long, to which he is obviously unaccustomed, propels me around a bend and into a square, brilliantly lit room.

"Here she is."

"The little witch!"

Miss Milleravage hoists her tonnage up from behind the steel desk facing the door.

The walls and the ceiling of the room are riveted metal battleship plates. There are no windows.

From small, barred cells lining the sides and back of the room I see Johnny Panic's top priests staring out at me, arms swaddled behind their backs in the white Ward nightshirts, eyes redder than coals and hungry-hot.

They welcome me with queer croaks and grunts, as if their tongues were locked in their jaws. They have no doubt heard of my work by way of Johnny Panic's grapevine and want to know how his apostles thrive in the world.

I lift my hands to reassure them, holding up my notebook, my voice loud as Johnny Panic's organ with all stops out.

"Peace! I bring to you . . ."

The Book.

"None of that old stuff, sweetie." Miss Milleravage is dancing out at me from behind her desk like a trick elephant.

The Clinic Director closes the door to the room.

The minute Miss Milleravage moves I notice what her hulk has been hiding from view behind the desk—a white cot high as a man's waist with a single sheet stretched over the mattress, spotless and drumskin tight. At the head of the cot is a table on which sits a metal box covered with dials and gauges.

The box seems to be eyeing me, copperhead-ugly, from its coil of electric wires, the latest model in Johnny-Panic-Killers.

I get ready to dodge to one side. When Miss Milleravage grabs her fat hand comes away with a fist full of nothing. She starts for me again, her smile heavy as dogdays in August.

"None of that. None of that. I'll have that little black book."

Fast as I run around the high white cot, Miss Milleravage is so fast you'd think she wore rollerskates. She grabs and gets. Against her great bulk I beat my fists, and against her whopping milkless breasts, until her hands on my wrists are iron hoops and her breath hushabyes me with a love-stink fouler than Undertaker's Basement.

"My baby, my own baby's come back to me . . ."

"She," says the Clinic Director, sad and stern, "has been making time with Johnny Panic again."

"Naughty naughty."

The white cot is ready. With a terrible gentleness Miss Milleravage takes the watch from my wrist, the rings from my fingers, the hairpins from my hair. She begins to undress me. When I am bare, I am anointed on the temples and robed in sheets virginal as the first snow.

Then, from the four corners of the room and from the door behind me come five false priests in white surgical gowns and masks whose one lifework is to unseat Johnny Panic from his own throne. They extend me full-length on my back on the cot. The crown of wire is placed on my head, the wafer of forgetfulness on my tongue. The masked priests move to their posts and take hold: one of my left leg, one of my right, one of my right arm, one of my left. One behind my head at the metal box where I can't see.

From their cramped niches along the wall, the votaries raise their voices in protest. They begin the devotional chant:

"The only thing to love is Fear itself.
Love of Fear is the beginning of wisdom.
The only thing to love is Fear itself.
May Fear and Fear and Fear be everywhere."

There is no time for Miss Milleravage or the Clinic Director or the priests to muzzle them.

The signal is given.

The machine betrays them.

At the moment when I think I am most lost the face of Johnny Panic appears in a nimbus of arc lights on the ceiling overhead. I am shaken like a leaf in the teeth of glory. His beard is lightning. Lightning is in his eye. His Word charges and illumines the universe.

The air crackles with his blue-tongued lightning-haloed angels.

His love is the twenty-story leap, the rope at the throat, the knife at the heart.

He forgets not his own.

The Fifteen-Dollar Eagle

Written: before 28 December 1958
Published: *The Sewanee Review* (Autumn 1960): 603–18[*]

There are other tattoo shops in Madigan Square, but none of them a patch on Carmey's place. He's a real poet with the needle and dye, an artist with a heart. Kids, dock bums, the out-of-town couples in for a beer put on the brakes in front of Carmey's, nose-to-the-window, one and all. You got a dream, Carmey says, without saying a word, you got a rose on the heart, an eagle in the muscle, you got the sweet Jesus himself, so come in to me. Wear your heart on your skin in this life, I'm the man can give you a deal. Dogs, wolves, horses, and lions for the animal lover. For the ladies, butterflies, birds of paradise, baby heads smiling or in tears, take your choice. Roses, all sorts, large, small, bud, and full bloom, roses with name scrolls, roses with thorns, roses with Dresden-doll heads sticking up in dead center, pink petal, green leaf, set off smart by a lead-black line. Snakes and dragons for Frankenstein. Not to mention cowgirls, hula girls, mermaids, and movie queens, ruby-nippled and bare as you please. If you've got a back to spare, there's Christ on the cross, a thief at either elbow and angels overhead to right and left holding up a scroll with "Mount Calvary" on it in Old English script, close as yellow can get to gold.

Outside they point at the multi-colored pictures plastered on Carmey's three walls, ceiling to floor. They mutter like a mob scene, you can hear them through the glass:

---

[*] Printed with the following contributor note: 'SYLVIA PLATH has published poems and stories in numerous magazines.' Typescript held by Lilly Library. Beneath the title on typescript, SP crossed out '(Conversation Piece At Carmey's)'. Typed at top right: 'Sylvia Plath / Suite 61 / 9 Willow Street / Boston 8, Massachusetts.' SP added by hand 'Sewanee R' at top left. In centre, in pencil by Constance Kyrle Fletcher, 'Published in Sewanee Review.' SP submitted also to *London Magazine*.

"Honey, take a looka those peacocks!"

"That's crazy, paying for tattoos. I only paid for one I got, a panther on my arm."

"You want a heart, I'll tell him where."

I see Carmey in action for the first time courtesy of my steady man, Ned Bean. Lounging against a wall of hearts and flowers, waiting for business, Carmey is passing the time of day with a Mr. Tomolillo, an extremely small person wearing a wool jacket that drapes his nonexistent shoulders without any attempt at fit or reformation. The jacket is patterned with brown squares the size of cigarette packs, each square boldly outlined in black. You could play tick-tack-toe on it. A brown fedora hugs his head just above the eyebrows like the cap on a mushroom. He has the thin, rapt, triangular face of a praying mantis. As Ned introduces me, Mr. Tomolillo snaps over from the waist in a bow neat as the little moustache hairlining his upper lip. I can't help admiring this bow because the shop is so crowded there's barely room for the four of us to stand up without bumping elbows and knees at the slightest move.

The whole place smells of gunpowder and some fumy antiseptic. Ranged along the back wall from left to right are: Carmey's worktable, electric needles hooked to a rack over a lazy Susan of dye pots, Carmey's swivel chair facing the show window, a straight customer's chair facing Carmey's chair, a waste bucket, and an orange crate covered with scraps of paper and pencil stubs. At the front of the shop, next to the glass door, there is another straight chair, with the big placard of Mount Calvary propped on it, and a cardboard file-drawer on a scuffed wooden table. Among the babies and daisies on the wall over Carmey's chair hang two faded sepia daguerreotypes of a boy from the waist up, one front view, one back. From the distance he seems to be wearing a long-sleeved, skintight black lace shirt. A closer look shows he is stark naked, covered only with a creeping ivy of tattoos.

In a jaundiced clipping from some long-ago rotogravure, these Oriental men and women are sitting cross-legged on tasseled cushions, back to the camera and embroidered with seven-headed dragons, mountain ranges, cherry trees, and waterfalls. "These people have not a stitch of clothing on," the blurb points out. "They belong to a society in which tattoos are required for membership. Sometimes a full job costs as much as $300." Next to this, a photograph of a bald man's head with the tentacles of an octopus just rounding the top of the scalp from the rear.

"Those skins are valuable as many a painting, I imagine," says Mr. Tomolillo. "If you had them stretched on a board."

But the Tattooed Boy and those clubby Orientals have nothing on Carmey, who is himself a living advertisement of his art—a schooner in full sail over a rose-and holly-leaf ocean on his right biceps, Gypsy Rose Lee flexing her muscled belly on the left, forearms jammed with hearts, stars and anchors, lucky numbers, and name scrolls, indigo edges blurred so he reads like a comic strip left out in a Sunday rainstorm. A fan of the Wild West, Carmey is rumored to have a bronco reared from navel to collarbone, a thistle-stubborn cowboy stuck to its back. But that may be a mere fable inspired by his habit of wearing tooled leather cowboy boots, finely heeled, and a Bill Hickok belt studded with red stones to hold up his black chino slacks. Carmey's eyes are blue. A blue in no way inferior to the much sung-about skies of Texas.

"I been at it sixteen years now," Carmey says, leaning back against his picture-book wall, "and you might say I'm still learning. My first job was in Maine, during the war. They heard I was a tattooist and called me out to this station of WACs . . ."

"To tat*too* them?" I ask.

"To tattoo their numbers on, nothing more or less."

"Weren't some of them *scared*?"

"Oh, sure, sure. But some of them came back. I got two WACs in one day for a tattoo. Well they hemmed. And they hawed. 'Look,' I tell them, 'you came in the other day and you knew which one you wanted, what's the trouble?'"

"'Well it's not what we want but where we want it,' one of them pipes up. 'Well if that's all it is you can trust me,' I say. 'I'm like a doctor, see? I handle so many women it means nothing.' 'Well I want three roses,' this one says; 'one on my stomach and one on each cheek of my butt.' So the other one gets up courage, you know how it is, and asks for one rose . . ."

"Little ones or big ones?" Mr. Tomolillo won't let a detail slip.

"About like that up there." Carmey points to a card of roses on the wall, each bloom the size of a Brussels sprout. "The biggest going. So I did the roses and told them: 'Ten dollars off the price if you come back and show them to me when the scab's gone.'"

"Did they come?" Ned wants to know.

"You bet they did." Carmey blows a smoke ring that hangs wavering in the air a foot from his nose, the blue, vaporous outline of a cabbage-rose.

"You wanta know," he says, "a crazy law? I could tattoo you anywhere," he looks me over with great care, "anywhere at all. Your back. Your rear." His eyelids droop, you'd think he was praying. "Your breasts. Anywhere at all but your face, hands, and feet."

Mr. Tomolillo asks: "Is that a *Fed*eral law?"

Carmey nods. "A Federal law. I got a blind," he juts a thumb at the dusty-slatted venetian blind drawn up in the display window. "I let that blind down, and I can do privately any part of the body. Except face, hands, and feet."

"I bet it's because they *show*," I say.

"Sure. Take in the Army, at drill. The guys wouldn't look right. Their faces and hands would stand out, they couldn't cover up."

"However that may be," Mr. Tomolillo says, "I think it is a shocking law, a totalitarian law. There should be a freedom about personal adornment in any democracy. I mean, if a lady *wants* a rose on the back of her hand, I should think . . ."

"She should *have* it," Carmey finishes with heat. "People should have what they want, regardless. Why, I had a little lady in here the other day." Carmey levels the air with the flat of his hand not five feet from the floor. "So high. Wanted Calvary, the whole works, on her back, and I gave it to her. Eighteen hours it took."

I eye the thieves and angels on the poster of Mount Calvary with some doubt. "Didn't you have to shrink it down a bit?"

"Nope."

"Or leave off an angel?" Ned wonders. "Or a bit of the foreground?"

"Not a bit of it. A thirty-five dollar job in full color, thieves, angels, Old English—the works. She went out of the shop proud as punch. It's not every little lady's got all Calvary in full color on her back. Oh, I copy photos people bring in, I copy movie stars. Anything they want, I do it. I've got some designs I wouldn't put up on the wall on account of offending some of the clients. I'll show you." Carmey opens the cardboard file-drawer on the table at the front of the shop. "The wife's got to clean this up," he says. "It's a terrible mess."

"Does your wife help you?" I ask with interest.

"Oh, Laura, she's in the shop most of the day." For some reason Carmey sounds all at once solemn as a monk on Sunday. I wonder, does he use her for a come-on: Laura, the Tattooed Lady, a living masterpiece, sixteen years in the making. Not a white patch on her, ladies and gentlemen—look all you want to. "You should drop by and keep her company, she likes talk." He is rummaging around in the drawer, not coming up with anything, when he stops in his tracks and stiffens like a pointer.

This big guy is standing in the doorway.

"What can I do for you?" Carmey steps forward, the maestro he is.

"I want that eagle you showed me."

Ned and Mr. Tomolillo and I flatten ourselves against the side walls to let the guy into the middle of the room. He'll be a sailor out of uniform in his peajacket and plaid wool shirt. His diamond-shaped head, width all between the ears, tapers up to a narrow plateau of cropped black hair.

"The nine dollar or the fifteen?"

"The fifteen."

Mr. Tomolillo sighs in gentle admiration.

The sailor sits down in the chair facing Carmey's swivel, shrugs out of his peajacket, unbuttons his left shirt cuff and begins slowly to roll up the sleeve.

"You come right in here," Carmey says to me in a low, promising voice, "where you can get a good look. You've never seen a tattooing before." I squinch up and settle on the crate of papers in the corner at the left of Carmey's chair, careful as a hen on eggs.

Carmey flicks through the cardboard file again and this time digs out a square piece of plastic. "Is this the one?"

The sailor looks at the eagle pricked out on the plastic. Then he says: "That's right," and hands it back to Carmey.

"Mmmm," Mr. Tomolillo murmurs in honor of the sailor's taste.

Ned says: "That's a fine eagle."

The sailor straightens with a certain pride. Carmey is dancing round him now, laying a dark-stained burlap cloth across his lap, arranging a sponge, a razor, various jars with smudged-out labels and a bowl of antiseptic on his worktable—finicky as a priest whetting his machete for the fatted calf. Everything has to be just so. Finally he sits down. The sailor holds out his right arm and Ned and Mr. Tomolillo close in behind his chair, Ned leaning over the sailor's right shoulder and Mr. Tomolillo over his left. At Carmey's elbow I have the best view of all.

With a close, quick swipe of the razor, Carmey clears the sailor's forearm of its black springing hair, wiping the hair off the blade's edge and onto the floor with his thumb. Then he anoints the area of bared flesh with Vaseline from a small jar on top of his table. "You ever been tattooed before?"

"Yeah." The sailor is no gossip. "Once." Already his eyes are locked in a vision of something on the far side of Carmey's head, through the walls and away in the thin air beyond the four of us in the room.

Carmey is sprinkling a black powder on the face of the plastic square and rubbing the powder into the pricked holes. The outline of the eagle darkens. With one flip, Carmey presses the plastic square powder-side against the sailor's greased arm. When he peels the plastic off, easy as skin off an onion, the outline of an eagle, wings spread, claws hooked for action, frowns up from the sailor's arm.

"Ah!" Mr. Tomolillo rocks back on his cork heels and casts a meaning look at Ned. Ned raises his eyebrows in approval. The sailor allows himself a little quirk of the lip. On him it is as good as a smile.

"Now," Carmey takes down one of the electric needles, pitching it rabbit-out-of-the-hat, "I am going to show you how we make a nine-dollar eagle a fifteen-dollar eagle."

He presses a button on the needle. Nothing happens.

"Well," he sighs, "it's not working."

Mr. Tomolillo groans. "Not again?"

Then something strikes Carmey and he laughs and flips a switch on the wall behind him. This time when he presses the needle it buzzes and sparks blue. "No connection, that's what it was."

"Thank heaven," says Mr. Tomolillo.

Carmey fills the needle from a pot of black dye on the lazy Susan. "This same eagle," Carmey lowers the needle to the eagle's right wing tip, "for nine dollars is only black and red. For fifteen dollars you're going to see a blend of four colors." The needle steers along the lines laid by the powder. "Black, green, brown, and red. We're out of blue at the moment or it'd be five colors." The needle skips and backtalks like a pneumatic drill but Carmey's hand is steady as a surgeon's. "How I *love* eagles!"

"I believe you *live* on Uncle Sam's eagles," says Mr. Tomolillo.

Black ink seeps over the curve of the sailor's arm and into the stiff, stained butcher's-apron canvas covering his lap, but the needle travels on, scalloping the wing feathers from tip to root. Bright beads of red are rising through the ink, heart's-blood bubbles smearing out into the black stream.

"The guys complain," Carmey singsongs. "Week after week I get the same complaining: What have you got new? We don't want the same type eagle, red and black. So I figure out this blend. You wait. A solid color eagle."

The eagle is losing itself in a spreading thundercloud of black ink. Carmey stops, sloshes his needle in the bowl of antiseptic, and a geyser of white blooms up to the surface from the bowl's bottom. Then Carmey dips a big, round cinnamon-colored sponge in the bowl and wipes away the ink from the sailor's arm. The eagle emerges from its hood of bloodied ink, a raised outline on the raw skin.

"Now you're gonna see something." Carmey twirls the lazy Susan till the pot of green is under his thumb and picks another needle from the rack.

The sailor is gone from behind his eyes now, off somewhere in Tibet, Uganda, or Barbados, oceans and continents away from the blood drops jumping in the wake of the wide green swaths Carmey is drawing in the shadow of the eagle's wings.

About this time I notice an odd sensation. A powerful sweet perfume is rising from the sailor's arm. My eyes swerve from the mingling red and green and I find myself staring intently into the waste bucket by my left side. As I watch the calm rubble of colored candy wrappers, cigarette butts, and old wads of muddily stained Kleenex, Carmey tosses a tissue soaked with fresh red onto the heap. Behind the silhouetted heads of Ned and Mr. Tomolillo the panthers, roses, and red-nippled ladies wink and jitter. If I fall forward or to the right, I will jog Carmey's elbow and make him stab the sailor and ruin a perfectly good fifteen-dollar eagle not to mention disgracing my sex. The only alternative is a dive into the bucket of bloody papers.

"I'm doing the brown now," Carmey sings out a mile away, and my eyes rivet again on the sailor's blood-sheened arm. "When the eagle heals, the colors will blend right into each other, like on a painting."

Ned's face is a scribble of black India ink on a seven-color crazy quilt.

"I'm going . . ." I make my lips move, but no sound comes out.

Ned starts toward me but before he gets there the room switches off like a light.

The next thing is, I am looking into Carmey's shop from a cloud with the X-ray eyes of an angel and hearing the tiny sound of a bee spitting blue fire.

"The blood get her?" It is Carmey's voice, small and far.

"She looks all white," says Mr. Tomolillo. "And her eyes are funny."

Carmey passes something to Mr. Tomolillo. "Have her sniff that." Mr. Tomolillo hands something to Ned. "But not too much."

Ned holds something to my nose.

I sniff, and I am sitting in the chair at the front of the shop with Mount Calvary as a backrest. I sniff again. Nobody looks angry so I have not bumped Carmey's needle. Ned is screwing the cap on a little flask of yellow liquid. Yardley's smelling salts.

"Ready to go back?" Mr. Tomolillo points kindly to the deserted orange crate.

"Almost." I have a strong instinct to stall for time. I whisper in Mr. Tomolillo's ear which is very near to me, he is so short, "Do *you* have any tattoos?"

Under the mushroom-brim of his fedora Mr. Tomolillo's eyes roll heavenward. "My gracious no! I'm only here to see about the springs. The springs in

Mr. Carmichael's machine have a way of breaking in the middle of a customer."

"How annoying."

"That's what I'm here for. We're testing out a new spring now, a much heavier spring. You know how distressing it when you're in the dentist's chair and your mouth is full of whatnot . . ."

"Balls of cotton and little metal siphons . . . ?"

"Precisely. And in the middle of this the dentist turns away," Mr. Tomolillo half-turns his back in illustration and makes an evil, secretive face, "and buzzes about in the corner for ten minutes with the machinery, you don't know what." Mr. Tomolillo's face smooths out like linen under a steam iron. "That's what I'm here to see about, a stronger spring. A spring that won't let the customer down."

By this time I am ready to go back to my seat of honor on the orange crate. Carmey has just finished with the brown and in my absence the inks have indeed blended into one another.

Against the shaven skin, the lacerated eagle is swollen in tricolored fury, claws curved sharp as butcher's hooks.

"I think we could redden the eye a little?"

The sailor nods, and Carmey opens the lid on a pot of dye the color of tomato ketchup. As soon as he stops working with the needle, the sailor's skin sends up its blood beads, not just from the bird's black outline now, but from the whole rasped rainbowed body.

"Red," Carmey says, "really picks things up."

"Do you save the blood?" Mr. Tomolillo asks suddenly.

"I should think," says Ned, "you might well have some arrangement with the Red Cross."

"With a blood bank!" The smelling salts have blown my head clear as a blue day on Monadnock. "Just put a little basin on the floor to catch the drippings."

Carmey is picking out a red eye on the eagle. "We vampires don't share our blood." The eagle's eye reddens but there is now no telling blood from ink. "You never heard of a vampire do that, did you?"

"Nooo . . ." Mr. Tomolillo admits.

Carmey floods the flesh behind the eagle with red and the finished eagle poises on a red sky, born and baptized in the blood of its owner.

The sailor drifts back from parts unknown.

"Nice?" With his sponge Carmey clears the eagle of the blood filming its colors the way a sidewalk artist might blow the pastel dust from a drawing of the White House, Liz Taylor or Lassie Come-Home.

"I always say," the sailor remarks to nobody in particular, "when you get a tattoo, get a good one. Nothing but the best." He looks down at the eagle which has begun in spite of Carmey's swabbing to bleed again. There is a little pause. Carmey is waiting for something and it isn't money. "How much to write Japan under that?"

Carmey breaks into a pleased smile. "One dollar."

"Write Japan, then."

Carmey marks out the letters on the sailor's arm, an extra flourish to the J's hook, the loop of the P, and the final N, a love-letter to the eagle-conquered Orient. He fills the needle and starts on the J.

"I under*stand*," Mr. Tomolillo observes in his clear, lecturer's voice, "Japan is a center of tattooing."

"Not when *I* was there," the sailor says. "It's banned."

"Banned!" says Ned. "What for?"

"Oh, they think it's *bar*barous nowadays." Carmey doesn't lift his eyes from the second A, the needle responding like a broken-in bronc under his masterly thumb. "There are operators, of course. Sub rosa. There always are." He puts the final curl on the N and sponges off the wellings of blood which seem bent on obscuring his artful lines. "That what you wanted?"

"That's it."

Carmey folds a wad of Kleenex into a rough bandage and lays it over the eagle and Japan. Spry as a shopgirl wrapping a gift package he tapes the tissue into place.

The sailor gets up and hitches into his peajacket. Several schoolboys, lanky, with pale, pimply faces, are crowding the doorway, watching. Without a word the sailor takes out his wallet and peels sixteen dollar bills off a green roll. Carmey transfers the cash to his wallet. The schoolboys fall back to let the sailor pass into the street.

"I hope you didn't mind my getting dizzy."

Carmey grins. "Why do you think I've got those salts so close to hand? I have big guys passing out cold. They get egged in here by their buddies and don't know how to get out of it. I got people getting sick to their ears in that bucket."

"She's never got like that before," Ned says. "She's seen all sorts of blood. Babies born. Bullfights. Things like that."

"You was all worked up." Carmey offers me a cigarette which I accept, takes one himself, and Ned takes one, and Mr. Tomolillo says no-thank-you. "You was all tensed, that's what did it."

378

"How much is a heart?"

The voice comes from a kid in a black leather jacket in the front of the shop. His buddies nudge each other and let out harsh puppy-barks of laughter. The boy grins and flushes all at once under his purple stipple of acne. "A heart with a scroll under it and a name on the scroll."

Carmey leans back in his swivel chair and digs his thumbs into his belt. The cigarette wobbles on his bottom lip. "Four dollars," he says without batting an eye.

"Four dollars?" The boy's voice swerves up and cracks in shrill disbelief. The three of them in the doorway mutter among themselves and shuffle back and forth.

"Nothing here in the heart line under three dollars." Carmey doesn't kowtow to the tight-fisted. You want a rose, you want a heart in this life, you pay for it. Through the nose.

The boy wavers in front of the placards of hearts on the wall, pink, lush hearts, hearts with arrows through them, hearts in the center of buttercup wreaths. "How much," he asks in a small, craven voice, "for just a name!"

"One dollar." Carmey's tone is strictly business.

The boy holds out his left hand. "I want Ruth." He draws an imaginary line across his left wrist. "Right here . . . so I can cover it up with a watch if I want to."

His two friends guffaw from the doorway.

Carmey points to the straight chair and lays his half-smoked cigarette on the lazy Susan between two dye pots. The boy sits down, schoolbooks balanced on his lap.

"What happens," Mr. Tomolillo asks of the world in general, "if you choose to change a name? Do you just cross it off and write the next above it?"

"You could," Ned suggests, "wear a watch over the old name so only the new name showed."

"And then another watch," I say, "over that, when there's a third name."

"Until your arm," Mr. Tomolillo nods, "is up to the shoulder with watches."

Carmey is shaving the thin scraggly growth of hairs from the boy's wrist. "You're taking a lot of ragging from somebody."

The boy stares at his wrist with a self-conscious and unsteady smile, a smile that is maybe only a public substitute for tears. With his right hand he clutches his schoolbooks to keep them from sliding off his knee.

Carmey finishes marking R-U-T-H on the boy's wrist and holds the needle poised. "She'll bawl you out when she sees this." But the boy nods him to go ahead.

"Why?" Ned asks. "Why should she bawl him out?"

"Gone and got yourself tattooed!" Carmey mimics a mincing disgust. "And with just a name! Is *that* all you think of me?—She'll be wanting roses, birds, butterflies . . ." The needle sticks for a second and the boy flinches like a colt. "And if you *do* get all that stuff to please her—roses . . ."

"Birds and butterflies," Mr. Tomolillo puts in.

". . . she'll say, sure as rain at a ball game: What'd you want to go and spend all that *money* for?" Carmey whizzes the needle clean in the bowl of antiseptic. "You can't beat a woman." A few meager blood drops stand up along the four letters—letters so black and plain you can hardly tell it's a tattoo and not just inked in with a pen. Carmey tapes a narrow bandage of Kleenex over the name. The whole operation lasts less than ten minutes.

The boy fishes a crumpled dollar bill from his back pocket. His friends cuff him fondly on the shoulder and the three of them crowd out the door, all at the same time, nudging, pushing, tripping over their feet. Several faces, limpet-pale against the window, melt away as Carmey's eye lingers on them.

"No wonder he doesn't want a heart, that kid, he wouldn't know what to do with it. He'll be back next week asking for a Betty or a Dolly or some such, you wait." He sighs, and goes to the cardboard file and pulls out a stack of those photographs he wouldn't put on the wall and passes them around. "One picture I would like to get." Carmey leans back in the swivel chair and props his cowboy boots on a little carton. "The butterfly. I got pictures of the rabbit hunt. I got pictures of ladies with snakes winding up their legs and into them, but I could make a lot of sweet dough if I got a picture of the butterfly on a woman."

"Some queer kind of butterfly nobody wants?" Ned peers in the general direction of my stomach as at some highgrade salable parchment.

"It's not what, it's where. One wing on the front of each thigh. You know how butterflies on a flower make their wings flutter, ever so little? Well, any move a woman makes, these wings look to be going in and out, in and out. I'd like a photograph of that so much I'd practically do a butterfly for free."

I toy, for a second, with the thought of a New Guinea Golden, wings extending from hipbone to kneecap, ten times life-size, but drop it fast. A fine thing if I got tired of my own skin sooner than last year's sack.

"Plenty of women *ask* for butterflies in that particular spot," Carmey goes on, "but you know what, not one of them will let a photograph be taken after the job's done. Not even from the waist down. Don't imagine I haven't asked. You'd think everybody over the whole United States would recognize them from the way they carry on when it's even mentioned."

"Couldn't," Mr. Tomolillo ventures shyly, "the wife oblige? Make it a little family affair?"

Carmey's face skews up in a pained way. "Naw," he shakes his head, his voice weighted with an old wonder and regret. "Naw, Laura won't hear of the needle. I used to think the idea of it'd grow on her after a bit, but nothing doing. She makes me feel, sometimes, what do I see in it all. Laura's white as the day she was born. Why, she *hates* tattoos."

Up to this moment I have been projecting, fatuously, intimate visits with Laura at Carmey's place. I have been imagining a lithe, supple Laura, a butterfly poised for flight on each breast, roses blooming on her buttocks, a gold-guarding dragon on her back and Sinbad the Sailor in six colors on her belly, a woman with Experience written all over her, a woman to learn from in this life. I should have known better.

The four of us are slumped there in a smog of cigarette smoke, not saying a word, when a round, muscular woman comes into the shop, followed closely by a greasy-haired man with a dark, challenging expression. The woman is wrapped to the chin in a woolly electric-blue coat; a fuchsia kerchief covers all but the pompadour of her glinting blonde hair. She sits down in the chair in front of the window regardless of Mount Calvary and proceeds to stare fixedly at Carmey. The man stations himself next to her and keeps a severe eye on Carmey too, as if expecting him to bolt without warning.

There is a moment of potent silence.

"Why," Carmey says pleasantly, but with small heart, "here's the Wife now."

I take a second look at the woman and rise from my comfortable seat on the crate at Carmey's elbow. Judging from his watchdog stance, I gather the strange man is either Laura's brother or her bodyguard or a low-class private detective in her employ. Mr. Tomolillo and Ned are moving with one accord toward the door.

"We must be running along," I murmur, since nobody else seems inclined to speak.

"Say hello to the people, Laura," Carmey begs, back to the wall. I can't help but feel sorry for him, even a little ashamed. The starch is gone out of Carmey now, and the gay talk.

Laura doesn't say a word. She is waiting with the large calm of a cow for the three of us to clear out. I imagine her body, death-lily white and totally bare—the body of a woman immune as a nun to the eagle's anger, the desire of the rose. From Carmey's wall the world's menagerie howls and ogles at her alone.

The Shadow

Ts,* 31 December 1958–7 January 1959, Lilly Library

The winter the war began I happened to fall in the bad graces of the neighborhood for biting Leroy Kelly on the leg. Even Mrs. Abrams across the street, who had an only son in technical college and no children our age, and Mr. Greenbloom, the corner grocer, chose sides: they were all for the Kellys. By rights, I should have been let off easy with a clear verdict of self-defense, yet this time, for some reason, the old Washington Street ideals of fairness and chivalry didn't seem to count.

In spite of the neighborhood pressure, I couldn't see apologizing unless Leroy and his sister Maureen apologized too, since they started the whole thing. My father couldn't see my apologizing at all, and Mother lit into him about this. From my listening post in the hall I tried to catch the gist of it, but they were having hot words off the point, all about aggression, and honor, and passive resistance. I waited a full fifteen minutes before I realized the problem of my apology was the last thing in their heads. Neither of them brought it up to me afterwards, so I guessed my father had won, the way he won about church.

Every Sunday, Mother and I set out for the Methodist church, passing the time of day, often as not, with the Kellys or the Sullivans, or both, on their way to eleven o'clock mass at St. Brigid's. Our whole neighborhood flocked to one church or another; if it wasn't church, it was synagogue. But Mother never could persuade my father to come with us. He pottered around at home, in the garden when the weather was fair, in his study when it wasn't, smoking and correcting papers for his German classes. I imagined he had all the religion he needed and didn't require weekly refills the way Mother did.

Give or take, my mother couldn't get enough of preaching. She was always after me to be meek, merciful, and pure in heart: a real peacemaker. Privately, I figured Mother's sermon about "winning" by not fighting back worked only if you were a fast runner. If you were being sat on and pummeled, it served less purpose than a paper halo, as proved by my skirmish with Maureen and Leroy.

◆

---

* Typescript with holograph corrections by SP. Typed at top right: 'Sylvia Plath / Suite 61 / 9 Willow Street / Boston 8, Massachusetts.' Submitted to *London Magazine*.

The Kellys lived next door to us in a turreted, yellow frame house with a sagging veranda and orange and purple panes in the window on the stair landing. For convenience, my mother classed Maureen as my best friend, although she was over a year younger than I and a grade behind me in school. Leroy, just my age, was a lot more interesting. He had built a whole railroad village in his room on top of a large plywood table, which left barely enough space for his bed and the crystal set he was working on. *Believe It or Not!* by Ripley clippings and drawings of green men with grasshopper antennae and ray guns, cut out of the several science fiction magazines he subscribed to, covered the walls. He had a lead on moon rockets. If Leroy could make a radio with earphones that tuned in on regular programs like *The Shadow* and *Lights Out*, he might well be inventing moon rockets by the time he got to college, and I favored moon rockets a lot more than dolls with open-and-shut glass eyes who wah-wahed if you held them upside down.

Maureen Kelly was one for the dolls. Everybody called her cute as a button. Petite, even for a girl of seven, Maureen had soulful brown eyes and natural ringlets that Mrs. Kelly coaxed around her fat, sausage finger every morning with a damp brush. Maureen also had a trick of making her eyes go suddenly teary and guileless, a studied imitation, no doubt, of the picture of St. Therese of the Child Jesus pinned up over her bed. When she didn't get her way, she simply raised those brown eyes to heaven and yowled. "Sadie Shafer, what are you *doing* to poor Maureen?" Somebody's mother, toweling her hands, flour-whitened, or wet from the dishpan, would appear in a doorway or at a window, and not a hundred straight-talking Girl Scout witnesses from around the block could convince her I wasn't plaguing Maureen above and beyond all human feeling. Just because I was big for my age, I came in for all the scoldings going. I didn't think I deserved it; no more than I deserved the full weight of blame for biting Leroy.

The facts of the fight were clear enough. Mrs. Kelly had gone down to Greenbloom's to get some gelatin for one of those jiggly, plastic salads she was always making, and Maureen and I were sitting by ourselves on the couch in the Kellys' den, cutting out the last of the wardrobe for her Bobbsey Twins paper dolls.

"Let me use the big scissors, now." Maureen gave a delicate, put-upon sigh. "I'm tired of mine, they make such little snips."

I didn't look up from the sailor suit I was trimming for the boy Bobbsey. "Oh, you know your mother won't let you use these," I said reasonably. "They're her best sewing scissors, and she said you can't use them until you're bigger."

It was then that Maureen put down her stub-ended Woolworth scissors and started to tickle me. Tickling made me have hysterics, and Maureen knew it.

"Don't be *silly*, Maureen!" I stood up out of reach on the narrow scatter rug in front of the couch. Probably nothing more would have happened if Leroy hadn't come in at that moment.

"Tickle her! Tickle her!" Maureen shouted, bouncing up and down on the couch. Why Leroy responded as he did I found out several days later. Before I could dart past him and through the door, he had whisked the scatter rug from under my feet and was sitting on my stomach while Maureen squatted beside me, tickling, craven pleasure written all over her face. I squirmed; I shrieked. As far as I could see there was no escape. Leroy had my arms pinioned and Maureen wasn't anywhere in range of my wild kicks. So I did the one thing I was free to do. I twisted my head and sank my teeth in the bare space of skin just above Leroy's left sock, which, I had time to notice, smelled of mice, and held on until he let go of me. He fell to one side, roaring. At that moment Mrs. Kelly walked in the front door.

The Kellys told certain neighbors my bite drew blood, but Leroy confessed to me, after the excitement died down and we were speaking to each other again, that the only sign he had been bitten was a few purplish teeth marks, and these turned yellow and faded in a day or two. Leroy had learned the scatter rug trick from a Green Hornet comic book he later loaned me, pointing out the place where the Green Hornet, at bay, the spy's gun a few feet from his nose, asks humbly to pick up a cigarette he has just dropped and please, may he enjoy his last smoke on earth. The spy, carried away by his certain triumph and neglecting to notice he is standing at the end of a narrow scatter rug, says, with fatal smugness, "Uff corss!" A deep knee bend, a flick of the wrist, and the Green Hornet has the rug out from under the spy, the spy's gun in his hand, and the spy flat on the floor, his word-balloon crammed with asterisks and exclamation points.

Maybe I'd have done the same thing if I'd had Leroy's chance. If the scatter rug hadn't been under my feet, Leroy would have no doubt scorned Maureen's silly screams and both of us coolly walked out on her. Still, however such breakdown of cause and effect may illumine a sequence of events, it doesn't alter the events.

That Christmas we did not get our annual fruit cake from Mrs. Abrams; the Kellys got theirs. Even after Leroy and Maureen and I had come to terms, Mrs. Kelly didn't start up the Saturday morning coffee hours with my mother which she had broken off the week of our quarrel. I continued to go to Greenbloom's for comics and candy, but there, too, the neighborhood cold front was apparent. "A little something to sharpen the teeth, eh?" Mr. Greenbloom lowered his voice although there was no one else in the shop. "Brazil nuts, almond rock, something tough?" His sallow, square-jowled face with the purple-pouched black eyes didn't crinkle up in the familiar smile but remained stiff and heavy, a creased, lugubrious mask. I had an impulse to burst out, "It wasn't my fault. What would you have done? What would you have had me do?" as if he had challenged me directly about the Kellys, when, of course, he had done nothing of the sort. Rack on rack of the latest gaudily covered comic books—*Superman*, *Wonder Woman*, *Tom Mix*, and *Mickey Mouse*—swam in a rainbowed blur before my eyes. I fingered a thin dime, extorted as early allowance, in my jacket pocket, yet I didn't have the heart to choose among them. "I-I think I'll come back later." Why I felt compelled to explain my each move so apologetically I didn't know.

From the first, I thought the issue of my quarrel with the Kellys a pure one, uncomplicated by any flow of emotion from sources outside it—whole and self-contained as those globed, red tomatoes my mother preserved at the end of every summer in airtight Mason jars. Though the neighbors' slights seemed to me wrong, even strangely excessive—since they included my parents as well as myself—I never doubted that justice, sooner or later, would right the balance. Probably my favorite radio programs and comic strips had something to do with my seeing the picture so small, and in such elementary colors.

Not that I wasn't aware of how mean people can be.

"Who knows what Evil lurks in the hearts of men?" the nasal, sardonic voice of the Shadow asked rhetorically every Sunday afternoon. "The Shadow knows, heh, heh, heh, heh." Each week Leroy and I studied our lesson: somewhere innocent victims were being turned into rats by a vicious, experimental drug, burned on their bare feet with candles, fed to an indoor pool of piranha fish. Gravely, in Leroy's room or my own, behind shut doors, or in whispers at recess on some patch of the playground, we shared our accumulating evidence of the warped, brutish emotions current in the world beyond Washington Street and the precincts of the Hunnewell School.

"You know what they do with prisoners in Japan," Leroy told me one Saturday morning soon after Pearl Harbor. "They tie them to these stakes on the ground over these bamboo seeds, and when it rains the bamboo shoot grows right up through their back and hits the heart."

"Oh, a little shoot couldn't do that," I objected. "It wouldn't be strong enough."

"You've seen the concrete sidewalk in front of the Sullivans, haven't you—all funny cracks in it, bigger and bigger every day? Just take a look what's pushing up under there." Leroy widened his pale owl eyes significantly. "Mushrooms! Little, soft-headed mushrooms!"

The sequel to the Shadow's enlightening comment on evil was, of course, his farewell message: "The weed of crime bears *bitter* fruit. Crime does *not* pay." On his program it never did; at least never for more than twenty-five minutes at a stretch. We had no cause to wonder: *Will* the good people win? Only: *How?*

Still, the radio programs and the comic books were a hard-won concession; I knew Mother would put her foot down once and for all at my seeing a war movie ("It's not good to fill the child's mind with that trash, things are bad enough"). When, without her knowledge, I saw a Japanese prison-camp film by the simple device of going to Betty Sullivan's birthday party which included treating ten of us to a double feature and ice cream, I had some second thoughts about Mother's wisdom. Night after night, as if my shut eyelids were a private movie screen, I saw the same scene come back, poisonous, sulfur-colored: the starving men in their cells, for days without water, reached, over and over again, through the bars toward the audibly trickling fountain in the center of the prison yard, a fountain at which the slant-eyed guards drank with sadistic frequency and loud slurps.

I didn't dare to call Mother or to tell her of my dream, though this would have relieved me greatly. If she found out about my harassed nights, it would be the end of any movies, comic books, or radio programs that departed from the sugary fables of the *Singing Lady*, and such a sacrifice I was not prepared to make.

The trouble was, in this dream, my sure sense of eventual justice deserted me: the dream incident had lost its original happy ending—the troops of the good side breaking into the camp, victorious, to the cheers of the movie audience and the near-dead prisoners. If a familiar color—the blue of Winthrop Bay, and the sky over it, or the green of grass, trees—suddenly vanished from the world and left a pitch-black gap in its place, I could not have been more bewildered or appalled. The old, soothing remedy, "It's not true, it's only a dream," didn't seem to work anymore, either. The hostile, brooding aura of the nightmare seeped out, somehow, to become a part of my waking landscape.

The peaceful rhythm of classes and play periods at the Hunnewell School was broken often now by the raucous, arbitrary ringing of the air-raid alarm. With none of the jostling and whispering we indulged in during fire drills, we would take up our coats and pencils and file down the creaking stairs into the school basement where we crouched in special corners according to our color tags and put our pencils between our teeth so, the teachers explained, the bombs wouldn't make us bite our tongues. Some of the children in the lower grades always started to cry; it was dark in the cellar, the cold stone bleakly lit by one bare bulb in the ceiling. At home, my parents sat a great deal by the radio, listening, with serious faces, to the staccato briefs of the newscasters. And there were the sudden, unexplained silences when I came within hearing, the habit of gloom, relieved only by a false cheer worse than the gloom itself.

Prepared as I was for the phenomenon of evil in the world, I was not ready to have it expand in this treacherous fashion, like some uncontrollable fungus, beyond the confines of half-hour radio programs, comic book covers, and Saturday afternoon double features, to drag out past all confident predictions of a smashing-quick finish. I had an ingrained sense of the powers of good protecting me: my parents, the police, the FBI, the President, the American Armed Forces, even those symbolic champions of Good from a cloudier hinterland—the Shadow, Superman, and the rest. Not to mention God himself. Surely, with these ranked round me, circle after concentric circle, reaching to infinity, I had nothing to fear. Yet I was afraid. Clearly, in spite of my assiduous study of the world, there was something I had not been told; some piece to the puzzle I did not have in hand.

My speculations about this mystery came into focus that Friday when Maureen Kelly hurried to catch up with me on the way to school. "My mother says it's not your fault for biting Leroy," she called out in clear, saccharine tones. "My mother says it's because your father's German."

I was astounded. "My father is not German!" I retorted when I had my breath back. "He's . . . he's from the Polish Corridor."

The geographical distinction was lost on Maureen. "He's German. My mother says so," she insisted stubbornly. "Besides, he doesn't go to church."

"How could it be my father's fault?" I tried another tack. "My father didn't bite Leroy. I did." This wanton involving of my father in a quarrel Maureen had started in the first place made me furious, and a little scared. At recess I saw Maureen in a huddle with some of the other girls.

"Your father's German," Betty Sullivan whispered to me in art period. I was designing a civil defense badge, a white lightning bolt bisecting a red-and-blue-striped field on the diagonal, and I didn't look up. "How do you know he's not a spy?"

I went home straight after school, determined to have it out with Mother. My father taught German at the city college, right enough, but that didn't make him any less American than Mr. Kelly or Mr. Sullivan or Mr. Greenbloom. He didn't go to church, I had to admit. Still, I could not see how this or his teaching German had the slightest relation to my row with the Kellys. I only saw, confusedly, that by biting Leroy I had, in some obscure, roundabout way, betrayed my father to the neighbors.

I walked slowly in through the front door and out to the kitchen. There was nothing in the cookie jar except two stale gingersnaps left over from the last week's batch. "Ma!" I called, heading for the stairs. "Ma!"

"Here, Sadie." Her voice sounded muffled and echoey, as if she were calling to me from the far end of a long tunnel. Although the winter afternoon light died early on these shortest days, no lamps were lit in the house. I took the steps two at a time.

Mother was sitting in the big bedroom by the graying window. She looked small, almost shrunken, in the great wing chair. Even in that wan light I could tell her eyes were raw-rimmed, moist at the corners.

Mother didn't act the least bit surprised when I told her what Maureen had said. Nor did she try to sweeten things with her usual line about how Maureen didn't know any better, being so little, and how I ought to be the generous one, forgive and forget.

"Daddy *isn't* German, the way Maureen said," I asked, to make sure, "is he?"

"In one way," my mother took me by surprise, "he is. He is a German citizen. But, in another way, you are right—he isn't German the way Maureen said."

"He wouldn't hurt anybody!" I burst out. "He'd fight for us, if he had to!"

"Of course he would. You and I know that." Mother did not smile. "And the neighbors know it. In wartime, though, people often become frightened and forget what they know. I even think your father may have to go away from us for a while because of this."

"To be drafted? Like Mrs. Abrams' boy?"

"No, not like that," Mother said slowly. "There are places out West for German citizens to live in during the war so people will feel safer about them. Your father has been asked to go to one of those."

"But that's not fair!" How Mother could sit there and coolly tell me my father was going to be treated like some German spy made my flesh creep. "It's a mistake!" I thought of Maureen Kelly, Betty Sullivan, and the kids at school: what would they say to this? I thought, in rapid succession, of the police, the

FBI, the President, the United States Armed Forces. I thought of God. "God won't let it happen!" I cried, inspired.

Mother gave me a measuring look. Then she took me by the shoulders and began to talk very fast, as if there were something vital she had to get settled with me before my father came home. "Your father's going away *is* a mistake, it *is* unfair. You must never forget that, no matter what Maureen or anybody says. At the same time, there is nothing we can do about it. It's government orders, and there is nothing we can do about them . . ."

"But you said God . . ." I protested, feebly.

Mother overrode me. "God will let it happen."

I understood, then, that she was trying to give me the piece to the puzzle I had not possessed. The shadow in my mind lengthened with the night, blotting out our half of the world, and beyond it; the whole globe seemed sunk in darkness. For the first time the facts were not slanted Mother's way, and she was letting me see it.

"I don't think there is any God, then," I said dully, with no feeling of blasphemy. "Not if such things can happen."

"Some people think that," my mother said quietly.

Sweetie Pie and the Gutter Men

Ts,* 2–18 May 1959, Lilly Library

Waiting on the front doorstep of the unfamiliar house for someone to answer the bell and listening to the shrill, musical intonation of children's voices from the open window upstairs, Myra Wardle remembered how little she had cared for Cicely Franklin (then Cicely Naylor) at college. In those days she had tolerated Cicely—few of the other girls did—as a well-meaning, if prudish and provincial classmate. Clearly, that same bare tolerance on Myra's part must have mellowed, in Cicely's mind, over the subsequent eight years, to a facsimile of friendship. How else to explain Cicely's note, their one communication in all that time, turning up in the Wardles' mailbox? "Come see our new house, our two little girls and cocker puppy," Cicely had written in her large,

---

* Typescript with holograph corrections by SP. Typed at top right: 'Sylvia Plath / Suite 61 / 9 Willow Street / Boston 8, Massachusetts.' SP later used a scene from this story in *The Bell Jar*. See also SP's poem 'Two Views of a Cadaver'.

schoolmarmish hand on the back of an engraved card announcing the opening of Hiram Franklin's obstetrical practice.

The card itself, until she'd discovered Cicely's note on the reverse side, gave Myra an unpleasant moment. Why should a new obstetrician in town (Myra hadn't recognized Cicely's husband's name) be sending her an engraved announcement unless to suggest, with the utmost subtlety, that the Wardles were not fulfilling their duty to the community, to the human race? Myra Wardle, after five years of marriage, had no children. It was not, she explained, in answer to the delicate queries of relatives and friends, because she couldn't have them, or because she didn't want them. It was simply because her husband Timothy, a sculptor, insisted that children tied one down too much. And the Wardles' relatives and friends, saddled with children, with the steady jobs, the mortgaged houses, the installment-plan station wagons and washing machines that form such an inevitable part of parenthood in the suburbs, couldn't have been in more gratifying agreement.

Myra pressed the doorbell again, faintly annoyed that Cicely should keep her waiting so long on the unshaded step in the humid August afternoon. The children's voices continued, a clear, sweetly discordant babble from the second-floor window. A woman's voice sounded among them now, a low counterpoint to the slenderly spun treble. Myra tried the handle of the screen door to get at the front door knocker, but the screen door seemed hooked from within.

Unwilling to raise her voice, to shout upstairs as if Cicely were a back-fence neighbor, she rapped loudly with her knuckles on the doorjamb. A bit of paint flaked off into the dry, sepia-colored shrubbery. The whole place looked in bad shape. White paint peeling away in blistered swatches, shutters down, stacked haphazardly at the end of the yard, the house had a curiously lashless albino expression—rather, Myra thought, resembling Cicely's own. For a moment she wondered if Cicely meant her to go away under the illusion that the bell didn't work. Then she heard the voices receding from the window. Footsteps clattered on a staircase in the depths of the house. The front door swung inward.

"Well, Myra." It was Cicely's voice, the same prosy Midwestern accent, the trace of a lisp lending a touch of primness. Shading her eyes against the glare of the white shingles, Myra peered through the screen, unable to make out much of anything in the dark well of the hall. Cicely opened the screen door then, and came out onto the step, carrying a chubby blonde child in her arms. A thin, lively girl of about four followed her, looking at Myra with frank interest. Flat-chested, her complexion pallid even in summer, Cicely still wore her wan blonde hair crimped tight, like a doll's wig.

"You weren't sleeping, were you?" Myra said. "Is this a bad time?"

"Oh no. Alison had just woken Millicent up anyway." Behind the tortoiseshell-rimmed glasses, Cicely's pale eyes shifted slightly to a point somewhere beyond Myra's right shoulder. "Let's go out and sit under the beech tree in the back. It's always coolest there."

Striped canvas chairs and child-size wicker chairs stood in a circle in the dense, russet-blue shade of the great tree whose comprehensive boughs arched over half of the small yard. A rubber wading pool, a swing, a metal slide, a wooden seesaw, and a yellow sandbox crowded the children's play area. Cicely set Millicent on her feet beside the wading pool. The child paused, teetering slightly, her plump belly rounding out over her pink seersucker pants like a smooth-skinned fruit. Alison jumped immediately into the pool and sat down hard; the water splashed up in a fine sheet of spray, dousing her close-cropped hair.

Cicely and Myra pulled up two canvas chairs and sat some little distance from the children. "Now Alison," Cicely said, rehearsing what was evidently an old lesson, "you can wet yourself and the toys, and the grass, but you mustn't wet Millicent. Let Millicent wet herself."

Alison did not seem to hear. "The water's *cold*," she told Myra, widening her gray-blue eyes in emphasis.

"Cud," Millicent echoed. Squatting beside the pool, she made gentle churning motions in the water with her hand.

"I often wonder if linguistic ability is hereditary," Cicely said, lowering her voice out of range of the children's hearing. "Alison spoke complete sentences at eleven months. She's amazingly word-conscious. Millicent mispronounces everything."

"Why, how do you mean?" Myra had a private pact with herself to "bring people out." She began by imagining herself a transparent vase, clearer than crystal—almost, in fact, invisible. (She had read somewhere that a certain school of actors pretended they were empty glasses when studying a new role.) In this way—purged of any bias, any individual color tint—Myra became the perfect receptacle for confidences. "How do you mean, 'word-conscious?'"

"Oh, Alison makes an *effort* to learn words. She works on changing her vocabulary. Once, for instance, I overheard her talking to herself in the playroom. 'Daddy will fix it,' she said. Then she corrected herself: 'No, Daddy will *repair* it.' But Millicent's hopeless . . ."

"Perhaps Alison subdues her?" Myra suggested. "Often when one child talks a lot, the other turns inward, develops a sort of secret personality all her own. Millicent may, don't you think, one day simply come out with a complete sentence?"

Cicely shook her head. "I'm afraid there's little chance of that. When we were in Akron, visiting Mother, Millicent learned to say 'Nana' and 'Daddy' quite clearly. Ever since we moved up here, though, she's confused the two. She comes out with 'Nada,' some weird combination like that. And she says 'goggy' for 'doggy' and so on."

"Ah, but that's quite natural, isn't it? Quite common?" Myra's fingers twiddled at the leaves of a low branch of the beech tree near the arm of her chair. Already she had shredded several of the glossy, reddish-black leaves with her nails. "Don't most children substitute some letters for others that way?"

"I suppose," Cicely said, her attention diverted momentarily by the children chattering and dabbling in the wading pool, "it's common enough."

"Why, I remember when *I* was a child," Myra said, "I couldn't pronounce 'l' for some reason. I used to say 'Night! Night!' when I wanted the hall light left on. This confused the women who used to babysit for me no end."

Cicely smiled, and Myra, heartened, was inspired to ad-lib. "I believe I also alienated a certain Aunt Lily from the family. She wouldn't accept Mother's explanation of my foible with 'l's. She insisted I'd overheard her called Aunt Ninny by my parents."

Cicely shook with dry, silent laughter. In her starched middy blouse, her beige Bermuda shorts and her flat brown walking shoes with the scalloped flaps over the ties, Cicely was undeniably plain, even dowdy. She possessed none of the fruity buxomness of the harassed working-class mothers Myra ran into in Woolworth's or the A & P. Then, a bit guilty about her brief lapse from impersonal glassiness, Myra steered the conversation toward Hiram and his obstetrical practice. With some relief, she became transparent, crystalline, again. But as Cicely talked on about the difficulties of starting an obstetrical practice in a strange town, Myra fell into a reverie of her own. Cicely's words faded away like the words of a television announcer after the sound track is shut off. Suddenly Myra felt a warm silkiness graze her ankle. She glanced down. The black cocker puppy lay stretched out under her chair, eyes shut, his tongue a scrap of pink felt lolling at the corner of his mouth.

". . . the Chamber of Commerce letters were mostly silly," Cicely was saying. "All about population, industry, things like that. Some of the towns had too many obstetricians. Some had none . . ."

"Why wouldn't a town with*out* any be a good place to start?"

Obligingly, Cicely launched into a detailed account of the animosity kindled in the hearts of general practitioners when an obstetrician invaded their town and stole away their clients by his specialty. "Then Dr. Richter wrote from here. He said there was a good opening, and a man was already thinking about moving in, so Hiram had better hurry if he wanted to come . . ."

At that moment, Cicely was interrupted. Millicent lay on her stomach in the wading pool, howling and spitting water, her round face twisted into an image of outrage.

"She must have fallen," Myra found herself saying, although she was reasonably sure Alison had pushed her sister into the water.

Cicely jerked up from her chair and went to pick Millicent out of the pool.

"Can you open this?" Coolly ignoring Millicent's cries, Alison handed Myra a black-enameled can with holes punched in the screw top. "It's stuck."

"I can try." The can felt oddly heavy. Myra wondered for a moment if she was reading her own suppressed pleasure into Alison's eyes—pleasure at the sight of plump, white-skinned Millicent whining on the grass, rubbing at her wet sunsuit pants, stained a deep crimson from the water. "What's *in* here?"

"Cake mix."

Myra tried to loosen the screw-top, but the can, glistening with wet, slithered around in her grasp. The lid would not budge. With a sense of mild chagrin, she handed the can back to Alison. She felt a little as if she had failed to pass a test of some sort. "I can't do a thing with it."

"Daddy will open the can when he comes home from the office." Cicely paused by Myra's chair, Millicent bundled under her arm. "I'm going in to make us some lemonade and change Millicent. Want to see the house?"

"Sure." Myra's hands were uncomfortably wet and gritty, even sore, from her efforts with the can. Taking a Kleenex from her purse, she dabbed at her palms. From the back steps of the house she glanced over at Alison, framed by the greenery around the wading pool. "What's in that can, anyway?" With a small beech twig, Alison was prodding the stomach of the sleepy cocker puppy. "It's heavy as lead."

"Oh," Cicely shrugged and gave Millicent a little jounce in her arms, "sand from the sandbox and water from the wading pool, I guess."

The interior of the Franklins' house smelled of varnish and turpentine, and the white-painted walls gave off a surgical light. An upright piano, a few armchairs upholstered in vague pastels, and a mauve sofa stood, desolate as rocks on a prairie, on the bare, freshly shellacked floor of the living room. The linoleum in the dining room, playroom, and kitchen, patterned with inordinately large black and white squares, suggested a modernized Dutch painting—bereft, however, of the umber and ocher patinas of polished wood, the pewter and brass highlights, and the benevolent pear and cello shapes which enrich the interiors of a Vermeer.

Cicely opened the icebox and took out a frost-covered can of lemonade concentrate. "Do you mind?" She handed Myra a can opener. "I'll just run up and change Millicent."

While Cicely was upstairs, Myra opened the can, poured the contents into an aluminum pitcher, and measured four cans of cold water into the lemonade base, stirring the mixture with a spoon she found in the sink. The sunlight glancing off the white enamel and chrome surfaces of the kitchen appliances made her feel dazed, far off.

"All set?" Cicely chirruped from the doorway. Millicent beamed in her arms, dressed in a clean pair of seersucker pants, exactly like the pink ones, only blue.

Carrying the aluminum pitcher of lemonade and four red plastic cups, Myra drifted after Cicely and Millicent toward the little oasis of chairs in the dark shade of the beech tree.

"Do you want to pour?" Cicely set Millicent on the lawn and dropped into her canvas chair. Alison wandered over to them from the wading pool, her short, sandy hair slicked back like an otter's.

"Oh, I'll let you do it." Myra handed Cicely the pitcher and the cups. With a curious, nerveless languor, she watched Cicely start to pour out the lemonade. The tree leaves, and the sun falling through the leaves in long pencils of light, went out of focus for a moment in a dappled green-and-gold blur. Then a quick flash caught her eye.

Alison had, in plain view, given Millicent a sudden, rough shove, tumbling her to the ground. There was a second of silence, expectant as the brief interval between the flash of lightning and the thunder-crack, and then Millicent howled from the grass.

Cicely placed the pitcher and the cup she was filling on the ground beside her chair, got up, and lifted the sobbing Millicent to her lap. "Alison, you've made a mistake." Cicely's tone was remarkably cool, Myra thought. "You know we don't hit people in this house."

Alison, wary, a small foxy creature at bay, stood her ground, her eyes flickering from Myra to Cicely and back again. "She wanted to sit in *my* chair."

"We don't hit people in any case." Cicely smoothed Millicent's hair. When the child's sobs had quieted, she set Millicent in one of the small wicker chairs and poured her a cup of lemonade. Alison, without a word, stared at Myra while waiting her turn, took the cup Cicely gave her, and returned to her chair. Her steady look made Myra uneasy. She felt the child expected something of her, some sign, some pledge.

The silence deepened, punctuated only by the irregular sound of four people sipping lemonade—the children, loud and unselfconscious, the grown-ups more discreet. Except for this tenuous noise, the silence surrounded them like a sea, lapping at the solid edges of the afternoon. At any moment, Myra thought, the four of them might become fixed, forever speechless and two-dimensional—wax-like figures in a faded photograph. "Has Hiram had any patients yet?" With an effort she broke the gathered stillness.

"Oh, Hiram's joined the charity ward in the hospital for the month of August." Cicely tilted her cup of lemonade and drained it. "Of course, he doesn't get paid for ward cases, but he's had four deliveries already this month."

"Four!" A vision of babies in pink and blue bassinets loomed in Myra's mind—three hundred and sixty-five babies in three hundred and sixty-five bassinets—each baby a perfect replica of the others, all lined up in a ghostly alley of diminishing perspective between two mirrors. "Why, that's about one a day!"

"That's about the average for this town. Hiram hasn't really had any patients of his own yet, any private patients. Still, a woman walked into his office yesterday, out of the blue. She asked for an appointment for today. I don't know how she heard of Hiram, maybe from the announcement in the paper."

"What sort of anesthesia does Hiram use?" Myra asked suddenly.

"Well, that depends . . ." Cicely's own frankness demanded that she answer, but she was withdrawing, Myra could tell, into that blithe evasiveness of so many mothers when questioned point blank about childbirth by childless women.

"I just meant," Myra said hastily, "there seem to be different schools of thought. I've heard some mothers talk about caudal anesthesia. Something that deadens the pain, but still lets you see the baby born . . .?"

"Caudal anesthesia." Cicely sounded a trifle scornful. "That's what Dr. Richter uses in *all* his cases. That's why he's so popular."

Myra started to laugh, but behind the sheen of her glasses Cicely looked dubious. "It only seems so amusing," Myra explained, "to raise your popularity rating by the kind of anesthesia you use." Still, Cicely did not appear to see the joke.

"Perhaps," Myra dropped her voice, with a cautious glance at Alison who was sucking up the dregs of her lemonade, "perhaps I'm so interested because I had an experience myself, once, years ago, seeing a baby born."

Cicely's eyebrows rose. "How ever did you do that? Was it a relative? They don't let people, you know . . ."

"No relative." Myra gave Cicely a slight, wry smile. "It happened in my . . . salad days. In college, when I was dating medical students, I went to lectures on sickle-cell anemia, watched them cut up cadavers. Oh, I was a regular Florence Nightingale."

Alison got up, at this point, and went over to the sandbox just behind Myra's chair. Millicent was kneeling by the wading pool, swirling a fallen beech leaf in the water.

"That's how I got into the hospital to watch a delivery in the charity ward. Camouflaged in a white uniform and a white mask, of course. Actually, it must have been about the time I knew you, when you were a senior and I was a sophomore." As she spoke, hearing her own voice, stilted, distant, as on an old record, Myra remembered with sudden clarity the blind, mushroom-colored embryos in the jars of preserving fluid, and the four leather-skinned cadavers, black as burnt turkey, on the dissecting tables. She shuddered, touched by a keen chill in spite of the hot afternoon. "This woman had some drug, invented by a man, I suppose, as all those drugs are. It didn't stop her feeling the pain, but made her forget it right afterwards."

"There are lots of drugs like that," Cicely said. "You forget the pain in a sort of twilight sleep."

Myra wondered how Cicely could be so calm about forgetting pain. Although erased from the mind's surface, the pain was there, somewhere, cut indelibly into one's quick—an empty, doorless, windowless corridor of pain. And then to be deceived by the waters of Lethe into coming back again, in all innocence, to conceive child after child! It was barbarous. It was a fraud dreamed up by men to continue the human race; reason enough for a woman to refuse childbearing altogether. "Well," Myra said, "this woman was yelling a good deal, and moaning. That kind of thing leaves its impression. They had to cut into her, I remember. There seemed to be a great deal of blood . . ."

From the sandbox Alison's voice began to rise, now, in a shrill monologue, but Myra, intent on her own story, did not bother to distinguish the child's words. "The third-year man delivering the baby kept saying, 'I'm going to drop it, I'm going to drop it,' in a kind of biblical chant . . ." Myra paused, staring through the red-dark scrim of beech leaves without seeing them, acting out once again her part in the remembered play, a part after which all other parts had somehow dwindled, palled.

" . . . and she goes upstairs in the attic," Alison was saying. "She gets splinters in her feet." Myra checked a sudden impulse to slap the child. Then the words caught her interest. "She pokes people's eyes on the sidewalk. She pulls off their dresses. She gets diarrhea in the *night* . . ."

"Alison!" Cicely yelped. "You be quiet now! You know better than that."

"Just who's she talking about?" Myra let her story of the blue baby lapse back, unfinished, into the obscure fathoms of memory from which it had risen. "Some neighborhood child?"

"Oh," Cicely said with some irritation, "it's her *doll*."

"Sweetie Pie!" Alison shouted.

"And what else does Sweetie Pie do?" Myra asked, countering Cicely's move to quiet the child. "I used to have a doll myself."

"She climbs on the roof." Alison jumped into her wicker chair and squatted on the seat, frog-fashion. "She knocks down the gutter men."

"*Gutter* men?"

"The painters took the gutters off the porch roof this morning," Cicely explained. "Tell Mrs. Wardle," she ordered Alison in the clear, socially constructive tones of a Unitarian Sunday School teacher, "how you *helped* the painters this morning."

Alison paused, fingering her bare toes. "I packed their things up. One was named Neal. One was named Jocko."

"I don't know what I'm going to *do* with Mr. Grooby." Cicely turned to Myra, pointedly leaving Alison out. "This morning he came to start painting at six-thirty."

"Six-thirty!" Myra said. "Why on earth?"

"And left at ten-thirty. He's got a heart condition, so he works all morning and fishes all afternoon. Each morning he's come earlier and earlier. Eight-thirty was all right, but *six*-thirty! I don't know what it'll be tomorrow."

"Sunup, at that rate," Myra said. "I guess," she added thoughtlessly, "you must be kept pretty much occupied just being a mother." She hadn't meant to say "just," which sounded disparaging, but there it was. Lately Myra had started wondering about babies. Young as she was, and happily married, she felt something of a maiden aunt among the children of her relatives and friends. Lately, too, she had taken to tearing off low-hanging leaves or tall grass heads with a kind of wanton energy, and to twisting her paper napkin into compact pellets at the table, something she hadn't done since childhood.

"Morning, noon, and night," Cicely said with an air, Myra thought, of noble martyrdom. "Morning, noon, and night."

Myra glanced at her watch. It was close to four-thirty. "I guess," she said, "I ought to be running along now." She would be staying on till suppertime, if she wasn't careful, out of sheer inertia.

"No need to go," Cicely said, but she rose from her chair, idly dusting off the seat of her Bermudas.

Myra tried to think of a good excuse to see her to the gate. It was too early to be preparing dinner, too late to plead last-minute shopping downtown. Her life all at once seemed excessively spacious. "I must go, anyway."

As Myra turned, she noticed a dark blue car pulling up outside the unpainted picket gate that closed the driveway and backyard off from the street. It would be Hiram Franklin, whom Myra had met only once or twice eight years ago at college. Already Cicely and the children were receding from her, behind the glass window of some heartless nonstop express, secure in their rosily lit, plush compartment, arranging themselves in loving attitudes about the young man of medium height now unlatching the gate. Millicent started, with uneven steps, toward her father. "Daddy!" Alison shouted from the sandbox. Hiram walked toward the women. As he approached, Millicent caught him about the knees, and Hiram bent to pick her up. "She's her daddy's girl," Cicely said.

Myra waited, the smile stiffening on her face as it did when she had to hold still for a photographer. Hiram looked very young to be an obstetrician. His eyes, a hard, clear blue, bordered by black lashes, gave him a slightly glacial expression.

"Myra Smith Wardle, Hiram," Cicely said. "An old college friend you should remember."

Hiram Franklin nodded at Myra. "Whom I should remember, but do not, unfortunately." His words were less an apology for forgetfulness than a firm denial of any prior acquaintance.

"I'm just going." Cicely's alliance with Hiram, powerful and immediate, shut out everything else. Some women were like that with their husbands, Myra thought—overly possessive, not wishing to share them, even for a moment. The Franklins would be wanting to talk about family matters, about the woman who had made the office appointment out of the blue for that afternoon. "Bye now."

"Bye, Myra. Thanks for coming." Cicely made no move to accompany Myra to the gate. "Bring Timothy over sometime."

"I will," Myra called back from halfway across the lawn. "If I can ever wean Timothy from the chisel."

At last the bunched shrubbery at the corner of the house shut out the Franklins' family portrait of togetherness. Myra felt the late afternoon heat wearing into the crown of her head and into her back. Then she heard footsteps thudding behind her.

"Where's your car?" Alison stood on the ragged grass-strip between sidewalk and the street, detached, willfully or for some other reason, from the family group in the yard.

"I don't have one. Not with me." Myra paused. The street and sidewalk were deserted. With an odd sense of entering into a conspiracy with the child, she bent toward Alison and dropped her voice to a whisper. "Alison," she said, "what do you do to Sweetie Pie when she is *very* bad?"

Alison scuffed her bare heel in the weed-grown grass and looked up at Myra with a strange, almost shy, little smile. "I hit her." She hesitated, waiting for Myra's response.

"Fine," Myra said. "You hit her. What else?"

"I throw her up in the sky," Alison said, her voice taking on a faster rhythm. "I knock her down. I spank her and spank her. I bang her eyes in."

Myra straightened. A dull ache started at the base of her spine, as if a bone, once broken and mended, were throbbing into hurt again. "Good," she said, wondering why she felt at such a loss. "Good," she repeated, with little heart. "You keep on doing that."

Myra left Alison standing in the grass and began to walk up the long, sun-dazzled street toward the bus stop. She turned only once, and saw the child, small as a doll in the distance, still watching her. But her own hands hung listless and empty at her sides, like hands of wax, and she did not wave.

Above the Oxbow

Ts,[*] 31 December 1958–7 January 1959, Lilly Library

On all the mountain that hot, August day Luke Jenness hadn't seen a thing moving. Traffic was slack on Mondays. The rickety remains of the old mountain top hotel, half of it blown away in the '38 hurricane, seemed oddly quiet after the lines of tourist cars grinding up the steep hairpin curves in first gear all that weekend, with the children piling out in the parking lot and running around and around the four-way veranda, buying root beer and popsicles and fiddling with the telescope on the north side. The telescope opened its magnifying eye on the Oxbow, the green flats of Hadley farms across the river, and the range of hills to

---

[*] Typescript has holograph corrections and additions by SP. Typed at top right: 'Sylvia Plath / Suite 61 / 9 Willow Street / Boston 8, Massachusetts.' See also SP's poem 'Above the Oxbow'. Submitted to the *Atlantic Monthly*.

the north, toward Sugarloaf. You could see up to New Hampshire and Vermont, even, on clear days. But today heat hazed the view, sweat didn't dry.

Luke leaned, arms folded, on the white-painted railing, looking down at the river. The raised scar running diagonally from his right eyebrow across his nose and deep into his left cheek showed white against his tan. Pale, almost dirty, the scar tissue had a different texture from the rest of his skin; it was smoother, newer, like plastic caulking a crack. At his feet, extending down to the halfway house below him, the gray, splintered timbers of the funicular railway lay bleaching in the sun in a fenced-off danger area, the warped flight of steps still intact, but ready to collapse any day now. Abraham Lincoln had stood where Luke was standing, and Jenny Lind, the famous singer. She'd called the view of the valley a view of Paradise. Visitors wanted to know things like that. What date did the hotel go up? What date did it blow down? How high was the mountain compared to Mount Tom, say, or Monadnock? Luke knew the facts: it was part of his job. Some people wanted to talk. Others paid him the fifty-cent parking fee, or the dollar on Sundays, like a tip, so he'd disappear and they could watch the view by themselves. Other people didn't seem to see him at all after they paid him; you'd think he was some kind of tree, just standing there.

Down in the clearing at the halfway house now, Luke saw two figures moving. A dark-haired boy in khaki pants and a girl in a blue jersey and white shorts were walking up the blacktop road, very slowly. From where he stood they seemed smaller than his thumb. Probably they'd parked their car somewhere a little below, in the brush at the side of the road, and walked up from there. He hadn't had a hiker for three weeks or more. People drove up, got out and looked at the view a few minutes, maybe bought a cold soda—the tap water was warm and full of air bubbles, hardly spouting high enough out of the chipped chrome fountain bowl for you to get a good gulp of it. Then they drove down. Sometimes they brought picnics for their noon meal and ate at the brown wooden tables in among the trees. Nobody walked up much anymore. It would be a good half-hour before the kids got to the top. They'd just strolled out of sight to the right and would be coming up the road around the south side of the mountain. Luke sat down in a frayed wicker rocking chair and propped his feet on the veranda railing.

When he heard voices coming up the ramp onto the rocky ledge below the hotel veranda he got up and leaned on the railing again. Far down there, the speedboats were making small V-shaped wakes of white foam on the dull gray surface of the river. A queer river, for all its broad, smooth back—full of rock reefs, just under the water, and sandbars. The kids weren't coming up on the veranda. Not yet, anyway. They had spread out a khaki raincoat on the orange shale ledge just beneath Luke, and they were resting.

"I feel better," he heard the girl say. "Much better now. We'll do this every day. We'll bring up books, and a picnic."

"Maybe it'll help," the boy said. "Help you forget that place."

"It might," the girl said. "It just might."

They were quiet for a moment.

"Not a wind moving." The boy pointed down at some black birds flying over the treetops. "Look at the swifts."

Luke felt the girl glance up at him then. He shifted, and stared straight ahead, not wanting to seem an eavesdropper. If they didn't come up to the veranda the way everybody did, if they started back down, he'd have to call after them and collect the parking fee. Maybe they'd come up to the veranda and want a drink.

The voices stopped. The boy was getting up. He helped the girl to her feet, bent, picked up the raincoat, and folded it over his arm. They started to climb the veranda steps. At the top, they paused by the railing, not far from Luke.

"You sure you're all right?"

"Yes." The girl tossed her lank, shoulder-length brown hair almost impatiently. "Yes, I'm all right. Of course I'm all right." There was a little pause. "How high is it here?" she asked, then, raising her voice as if she meant Luke to answer, not the boy.

Luke glanced in her direction and saw she was, in fact, looking at him and waiting. "About eight thousand feet," he said.

"What can you see from this side?"

"Three states, if the weather's clear."

They said nothing about paying him. "Is there any water?" the boy asked. The kid hadn't shaved for a day, and the stubble made a green shadow on his square chin.

Luke jutted a thumb back over his shoulder. "In there. There's cold soda, root beer, too," he added. "If you want it."

"No," the boy said. "Water's fine."

The boards sounded hollow under their feet, creaking and echoing as they went inside to the water fountain. He'd have to get the money from them sooner or later. The sign inside said people without cars paid fifteen cents each. It was a new State regulation; they hadn't charged for hikers before this year. Maybe the kids would try to get out of paying the fifty-cent parking fee when they noticed that sign and see if they could get away with the thirty cents.

◆

"You both walk all the way up?" Luke asked when they came out again, keeping his voice casual. The girl wiped the water drops from her chin with the back of her hand, leaving a small, triangular smear of dirt. She didn't seem to be wearing any makeup, and her skin had a queer, indoor pallor. Little beads of sweat stood out on her forehead and upper lip.

"Sure we walked," she said. "It's a tough walk, too. A lot of work."

The boy didn't say anything. He had draped the raincoat over the railing and was looking through the telescope.

"Where'd you leave your car?"

"Oh, down there." The girl waved vaguely toward the foot of the mountain where the State Park road started, sloping gradually up past a hayfield and a chicken farm before beginning the steep climb. "At the bottom. Right inside the gate."

"You'll have to pay for that," Luke said.

The girl looked at him. "But we walked up." She seemed to be confused about what he meant. "We walked up the whole way."

Luke tried again. "Didn't you see the sign down there?"

"At the gate? Sure we saw. It says fifty cents for parking up here. But we left the car and walked up."

"You'll have to pay anyway," Luke said. He'd have to get them to put that new bit about the fifteen cents on the old gate-sign down there, too, to make things plain. "Even if you parked just inside the gate."

The boy came away from the telescope. "Well, where *can* you park the car free?" He seemed a lot easier-going than the girl. "And just walk up?"

The girl bit her lip. With a sudden, quick jerk of her head, she looked away from Luke and the boy, out over the green treetops that sloped down toward the river.

"Nowhere." Luke kept to his point. He couldn't see the girl's face. What some people wouldn't do to save twenty cents: leave their cars hidden in the brush and walk up a little way. "Nowhere in park bounds."

"What about *walk*ing, though?" The girl's voice rose in an odd way as she turned to him. "What if we just *walked* up with no car anywhere at all?"

"Look, lady," Luke said in a reasonable, even tone, "you yourself just now told me you parked your car inside the gate, and that sign in the lookout there says fifty cents for parking, regardless, and a dollar on Sundays . . ."

"But I don't *mean* parking. I mean if we *walked*."

Luke sighed. "Walkers pay too, lady. That sign in there says fifteen cents for walkers, fifteen cents a*piece*." He felt she was somehow getting him off the track. "Only maybe you didn't notice, maybe you want to see it?"

"You go," she said to the boy.

Doggedly, the back of his neck flushed hot, Luke led the boy into the hotel lobby. The girl stayed out on the veranda.

"It really does say fifteen cents," the boy told her when he came out again. "Fifteen cents for walking, for each person."

"I don't care *what* it says." The girl hung onto the railing and kept her back to him. "It's dis*gust*ing. Making money, that's all they want. I mean, they ought to *pay* people who care enough to walk all the way up here."

Luke waited just inside the door. She sounded as though she might fly off the handle any minute; her voice was getting shriller and shriller. He'd done his job. Most of it. He'd told them what was what. Now he just had to collect the money. Slowly he walked out toward them.

"I can see the *park*ing fee." The girl whirled on him so suddenly, he wondered did she have eyes in the back of her head. "Even for parking way down there at the gate." A fleck of saliva showed at the corner of her mouth. For a second Luke thought she actually meant to spit at him. "But to pay for *walk*ing!"

Luke shrugged. "State law, lady." Squinting off into the green distance, to the far hills that melded, one into the other, in the August haze, he jingled his pouch of silver coins. What was she blaming him for? What was thirty cents, fifty cents? "Besides," he added, spacing his words carefully, the way one explains a problem to a difficult child, "you pay parking, not walking, today. So what do you want to bother yourself about the price of walking for, lady?"

"But we were going to *walk* . . ." The girl broke off. Turning from him with surprising swiftness, she rounded the corner of the hotel to the west side of the veranda, out of sight. The boy followed her.

Luke cut through the inside of the hotel and out onto the back porch where he could see if they tried to get off down the south side of the mountain. You couldn't tell what kids like that would try to do. If they didn't want to pay, the way everybody paid, they'd probably want to get off scot-free.

The girl was standing on the top of the west staircase down to the parking lot with the boy facing her, his back to Luke. She was crying, of all things, crying and dabbing at her face with a white handkerchief. Then she glanced up and saw Luke. She bent her head; she seemed to be hunting for something she had lost through the spaced cracks of the floorboards. The boy reached out to touch her shoulder, but she dodged, in that quick way of hers, and started down the steps.

The boy let her go and came around the veranda to Luke, a battered brown leather wallet open in his hand. "How much is it, now?" He sounded tired. Whatever he thought, he must be sorry about the girl, making a scene like that. Over something nobody's fault to begin with.

"Fifty cents," Luke said, "if your car's on the park grounds."

The boy counted out a quarter, two dimes, and a nickel into Luke's broad palm and went round to pick up the raincoat from the north railing where he had left it.

Dropping the coins into his money pouch, Luke followed the boy. "Thanks," he said.

The boy didn't answer, didn't apologize for the girl or anything, just took off down the stairs after her on the double-quick, the raincoat flapping out behind him like a hurt bird.

"Well," Luke said aloud, wonderingly, to nobody but himself. "Well, you'd think I was a gosh-darn *crim*inal." Down on the bland surface of the river the toy-size speedboats were zigzagging still, skirting the unseen reefs. Luke stared at them blankly for a bit, and then went round to the south side of the veranda. The two figures were dwindling on the road below him—the girl a little ahead, and the boy gaining on her; but before the boy could overtake her, they were lost to sight where the road vanished into the densely wooded mountainside. "A gosh-darn honest-to-Pete *crim*inal," Luke said.

And then he gave it up, washed his hands of the whole affair, and went inside the sun-blistered lookout to treat himself to a cold soda.

The Daughters of Blossom Street

Written: 17–31 May 1959
Published: *London Magazine* (May 1960): 34–48[*]

As it turns out, I don't need any hurricane warnings over the seven a.m. news-and-weather to tell me today will be a bad day. First thing when I come down the third-floor hall of the Clinics Building to open up the office I find a pile of patients' records waiting for me just outside the door, punctual as the morning paper. But it is a thin pile, and sure as Thursday's a full day with us, I know

---

[*] Printed with a biographical sketch: 'Sylvia Plath was born in Boston, Mass. She graduated from Smith College in 1955 and attended Newnham College, Cambridge, from 1955–57. She is the wife of Ted Hughes. Her poems have often appeared in *The London Magazine*, but the story printed in this issue is the first she has had published in England.'

I'll have to spend a good half-hour phoning every station in the Record Room to chase those missing records down. Already, so early in the morning, my white eyelet blouse is losing starch, and I can feel a little wet patch spreading under each arm. The sky outside is low, thick, and yellow as hollandaise. I shove open the one window in the office to change the air; nothing happens. Everything hangs still, heavier than wet laundry in a basement. Then I cut the string around the record folders and, staring up at me from the cover of the top record, I see stamped in red ink: DEAD. DEAD. DEAD.

I try to make the letters out to read DEAF, only it doesn't work. Not that I'm superstitious. Even though the ink is smeared rusty as blood on the cover of the case history, it simply means Lillian Ulmer is Dead, and Number Nine-one-seven-oh-six cancelled in the Record Room's active file for once and forever. Grim Billy at Station Nine has mixed the numbers up again, meaning me no harm. Still and all, with the sky so dark, and the hurricane rumbling up the coast, closer every time I turn around, I feel Lillian Ulmer, rest her soul, has started my day off on the wrong foot.

When my boss Miss Taylor comes in, I ask why they don't burn the records of the people gone to Blossom Street to save room in the files. But she says they often keep the records around a bit, if the disease is interesting, in case there might be a statistical survey of patients who lived or died with it.

It was my friend Dotty Berrigan in Alcoholic Clinic told me about Blossom Street. Dotty took it on herself to show me around the Hospital when I first signed on as Secretary in Adult Psychiatric, she being right down the hall from me and we sharing a lot of cases.

"You must have a lot of people dead here every day," I said.

"You bet," she said. "And all the accidents and beatings up you could want from the South End coming into Emergency Ward steady as taxes."

"Well, where do they keep them, the dead ones?" I didn't want suddenly by mistake to walk into a room of people laid out or cut up, and it seemed only too easy at that point for me to get lost in the numberless levels of corridors in the greatest General Hospital in the world.

"In a room off Blossom Street, I'll show you where. The doctors never say anyone *died* in so many words, you know, because of making the patients morbid. They say: 'How many of yours went to Blossom Street this week?' And the other guy'll say: 'Two.' Or, 'Five.' Or however many. Because the Blossom Street exit's where the bodies get shipped off to the funeral parlors to be fixed up for burying."

You can't beat Dotty. She's a regular mine of information, having to go about, as she does, checking for alcoholics in Emergency Ward and comparing notes with the doctors on duty in Psychiatric Ward, not to mention her dating various members of the Hospital staff, even a surgeon once, and another time a Persian intern. Dotty is Irish—shortish, and a little plump, but she dresses to make the best of it: always something blue—heaven blue to match her eyes, and these snug black jumpers she runs off herself from *Vogue* patterns, and high pumps with the spindly steel heels.

Cora, in Psychiatric Social Service down the hall from Dotty and me, is nowhere near the person Dotty is—pushing forty, you can tell it by the pleats around her eyes, even if she does keep her hair red, thanks to these colored rinses. Cora lives with her mother, and to hear her talk you'd think she was a green teenager. She had three of the girls in Nerve Clinic over her place one night, for bridge and supper, and stuck the casserole into the oven with the frozen raspberry tarts and wondered an hour later they weren't warm, when all the time she hadn't thought to turn the oven on. Cora keeps taking these bus trips to Lake Louise and these cruises to Nassau in her vacations to meet Mr. Right, but all she ever meets is girls from Tumor Clinic or Amputee Clinic, and every one of them on the selfsame mission.

Anyhow, the third Thursday of the month being the day we have our Secretaries' Meeting in the Hunnewell Room on the second floor, Cora calls for Dotty and the two of them call for me, and we click-clack in our heels down the stone stairs and into this really handsome room, dedicated, as it says on a bronze plaque over the door, to a Doctor Augustus Hunnewell in 1892. The place is full of glass cases crammed with old-fashioned medical instruments, and the walls are covered with faded, reddish-brown tintypes of Civil War doctors, their beards bushy and long as the beards of the Smith Brothers on those cough-drop packets. Set in the middle of the room, and stretching almost from wall to wall, is a great, dark, oval walnut-wood table, legs carved in the shape of lions' legs, only with scales instead of fur, and the whole top polished so you can see your face in it. Around this table we sit smoking and talking, waiting for Mrs. Rafferty to come in and start the meeting.

Minnie Dapkins, the tiny white-haired receptionist in Skin, is handing around pink and yellow referral slips. "Is there a Doctor Crawford in Nerve?" she asks, holding up a pink slip.

"Doctor Crawford!" Mary Ellen in Nerve bursts out laughing, her black bulk jiggling like a soft aspic in the flowered print dress. "He's dead six, seven years, who wants him?"

Minnie purses her mouth to a tight pink bud. "A patient *said* she had Doctor

Crawford," she returns coldly. Minnie can't stand disrespect for the dead. She's been working at the Hospital since she was married in the Depression and just got her Twenty-five Year Silver Service Pin at a special ceremony at the Secretaries' Christmas Party last winter, but the story goes she hasn't cracked a joke about a patient or a dead person in all her time. Not like Mary Ellen, or Dotty, or even Cora, who isn't above seeing the humor in a situation.

"What are you girls going to do about the hurricane?" Cora asks Dotty and me in a low voice, leaning across the table to dab off her cigarette ash in the glass ashtray with the Hospital seal showing through the bottom. "I'm worried blue about my car. That motor gets wet in a sea breeze, it stops dead."

"Oh, it won't hit till after we're well through work," Dotty says, casual as usual. "You'll make it home."

"I still don't like the look of the sky." Cora wrinkles her freckled nose as if she smelt something bad.

I don't much like the look of the sky either. The room has been darkening steadily since we came in, until we are now all sitting in a kind of twilight, smoke drifting up from our cigarettes and hanging its pall in the already dense air. For a minute no one says anything. Cora seems to have spoken out loud everybody's secret worry.

"Well, well, well, what's the *mat*ter with us, girls! We're gloomy as a funeral!" The electric lights in the four copper lamp bowls overhead flash on, and, almost magically, the room brightens, shutting the stormy sky off in the distance where it belongs, harmless as a painted stage backdrop. Mrs. Rafferty steps up to the head of the table, her silver bangles making a cheerful music on each arm, her pendant earrings, exact replicas, in miniature, of stethoscopes, bouncing gaily from her plump earlobes. With an agreeable flurry she sets her notes and papers down on the table, her tinted blonde chignon gleaming under the lights like a cap of mail. Even Cora can't be sour-faced in front of such professional sunniness. "We'll get our affairs cleared up in a jiffy and then I've told one of the girls to send in the coffee machine and we'll have a little pick-me-up." Mrs. Rafferty glances around the table, absorbing, with a gratified smile, the exclamations of good feeling.

"Give her credit," Dotty mutters in my ear. "The old girl ought to market it."

Mrs. Rafferty starts out with one of her jolly scoldings. Mrs. Rafferty is really a buffer. A buffer between us and the hierarchies of Administration, and a buffer between us and the Doctors, with their odd, endless follies and foibles, their illegible handwriting ("I've seen better in *kind*agarten myself," Mrs. Rafferty is reported to have said), their childlike inability to paste prescriptions and reports on the right page in the patients' record books, and so on. "Now girls," she says, raising one finger playfully, "I'm having all sorts of complaints about the daily statistics. Some of them are coming down without the Clinic stamp or date." She pauses, to let the enormity of this sink in. "Some aren't added correctly. Some," another pause, "aren't coming down at *all*." I lower my eyes and try to will away the blush I feel rising to heat my cheeks. The blush is not for myself, but for my boss, Miss Taylor, who confided to me shortly after my arrival that, to be perfectly open and above board, she *hates* statistics. Our patients' interviews with the staff psychiatrists often run over the Clinics' official closing time, and of course Miss Taylor can't get the statistics turned in downstairs every night unless she's going to be more of a martyr to the Office than she is anyway. "Enough said girls."

Mrs. Rafferty glances down at her notes, bends to make a check mark with her red pencil, and straightens, easy as a reed. "Another thing. Record Room says they're getting a lot of calls for records you already have on hand in your Hold Boxes, and they're simply in*furi*ated down there . . ."

"Infuriated is right," Mary Ellen groans good-naturedly, rolling her eyes so for a minute nothing but the whites are showing. "That guy what's-his-name at Station Nine acts like we shouldn't call in at all anyhow."

"Oh, that's *Billy*," says Minnie Dapkins.

Ida Kline and a couple of the other girls from the Typing Pool in the First Basement titter among themselves, and then hush up.

"I guess you girls all know by now," Mrs. Rafferty sends a meaning smile around the table, "Billy's got troubles of his own. So let's not be too hard on him."

"Isn't he seeing somebody in your Clinic?" Dotty asks me in a whisper. I just have time to nod, when Mrs. Rafferty's clear green eye silences us like an ice bath.

"I've got a complaint myself, Mrs. Rafferty," Cora puts in, taking advantage of the interruption. "What's going *on* down there at Admissions, I wonder? I tell our patients to come in an hour early for appointments with the girls in Social Service, so they'll have plenty of time to get through the line downstairs and pay the cashier and all, and that's *still* not early enough. They call up frantic from downstairs, ten minutes late already, and say the line's not moving for half an hour, and the Social Service girls on my end are waiting too, so what should I do in a case like that?"

Mrs. Rafferty's eyes drop, for the briefest moment, to her notes, as if she had the answer to Cora's question outlined there. She seems almost embarrassed.

"Some of the other girls have complained of that too, Cora," she says finally, looking up. "We're short a girl at Admissions, so it's a terrible job to do all the processing . . ."

"Can't they *get* a guhl?" Mary Ellen asks boldly. "I mean, what's holding them up?"

Mrs. Rafferty exchanges a quick look with Minnie Dapkins. Minnie rubs her pale, papery hands together and licks at her lips in that rabbity way she has. Outside the open windows a small wind has suddenly risen, and it sounds as if it is beginning to rain, though it is probably only the rustle and scrape of papers starting to blow about down in the street. "I guess I may as well come straight out and *tell* everybody," Mrs. Rafferty says then. "Some of you know already, Minnie here knows, the reason we're holding up filling that position is . . . Emily Russo. You tell them, Minnie."

"Emily Russo," Minnie announces with funereal awe, "has got *can*cer. She's in this Hospital right now. I want to tell you, anybody who knows her, she might like company. She still can have visitors on account of she's got no kin to stand by . . ."

"Gee, I didn't know that," Mary Ellen says slowly. "That's a shame."

"It was the last Cancer Check showed it up," says Mrs. Rafferty. "She's just hanging on by a *thread*. Those new drugs help with the pain, of course. The only thing is, sick as she is, Emily's *count*ing on coming back to her job. She *loves* that job, it's been her life these forty years, and Doctor Gilman doesn't want to tell her the hard facts as to how she isn't ever going back for fear of giving her a shock and all. Everybody who comes in to see her, she asks, 'Is the job filled yet? Have they got anybody yet down in Admissions?' The minute that job's filled Emily'll think it's her own death warrant, plain and simple."

"How about a substitute?" Cora wants to know. "You could say whoever-it-was was pinch-hitting, sort of."

Mrs. Rafferty shakes her smooth, gilded head. "No, Emily's to the point she wouldn't believe it, she'd think we were just jollying her along. People in her state get *aw*fully keen. We can't risk that. I go down to Admissions myself, when I can, and lend a hand. It's only," her voice drops, sober as an undertaker's, "a little while now, Doctor Gilman says."

Minnie looks about to cry. The whole meeting is in a worse state than when Mrs. Rafferty walked in, everybody bowing their heads over their cigarettes or picking away at their nail polish. "Now, now, girls, don't take on so," Mrs. Rafferty says, with a bright, rallying glance round. "Emily couldn't be in a better place for care, I'm sure we'll all agree, and Doctor Gilman is like a relative to her, she's known him these ten years. And you can go visit her, she'd love that . . ."

"How about flowers?" Mary Ellen puts in. There is a general murmur of approval. Every time anybody in our group gets sick, or engaged, or married, or a baby (though that is a lot rarer than the rest) or a Service Award, we chip in and send flowers, or a suitable gift, and cards. This is the first terminal case I've been in on, though; if I do say so, the girls couldn't have been sweeter about it.

"How about pink, something cheerful?" Ida Kline suggests.

"A wreath, why not?" a recently engaged little typist from the Pool says softly. "A big pink wreath, carnations maybe."

"Not a *wreath*, girls!" Mrs. Rafferty groans. "With Emily so touchy not a *wreath*, for heaven's sake!"

"A vase, then," says Dotty. "The nurses are always complaining about no vases. A real nice vase, maybe from the Hospital Gift Shop, they have these im*por*ted vases, and a mixed bouquet in the vase from the Hospital Florist's."

"Now that is a very good idea, Dorothy." Mrs. Rafferty sounds relieved. "That's much more the type of thing. How many of you girls agree on a vase with a mixed bouquet?" Everybody, including the little typist, raises their hands. "Now I'll just put you in charge of that, Dorothy," Mrs. Rafferty says. "Leave your contributions with Dorothy, girls, before you go, and we'll send around a card this afternoon for everyone to sign."

The meeting breaks up, then, everybody talking to everybody else, and some of the girls are already digging dollar bills out of their bags and shoving them across the table at Dotty.

"Quiet!" Mrs. Rafferty calls out. "Quiet, please, one more *min*ute, girls!" In the hush that follows, the siren of a nearing ambulance raises and lets fall its banshee wail, passing under our windows, fading around the corner, and ceasing at last at the Emergency Ward entrance. "I meant to tell you. About the *hur*ricane, girls, in case you were wondering what the procedure is. The latest bulletin from the Head Office says things may start blowing up around noon, but you're not to *wo*rry. Keep calm. Business as usual" (amused laughter from the Typing Pool) "and above all don't show any con*cern* you may have over the hurricane to the patients. They'll be nervous enough without that. Those of you who live far out, if it's too bad, can stay over in the Hospital tonight. Cots are being set up in the halls of the Clinics Building, and we have the third floor all marked out for you girls, barring any emergency."

At this point, the swinging doors open with a bump, and a nurse walks in pushing the coffee-maker on a metal food-cart. Her rubber-soled shoes creak as though she was stepping on live mice. "Meeting adjourned," says Mrs. Rafferty. "Coffee, everyone."

Dotty draws me away from the crush around the coffee urn. "Cora's bound to have coffee, but that stuff's so bitter I can't stomach it. And in paper cups, yet." Dotty makes a little grimace of distaste. "Why don't you and me go blow this money on a vase and flowers for Miss Emily right here and now."

"Okay." Leaving the room with Dotty, I notice she is walking with short choppy strides. "Say, what's with you? You don't *want* to buy a vase?"

"It's not a *vase* I mind, it's the thought of that old lady up there being fed all this soft soap. She's going to die, she should have decent time to get used to the idea, see a priest, not hear everything's finesy-winesy." Dotty started taking a novitiate, she told me once, before she knew what the world was about, only, she said, she could no more keep her eyes down and her hands folded neatly in her sleeves or her tongue still than she could stand on her head and recite the Greek alphabet backwards. Every now and then, though, I feel her convent training showing through, like the sheen of her fair skin under the pink and peach-colored powder she uses.

"You should have been a missionary," I say. By this time we are up to the Gift Shop, a spiffy bandbox of a place, with fancy goods stacked from floor to ceiling—fluted vases, breakfast cups enameled with hearts-and-flowers, wedding-dress dolls and china bluebirds, gilt-edged card decks, cultured pearls, all you can think of, and every bit of it priced too high for anybody but a loving relative with his mind on something besides his pocketbook. "She's better off not knowing," I add, since Dotty doesn't say anything.

"I've got half a mind to *tell* her." Dotty picks up a big purple bubble-glass vase with a wide ruffle of glass around the rim and glares at it. "This We-know-better-than-you-do business around here gives me the creeps every so often. I sometimes think if there *weren't* any Cancer Checkups or any National Diabetes Weeks with booths in the hall for you to test your own sugar, there wouldn't be so much cancer or diabetes, if you see what I mean."

"Now you're talking like those Christian Science types," I say. "And by the way, I think that vase is too loud for an old lady like Miss Emily."

Dotty gives me an odd little smile, takes the vase up to the saleslady at the counter and plonks down six dollars for it. Now instead of keeping to the kitty money she has left over after blowing most of it on the vase, Dotty adds a couple of dollars of her own, and, I must admit, so do I, without much prodding on her part. When the florist next door comes up, rubbing his hands and looking equally ready for congratulations or condolences, to ask what we want, a dozen long-stemmed roses, or maybe a bachelor's-button and babies'-breath corsage with silver ribbon, Dotty holds out the purple bubble-glass vase. "Something of everything, buster. Fill her up."

The florist peers at Dotty, one side of his mouth skipping up in a little smile, the other side waiting until he can be sure she's just joshing him. "Come on, come on." Dotty thumps the vase up and down on the glass counter, causing the florist to wince and rapidly relieve her of it. "Like I said. Tea roses, carnations, some of those whatyamacallums . . ."

The florist's eyes follow Dotty's finger. "Gladioluses," he supplies in a pained tone.

"Gladolus. Some of them, different colors—red, orange, yellow, you know. And a couple of those purple irises . . ."

"Ah, they'll match the vase," the florist says, starting to get into the spirit of the thing. "*And* an assortment of anemones?"

"That too," Dotty says. "Except it sounds like a rash."

We are out of the florist's in short order, through the covered passageway between the Clinics Building and the Hospital proper, and up on an elevator to Miss Emily's floor, Dotty bearing the purple vase jammed with this bouquet.

"Miss Emily?" Dotty whispers as we tiptoe into the four-bed ward. A nurse glides out from behind the curtains drawn around the bed in the far corner by the window.

"Shh." She puts her fingers to her lips and points back at the curtains. "In there. Don't stay too long."

Miss Emily is sunk back into the pillows, her eyes open and filling most of her face, her hair spread out in a gray fan on the pillow round her head. Bottles of all sorts are on the medicine table, on the floor under the bed, and hung up around the bed. Thin rubber tubes lead off from a couple of the bottles, one tube disappearing under the bedcovers and one tube going right up into Miss Emily's left nostril. There is no sound in the room but the dry rustle of Miss Emily's breathing, no motion but the faint heave of the sheet over her chest and the air bubbles sending up their rhythmic silver balloons in one of these bottles of fluid. In the unhealthy storm-light from the window Miss Emily looks like a wax dummy, except for her eyes, which fix on us. I can almost feel them burning into my skin, they are so keen.

"We brought these flowers, Miss Emily." I point to the enormous, multi-colored vaseful of hothouse blooms Dotty is setting down on the medicine table. The table is so small she first has to clear away all the jars and glasses and pitchers and spoons on to the bottom shelf to make room.

Miss Emily's eyes slide to this heap of flowers. Something flickers there. I feel I am watching two candles at the end of a long hall, two pinpoint flames blowing and recovering in a dark wind. Outside the window the sky is blacker than a cast-iron skillet.

"The girls sent them." Dotty takes Miss Emily's inert, waxen hand from where it lies on the coverlet. "The card'll be up later, everybody's signing it, only we didn't want to wait with the flowers."

Miss Emily tries to speak. A faint hiss and rattle escape her lips, no words you can make out.

Still, Dotty seems to know what she means. "The job is there, Miss Emily," she says, spacing her words clear and slow, the way you explain things to a very young child. "They're holding it open." The selfsame words Mrs. Rafferty would use, I thought wonderingly. Only Mrs. Rafferty would add something to spoil it: You'll be up and around in a jiffy, Miss Emily, don't you fret. Or, You'll be getting your Gold Fifty Year Service Bracelet yet, Miss Emily, just you wait and see. The queer thing is, Dotty doesn't give any impression of twisting the facts into a fib. She is telling the honest truth, saying: Everybody is flying around like chickens with their heads off in Admissions, Miss Emily, because they want you to know you aren't replaceable. Not so soon, not so fast.

Miss Emily lets the lids droop over her eyes. Her hand goes limp in Dotty's palm, and she sighs, a sigh that passes with a shudder through her whole body.

"She knows," Dotty says to me as we leave Miss Emily's bed. "She knows now."

"But you didn't *tell* her. Not in so many words."

"Whaddayou think I am?" Dotty is indignant. "No heart or something? Say," she breaks off suddenly, as we step out of the doorway into the hall, "who's that?"

A lean, slight figure is propped up against the wall in the empty corridor a short way down from Miss Emily's door. As we approach, the figure flattens back against the wall, as if it could by some miracle become part of the pale, green-painted plaster material and vanish from sight. In the dim corridor, the electric lights give the effect of early nightfall.

"Billy *Moni*han!" Dotty exclaims. "What in the name of goodness are *you* doing here?"

"Wuh-wuh-waiting," Billy manages to squeak, his face flushing a painful shade of red under the crimson overlay of pimples and boils. He is a very short boy, almost as short as Dotty, and extremely thin, although he has attained his full growth and has nothing more to expect in that line. His long black hair is slicked back with some sort of redolent hair oil and shows the furrows of a comb drawn recently through the glossed, patent-leather surface.

"Just what," Dotty straightens to her full height, and in her heels she has the edge on Billy, "do you think you're doing hanging around up here?"

"Juh-just . . . wuh-waiting." Billy ducks his head to avoid Dotty's gimlet eye. He seems to be making an effort to swallow his tongue so as to be beyond all communication whatsoever.

"You should be trotting up records from Record Room in the Clinics Building right this minute," Dotty says. "You don't know Miss Emily from Adam, you leave Miss Emily alone, hear?"

A weird, indecipherable gurgle escapes from Billy's throat. "Shuh-shuh-she suh-said I cuh-could come," he gets out then.

Dotty gives a sharp, exasperated snort. Still, something in Billy's eye makes her turn away and leave him to his devices. By the time the elevator stops for us, Billy has melted, pimples, slick hair, stutter, and all, into Miss Emily's room.

"I don't like that boy, that boy's a regular," Dotty pauses for the right word, "a regular *vul*ture. There's something funny with him these days, let me tell you. He hangs around that Emergency Ward entrance, you'd think the Lord God himself was supposed to come in that door and announce Judgment Day."

"He's seeing Doctor Resnik in our place," I say, "only I haven't got any of the Audograph records on him to type up yet, so I don't know. Did it come on sudden, this vulture business?"

Dotty shrugs. "All I know is, he scared Ida Kline sick in Typing Pool last week, telling her some story or other about a woman came in to Skin Clinic all purple and swollen fat as an elephant in a wheelchair with this tropical disease. Ida couldn't eat her lunch for thinking of it. They've got a name for it, these people who hang around bodies and all. Nega . . . negafills. They get real bad, they start digging up bodies right out of the graveyard."

"I was doing an Intake Report on a woman yesterday," I say. "She sounds something like that. Couldn't believe her little girl had died, kept seeing her around, at church services, in the grocery store. Visited the graveyard day in, day out. One day, she says, the little girl comes to see her, dressed in this white lace smock, and says not to worry, she's in heaven and well taken care of, doing just fine."

"I wonder," Dotty says. "I wonder how do you cure that?"

From the hospital cafeteria where we are sitting around one of the big tables over dessert and signing Miss Emily's Get-Well-Quick card, I can see the rain swatting in long lines against the windows overlooking the Garden Court. Some wealthy lady had the Court built and filled up with grass and trees and flowers so the doctors and nurses could have something prettier than brick walls and gravel to look at while they ate. Now the windows are streaming so you can't even see the color green through the sheets of water.

"You girls going to stay over?" Cora's voice is wobbly as the Jell-O she is spooning up. "I mean, I don't know what to *do* with Mother home alone. What if the lights go out, she might break a hip hunting around for candles in the cellar in the dark, and the roof shingles are none too good, they leak through in the attic even if it's just a shower . . ."

"You stay, Cora," Dotty says with decision. "You try going home in *this* soup, you'll be drowned silly. You call up home tomorrow morning, you'll find your mother happy as a cricket with the storm blowing itself out a hundred miles away up Maine someplace."

"Look!" I say, partly to distract Cora. "Here's Mrs. Rafferty just come in with her tray. Let's get her to sign." Before any of us can wave, Mrs. Rafferty spots us and comes over, a white sloop in full sail, her stethoscope earrings bobbing on either side of a face that means nothing but bad news.

"Girls," she says, seeing the card lying open there on the table in front of us, "girls, I don't like to be a bearer of sad tidings, but I have to tell you that card won't be needed."

Cora turns the color of putty under her freckles, a spoonful of strawberry Jell-O suspended halfway to her mouth.

"Emily Russo passed away not an hour ago." Mrs. Rafferty bows her head for a second, and lifts it with a certain fortitude. "It's all for the *best*, girls, you know that as well as I do. She passed on easy as could be, so don't let it get you down now. We've got," she nods her head briskly at the blind, streaming panes, "other people to think of."

"Was Miss Emily," Dotty asks, stirring cream into her coffee with an odd absorption, "was Miss Emily *alone* at the last?"

Mrs. Rafferty hesitates. "No, Dorothy," she says then. "No. She was *not* alone. Billy Monihan was with her when she passed on. The nurse on duty says he seemed *very* affected by it, very moved by the old lady. He said," Mrs. Rafferty adds, "he said to the nurse Miss Emily was his aunt."

"But Miss Emily doesn't have any brothers or sisters," Cora protests. "Minnie told us. She doesn't have *any*body."

"Be that as it may," Mrs. Rafferty seems eager to close the subject, "be that as it may, the boy was very moved. Very moved by the whole thing."

With it raining cats and dogs, and a wind blowing to flatten the city itself, no patients come in to the office all that afternoon. Nobody, that is, except old Mrs. Tomolillo. Miss Taylor has just gone out to get two cups of coffee at the dispenser down the hall when Mrs. Tomolillo walks in on me, furious and wet as a witch in her black wool year-round dress, waving a soggy lump of papers. "Where's Doctor Chrisman, Doctor Chrisman, I want to know."

The soggy lump of papers turns out to be Mrs. Tomolillo's own record book which patients are never under any circumstances allowed to get hold of. It is a fine mess, the red, blue, and green ink entries of the numerous doctors in the numerous Clinics Mrs. Tomolillo frequents blurring into a wild rainbow, dripping colored beads of water and ink even as I take it from her hands. "Lies, lies, lies," Mrs. Tomolillo hisses at me, so I can't get a word in. "Lies."

"What lies, Mrs. Tomolillo?" I ask then, in a clear, loud voice, for Mrs. Tomolillo is notably hard of hearing, although she refuses to learn to operate an aid. "I'm sure Doctor Chrisman . . ."

"Lies, lies he's written in that book. I am a good woman, my husband dead. You let me just get my hands on that man, I'll teach him lies . . ."

I glance quickly out into the hall. Mrs. Tomolillo is flexing her strong fingers in an alarming fashion. A man on crutches, one pants leg empty and folded up in a neat tuck at the hip, is swinging along past the door. After him comes an aide from Amputee Clinic, lugging a pink, artificial leg and half an artificial torso. Mrs. Tomolillo quiets at the sight of the little procession. Her hands fall to her sides, losing themselves in the folds of her voluminous black skirt.

"I'll tell Doctor Chrisman, Mrs. Tomolillo. I'm sure there's been some mistake, don't you get upset." Behind my back, the window rattles in its frame as if some great drafty giant out there is trying to shoulder into the light. The rain is striking the pane now with the force of pistol cracks.

"Lies . . ." Mrs. Tomolillo hisses, but more placidly, rather like a kettle just coming off the boil. "You tell him."

"I'll tell him. Oh, Mrs. Tomolillo . . ."

"Yes?" She pauses in the doorway, black and portentous as one of the Fates, caught in a squall of her own making.

"Where shall I tell Doctor Chrisman the record book came from?"

"Down there in that room," she says simply. "That room where all the books are. I ask for it, they give it to me."

"I see." The number on Mrs. Tomolillo's record, printed in indelible ink, reads Nine-three-six-two-five. "I see, I see. Thank you, Mrs. Tomolillo."

◆

The Clinics Building, big as it is, founded solid on concrete and built of brick and stone, seems shaken to its roots as Dotty and I cross through the first-floor halls and down the passageway to the cafeteria in the main Hospital for a hot supper. We can hear the sirens, loud and faint, in and around the city—fire engines, ambulances, police wagons. The Emergency Ward parking lot is jammed with ambulances and private cars pouring in from the outlying towns—people with heart attacks, people with collapsed lungs, people with galloping hysteria. And to top it off, there is a power failure, so we have to feel our way along the walls in the semi-dark. Everywhere doctors and interns are snapping out orders, nurses gliding by white as ghosts in their uniforms, and stretchers with people bundled on them—groaning, or crying, or still— being rolled this way and that. In the middle of it all, a familiar shape darts past us and down a flight of unlit stone steps leading to the First and Second Basements.

"Isn't that him?"

"Him who?" Dotty wants to know. "I can't see a thing in this pitch, I should get glasses."

"Billy. From the Record Room."

"They must be having him whip up records on the double for the Emergency cases," Dotty says. "They need all the extra hands they can get when things are thick as this."

For some reason I can't bring myself to tell Dotty about Mrs. Tomolillo. "He's not such a bad kid," I find myself saying, in spite of what I know about Mrs. Tomolillo, and Emily Russo, and Ida Kline and the elephant woman.

"Not bad," Dotty says, ironically. "If you happen to like vampires."

Mary Ellen and Dotty are sitting cross-legged on one of the cots in the third-floor annex, trying to play social solitaire by the light of a purse flashlight somebody has dug up, when Cora comes flying down the hall toward the row of us propped in the cots.

Dotty lays a red nine on a black ten. "You get hold of your mother? The roof still on at your place?"

In the pale, luminous circle cast by the flashlight, Cora's eyes are wide, wet around the edges.

"Say," Mary Ellen leans toward her, "you haven't heard anything bad? You're as white as a sheet, Cora."

"It's not . . . it's not my *mother*," Cora brings out. "The lines are down, I couldn't even get through. It's that boy, that *Billy* . . ."

Everybody is very quiet all of a sudden.

"He was running up and down these *stairs*," Cora says, her voice so teary you'd think she was talking about her kid brother or something. "Up and down, up and down with these records, and no lights, and he's in such a hurry he's skipping two, three steps. And he *fell*. He fell a whole flight . . ."

"Where is he?" Dotty asks, slowly putting down her hand of cards. "Where is he now?"

"Where *is* he?" Cora's voice rises an octave. "Where is he, he's dead."

It's a funny thing. The minute those words are out of Cora's mouth, everybody forgets how little Billy was, and how really ridiculous looking, with that stammer and that awful complexion. With all this worry about the hurricane, and nobody able to get through to their folks, memory throws a kind of halo around him. You'd think he'd laid down and died for the whole bunch of us sitting there on those cots.

"He wouldn't of died," Mary Ellen observes, "if he hadn't been helping out other folks."

"Seeing how things are," Ida Kline puts in, "I'd like to take back what I said about him the other day, about him and that woman with the elephant sickness. He didn't know what a bad stomach I've got or anything."

Only Dotty is silent.

Mary Ellen turns out the flashlight then, and everybody takes off their dresses in the dark and lies down. Dotty climbs into the cot at the far end of the row, next to mine. All along the corridor you can hear the rain, quieted now, drumming steadily against the panes. After a while the sound of regular breathing is rising from most of the cots.

"Dotty," I whisper. "Dotty, you awake?"

"Sure," Dotty whispers back. "I've got asomnia like nobody's business."

"So Dotty, what do you think?"

"You want to know what I think?" Dotty's voice seems wafted to my ears from a small, invisible point in a great darkness. "I think that boy's a lucky boy. For once in his life he's got sense. For once in his life, I think that boy's going to be a hero."

And what with the newspaper stories, and the church ceremonies, and the Posthumous Gold Medal awarded by the Hospital Director to Billy's parents after the storm is blown over, I have to give Dotty credit. She's right. She's absolutely right.

The It-Doesn't-Matter Suit

Ts,* before 16 September 1959, Lilly Library

Max Nix was seven years old, and the youngest of seven brothers. First came Paul, the eldest and tallest of all seven. Then came Emil. Then Otto and Walter, and Hugo and Johann. Last came Max. Max's whole name was Maximilian, but because he was only seven he did not need such a big name. So everybody called him just Max.

Max lived with Mama and Papa Nix and his six brothers in a little village called Winkelburg, halfway up a steep mountain. The mountain had three peaks, and on all three peaks, winter and summer, sat caps of snow, like three big scoops of vanilla ice cream. On nights when the moon rose round and bright as an orange balloon you could hear the foxes barking in the dark pine forest high above Max's house. On clear, sunlit days you could see the river winking and blinking far, far below in the valley, small and thin as a silver ribbon.

Max liked where he lived.

Max was happy, except for one thing.

More than anything else in the world, Max Nix wanted a suit of his own.

He had a green sweater and green wool socks and a green felt hunting hat with a turkey feather in it. He even had a fine pair of leather knickers with carved bone buttons. But everybody knows a sweater and a pair of knickers are not the same thing as a suit—a made-to-order suit with long trousers and a jacket to match.

Wherever Max Nix looked in Winkelburg—east and west, north and south, high and low and round about—he saw people wearing suits. Some people had suits for work, and these were very sturdy suits of brown or gray cloth. Some people had suits for weddings, and these were very handsome suits with striped silk waistcoats. Some people had suits for skiing, and these were gay blue or red suits with rows of snowflakes or edelweiss embroidered on the cuffs and collars. Some people had summer suits of linen, white and crisp as letter paper. Papa Nix and Paul and Emil and Otto and Walter and Hugo and Johann all had suits. *Everybody* on the mountain had some sort of suit except Max.

---

* Typescript has typed and holograph additions and corrections by SP. Typed at top right: 'Sylvia Plath / 26 Elmwood Road / Wellesley, Massachusetts.' SP annotated at top left: 'Knopf: Sept 16.' Beneath the title, SP added by hand '(Max Nix & the Mustard Suit)'.

Now Max did not want a suit *just* for work
  (that would be too plain)
or *just* for weddings
  (that would be too fancy)
or *just* for skiing
  (that would be too hot)
or *just* for summer
  (that would be too cool).
He wanted a suit for All-Year-Round.
He wanted a suit for doing Everything.

Not too plain a suit for birthdays and holidays, and not too fancy a suit for school and calling the cows home. Not too hot a suit for hiking in July, and not too cool a suit for coasting in the snow.

If Max had a suit for All-Year-Round, the butcher and the baker, and the blacksmith and the goldsmith, and the tinker and the tailor, and the innkeeper and the schoolteacher, and the grocer and the goodwives, and the minister and the mayor, and everybody else in Winkelburg would flock to their doors and windows when he went by. "Look!" they would murmur to one another. "There goes Maximilian in his marvelous suit!"

If Max had a suit for doing Everything, the cats in the alleys and the dogs on the cobbles of Winkelburg would follow him uptown and downtown, purring and grrring with admiration.

That was the sort of suit Max wanted.

That was the sort of suit Max was dreaming about the day the postman of Winkelburg knocked on the Nixs' door and delivered the big package.

The package was shaped like a long, flattish box.

It was wrapped round with heavy brown wrapping paper.

It was tied with red string.

Across the top of the package Max spelled out N-I-X in large black letters. The first name had been rained on and not even the Postmaster of Winkelburg could read it. So nobody knew *which* Nix the package was for.

The package might be for Papa Nix or Mama Nix, or Paul or Emil, or Otto or Walter, or Hugo or Johann. It might even be for Max. Nobody could tell for sure.

Mama Nix had just baked a batch of apricot tarts. Everybody sat around the kitchen table, wondering who the package was for, and who it was from, and what was in it, and eating up the apricot tarts one by one.

It was not Christmastime, so it was not a Christmas present.

It was not near anybody's birthday, so it was not a birthday present.

"It is too short," said Paul, "to be a pair of skis."

"It is too small," said Emil, "to be a toboggan."

"It is too light," said Otto, lifting the package easily, "to be a bicycle."

"It is too wide," said Walter, "to be a fishing rod."

"It is too large," said Hugo, "to be a hunting knife."

Johann put his ear to the package and gave it a little shake. "It is too quiet," he said, "to be a cow bell."

Max did not say anything.

It is too fine, he thought to himself, to be for me.

At last the apricot tarts were all gone, and still nobody could guess what was in the package.

"Let us open it," everybody said.

Papa Nix untied the knot in the red string. Mama Nix unwrapped the brown paper. Inside the brown paper was a gray cardboard box. Paul lifted the lid off the box. Inside the gray box was a lot of white tissue paper. Emil and Otto and Walter and Hugo and Johann and Max all helped to pull away some of the tissue paper.

And there in the gray box with a wreath of white tissue paper around it lay a

> woolly
> whiskery
> brand new
> mustard-yellow
> suit

with three brass buttons shining like mirrors on the front of it, and two brass buttons at the back, and a brass button on each cuff.

"What a strange suit," said Papa Nix. "I have never seen anything quite like it."

"It is made of good strong cloth," said Mama Nix, feeling the yellow wool between thumb and forefinger. "*This* suit will not wear out in a hurry."

"It is a handsome suit!" said Paul.

"Light as a feather!" said Emil.

"Bright as butter!" said Otto.

"Warm as toast!" said Walter.

"Simply fine!" said Hugo.

"Dandy!" said Johann.

"O my!" said Max.

Every one of the seven brothers wished he owned just such a suit.

But the suit looked as if it might be Papa Nix's size. So Papa Nix tried it on. The jacket was wide enough, and the trousers were long enough. The suit fit Papa Nix to a T.

"I shall wear the suit to work tomorrow," he said.

Papa Nix worked in a bank. He thought how it would be to wear the woolly, whiskery, brand new, mustard-yellow suit to work. Such a suit had never been seen before in all Winkelburg. What would the people say? Perhaps they would think the suit was too gay for a sensible banker. Those brass buttons would flash out like big coins. All the other bankers wore dark blue or dark gray suits. None of them ever wore a mustard-yellow suit.

At last Papa Nix sighed and said, "I am too big to wear a mustard-yellow suit."

Paul held his breath.

"I will give the suit to Paul," said Papa Nix.

So Paul tried on the mustard-yellow suit. Paul was as tall as Papa Nix, so the trousers were the right length. He was not as broad as Papa Nix around the middle though, so the jacket hung about him in loose, flapping folds. But Mama Nix was clever with needle and thread. She took a tuck here and a stitch there. When she was through, the suit fit Paul to a T.

"I shall wear the suit skiing tomorrow," he said.

Paul often went skiing with his friends. He thought how it would be to wear the woolly, whiskery, brand new, mustard-yellow suit skiing. Such a suit had never been seen before in all Winkelburg. What would his friends say? Perhaps they would think yellow was a silly color for a ski-suit. He would look like a meadow of sunflowers against the snow. All his friends wore red ski-suits or blue ski-suits. None of them ever wore a mustard-yellow suit.

At last Paul sighed and said, "I, also, am too big to wear a mustard-yellow suit."

Emil held his breath.

"Let Emil try on the suit," said Paul.

So Emil tried on the mustard-yellow suit. Emil was as broad as Paul, but shorter. The cuffs of the jacket covered his hands, and the cuffs of the trousers folded down over his shoes. But Mama Nix took a tuck here and a stitch there. When she was through the suit fit Emil to a T.

"I shall wear the suit in the toboggan race tomorrow," he said.

Emil was a member of the Winkelburg toboggan team. Once a month the Winkelburg team raced the team of a town on the other side of the mountain. He thought how it would be to wear the woolly, whiskery, brand new, mustard-yellow suit in the toboggan races. Such a suit had never been seen before in all Winkelburg. What would his teammates say? Perhaps they would think he was trying to show off in the mustard-yellow suit. He would look like a streak of lightning going down the toboggan track. All his teammates wore brown zipper jackets and brown pants. None of them ever wore a mustard-yellow suit.

At last Emil sighed and said, "I, also, am too big to wear a mustard-yellow suit."

Otto held his breath.

"Maybe the suit will be right for Otto," said Emil.

So Otto tried on the mustard-yellow suit. Otto was almost as tall as Emil, only his shoulders were not quite so broad. The jacket drooped a little. But Mama Nix took a tuck here and a stitch there. When she was through the suit fit Otto to a T.

"I shall wear the suit on my paper route tomorrow," he said.

Otto delivered newspapers on his bicycle. He thought how it would be to wear the woolly, whiskery, brand new, mustard-yellow suit on his paper route. Such a suit had never been seen before in all Winkelburg. What would his customers say? Perhaps they would think the suit was too fancy for a paperboy. He might splash mud on it or be caught in the rain, and then what a sorry sight he would be! All the other paperboys wore their old clothes when they delivered papers. None of them ever wore a brand new mustard-yellow suit.

At last Otto sighed and said, "I, also, am too big to wear a mustard-yellow suit."

Walter held his breath.

"If the suit fits me, it should fit Walter," said Otto.

So Walter tried on the mustard-yellow suit. Walter was a little shorter than Otto, and a little thinner. But Mama Nix took a tuck here and a stitch there and moved the brass buttons over an inch. When she was through the suit fit Walter to a T.

"I shall wear the suit ice-fishing tomorrow," he said.

Walter often went ice-fishing in Winkelburg Lake in the winter. He thought how it would be to wear the woolly, whiskery, brand new, mustard-yellow suit ice-fishing. Such a suit had never been seen before in all Winkelburg. What would the fish think? Perhaps the suit would frighten them away. It would glow through the ice like a bright sun. The other fishermen all wore green suits in the summer so the fish could not tell them from leaves, and brown suits in the winter so the fish could not tell them from tree trunks. None of them ever wore a mustard-yellow suit.

At last Walter sighed and said, "I, also, am too big to wear a mustard-yellow suit."

Hugo held his breath.

"Perhaps Hugo might like to wear it," said Walter.

So Hugo tried on the mustard-yellow suit. Hugo was a good deal shorter than Walter, but Mama Nix snipped a bit here and trimmed a bit there with her scissors and turned the thread-ends under. When she was through the suit fit Hugo to a T.

"I shall wear the suit hunting tomorrow," he said.

Hugo often went fox-hunting in the forest above Winkelburg, for the foxes stole the plump Winkelburg chickens. He thought how it would be to wear the woolly, whiskery, brand new, mustard-yellow suit fox-hunting. Such a suit had never been seen before in all Winkelburg. What would the fox think? Perhaps the fox would just hide in a hole and laugh at him. The brass buttons would beam like lanterns from far off and warn the fox he was coming. All the other hunters wore checked and speckled suits so the fox could not see them easily in the checked and speckled shade of the forest. None of them ever wore a mustard-yellow suit.

At last Hugo sighed and said, "I, also, am too big to wear a mustard-yellow suit."

Johann held his breath.

"Let's see how the suit looks on Johann," said Hugo.

So Johann tried on the mustard-yellow suit. Johann was shorter and rounder than Hugo, but Mama Nix snipped here and clipped there and moved the buttons back to the edge of the jacket. When she was through the suit fit Johann to a T.

"I shall wear the suit for milking the cows tomorrow," he said.

Johann took turns with his six brothers milking Papa Nix's cows. He thought how it would be to wear the woolly, whiskery, brand new, mustard-yellow suit for milking the cows. Such a suit had never been seen before in all Winkelburg. What would the cows think? Perhaps they would take him for a bundle of whiskery yellow hay and nibble at his collar. Everybody else wore blue overalls for milking cows. Nobody ever wore a mustard-yellow suit.

At last Johann sighed and said, "Even *I* am too big to wear a mustard-yellow suit."

Max could hardly keep from jumping up and down, but he held still as a mouse and waited to see what would happen.

"Max has no suit," said Johann.

"Goodness!" said Papa Nix.

"Gracious!" said Mama Nix.

"Let it be Max's suit," everybody said, nodding and smiling.

So Max tried on the mustard-yellow suit. Max was the shortest and thinnest of all the Nix brothers, but Mama Nix snipped and stitched and took tucks and moved buttons. When she was through the suit fit Max as if it was made-to-order.

"I shall wear the suit," Max said, "today and tomorrow and the day after that."

Max went to school in his mustard-yellow suit. He walked straight and he sat tall, and pretty soon the schoolchildren began to wish they had suits like the suit Max wore. So even though nobody in Winkelburg had ever seen such a suit before

IT DIDN'T MATTER.

Max went skiing in his mustard-yellow suit. He slipped and slid for a way on the seat of his pants, but the cloth of the suit was very strong and didn't rip so

IT DIDN'T MATTER.

Max rode his bicycle in his mustard-yellow suit. He got caught in the rain, but the drops ran right off the whiskery suit like drops off a duck's back so

IT DIDN'T MATTER.

Max went ice-fishing in his mustard-yellow suit. The fish came swimming up to see what gleamed so bright on the other side of the ice, and Max caught enough for supper. He got some fish scales on his suit, but everybody was so busy admiring Max's fish that they never noticed so

IT DIDN'T MATTER.

Max went coasting in his mustard-yellow suit. He tipped over once or twice and landed in a cold snowbank, but the woolly suit was very warm so

IT DIDN'T MATTER.

Max went fox-hunting in his mustard-yellow suit. The fox saw something yellow through the trees and thought it was a fat yellow Winkelburg chicken. His mouth started to water and he came running. Max caught the fox. He lost a brass button in the bushes, but the button shone out like a star in the dark forest and he found it again, so

IT DIDN'T MATTER.

Max milked the cows in his mustard-yellow suit. The suit's sunny color made the cows dream of buttercups and daisies in the spring meadows, and they mooed for happiness. When Max finished milking he had three pails full

of the creamiest milk ever seen in Winkelburg. Some pieces of hay stuck to the suit, but the hay was yellow and the suit was yellow and the hay didn't show so
 IT DIDN'T MATTER.

Max walked uptown and downtown and round about Winkelburg in his mustard-yellow suit. When he went by, the butcher and the baker, the blacksmith and the goldsmith, the tinker and the tailor, the innkeeper and the schoolteacher, the grocer and the goodwives, the minister and the mayor all leaned out of their doors and windows.

"Look!" they murmured to one another. "There goes Maximilian in his marvelous suit."

And the cats in the alleys and the dogs on the cobbles of Winkelburg followed at his heels, purring and grrring with admiration for Max Nix and his

>wonderful
>woolly
>whiskery
>brand new
>mustard-yellow
>IT-DOESN'T-MATTER
>SUIT.

The Fifty-ninth Bear

Written: 16 September 1959[*]
Published: *London Magazine* (February 1961): 11–20

By the time they arrived, following the map of the Grand Loop in the brochure, a dense mist shrouded the rainbow pools; the parking lot and the boardwalks were empty. Except for the sun, already low above the violet hills, and the sun's image, red as a dwarf tomato lodged in the one small space of water visible, there was nothing to see. Still, enacting as they were a ritual of penance and forgiveness, they crossed the bridge over the scalding river. On either side, ahead and behind, columns of steam mushroomed above the surface of the

---

[*] SP also submitted to the *Atlantic Monthly* in the US. Smith College holds two typescripts of the story: one (heavily revised) with her Wellesley address and one with her Chalcot Square address. The version printed in *Johnny Panic and the Bible of Dreams* cut several hundred words and more closely matches the later typescript copy.

pools. Veil after veil of whiteness raveled across the boardwalk, erasing at random patches of the sky and the far hills. They moved slowly, enclosed by a medium at once intimate and insufferable, the sulfurous air warm and humid on their faces, on their hands and bare arms.

Norton dallied then, letting his wife drift on ahead. Her slender, vulnerable shape softened, wavered, as the mists thickened between them. She withdrew into a blizzard, into a fall of white water; she was nowhere. What had they not seen? The children squatting at the rim of the paintpots, boiling their breakfast eggs in rusty strainers; copper pennies winking up from cornucopias of sapphire water; the thunderous gushers pluming, now here, now there, across a barren ochre-and-oyster moonscape. She had insisted, not without her native delicacy, on the immense, mustard-colored canyon where, halfway down to the river, hawks and the shadows of hawks looped and hung like black beads on fine wire. She had insisted on the Dragon's Mouth, that hoarse, booming spate of mud-clogged water; and the Devil's Cauldron. He had waited for her habitual squeamishness to turn her away from the black, porridgey mass that popped and seethed a few yards from under her nose, but she bent over the pit, devout as a priestess in the midst of those vile exhalations. And it was Norton, after all, bareheaded in the full noon sun, squinting against the salt-white glare and breathing in the fumes of rotten eggs, who defaulted, overcome by headache. He felt the ground frail as a bird's skull under his feet, a mere shell of sanity and decorum between him and the dark entrails of the earth where the sluggish muds and scalding waters had their source.

To top it off, someone had stolen their desert water bag, simply pinched it from the front fender of the car while they were being elbowed along by the midday crowds on the boardwalk. Anybody might have done it: that man with a camera, that child, that Negress in the pink sprigged dress. Guilt diffused through the crowd like a drop of vermilion dye in a tumbler of clear water, staining them all. They were all thieves; their faces were blank, brutish, or sly. Disgust curdled in Norton's throat. Once in the car he slumped down, closed his eyes, and let Sadie drive. A cooler air fanned his temples. His hands and feet seemed to be lifting, elongating, pale and puffed with a dreamy yeast. Like a vast, luminous starfish he drifted, awash with sleep, his consciousness fisted somewhere there, dark and secret as a nut.

"Fifty-six," Sadie said.

Norton opened his eyes; they stung and watered as though someone had scoured them with sand while he drowsed. But it was a fine bear, black-furred and compact, purposefully skirting the edge of the forest. To left and right, the tall, mottled boles of pines speared skyward, spreading out, far overhead, their dark thatch of needles. Although the sun stood high, only a few splinters of light pierced the cool, blue-black mass of the trees. The bear-counting started as a game on their first day in the park, and continued still, five days later, long after they stopped listing license plates from different states and noticing when the mileage showed four, or five, or six identical figures in a row. Perhaps it was the bet that kept it going.

Sadie bet ten dollars on seeing fifty-nine bears by the end of their stay. Norton had set his figure carelessly at seventy-one. In secret, he hoped Sadie would win. She took games seriously, like a child. Losing wounded her, she was so trusting; and above all, she trusted her luck. Fifty-nine was Sadie's symbol of plenitude. For Sadie there were never "hundreds of mosquitoes," or "millions," or even "a great many," but always fifty-nine. Fifty-nine bears, she predicted breezily, without a second thought. Now that they were so close to that total—having numbered grandfather bears, mother bears and cubs, honey-colored bears and black bears, brown bears and cinnamon bears, bears up to their middles in trash cans, bears begging at the roadside, bears swimming the river, bears nosing around the tents and trailers at suppertime—they might well stick at fifty-nine bears. They were leaving the park the next day.

Away from the boardwalks, the spiels of rangers, the popular marvels, Norton revived a little. His headache, withdrawn to the far edge of awareness, circled and stalled there like some thwarted bird. As a boy, Norton had developed, quite by himself, a method of intense prayer—not to any image of God, but to what he liked to think of as the genius of a place, the fostering spirit of an ash grove, or a shoreline. What he prayed for was, in one guise or another, a private miracle: he contrived to be favored, by the sight of a doe, say, or the find of a lump of water-polished quartz. Whether his will merely coincided with circumstance, or really did force tribute, he could not be sure. Either way, he had a certain power. Now, lulled by the putter of the car, and feigning sleep, Norton began to will toward him all the animals of the forest—the fog-colored, delicately striated antelope, the lumbering, tousled buffalo, the red foxes, the bears. In his mind's eye he saw them pause, startled, as by some alien presence, in their deep thickets and noonday retreats. He saw them, one by one, turn and converge toward the center where he sat, fiercely, indefatigably willing the movement of each hoof and paw.

"Elk!' Sadie exclaimed, like a voice out of the depths of his head. The car swerved to a halt at the side of the road. Norton came to with a start. Other cars were pulling up beside them and behind them. Timorous as Sadie was, she had no fear of animals. She had a way with them. Norton had come upon her once, feeding a wild stag blueberries out of her hand, a stag whose hooves could, in one blow, have dashed her to the ground. The danger simply never occurred to her.

Now she hurried after the men in shirtsleeves, the women in cotton print dresses, the children of all ages, who were crowding to the verge of the road as to the scene of an astounding accident. The shoulder dropped steeply to a clearing in a thick growth of pines. Everybody carried a camera. Twirling dials, waving light meters, calling to relatives and friends above for fresh rolls of film, they plunged over the slope in a wave, slipping, lapsing, half-falling, in an avalanche of rust-colored pine needles and loose turf. Great-eyed, kingly under the burden of their spreading, dark-scalloped antlers, the elk knelt in the damp green bottom of the little valley.

As the people came charging and crying toward them, they rose with a slow, sleepy amazement and moved off, unhurried and detached, into the pathless wood beyond the clearing. Norton stood on the top of the slope with a quiet, insular dignity. He ignored the people about him, disgruntled now, and barging about noisily in the underbrush. In his mind he was forming an apology to the elk. He had meant well.

"I didn't even have time for a shot," Sadie was saying at his elbow. "It was pitch-dark down there anyway, I guess." Her fingers closed on the bare flesh of his upper arm, soft-tipped as limpets. "Let's go see that pool. The one that comes to a boil every fifteen minutes."

"You go," Norton said. "I have a headache, a touch of sunstroke, I think. I'll sit and wait for you in the car."

Sadie did not answer, but she ground the car into gear with an unmistakable wantonness, and Norton knew he had disappointed her. More and more during the second year of their marriage she seemed unwilling to go anywhere without him—to the market, to the bank, to the park. She clung to him, shy as a child, as if he provided a sanctum outside which she would be ruined, undone by brutal elements. He read her like a book. Even her tantrums were infantile, transparent. A prolonged din of pot-lids in the kitchen, a glass hurled to smithereens in the fireplace, a slammed door—these naïve stage effects testified to some straw too many in her slight load. The simplest question would free her tongue, her tears, and, after a decent interval, embraces, the act of love, would heal the last of her hurt.

Now, with a sense of impending storm, Norton watched Sadie stalk away from the car in the peaked straw hat with the red ribbon bow under the chin, her underlip set, pink and glistening, in a grieved pout. Then she passed, with the line of other tourists, over the glaring white horizon.

Often, in daydreams, Norton saw himself in the role of a widower: a hollow-cheeked, Hamletesque figure in somber suits, given to standing, abstracted, ravaged by casual winds, on lonely promontories and at the rail of ships, Sadie's slender, elegant white body embalmed, in a kind of bas relief, on the central tablet of his mind. It never occurred to Norton that his wife might outlive him. Her sensuousness, her simple pagan enthusiasms, her inability to argue in terms of anything but her immediate emotions—this was too flimsy, too gossamery a stuff to survive out from under the wings of his guardianship.

As he had guessed, Sadie's jaunt on her own was anything but satisfactory. The pool boiled up, right enough, a perfectly lovely shade of blue, but a freakish shift in wind flung the hot steam in her face and nearly scalded her to death. And somebody, some boy or group of boys, had spoken to her on the boardwalk and spoiled the whole thing. A woman could never be alone in peace; a solitary woman was a walking invitation to all sorts of impudence.

All this, Norton knew, was a bid for his company. But since the incident of the water bag, a revulsion from the crowds of tourists had been simmering at the base of his skull. When he thought of going out into the mobs again, his fingers twitched. He saw himself, from a great distance, from Olympus, pushing a child into a steaming pool, punching a fat man in the belly. His headache stabbed back out of the blue like a vulture's beak.

"Why don't we leave the rest till tomorrow?" he said. "Then I'd feel up to walking round with you."

"Today's our last *day*."

Norton couldn't think of an answer to that.

It was only when they passed the fifty-seventh bear that he realized how upset Sadie was. The bear lay stretched into the road ahead of them, a ponderous brown Sphinx occupying a pool of sunlight. Sadie could not have missed seeing him: she had to pull out into the left lane to get round, but she set her lips and said nothing, accelerated, and shot them past a bend in the road. Norton remembered hearing of a child who never turned his anger on the objects or people around him, but threw himself on the floor, kicking and crying, "I'll break my legs, I'll break my legs." Sadie was driving recklessly, now. When they came to the junction near the great rainbow pools, she drove by so fast that a group of people about to cross the road jumped back in alarm, and the ranger with them yelled out angrily, "Hey, slow down there!" A few hundred yards beyond the junction Sadie began to cry. Her face puckered up and her nose reddened; tears streamed into the corners of her mouth and over her chin.

"Pull up," Norton ordered at last, taking the reins in hand. The car bumped off on to the shoulder of the road, bucked once or twice, and stalled. Sadie collapsed like a rag doll over the steering wheel.

"I didn't ask anything else," she sobbed vaguely. "All I asked was the pools and the springs."

"Look," Norton said, "I know what's the matter with us. It's about two o'clock, and we've been driving around six hours without a bite."

Sadie's sobs quietened. She let him untie her straw hat and stroke her hair.

"We'll go along to Mammoth Junction," Norton went on, as if he were telling a soothing bedtime story, "and we'll have hot soup and sandwiches, and see if there's any mail, and we'll climb all the hot springs and stop at all the pools going back. How's that?"

Sadie nodded. He felt her hesitate for a second. Then she blurted, "Did you see the *bear*?"

"Of course I saw the bear," Norton said, hiding a smile. "How many is that, now?"

"Fifty-seven."

With the waning of the sun's force, the pleasant, pliable shape of Sadie's waist in the crook of his arm, Norton felt a new benevolence toward humanity bloom in him. The irritable flame at the base of his skull cooled. He started the car with a firm, complacent mastery.

Now Sadie strolled, well fed and at peace, a few yards ahead of him, invisible, swathed in a mist, but surely his as a lamb on a leash. Her innocence, her trustfulness, endowed him with the nimbus of a protecting god. He fathomed her; enclosed her. Still, he had never quite lost his awe of her body. Each time he undid her dress, unsheathed her from her electric silks and crisp laces he felt unaccountably bearish, a violator of her whiteness. He did not see, or did not care to see, how her submissiveness moved and drew him. Night after night she would turn to him with the full, somnambulant abandon of a deep-throated flower. Yet in the very act of love he was unmanned; he nuzzled and drowsed at her breast like a child searching out its mother. And now, through the steaming, suffocating baths of mist, she led him, and he followed, though the rainbows under the clear water were lost.

Dark came upon them without warning. By the time they completed their circuit of the boardwalk, the sun had gone under the hills and the tall pines walled the deserted road with shadow. As he drove, a touch of uneasiness made Norton glance at the gas meter. The white pointer registered empty. Sadie must have seen it, too, for in the obscure, fading light she was watching him.

"Do you think we'll make it?' she asked, with a curious vibrancy.

"Of course," Norton said, although he was not at all sure. There were no gas stations until they got to the lake, and that stretch would take over an hour. The tank had a reserve, of course, but he had never tested it, never let it run below a quarter full. The upset with Sadie must have taken his mind off the meter. They could easily have filled up at Mammoth Junction. He switched on the long beams, but even then the little cave of light moving ahead of them seemed no match for the dark battalions of surrounding pines. He thought how pleasant it would be, for a change, to see the beams of another car close behind him, reflected in the rear-view mirror. But the mirror brimmed with darkness. For one craven, irrational moment, Norton felt the full weight of the dark: it bore down on top of his skull, pressed in upon him from all sides, brutally, concentratedly, as if intent to crush the thin, bone-plated shell that set him apart.

Working to moisten his lips, which had gone quite dry, Norton started to sing against the dark, something he had not done since childhood.

"You wanderin' boys of Liverpool
I'll have you to beware
When you go a-huntin'
With your dog, your gun, your snare . . ."

The plaintive cadences of the song deepened the loneliness of the night around them, as if they, too, were marooned on a continent on the dark underside of the world.

"One night as I lay on my bunk
A-dreamin' all alone . . ."

Suddenly, like a candle in a draft, Norton's memory flickered. The words of the song blacked out. But Sadie took it up.

"I dreamt I was in Liverpool
Way back in Marylebone . . ."

"With my true love beside me
And a jug of ale in hand
And I woke quite broken-hearted
Lying off Van Diemen's Land."

They finished in unison. Forgetting the words disturbed Norton; he had known them by heart, surely as his name. His brain felt to be going soft.

In half an hour of driving they passed no landmark they recognized, and the pointer of the gas meter was dipping well below empty. Norton found himself listening to the tenuous whirring of the motor as to the breathing of a dear, moribund relative, his ears cocked for the break in continuity, the faltering, the silence.

"Even if we make this," Sadie said once, with a taut little laugh, "there will be two more bad things. There'll be a trailer parked in our car space and a bear waiting at the tent."

At last the lake loomed before them, a radiant, silvery expanse beyond the dark, cone shapes of the pines, reflecting the stars and the ruddy, newly risen moon. A flash of white crossed the headlights as a stag galloped off into the brush. The faint, dry reverberation of the stag's hooves consoled them, and the sight of the open water. Across the lake, a tiny crownlet of lights marked the shops of the camp center. Twenty minutes later, they were driving into the lit gas station, chuckling like two giddy adolescents. The engine died five yards from the pump.

Norton hadn't seen Sadie so merry since the start of their trip. Sleeping out, even in state parks, among other tents and trailers, unnerved her. One evening when he had walked off along the lake shore for a few moments, leaving her to finish up the supper dishes, she had become hysterical—run down to the shore with her dishtowel, waving and calling, the blue shadows thickening around her like water, until he heard her and turned back. But now the safely passed scare of darkness, the empty tank, and the unpeopled road was affecting her like brandy. Her exhilaration bewildered him; he shouldered the burden of her old cautions, her rabbitish fears. As they drove into the campground and around D-loop to their site, Norton's heart caught. Their tent was gone. Then, flushing at his own foolishness, he saw that the tent was merely hidden behind the long, balloon shape of an unfamiliar aluminum trailer which had moved in on them.

He swung the car into the parking space behind the trailer. The headlights fixed on a dark, mounded shape a few yards from their tent. Sadie gave a low, exultant laugh. "Fifty-eight!"

Distracted by the bright lights, or the noise of the engine, the bear backed away from the garbage can. Then, at a cumbersome lope, it vanished into the maze of darkened tents and trailers.

Usually Sadie did not like to cook supper after dark, because the food smells attracted animals. Tonight, though, she went to the camp ice chest and took out the pink fillets of lake trout they caught the day before. She fried them, with some cold boiled potatoes, and steamed a few ears of corn. She even went through the ritual of mixing Ovaltine by the yellow beam of their flashlight, and cheerfully heated water for the dishes.

To make up for the loss of the water bag and his carelessness about the gas tank, Norton was especially scrupulous about cleaning up. He wrapped the remains of the fried fish in wax paper and stored it in the back seat of the car, along with a bag of cookies, some Fig Newtons and the ice chest. He checked the car windows and locked the doors. The trunk of the car was packed with enough canned and dry goods to last them two months; he made sure that was locked. Then he took the bucket of soapy dishwater and scrubbed down the wooden table and the two benches. Bears only bothered messy campers, the rangers said—people who littered food about or kept food in their tents. Every night, of course, the bears travelled throughout the camp, from garbage can to garbage can, foraging. You couldn't stop that. The cans had metal lids and were set deep in the ground, but the bears were sly enough to flip up the tops and scoop out the debris, rummaging through wax paper and cardboard cartons for stale breadcrusts, bits of hamburgers and hotdogs, jars with honey or jam still glued to the sides, all the prodigal leavings of campers without proper iceboxes or storage bins. In spite of the strict rules, people fed the bears, too—lured them with sugar and crackers to pose in front of the camera, even shoved their children under the bear's nose for a more amusing shot.

In the furred, blue moonlight, the pines bristled with shadow. Norton imagined the great, brutish shapes of the bears padding there, in the heart of the black, nosing for food. His headache was bothering him again. Together with the headache, something else beat at the edge of his mind, tantalizing as the forgotten words to a song: some proverb, some long-submerged memory he fished for but could not come by.

"Norton!' Sadie hissed from within the tent.

He went to her with the slow, tranced gestures of a sleep-walker, zipping the canvas door with its inset window of mosquito netting behind him. The sleeping-bag had taken warmth from her body, and he crawled in beside her as into a nest, burying his face in the hollow of her throat, searching, like some schooled dowser, for the springs of forgetfulness.

The crash woke him. He dreamed it first, the tearing smash, the after-shattering tinkle of glass, then woke, with a deadly clear head, to hear it going on still, a diminished cascade of bells and gongs.

Beside him Sadie lay taut as a strung bow. The breath of her words caressed his ear. "My bear," she said, as if she had called it up out of the dark.

After the crash the air seemed preternaturally still. Then Norton heard a scuffling in the vicinity of the car. A bumping and clattering set in, as if the bear were bowling cans and tins down an incline. It's got into the trunk, Norton thought. It's going to rip open all our stews and soups and canned fruits and sit there all night, gorging. The vision of the bear at their stores infuriated him. The bear was to blame for the filched water bag, the empty gas tank, and, as if that were not enough, he would eat them out of two months' supplies in a single night.

"Do something." Sadie huddled down into the nest of blankets. "Shoo him away." Her voice challenged him, yet his limbs were heavy, recalcitrant as ice.

Norton could hear the bear snuffling and padding along beside the tent. The canvas luffed like a sail. Gingerly, he climbed out of the sleeping-bag, reluctant to leave the dark, musky warmth of his bed. He peered through the netting of the door. In the blue drench of moonlight he could see the bear hunched at the left rear window of the car, shoving its body through a gap where the window should have been. With a crackle, like the listing of a ball of paper, the bear brought out a little bundle of straw and trailing ribbons.

A surge of anger beat up in Norton's throat. The damn bear had no right to his wife's hat, mangling it like that. The hat belonged to Sadie as indissolubly as her own body, and there was the bear, ravaging it, picking it apart in a horrid, inquisitive way.

"You stay here," Norton said. "I'm going to drive that bear off."

"Take the light," Sadie said. "That'll scare it."

Norton felt for the cold, cylindrical shape of the flashlight on the floor of the tent, unzipped the door, and stepped out into the pale blur of moonlight. The bear had got the fried fish out of the bottom of the car now, and stood reared, preoccupied, fumbling with the wax paper wrappings. The remains of Sadie's hat, a grotesque crumple of straw, lay at the bear's feet.

Norton aimed the beam of the flashlight straight at the bear's eyes. "Get out of here, you," he said.

The bear did not move.

Norton took a step forward. The shape of the bear towered against the car. Norton could see, in the glare of the light, the jagged teeth of glass around the hole gaping in the car window. "Get out . . ." He held the light steady, moving forward, willing the bear to be gone. At any moment the bear should break into a shuffle and be off. "Get out . . ." But there was another will working, a will stronger, even, than his.

The darkness fisted and struck. The light went out. The moon went out in a cloud. A hot nausea flared through his heart and bowels. He struggled among petals, waxy white and splotched with red, tasting the thick, sweet honey that filled his throat. As from a rapidly receding planet he heard Sadie's cry—whether of terror or triumph he could not tell.

It was the last bear, her bear, the fifty-ninth.

The Lucky Stone

Ts, autumn 1960–winter 1961, Smith College[*]

Joanna lay on the boardinghouse bed, trying to calm the trip-hammer of her heart. As she looked round the unfamiliar room at the sturdy, rush-bottomed chairs, the wardrobe, the white walls, bare except for a small, luminous watercolour of a rain-wet beach, she seemed suspended in time and space – she might even be home in Canada again, with the clear sea-light pouring in through the window, about to go down and put the kettle on for the family tea. But together with this image came the inevitable sequel: the late-night phone call, word of the car crash, the chill, midwinter chapel service, and the bleak arrangements with her parents' solicitors for the sale of the house, the furniture, the little oddments that had meant so much. Once more Joanna fought the brimming tears. *No, no: that's over, I've mourned enough. I'm starting a*

---

[*] Typescript has holograph and typewritten corrections and additions by SP. Typed at top right: 'Sylvia Plath / 3 Chalcot Square / London N.W.1'. SP wrote 'Sold £15.15.0 by Jennifer Hassell', her agent at A. M. Heath, at the top of the first page. Published as 'The Perfect Place', *My Weekly* (28 October 1961): 3–7, 31. Printed with the following leading sentence: 'Where love dwelt—and laughter and happiness, with all the world shut out . . . and she herself shut out . . .' The printed version cut four hundred or so words, making a marked difference to the development of the story.

new life now, in a new country. A chair scraped on the floor of the room overhead. *With Kenneth,* she reminded herself a bit too deliberately.

And as Joanna remembered all Kenneth had done for her since her parents' death, she felt ungrateful, ashamed of her present surge of disappointment in him. They had met in Canada over a year ago at the house of a mutual friend and managed a brief flurry of dinners, dances and sightseeing trips together before Kenneth's law firm called him home to England. At the time, Joanna hadn't really thought of their relationship as anything very serious, but weeks later, after the accident, when Kenneth's letter came asking her to be his fiancée – the one heartwarming note in her frostbitten world – she felt a deep need to read love into that short Canada encounter.

Now their marriage loomed ahead: white lace, candles, flower girls, photographers – all the imposing, traditional fanfare Kenneth's family would expect at the wedding of their only son. Joanna's half-wistful suggestion of a simple, private ceremony had been laughingly but firmly brushed aside by Kenneth's mother.

'Really, Joanna,' she had said, not unkindly, 'we can't allow you to go on playing the shy violet. Oh, don't think I'm not aware of your feelings! You're hesitant because of your parents, of course. But haven't you already delayed your marriage long enough on their account? Think how happy it would make them to see you coming down the aisle, by candlelight, crowned by flowers . . .'

So Joanna had given in, and with a queer, almost hypnotic languor let Kenneth's mother plan the wedding down to the last, fashionable detail, even to the choice of a London designer for her bridal dress. At such a decisive point in her life, Joanna hungered for some comforting talisman, some reminder of home, and it was as a sort of reward for her compliance, she suspected, that Kenneth had humoured her impulse to visit this remote fishing village on the north coast.

But already, on their first day at the shore, Kenneth had shown how the place bored him. Wasn't he at that very minute lingering upstairs in his room over the briefcase full of papers he insisted on bringing along, while the superb, early summer evening went to waste outside? Swamped by homesickness, Joanna listened to the shrill catcalls of the gulls as they wheeled above the chimneys. With an effort, she tried to put herself in Kenneth's position. Of course, after the rich distractions of the city – plays, concerts, dinner parties and so on – he would find the seaside village tedious. After all, no one knew him here, or gave him the instinctive deference he was used to as the junior partner of a prosperous law firm. Still, did he have to be quite so intent on quenching her enthusiasm? It was almost as if he resented anything that might bring her past to life. And she remembered their morning walk.

Joanna had tucked into the ample boardinghouse breakfast with unaccustomed appetite and made no secret of her excited plans for the day, to the amusement of Mrs Welbeck, the owner, and her son, Simon.

'Have a spot more tea, love.' Mrs Welbeck reached over to refill the oddly delicate blue-rimmed cup. Its hollowed-out pattern of rice grains let the light through with a milky radiance. Chinese, Joanna guessed vaguely, and wondered whether Mrs Welbeck or Simon was to be credited for the tea-set and other touches which made the boardinghouse seem a strikingly distinctive home, not the usual dreary public affair of sallow wallpaper, liverish-stained veneer furniture and tasteless 'white' meals of potato, cauliflower and fish lumped together unimaginatively on the same plate. The very word 'love' echoed warmly in her ears, although she knew it was only a way of speaking.

'Now, if you're *really* going to see our place properly,' Mrs Welbeck went on in a motherly manner, 'you ought to take a glance at the rock pools. You might even run into Simon balancing his easel on some cliff or other!'

'So you're the one responsible for that lovely rainstorm in my room.' Joanna turned to Simon, who poised his empty teacup between angular fingers, not out of idleness, but as if drawing some fine essence from the frail china itself. 'The minute I saw it, I felt I was looking out of a window at home.'

Joanna noticed Kenneth's lips tighten as he industriously buttered a slab of toast. Kenneth suspected all artists of self-indulgence and irresponsibility. Some of them, he once observed, even had the callousness to subject wives and children to their unheated garrets: a grown man had to consider others. A vision of their carefully chosen flat floated before Joanna's eyes: discreet, impeccable, theirs but for the signing of the lease. Yet the prospect of selecting carpets, drapes and furniture to meet Kenneth's exacting taste settled on her heart like a weight. She shrugged it aside and concentrated on what Simon was saying.

'Mother wondered if the guests mightn't find a grey day on the wall a bit grim in addition to the frequent grey days framed by the window.' As Simon's dark eyes appraised her, Joanna flushed. *He's examining me like the china, to see if I ring true.* 'But so far no one's objected.'

Kenneth had agreed to the rock pools. When they met in the hall a short time later, Joanna noticed with mild surprise that he hadn't bothered to change from the crisp linen suit and slippery-soled summer shoes he had worn on the trip down on the train and to breakfast that morning.

'Well, *you* look comfortable,' Kenneth said dryly, eyeing her thick fisherman's sweater and the salt-stained tennis shoes she hadn't worn since scaling the shore rocks in Canada two summers ago to gather the mussels that clustered there, blue as grapes.

'I am comfortable,' Joanna returned amiably, and tucked her hand under his elbow. It was early still, with a pale, rinsed sky. The few summer visitors had not yet come down to stroll along the harbour front where the fishing fleet anchored or across the bridge leading to the old section of the town under the ruined abbey perched atop its headland like a great, grey seabird. As Joanna gulped in long draughts of the moist, salt air, she felt a constricting band around her loosen for the first time in over a year. 'How I'd love a summer place here!' she sighed, taking in the angular red-tiled gables of the tiny houses crowding the opposite shore, their yellow, pink and blue plaster walls gleaming like freshly washed up shells.

'How you can think of a summer place when we haven't even made the final arrangements for our year-round house, I don't know,' Kenneth countered. 'Don't be such an escapist, darling. I want to talk to you about that problem wall in the lounge. I'm really not satisfied with the fleur-de-lis paper we picked out last week.'

'No, that fuzzy maroon pattern would just catch dust, wouldn't it?' Joanna agreed absently, admiring the bright orange and yellow cork floats on the decks of the moored boats. 'Why not simply put up a plain nubbly paper, paint it white, and buy a few good paintings? That would let the light in.'

Kenneth sighed. 'That wasn't quite what I mean, Joanna. After all, we're not furnishing some Chelsea studio. We've been over it a dozen times – something elegant and yet substantial. A responsible lawyer can't afford to indulge in jazzed-up modern stuff. It just wouldn't go.'

As they crossed the bridge, Joanna gazed down at the reflections of boats and houses sparkling on the dull green water. *Fine for our guests, Kenneth*, she almost said, *only what about me?* But she stopped in time and made her tone casual: 'What do you have in mind, dear? I'm relying on you to tutor me, you know.'

Kenneth seemed pleased. 'We really need to go back to the shop and pore over those sample books again, I think.'

Joanna bit her lip at the thought of the long, stuffy afternoon spent turning the pages of expensive wallpaper from one cold, pompous pattern to another. *I should be loving this*, she had chided herself, *yet I feel stifled, hemmed in.*

'I noticed a rather nice piece – Grecian urns in white and silver on a dark green ground,' Kenneth was saying. 'That would mean giving up the idea of the gold brocade drapes, of course . . .'

He broke off as the cobbled lane petered out in a flight of rough stone steps leading to the beach. Joanna moved easy as a cat along the rugged, shelving rock which in a few hours would be veiled with a white froth of foam, but Kenneth kept his eyes down, finding his footing with effort, his face tight and humourless, as she had seen it when he was working out the details of some complicated law case. *He's clever, a good provider, even handsome, in his reserved way. I couldn't ask for more, yet why does he make me want to smile? Like a silly, irreverent little girl in the middle of a chapel service?*

'Are you really set on trekking to those rock pools?' he asked her now.

'I wouldn't miss them for the world!' Joanna exclaimed, although Kenneth obviously wanted to turn back. 'You take your time and I'll just nip ahead and find out how much further they are.'

With something peculiarly close to relief, she struck out on her own. As she rounded a bend in the shore, a vista of deserted rock flats spread out before her under the blue vault of the sky – deserted except for a distant figure in a red sweater standing on a stony rise before something that looked rather like a witch's tripod.

Simon waved as she came up. 'Have you seen the starfish?'

'Starfish?' Joanna paused to catch her breath, brushing back a lock of blown brown hair. 'Not a one. Only the most sober-suited periwinkles.' She peered at the nearly finished seascape tacked to the easel. 'What a marvellous wave! It's green as a bit of bottle-glass held up to the light.'

'You sound like a regular beachcomber,' Simon grinned, and Joanna found herself admiring the frank, open set of his features. *He's isn't thinking of the impression he's making, that's why his paintings have that queer spontaneous light I'm learning to recognise like a signature.* 'Confess now – haven't you spent a childhood hunting for driftwood and coloured pebbles?'

'I admit it,' Joanna smiled, and added a little ruefully, 'I suppose I still act childish enough when I'm back by the sea.'

'How do you mean?'

'Oh, I want to dig wells in the sand and collect things – sprigs of seaweed, the sort you can pop, and lucky stones with a ring round the middle . . .'

Simon laughed. 'I think there's a lucky stone in a pool near here. Come on, I'll show you.' And he jumped down to a lower level of the rock, holding out his hand to help her after him.

Joanna was squatting opposite Simon over a shallow pool watching a red-speckled crab stalk across the brilliant pebbles, when a small, rattling avalanche sounded behind her.

'Oof,' Kenneth said, and she turned in time to see him slip and sit down suddenly in a patch of wet sand. Surprise blotted out the disapproval on his face. The lucky stone Simon had found for her, deep purplish and ringed with white, dropped from her fingers like a guilty token.

'I say,' Simon was helping Kenneth to his feet, 'you're not hurt, are you?'

'Hurt? Of course not! But my suit's ruined.' Kenneth brushed irritably at the grit and tar streaking the expensive material. 'I think we've had enough for one morning, Joanna.' Slowly, like a child caught playing out too late by an impatient parent, Joanna rose and resigned herself to accompanying him back to the boardinghouse.

'If you'll just wait a second,' Simon offered, 'I'll pack up my things and go home with you. I've some dry clothes you could change into.'

'I suppose I will need something to wear,' Kenneth said grimly. 'I hadn't counted on getting mucked up the minute we arrived.'

Luncheon, Joanna recalled, had been pretty awful. At first she tried to make up for Kenneth's silence by chattering with Mrs Welbeck, but the sight of his preoccupied face and his only-too-evident discomfort at wearing a pair of Simon's old cord trousers and a weathered sports coat reduced her to wordless embarrassment. *Oh, why can't he unbend, make light of it: it's only a suit, after all.* Yet she knew by now what value Kenneth placed on his few costly possessions. To make things worse, the fair morning sky was already curdling with clouds. Even the weather seemed set against her.

Simon, sensing her humiliation, did his best to relieve the tension in the air. 'I'm going up the coast this afternoon to deliver a painting. Why don't you two come along for the drive? There isn't much doing here in bad weather.'

'That's very kind of you,' Joanna ventured. 'I'm sure we'd love to come.'

'You two go.' Kenneth pushed back his chair and rose briskly. 'I've some work that need attending to and some phone calls to make.'

Ironically, that afternoon in Staithes had been the first really carefree event of their stay, and Kenneth had missed it. Joanna brushed aside the disquieting possibility that Kenneth's very absence enabled her to enjoy herself to the full. As the small second-hand car negotiated the hairpin turns along the shore, climbing inland between brilliant green pastures before plummeting down the almost perpendicular road into the little harbour town, the rain broke in cascades around them, like a waterfall, shrouding the landscape in a grey blur.

'You're smiling,' Simon cast a side glance at her. 'Doesn't the rain bore you?'

'I love it,' Joanna said simply. 'I used to walk out in the rain at home, in this same old oilskin, listening to the foghorns off the coast hooting like lost owls. I . . . I . . .' And she ducked her face to hide the sudden tears.

But Simon seemed to accept her outburst of emotion – a weakness she never allowed herself in Kenneth's presence – as perfectly natural. He talked on easily, waiting until she recovered her composure. 'I guess you feel the way I do about this sort of place. For some people the sea's a native habitat – they take to it like fish. During the years I saw nothing but city pavements, I made up my mind I'd move to the north coast as soon as I'd sold enough paintings to manage it. Luckily for me, my first one-man show bought our house – much too big for just Mother and me, so she takes in a few guests because she enjoys company. She has a day-girl to help, so it's no work for her, and I, as you see, have my very comfortable garret to work in.'

Joanna flushed as she thought how Kenneth misinterpreted Simon's living with his mother. How had he put it? – 'Sponging off the woman while she works herself to the bone to support him.'

In the course of the afternoon, Joanna found herself confiding all sorts of details about her homelife in Canada to Simon, even the difficult story of her parents' death. They left the painting, an oil portrait swaddled from the rain in thick canvas, at the whitewashed cottage of a retired fisherman.

'He seemed so delighted with it,' Joanna observed, as they tramped the labyrinth of narrow streets that rayed out from the clear green bay, eating mussels from a newspaper and listening to the gulls mewing overhead, invisible in the blown mist. 'Did you notice the space ready for it on the wall over the fireplace?'

'I've done a series of paintings of him,' Simon smiled, roused by her interest. 'You should hear his stories about the rare days before automobiles and television. They're a treat.'

After exploring the streets and the harbour quay, almost deserted that wet afternoon, they stopped for tea at a little shop on the waterfront where the woman who served them wore one of the traditional mobcaps that seemed part of the village costume. By the time they emptied the generous china pot and devoured the last of the buttered scones and honey, the rain had thinned and the sky was beginning to clear.

'You're already looking better for the salt air,' Simon said appreciatively. 'You seemed . . . I don't know . . . sort of pale and sorrowful last night when you arrived. I hope you don't think I'm impertinent to say so.' And his eyes lingered briefly on her left hand where the sizeable diamond glittered like a frozen, many-faceted tear.

Kenneth and Mrs Welbeck were sitting down to supper when they returned. 'I think we'll have to start back earlier than we planned, Joanna,' Kenneth said by way of greeting. 'I've just been on the phone with Sam Carter, and he says there are some new developments in the libel case I'd better look into. So I've arranged for us to leave first thing tomorrow. I know you'll be sensible about it. It's very important.'

I know it's important. Lying on the neat white bed, Joanna felt her heart pulse like some impetuous, snared bird. *Kenneth's career comes first, that's only natural. What must I feel so rebellious? What's happening to me?* Dimly she realised that the numb fog of grief was beginning to lift from her spirit, letting in the light. *I'm only just learning who I am and what I want. I'm not ready to go back, I'm not ready . . .*

Restlessly, she jumped up, straightened her hair in front of the mirror, and dashed on some fresh lipstick. *I'll just go down to the living room for a magazine to pass the time. Kenneth's sure to be through any minute now, and then we'll walk up to the abbey together by moonlight . . .*

Simon met her on the stair. 'Going out?'

'I thought of climbing up to the abbey,' Joanna admitted, 'but Kenneth is buried in his papers and I don't know when he'll be through.'

'I suggest you be off while the sky's clear. We're due for another cloudburst tonight . . . it's one of those fickle days.'

'I guess I'd better wait for Kenneth.' Joanna hesitated, half-tempted to stroll to the abbey alone in the luminous blue evening.

'If you have a few minutes to spare,' Simon offered, 'why don't you glance into my studio. I'm just putting the finishing touches on a night-study of the abbey. It won't take the place of the real thing, of course, but it might amuse you.'

This is one garret Kenneth couldn't complain about, Joanna thought with an odd flash of triumph as she stepped into the large, low-beamed studio running the length of the house. Thick white rugs padded the floor, and spacious windows let in the gilded after-sunset glow, but Joanna's attention centred immediately on the drawings and paintings – some sombre, some vivid as stained glass – that crowded the walls and stood stacked in the bare alcove where Simon had his easel.

'How can you ever bear to part with these?' She made a slow circuit of the room and came to a halt before the night-study.

'Oh, I keep the best ones . . .' Simon said, but Joanna was already lost in the dark vaults and moon-blued arches of the ruined abbey.

'How lonely it looks! Did you see any ghosts?'

'No, but I think I heard one,' Simon replied, with a glint of mischief. 'The churchyard is full of stones in memory of local captains who went down with their ships. On a windy night the air fairly vibrates with voices.' There was a pause. In those few moments, the radiance had paled from the sky and the room foundered in shadow. A few heraldic drops of rain tapped on the roof. Then Joanna flinched in surprise. Simon's hand closed on her arm. 'Look,' he spun her round toward him, all at once serious. 'I know I have no rights in this matter, but if for any reason you'd like to stay on here a bit, Mother and I would be happy to have you . . . as our guest.'

For one crazy second, Joanna felt the floor sway under her feet, and she wanted to bury her face on Simon's comfortable shoulder and cry out, *Let me stay, let me stay*. Yet even as she wavered, she heard Kenneth's voice on the stair landing, calling her name. He must have knocked on her door and found the room empty.

'I'd better go now,' she managed. 'Thank you. I promise I'll . . . I'll think it over.' And as the door of Simon's studio swung shut behind her, she heard the rain strike up its dulcet, drumming lullaby on the broad roof.

Kenneth was waiting for her at the foot of the stair, a tall, unbending shape in the brilliantly lit hall. One glimpse of his exasperated face told Joanna he would never understand, or make an effort to understand, the painful changes taking place in her heart.

'I'm not going to ask what you've been doing up there all this time,' he began in a low, insistent voice, 'but I do ask that you show a little more consideration . . .'

'Please,' Joanna struggled to edge past him as he stood there, obdurate as a building or a tree – a solid, commonsensical object blocking out the view of everything that mattered to her. 'I'm going up to the abbey. I need to think things over.'

'Has the sea air bewitched you completely? You can't go to the abbey – it's raining rivers outside.' Kenneth tracked her downstairs into the front hall where the coats hung on a row of hooks near the door. 'Listen, darling,' his voice took on a cajoling tone, 'I know you're upset, but we'll be back in the city again tomorrow, and you'll forget all the memories this place has stirred up.'

'I don't *want* to forget!' Joanna cried, shoving her arms blindly into her oilskin. 'Can't you see?' And with a great effort she pulled the cold emblem of security and affluence off her left hand and slipped it into Kenneth's palm. 'I'm sorry,' she said simply, 'but in all honesty I can't continue to wear this.' Then she wheeled from him, opened the door, and stepped out into the enveloping rain.

For a while she walked rapidly, head down, numb and confused, without noticing anything around her, but bit by bit her spirit lightened, and she began to enjoy the wind whipping the rain in sheets and flickering reflections of the street lamps on the wet pavement. Not a soul passed her as she crossed the bridge to the old town, its tiles and cobbles gleaming as in some quaint, rainswept village out of Dickens. It was only when she began the breathtaking climb up the steps to the floodlit abbey that she realised she was being followed.

A silly panic made her quicken her pace. Then, in an attempt to reassure herself and seem casual, she thrust her hands into her pockets. Her right hand encountered a round, hard object. Curious, she drew it out and examined it in the glow of the abbey lights. It was the lucky stone. Simon must have picked it up after she dropped it and stowed it away in the pocket of her oilskin on the hook in the hall. Calmed and encouraged, she turned to meet the figure, still veiled in rain, coming toward her out of the dark.

'You're hard to catch,' Simon said. 'I thought you might well be in danger of falling off a cliff up here. It's pretty rough country at night.'

'I was afraid . . .'

'Afraid I was someone else?' Simon paused. 'I suppose you know he's packing.'

'Yes,' Joanna said, thinking with a strange little surge of relief: *Kenneth will be more worried about undoing all our plans and arrangements than he is about losing me.* 'Yes,' her voice sounded serene, sure of itself, 'I know.'

'There's a small pub at the bottom of the hill.' Simon took her arm with sudden firmness. 'I recommend a thorough drying out and perhaps a sip of brandy to steady the nerves.'

The pub door opened on a blaze of light, dazzling after the wet, black streets, and a crescendo of piano music and chorusing voices met them as they stepped in, dripping, out of the rain. Joanna's heart lifted, and she let Simon guide her to a corner table.

'Hel-lo!' croaked the shrewd, green parrot from its cage at the end of the bar. 'Hel-lo.'

'Staying?' Simon asked, reaching for her hand.

'Staying.' Joanna smiled, her eyes bright.

'Hello yourself,' she said to the parrot.

Day of Success

Ts,[*] February–August 1961, Smith College

Ellen was on her way to the bedroom with an armload of freshly folded nappies when the phone rang, splintering the stillness of the crisp autumn morning. For a moment she froze on the threshold, taking in the peaceful scene as if she might never see it again – the delicate rose-patterned wallpaper, the forest-green cord drapes she'd hemmed by hand while waiting for the baby to come, the old-fashioned four-poster inherited from a loving but moneyless aunt, and, in the corner, the pale pink crib holding sound-asleep six-month-old Jill, the centre of it all.

Please don't let it change, she begged of whatever fates might be listening. *Let the three of us stay happy as this for ever.*

Then the shrill, demanding bell roused her, and she stowed the pile of clean nappies on the big bed and went to pick up the receiver reluctantly, as if it were some small black instrument of doom.

'Is Jacob Ross there?' enquired a cool, clear feminine voice. 'Denise Kay speaking.' Ellen's heart sank as she pictured the elegantly groomed red-headed woman at the other end of the wire. She and Jacob had been to lunch with the brilliant young television producer only a month before to discuss the progress of the play Jacob was working on – his first. Even at that early date, Ellen had secretly hoped Denise would be struck by lightning or spirited to Australia rather than have her thrown together with Jacob in the crowded, intimate days of rehearsal – author and producer collaborating on the birth of something wonderful, uniquely theirs.

'No, Jacob's not home at the moment.' It occurred to Ellen, a bit guiltily,

---

[*] Typescript has holograph and typewritten corrections and additions by SP. Typed at top right, 'Sylvia Plath / 3 Chalcot Square / London N.W.1.' Published posthumously in *Bananas* (1975): 11–13.

how easy it would be to call Jacob down from Mrs Frankfort's flat for such an obviously important message. His finished script had been in Denise Kay's office for almost two weeks now, and she knew by the way he ran down the three flights of stairs each morning to meet the postman how eager he was to hear the verdict. Still, hadn't she promised to behave like a model secretary and leave his hours of writing time uninterrupted? 'This is his wife, Miss Kay,' she added, with perhaps unnecessary emphasis. 'May I take a message, or have Jacob call you later?'

'Good news,' Denise said briskly. 'My boss is enthusiastic about the play. A bit odd, he thinks, but beautifully original, so we're buying it. I'm really thrilled to be the producer.'

This is it, Ellen thought miserably, unable to see anything for the vision of that smooth-sheened coppery head bent with Jacob's dark one over a thick mimeographed script. *The beginning of the end.*

'That's wonderful, Miss Kay. I . . . I know Jacob will be delighted.'

'Fine. I'd like to see him for lunch today, if I may, to talk about casting. We'll be wanting some name actors, I think. Could you possibly ask him to pick me up in my office about noon?'

'Of course . . .'

'Righto. Goodbye, then.' And the receiver descended with a businesslike click.

Bewildered by an alien and powerful emotion, Ellen stood at the window, the confident, musical voice that could offer success casually as a bunch of hothouse grapes echoing in her ears. As her gaze lingered on the green square below, its patch-barked plane trees thrusting into the luminous blue sky above the shabby housefronts, a leaf, dull gold as a threepenny bit, let go and waltzed slowly to the pavement. Later in the day, the square would be loud with motorbikes and the shouts of children. One summer afternoon Ellen had counted twenty-five youngsters within view of her bench under the plane trees: untidy, boisterous, laughing – a miniature United Nations milling about the geranium-planted plot of grass and up the narrow, cat-populated alleys.

How often she and Jacob had promised themselves the legendary cottage by the sea, far from the city's petrol fumes and smoky railroad yards – a garden, a hill, a cove for Jill to explore, an unhurried, deeply savoured peace!

'Just one play sale, darling,' Jacob had said earnestly. 'Then I'll know I can do it, and we'll take the risk.' The risk, of course, was moving away from this busy centre of jobs – odd jobs, part-time jobs, jobs Jacob could manage with relative ease while writing every spare minute – and depending solely on his chancy income from stories, plays and poems. Poems! Ellen smiled in spite of herself, remembering the gloomy, bill-harassed day before Jill's birth, just after they'd moved into the new flat.

She'd been down on her knees, laboriously slapping light grey lino paint on the depressing, chewed-up, hundred-year-old floorboards when the postman rang. 'I'll go.' Jacob laid down the saw he was using to cut bookshelf lengths. 'You want to save yourself stairs, love.' Ever since Jacob had begun sending manuscripts to magazines the postman, in his blue uniform, was a sort of possible magic godfather. Any day, instead of the disheartening fat manila envelopes and the impersonal printed rejection slips, there might be an encouraging letter from an editor or even . . .

'Ellen! Ellen!' Jacob took the steps two at a time, waving the opened airmail envelope. 'I've done it! Isn't it beautiful!' And he dropped into her lap the pale blue, yellow-bordered cheque with the amazing amount of dollars in black and the cents in red. The glossy American weekly she'd addressed an envelope to a month before was delighted with Jacob's contribution. They paid a pound a line and Jacob's poem was long enough to buy – what? After giggling over the possibility of theatre tickets, dinner in Soho, pink champagne, the cloud of common sense began to settle.

'You decide.' Jacob bowed, handing her the cheque, frail and gay as a rare butterfly. 'What does your heart desire?'

Ellen didn't need to think twice. 'A pram,' she said softly. 'A great, big beautiful pram with room enough for twins!'

Ellen toyed with the idea of saving Denise's message until Jacob came loping downstairs for lunch – too late to meet the attractive producer at her office – but immediately felt profoundly ashamed of herself. Any other wife would have called her husband to the phone excitedly, breaking all writing-schedule rules for this exceptional news, or at least rushed to him the minute she hung up, proud to be the bearer of such good tidings. *I'm jealous,* Ellen told herself dully. *I'm a regular jet-propelled, twentieth-century model of the jealous wife, small-minded and spiteful. Like Nancy Regan.* This thought pulled her up short, and she headed purposefully into the kitchen to brew herself a cup of coffee.

I'm just stalling, she realised wryly, putting the pot on the stove. Still, as long as Jacob remained unaware of Denise Kay's news, she felt, half-superstitiously, she would be safe – safe from Nancy's fate.

Jacob and Keith Regan had been schoolmates, served in Africa together, and come back to post-war London determined to avoid the subtle pitfalls of full-time bowler-hat jobs which would distract them from the one thing that mattered: writing. Now, waiting for the water to boil, Ellen recalled those down-at-heel yet challenging months she and Nancy Regan had swapped budget recipes and the secret woes and worries of all wives whose husbands are unsalaried idealists, patching body and soul together by nightwatching, gardening, any odd job that happened to turn up.

Keith made the grade first. A play staged in an out-of-the-way theatre catapulted through the hoop of please-see-it! reviews into the West End and kept going like some beautiful, lucky-star-guided missile to land smack in the middle of Broadway. That's all it took. And as at the wave of a wand, the beaming Regans were whisked from an unheated, cold-water flat and a diet of spaghetti and potato soup into the luxuriant green pastures of Kensington with a backdrop of vintage wines, sports cars, chic furs and, ultimately, the more sombre decor of the divorce courts. Nancy simply couldn't compete – in looks, money, talent, oh, in anything that counted – with the charming blonde leading lady who added such lustre to Keith's play on its debut in the West End. From the wide-eyed, adoring wife of Keith's lean years, she had lapsed gradually into a restless, sharp-tongued, cynical woman-about-town, with all the alimony she could want, but little else. Keith, of course, had soared out of their orbit. Still, whether out of pity or a sort of weatherproof affection, Ellen kept in touch with Nancy, who seemed to derive a certain pleasure from their meetings, as if through the Ross's happy, child-gifted marriage she could somehow recapture the best days of her own past.

Ellen set out a cup and saucer on the counter and was about to pour herself a large dose of scalding coffee when she laughed, ruefully, and reached for a second cup. *I'm not a deserted wife yet!* She arranged the cheap tin tray with care – table napkin, sugar bowl, cream pitcher, a sprig of gilded autumn leaves beside the steaming cups – and started up the steeply angled steps to Mrs Frankfort's top-floor flat.

Touched by Jacob's thoughtfulness in lugging her coal buckets, emptying her trash bins and watering her plants when she visited her sister, the middle-aged widow had offered him the use of her flat during the day while she was at work. 'Two rooms won't hold a writer, his wife and a bouncing baby! Let me contribute my mite to the future of world literature.' So Ellen could let baby Jill creep and crow loud as she liked downstairs without fear of disturbing Jacob.

Mrs Frankfort's door swung open at a touch of her fingertips, framing

Jacob's back, his dark head and broad shoulders in the shaggy fisherman's sweater whose elbows she had mended more times than she liked to remember, bent over the spindly table littered with scrawled papers. As she poised there, holding her breath, Jacob raked his fingers absent-mindedly through his hair and creaked round in his chair. When he saw her, his face lit up, and she came forward smiling, to break the good news.

After seeing Jacob off, freshly shaven, combed and handsome in his well-brushed suit – his only suit, Ellen felt strangely let down. Jill woke from her morning nap, cooing and bright-eyed. 'Dadada,' she prattled, while Ellen deftly changed the damp nappy, omitting the customary game of peekaboo, her mind elsewhere, and put her to play in the pen.

It won't happen right away, Ellen mused, mashing cooked carrots for Jill's lunch. *Break-ups seldom do. It will unfold slowly, one little telltale symptom after another like some awful, hellish flower.*

Propping Jill against the pillows on the big bed for her noon feed, Ellen caught sight of the tiny cut-glass vial of French perfume on the bureau, almost lost in the wilderness of baby powder cans, cod liver oil bottles and jars of cotton wool. The few remaining drops of costly amber liquid seemed to wink at her mockingly – Jacob's one extravagance with the poem-money left over from the pram. Why had she never indulged wholeheartedly in the perfume, instead of rationing it so cautiously, drop by drop, like some perishable elixir of life? A woman like Denise Kay must have a sizeable part of her salary earmarked: Delectable Scents.

Ellen was broodily spooning mashed carrot into Jill's mouth when the doorbell rang. *Darn!* She dumped Jill unceremoniously in her crib and made for the stairs. *It never fails.*

An unfamiliar, immaculately dressed man stood on the doorstep beside the clouded battalion of uncollected milk bottles. 'Is Jacob Ross in? I'm Karl Goodman, editor of *Impact*.'

Ellen recognised, with awe, the name of the distinguished monthly which only a few days ago had accepted three of Jacob's poems. Uncomfortably aware of her carrot-spattered blouse and bedraggled apron, Ellen murmured that Jacob wasn't at home. 'You took some poems of his!' she said shyly, then. 'We were delighted.'

Karl Goodman smiled. 'Perhaps I should tell you what I've come for. I live nearby and happened to be home for lunch, so I thought I'd come round in person . . .'

Denise Kay had phoned *Impact* that morning to see if they couldn't arrange to publish part or all of Jacob's play in time to coincide with the performance. 'I just wanted to make sure your husband wasn't committed to some other magazine first,' Karl Goodman finished.

'No, I don't think he is.' Ellen tried to sound calm. 'In fact I know he's not. I'm sure he'd be happy to have you consider the play. There's a copy upstairs. May I get it for you . . . ?'

'That would be very kind.'

As Ellen hurried into the flat, Jill's outraged wails met her. *Just a minute, love*, she promised. Snatching up the impressively fat manuscript she had typed from Jacob's dictation through so many hopeful teatimes, she started downstairs again.

'Thank you, Mrs Ross.' Abashed, Ellen felt Karl Goodman's shrewd eyes assess her, from the coronet of brown braids to the scuffed though polished tips of her flat walking shoes. 'If we accept this, as I'm almost sure we shall, I'll have the cheque sent to you in advance.'

Ellen flushed, thinking: *We're not that desperate. Not quite.* 'That would be fine,' she said.

Slowly she trudged upstairs to the shrill tune of Jill's cries. *Already I don't fit. I'm homespun, obsolete as last year's hemline. If I were Nancy, I'd grab that cheque the minute it dropped through the mail slot and be off to a fancy hairdresser's and top off the beauty treatment by cruising Regent Street in a cab loaded with loot. But I'm not Nancy,* she reminded herself firmly, and, mustering a motherly smile, went in to finish feeding Jill.

Thumbing through the smart fashion magazines in the doctor's office that afternoon, waiting for Jill's regular check-up, Ellen mused darkly on the gulf separating her from the self-possessed fur, feather and jewel bedecked models who gazed back at her from the pages with astoundingly large, limpid eyes.

Do they ever start the day on the wrong foot? she wondered. *With a headache . . . or a heartache?* And she tried to imagine the fairy-tale world where these women woke dewy-eyed and pink-cheeked, yawning daintily as a cat does, their hair, even at daybreak, a miraculously intact turret of gold, russet, blue-black or perhaps lavender-tinted silver. They would rise, supple as ballerinas, to prepare an exotic breakfast for the man-of-their-heart – mushrooms and creamy scrambled eggs, say, or crabmeat on toast – trailing about a sparkling American kitchen in a foamy negligee, satin ribbons fluttering like triumphal banners . . .

No, Ellen readjusted her picture. They would, of course, have breakfast brought to them in bed, like proper princesses, on a sumptuous tray: crisp toast, the milky lustre of frail china, water just off the boil for the orange-flower tea . . . And into the middle of this fabulous papier-mâché world the upsetting vision of Denise Kay insinuated itself. Indeed, she seemed perfectly at home there, her dark brown, almost black eyes profound under a ravishing cascade of coppery hair.

If only she were superficial, empty-headed! Ellen was momentarily swamped by speculations unworthy of a resourceful wife. *If only* . . .

'Mrs Ross?' The receptionist touched her shoulder, and Ellen snapped out of her daydream. *If only Jacob's home when I get back,* she changed her tack hopefully, *his feet up on the sofa, ready for tea, the same as ever* . . . And, hoisting Jill, she followed the efficient, white-uniformed woman into the doctor's consulting room.

Ellen unlatched the door with deliberate cheerfulness. Yet even as she crossed the threshold, Jill drowsing in her arms, she felt a wave of dismay. *He's not here* . . .

Mechanically, she bedded Jill for her afternoon nap and started, with small heart, to cut out the pattern of a baby's nightgown she planned to run up on a neighbour's hand-wind sewing machine that evening. The clear blue morning had betrayed its promise, she noticed. Looming clouds let their soiled parachute silks sag low above the small square, making the houses and sparse-leaved trees seem drabber than ever.

I love it here. Ellen attacked the warm red flannel with defiant snips. *Pouf to Mayfair, pouf to Knightsbridge, pouf to Hampstead* . . . She was snuffing out the silver spheres of luxury like so many pale dandelion clocks when the phone rang.

Red cloth, pins, tissue pattern pieces and scissors flew helter-skelter onto the rug as she scrambled to her feet. Jacob always called if he was held up somewhere, so she wouldn't worry. And at this particular moment, some token of his thoughtfulness, however small, would be more welcome than cool water to a waif in the desert.

'Hallo, darling!' Nancy Regan's cocky, theatrical voice vibrated across the wire. 'How are things?'

'Fine,' Ellen fibbed. 'Just fine.' She sat down on the edge of the chintz-covered trunk that doubled as wardrobe and telephone table to steady herself. No use hiding the news. 'Jacob's just had his first play accepted . . .'

'I know, I know.'

'But how . . . ?' *How does she manage to pick up the least glitter of gossip? Like a professional magpie, a bird of ill-omen . . .*

'It was easy, darling. I ran across Jacob in the Rainbow Room tête-a-tête with Denise Kay. You know me. I couldn't resist finding out why the celebration. I didn't know Jacob went in for Martinis, darling. Let alone redheads . . .'

A crawling prickle of misery, rather like gooseflesh, made Ellen go hot, then cold. In the light of Nancy's suggestive tone, even her worst dreads seemed naïve. 'Oh, Jacob needs a change of scenery after all the work he's been doing.' She tried to sound casual. 'Most men take the weekend off, at least, but Jacob . . .'

Nancy's brittle laugh rang out. 'Don't tell me! I'm the expert to end all experts when it comes to newly discovered playwrights. Are you going to have a party?'

'Party?' Then Ellen remembered the spectacular fatted calf the Regans had served up by way of commemorating their first really big cheque – friends, neighbours and strangers cramming the small, smoke-filled rooms, singing, drinking, dancing till night blued and the dawn sky showed pale as watered silk above the cockeyed chimney pots. If bottles with awe-inspiring labels and dozens of Fortnum and Mason chicken pies and imported cheeses and a soup plate of caviar were any measure of success, the Regans had cornered a lion's share. 'No, no party; I think, Nancy. We'll be glad enough to have the gas and electric bills paid a bit in advance, and the baby's outgrowing her layette so fast . . .'

'Ellen!' Nancy moaned. 'Where's your imagination?'

'I guess,' Ellen confessed, 'I just haven't got any . . .'

'Excuse an old busybody, but you sound really blue, Ellen! Why don't you invite me round for tea? Then we can have one of our chats and you'll perk up in no time . . .'

Ellen smiled wanly. Nancy was irrepressible, you had to say that for her. No one could accuse *her* of moping or wallowing in self-pity. 'Consider yourself invited.'

'Give me twenty minutes, darling.'

'Now what you really should do, Ellen . . .' Stylish, if a bit plump, in the dressy suit and fur toque, Nancy dropped her voice to a conspiratorial whisper and reached for her third cupcake. 'Mmm,' she murmured, 'better than Lyons. What you really should do,' she repeated, 'if you'll pardon me for being frank, is assert yourself.' And she sat back with a triumphant expression.

'I don't quite see what you mean.' Ellen bent over Jill, admiring the baby's clear grey eyes as she sipped her orange juice. It was getting on toward five, and still no word from Jacob. 'What have I got to assert?'

'Your inner woman, of course!' Nancy exclaimed impatiently. 'You need to take a good, long look at yourself in the mirror. The way I should have, before it was too late,' she added grimly. 'Men won't admit it, but they do want a woman to look *right*, really *fatale*. The right hat, the right hair colour . . . Now's your chance, Ellen. Don't miss it!'

'I've never been able to afford a hairdresser,' Ellen said lamely. *Jacob likes my hair long*, a small, secret voice protested. *He said so, when was it? Last week, last month . . .*

'Of course not,' Nancy crooned. 'You've been sacrificing all the expensive little feminine tricks for Jacob's career. But now he's arrived. You can go wild, darling. Simply wild . . .'

Ellen entertained a brief vision of herself leaning seductively out of the window of a Silver Wraith, swathed in furs and studded with priceless hunks of jewellery, green eyeshadow heavy enough to astound Cleopatra, one of the new pale lip colours, a coquettish feather cut complete with kiss curls . . . But she wasn't deceived – at least not for more than a few seconds. 'I'm not the type.'

'Oh rubbish!' Nancy waved a ring-winking, vermilion-tipped hand that resembled, Ellen thought, a bright, predatory claw. 'That's your trouble, Ellen. You've no self-confidence.'

'You're wrong there, Nancy,' Ellen returned with some spirit. 'I've about two bob's worth.'

Nancy dumped a heaping spoon of sugar into her fresh cup of tea. 'Shouldn't,' she chided herself, and then rattled on without looking at Ellen, 'I don't wonder if you're a tiny bit worried about Denise. She's a legend, one of those professional homewreckers. She specialises in family men . . .'

Ellen felt her stomach lurch, as if she were on a boat in a gale. 'Is she married?' she heard herself say. She didn't want to know. She wanted nothing more than to put her hands to her ears and flee into the comforting rose-patterned bedroom and find some outlet for the tears that were gathering to a hard lump in her throat.

'Married?' Nancy gave a dry little laugh. 'She wears a ring, and that's covered a good deal. The current one – her third, I think – has a wife and three children. The wife won't hear of a divorce. Oh, Denise is a real career girl – she always manages to land a man with complications, so she never ends up drying dishes or wiping a baby's nose.' Nancy's bright chatter slowed and began to run down, like a record, into an abyss of silence. 'Pet!' she exclaimed, catching sight of Ellen's face. 'You're as white as paper! I didn't mean to upset you – honestly, Ellen. I just figured you ought to realise what you're up against. I mean, I was the last to know about Keith. In those days,' and Nancy's wry smile didn't succeed in hiding the tremor in her voice, 'I thought everybody had a heart of gold, everything was open and above board . . .'

'Oh Nan!' Ellen laid an impulsive hand on her friend's arm. 'We did have good times, didn't we!' But in her heart a new refrain sang itself over and over: *Jacob's not like Keith, Jacob's not like Keith . . .*

'"The days of auld lang syne . . ." Huh!' With a delicate snort Nancy dismissed the past and began to draw on her admirably classic mauve gloves.

The moment the door closed on Nancy, Ellen started to behave in a curious and completely uncharacteristic fashion. Instead of putting on her apron and bustling about in the kitchen to prepare supper, she stowed Jill in her pen with a rusk and her favourite toys and disappeared into the bedroom to rummage through the bureau drawers with sporadic mutterings, rather like a female Sherlock Holmes on the scent of a crucial clue.

Why don't I do this every night? she was asking herself half an hour later as, flushed and freshly bathed, she slipped into the royal blue silk Japanese jacket she had been sent several Christmases ago by a footloose schoolfriend circling the globe on a plump legacy, but never worn – an exquisite whispery, sapphire-sheened piece of finery that seemed to have no business whatsoever in her commonsensical world. Then she undid her coronet of braids and swept her hair up into a quite dashing impromptu topknot which she anchored precariously with a few pins. With a couple of tentative waltz steps she accustomed herself to her holiday pair of steep black heels and, as a final touch, doused herself thoroughly with the last drops of the French perfume.

During this ritual, Ellen resolutely kept her eyes from lingering on the round moonface of the clock which had already inched its short black hand past six. *Now all I have to do is wait . . .*

Breezing into the living room, she felt a sudden pang. *I've forgotten Jill!* The baby was sprawled sound asleep in the corner of her playpen, thumb in mouth. Gently Ellen picked up the warm little form and carried her into the bedroom.

They had a wonderful bathtime. Jill laughed and kicked until water flew all over the room, but Ellen hardly noticed, thinking how the baby's dark hair and serene grey eyes mirrored Jacob's own. Even when Jill knocked the cup of porridge out of her hand and onto her best black skirt she couldn't get really angry. She was spooning stewed plums into Jill's mouth when she heard the click of a key in the front door lock and froze. The day's fears and frustrations, momentarily brushed aside, swept back over her in a rush.

'Now that's what I like to see when I come home after a hard day!' Jacob leaned against the doorjamb, lit by a mysterious glow that didn't, somehow, seem to stem from Martinis or redheads. 'Wife and daughter waiting by the fireside to welcome the lord of the house . . .' Jill was, in fact, treating her father to a spectacular blue ear-to-ear smile, composed largely of stewed plums. Ellen giggled, and her desperate silent prayer of that morning appeared close to being granted when Jacob crossed the room in two strides and enveloped her, sticky plum dish and all, in a hearty bear hug.

'Mmm, darling, you smell good!' Ellen waited demurely for some mention of the French perfume. 'A sort of marvellous homemade blend of Farex and cod liver oil. A new bedjacket too!' He held her tenderly at arm's length. 'You look fresh from the tub with your hair up like that.'

'Oooh!' Ellen shook herself free. 'Men!' But her tone gave her away – Jacob obviously saw her as the wife and mother type, and she couldn't be better pleased.

'Seriously, love, I've a surprise.'

'Isn't the play enough for one day?' Ellen asked dreamily, tilting her head to Jacob's shoulder and wondering why she didn't feel in the least like making a scene about his luncheon with Denise or his unexplained absence all the tedious, worrisome afternoon.

'I've been on the phone to the estate agent.'

'Estate agent?'

'Remember that funny out-of-the-way little office we stopped at for a lark on our holiday in Cornwall, just before Jill came . . . ?'

'Ye-es.' Ellen didn't dare let herself jump to conclusions.

'Well, he still has that place for sale . . . that cottage we rented overlooking the inlet. Want it?'

'*Want* it!' Ellen almost shouted.

'I sort of hoped you did, after the way you raved about the place last spring,' Jacob said modestly. 'Because I've arranged to make the down payment with the cheque Denise handed me at lunch . . .'

For a second, the merest snag of foreboding caught at Ellen's heart. 'Won't you have to stay around London for the play . . . ?'

Jacob laughed. 'Not on your life! That Denise Kay is a career woman with a mind of her own – a regular diesel engine. Catch me crossing her path! Why, she's so high-powered she even fuelled up on the Martini she'd ordered for me when I told her I never touch the stuff on weekdays . . .'

The phone, curiously muted, almost musical, interrupted him. Ellen bundled Jill into his arms for her goodnight lullaby and tucking-in and floated into the living room to answer.

'Ellen, darling.' Nancy Regan's voice sounded giddy and thin as tinsel over a raucous background of jazz and laughter. 'I've been racking my brain for what I could do to pep you up, and I've made you an appointment with my Roderigo for Saturday at eleven. It's amazing how an utterly new hairdo can raise your morale . . .'

'Sorry, Nan,' Ellen said gently, 'but I think you'd better cancel my appointment. I've news for you.'

'News?'

'Braids are back in style this season, love – the latest thing for the country wife!'

Shadow Girl

Ts,[*] before 13 October 1961, Smith College

The girl in the smoke-coloured coat paused on the doorstep, her finger an inch from the bell, then noticed the door was open. Not wide open, but just ajar. What fun it would be to slip in secretly and leave the orange chrysanthemums she had brought for Angus on the hall table – a May basket in November. He would come downstairs, whistling after his third cup of black coffee. He would find the flowers, wonder how they had come there, then think, inevitably, of her . . .

The frosty morning made her draw her wool scarf snug and fluff up her fine, reddish hair like a chilled robin. A passer-by, seeing her framed there against the cream housefronts – slim, dark-clad, with bright hair and an armload of

---

[*] Typed at top right of typescript: 'Sylvia Plath / Court Green / North Tawton, Devon.' SP submitted 'Shadow Girl' and 'The Beggars' (an earlier story written in autumn 1959 at Yaddo and presumed lost) to her agents, A. M. Heath, on 13 October 1961. She also submitted these to *Woman's Realm*. On 28 December 1961 SP submitted 'Shadow Girl' and 'A Winter's Tale' to *My Weekly*, who rejected them on 19 January 1962.

flowers, might have said to himself: Wow! Or: What a picture! Or simply walked on warmed, as if by fire-glow.

But no such elevated notion of her looks emboldened Jenny Evans. She was too busy tiptoeing into Angus's front hall. The rustle of the stiff-stemmed chrysanthemums sounded louder than the pounding of her heart. Surely he could hear her!

But before she could take another step, she heard *him*. Instinctively, Jenny held back. Company at that early hour? Then, hearing no other voice, only spaces of silence, between Angus's remarks, she smiled. He would be on the telephone in the study.

She decided not to call out or to interrupt him, but to leave the flowers on the hall table and wait until their luncheon date to find out about his trip to Lancashire.

As Jenny crept toward the table – perilously near the open study door, clear snatches of what Angus was saying drifted out to her. And instead of shutting her ears, without really meaning to, she listened in.

With Jenny, listening in was an old habit.

She had been listening in, in one way or another, all her life. That's what happened when you had a father like Jonathan Evans. People with important, familiar-sounding names were always chatting in the library or arguing hotly at dinner – for Jonathan Evans was nothing if not argumentative, or ringing up and leaving tantalising messages.

Where did the listening in begin?

It began with a small, sleepless girl in a pink flannel nightgown sitting barefoot at the top of the stairs, listening to the laughter and the chink of glasses and silverware from the lit rooms below. It began with a very tall, very bristly man bursting out into the hall with a blonde lady in satin, spotting her and saying, *Here's a girl who needs a story told her, I can see by her lorn, great eyes.* And without time to draw breath, the young Jenny was swept up onto two mountainous knees and a wonderful, right voice rumbled: *Once upon a time . . .*

That's what happened when your father was a publisher. You were always, merely by being there, hearing stories. And with no mother, only the pale, sweet shadow-memory of a mother, you often didn't go to bed when young girls should, but sat up into the evening, forgotten about, listening with wide, still eyes.

Listening . . .

'It's got to end sometime,' Angus was saying. 'It's like being followed a devoted cocker spaniel. Those big, soulful eyes . . .'

A slow flush reddened Jenny's cheeks. All at once she saw the absurdity of her position. There she was, in the hall of the one man in the world she loved and trusted, listening in to his phone conversation like some brazen lady spy.

Not listening. *Eaves*dropping.

And who was Angus talking about? Why who could it possibly be but Jenny herself!

'It's not as if I gave any encouragement,' the pitiless voice went on. 'It's got to end. I'll break it off this week . . .' A little laugh. 'If I ever can.'

Jenny almost dropped the bundle of chrysanthemums. *A devoted cocker spaniel . . .*! Was that what Angus thought of her? Of course – with her reddish hair and dark eyes. The perfect description! How had she ever thought he loved her! Hadn't he simply been – as he was with all his admirers – too kind to turn her away?

Jenny's distracted gaze swept the mail table – the crisp litter of long envelopes, newspapers and bulky brown-wrapped parcels that would be books. There was no room for her chrysanthemums. And besides, men were supposed to be the ones who brought you flowers. Another sample of her foolish devotedness!

Angus seemed to be nearing his goodbyes.

Hugging the bouquet to her like a loved, spurned child, Jenny fled into the street.

Cold air soothed her hot cheeks. Blindly she climbed the steep green dome of the hill in the park from which she and Angus had so often admired the view. No one met her but a solitary pipe-smoker, walking his dog. All the city lay at her feet, and the sun, round and orange as one of her own chrysanthemums, poked feebly through a white fur haze. To Jenny, the ghostly landscape of domes and chimneys seemed frozen and bitter as her heart.

What had she done wrong?

The chrysanthemums irritated her now. They got in her way – brushing her face and reminding her for whom they were meant. Briefly she considered junking them in a litter bin. But then she thought how they would enliven the drab Adoption Office and tightened her hold on them resignedly.

It was Jenny's Saturday morning in. Her first appointment was for ten o'clock. She could imagine in advance the couple she was scheduled to interview. They would be young, yet not too young – the woman eager, carefully dressed in her best autumn suit, and the man a bit shy, tense, fingering his key chain or his hat. And behind them would be the new home, the redecorated flat, with the extra, empty room.

To the young couples who came to the Adoption Office, she was simply Miss Evans, the stepping stone to a warm, wonderful bundle ribboned in pink or blue – the baby they had been wanting so long, but could not have.

Jenny didn't mind being that sort of stepping stone. She loved it.

It was the sort of stepping stone she had been at her father's publishing firm that she minded. The stepping stone for people like . . . well, face it . . . Bruce Seymour.

In spite of herself, Jenny winced, although the name had long since lost its magical power to hurt. Bruce was the main reason she had moved out of the world where she was 'Jenny Evans – you know, Jonathan Evans' daughter' to one in which she was plain Miss Evans, lost and anonymous among all the other plain Miss Evanses in the city phone directory.

Her new basement flat, with the infinitesimal garden and its sunburst of chrysanthemums, her new job – these were part of her attempt to free herself from her father's shadow.

'I need a confidential clerk, Jenny,' her father had announced at dinner one night, 'now that Miss Morton is deserting me for her young whippersnapper of a fiancé. I've a crowd of young hopefuls queueing up for this job, but I don't see why my new Girl Friday shouldn't be you.'

And when Jenny held her breath, her father went on with a wave of his imperious, fine-boned hand: 'Who better, in fact? You know my authors, my business, my bothers. If the university's done its job properly, you know *every*thing.'

So Jenny, without any of the usual pavement trudging and scanning of newspaper ads, slipped into the front room of her father's publishing firm with the thick Oriental carpet and the high blue ceilings.

And she went on listening.

She listened to authoresses, just back from Kenya or Alaska, confirming newspaper interviews and literary luncheons. She listened to authors with expanding families wondering whether they could have an advance on their spring royalties. And one day, she found herself listening to a tall, plausible young man with a calfskin briefcase full of neatly typewritten chapters.

To be fair, the calfskin briefcase didn't appear until after a month – or was it six weeks? – of dinner dates and theatre parties. Bruce had shouldered up to Jenny at a crowded tea dance, scarcely giving her time to take in the dark hair and the oddly compelling yellow-green eyes, before he said:

'You're Jenny Evans?' It was more a statement than a question.

'Caught!' Jenny smiled. 'How did you know?'

She waited for the usual, *Oh everybody knows Jonathan Evans' daughter*. But it didn't come.

'I just asked our hostess: Who's that girl with the flamethrower hair. And she said . . .'

'Jenny Evans!' they chorused, and burst out laughing.

But of course Bruce had known about Jenny's father all along.

By the time the calfskin briefcase appeared one rain-jewelled April Saturday in an espresso bar, Jenny was so much under the spell of those profound, tigerish eyes that she found herself saying:

'Of course I'll read your novel, Bruce. And if I think it's good, would it be all right for me to show it to Father?'

'Well . . .' Bruce seemed to hesitate, 'if it wouldn't be too much trouble . . .'

'No trouble at all, love. He'll read it that much faster if I slip it straight onto his desk.'

Bruce seemed to think so too.

'Whatever would I do without you, Jenny!' he smiled, his hand closing over hers.

'Oh I'm not such a pushover for every hopeful author,' Jenny laughed back fondly. 'Just you.'

It wasn't until her father had read Bruce's novel – read it and come exploding into the outer office ('Where have you been hiding that young man of yours, Jenny? Ring him up! Call him in!') – that Bruce's attentions began, mysteriously, to slacken. It was his work, the rewriting, he told her, that kept him so infernally busy.

Then one afternoon Bruce breezed in to sign the final contract, and Jenny, smiling with happiness for him, ushered him in to her father's office. When he came out, she thought, they would go to some quiet little restaurant to celebrate. A good steak. Champagne, maybe . . .

Idly she drifted to the window. And there below, at the kerb, she read the evidence of her betrayal – the white sports car, the girl in the silk scarf, waiting.

Then the car and the girl and the green square beyond, with its bright carpet of daffodils, wavered in a mist. Jenny slipped into the Ladies' Room and cried her way silently through half a purse packet of Kleenex before she heard the door to her father's office open and shut, and Bruce's footsteps fade out of her life.

The engagement made the gossip columns, of course. The cover girl from Kensington and the rugged novelist were married, Jenny felt grimly sure, on the fat royalties from that first, fine-fated novel. For a few grey weeks she found herself imagining the sort of carpets and curtains they would be buying on their combined salaries.

Then Marla stepped in. Marla – the wise, wry publicity manager who had been with the firm almost since Jenny could remember, and who doubled as a mother for Jenny when Jenny badly needed mothering.

'Look, Jenny love,' Marla raked a hand through her crisp, white-tipped hair, 'you have a job here most girls would give their eyeteeth for, but where is it getting you? Shall I be frank?'

Jenny nodded, savouring the after-hours calm of the Publicity Office, quiet now, and deserted but for the two of them. 'Of course, Marla.'

'Well for the last weeks you've been moping about like a shadow. It isn't good – this hanging in the background all the time, holding your dad's hat.'

'It's not that . . .' Jenny started to object.

'Oh I know, I know,' Marla grinned and waved her silent. 'It's that young man . . . that what's-his-name whose soulful picture I've been sending to the ends of the earth!'

Jenny flushed, but couldn't help smiling a little. Marla had a way of cutting things down to size.

'You need,' Marla forged on, 'to stop being your father's daughter for a bit. Now there's a friend of mine who's wanting to let a very pleasant basement flat . . .'

And so it started, Jenny's move out from under her father's wide, overshadowing wing into a world of her own. A world in which Angus was the best part. Angus . . . !

'What lovely chrysanthemums!' The young woman's fingers reached out and caressed a petal, and Jenny, pen poised over the application blank, thought: she's gentle, she's kind.

'Oh that's too bad, here's one that must have broken off.' The woman pointed at a headless chrysanthemum, and Jenny said absently, 'Yes, I must have lost a bloom on the way to the office.' Then, with an effort, she turned to the business at hand, forcing Angus into an uncomfortable cubbyhole in her mind until the couple left.

The couple – a Mr and Mrs Lane – floated out on an almost visible pink cloud, with an appointment, after months and months of waiting, to see a baby girl in the Adoption Ward that same afternoon.

With ten minutes before her next interview, Jenny brewed herself a cup of black, bitter tea.

'Just what I needed,' she thought, grateful for the scalding warmth. 'Just what Angus would focus his camera on for the final shot in a documentary about adopting babies . . .'

And with that, Angus was back with a vengeance – all her thoughts of him plagued by the miserable refrain *It's got to end sometime . . . It's got to end . . . it's got to end.*

Why, she was worse off than Joel Hyde, that seedy and unshakable man who deluged Angus with useless documentary scripts in blank verse and sonnet sequences for twenty-minute close-ups of the sea.

'Why don't you just get rid of him once and for all,' Jenny asked Angus once, after Joel had buttonholed them in a pub and talked through several pints of bitter (paid for by Angus) about his plans for a TV play based on his own adaptation of several Japanese ghost stories. 'The man's impossible!'

'Almost impossible,' Angus laughed. 'But he may come up with something . . . someday . . .'

'And you'll wait!'

'I'll wait,' Angus had turned to her with sudden intentness, 'for a lot of things.'

And I thought he meant me, Jenny mused. How could I have been so mistaken!

Yet today she was seeing Angus for lunch . . . he *had* asked her for lunch, she hadn't made that up. They were meeting in front of the Small Mammal House at the Zoo.

Jenny giggled. She couldn't help it. That was one of the wonderful things about Angus – the queer, unexpected insights into life that his profession brought him. Or that he brought his profession. What was he filming this time? A new armadillo?

She pictured him, rapt, intent, utterly unaware of himself except as a clear lens through which the strangeness and wonder of the world revealed itself to millions of people. Angus, surrounded by his cameramen, his film cutters, his 'team'.

Where did she fit in?

Was Angus just interested in her because of her job? 'Your work,' he'd told her once, '*that's* real. That's something people should know about . . .' Perhaps Angus was only waiting to make a film of the Adoption Office before he vanished for good. Perhaps somewhere he, too, had a white car, a girl in a silk scarf . . .

Then Jenny remembered the first time Angus had kissed her – on the deserted top deck of a 53 bus. They were riding up at the front, gay as children, admiring the city lights, when all at once Angus turned to her.

'Sometimes I think I'm riding on top of the world, Jenny, all by myself, hunting and hunting for something I can't quite pin down. But tonight it's not like that. You're here . . .'

Yet now, in the light of the words she had overheard that morning, his kiss seemed shadowy and unreal as her memories of Bruce Seymour. The only difference was, Angus had no idea her father was Jonathan Evans. Angus knew her for herself alone, unglamourised by family connections. And that, at least, had been a step in the right direction.

The buzzer sounded twice before Jenny pulled herself together and admitted the couple at the door. They were soft-spoken, eager. Maybe they would like a cup of tea . . .

Under the bleached glare of the TV camera lights, the armadillo dozed like a fat, pink prima donna.

At the outskirts of the film group, Jenny waited for Angus to notice her. *If I hadn't stopped by his place this morning*, she thought wistfully, *I'd be all warm and happy now, without a worry in the world.*

The cameramen were coiling up their wires. One by one the great white lights blinked out, and by contrast the light of day seemed wan and dusty.

Angus paused, spoke a few words to a smart, sharp-faced girl at his elbow, who jotted something down on a yellow pad, then came straight for Jenny as if he'd seen through the back of his head she'd been there all along.

'Ready for lunch?'

Was it Jenny's imagination, or was Angus paler than usual, more preoccupied? She felt a sudden pang. Maybe Angus wasn't even going to bother with a film of the Adoption Office. Maybe today was the day of his ultimatum, the end of the world . . .

'How was Lancashire?' Jenny propped her elbows on the linen tablecloth and hoped Angus wouldn't notice the hollow void below the bright chatter.

But Angus seemed completely absorbed by the menu.

'Did the writer come out of his shell?' Angus had been shooting a taciturn Lancashire author, reciting and tale-telling in the moor country of the stories which had made him famous.

'Hmm?' Angus glanced up. 'Oh the writer! Yes, yes. He was superb. The places we went – the crags, the farms, the pubs – carried him away. I didn't have to do a thing.'

In spite of herself, Jenny's eyes brimmed. *This isn't what I want to talk about, this isn't it at all!* she almost cried. But still she made an effort to keep the gay smile pasted on her face, afraid that any minute it would crack.

If only Angus wouldn't stare at her so!

'I have a confession to make, Jenny.'

The soup had come, a clear, hot chicken broth, but Jenny could scarcely swallow. Her heart thudded dully in her ears: *This is it, this is the end.*

'What sort of a confession?'

'Something I should have told you long ago . . .'

Jenny waited, unable to say a word.

'Your father,' Angus said, 'is publishing a book of mine.'

'*What!*' The news was so completely unexpected, so different from what she had feared, Jenny thought for a minute she must be hearing a voice out of the past, and not Angus at all. 'But I didn't know you knew my father,' she stammered. 'I mean I didn't know you knew my father was my father . . .'

'Well I do know your father. And I also know that for some reason you haven't wanted me to know he was your father – or why would you never mention him, not once! But the book will be out soon – it's a collection of documentary scripts – and I thought it might be awkward if you saw it in a shop and thought I'd been hiding something.'

Angus gave his words time to sink in. Then he grinned.

'And while we're on the subject of books, somebody else you know is having a book published.'

'I give up!' Jenny hardly dared trust her first rush of relief. 'Who?'

'Joel Hyde.'

'Joel! Has he done it at last!'

'He not only has one publisher. He has two.' And Angus told how Joel had left the same manuscript with two separate publishers, been accepted by both, and demanded that both his advances be delivered to him in a certain pub at a certain hour. Now the two publishers, having discovered Joel's duplicity, were arguing as to which contract was signed first. 'So I'm parting company with Joel,' Angus finished. 'He's on his own two feet now. This is the end.'

This is the end. The words woke a familiar echo in Jenny's heart. The pieces of the shattered day fell into place. Joel Hyde, with his big, soulful eyes. Joel Hyde, with his floppy, cocker-spaniel hair . . .

'And now,' Angus breathed, 'that I've explained so much, how about you explaining something, Miss Jenny Evans.'

'But what can I explain?' Jenny wondered.

Angus fumbled in his breast pocket and withdrew a crumpled, orange shape which he laid like Exhibit A on the white cloth.

'This!'

Jenny just stared.

'I thought,' Angus went on agreeably, 'you might happen to have some idea where it came from. I found it on the doormat this morning, and as I know of no other young woman with a fondness for orange chrysanthemums . . .'

'I dropped it,' Jenny confessed.

'Not by accident, I hope.'

Jenny flushed.

'You know,' Angus observed, 'when you turn pink like that you look ravishing enough to have a book dedicated to you.'

Jenny's colour deepened.

'Or would that bore you? Daughter of a great bookman as you are?'

'No,' Jenny managed faintly, 'it wouldn't bore me.'

And as Angus reached for her hand, Jenny felt herself shedding the last, tattered shadows of self-doubt and stepping into the serene, clear light of her own world – her world with Angus.

A Winter's Tale

Ts,[*] autumn 1961, Smith College

A smothery cloud from Irene's after-breakfast cigarette sent me to the cottage window where I stood for a minute, drinking in the surprising green of the December fields under the moortops. It was a landscape without blandishments – stark, snow-chalked and cold. Yet on this particular morning I found it curiously refreshing.

So I lingered, reluctant to face the untidy breakfast trays – the plates scummy with egg yolk, the bacon fat whitening under a peppery mess of toast crumbs. Usually, by this late hour, I'd put breakfast half a day behind me and returned from a stroll on the road that linked the sparse, hilltop farms. But what schedule, however settled, could withstand a visit from Irene!

---

[*] Typescript has holograph and typewritten corrections and additions by SP. Typed at top right, 'Sylvia Plath / Court Green / North Tawton / Devon.' In a letter to her mother written on 24 December 1960, SP wrote 'Ted & I wrote out the plot for a romance set up here on the moors', which may be the genesis of this story (*The Letters of Sylvia Plath, Volume* 2: 555).

Vivid as a leftover Christmas ornament in her red, quilted robe, she nursed her third cup of coffee like a sweet, necessary medicine. But Irene wasn't spending the winter holidays in the country for her health. Nothing less than Operation Rescue had dragged her up from the city. And the person she intended to rescue was me.

I turned, trying to bridge the silence between us. 'Do you think he'll come?'

'The faithful Wilfred!' Irene smiled. 'Is there a chance he *won't* come!'

'No chance,' I sighed. 'Knowing Wilfred.'

'Well at long last you've invited him. He was tickled pink.'

A vision of Wilfred – tall, earnest and tickled pink – made me stifle a little laugh. Thank heaven I could laugh! Ten months ago I couldn't even manage that.

Ten months ago. I didn't like to think of it – of the bleak, hateful flight north to the cottage Spencer and I had fitted out so snugly as a retreat from the bustle and obligations of the city. The cottage reminded me of him, of course – what didn't! But in a different and easier way than the town house, with his library, his desk, and the countless emblems of his life and work.

'You're mad, Kate,' everybody had said then. 'Mad to hide yourself away up north with nothing to do but brood and be lonely. What's the good? Down here in town you can carry on Spencer's work, see your old friends, and mend, mend . . .'

But I didn't believe in mending. If the heart was fragile, like a porcelain cup, and a great loss shattered it, all the time and kindness in the world couldn't hide the ugly cracks. Once the precious liquid of love had seeped away, you were left dry. Dry and empty.

'There!' Irene's voice scattered my thoughts. 'You've done it again!'

'Done what?'

'Gone off. We'll be talking along, and then, suddenly, your eyes go all funny and far, as if you were looking straight through me to something a hundred miles away.'

'Surely I'm not *such* a bad hostess!' I joked. But I knew what was coming.

'Just as I thought,' Irene pursued. 'This place is doing you no good. It's making you more broody, not less. You know, Kate, from infant school on, you were always rather too broody . . .'

The evocation of infant school made me smile.

'Come back with me!' Irene reached out an impulsive hand. 'Come back with me and Wilfred. You could stay at my flat until you've found a little place of your own. You could start up work again. Wilfred's often said the publishing house hasn't been the same without you, the verve's gone out of it . . .'

'The verve!' I shook my head, and in spite of all my fine, firm resolutions, a wave of emptiness ached up into my throat. 'I'm afraid the verve was Spencer's.'

But still I took it up, examined it – the idea of a comeback, as I so often had in the black vacancy between midnight and morning. It glittered and shone like one of those glass paperweights with a miniature village inside it. There would be talk, cocktails, laughter, gossip and news of friends to fill the empty spaces. Oh it was beguiling, all right, that bright, tight, self-enclosed globe.

Only I couldn't fool myself. I had come to savour loneliness. It was a part of Spencer's legacy, after all – cold as mountain water, and more constant than anything in this world, after Spencer's love . . .

But Irene was waiting.

'You forget.' I started briskly to stack the breakfast plates.

'I like it here. Besides, Wilfred sends me books to read for the firm, so I keep my finger in.'

'But these people! These – these villagers!' Irene exploded. 'What have you in common with them?'

I was careful not to hesitate. 'They're pleasant enough.'

'Do you call people like that man on the hill, that what's his name . . .'

'Mr Blake,' I supplied serenely.

'Do you call *him* pleasant?'

I couldn't help smiling. Trust Irene to pick on the local curmudgeon. Of course Justin Blake couldn't properly be called local – he didn't have aunts and uncles and cousins and in-laws perched on all the surrounding hillsides, nor the moss-eaten stones of ancestors in the village graveyard. When the neighbourhood manor had been put up for auction some five or six years ago, he had simply appeared out of the blue and prevented the grim stone mausoleum from becoming a boys' school and a torment to a lot of innocent youngsters by buying the place himself.

Justin Blake's arrival preceded mine by a long way, but after picking up a word here and a detail there, I pieced together a story too like my own for comfort. Blake had buried a young wife, dead of leukaemia, in the dour Welsh hills, then vanished on a long, botanical study of the grasses in Africa, South America and other outlandish corners, until the day came when he chose to cloister himself under the moors in a house bleak and scowling and echoingly lonely as his own temperament.

Irene had run into what she termed 'a very rude man' in the village while buying some Christmas greens for the mantel – decorations which had already begun to strew their dried brown needles over the hearthrug as if unable to face the onslaught of the New Year.

The man's 'rudeness' followed upon Irene's asking about walks over the neighbouring moors to places of interest such as Wuthering Heights. Instead of being helpful – taking her aside and mapping out a few strolls, I guess – the man had growled that only a nitwit would traipse about up there at this season, not knowing the landmarks and danger spots.

Of course, there was a good bit of truth in this rather blunt advice, but that wasn't really what piqued Irene. If Irene had a weakness, it was wanting to be the centre of things, especially the centre of a man's attention. That was something *I* knew from infant school!

And Justin Blake simply couldn't stand women. Or so the villagers would have one believe. It was almost as if he felt each live and blooming woman had usurped the place of the wife whose frail shadow seemed to accompany him wherever he went and shroud him from contact with the world.

But Irene knew nothing of this. For her, Justin was one more eligible male – the more interesting, perhaps, because so unlike the groomed, chivalrous city type to which she was accustomed.

'I'm sure Mr Blake didn't mean to be rude,' I told Irene, although of course I wasn't sure at all what went on behind that taciturn face I glimpsed so seldom. 'It's only the gruff way he has.'

But Irene wasn't mollified. 'He needs taking down a peg,' she said. 'That's my guess.'

'You wouldn't say that if . . .' But I broke off. For some reason it didn't seem right to share Blake's story out like common bread.

'Mind you, I didn't let him think he'd convinced me!' Irene finished. 'I told him I'd be seeing those old ruins on the first fair day, no matter what!'

And whether it was this conversation that put the idea in our heads, or desperation as to what to do with Wilfred, or just that the good weather held, the last day of the old year found the three of us tramping in single file along the narrow path from Haworth to the moors, Irene leading, me in the middle, and Wilfred bringing up the rear.

It seemed we had hardly started when Wilfred asked, 'Is it very far?' Since Wilfred's main exercise was being whisked effortlessly up and down by elevators and escalators, I began to wonder if the strenuousness of our little journey wouldn't prove too much for him.

'Not very far,' I smiled back.

All the way to Haworth on the bus, Wilfred had peered down at me in his kindly, near-sighted way, chatting on about the firm and how business was going. I should have felt grateful for his solicitude, I guess, but somehow I couldn't be easy with Wilfred any more, as I could when he was simply Spencer's friend and right-hand man.

Wilfred was a bachelor, and I knew perfectly well that all our mutual friends had been matching us up since Spencer's death – after a decent interval, of course. I also know that no interval at all, be it an ice age, could make me think of Wilfred as anything but a dear, good friend.

Irene showed little tact, I thought, in her obvious manoeuvring to keep out of our path. Already her red hood bobbed a bend or two ahead.

As the green farms fell away behind us, we entered a rust-coloured world of bracken and heather, hushed and still in the watery noon light. Now that the village had dropped from view, the moors looked identical, without tree or house to signpost us on our way.

'Come on, slowpokes!' Irene funnelled her voice back to us between two fur-mittened hands. I was thinking how bright and lithe she looked against the sombre backdrop, when the white mittens flew apart. For a moment they fanned the air in an odd way, as if Irene were attempting to fly. Then her whole figure crumpled out of sight.

Immediately I broke into a run. The dull thump of my boots on the frozen turf vied with the loud beat of my heart as I slipped and slid to where Irene lay in a deep pothole at the side of the path.

'Are you all right?' I knelt beside her. 'What happened?'

'Just turned my ankle. I'll be fine in a minute.' Irene lowered her voice to a conspiratorial whisper. 'How's Wilfred?'

I felt myself blushing like a schoolgirl and said, a bit crossly, 'Don't get any wild ideas, Irene.'

Then Wilfred was upon us. 'Is the walk too much for you girls?' he asked hopefully. 'Do you want to turn back?'

'Not a bit of it!' Irene winced as I helped her up, but then she smiled, and I figured she must be all right.

I had to admit the black stone ruins seemed a lot farther from town than when I had trekked out to it on a guided tour that summer. Wilfred was making repeated references to cream cakes and Brontë steaks by the time the rooftree rose ahead of us – the prow of a ghost ship in a frozen wilderness.

Now it was the literary associations of the place that drew Wilfred on, while I saw with misgiving that the sun had shrouded itself in grey clouds and smelt the damp chill on the wind that heralds snow.

The first flakes were hissing into the dried grasses as Irene took me aside and murmured: 'I don't want to be spoil-sport, love, but I do think I've damaged my ankle. It's like walking on needles and pins.'

Without more ado, I sat Irene down on a cushion of turf and gently removed her red leather boot with its high, fashionable heel. My heart sank when I saw her ankle. It was double in size and an alarming shade of purple, tinged with yellow-green.

'A bad sprain, I'd say,' Wilfred pronounced cheerfully at my elbow. 'Shouldn't walk another step on that.'

'Oh, don't be so gloomy!' I exclaimed in exasperation. Then I bit my tongue. What right had I to give way to my apprehensions? I was responsible for my two friends, after all – Irene with a sprained, possibly broken ankle, and Wilfred – Wilfred! He was muttering something about going back to get a sledge.

'You can't get a sledge out here.' Irene looked close to tears. 'There's no snow.'

'There'll be snow enough by the time I get back to the village,' Wilfred said seriously.

The ground was certainly whitening fast. With Irene's lameness, we'd take twice as long going back as we had in coming. By that time it would be night, or nearly, and the snow a perilous impediment. At least there was a path. A path! My heart jumped a beat. At this rate there wouldn't be a path for long!

Stories of a local woman caught on the moors in a blizzard floated back to me. She had wandered round and round in circles, then sat in the shelter of a ruined wall and smoked one cigarette after another. How had it ended? Frozen to death or rescued – I couldn't for the life of me remember which.

Then, from the cold, polar gloom of my thoughts, I heard Wilfred and Irene arguing.

'Get back to the village!' Irene's voice rose shrilly. 'You're not going to leave the two of us out here to freeze to death!'

'Why I don't see how else I can get help . . .'

'Help! You and Kate will have to be the help. I'll put one arm round your neck and one arm round Kate's neck and hop back on one foot if I have to. Better still, you can carry me . . .'

'I'm afraid there's no question of that,' Wilfred said sadly. 'I've a slipped disc, and I'm under doctor's orders not to put any weight on it. That's why I think I'd better start off for the village and get some men.'

I don't know how to describe the queer feeling I had then – as if I stood far off, on a star or a cloud, watching three tiny characters in a play a million miles below. The distance between me and the reality of our situation frightened me a little, a trick of numbness learned since Spencer's death which protected me from hurtful involvements.

Then Irene stood up and tried to walk, and I think it was the genuine pain in her face that dropped me back to earth.

'We'd better let Wilfred go for some men,' I said, making her sit down again in the shelter of the stone doorway. 'They'll be here in no time with a stretcher and blankets and hot coffee. Meanwhile we'll build a fire and sing songs to keep the wolves away.'

If my words had a hollow ring, Irene didn't seem to notice. She beamed at me gratefully. It was only as Wilfred bade us to take care and started off into the swirling twilight that I realised what a comfort his presence had been.

There's something almost selfish about sorrow. I'd been thinking of myself as alone and bereft for so long I found it more and more difficult to interest myself in the feelings of others. Wilfred's affection had always seemed unreal to me, even a touch ridiculous. Now I found myself moved to tears by his setting out over the unfamiliar moors to get help.

'A fine New Year's Eve!' Irene muttered, as with numb fingers I gathered up bits of dry timber. 'If I were in town now, I'd be sitting in a hot tub breathing in Gardenia Essence and wondering whether to wear my red satin or the white lace.'

New Year's Eve! I hadn't even thought of it. Then I realised it was nearer the truth to say I'd made every effort not to think of it. My first year without Spencer wasn't a thing to dwell on, much less celebrate. The traditional image of couples kissing under mistletoe at the stroke of twelve seemed sweet and unattainable as a scene glimpsed through the window of a stranger's house.

'We need a Yule log,' Irene observed, as I piled my scanty harvest of dry sticks against the house wall, out of the wind. 'Or a Saint Bernard, complete with brandy.'

'To be even more practical, we need a match.'

Irene fumbled in her jacket and produced a monogrammed lighter.

I flicked the lighter once, twice, three times. Nothing happened.

'Here, let me try.' At last a small flame leapt into life, and Irene set it to the pile of tinder.

My heart rose with the sparks that crackled skyward. If only the fire would keep alight, we could warm our hands and spirits until Wilfred's return. But within minutes, the sparse pile of sticks consumed itself, and we were left contemplating a handful of red embers.

There was a little pause.

'I'm frozen to the bone,' Irene said then.

'Me too,' I admitted. 'I suppose we ought to move about to keep from getting frost-bitten . . .' But I remembered Irene's ankle and fell silent.

The gap in our talk accentuated the weird noise of the wind. It had a ghostly, half-human sound, as if it were trying to warn us in some way. Already the whiteness was swathing in about us like a sinister muffler.

I was wondering if I would ever see the glow of my coal fire again, when we heard the footsteps. Both of us started, scarcely breathing. Something was wrong. There were no voices or encouraging halloos, as there would be with a group of rescuers and Wilfred at their head. Only one person was creaking toward us through the snow.

'It's too soon for Wilfred to be back,' Irene whispered, clutching my hand, her eyes wide with fear.

I felt a cold foreboding. What sort of person other than a ghost, or madman, would be wandering the moors so silently that snow-filled evening?

Instinctively, Irene and I shrank together in the shadow of the doorway as the beam of a torch angled round the side of the cottage and came to rest in a white glare at our feet.

'I thought as much!'

Behind the light a figure loomed, but dazzled as we were, it was impossible to make out his features. Still, he sounded sane and sensible, though hardly friendly.

'Have you come from the village?' I spoke up a bit defensively. 'We sent someone back for help. My friend here's hurt her ankle.'

'I don't know about that,' the man said. 'All I know is a farmer told me he'd seen three people passing behind his barn in the direction of the moors earlier today, and he hadn't seen them since. So I thought it would do no harm, in this foul weather, if I trekked up for a look . . .'

Beside me, Irene caught her breath. At first I thought her ankle must have given a twinge. Then the man went on: 'I figured nobody roundabout would be giddy enough to try the moors this time of year, so it must be strangers, and strangers are that much more likely to get themselves lost . . .'

And I knew Irene had recognised his voice.

Whether at Justin Blake's patronising tone or at his standing there and lecturing us while we slowly froze to death, anger surged up in my heart. I fairly glowed with it.

'It's very kind of you to come out, I'm sure, Mr Blake,' I said tartly. 'But perhaps you'd give me a hand with my friend first, and scold us later. As I said, she's hurt her ankle . . .'

'I believe Mr Blake and I have met,' Irene said meekly.

The torch light approached and took us in, and a strange thing happened. Justin Blake laughed. It wasn't a mocking laugh, nor yet a happy laugh, and it was a bit harsh and rusty from disuse, but for a man reputed never to have laughed in his life, it was an encouraging sound.

'I should think we've met!' Justin Blake said. 'And here you are, cold as a church mouse, just as I said you'd be if you insisted on facing bog holes and blizzards this time of year!'

'Well, now that I've been so good as to prove you right,' Irene murmured, 'perhaps you'll help me back to the village. Then I won't trouble you further.'

'It's no trouble,' said Justin Blake. 'If your friend here will just hold the torch . . .'

I took the torch, struck by the new undercurrent of gentleness in his tone and feeling, more than ever, outside the lighted window, looking in.

We made a queer procession in the grey gloom – Irene slung over Justin Blake's shoulder in a fireman's carry, and me bringing up the rear with the torch. It wasn't until I saw two figures waving from the stile gate of the first farm that I realised I had completely forgotten Wilfred!

'Halloo!' came his cheerful voice. 'Everybody all right?'

It occurred to me that Wilfred must have been warming himself by a kitchen fire for a good hour. Not that I grudged him the comfort, but it gave me pause. And surely it was my imagination that credited him with an extra plumpness – the sort of plumpness conferred by buttered scones with liberal dollops of cream and jam.

The farmer with Wilfred spoke first to Justin Blake. 'I found this one knocking about the cowsheds soon after you left . . .'

Wilfred had the grace to look sheepish.

'. . . so I brought him in and told him you'd gone to fetch the rest of the party.' Then he turned to Irene and me. 'My wife's got some hot tea ready. I expect you could use it, if you're half as hungry as *him*.'

Later, as we sipped our mugs of sweet, scalding tea round the kitchen fire in the company of the farmer and his wife and a big ginger cat, I began to wonder if a stranger's kitchen wasn't as good a place to spend the New Year's Eve as any.

I was careful to keep my eyes on my teacup, or on the cat, or on the fire

– anywhere but on the face of Justin Blake. I'd never seen him at close quarters before. In the leaping firelight I couldn't tell the colour of his eyes, but I knew they would be clear, and still, and full of reflections. And while I listened to him speaking to the farmer and his wife – and to Irene – I tried to trace the odd sense of annoyance I felt. As if Justin Blake, a perfect stranger, had betrayed me in some way.

It was only as we jolted home over the dark, snow-muffled moor road in the farmer's van – Irene between the farmer and Justin in front, and Wilfred and I crouched on some sacking at the back – that I realised what the trouble was.

I had wanted Justin Blake to stand apart, morose and proud in his grief. And instead, here he was – thoughtful and talkative. He had bound up Irene's sprained ankle like a gentle doctor.

In a wild and disconcerting fantasy, I imagined Justin Blake thawing out altogether, altering, marrying Irene. Not that Irene would ever marry – she was too fond of her freedom and her career for that. Or so I'd always imagined . . .

Ruthlessly I dragged out my secret vision: Justin Blake on one lone moortop and me on the other, united in our constancy to the ghosts that roamed there. But then I began to wonder if the proper place for ghosts wasn't a bleak place, like Wuthering Heights, rather than the hearts of the living.

'Kate . . .' Wilfred whispered, and I came to with a start. The snow had stopped, I noticed, and a few early stars were showing.

'Yes, Wilfred?'

'I've to be back in town tomorrow. There's so little time. Is there any chance . . . any chance at all, of your coming back with me?'

This is it! said a commonsensical inner voice. Your chance to take a hold on life again. And isn't a hold, however partial, better than nothing? Better than the miles and miles of nothingness stretching away on either side of the starlit road.

But I knew the answer, even before I heard myself say gently: 'No, Wilfred, I'll be staying on up here. I've grown so used to it now, it's a kind of home.'

Wilfred heaved a deep, dubious sigh. 'Well, if you're sure . . .'

'I'm sure.'

New Year's Day dawned as it should – beautiful, cold and pure. It was a day of departures. Irene and Wilfred left together on the early train, and I could see how the prospect of the city cheered them after the unrelieved solitude of the moortops. Resolutely, I started to sweep up the traces of their stay.

I emptied the ashtrays, fed the withered greens to the fire, put the breadcrumbs out for the birds and did the washing up. And still the whole morning stretched ahead, virginal and fresh. Idly I picked up a book from the pile of new novels Wilfred had left. Then, after scanning three pages without taking in a word, I set it down again.

I didn't feel sad. I didn't even feel lonely, the way I had expected to, after all the goodbyes. I felt *odd*, as if a weight had shifted somewhere deep inside, lending me a new, disturbing buoyancy. I considered taking a walk in the crisp snow. But I didn't. I did something quite ridiculous instead.

I baked a huge and very fancy coffee cake.

The cake was much too big for one person and would go stale before I could eat half of it. I should, of course, have made it before Irene and Wilfred left.

I set the cake, still warm, on my best china plate and admired the honey glaze, the holiday bits of fruit peel, and the elaborate pattern of pecans. Was there any poor or starving family nearby I could enrich with it?

Then I had to laugh. I laughed so hard the tears came. Every family in my village was well fed, even stuffed by now, on turkey and Christmas pudding. If anybody needed a treat like that coffee cake, it was the solitary widow on the hill. And that was me.

I brewed a fresh pot of coffee and was about to carve myself an extra thick wedge of cake when I heard the gate latch click. The post, I thought, cake knife poised in midair. Then I thought: No, not the post, it's a holiday. And I put down the knife and started for the door.

I could hardly see Justin Blake for the great armload of holly.

I didn't welcome him. I didn't even smile. After all, we were nearly perfect strangers.

'She's gone,' I said. 'Irene left for London this morning on the early train.'

'So she told me she would do.'

'Well then . . . ?' The words hung stupidly on the clear air.

'I suppose I should explain *this*.' Justin Blake glanced down at the holly. 'But I'm not sure I can explain it myself. I got up this morning, and I felt so good after last night – just for *doing* something, for being of use some way, that I went out and picked all the holly from the woods behind my house.'

I could feel the corners of my mouth beginning to twitch.

'And I couldn't think what to *do* with the blasted stuff after I picked it,' Justin Blake finished. 'Except give it to somebody.'

'And you thought of me?'

Justin Blake nodded.

'Well, I have a similar problem, Mr Blake,' I said. 'Only it's about a coffee cake. Perhaps, if you'd care to step in for a minute, we could discuss it.'

And as I took my New Year's bouquet from Justin Blake, the dazzle of the snowy moortops filled my heart. The moors were clean and white and full of promise, like the first page of a chapter not yet written.

Mothers

Ts,[*] 1961–2, Smith College

Esther was still upstairs when Rose called in at the back door. 'Yoohoo, Esther, you ready?' Rose lived with her retired husband Cecil in the topmost of the two cottages in the lane leading up to Esther's house – a large, thatched manor farm with its own cobbled court. The cobbles were not ordinary street cobbles, but pitch cobbles, their narrow, oblong sides forming a mosaic melted to gentleness by centuries of boots and hooves. The cobbles extended under the stout, nail-studded oak door into the dark hall between the kitchen and scullery, and in Old Lady Bromehead's day had formed the floor of the kitchen and scullery as well. But after old Lady Bromehead fell and broke her hip at the age of ninety and was removed to a Home, a series of servantless tenants had persuaded her son to lay linoleum in those rooms.

The oak door was the back door; everybody but the random stranger used it. The front door, yellow-painted and flanked by two pungent bushes of box, faced across an acre of stinging nettles to where the church indicated a grey heaven above its scallop of surrounding headstones.

The front gate opened just under the corner of the graveyard.

Esther tugged her red turban down around her ears, then adjusted the folds of her cashmere coat loosely so that she might, to the casual eye, seem simply tall, stately and fat, rather than eight months pregnant. Rose had not rung the bell before calling in. Esther imagined Rose, curious, avid Rose, eying the bare floorboards of the front hall and the untidy strewing of the baby's toys from front room to kitchen. Esther couldn't get used to people opening the door and calling in without ringing first. The postman did it, and the baker, and the grocer's boy,

---

[*] Typescript with holograph corrections and additions by SP. Typed at top right of typescript: 'Sylvia Plath / Court Green / North Tawton / Devonshire, England.' Published as 'The Mothers' Union', *McCall's* (October 1972): 81, 126, 128, 130, 142, with the following leading paragraph: 'Esther was a newcomer—and an American besides. What would it take, she wondered, for these conventional villagers to accept her?'

and now Rose, who was a Londoner and should have known better.

Once when Esther was arguing loudly and freely with Tom over breakfast, the back door had popped open and a handful of letters and magazines clapped onto the hall cobbles. The postman's cry of 'Morning!' faded. Esther felt spied on. For some time after that, she bolted the back door from the inside, but the sound of tradesmen trying the door and finding it bolted in broad day, and then ringing the bell and waiting until she came and noisily undid the bolt, embarrassed her even more than their former calling in. So she left the bolt alone again, and took care not to argue so much, or at least not so loudly.

When Esther came down, Rose was waiting just outside the door, smartly dressed in a satiny lavender hat and checked tweed coat. At her side stood a blonde, bony-faced woman with bright blue eyelids and no eyebrows. This was Mrs Nolan, the wife of the pub keeper at the White Hart. Mrs Nolan, Rose said, never came to the Mothers' Union meetings because she had no one to go with, so Rose was bringing her to this month's meeting, together with Esther.

'Do you mind waiting just another minute, Rose, while I tell Tom I'm off?' Esther could feel Rose's shrewd eyes checking over her hat, her gloves, her patent leather heels, as she turned and picked her ginger way up the cobbles to the back garden. Tom was planting roller berries in the newly spaded square behind the empty stables. The baby sat in the path on a pile of red earth, ladling dirt into her lap with a battered spoon.

Esther felt her little grievances about Tom's not shaving and his letting the baby play in the dirt fade at the sight of the two of them, quiet and in perfect accord. 'Tom!' She rested her white glove, without thinking, on the earth-crusted wooden gate. 'I'm off now. If I'm late getting back, will you boil the baby an egg?'

Tom straightened and shouted some word of encouragement that foundered between them in the dense November air, and the baby turned in the direction of Esther's voice, her mouth black, as if she had been eating dirt. But Esther slipped away, before the baby could heave up and toddle after her, to where Rose and Mrs Nolan were waiting at the bottom of the court.

Esther let them through the seven-foot-high stockade-like gate and latched it behind them. Then Rose crooked out her two elbows, and Mrs Nolan took one, and Esther took the other, and the three women teetered in their best shoes down the stony lane past Rose's cottage and the cottage of the old blind man and his spinster sister at the bottom, and into the road.

'We're meeting in the church today.' Rose tongued a peppermint drop into her cheek and passed the twist of tinfoil round. Both Esther and Mrs Nolan refused politely. 'We don't always meet in church, though. Only when there's new members joining up.'

Mrs Nolan rolled her pale eyes skyward, whether in general consternation or simply at the prospect of church, Esther couldn't tell. 'Are you new in town, too?' she asked Mrs Nolan across Rose's front, leaning forward a little.

Mrs Nolan gave a short, joyless laugh. 'I've been here *six years*.'

'Why, you must know everybody by now!'

'Hardly a *soul*,' Mrs Nolan intoned, causing misgivings, like a flock of chilly-toed birds, to clutter at Esther's heart. If Mrs Nolan, an Englishwoman by her looks and accent, and a pubkeeper's wife as well, felt herself a stranger in Devon after six years, what hope had Esther, an American, of infiltrating that rooted society ever at all?

The three women proceeded, arm in arm, along the road under the high, holly-hedged boundary of Esther's acre, past her front gate and under the red cob wall of the churchyard. Flat, lichen-bitten tombstones tilted at the level of their heads. Worn deep into the earth long before pavements were thought of, the road curved like some ancient riverbed under its slant banks.

Along past the butcher's window, with its midweek display of pork hocks and cartons of drippings, and up the alley by the constabulary and the public conveniences, Esther could see other women converging, singly and in groups, at the lychgate. Burdened by their cumbersome woollens and drab hats, they seemed, without exception, gnarled and old.

As Esther and Mrs Nolan hung back at the gate, nudging Rose ahead, Esther recognised the uncommonly ugly person who had come up behind her, smiling and nodding, as the woman who sold her an immense swede for one-and-six at the Harvest Festival. The swede had bulged like a miraculous storybook vegetable above the rim of Esther's shopping basket, filling it entirely; but when she got round to slicing it up, it turned out to be spongy and tough as cork. Two minutes in the pressure cooker, and it shrank to a wan, orange mash that blackened the bottom and sides of the pot with a slick, evil-smelling liquor. I should have simply boiled it straight off, Esther thought now, following Rose and Mrs Nolan under the stumpy, pollarded limes to the church door.

The interior of the church seemed curiously light. Then Esther realised she had never been inside before except at night, for Evensong. Already the back pews were filling with women, rustling, ducking, kneeling and beaming benevolently in every direction. Rose led Esther and Mrs Nolan to an empty pew halfway up the aisle. She pushed Mrs Nolan in first, then stepped in herself, drawing Esther after her. Rose was the only one of the three who knelt. Esther bowed her head and shut her eyes, but her mind remained blank; she just felt hypocritical. She opened her eyes and looked about.

Mrs Nolan was the one woman in the congregation without a hat. Esther caught her eye, and Mrs Nolan raised her eyebrows, or rather, the skin of her forehead where the brows had been. Then she leaned forward. 'I never,' she confided, 'come here much.'

Esther shook her head and mouthed, 'Neither do I.' That was not quite true. A month after her arrival in town, Esther had started attending Evensong without a miss. The month's gap had been an uneasy one. Twice on Sundays, morning and evening, the town bell-ringers sent their carillons pounding out over the surrounding countryside. There was no escape from the probing notes. They bit into the air and shook it with a doggy zeal. The bells had made Esther feel left out, as if from some fine local feast.

A few days after they had moved into the house, Tom called her downstairs for a visitor. The rector was sitting in the front parlour among the boxes of unpacked books. A small grey man, with protruding ears, an Irish accent and a professionally benign, all-tolerating smile, he spoke of his years in Kenya, where he had known Jomo Kenyatta, of his children in Australia and of his English wife.

Any minute, now, Esther thought, he's going to ask if we go to church. But the rector did not mention church. He dandled the baby on one knee and left shortly, his compact, black figure dwindling down the path to the front gate.

A month later, still perturbed by the evangelical bells, Esther dashed off, half in spite of herself, a note to the rector. She would like to attend Evensong. Would he mind explaining the ritual to her?

She waited nervously one day, two days, each afternoon readying tea and cake which she and Tom ate only when the tea hour was safely past. Then, on the third afternoon, she was basting a nightdress of yellow flannel for the baby when she happened to glance out the window toward the front gate. A stout, black shape paced slowly up through the stinging nettles.

Esther welcomed the rector with some misgiving. She told him right away that she had been brought up a Unitarian. But the rector smilingly replied that as a Christian, of whatever persuasion, she would be welcome in his church. Esther swallowed an impulse to blurt out that she was an atheist and end it there. Opening the Book of Common Prayer the rector had brought for her to use, she felt a sickly, deceitful glaze overtake her features; she followed him through the order of service. The apparition of the Holy Ghost and the words 'resurrection of the flesh' gave her an itchy sense of her duplicity. Yet when she confessed that she really could not believe in the resurrection of the flesh (she did not quite dare to say 'nor of the spirit'), the rector seemed unperturbed. He merely asked if she believed in the efficacy of prayer.

'Oh yes, yes, I do!' Esther heard herself exclaim, amazed at the tears that so opportunely jumped to her eyes, and meaning only: How I would like to. Later, she wondered if the tears weren't caused by her vision of the vast, irrevocable gap between her faithless state and the beatitude of belief. She hadn't the heart to tell the rector she had been through all this pious trying ten years before, in Comparative Religion classes at college, and only ended up sorry she was not a Jew.

The rector suggested that his wife meet her at the next Evensong service and sit with her, so she should not feel strange. Then he seemed to think better of it. She might prefer, after all, to come with her neighbours, Rose and Cecil. They were 'churchgoers'. It was only as the rector picked up his two prayer books and his black hat that Esther remembered the plate of sugared cakes and the waiting tea tray in the kitchen. But by then it was too late. Something more than forgetfulness, she thought, watching the rector's measured retreat through the green nettles, had kept back those cakes.

The church filled rapidly now. The rector's wife, long-faced, angular, kind, tiptoed back from her front pew to pass out copies of the Mothers' Union Service Book. Esther felt the baby throb and kick, and placidly thought: I am a mother; I belong here.

The primeval cold of the church floor was just beginning its deadly entry into her footsoles when, rustling and hushing, the women rose in a body, and the rector, with his slow, holy gait, came down the aisle.

The organ drew breath; they started on the opening hymn. The organist must have been a novice. Every few bars a discord prolonged itself, and the voices of the women skidded up and down after the elusive melody with a scatty, catlike desperation. There were kneelings, responses, more hymns.

The rector stepped forward and repeated at length an anecdote which had formed the substance of his last Evensong sermon. Then he brought out an awkward, even embarrassing metaphor Esther had heard him use at a baptism ceremony a week earlier, about physical and spiritual abortions. Surely the rector was indulging himself. Rose slipped another peppermint between her lips, and Mrs Nolan wore the glazed, far look of an unhappy seeress.

At last three women, two quite young and attractive, one very old, came forward and knelt at the altar to be received into the Mothers' Union. The rector forgot the name of the eldest (Esther could feel him forgetting it) and had to wait until his wife had the presence to glide forward and whisper it in his ear. The ceremony proceeded.

Four o'clock had struck before the rector allowed the women to depart. Esther quitted the church in the company of Mrs Nolan, Rose having caught up with two of her other friends, Brenda, the wife of the greengrocer, and stylish Mrs Hotchkiss who lived on Widdop Hill and bred Alsatians.

'You staying for tea?' Mrs Nolan asked, as the current of women ferried them across the street and down the alley toward the yellow brick constabulary.

'That's what I came for,' Esther said, 'I think we deserve it.'

'When's your next baby?'

Esther laughed. 'Any minute.'

The women were diverting themselves from the alley into a courtyard at the left. Esther and Mrs Nolan followed them into a dark, barnlike room which reminded Esther depressingly of church camp-outs and group-sings. Her eyes searched the dusk for a tea urn or some other sign of conviviality, but fell on nothing but a shuttered upright piano. The rest of the women did not stop; they filed ahead up an ill-lit flight of steps.

Beyond a pair of swinging doors, a brightly lit room opened out revealing two very long tables, set parallel to each other and swaddled with clean white linen. Down the centre of the tables, plates of cake and pastries alternated with bowls of brass-coloured chrysanthemums. There was a startling number of cakes, all painstakingly decorated, some with cherries and nuts and some with sugar lace. Already the rector had taken a stand at the head of one table, and his wife at the head of the other, and the townswomen were crowding into the closely spaced chairs below. The women in Rose's group fitted themselves in at the far end of the rector's table. Mrs Nolan was jockeyed unwillingly into a position facing the rector, at the very foot, Esther at her right and an empty chair that had been overlooked at her left.

The women sat, settled.

Mrs Nolan turned to Esther. 'What do you *do* here?' It was the question of a desperate woman.

'Oh, I have the baby.' Then Esther was ashamed of her evasion. 'I type some of my husband's work.'

Rose leaned over to them. 'Her husband writes for the *radio*.'

'I paint,' said Mrs Nolan.

'What in?' Esther wondered, a little startled.

'Oils, mainly. But I'm no good.'

'Ever tried watercolour?'

'Oh, yes, but you have to be good. You have to get it right the first time.'

'What do you paint then? Portraits?'

Mrs Nolan wrinkled her nose and took out a pack of cigarettes. 'Do you suppose we can smoke? No, I'm no good at portraits. But sometimes I paint Ricky.'

The tiny, extinguished-looking woman making the rounds with tea arrived at Rose.

'We can smoke, can't we?' Mrs Nolan asked Rose.

'Oh, I don't think so. I wanted to the worst way when I first came, but nobody else did.'

Mrs Nolan looked up at the woman with the tea. 'Can we smoke?'

'Ooh, I shouldn't think so,' the woman said. 'Not in the church rooms.'

'Is it a fire law?' Esther wanted to know. 'Or something religious?' But nobody could say. Mrs Nolan began to tell Esther about her little boy of seven, named Benedict. Ricky was, it turned out, a hamster.

Suddenly the swinging doors flew open to admit a flushed young woman with a steaming tray. 'The sausages, the sausages!' pleased voices cried from various parts of the room.

Esther felt very hungry, almost faint. Even the ribbons of clear, hot grease oozing from her sausage in its pastry wrapper didn't stop her – she took a large bite, and so did Mrs Nolan. At that moment everybody bowed their heads. The rector said grace.

Cheeks bulging, Esther and Mrs Nolan peered at each other, making eyes and stifling their giggles, like schoolgirls with a secret. Then, grace over, everybody began sending plates up and down and helping themselves with energy. Mrs Nolan told Esther about Little Benedict's father, Big Benedict (her second husband), who had been a rubber planter in Malaya until he had the misfortune to fall sick and be sent home.

'Have some dough bread.' Rose passed a plate of moist, fruity slices, and Mrs Hotchkiss followed this up with a three-layer chocolate cake.

Esther took a helping of everything. 'Who made all the cakes?'

'The rector's wife,' Rose said. 'She bakes a lot.'

'The rector,' Mrs Hotchkiss inclined her partridge-wing hat, 'helps with the beating.'

Mrs Nolan, deprived of cigarettes, drummed her fingers on the tabletop. 'I think I'll be going soon.'

'I'll go with you.' Esther spoke through a doughy mouthful. 'I've to be back for the baby.'

But the woman was there again, with refills of tea, and the two tables seemed more and more to resemble a large family gathering from which it would be rude to rise without offering thanks, or at least seeking permission.

Somehow the rector's wife had slipped from the head of her table and was bending maternally over them, one hand on Mrs Nolan's shoulder, one on Esther's. 'This dough bread is delicious,' said Esther, thinking to compliment her. 'Did you make it?'

'Oh, no, Mr Ockenden makes that.' Mr Ockenden was the town baker. 'There's a loaf over, though. If you like, you could buy it afterwards.'

Taken aback by this sudden financial pounce, Esther almost immediately recollected how church people of all orders were forever after pennies, offertories and donations of one sort and another. She had found herself walking out from Evensong recently with a Blessings Box – an austere wooden container with a slot into which one was apparently intended to drop money until the next year's Harvest Festival, when the boxes would be emptied and handed round again.

'I'd love a loaf,' Esther said, a bit too brightly.

After the rector's wife returned to her chair, there was a muttering and nudging among the middle-aged women in best blouses, cardigans and round felt hats at the table's foot. Finally, on a spatter of local applause, one woman rose and made a little speech calling for a vote of thanks to the rector's wife for the fine tea. There was a humorous footnote about thanking the rector, too, for his help – evidently notorious – in stirring the batter for the cakes. More applause; much laughter, after which the rector's wife made a return speech welcoming Esther and Mrs Nolan by name. Carried away, she revealed her hopes of their becoming members of the Mothers' Union.

In the general flurry of clapping and smiles and curious stares and a renewal of plate-passing, the rector himself left his place and came to sit in the empty chair next to Mrs Nolan. Nodding at Esther, as if they had already had a great deal to say to each other, he began speaking in a low voice to Mrs Nolan. Esther listened in unashamedly as she ate through her plate of buttered dough bread and assorted cakes.

The rector made some odd, jocular reference to never finding Mrs Nolan in – at which her clear blonde's skin turned a bright shade of pink – and then said, 'I'm sorry, but the reason I've not called is because I thought you were a divorcée. I usually make it a point not to bother them.'

'Oh it doesn't matter. It doesn't matter now, does it,' muttered the blushing Mrs Nolan, tugging furiously at the collar of her open coat. The rector finished with some little welcoming homily which escaped Esther, so confused and outraged was she by Mrs Nolan's predicament.

'I shouldn't have come,' Mrs Nolan whispered to Esther. 'Divorced women aren't supposed to come.'

'That's ridiculous,' Esther said. 'I'm going. Let's go now.'

Rose glanced up as her two charges started to button their coats. 'I'll go with you. Cecil will want his tea.'

Esther glanced toward the rector's wife at the far end of the room, surrounded now by a group of chattering women. The extra loaf of dough bread was nowhere in sight, and she felt no desire to pursue it. She could ask Mr Ockenden for a loaf on Saturday, when he came round. Besides, she vaguely suspected the rector's wife might have charged her a bit over for it – to profit the church, the way they did at Jumble Sales.

Mrs Nolan said goodbye to Rose and Esther at the Town Hall and started off down the hill to her husband's pub. The river road faded, at its first dip, in a bank of wet blue fog; she was lost to view in a few minutes.

Rose and Esther walked home together.

'I didn't know they didn't allow divorcées,' Esther said.

'Oh no, they don't like 'em.' Rose fumbled in her pocket and produced a packet of Maltesers. 'Have one? Mrs Hotchkiss said that even if Mrs Nolan wanted to join the Mothers' Union, she couldn't. Do you want a dog?'

'A what?'

'A dog. Mrs Hotchkiss has this Alsatian left over from the last lot. She's sold all the black ones, everybody loves those, and now there's just this grey one.'

'Tom *hates* dogs.' Esther surprised herself by her own passion. 'Especially Alsatians.'

Rose seemed pleased. 'I told her I didn't think you'd want it. Dreadful things, dogs.'

The gravestones, greenly luminous in the thick dusk, looked as if their ancient lichens might possess some magical power of phosphorescence. The two women passed under the churchyard, with its flat, black yew, and as the chill of evening wore through their coats and the afterglow of tea, Rose crooked out one arm, and Esther, without hesitation, took it.

PART II
NON-FICTION

Sylvia Plath
Whitstead
4 Barton Road
Cambridge, England

Poppy Day At Cambridge

    At 9:30 a.m. on Saturday, November 10th, we strolled out of our Barton Road rooms under dove-gray Cambridge skies and through spasmodic showers of rain, umbrella in hand, to take a look at Poppy Day. Directly in front of our driveway, a road block of wooden crates was stopping cars entering Cambridge from Granchester while five or six Cambridge University students, each one uniformed in white coat and red fez, were supplying artificial red poppies and a rapid car-polishing in return for contributions from the drivers. Already, all cars coming from the town bore red poppies twined about their front fenders or prominently displayed on hood or windshield. Waylaid by a black-masked horseman on a white stallion, we meekly handed up most of our loose change of copper pennies, received a poppy for the buttonhole, and, thus armed, proceeded on toward the center of town.
    Each year, on the anniversary of the 1918 armistice, throughout England, in every city, town and village, there are funereal processions, laying on of laurels, hymns, and in the morning at 11, for two whole minutes, a national silence; but in Cambridge, from 9 in the morning onwards, anywhere within half a mile of the market place, you have to shout to hear yourself speak. While today, all over England, charitable volunteers are moving patiently from door to door, each with a tray of poppies, each holding out a collecting box with its prominent "For The Red Cross", in Cambridge thousands of University undergraduates are transforming the narrow

Hike to Lovell River

Published: *Weetamoe Megaphone* (18 July 1943): 1*

This week Oehda went on a hike to Lovell River, carrying picnic suppers with us. When we arrived we talked for a few minutes, but soon our hunger overcame us as we ate our fill.

Two girls and I decided to walk around the river and get on a rock opposite the other girls. When we finally got there, panting and perspiring after laboriously climbing through barbwire, it was time to go home. We went right to bed after a happy day!

Girl Scout News: Troop 5 Valentine Party

Written: 21 February 1944
Published: *The Townsman* (10 March 1944): 4†

Monday, February 21st, all of the girls in Troop 5 and four adults met at Betsy Powley's outdoor fireplace to prepare our lunch. We cooked American Chop Suey and cocoa. Our appetites were sharp as we had been playing games. Everybody had second and third helpings. Mrs. Powley and Betsy's cousin came out to see how we were getting along. After lunch we walked over to Reed's Pond to skate. It was a lovely day and full of fun.

Sylvia Plath, Scribe

---

* SP was a camp reporter for her unit, Oehda. In the second issue of the *Megaphone*, printed on 31 July 1943, she is listed as a reporter along with Louise Anthony. While there are two reports about Oehda, neither is attributed to a specific writer.

† SP's summary appeared with another Girl Scout's, Marcia Egan. Upon publication, SP wrote in her diary, 'Marcia and I got our stories printed in the Townsman. I am very proud of my names in the papers.'

Seventh-grade Girls

Written: 23 October 1944
Published: *The Phillipian* (November 1944): 16

In after-school sports the seventh-grade girls are playing beat ball. Miss Ely is overseeing the games. All of the rooms hope to win the banner, but it seems that Room 21 is ahead and that Room 15 is close behind. Room 18 has lost every game and looks longingly at the banner, still hoping at least to get honorable mention. Very few showed up to play at first, but now the girls are really enthusiastic about the games, and many more are playing.

Assembly Lineup: January 30

Written: 30 January 1946*
Published: *The Phillipian* (February 1946): 12

January 30—Miss Ely's physical education assembly was of special interest. A group of eighth-grade hillbillies performed three folk dances. Following this, a seventh-grade group of tumblers performed to the accompaniment of piano and drum. To add a finishing touch to the athletic trend, an interesting and exciting movie on skiing was shown.

Cove Unit Report

Written: *c.*23 July 1946†
Published: *c.*25 July 1946

On June 30, the first Storrow campers arrived. Twenty-four of them came one

---

* On 30 January 1946, SP wrote in her diary, 'In assembly we had a wonderful show. First three square dances were done by eighth grade girls. Then a marvelous acrobatic show was performed by the seventh grade girls. They did everything to time and drumbeats. They did cartwheels, handstands, double somersaults, rope jumps and many other admirable acts. I "covered" it for a Phillipian report.'

† SP wrote in her diary on 23 July 1946: 'I began to work furiously on the speech that I am to

by one to the Cove Unit. I will now pick out some of the highlights of this month which has so quickly passed by.

On Monday evening, Cove entertained Woods with a hilarious barn dance. I'm sure that we will always remember Red and her "piana."

On Independence Day, Cove joined the camp around a campfire on the beach. The beautiful evening was further commemorated by the fact that ice cream was served in the dining hall.

We then began to rehearse for our minstrel show that we were to give to Ridge. How it gradually turned from a minstrel to a variety show, no one knows. One of the favorites was Gloria's and Betsy's original interpretation of "Swance." The unit had already become familiar with this graceful little dance before, as the stars had thumped it out on almost every cabin floor.

After the show the performers donned pajamas and headed for Skipper's party. There we heard most of the hits on the Hit Parade, and had some delicious punch and cookies.

We all enjoyed an evening boat trip and supper across the lake on July 8th.

On July 9th, Gayle's brother was born.

We were invited to Hilltop's Masquerade. We had a delightful time and the wedding that they staged was most realistic.

The day that half of the unit was supposed to hike to Fisherman's Cove turned out cold and cloudy, so they started to hike around the lake instead. By some grave mistake they took the wrong road, and followed an old dirt road without a house on it, for miles. Finally they came to a paved road, and after a long hike of at least eight miles; they gratefully turned in on the Storrow road and hobbled back to their cabins.

Friday, July 12th, was marked by the arrival of Elmer and Bill. They gave each unit some very interesting nature lectures. Of course, nature was not the only interest.

On Sunday, the 14th, the unit was made ready for the next set of two-week campers. On the following day one of the more ambitious campers was searching for wood, when an angry bee flew by and stung her on the lip good and

---

give at the banquet on Thursday. It is coming along superly.' Two days later, she wrote, 'Today we had our long anticipated banquet. The tables were arranged like this: U. Skipper sat at the head table, and I did too, for I had to get up and make my Cove Unit Report after the meal, which was yummy! Roast beef, corn on the cob, apple salad, mashed potatoes, grapefruit, gravery, rolls, butter, and icecream. My report was evidently enjoyed the most, because they laughed in all the right places, and I got plenty of applause.' Typescript, published by 'Rita Hunt, Inc.', has holograph corrections by SP. Verso contains reports from the Ridge Unit and the Woods Unit which have been crossed out in pencil by an unknown hand.

hard. Her mouth and cheek swelled up until she looked like something between a chipmunk and Mortimer Snerd. However, after a few days the swelling went down and she began to look natural once more.

On the night that the unit slept out on the beach, strange visions in yellow nightgowns and pink pajamas were seen flying across the sky.

The whole unit enjoyed the trip to the blueberry farm immensely. After working for four hours, stopping only for lunch and rest hour, we found that as a unit, we had earned $17.60.

From now on all "pistol shots" heard at night will be contributed to the banging of doors in the Cove. The whip-poor-wills, bobwhites, and phoebes sing back and forth all night without tiring.

Cove has had great success in the softball games, having beaten first Ridge (23–4) and then Woods (7–6).

All our experiences here at camp will be stowed away in our pack of treasured memories, as the sun sets on these last days at Storrow.

Junior High Briefs

Written: 9 October 1946[*]
Published: *The Townsman* (17 October 1946): 4

Thank You Program

On October 9th the long-anticipated "Thank You Assembly" was presented by the seventh graders as an acknowledgment of the "Welcome Assembly" given two weeks previously by the upper classmen. The latter always look forward to this assembly each year with a brotherly interest in the use of new talent in the school. There were many excellent performances, all proving that the new seventh grade is indeed a gifted one. The Mistress of Ceremonies was Judith Miller who introduced the following numbers:

Reading—Elizabeth Becker
Piano Solo—Dorothy Barnes
Reading—Eunice Nevins
Choral Singing and Reading—Room 15

---

[*] On 9 October 1946, SP wrote in her diary, 'Today we had the long awaited welcome assembly . . . I had to write up this assembly for the newspaper.'

Original Song—William Lloyd, John Cahill, Lindsey Rice, Bradford Count, John Leyon, and Robert Mills
Song (with gestures)—Jay Bailey
Piano Solo—Ruth Garron
Harmonica Solo—Georgia Emerson
Skit—Marcie Govoni, Ellen Child, Helen Benjamin, Patricia O'Brien, Patricia Kelly
Vocal Trio—Susan Leach, Stanley Woodward, Carolyn Paul
Tap Dance—Jerry Mullen
Piano Solo—Allen Balsbaugh
Accordion Solo—Bruno Mortarelli

World Series

The exciting World Series games have provided interesting material for projects and assignments undertaken by two groups in the Junior High School.

The Indoor Games Club is making a chart that follows each game play by play. The members have learned how to fill in and interpret the games as they are broadcast over the radio.

One of the seventh-grade English classes is having fun keeping a bulletin board, making notebooks and writing biographical sketches of the players. These proceedings are certainly keeping everyone well informed as to the outcome of each game.

Visual Aid

Mr. John D. Provasoli, director of visual education in the Junior High School, gives instruction to the teachers each Wednesday afternoon in the value and uses of the many visual aid education materials in the school. The topics dealt with thus far have been the theory behind visual education, practice in the use of various machines, and a movie, *Visual Education in the Schools*, which was followed by a discussion period.

Physical Exams

During the past week the ninth-grade boys have been given physical examinations by Dr. Lyman.

Club Doings: Book Lovers and Recreational Reading Club

Written: *c.* 3 October 1946*
Published: *The Phillipian* (November 1946): 14

The first meeting of the Book Lovers and Recreational Reading Club was begun by having every member write his reasons for joining the club. The papers were then read aloud, and a lovely book by Joseph C. Lincoln was presented to the writer of the paper voted the best. Some of the members have brought in books for the others to read. Recently we have made book jackets and discussed the Book Fair. We all look forward in pleasant anticipation to the meetings ahead.

Club Doings: Book Lovers

Written: before 21 February 1947
Published: *The Phillipian* (February 1947): 18

Book Lovers—Miss Craig

Ben-Hur .... *Lew Wallace*
COunt of Monte Cristo .... *Dumas*
TwO Years Before the Mast .... *Dana*
BooK of Marvels .... *Halliburton*
LittLe Women .... *Alcott*
NatiOnal Velvet .... *Bagnold*
OliVer Twist .... *Dickens*
ThE Kid Comes Back .... *Tunis*
PRide and Prejudice .... *Austen*
Salute to the Marines .... *White*

---

* On 3 October 1946, SP wrote in her diary, 'I'm in the Recreational Reading Club and sit next to Pris. Imagine! I won a book in club by writing the best paragraph on why I joined it (class voted.) I was thrilled to get a beautifully illustrated copy of "Cape Cod Yesterdays by Joseph C. Lincoln.'

These books are among those that have been read, or are being read, by the members of our club.

During the past term we have had two quizzes about books. One was a pictorial quiz on well-known book titles. Everyone drew a title in pictures on the blackboard and the rest of the class guessed the name of the book. A box of notepaper was given to the winner of the second quiz about books.

We plan to spend many more enjoyable periods reading new books and sharing our favorite books with each other.

Introducin'

Written: 2 October 1947[*]
Published: *The Bradford* (30 October 1947): 3

The name "Coletta" is familiar to many of you since Mrs. Coletta taught last year the same subject that her husband teaches this year, namely Art. Born in Italy, Mr. Coletta came to America in 1930 and attended high school here. Upon graduating, he studied at the Massachusetts School of Art. He joined the service for four years and then finished his last year at the School of Art and continued exhibiting his work. Mr. Coletta states that he has enjoyed his work at high school so far and is sure that he will continue to do so.

The Atomic Threat

Published: *The Bradford* (26 April 1948): 1

"The atom bomb is not just another weapon, but the greatest cataclysmic force ever released on earth."

Thus speaks Mr. William Laurence, who has witnessed four out of the five atomic bomb explosions.

In a third world war, the atom bomb would, in all probability, be used as a weapon. Reliable scientists state that, once a city is the target of atom bombs,

---

[*] From SP's diary for 2 October 1947: 'Today we had a *Bradford* meeting. I joined at the last minute and am on the feature staff. My assignment is to do a brief write-up about Mr. Coletta, the school's new art teacher.' Other teachers were written up in the feature but not have not been included here.

only a bare fourth of the people would be left alive. The cultural facilities to which we are accustomed would be long in becoming a part of our lives again. Millions of thinkers upon whom our advance depends would be killed, and the world, as we know it, would not be rebuilt for generations. Such a war would not culminate in the victory of one nation. All nations would be so devastated by atomic warfare that none could afford to take over the world. A catastrophe like this must be avoided at all costs.

Some think that a defense can be made against the bomb. Professor Hand, editor of the booklet *Living in the Atomic Age*, writes:

"There has never been a defense against *any* weapon that has been 100 per cent effective and, to be adequate, atomic defense *must* be 100 per cent effective . . . It is very doubtful if our civilization could survive an atomic war and therefore imperative that steps be taken to prevent such a happening."

We, the citizens of the United States, are faced with a variety of plans for preventing atomic war, but all of these proposals have their particular pitfalls. Nevertheless, let us examine them.

First, there is isolation. However, this is no longer possible in a world where the farthest country can be reached in a few hours' travel time by plane.

Treaties might answer our need for securing world peace, but past experience has not been encouraging in this respect.

At the present time the United States is comparatively powerful enough to start out and conquer the world with the atom bomb, but it is hardly believable that our people, while upholding Christian principles, would support this plan of aggression.

The United Nations is a possible way out of our dilemma—that is, if all nations continue to support it wholeheartedly and do not withdraw for personal interests.

It has been suggested that an International Atomic Development Authority be established to make sure that atomic energy is used solely for peaceful, commercial purposes. Again, this would depend upon the universal support of all nations.

An international police force would depend upon the same universal support.

A world government seems to be the most likely—a government that would deal with people as individuals, not as members of different nations. To achieve this, we must be willing to conform to our own professed belief that all men are created equal. We must also realize that in moving forward in our evolutionary society, we must be willing to forfeit some of our past national privileges to make way for a plan that will bring about good for all the peoples of the world.

As Professor Hand so ably reasons: "In bygone times, families were warring groups until this resolved in the clan. War between clans was finally resolved in the city-state and war between city-states was resolved in the nation. Would not the next logical step be to resolve war between nations by the organization of a world government?"

Who Are They???*

Published: *The Bradford* (4 February 1949): 2

1. This pert sophomore has a passion for music and enjoys playing the piano. (She's one of the five pianists in the orchestra!) However, music isn't her only forte. As chairman of Room 213 this gal is a popular member of the Student Council. She was also co-chairman of the successful Football Dance. Seniors will remember her sister Ginny (class of '47), and all should know this petite, attractive Soph.
2. A member of the senior class, this guy is well known for his prodigious mastery (??) of the French language, his dramatic ability—"Are We Dressing?", and his hockey playing. This *Bradford* editor (that gives it away!) is also frequently seen driving a moss-green convertible. Finally, this wizard is noted for his wit and his sometimes startling observations in physics.
3. This attractive junior participates in many extracurricular activities. Being a sports enthusiast, she is a member of the field hockey, basketball, and tennis teams, while her favorite recreation is ice skating. Popular and energetic, this member of Room 314 is well known for her struggles with geometry and her baby sister who bawls every morning at six o'clock. Her ambition is to fly to Florida.

---

* SP was credited for contributing to the features and art in the 4 February 1949 issue of *The Bradford*. The only art printed in the newspaper are three silhouettes of the students' heads accompanying these descriptions. The students described were 1. Janet Seely. 2. Mike Moore. 3. Jeanne Woods.

High School Highlights

Written: *c.*9 September 1949
Published: *The Townsman* (15 September 1949): 3

On Thursday, September 8, the pupils of the Gamaliel Bradford Senior High School came flocking back from various summer resorts and summer jobs to begin another school year. All is as it was before . . . well, almost. As Mr. Graves remarked in the assembly on Friday, "Something new has been added." The Juniors and Seniors welcomed into their midst the class of 1952. Then Mr. Davidson, the Chairman of the School Committee, introduced another addition to the student body, Mr. Lyman B. Owen, our new superintendent. Mr. Owen stated that his experience in Wellesley thus far had been pleasant and that he had been helped a great deal by the girls in the office. We also learned that Mr. Owen skis and plays the accordion. The students can testify as to the merit of this last accomplishment, for in parting he entertained us with a "subdued classical selection" known as "Twelfth Street Rag." Mr. Owen left the students and faculty anticipating an enjoyable school year ahead.

With the arrival of fall comes also the football season. From the field after school one may hear the shouts of the squad hard at practice. Mr. Bragdon has scheduled eight films on football techniques to show the boys on the teams. Films for other sports, such as track, are also being lined up . . . And the student council is busy, as always, planning the annual campaign for the football ticket drive.

When I'm a Parent

Published: *Seventeen* (November 1949): 77[*]

I will not pry, but I will never go to the opposite extreme and be indifferent to my child's experiences outside of the home.

---

[*] Unattributed. SP wrote to *Seventeen* magazine in reply to what teenagers' attitudes are about certain aspects of parenting including raising a family. See letter from Margot Macdonald to Sylvia Plath, 4 October 1949, held in SP's Publications Scrapbook, Lilly Library. SP received $2 for her thoughts.

Bradford Editors Attend Boston Tea Party!!

Printed: c. December 1949–January 1950*

No, your editors didn't *quite* make history by parading through the Copley Plaza in full war paint. Instead, we made a rather conventional entrance into the plush elegance of the lobby. This was to be our initiation into the mystery of editors' teas; so we didn't know just what to expect. Would there be footmen perhaps? Or heralds to proclaim our arrival by tooting golden trumpets?

We were somewhat relieved to find ourselves part of a large, chattering throng of other teenagers, amazingly like ourselves. Borne into the dining room on the current of this talkative human tidal wave, we found ourselves seated at a table, listening to Mr. John I. Taylor of the *Boston Globe* introduce himself and explain the general idea of these gatherings. We learned first about the Annual High School Newspaper Competition sponsored by the *Boston Globe*. We must admit we became a bit starry-eyed at the thought of the prizes offered and resolved then and there to scout around for local talent in writing—stories, poems, essays, and news stories are acceptable.

Mr. Taylor then proceeded to answer most of the questions that have had your editors growing gray for the past month. How to get subscribers? Contributors? The solution to this first problem is primarily publicity . . . and, of course, a first-rate publication. Another trade secret, which we fell upon eagerly, is the idea of sending postcards to the parents of those students featured in the issue. We've also found that selling papers in the cafeteria at lunchtime lures a lot of curious individuals into purchasing a copy before the official distribution to subscribers after school. Getting contributors is something else again. This dilemma can be solved partially by announcing names over the public address system and by giving the budding writers a big byline . . . (There's *something* about having one's name in print!)

---

* Unattributed. SP was co-editor of *The Bradford* in the 1949–50 academic year. A printed clipping was located in SP's High School Scrapbook, page 63, held by Lilly Library. SP annotated the page: '↓ For this little review, yours truly received $10 in cool, cool cash!' The event was held on 12 November 1949 and received regional coverage in 'High School Editors Party', *Boston Globe* (13 November 1949): B1. SP's name is listed in the article 'Globe Party for Editors Features Miss Woodward', *Boston Globe* (28 January 1950): 1, 3. A review of all issues of *The Bradford* – the type and font of which matches that of the clipping – during SP's high school years did not uncover this article. The article may have been specially printed for submission. It might be that the clipping was a 'dummy', which SP refers to in 'The All-Round Image', printed later in this section.

While we begin to glow with enthusiasm, realizing that there were *other* editors in the world besides ourselves who had troubles, Mr. Taylor went around the room answering individual questions. Quite a fellow, we thought. Even printing presses seem to have their guardian angels!

Naturally, no program is complete without entertainment, but we were quite overcome by the imposing personages who confronted us.

Mr. Metcalfe, poet extraordinaire of the *Boston Globe*, regaled us with a colorful account of his change from the role of federal investigator to that of a poet. He can make a better living with a pen than with a pistol, he tells us.

Our second guest was James Melton, Metropolitan Opera star, who won us over immediately with his gracious manner and good humor. He delighted us by singing "The Surrey with the Fringe on Top." Attractive, blonde Lillian Murphy followed this with a lilting selection called "Romance," by Romberg. These two then blended their voices in a memorable duet from *Maytime*.

At the close of the afternoon, Mr. Taylor bade us goodbye, and we left, anticipating with pleasure our next editors' tea.

(P. S. For those of you who are sticklers for detail and are now demanding loudly how your undernourished editors sustained themselves—we had pink ice cream, a square of cake (3" by 3"), and tea for refreshments. So there!)

Youth's Plea for World Peace

Published: *Christian Science Monitor* (16 March 1950): 19[*]

Since one of the many advantages of a democracy is free speech, we would like to take the opportunity to speak out concerning the President's direction to the Atomic Energy Commission to continue its work on the hydrogen bomb.

At first glance, it seems inconsistent to undertake the construction of a weapon designed to kill more people more efficiently, and yet maintain that this plan of action is consistent with the objectives of our program of peace and security. Let us examine this apparent paradox.

The following logic may be used to support the production of the H-bomb. If Russia succeeded in perfecting a more powerful bomb before we did, she might very well use it to destroy us or to frighten us into submission. Therefore

---

[*] The byline reads, 'Sylvia Plath, Perry Norton / English 11, Wellesley Senior High School, Wellesley, Mass.'

we must not let Russia get ahead of us. But, on the other hand, if we Americans remained one jump ahead of the USSR in bomb production, there would be no danger of destruction because a nation such as ours which follows humanitarian principles would never be the aggressor or use the bomb to kill anyone. Thus we would have the double advantage of insuring peace for the world and inner security for ourselves.

We wish to spread democracy and the capitalistic system, since we believe that our society is more nearly ideal than any other existing at the present time. Certainly we need force to sustain a political and economic state, but the question is, are we right in assuming that this force must inspire fear in order to be effective? Could we not achieve peace by the power of attraction rather than by the power of dread or repulsion?

In postulating that possession of the H-bomb will help our security, we are resorting to the naïve concept that we must have a military power "second to none" to defend our state. At first we believed that the atomic bomb was sufficient threat to dissuade any advocate of further warfare. Now that Russia has developed the bomb, America can't stop there. She must find a more powerful weapon with which to menace her enemy. She must have an even greater weapon to wield in power politics. And when the USSR catches up with her, no matter: there will always be a more potent instrument of destruction to work on. Once again two nations are attempting to reach the impracticable goal of world supremacy in military reserves.

Already we have succeeded in killing and crippling a good part of humanity, and destruction, unfortunately, is always mutual. Is it any wonder, then, that some of us young people feel rebellious when we watch the futile armaments race beginning again? How much experience do we need to realize that war solves no problems, but creates them instead?

An asset to any nation is the potential energy of its youth. Why not do more to support those of our young men and women who are essentially idealistic, believing firmly in the possibilities of world peace? These people can see beyond the present dilemma of nationalism to the basic brotherhood of all human beings. Witness the organization of World Federalism . . . the experiments in international living.

These movements, even if they do not and cannot fulfill their ends, exemplify the strong hope for world peace. Let us devote our money and our energy to the education and support of a positive force which comes from our youth groups, rather than spending our strength in developing weapons which we never plan to use.

For those of us who deplore the systematic slaughter legalized by war, the hydrogen bomb alone is not the answer.

The International Flavor

Ts,* summer 1950, Smith College

This has been quite a summer for travel abroad. Not only did several of my close friends set out last June on ships bound across the Atlantic, but a group of students at high school was organized to make a tour of Europe under the guidance of my favorite instructor. You may well imagine how tantalizing it was for me, a victim of wanderlust, to realize that I would be working at home while my friends were in Europe visiting foreign capitals and making stimulating new acquaintances. At that time, however, I was completely unaware of the delightful characters I would meet during my days at the Farm.

I am now firmly convinced that farm work is one of the best jobs for getting to know people as they really are. As you work side by side in the rows, your hands move automatically among the leaves and your thoughts are free to wander at will. What, then, is more natural than to drift into conversation with your neighbor? It is really amazing what a receptive ear can do by way of encouraging confidences.

First, of course, I became acquainted with the girls in my crew. They came from high schools in neighboring towns and were a friendly crowd. There was Carol Ann, with the Dutch bob, the twinkling green eyes, and the pert snub nose. There was Betsy, irresistibly comic, with red blonde hair and the pale white skin. There was Lucy, the foreman's daughter with the impish smile; Joan, who wanted to have her own horse more than anything; and fragile, black-haired Alison who dated the soda jerk at the corner drugstore. There were shared secrets, amusing anecdotes, and laughter clear and fresh as well water.

I still remember the day I met Agnar, the DP from Latvia. It was the afternoon we set strawberry plants. As we moved slowly up and down the rows, weeding and setting the runners to the ground with little stones to hold them in place, we began to talk together.

Agnar had been bending over the row on one knee, sun gleaming on his bronzed back, his blonde hair tucked up under a white handkerchief, merriment

---

* Typed at top right: 'Sylvia Plath / Wellesley, Mass.'

flickering in his blue eyes. He seemed to be concentrating very hard on something. Suddenly he asked, "You go to college next year?" His voice was blurred by strong traces of a German accent.

"Yes," I said. "I'm going to study English and Art."

"Art? Drawing?" He sounded pleased. It turned out that he had studied art in Europe. For the rest of the afternoon we discussed artists, poets, and composers while we worked. There were books we both had read, he in the German original, I in the English translation. Art transcended barriers of language and homeland.

Then, all at once, it was five o'clock. The sun was lower, the shadows longer. Agnar stood up and stretched, the muscles flowing smoothly under his fine browned skin. He flashed a smile. "Someday I draw a picture for you."

At times we would have for our crew boss talkative old Ted, New England born and bred. We would fill our wicker baskets with beans as we listened to him. His conversation consisted of long repetitions of magazine articles he had read concerning politics, cattle ranching, and the water supply in New York. His oratory was punctuated by little jokes everyone had read in last month's *Reader's Digest*. Although we smiled now and then at Ted's loquacity, we all had a soft spot in our hearts for him.

We became fond of many other people, too. There was the thin, spry woman who lived over the washroom with her family of five little girls. It was a mystery to us how she cooked for them, working in the fields, and was cheerily hanging out her daily wash by the time we arrived at eight in the morning. There were the two small Negro children who played in the fields while their parents worked. It got so we looked forward to seeing Rosalie and her younger brother peeping out at us from behind the barn, their black eyes round and mischievous, their mouths stained red with berry juice. There was the young Polish boy with the high cheekbones and the clean-cut features. There was Roy, with the sharp blue eyes, the weather-beaten face, and the Cockney accent.

Yes, I could go on and on, telling you about the people at the Farm. Best of all though, were the times when I would stand up to rest for a moment, in the tomato patch perhaps, and look across the surrounding fields. I'd have a warm feeling inside as I saw Agnar's bronze back bending over the celery with old Ted. Roy and the foreman were spraying the apple orchard. There was the Polish boy weeding lettuce with his crew. And singing in a husky contralto as she helped me pick tomatoes was Mary Lou, the mother of the Negro children.

I would turn back to work, wondering why I had ever dreaded staying at home when so much of the world was in my own backyard.

Rewards of a New England Summer

Written: *c.* August 1950
Published: *Christian Science Monitor* (12 September 1950): 15

Of all my summers, I choose to remember this, my seventeenth, with a bit more tenderness than the rest. There has been something unique about these past three months, full of sensations I may never have again, never so keen, never so poignant.

I reported for work at Lookout Farm shortly after graduating from high school in June. The Farm is on a hilltop in a neighboring town, and from the fields you can see the encircling green hills blending, fold on fold, into the blue distance.

I would leave the house at seven in the morning and bike the five miles to the Farm. At that isolated hour, I became aware of minute details as I had never been before in the heat of the day when the cars raised clouds of dust along the road.

A wetness, a virgin freshness was in the air. Biking leisurely through the Wellesley College campus, I caught the chill spicy smell of pine needles; the sound of a bird fluttering for cover in the brush; a rush, a scrabble, the flick of a gray tail, and a squirrel eyed me from the safety of his tree. All this, and the delightful morning shadows, the light a silky golden sheen across the grass.

There were the days in the radish fields, where the dirt was black and rich, so wet that we sank in ankle-deep. We knelt, reaching in among the leaves, pulling up the bunches swiftly with one hand, snapping the elastics around with the other. There is so much to remember, so many little, yet important things . . . the smell of freshly harrowed earth; the smooth, slender feel of wax beans; the cool metallic taste of water from the tin pail.

I recall the green rosettes of New Zealand spinach leaves, bunched in tiers in the bushel baskets; the long, languid afternoons; the wind rustling huskily in the corn under a blazing Technicolor-blue sky.

There were the days spent in the dark cavern of the washroom, washing celery in the tubs. We fished out the stalks as the trimmers chucked them in, scrubbed them squeakily clean with the brush, and laid them to be wrapped, the leaves glittering and cold with water. I remember how the skin of our hands looked at the end of the day, whitened and wrinkled.

There was the pride of walking into the stand at lunch to see the vegetables we picked that morning being sold to the customers who came flocking up in cars. "A dozen ears of corn; two pounds of tomatoes." And the cash register would ring, sounding out its musical little note of triumph. We stood there, behind the counter in our faded blue jeans and plaid cotton shirts, munching early green apples with a proprietary air.

The colors in the stand were easy, pleasing to the eye. We could almost see our reflection in the polished purple-black surface of the eggplant. There was the red of radishes and tomatoes; the pale yellow-green of string beans; the tawny orange of peaches; the warm, sunlit yellow of summer squash.

And then, suddenly, it was the end of August—my last day of work. I could hardly believe I wouldn't be biking up to the Farm anymore. All the days of my ten weeks there had flowed together, melted into each other so that only one solid impression remained, a blend of blue skies, sunlight, and green fields.

My tan will fade with the coming of autumn; the money I earned will be used for college expenses; the people I knew will go about their business of living, apart from me, far off. But I will not forget. When you see me pause and stare a bit wistfully at nothing in particular, you'll know that I am deep at the roots of memory, back on the Farm, hearing once more the languid, sleepy drone of bees in the orange squash blossoms, feeling the hot, golden fingers of sun on my skin, and smelling the unforgettable spicy tang of apples which is, to me, forever New England.

In Retrospect: A Plea for Moderation

Written: 19 March 1951
Published: *Princeton Tiger* (5 May 1951): 14–15[*]

We think we are relatively well-rounded (figuratively—whoops . . .). Well, anyway, we possess a variety of psychogenic interests and can wax informed on Kafka or labor unions or stock-car racing. To wit: we are perhaps hybrids of pseudo-sophistication, nebulous intellect, and a faint tinge of that healthy American type. We are also liberal. The purpose of this lengthy introduction is to establish evidence of our adaptability to persons and situations (or so we thought).

Recently while contemplating a panacean whiskey sour, we got to (perhaps nostalgically, perhaps not) reminiscing about the social year, i.e. those males

---

[*] Co-authored by Marcia Brown Stern.

who have barged, sidled, crawled, staggered, or even walked upright in the door as our dates. As freshmen we started out with an average number of active or passive contacts at various male institutions. Also as freshmen we hastened to broaden our field. Utilizing various schemes of dubious ethical merit (even, in a whisper, blind dates) we have.

From this evening of looking backward, a rather disturbing categorical result was evolved. The following then, is an unasked for, unprecedented, purposely malicious classification in which, if scrutinized too carefully, you might find a disturbingly familiar character.

To begin with, we found almost simultaneously, a large number of SUPER-EGOED RAH-RAHS. The kind who, in twenty years, will have a doorbell which, at a gentle push, will sing out "for God, for country, *or* Yale." In his wardrobe rests everything that the well-dressed college man should wear but not all at once—tattersall vest, plaid tie, hounds-tooth jacket, raccoon coat, argyle socks, white bucks, and a Douglas clan golf cap.

Perhaps while prepping at St. Marks or Taft, he was restricted in alcohol content. Still, stretching liberalism to the breaking point, we fail to see side-splitting humor in sea breezes down the front of an impressively décolleté dress. (That whole evening, incidentally, was tinged with failure. He made the rounds before coming to fetch. His greeting was touching: shook hands with the bridge lamp and ground his cigarette on the head of our housemother who was reading in the living room. Collegiate casualness—well, no comment.)

The upper classmen in the house have been especially thoughtful in procuring us COUSINS, BROTHERS, and CAST-OFF SUITORS for an evening's entertainment. We recall one well-meaning soul who smiled with mischievous cupidity and purred, "I've got just the man for you: fine, philosophical, sensitive—simply a dear!"

We were in the market for a basic character—either out of lack of one ourselves or a desire for understanding. He turns up one dismal Sunday afternoon bearing his horn-rimmed spectacles, looking promising. We sit on the couch brightly discussing ourselves:

HE: "I suppose you like to walk in the rain."
WE: "Oh yes!"
HE: "At night in the city?"
WE: "Why, however did you know?"

And on and on. We are in the midst of baring our souls (we females mentally carrying this on for a long-range program) when an absolutely saccharine, dumb, adorable friend from across the hall walks in.

SHE: "Oops, sorry." Leaves languidly.

HE: "WHO IS SHE?" Mute adoration.

We tell, he goes, leaving Edith Sitwell's poetry unread. We've still got the book—she's still got him.

THE ATHLETE deserves a paragraph of his own particularly if he is one whose activity is not confined to team play exclusively. After a motley variety of wrestling matches and chinning the bar all weekend, nature boy plans an invigorating Sunday. Sleep? Hell, we go on a seven-mile hike up the local Mt. Everest. We are such good sports. Outfitted in his old sneakers and dungarees, we somehow are disinclined to respond cheerfully to his sprightly monologue on geological formations. He forges masterfully ahead through the bracken, but ho! two can play. We take the lead and somehow (pure carelessness) manage to snap a healthy branch of *Robinia pseudoacacia* back into his unsuspecting physiognomy. Score!

We have oft been accused of possessing officious brains which we wittingly impose on unsuspecting and annoyed males. Moreover, we have alternately been praised or damned for our moral values, elastic views, etc. But upon a few occasions we have felt terribly, terribly void of knowledge of any type. THE RESPONSIBLE cannot be typed. And he is the first to so inform us. Yes, he smiles sweetly and benignly; not only is he concerned with such weighty topics as "Is-there-a-point-of-total-knowledge?", but he can quote the football scores for the last two decades. (At this point we pant with glee.)

He disdains not intellectual solitude, nor bout with synthetic Cubism, yet he is master of the samba and the cross-ruff. He is the enigmatic example—the synthesis of *all* types. A versatile conglomerate of virtues. A free spirit (that's fine if you are partial to free spirits and who isn't to a point?). But, alas, more often than not, after spirits, he proposes free love. (*So?—Ed.*)

By way of passing we mentioned MOTHER'S BOY who, fresh from an Indiana high school, just . . . well, he worries us. He doesn't smoke nor drink nor swear nor say suggestive things, and evokes in us a disarming feeling of wickedness. His faintly disapproving leer, if verbalized, seems to mean "Get thee hence to a nunnery!" We then feel old, worldly, and slightly maternal.

Ah—we have had our times, i.e., our horizons have been lengthened, our experience augmented, our shining expectations slightly dulled. But, with the unfailing idealistic spirit of youth (freshmen, that is) we swallow all bitterness with the last sip of whiskey sour and hopefully, but cynically, look forward to next weekend. Who knows?

As a Babysitter Sees It

Written: 10 October 1951
Published: *Christian Science Monitor* (6–7 November 1951): 19, 21[*]

Along about winter time, every college girl who works for a living during vacation is faced with the same dilemma: What will I do for my summer job this year? Last spring I found myself in a rather undecisive position. I needed money, yet I wanted a vital job, something more than adding up figures from nine to five in an office all summer: something more than feeding and serving large masses of humanity come meal time. My practical skills were negligible, and since routine work did not appeal to me anyway, I was at a complete loss as to ideas concerning lucrative, as well as challenging, positions.

At last, however, an idea began to dawn, strange and full of potentialities. I would hire myself out as a babysitter and governess of sorts. If only I could find a congenial family, I would be able to live outdoors most of the summer, go to the beach often, and draw a good salary to boot. I had visions of spending days in the sun, reading, swimming, and all the while keeping a watchful eye on my juvenile charges.

This ideal situation took a more tangible form when I applied to the vocational office at school. As a result I was deluged with the usual mimeographed notices sent to all hopeful students wishing a summer job. The position which appealed to me most was one which involved a family with three children living on the North Shore of Massachusetts. A devotee of the New England shore, I walked to my interview with great hopes. Out of a group of twenty other girls, I was the one fortunate enough to walk away with the job.

Among the many advantages my employer listed was a tennis court, available in her backyard, a yacht which took the children for cruises, and a beautiful sandy beach at the end of her front lawn. I wax exuberant, filled with curiosity about the children who were to be in my charge for the next three months, excited by the beauty of my new surroundings. For taking care of the children, their rooms, their clothes, their meals, I was to receive board and room, a good weekly wage, and one day off a week. This seemed like a flawless arrangement as far as I was concerned.

---

[*] Published in two parts; with two sketches by SP in the first part and one in the second part. Captioned 'Judy loved the beach' and 'Alice posed for the author' and 'Eric, as the author sees him'. When printed, the article split between paragraphs nine and ten.

When I arrived at the Johnsons' house in June, I was even more amazed than I had expected to be. The eleven-room white home stood on top of a green hill which sloped down to the sea in a landscaped curve of freshly mowed lawns and close-clipped hedges. There was a vegetable garden and a small orchard of fruit trees at the side of the house, and a great yard with a playhouse especially for the children. My room on the second floor was about as big as the whole first floor of my own little white home, and best of all, my windows overlooked the sea, which showed blue and glittering through the starched white curtains.

Breathless with eagerness and curiosity, I met the three children. Alice was a chubby little blonde toddler, almost two years old; Judy was a pretty, thin child of four; Eric was a talkative and imaginative lad of six. I loved them dearly from the moment I saw them, and was touched to have them crowd around me as I unpacked, saying, "Oh, we just couldn't wait to have you come."

Supper was my first chore, and I found myself quite lost in the big unfamiliar kitchen, with its lovely blue linoleum, white woodwork, and what seemed to me to be miles of counter space. At last, under the friendly guidance of Mrs. Johnson, the baby was in her high chair and the two oldest were seated at the table contentedly devouring soup, toast, and milk. Bedtime and baths came next, with an added bonus of two stories.

The days that followed were full of adventures, adjustments, and amusement. I was not trained as far as domestic chores were concerned, and found myself getting on companionable terms with the stove, which had hitherto been hardly a speaking acquaintance. I found that children respond wonderfully to special attention, especially when it involves "making something." So rainy-day quarrels were averted, along with boredom, by periodic cookie baking in the kitchen. Very benevolent, very maternal, I felt, when asked for favors: "May I lick the spoon?" or "Please, can I beater up the eggs?"

Every day, while involving a basic routine, brought something new in the way of experience. Living with the children is in itself a continually variable and unpredictable existence. In the morning I would get up at seven and go downstairs to prepare the oranges, get bacon and eggs and toast ready. I would also manage to get the children dressed in between, a process allowing no system or schedule.

After breakfast the children would play in the house while I did the dishes, the beds, and the laundry. In mid-morning I would take the children to the beach, or watch them playing in the neighborhood. This job was nowhere near the rest I had anticipated. At the waterfront one must be constantly vigilant:

even when a baby is playing, she must be watched lest she wander off.

A hot lunch followed a long and strenuous morning, and then came that blessing granted to all guardians of young children—nap time. While the children rested or slept, I finished up the dishes, did the ironing, and caught my breath before the next onslaught. The afternoon brought more beach or more play, and supper was a quieter meal. Alice was bathed and put to bed after she had eaten, while Judy and Eric stayed up later, not retiring until about eight o'clock.

You may imagine that by this hour I welcomed a little solitude. Often I would go upstairs and prop myself up on the big four-poster bed, with my view of the ocean there anytime I chose to glance up from my reading. Sometimes, when the children's parents were home for the evening, I would take a walk along the beach, or go for a night swim, or visit with other babysitting friends of mine. Early bedtime was a necessity, especially as a bright cheerful face proved an essential for greeting the children every morning.

When the summer was over, a good friend of mine asked me: "Well, what did you get out of your summer? What did it do for you?"

For a moment I was nonplussed. How to convey the wealth of experience, of new ideas, of fresh capabilities that I had added up during the summer months? In the first place, from a purely practical point of view, I felt that I could be completely responsible for three young children, their physical, mental, and emotional needs. I had proved to myself that I could cook, iron, do laundry, and pretty much run a home. This was an education not to be received at a liberal arts school, and therefore all the more invaluable.

In the second place, my whole conception of life was considerably broadened by the actual opportunity to live with and to observe a family living on a scale to which I was completely unaccustomed. My desire to open new horizons, as well as new awareness of life and of human beings, was thus filled.

I also came away with a glowing tan, acquired from being outside with the children for most of the day. And then of course there is the store of incidents, each one precious in itself, which came from the summer's experience.

I remember the night that Judy hugged me wistfully as I tucked her into bed, saying, "I wish you could stay here till next year." I remember how she liked "April syrup" on her pancakes. I remember all the little endearing ways in which the three children emerged as individuals, each one with special needs, special concerns, all of which I grew to know and care for.

My reply to my friend's inquiry involved all these factors, including a vehement assertion that the summer had been the most valuable one possible in the way of a vivid and many-sided experience.

To those of you readers who are interested in obtaining a job like mine, involving living and working with a family with children, I have a few bits of advice.

For one thing, be sure that the family you work for will be kindly and congenial. There is a great and intangible difference between being a near part of the family and being merely hired help. Then, too, ask about time off during the day. Even though child care is entertaining and stimulating, it can also be quite exhausting.

Lastly, make sure just what jobs you will be required to do in addition to caring for the children. In this way you won't be imposed upon by an employer who thinks you might just as well wash dishes after her dinner parties, and bake and iron for her as well as for the children.

In conclusion, I would like to recommend the job of babysitter to all of you who are desiring an exciting and challenging job with variety and opportunity for new experiences. May your summer prove as delightful as mine did!

Suburban Nocturne

Ts,[*] 11 November 1951, Lilly Library

There is a certain unique delight about walking down an empty street alone at night. A queer off-focus light is cast by the moon, illumining the bare stage I am wandering through. No one is around to hear me, so I will talk aloud and let the strangeness of being no one in particular and everyone in general increase inside me. From one place to another I am walking, and there is a metamorphosis occurring in between.

I am walking down this street and I am being propelled by a force too

---

[*] Typescript has holograph additions by SP. In a letter to her mother written on 13 November 1951, SP wrote: 'Sunday I wrote an essay for English on a nebulous walk down a street at night. I realized with horror today that it was much too seamy to pass in, and so have composed another one about my summer job on the typewriter tonight. Much more concrete and sarcastic' (*The Letters of Sylvia Plath, Volume 1*: 395–6). The second piece was 'Somebody and We'. Both written for English 220a, Practice in Various Forms of Writing.

powerful for me to break because nineteen years of walking down streets has conditioned me to the inevitable routine of going from one place to another, always repeating the circle or line and returning home.

In all these blind box houses there is no one to listen to me or to hear my feet clicking on the pavement. But perhaps behind one of those gaping black bedroom windows someone lies on the brink of sleep, and my footsteps are grinding impersonal anonymous sounds along the edges of oblivion. Footsteps without feet or legs or body.

But I have a body, and I am curled up in its neat and miraculous network of muscles, bones, and nerves, woven inextricably into a snug cocoon of flesh and blood. A curious amusement I feel as my feet move me on, and as the world slips by, and houses never stop, but turn a side foreshortening to a front and lapsing to a side again, always moving as I move.

I wonder if I could will myself to stop. There. There. Now I am standing still, and my feet have stopped their clicking. They are waiting docilely in their snail-like leather houses. I have willed myself to stop, but I could not will myself to turn and walk back into the night. No, the lessons ingrained in me these nineteen years are too strong for that. But some night I will break the pattern of always walking home and turn away from the magnet that pulls and attracts me as if I were a scrap of metal merely.

Now I am walking again, but I will take this road home instead of that. I will assert myself feebly and approach from a less frequented path.

These houses have shadows strange across their faces. I would like to go up to the door and knock and say to the one who answers: Let me come in and suck your joys and sorrows from you as a leech sucks blood; let me gorge myself on your sensations, your ideas, your dreams; let me crawl inside your entrails and live like a tapeworm for a while, assimilating your life substance into myself.

But the houses have strange leaf shadows on their faces. They draw their tree leaves like a veil across their faces, and I walk in the middle of the road. I think I could be strangled by those shadows.

So I walk on. Down the corridors of my mind the footsteps echo. On either side are doors, avenues of doors. Tonight I shall wander through the rooms of my mind at will. Backwards I shall go, in quest of time past.

I could bring a yesterday to life on this quiet wind. It blows my hair across my mouth the way it did one March night when I was seventeen. If I wait long enough, if I am very still, I will begin to retreat from the extremities of my body (which will keep on walking). I will withdraw entirely into the vivid little room in my mind where the wind awaits me, and the boy whose name I have forgotten.

Walking home after the dance we are, a mile or so, and the air like gulps of cold water between our teeth. Stride and stride and stride, freely walking, hand in hand. The circle of white net whips and darts about my quickly moving silver feet. Strong and together the two of us along the bare streets. And scornful of the taxis, empty, waiting. Stride and stride. Then stop.

Heads tilt back to stars. Words now, about the legends, and nimble lines of fire race around the sky, drawing in Orion and Cassiopeia, and Castor and Pollux, the heavenly twins. There is silence, growing loud and louder, more loudly than a roaring sea, pressing inward. Dry leaves rattle in the gutter, and the wind rushes by and by and ever by.

Always the wind is at my back, and always I am going home. The wind whistles me again to the emptiness of this street, with the alien shadows that can clutch and trip me; I am wading knee-deep in a marsh of shadows, with the wind laughing in my ear.

Laugh, wind. Go ahead and laugh. Shake the window frames and shiver the glass with your great gusts of laughter. I left my name in the house that I am coming from, and I go to greet myself in the house that I am going to. In between, I tell you, I am nobody, everybody.

All the people in the world are swarming like ants in my head, and daily their million voices babble for attention. I can lift the lid of any cranium like that of a teapot and blow on the little scraps inside. All inclusive I am, wind, wind, and the solar system tilts and spins inside my head.

I can make a yesterday jerk into life like a puppet on a string, and I can coax tomorrow to parade like a mechanical toy. Dance, dance, I tell them, until there is no past, no future, only the now, the great stage where the wind laughs always behind the scenes, and the footsteps without feet, without legs, without body, strut to and fro somewhere in the distance.

But there is a body, and I am curled inextricably within it. So laugh, wind, at my finitude. I might have been a lesser god, I tell you, had not the leaves read otherwise, the fates deceived, and the cards spoken false.

Like Ulysses, I am a part of all that I have met. But the film of my nights and days is wound up tight in me, never to be re-run. The occasional flashbacks give me mere glimpses of the rooms that I have traveled through.

I think that I am lost in the corridors of my mind, doomed to wander forever down the empty hallways, opening door after door. There is no exit.

One room says: Once the wind blew a warm yellow moon up over the sea; a bulbous moon which sprouted in the soiled indigo sky and grew there forever like a tulip.*

Another room says: In the garden the old man bends his creaking back over the lettuce heads and tweaks the weeds from the soil. His open shirt shows a brown stained neck, and muscles loose hanging, wrinkled like a walnut shell.

A third room says: From here to happiness is a road leading down blue pajamas to feet, to bed post, to screen door, to wet puddled porch roof, to a road, to a line of sand, to a gray rain-beaten sea.

I could cry for all the people behind all the shut doors that I may never have time to open. For I have found at last the thread to lead me from the labyrinth, and the present tugs at the other end impatiently.

Now, as I am walking, the houses are turning still. There are a few rooms yet lit, and I can see into squares of warm yellow light where little people revolve inside their brightly papered boxes.

I would like to walk and talk aloud to myself all night, but that I cannot do, because my feet have brought me to the door. I know instinctively, like the rat in the maze, that this door opens, this of all doors. Of all the houses turning after me as I passed, this is the one where I was young, and where I turned through time.

From one place to another I have been going, and in between I was nobody, anybody. But there has been no metamorphosis after all, because I am again at the same door, and the rooms I have wandered through this night are as nothing. Always going out, I meet myself eternally coming in.

My feet know this is the door; my eyes know, and there is no doubt whether it will be the lady or the tiger, because here I sever the thread of aloneness and

---

* This image appears in SP's journal entry 110. See *The Journals of Sylvia Plath*: 87. SP turned this journal entry into a poem entitled 'august night' (typescript held by Lilly Library):

and the wind has blown
a warm yellow moon
up over the sea:

a bulbous moon
which sprouts
in the soiled indigo sky

and spills winking white
petals of light

upon quivering black plains
of ocean water.

enter the ritual that is the family, the rooms that are the home. My umbilical cord has never been cut cleanly, so I press thumb down on the latch and step up into light, into tomorrow. The door closes behind me, and I turn the lock with a final click that shuts out the wasteland of sleeping streets.

Somebody and We

Ts,[*] 13 November 1951, Lilly Library

At one time or another in the course of years, one is faced with a dilemma which seems insoluble. The conflict may be as trivial as deciding which color of fingernail polish to buy, or it may present itself in terms of a more serious nature, involving, perhaps, the choice of a career or a potential husband. This summer I found myself in just such a position of frustration, with the exception that my case concerned three young children and a stove.

For several months I had been considering the pros and cons of a job as babysitter for a family, any family, near the ocean. To my naïve nature, a more idyllic arrangement could hardly be desired. Not only was I overflowing with patience and creative imagination, but I cherished a great love for children, resulting no doubt from a singular lack of exposure to the infants of the human race. What more fertile field could I choose for a lucrative summer pursuit than the care of several small and malleable beings?

With ardor I entered upon an interview, and by depicting my storytelling abilities and my theories of creative play in heroic terms, I so impressed the woman who had been questioning me that I was hired on the spot. Amid the flurry of rather incoherent practical details which followed, I received the distinct impression that I would be living in a white mansion overlooking the sea, with the attendant accessories of yachts, tennis courts, and swimming pools, all of which combined to make living gracious. The fact that I was to make light suppers for the three children, to clean up their rooms, and to amuse them, was glossed over lightly as a mere formality, and a rather distressingly bourgeois formality at that.

During the month that remained before I was to set out on my first venture at working away from home, I lived in a world of hopeful and thoroughly nebulous idealism. It did not occur to me to inquire about hours off during

---

[*] Typescript with holograph corrections by SP and instructor's comments.

the day, or to ask for a precise definition of my status in the home. Indeed, I blithely assumed that I would be spending most of my days lolling on the beach, swimming when the spirit moved me, writing sonnets, and keeping an occasional vigilant eye on the children, who would of course play cheerfully among themselves.

Never in the course of individual history have human beings suffered a ruder awakening than I did after my first few days of labor. Adam's dismay as he choked on the fatal apple, Marie Antoinette's horrified surprise as the tumbril pulled up before the guillotine . . . all these emotional revelations pale to insignificance beside my realization of what my summer entailed.

Every morning, as the first rays of red morning sun spilled into my luxurious bedroom, I would be awakened by the gradually increasing howls of the baby, Joanne. I would leap out of bed and charge to the scene of the tumult, waving my flag of truce, a dry diaper. All sleep from that time on was a laughable gamble. Pinny, the four-year-old girl, developed the regrettable habit of climbing into bed with me whenever she chanced to wake up, and she spent her last forty winks kicking me in the shins, unconsciously, no doubt.

Freddy, a volatile six-year-old with a stubborn penchant for socks and jerseys with matching stripes, invariably slept late and wandered down to breakfast when his sisters were already well submerged in the sticky intricacies of egg yolk.

It developed with the rapidity of a poisonous mushroom that I, who had never cooked an egg in all my young life, was to provide for my own meals and those of the children. I even was to make breakfast for the whole family. During that first horrible week I cut my finger badly while slicing oranges, burnt myself on the iron while pressing a ruffled Paris original dress for the baby, and succeeded in thoroughly alienating Mr. Johnson by putting the coffee on to percolate without any water in the container.

Wrestling with unfamiliar mechanical tasks soon proved to be the most relaxing part of my day. I grew to look forward to the damp and blissful silence of the cellar where I did the daily mountain of laundry. There was a plethora of sheets, diapers, dresses, and pants. Mrs. Johnson believed in starting the day cotton fresh from the skin out. I also enjoyed ironing, after I got used to the idea of pressing the wrinkles out, instead of in. Even washing dishes, making beds, mopping and dusting, came to be pleasant escapes from the formidable task which I had apparently been hired for: supervision and maintenance of the children.

At first, I must admit, I was emotionally spent at the end of the day, after having extracted the baby toddler from near death several times, and having pulled the two oldest children apart from frequent physical combat. Eventually I got used to laughing gaily when I heard the shrill scream of one of my charges rise with all the ominous connotations of an air-raid siren. One swiftly grows able to differentiate between the cry of rage and that of pain.

My status in the family was vague and often uncomfortable. As a college girl, I was presumably above the caste level of outright maid and governess. My relations with Mr. and Mrs. Johnson had a liberal, even intellectual aura. For example, when I evinced an embryonic interest in writing, I was introduced to a supercilious maiden aunt who had published several bad melodramatic novels. My employers often suggested that I take in an evening movie. They found it hard to understand that after coping with their children and their kitchen for twelve hours a day I preferred to retire to the solitude of my room and meditate or read before going to bed.

There was no time during the day when I had a legitimate hour to rest, free from disturbance. Even when the children were taking naps and my other chores were completed, Mrs. Johnson seemed disturbed to find me sitting down, book in hand. Invariably she would suggest that I try a new recipe for cake or pie, one so easy that "any child could bake it." The inference was not, as you may imagine, a pleasant one.

Strange as it may seem, I grew to love the children fully as much as I disliked their tantrums and spoiled attitudes. They were a beautiful trio, with firm clear skin, brown eyes, and neatly formed little bodies. At times they adopted me as a mother; at other times, they would cry smugly, "You can't boss me. You don't live here." Daily attitudes changed at the slightest provocation. I never knew whether amity or animosity would greet in the morning.

No matter what my mood was, whether one of weariness, anger, or depression, I managed to keep a bright amenable front. My sense of humor increased as the days went by, and I was able to amuse myself by laughing off my domestic blunders silently, and by considering the children's tyrannies in the light of mirth, rather than that of maniac despondency. Perhaps my most enjoyable outlet was the fraternizing with the other hired help.

In order to keep the several adjoining mansions in good working order, a crew of specialized individuals was necessary. I liked to listen to Louie, the chauffeur, embroider at length upon the history of the family while he drove the children and myself to the beach or to the swimming pool. The six men who took care of the vegetable gardens and the grounds became friendly acquaintances. There was Bill, who mowed the acres of lawn and clipped hedges eternally. Harry came to the back door every day with an assortment of vegetables fresh from the garden. Fred, Tom, Jake, and Allen tended the flowers in the hothouse, swept off the terrace after Mrs. Johnson had fixed flowers for the house vases, and polished the brass ornaments.

I will pass over the tall, tubercular old seamstress who came once a week. I will leave out the crew aboard the yacht. I never really had a chance to cultivate those particular individuals. My two favorites were Katherine, the part-time cook, and Helen, the laundress who won the Irish sweepstakes in 1932.

Katherine had thick glasses from which one eye glanced out sideways and the other straight ahead. I remember her as a gaunt, crooked figure in a dirty apron, her voice cracked and querulous, her caviling hiding a deep and pathetic loneliness. A loneliness born of lack of her own kind, born of no one to talk to. So old she was that she could not remember the year of her birth. Ireland and her girlhood had vanished as if they never were. No doubt she still ambles arthritically around the Johnsons' kitchen burning batches of Toll House cookies and rattling among her bent aluminum saucepans on the ugly black stove.

Opposing Katherine's melancholic humors was Helen's jovial Irish wit. I recall the day we took the children to the beach together. It was so hot that Helen insisted that the baby go in for a dip, even though she was just getting rid of a cold. A few minutes later, Helen came up from the water carrying a dripping, bewildered Joanne.

"Lord," Helen chortled, "you should of seen that wave. It come in over her head and she was choking for breath when she come up. The water ran out of her for ten minutes straight, streamin from her nose and mouth. An I said: there goes the cold. Salt water'll wash it out good."

I laughed with Helen over her therapeutic measures as she laughed with me over the peculiarities of the family we worked for. Moreover, I fell into the habit of using the impersonal pronoun to refer to the members of the household, as the rest of my more subordinate comrades did. Mrs. Johnson was always referred to as "She." Thus vindictive or resentful remarks about our mistress always had a pleasantly indefinite flavor. When discussing the evil tempers of the children we would wink and say, "Somebody sure is in a bad mood today." As for ourselves, the editorial "We" had the effect of making us seem to be a co-operative federation of capable and magnanimous workers, united against would-be oppressors.

In retrospect, the summer was a combination of obstacles, internal conflict, indignities, and compensations. On the debit side was the evening that I cleaned up after a cocktail party of fifty people. It took me over two hours to wash and put away the last glass, to brush the cigarette ashes off the remaining hors d'oeuvres, and to collect the whiskey-saturated maraschino cherries from under the couch.

On the credit side were memories of the children in their more docile moods. Joanne liked to play in her crib before going to sleep, so I would lean over and let her tweak my nose and cheeks with her plump little hands, and she would smile and gurgle with delight. Pinny used to ask me gravely for a love pat and a pillow case to hug . . . "a soft little one." Freddy was tucked in last. After a tale about a crooked mouse, he responded to my usual question, "Going to give me a goodnight hug?" with a kiss on one eyelid. "Now I have to kiss the other eye," he said. "Then mouth." His little mouth smacked softly. "I have to give your forehead three because it's so large." And so to bed.

Another compensation was the Day Off, one a week. Somehow the sun always shone, and I spent long hours biking along the shore, swimming, and sketching. Burned a deep brown I was by the end of the summer. When I packed my bags and went home at last, my friends would survey my tan and say, "What have you been doing? Lying out on the beach all summer?" My answering smile was pregnant with the pained reproach which one bestows on a backward child.

In summary, I consider my summer job in many lights. The main achievement on my part was one of adjustment, or resolving an ideal with a reality, and in making the solution a workable one. To be sure, I overcame my lack of domestic proficiency, increased my bank account, and learned to subordinate my personal moods under a necessary veneer of bright willingness. But I am most pleased with the fact that I could make a stimulating and vital relationship exist between "somebody and we."

TV or Not TV

Published: *Campus Cat* (Commencement 1952): 1[*]

We have a friend who is a non-conformist. If anybody else likes anything, she always doesn't, and vice versa. Recently she went to a lecture by Ogden Nash and

---

[*] In SP's 1952 calendar, she wrote on 3 May: 'Eve – Wrote for *Campus Cat*,' the Smith College humour magazine. She attended meetings on 7 and 14 May. The latter date says she has a 'story due'. Contributions to the *Campus Cat* were anonymous but the two pieces included in this volume print two of SP's poems. The poem in this article was titled 'Virus TV: (We Don't Have a Set Either)' in typescript; held by Lilly Library. In line 2 of the poem, the reference is to Milton Berle, an American actor and comedian.

she liked him. However, so did everybody else. This has been bothering her for days. She has been sitting in a dark booth at Toto's for a week now, drinking milk and mulling; mulling and drinking milk. Everybody else drinks coffee. We are afraid that her philosophy of life has been shaken. One day she beckoned to us with a sinister finger from her booth. Leaning forward with a bleak smile she said in a hoarse whisper, "Listen, I know there are nasty rumors going around about me not being a non-conformist, but they're all lies, lies I tell you. I hate Nash. I hate bridge games. I hate coffee. I hate Eisenhower. I especially hate television. I even make up horrid poems about it. Look!" With this she thrust a crumpled napkin at us with verses scrawled upon it. The influence was Obvious, Ludicrous, Pathetic. The rhyme was cracked. The rhythm would be next to go. It read:

> Oh, why is it that I recoil
> Each time I sit through Milton Boil?
> What is it makes my stomach assidy
> When children tune in Hopalong Cassidy?
> Why do my eyes reveal fateague
> When I teleview the Baseball League?
> Alas, I do not give a damn
> Which boxer gets the knockout slamn.
> I really wish I never hurda
> The ten-inch square of crime and murda.
> I'd rather live in the Tunnel Hoosac
> Than see an open mouth make moosac.
> My diagnosis of this condition?
> I was not meant for television.
> (Therefore when I sit bored sans TV fixture,
> I go and see a moving picture!)

Be Mine—For Now

Published: *Campus Cat* (Commencement 1952): 3[*]

Every now and then our roommate gets an inspiration out of season. This one she is sending to the shoeiest of white-shoe Yalies next February 14:

---

[*] The poem was titled 'Valentine: Lines for a Rich Bachelor' in typescript; held by Lilly Library.

If you'll be my Valentine,
I'll not covet Bordeaux wine;
I'll not crave a Southern villa,
Caviar or soft chinchilla.
After none of these I'll pine,
If you will say you will be mine.
(On the other hand, I think,
That if I come into a mink;
If by chance I should inherit
A gold bracelet, pure in carat;
Or if somehow I acquire
A limousine with white-walled tire,
I'd change these lines to read, I fear:
"You may go to hell, my dear.")

The Ideal Summer

Ts, *c.*17 February 1953,* Lilly Library

Millionaire uncles have maintained a stolid silence as far as I'm concerned. I have received no word, no magic postcard saying: "Here, Sylvia, a million dollars with only one stipulation: you must spend it on a summer after your own heart." But suppose, just for the sake of argument, that I received a sudden message from the powers-that-be at Smith College Hall—a mysterious unknown individual is paying my college expenses for the whole next year and wants me to take a rest this summer, to do what I want to do most in the world: loaf, travel, go to summer school, surf bathe on the Riviera, climb Mount Fuji, shoot Niagara in a barrel, ski in the Tyrolean Alps, or live on mangoes and papayas in Hawaii. What would I do? Where would I go?

In the past, my summer activities have been dictated mainly by necessity. Working my way through Smith on a combination of summer job earnings and scholarships, I find my main problem has always been one of earning enough

---

* SP's calendar reads 'MLLE – Summer ideal' on 17 February 1953. She sent a draft copy to her mother to be typed the following day (see letter of 18 February 1953, *The Letters of Sylvia Plath, Volume 1*: 563). Typed at top right: 'Sylvia Plath / Smith College / Assignment II.' Written for the *Mademoiselle* College Board contest. The final copy of the assignment was typed by Aurelia Schober Plath and posted to *Mademoiselle* on 27 February 1953.

money in the most stimulating manner possible under the circumstances. And I think, on looking back, that I've had a maximum of unique adventures in the June-to-September period of the last three years: picking vegetables on a truck farm, governessing for three children in a doctor's family, and waitressing at a big Cape Cod hotel.

It's been my philosophy for a long time now that attitude is all important: that you can be creative and alert about a trip to the Acme Market, and often live a lot more fully, even if finances are strictly limited, than the blasé globe-trotter who is no more eager and animated in Bombay than she was in her own backyard. And so I found in my summer jobs the novelty, the rewarding mélange of characters, the delight in mastering a trade capably, that made what might have been drudgery and dull routine become (presto!) a continually stimulating adventure.

But now that I am free to dream, to squander the luxurious funds of my mythical fairy godmother on an ideal summer, the major difficulty is to narrow my desires to the time and space of three months. Let's have a look at the possibilities.

I have never traveled out of the New England states except for a brief exciting champagne-sip of New York. Shall I travel, then? Shall I become a female Richard Halliburton and follow the Royal Road to Romance? On the other hand, I have always wanted to go to summer school to take some of those enticing courses I will never be able to crowd into my schedule, even during these four years at Smith. Shall I take writing, poetry, and modern literature courses at the green haven of Bread Loaf? Or how about Columbia, in New York, where I could haunt the theaters, the cream of restaurants, the art museums, Central Park, and learn to know the byways of the tall, concrete, multi-colored mecca I have worshipped so long from afar?

Oh, it is almost unbearable to have to choose one of these attractive possibilities, for a choice, of necessity, precludes all the other diverging roads. Yet choose I must. What is it, I ask myself, that I want most? Obviously, that which is most impossible and dubious in the actual financial austerity of my life. Normally forced to be intensely practical, I find myself exploding forth with ideas like extravagant colored fireworks when the match is touched to the fuse of my imagination.

Travel, I think, is the order of the day. Altering Housman slightly, I exclaim: "Towns and countries woo together, / Forelands beacon, belfries call; / Never lass that trod on leather / Lived to feast her heart with all."* I choose to go to Europe.

The tour I want to take will not be a stereotyped superficial snapshot-taking circuit of the high spots of European culture merely. It will be, rather, a unique journey calculated to increase my knowledge, understanding, and appreciation of the world beyond my small circle of experience that radiates modestly from the hub of Boston.

As far as I'm concerned, the most important choice to make about this tour is not where to go, but rather whom to choose as a traveling companion? For although I enjoy meeting new people and settling forth on adventures by myself, I feel that new experiences are intensified and enhanced by sharing them with an understanding partner.

I have run through my roster of friends, relatives, and favorite professors, and my choice for a fellow wanderer is, strange as it may seem, my eighteen-year-old brother, Warren! In the first place, I have narrowed my choice to one, because with two people a flexibility of plans is possible as it never is with a larger group. In the second place, Warren and I have a rather wonderful friendship and enjoy each other as if we were chosen comrades, not merely related. Furthermore, Warren starts Harvard on scholarship next fall, and as a culturally and intellectually stimulating companion, then, he is also ideal.

My projected account of the unusual summer will be an impressionistic outline at best; details will fill themselves in as I travel. This will be, then, a whimsical brief whirl at wish-fulfillment.

The trip we take will be scheduled according to the dictates of our moods. We shall linger as long as we like wherever we choose. Our itinerary will be planned out with the help of friends who know the artistic and historic attractions of the continent. Our program will be versatile, including everything from dining and dancing in Paris to bicycling through the Irish hills. We shall be reading, writing, sketching, sunning, swimming, talking, observing, learning, and working along the way: a rich compote of activity and contemplation is in the offing.

And so we start. We both have purchased wardrobes ideal for the scope of our travels: lightweight clothes ranging from dinner jackets (for him) and a flurry of classical, simply cut cocktail dresses (for me), not to mention bathing suits, dungarees, and hiking shoes. In addition, we have a large supply of books for rainy days and quiet evenings. French books, too, because Warren

---

* A. E. Housman, *A Shropshire Lad*. <SP's footnote.>

is helping me dredge up my rusty French in preparation for Paris. And both of us will find someone on shipboard who will teach us the elements of beginning German. We would like to know as much of language and history as we can in order to most fully appreciate the places we visit.

We shall leave New York in June aboard a student ship, because we want to savor the novelty of ocean travel. Ten days on shipboard, then, getting to know the other passengers, swimming, playing deck tennis, sitting up for trenchant midnight bull sessions on everything from seafood to sex to Siberia. We plan to learn actively along the way, not just looking at surfaces, but trying to get behind the places and the people and to appreciate and understand them: education in living is not confined to the groves of Academe.

Landing in England, we shall explore the city of London, traveling out from there to all the spots we wish to see. We shall stop in at Cambridge and Oxford and linger to watch cricket matches, to read Shakespeare aloud on the river Cam, to eat buttered scones and strawberries and clotted cream, and pay a literary pilgrimage to T. S. Eliot. Crossing to Ireland, we shall bicycle through the Killarney lake region, pausing in Dublin to ramble down the streets of James Joyce's *Ulysses*.

Then we shall cross the straits to France, spending a good deal of time in Paris, going to theaters, concerts, obscure nightclubs, meeting people everywhere, sipping aperitifs on the Champs-Élysées, and sketching in the parks. Tearing ourselves away at last with the promise to return, we shall head down through France, highlighting our trip with visits to Fontainebleau, Mont Saint-Michel, Chartres, steeping ourselves in history and culture and folkways. Then Rheims, Orléans, Cluny, Lyon, and a sojourn on the Riviera. The very names are lovely as cathedral bells.

Next on the agenda are Switzerland and Austria: Geneva, and then Vienna and the Tyrol, where our grandparents were born. Here we shall stay in the ancestral inn that our relatives still run, and we shall spend days with them, skiing in the mountains.

Italy follows, where we shall go gondoling in Venice, swimming in the Blue Grotto, sightseeing in Rome. Crossing to Greece, we shall put ourselves in the capable hands of a Smith friend who lives in Athens, and she will introduce us to the Parthenon and picnics in olive groves. From there we'll take a quick plane trip to Egypt and the Nile. (We have always wanted to see the pyramids and the Sphinx since we first saw the photographs in our fifth-grade geography books. And I think that we shall both go for a ride on a camel.) A plane ride to Spain, then, for time is getting short, and we shall pick oranges, watch bullfights, and travel up from Cadiz to Valencia and Barcelona. Back to Paris, where a week or so shall be spent in refined hedonism, saying farewell to friends, visiting favorite haunts for the last time, and steeling ourselves for the return trip.

After prolonging our stay in Paris until the last possible moment, we shall fly back to the States. It will be a clear September evening when we come into New York, and the skyline of the lighted city will stab at us with a sharp poignance. We are not sentimental; we are yet too young to want to halt our wanderlusting ways. But this is home. America: the big sprawling wonderland we live in.

We want so desperately to know the world; to love the million myriad people, to write, to paint, to learn as long as we live. And this summer has been a miraculous continuation of what we have begun at home—the extension of horizons.

The ideal summer has been dropped like a ripe purple plum in our laps, and we have eagerly devoured the exotic fruit. But this fall, more alive, more aware, more understanding, we will return to our local heritage and appreciate as we never did before the tang of early green New England apples.

Smith Review Revived

Written: *c.*26 May 1953[*]
Published: *Smith Alumnae Quarterly* (Fall 1953): 26

The roster of extracurricular activities at Smith College is as varied and inviting as a Swedish smorgasbord, and the menu fluctuates from year to year with the changing tastes of Smith students. Since the very presence of an organization on campus testifies to a special need and interest, the appearance the past year of the revitalized literary magazine, the *Smith Review*, is evidence in itself of a growing desire for a regular publication featuring undergraduate stories, essays, and poetry.

Naturally, when considering the quantity (and quality!) of Smith students, it is obvious that there is plenty of writing going on during the year: stories and poems are being produced for creative writing courses; critical essays are being written for units and seminars; at the end of each year, at the award assembly,

---

[*] SP wrote 'Alum Q ed' on 26 May 1953 in her calendar; held by Lilly Library.

prizes are given for poetry, stories, and essays written in many departments. Considering the interest and emphasis on writing at Smith, it comes as somewhat of a shock to realize that, since the flourishing days of the old *Monthly* (which was revived for a few years in the 1940s) there has been no solidly established literary magazine at Smith for approximately twenty years. Let's just take time out for a bird's-eye view of Smith's literary publications.

First Literary Publication

Back in the days of gas lamps and Gibson girls, the first Smith College publication was launched on its career. When the *Smith College Monthly* made its debut in October 1893, its editors announced that it was to be "not so much a literary production as an expression of the general life of the college, intellectual, social, and religious." Miss Mary A. Jordan of the English Department, a faculty member well-known to many alumnae of the classes of '84 to '24, was the founder of the *Monthly*, as well as its "champion, critic, and friend," and Bertha Alice Watters '94 (now Mrs. John L. Tildsley) was the first editor-in-chief.

In the second issue, the purpose of the paper and its principles were announced to be of practical value, since the *Monthly* would act as a "stimulus to good writing." Operating on the principle of competition, it would be "an incentive to clear thinking and spirited writing."

Among the several sections of the *Monthly* which included a contributors' club for "shorter papers, generally in a lighter vein," was the Alumnae Department which hoped to have at least one article an issue by a graduate student. (In 1909, when the increasing size of the College made it impossible for one paper to handle both the alumnae news and the undergraduate literature, the *Alumnae Quarterly* was founded.)

The *Monthly* flourished until June 1930, when it was announced in the *Smith College Weekly* (the newspaper established in 1911) that the traditional magazine was to be transformed into a new literary quarterly. In the fall of 1930, *Sequence* was heralded by the *Weekly* which asserted: ". . . it seems likely, if the College contributes its best, that the new quarterly will make itself a real mirror of undergraduate thought and perception."

However, in spite of this optimistic forecast, the quarterly was discontinued after a year of life and there was a lull in Smith literary publication until 1940, when the *Monthly* was revived by Smith College students who recognized a real need for a literary magazine among campus publications.

Editorial policy for the magazine modeled both content and format after the *Atlantic Monthly* and *Harper's* and aimed to "reflect student trends of thought through essays, short stories, poetry, critical articles, and editorials . . . [with] occasional contributions from faculty members." The magazines thrived for approximately four years as the *Monthly*, and then gave way to the sporadically published *Smith Review*.

Last fall a group of students determined to establish the literary magazine on a firm foundation, to publish a magazine which would print the best of the stories, essays, and poems being written at Smith during the year. The revitalized *Smith Review* appeared twice last year and managed to pay off a series of back debts and to balance books. This coming year the *Review* hopes to appear at least twice, perhaps three times, if the response to the drives for literary contributions and subscriptions is encouraging.

The contents of the magazine will include stories, poems, and essays by Smith students, a guest faculty spot (last year the *Review* was proud to publish essays by Mary Ellen Chase and by Martha Winburn England of the Smith College English Department), as well as artwork by Smith students. The magazine wants, as did the *Monthly*, to encourage young writers and artists on the Smith campus and believes that publication provides both stimulus and satisfaction for creative activity, as well as entertainment for the campus as a whole.

(Alumnae interested in subscribing or contributing to the *Smith Review* this coming year may address requests for appropriate blanks to Marie Gillette, Morris House.)

We Hitch Our Wagons: Elizabeth Bowen and Sylvia

Written: *c.*26 May 1953
Published: *Mademoiselle* (August 1953): 282[*]

The writer, according to the author Elizabeth Bowen, "should move about the world, in contact with people," keep away from jobs that waste his creative energies and write out of his own sensations and feelings. Her own work often grows out of her visual impressions, reaches print only after a great deal of rewriting. Miss Bowen counts "criticism and encouragement" as the two most important

---

[*] SP interviewed and was photographed with Elizabeth Bowen on 26 May 1953, at the house of May Sarton in Cambridge, Massachusetts.

aids to the young writer, says she began writing stories after she "had failed to be a poet," still prefers the form of the short story to that of the novel.

Poets on Campus

Written: *c.*1 June 1953
Published: *Mademoiselle* (August 1953): 290–1

Five talented young men combine poetry and the classroom

"*Poets are not born but make themselves*"

"I encourage students to concentrate on words as excitement in themselves, to concentrate less on *what* they have to say since that will change as they grow," claims Alastair Reid, a twenty-seven-year-old Scotsman whose first book of poetry, *To Lighten My House*, was published this year. He adds: "You can teach students to make words do what they want them to do, but you can't teach them what to say." Reid grew up in a fishing village on the island of Arran, off the west coast of Scotland, and studied at St. Andrews University, taking his MA in philosophy. As an undergraduate he began publishing in Scottish literary magazines; in America his poetry has appeared in the *Atlantic Monthly* and the *New Yorker*. Reid just finished a children's book about "a strange conglomeration of people and animals that I like." Work in progress: a poetic play about Icarus. Come fall, Reid celebrates his fourth year in the US at Sarah Lawrence, where he gives courses in poetry reading and literature.

"*Teaching and writing are not inimical*"

Anthony Hecht, alumnus of and teacher at Bard, believes that poetry and the classroom involve the same kind of living and thinking. Of the demands of his creative work the thirty-year-old poet says: "When I am writing, I like to feel I can skip meals and everything else till I've bogged down or finished." After taking his MA at Columbia, Hecht went to Europe, won the Prix de Rome in literature from the American Academy of Arts and Letters in 1951, and moved to the Academy. Here his translations from Rilke (*A Parable of Death*) were set to music by composer Lukas Foss. Commissioned by the Louisville Symphony Society and performed there for the first time, the work made its debut in New York last April under the direction of Robert Shaw, was performed at

Tanglewood this summer and has been recorded by Columbia. Hecht's first book of poetry will be out early in 1954.

"The worst trap is careerism"

"I'm less interested in the chance that students might turn out to be professionals than in the fact that numerous students of mine, who will never publish, have simply by writing and writing become more coherent," states Richard Wilbur, poet and English professor at Harvard. "I think the primary function of the writing course is to be a goad and a go-ahead for students who are moved to write. There are certain temperaments, some of the best, for which muteness is sickness." Educated at Amherst and Harvard, Wilbur became a member of the Society of Fellows there in 1947. His two published books of poetry, *The Beautiful Changes* (1947) and *Ceremony* (1950), met with critical acclaim. The thirty-two-year-old poet has won the Harriet Monroe Prize and the Oscar Blumenthal Prize from *Poetry*. Wilbur spent the last year in New Mexico as Guggenheim Fellow.

"Modern writers whine too much"

Parisian-born F. George Steiner dislikes writers who moan "what a miserable time is ours." Taking a positive approach, the twenty-three-year-old poet asserts: "Literature has one purpose: to enlarge the mind of man and to keep his heart pliant and rebellious." Staff member of the London *Economist* during the past year, Steiner received his BA at the U. of Chicago, where he began grad work under McKeon and Tate. Commenting that he really spent that year with four great masters (Aristotle, Pound, Henry James, and Racine), he adds: "Poets need not know many books, but those that they do they must know like their own dreams." At Harvard Steiner took his MA, won the Bell Prize in American Literature, and studied poetry with MacLeish, "who remains my most respected teacher and friend." On a Rhodes Scholarship at Oxford, he was awarded the Chancellor's Essay Prize in 1952 and has been completing requirements for this PhD. Williams welcomes Steiner as instructor in English this fall.

"The frontier is everywhere!"

William Burford sees the excitement of writing today in the opportunities open to talent. "Read the good poets of the past as well as of the present," advises the twenty-six-year-old poet-teacher at Southern Methodist University. "Pope teaches us, better than anyone else in English poetry, how to take our first steps." With his father and grandfathers all in the oil business, Burford spent summer vacations working in a Gulf Coast refinery. An Amherst man, he was invited to Yaddo through Newton Arvin, then teaching at Smith. Winner of a Fulbright to Paris, Burford has had his verse published in *Botteghe Oscure* (Rome), *Merlin* (Paris), and in little magazines here. Awards include the Kathryn Irene Glascock Memorial Prize in 1949, presented yearly to an undergrad American poet; in 1953, the first annual poetry prize given by the Philadelphia Art Alliance to an American poet under thirty.

MLLE's Last Word on College

Written: *c.*5 June 1953
Published: *Mademoiselle* (August 1953): 235[*]

We're stargazers this season, bewitched by an atmosphere of evening blue. Foremost in the fashion constellation we spot *MLLE*'s own tartan, the astronomic versatility of sweaters, and men, men, men—we've even taken the shirts off their backs! Focusing our telescope on college news around the globe, we debate and deliberate. Issues illuminated: academic freedom, the sorority controversy, our much labeled (and libeled) generation. From our favorite fields, stars of the first magnitude shed a bright influence on our plans for jobs and futures. Although horoscopes for our ultimate orbits aren't yet in, we Guest Eds. are counting on a favorable forecast with this send-off from *MLLE*, the star of the campus.

The Neilson Professor

Written: *c.*19 October 1954
Published: *Smith Review* (Fall 1954): 12

Smith College is fortunate to welcome Alfred Kazin, talented writer and critic, as William Allan Neilson Professor this year. Author of *On Native Grounds* (1942) and of *A Walker in the City* (1951), Mr. Kazin has also edited a volume of Blake

---

[*] The text is accompanied by a photograph of the twenty guest editors holding hands and in the shape of a star at the Bethesda Terrace, Central Park, New York. SP is numbered 1 and is situated at the top of the formation.

and a book on F. Scott Fitzgerald and has written numerous critical essays.

A teacher, too, though he calls himself "nomadic," Mr. Kazin has taught at Black Mountain College (1943–4), the University of Minnesota (1946, 1950), the Salzburg Seminar in American Studies, and the University of Cologne (1952). He has lectured at Columbia, The New School, and Harvard, and was a Fulbright lecturer at Cambridge University in the summer of 1953.

Mr. Kazin has twice received Guggenheim fellowships (in 1940 and 1947) and has been awarded a Rockefeller fellowship "to study popular education movements in the British Army and trade unions during the war." In 1949 he won an award for literature from the National Institute of Arts and Letters.

While Mr. Kazin does not like to consider himself as any one particular type of writer, the majority of his works have been literary criticism. He started publishing articles in the *New Republic* while still a senior at the College of the City of New York, and has been writing ever since. At present, he is gathering a collection of his selected essays and working on a study of the influence of Italy on non-Italian writers. Mr. Kazin has also collaborated recently on a volume about Theodore Dreiser which the Indiana University Press will publish in the coming year.

In his book *On Native Grounds* Mr. Kazin presents a definitive interpretation of American literature. He prefaces it with these words:

> Our modern literature came out of those great critical years of the late nineteenth century which saw the emergence of modern America, and was molded in its struggles. It is upon this elementary and visible truth—almost too elementary and visible, so close are we still to its crucible—that this book is based; and it was the implications following upon it that gave me some clue to the patterns of the writing that came after.

In *A Walker in the City*, his more recent book, Mr. Kazin describes the vivid odyssey of a young American "walking into the world, learning on his skin what it is like."

At Smith College, Mr. Kazin is teaching a first-semester course in advanced composition. When asked about his theories of teaching creative writing, Mr. Kazin would only say that the important thing is "not to have theories." In his composition course he emphasizes individual criticism in private conferences and considers that the teacher's chief job is to "release the unexplored talents of the student."

The teacher can help the student in two ways, Mr. Kazin points out: first, to have confidence in her own individuality; and, second, to learn that all literature is discipline. Seasoned writers can break all the rules and still be successful, states Mr. Kazin, but young writers need to learn the discipline of different genres before they strike out on their own.

During the course of the year, Mr. Kazin will give two lectures open to the whole college. On December 1 he will lecture on "The Opera House of Parma," a study of Stendhal and Italy, and in the spring he will lecture for a second time at a Smith College symposium on American Literature. In the second semester Mr. Kazin will teach a course in the Twentieth-Century American Novel.

Speaking of his impressions of this valley, Mr. Kazin confides that he and his wife are "enchanted by Northampton" and that the view of the leaves and mountains from their home overlooking Paradise Pond is truly "paradisiacal."

Articles for *Vogue*'s Prix de Paris Competition[*]

Wardrobe for Six Weeks in Europe

Ts,[†] *c*.31 December 1954, Lilly Library

"To travel best," the experts chorus, "travel light!" Forty-four pounds of luggage for six weeks in Europe seemed most inadequate to me at first, in spite of

---

[*] SP enrolled in the contest by its 15 October 1954 entry deadline. Three poems, 'Closet Drama', 'The Desperate Hours' and 'Checkmate', are in the folder with the Prix de Paris materials but they do not appear related to the contest. Typed in the top-right corner of each poem: 'Sylvia Plath / 26 Elmwood Road / Wellesley, Massachusetts.'

Questions to which SP responded for *Vogue*'s twentieth Prix de Paris contest appeared in the December 1954 issue and were due by 14 January 1955. The quiz, based on the contents of the December issue, asked for two answers out of four possible questions in the fields of Fashion and Feature. In Fashion, SP's 'Wardrobe for Six Weeks in Europe' was a response to question 1: 'What would you take on a six week's trip to Europe if your luggage weight was limited to 44 lbs.? In 500 words, outline your wardrobe and tell how you would make it work' (73). SP's 'Children's Fashion' was a response to question 4: 'Suggest a way to presenting children's fashions. Include layout and copy.' For the Feature section, 'Try a Talent Party' and 'Party for a Princess' were potential responses to question 2: 'Write a feature article on giving a party. Include your plans for decorations, menu, and state whether you plan special entertainment for the guests and what that entertainment would be (music, cards, dancing?). If you would not plan special entertainment, state why' (73). SP's second Feature response was to question 3: 'Why did you enter the Prix de Paris?"

[†] Typed in top-left corner: 'Fashion: Question 1.' Typed in the top-right corner: 'Sylvia Plath / Lawrence House / Smith College.' All five typescripts comprising the submission contain holograph revisions by SP. SP made it to the finals and was one of twelve winners awarded a $25 prize.

this advice. But then my four years of college training at disciplined traveling came to my rescue. It has taken me that long to combat the lavish urge which argues persuasively over each extra piece of clothing: "Oh, yes, put that in too. You just *might* decide to wear it, and you never can tell what will come up." What came up usually was the need of a camel caravan to transport my excess baggage!

Then I learned a few tricks, such as packing an ensemble of clothes that have a basic color harmony and combine no matter what. This means making a stern selection between my favorite pink linen duster and my red dress, my mauve suit and dramatic tangerine beads. While clashes lend variety to my college closet, it only makes compact travel difficult. So for my forty-four pounds, I'll pack a wardrobe which, when spread out altogether on a bed, dovetails to the last earring. Gray, black, and white are my backgrounds, and my pet color accents are aquas and reds.

The foundation of our wardrobe is a gray wool flannel suit, exquisitely tailored, with a matching topcoat, a welcome wrap on chilly days for every other outfit we bring. Color accessories can spice this practical and pretty ensemble (which we'll wear setting off) so we'll add an aqua peasant-print nylon blouse to the classic white one. An aqua knitted dress (or suit) is the next item. Wonderfully wrinkle-free, suitable for tea or travel, knits are versatile and stand up spunkily to both packing and peregrinating.

A cocktail dress goes into the suitcase next, this one of black tie-silk (black being eternal as the Mona Lisa smile!). This dress is strapless, for evening dancing, with a cover-up jacket for afternoon cocktails, cathedral going. We like rhinestones, star-shaped earrings, matching necklace, to spark black. (Believe us, if we had diamonds, to glitter in, we'd wear them!) Another cocktail dress breaks into a bold black-and-brown Mexican print on a sun-yellow background: a striking sheath. For cool terraces or special evening occasions, we'd pack a woolen stole, white or black, or two of those ubiquitous little shrug bolero sweaters (also white and black) that go over everything with equal savoir faire.

Because we can perform amazing arithmetic with separates, our sports and traveling "dresses" are two pieces. A mix-and-match challenge for a girl with a strict budget and strict luggage limitations. We'll bring a straight black skirt with a matching boat-necked top, dress it up with a long strand of aqua-and-silver beads, draped several times around the neck, or with a red-and-white polka dot cummerbund, both simple to pack, marvelous for variety. The cummerbund for example can go with the black skirt and white halter blouse, more informally, and the beads with the aqua knit dress. Another skirt, dirndl this time, is flared bright red with a white V-neck, bare-backed halter top. One bathing suit for swimming and sunning should be added. Because we love what white does for a honey-colored tan, we choose a classic white two-piece suit with tailored top and pants; it also makes a smart combination with the checked beachcoat. Add a pair of aqua shorts, and we have a sundeck wardrobe ready! The white bathing suit shorts go with either white or black tops, the aqua shorts combine well too. A tailored reversible cotton robe, white on one side, black-and-white check on the other triples as beach coat, housecoat, and bathrobe. We are now set for sunning and shopping, touring and traveling, dining and dancing.

The next items are more practical accessories. Shoes take up much room and weight, and we feel well-equipped with a pair of white linen shell pumps, a pair of black patent leathers, and a good pair of red walking shoes, for museums and jaunts on foot. For a hat, we'll take that wispy black veil type that clips on with a black headband and takes up less room than a Kleenex. A white pocketbook and a black patent leather box pocketbook, two pairs of white washable gloves for that always spic-and-span look, and our favorite red beads, earrings, and necklaces.

Because we are active and always manage to run stockings, we'll bring eight to ten pairs, all the same color, which will give us twice the life, as we can dub in a new stocking every time we run one. All-nylon underwear is the cry, and since we can wash and dry it overnight, we absolutely don't need more than two of everything: two nylon bras (an extra strapless one might come in handy), two nightgowns, aqua print and then white (or black if we're feeling wicked), one full slip, one half slip, two nylon pantie girdles, and two pairs of nylon pants. There it is. Oh, yes, one of those plastic raincoat-and-rubber sets, packed space-savingly in a travel kit, to be ready for the deluge.

For a cosmetic case or overnight bag, we'd remember those wonderful individual sealed packages of soap flakes for lingerie, and plastic containers for perfume, lotion, deodorants, to make for unbreakable, lightweight traveling. In any case, we believe that we can synchronize our wardrobe so that we can be versatile and vivid under the forty-four-pound limit. Our tour is a middle-of-the-road tour, and so we pack no bouffant formals for first-class ship wear, nor hobnailed boots for mountain climbing. We will be sunning, touring, dining, dancing, and sightseeing during the summer in Europe, and we firmly believe that we can get along admirably on this selective wardrobe. We also believe we'll be happier than if we'd dragged a trunk of extra outfits, just "in case" we went skiing or on a safari. We picked our favorite dresses, our most comfortable shoes, our most versatile accessories. And we find a pleasure in the classic quality of our selection; we will be feeling comfortable, compact, and well-clad during our six weeks in Europe.

Children's Fashions

To present children's fashions, we suggest a literary theme to hold the display together. The idea could be worked out in several ways. For example, brief appropriate quotations from favorite children's books could be blurbs for the fashion shots and their backgrounds. In every case, the mood of the layout should grow naturally from the type of children's fashions presented.

Enclosed, a rough outline for a spread of play-clothes for picnics, beach, or backyard. We like the setup of one big full-page picture on the left, and two smaller ones, plus copy, on the right, because it gives us a large, spacious picture-book feeling and (as in pages 148–9 and 152–3 in *Vogue*'s Christmas issue) allows for artistic photos of dress, model, and mood setting.

For the picnic spread, we offer two approaches. On the left, a full-page photograph of two children playing with pail and shovel at the water's edge in bathing suits. The shot should not only capture the color and line of the suits, but also the charm of the children, the mood of the setting, so it would be, as are most of the photographs in *Vogue*, a work of art. A few lines from Robert Louis Stevenson's *A Child's Garden of Verses* printed on the lower corner of the page could sum up: "When I was down beside the sea / A wooden spade they gave to me / To dig the sandy shore." Two shots of children in sun suits and play-clothes on the right-hand page could be headed by similar quotes: from the *Wind in the Willows*, for instance, with Rat's classic remark about the contents of his picnic basket. The quotes should not be cute or coy, but rather words from songs and stories that express the fresh delight of children at play while appealing to the external nostalgia in grown-up mothers who find pleasure in reading *The Little Prince* or *Winnie-the-Pooh* over again and again to their eager offspring. Fashion copy would appear also on the right-hand page.

Another idea for this layout is to blow up photographs of the book illustrations themselves and superimpose the children on these, with quotations from the book. The black-and-white drawings for *Alice in Wonderland*, for example, might be the background for one spread of party dresses. The theme might be Alice Through the Looking-Glass, with little girls in party dresses standing against a tapestry-like background of Looking-Glass figures.

Or it might even be possible to have contemporary illustrators of children's books do a series of backdrops for these children's fashions. In any case, the central idea we'd like to emphasize is that the fashions presented through the words and pictures of the children's storybook world itself, a world that appeals to children and grown-ups alike, because it touches at the very roots of life, because it is, as long as there are children, eternal.

Try a Talent Party

What makes a party, any party, is the people. A party can be a celebration, whether birthday or bridal, Christmas or anniversary. A party can be a mustard-and-relish picnic or a candlelight-and-champagne affair. A party is like a casserole: it may be garnished with mushrooms, or served up with sherry, but the real secret of its success is in the expert blending of basic ingredients. And any clever hostess knows that her guest list is the indispensable recipe for her social *chef d'œuvre*.

In the midst of the holiday season, when hospitality is the keynote of the day and colored lights spill out across the snow to welcome all comers, we want to suggest a special kind of party for special people. Because it can be made simple or elegant, small or expandable, it will stimulate the imagination of the creative hostess. This is a party that is as versatile as those who go to it. For this party depends upon the selection of performers, not professional, but amateur: it is a talent party.

Invitations to the talent party are handmade by the hostess: if she is artistic, a sketch or cartoon of each guest in the act of painting, dancing, or crocheting antimacassars will liven the card that states time, place, and type of party. "Bring your favorite talent!" is the one requirement for admission.

Now *everybody* has a favorite talent. Talent may be public, like singing or storytelling, or it may be private, like writing villanelles or copying Dior dresses on grandmother's sewing machine. Perhaps in this era of nationwide professional entertainment, we have become a little too inclined to be bashful about our own abilities. At any rate, a talent party is designed to bring back the pioneer spirit of old days when families had to perform in their own instrumental groups instead of turning on the radio or invent charades to while away long winter nights instead of sitting silently around the television set. At a talent party, the guests themselves are the entertainment.

The atmosphere of our talent party is gay and convivial. There is a buffet dinner to which a domestic guest may contribute her talent in the form of an exotic cake or platter of strikingly iced cookies. There are decorations "in season" which may be created beforehand by the hostess or an artistic guest: blue-and-silver balls and pine boughs dusted with sparking snow, and cutout silver snowflakes may be hung about for a winter party; a crepe-paper wreath of leaves and flowers to laurel the head of each guest might welcome in the spring. Decorations are variable with the time of year and the temperament of the hostess. Ingenuity is the one demand, and this very word sums up the essence of the talent party.

Just for fun, run arbitrarily through the names of a group of friends and see if you aren't surprised at the potentialities for a talent party of your own. We tried it, and came up with a young man who is a superlative accordionist, a bright girl who has a singing voice, a Jerry Lewis-type fellow who draws personal caricatures to help earn his way through college. And then there is the homebody who will stitch up novelty aprons: frivolous plaid cocktail ones for the women, denim steak aprons for the men. The boy next door can do creditable imitations of Tom Lehrer, and a mother of two exacting children can whip up a "made-to-order" story that rivals O. Henry.

This is a mere sampling to overcome the initial, shocked "But what can *I* do?" attitude that may greet the first request to perform. Given enough time to mull over the challenge of the invitation (which may take the shape of a silver gauntlet!), even the most reticent party-goer will arrive armed for combat.

In order to avoid duplication (after all, you can't have eight renditions of "Greensleeves" on a guitar!) the hostess should ask each guest to send her a description of his or her talent a few days before the party. Then she can make up a program according to her own discretion and serve as moderator.

Our favorite number of guests for a talent party concedes to our budget and the size of our apartment: four couples for a congenial buffet is excellent, and provides a full evening of entertainment. Indeed, the hostess herself may be surprised at the skills of her guests! The talent party appeals to the innate desire everybody has to be the center of the stage, to be appreciated in a very special way.

The buffet, by the way, is arranged by the hostess to display her own talents at cookery. We have a predilection for beginning with cocktails and a smorgasbord of hors d'oeuvres (ranging from salted nuts to anchovy-paste-and-cream-cheese) and progressing to a steaming shrimp casserole with onions and cheese (page 126 in *Joy of Cooking*), the favorite tossed-salad-of-the-house and hot homemade biscuits. For dessert, a make-your-own sundae is always fun, with ice cream as base and serving dishes of nuts, frozen strawberries, and butterscotch and chocolate sauce to add to taste. It inspires the inventive spirit!

And there you have it, ladies and gentlemen. The talent party. The outline is ours, the originality is yours. Pick your guests, plan your program, and we guarantee you an evening of entertainment that will spread a creative glow throughout the whole company: that wonderful spirit of warmth which comes when very special people have all participated in that "gathering together for social pleasure" which Webster calls "a party."

Party for a Princess

Storybook setting for a special event . . . birthday or tea, that particular enchanted look for a party-goer. Here, a party dress that will bewitch the most discriminating young miss. A pale yellow dress of daffodil crisp nylon patterned with tiny white stars.

Summertime goes with a shepherdess. A forest-green cotton bodice that laces over a full-skirted frock of white, bordered with a print of laurel leaves. Straw hat ties with green bow, tilts back wide brimmed, wreathed with daisies.

Beachwear for the shore patrol: a picnic basket of fashion, both practical and pretty. On a Picnic We Will Go. "There's cold chicken inside it," replied the Rat briefly: "coldtonguecoldhamcoldbeefpickledgherkinssaladfrenchrollscresssandwichespottedmeatgingerbeerlemonadesodawater—"

When I was down beside the sea
A wooden spade they gave to me
To dig the sandy shore.
My holes were empty like a cup.
In every hole the sea came up,
Till it could come no more.
    Robert Louis Stevenson

New shoes, new shoes,
    Red and pink and blue shoes
Tell me, what would *you* choose
    If they'd let us buy?
    Ffrida Wolfe

Beachwear for the younger set, perfect for swimming and sunning, borrows from the navy blues, shows splashes of liberal accents of red, shows a fondness for sturdy fabrics, and bright colors, sun-yellows, sail-whites.

Facing page: big sister sports reversible terrycloth beach coat that can double as bath robe: vivid white faced by a diamond-pattern of navy blue and white. Blazing red bathing suit to match, with snug halter top and flared skirts that bob over lollypop pants. Little sister in a sun-yellow romper suit stitched about with moss green.

Above right: A three-piece delight for picnic or beach party in water-blue denim, bordered with spunky white braid. Halter top with scooped neck; flaring skirt covers a pair of trim matching shorts.

Directly right: A striped jersey, red-and-white, and, for the discriminating young man, socks to match. Shorts are navy blue denim, stitched round with red.

Why I Entered the Prix de Paris

One of the main reasons why I entered the Prix de Paris is so that I would have the challenge of answering questions like this one! The Prix de Paris demands a good deal of us in the way of time and talent, ideas and ingenuity; it also offers much that is not mere glitter, but genuine advantage to the college senior. Such as experience in writing articles, analyzing layouts, inventing features and fashion displays that will attract the *Vogue* reader. This is not mere nebulous dreaming: this is practical experience.

I would be equivocating if I pretended the actual prizes *Vogue* offers to the winners weren't an important incentive: as a typically active college girl, plunged in Dostoevsky thesis, poetry and story-writing courses, co-operative house jobs, postgraduate applications, and the usual plethora of extracurricular obligations, I distribute my time with more care than I use in selecting Christmas presents for the man in my life. So *Vogue*'s Prix is the golden apple on top of the glass hill in the fairy tale. I like riding up glass hills, only the golden apple crowns the whole venture and gives it the requisite spice.

Now, for the reasons I enjoy *working* for the Prix. First of all, there is that bewitching tangible: experience. My personal plans for the future will be indefinite till late next spring, when I find out the outcome of Fulbright applications and so on. I *do* know, however, that writing is my central interest. Whether freelance or professional, I will be writing short stories, poems, and feature and news articles for the rest of my life. The opportunity to direct my love for the English language along specific lines, such as the *Vogue* assignments, is invaluable. My American heritage shows my pragmatism: I may be poetic, but pragmatically so! Experience in writing for a professional magazine with highly selective standards, then, is a very actual reason for my participation in the Prix de Paris.

Another reason for my work for the Prix has revealed itself more completely as I've gone along. I have learned a good deal more about myself than I knew when I began! And that is all to the good. When one is asked to describe oneself in a few hundred words, one learns discipline! My first reaction was: why, I could write a book! And then I began to sift, to select, to try for representative specific details that could somehow present all the diverse qualities that go to make up an identity. The *Vogue* questions have helped me organize my opinions (about college room decorations, party giving, Smith fashions, life in general and in particular) and attempt to portray them vividly, with as much versatility as possible. I was sure that the Prix would stimulate my thinking when I entered, and indeed answering the questions has been like working out creative charades!

At the outset I felt that the Prix de Paris would help me grow in several ways, and I certainly haven't been disappointed! I have had as much fun arranging the words in my articles as jewelers must have in setting rare stones! I have thought over questions and talked about them with friends and thoroughly enjoyed myself in writing up features and arranging amateur layouts. The enterprise has been just what I hoped it would: a challenging enterprise which, in the aesthetic sense, is its own reward!

Social Life Without Sororities: A Profile of Smith College

Ts, 10 January 1955, Smith College and Lilly Library[*]

Let us begin with two incontestable statements. First, social life at Smith is superlative. Second, social life proceeds in full swing without sororities. The thesis of this article is that Smith College meets its problems of social organization in a way which approaches perfection[†] and attains all the advantages a sorority system might have without any of the disadvantages.

With an enrollment of 2,192 undergraduates, Smith is the largest resident women's college in the world. Naturally the challenge here is to create a warm,

---

[*] Typed at top right: 'Sylvia Plath / Lawrence House / Smith College.' Written for the Yale *Gargoyle*. The Smith College typescript is six pages and is incomplete. The Lilly Library typescript is eight pages with holograph revisions by SP (reflected in the Smith typescript) as well as comments by Aurelia Schober Plath. As such it was necessary to use both typescripts in order to produce a final copy of the piece. It is noted in the article where the Lilly Library's typescript takes over from Smith's.

[†] It becomes suddenly relevant to state that the authoress is a Smith senior with a vehement bias (which she maintains is valid) in favor of the non-sorority system as it operates at Smith. This article is an attempt at presenting a positive, factual account of social life at Smith; criticism of the sorority system, if not always merely implicit, may reflect general opinion, but does not pretend to represent it. <SP's footnote.>

closely knit, personalized community where the individual doesn't feel she is drowning in a sea of human beings who don't seem to know she exists. The organization of social life at Smith College—the small house system, the recreational program, the multitude of extracurricular activities—manages to achieve just this aim: a campus life where each girl is a unique, indispensable part of that enormous collective entity known as "Smith."

As is the case everywhere, home is the center of activity which radiates outward, and at Smith the core of life is the "cottage system of houses." Statistically, Smith girls live in thirty-five different dormitory units in groups averaging fifty-seven girls. Most houses have their own dining rooms, and each house contains girls from all four classes and all parts of the country. The advantages of this small house system far outweigh the expense involved in the upkeep of the many dormitories, and part of Smith's charm results from the unique heritage and traditions of each house. This is where Smith's social organization begins.

Take the social life of a typical Smith freshman. It starts the day she steps over the threshold of her dormitory. She'll find that her housemates are a congenial group, small enough to allow acquaintance with all, large enough to offer several close friends who share her interests. "House spirit" is strong. Interhouse athletic tournaments rally students to sports ranging from tennis to crew.

Each house has a social chairman who supervises the house dances, parties, and celebrations, and who works closely with the college Recreational Council, which promotes social activities at Davis Student Center. House customs are part of the Smith girl's heritage. Whether it is the annual hunt for the secret staircase at Sessions House, the Halloween charades, or Christmas caroling by candlelight early the last morning before winter vacation, each Smith girl participates in traditions that involve her in a very personal way with the life of her college, past and present.

Housing assignments are planned by the Warden's office and are "impersonally decided, with personal considerations." While interviewing Miss Helen Russell, the acting Warden at Smith, we were amazed by the intricacy of considerations here. The freshman requests houses preferentially, double or single rooms, and sometimes even a particular roommate. From here on in, rooms are distributed with an eye to stated preferences, varied geographical representation, a mixture of public and private school graduates, and a blend of common and contrasting interests. In no case is there a stigma attached to not "making" the house of her first choice, as there often is on a campus which has sororities.

Because of the rich diversity of girls in each house, there is no valid list of the "best" houses on campus. Preferences for houses vary from year to year, with students often being advised by relatives or older friends in college. Every house has its exceptional members; each individual makes her own reputation without the debits or credits of a particular Greek label. No feelings are trampled, as in the sorority "rush," and no girl is considered unfortunate because she didn't make a student-run gauntlet which leads to the top sorority.

Interestingly enough, the few complaints about not getting into the house of her choice at Smith generally come before the freshman has moved in. Once she is settled in her assigned room, wild Princeton tigers couldn't shake her conviction that hers is "the greatest house on campus." And at Smith, there are thirty-five of "the greatest houses."

Perhaps one of the most successful aspects of housing arrangements at Smith is the immediate contact of the freshman with upperclassmen. Our Smith freshman is not quarantined to a dormitory with five hundred other freshmen exactly as green as she is, or made to feel apart from the rest of the upperclassmen by social distinctions. Assimilation of the freshman is rapid. Each girl has her own upperclass adviser, a sort of "big sister" who sees her through the first weeks of orientation and who may assist her, during the year, with anything from room decorating to deciphering the train schedule to New Haven. By being initiated immediately into a four-class cross-section of campus life, the freshman learns fast, socially and academically. Constructive help, not hazing, is a keynote in the attitude toward the freshman at Smith.

Almost simultaneously with her entrance through the Grécourt gates, our freshman will begin weekend dating, which is naturally an important part of social life at Smith. If she doesn't already have contacts from home, the Smith College Recreational Council, a student committee of sixteen, sponsors two freshman "mixers" in the fall at Davis Student Center. Guests flock to Northampton from Amherst, Dartmouth, Trinity, Wesleyan, Williams, and Yale, to mention only a few. (If challenged, we could draw you a social map of the eastern coast and prove that Smith College is the hub of a huge wheel that radiates out to every men's college within reasonable commuting distance. "Reasonable," here, can even mean California!)

Upperclassmen often provide a stream of brothers, cousins, or other distant relatives as "blind dates" for the freshman. In every case, active attention is given to the social life of the incoming class. Lawrence House, for example, held a jazz concert and reception for its freshmen this fall, to which every male acquaintance available was invited, as a sort of "debut" party for the new girls in the house. This kind of activity is the rule, and not the exception, at Smith.

Among the most popular social affairs at Smith are the house dance weekends, which take place just before Christmas and then again in the spring. Traditional events, such as Christmas Vespers and the annual tree-trimming party at Davis, are open to the college, while each house puts forth its special brand of hospitality, including dinners, dances, concerts, and Sunday brunch.

The intimacy and conviviality of these house dances make them high points of the social year. Practically every dance or party at Smith imports entertainment from the men's colleges. The Whiffenpoofs and Amherst DQs did the honors at the two freshman mixers this fall, while our 1954 house dances featured, among other groups, the Princeton Boomerangs, the Amherst Zumbas, the "Bards" of Columbia, and the Baker's Dozen from Yale. The conclusion is obvious: Smith social life is varied, as well as vital.

Then, of course, there are the larger class dances, foremost among which is the Junior Prom. Charity Ball, the only all-college formal dance, generally takes place on Rally Day weekend. (Rally Day, Smith fans will recall, is the celebration of George Washington's birthday at Smith. It involves, among its more amusing features, variety shows by the three upper classes.) Last year, Charity Ball weekend featured the Princeton Nassoons, a jazz concert by the Wesleyan High Street Five, and excerpts from the 1953 Princeton Triangle Show "Malice in Wonderland."

Men, as you have no doubt noticed by now, are always around at Smith. In fact they are so plentiful that sometimes they are even auctioned off. This fall the Amherst DQ singing group went to the house bidding the highest at Sophia's Circus, the annual outdoor festival for the benefit of Service Fund, the campus equivalent of Community Chest. Indeed, with Amherst merely a brief knot or two away across the Connecticut River, study dates are frequent, and casual, companionable relationships exist which balance the glitter and flare of the Big Weekends.

Davis Student Center is the modern, convenient rallying ground for all extracurricular activities at Smith and a good place to take dates on the weekend. Equipped with a colorful snack bar, a lounge, and a maze of committee rooms, Davis also sports a ballroom (with ping pong and bridge tables) which is often used for informal dances, proms, and jazz and octet concerts. A jukebox provides background music for the food shop, while the lounge boasts a large fireplace, grand piano, radio Victrola, and current magazines. And just to prove what a fixture men are in the social life at Smith, Davis even has a men's shower room for the particular convenience of Smith dates!*

---

* The Smith College typescript ends here; the following is taken from the Lilly Library typescript.

One of the most satisfying aspects of social life at Smith is the extracurricular activities, a smorgasbord of about fifty clubs and societies open to those interested or talented in arts, sports, politics, and so on. The programs of these varied associations are coordinated by Activities Board, a group composed of the heads of the extracurricular organizations, which works out general policies, plans forums, and considers the overall extracurricular scene at Smith.

A democratic distribution of offices is assured by Point System, a student-run organization which limits the number of offices one girl may hold in a year. Each Smith student is given a rating for her health and academic work, and ratings for extracurricular activities are given according to the time and responsibility of the job involved. Another example of the efficiency and democratic method of extracurricular elections at Smith is Electoral Board, a student committee which interviews and carefully screens each member of the junior class in preparation for the college-wide election to the big campus offices. In this way, no girl of ability and promise is overlooked.

One of the major attractions of the clubs at Smith is that they emphasize intercollegiate activity. As a case in point, the girl who is interested in radio will join WCSR, the Smith student-owned and operation radio station. There she will not only work with other Smith girls who share her interests, but she will play hostess to guests from the radio stations at men's colleges. This October, Dartmouth presented a program over WCSR, and, during the year, Smith delegates will be guests at other college radio stations, including Dartmouth, Harvard, and Yale.

Intercollegiate contacts through extracurricular activities are frequent at Smith, offering the stimulation of shared experiences, the basis of common interests. Smith singing groups combine with the male glee clubs for concerts and broadcasts. The Amherst College Glee Club participated in our annual Christmas Vespers this year, while our Smith College Glee Club has put on benefit concerts with Harvard, Yale, and Williams. The Smith Chamber Singers are known throughout Europe from their summer tours, and during the summer of 1953, they were the guests of the Air Force and sang their way through Newfoundland, the Azores, and Iceland.

Uniformed in red blazers and gray skirts, the Huff 'n Puffs, Smith College band, not only provide a Sousa flourish to campus affairs, but appeared in New Haven this fall to participate in a Variety Show sponsored by the Yale Band. This is only one more example which represents the general tone of life at Smith, a campus where the individual is free to develop her interests and talents in the fullest way possible, under an organization which encourages all and excludes none.

Smith College social life, then, is hardly provincial. It is, to all practical purposes, universal. Organized around the small house system and clubs which are open to all with the interest or ability to join, social activity extends from the informal tête-à-tête date over a sundae at Davis to the gala formality of the all-college Charity Ball, from the co-ed work weekends at Rabbit Hollow to the intercollegiate Debating Club tourneys. Sororities are nonexistent at Smith; social life is everywhere, available for everyone. To steal a line from Robert Frost, we "don't know where it's likely to go better!"

The Arts in America: 1954: Collage by a Collegian[*]

Ts, 28 February 1955,[†] Lilly Library

Where does the observation of art begin? At Smith College, more often than not, we start to dream at a distance over the theater section of the *Sunday Times* or the art news in the *New Yorker*. Taking our black coffee and hot-cross buns in a sunny studio-bedroom, we plot like buccaneers preparing to conquer a new tropical isle. Colors and sounds shape themselves in our imagination with the revolving intrigue of a Calder mobile. So one fine day we pack

---

[*] This piece was written for *Vogue*'s Prix de Paris contest and is in response to the following requirement: 'The AMERICANA issue of *Vogue* stresses different aspects of the American scene. Write a feature for such an issue on your observations of the arts this year. What have you found most exciting in the American theatre, books, music, et cetera' (201).

[†] According to SP's calendar she finished and mailed 'The Arts in America: 1954' by 28 February 1955. The typescript contains holograph and typewritten corrections. In SP's hand at the top is 'To *Vogue* – 1955'. Typed at top right: 'Sylvia Plath / Lawrence House / Smith College / Northampton, Massachusetts.'

SP visited the Whitney Museum on 8 February 1955, and wrote three poems based on this visit under a collected title of 'Wayfaring at the Whitney: A Study in Sculptural Dimensions' (c.28 February 1955). The individual poems were: 'Kafka by Sahl Swarz', 'Daedalus and Icarus by Lindsay Daen' and '"Three Caryatids Without a Portico" by Hugh Robus'. SP wrote her poem 'Black Pine Tree in an Orange Light' (8 March 1955) based on Gregorio Prestopino's painting; saw William Inge's *Picnic* at the Music Box Theatre, New York City, on 29 March 1954; saw Maxwell Anderson's *The Bad Seed* at the 46th Street Theatre, New York City, on 11 December 1954; and saw T. S. Eliot's *The Confidential Clerk* twice: at the Colonial Theatre, Boston, on 22 January 1954, and at the Morosco Theatre, New York City, on 28 March 1954. SP heard Dylan Thomas read on 20 May 1953 at Amherst College, Massachusetts, and attended Mary Ellen Chase's book event on 5 November 1954. The quote concluding the essay is from Psalm 118.

our theories along with our tweed suit and head toward that nearest Mecca of contemporary art, New York City.

Let it be said, as the 9:25 train pulls out of Northampton in a syncopation of sunlight and excitement, that we call ourselves cultural vagabonds. With time and theses both of the essence at Smith, we sample extracurricular arts with the speed, economy, and yet, paradoxically, the intense delight, of a beachcomber with a tidal deadline, searching for silver twists of driftwood and rare scallops in a labyrinth of blazing sand and sun. We are looking for that particular "shock of recognition," that re-vision of the usual world, which is the experience of art and comes as many colors as a versatile chameleon.

The experience of art is universal as the samba of spring across the countryside, yet personal as our favorite tossed salad recipe: we all experience art, but our own experience is uniquely private. So the present odyssey is no world-circling jaunt, but rather a series of brief verbal snapshots of our favorite artistic islands where perhaps a certain arrangement of watermelon red, black, and white catches our fancy or where a Dufy-blue song makes diamonds jangle in our blood. This is a journey through the kaleidoscope of the mind's eye: a Smith girl's 1954 collage of contemporary art.

Let us begin where there is light, very much light, at the Whitney Museum of American Art. The 1955 Annual Exhibition—a comprehensive cross-section of paintings, sculpture, watercolors, and drawings—blazes in an atmosphere of immaculate high-voltage brilliance. We feel as if we are watching the vivid world go by from the heart of a glittering diamond: we can almost cut the air into facets, it is so bright, so hygienic.

Sculpture is on the first floor, where Robert Cook's *Rodeo*, a jagged bronze of man and horse, poised in a plunging tension of tendons. Nearby, Hugo Robus' *Three Caryatids Without a Portico* curve with the lyric calm of plaster, a trio of supple pillared maidens. Joseph Cornell's deft box construction, *Midnight Carousel*, opens on a black window barred with chalk-white wire; a flying horse diagrammed with astrological finesse gives a sense of revolving in a black-and-white circuit of zodiacal discipline.

In Lindsay Daen's fragile bronze *Daedalus and Icarus*, two slender greenish beings poise, one above the other, like tenuous dragonflies, relating the worlds of vegetable and insect, bird and human, in a delicate equilibrium of green. *Snakes and Birds* by Chaim Gross, is a tall totem of lignum vitae where, twining through yellow and brown rings of wood, bird plumage and snake coils undulate upward. On a boulder, Lorrie Goulet has sketched a pony *Bestia* who looks most impish about being revealed in his natural stable of stone, while from a flat slab of black granite, Jane Wasey has evoked a malevolent *Serpent* which meanders in perilous Gordian knots.

Ruth Vodicka's *Fulfillment* of welded bronze and brass reveals a slender, demure couple, lyrically enclosing the space between them, linked by a shy handclasp and an air of bucolic diffidence. In sharp contrast to this mellow golden mood and starkly haunting is Sahl Swarz's fierce head of *Kafka* in steel and mosaic. The blue mosaic squares give the face a complexion of cubed infinity, diagrammed with stylized lines like planet tracks; bristling metallic eyebrows and hair flow stiffly backward as if blown through by winds from outer space.

Upstairs, we pass by José de Rivera's slick *Construction in Red and Black* (plugged into the wall, no less), which turns with the slow narcissistic satisfaction of an apple paring. Now, the paintings. Edward Hopper's powerful *Sea Watchers* links tawny tones of sand to human flesh, and spare aesthetic blue of sea with land shadows in a correspondence of color and clean strength.

Among the Abstract Expressionists, Hans Hofmann's vital *Fantasia* almost leaps from the canvas in three-dimensional daubs of blue and white on a background of orange and black. Strictly abstract is *The Eight Categories of Fate* by Charmion von Wiegand, a geometrical arrangement of eight color-squares leading in a rainbow of progression to a vortex of black.

We like especially the range of nature paintings, both abstract and representational. Dylan Thomas might be reading "The force that through the green fuse drives the flower" to parallel the pastel mood of *Atomic Spring* by Russell Twiggs (we can't help wondering if his name is a painter's pun!). Here, a whitish canvas is interwoven with the pale greens and lemon yellows of plant veins in a tapestry of fluid roots and leaves; all is soft, undefined, as if the first subtle network of creation were taking place in the mind of a dreaming pagan god. Recognizable, yet transformed in a pale fury of fertility, Charles Burchfield's *Pussy Willows in the Rain* erupts green growth under the forking lash of white rain. John Ferren's *Spring Fronds* is a sprouting of yellow, brown, and orange roots and seeds in a whitish medium, where the force of life thrusts outward through incorrigible shoots and tendrils. *March 1954* by Boris Margo shows the rich bark-brown of colossal tree trunks sliced down by a yellow shaft of knifing sunlight. Georgia O'Keeffe's *Winter Tree III* is a symphonic fountain of white frost.

Intellectually, as well as sensuously, we are attracted by the dream-photography of the surrealists. Ivan Albright's *Whiskey Mountain* is a swarming canvas of predominant leather-browns and shingle-grays where ropes and harnesses tangle with the meticulous precision of snakes about a camouflaged horse grazing to right of center. In drastic opposition to this masculine painting, which fairly reeks with the pungence of tobacco and horse dung, is Peggy Bacon's sensitive interpretation of *Lingering Memories*. A ramshackle gray house set in a plot of trees and grass glimmers in a weird gloom of greenish-yellow. Around the house, the figures of the inhabitants are frozen in attitudes of grief and love, solitary ghosts united only by the eerie wash of light that seeps in from another world and captures all in a phosphorescent trance.

At this point we are interrupted by a polite puzzled gentleman who asks: "Say can you figure out Number 144?" Whether or not we can figure out Number 144 (John Wilde's high key *Apotheosis of Marie-Henri Beyle*) we are fascinated by this orange, pink, and fuchsia fantasia of tree avenues and wild young women who are running, dancing, floating, climbing saplings, or lying exquisitely dismembered on a tangerine ground covered with bright pebbles of colored glass.

Moving from the landscape of nature and the photographic intricacy of neuroses, we come to the twentieth-century city, that paradoxical wasteland of mechanized men, that garden of flowering neons. Richard J. Bové's *The Riders* captures a row of expressionless faces on a jolting subway train in heavy gray, black and white stroboscopic forms that are men already half gone on their metamorphosis into mindless machinery. In *City, Night and Day*, Byron Goto anatomizes the long skeleton of a city in black and white on a beige ground, recalling the intricate relics of some prehistoric monster. Dong Kingman, in his *Factory X*, creates a witty cityscape where faces, clocks, birds, and musical instruments emerge in greater numbers the more one looks.

Our favorite among all the paintings exhibited is Siegfried Reinhardt's *Winter*. Against an inexorable black sky is frozen the disc of a chalk-white moon; in strict geometric areas there is a black-and-white lace as of blackbird feathers seen through snowflake crystals; then, a delicate tilted abacus of lavenders and aquas, essence of snow shadows at twilight and the pallor of ice: all hangs in perfect balance, transfixed by the gorgon's eye of winter.

Before leaving, we'd like to mention John Altoon's *Archaic Visitors*, two crude stony birds done in a lichen-gray-green just barely tinged with pink, like sunset on marble; Ynez Johnston's calligraphic *Statues at Midnight*, a whimsical network of lines texturing stolid maroon-and-brown forms with pink; Gregorio Prestopino's *Pine Tree*, a weird Rorschach-blot of twisted black on orange with the creaking rhythms of an umber plow in the foreground; and Charles Sheeler's serene, dynamic *Lunenberg*, a pure abstraction of farm buildings.

Walter William's *New Day* brings us to the Exit door. This strong canvas glows with the hot pinks, oranges, reds, and yellows of another fruit-stand where colors are kindled in the flame of morning sun and range from elliptical yellow of lemons to elegant mahogany of the negro proprietor's skin.

It's a simple switch from the curb of the Whitney to a passing yellow cab. With luck and an obliging taxi driver we can cut a few neat corners in time and recapitulate some of our theater discoveries this past year. We won't attempt a resume of plot and character, because our mind's eye is definitely not encyclopedic but eclectic. We will recall a mood here, a tableau there, or the Martini-textured voice of a certain character actress, as our turning diamond-facets reflect the neon glitter of Broadway boogie-woogie.

Take an early Labor Day morning in a small Kansas town, with the mists rising and autumn nipping at the green heels of summer. Imagine a backyard sandwiched between two shabby houses, add a handsome young vagabond named Hal Carter (Ralph Meeker) and a beautiful redhead, Madge Owens (Janice Rule), and call it a *Picnic*. We are captivated by the characters here, real and colloquial as a hometown Thanksgiving dinner. There is an urgency in the love of Hal and Madge that cuts across the practicality of Madge's mother, who bristles to keep her daughter from the mistakes and heartbreak she herself has found in romance. But the important thing in life, as the gaudy schoolmarm, Rosemary Sydney (Eileen Heckhart) realizes, is a man to love, a man to marry. No matter what.

Now Eileen Heckhart, our favorite character actress, leads us to a play of very different mood, one that chills the blood: *The Bad Seed*. Here Miss Heckhart drew spontaneous applause in her creation of the raw-voiced, tissy mother of the drowned boy, Claude Daigle. The audience atmosphere is electric: there is a sense of participation in horror that breaks barriers: the svelte black-clad beauty next to us, with huge diamonds dangling through pierced ears, turns a blinding smile of complicity in our direction as the tension builds unbearably and then breaks with a nervous laugh.

Eight-year-old Rhoda Penmark (Patty McCormack) is the coolest little murderess going, all the more terrifying for her innocent-as-peppermint-candy appearance. Leroy (Henry Jones), the simple hired man, gives one of the top supporting performances of the season, taunting Rhoda in a macabre scene about "a little blue electric chair" especially designed for young murderers.

NON-FICTION | 549

Against Nancy Kelly's sensitive portrayal of the gradually enlightened and appalled mother, Christine Penmark, Rhoda marches diabolically to her third murder. While Leroy burns, Rhoda plays her glittering piano at a faster and faster tempo, with all the detachment of Nero on the walls of Rome.

The controlled and probing study of the psychopathic personality, adapted from William March's novel by Maxwell Anderson, is all too credible. It concentrates in its dynamic tension the echoes of recent newspaper headlines about wanton juvenile murderers. It makes us stare with a shiver of misgiving at the precocious little blonde girl across the street who has pigtails just like Rhoda's.

Looking backward, now, we conjure up the sedate poetry of T. S. Eliot's *Confidential Clerk*, which has had countless critics scrambling around like housewives during a January sale, hunting for symbols and ulterior meanings. Sir Claude Mulhammer (Claude Rains) is beautifully articulate about second-rate potters and the aftermath of true creation: "That state of utter exhaustion and peace / which comes in dying to give something life."

Into the midst of the Mulhammer study (which toward the end of the play is almost palpably furnished with unfulfilled dreams) comes Mrs. Guzzard (Aline MacMahon), her pocketbook apparently full of crystal balls and tea leaves. With the calm savoir faire of a fairy-godmother incognito, Mrs. Guzzard proceeds to grant wishes right and left by simply straightening out a tangled forest of family trees.

We find ourselves thoroughly enchanted by the subtle interplay of personalities in the drawing-room arrangements where talk ranges from champagne-bubbling banter to profound philosophy, where the sandy voice of Lucasta Angel (Joan Greenwood) and the chicly clad non sequiturs of Lady Mulhammer (Ina Claire) give a vivid feminine dimension to the more somber background of the four men, each one most deft at packing household words with rich levels of meaning. The *Confidential Clerk* takes us, in the words of Sir Claude, "through the private door / Into the real world."

Another dimension of this world builds its facets from a spinning platter. Because we think in terms of synesthesia, we like to visualize and verbalize music. Our ear isn't tutored to hear music in its own pure terms alone: as we listen, tones turn to color, chords vibrate into words. So we shan't indulge in esoteric palaver about recent "approved" records here. Very simply, we come, we listen, we know what we prefer and that, as Cleopatra said, is that.

For jazz, there is no one like Dave Brubeck. When *Jazz Goes to College*, we go along to a blue-beat heaven. "Balcony Rock" is honest blues at its best, with

Paul Desmond on the alto sax sauntering over a rockaby rhythm coming from Bob Bates on bass, Joe Dodge on drums. The improvisations of this quartet are like snowflakes, no two alike. When Desmond turns oriental in "Le Souk," his imagination builds tonal pagodas and the pounding background beat rocks our blood like the China Sea. "Take the A Train" begins with a plaintive pulse beat by Joe Dodge and weaves an elegy of autumn leaves and empty stations. As a classical-enthusiast friend of ours remarked: "Brubeck shoots the moon like he was first Bach and then maybe Stravinsky."

Luis Sandi's *Ballet Bonampak* gives an offbeat color cruise with lovely weird Indian percussion effects. On RCA Victor, the Mexican National Symphony Orchestra creates the eighteenth-century city of Bonampak, threatened by war. The mood is metallic, from the silver jangle of tribal invocations to the brazen gongs of the conquering sun god. On reverse side, Sarita Gloria enchants with thirteen Brazilian songs, her phrasing clear and lyrical as mission bells. We like especially the archness of "Côco Peneruê," and the fluid reverence of "O Kinimbá." Anthony Chanaka provides the piano setting for this soprano jewel.

Of the recent recorded musicals, we tune in on *Pajama Game*, where Richard Adler and Jerry Ross render one tour de force after another. For novel fun, Eddie Foy, Jr., and the ensemble mimic our quick-ticking time-study age with the urgent point-counterpoint of "Racing With the Clock." The "Steam Heat" routine is a showstopper, while John Raitt makes his "Once a Year Day" the buoyant vocal vaulting of a gay blade over red-letter hydrants. So we're sentimental, so we like Raitt's husky "Hey There" with the Dictaphone echo. For brass, for verve, for vernacular, it is very definitely "The Pajama Game."

There's something irresistible about a virtuoso turned comedienne. Anna Russell's latest *Guide to Concert Audiences* is her third whirl on Columbia Masterworks, and her esoteric accent makes her interim patter incredibly funny. Designed to clarify concerts to concert-goers who *hate* concert-going, Anna Russell's take-offs are hysterically accurate. Every fan has a favorite port on this "voyage musical," whether it is the chill, sexless ripples of "Oh! Night Oh! Day," English version: "utterly disembodied or angel-chorus kind of singing" or the trio of French songs: "like a soufflé, delicate in texture and if not in exactly the right atmosphere, they fall completely flat."

Among the *chefs d'œuvre* of Caedmon, we rank the poetry of Edna St. Vincent Millay. Judith Anderson's cello voice is just right for the range of lyrics here. "Renascence" alone is worth the record. "Wild Swans" and the sonnet "I know I am but summer to your heart" are perfect examples of that clean sedate Millay line.

Caedmon provides a link to the facets of literature, too. A voice we cherish on record still, although the owner has already gone into "that good night," is Dylan Thomas. It is spring 1953 in the Connecticut Valley, we remember. In the Amherst chapel a plump, cherubic poet with curly red hair and a blue suit reads aloud with the voice of a whimsical angel from his new verse play *Under Milk Wood*.

Somehow the clean sunlight on the white pews of the New England church is right for the holy music of this voice that rocks us to tears, to shivers, on lilting cadences of sounds: "It is spring, moonless night in the small town, starless and bible-black, the cobblestreets silent and the hunched, courters'-and-rabbits' wood limping invisible down to the sloeblack, slow, black, crowblack, fishingboat-bobbing sea." We love the verbal calisthenics of the lyric Welsh townspeople, from the poetic Reverend Eli Jenkins for whom the breeze is a "greenleaved sermon on the innocence of men" to uxoricidal Mr. Pugh who "Alone in the hissing laboratory of his wishes . . . minces among bad vats and jeroboams, tiptoes through spinneys of murdering herbs, agony dancing in his crucibles, and mixes especially for Mrs Pugh a venomous porridge unknown to toxicologists . . ." With the death of Dylan Thomas, the world loses the poetry of its most lyrical lover.

In the Hampshire Bookshop one clear topaz evening, Smith students and Northampton friends meet to celebrate the publication of Mary Ellen Chase's new book *The White Gate*. It is a happy time. Those who made the book are here. Mr. Lunt, of W. W. Norton, tells about the details of publishing and rings the ancient bookshop bell to herald this story of a Maine childhood told with the simplicity of mountain water. Nora S. Unwin, the quaint little British illustrator, describes her jaunts about New England to sketch country stoves and hay lofts and signs our books with the symbolic blueberry spring. Mary Ellen Chase recaptures the evanescent quality of childhood in her informal speech as she does in the pages of *The White Gate*. Our favorite chapter, if it is possible to choose, is "Words," where Miss Chase describes the "discovery of words as entities" by a sensitive child. "One memorable rainy afternoon," she writes, "I suddenly perceived that words with long L's in them were filled with light and thereupon wrote down a list of them, beginning with *light* itself."

With the rewarding deluge of paperbacked books on the newsstands these days, we can at last browse with a sense of *discovery* and *New World Writing*. The latest pieces by well-known names are generously balanced by "firsts." Free from the restrictions of the plotted slick markets, prose can punch below the belt, poetry can go rollickingly experimental, as in Jack Jones' "Plumpity," in *discovery*, Number 4. In this same issue, we were struck by Barbara Donnelly's sorority tale "Sweetie and Bobo." Ever look at yourself in the wavering glass mirror of a fun house? Well, there are the same shocks of recognition here. "The moon's pale eye stares at nothing at all" over this "fun house of the soul," while the grotesque lives of the slovenly Sweetie and the house-brain Bobo fuse for a brief while in their talk, talk that reveals their implicit hungers and fears which are vital as protoplasm, neglected as a tangle of garbage.

For a rigadoon of life dramatic as a newsreel, flaring as the brandy on a rich plumcake, we vote for Ben Hecht's autobiography *A Child of the Century*. We wander around in this colossal circus of life feeling somewhat as we did during Tennessee Williams' *Camino Real*: aroused and stunned, delighted and angry. In any case, this is a great book for browsing, even if it's too much Ben Hecht for us to toss down from start to finish with a stiff wrist. If you like to sit in on personal tête-à-têtes with famous actors, writers, and newspaper men, step right up. We think a most moving piece is the chapter about John Barrymore's waning days, "A Last Performance." It has something to say to us all, ending with a catch in the throat, a birthday cake blazing with candles "like a triumphant row of footlights."

A slim, yellow-clad book, striated with black, is the 1954 offering of the Yale Series of Younger Poets, an admirable choice: Daniel G. Hoffman's *Armada of Thirty Whales*. His lyric discipline is subtle, a study in the nuances of consonance and assonance. Nature is the primary inspiration here, not the intimate speaking nature of Wordsworth's day, but the landscape of the twentieth century, beautiful in its sheer being, yielding meanings that are often sobering or tinged with what W. H. Auden calls "skeptical caution." Here again, our words can't approximate the voice of Mr. Hoffman himself.

Take the exquisite verbal precision of "Lobsterpot Labyrinths": "Ternmewed winds pour past their ribs / gathering old fishheads gaping // with the smell of death; there is a splendour / in their ramshackle spined ridgepoles / structural as architecture." Hoffman's mood ranges from the taut rhythmic wit of the "Dancing-Master of the Pussycats," who "rapped his viol da gamba / & played a courtly air, // Played Buxtehude's minuets," to the accurate recording of "Ephemeridae" where the meaning is implicit in the description: "out of nowhere whirled the nebulae, // gadding gilded, all green energy, toward death."

The bright saucy lilt of *The Love Letters of Phyllis McGinley* is among our favorite baubles on the 1954 Christmas tree. Miss McGinley is the modern college girl's Dorothy Parker, but with what perspicacity and verve she plies her poetics! Our intellect, our imagination, and best of all, our sense of humor and perspective, are kindled by her impudent, yet often paradoxically reverent rhymes. We conclude our collage of the 1954 arts in America by joining in to chorus a stanza of her magnificent poem "In Praise of Diversity":

Praise *con amor'* or *furioso*
The large, the little, and the soso.

Rejoice that under cloud and star
   The planet's more than Maine or Texas.
Bless the delightful fact there are
   Twelve months, nine muses, and two sexes;
And infinite in earth's dominions
Arts, climates, wonders, and opinions.

These words *are* Americana: they laud the diversity of our life and landscape, they consecrate the clash and concord of our contemporary arts. And we are "glad and rejoice therein."

Tea With Olive Higgins Prouty

Ts,* 19 July 1955, Smith College

"It's our custom," the smiling woman in the college scholarship office told me, "to have our students write personal letters to their benefactors. We feel this helps create a friendly relationship, not just a financial one."

In those first green freshman days, I knew only that my scholarship was endowed for "a girl interested in writing." I had no idea of its origin, but it made up the large difference between college expenses and my scanty summer earnings. Perhaps most important, the scholarship encouraged me to go on writing in face of the rejection slips that were already flooding in.

"I've typed out the name and address of your benefactress," the woman went on. "Just write an easygoing letter about what being here in college means to you." She handed me a slip of paper.

"Thank you very much," I said, looking down at the name on the paper

---

* Typed at top right: 'Sylvia Plath / 26 Elmwood Road / Wellesley, Massachusetts.' The letter SP mentions writing to Olive Higgins Prouty is in *The Letters of Sylvia Plath, Volume 1*: 232–6. Prouty's reply to SP, 6 December 1950, is held by the Lilly Library. SP later references her story 'Initiation'.

in my hand. I gulped and did a double-take. The name read: Olive Higgins Prouty. "B-but," I stammered, "she's famous! I've heard of her! Isn't she the one who wrote *Stella Dallas*?"

"Yes," the woman across the desk said kindly. "But remember, she was a beginner once, too. And this is the college where she started writing."

I walked back to my dorm on air. Already I felt some sort of magical kinship to this woman. Throughout my childhood the name Olive Higgins Prouty had been a household word. Every day the radio serial announced that *Stella Dallas* was "adapted from the novel of that name by Olive Higgins Prouty." And now this very woman was personally responsible for my being in college!

The letter formed itself with the ease of a dream under my fingertips, running on for many pages. It was not just a thank-you note. With every word I tried to describe how it felt, looked, tasted to be a freshman at my beautiful New England college. It was only when I addressed the envelope that I realized Olive Higgins Prouty lived in the town next to mine.

During the crisp autumn days which followed, freshman courses and activities kept me in a whirl. Every time I thought of the letter I'd written, I felt a warm joy in my heart, but gradually I allowed the letter to slip from my mind. After all, I didn't really expect an answer.

Several weeks later, however, I received a thick gray envelope addressed to me in an unfamiliar, strongly individual hand. I looked casually at the return address, then ran upstairs two at a time to open it in the quiet of my room. It was from Olive Higgins Prouty.

As I read the letter, I felt I could almost hear her talking, clearly, directly, her remarks often sparkling with a vital sense of humor. The words blurred before my eyes. Since by coincidence we lived so close together, she wrote, she was inviting me to tea during my Christmas holidays!

But then I felt a slight chill of misgiving. Olive Higgins Prouty was such a *successful* writer. How could she ever think my beginning stories and articles were worth her generous scholarship? I should be producing work like Jane Austen or Willa Cather, or like . . . like Olive Higgins Prouty! And suddenly my few stories and poems published in *Seventeen* magazine seemed very small in face of a shelf of novels that had been made into movies (one starring Bette Davis!), a play, and a radio program.

Nevertheless, I prepared for my Christmas visit by reading all of the novels by Olive Higgins Prouty which I could find on the library bookshelves. And there were a good many of them! I got in the habit of reading a few chapters every night after I'd finished my homework.

Gradually the vital people in these books came alive for me. They were remarkably unlike the bitter, depressed characters I read about in my modern novel course at college. Behind the honest description of their human joys and struggles I felt the same warm heart that was present in Olive Higgins Prouty's letter.

The first afternoon of Christmas vacation, I dressed very carefully at home in my best wool suit, the only one I had. I checked and re-checked the seams in my stockings. I reviewed the directions Mrs. Prouty had written me. Then I gripped my limp white gloves in a nervous hand and set out.

During the half-hour bus ride I didn't notice the passing scenery. I was too busy concentrating on what I would say to this famous writer. Again the old insecure fears came back.

What if I never became a good writer? What if they took away my scholarship and gave it to some senior who was writing a best-selling novel? Worst of all, what if Olive Higgins Prouty was disappointed in me? My thoughts were bogged down at this point when the bus driver called out my stop.

As I walked up the curving driveway to Olive Higgins Prouty's large, graceful white house, I was awestruck. It was so big, with all that landscaping, that she would be sure to have several maids. I didn't know how to behave with maids, because I had never seen one. Trembling at the imposing entrance, I rang the doorbell.

For what seemed an ice age I waited in the chill gray December afternoon. Distantly, inside the house, I heard a dog bark in short yips. Then footsteps. Slowly the big door swung open and a white-aproned maid beckoned me to the living room.

"Mrs. Prouty will be right down," she said and vanished like the genie in Aladdin's lamp.

I stood stiff as the andirons in the fireplace where a cheerful red blaze was crackling. The room was lovely, I noticed, relaxing a bit. Sky-blue walls with textured gold curtains and wonderful French windows that could open on a terrace in the summer . . .

"Why, you must be Sylvia!" I heard a warm, musical voice behind me. Startled, I wheeled. I'd been so wrapped up in my own thoughts that I hadn't heard anyone come in. A tall, attractive, elderly woman came toward me, holding out her hand in greeting.

As soon as I took hold of that firm, friendly hand, all my misgivings dropped away. I was aware only of a pair of merry sky-blue eyes smiling into mine. I smiled back, and Olive Higgins Prouty and I sat down together on the sofa.

To my great relief, she didn't immediately challenge me to produce samples of my writing. Instead, she busied herself over the silver tea things.

"Oh, cucumber sandwiches!" I blurted out involuntarily, adding in a more ladylike tone: "They're my favorite."

Mrs. Prouty threw her head back and laughed. "I rather like them, too," she said.

Then she began to ask me about my family, and I found myself talking easily about the things I knew best.

"Mother began teaching after Daddy died," I said, helping myself to the cucumber sandwiches, "and my brother is working his way through school too."

"Is he interested in writing, like you?"

"Oh, no. He's the scientific one." I couldn't help sounding proud.

"Have you ever written about your family?" Mrs. Prouty asked casually.

"No," I said, feeling for words, "we're so . . . so ordinary!"

"For you, perhaps," Mrs. Prouty smiled, "but not for me, not for others. Think of the material you have there!"

I thought about it. Somehow, I had always wanted to write about something very grand and complicated, very important and world-shaking. Home seemed so close, so familiar, that I took it for granted.

"That's something that's been bothering me," I admitted. "I'd like to write about travel and exciting action, but when I make it up it just doesn't sound real. I never climbed volcanoes or shot tigers, and what *does* happen to me is so ordinary I'm sure no one would really want to read about it."

"Wait a minute," Mrs. Prouty said, pouring me another cup of steaming tea. "Isn't there any time in your life you've had a problem, and real conflict which seemed terribly important to you at that moment?"

"Well, yes." I thought back. "There was the time I wanted to get into the high school secret sorority. I thought about it night and day."

"And did you get in?"

"Yes," I laughed, remembering. "But when I got through all the initiations, I found out what a purposeless club it was, so I dropped out with several of my friends. Soon after that the sorority came to an end and so did a lot of unnecessary unhappiness among the girls who had been left out."

"Seems to me there's a story there," Mrs. Prouty said. "An interesting one, too."

There really was, I thought, recalling the conflict and heated arguments among the girls at school in those days when belonging to the crowd seemed the most important thing in the world. Seeds of a plot began to form in my mind.

"You see," Mrs. Prouty smiled.

"Yes," I said enthusiastically, "yes, I guess there is!"

By this time, the cold, slick feeling in the pit of my stomach had vanished completely. To my surprise, I was enjoying myself to the hilt. After my fifth cucumber sandwich, I felt bold enough to ask the question that had been on the tip of my tongue for weeks.

"How did *you* begin to write?" I asked, leaning forward. I had always suspected that every famous writer had some complicated secret of success and now, at last, I might have a chance to find out about it.

Olive Higgins Prouty's eyes grew reminiscent. "I started very simply," she said, "with something I knew about. I wrote a series of short stories about one particular family. The editors at *McClure's*, now the *American*, liked them and published them. Finally, one publisher suggested that I gather them into a novel. And," she looked at me with a disarming smile, "there I was."

"Oh," I breathed, spellbound, "how wonderful!"

"Not so amazing," Mrs. Prouty countered. "You were beginning to think up a story just now, about the sorority at high school. Why not just be yourself and write simply, directly, the way you talk to me. We always want to hear about people, real people, like ourselves."

Then I saw that by answering Mrs. Prouty's questions I had been talking to myself, too. Mrs. Prouty hadn't written about the castles in Spain or safaris in Africa. She had created heroines who were believable, living in her own home city. How vivid life seemed after all, when you looked for the human interest stories lurking all around you!

Just then, the clock struck six. Shocked, I realized that I had been talking with Mrs. Prouty for over an hour. Never outstay your welcome, Mother had warned me. So, reluctantly, I stood up to say goodbye.

"You'll be coming to visit me again," Mrs. Prouty assured me at the door. "And by the way, send me some of your stories. I'd like to see them."

I walked away down the gravel path with a warmth spreading all through me. It wasn't just from the tea, either. It was from a very special kind of admiration and love.

Suddenly I felt an enormous freedom. It didn't matter if I became a world-famous writer after all. Not if I could simply be myself and say honestly the things I believed and loved about life as I knew it. Why, if everyone looked at daily life for hidden stories and human interest, how fascinated they would be!

A trip to the grocery store could seem as colorful as a jaunt to Tibet. The difference was only in a way of looking, in developing a sense of drama and daily adventure. Writer or not, the secret could be learned. From that day forward, whenever I was discouraged or dull I remembered Olive Higgins Prouty's words: "Take life! Think of the material you have there!"

Cambridge Vistas

Written: 13–15 January 1956
Published: *Institute of International Education News Bulletin* (December 1958): 22, 24–8[*]

When an American college graduate sails from the United States to study at Cambridge University in England, the experience of transition is in some respects like turning back a time machine. To be sure, the modern world has not left Cambridge untouched: narrow one-way streets are precariously jammed with a steady traffic of motorcycles, bicycles, cars and tomato-red two-storey buses, while jet planes scrawl white trails against the sky. But in spite of twentieth-century innovations, the town of Cambridge maintains its unique atmosphere of country calm.

Situated on the edge of the Fens, Cambridge has a flat landscape which, when the mists rise at twilight, takes on the muted green and silver-grey tones of a Corot painting. From the western gable window of Whitstead, a small house for foreign students on the grounds of Newnham College, one sees a vista of peaked orange-tile rooftops with chimney pots, a diminishing perspective of kitchen gardens and, of course, those ubiquitous large black ravens,

---

[*] The only known publication with the byline 'Sylvia Plath Hughes'. Printed with a biographical sketch: 'Sylvia Plath Hughes spent two years at Newnham College, Cambridge, as a Fulbright student. Her poems have won prizes both in England and in this country, where they have appeared in *The Atlantic Monthly* and *The New Yorker*. She is a graduate of Smith College.' Printed with two drawings by SP, one with the caption 'The isolated tumble-down remains of "Wuthering Heights" in Brontë country . . .' The second drawing is of a thistle.

Originally published in two parts as 'Leaves from a Cambridge Notebook', *Christian Science Monitor* (5–6 March 1956): 17, 15, with a sketch by SP in the first part captioned 'Cambridge: A vista of gables and chimney pots'. The second part included a brief biographical note: 'Our author, an American college graduate, who is at present studying at Cambridge University, England, has jotted down some of her observations. The first part appeared in the Youth Section on Monday.' When printed, the article split between paragraphs nine and ten. The quote concluding the article is from William Shakespeare, *The Tragedy of King Richard the Second*.

lurching along the ground with a sinister air or hunching darkling in the trees, muttering perhaps, if one listens closely, 'Nevermore.'

To the writer, to the artist, Cambridge is the centre of fresh images, fresh colours – as are the special corners of England visited in vacation-time. The rooks, bare moors, emerald fields, meadow flowers and intricate webbing of black stone walls in Yorkshire, for example, find their way into poems and sketches. Whether viewing the isolated tumble-down remains of 'Wuthering Heights' in Brontë country or the jewel-bright stained-glass windows of King's Chapel, Cambridge, one feels a sense of deep-rooted history and tradition – the paradoxically new stimulus of antiquity which may enrich one's creative work and become an integral part of it. And to the eye of a poet, or the eye of an artist, Cambridge and its environs offer memorable vistas.

One of the loveliest walks in the surrounding countryside leads across green meadows along the river to Grantchester. Here, on brisk winter afternoons, tea may be had beside a glowing coal fire at The Orchard. A picture of Rupert Brooke looks down from the wall, and the hands of the clock are stopped at the hour mentioned in his poem 'The Old Vicarage, Grantchester': 'Stands the Church clock at ten to three? / And is there honey still for tea?' There is. And most delectable, fragrant honey it is, too.

On the dark waters of the river Cam, swans float in pale feathery clouds, bobbing for apples fallen from overhanging fruit trees. Fleets of quacking ducks outmanoeuvre the daily armada of punts, canoes and rowing shells which crowd the narrow stream. From the vantage point of a punt, the scenic panorama of the 'Backs' unfolds: the rough, angular wooden bridge of Queens' College, the incredibly green lawns under the Gothic spires of King's Chapel, the covered 'Bridge of Sighs' joining the old and new courts of St John's. All along the Backs there is the green peace of arched willows and quiet lawns; the sunlit air has the clear, sweet quality of Cambridgeshire honey.

Market Hill, at the centre of town, while not a hill at all, is certainly the most lively of country markets. Every day of the week in the cobbled square, row upon row of open stalls display their wares, ranging from vegetables, flowers, fruit, antique brass, and second-hand books to puppies and parakeets. Each booth spills over with colour: bunches of green grapes, hands of yellow bananas, spiky pineapples; carrots, cabbages and beets with garden earth still clinging to the roots; banks of white and russet chrysanthemums in the fall. And, in the cold heart of winter, the flower stands explode into springtime with bouquets of daffodils, yellow as sunlight, pots of pink and grape-coloured hyacinths, and the delicate white snow-star of the narcissus.

From the tale of the group of Oxford students who migrated to Cambridge in 1209 hoping to avoid town and gown feuds, to the spires of King's Chapel begun by Henry VI in the fifteenth century, the Cambridge undergraduate is aware of a rich historical past. Each college boasts its roster of famous names and there is a certain intimacy felt for these illustrious Cambridge students of former days: Milton's mulberry tree flourishes in the garden of Christ's College; at the bend in the river above Grantchester is the pool where Lord Byron swam. Contemporary student life moves against the mellow background of centuries of tradition.

While the 'campus' is an important part of the American college scene, it is literally impossible to divide Cambridge University from the town. In a sense, the University *is* the town and vice versa. Clusters of colleges, each one with green courts, gardens, architecture and customs all its own, are separated by cobbled lanes lined with colourful shops, inns, banks and public buildings. During the eight-week terms the streets are crowded with thousands of students, clad in the traditional black gowns, on their way to classes in the morning, sports fields or tea shops in the afternoon, and theatre or club activities at night.

Amid the tempting variety of extracurricular offerings which fill the term – plays, visiting speakers, ballet, concerts, debates, foreign films and balls – the Cambridge student must constantly make the difficult choice between studies and the rich cultural life at hand. Although required to take only two sets of examination papers during his three years, and free to attend lectures as he pleases, there is nonetheless the tacit assumption that he will spend a good part of the three brief eight-week terms – and the long between-term vacations themselves – in serious study.

Long lists of set examination books are published two years ahead, and except for the papers and discussions prepared for weekly supervisions with a Faculty don, the student arranges his own tempo and scope of work. Since there are none of the tests and check-up quizzes so frequent in American universities, the ultimate responsibility for his education rests in the student's own hands.

For the American college graduate fresh from the general elective programme of a 'liberal arts' education, the intense specialisation of a British undergraduate seems to begin surprisingly early. Before coming to the university, he must choose his particular Faculty, and, once there, takes no courses outside his department. Thus, by the end of three years, he has a thorough knowledge of his subject and is well-prepared for the series of comprehensive final exam papers, called 'triposes', in his field. This concentration is somewhat similar to graduate work in America.

However, the British student has already received his 'liberal' education in the highly selective preparatory schools and, by the time he is ready for the university, is considered mature enough to start scholarly specialisation in his chosen subject. Limiting as this may seem at first glance to an American, one soon discovers that British undergraduates have a remarkable awareness of politics, theatre and music – interests acquired not through college courses, but independently.

On the other hand, in contrast to the advanced level of their academic maturity, British students seem rather younger in their social relationships than their American counterparts of the same age. Separated until seventeen or eighteen in preparatory schools, boys and girls begin to learn in college the casual, daily friendships already taken for granted in co-educational American high schools.

Nevertheless, even the stricter social disciplines at Cambridge have a certain appeal. Biking in haste down a nearly deserted street before midnight, black gown flying, I caught a glimpse of three imposing gentlemen standing on the corner, costumed like characters fresh from the *Pickwick Papers*: the Proctor, in academic gown and hood, carrying a mace, and his two 'bulldogs', wearing full morning dress complete with top hats. These officials maintain order among the undergraduates in the town, and breaches of conduct incur penalties ranging from fines to 'rustication' or expulsion.

Curfew for Cambridge students is on the stroke of twelve. After dark, the gates of the college grounds are locked and the porter's lodge remains the only entrance until midnight, when the college buildings assume the character of an impregnable fortress. Night-climbing is, of necessity, a secret and hazardous occupation. At every strategic climbing point the belated undergraduate finds ingenious revolving spikes, metallic teeth and thorny tangles of wire, bearing a strong resemblance to medieval torture instruments. The only alternative to success, it would seem, is the rather unpleasant fate of being impaled until dawn on spears of rusty iron.

Perhaps the most marked change in the daily climate of the American student at Cambridge is occasioned by the penetrating cold. Rumour has it that a continuous blast of freezing wind sweeps directly to Cambridge from the Russian steppes. At any rate, the lack of central heating and the near equation of indoor and outdoor temperatures in England encourage a spartan attitude.

It took me a few weeks to get used to seeing my breath hanging in white puffs on the air, like Indian smoke signals, while I took a bath. The heat radius of the gas fires, which ravenously devour shillings in students' rooms, is small enough so that butter, stored in a tea cupboard a few feet away, remains as fresh and rock-hard as on the day it was bought. It is easy to understand the rarity of iceboxes in England; mere cupboards harbour the chill of polar regions.

Yet these very differences, large and small, combine to make the special texture of life at Cambridge. When I found myself expertly piling peas on the back of my left-hand fork, looking forward to stewed tomatoes and fried bread for breakfast, toasting scones before the gas fire, and sensing a sudden warm loyalty and admiration surge from the heart as lovely, radiant Queen Elizabeth and the smiling Duke walked through our dining hall on their royal visit to Newnham – then I knew how very much I had grown to feel a part of 'This blessed plot, this earth, the realm, this England.'

Fulbright Scholar Sylvia Plath Describes Her Impressions As . . . An American in Paris

Written: 15 April 1956
Published: *Varsity* (21 April 1956): 6–7[*]

April in Paris: visions of holiday tables under the trees and that most particular magic of the Left Bank. What happens really? A different Paris for each pair of eyes. We set out by Simca from Calais on March 24 to discover the city, not merely by café-hopping and swinging from the girders of the Eiffel Tower, though that was all part of it, but by living simply as a starving student for two weeks in a six-flight walkup, sketching along the Seine, sauntering myriad miles a day, and speaking merry if mangled French to shopkeepers, children and poodles.

Here is how it was. A blur of impressions, first like watercolour jottings: street perspectives incredibly white-grey, after Utrillo; gay pink, yellow and green posters on the baroque kiosks; folderol wrought-iron balconies droll as a pen-sketch by Steinberg. From the attic-window of our room in the Hotel Béarn on Rue de Lille (right across from the Louvre, one street from Seine and bookstalls) we could see a vista of grey-blue tile gables, ubiquitous orange chimney pots and artists' skylights.

---

[*] Printed with two sketches by SP and one by Donald Stevens. SP's are captioned 'Kiosque by Louvre' and 'Tabac opposite the Palais de Justice'.

Every morning after café au lait and croissants so light they hovered above the bed, we sketched versions of our view. Directly opposite us lived a mammoth tiger cat which used to crouch and glare out of wild green eyes from its windowsill as we drew and spoke to it in intimate, conversational French.

In our hotel we met Giovanni Perego, an Italian communist and Paris correspondent for *Paese-Sera*, a left-wing Roman newspaper. Spent hours in cheap restaurants so small that everything had to be served in one soup plate, drank red wine, white wine, managed to discuss communism in Italy, the art of De Chirico, De Staël, novels of Melville, poems of Verlaine – all this in French as we could understand no Italian, Perego no English. Rainy mornings we borrowed his Olivetti to pound out notes.

Days finishing March were warm and blue. Each morning we set out with sketchbook and a volume of Anouilh or Cocteau while the day was new, down the Rue des Saints-Pères past private art salons and antique shops, across the Seine where we walked along the Quais until a view took our fancy. In the Tuileries – a park full of precocious children riding in donkey carts, sailing ships or screaming with excitement at the puppet show (which we attended with equal delight) – we rented a chair for five francs to draw a green citronnade stand with orange awnings. Beyond, up the geometrical avenues of black trees just breaking into bud, past countless white marble statues, sprouted the obelisk in the Place de la Concorde, with its weird birds, eyes and hieroglyphics, and, behind it, the Arc de Triomphe, misted grey.

By utter accident we met several friends from Cambridge while thus outdoor sketching and so were squired on more conventional trips through tourist centres. We climbed the Tour Eiffel which rose in a great upward swoop of angled girders over our heads like a mechanical Martian monster ready to lumber off on four skeletal legs. The wind-whipped view was fine: below lay the snaky grey-green crooks of the Seine; we spotted the spires of Notre Dame and the brownish smutch of Bois de Boulogne. From the hill of Montmartre, the white domes of Sacré-Cœur shone like a frosted Byzantine wedding cake.

Later, walked along the wide affluent Avenue of the Champs-Élysées; crossed the deadly whoosh of traffic in the Place de la Concorde by the sprouting dolphin fountains and browsed in elegant shop windows along the Rue Royale by the Église de la Madeleine. From there, up the Rue de la Paix, glancing at small choice windows full of glittering diamonds, furs and delicate red shoes, orange and smoky-blue shoes, gold mandarin shoes and shoes made of fish-scales and bird-wings. The best things in life are free, we muttered as we strode along to the Jardin des Plantes in our comfortable soiled mackintosh and sat for an hour in gathering dusk resting our feet, watching the children roll hoops and listening to the goats baa in the wooden chalet-pens.

Spent one whole hot day with a Cambridge friend and climbed the steep quirked roads of Montmartre. The shops were dark holes reeking of garlic and stale tobacco; yet, in the sun, even decay was magic: scabbed pastel posters, leprous umber walls, flowers sprouting out of filth. Scaled a series of angled steps to the Place du Tertre which was chock full of tourists and bad, bad artists in various self-conscious stances doing charcoal portraits or muddy paintings of the domes of Sacré-Cœur.

We shouldered through clots of tourists with cameras staring at other tourists with cameras until a little wandering silhouette-cutter offered to immortalise our profile 'comme un cadeau'. So we stood in the sun as a collecting crowd ohed and ahed over the difficulty of cutting eyelashes and hair ribbon with polka dots.

Waiters moved among the trees serving lunch at tables set out in the square under tilted orange and blue umbrellas. A bearded bohemian with a picture-frame and garland of paper flowers around his head rode an antique giant-wheeled cycle around the street while his comrade ground out plinky music on a hand organ.

We stood then in front of Sacré-Cœur, looking out over the city, watching the tourist buses grunt up the hill, full of deadpan people sheltered by sun-proof, windproof, bulletproof glass domes. Inside the church it was cool and dark as a well with red patches swimming in the air.

Leaving the sweating mobs in the square, we lunched delectably at the vine-grown Auberge du Coucou just around the corner, where lilting violin music came wafting to us for free. Had fine tomato salads, miraculous veal sauté in mushrooms, and a bottle of iced white wine which sent us floating into the afternoon like larks, sniffing a bouquet of violets someone had bequeathed us in transit.

After stalking the immense dark halls of Notre Dame and marvelling at the great rose windows in the transept, we bought a triple-decker ice-cream cone outside, and craned our necks to see the most whimsical and grotesque of Paris gargoyles. Spent an hour in Sainte-Chapelle, our favourite holy place, rejoicing at the gilded fleur-de-lis and stars on the blue ceiling downstairs, and then the brilliant jewelled light of the sun-shot upper chapel with its hundreds of vivid biblical scenes, and, on the doors outside, the bas reliefs of the creation, the fall and Noah's ark complete with quaint two-by-two animals.

Another day we reverted to the age of innocence in the Tuileries, where a friend bought us the most enormous blue balloon in the world from a brown, wrinkled gypsy woman who vanished in a puff of smoke immediately thereafter. It was a clear lovely colour, helium-filled, caught in a loose mesh of red string with little tri-colour streamers and a long string. As we walked through the parks and along the Quais, the balloon bobbing overhead, children followed us like the Pied Piper, wide-eyed, reaching up and saying in wonder: 'Ballon!' People smiled and grew benevolent; cats stared with yellow eyes from first-floor balconies. That night we went to see *Snow White (Blanche Neige et Les Sept Nains)* in French.

And so it went: with debates in cafés, lights and colour, and the miraculous chance to simply walk, look, talk – and even skip when the air tasted close to champagne; plays and people, mottled sycamores along the Seine and mad clowns begging for tins of soup. With camera switched for sketchpad, Chaucer's tongue for Cocteau's, water for wine, we hacked out fourteen enchanted Parisian days and nights. Now, most spartan, most martyred, we return to cabbage and custard sauce and the little quais along the Cam.

Smith College in Retrospect

Written: 30 April 1956
Published: *Varsity* (12 May 1956): 6–7

With an enrolment of 2,192 undergraduates, Smith College in Northampton, Massachusetts, is the largest resident women's college in the world. Situated on a green campus amid the easy-going hills of the Pioneer Valley, Smith's crowded dormitories and lectures halls (displaying polyglot architecture ranging from Victorian to Georgian to Frank Lloyd Wright in style) overlook Paradise Pond, so named by Jenny Lind during her visit shortly after the founding of the college in 1871.

Academically, Smith ranks top in standard among the Big Seven women's colleges in the East. Rigorously screened by entrance exams, and interviews, Smith girls come from every state in the union and from countries all over the world.

One of the most startling differences in social structure between Smith College and, say, the women's colleges at Cambridge, is the intensely centralised social 'organisation' at Smith. All rules and reprimands are administered by the Student Government, which is divided into four main branches: Student

Council (executive), House of Representatives (legislative), Judicial Board (social honour system) and Honour Board (the only organisation including faculty members as well as students, dealing with infringements of the academic honour system).

Extracurricular activities at Smith offer a smorgasbord of choices for enthusiasts in everything from athletics to aesthetics. Our crew shells compete on the river; we play golf, tennis, swim in the college pool, ride horseback, shoot arrows and even have a student–faculty baseball game each spring.

With the usual American concern for the pragmatic, girls often begin working into professional jobs while still in college. Those interested in TV and radio, for example, may begin training on WCSR, the Smith student-owned and operated radio station. Writers gravitate to the college literary magazine and weekly newspaper, while more serious reporters join Press Board, the student branch of the College News Office, which pays its student correspondents to write coverage of all college news to local and national newspapers.

Men at Smith, by the way, are almost as ubiquitous as they are at Cambridge. In fact, they are so plentiful that sometimes they are even auctioned off. An Amherst College singing group recently went to the house bidding highest at Sophia's Circus (named after Sophia Smith, college founder), the annual outdoor festival for the benefit of Service Fund, the campus equivalent of Community Chest.

During the Monday-to-Friday week, the Smith girl plunges into classes, papers, extracurricular activities. (Weekday costume: grey flannel Bermuda shorts, wool knee socks, pink Brooks Brothers shirts for lectures; tweed skirts and sweaters for dinner and faculty appointments). With the coming of Friday and the Weekend, however, Plato is packed in the suitcase along with a devastating black cocktail dress and the Northampton train station is flocked with attractive, smart young women who look more like *Vogue* models than Marie Curie. All the nearby men's colleges – Harvard, Yale, Columbia, Williams, Amherst, Princeton and Dartmouth, among others – offer fall football weekends, winter ski carnivals, and spring balls and beach parties.

Although not even a century old, Smith College already has made traditions and customs. Among the most colourful are Float Night, a spring evening when Paradise Pond is illuminated for a procession of elaborate canoe-floats steered by the year's forty outstanding freshmen; International Students' Day, when Smith students from countries all over the world dress in national costume and run a day-long bazaar for charity with songs, skits, national dishes and a Left Bank luncheon; Father's Day, a Smith institution when harassed, bill-paying fathers are treated to a weekend as guests of honour; they attend classes, go to teas and discussions, inspect the complicated boiler rooms, and finish off with a father-and-daughter dance.

Smith College life, then, is hardly provincial. It is, to all practical purposes, universal – including classes and theses, community and campus clubs, sports and a vital social and cultural life.

After four years of trying out her keenest interests and talents, Smith girls don black gowns for the first time at Commencement and enter that world for which they have been preparing all along, where they will combine theory and practice as they have been doing throughout college: becoming teachers and laboratory technicians, civic leaders and writers, secretaries and social workers, and, eventually, most of them, wives and mothers.

B. and K. at the Claridge

Written: 3 May 1956
Published: *Smith Alumnae Quarterly* (November 1956): 16–17[*]

We were sitting on the floor by the gas fire in our gable room at Newnham College one chilly April afternoon, idly tracing the route of the Soviet cruiser *Ordzhonikidze* on Bartholomew's *Political Map of Europe and the Mediterranean*. Just as we finished following its trail through the azure Kattegat and Skagerrak to a rather suspiciously pink-outlined Britain, Timothy Green, feature editor of *Varsity*, the Cambridge weekly undergraduate newspaper, walked in the door.

'How', he said without ado, 'would you like to cover the reception for Bulganin and Khrushchev at the Claridge Tuesday night?'

'Slowly,' we said. Our hands shook slightly, but only enough to slosh a bit of Typhoo tea into the Zaalberg pottery saucer. 'Once more?'

Tim grinned. 'Bulganin and Khrushchev,' he said more slowly, once more. 'Vodka and caviar.'

That was all we needed. 'When do we start?' we asked, mentally rolling up

---

[*] Printed with a biographical sketch: 'Sylvia Plath, 1955 honors graduate, published poet, now at Cambridge University with a renewed Fulbright grant, working for an Honours B.A. next spring.' The two *Guardian* articles SP references are: 'Soviet Leaders in London', *Manchester Guardian* (19 April 1956): 1, and 'First Talks With the Visitors', *Manchester Guardian* (20 April 1956): 1.

khaki shirtsleeves for business and invoking the spirit of Marguerite Higgins.

We started at 3 p.m. on the afternoon of April 24 in the company of three staunch Britons: Timothy Green, Barry Wagg, staff photographer, and reporter Josephine Scarr. Armed with back copies of the *Manchester Guardian*, which gave a colourful coverage of the Russian leaders' visit (describing Khrushchev in bright vegetable-and-fruit terms: 'the familiar bald head gleams like a peeled beetroot, the familiar grin stretches wide as a slice of melon'), we left Cambridge in a small rented Morris, green as an avocado.

As we drove along Route A-1 through the flat yellow-green landscape under a dour sky, we learned that *Varsity* had offered to arrange a reception and tour for Bulganin and Khrushchev if they would come to Cambridge. B. and K. chose Oxford instead, hence two consolatory invitations from Madame Malik for Mr and Mrs Timothy Green and Mr and Mrs Barry Wagg. Lacking wives, Mr Green and Mr Wagg decided to adopt the only two women reporters *Varsity* offered for the occasion.

Within an hour we hit the outskirts of London. By 4:30 we had found a parking place near the Claridge and were seated together in one of the ubiquitous Lyons Corner Houses drinking hot tea and eating apple flans. The air was taut.

Shortly before 6 p.m. we left Lyons and walked toward the Claridge. At the corner of Brook Street and Davies Street, in the City of Westminster, a small crowd had gathered on the pavement opposite the side entrance to the hotel. With half an hour to spare before the reception began, we mingled in the throng, hoping for a full view of the Russians' grim black motorcycle escort (which reminded the imaginative and cultured *Manchester Guardian* correspondent of the messengers of death in Cocteau's *Orphée*).

The crowd was thin, made up chiefly of young people and thick burly men who, we felt sure, were bodyguards. Above each of the two Claridge entrances a red and yellow hammer-and-sickle flag flapped in the cold wind, flanked boldly by two Union Jacks. Sober black London taxis continued to drive up and discharge customers in front of the hotel; a bright red Royal Mail truck, marked with gilt crown, rolled past.

Mustering initiative, we walked across the street and accosted one of several bobbies stationed outside the front entrance of the hotel. 'Excuse me, sir. What door will they use?'

The bobby stiffened. 'Can't say a word, lady.'

On our return to the opposite kerb, Timothy said, 'Looks like they're already in there.'

'But how?' we asked, incredulous.

'Chap who's head of the police squad told me they'd come twenty minutes ago. We must have just missed them.'

'Oh well,' Josephine consoled, 'soon we'll simply walk in the front door past all those policemen with our invitations.' There was among us a pleasant sense of being one up on the crowd of onlookers, at once anonymous and initiate.

Large, affluent black cars decorated with crests and coats of arms now began to pull up to the front entrance of the Claridge. We glimpsed gold braid, Slavic cheekbones. Timothy pointed out one especially elegant limousine: 'There's the Dean of Canterbury.'

Promptly at 6:30 we joined the crowd of guests outside the Claridge ballroom. We were nudged and pushed through the revolving doors into a narrow hallway with steps leading up into the lobby. It was already a crush. For fifteen minutes we stood jammed among distinguished grey-haired men, uniformed Russian officers, brightly painted young women in black lace and roses, and ancient, weathered women in mink wraps and wispy straw hats.

'You might know,' a pragmatic American voice remarked out of the depths of the throng, 'always a queue in Britain!'

We were among the first to make the door into the lobby where an elderly man, lids drooping low over his eyes, took our mammoth invitations, checked us off on a list, and added the invitations to a large pile on his table. 'Ladies' room to the right,' he whispered hoarsely, anticipating our desire to shed the soiled mackintosh which made us feel rather like Scotland Yard, but hardly fit for caviar.

'May we please,' we wheedled, 'keep the invitations for photostatic copies?'

The old man shook his bald head ever so slightly. 'We must keep them for a check.'

Accompanying Josephine to the ladies' room, we gave our mackintosh to a black-clad attendant, and, on second thought, added our black velvet beret which seemed all at once out of season. Then, after Josephine had straightened the hem of her green taffeta skirt, we joined our temporary husbands in the lobby.

A majordomo in lobster red asked our names while another seemed to be clocking the proceedings with a large stopwatch. Once past the perils of the invitation desk, we assumed our maiden name again and strolled up to shake hands with our host Mr Malik, Soviet ambassador, and his hefty, dark-haired wife.

Floodlights glared from all corners creating an atmosphere of most unnatural brilliance. Blinking into the blaze of the first of six reception rooms, we were stopped by a waiter with four kinds of drinks: 'Sweet sherry, dry sherry, ruby port or vodka, mum?' Bound to enter into the Russian spirit of the party, we lighted a goblet of clear vodka and moved over to the refreshment tables which stretched the length of the room, laden with luxury fare.

The waiter helped us to cold turkey, a batch of small hot sausages and lobster puffs. Then we saw the caviar, red and black, specially flown from Russia. Not satisfied with discreet dabs of black caviar on Ritz crackers, we took a soupspoon and surreptitiously ladled a large quantity from a cut-glass bowl onto our cold turkey.

'You missed them!' Timothy Green hissed as we turned away from the refreshment table. 'They just came in.' To pay for our gluttony, we had forfeited the sight of Bulganin and Khrushchev entering the room, but we could follow their progress by the stream of guests thrusting after as if hauled along a wind tunnel. By now it was difficult to move about at all in the crowd numbering at least a thousand, so we decided to investigate the motley guests before fighting for a view of the elusive Russian leaders.

Curious about numerous men with ribbons and coloured medallions around their necks, we discovered that these were the mayors of the boroughs of London and surrounding towns. 'Excuse me,' we said to a spare, lively, grey-haired man beached next to us by the tide of the crowd, 'but would you mind telling us what town you're mayor of?'

'Not at all,' he beamed, holding out his chain of office for our inspection, 'Northampton.'

'Northampton!' we exclaimed. 'Why we're from Northampton, Massachusetts. At least we went to Smith College there. Have you ever heard of it?'

'Of course. The mayor of your Northampton is coming to visit us this May. We've had a fine exchange of letters.'

As we were still standing near the main entrance, we saw a familiar face. 'Isn't that Clement Attlee?' It was, with Sir Anthony Eden close by.

At this juncture, the plump, pink mayor of Paddington came up with a handful of chocolates. 'Have one,' he said.

We all had a round and, unable to find a waiter with vodka, settled for Russian white wine. 'I know what you'd like,' the waiter grinned at us, 'a dry Martini or Scotch on the rocks.'

Gradually we found ourselves being carried through the room on a fresh wave of guests bearing in its midst a bald, smiling Khrushchev and a white-bearded, benevolent Bulganin. Strong-arm guards tried to bar the doorway to prevent the crowds from crushing Bulganin, whose interpreters translated as people shoved close to shake the Marshal's hand.

B. and K. soon left the public halls for dinner in a separate room and we managed to snag a refill of vodka. A pale youth in Claridge uniform was dispensing cigarettes from a silver tray.

'And what do you think of all this?' we asked.

'I'm on the management training staff,' he replied, straightening up with no small pride. 'This is just usual to us. We're always having big receptions and parties for our famous guests. But', he added, 'we're very proud of this.'

In the corner of the main room, a smiling coloured man in a bright red fez, and his jovial wife, caught our eye; they looked like a royal couple out of *The King and I*. Kneeling down beside the third member of their party, a fine doughty specimen of British womanhood, we inquired about them.

'I'm Lady Catherine McEntee,' she informed us, 'mayor of Walthamstow.' We said we didn't know there were women mayors in England.

'Oh, yes. And in July and August I'm going to your country for the Soroptimists' convention at the Waldorf-Astoria.'

Walthamstow, we learned, was the birthplace of William Morris, English poet, artist and socialist.

Lady McEntee introduced us to her companions, Chief Okorodudu, commissioner for Western Nigeria, and his wife. We were enchanted by their impulsive warmth, their perfect English. 'It's nice to see someone excited about all this,' Mrs Okorodudu grinned at us, and broke into a rich laugh.

On a fresh foray for vodka, we met an American radio man from North Adams, Massachusetts; the wife of a BBC reporter who confided: 'I generally don't go to these things, but this looked like something special'; and a Russian artillery officer resplendent in gold braid who said that foreigners seem to know only three Russian authors, Tolstoy, Dostoevsky and Chekhov. 'Have you ever heard of the brilliant critic, D. S. Mirsky?' we asked, loading the dice. 'I must be going,' the officer said, and hurried off.

Next we ran into a cheerful group of Russian businessmen. One, blonde, blue-eyed and very jolly, spoke English better than his friends and said how curious they were about America and what a good thing it was for Russians and Americans to get together personally and find out about each other. 'If we exchanged a thousand students on each side,' he said, 'there would be no trouble. We don't want a war either; we want to go on living and working, with our families.'

'Guess what,' an excited young man told us for no apparent reason, 'Bulge and Krush are talking with Charlie Chaplin in that room in there.'

At our elbow, a news reporter was talking into a portable microphone: 'Ladies and gentlemen, I've been to lots of diplomatic parties in my time and this is the biggest blast of them all.'

Suddenly the doors of the private dining room flew open and a fed, smiling Bulganin was catapulted toward us into the crowd, waving his two fingers and looking innocent as a white Russian teddy bear. Cheers burst around us, and we joined in a chorus of 'For he's a jolly good fellow.'

'They'll never let you back in the States if you sing like that,' a dry British voice remarked in our ear.

All at once, we were shaking hands with Bulganin, firmly, with much joy. 'You must come to Cambridge,' we said fervently. 'Cambridge, Cambridge,' hissed the interpreters, giving it a Russian inflection, with lots of extra consonants, especially k's.

Bulganin smiled ahead blandly and went on into the crowd. Outside the Claridge we fell into a cab muttering: 'Just shook hands with Bulganin.'

Imperturbable, most British, the cabbie grinned. 'Don't wash that one for a week,' he said.

Cambridge Letter

Written: 9 May 1956
Published: *The Isis* (16 May 1956): 9[*]

'Guess Where It's Heaven to be a Girl!' the *Woman's Sunday Mirror* gushed a short while back; we couldn't, so read on. Cambridge University, it seems, is this very green Eden, offering women students a 'crazy mixed-up social whirl, with an average of five hundred bottle parties per eight-week term.' Slightly staggered by such statistics as 'In her forty-five weeks at Cambridge she has had 180 dates with forty-five different men', we skimmed through an account of dating life that would have made the Alpha maidens in *Brave New World* take to soma, wild with envy.

Varsity, admitting that the *Mirror* account contained nothing 'specifically

---

[*] Articles referenced in this piece are Pat Alexander, 'Guess Where It's Heaven to be a Girl!', *Woman's Sunday Mirror* (29 April 1956): 1, 24 and 'Our Blue Heaven', *Varsity* (5 May 1956): 1.

untrue', cleverly criticised the exaggerated effect arising from the 'subtle technique of leaving out'. Leaving out, no doubt, those bluestockinged Cambridge women who brood in the University Library until closing time. Or also, the advice given by the main speaker at a women's college dinner: cloister yourself in 'research' during these three precious academic years; avoid, if possible, anything so distracting as summer jobs; 'You can always get out in the world later.'

Fresh from the easy-going co-educational school system in America, where boys and girls are not immured in segregated public schools during adolescence until they come upon the 'opposite sex' with some of the self-consciousness and awe of an amateur anthropologist confronting, for the first time, a mob of orangoutangs (or vice versa), we paused to reflect upon the position of women in Cambridge, upon the man/woman relationship, even.

Apparently, the most difficult feat for a Cambridge male is to accept a woman not merely as feeling, not merely as thinking, but as managing a complex, vital interweaving of both. Men here are inclined to treat women in one of two ways: either (1) as pretty beagling frivolous things (or devastating bohemian things) worthy of May balls and suggestive looks over bottles of Chablis by candlelight, or, more rarely, (2) as esoteric opponents on an intellectual tennis court where the man, by law of kind, always wins.

Is this drastic split in the functions of a whole woman (matter versus mind, one might say) a flaw in the male approach, or does it stem from some lack on the woman's side? Perhaps a little of both. We shall deal, however, with the former. A debonair Oxford PPE man demurred, laughing incredulously: 'But really, talk about philosophy with a *woman*!' A poetic Cambridge chap maintains categorically: 'As soon as a woman starts talking about intellectual things, she loses her feminine charm for me.' By complaining about such remarks here, we are not advocating abstruse discussions about the animal symbolism in *The Garden of Delights*, by Hieronymus Bosch, but only a more natural and frequent commerce between male and female minds on their favourite subjects; perhaps in supervisions, perhaps in coffee shops: a sense of fun, not artificial posturing, in playing with ideas where a woman keeps her female status while being accepted simultaneously as an intelligent human being.

In a society where men outnumber women ten to one, women are, admittedly, in an artificial position; competition is keen, even deadly, and the difficulty of acquiring a date induces many Cambridge men to draw on the reservoir of blonde, monosyllabic Scandinavian girls at the English schools, favouring what is often the prettier, less complicated, side of the pass.

Perhaps a restoration of the old French salon, with each Cambridge girl presiding like Madame Récamier over her ratio of ten men, would enrich male/female relationships. More likely, co-educational public schools would make intelligent sharing of ideas easier, less self-conscious from an earlier age. At least co-ed university activities such as political clubs, newspaper work, and acting, make it possible for men and women to meet on a sounder basis than the superficial sherry party where a girl is just that, and, alas, not much more.

Sylvia Plath Tours the Stores and Forecasts May Week Fashions

Written: 22 May 1956
Published: *Varsity* (26 May 1956): 1, 6–7[*]

With May Week just around the corner like some fair Country of Cockaigne – but barely visible through the present smog of Tripos exams – we set out to discover what the well-dressed Newnhamite or Girtonian might wear for punting, cocktails and balls.

From large department stores to small specialty shops, Cambridge offers a fine, colourful selection of spring fashions which should enable our Cambridge undergraduates to rival the most chic and charming of imported London models.

We chose a different Cambridge shop to outfit us for each occasion and picked featured and favourite styles for photographs. While aware that our assignment was for a newspaper article rather than for private purchase, department managers kindly donated advice, information and much time, treating us, indeed, like a Saturday Cinderella.

To begin with bathing suits, perfect for beach holidays and very safe punting. At Robert Sayle's on St Andrew's Street we found this bright white one-piece, peppered with black polka-dots, bow-tied over each hip, by Aqualine in elasticated rayon batiste (at 79/6). Also on the rack and worthy of note: a vivid red

---

[*] With four photographs of SP captioned 'Bought your May Week outfit yet? Sylvia Plath, American Fulbright Scholar at Newnham, reviews May Week fashions on the entire page' (1); 'Strapless Frank Usher ball gown' (6); 'Strapless white cocktail dress' (6); and 'White one-piece with black polka dots, bow tied over each hip' (6–7).

NON-FICTION | 575

swimsuit by Slix in rayon lastex, bordered narrowly at bodice and hem by a woven cotton design of blue hearts and red rickrack on a white ground (67/9).

For the sleekest of black suits to set off a tan, we liked a rayon lastex model by Trulo, cut close with straight princess lines and two small darts sliced in the cuffed top (99/6).

Valuable beach accessories also at Robert Sayle's: a wide-brimmed raffia sun-hat, gaily beaded in red (27/9); a stylish Italian beachbag in black straw, embroidered with white raffia flowers, to carry everything from picnic to sunglasses (12/6); a flamboyant red-and-white striped towelling stole with big pockets and black-tasselled fringe (24/9); and finally, to complete the whole ensemble, a white terrycloth beachcoat with attractive full circular yoke (73/6). Happy swimming, everyone!

Our cocktail and dance dress featured at Joshua Taylor's is a strapless white cotton by Jean Allen, patterned with pink rosebuds and green leaves; the marvellous pouf skirt billows most bouffant over its triple crinoline petticoats (£10 12s. 6d.). Draped from the front to a pert bow in back, this gala outfit sports its own cover-up bolero and so becomes suitable for afternoon garden parties or champagne soirées overlooking Great Court, Trinity.

Runners-up: A poppy-red button-down jumper dress in French cotton put out by Continentals (at £4 7s. 6d.), with square open neck and cool, clean-cut flared skirt; also, a green-and-white striped cotton dress by Estrava, fresh as a mint julep, with off-the-shoulder boat neck, cuffed pockets at hip (£4 10s.).

Rembrandt Originals are showing a versatile tan cotton dress, its skirt printed in a stunning black design; definitely to be seen in motion, the accordion-pleated skirt flares out, changing the pattern with every walking step; sleeveless, buttoned neatly down the front and trimmed by a slim black belt, this dress is fitted for casual afternoons about town (£5 19s. 6d.).

For the ultimate in exquisite ball gowns, we visited Vogue's elegant shop just opposite Emmanuel and chose a strapless Frank Usher model in floating white nylon sketched over lightly with a delicate black pattern and banded once about the bodice, twice about the full skirt, with black lace and velvet ribbon (17 guineas).

Pick your partners, men; we propose a toast to the best May Week yet.

Sketchbook of a Spanish Summer

Written: 3 September 1956
Published: *Christian Science Monitor* (5–6 November 1956): 15, 19[*]

After a bitter British winter, we sought the heart of the sunlight in the small Spanish fishing village of Benidorm on the border of the Mediterranean for a summer of studying and sketching. Here, in spite of the tourist hotels along the waterfront, the natives live as simply and peacefully as they have for centuries, fishing, farming, and tending their chickens, rabbits, and goats.

We woke early each morning to hear the high, thin jangle of goat bells as the goatherd across the street led his flock of elegantly stepping black goats to pasture.

"Ya hoi!" came the cry of the little bread woman as she strolled by with a great basket of fragrant fresh rolls over her arm. Daily, after breakfast, we walked downtown to shop at the peasant market.

Spanish kitchens are a far cry from those in America: only the wealthy possess iceboxes, which are proudly displayed in the living room; dishes are washed in cold water and scrubbed with tangles of straw; and a one-ring petrol stove must cope with everything.

The open-air peasant market begins at sunup. Natives set out their wares on little wooden tables or rush mats at a hilly crossroads between white pueblos that sparkle like salt crystal in the sun. Black-clad peasant women bargain with the vendors for watermelons, purple figs wrapped in their own scalloped leaves, yellow plums, green peppers, wreaths of garlic, and speckled cactus fruit. Two straw baskets hung on a balance serve as scales and rough stones are used as weights.

One woman holds a squawking, flapping black chicken while she calmly goes about the rest of her shopping. Strung upon wires against the pueblo walls are gaudy striped beach towels, rope sandals, and delicate white cobwebs

---

[*] Published in two parts with four sketches by SP. Drawings in the first part captioned 'Sardine boats and lights patterned the beach during the daylight hours' and 'At sunup, the banana stand at the peasant market in Benidorm opened for business'. Drawings in the second part captioned 'Palms and pueblos on the sea cliffs at Benidorm, Spain' and 'Arched stairway to Castillo, in Benidorm'. The second part included a brief introduction: 'Today our contributor continues her account of a delightful summer in a small Spanish village on the Mediterranean. The first part of her article appeared in the Youth Section yesterday.' When printed, the article split between paragraphs nine and ten.

of handmade lace. Higher on the hill, a man is selling petrol stoves, earthenware jugs, and coat hangers.

The fish market is a fresh adventure every day, varying according to the previous night's catch. Every evening at dusk the lights of the sardine boats dip and shine out at sea like floating stars. In the morning counters are piled with silvery sardines, strewn with a few odd crabs and shells. Strange fish of all shapes and sizes lie side by side, speckled or striated, with a rainbow sheen on their fins. There are small fish with black streaks on shimmering pale blue scales, fish glinting pink and red, and a Moray eel with black eyes and a splendid yellow brocade patterning its dark back. We never quite had the courage to select our dinner from the pile of baby octopuses, their long legs tangled and twined like a heap of slippery worms.

All our food and drink came from the farms around us. When we needed extra milk for supper one evening, we crossed the street to wait for the goatherd. Soon a musical tinkling sounded in the distance, and the flock of aristocratic black goats rounded the wall of the corral, followed by the goatherd, who resembled a smiling Spanish leprechaun in patched, faded dungarees, rope sandals, and a sombrero. He invited us into the corral to watch the milking, clucking and shooing his goats into what he called "their little *casa*." Stepping after him into the dark, musky, pleasant interior, we found the ground softly carpeted with confetti-like strips of freshly dried seaweed. Then the goatherd began milking one of the black goats, squirting out a thin, powerful stream of milk which hissed and rang in the bottom of our aluminium pail.

Modern innovations in Benidorm on the border of the Mediterranean have not disturbed the rhythm of native customs. Although motor-scooters and a few large, grand tourist cars now crowd the narrow streets, the main traffic is donkey carts, loaded with vegetables, straw, or jugs of oil and water. Delivery men continue to bicycle along their routes, one with a crate of red-crested cocks, another with a large slab of swordfish in his basket.

By noon, the glare of the Spanish sun is so bright that it is difficult to raise one's eyes. All glitters white: sky, streets, and house seem to glow with an inner radiance. From three to five, after a late lunch, all shops are closed and work halts for siesta time. Later, in the cool of the day, the tanned, elderly women sit outside their doorways in wooden chairs, backs to the street, weaving nets of thick rope or fine mesh. In spite of the heat, they are always clad completely in black: shoes, stockings, dresses, and for town shopping, often a black mantilla.

Only once in our whole summer of clear blue sunny days did a rain cloud pass. During the sudden, brief shower the lighting effects were startlingly beautiful. As we looked through a silver sheet of rain toward the sun, which was still visible, we saw a dazzling drenched street between dark pueblos; in the opposite direction, against a backdrop of dark clouds, white pueblos shone under the arch of a perfect rainbow, one end rooted in the mountains, the other in the sea.

Every vista in Benidorm was brilliant with colour. From the front porch of our house, latticed by an arbour of purpling grapes and green leaves, we could glimpse an azure corner of the Mediterranean, glossy as peacock feathers. Behind the village, the encircling hills rose in a scrim of mist against the still blue sky. Our garden itself was like a painter's palette: white daisies and pungent red geraniums sprouted under the jagged green fronds of a palm tree, while vivid indigo morning glories hung a tapestry of leaves and flowers along the wall.

Late one afternoon we walked up into the hills for a twilight view of the sea. The rows of white pueblos gave way to almond groves, each tree thick with ripe nuts. The green furry pods were split open, showing the pocked brown shell inside. We shook down a few nuts, cracked them between two stones, and munched the kernels as we went along. Farther on, the dusty reddish soil was spiked with dry yellow grass and scattered with stones; twisted scrub pines grew on the bare summits of the hills. As we climbed, the bay of Benidorm spread out beneath us, a wide crescent of blue.

Crossing the tracks of the little railway station where hens scrabbled and scratched, we sat under a large pine, listening to the wind sough in the branches and watching the sea darken as the sun sank lower behind the purple hills at our back. Clouds scudded luminous across the brightening white moon which laid a paving of platinum light on the ocean. The little green neons on the waterfront blinked on and the bells of the clock tower were striking as we descended.

Now, back in the midst of a chilly British autumn, with drifting grey mists and bleak winds, the memory of this Spanish summer turns in our mind with a blaze of colour and light like an inward sun, to warm us through the long winter.

Poppy Day at Cambridge

Ts,* 11 November 1956, Lilly Library

At 9.30 a.m. on Saturday, November 10th, we strolled out of our Barton Road rooms under dove-grey Cambridge skies and through spasmodic showers of rain, umbrella in hand, to take a look at Poppy Day. Directly in front of our driveway, a roadblock of wooden crates was stopping cars entering Cambridge from Grantchester while five or six Cambridge University students, each one uniformed in white coat and red fez, were supplying artificial red poppies and a rapid car-polishing in return for contributions from the drivers. Already, all cars coming from the town bore red poppies twined about their front fenders or prominently displayed on hood or windshield. Waylaid by a black-masked horseman on a white stallion, we meekly handed up most of our loose change of copper pennies, received a poppy for the buttonhole, and, thus armed, proceeded on toward the centre of town.

Each year, on the anniversary of the 1918 armistice, throughout England, in every city, town and village, there are funereal processions, laying on of laurels, hymns, and in the morning at 11, for two whole minutes, a national silence; but in Cambridge, from 9 in the morning onwards, anywhere within half a mile of the marketplace, you have to shout to hear yourself speak. While today, all over England, charitable volunteers are moving patiently from door to door, each with a tray of poppies, each holding out a collecting box with its prominent 'For The Red Cross', in Cambridge thousands of University undergraduates are transforming the narrow streets – usually crowded with black-gowned students biking to and from classes and staid townspeople going about their shopping and official business – into a noisy, rollicking carnival of floats, fair competitions and dramatic skits with one common aim: to collect money from passers-by for the Earl Haig Poppy Day Fund. The year's Poppy Day organiser, Mr P. R. M. Harbottle, of Trinity Hall, and his assistant, Mr M. Oatley, of Trinity College, determined to surpass last year's record total of £6,127, have set the 1956 Poppy Day target at £6,500; in a letter to *Varsity*, the Cambridge undergraduate weekly newspaper, Mr Harbottle promised that every penny raised over the target total would go to Hungarian relief.

---

* Typed at top right: 'Sylvia Plath / Whitstead / 4 Barton Road / Cambridge, England.' The typescript has several holograph revisions by SP.

Except for several road workers at the crossing of Queen's Road and Silver Street flaunting red poppies on their navy blue sweaters as they laid fresh gravel and tar over the ubiquitous potholes, we spotted nothing out of the ordinary in the heavy Saturday morning traffic of trucks, automobiles, and motorcycles. We turned up Silver Street, passed the curved redbrick façade of the new buildings of Queens' College, and were halted by another roadblock on the Silver Street bridge arching across the green waters of the River Cam. A motley group of students dressed in yellow-and-black striped football jerseys and raffia hula skirts held up traffic with a rope, demanding toll. Our poppy in evidence, we were let pass unmolested. For a moment we paused on the bridge to survey one of our favourite Cambridge scenes; to the right: the pale blue buildings of the Anchor pub overhanging the river, the punt landing, Mill Lane bridge above the white froth of the mill race where students lunch on beer and sandwiches in fair weather, and then the backdrop of poplars and brindled cows grazing on Sheep's Green; to the left: the beginning of the Backs, with the quaint arched wooden bridge joining the old and new courts of Queens' College, beyond which, a diminishing vista of grassy riverbanks and sallow, autumnal willows.

Continuing up Silver Street where the passage of double-lane traffic is hazardous at best, we met a light-blue brewery wagon lumbering slowly toward the bridge, its open truck platform thronged by black-draped figures masked behind grimacing skulls and dog's heads; tin collection cans dangled on long poles over the sides of the truck within reach of pedestrians. Between the dark buildings of old Queens' and the University Press, the luminous sky reflected its grey light in the puddled street. We pivoted left onto King's Parade. Where else in the world at this time can one see, within fifty yards, Little Red Riding Hood, an undulating green dragon with a human head under each hump, George Washington, a walking Chinese pagoda, a gang of blue Martians, a baby in a bathtub, and a traction engine dragging a load of ravishing Sabine women?

Traffic moved at a snail's pace, keeping time with the cumbersome floats. We easily outdistanced a lorry on which three pairs of dancers jitterbugged to jazz throbbing out of a gramophone. In front of St Catherine's, glass cases presented stuffed ducks, pheasants and owls for sale; nearby a student loudly hawked his sticky display of toffee-apples. Across the street, in front of the pale orange stone walls of Corpus Christi, a mile of pennies began, running along the inner edge of the sidewalk, overleaping Bene't Street, and reaching, at the time we passed, to the doors of Miller's Wine Parlour. Pink, orange and green balloons studded the sky above the elaborate clock tower and main gate of King's College; at King's Lane, the balloon marathon was in full swing; each balloon sent up bore the name of the buyer and a plea 'return to Queens'; a prize awaited the contestant whose balloon landed farthest afield. We brushed elbows with a costumed monkey, winced at the nasal threnody of a bagpipe rendering its version of 'Over the Sea to Skye', and thrust forward.

Only recently grown accustomed to the formal Cambridge University teas, the often painful reserve between men and women undergraduates, and the conservative dress (black gowns worn to academic appointments and after dark), we were rather startled to find decorum turned, as it were, completely topsy-turvy: to see students parading in pyjamas and paisley dressing-gowns under the pinnacles of King's Chapel, to observe chamber pots and red paper-link necklaces adorning the sober statues staring down upon Senate House Passage from their lofty vantage point high on the walls of Caius (pronounced 'keys') College.

On the sidewalk before the august white pillars of the Senate House itself (where degrees are awarded to undergraduates and honorary degrees to the illustrious), chalk artists held out hats for donations. A tribe of Maoris in war paint proffered the hollow legs and busts of store dummies as receptacles for pennies. At the traffic-jammed juncture of Trinity Street and Great St Mary's Street, a red British Road Service truck bearing an eight-piece jazz band midway through the 'Darktown Strutters' Ball' slowly turned the corner into Market Hill, while, in the doorway of Bowes and Bowes bookshop, a salesgirl stood, jiving gently on the spot in time to the syncopated music.

Although the commotion in the open cobbled square of Market Hill rivalled Mardi Gras, the little canvas-roofed stalls were carrying on business as usual in the Saturday rush, salespeople grinning at the student floats as they sold their daily wares: rabbits, antique brass, dahlias, turnips, sausages, costume jewellery and tanks of goldfish. Our overall impression was one of total and blatant chaos. We backed into a cabbage stand, apologised, and watched the floats pass: a mock Liberace in full evening dress bowed from the top of a grand piano on a coal wagon, flourishing a silver candelabra and tossing dazzling smiles into the crowd while his buxom washerwoman mum glared grimly at the streets jam-packed with people, students out staring, visitors, locals in from the other side of town for the yearly show, and all stirred slowly like an immense soup near the boil by the lorry-loads of performers and marvels. Well-tempered Cambridge bobbies wearing their traditional navy-blue sugar-loaf helmets tried to keep the crowds moving at least as fast as cold molasses.

'We're hunting for a Flook!' a slouched khaki-clad individual informed us, pointing at a huge Teddy-bearish animal with round white eyes and a protruding snout just vanishing into the Victoria Cinema. On the steps of the Guildhall, several Arabs turbaned in Downing College's purple-and-black striped scarves were auctioning off a bevy of slave girls trapped in a wire cage. We arrived just as a pretty blonde in a camel's hair coat and pink high heels went to a bidder for the unprecedented sum of half a crown; two stocky girls plodded out on the stand next, giggling and casting mute, helpless looks at each other. 'To be sold by the pair,' the auctioneer announced; the bidding was up to one penny from a ha'penny when we left for the more pressing attractions of King's Backs where a battle between the Greeks and the Trojans was scheduled for 11 a.m.

A thumping brass band streamed by us in Great St Mary's Passage where Clare College was offering skittles, coconut shies, and a portable boxing ring as attractions. 'The referee wins!' shouted an enthusiastic onlooker as we sidled past the latter, joining the multitudes pushing through the King's gates. Past the elegant buttresses of King's Chapel we sauntered, down to the river where crowds already packed the sloping banks, about twenty-five yards apart, on either side, between King's Bridge and the lovely, slightly canted bridge of Clare. As we took a stance commanding a good view of the river, the chameleon weather changed all at once for the worse, and, under a sudden downpour of rain, black umbrellas mushroomed open. The Trojan ship, constructed out of wood and lavishly painted cardboard flats upon two punts, waited at one bank; a lorry drove up the Greek ship, its unwieldy prow painted in a likeness of a red, white, and black animal head vaguely reminiscent of a kangaroo. Willing hands responded to a megaphoned plea for help from the master-of-ceremonies, and with a few ominous tilts and lurches, the huge craft was lowered into the water. The rain stopped as suddenly as it began; flights of pigeons wheeled against the lightening sky above King's; a jet plane roared overhead and disappeared. Helen, clad in white sheets and a plethora of gold bracelets, stepped aboard the Trojan boat amid hearty cheers. The boat zigzagged toward Clare Bridge and the turrets of Troy. Landing under a drooping yellow willow, Helen and her captors proceeded to clamber atop Clare Bridge by a ladder and revel, guzzling from wine bottles and emitting gleeful cries, whereupon the Greek ship, loaded with purple-and-white jerseyed galley slaves and a remarkably effective catapult, rowed after; the battle was on. Forcing a landing, the Greeks seized Clare Bridge and, with Indian war whoops, carried off Helen, who was left shivering on the bank among spectators during the subsequent rough-and-tumble encounter. Manning ships again, both Trojans and Greeks attacked each other with ammunition of flour bombs and ripe tomatoes. The placid river, usually disturbed by nothing more violent than languidly gliding punts and quacking squadrons of mallards and swans, seethed with flour sacks, split tomatoes, and men knocked flailing overboard. Flour bombs broke, sending up a dense white haze; both crews were soon whiter than snowmen. At the height of battle, a float of Trinity 'police' sailed out from under Clare Bridge to break up the flight. Their placards, reading: 'Not War! Armed Conflict!' and 'Is This A Forest Fire?' were one of the few reminders of the vehement debates, public meetings and rallies that have raged in Cambridge during the past week over the British action in Egypt. At 11.45 the sun came out, striking King's Chapel, Clare, and Clare Bridge with light; the green impeccable lawns shone, almost incandescent. In a few minutes both Greek and Trojan ships swamped, and the Cam was awash with shattered crates and bedraggled swimmers. A punt skirted the banks of the river from which Helen collected money in a saucepan.

We left the gates of King's, bought a hot dog (alias *chien chaud* and *warme hunde*) at the flaming coal brazier, tossed a penny to an Indian on a praying rug and struggled out again into the crowds on King's Parade, running smack into a South American band giving an energetic rendition of 'The Wedding Samba.' Spaniards on donkeys and allegorical figures of the Seven Deadly Sins waved their Poppy Day collection cans. Towering overhead, high as the second-storey windows, Wilberforce, Pembroke's Trojan horse, halted the traffic of floats and double-decker red buses while a door in its side opened onto a neighbouring car hood, ejecting a band of soldiers armed with shields in the form of garbage-can lids in which they began collecting pennies. Bagpipes still skirled above the general bedlam, the heavens were thick with coloured balloons. We kept pace with a float representing the 'Bolshoi Ballet' for a few minutes, watching a muscular ballerina in white tutu revolve in the consecutive embraces of three bearish, fur-hatted Cossacks to the lyric strains of a violin, oboe, and clarinet.

Slipping into the relative halcyon quiet of the Eagle Pub, in its cobbled courtyard off Bene't Street, we lunched by a comfortable coal fire and craned our necks at the ceiling, a veritable palimpsest of air squadron numbers scrawled in candle-smoke during the last war, and varnished in tawny orange. After fortifying ourselves with half a pint of Merrydown cider, we journeyed forth once more, this time past King's and up Trinity Street. High in the air, an undergraduate in a bosun's chair, strung on rope and pulley, from the third floor of Caius to the windows across the way, fished for pennies in a wicker basket. Outside the Great Gate of Trinity (the biggest of the colleges, boasting its share of royalty in undergraduate enrolment), beneath the niched statue of Henry VIII, coloured triangular pennants flapped in the wind, a husky-voiced songstress crooned from microphones suspended in the bare trees, and a valiant Trinity man sat on a ducking stool over a water trough, ready to be soused by any member of the surrounding crowd who could throw a ball through a small hole and release the mechanism which would plunge him in. We left him shivering on his precarious perch. As Trinity Street metamorphosed into St John's Street (not changing its direction, only its name), a jaunty group of Alpine climbers marched out from All Saints' Passage, bells jingling on their knees, in front of the Indian restaurant euphemistically called the Taj Mahal, where undergraduates dine on piquant curries, pilaus, canned mangoes, and lychees when desiring a change from college diet.

At the congested crossing of St John's Street and Bridge Street we were momentarily cowed by Downing's Diabolical Differential Dirt Distributor, a monumental construction of rubber tubing, pipes, bathtubs and hoses rising to support a great revolving paddle-wheel, each spoke culminating in a tin can; black smoke belched from a twenty-foot chimney stack while white-coated students leaned over to catch money thrown by admiring sidewalk spectators. We progressed down Sidney Street, past Woolworth's and Lloyds Bank to St Andrew's Street; at the gateway of Christ's College, under the stone heraldry of gold-spotted antelopes rampant and pink Tudor roses, a student begged pennies to cover the college seal drawn in coloured chalk on the flagstones.

Crowds of children were yelling with delight around the low walls in front of Emmanuel where a genial fellow in a black felt hat grinned out from under a jet of water showering upon him, apparently insensible to the chill November wind. Next to him, Emmanuel's Electronic Brain flashed its coloured lights; dials whirred and a bodiless breathy voice murmured 'Three . . . four . . . seven . . .' in the throes of predicting this week's football pools.

It was shortly after 4 p.m. The rain began to pour down in earnest. Townspeople turned tail, heading for home; drenched student demonstrators retreated to their colleges. As we hastened along Downing Street, a single undergraduate in rugby regalia held out a lacrosse stick to us; we parted with our penny. The Geology and Economics buildings on the left, the Medical School and Chemistry buildings on the right, bulked bleak and forbidding in the twilight; street lamps reflected in the wet pavements. Down Free-School Lane from beyond the gloomy, glowering Cavendish Laboratory sounded the faint jazz strains of 'Alexander's Ragtime Band.' Raising the collar of our mackintosh against wind and weather, we hurried, head lowered, past Pembroke and the Mill Lane lecture rooms, over the Mill Lane bridge. In front of the glowing dining rooms of the Garden House Hotel, across the river, stood a row of imperturbable mallard ducks, heads tucked under their wings. The orange streetlights along the Fen Causeway shed an unhealthy phosphorescence over the fens, giving the straggling pedestrians ghastly Toulouse-Lautrec complexions. Our red poppy drooping soggy in our buttonhole, we strode over the muddy paths of the Lammas Land Recreation Ground to our rooms and the hedonistic delight of hot tea, gas fire, and for supper, likely as not, cold pork pie, stewed prunes, and custard sauce.

Beach Plum Season on Cape Cod

Written: *c.* early August 1958
Published: *Christian Science Monitor* (14 August 1958): 17[*]

In the quiet scrub pine woods along Cape Cod, with their floor of tawny needles, and in peaceful inlets where the tides are gentle, an observant walker may find the chipmunks, or fiddler crabs, livelier entertainment than any movie at the summer drive-in theaters on the main traffic routes. The vivid black-and-white stripe on the chipmunk's reddish coat, the jade-greens of seaweed, and the delicate mottle of crab-backs, the beach plums yellowing toward their ripe red-purple—all these offer live color enough for the most demanding eye.

At "Hidden Acres," a small group of cottages, each one concealed in its grove of pines, we lived near a family of chipmunks. Glancing out of the kitchen window when the early-morning sun lent the fallen pine needles a russet light of their own, I saw a quick flash of red on the rough brown bark of a pine tree. A chipmunk, cheeks bulging, paused for a moment at the tree root, then vanished into a dark hole well camouflaged by pine needles.

The chipmunk had discovered a bag of corn-ears left over from the previous night's dinner and evidently enjoyed the seasonal dish as much as we did. From that time on, we invited the chipmunks to share our corn feasts and, in return, the chipmunks, brazen as their coats were brilliant, let us watch them turning the cobs of corn over and over in their paws as they deftly gleaned the last corn grains with their quick teeth.

---

[*] Printed with two sketches by SP captioned: 'Picking over beach plums under the pines' and 'Potted plants and a wheelbarrow of beach plums.'

To summer visitors who winter in the city among park pigeons and alley cats, a far stranger sight than chipmunks are the colonies of fiddler crabs that inhabit the shifting provinces between land and sea. We discovered our first fiddler crabs by accident while hunting for the blue mussels growing in clusters at the grass-roots of pools that empty and fill with the ebb and flow of the tidal river near our cottage.

A peculiar sound met our ears as we approached the nearest of these pools. The tide stood dead low and only a trickle of water showed in the riverbed. A dry, crusty scrabbling noise came steadily from the pool bed. At first glance, we thought the whole green-brown mud bottom of the pool had heaved into motion.

From tiny burrows in the fringe of grass and in the sloping pool sides, small crabs, each with one large claw almost equaling them in size, filed to join forces. They marched in a slow, continuous stream toward the place where the pool joined the river. As we began to walk about the rim of the pool, the crabs must have heard our sneakers crashing in the grass like thunder, our steps shaking the earth, for they halted. Those near their burrow doors sidled to shelter. Others farther from home took cover in impromptu mud trenches. The hush of the grasses, the muteness of the mud, made a morning silence. We waited, hoping to outwait the fiddler crabs.

Slowly the rustle started up again. One by one, the crabs emerged from the burrows and from the mud, wearing their own camouflage as the chipmunk, russet among the russet needles, had worn his. But the crabs' color was of grass and green sea, mingled with the brown of earth and sand. Their big single claws held stiffly in front of them like ceremonial shields, the fiddler crabs advanced, their smaller claws rapidly picking up invisible algae from the mud to eat on the march.

We stood watching them, ourselves silenced now by their rhythm, their order, their purpose—a purpose unknown to us, utterly alien. The world of automobiles, jet planes, and supermarkets suddenly seemed to dwindle—a recent innovation sprung up on the edge of the immeasurably older and larger world living in and around the sea.

At low tide, wading through the translucent water we located small clams near the surface of the sand by the green plumes of seaweeds attached to their shells, waving to and fro like signal flags in the rippling currents. A hermit crab scuttled past our bare toes wearing a barnacle-encrusted snail shell, trailing feathers of sea moss, masquerading under the most elaborate disguise in the little bay.

Children soon learn how seashells lose their mother-of-pearl gloss, and how sea-smoothed bits of colored glass lose their jewel-like brightness when taken out of the water and transferred to dry land, to bookshelves, and to boxes. Perhaps words or pictures can best capture and keep some of the color and fullness of the transient summer season and safeguard it through the sooty snowfalls of city winters.

Perhaps even those who have simply spent long afternoons under blazing Indian-summer skies, picking beach plums from the waist-high bushes and hearing them ring with a pleasant metallic sound in the bottom of tin pails, can once more savor the fragrant grasses and the richness of the early harvest air in the clear, red sweetness of homemade beach-plum jelly—preserved not only as breakfast food, but as food for memories of a Cape Cod summer also.

Kitchen of the Fig Tree

Written: *c.* April 1959
Published: *Christian Science Monitor* (5 May 1959): 8*

Most people enjoy "a room with a view." I am even more particular: I prefer "a kitchen with a view," and at present I am fortunate enough to have one. At any moment, in the midst of the commonest kitchen chores—while poking at a pan of sizzling bacon or stirring up the custard filling for a lemon meringue pie—I may glance out of my sixth-story window across a "front yard" of slate roof tops, orange chimneys and chimney pots to the blue waters of the Charles River Basin and watch the white sails catching the sunlight as they tilt back and forth.

The feathery treetops of Boston's Public Garden to my left are just coming into leaf: behind the screen of distant branches I glimpse a moving spot of white. A swanboat? I like to think so. To my right, a spring bouquet in the bowl of brick buildings, blooms the green and gold of Louisburg Square, forsythia a delicate fountain of nodding yellow flower-sprays. Overhead (and often, I feel, around my head) echo gull cries as the gray birds drift by on the wind, close and neighborly as the park pigeons and sparrows, bringing with them a tang of salt and the fish piers and wharves along Atlantic Avenue.

---

* A portion of this article was reprinted as 'A Kitchen With a Fig Tree', *Buckingham Post* (29 May 1959): 7.

In a flash I am lifted from the position of an aproned housewife at a stove: I become a voyager on the deck of a ship, an airplane passenger looking down at a familiar map of streets and parks, poised high above it all. I begin to number and remember the kitchens I have known, the way travelers in foreign countries recollect the monuments and landmarks they have visited.

Now, alas, I am a bit spoiled as far as kitchens go: I have a sixth-story view of treetops and sailboats, a panorama of sunset every evening, not to mention all the American conveniences—icebox, canned and frozen foods, hot water at the tap, a stove with an even temper which does not scorch this side of the cake and leave that side doughy. And yet the other kitchens I remember, although both of them lacked iceboxes and sundry other conveniences an American housewife learns to expect, had special advantages of their own.

I had serious doubts about the kitchen in England when I first stepped into it. It was just big enough to step into and turn about in, added on, like a commonsensical afterthought, to the back of the house on the ground floor, very dim the day round, with only one small window of opaque glass over the little sink. Primitive, I thought sadly as I looked at the spindly black stove. A stove which had never, to judge by its expression, turned out a batch of orange icebox cookies or a fluffy spongecake in all its long years of service.

A strange edifice in the corner took up the remaining floor space: a block of stone, table-height, with a great bowl-shaped hollow carved out of it. A friend suggested that this hollow had probably been used for kneading bread, but I never was quite sure about it. It might, I suspected, have served as a laundry tub, or even as a mortar for the grinding of corn. Who knew what the British housewives of old had endured? I finished by covering it with some clean-scrubbed planks and calling it a kitchen table.

The kitchen itself I named the Kitchen of Doors. All the wall space not taken up by sink, stove, or stone block had been devoted to doors: a door into the main part of the house, a door into the coal shed, a door into the pantry, and a door into the kitchen garden.

It was this garden that saved the kitchen for me—one of those narrow back gardens between high board fences which are everywhere in England. I did not inherit cabbages or herbs, but a wall of roses and an apple tree. So in the warm weather I cooked with the kitchen door to the garden open, and the scent of apple blossoms and roses mingled with the spicy odors of pies and stews. Thrushes and diminutive English robins came to my doorstep for crumbs, or to knock snail shells against the hard stone paving.

When I look back on this kitchen, I am inclined to forget its smallness and almost underwater shadowiness and think of the garden at my door. In winter my icebox problem was neatly solved, too. The milk left on the shelves of the pantry solidified to a kind of Eskimo pudding, and the butter sticks snapped in half, crisp as carrots from the deep cold which even in summer never quite left the stone-floored larder.

In Spain I enjoyed my largest, and yet perhaps my most primitive, kitchen. No cool weather substituted for my icebox. I marketed every morning in the village for fresh fish and eggs and melons and bananas. This kitchen also had one window, but even on the rare cloudy days seemed flooded with light, light that glanced from the bare whitewashed walls and the spacious red-tiled floor.

I possessed, my landlady the Widow Mangada informed me, the great luxury of a sink with cold running water. The wives of the goatherd and the fishermen down the street had no such comforts and used tin pails of well water for washing up, emptying them afterward at the doorstep, suds and all, to settle the dust. Drinking water I did draw from a well built into the house. I looked forward to letting down the rope of the bucket, hearing the echoes multiply as the bucket clanged against the narrow walls of the shaft and splashed at last into the cool, delicious water invisible in the darkness below.

My Spanish kitchen came "furnished" with dishes, glassware and cutlery, a frying pan, a stew pot, and a milk can which I left on the back doorstep every evening to be filled by the goatherd across the road before he took his herds to pasture in the hills at dawn. A bottle of oil, a bottle of vinegar, a petrol stove with one burner, and I had all the essentials of a Spanish kitchen.

Widow Mangada, who kindly supervised my settling in, seemed shocked when I began to heat a pot of water for the lunch dishes. "This is how we do it," she offered, and began to scrub the dishes clean under the cold water faucet, rubbing them vigorously with a handful of fresh straw.

Not too long afterward I discovered what must be the very old housewifely pleasure of laying sheets, pillowcases, and white clothes (washed in cold water also) in the morning sun and seeing them take on an almost miraculous whiteness by noon.

That summer I lived on a diet consisting of all manner of combinations of eggs, potatoes, tomatoes, fish, and fresh fruit. At night I could see the lights of the sardine boats from my porch, low-hung stars in the outer reaches of the harbor. Our village was truly a fishing village. In the daytime the women on my street would set out their chairs in the doorways, chatting together and mending the large-webbed fish nets. In almond season, they would sit out with neighbors and relatives, a roomful of nuts between them, pyramided to the low ceiling, their hands rapidly splitting off the green fruitlike covering of the almonds.

When August came, I looked longingly at the field of corn, tassels waving outside my pantry window, and thought of the fresh buttered corn-on-the-cob my friends in America would be biting into. But corn in Spain fattened the pigs and chickens; I never did see the harvest of that neighbor's field appear in the marketplace.

My prize kitchen accessory that summer was neither sailboats and gulls nor robins and roses but a fig tree. I would step out of my kitchen door, in the cool of the day before sunrise, when the mountains behind our house, half-wrapped still in a pale, raveling mist, took on the pink and orange tint of the sun rising over the sea, or when the Spanish women walked out in the white, glittering radiance of high noon under the shelter of big black umbrellas—and there the fig tree would be, offering me its own umbrella of broad green leaves with the green fruit studded among them, beginning to purple. Later in the season I would go out and pick my dessert from the branches and eat it from the natural plate of the leaf.

When the time came for me to travel north, back to the Kitchen of Doors and the wintry larder, Widow Mangada stopped me on the front porch. "One minute, señorita!" Balancing herself with fine dexterity in her voluminous black skirts, she climbed onto the seat of the big rocking chair, reaching up to pick me the first clusters of ripe grapes from the green, leaf-tapestried lattice shading the porch.

If ever asked to choose among my kitchens the one where I would spend the rest of my cooking days, I think I would ask for a composite kitchen, made up of the best of all of these. But if that were impossible, I have a suspicion that I would choose the Kitchen of the Fig Tree, and make a private arrangement with the farmer next door for a tithe of his corn when it came in season.

A Walk to Withens

Written: *c.*25 April 1959
Published: *Christian Science Monitor* (6 June 1959): 12

There are as many ways to walk to Withens, I suppose, as there are compass points. I have only tried two of them—the traditional and easily followed route from the steep, stonebuilt town of Haworth, and then a wild, uncharted track over the moors from a fixed point in the opposite direction—another black stone village, Heptonstall Slack, perched high above the River Hebden.

The path from Haworth, from the old rectory where the Brontës lived and the Church of St. Michael and All Angels, starts out disarmingly enough, and many visitors like myself, with the best intentions in the world, start with it.

The rectory is hard to leave: it is less a memorial to the Brontës than the home of a tribe of creative young people who are simply not in for tea. Here a blue book and a sprig of heather on Emily's horsehair sofa, and wafers of brown and cream-colored sealing wax on her rosewood writing desk, wait for her return. There lies Charlotte's morocco workcase, full of reels of embroidery thread, next to a silvery Paisley shawl with pink and green figures woven into the sheen of it. Then there are all those miniature drawings and books in microscopic script the children made.

Surely Withens, that stark, stormy setting for *Wuthering Heights*, can scarcely be farther than over the next green hill, so benevolent and mild is the clear weather. "What is there to see out there, exactly?" a fellow American asks me in a low voice as we come down the rectory steps and turn to the left to begin our walk with a scattering of other visitors. I have to confess that I do not know. I do not know, either, just what I expect to find there.

Keeping pace beside my curious friend I skirt pastures of an emerald-green intensity unrivaled elsewhere, bordered by black stone walls. From the distance, the green hills of Yorkshire seem to have a net of these walls cast over them, neatly marking off one square of grazing land from another.

At the stiles we pause, going single file up and down the steps. We come, then, to a long, narrow cataract, a white scarf fluttering down from a rocky height beside the path and flowing away under a footbridge ahead.

Here, our guide tells us, the road roughens. Here, too, the sheep are separated from the goats. With some remarks about the exquisite waterfall, the view of the moors swimming in a mist of heather ahead, at least half of our party lingers, waiting for the rest to go on before they turn back. Not quite sure whether I am a sheep or a goat, I say goodbye to my companion of an hour and cross the wooden footbridge into wilder country.

A hundred years ago, in more spacious days, a carriage road ran where now only the shaggy, yellow-eyed moor sheep browse, crisscrossing their own paths in the long grasses. Under our feet the old road, sunken to a grass-grown rut, leads past cellar holes and gate pillars opening on nothing but vistas of moorland—sheep country, grouse country. At last we see a roof rising, like the prow of a far-off ship, over the slope of the hill ahead of us.

Now, distanced in space and time, I remember Withens as I found it then—a surprisingly small house of black stone far out on the moors. The ridgepole of the roof broken, slates fallen to reveal the framework of the wooden beams beneath, it is nothing like the great, frowning, stalwart black mansion I had pictured as a young girl, munching on walnuts and apples beside a birch log fire on a wuthering winter evening and reading about the trials of Cathy and Heathcliff.

And yet, so strong were my impressions of the book, I felt at Withens that the presence which endows places long loved and lived in with a radiance subject to no alteration or ruining by wind and rain. Withens stands, and stands alone, ringed by the moors, like the center of a pie, approachable from all directions.

Two sizable trees rise like natural pillars before the house, oddly tall in the lee of the windswept hill where nothing else grows higher than a gorse bush. In the late afternoon sun the moors are reddish-brown, warm as burnt sugar. Suddenly a phrase from Dylan Thomas springs to mind—"the bracken kitchens rust." Bracken rust-colored indeed grows now where housewives of a century ago tended their kettles and roasts over fires bright as today's grouse and rabbit-peopled hills.

Some weeks after my first trip, my husband and I set out for Withens from Heptonstall Slack by the trackless route over the moors. Fortified with a brown paper bag of bread-and-honey sandwiches and hard-boiled eggs, we stomp awkwardly along the well-tarred roads in our Wellington boots.

When we reach the clear, peat-brown River Hebden, we cross the stepping stones leading in the general direction of Withens. Gradually we leave behind us the houses, the tearooms, the green fields of spotted nursery-rhyme cows and chickens white as daisies in the distance. Climbing steadily upward we seem at last to be emerging on top of the world; the country is so unpeopled, so close to the sky.

"How do you know which way Withens is?" I ask, stopping to catch my breath and looking curiously at the endless slopes of gorse and bracken surrounding us. But Ted only glances wisely at the sun, just past the peak of its noon arc and already starting to descend in what I assume is the west, and I know he knows and all will be well.

How bogs and swampland come to flourish on the tops of moors I cannot understand, yet here we are, balancing on slippery tussocks, sliding into plashy quags of water and mud, almost, not quite, up over the rims of our Wellington boots. Already my appetite is sharpened by the keen blue air. I am eager for bread and honey. Surely Withens will be over the next hill, I console myself. Of course Withens is nowhere at all by this time; it is a figment, a castle in the clouds. We aim toward the horizon, and when we arrive there, bland and identical, another horizon beckons us on, no ridgepole of a house to be seen over the spindling blue gorse and brown, cloud-mirroring pools.

"Why don't we," I suggest somewhat timidly, too concerned with tea to be very adventurous, "eat the bread and honey *now* and have *another* tea in Haworth?" The pale sun seems perilously low in the sky and I do not like to think of spending the night poised on a grass tussock in the middle of a bottomless moor-pool with a mere hard-boiled egg to see me through till dawn. We do eat then, sitting in a dry clearing among the prickly gorse bushes. We do not even save the hard-boiled eggs in case of emergency.

"Are we lost?" I am pleased that my voice does not quaver.

"Goodness no! Withens'll be just over that way," Ted reassures me with a fine, vague gesture of his arm. Our words challenge a silence unbroken, to judge by its depth and immensity, for centuries. But then the silence closes in again, like water over a dropped stone.

We come to Withens before sundown, by a direction rather different from the one we had plotted on the Ordnance Survey map by the coal fire at home the previous evening. And later we do have a second, much higher tea in Haworth, with tiers of triangular and diamond-shaped sandwiches and pink-and-white frosted cakes.

An American woman is sitting at the table next to ours, wholesome and ruddy-cheeked in tweeds and walking shoes, enough like the lady I parted from at the cataract to call up those memories again. She sips quietly with a calm and delicacy that suggest she, at least, has not walked too far for comfort today, and while she sips she leafs slowly through a sheaf of tinted postcards of Haworth and environs.

Seeing us glance in her direction, the woman smiles and holds up a colored picture of Withens for our inspection. "A lovely purple, that heather."

"It is," I say, gently easing my mud-caked Wellington boots off under cover of the trailing white tablecloth and smiling back, "isn't it!"

Watching the Water-Voles

Ts, *c.*3–15 May 1959,* Lilly Library

To this day I am not quite sure whether I began by watching the water-voles, or whether it was the water-voles that began by watching me. I have a suspicion that a water-vole managed to spy me out first. These were not just ordinary water-voles, but Grantchester Meadow Water-Voles, made tamer than most by living on the left bank of a river much traveled by punts and canoes, opposite a reed-fringed right bank of cow pastures, a bank thronged by black-gowned students and tweed-clad townspeople—walkers, talkers, readers, sitters, meditators, and occasional water-vole watchers like myself. The meadows of Grantchester are an almost legendary green. Perhaps there is something about the shifting, watery lights of the sky above the meadows—iridescent gray or a delicate, lucent blue—which endows the long meadow grasses with their color, a green so brightly sheened in the sun, and even in showery weather, that it seems to float, a lake of pure color, a little above the grasses themselves.

As final exams approached together with the fair May weather I came to the Meadows to stroll, or to sit in the shade of an elder bush and read. But the pages of white, however absorbing, couldn't rival the daisy petals in the meadow. Even the most logical arguments of Plato turned to black crow's-foot prints under those luminous skies, and there was nothing for it but to look up among the willow leaves for a baby owl or to gaze across the river at the cloudlike jostling of the lambs whose baaing filled the quiet country air.

It was at just such a peak of spring laziness that I became aware I was being watched. Watched, as it happened, by a water-vole.

Now to enter Grantchester Meadows from Cambridge, one passes down a narrow, greenly shaded gravel lane, flanked on the right by hedgerows studded with trimly woven robins' nests—those small, sparrow-size editions of our American robin, with their muted olive-colored backs and discreet orange bibs. On the left, from a meadow of feathery green sedge, rises the miniscule chittering of shrews. A wooden stile gate swings open and shuts behind one,

---

* Typed at top-right corner: 'Sylvia Plath / Suite 61 / 9 Willow Street / Boston 8, Massachusetts.' In her journals, SP wrote about the idea for the article on 3 May 1959. The *Christian Science Monitor* rejected it between 13 and 18 May 1959. SP quotes from the nursery rhyme 'Tweedle-Dum and Tweedle-Dee'.

and there, to the left, the meadows stretch, hazed golden with buttercups, to the margin of the river.

A dense hedge of hawthorn borders the right of the path for some little way, screening with a lattice of white blossoms the allotment gardens lying beyond. All summer long, local gardeners tend with care the great, greeny-blue cabbage heads which seem, at times, the sole vegetation in the allotments—to be protected at all costs from the spry brown rabbits that live not by dozens, but by dynasties, in the meadow hedges. The meadows proceed, linked by wooden gates and fenced by thick-leaved hedges, to the town of Grantchester itself—teatime destination of punters and walkers from the country round.

It became my habit to leave the paved pathway just after the stile gate and to strike out to the left through the first meadow to the bank of the river. Once there, I would follow another, rougher path through the trodden grasses along the river's brim until I came to a likely spot for sitting.

Another quality of the air in Grantchester Meadows, besides its strangely radiant lighting effects, is its odd hush, a hush in which sounds are small, but uniquely clear, easily separated, one strand from another. The lambs baa. A hound barks in the distance. The river lisps clear and brown over its underwater shrubbery of reeds and cabbagey water-plants. Occasionally a swan or two will take wing and clatter loudly, wing tips just grazing the surface of the river, down the ripple-cobbled thoroughfare.

One day a raucous uproar dominated the scene for a few moments: across the water two black crows, like angry specks of pepper, were mobbing a blue heron. The large bird rose awkwardly, a misty apparition of long neck and flapping wings, and moved elsewhere in the marsh. In the stillness following this encounter, I heard, among the reeds in the water just to my left, the unmistakable sound of munching: a sound I never would have noticed in the street or in the town. But here, in the windless quiet, it came to my ear with great clarity: the sound of a child eating a raw carrot, or of a rabbit at the prize cabbages.

Almost at the same moment—I had made a slight move and craned my neck in the direction of the noise—I felt I was being watched. Methodically my eyes scanned the reeds. Everything seemed in order. Then I saw one reed had apparently broken off. This struck me as a little odd: reeds were supposed, according to the old maxim, to bend, not break. Behind the reed two liquid black eyes held mine. My first water-vole.

Just the nose and the top of the little animal's head showed above the water. I kept very still. So did the water-vole. At last, deciding, perhaps, that I was a safe sort of water-vole watcher, the water-vole took the reed in its teeth and began paddling to the opposite bank. In the process of watching I felt my eyes becoming a good deal keener. The vole was swimming toward a dark, roundish hole half-concealed among the grasses drooping over the water, a hole I had never noticed before. Climbing up on the door-stoop, the vole poked the reed into its hole and heaved its plump, furry body in after it. Almost immediately I saw a snout and two bright eyes peer out, as if to make sure I wasn't going to be rash and plunge into the water in pursuit, and then they were gone.

The whole opposite bank of the river, I discovered in the course of that spring, was a tunneling of water-vole apartments, some opening underwater, some with porches commanding a fine view of the river and cow pastures. When many walkers and punters were about, the voles grew shy and secretive. Only a little "plop" and a spreading circle of ripples under the far bank would give a clue to their presence. At other times, however, if I sat quietly, I could follow their noses as they swam from one hole to another, from a bank-hole to one hidden under a willow-root. Often a whole family would waddle out into the grass and have a vegetarian picnic, nibbling and munching and showing their progress by a small stir among the grass heads, as though a very local breeze were worrying the blades.

Gradually I began to become familiar with other birds and animals in the meadows besides the water-voles.

Just after the sun had set, countless bats of all sizes started nip-and-tucking back and forth over the fields, black scissoring shapes in the deep blue dusk. The leathery crick-crick of their wings was audible, as were the hootings of the owls, larger shapes silhouetted against the flittering zigzag of the bats.

My husband enjoys calling animals, and often, to my delight, they come to the call. Once he started a whole field of browsing rabbits loping cautiously toward us, until they scattered at the chatter of a jenny-wren. This particular twilight, I remember, he started hooting at the owls outside a dark, clumped wood bordering Grantchester Meadows. The owls did seem to be answering Ted as well as each other. My eyes were fixed on the wood when suddenly a vast winged shape rose up out of the darkness directly in front of us, "big as a tar barrel," against the paler sky. We ducked, waving our arms, and the owl flapped silently up, just over Ted's head, and away into the night, probably as startled as we had been at seeing it, to find Ted's head a man's head and not a roosting post for another owl.

Amused and challenged by Ted's gift of attracting rabbits and owls within hand-shaking distance, I forgot all dignity one morning and mooed at a

Grantchester Meadows cow. The cow mooed back obligingly and started to follow me with some interest. Several other brown-and-white cows looked up from their lunch of buttercups, and I mooed again. They too began to follow me. I soon felt rather awed. The whole field of cows was pacing after me at a leisurely rate, following my trail of moos. In my new role as Pied Piper of Grantchester Meadows, I came to a wooden stile and climbed over it, perching on the first rung of the railing. I looked back.

About twenty cows stood in a close flock on the other side of the stile, jaws rotating, their kind brown eyes watching me expectantly. I felt called upon to give some excuse for my mooing. Before I quite knew what I was doing, I began to recite in clear, cowishly resonant tones: "Whan that Aprille with his shoures soote . . ." The cows gazed up with unflagging interest, not letting out one moo to interrupt, until I had recited the thirty or forty lines of Chaucer's Prologue to *The Canterbury Tales* I knew by heart. A year later, I was to find a similar attentiveness in my college classes of freshman English, but nothing surpasses the great, gentle calm of those cows. I never did try reading aloud to the water voles. I think they might well prove too shy for such entertainment. And then too, perhaps Chaucer would be not quite to their taste.

Mosaics—An Afternoon of Discovery

Written: before 14 September 1959
Published: *Christian Science Monitor* (12 October 1959): 15[*]

The advantages of a motionless subject to a person rather slow with pen and pencil are obvious: the pattern is a constant one, changing only with the light, as shadows shorten or lengthen, emphasizing line, or mass.

After attempts at following some of the slower animals—such as cows—with my drawing pad, and some of the slower people—those lingering at a market counter, for example—I decided to try subjects that were perfectly stationary. (The donkeys always walked away or turned their back at an inconvenient moment; the lady in the fine black lace shawl picked up her bag and left the tomato stand while she was still in barest outline on my page.) I gave up people

---

[*] Printed with two sketches by SP and captioned 'White plaster tenements on a cliff overlooking the fishing harbor at Benidorm, Spain' and 'A Spanish kitchen range with a petrol stove, oil bottles, milk can, and a stewpot'.

and animals on the move with some regret. But there were compensations.

The design of windows in a row of houses began to interest me. Some windows were dark, some boarded-up, some full of stained glass, some oblong in shape, some with a Moorish keyhole outline. In fact, I spent a whole afternoon discovering that the windows, balconies, doors, and chimneys of the houses at the fishing harbor formed a kind of mosaic, with the oblong white walls balanced, broken and tilted in harmonious patterns.

I found scallops in the roof tiles, wheel designs in the railings, stippled patches on the surface of the plaster itself. Awnings and lines of laundry added dips and a larger rhythm of scallops. After this experience, I began to look at the familiar streets as if I had never seen them—really seen them—before.

In time, my kitchen counter became the subject of a drawing. Against the glossy white tile backdrop, the glass bottles of oil and vinegar, the milk tin, the butter dish, the rotund metal stewpot, the all-purpose black frying pan, and even the recalcitrant one-burner petrol stove took on a fine dignity—a pantry battalion posing in full dress. The dark cylinder of the stovepipe at the left of the red-tiled shelf loomed purposeful as a Greek column, or the funnel of a liner.

So, instead of hunting for outlandish or conventionally picturesque subjects, I rediscovered a row of back porches and my own kitchen range. And indeed, a teakettle or a thistle, an umbrella or a chestnut have personalities all their own. When the tendency to take them for granted is put aside, they assume a fresh luster. Details emerge which were never noticed before; bumps, quirks, dents which impart a specific character. But then, it is not that the objects are rare and strange, only that one has tried on a way of looking.

Explorations Lead to Interesting Discoveries

Written: before 14 September 1959
Published: *Christian Science Monitor* (19 October 1959): 17[*]

Outworn objects have a way of keeping strange company. Whether in barns or basements, attics or antique shops, they leave behind their natural environment

---

[*] Printed with two sketches by SP and captioned 'A colorful pattern of rounds and oblongs, knobs and wheels, legs and handles' and '"Each object has a line, a tint, a character of its own—the older and odder the better."' SP quotes from Lewis Carroll, 'The Walrus and the Carpenter', *Through the Looking-Glass* (1871).

and form nodding acquaintances with all manner of strangers.

While exploring in the country one summer day, I rounded the corner of a weed-grown garage long fallen out of use and discovered, near a large pile of quahog shells, a whole clan of these once-serviceable, discarded objects basking in the bright sunlight. Jumbled together with apparent abandon they formed a colorful pattern of rounds and oblongs, knobs and wheels, legs and handles.

There, four feet planted firmly in the crab grass and purple vetch, a rusted iron stove stood, subject to any whim of the weather. A stippling of orangey red warmed the once-black surface to a glow worthy of an oil painter.

Next to the stove a sun-silvered wooden chest took the air, empty now, but stirring the imagination: what had it held and guarded in its day? Fine linens, a carpenter's tools, a pirate's coins? And how did it come at last to sit beside a rubber tire, round as a donut, an upended wheelbarrow, and a pump?

All of these objects silhouetted against the weathered, oyster-white shingles of the garage had seen their heyday and come to rest, unsung, dimly remembered by their owner, if at all; and yet, not without a certain shapeliness, an honorable patina conferred by time and wear.

The value of these objects is sometimes only in the eyes of the beholder. However, the choicest of them often appear—still in motley company but with a price tag matching their age and rarity—in antique shops.

Here I found an old-fashioned sleigh on holiday, its snow-cutting runners framing the scrolls and plumes of summer greenery, bearing no wind-nipped children of the nineties, but a crew of jugs and tins. The jugs of sturdy earthenware, mottled gray, buff, and a glossy molasses-brown, perched fat and complacent on the back of the sleigh as on any pantry shelf.

Once one becomes a hunter of odds and ends, of "shoes and ships and sealing wax," or whatever may turn up, no long-neglected corner is safe from the curious eye. Each object has a line, a tint, a character of its own—the older and odder the better.

One does not need to become a buyer of antiques to savor these age-polished, wear-smoothed jugs, and barrows and boxes and stoves and sleighs. One can try to capture them with a few lines of the pen, or, lacking cupboard space, store them in a niche of words.

Introduction

Written: 17 October 1961
Published: *American Poetry Now* (1961): 2

American Poetry Now is a selection of poems by new and/or youngish American poets for the most part unknown in Britain. I'll let the vigour and variety of these poems speak for themselves. Unfortunately it was not possible to obtain permission to print a poem by Gregory Corso.[*]

'Context'

Written: after 9 November 1961
Published: *London Magazine* (February 1962): 45–6[†]

The issues of our time which preoccupy me at the moment are the incalculable genetic effects of fallout and a documentary article on the terrifying, mad, omnipotent marriage of big business and the military in America – 'Juggernaut,

---

[*] SP included poems by Daniel G. Hoffman, Howard Nemerov, George Starbuck, William Stafford, Denise Levertov, Louis Simpson, Barbara Guest, Richard Wilbur, E. Lucas Myers, Adrienne Rich, Anthony Hecht, Hyam Plutzik, W. S. Merwin, Edgar Bowers, Robert Creeley, Anne Sexton and W. D. Snodgrass.

[†] 'Context' is a collective title given to six questions sent to a number of poets by *London Magazine*: a) Would poetry be more effective, i.e. interest more people more profoundly, if it were concerned with the issues of our time?; b) Do you feel your views on politics or religion influence the kind of poetry you write? Alternatively, do you think poetry has uses as well as pleasure?; c) Do you feel any dissatisfaction with the short lyric as a poetic medium? If so, are there any poems of a longer or non-lyric kind that you visualize yourself writing?; d) What living poets continue to influence you, English or American?; e) Are you conscious of any current 'poeticization' of language which requires to be broken up in favour of a more 'natural' diction? Alternatively, do you feel any undue impoverishment in poetic diction at the moment?; and f) Do you see this as a good or bad period for writing poetry? The responses were submitted by the following (in order of appearance in the issue): Robert Graves, George Seferis, Stephen Spender, C. Day Lewis, Philip Larkin, Lawrence Durrell, Roy Fuller, Robert Conquest, Laurie Lee, Thomas Blackburn, Derek Walcott, Judith Wright, D. J. Enright, Thom Gunn, Charles Causley, Bernard Spencer, Vernon Watkins, Ted Hughes, SP, Edwin Brock, Hugo Williams, John Fuller, Julian Mitchell, Elizabeth Jennings, Anthony Thwaite and Norman Nicholson. In the piece, SP refers to Fred J. Cook, 'Juggernaut: The Warfare State', *The Nation* (28 October 1961): 299–307, and Stevie Smith, 'The New Age', in *Not Waving But Drowning* (London: Andre Deutsch, 1957).

The Warfare State', by Fred. J. Cook in a recent *Nation*. Does this influence the kind of poetry I write? Yes, but in a sidelong fashion. I am not gifted with the tongue of Jeremiah, though I may be sleepless enough before my vision of the apocalypse. My poems do not turn out to be about Hiroshima, but about a child forming itself finger by finger in the dark. They are not about the terrors of mass extinction, but about the bleakness of the moon over a yew tree in a neighbouring graveyard. Not about the testaments of tortured Algerians, but about the night thoughts of a tired surgeon.

In a sense, these poems are deflections. I do not think they are an escape. For me, the real issues of our time are the issues of every time – the hurt and wonder of loving; making in all its forms – children, loaves of bread, paintings, buildings; and the conservation of life of all people in all places, the jeopardising of which no abstract doubletalk of 'peace' or 'implacable foes' can excuse.

I do not think a 'headline poetry' would interest more people any more profoundly than the headlines. And unless the up-to-the-minute poem grows out of something closer to the bone than a general, shifting philanthropy and is, indeed, that unicorn-thing – a real poem – it is in danger of being screwed up as rapidly as the news sheet itself.

The poets I delight in are possessed by their poems as by the rhythms of their own breathing. Their finest poems seem born all-of-a-piece, not put together by hand: certain poems in Robert Lowell's *Life Studies*, for instance; Theodore Roethke's greenhouse poems; some of Elizabeth Bishop and a very great deal of Stevie Smith ('Art is wild as a cat and quite separate from civilisation').

Surely the great use of poetry is its pleasure – not its influence as religious or political propaganda. Certain poems and lines of poetry seem as solid and miraculous to me as church altars or the coronation of queens must seem to people who revere quite different images. I am not worried that poems reach relatively few people. As it is, they go surprisingly far – among strangers, around the world, even. Farther than the words of a classroom teacher or the prescriptions of a doctor; if they are lucky, farther than a lifetime.

A Comparison

Written: *c.*26 June 1962[*]
Broadcast: 7 July 1962

How I envy the novelist!

I imagine him – better say her, for it is the women I look to for a parallel – I imagine her, then, pruning a rosebush with a large pair of shears, adjusting her spectacles, shuffling about among the teacups, humming, arranging ashtrays or babies, absorbing a slant of light, a fresh edge to the weather, and piercing, with a kind of modest, beautiful X-ray vision, the psychic interiors of her neighbours – her neighbours on trains, in the dentist's waiting room, in the corner teashop. To her, this fortunate one, what is there that *isn't* relevant! Old shoes can be used, doorknobs, airletters, flannel nightgowns, cathedrals, nail varnish, jet planes, rose arbours and budgerigars; little mannerisms – the sucking at a tooth, the tugging at a hemline – any weird or warty or fine or despicable thing. Not to mention emotions, motivations – those rumbling, thunderous shapes. Her business is Time, the way it shoots forward, shunts back, blooms, decays and double exposes itself. Her business is people in Time. And she, it seems to me, has all the time in the world. She can take a century if she likes, a generation, a whole summer.

I can take about a minute.

I'm not talking about epic poems. We all know how long *they* can take. I'm talking about the smallish, unofficial garden-variety poem. How shall I describe it? – a door opens, a door shuts. In between you have had a glimpse: a garden, a person, a rainstorm, a dragonfly, a heart, a city. I think of those round glass Victorian paperweights which I remember, yet can never find – a far cry from the plastic mass-productions which stud toy counters in Woolworths. This sort of paperweight is a clear globe, self-complete, very pure, with a forest or village or family group within it. You turn it upside down, then back. It snows. Everything is changed in a minute. It will never be the same in there – not the fir trees, nor the gables, nor the faces.

---

[*] Title supplied from typescript. Written for the BBC and broadcast as 'Sylvia Plath Speaks on a Poet's View of Novel Writing', *The World of Books*, BBC Home Service (7 July 1962); re-broadcast 13 July 1962; recorded 26 June 1962. Published as 'The Novelist and the Poet', *The Listener* (7 July 1977): 26. In the piece, SP cites Ezra Pound, 'In a Station of the Metro', *Poetry* (April 1913): 12. Reprinted in *Brick* (Winter 2006): 140–1.

So a poem takes place.

And there is really so little room! So little time! The poet becomes an expert packer of suitcases:

The apparition of these faces in the crowd:
Petals on a wet, black bough.

There it is: the beginning and the end in one breath. How would the novelist manage that? In a paragraph? In a page? Mixing it, perhaps, like paint, with a little water, thinning it, spreading it out.

Now I am being smug, I am finding advantages.

If a poem is concentrated, a closed fist, then a novel is relaxed and expansive, an open hand: it has roads, detours, destinations; a heart line, a head line; morals and money come into it. Where the fist excludes and stuns, the open hand can touch and encompass a great deal in its travels.

I have never put a toothbrush in a poem.

I do not like to think of all the things, familiar, useful and worthy things, I have never put into a poem. I did, once, put a yew tree in. And that yew tree began, with astounding egotism, to manage and order the whole affair. It was not a yew tree by a church on a road past a house in a town where a certain woman lived . . . and so on, as it might have been in a novel. Oh no. It stood squarely in the middle of my poem, manipulating its dark shades, the voices in the churchyard, the clouds, the birds, the tender melancholy with which I contemplated it – everything! I couldn't subdue it. And, in the end, my poem was a poem about a yew tree. That yew tree was just too proud to be a passing black mark in a novel.

Perhaps I shall anger some poets by implying that the *poem* is proud. The poem, too, can include everything, they will tell me. And with far more precision and power than those baggy, dishevelled and undiscriminate creatures we call novels. Well, I concede these poets their steamshovels and old trousers. I really *don't* think poems should be all that chaste. I would, I think, even concede a toothbrush, if the poem was a real one. But these apparitions, these poetical toothbrushes, are rare. And when they do arrive, they are inclined, like my obstreperous yew tree, to think themselves singled out and rather special.

Not so in novels.

There the toothbrush returns to its rack with beautiful promptitude and is forgot. Time flows, eddies, meanders, and people have leisure to grow and alter before our eyes. The rich junk of life bobs all about us: bureaus, thimbles, cats, the whole much-loved, well-thumbed catalogue of the miscellaneous which the novelist wishes us to share. I do not mean that there is no pattern, no discernment, no rigorous ordering here.

I am only suggesting that perhaps the pattern does not insist so much.
The door of the novel, like the door of the poem, also shuts.
But not so fast, nor with such manic, unanswerable finality.

The All-Round Image

Ts, c.20–2 January 1963[*]

I went to public schools – genuinely public. *Everybody* went: the spry, the shy, the podge, the gangler, the future electronic scientist, the future cop who would one night kick a diabetic to death under the mistaken impression he was a drunk and needed cooling off; the poor, smelling of sour wools and the urinous baby at home and polyglot stew; the richer, with ratty fur collars, opal birthstone rings and daddys with cars ('Wot does *your* daddy do?' 'He don't woik, he's a bus droiver.' Laughter.) There it was – Education – laid on free of charge for the lot of us, a lovely slab of depressed American public. *We* weren't depressed, of course. We left that to our parents, who eked out one child or two, and slumped dumbly after work and frugal suppers over their radios to listen to news of the 'home country' and a black-moustached man named Hitler.

Above all, we did feel ourselves American in the rowdy seaside town where I picked up, like lint, my first ten years of schooling – a great, loud cats' bag of Irish Catholics, German Jews, Swedes, Negroes, Italians and that rare, pure *Mayflower* dropping, somebody *English*. On to this steerage of infant citizens the doctrines of Liberty and Equality were to be, through the free, communal

---

[*] Accepted by *Punch* editor Bernard Hollowood in a letter to SP dated 23 January 1963. Published as 'America! America!', *Punch* (3 April 1963): 482–4, with a biographical sketch: 'Sylvia Plath, who died earlier this year at the age of 30, was educated at Smith College and Cambridge University. She was a poet with a clear, original and very effective style and had also written a novel.' In their 20 February 1963 issue, *Punch* advertised that this piece was to be printed in their next issue, 27 February 1963. However, due to SP's death it was delayed. SP refers to 'October's Bright Blue Weather' by Helen Hunt Jackson, one of many poems she copied into a notebook which is held by the Berg Collection, New York Public Library.

NON-FICTION | 605

schools, impressed. Although we could almost call ourselves Bostonian (the city airport with its beautiful hover of planes and silver blimps growled and gleamed across the bay), New York's skyscrapers were the icons of our 'homeroom' walls, New York and the great green queen lifting a bedlamp that spelt out Freedom.

Every morning, hands on hearts, we pledged allegiance to the Stars and Stripes, a sort of aerial altarcloth over teacher's desk. And sang songs full of powder-smoke and patriotics to impossible, wobbly soprano tunes. One high, fine song 'For purple mountain majesties above the fruited plain' always made the scampi-size poet in me weep. In those days I couldn't have told a fruited plain from a mountain majesty and confused God with George Washington (whose lamblike granny-face shone down at us also from the schoolroom wall between neat blinders of white curls), yet warbled, nevertheless, with my small, snotty compatriots 'America, America! God shed His grace on thee, and crown thy good with brotherhood from sea to shining sea.'

The sea we knew something about. Terminus of almost every street, it buckled and swashed and tossed, out of its grey formlessness, china plates, wooden monkeys, elegant shells and dead men's shoes. Wet salt winds raked our playgrounds endlessly – those Gothic composites of gravel, macadam, granite and bald, flailed earth wickedly designed to bark and scour the tender knee. There we traded playing cards (for the patterns on the backs) and sordid stories, jumped clothes rope, shot aggies, and enacted radio and comic book dramas of our day ('Who knows what evil lurks in the hearts of men? The Shadow knows – nyah, nyah, nyah!' or 'Up in the sky, look! It's a bird, it's a plane, it's Superman!') If we were destined for any special end – grooved, doomed, limited, fated – we didn't feel it. We beamed and sloshed from our desks to the dodgeball dell, open and hopeful as the sea itself.

After all, we could be anybody. If we worked. If we studied hard enough. Our accents, our money, our parents didn't matter. Did not lawyers rise from the loins of coal-heavers, doctors from the bins of dustmen? Education was the answer, and heaven knows how it came to us. Invisibly, I think, in the early days – a mystical infrared glow off the thumbed multiplication tables, ghastly poems extolling October's bright blue weather and a world history that more or less began and ended with the Boston Tea Party – Pilgrims and Indians being, like the eohippus, prehistoric.

Later, the college obsession would seize us, a subtle, terrifying virus. Everybody had to go to *some* college or other. A business college, a junior college, a state college, a secretarial college, an Ivy League college, a pig farmer's college.

The book first, then the work. By the time we (future cop and electronic brain alike) exploded into our prosperous, post-war high school, full-time guidance counsellors jogged our elbows at ever-diminishing intervals to discuss motives, hopes, school subjects, jobs – and colleges. Excellent teachers showered on to us like meteors: Biology teachers holding up human brains, English teachers inspiring us with a personal ideological fierceness about Tolstoy and Plato, Art teachers leading us through the slums of Boston, then back to the easel to hurl public school gouache with social awareness and fury. Eccentricities, the perils of being *too* special, were reasoned and cooed from us like sucked thumbs.

The girls' guidance counsellor diagnosed my problem straight off. I was just too dangerously brainy. My high, pure string of straight As might, without proper extracurricular tempering, snap me into the void. More and more, the colleges wanted All-Round Students. I had, by that time, studied Machiavelli in Current Events class. I grabbed my cue.

Now this guidance counsellor owned, unknown to me, a white-haired identical twin I kept meeting in supermarkets and at the dentist's. To this twin, I confided my widening circle of activities – chewing orange sections at the quarters of girls' basketball games (I had made the team), painting mammoth L'il Abners and Daisy Maes for class dances, pasting up dummies of the school newspaper at midnight while my already dissipated co-editor read out the jokes at the bottom of the columns of the *New Yorker*. The blank, oddly muffled expression of my guidance counsellor's twin in the street did not deter me, nor did the apparent amnesia of her whitely efficient double in the school office. I became a rabid teenage pragmatist.

'Usage is Truth, Truth, Usage,' I might have muttered, levelling my bobby socks to match those of my schoolmates. There was no uniform, but there *was* a uniform – the pageboy hairdo, squeaky clean, the skirt and sweater, the 'loafers', those scuffed copies of Indian moccasins. We even, in our democratic edifice, nursed two ancient relics of snobbism – two sororities: Subdeb and Sugar 'n' Spice. At the start of each school year, invitation cards went out from old members to new girls – the pretty, the popular, the in some way rivalrous. A week of initiation preceded our smug admittance to the cherished Norm. Teachers preached against Initiation Week, boys scoffed, but couldn't stop it.

I was assigned, like each initiate, a Big Sister who systematically began to destroy my ego. For a whole week I could wear no make-up, could not wash, could not comb my hair, change clothes or speak to boys. By dawn I had walked to my Big Sister's house and was making her bed and breakfast. Then, lugging her intolerably heavy book, as well as my own, I followed her, at a dog's distance, to school. On the way she might order me to climb a tree and hang from a branch till I dropped, ask a passer-by a rude question or stalk about the shops begging for rotten grapes and mouldy rice. If I smiled – showed, that is, any sense of irony at my slavishness, I had to kneel on the public pavement and wipe the smile off my face. The minute the bell rang to end school, Big Sister took over. By nightfall I ached and stank; my homework buzzed in a dulled and muzzy brain. I was being tailored to an Okay Image.

Somehow it didn't take – this initiation into the nihil of belonging. Maybe I was just too weird to begin with. What did these picked buds of American womanhood do at their sorority meetings? They ate cake; ate cake and catted about the Saturday night date. The privilege of being anybody was turning its other face – to the pressure of being everybody; ergo, no one.

Lately I peered through the plate-glass side of an American primary school: child-size desks and chairs in clean, light wood, toy stoves and minuscule drinking fountains. Sunlight everywhere. All the anarchism, discomfort and grit I so tenderly remembered had been, in a quarter century, gentled away. One class had spent the morning on a bus learning how to pay fares and ask for the proper stop. Reading (my lot did it by age four off soapbox tops) had become such a traumatic and stormy art one felt lucky to weather it by ten. But the children were smiling in their little ring. Did I glimpse, in the First Aid cabinet, a sparkle of bottles – soothers and smootheners for the embryo rebel, the artist, the odd?

Snow Blitz

Ts,[*] after 26 January 1963, Smith College

In London, the day after Christmas (Boxing Day) – it began to snow: my first snow in England. For five years I had been tactfully asking 'Do you ever have snow at all?' as I steeled myself to the six months of wet, tepid grey that

---

[*] Typed at top right of typescript: 'Sylvia Plath / 23 Fitzroy Road /London N.W.1.' Date assigned from internal evidence.

Electrical worker strikes commenced on 3 January 1963 due to the 'work-to-rule' campaign and overtime ban. SP references the death of a baby which took place during the first power cut on 3 January at Wanstead Hospital. An article appeared in *The Times* on 9 January 1963 in advance of the inquiry to the tragedy. Power cuts were still in effect on 10 and 14 January, and a big blackout took place on the 18th. On several days, from 17 January to 2 February, *The Times* published Letters to the Editor under the title of 'Not Enough Power'.

make up an English winter. 'Ooo I do remember snow,' was the usual reply, 'when I were a lad.' Whereupon I would enthusiastically recall the huge falls of crisp and spectacular white I snowballed, tunnelled in and sledded on in the States when *I* was young. Now I felt the same sweet chill of anticipation at my London window, watching the pieces of darkness incandesce as they drove through the glow of the streetlight. Since my flat (once the home of W. B. Yeats and so marked on a round, blue plaque) has no central heating, my chill was not metaphorical but very real.

The next day the snow lay about – white, picturesque, untouched, and it went on snowing. The next day the snow still lay about – untouched. There seemed to be a lot more of it. Bits plopped in over my boot tops as I crossed the unploughed street. The main road had not been ploughed either. Random buses and cabs crawled along in deep white tracks. Here and there men with newspapers, brooms and rags attempted to discover their cars.

Most of the local shops still foundered in a foot or two of fluff, the customers' footsteps like birdtracks looping from door to door. A small space in front of the chemists had been cleared. Into this I gratefully stepped.

'I suppose you don't *have* snowploughs in England, heh, heh!' I joked, loading up with Kleenex, Paddi Pads, blackcurrant juice, rosehip syrup and bottles of nose drops and cough medicine (labelled The Linctus in Gothic script) – those sops and aids to babies with winter colds.

'No,' the chemist beamed back, 'no snowploughs, I'm afraid. We in England are simply not prepared for snow. After all, it falls so seldom.'

This seemed to me a reasonable, if ominous reply. If England was due for a new ice age, what then?

'Shall I', the chemist leaned forward with a confidential smile, 'show you what *I* have found helpful?'

'Oh yes, do,' I desperately said, thinking of tranquillisers.

The chemist lifted, shyly and proudly, a rough six-foot plank from behind a counter of Trufoods and cough pastilles.

'A board!'

'A board?'

The chemist closed his eyes and gripped the plank, blissful as a housewife with a rolling pin.

'With this board I simply *push* the snow aside.'

I stumbled out with my bundles. I smiled. Everybody smiled. The snow was a huge joke, and our predicament that of Alpine climbers marooned in a cartoon.

Then the snow hardened and froze. Sidewalks and streets became a rugged terrain of ice over whose treacherous crevices old people teetered, clutching dog leads or steered by strangers.

One morning my doorbell rang.

'Shovel your steps, lydy?' asked a small cockney with a vast canvas pram.

'How much?' I cynically wondered, not knowing the going rate and expecting extortion.

'Oh, thruppence. A penny.'

I melted and said all right.

Then, foreseeing slackness: 'Mind you chip off the ice!'

Two hours later the boy was still working. Four hours later he rang to borrow a broom. I glanced out the window and saw a pram full of tiny icebergs. Finally he had finished. I inspected the job. He seemed to have cleaned between the railing struts with a chisel. 'Looks like it might snow again.' Hopefully he surveyed the low grey sky. I gave him sixpence and he vanished in an avalanche of thanks with the snow-mountained pram.

It did snow again. Then came the cold.

The morning of the Big Freeze I discovered the bathtub half full of filthy water. I could not understand it. I do not understand plumbing. I waited a day; maybe it would go away. But the water did not go away, it increased, both in depth and dirtiness. The next day I woke to find myself staring at a stain in my beautiful new white ceiling. As I looked, the ceiling discharged, at various spots, drops of viscous liquid that splopped onto the rug. The ceiling paper sagged at the seams.

'Help!' I cried to the house agent from a puddle of black water in the telephone kiosk. I had no home phone because getting one took at least three months. 'My ceiling is leaking and the bathtub is full of dirty water.'

Silence.

'Not *my* dirty water,' I hastened to add. 'Water that floods up into the tub of its own accord. I think there is snow in it. Maybe it's the roof water.'

This last information was a bit apocalyptic. *Had* I seen snow in the tub water? It certainly sounded more dangerous.

'The water may well be from the roof,' the agent faintly said. Then, more sternly, 'You realise there is not a plumber to be had in London. Everyone has the same trouble. Why, I have had three burst pipes in my flat.'

'Yes, but you know how to fix them,' I resolutely cooed. 'There is no cold water in the cold water taps either. What does *that* mean?'

'We', muttered the agent, 'shall soon see.'

The builders and the agent's assistant arrived within the hour, booted and puffing and tracking up black muck. With shovels and picks they crawled through the attic trapdoor and soon great masses of snow were thunking from the roof into the yard.

'Why does the roof leak?' I asked the agent's assistant.

'These are old roofs. It's all right when it rains, but when it snows, the snow piles up and up behind the gutters. It's all right as long as it stays cold.' He smiled. 'But when it melts!'

'But where I come from there is snow every winter and the roofs *never* leak.'

The agent's assistant blushed. 'Well, there *is* a faulty gutter just over your bed.'

'Over my bed! Hadn't you better repair it? If it snows and melts any more I'll wake up in a mess of wet plaster. Or maybe I won't even wake up.'

The agent's assistant didn't look as if he had seriously considered repairing the gutter. After all, I could see him hoping, there might not be any more snow.

'You better repair it. I don't want to have to bother you *again*!'

The men descended and began to swab the discoloured and still dripping ceiling with a general air of having things fixed. I ran into the babies' room in answer to a crash and a scream. My son, in an access of energy, had just shaken his cot apart, snapping all the screws. When I returned, coddling his sobs, I heard the men mumbling and saying 'Whoops' to one another. They were holding a yellow plastic bucket to a geyser of ceiling water with the embarrassed air of covering some obscenity.

'How long', I demanded, 'is this leakage going to go on? You know it's like Chinese water torture, don't you, drip drip drip all night. Can't you put a bucket up in the attic?'

'Ooo mum, there's not room to stand a candle in that attic. The gutter lays straight atop your ceiling.'

They left the bucket on the floor, just in case, and with promises to repair the gutter before the weekend, stumped off.

I have not seen them since.

Then the agent himself arrived, with bowler and moisture detector, to see about my leakage, the failure of cold water and the tub full of Alpine fluid.

With the moisture detector he pricked the bedroom ceiling and assured me that it would not, in the immediate future, fall.

'You realise, though, that you are in danger of having no drinking water.'

I said no, I had not realised it. Why?

'The builders haven't properly layered the pipes to the house and they are frozen. I would turn off your immersion heater in case it burns out the empty tank. When the water in the upstairs cistern is finished, that's the end.'

I tried to recall some of the things one cannot do without water besides washing one's face and making tea. There were many.

'I'll try to get the pipes fixed by tonight,' the agent promised. 'The drinking water situation is more important than your tub.'

He stepped onto the snowy balcony to survey the maze of ancient pipes against the wall, then went in to fiddle with the water taps in the kitchen. 'Aha!' he finally said. 'At first I thought the plumbers might have connected a pipe wrong and that the tub water could indeed be coming from the roof. But look!' He instructed me to stand and watch the tub full of water while he went into the kitchen and ran the hot tap.

Bubbles and rings plopped up from the open drain hole.

'You see,' the agent accused, 'it is *your own water* filling the tub. You have a frozen waste pipe, so it can't escape.'

Then he invited me out on the balcony.

With dazzling glibness he rattled off the sources and origins of the twining pipes. 'That is your sink pipe, that is your bath pipe, those going up into the air are the air pipes.' I stared in despair. The bath waste pipe alone ran some twenty feet down the wall and along the balcony before it bent to drop its load into an open drain below.

'Somewhere the bath waste pipe is frozen.'

'What happens', I asked, 'if you run hot water in the tub?'

'Oh it just melts the top bit of ice and freezes again.'

'Then what can I do?'

'Hold candles to the pipe. Or pour hot water on it. Of course I *could* have the builders put a blowtorch to it, but you'd have to have it done at your own expense.'

'But *you* are responsible for the outside repairs, and the pipes are outside the house.'

'Ah but', the agent evilly gleamed, 'the *bath* is inside. Have you been plugging your drains every night to prevent water escaping and freezing?'

'No-o. Nobody told me to. But I always turn off the taps very tightly.'

I felt cornered. 'Granted,' said the agent loftily, 'the Water Board should have sent round leaflets telling what to do in such an emergency.'

'What do *you* do at *your* flat?'

'Oh, I run great douches of boiling water through several times a day and bung up the drains at night. Terrible waste of electricity, of course, but it seems to work.'

After the agent had folded himself into muffler, gloves and bowler and left with his moisture detector, I pondered his advice. Douches of boiling water would do nothing if the pipes weren't already cleared, and I had a limited, perhaps even now extinct supply of water. The candle cure seemed miserably Dickensian. Still, to be doing something, I filled a bucket with hot water and shivered out onto the balcony. At random I emptied the almost immediately lukewarm water onto a spot of black, recalcitrant pipe. Then went in to look at the tub, hoping for a miracle. There wasn't any.

The dirty stuff didn't stir.

All that materialised was the downstairs tenant.

'Did you happen to empty some water on your balcony just now?'

'The agent told me to,' I confessed.

'The agent's a fool. There is a puddle leaking through onto my kitchen floor. And my front walls are dripping. *That* of course is not your fault. But how can I lay carpets over a whole lot of water?'

I said I had no idea.

In the street that evening I passed great frozen fields of water. From, I presumed, burst pipes. At a tap newly raised from the sidewalk at one corner, an old age pensioner stooped to fill a fat flowered china pitcher.

'Is that *drinking* water?' I called above the mean east wind.

'I suppose,' he croaked, 'they put it there for that purpose.'

'Shocking!' we both cried at the same moment, and passed in the darkness like sad ships.

Later that night I heard the noise of a Niagara overhead and feet thudding up my hall stairs and a frenzied knocking. The taps gurgled and choked. I flung open the door and a ruddy young plumber rushed in. 'Is the water coming?'

I covered my eyes and pointed up to the roaring. 'You look. I can't. Will it flood everything?'

'Oh it's just filling the cistern. It's all right.'

And it was. We had water to drink, we were lucky.

As for the tub, I decided to wait until the thaw – that mystical, unpredictable date when affairs would better. Every day I emptied its dirty contents by bucket into the toilet and flushed them away.

Oddly enough, no one really beefed.

I asked a man holding a small blue gas flame to a button of pipe at the side of the house if the flame helped. 'Hasn't yet,' he cheerfully said.

The cheer seemed universal. We were all mucking in together, as in the Blitz. An Indian girl in the Chalk Farm tube told me her house had been without any water for three weeks, when the pipes burst and flooded the lot. They had to go out to eat, and the landlady rationed out buckets of water each day.

'Sorry to get you out of the warm,' the milkman apologised, calling for his weekly ten and six. 'What we got now is nine months of winter and three of bad weather.'

Then came the power cuts.

One soot-coloured and frigid dawn I snapped on the two buttons of the electric heater the builders had stuck, like a Martian surgical mask, in the middle of my otherwise beautiful Georgian wall. A red, consoling glow – two bars of it. Then nothing. I snapped on a light. Nothing. Had I blown a fuse with my piecemeal heating – the little mushroom-shaped childproof electric fan heaters I lugged around from room to room (there were never enough)? *They* had been going defunct lately, one by one, fanning out icy air. I peered into the grey street. No light showed anywhere. My personal concern must be universal. Still, I felt dismal. What had happened? How long would it last?

I knocked at the flat downstairs. A warm oil stench flooded the hall, from one of those paraffin heaters I would never buy because of my fear of fire.

'Oh, didn't you know, there's a power cut,' said the tenant, who read newspapers.

'Why?'

'Strikes. A baby died in hospital because of it.'

'But what about *my* babies? They've got flu. They can't do this to us, it isn't right.'

The tenant shrugged with a resigned and helpless smile. Then he loaned me a green rubber hot water bottle. I wrapped my daughter in a blanket with the hot water bottle and set her over a bowl of warm milk and her favourite puzzle. The baby I dressed in a snowsuit. Luckily I cooked by gas.

Hours later my little girl crowed 'Fire on.' And there it was – dull, red, ugly, but utterly wonderful.

The next power cut came unannounced a few days later, at tea. By this time I had flu too – that British alternation of fever and chills for which my doctor offered no relief or cure. You either die or you don't.

A neighbour popped in with prize booty – night lights. To see by. The shops were sold out of tapers, candles, everything. She had stood in a queue to get these. In the street old people were being helped down the perilous steps of cellar flats by candlelight. Candles filled the windows, mellow and yellow; the city flickered.

Even after the power cut, the instinct to hoard remained. One ironmonger simply wrote CANDLES in his window and sold out the piles of red and white boxes from some secret source – no other ironmonger had refills yet – in a few minutes. I bought a pound of wax fingers and stuffed my pockets.

An electrician told me the generators simply weren't equipped to take care of the load of new electrical appliances. They were building new generators, but not fast enough. The statisticians hadn't envisioned the demand.

Then, just a month after the first snowfall, the weather relaxed. Eaves began to drip. With a sordid gurgle my bathtub emptied of its own accord. In the street I saw official-looking men sprinkling shovelfuls of powder on the already half-melted ice.

'What's that?' I demanded.

'Salt and sawdust. To make it melt.'

I also saw my first London snowplough – small, doughty, with a crew of men helping it along by chipping and chopping the truculent remnants and dumping them into an open van. 'Where have you been all month?' I asked one of them.

'Oh, we've been coming.'

'How many ploughs do you have in all?'

'Five.'

I didn't ask whether the five served our zone only, or the whole of London. It didn't really seem to matter.

'What do you do with the snow?'

'We empty it down the sewers. Then there's floods.'

'What will you do if this happens every year?' I asked my agent.

He blenched. 'Oh it's not been this bad since nineteen-forty-seven.'

I could tell he didn't want to think about it – the possibility of an annual snow blitz. Dress up warm, lots of tea and bravery. That seemed the answer. After all, what but war or weather breeds such comradeliness in a big, cold city?

Meanwhile, the pipes stay outside. Where else?

And what if there *is* another snow blitz?

And another?

My children will grow up resolute, independent and tough, fighting through queues for candles for me in my aguey old age. While I brew waterless tea – *that* at least the future should bring – on a gas ring in the corner. If the gas, too, is not kaput.

NON-FICTION | 615

Landscape of Childhood

Ts,[*] c.28 January 1963, privately owned

My childhood landscape was not land but the end of the land – the cold, salt, running hills of the Atlantic. I sometimes think my vision of the sea is the clearest thing I own. I pick it up, exile that I am, like the purple 'lucky stones' I used to collect with a white ring all the way round, or the shell of a blue mussel with its rainbowy angel's fingernail interior, and in one wash of memory the colours deepen and gleam, the early world draws breath.

Breath, that is the first thing. Something is breathing. My own breath? The breath of my mother? No, something else, something larger, farther, more serious, more weary. So behind shut lids I float awhile, a small sea captain, tasting the day's weather – battering rams at the seawall, a spray of grapeshot on my mother's brave geraniums, or the lulling shoosh-shoosh of a full, mirrory pool that turns the quartz grits at its rim idly and kindly, a lady brooding at jewellery. There might be a hiss of rain on the pane, there might be wind sighing and trying the creaks of the house like keys. I was not deceived by these. The motherly pulse of the sea made a mock of such counterfeits. Like a deep woman, it hid a good deal; it had many faces, many delicate, terrible veils. It spoke of miracles and distances; if it could court, it could also kill. When I was learning to creep, my mother set me down on the beach to see what I thought of it. I crawled straight for the coming wave and was just through the wall of green when she caught my heels.

I often wonder what would have happened if I had managed to pierce that looking-glass. Would my infant gills have taken over, the salt in my blood? For a time I believed not in God nor Santa Claus, but in mermaids. They seemed as logical and possible to me as the brittle twig of a seahorse in the Zoo aquarium or the skates lugged up on the lines of cursing Sunday fishermen – skates the shape of old pillowslips with the full, coy lips of women.

Mermaids! What if, like the coelacanth, I had never seen one! I adored the

---

[*] Typed in top-right corner: 'Sylvia Plath / 23 Fitzroy Road / London N.W.1.' Published as 'Ocean 1212-W', the title of which was suggested by Leonie Cohn of the BBC in a letter to SP dated 8 February 1963. Printed in *The Listener* (29 August 1963: 312–13) with the biographical note: 'Sylvia Plath died in February this year. She published one book of poems, *The Colossus*.' The typescript was owned by the late Elizabeth Sigmund and sold at a Bonhams auction on 26 June 2019.

beautifully morbid story of the little mermaid who fell in love with a land prince and traded her tongue to the sea witch for a pair of feet on which she could dance for him, utterly dumb, and pained and faint with the feel of needles. And I recall my mother, a sea-girl herself, reading to me and my brother – who came later – from Matthew Arnold's 'Forsaken Merman':

> Sand-strewn caverns, cool and deep,
> Where the winds are all asleep;
> Where the spent lights quiver and gleam,
> Where the salt weed sways in the stream,
> Where the sea-beasts, ranged all round,
> Feed in the ooze of their pasture-ground;
> Where the sea-snakes coil and twine,
> Dry their mail and bask in the brine;
> Where great whales come sailing by,
> Sail and sail, with unshut eye,
> Round the world for ever and aye.

I saw the gooseflesh on my skin. I did not know what made it. I was not cold. Had a ghost passed over? No, it was the poetry. A spark flew off Arnold and shook me, like a chill. I wanted to cry; I felt very odd. I had fallen into a new way of being happy.

Now and then, when I grow nostalgic about my ocean childhood – the waul of gulls and the smell of salt – somebody solicitous will bundle me into a car and drive me to the nearest briny horizon. After all, in England, no place is what? more than seventy miles from the sea. 'There,' I'll be told, 'there it is.' As if the sea were a great oyster on a plate that could be served up, tasting just the same, at any restaurant the world over. I get out of the car, I stretch my legs, I sniff. The sea. But that is not it, that is not it at all.

The geography is all wrong in the first place. Where is the grey thumb of the water tower to the left and the sickle-shaped sandbar (really a stone bar) under it, and the Deer Island prison at the tip of the Point to the far right? The road I knew curved into the waves with the ocean on one side, the bay on the other, and my grandmother's house, halfway out, faced east, full of red sun and sea lights.

To this day I remember her phone number: OCEAN 1212-W. I would repeat it to the operator, from my home on the quieter bayside, an incantation, a fine rhyme, half expecting the black earpiece to give me back, like a conch, the susurrus of the sea out there as well as my grandmother's Hello.

The breath of the sea, then. And then its lights. Was it some huge, radiant animal? Even with my eyes shut I could feel the glimmers off its bright mirrors spider over my lids. I lay in a watery cradle, sea gleams finding the chinks in the dark green window blind, and playing and dancing, or resting and trembling a little. At naptime I clinked my fingernail on the hollow brass bedstead for the music of it and once, in a fit of discovery and surprise, found the join in the new rose paper and with the same curious nail bared a great bald space of wall. There was a scolding for this, a spank, too, and then my grandfather extracted me from the domestic furies for a long beachcombing stroll over mountains of rattling and cranking purple stones.

My mother, born and brought up in the same sea-bitten house, remembered days of wrecks where the townspeople poked among the waves' leavings as at an open market – teakettles, bolts of soaked cloth, the lone, lugubrious shoe. But never, that she could remember, a drowned sailor. They went straight to Davy Jones. Still, what mightn't the sea bequeath? I kept hoping. Brown and green glass nuggets were common, blue and red ones rare: the lanterns of shattered ships? Or the sea-beaten hearts of beer and whisky bottles. There was no telling.

I think the sea swallowed dozens of tea-sets – tossed in abandon off liners, or consigned to the tide by jilted brides. I collected a shiver of china bits, with borders of larkspur and birds or braids of daisies. No two patterns ever matched.

Then one day the textures of the beach burned themselves on the lens of my eye for ever. Hot April. I warmed my bottom on the mica-bright stone of my grandmother's steps, staring at the stucco wall, with its magpie design of egg-stones, fan shells, coloured glass. My mother was in hospital. She had been gone three weeks. I sulked. I would do nothing. Her desertion punched a smouldering hole in my sky. How could she, so loving and faithful, so easily leave me? My grandmother hummed and thumped out her bread dough with suppressed excitement. Viennese, Victorian, she pursed her lips, she would tell me nothing. Finally she melted a little. I would have a surprise when Mother came back. It would be something nice. It would be – a baby.

A baby!

I hated babies. I who for two and a half years had been the centre of a tender universe felt the axis wrench and a polar chill immobilise my bones. I would be a bystander, a museum mammoth. Babies!

Even my grandfather, on the glassed-in veranda, couldn't woo me from my huge gloom. I refused to hide his pipe in the rubber plant and make it a pipe tree. He stalked off in his sneakers, wounded too, but whistling. I waited till his shape rounded Water Tower Hill and dwindled in the direction of the sea promenade; whose ice cream and hotdog stalls were boarded up still, in spite of the mild pre-season weather. His lyrical whistle beckoned me to adventure and forgetting. But I didn't want to forget. Hugging my grudge, ugly and prickly, a sad sea urchin, I trudged off on my own, in the opposite direction toward the forbidding prison. As from a star I saw, coldly and soberly, the *separateness* of everything. I felt the wall of my skin: I am I. That stone is a stone. My beautiful fusion with the things of this world was over.

The tide ebbed, sucked back into itself. There I was, a reject, with the dried black seaweed whose hard beads I liked to pop, hollowed orange and grapefruit halves and a garbage of shells. All at once, old and lonely, I eyed these – razor clams, fairy boats, weedy mussels, the oyster's pocked grey lace (there was never a pearl) and tiny white 'ice cream cones'. You could always tell where the best shells were – at the rim of the last wave, marked by a mascara of tar. I picked up, frigidly, a stiff pink starfish. It lay at the heart of my palm, a joke dummy of my own hand. Sometimes I nursed starfish alive in jam jars of seawater and watched them grow back lost arms. On this day, this awful birthday of otherness, my rival, somebody else, I flung the starfish against a stone. Let it perish. It had no wit.

I stubbed my toe on the round, blind stones. They paid no notice. They didn't care. I supposed they were happy. The sea waltzed off into nothing, into the sky – the dividing line on this calm day almost invisible. I knew, from school, the sea cupped the bulge of the world like a blue coat, but my knowledge somehow never connected with what I *saw* – water drawn halfway up the air, a flat, glassy blind; the snail trails of steamers along the rim. For all I could tell, they circled that line for ever. What lay behind it? 'Spain,' said owl-eyed Harry Bean, my friend. But the parochial map of my mind couldn't take it in. Spain. Mantillas and gold castles and bulls. Mermaids on rocks, chests of jewels, the fantastical. A piece of which the sea, ceaselessly eating and churning, might any minute beach at my feet. As a sign.

A sign of what?

A sign of election and specialness. A sign I was not for ever to be cast out. And I *did* see a sign. Out of a pulp of kelp, still shining, with a wet, fresh smell, reached a small, brown hand. What would it be? What did I *want* it to be? A mermaid, a Spanish infanta?

What it was, was a monkey.

Not a real monkey, but a monkey of wood. Heavy with the water it had swallowed and scarred with tar, it crouched on its pedestal, remote and holy, long-muzzled and oddly foreign. I brushed it and dried it and admired its delicately carved hair. It looked like no monkey I had ever seen eating peanuts and moony-foolish. It had the noble pose of a simian Thinker. I realise now that the totem I so lovingly undid from its caul of kelp (and have since, alas, mislaid with the other baggage of childhood) was a Sacred Baboon.

So the sea, perceiving my need, had conferred a blessing. My baby brother took his place in the house that day, but so did my marvellous and (who knew?) even priceless baboon.

Did my childhood seascape, then, lend me my love of change and wildness? Mountains terrify me – they just sit about, they are so *proud*. The stillness of hills stifles me like fat pillows. When I was not walking alongside the sea I was on it, or in it. My young uncle, athletic and handy, rigged us a beach swing. When the tide was right you could kick to the peak of the arc, let go, and drop into the water.

Nobody taught me to swim. It simply happened. I stood in a ring of playmates in the quiet bay, up to my armpits, rocked by ripples. One spoilt little boy had a rubber tyre in which he sat and kicked, although he could not swim. My mother would never let my brother or me borrow water wings or tyres or swimming pillows for fear they would float us over our depth and rubbish us to an early death. 'Learn to swim first,' was her stern motto. The little boy climbed off his tyre, bobbed and clung, and wouldn't share it. 'It's mine,' he reasonably said. Suddenly a cat's paw scuffed the water dark, he let go, and the pink, lifesaver-shaped tyre skimmed out of his grip. Loss widened his eyes; he began to cry. 'I'll get it,' I said, my bravado masking a fiery desire for a ride. I jumped with a sideflap of hands; my feet ceased to touch. I was in that forbidden country – 'over my head'. I should, according to Mother, have sunk like a stone, but I didn't. My chin was up, hands and feet milling the cold green. I caught the scudding tyre and swam in. I was swimming. I could swim.

The airport across the bay unloosed a blimp. It went up like a silver bubble, a salute.

That summer my uncle and his petite fiancée built a boat. My brother and I carried shiny nails. We woke to the tamp-tamp of the hammer. The honey-colour of the new wood, the white shavings (turned into finger rings) and the sweet dust of the saw were creating an idol, something beautiful – a real sailboat. From the sea my uncle brought back mackerel. Greeny-blue-black brocades unfaded, they came to the table. And we did live off the sea. With a cod's head and tail my grandmother could produce a chowder that set, when chilled, in its own triumphal jelly. We made suppers of buttery steamed clams and laid lines of lobster pots. But I never could watch my grandmother drop the dark green lobsters with their waving, wood-jammed claws into the boiling pot from which they would be, in a minute, drawn – red, dead and edible. I felt the awful scald of the water too keenly on my skin.

The sea, then, was our main entertainment. When company came, we set them before it on rugs, with thermoses and sandwiches and coloured umbrellas, as if the water – blue, green, grey, navy or silver as it might be – were enough to watch. The grown-ups in those days, still wore the Puritanical black bathing suits, redolent of salt and mothballs, that make our family snapshot albums so archaic.

My final memory of the sea is of violence – a still, unhealthily yellow day in 1938, the sea molten, steely-slick, heaving at its leash like a broody animal, evil violets in its eye. Anxious telephone calls crossed from my grandmother, on the exposed oceanside, to my mother, on the bay. My brother and I, knee-high still, imbibed the talk of tidal waves, high ground, boarded windows and floating boats like a miracle elixir. The hurricane was due at nightfall. In those days, hurricanes did not bud in Florida and bloom over Cape Cod each autumn as they now do – bang, bang, bang, frequent as firecrackers on the Fourth and whimsically named after women. This was a monstrous specialty, a leviathan. Our world might be eaten, blown to bits. We wanted to be in on it.

The sulphurous afternoon went black unnaturally early, as if what was to come could not be starlit, torchlit, looked at. The rain set in, one huge Noah douche. Then the wind. The world had become a drum. Beaten, it shrieked and shook. Pale and elate in our beds, my brother and I sipped our nightly Ovaltine. We would, of course, not sleep. We crept to a blind and hefted it a notch. On a mirror of rivery black our faces wavered like moths, trying to pry their way in. Nothing could be seen. The only sound was a howl, jazzed up by the bangs, slams, groans and splinterings of objects tossed like crockery in a giant's quarrel. The house rocked on its root. It rocked and rocked and rocked its two small watchers to sleep.

The wreckage the next day was all one could wish – overthrown trees and telephone poles, shoddy summer cottages bobbing out by the lighthouse and a litter of the ribs of little ships. My grandmother's house had lasted, valiant – though the waves broke right over the road and into the bay. My grandfather's seawall had saved it, neighbours said. Sand buried her furnace in golden whorls, salt stained the upholstered sofa and a dead shark filled what had been the geranium bed, but my grandmother had her broom out, it would soon be right.

And this is how it stiffens, my vision of that seaside childhood. My father died, we moved inland. Whereon those nine first years of my life sealed themselves off like a ship in a bottle – beautiful, inaccessible, obsolete, a fine, white flying myth.

PART III
SMITH COLLEGE PRESS BOARD

monthly meeting —
Day-school parent teacher's association
Dr. Gesell - before 6., children didn't develop cycles of
"Child Development"
Theme involves all of us. Infant, toddler, school child, adolescent, mom & dad, grandparents. Cycles overlap - create interesting situations accomodate better to overlay in cycles if we understand

Growth a concept to conjure with —
E. Dickinson — "can you teach me how to grow, or is it unconveyed like melody + witchcraft?" "Growth of man like growth of nature gravitates within, ... it stirs alone."

Withinness of growth — "gravitates" suggests universal law, gravity — as forces of growth should suggest — growth, like gravity came out of cosmos — all living things grow. Every newborn infant — focal endproduct of countless ages of evolution — endowed with prodigious powers of growth & many unknown potentials.

Says Capitalism May Save Asia

Written: 15 November 1951*
Published: *Daily Hampshire Gazette* (16 November 1951): 10

"Capitalism may save Asia," asserted Sir George Samson, director of the East Asian institute at Columbia, in his lecture on "Conflicts of Interest and Power in Asia" which concluded the Far Eastern lecture series at Smith College Wednesday evening.

"There is no irreconcilable clash of interest between Asia and the West," claimed Sir George, that could not be resolved through patience and conciliation.

Sir George went on to emphasize the urgency of organizing an ideological offensive of our own to combat the appeal of Communism in Asia. He also stressed the necessity of offering Asia our technical experience and resources to help her become industrialized. In this way we can gain an important influence over the minds of Asian men and at the same time guide the delayed development of the industrial revolution in Asia.

Sir George mentioned that one of the possible causes of misunderstanding between Asia and the Western world was the different standard of material life. "Poverty is inherent in the traditional agrarian economy of Asia," he pointed out. Western capitalism could bring about mutual advantages by offering Asia more positive help such as that given in the Point Four and Colombo Plans.

"The antagonism between the Soviet and the Western worlds is another hindrance to the solution of an otherwise soluble problem," Sir George stated. Thus we must not be deterred from aiding governments because they are socialist, for socialism has proved to be one of the most promising forces opposed to Communism today.

The role of Japan, Sir George continued, is a key to the strategy in Asia. Although Japan at present is relatively weak compared to the powerful states on the Asian mainland, she still has industrial strength. With strong backing, her military strength might be sufficient to maintain the balance of power in Eastern Asia.

Sir George concluded by saying that in spite of practical difficulties and fearful obstacles, collaboration between Asia and the Western world is possible if common interests are discovered, created, and pursued.

---

* Unattributed. SP's notes on the lecture are held by the Lilly Library. In SP's 1951 calendar, she wrote on 14 November: 'Lecture-8' and on the next day 'Press Board 9'.

Can Benefit by the Writing of the Satirists

Written: 20 November 1951*
Published: Daily Hampshire Gazette (21 November 1951): 3

The satirist hopes to improve society by exposing its vices and holding them up to ridicule, said Gilbert Highet, professor of classics at Columbia University, in a lecture Tuesday evening at Smith College.

"Satire is a separate form of writing," Prof. Highet explained, "though many forms of literature contain satirical qualities. The satire as a monologue is with us today in the form of newspaper columns written by men like Philip Wylie and Westbrook Pegler. The wildly distorted and exaggerated narrative was used by Swift in his *Gulliver's Travels*, while parody was used to perfection by Charles Dickens in books like the *Pickwick Papers*."

The author often makes fun of his audience, continued Prof. Highet, pointing out the stylistic devices employed by satirists. To shock the reader into remembering the message of the satire, the writer often includes obscenities and violence. Distortion is always present in satire, said Mr. Highet, and is many times emphasized by use of colloquial expressions.

Satire, stated the lecturer, usually produces a combination of laughter at the foolish person and hatred of the scoundrel, both of which imply a judgment on the morals of the times.

"The democracies," concluded Mr. Highet, "wince under the probing of satirists but if they are wise they will accept and benefit by it."

Smith Girls to Take Exams in Civil Service

Written: 4 December 1951†
Published: Daily Hampshire Gazette (5 December 1951): 3

Approximately a hundred Smith girls will take the annual civil service exams next Saturday at Sage Hall. At the present time there is an emergency need for top government employees and all qualified seniors have been urged to take

---

* Unattributed. SP's notes on the lecture are held by the Lilly Library.
† Unattributed. SP's notes for this article held by Lilly Library. In SP's 1951 calendar, she wrote on 4 December: 'Press Board Due.'

the exams. Every year the government examines thousands of applicants for these executive positions and places the high ranking candidates in intern programs in Washington, D.C.

Civil service exams are not the only way of entering government employment. Some intelligence agencies have special permission to make appointments outside of civil service, and twenty-five of last year's graduates from Smith College are working for these agencies at the present time.

'True Health' Lecture Topic at the College

Written: *c.*12 December 1951[*]
Published: *Daily Hampshire Gazette* (14 December 1951): 7

"True health is a state of mind apart from the condition or structure of the physical body," asserted Margaret Morrison of Boston in the Smith College Little Chapel this week in her lecture, "Christian Science: The Voice of Truth."

Miss Morrison illustrated the science of healing through the mind of selected readings from Mary Baker Eddy's Christian Science textbook, *Science and Health*. True health, according to Miss Morrison, is never affected by the illusions of the senses, or governed by so-called material laws. This concept of Christian Science is revealed in the scientific healing power as practiced by Jesus Christ.

At a time when a great part of the world believes that man depends on matter alone for life, health and sustenance, faith in joy, peace, intelligence, love and health come from the divine mind of God. These qualities, Miss Morrison continued, are indestructible and transcend the mere physical limitations of the flesh.

The higher mission of Christian Science, Miss Morrison further stated, is to redeem individuals from the illusive passions of the senses. This must be done by revealing to mankind the divine qualities which are the source and law of his being.

In this way, man will no longer be a slave of the body and its ills. He will come to understand that he is a spirit of God's creation, not a prisoner of the flesh. "It is this truth of Christian Science which will make us free," Miss Morrison concluded.

---

[*] Unattributed. SP's notes on the lecture are held by the Lilly Library. In SP's 1951 calendar, she wrote on 11 December: '7:45 Press Board.'

Says Music Can Illustrate Cultural Life of a Nation

Written: 15 January 1952*
Published: *Daily Hampshire Gazette* (17 January 1952): 8

"Music can illustrate the cultural life of a nation," asserted Waclaw Jedrzejewicz, associate professor of Russian at Wellesley College in his lecture "Literature and History Through Music" this week at Smith College. Mr. Jedrzejewicz illustrated his theme by playing six musical recordings. The first four selections were by Tchaikovsky, who Mr. Jedrzejewicz said expressed the Russian soul.

"The 1812 Overture," said the lecturer, could represent the same ideas as these represented by Leo Tolstoy in his novel *War and Peace*. The Orthodox Russia of peasants and gentry at the beginning of the overture changes suddenly as the War of 1812 begins and Napoleon's army nears. At the end, however, "we note the triumph of Russian orthodoxy and monarchy as we hear the solemn motif of the Russian national anthem 'God Save the Tsar.'" This music, declared Mr. Jedrzejewicz, emphasizes the importance of autocracy, orthodoxy, and nationalism in the Russian life of the time.

The next selection, "Marche Slave," claimed Mr. Jedrzejewicz, is a wonderful interpretation of the Russian state of mind and the political atmosphere during the Serbo-Turkish War of 1877. Here the current of Pan-Slavism is shown musically by the mingling of a Serbian melody with the Russian national anthem.

Tchaikovsky's Concert in D Major for Violin and orchestra was next on the program. "This music presents the chief characteristic of the Russian soul: a deep melancholy changing to gaiety," remarked Mr. Jedrzejewicz. This is the same "laughter through tears" which is often seen in Russian literature by Gogol, Chekhov, and others, he continued.

The speaker compared the fourth selection, Tchaikovsky's Symphony No. 6 in B Minor (Pathetique), to "works by Dostoev-† others where the tragic Russian soul is presented."

---

* Unattributed. SP's notes on the lecture are held by the Lilly Library. In SP's 1952 calendar, she wrote on 14 January: 'lecture – Sage' and on 15 January 'press Board ass. Due 9:00'.

† The printed article is missing at least one line at 'works by Dostoev- / others where the tragic . . .' Where SP mentions Dostoevsky in her lecture cover notes, she lists two additional authors: Pushkin and Turgenev.

Next, Mr. Jedrzejewicz played a Czechoslovakian piece by Bedrich Smetana, "My Country," to show the characteristic Slavic spirit of the author.

The final recording was Chopin's Polonaise in A Flat Major. "Polish music," affirmed the lecturer, "reflects the psyche of the Polish soul."

In conclusion, Mr. Jedrzejewicz said that he was practicing the theory that music reflects the culture of a nation at Wellesley College, where he gives musical sessions especially prepared to cover his course in Russian literature.

The lecture was followed by an informal reception at Hatfield Hall.

Universal Faith Has the Answer, Dr. Niebuhr Says

Written: 4 February 1952[*]
Published: *Springfield Union* (5 February 1952): 21

Northampton, Feb. 4—The present crisis offers an opportunity for faithfulness, was the assertion made tonight by Rev. Richard Niebuhr, professor of Christian ethics at Yale University, in his lecture "The Cultural Crisis," which opened the Religious Association forum at Smith College. The theme of the forum is "The Shaping of the Foundations."

"Our proper response," Rev. Niebuhr said, "is openness of mind and willingness to recognize the errors of the past. It is confidence in the fact that we are participants in a universal, meaningful, creative process which has life as its purpose."

Rev. Niebuhr went on to consider the aspect of the crisis. "Part of our uncertainty," he observed, "has to do with the world of faith. We realize that our planetary system is part of a minor one even in an infinite universe, and therefore we feel very small. In contrast," Rev. Niebuhr continued, "our own living space is contracting. There are no longer any frontiers left in the world."

"Another aspect of the cultural crisis," Rev. Niebuhr remarked, "is that the material world has grown unstable. Once we counted on the laws of nature, the clock of the universe, and now we are living in a world of chance.

"In comparison to the billions of years that time extends back in history, our lives seem once more contracted and our future small," Rev. Niebuhr said.

---

[*] Unattributed. SP's notes on the lecture are held by the Lilly Library. In SP's 1952 calendar, she wrote on 4 February: '8:00 Niebuhr – early – writeup phone to S. Union by 11 p.m.'

"There is the tension of the will to exist in the face of the nothingness that surrounds us. We fear to be forgotten in its finity."

"There are several means of dealing with this crisis," Rev. Niebuhr averred. First, one can assume a defensive attitude towards the old way of life which does not allow for any adjustments. In contrast there is the path of appeasement which yields to threats and lets things slide. Nihilism is the third approach to the crisis and it holds the absolute liberty of man to do what he pleases. This attitude was evident in Germany in the 1930s, he said.

"The answer that the forum will give to this crisis," he stated, "is the answer to the religious traditions of Judaism, Protestantism, and Catholicism."

"We are confronting a genuine threat," Rev. Niebuhr affirmed. "It is not the threat of chance, but the solid permanent structure of things. It involves realizing the new possibilities of infinite variety and the creative goodness which is the foundation of creation."

"We can only begin by being faithful to each other," he stated. "We have certain duties to ourselves, our parents, our country, and our neighbors.

"We go forward," Rev. Niebuhr concluded, "on the foundations of such faith."

'Crisis' Is Topic of Dr. Niebuhr in Northampton

Written: 5 February 1952[*]
Published: *Springfield Union* (6 February 1952): 21

Northampton, Feb. 5—"There is more personal crisis in our time because people are not vaccinated against personal crises. We try to make things easy for ourselves so that we won't have to face the question of the meaning of life."

So said the Rev. Richard Niebuhr, professor of Christian ethics at Yale Divinity School at Smith College tonight. His lecture, on the subject of "Personal Crisis" was the second in the annual religious forum conducted by the Smith College Religious Association.

"We have turned away from the idea that life is crisis and that we have got to meet crisis," Dr. Niebuhr asserted. "We have organized our skepticism about life's meaningfulness. We have organized our beliefs that man is after all a pretty petty little creature that can be satisfied with little things.

---

[*] Unattributed. SP telephoned her lecture cover to the *Springfield Union*. See letter to Aurelia Schober Plath, 6 February 1952, *The Letters of Sylvia Plath, Volume 1*: 411–12.

"We have lost our sense of participation in nature, and have substituted a mechanical supernaturalism for our social and personal supernaturalism."

Instead of seeing nature as a great brotherhood united by love, he explained, we see "numbers related to each other without value, parts of a mechanical thing related to each other by power."

Dr. Niebuhr said, "when we meet personal crisis we are no longer dealing with man's mind, we are dealing with individuality. In all personal crises there is a sense of the meaningfulness of life, a sense of self-deception, and a sense of inevitability.

"Those people who have come through personal crises, however, have in some way accepted reality and come to regard it as good," Dr. Niebuhr declared. "Where there is victory in personal crisis there is reconciliation and acceptance of reality. There is a socialization and the individual no longer feels himself alone. There is a feeling that life is victorious, that all things pass away, but all things become new."

This was the second lecture in a series sponsored by the Smith College Religious Association on "The Shaping of the Foundations." Dr. Niebuhr discussed "the cultural crisis" in a talk on Feb. 4. The forum will be continued tomorrow as Frank J. Sheed, president of Sheed and Ward Publishing Co. discusses "The resources of Roman Catholicism" and John A. Hutchison, professor of religion at Williams College speaks on "The resources of Protestantism." The final lecture in the series, "The resources of Judaism" will be given Thursday by Rabbi Arthur J. Lelyveld, national director of the B'nai B'rith Hillel.

Smith Students Have Service of Koffee Klatch

Written: 13 February 1952[*]
Published: *Daily Hampshire Gazette* (20 February 1952): 3

Between morning classes Smith girls are often seen hurrying from building to building with a donut in hand, or a cup of steaming coffee balanced along with an armload of books. The source of this morning snack is the Koffee Klatch, an indispensable Smith institution, which is located in Seelye Hall where many classes are held.

---

[*] Unattributed. SP's notes held by Lilly Library. In SP's 1952 calendar, she wrote on 13 February: 'feature write-up on Koffee Klatch due.'

The Koffee Klatch was operated as part of the Smith College seventy-fifth Anniversary Fund drive. Since 1950, when that anniversary was celebrated, the money raised by this snack bar has been given to Service Fund. The proceeds, almost $1,000 last year, are used for foreign student scholarships.

Margaret Kent, a junior from Berkeley, California, and head of the Koffee Klatch, explains that the food is obtained at wholesale rates from the merchants of Northampton. In an average day, twenty to twenty-five dozen donuts, eighteen dozen cookies, sixty cups of coffee in addition to milk, tomato juice, and brownies are sold. The Koffee Klatch is staffed by thirty volunteers who give an hour a week of their time in order to keep this popular institution going.

Dr. A. Gesell Gives Lecture for Day School PTA

Written: 1 March 1952[*]
Published: *Daily Hampshire Gazette* (3 March 1952): 16

"Every child has a unique pattern of growth which is the key to its individuality," asserted Dr. Arnold Gesell of the Gesell Institute of Child Development at New Haven, in his lecture "The Cycle of Child Development" sponsored by the Smith College Day School Parent–Teacher Association and presented at the college Friday evening.

"Every newborn infant," Dr. Gesell maintained, "is the focal end product of countless ages of evolution," and is endowed with vast powers of growth and many unknown potentials of both body and mind. "The development philosophy," explained Dr. Gesell, "sees the child in a vista of a long spiraling cycle of growth." This outlook gives parents an understanding and respect of the dignity of the growing personality which harmonizes with the spirit of democracy.

Dr. Gesell stated that he had had a rare opportunity to observe growth in both normal and abnormal children at the clinic of child development at Yale University School of Medicine. He illustrated his lecture with slides from the Yale photographic research library and a color film titled *The Embryology of Human Behavior*, which was based upon the work of the speaker and his associates at the Yale clinic.

In the film, Dr. Gesell, the narrator, traced the patterns of behavior in the

---

[*] Unattributed. SP's notes on the lecture are held by the Lilly Library. In SP's 1952 calendar, she wrote on 29 February: 'Child development lecture.'

child from its embryonic beginnings through early infancy and into the preschool years.

The film demonstrated the techniques used by the Yale clinic of child development to evoke behavior patterns revealing the normality of the child's action system. The behavior patterns of normal and deficient children at comparable ages were contrasted. Growth was proved to be a key concept for interpreting the nature and needs of all types of children, whether normal or handicapped.

Following the lecture an informal reception for Dr. Gesell was held at the day school.

'Heresy Hunts' Menace Liberty; Struik Claims

Written: 3 March 1952*
Published: *Springfield Union* (4 March 1952): 2

Northampton, March 3—"The attack on academic freedom is part of an attack on the civil liberties of American people as a whole," declared Dr. Dirk Jan Struik, lecturing at Smith College tonight on the subject of "Academic freedom and the trend toward conformity."

Dr. Struik, for twenty-five years a professor of mathematics at Massachusetts Institute of Technology, temporarily was discharged from the faculty this year, pending the outcome of a case brought against him by the State of Massachusetts, which charged him with teaching Marxism.

Dr. Struik said that attacks on academic freedom in many American colleges threaten all levels of the population, farmers, clerks, workers, and scientists as well as teachers. "Politicians have tried to throw me out in the hopes that it will frighten others into conformity," he said.

"All these heresy hunts make the university suffer, in the sense that the heresy hunts affect the very purpose for which the university was founded—for the search of truth and the betterment of man's physical and spiritual welfare," Dr. Struik concluded.

---

* Unattributed. SP's notes on the lecture are held by the Lilly Library. In SP's 1952 calendar, she wrote on 3 March: 'cover Struik lecture – 7:45 Browsing Room.'

Life University Second Program Slated Sunday

Written: 6 March 1952*
Published: *Springfield Union* (7 March 1952): 30

Northampton, March 6—Rev. Dr. David Roberts, dean of the Union Seminary in New York City, will be guest speaker at the second of six University of Life programs, Sunday night. His talk will be given in John M. Greene Hall at a joint session of University of Life registrants and Smith College students.

The adult courses will be conducted in the First Methodist Church and supper will be served by women of St. John's Episcopal Church. Supper will be at five fifteen, the classes at six and the worship period in John M. Greene Hall from seven to eight. The courses for young people will be in St. John's Episcopal Church with the subject "Hosea, the Prophet of God's Love."

Rev. Mr. Roberts Will Be Vespers Speaker

Written: 6 March 1952†
Published: *Daily Hampshire Gazette* (7 March 1952): 6

The Rev. David Roberts, professor of philosophy and religion at the Union Theological Seminary, will speak on "The Grandeur and Misery of Man" at the Smith College Sunday vespers, at seven in John M. Greene Hall.

Mr. Roberts, who has spoken at Smith before, specializes in the fields of theology, psychiatry, and existentialism. Much of his time is devoted to writing, and he is the author of the book titled *Psychotherapy and a Christian View of Man*. Last year, at the Colgate Rochester Divinity School, he gave a series of lectures which will be published in book form.

Mr. Roberts is a graduate of the Occidental College in California and of the Union Theological Seminary. He received his Ph.D. from Edinburgh, and for ten years was dean of the Union Theological Seminary.

---

* Unattributed. SP's notes on the event held by Lilly Library. In SP's 1952 calendar, she wrote on 6 March: 'Vespers advance due.' Two articles were published and both are included here.

† Unattributed. SP's notes on the event held by Lilly Library. In SP's 1952 calendar, she wrote on 6 March: 'Vespers advance due.' Two articles were published and both are included here.

Misery of Man Is Due to His Defects

Written: 10 March 1952*
Published: *Daily Hampshire Gazette* (11 March 1952): 5

"In Christ we are made aware of the misery of man when separated from God and the grandeur of man when restored to God," declared Rev. David Everett Roberts, professor of the philosophy of religion at Union Theological Seminary in New York, in his vespers sermon Sunday evening at Smith College.

Christianity, as the 17th-century philosopher Pascal said, bids man to recognize that he is vile and yet tells him that he should aspire to be like God. The modern view, according to Mr. Roberts, splits man into the "innocent automaton," who is the victim and not the doer of evil, and the "amazing potential godling," who is capable of directing a just, stable civilization if only he can trust himself enough.

The modern refusal to admit that man is vile arises from the confidence in human possibilities and a faith in the power of science to control nature and human affairs, the speaker explained. Our modern age has not avoided delusions of grandeur, however, by seeing no need to be like God. If men don't worship the Almighty, they will worship at the shrine of some leader, party, or system.

The refusal of governments of the East and West to admit guilt stems from a religious defect of contrition, claimed Mr. Roberts. "We as peoples have lost touch with the strength of genuine repentance and the dreadful courage of looking at our policies in the light of God's righteousness. We should acknowledge our own violences in the sphere of international relations."

"Only by recognizing the evil in himself can man find compassion for others," concluded the speaker. Men must first become brothers in mutual contrition before they can become brothers in trust.

---

* Unattributed. SP's notes on the lecture are held by the Lilly Library. In SP's 1952 calendar, she wrote on 9 March: 'vespers cover 7:00 J. M. Greene.'

Marxism Seeks to Replace God, Lecturer Says

Written: 12 March 1952[*]
Published: *Springfield Union* (13 March 1952): 30

Northampton, March 12—"The main tendency of Marxism is to make man the center of everything, to replace God with what Marxists call the ultimate reality—matter," said Prof. Max Salvadori, associate professor of history at Smith College tonight in a lecture, "The Rise of Modern Communism."

Prof. Salvadori spoke at Smith College on "Marxism and Religious Beliefs," in the second of a series on "Modern Thought and Religious Belief," sponsored by Hillel Foundation, an organization of Jewish students on campus.

Prof. Salvadori explained that the eighteenth-century French materialism became one of the main bases of Marx's "intellectual system." "Marxists denied the existence of God and tried to destroy organized religion because they maintained that, through proper use of reason, man can understand everything in the universe," he said.

"Although they sincerely believed that they were going to free mankind by destroying the concept of God, the Marxists discovered that as they destroyed one religion, they had to create another. Materialism could not explain everything," Prof. Salvadori declared.

In the search for security, Marxism has developed a myth which has its prophets, law-givers, clergy, and ritual, "all the paraphernalia of religion which the Marxists had rejected."

"Can this religion survive?" Prof. Salvadori asked. "The religion which is nothing else but form and not substance, which is a ritual without the soul that is required to keep religion alive, is not going to live a long time," Prof. Salvadori answered. "The day will come when people will ask, 'where is the salvation we have been promised on earth?' and this will weaken considerably the Marxist belief," the lecturer concluded.

---

[*] Unattributed. SP's notes on the lecture are held by the Lilly Library. In SP's 1952 calendar, she wrote on 12 March: '7–10 Cover Salvadori lecture.'

Smith Hears Frost in Muse and Views

Written: 10 April 1952*
Published: *Springfield Union* (10 April 1952): 31

Northampton, April 9—Robert Frost read his poetry and discussed his ideas to a capacity audience at Smith College tonight. Invited to present a lecture for the benefit of SCADS, a college scholarship drive, Mr. Frost spoke of the world, its confusion, and its problems.

"People say that it is strange for me to write poetry in a materialistic and confused country," he said. "But look at the encouragement we poets receive—this audience, for example."

Mr. Frost insisted on the simplicity of most of his poetry. He said he thinks that people "read things into his lines that are startling and terrible." The poet recited "Stopping by Woods on a Snowy Evening."

"What does it mean?"

"I simply mean that the woods are very lovely."

Frost Presents Poetry Readings

Written: 10 April 1952†
Published: *Daily Hampshire Gazette* (11 April 1952): 12

Robert Frost, well-known American poet, presented a varied selection of readings in a benefit lecture sponsored by the Smith College annual drive for scholarships at Smith College, Wednesday evening.

The poet-interpreter of New England entertained his audience with representative readings from his own poetry, spicing his talk with anecdotes and shrewd observations of the contemporary scene.

Among the themes running through his work, Frost stated, was the question of "who we are and what we are." He illustrated his point by reading "The Star-Splitter," a poem concerning a man who bought a telescope "to

---

* Unattributed. SP's notes on the lecture are held by the Lilly Library. In SP's 1952 calendar, she wrote on 10 April: 'Lecture cover due.' Two articles were published and both are included here.
† Unattributed. SP's notes on the lecture are held by the Lilly Library. In SP's 1952 calendar, she wrote on 10 April: 'Lecture cover due.' Two articles were published and both are included here.

satisfy a life-long curiosity about our place among the infinities."

Robert Frost read the prophetic words "It looked as if a night of dark intent was coming, and not only a night, an age," from his poem "Once by the Pacific," and revealed that they were written previous to the two world wars.

In "The Gift Outright," Frost said that he had presented the history of the revolution in a few lines of blank verse. Here, the love of country is expressed by a salvation of faith, a surrender to the land. "Such as she was, such as she would become."

Among the best-known poems, Frost read the lyric "Stopping by Woods on a Snowy Evening," "The Road Not Taken," "Birches," "Mending Wall," and "West-Running Brook."

In conclusion, Frost read "Departmental," or "The Death of My Ant Jerry," a frankly comic tale, and "A Considerable Speck" where he announced, with a twinkle in his eye, that the poet was glad to find "on any sheet the least display of mind."

Smith College

Written: 17 April 1952[*]
Published: *Daily Hampshire Gazette* (18 April 1952): 13

A fairy wand, a magic slipper, and a sparkling pumpkin coach, otherwise known as a "car," will appear this coming weekend when the juniors at Smith College become modern Cinderellas at their long-anticipated junior prom.

The highlight of a weekend of planned activities, the junior promenade will be held Saturday evening from 9 until the stroke of midnight at Scott Gymnasium, Smith College. Music will be played by Herb Sulkin's orchestra, and intermission entertainment will be provided by the O's and B's, a singing group from Yale University.

The storybook theme of Cinderella will be carried out through the decorations. A magic slipper prize, but not of glass, will be awarded to the lucky Cinderella whose foot fits the traditional shoe.

Under the general chairmanship of Miss Virginia Rutledge, a junior from Louisville, Ky., the entire prom weekend offers a variety of festivities. On Friday night the juniors will have a chance to dine and dance at the Club 53 in the

---

[*] Unattributed. In SP's 1952 calendar, she wrote on 17 April: 'Press Board – Jr. Prom Story.'

Hotel Northampton. Miss Phyllis Penney, from Wilmette, Ill., has been named as chairman for the dinner-dance.

Miss Katharine Davies, from Chicago, Ill., has planned the garden party, which will be held at Laura Scales and Franklin King houses on campus Saturday afternoon preceding the promenade. Finally, rounding out the weekend, is a picnic at Look Memorial Park and a jazz concert at Davis Student Center on Sunday afternoon.

Ogden Nash's Rhyming Knack Makes Up for His Talent Lack

Written: 1 May 1952*
Published: *Springfield Union* (1 May 1952): 30

Northampton, April 30—"I came here tonight to enjoy the very real pleasure of talking about myself," Ogden Nash, well-known poet and author, told an enthusiastic audience at Smith College tonight in John M. Greene Hall.

Mr. Nash, who was invited to speak for the benefit of the Smith College annual drive for scholarships, admitted that he defined himself as the "candy is dandy, but liquor is quicker" kind of man.

"These lines were written in my unregenerate days and they are the only two lines of my poetry that I do not fully understand," he confessed. "I read them for the first time in Evanston, Ill., but at the time I didn't realize that temperance leaders would be celebrating their 75th anniversary," he added.

Mr. Nash remarked that he had no political or social message to relate because, "My life happens to have been a purely personal one." Mr. Nash brought the audience up to date on his biography. He described himself as having reached middle age and then explained that he knew that he had reached this period of life because one of his daughters had admonished him for getting thin on top and the other had sadly informed him that he was getting thick around the middle.

Mr. Nash quoted from his early poetry that he wrote when he was "a nasty tot." After mentioning that he had been at Harvard for one year, he described

---

* Unattributed. SP's notes on the lecture are held by the Lilly Library. In SP's 1952 calendar, she wrote on 30 April: 'Ogden Nash: 8:00 – cover.' Two articles were published and both are included here.

his job at a publishing house. During his tenure of office there, Mr. Nash said that he had read a fantastic amount of bad poetry that was submitted to the editors.

After six or seven years, he concluded that he was an expert on the subject of bad poetry. "I wondered what would happen," the speaker said, "if someone who knew the rules of poetry broke the rules consciously. It would be both bad and funny at the same time," he said.

Although Mr. Nash declared that he had a lack of talent, he said that he had a knack for rhyming and versification. "The knack is nothing special," he said. "It's the same thing as having a knack for making a four spade vulnerable bid in bridge."

Mr. Nash told how he submitted his literary efforts to several editors and met with luck, which he claims is an invaluable asset. "After receiving a letter from the *New Yorker* encouraging me to continue my minor maulings of the mother tongue," Mr. Nash said, "I decided that I would continue to persuade the English language to adjust itself to me, instead of adjusting myself to the English language."

Mr. Nash concluded his talk by quoting from what he called a "helter-skelter assortment" of poems. They provided another equally amusing source of details on the life of the poet.

Ogden Nash Is Speaker

Written: 1 May 1952[*]
Published: *Daily Hampshire Gazette* (2 May 1952): 6

"I was born a nasty tot with an ambition to write," said Ogden Nash in his lecture at Smith College last Wednesday evening. Well-known writer of unique light verse, Mr. Nash entertained his audience with humorous anecdotes and readings from his verse, which has appeared in leading magazines such as the *New Yorker*. Spicing his talk with amusing incidents about his life, which he considers "a purely personal one," the speaker remarked that he had always been able to express himself more effectively in doggerel than in prose.

---

[*] Unattributed. SP's notes on the lecture are held by the Lilly Library. In SP's 1952 calendar, she wrote on 30 April: 'Ogden Nash: 8:00 – cover.' Two articles were published and both are included here.

As a writer, Mr. Nash claimed he needed something more than his "simple lack of talent." Luck was provided by the fact that the *New Yorker* was a young magazine open for newcomers when Mr. Nash began sending in his verse. Encouraged by the *New Yorker*, which requested more of his "minor maulings of the mother tongue," Ogden Nash set his feet on "the long winding path through eleven volumes of verse."

Smith Library Displaying 'Fanny Fern Collection'

Written: *c.*4 May 1952[*]
Published: *Daily Hampshire Gazette* (5 May 1952): 8

"The Fanny Fern Collection," a recent addition to the Sophia Smith collection of books, pamphlets, letters, and photographs, now on display at the William Allan Neilson Library, Smith College, reflects the "current interest in the subject of women in history and their many contributions to society." Presented to the college by James Parton, grandson of Mrs. Sara Willis Parton, who wrote under the pseudonym "Fanny Fern," the collection includes letters from family, friends, such as Harriet Beecher Stowe; contracts with publishers of her books; and a volume of the *New York Ledger*, which contains her "Fern Leaves" column.

The exhibition marks the Tenth Anniversary of the Sophia Smith collection, which has gathered throughout the years records of the part women have played in the history of the world and the development of civilization. Named in honor of the founder of Smith College, the collection is a special project of the Society of Friends of Smith College Library, which was inaugurated by President Herbert Davis in 1942, and which has grown from a membership of 125 alumnae to over a thousand contributors within the last 10 years.

---

[*] Unattributed. SP's notes on the event held by Lilly Library.

15 Area Girls to Graduate from Smith College June 9

Written: *c.*12 May 1952
Published: *Daily Hampshire Gazette* (27 May 1952): 9

Four hundred and fifty-three Bachelor of Arts degrees will be conferred at the 74th Smith College Commencement exercises on June 9. Sir Oliver Franks, British ambassador to the United States, will be the commencement speaker. Graduation, which will be held out of doors in the Quadrangle, will be the climax of a weekend of activities which includes a baccalaureate service on June 8 and the traditional Ivy Day ceremonies on June 7.*

Miss Judith Atwater was a member of WCSR, the student-owned and operated Smith College radio station, for three years, and in her senior year she was her house representative of St. John's Church student chapter. She majored in education, and plans to attend the Yale School of Nursing after graduation.

Miss Margaret Berry, a graduate of Northampton High School, majored in psychology. She was the Hampshire House senior class representative, and a member of the Pan-American Club for three years. In her freshman and sophomore years she was a member of her class choirs.

Miss Alice Ann Dunn, also an alumna of the Northampton High School, majored in English. She was on the Dean's list for four years and a first group Dwight Morrow scholar in her junior year. In her sophomore year she was publicity director of Newman Club, and in her senior year she was elected to Phi Beta Kappa.

Miss Janett Louise Forsander, an English major, prepared for college at Northampton High School, and plans to teach English in secondary school after graduation. She was president of Hampshire House in her senior year, and a member of Newman Club for four years. She was also on the advertising staff of the *Campus Cat* humor magazine.

Miss Elizabeth B. King graduated from Northampton High School and majored in chemistry. She plans to work in the research laboratories of the American Cyanamid Company in Stamford, Conn., after graduation. In her senior year she was president of Franklin King House and will be chairman of outdoor Ivy Day at commencement. In her junior year she was business

---

* A long list of students, parents and addresses follows in the original text, redacted here.

manager for the *Freshman Handbook* and one of the junior ushers who carry the ivy chain at commencement. She was in the Glee Club her last two years.

Miss Martha E. Longpre majored in government and is an alumna of Northampton High School. She was on the Dean's list her senior year, and on the decorations committee for senior promenade. She was on the advertising staff of *Current*, a weekly student newspaper, and her house representative to curriculum committee, and undergraduate group which acts as liaison between the faculty and students in matters concerning the course of study.

Miss Eileen M. Maher, who majored in Spanish, graduated from the Northampton High School and will receive a commission in the Marine Corps after graduation. She was a member of Newman Club for four years and on the Dean's list in her junior year.

Miss Mary Elizabeth McBreen majored in education and will teach in West Hartford, Conn., after graduation. She was on the Dean's list for four years and a member of Newman Club for four years. In her junior year she was editor of *Who's Who in 1954* and president of Hampshire House for the second half of the year. In her senior year she was head of the children's department in the community service program at the People's Institute sponsored by the Religious Association.

Miss Martha Morrell majored in zoology and in her senior year was the program chairman for the Biology Club. She was on the Dean's list in her junior and senior years.

Miss Doris May O'Brien graduated from the Northampton High School and majored in education and child study. She was a member of Newman Club for four years.

Miss Muriel Irene Post majored in sociology at Smith, for which she prepared at the Northampton High School. She was a member of her house council in her sophomore year and her class representative from the house in that year. She was a member of the Christian Association, and on the Dean's list in her sophomore year.

Miss Anne Robinson is an alumna of the Northampton School for Girls and majored in music. In her freshman year she was president of the freshman choir, and in her sophomore year she was elected to the musical Clef Club. In her senior year she was the publicity manager of Clef Club and treasurer of the Glee Club.

Mrs. Robert S. Wicks, the former Miss Barbara Bruce, majored in art at Smith and graduated from the Northampton School for Girls. She was in her class choirs in her first two years and in the Glee Club her junior and senior years. In her freshman year she was the freshman representative from Washburn House.

Miss Elizabeth Yates prepared for college at the Northampton School for Girls and majored in sociology at Smith.

Miss Tatiana N. Glaskovsky, an art major, is an alumna of the Northampton School for Girls. She was elected to Alpha Phi Kappa Psi, an honorary society which recognizes talent and creative ability in the arts.

Smith Freshman Given Welcome

Written: 27 September 1952*
Published: *Springfield Daily News* (29 September 1952): 22

Northampton, Sept. 29—Blue skies and clear autumn weather heralded the annual freshman day held at Smith College Saturday, when a special welcome to the incoming class of 1956 was extended, and returning alumnae and pre college guests were also entertained.

Saturday morning activities for the guests included a chance to attend classes and to view the exhibit on "calligraphic and geometric art" in the Tryon Art Gallery, as well as two exhibits at the William Allan Neilson Library entitled "Smith Opens and Develops into a Four Class College, 1875–1879," and "Women of Japan Today," from the Sophia Smith collection.

Freshmen were escorted to their activities by their upper class advisers, and class teams gave demonstrations of soccer, hockey, volleyball, archery, and golf. Tennis matches followed on the exhibition courts, and there was a round of freshmen interhouse softball games.

Crew races on Paradise Pond were followed by a picnic supper on the banks of the pond, and the day's celebration ended with a Step Sing at Students' Building.

---

* Unattributed. In SP's 1952 calendar, she wrote on 27 September: 'feature on Freshman Day.' An unattributed, advance article appeared as 'Smith College Freshman Day Slated Today', *Springfield Union* (27 September 1952): 23. It is unclear if SP wrote it and is therefore not included.

Freshmen at Smith Will Meet Local Ministers

Ts,* 30 September 1952, Smith College

Northampton, October 1—Smith College Freshman will have the opportunity to meet the ministers of the Northampton churches at a tea given by the Smith College Christian Association on Thursday afternoon, October 2nd, at the Religious Center, 7 College Lane. Clergymen present will include the Reverend Mr. David Cochran of the Episcopal Church, the Reverends Mr. Byron Whipple and Mr. Benjamin Andrews of the two Congregational Churches, the Reverend Mr. Bernard Graves of the Methodist Church, the Reverend Mr. Nathaniel Lauriat of the Unitarian Church, and the Reverend Mr. Gerhard Leverenz of the Lutheran Church in Easthampton.

Miss Virginia Davidson, a senior from Miami Beach, Florida, and President of the Smith College Christian Association, and the members of the cabinet of the Christian Association will be hostesses at the tea.

Can Rent Reproductions

Ts,† 2 October 1952, Smith College

Northampton, October 2—Among the bargains offered Smith College students upon their return to Northampton is the chance to rent framed reproductions of masterpieces at the Hillyer Art Gallery. The pictures vary in size and are representative of all schools of painting. Ranging from Japanese mats and black-and-white etchings to full-color landscapes and portraits, they include works of Degas, Rouault, Marin, Picasso, and Grandma Moses.

Students who browse through the Art Lending Collection are sure to find at least one reproduction to their liking. Calculated to fit into the limited student budgets, the rental fees for the pictures range from a quarter to a few dollars a year.

---

* The Smith College Archives holds a press release typescript with SP's name typed on it. According to SP's 1952 calendar, on 30 September 1952 she noted 'RA <Religious Association> writeup due'. Title assigned from one of the two articles published: 'Freshmen at Smith Will Meet Local Ministers', *Daily Hampshire Gazette* (1 October 1952): 9, and a shorter version: 'Freshmen to Greet Pastors of Churches', *Springfield Daily News* (1 October 1952): 32.
† The Smith College Archives holds a press release typescript with SP's name typed on it. Title is from published article: 'Can Rent Reproductions', *Daily Hampshire Gazette* (2 October 1952): 15.

Smith Events

Ts,* 2 October 1952, Smith College

Northampton, October 2—Celebrating the happy completion of the harvest, and the never-interrupted sojourn of men under God's wing, the Hillel Foundation of Smith College will commemorate the ancient Hebrew holiday of Succoth on Friday evening, October 3, in the Religious Center. Rabbi Louis Ruchames, advisor to the Hillel group, will speak on "A Festival of Joy and Hope."

Covering a period of nine days, Succoth is also called the festival of the Tabernacles. Simchat Torah, the final day of the holiday, symbolizes the rejoicing in the completion of the yearly reading of the Bible, and the re-beginning in the Synagogue of the annual cycle of the reading of the five books of Moses. In accord with the traditional spirit of rejoicing in the end of the harvest season, and the beginning of a new year, the Religious Center will be decorated with fruits of all varieties.

Faith Groups Open Center

Ts,† 6 October 1952, Smith College

Northampton, October 6—This year, for the first time, Smith students have a central location for their Religious Association on campus. The attractive white house at 7 College Lane has been redecorated and converted into a Religious Center for the whole college, meeting a long-felt need for a unified headquarters to coordinate Association activities.

Situated at the top of the hill overlooking Paradise Pond, the newly furnished Center has a comfortable and dignified decor. On the first floor there are three main rooms: two living rooms for meetings, teas, and informal gatherings, and a kitchen, available for the preparation of refreshments for receptions.

---

* The Smith College Archives holds a press release typescript with SP's name typed on it. Title assigned from one of the two articles published: 'Smith Events', *Daily Hampshire Gazette* (2 October 1952): 15, and a shorter version: 'Succoth Service', *Springfield Daily News* (2 October 1952): 32.

† The Smith College Archives holds a press release typescript with SP's name typed on it. Title assigned from one of the two articles published: 'Faith Groups Open Center', *Springfield Daily News* (6 October 1952): 26, and a shorter version: 'Central Spot for Religion Groups at Smith', *Daily Hampshire Gazette* (7 October 1952): 16.

Upstairs is the office of the new Chaplain, Rev. Stephen Crary, where every student is invited to drop in for counsel or conversation during office hours or by special appointment.

One of the distinctive features of the Center is the library where every student in the college is free to come and browse. Here are collected the libraries of the three fellowship groups: Newman Club, Hillel, and Christian Association. Recent books in the field of religion will be added gradually under the guidance of faculty advisors.

Among the activities which will be held at the center during the year are Religious Association discussion groups, club meetings, teas, and receptions for the visiting speakers after Sunday vespers. A bulletin board in the front hall will greet the interested student visitor with a complete calendar of Religious Association events so that she may find out when the various groups meet and what their specific activities are.

Community service is one of the most important projects of the Religious Association. Every year a large group of Smith students put their faith into action by doing volunteer work for the social agencies in Northampton. At the Cooley Dickinson Hospital, students serve as nurses' aides, and they assist with recreational therapy and entertainment at both the Veterans' Hospital and the Northampton State Hospital. Those interested in children may work at the Community "Y," the Children's Home, or the People's Institute, where they teach afternoon classes. Adult evening classes at the Institute are conducted by Smith volunteers. Students also participate in the Red Cross Blood Program and the annual T.B. Christmas Seal Drive.

Now that the Religious Association has an actual "home," it is felt that interaction between worship and community service will be stronger than before.

Smith Outing Club Will Bike to Hatfield

Ts,[*] 15 October 1952, Smith College

October 15—Members of the Outing Club at Smith College will bicycle to the Smith College cabins in the vicinity of Hatfield for a weekend of cookouts,

---

[*] The Smith College Archives holds a press release typescript with SP's name typed on it. Title assigned from published article: 'Smith Outing Club Will Bike To Hatfield', *Springfield Daily News* (15 October 1952): 32. In SP's 1952 calendar, she wrote on 14 October: 'writeup on Outing Club due.'

song fests, and hiking parties beginning Saturday, October 19.

Designed to sponsor hale and hearty events like this throughout the year, the Outing Club opened its activities this fall by participating in a gala weekend at Lake George last Saturday and Sunday. Over three hundred students from outing clubs at other colleges combined for a weekend of canoeing, camping, hiking, and mountain climbing.

On the agenda for the coming year, the Outing Club will sponsor intercollegiate square dances, a Sunday out at Amherst, a trip to the Yale Engineering Camp near Old Lyme, Conn., and ski weekends at nearby resorts.

Outing Club activities are open to every Smith student and are planned and directed by a group of twenty-five Board members. Officers of the club this year are as follows: President, Hazel Burton, a senior from Wayzata, Minn.; Vice President, Ann Brooks, a senior from Needham, Mass., and Intercollegiate Secretary, Elizabeth Haddock, a junior from Manchester, NH.

Varied Religious and Cultural Program Planned for Smith College Students

Ts,[*] 16 October 1952, Smith College

Northampton, October 17—A varied program of religious and cultural services is being provided for local students by the Smith College Hillel Foundation.

A series of four lectures dealing with Religious Thought and the Dilemma of Modern Man is planned for the semester. The first of the monthly lectures was held last Monday when Professor James A. Martin, Jr., of the Amherst College Religion Department addressed an open meeting in the Browsing Room of the Smith College Library.

Future lectures include an address on November 5 by Carl Cohn entitled "Philosophy of Reason in Medieval Jewish Thought." Mr. Cohn, Director of math refresher courses at Harvard University, has written several papers on Hebrew grammar as well as having taught at Wheaton, Radcliffe, and Harvard.

On December 4, a lecture on Spinoza is planned and on February 25 the

---

[*] The Smith College Archives holds a press release typescript with SP's name typed on it. Title assigned from one of the two articles published: 'Varied Religious And Cultural Program Planned For Smith College Students', *Daily Hampshire Gazette* (17 October 1952): 6, and 'Lectures Arranged by Hillel Foundation', *Springfield Daily News* (17 October 1952): 32.

noted Jewish author, Will Herberg, is scheduled to speak on "Judaism in Modern Life."

The Smith College Hillel Foundation is also presenting a series of fortnightly Sabbath Evening Services. On October 31, Ralph S. Harlow, professor of Religion at Smith, will speak on the topic "Various Philosophies Facing Youth Today." The Chaplain of Smith, Stephen T. Crary, will address the group on November 14, while Rabbi Louis Ruchames will give a sermon on the Kibbutz in Israel this Friday evening at 7:15 p.m. in the Religious Association Center.

Further Hillel activities include a Dance and Brunch on November 8–9, visits to various communities in this area, and classes in Hebrew, Yiddish, and basic Jewish beliefs.

First Recital at Smith College Is Sunday at 8:30

Ts,[*] 23 October 1952, Smith College

Northampton, October 24—The first recital in the Sunday evening series by members of the department of music of Smith College will be given in Sage Hall, Sunday, October 26, at 8:30 p.m., by Miss Louise Rood, violinist, and John Duke, pianist and composer. This recital for violin and piano will present one of Mr. Duke's own compositions and three sonatas by Pergolesi, Mozart, and Brahms.

The program will open with the rarely heard First Sonata in G major by the early eighteenth-century Italian composer, Pergolesi. This sonata is known as one of the finest examples of rich melodic writing especially for violin. This will be followed by the C major Sonata K. 296 of Mozart, an example of the development of the later eighteenth-century writing for piano and violin. The Brahms G major Sonata op. 78 brings out the full sonority of both the piano and violin.

Mr. Duke's Fantasy in A minor, an early work composed in 1936, is a favorite among violinists because of its range of melody and its brilliant rhythmic passages.

The Sunday evening recitals are open to the public without charge.

---

[*] The Smith College Archives holds a press release typescript with SP's name typed on it. Title assigned from one of the two articles published: 'First Recital At Smith College Is Sunday At 8:30', *Daily Hampshire Gazette* (24 October 1952): 15, and a shorter version: 'First Recital Sunday', *Springfield Daily News* (24 October 1952): 30.

Smith College Holds Clinic

Ts,* 23 October 1952, Smith College

Northampton, October 24—Connecticut high school teachers of physical education will collaborate with the physical education instructors of the Smith College department of physical education at the annual sports clinic, Saturday, October 25 at the college.

The program will consist of sessions of rhythmic gymnastics, volleyball technique and training, speedball officiating and playing, and folk and square dancing. Miss Dorothy Ainsworth, director of the Smith College physical education department, and Miss Doris Hinson, Miss Marjorie Harris, and Miss Phyllis Ocker, of the same department, will direct these activities, while other teachers participate in them.

The clinic was initiated six years ago at the request of the Connecticut state organization of physical education teachers for the purpose of learning new ideas and methods of teaching athletics in its schools.

At the close of each session, the teachers choose the sports they would like to emphasize at the sports clinic the following year. Swimming, tennis, basketball, badminton, hockey, soccer, and modern dance have been the activities of the clinic during its six years of existence.

Friday evening, the members of the sports clinic will have dinner at Wiggins Tavern.

Cheers, Jeers Promised for Smith Game

Ts,† 26 October 1952, Smith College

Northampton, October 27—Cheers and jeers will spur the student and faculty teams on to victory at the Student–Faculty soccer game, Tuesday, October 28, at 4 p.m. at the Smith College Athletic Field.

---

* The Smith College Archives holds a press release typescript with SP's name typed on it. Title assigned from one of the two articles published: 'Smith College Holds Clinic', *Daily Hampshire Gazette* (24 October 1952): 17, and 'Sports Clinic at Smith', *Springfield Daily News* (24 October 1952): 30.

† The Smith College Archives holds a press release typescript with SP's name typed on it. Title

Dating as far back as soccer records go—to 1937—the annual soccer contest has inspired members of both teams to demonstrate their soccer skill at the "off the record" game.

Fighting for the faulty are: George Swinton, instructor in art and captain of the team; David Coffin, instructor in Classics; Stephen T. Crary, assistant professor of Religion and Chaplain of Smith; Deming Hoyt, instructor in education; Jacob Rietszema, Plant physiologist; Klemens von Klemperer, assistant professor of history; Theodore Kazanoff, instructor in the theatre department; William Campbell, Horticulturist; William F. May, instructor in Religion; James L. McPherson, instructor in sociology; Donald S. Sheehan, assistant professor of history; Robert P. Creed, instructor in English; Wendell S. Johnson, instructor in English; James H. Durbin, Jr., instructor in English, and Daniel Aaron, associate professor in English.

Upholding the students will be the following seniors at Smith: Miss Margaret F. Allyn of Framingham Center, Mass.; Miss Anabel Carey of Denver, Colo.; Miss Mary F. Morrison of Reading, Pa.; Miss Florence Treadwell of Obispo, Cal.; Miss Holly Blanton, of Irvington, NY; Miss Gayle Walter of San Mateo, Cal.; Miss Julie Jones of Rochester, NY; Miss Jeanie Clark of Farmington, Ct.; Miss Ann Watson of Mamaroneck, NY; Miss Ann Roesing of Glencoe, Ill.; and Miss Isabel Brown of Houston, Texas.

Week-End Dance

Ts,* 6 November 1952, Smith College

Northampton, November 7—A dance and breakfast this weekend at the Fieldhouse have been planned by the Smith College Hillel group as their first social function of the year. The dance will be held Saturday evening and breakfast Sunday morning. Members of Hillel groups from several neighboring men's colleges have been invited to join in the program.

---

assigned from one of the two articles published: 'Cheers, Jeers Promised for Smith Game', *Daily Hampshire Gazette* (27 October 1952): 8, and 'Smith Girls Will Get Chance to Jeer Faculty', *Springfield Daily News* (27 October 1952): 30.

* The Smith College Archives holds a press release typescript with SP's name typed on it. Title assigned from one of the two articles published: 'Week-End Dance', *Daily Hampshire Gazette* (7 November 1952): 5, and 'Hillel Group Plans First Social Function', *Springfield Daily News* (7 November 1952): 32.

With dancing and refreshments, the "Fall Fling" will last from eight p.m. to twelve a.m., under the direction of the Social Chairman, Miss Marianne Mosbacher, a sophomore of Forest Hills, New York. The breakfast, featuring bagels and lox, will be from 10 a.m. to 12 noon. A couple from Northampton will perform several folk dances as part of the breakfast entertainment program.

During the fall, members of Hillel have participated in joint religious services with Hillel of Amherst College each week and have also sponsored lectures and discussions, held periodically in the college library. Miss Lois B. Sitrin, a senior, of Utica, New York, is this year's president.

Smith Provides Writing Clinic

Written: *c.*8 November 1952[*]
Published: *Springfield Sunday Republican* (9 November 1952): 10D

Northampton, Nov. 8—The Writing Clinic at Smith College is a voluntary educational aid designed to provide free tutorial service for any of the 2,266 Smith College students who need help in written English. The three members of the committee on written English offer instruction through individual conferences.

Students who are having trouble with organization or expression in prepared papers or examinations are sent to the clinic by members of the faculty of their class deans. Some attend voluntarily. Instruction is based on a particular examination or paper which is the source of the student's difficulty. The Writing Clinic aids students in many courses, among them philosophy, history, economics, religion, and literature, where coherent expression in examinations and papers is especially important.

Organization and accuracy of expression are stressed by the committee in their work with students from all four classes, and with transfer, foreign, and graduate students. Several students who have taken advantage of the Writing Clinic have had their academic standing raised from below diploma grade to "B." Foreign students have been helped in their knowledge and fluency in written English.

The Committee for Special Assistance in Written English was established

---

[*] Unattributed. In SP's 1952 calendar, she wrote on 4 November: 'Writing Clinic feature.'

at Smith College in 1921, at the suggestion of Miss Elizabeth D. Hanscom, now professor emeritus of English. During the first year, sixty-five students were helped. Last year eighty Smith students came to the clinic, fifty-seven in 1950–1, and seventy in the year 1949–50. This year, the Committee on Written English is composed of Mrs. Ruth E. Hill, chairman, Mrs. Martha England, and Miss Marlies Kallman, instructors in English.

More Than a Hundred Varieties Of Chrysanthemums Will Be Seen at Lyman Plant House

Ts,* 10 November 1952, Smith College

Northampton, November 11—Over 100 varieties of plants with blossoms from less than an inch to over nine inches in diameter will be featured at the annual fall exhibit of Chrysanthemums at the Lyman Plant House, Smith College, Monday through Sunday this week, from 2 to 5 p.m. each afternoon. The showing, organized by the Botany department, is under the direction of Mr. William Campbell, horticulturist.

Twenty of these plants were hybridized by students in past years in the Botany department course in horticulture, which Mr. Campbell teaches. After cross-pollenization, the plants take a year to blossom, and many students return in the fall to see the first blossoming of their work. These plants are named for the students who did the pollenization.

Among the students now at Smith College who will have their plants on display in the Plant House are: Miss Margaret Knecht, a senior of Allentown, Pa.; Miss Jean Richmond, a senior of Kenilworth, Ill., and Miss Bernice Low, a senior of Singapore, British Malaya.

In conjunction with the exhibition, there will be a display of cuts from plants bearing student names in the Botany Showcase in Burton Hall. Next week, there will be a display of some of the parent plants, with the progeny resulting from the cross-pollenization.

---

* The Smith College Archives holds an incomplete press release typescript with SP's name typed on it. Title assigned from one of the two articles published. The first four paragraphs here are from the typescript; the last three are from the published article: 'More than 100 Varieties of Chrysanthemums Will Be Seen at Lyman Plant House', *Daily Hampshire Gazette* (11 November 1952): 6. A shorter version was printed as: 'Chrysanthemums Are on Display at Smith', *Springfield Daily News* (11 November 1952): 9.

The fall Chrysanthemum display is one of the two major flower exhibits given each year. An annual feature for over fifty years, the exhibition was first started under Dr. William F. Ganong, head of the Botany department, and Mr. E. G. Canning, head of the Garden department. The second flower showing is the Spring Bulb Exhibit in March.

Many of these plants on display at the Smith College Chrysanthemum Show were entered at the annual University of Massachusetts Flower Show in Amherst, which 20,000 people attended over the past weekend.

One of the special features of the exhibit is chrysanthemums trained into Cascade Growth. This form, originated in Japan to represent a waterfall, grows from cuttings and is trained over chicken wire.

Mrs. L. Diem of Cologne Visiting Smith

Ts,* 10 November 1952, Smith College

Northampton, November 11—Mrs. Liselotte Diem, director of the women's physical education department at the Sportschule, Cologne, Germany, is visiting Smith College Monday and Tuesday of this week. While here she will attend gym classes, observing the type of work and facilities of the Smith College Physical Education department.

Coming here under the sponsorship of the National Welfare Association, Mrs. Diem will spend three months in the United States viewing physical education techniques in a cross-section of the nation's colleges. Both she and her husband, Dr. Carl Diem, director of the Sportschule in Cologne, were present at the Olympic Games in Helsinki this summer. Dr. Diem, who has been a consultant for the past three Olympic games, was honored at a dinner given there by the American Academy of Physical Education.

---

* The Smith College Archives holds a press release typescript with SP's name typed on it. Title assigned from published article: 'Mrs. L Diem of Cologne Visiting Smith', *Daily Hampshire Gazette* (11 November 1952): 5.

Newly Revised Edition of *Smith Review* Has Articles by Students

Ts,* 12 December 1952, Smith College

Northampton, December 12—Essays, stories, and poems written by Smith College students appeared recently in the fall issue of the *Smith Review*, the students' semi-annual literary magazine which has been revived on campus this year. Operating under a revised constitution, the staff of *Smith Review* has remodeled the magazine and added new features to attract the interest of more Smith students. Any member of Smith College is eligible to submit material for publication.

The contents of the 1952 fall issue spotlighted a short article by Mary Ellen Chase, Professor of English at Smith College. Miss Chase is the distinguished authoress of many novels as well as critical writings and commentaries on the Bible and biblical literature. A similar "guest feature" written by different members of the Smith faculty will appear in every issue of the *Review*.

Among the other leading articles in the magazine was an essay on "The Theme of Government in Shakespeare's Plays," written by Miss Ruth Barnes of Wallingford, Connecticut, the first freshman in the history of Smith College to win the annual prize for an essay on a Shakespearian subject. A play entitled "Come Home Bringing Me Laughter," written by Miss Patience Cleveland, a senior in last year's graduating class, was also featured. The play won the annual prize for the best creative writing done at Smith last year and also received two theater awards. "Sunday at the Mintons'," a story which won one of the two five-hundred-dollar prizes in the annual college short-story competition sponsored by *Mademoiselle* magazine, is among the three stories appearing in the *Review*. The story was written by Miss Sylvia Plath, a junior from Wellesley, Mass., who is also a member of the editorial board of the magazine.

The artwork for the fall issue of the *Smith Review* was done by students in the art department of the college and includes black-and-white ink drawings

---

* The Smith College Archives holds a press release typescript with SP's name typed on it. Title assigned from one of the two articles published: 'Newly Revised Edition of "Smith Review" Has Articles By Students', *Daily Hampshire Gazette* (12 December 1952): 7, and 'Student's Prize Story Featured in Review', *Springfield Daily News* (12 December 1952): 32. The Smith College Archives also holds an unattributed press release typescript specifically for the *Springfield Union* with similar content.

and the reproduction of a woodcut. The cover of the magazine was a winning design submitted to the art department in a class competition. The cover design competition will be another regular feature sponsored by the publication.

The staff of twelve editors and board members is under the direction of Miss Sally Rosenthal, a junior from Washington, DC.

College Group Will Debate on February 11

Ts,* 12 December 1952, Smith College

Northampton, December 12—"Christian Responsibility in the Field of Social and Political Activity" was discussed at the Smith College Religious Center this week. Sponsored by Christian Action, a new organization formed recently at Smith College, the discussion centered on the need for some definite action on the part of religion for the betterment of society and the world today.

The Christian Action group feels that suggestions made and action taken on ethical issues will help to make other people aware of current problems. In order to insure this, activities of the group will be posted in the college and pamphlets will be kept at the Religious Center.

Christian Action is now sponsoring a drive to send books to India and recently the group wrote a letter to President-elect Dwight D. Eisenhower requesting that Chester Bowles be kept on as US Ambassador to India. On February 11 the group will participate in a discussion on civil rights with the Inter-race Council at Smith College.

Christian Action plans to send Smith College students on deputations to the Massachusetts Council of Churches which hopes to inform the people in Massachusetts on some of the civil rights issues.

By means of church activities and through political organizations such as the National Students' Association, Christian Action intends to give religious ideas some form of concrete expression.

Miss Claiborne Philips, a junior from Washington, DC, led the discussion at the Religious Center. Stephen T. Crary, Chaplain of Smith College, and Mrs. Crary, were among those present.

---

* The Smith College Archives holds a press release typescript with SP's name typed on it. Title assigned from published article: 'College Group Will Debate on Feb 11', *Daily Hampshire Gazette* (13 December 1952): 7.

Drive For Hymnals at Smith College

Ts,* 12 March 1953, Smith College

Northampton, March 12—Widespread student enthusiasm greeted a recent bulletin from the Smith College Vespers Board announcing a drive for new hymn books on campus. Smith College has been labeled a school where everybody sings, and even those students that are not members of the All-Smith Choir, the Smith Glee Club, the Chamber Singers, and the three octets still join in on the musical activity when they attend Sunday night Vespers services and Wednesday morning chapel.

The campaign has as its first goal the purchase of enough hymn books to use during the Vespers services. The hymn book which has been selected is *The Hymnal*, published under the auspices of the Presbyterian Church, since it has been found that the words and music contained in the selection are those more enjoyed by a majority of students of all denominations and are appropriate for congregational participation.

When enough hymnals have been obtained to serve those attending Vespers services, a second drive will commence which will aim at supplying enough books for use on Wednesday mornings, when the entire student body attends chapel in John M. Greene Hall.

The announcement of this activity was made by Miss Celia Allison, a senior from Winnetka, Ill. and Head of the Vespers Board. Several college houses are donating books to be inscribed with their name. There will be an opportunity to contribute before and after the Vespers service on March 15th.

Passover Will Be Marked Monday at Smith College

Ts,† 21 March 1953, Smith College

Northampton, March 21—Passover, or the Festival of Freedom, commemorating the flight of the Jews from Egypt thousands of years ago, will be celebrated

---

* The Smith College Archives holds a press release typescript with SP's name typed on it. Title assigned from published article: 'Drive For Hymnals at Smith College', *Daily Hampshire Gazette* (13 March 1953): 8.

† The Smith College Archives holds a press release typescript with SP's name typed on it. Title

at a Smith College Seder, to be held by members of Hillel foundation on Monday evening, March 23, in the Alumnae House.

The symbolic matzoth, or unleavened bread, will be one feature at the dinner, celebrating the eating of unleavened bread during the forty-day sojourn of the Jewish people in the desert. A traditional religious service will be held by Rabbi Ruchames, Director of the Smith, Amherst, and the University of Massachusetts Hillel groups. Songs will be presented by the Hillel Choir. More than two hundred students, many of them Christian friends of Hillel members, as well as a number of faculty members from the Smith department of religion, will be present at the feast.

Fencing Techniques to be Demonstrated

Ts,[*] March 1953, Smith College

Northampton, March 21 – Beginning techniques in drill and bouting and advanced techniques in duel form will be presented by members of the Fencing Club at a demonstration in Scott Gymnasium Monday, March 23, at 7.30 p.m. This exhibition will be served at the close of the program.

All of the fencing will be done with foils, and Miss Ettie Chin, Assistant Professor of Physical Education will explain the various techniques as they are being presented. Afterwards, Miss Chin will give class emblems to the first teams and announce the All-Smith teams. The results of the class tournament will be given and two cups presented, one to the beginner who has won the beginners' tournament and the other for the winners of the open college tournament. Bouts between classes will close the program.

---

assigned from one of the two articles published: 'Passover Will Be Marked Monday at Smith College', *Daily Hampshire Gazette* (21 March 1953): 4, and 'Smith College Seder', *Springfield Daily News* (21 March 1953): 7.

[*] The Smith College Archives holds a press release typescript with SP's name typed on it. Title assigned from published article: 'Fencing Techniques to be Demonstrated', *Springfield Daily News* (21 March 1953): 7.

Shale that Is 400 Million Years Old at Smith Lab

Ts,* 14 April 1953, Smith College

Northampton, April 14—Ten pounds of fossil-bearing shale were brought back for the Smith Geology Laboratory from the annual meeting of the Association of Geology Teachers in Troy, New York, last week, by Marshall Schalk, assistant professor of geology at Smith. The New England section of the Association, organized last fall, met as guests of the older Eastern Section at Rensselaer Polytechnic Institute. About forty teachers from New York, Pennsylvania, West Virginia, Ontario, and New England attended the sessions. Concerned with the teaching of the earth sciences at the high school as well as the college level, the Association holds meetings to exchange ideas and teaching methods, to demonstrate new laboratory equipment, and to share illustrative materials.

Friday morning the group toured the shops of the W. & L. E. Gurley Company, 108-year-old makers of mapping and surveying instruments. Papers were scheduled Friday afternoon and all day Saturday. No field trip had been planned, but when the weather looked good Friday night, the local chairman announced he would be at the hotel Saturday morning at seven, breakfast over, and take anyone who wanted to go to a geologically famous locality five miles north of Troy. Nine members took the trip into Deep Kill Ravine and were back in time for the meeting at 9:30. The shale brought back was roughly 400 million years old and the fossils look like fine pencil markings on the black rock. Called "graptolites," they are remarkable in that identical fossils are found in rocks of similar age as far away as Australia.

---

* The Smith College Archives holds a press release typescript with SP's name typed on it. Title assigned from published article: 'Shale that Is 400,000,000 Years Old at Smith Lab', *Daily Hampshire Gazette* (14 April 1953): 12.

John Mason Brown Lectures on Writer's Responsibility

Written: 14 April 1953[*]
Published: *Daily Hampshire Gazette* (15 April 1953): 18

"Writers enjoy no exemption from citizenship," asserted John Mason Brown, noted critic, writer, and lecturer, in his lecture "Seeing Things" Tuesday at Smith College. "Writers have a special responsibility because of their gift (or curse) of articulation." They know the same anguishes as we do, and are able to phrase their sorrows. We find solace in their words.

The greatest privilege and obligation in a free society, Mr. Brown continued, is the right of dissent. "The artist sticks his neck out in pursuit of truth.

"In order to get the right answers," Mr. Brown went on, "we must ask the right questions. Five questions that are continually being asked by man are: How can man find a way of living with himself? With his neighbors? With the world beyond his neighbors? And with God, or the forces in Nature?" The fifth and most pressing question is "How can individual man achieve inner security in these days when uncertainty is the only certainty?"

Mr. Brown pointed out man's relation to himself, his neighbors and God as expressed in recent plays and novels. He cited George Bernard Shaw's "Don Juan in Hell" as a "brilliant performance" that portrayed "man as what he was and what he must become in order to survive."

Speaking of Ernest Hemingway's novel *The Old Man and the Sea*, Mr. Brown stressed the old man's heroic belief in his hero, Joe DiMaggio, who kept on playing in spite of a painful bone spur in his heel. Mr. Brown considered the novel "an affirmation to the question of how man must work with agents controlling his being."

John Steinbeck, in his novel *East of Eden*, was trying to say the same affirmative thing, the speaker revealed. Steinbeck wrote that there is only one main story, "built on the never-ending contest in ourselves of good and evil."

As for the fifth theme, the question of serenity, Mr. Brown maintained that these are uneasy times for writers, and for all of us. The threat of war breeds fear. The "cry of anguish" and the "roaring credo" of the young writers had temporarily disappeared in a kind of fright at the finger of suspicion pointed by the Communist investigations, he said.

---

[*] Unattributed. In SP's 1953 calendar, she wrote on 14 April: 'Cover John Mason Brown – 8 ★'.

Summarizing the nearest solution to finding serenity in an age of possible total destruction, Mr. Brown quoted an excerpt from Alistair Cooke's book *One Man's America*. The ominous eclipse of the sun in 1789 struck terror in the Connecticut House of Representatives which was in session. Rising to calm the furor, the speaker of the House said, "Either the Day of Judgment is approaching or it is not. If it is not, there is nothing to worry about. If it is, I wish to be found doing my duty." This is the only dignified pattern of behavior, the speaker concluded.

Literary Speakers Mark Symposium at Smith College

Ts,* 24 April 1953

For Immediate Release
By Sylvia Plath, Smith College Correspondent

Northampton, April 24—The literary panel speakers at the Smith College Symposium on "Art and Morals" tonight stressed the close relationship of art and morals. Speakers were W. H. Auden, Neilson Professor of English, Allen Tate, critic, poet, professor of English at the University of Minnesota, and Lionel Trilling, professor of English at Columbia.

The Symposium opened this afternoon with an address by Archibald MacLeish, Boylston professor at Harvard who stressed the responsibility of the artist toward society.

W. H. Auden said that only by our artistic imagination being caught is our conscience aroused; imagination makes moral judgment. Among the presuppositions concerning the artistic imagination is the assumption that the living being is not a puppet but has freedom to choose for itself. The artist understands the vow, which applies equality at all times. Propaganda is repugnant to the imagination for its effect makes obedience a mere reflex. Auden asserted

---

* The Smith College Archives holds a press release typescript with SP's name typed on it which was brought to my attention by Amanda Golden. Title assigned from published article: 'Literary Speakers Mark Symposium at Smith College', *Daily Hampshire Gazette* (24 April 1953): 1, 12. Published article includes more text which was taken from a different press release written by an unknown person. SP mentioned covering the symposium: 'I'm covering the whole whoopedo for the Hampshire Gazette and having all kinds of fun doing it.' (Letter to Warren Plath, 24 April 1953, *The Letters of Sylvia Plath, Volume 1*: 601.)

that "as long as art is produced at all" it is itself an assertion of value, the personal, and free will.

Allen Tate claimed that "art is a form of conduct which will lead to moral implications but the end is not necessarily morality." The end of a work of art is to be a work of art. Even if all men could agree on the moral soundness of a poem as a standard of conduct. Art should enrich our understanding of the varieties of being. It is an absurd supposition that poetry should be an inculcation of morality.

"Art and morality are in actuality the same," said Lionel Trilling. "No living practitioner of literary art in actual practice is against morality." Moral life, in all its pain, is the greatest subject of art. Yet the artistic spirit, in choosing whatever shape it wills, never stoops to a mechanical or servile shape.

Laughton Holds Audience Spellbound with Readings

Written: 5 May 1953[*]
Published: *Daily Hampshire Gazette* (6 May 1953): 3

Charles Laughton, well-known actor, held a near-capacity crowd spellbound for two hours last evening (Tuesday) at John M. Greene Hall, Smith College, with his program of readings.

As the lights dimmed, hearty applause heralded Mr. Laughton, who crossed to the front of the stage to the microphone with an armful of books which he used as props for the readings.

In tones that ranged from the thundering rhythms of the biblical story of the fiery furnace to the hushed, whispered conclusion of Hans Christian Andersen's story of "The Emperor and the Nightingale," Mr. Laughton's versatile voice and dramatic characterizations completely captivated his audience.

The speaker presented and cited two selections as pertinent to modern times, although written far from recently.

The first selection was the Devil's speech concerning the tremendous and ingenious destructive instruments of man, and it was taken from the "Don Juan in Hell" dream sequence of George Bernard Shaw's play, *Man and Superman*, written in 1901. Mr. Laughton was recently cast as the Devil in the

---

[*] In SP's 1953 calendar, she wrote on 5 May: 'Charles Laughton – cover.' SP's initials conclude this article.

performances of "Don Juan in Hell" by the First Drama Quartet, which also included actress Agnes Moorehead, and actors Charles Boyer and Sir Cedric Hardwicke.

The second reading was from Charles Dickens' book, *Little Dorrit*, written in 1835, and it concerned the red tape and deceit in government offices.

Two modernized fairy tales by James Thurber, "Red Riding Hood and the Wolf" and "The Bear Who Could Leave It Alone," highly amused the audience with their final humorous moral twists.

Mr. Laughton also recited two moving descriptive passages, one from a movie he appeared in, entitled *Rembrandt*, the other a selection from the writings of Thomas Wolfe.

The dramatic and entertaining evening presented by the veteran screen, stage, radio, and television star was concluded with a resonant and moving recitation of Lincoln's Gettysburg Address.

Mr. Laughton was introduced by Miss Carol Scharmett, a senior from Bridgeport, Conn., and head of SCADS, which sponsored the "Evening With Laughton" last night and also the lecture by John Mason Brown last month for the benefit of the Smith College Annual Drive for Scholarships.—S.P.

Smith Christian Group Points to Achievements

Ts,[*] 14 May 1953, Smith College

"Faith, fellowship and action" has been the motto of the revitalized Christian Association at Smith College this year. The program of Christian Association has been extended in an attempt to reach all the Protestant students on the Smith campus and coordinate them into an active group.

The activities of CA range from Little Chapel, a daily morning worship service held in the Little Chapel of the Library, to the Committee on Christian Action, which has attempted to reawaken the public's interest in politics, both through deputations sent on request to local churches and by letters written to congressmen and to women in public life.

Among the other activities of CA which are designed to emphasize the

---

[*] The Smith College Archives holds a press release typescript with SP's name typed on it. Title assigned from published article: 'Smith Christian Group Points to Achievements', *Daily Hampshire Gazette* (14 May 1953): 23.

part which Smith plays in the Northampton community, are the babysitting plan, which takes care of faculty children one day a week, and the Church co-operation Committee, which provides Sunday School teachers for Northampton churches and aids various church committees with church dinners and rummage sales.

Christian Association also works with the Vespers Board to sponsor the open houses which are held after each Sunday evening Vespers service. These open houses provide a chance for further discussion with the visiting minister.

CA also participates in the more extensive program of the New England Student Christian Movement. This larger organization sponsors, among other activities, the Northfield Conference in February, which is designed to strengthen the faith of each student who attends the conference through discussions, panels, and informal sessions.

O-at-Ka, the second major conference sponsored by the Student Christian Movement, is held in Maine the first week in June. This conference is designed to give the students who attend the camp a fuller understanding of the relationship between faith and action.

This year a series of weekend work camps held at Yale in an effort to clean up the New Haven slums have helped recreate the motto of "Faith, fellowship and action."

The Religious Association, composed of Christian Association, the Hillel Foundation for Jewish students, and Newman Club for Catholic students, is the coordinator for the many activities of these faith groups.

Each year a Forum is held in February at which an eminent member of each faith group lectures on a vital issue. The subject of the Forum this year was "Faith on Trial."

The new officers of Christian Association are: Miss Louise Giesey, a junior from Wellesley Hills, Mass., president; Miss Margot Lambert, a junior from Omaha, Neb., vice president; and Miss Sally Clise, a freshman from Port Blakely, Wash., secretary.

An open house was held at the Religious Center, Monday evening, to honor the new officers. The open house was followed by a candlelight service in the Little Chapel.

Smith College Field Events Saturday Afternoon, Night

Ts,[*] 14 May 1953, Smith College

Smith College students and faculty will celebrate the last weekend before final examinations by viewing and participating in the annual Smith College Field Day activities on Saturday afternoon, May 16, and by gathering on the banks of Paradise Pond to watch the crew races and the gala procession of canoes, decorated and maneuvered by prominent members of the freshman class, at the Float Night celebration that evening.

During the afternoon three sports finals will be played: the tennis doubles finals, the interclass archery finals, and the interhouse finals. There will also be a lacrosse exhibition. A golf competition for beginners and advanced students will be open to all interested.

One of the highlights of the afternoon will be the horse show. Members of the riding classes will be the participants. Riding, jumping, an exhibition drill, and an exhibition tandem (in which each student will ride a horse, driving another horse before her) will be included in the program.

The program will be culminated by the awarding of two cups, the Improvement Cup to be awarded to the student showing the most improvement in her riding class; and the Anna K. Brown Memorial Cup to be awarded to the student who shows her horsemanship by her expert handling of the horses and her love for them. Mr. Carl Bauer, riding instructor at Skidmore College, will be the guest judge.

Another highlight of the afternoon will be the faculty "All Stars" softball game between the students and the faculty. Daniel Aaron of the English department will captain the faculty team. The tentative line-up of this team is: David Coffin, classics dept.; William May, religion dept.; Leonard G. Miller, philosophy dept.; Michael S. Olmstead, sociology dept.; George H. Cohen, art department; Clifford R. Bragdon, education dept.; Irving I. Kofsky, physics dept.; and N. Deming Hoyt, education and child study department.

On Saturday, May 16, Smith College's Paradise Pond will be the scene of extraordinary activity. After dark, strangely decorated canoes with crews of

---

[*] The Smith College Archives holds a press release typescript with SP's name typed on it. Title assigned from one of the two articles published: 'Smith College Field Events', *Daily Hampshire Gazette* (15 May 1953): 1, 12, and 'Float Night At College', *Springfield Daily News* (15 May 1953): 9.

three will slide through the waters, spotlighted from shore for the benefit of the audience on land. The occasion for the evening water exhibition is Smith's annual Float Night.

First initiated in 1917 as Regatta Night, the pageant was a canoe parade made up of floats representing different artistic settings. The theme of the first show was "Allied Countries" and the floats, emphasizing the war, were U-boats, battleships, and Red Cross ships.

In 1933 the event was officially given to the freshman class to present and ever since then the freshmen have sponsored the project. In past years they presented such varied themes as "See America First" with floats of Coney Island and a ghost town, and "News Today," showing daily newspaper features: the society page, sports, the stock exchange report, and the comics.

In 1939 a group of Amherst students tried to enter a float they had built secretly in a garage, but they were apprehended on the way to the pond by the police and the traditional Smith pageant proceeded as usual.

Each year, before the decorated canoes make their appearance to compete for prizes of "prettiest" and "most original," there are several crew demonstrations and races.

After the races, the theme, which has been kept a secret during weeks of preparation, is revealed and the water pageant begins. This year there will be thirteen canoes and thirty-nine students participating. The crews are composed of outstanding freshmen who have made "contributions to house, class, and college."

Smith College Play Delights 'Hamp Audience

Written: 14 May 1953[*]
Published: *Springfield Union* (15 May 1953): 31

Northampton, May 14—The gay French farce, *Ring Round the Moon*, written by Jean Anouilh and adapted by Christopher Fry, delighted playgoing audiences at Smith College week.

A combination of excellent character acting, colorful costumes, and a

---

[*] Unattributed. SP wrote, 'Last night I ushered at a delightful performance of "Ring Round the Moon" and tonight I wrote up a review of it and phoned it collect just now to the Springfield Union, where I read it word by word to the man at the teletype.' (See letter to Aurelia Schober Plath, 14 May 1953, *The Letters of Sylvia Plath, Volume 1*: 624.)

versatile winter garden set, imaginatively varied by the use of scrims, made this year's final production of the Smith College Theater Department a sparkling satirical diversion.

Dealing with social distinction and financial intrigue, *Ring Round the Moon* treats with wit and aplomb the central situation of a beautiful and poverty-stricken young ballet dancer made queen for a night at a spectacular ball in a palatial chateau.

Lilting music by Richard Addinsell provided a bewitching background for the performance.

The entire cast had an opportunity to demonstrate individual acting ability in the whimsical and often hilarious character parts. Among highlights was an extravagant conversational tango executed by finesse by Rita Parr and William White.

Ted Kazanoff manipulated his tricky dual dole as twin brothers Hugo and Frederic with convincing dexterity. Joan Ford evoked laughter and applause in her brilliant performance as the poor but ambitious mother of a lovely ballet dancer, who is played with starry-eyed simplicity by Joan Bryan.

Constance Eddy, the dictatorial dowager, ruled the stage from her wheelchair, and Marlene McKay provided an appropriate contrast as her soft, sentimental and skittish companion.

The *Ring Round the Moon* set was designed by Sonya Levene and costumed by Gene Jones, both graduate students. George Brendan Dowell's well-cast, well-knit production will be performed again at Commencement.

Austrian-Born Junior Enlists in Women's Marine Corps, 'Can't wait to get there'

Written: *c.*12 May 1953
Published: *Daily Hampshire Gazette* (16 May 1953): 2[*]

"I'm joining the Women's Marine Corps mainly because of the wonderful opportunities the service offers," said petite, attractive Antoinette Willard, Smith College junior, when interviewed on the steps of Baldwin House at Smith.

Antoinette, daughter of Mr. and Mrs. Paul A. Willard of 173-25 Croydon Rd.,

[*] Article printed with 'Sylvia Plath' as a byline.

Jamaica Estates, Long Island, NY, has just been accepted in the Marine Corps woman officer training class, and went to Hartford, Conn., last week to enlist.

"I first began to think seriously about joining the Women's Marine Corps last winter," explained Antoinette, "when First Lt. Patricia Maas of the Boston women officer procurement office came to Smith to talk about the Marines to girls who were interested.

"Besides," added the pretty brunette, "my older sister, Mrs. George Russell, was a cadet nurse at Fort Devens during the last war, and so the service has always intrigued me."

"This summer I'm going to attend training school at Quantico, Va.," Antoinette continued enthusiastically. "All expenses paid, too! I'll be taking two six-week sessions of training. The first six weeks will be mainly marching, drill, sports, and classes on the history of the Marines, for example. The second week will be pretty much devoted to classes."

Antoinette gave a glowing account of her planned activities for the summer at Quantico. They include sports such as sailing, riding, tennis, swimming, and golf.

"There are really tremendous opportunities offered by the Marine Corps," the energetic Smith girl maintained. "Good pay, a chance to meet interesting people and to see some of the world."

Antoinette herself already has seen a good deal of the world. Born in Vienna, Austria, she has traveled widely over Europe and attended schools in France, Switzerland, and Italy. She spoke fluent German and French long before she learned English.

In 1939, with the growing danger from the Nazis rising to power in Europe, Antoinette and her family sailed to America. Here Antoinette learned to speak English and became an American citizen in 1944. Before coming to Smith, she attended the Lincoln School in Providence, RI, for seven years.

"I'm a government major at Smith," Antoinette informed us, "and since I can speak both French and German, I hope I can eventually get a job in the foreign service. That's my main ambition."

"After my service in the Marines, I'd like to go to graduate school on the GI Bill and then work in the foreign service abroad," she said, adding with a grin, "After all, Vienna's really my old 'home town.'"

Among the qualifications for officers in the Women's Marine Corps is good standing in college, leadership ability, and extracurricular activities, and Antoinette certainly fills the bill in all these fields.

At Smith, Antoinette has been active for three years as her house representative to the National Students' Association. She has also worked for the junior class Rally Day show and the annual Smith College celebration of George Washington's birthday. In addition, Antoinette has participated in the student activities at St. John's Church. She taught Sunday School there last year.

After her training period this summer, the versatile Smith junior will return to college for her senior year and receive her diploma in June 1954. In previous summers, Antoinette has worked as a waitress in Boothbay, Me., to pay for college expenses, and she also spent a summer making reservations for the American Airlines in New York.

Upon enrollment in the officer training program, Antoinette will be listed, with the other candidates, as a private and immediately promoted to corporal, with a pay of $99.37 per month.

At the end of the first six-week session, she will be promoted to sergeant, with pay of $122.30 per month. Earnings for the three-month training period will amount to $332.50, which is practically "clear profit," since food, clothing, shelter, and transportation are provided.

Antoinette was especially impressed by the fact that the Women's Marine Corps is the only branch of the services that lets a candidate change her mind about entering after training. "Any candidate who wishes may resign either from the program or from the Marine Corps Reserve altogether, at any time prior to acceptance of a commission," Antoinette read from her pamphlet, entitled "Your Future as a Woman Marine Officer."

"If a candidate resigns from the Marine Corps, she is honorably discharged with no strings attached and no mark against her record either for job references or any future association with any of the armed forces."

If Antoinette accepts a reserve commission, she will agree to keep that commission for at least six years. At the present time this means that she will spend two years on full-time active duty and four years as a "civilian Marine." If she wishes, she may apply for an extension of active duty or a commission in the regular Marine Corps.

"As a woman officer, I'll be assigned to any of the noncombatant jobs open to male officers," said Antoinette. Current assignments include administrative and staff jobs, communications, special services such as recreation and education, instructing, disbursing, Marine Corps Exchange, personnel, public information, legal work, and supply.

"Now that I'm accepted and enlisted in the Marine Corps women officer training class," Antoinette finished, "all I have to do is wait to receive my orders to report to Quantico on June 18. And, frankly," she added, smiling, "I can't wait to get there!"

Many Area Students Are Among the 464 Who Will Get Smith Degrees on June 8

Written: *c*.14 May 1953
Published: *Daily Hampshire Gazette* (20 May 1953): 8[*]

Four hundred and sixty-four Bachelor of Arts degrees will be conferred at the seventy-fifth Smith College Commencement exercises on June 8. John J. McCloy, former US high commissioner for Germany, now chairman of the board of the Chase National Bank, will be the commencement speaker. Graduation, which will be held out of doors in the Quadrangle, will be the climax of a weekend of activities which include a baccalaureate service on June 7, and the traditional Ivy Day ceremonies on June 6.[†]

Miss Betty Lou Bowry, who is majoring in American studies, is the Ellen Emerson House representative to the House of Representatives this year. In her junior year she was a member of the Outing Club board.

Miss Mary Margaret Clark is her senior class representative to the House of Representatives. In her junior year she was a member of the advertising staff of the *Campus Cat*, the Smith College humor magazine.

Miss Jane Cowen is a member of the advertising staff of the *Hamper*, Smith College yearbook, as well as head of securing commencement rooms for parents and guests. Miss Cowen is also a member of the curriculum committee, an undergraduate group which acts as liaison for the faculty and students, dealing with matters concerning the course of study. This year she is on the Dean's list.

Miss Nancy Ann Dragon, who is majoring in sociology, did community service at the Northampton People's Institute during her junior year, when she was also a member of the advertising staff of the *Campus Cat*.

Miss Karen Duke, a music major, is president of Clef Club, a small group of students interested in writing and performing music. She is also secretary of Alpha Phi Kappa Psi, an honorary society which recognizes outstanding talent and creative ability in the arts. This year she was elected to Phi Beta Kappa and received the annual Alpha award for excellence in music.

Miss Margaret Frances Hennessy, a government major, spent her junior year at the University of Toronto, where she was a member of the Political Science

---

[*] Article printed with 'Sylvia Plath' as a byline.
[†] A long list of students, parents and addresses follows in the original text, redacted here.

Club. This year she took park in the International Students' Day bazaar. Miss Hennessy was on the Dean's list in her sophomore and junior years.

Miss Joan Alexandra Houston, an art major, was head of the decoration committee for the International Students' Day bazaar this year, as well as her Henshaw House representative to the College Relief Committee and the World Service Fund. A member of the Art Studio Club, Miss Houston also participated in the All-Smith choir and the Smith College orchestra.

Miss Priscilla Ann Ketchell was the president of Hampshire House this year. In her junior year she was head of the Hampshire House freshman advisers and did community service work at the People's Institute.

Mrs. David Lawrence, the former Miss Beverlee Sender, was publicity chairman for the political committee this year, and has been a member of the Liberal Association and the United World Federalists. In her junior year she was on the Dean's list.

Miss Shirley Ann Lemon, an art major, has been art editor of *Who's Who*, the freshman picture directory, for the past three years. In her senior year she has done artwork of the *Alumnae Quarterly* and served on the publicity committee for Rally Day, the traditional Smith College celebration of George Washington's birthday, and Charity Ball. For the last two years Miss Lemon has been on the Dean's list.

Miss Joan MacRae, who was vice president of Hampshire House this year, was also a member of the advertising staff of the *Hamper*, the Smith College yearbook. Miss MacRae was co-editor of *Who's Who in 1955*.

Miss Mary Angela Maher was a representative to curriculum committee this year. She also participated in the International Students' Day bazaar. In her junior year she was advertising manager for the *Campus Cat*, the college humor magazine. Miss Maher has done community service work at the People's Institute.

Miss Nancy Claire Major, an education and child study major, has taught classes in handicraft at the People's Institute. This year she was elected to Phi Beta Kappa.

Miss Marilyn Mirkin, an education major at Smith, has been a member of the Hillel Foundation and Inter-Race Club during her four years at college.

Mrs. Walter D. Munro, the former Miss Ruth Belding, an education and child study major, has been a member of the Smith College Glee Club and the Religious Association.

Miss Kathrine Margaret Ockenden is a member of Gold Key, a group of official student guides who conduct visitors about the campus. She is also a member of the Christian Association cabinet. In her junior year, Miss Ockenden was a member of junior ushers, a group of juniors who carry the ivy chain at commencement time. She served on the Outing Club board, as well.

Miss Amanda Sophronia Rogers, a French major at Smith, is on the Dean's list. In her sophomore and senior years she was a member of the college relief committee. Miss Rogers participated in the Smith College band in her sophomore year.

Miss Sarah Sessions, a music major, is vice president of Clef Club and a member of the Smith College orchestra. She was also vice president of Sessions House.

Miss Julia Eve Tessier has been senior advertising manager for the Smith College yearbook, the *Hamper*. She is also a Gold Key guide. In her junior year she was vice president of Hampshire House and a junior usher. Miss Tessier was co-editor of *Who's Who in 1955*, the freshman handbook for the class of 1955.

Miss Beverly Ann Vigneault is majoring in French at Smith. In her junior year she was yearbook representative for Hampshire House. In her freshman year she was a member of the freshman choir.

Mrs. Hillary B. Waugh was president of press board, the student branch of the college news office. In her junior and senior years she was a Gold Key guide, an official student guide who conducts visitors about the campus. She has been on the Dean's list for four years and this year was selected to Phi Beta Kappa.

Miss Marie Yates is an English major at Smith. She has been Athletic Association representative to Northrop House in her sophomore and junior years.

14 Colleges to Take Part in Poetry Reading Festival

Written: *c.*5 May 1954
Published: *Daily Hampshire Gazette* (6 May 1954): 9[*]

Faculty and student representatives from fifteen Eastern colleges and universities will attend the twenty-fifth annual Intercollegiate Poetry Reading Festival which will be held at Smith College on Saturday, May 8, at the Alumnae House.

---

[*] The Smith College Archives holds an incomplete press release typescript with SP's name typed on it with significant edits in an unknown hand. The typescript includes a full programme of events. Due to the incompleteness of the typescript, the text here is from the printed article. Title assigned from published article.

Miss Elizabeth Drew, visiting professor of English at Smith College, will discuss "The Byzantium Poems of W. B. Yeats" at 3 p.m. in the lounge of the Alumnae House.

Miss Charlotte H. Fitch, chairman of the department of speech at Smith College, is general chairman of the festival. She is assisted by Miss Catherine Hanifan and Miss Blanche Muldrow, both speech instructors, and Miss Mildred Steele a senior, who is chairman of the student hostess committee.

Charles J. Hill, acting dean, will welcome the student and faculty delegates at a festival dinner to be held in the Dutch Room of the Alumnae House at 6:15. Miss Vera Sickels, professor emeritus of speech at Smith, and Miss Helen Hicks of Hunter College will review the "History and Highlights of the First Twenty-Five Years of the Intercollegiate Poetry Reading Festival."

Poems by Dylan Thomas, T. S. Eliot, E. E. Cummings, Amy Lowell, Robert Frost, and others will be read by the students representing the fifteen Eastern colleges at Alumnae House lounge at 8 p.m.

Miss Jo Taub, a senior from Hopewell Junction, NY, will represent Smith College at the festival readings. Miss Doris Abramson will represent the University of Massachusetts and Miss Nadine Shepardson will represent Mount Holyoke College.

Other colleges represented will be Adelphi College, Brooklyn College, Connecticut College, Dartmouth College, Hunter College, Long Island University, Orange County Community College, Pennsylvania State College, Queens College, Russell Sage College, Wellesley College, and Wesleyan College.

PART IV
BOOK REVIEWS

Sylvia Plath
Court Green
North Tawton
Devonshire

Lord Byron's Wife. By Malcolm Elwin. (Macdonald, 45s.)

In his splendid account of Byron's marriage and separation, based on that beautifully plummy accumulation of unpublished letters and documents known as the Lovelace Papers, Mr. Malcolm Elwin begins, as might many a shrewd marriage counselor, with a meticulous investigation of the bride's mother. Judith Milbanke was certainly formidable enough for anyone's Mother-in-law. Skilled whist player, markswoman and unflagging canvasser for her husband, she weathered the ghastly hazards of childbirth in her era to produce, at the age of 40, an only daughter, Annabella. From the start, her spry, gossipy letters about 'little Madam' reveal the fanatic and ominous fondness which flare with a crackling italics at the Byrons' separation after a mere year of marriage:

> Wonder not that I write Strongly, who could see that Suffering Angel Sinking under such unmanly and despicable treatment, and not feel? Ld Byron is sending her Parents also with Sorrow to the Grave---let him glory also in that--- and that he has three Lives to answer for at the great account.

And the 'Suffering Angel' could write 'I have escaped from the greatest Villain that ever existed.' Something of the Grand Guignol shows in these extremes of white and black. Byron himself had only praise for his 'Dearest Bell' ('She has ever appeared to me as one of the most amiable of beings---& nearer to Perfection than I had conceived could belong to Humanity in its present existence'), excused his morbidities by a press of money worries and liver trouble, and begged her back. But a sudden muzz of camp followers and rhetoric had swallowed Annabella. One is snowbound in the end, if not brainwashed, by the humourless gobbledygook of past wrongs upon which she was to embroider until her death. Against these boringly marmoreal 'Justifications' with their Saharas of jargon, Byron's few letters refresh like genuine water.

Miss Palmer's Treasures

Published: *The Bradford* (6 February 1948): 3

Which do you like to read most—humor or tragedy? mystery or adventure? fact or fiction? poetry or prose? No matter what type of literature you prefer, you are sure to be satisfied in *Treasures*, the third book in the series, *Adventures in Reading*.

Dora E. Palmer, an English teacher in our Wellesley High School, and Dorothy Nell Knolle worked together on this admirable collection of poems, short stories, and excerpts from well-known classics. The book is divided into four sections, each covering a wide range of subject matter. The first division, "What Would You Do?" contains stories about people with problems to solve and troubles to straighten out. In "Take an Easy Chair" one may find delightful, entertaining stories of mystery, humor, and adventure by such famous writers as O. Henry, Frank Stockton, and Oliver Wendell Holmes. Section Three, "Wingéd Words," traces the progress of communication down through the ages. The excerpts contain a section centered about World War II and include a poem, not previously published, by Edna St. Vincent Millay, which was read by Ronald Colman on D-Day on the radio. Lastly, contained in "Enduring Words," are literary contributions by such internationally representative authors as Alexandre Dumas, Mark Twain, Washington Irving, Charles Dickens, Victor Hugo, and Leo Tolstoy.

Treasures not only contains many complete stories, but by presenting thrilling excerpts from world-famous classics, this book encourages the reader to turn to the original classics and thereby to extend his range of reading experience.

Dora Palmer and Dorothy Knolle deserve high praise for their carefully compiled edition of *Treasures*.

Review of *The Stones of Troy* by C. A. Trypanis

Written: 17 March 1957
Published: *Gemini* (Summer 1957): 98–103

'Theonichos, Mnesarete': the first two words of the first poem in *The Stones of Troy* give us the key to the subject matter of most of the poems to follow. Mr Trypanis derives his places, characters and incidents chiefly from Greek history and Greek myth. The last thirteen poems of the book form a 'Homeric Sequence' – poetic footnotes, as it were, to lines from the *Iliad*.

Borrowing from the classical myths and re-working the mythological material into modern frames of reference is nothing new. Contemporary novelists, poets, and playwrights (James Joyce, T. S. Eliot, and Cocteau, et cetera) have used the 'mythical method' to advantage in their work. As T. S. Eliot wrote in his review of *Ulysses* (*The Dial*, November 1923):

> In using the myth, in manipulating a continuous parallel between contemporaneity and antiquity, Mr Joyce is pursuing a method which others must pursue after him ... It is simply a way of controlling, of ordering, of giving a shape and a significance to the immense panorama of futility and anarchy which is contemporary history.

In *The Stones of Troy*, the starting point of a poem is often a reference to a richly alive, richly heroic past. By juxtaposing this past with more recent days, Mr Trypanis shows how far we have fallen from the ancient grandeur and vigour:

> 'We need heroes, heroes,' muttered the old
> Grammarian, Plutarch's text and the jumping
> Dolphin of an exquisite lamp
> Mirrored in his eyes.

We must have heroes, the grammarian concludes, 'to read in them / All we dare not attribute to ourselves'. In 'Herodotus Logomimus', the writer (like any present-day author of pot-boilers) vows:

> ... I will write for the many, the crooks,
> The riff-raff, not like Zenodotus. I am no fool.
> What are the classics? Unfashionable books,
> Scattered on dusty shelves after we finish school.

But the latter days do not always come off so shoddily: they are not merely the province of dry grammarians and cheap hack writers. In 'Songs', Mr Trypanis tells us that 'Quality can be a matter of circumstance':

> Athenian prisoners, they tell,
> Were freed from the quarries of Sicily,
> Because they could sing Euripidean choruses:

'Winds, sea winds that drive the swift,
Surf-furrowing ships across the swollen water,
Where will you carry my misery . . . ?'

If a later generation 'pours its heart / Into a tinsel song' like 'Marleen', the results, while hardly enough to free the prisoners of war, managed to sustain prisoners of boredom, disillusion, and pain, equalling thus 'a grand tragic chorus'. And while it may be well-nigh impossible for a soldier to die heroically today, particularly if he is fighting 'Another man's battle', Mr Trypanis asserts, in 'Thermopylae 1941':

. . . He was brave, the Australian
Farmer who fell there in nineteen forty-one
With an oath that lashed the rock.

The vehemence of the verb 'lashed' here raises the stature of the foreign farmer to match that of the native hero. Although Leonidas 'Had made his inimitable stand', the visitor to Sparta:

. . . will
Announce also the death of the Australian farmer
Leonidas is only a matter of precedence.

Often, meditations on the past are occasioned by the digging up of some ruins. The corpses of a Christian boy and a pagan girl buried side by side suggest an imagined conversation between the two. In 'Fragment of a Cylix', the spade turns up

Fury-bound joy and death, stamped on a lip of clay.

Tourists in Pompeii are advised not to ask questions, but to 'joke and bask / In the sun', 'look swiftly at a site / And then leave smiling'. Moral distinctions prove irrelevant in face of vitality: both vile and virtuous alike are charred to ash. The aloof archaeologist picks about in the ruins, the tourist glances around casually: these, too, will have to 'give it up at night'. The epigram on the temple of Arsinoe-Aphrodite-Zephyritis ('Pure daughters of the Greeks come here to pray . . .') gives rise to an ironical account of Queen Arsinoe's bloody history. With terse economy, Mr Trypanis outlines the events after her marriage to Lysimachus:

> She murdered his son. And when the king, broken, was dead
> She married his enemy Ptolemy Ceraunus,
> Her own step-brother. From him she flew,
> Wanting a richer man, and so came to Egypt,
> To her weak, wealthy full-blood-brother Ptolemy
> The second. She married him. She won his wars,
> Intrigued, murdered, outwitted, tied in knots
> The haughty Hellenistic world.

Mr Trypanis appreciates vitality, even in the guise of Queen Arsinoe II.

In *The Stones of Troy*, we read most frequently poems about other poems, about tomb epigrams, about paintings ('Pictures of the Nativity in the Church of Krena in Chios'), about historic notes ('Varazdates'), about authors ('We have both loved Homer'). It is naturally absurd to claim that a poet cannot write about a vividly realised poem 'about' subjects (war, love, death, etc.) which he experiences keenly through the medium of another's art, another's historical account. However, there is always the danger that the poet will not transform the material, will not, in some way, make it freshly his own and ours. In 'Imbrius', although a newly slanted moral is extracted ('For only in giant disasters / True-born and bastards count for the same'), the imagery remains distressingly undigested. After reading the words of Mr Trypanis:

> . . . you feel like an ash, a landmark
> For years till the axe crashes it down,
> And the hammered bronze rang upon you.

one turns at random to a modern translation of the *Iliad* and reads:

> . . . and he dropped like an ash tree
> which, on the crest of a mountain glittering far about, cut down
> with the bronze axe scatters on the ground its delicate leafage;
> so he dropped . . .

The alteration of third to second person does little to bring us closer to Imbrius. Indeed, one may well prefer the translation, with its long, powerfully sustained lines. These poems, in *The Stones of Troy* sequence, when unsuccessful, remain mere 'Flowers pressed between the pages of their books'. Although morals are drawn (most deftly, perhaps, in 'Habit'), more often they fall flat, with a sing-song cadence, and one wishes they had been left where they were: implicit in the *Iliad* – as with the close of 'Axylus':

> Your friends made other friends. Though that be true,
> Were not your friends the greatest joy you knew?

Historic and mythic 'realms of gold', however, are not the only lost kingdoms: several poems look back nostalgically, if also rather sentimentally, at vanished childhood. The dead boy-king Tutankhamun 'In holy sleep ... yearns to touch his golden toys'. In 'Chios Revisited' the poet describes how:

> My childhood, like the sand-castles I built
> With flags and draw-bridges on this Aegean beach
> Was flattened by a storm that left the silt
> Covered with salty litter ...

The futility of trying to recapture the child's keen, immediate sense of experience with an 'adult's hand / That blindly flutes the wind' is expressed by the shift to a hard, cruel image:

> ... the steel
> Stars nail the night against the East.

But then the poem weakens: mere whimsy invalidates the effect of the stern stars:

> And the warm moon, hurrying to a feast,
> Halts over the carnations and slips
> Her arm in mine ...

The personification of the moon seems lax, uncritical: it blurs the force of the end lines which seek to freeze life in a stasis of reminiscence:

> ... and seal in carved stone the flight
> Of the past – my heart, a painted bird.

It is of interest at this point to consider the cadence and diction of these poems in more detail. As is evident in most of the above quotations, Mr Trypanis prefers understatement. His end lines are frequently simple, unadorned statements of fact:

A god should know what to protect you from.
A sham illness is now the one way out.
'Queen Stratonice is completely bald.'

At best, this method of writing may be trenchant and dramatic. At worst, it is merely flat, without tension or striking power, as in 'A sad, dusty gaiety stirs the town.'

Now and then, too, the choice of words in these poems is questionable, and sometimes unfelicitous: waves roll 'dimpling' into the night; holy light 'hugs' darkness every dawn. 'Dimpling' sounds unfortunately diminutive after the heroic 'roll'. 'Hugs' seems uncomfortably colloquial here. And occasionally Mr Trypanis falls back into tired adjective-noun combinations which do nothing to re-create experience, but underline it in the old grooves. Such pairs are both stereotyped ('aching heart', 'living flesh', 'low cunning', 'rich warm lips', 'dusty grey') and over-romanticised ('jasmine throat', 'fragrant oil', 'ivory chariots', 'haunted gardens', 'golden toys'). Other hyphenated adjectives have the vague aura of conventional translation epithets from heroic poetry: 'foam-stung sail', 'foam-clawed sand', 'wind-wrapt, luminous waves', 'sky-tall trees', 'tower-tall sons of kings'. 'Marble' is a favourite adjective, but used unimaginatively ('marble Ephebes', 'marble sleep', 'marble stage', 'marble steps'). Extended metaphor is avoided in most of these poems, and perhaps for the best, since the occasional flights often come to grief:

And the earth, scorched like a rusk,
Panted in breaths of thyme...

The incongruity of tone here, coming in the midst of a serious poem, makes for unease verging on levity. 'Rusk' is surely out of place in the dignified scope of the whole; 'panted' is overstated, and 'thyme', unfortunately, may be read as a weak pun. The subsequent image of the west as 'a smashed amethyst rose-bowl' seems forced, as does the sky's 'giant star-wrought chandelier'. The balance between heroic or romantic and colloquial diction is not happily struck in these particular spots.

On the other hand, at his best, Mr Trypanis fuses words and meaning in markedly successful poetry. In 'Icarus', for example, he chooses to view the shadow cast by the winged man and draw a private inference from the myth:

> The dark patch on the rock was the shadow
> Of wings. It swung to the terraced fields,
> To the leaning maize and poppies. It climbed
> The white-washed wall, the line of cypress trees,
> Swerving to the cold headlands,
> Where the North wind hangs his mask . . .

The verbs, powerful and exact, follow the motion of the shadow which 'swung', 'climbed', 'swerving' to pass over the poet's home territory. The moving shape is deftly contrasted with the 'stucco / Cupids of the porch':

> But the dark shape returned. It circled
> The paved yard of my house, rolled round the stucco
> Cupids of the porch, windscratched, unable to fly,
> And flashed through the latched iron gate.
> There was no summer in the reeds of the beach,
> No wisteria in my garden. Only the skeletons
> Of trees and ageing hands.

Every poet has his own Icarus: Mr Trypanis here concerns himself solely with the graphically imaged passing shadow, making it a metaphor (as he does with the classical subject matter in many of his poems) for a present perception:

> I did not hear the cry, nor the splash.
> I did not see the waxen tears. Only the shadow
> Of wings moving across the landscape,
> Hollow footfalls of those we loved,
> Who passed so strangely beyond our life –
> Grooves of yesterday's wind.

A similar sense of fresh, first-hand observation and reaction is revealed in 'Chartres'. Again, we are contemplating a work of art: this time, the architecture and stained-glass windows of a French cathedral. The metaphor-moral is intrinsic to the poem, working back and forth on itself, not expressed prosaically at the close, like the moral in a fable. And in spite of the questionable simile 'as free of flesh as sin' (isn't sin, *ipso facto*, inherent in the flesh?), the words and rhythms of the poem make the church leap alive in colour and light. The painted glass smashes 'the sunshine into brilliant stains': here, the vigorous verb 'smashing' reveals the violence done to the truths 'closed out' by the beauty of art, which 'deceiving points, curves, dyes'. The verbs do double-duty, describing both the scene and the sense of the poem. In Yeats' 'Sailing to Byzantium', the corrupt, dying nature of the sensual world sent him to invoke the sages standing in the 'gold mosaic of a wall' and ask to be gathered 'into the artifice of eternity'. Mr Trypanis takes a rather more ambivalent attitude to the windows of art and the weather of life behind them in 'Chartres'. The wind and autumn rains (metaphors for sorrow, no doubt, and not actual phenomena in the sunlit setting throughout) complain 'behind the silent aura-ring / Of king and saint and martyr on their panes'. One may well wish to forget life's sorrow by turning to art. It is more difficult to understand precisely why the poet wants to forget

> The sun, wading through pagan fields thigh-deep,
> The fragrance of newly-nibbled grass.

These closing images seem inviting, innocuous and free from pain: they are evidently part of the 'naked sunlight' of truth. And while the 'blazing glass' presents

> . . . a world that stabs the eyes –
> The royal blood, the golden glazes sting.

in spite of its violent beauty (also painful in its way), it none the less falsifies:

> Stained windows can't look out, and don't let in
> The naked sunlight.

The weakest poems in *The Stones of Troy* are those where the gap between 'contemporaneity and antiquity' is uncomfortably straddled: where the mythical material remains inorganic and untransformed in the context of the modern poem; where the parallel between old and new is pointed at, rather than realised in the poems' shape and texture. Mr Trypanis achieves his finest effects in poems like 'The Purple Cloak', 'Queen Arsinoe II', 'Thermopylae 1941', 'Icarus', 'Chartres', and 'The Carnival'; in these poems, his terse, witty style gives fresh insight and impact to history and legend, and his powers of sensuous observation create a poetic experience uniquely his own.

General Jodpur's Conversion

Written: 1 November 1961
Published: *New Statesman* (10 November 1961): 696, 698

The General. By Janet Charters. Illustrated by Michael Foreman. Routledge. 12s. 6d.
A Wish for Little Sister. By Jacqueline Ayer. Collins. 10s. 6d.
Joba and the Wild Boar. By Gaby Baldner. Pictures by Gerhard Oberländer. Constable. 12s. 6d.

Out from among the smiling horses and cats and suns, the prancing dragons and the sugar-cookie children, the General seems to rise of his own accord, his huge, richly plumed red uniform starred and crossed and circled with innumerable medals. In this first book, Janet Charters and Michael Foreman – a young couple new to the roster of venerable old hands – have brought off something profound, flamboyant and original. Essentially and satisfyingly a children's book, *The General* is simply told, with an eye for the small, specific detail and a luminous awareness of the world of smells and colours and recurring rhythms. It is also – in these days when more and more poisons are fisting themselves in the upper atmosphere – a uniquely meaningful book for parents: a sort of Age of Anxiety wish-fulfilment.

General Jodpur wants to be the most famous general in the world. His soldiers endlessly drill, polish and practise. But one day the General is thrown by his runaway horse and has to walk back to camp. He begins to listen and look; he comes to a field of flowers and sits down. A change of career follows a change of heart, and General Jodpur becomes the most famous general for principles very different from his original ones.

The layout of *The General* is large and bold, and the illustrations – in hot reds, sky blues and a vibrant shade of plum – oddly moving and amusing. Michael Foreman uses mosaic effects to fine advantage for his armies, flower banks and countrysides and in one admirable scene where the General, red and round as a Christmas ornament, meditates in his flower field in winter under a violet sky crammed with snow crystals.

What happens to book design after the picture-book age, anyway? Illustrations dwindle to drab, scratchy blacks-and-whites for the early teens. And after suffering the muddily lurid covers of many adult paperbacks and the dull, informational jackets of most hardbacks, I regress with joy to the delicately drawn world of Jacqueline Ayer's Siam in *A Wish for Little Sister* (also the setting for her first book, *Nu Dang and His Kite*). A mynah bird grants Little Sister one birthday wish, and all day she tries on the exotic and fanciful wishes of her friends and relatives until she finds a wish of her own. These fragile drawings of people at work, at play, in repose or floating in Little Sister's imagination – ochre-patterned, with touches of fuchsia, aqua, lavender and green – call to mind the dreamy brilliance of an Eastern brocade.

From another part of the world altogether comes *Joba and the Wild Boar* (English and German texts side by side) about a little girl who is carried off by a wild boar she has brought up as a pet. The night pieces are a beautiful, thunderous blue, bristling with Black Forest murk and studded with the lantern-eyes of crows and owls – a handsome contrast to the yellow pumpkin-orange day scenes.

Also recommended:

The theme of children (or animals) lost, stolen or strayed is a favourite one and also underlies the circus adventures of Madeline and her friend Pepito in Ludwig Bemelmans' *Madeline and the Gypsies* (Deutsch. 15s.). The sumptuous illustrations in this addition to the Madeline series have a curiously baroque air – all red plush and fanfare: Madeline's escapades take place against such elegant backdrops as Notre Dame, Chartres, Mont Saint-Michel and Deauville. *Charlie on the Run* (Faber. 12s. 6d.) is another escapee from routine – a fat, white farm horse sold to a scrap dealer when his farmer buys a tractor. Gerald Rose's sprightly drawings and meadowy, yellow-green colour spreads illustrate this story by Elizabeth Rose. Two kittens are stolen in *The Cat Thief* (Abelard-Schuman. 12s. 6d.), by Joan Cass, causing William Stobbs's magnificent cats – blue, black, tortoiseshell, Siamese, tangerine and tiger – to surge to the rescue. *A for the Ark*, by Roger Duvoisin, both an alphabet and an animal book, includes such *recherché* creatures as the Izard, the Jacana and the Zebu in the more familiar congregation Noah called on board before the rains fell. (Bodley Head. 10s. 6d.) Françoise also has a catalogue, a simpler one for very little children, in *The Things I Like* (Brockhampton Press. 12s. 6d.) – a soft, pastel world full of Easter-egg boys and girls and animals.

This is Venice (W. H. Allen. 15s.), another in the M. Sasek series, is a big, splendid book, combining lively vignettes, waterscapes and palazzo façades with delicacy, wit and historical fact – a grand gift book, as are the rest in this series. Selected and arranged by the composer Elizabeth Poston, *The Children's Song Book* (Bodley Head. 30s.), offers some six dozen winning songs ranging from 'Oranges and Lemons', 'Once in Royal David's City' and 'Greensleeves' to a finale of songs from foreign countries, and is embellished with lyrical French-blue drawings by Susan Einzig.

Pair of Queens

Written: *c*.17–18 March 1962
Published: *New Statesman* (27 April 1962): 602–3

A Queen of Spain. By Peter de Polnay. Hollis & Carter. 30s.
Joséphine. By Hubert Cole. Heinemann. 30s.

A Queen of Spain whips willy-nilly through a good bit of history of the survey sort ('Now Napoleon bursts on the scene') before Isabella the Second appears as a child of three, receiving the oath of allegiance in Madrid. Unsettled by the crowds and hand-kissing, she cries, is 'pacified . . . by sugar plums', then vanishes in the smoke of the Carlist wars. Isabella's thirty-six-year reign seems not much more than a backdrop to the jack-in-the-box bouncings of generals and politicians, intrigues, rebellions and turbulence. It must be admitted that Isabella herself has left few signs of life. Sloppy, lazy, a hater of books, she soon flattens to a stereotype: a fat, lustful queen. Perhaps the best thing in the book is a photograph of Isabella, elephantine and heavy-eyed, festooned in a Spanish-Victorian lampshade of a dress, with her willowy, dapper little son Alfonso at her side. Mr de Polnay's biography is a sustained barrage of broad facts, potted personalities and headline events, under which, like a sleight-of-hand phantom, Isabella flickers and faces.

Hubert Cole's *Joséphine*, in contrast, recreates with a beautifully steady luminousness the sense of what it means to be a certain person in a certain period. Marie-Joseph-Rose Tascher de la Pagerie, Napoleon's wife, was born in Martinique in the year of the ants. The description of the ants' invasion is only one of the many brilliant little particulars which give this account its immediacy and weight. History looms, but never overwhelms the features of life. Marie-Rose's first marriage – to the political dandy, Alexandre de Beauharnais, in France – was arranged and unhappy. Alexandre, embarrassed by his creole bride's lack of education, left her very much alone, urging her by post to read selected passages from the poets, memorise speeches from the classical playwrights and study history and geography if she wished to inspire him with more 'solid and durable sentiments'. But it was not till her sojourn at a convent in the Faubourg Saint-Germain, while awaiting a legal separation from Alexandre, that this originally somewhat giddy flirt laid the foundations of the culture that was to surprise both Napoleon and his court. Under the

Terror, Alexandre went to the scaffold; Marie-Rose evaded his fate by flukes and, later, the death of Robespierre. The clerk who 'claimed to have saved many victims from the guillotine by chewing up and swallowing their dossiers' is credited with having in the same curious way served her.

Napoleon renamed her Josephine, and as this much more important person, she very properly becomes much more interesting. In this book he and she are not really to be considered apart. The scenes of Napoleon's household are meticulous as a Dutch interior, and the later elaborations of etiquette finely rendered – the compulsory stag hunts in the rain in coats of green and gold, or purple, blue, pink, lilac and silver, according to the retinue, and the ponderous routine of Fontainebleau. The portrait of Napoleon, growing from the fresh genius, the passionate lover and husband (never so loving that it could make his ambition tremble), into the Emperor and godhead of France, comes completely alive in the mirror of Josephine's devotion. Even in the glare shed by these two luminaries, minor characters emerge vividly – notably Eugene and Hortense, Josephine's children by her first marriage. She and her children have a blessed strength: their loyalty to each other is an odd constant in the public tumult of vacillations and defections. It persists undiminished, just as Josephine's loyalty to Napoleon persisted – even after the notorious divorce and throughout the draughty, scabrous damps of Navarre, to which he relegated her, and her final grandmotherly mellowing at Malmaison.

Oblongs

Written: c.0–9 May 1962
Published: *New Statesman* (18 May 1962): 724[*]

The Emperor's Oblong Pancake. By Peter Hughes. Abelard-Schuman. 12s. 6d.
The Three Robbers. By Tomi Ungerer. Methuen. 12s. 6d.
The Funny Thing. By Wanda Gág. Faber. 8s. 6d.
Dr Spock Talks with Mothers. Bodley Head. 18s.

Once there was an Emperor who was a pancake addict. His breakfast pancakes were six in number – great big yellow ones, a little bit brown on top and

---

[*] SP's review of *The Funny Thing* was quoted on the rear jacket flap of Gág's *The ABC Bunny*. Her review of *The Big River* was quoted in the *Observer* (17 June 1962): 27.

very round. The appearance of a mysterious oblong pancake in the ordinary lot on the Emperor's birthday triggers the rage of a tyrant who loves his symmetry, but the *idea* of oblongs turns out to be irresistible. An oblong régime is in order: oblong pancakes cry for oblong plates, and these are only properly accompanied by oblong cups and saucers, and these in turn hurry in oblong pies and oblong hats and oblong wheels and oblong eggs. The lovely logic of this oblong empire is confounded only by the intolerable rotundity of the sun. The Emperor makes assault after assault and repeated journeys to the ends of the earth, but the sun comes up round as ever. The people have already begun to slip back into their old round habits when the Emperor returns in triumph, having learned a little from Machiavelli and a lot from Columbus: the empire is allowed to revert to roundness, although the Emperor does retain his oblong pancakes and a taste for a small, regular amount of the various. Gerald Rose's illustrations in a pancakey ochre, jazzed up on every other page with royal red and blue, are, as ever, humorous and deft.

 The taming of tyrants is also the subject of the next two books. Tomi Ungerer's three robbers move by owl-light through a fine, midnight-blue murk, their eyes glittering bright as scimitars between ominously humped black hats and batlike capes. Their weapons are a blunderbuss, a pepper-blower and a large red axe (used for chopping carriage wheels, not heads), and with this elaborate armoury, they prowl the roads, looking for loot. One night they turn up nothing but a golden-haired orphan named Tiffany. Tiffany is, like most children, beautifully pragmatic. One shrewd question about the *use* of the trunks of treasure in the robbers' cave, and she converts the three mountain-hatted highwaymen into collectors of lost, unhappy or abandoned little ones. A castle is bought, word gets round, and children land daily as mail on the doorstep. This witty and satisfying story is simply told with big, bold colour spreads.

 It takes a very strong black-and-white book to compete with the blaze and vibrancy of a book in full colour, but Wanda Gág's drawings do just that. There is a charming, idiosyncratic solidity about her people and animals and hills and flowers, rather as if they were carved lovingly out of wood. Her clouds have the body of floating stones and her bluebells ring sturdily as bells in a tower. Bobo, the man of the mountain, lives in a hobbitish sort of tunnel-house and, like Bilbo Baggins himself, is devoted to food – nut cakes, seed puddings and the like – which he spreads for the animals and birds. His ingenuity when one day confronted by a Funny Thing ('something like a dog and also a little like a giraffe') who enjoys a diet of children's dolls makes an excellent read-aloud adventure for very young children, and has all the finality of a good fable.

Dr Spock, of course, is by now almost apocalyptic; he makes splendid sense. In case of crisis, minor and major, his fine, wise voice (made immediately accessible by a convenient index) is both sedative and salubrious. This is a complementary volume to his *Baby and Child Care*, and covers general health, a child's position in the family, discipline, behaviour problems, attachments and anxieties – and more. An admirable aid to weathering the horrors and astonishments of parenthood.

Also recommended:

The Big River. By Elizabeth and Gerald Rose. Faber. 12s. 6d. A clear poetic account of a river's genesis and progress to the sea, superb illustrations, which capture the creatures in and around the river with verve and an apt feeling for colour and mood: blue and white water, slow or furious, the umber bulk of earth, and a delicate fretwork of ferns, waterweeds and waves.

The Cat Show. By Joan Cass and William Stobbs. Abelard-Schuman. 12s. 6d. A worthy successor to their *Cat Thief*. The handsomely patterned pages swarming with the same redoubtable cats, this time on their way to a cat competition in which virtue is more than its own reward and bad-mannered beauty still wins its points as beauty.

Oregonian Original

Written: *c.*1 November 1962
Published: *New Statesman* (9 November 1962): 660

Opal Whiteley. By E. S. Bradburne. Putnam. 25s.
The Wonderful Button. By Evan Hunter. Abelard-Schuman. 12s. 6d.
Little Blue and Little Yellow. By Leo Lionni. Brockhampton. 12s. 6d.
Punch and Judy Carry On. By Elizabeth and Gerald Rose. Faber. 13s. 6d.

Opal Whiteley's diary of life in the Oregon backwoods, written in her sixth and seventh years and published in 1920 when she was twenty-two, is now reprinted with a splendid and curious introduction. The four-page list of 'characters' in the diary made me cringe, I confess. I dreaded the fey, the breathless, the pretty. Not a bit of it. This record of home, barnyard and woodland in the days of sunbonnets and castoria is stunningly authentic. If Opal Whiteley 'forged' the diary at a riper age, as some have suggested, she is nonetheless blessed, as was Sarah, at ninety. But the style of the diary, so oddly archaic, yet so utterly unaffected, bears a strong resemblance to essays I have read by secondary modern pupils: a crow-line direct to the object, and the object itself gleam-new. Opal Whiteley is a sort of articulate Bird Girl, a Girl of the Limberlost, raising mosquitoes in the rain-barrel for pet bats, saving a cow track in a drawer and looking long looks at lichens ('lichen folk talk in grey tones. I think they do talk more when come winter days'). Here she is on potatoes:

> I have thinks these potatoes growing here did have knowings of star-songs. I have kept watch in the field at night and I have seen the stars look kindness down upon them. And I have walked between the rows of potatoes and I have watched the star-gleams on their leaves. And I have heard the wind ask of them the star-songs the star-gleams did tell in shadows on their leaves. And as the wind did go walking in the field talking to the earth-voices there, I did follow her down the rows. I did have feels of her presence near. And her goings by made ripples on my night gown.

A Douanier out-of-doors, indoors Opal Whiteley is pure Vermeer. Whether cutting ham ('After I did hang that slice of ham on a nail by the door, I did cut another slice. It was not so wide but it had more longness and some strings on it like the little short strings on the nightcap of Jenny Strong') or broom-sweeping or baby-minding or dyeing the Plymouth Rock hen in the blueing vat or analysing the feel of a spank, she dazzles.

Here and there the diary is larded with French phrases – lists of birds, flowers and suchlike, which one reader saw spelled out, in acrostics, the name of Henri d'Orléans. There are also references to an Angel Father and an Angel Mother who left two books with Opal from which she drew the weird names of her animals and other wisdom, even as the founders of Mormonism drew on the mysterious Urim and Thummim for their translations of holy writ in upper New York State. The manuscript was in thousands of pieces. It took Opal nine months to sort it out and stick it all together for Ellery Sedgwick, the Editor of the *Atlantic Monthly*, where the diary first appeared. In photograph, it looks for all the world like an American Rosetta stone – great jammed, skew, childish capitals. Now Opal certainly did have a spank-happy and crude mother, but whether her dreams of royal French parentage, of being, in fact, a princess – which she lived out so astoundingly in later life – were real or apocryphal, the diary does not give evidence. I myself found the French bits inorganic and patchy. They very quickly fall away – dress-up cloaks, fake jewellery. What does magnificently remain is the real princess, the Oregonian original, with pockets for toads in her underskirts and her pet, Felix Mendelssohn, 'a mouse that has likes for soft feels to go to sleep in'.

The wonderful button – the biggest, brightest, most beautiful in the world – has a large red ruby in the middle, and a circle of pearls around that, and a circle of emeralds around that, and a circle of sapphires around that, and lots of diamond clusters around *that*. The button belongs to King Tinki-San, and to his people it means hand-tooled sandals with silk thongs, quilted trousers with pearls, a velvet tunic, a spun gold cape, jewel chests, a crown, a kingdom. Everybody wants the wonderful button . . . and all it means. Nobody wants Tinki-San. Totally eclipsed by his archetypal status symbol, the king is as sad and lonely as, I imagine, the man in the Louis Roth suit in the *New Yorker* ads – all those glamorous women ogling him, and then cynically asking one another 'or could it be his Louis Roth suit?'

But whereas the man in the Louis Roth suit is no doubt for ever doomed to melt to a brand name on the lips of status-conscious women, King Tinki-San is more fortunate. He manages to get off in the woods to be alone with his thoughts and meets Ling, a fine, free Eastern nature boy – a type inaccessible to the Louis Roth man, I should think, even in the bracken of Connecticut. Ling is well and soundly in touch with his five senses – a natural: truly rich. Immediately he sees that Tinki-San, open-caped in the snow, is about to freeze, and tries to warm the incognito king by a bracing course of runs and slides. The two new friends exchange capes, and the king, stunned by Ling's imperviousness to the status symbol, hands it over. The wonderful button becomes a fishing lure.

Once the troublesome button is out of the way, greed and envy vanish – the people see their king for the man he is: wise, good and handsome. 'Why the king is just a person,' they whisper. And they begin to smile – seeing themselves (just 'persons' too) as kings. Quentin Blake's drawing splash their Oriental golds, fuchsias and blues about with superb abandon. Evan Hunter wrote *The Blackboard Jungle*; and the worry caused by that button does seem exceedingly American.

Little Blue and Little Yellow are inspired colour blobs – little nursery Rorschachs – and the best of friends. Their games and adventures and the crisis of identity which they suffer when they hug too hard may seem amoeba-simple, yet this makes one of the most *visually* exciting of picture books – full of wit and brio, with the leaning Stonehenge shapes of parents over the ego-balls of the little ones, and the whole spectrum of playmates tossed through space by a wonderfully skilled juggler, Leo Lionni.

A more familiar homunculus is the humped and hook-nosed Punch of *Punch and Judy Carry On*. Punch, a veteran wife-beater, scrams like the coward and bully he is when Judy lands him a few smacks. Gerald Rose manipulates his minute adventurer through superbly evocative bluey-green beach scenes – a real harlequin's Brighton. Punch's return to the old wife-beating racket ('a job he KNEW he could do') comes, at the summit of these mad exploits, as a bit of a let-down, but then the show must go on.

Also recommended:

The Mellops Go Flying. By Tomi Ungerer. Methuen. 10s. 6d. A flawless and logical fable for the very small about a father pig and his four boys who build and fly an aeroplane, fall down a mountain and encounter some sardonic and unkind Indians, but manage to wing home to whipped cream cake.

Achilles the Donkey. By H. E. Bates. Dobson. 15s. The adventures of a donkey, sold into servitude and liberated by an apocalyptic pelican.

Horton Hatches the Egg. By Dr Seuss. Collins. 12s. 6d. Horton was hatching it in America when I was eight, and twenty-two years later, on his arrival in Britain, I *still* have by heart the trump couplet. The reward of the harassed elephant, sitting-in for a flighty Mayzie bird, is that proper to a true father – a fledgeling with ears and a tail and a trunk just like his. Wings, too, of course.

The Penguins of Penguin Town. By Gaby Baldner. Pictures by Gerhard Oberländer. Heinemann. 12s. 6d. Capitalism among the penguins! Pengo and Penga and their two children move through a blue-green world of polar ice cubes, but dream of dresses, money and a big house.

The Creation. Illustrated by Reinhard Herrmann. Macmillan. 9s. 6d. The fourth book in this series – stark, radiant renderings of plants, planets, fish, birds and animals, worthy of the words.

Suffering Angel

Written: *c*.28 November 1962
Published: *New Statesman* (7 December 1962): 828–9

Lord Byron's Wife. By Malcolm Elwin. Macdonald. 45s.

In his splendid account of Byron's marriage and separation, based on that beautifully plummy accumulation of unpublished letters and documents known as the Lovelace Papers, Mr Elwin begins, as might many a shrewd marriage counsellor, with a meticulous investigation of the bride's mother. Judith Milbanke was certainly formidable enough for *anyone's* mother-in-law. Skilled whist-player, markswoman and unflagging canvasser for her husband, she weathered the ghastly hazards of childbirth in her era to produce, at the age of forty, an only daughter, Annabella. From the start, her spry, gossipy letters about '*little* Madam' reveal the fanatic and ominous devotion which flared with crackling italics at the Byrons' separation after a mere year of marriage:

> Wonder not that I write *Strongly*, who could see that Suffering Angel Sinking under such *unmanly* and *despicable* treatment, and not feel? Ld Byron is sending her Parents also with Sorrow to the Grave – let him *glory* also in *that* – and that he has three Lives to answer for at the great account . . .

And the 'Suffering Angel' could write: 'I have escaped from the greatest Villain that ever existed.' Something of the Grand Guignol shows in these extremes of white and black. Byron himself had only praise for his 'Dearest Bell', excused his morbidities by a press of money worries and liver trouble, and begged her back. But a sudden muzz of camp followers and rhetoric had swallowed Annabella. One is snowbound in the end, if not brainwashed, by the humourless rhetoric of past wrongs which she was to sustain until her death. Amid these 'Justifications', with their Saharas of jargon, Byron's few letters refresh like water. Annabella's refusal to grant her spouse an interview (she never saw Byron again), let alone try to make a second go of it, seems due less to his cruelty, adultery, incest and the rest than to the 'formidable apparition' of that consistency Byron had observed in her before their marriage – a consistency fixed by the ego-screws of pride and a need to be for ever, like Milton's God, tediously in the right.

Annabella aside, Byron the lion was undeniably poor husband-stuff. One shudders to read his fiancée's complacent expectations of 'the most rational happiness'. For it was when scavenging for an escape from the advances of Lady Caroline Lamb (her improprieties included a gift of pubic hair) that Byron first proposed to Annabella – to be rejected, then eventually snared by letters which bear down on their prey like some terrifyingly grey, pietistic Gorgon. The account of the wedding is chilling.

> As soon as we got into the carriage his countenance changed to gloom and defiance. He began singing in a wild manner as he usually does when angry . . . At the Inn at Rushyford he turned to me with a bitter look and said 'I wonder how much longer I shall be able to keep up *the part I have been playing*.'

The 'part' to come was theatrically infantine: unbridled brandy-drinking, fiddling with loaded pistols, 'studiously and maliciously' telling Annabella of his visits to a mistress during her pregnancy. Byron's own loyal sister Augusta worried that he

> appeared to feel the greatest hatred towards his Wife and the unborn child that he sometimes said he hoped they would both die and then he should be at Liberty that he never would see the Child or her after she was brought to bed but should go abroad immediately.

Add this to Byron's crude incestuousness – getting wife and sister by turns to kiss him on the sofa, and so on. What surprises is the fabulous malleability of the two women: did neither one dream of walking out? Jealousy of Augusta did, for the minute, simplify Annabella's memoirs ('the thought of his dagger lying in the next room . . . crossed my mind – I wished it in her heart') and one is grateful for the enlivened style; but this is jealousy recollected in tranquillity. On the spot, Augusta's role as Annabella's tender defender appears to have neutralised such acidulous thoughts. In fact the women often have the air of conspiring to manage a dangerous ape. 'His misfortune,' noted Annabella, with one of her rarely wifely insights,

> is an habitual *passion for Excitement*, which is always found in ardent temperaments, where the pursuits are not in some degree organised. It is the Ennui of a monotonous existence that drives the best hearted people of this description to the most dangerous paths . . .

'You know his way is to fast till he is famished & then *devour* more than his stomach in that *weak* state can bear,' Augusta even more astutely wrote: 'do hide YOUR *Brandy Bottle*.'

To the bitter end Augusta acted the hectic if unsuccessful Pandarus. Her portrait of Annabella after the separation cuts oddly across the latter's pompous letters:

> She is positively reduced to a Skeleton – pale as ashes – a deep hollow tone of voice & a calm in her manner quite supernatural.

How clearly one sees the killing dybbuk of self-righteousness in possession! And what better luck this cherished, sympathetic sister might have had as Byron's wife.

Sylvia Plath on *Contemporary American Poetry*

Ts,* 10 January 1963, Smith College

A new spirit is at work in American poetry. I won't say it's a wave, I won't say it's a trend – that's convenient and military and I'll leave the bore of tags to the men on *Time*. Whatever it is, has been happening, like breathing, quietly and spontaneously among individual poets for some while now, and a good sampling of it is in Donald Hall's Penguin Anthology of *Contemporary American Poetry*. Flip through Lowell's early poems – as fine and wild and rich and stiff as the animal room at the Vatican – to the intimate disarmament of this:

> Only teaching on Tuesdays, book-worming
> in pajamas fresh from the washer each morning,
> I hog a whole house on Boston's
> 'hardly passionate Marlborough Street,'
> where even the man
> scavenging filth in the back alley trash cans,
> has two children, a beach wagon, a helpmate,
> and is a 'young Republican'.

The shift in tone is already history: the flashing, elaborate carapace of *Lord Weary's Castle* dropped for *Life Studies* – walking the tightrope of the psyche naked. Snodgrass does something similar, albeit in watercolours, in *Heart's Needle*. There's no exhibitionism about it, no thunder and lightning. The voice is quiet, colloquial, laconic, wry. As often as not, it's the voice of the solipsist:

> I myself am hell;
> Nobody's here –

The *inwardness* of these images, their plummeting subjectivity is what Mr Hall points to as genuinely new to the American scene – the uncanny faculty of

---

* BBC transcript marked 'Not checked in Talks Department with "As Broadcast" script' with holograph corrections and deletions by SP. Produced by George MacBeth, the review was broadcast on the Third Programme. The recording was published in *The Spoken Word: Sylvia Plath* (London: British Library, 2010): Track 23. Three sections were marked for deletion in an unknown hand, presumably for time considerations of the broadcast; however, they are included here.

melting through the leaves of the wallpaper through the dark looking glass into a world one can only call surrealistic and irrational. The analyst's couch has played its role here, I think – that important and purgatorial bit of American literary furniture. Certainly the claustrophobic flow of nightmare and the startlements of free association inform passages like this from Louis Simpson's poem 'There Is':

> I have the poor man's nerve-tic, irony.
> I see through the illusions of the age!
> The bell tolls, and the hearse advances,
> and the mourners follow, for my entertainment.
>
> I tread the burning pavement,
> the streets where drunkards stretch
> like photographs of civil death
> and trumpets strangle in electric shelves.
>
> The mannequins stare at me scornfully.
> I know they are pretending
> all day to be in earnest.
> And can it be that love is an illusion?
>
> When darkness falls on the enormous street
> the air is filled with Eros, whispering.
> Eyes, mouths, contrive to meet
> in silence, fearing they may be prevented.

Now this is a far cry from the early pastoral and courtly Simpson – the shepherds shouting 'Ut Hoy' for intellectual joy, the caravels sailing to Cathay. Eyes and mouths, amputated of humanity, fabricate their contacts like neurotic cuttlefish, in a cloud of ink. The word 'Eros' falls with the hiss of some disease. Most of Simpson's recent poems possess this curious tension and inevitability. Their electric charge does not seem to depend on any special word or image, it's roused rather as emotion is roused in much modern cinema – by the juxtaposition of images, without editorialising. The images jostle and touch. The spark that springs – horror, tenderness, whatever – is the response of the viewer. I say viewer, because so much of this poetry is visual. Take these lines from 'Sunday in Glastonbury' by Robert Bly:

It is out in the flimsy suburbs,
Where the light seems to shine through the walls.

My black shoes stand on the floor
Like two open graves.

The curtains do not know what to hope for,
But they are obedient.

How strange to think of India!
Wealth is nothing but lack of people.

The act, not committed here, of stepping into those shoes broods over the poem like a little doom. The very weight and hang of the curtains is personal – personified, and this *in*-feeling, this identification with light, trees, water, *things* – this is another aspect of the new poetry – everything is listening, trembling, sentient. There's no sure objective ground – stillness and motion, near and far, telescope upsettingly, they become one. As James Merrill asks in his poem 'After Greece':

But where is home – these walls?
These limbs? The very spaniel underfoot
Races in sleep, toward what?
It is autumn. I did not invite
Those guests, windy and brittle, who drink my liquor.
Returning from a walk, I find
The bottles filled with spleen, my room itself
Smeared by reflection onto the far hemlocks.
I some days flee in dream
Back to the exposed porch of the maidens
Only to find my great-great-grandmothers
Erect there, peering
Into a globe of red Bohemian glass.

James Wright's new poems seem so pure and clear they might be documentaries, yet there's a darkness in this poem of his on 'Miners' and the images drift into something at once subconscious and archetypal.

The police are dragging for the bodies
Of miners in the black waters
Of the suburbs.

Below, some few
Crawl, searching, until they clasp
The fingers of the sea.

Somewhere,
Beyond ripples and drowsing woodchucks,
A strong man, alone,
Beats on the door of a grave, crying
Oh let me in.

Many women mount long stairs
Into the shafts,
And emerge in the tottering palaces
Of abandoned cisterns.

In the middle of the night,
I can hear cars, moving on steel rails, colliding
Underground.

Is it a coincidence that so many American poets should all at once cast off the old, stiff suits of the early styles? – Lowell, Simpson, Adrienne Rich, Anthony Hecht and W. S. Merwin for example. In Merwin's 'Small Woman on Swallow Street' the world buckles and warps like a flame in a mad draft:

> A big coat
> Can help save you. But eyes push you down; never
> Meet eyes. There are hands in hands, and love
> Follows its fuss into shut doors; who
> Shall be killed first? Do not look up there:
> The wind is blowing the building-tops, and a hand
> Is sneaking the whole sky another way, but
> It will not escape. Do not look up. God is
> On High. He can see you. You will die.

What I don't think is a coincidence is that so many of these poets should themselves be translators – very considerable and original translators – of foreign poets such as Pasternak, Montale, Neruda, Trakl and so on. It would be naïve to claim that this new surrealism had jumped, full-blown if slightly manic from the collective American poetic brain. I do think the voice in the poems I've been reading is uniquely American, that's where it lives, but it's not all that miraculously without its influences.

What happens to the freer sort of poetry when the feeling is lacking or forced or suspect is that the poem fizzles like a wet squib. And there are enough duds here – flat, prosy, pompous. Stafford and Nemerov, two fine poets, could have been better represented, Reed Whittemore's variety turns look pretty over-exposed and the elegant Wilbur comes off curiously bloodless. The one poet whose absence does glare out of the collection is Anne Sexton. The poems in her remarkable second book *All My Pretty Ones* could stand up to the best of anything here.

Galway Kinnell has a line describing dawn in New Hampshire: 'And the dimension of depth seizes everything'. That is, I think, what's been happening in a lot of American poetry. Let me close with a passage from Kinnell's 'Flower Herding Pictures on Mount Monadnock.' Here are two passages from it:

I kneel at a pool,
I look through my face
At the bacteria I think
I see crawling through the moss.

My face sees me,
The water stirs, the face,
Looking preoccupied,
Gets knocked from its bones.

In this last passage, the man of suits and attitudes seems vaporised in the fumes being given off by a flower. The flower takes his place – a totem, a small fierce deus.

In the forest I discover a flower.

The invisible life of the thing
Goes up in flames that are invisible,
Like cellophane burning in the sunlight.

It burns up. Its drift is to be nothing.

In its covertness it has a way
Of uttering itself in place of itself,
Its blossoms claim to float in the Empyrean,

A wrathful presence on the blur of the ground.

The appeal to heaven breaks off.
The petals begin to fall, in self-forgiveness.
It is a flower. On this mountainside it is dying.

Appendix I: Story Fragments

Stardust

Ts, June 1946–May 1947,[*] **Lilly Library**

Chapter 1

Nancy awoke with the pleasant sensation that a whole, unbroken stretch of summer vacation lay ahead of her—no more tutors, no more lessons for ever and ever so long. She turned over and yawned luxuriously.

A soft breeze blew the lacy white curtains away from the screened windows. Sunbeams made their way through the blinds and gave the room a warm, golden glow. Outside a lawnmower clacked monotonously. A milk truck stopped, and Nancy heard the clinking of the bottles as the milkman carried them to the doorstep. The truck started up again. Brrrooomm, it went, and caught its breath. Brrrrrrooomm—and it was gone. The rasping drone of a locust predicted a hot day, and the sparrows and robins were having a gay conversation in the apple orchard.

Nancy was debating to herself whether she should tiptoe out into the fresh dawn of early morning or stay drowsing in bed until breakfast, when her thoughts were interrupted by a tiny voice at her elbow.

"Hello, Nancy," it said.

Nancy stopped right in the middle of deciding that she would take a jam sandwich with her when she went out, and the voice repeated a little louder, "Hello, Nancy."

This time it came from right next to Nancy's ear. Cautiously she opened one eye. What she saw made both of her blue eyes fly open wide.

Standing on her pillow was a tiny little fairy! She was clad in shimmering yellow gauzy material, and she had fluttering, rainbow-tinted wings. Her

---

[*] SP began work on 'Stardust' in June 1946. A holograph chapter outline, which sold via a Bonhams auction on 16 March 2016, indicates she planned for twelve chapters, writing one per month. Only chapters 1–4 and 9 appear to be extant. SP drafted a first chapter, in holograph, in the same writing pad as 'The Thrilling Adventures of a Penny', held by Smith College.

golden hair rippled to her waist, and a gold star glinted on the end of her magic wand. A perfect fairy if you ever saw one!

Now, Nancy had read many fairy stories, but she had only dared to dream about seeing one of these magic little people—and here was one standing on her very pillow.

The fairy spoke to Nancy in a low, soft voice that sounded like pine trees sighing in the wind, or like a brook slipping through grassy meadows.

"I am Star," she explained. "Once in every generation, my Queen chooses one child on earth whom she thinks has the strongest belief in fairy magic, and one out of her fairy band to reward that child by showing him all the good magic that exists in the world today. You are that child, and I am the fairy who has been given the special power to take you on many travels to magic lands all over the world. But first I must clear away the invisible film that covers your eyes and that prevents you from seeing the fairy miracles which happen each day."

Thereupon the fairy passed her tiny wand across Nancy's forehead, and then, before Nancy could utter a word, Star gave her a smiling nod and faded away into thin air. All that was left where Star had been was a silver puff of vapor, and as Nancy reached out to touch it, that, too, vanished.

Chapter 2

Nancy sat upright in bed staring at the spot where the fairy had vanished. She knew that she had not been dreaming because Star certainly must be real.

"Well," thought Nancy, "I guess that I had better not think about it now. If Star comes back I'll be so happy, and if she doesn't I will try to forget her, though I know I never will be able to."

She dressed hurriedly, and then tiptoed down the curving staircase into the kitchen where savory odors announced the fact that Aunt Lucy was making breakfast.

"Aunt Lucy . . ." Nancy began, but thought better of telling her elderly maiden aunt about the fairy, because she would undoubtedly smile and call it a result of imagination.

"Yes, child?" said Aunt Lucy crisply.

"I have already made the two beds," replied Nancy truthfully, because she had just finished before coming downstairs.

"That is very nice of you, dear," exclaimed Aunt Lucy in a pleased manner, "By the way, your cousin sent you a new book. I left it on the table."

Nancy immediately ran to get it and found a beautifully illustrated copy of *Alice in Wonderland*. With a cry of joy she put the book down and quickly ate her breakfast. Her aunt excused her from her morning tasks, so Nancy ran out in the yard, lovingly clasping her book. She climbed high up in the apple tree and settled comfortably in her favorite perch. Carefully opening the book, she began to read.

"I wonder if this really happened," she thought, after completing the first few chapters. Nancy looked dreamily through the screen of leaves and pale white apple blossoms. Her thoughts turned to the natural beauty about her. One of the apple buds opened slowly before her very eyes. Nancy blinked, and saw a tiny winged creature emerge.

"Oh, Star," she whispered, "I knew you'd come."

"I was hoping that you wouldn't think I was a dream," said Star, for that's who it was, "because then I could never come back to see you."

"I've just begun to read *Alice in Wonderland*," said Nancy, but she received no reply. Nancy saw, to her amazement, that Star was growing steadily larger, or was she growing smaller? She couldn't tell. It was very warm, so Nancy closed her eyes. Then she felt a cool breeze and smelled the salty tang in the air.

Upon opening her eyes, Nancy saw that she was on a sandy beach that stretched a golden arm into the green waters of the ocean. She heard the roar of the waves as they pounded on the shore. Their crests were flecked with airy foam, and the water made a pleasant sound as it washed among the pebbles. The shrill cries of the seagulls echoed as they circled over the vast expanse of shimmering water. Now and then one would plunge down into the depths and come up triumphantly grasping a silvery fish in its strong beak. Lying on the smooth swept sand were many lovely scalloped shells and rounded stones.

"Well," said Star from her seat on a little fairy-boat shell, "how do you like it?"

Nancy turned and said, "Why I never thought that the ocean could be so wonderful! I have never seen anything so powerful and so beautiful!"

"Now," said the fairy, "How would you like to go *under* the ocean to visit the Queen of the Sea?"

"I'd love to," Nancy exclaimed, "but how will we get there?"

"Just follow me," replied the fairy, as she fluttered down to the water's edge. For a moment Nancy hung back timidly, but when she saw that nothing happened to Star, she followed her into the breakers. Strangely enough, the water was not at all wet, but felt very comfortable. They walked deeper and deeper, until Nancy could look up and see only clear green water above her head.

Wavy streamers of seaweed had anchored their roots in the sand. Lacy green fronds of other submarine plants floated about. Schools of rainbow fish scuttled by, and occasionally one was caught in the long arms of the flowerlike sea anemone. Pointed starfish lay quietly on the ocean floor. As Nancy followed the fairy, she heard liquid music that rippled louder and louder as they went on. Soon she saw some graceful pink coral spires rising in the distance. "The Sea Queen's palace," she thought, as they walked on.

They reached the palace sooner than she expected. It certainly was beautiful—the doorways were arched, and the windows shone transparently. Sea flowers and seaweed climbed over the wall. Evidently they were expected, because the gates were thrown open. As they walked through into the palace, Nancy saw that the music poured out of a shining harp that played by itself as it stood in the hall. They passed down a long corridor before they paused in the doorway of the Queen's courtroom. The glimmering blue walls were patterned with pearls, and, in one end of the room, there was a cushioned throne upon which the Sea Queen reposed, staring pensively into the distance. Her long black hair hung listlessly down on each side of her pale, expressionless face; her green eyes matched her trailing robes that flowed around her. Her skin was so pale that it almost had a bluish tinge, and her head rested in her cupped white hand. Around the Queen were gathered groups of mermaids, as motionless as marble statues. In their laps slept small merchildren, indistinct in the fading light. They all had a rather tiresome similarity.

"You see," said Star, "they sit silently like this until the sunlight is gone. Then all the lights go on, and the palace is filled with life and laughter. Down here it gets dark very early."

Just as she finished speaking the last long ray of sunlight disappeared and there was a moment of darkness before the lights flashed on. Hundreds and hundreds of them were suspended from crystal chandeliers. They sent twinkling beams of light to chase the shadows out of the gloomy corners, and under the white brilliance the room glowed softly. A rosy flush appeared on the lifeless faces and the mermaids began to stir; the merchildren awoke. The faint music grew louder and as it swelled into a burst of song, the Sea Queen rose slowly from her throne. She walked to the doorway and graciously greeted Nancy and Star, a lively sparkle in her clear, sea-green eyes, and a happy smile playing about her lips.

When she spoke, her resonant voice flowed on like softly running water. "We are having a banquet in honor of your visit," she said, leading them over to a white-clothed table that was heavily laden with food, none of which, oddly enough, came from the sea. There were exotic tropical fruits and strange, delicious meats that Nancy had never tasted before. After seeing that her guests had partaken generously of the feast, the Sea Queen led them out of the banquet hall. They left behind the clinking of silver and goblets and the laughter of the merpeople as they followed the Queen down winding passageways and twisting staircases. She paused at last in front of a barred doorway. Taking out a tiny gold key, she unlocked it and motioned them to go in. The splendor that met their eyes can hardly be described—the room was not lighted, but the light from the hall was sufficient to see the large piles of jewels that gave off a light of their own. There were creamy white pearls, warm red opals, flashing diamonds that gave off white fire, pale violet amethysts, gleaming blue sapphires, and translucent green emeralds. In one corner piles of silver shone with a cold blue light. There were stacks of ruddy gold pieces as well as a small heap of rare shells that had evidently been gathered from the very heart of the ocean.

"This," said the Queen, "is my treasure chamber. These gems are priceless. You see, my treasures are gathered from sunken ships or from the sea itself. My domain is exceedingly great."

The Sea Queen made her way to the heap of shells and picked up one of the loveliest ones. Seeing Nancy gazing at it in awed admiration, the Queen smilingly held it to her ear. Nancy's eyes widened. She heard the "Sshh-h-h-h, Ssshh-h-h-h" of the ocean waves so plainly that she could fancy herself on the beach again.

"I see that you are so fascinated by my Listening Shell that I will give it to you to keep as a remembrance," said the Queen as she handed Nancy the vivid yellow shell with the colored edge and brown spots.

Nancy was so overwhelmed that she could scarcely voice her thanks. The Queen laughed softly in her tinkling way, and led them out of the room, locking the door behind them.

"It's time that we were getting back," said Star.

"All you have to do is catch an ingoing current," replied the Queen, as she opened a door labeled "IN" and showed them the water flowing by. Nancy and Star stepped out in the current and were immediately swept along with it. They could hear the voice of the Queen rising faintly after them: "Good-b-y-e-e-e," she called.

Nancy felt a soft thud as a big wave landed her on the shore. Star landed beside her on a dash of spray. Surprisingly enough, neither of them was the least bit wet. Feeling overcome by a peculiar drowsiness, Nancy closed her eyes.

When she opened them, she found herself back in the apple tree, the copy of

Alice in Wonderland open in her lap. She was brought back to reality by her aunt's voice calling, "Nancy! Come in for lunch!"

Nancy wondered if she had been dreaming, but as she swung down from the tree, she found that her hand still clutched the Listening Shell. Pausing a moment on the way to the house, she held it to her ear. The country seemed to vanish and she could hear the ocean waves and almost smell the salty breeze.

When Nancy entered the house, her aunt asked, "How did you like the book," and then she noticed the shell. It seemed to have a strange influence upon her, for she did not ask where Nancy had got it, but merely said, "I can still remember stories told when I was a child, about the great tidal wave that once descended on this part of the country and swept all the neat white farms out to the sea. It took years before the terrible scene of waste and destruction again regained the rich top soil, and before the waving fields of wheat and corn were replanted. Ah, yes! Long were the seasons of want before the lands were built up again."

Nancy gazed in wonder at her aunt, whose rather sharp features were softened with memories. With an effort Aunt Lucy recalled herself to the present, and said in a kinder voice than she usually used, "Wash up, now, and put your things away before you eat."

Rather than break this strange yet more agreeable mood by talking, Nancy ran upstairs, and laid the shell carefully on the top shelf of her bookcase. Stepping back to admire it, she saw that the darkly varnished wood of the case made a striking background for the twisting shape of the gleaming, rainbow-colored shell.

Suddenly Nancy realized joyfully that she would be able to return to the ocean beach any time that she wished, just by holding the shell to her ear and listening to the wash of the waves among the pebbles.

Chapter 3

The old garden was looking more lonesome than usual that cool afternoon as Nancy made her way along the uneven, grassy paths. The late autumn sun sent long rays of faint, lukewarm light over the flowerbeds where only a few clumps of faded zinnias raised their proud heads above the dried-out stalks of former blooms. The ground was still soft underfoot, but the grass and the maple trees had lost the fresh green of summer.

Nancy sighed deeply as she paused by the zinnia bed and began to clip the flowers with Aunt Lucy's garden shears.

"All the pretty flowers are gone, and these dry old zinnias are the only ones left," she thought to herself as she regarded the stiff reddish-brown and dusty orange blossoms with their petals arranged in prim, orderly frills.

"Aunt Lucy said there was going to be an early frost tonight," she remembered as she finished cutting the last of the zinnias. Before going back to the house, Nancy stood in the midst of the garden, noticing the sunset. The sky was clear, and it seemed to have absorbed all the colors in the world to make its own hues so intense. The rosy violets, pale apple-greens and soft yellows blended together in perfect harmony. The sun, sinking slowly over the horizon, seemed like a brilliant gold coin. For a moment, Nancy was caught in the enchanting spell cast just between sunset and twilight. Something foreign *was* in the air, she admitted silently, shivering a bit at the suggestion of a mysterious presence.

Then, tightly gathering the sheaf of zinnias in her arms, she ran quickly toward the comforting warmth of the house.

Later that night, while snuggled deep in her bed, Nancy was awakened by a muffled commotion outside her window. When she peeked across the darkened room, it seemed too far a distance to walk in the wintry air. Just then, the full moon rounded a corner of the house and sent a beam of light gleaming across the chilly hardwood floor right to Nancy's bed. Overcome by curiosity, and trying to ignore the cold, the little girl threw back her covers. Before she could change her mind, she rushed to the window, pulled up the blind, and fumbled with cold fingers at the lock. After she had succeeded in getting it open, she leaned out over the sill and looked around. Her breath was suspended in a cloud of white vapor against the sky. Down below, the garden lay quiet, suffused in frosty moonlight. The disturbance was coming from the maple tree beside the house. It appeared to be the center of a minor tempest, for the leaves were blowing furiously, and their rustling became louder and louder. It sounded as if a thousand voices were whispering unintelligible words to one another. As Nancy listened, she heard the whispering voices more distinctly, and fancied that she could understand a few words here and there.

"When is he coming?" one shrill voice questioned.

"It's time now," replied a second.

"Tonight's the night—he promised us!" a third exclaimed breathlessly.

There was a brief pause, and then more incoherent voices swelled up into a veritable tumult of sound. Nancy stared at the shadowy depths of the maple tree. It must be the leaves, talking, she decided.

"Hello, Nancy," a rustly voice whispered in her ear.

"Oh, Star," said Nancy to the fairy that had flitted to her side on the windowsill. "What on earth is all this noise about?"

"Don't tell me you haven't heard!" Star widened her eyes in mock dismay. "Jack Frost is due tonight and . . ."

"He's the one who paints the leaves, isn't he?" interrupted Nancy.

"The very same," replied Star. "Here he comes now. Listen."

A shiver of expectancy traveled up Nancy's spine, and she listened. The leaves, too, had ceased their chatter and only rustled softly to and fro.

An eerie sighing sound filled the darkness, and almost immediately a blast of cold air made Nancy draw her woolly nightgown more tightly about her.

"That's the North Wind that heralds his coming," Star whispered.

Nancy saw a silver gleam in the darkness. As it approached, it took shape, and Nancy caught her breath. Never had she seen such a handsome youth. He gleamed silvery in the pale moonlight, and his wings sparkled and shimmered as he glided toward them.

"Hello, Star," he called in a clear, sweet voice, and then, "Hello, Nancy."

"Hello, Jack Frost," Nancy replied politely, as he seated himself gracefully on a maple branch. He was made entirely of smooth, shining ice, and Nancy could hardly take her eyes off his strong young face. Only his twinkling blue eyes appeared warm and lifelike.

"I'm a little late tonight," he began with an engaging smile, "but it took a long time to mix my paints. It's a little difficult to catch up with the Aurora Borealis, you know. They are so playful. Then too, this is one of my last stops for the night."

"Do you really get your paints from the Northern Lights?" Nancy questioned as, for the first time, she noticed the paintbrush and palette that he carried.

"Oh, yes," the boy replied, "where else!" As he glanced down to the garden he added a little disappointedly, "You've left no flowers for me to nip in the bud, I see."

"But there are so many leaves waiting," Star reminded gently.

"That's so," admitted Jack, brightening up a bit and daubing his brush into some scarlet paint.

Nancy watched admiringly as he tinted the leaves gold, orange and brown. With swift, deft strokes, he painted the entire tree in only a few minutes. The leaves rustled complacently, satisfied with their new costumes.

Jack laughed softly as he whispered to Nancy, "See how contented the poor things are. North Wind will have blown them all down in a day or two and *then* where would they be!"

"I don't know what you have to go to all this work for, then," said Nancy, adding indignantly, "Why do the leaves have to be blown down anyway?"

"Why," replied Jack, regarding her with astonishment, "that's just the way things are. *We* can't change them."

"Oh," said Nancy, still puzzled.

"I know what," began Jack in a wheedling tone as he turned to Star. "Let Nancy come with me on the rest of my trip. I've only a few more houses to go to, and we'll be right back."

Nancy looked at Star with pleading eyes, and the fairy smiled her consent.

Nancy took Jack's outstretched hand.

"Ouch!" Nancy gave a little scream of pain as she drew back. "Your hand," she said. "It burns."

"I'm so sorry," Jack said contritely. "I forgot you were mortal. I'm made of ice, you see, and it burns like fire when a human being touches it."

"It's quite all right," Nancy hastened to say. "I was a little surprised, that's all."

"Jump down," he called, as she hesitated on the windowsill. "The North Wind will catch you."

Nancy did as Jack Frost instructed, and immediately she felt the wind bear her upward. Side by side, she and the boy skimmed along with the wind behind them. It didn't feel so cold from the back, Nancy reflected.

The two paused an instant by a small pond. As the youth breathed upon it, a thin film of ice covered the waters. He then leaned over and playfully tweaked the petals of a late aster, and it withered beneath his touch.

"Don't look so sad," Jack told Nancy. "I don't kill things. I just prepare the seeds and roots so they'll live through the winter and be ready for the Great Awakening next spring."

"I see," said Nancy, relieved.

After Jack had stopped a second time to color a small clump of bushes he had somehow neglected, Nancy said wistfully, "Do you suppose *I* could paint something?"

"Try a window," grinned Jack as they came to a brown cottage. He handed her a brush covered with frosty white. Nancy perched on the branch of an elm and began to paint little patterns on the glass. First a hill, then some trees and flowers.

"There," she said proudly as she leaned back to survey her work.

"Very good," agreed Jack. "You're quite artistic, aren't you!"

"I never know who painted those lovely scenes on my window pane all last winter," Nancy smiled, "but now I'm sure it was you."

"Listen," exclaimed Jack, suddenly eager, "why don't you come up North with me. We'd live in a huge ice palace, and it would be such fun! There's no one for me to play with up there," he added sorrowfully. "No one except the Northern Lights, I mean, and all they ever want to do is play tag with each other."

"Oh," breathed Nancy, taken aback. It *would* be nice for a while, she thought. But then she remembered the pond, encased in ice.

"Oh," she said again, "I really couldn't."

"You'd come down with me each fall and see everyone again. It gets lonesome when I'm up there all by myself," the boy said, looking at her sadly. "Do say yes!"

"I'd love to," Nancy replied gently, "but I'd never live through the cold weather up there. Besides, *you* can visit *me* each year, you know."

"I suppose you're right," he sighed, and then added briskly, "Well, my job's done down here, so let's go back to your house."

Soon they were again at Nancy's windowsill. She was sorry to say goodbye to Jack Frost. He was *so* nice.

"Let me know if you've changed your mind when I come down next fall," he was saying.

"I will," promised Nancy. She heaved a little sigh as the young boy sped off into the night on wings of the wind.

"Farewell, farewell," his voice drifted back faintly, and he was gone.

The next morning, Nancy ran to the window as soon as she awoke and peered out through the frost-patterned glass.

In the sharp radiance of the morning sunlight, the trees were resplendent in crimson and gold. The grass was stiffened under a sprinkling of frozen dewdrops, and the air was crisp and cool. The picture seemed perfect. I hope it lasts forever, Nancy thought. And then a feeling of desolation overcame her as she recalled Jack's words—"only for a day or two, a day or two."

It was at that moment she noticed a small red leaf tucked under the crack between the window and the sill. The girl picked it up aimlessly, and then smiled.

"See you next fall! Don't forget!" was printed on it in neat white letters.

Chapter 4

Nancy sat among the soft cushions on the window seat one snowy Saturday afternoon. Her aunt was taking an afternoon nap, and the old house was dim and quiet. Outside it was quiet too. Large, lacy flakes of snow drifted lazily to the ground, and all Nancy could see as she looked up into the bleak gray sky were hundreds and hundreds of little snowflakes floating down. The snow softened the bare tree branches with cottony ruffles, and it piled up over the wheelbarrow in the orchard so that only the handles could be seen.

As Nancy stared through the window, her chin cupped in her hands, the glass pane melted away, and nothing was left between her and the hushed world outside. The snow sifted ceaselessly through the gnarled black branches of the trees in the apple orchard. Nancy felt a cold caress on her cheek. Why, the snowflakes were flying around her all whirly and white! They caught in her hair and on her eyelashes and lay there like glimmering diamonds. Then Nancy noticed one large snowflake floating around her head in a peculiarly jolly manner. It was Star, dressed in a specially beautiful snowflake costume. Nancy laughed delightedly and skipped over the snow after the fairy, who danced away on a little breeze. Star flew high above Nancy's head and her silvery voice called, "Follow me."

"Now how can I do that?" puzzled Nancy, as Star lost herself among the other snowflakes. Almost as if Star had mentally answered her question, she thought joyfully, "Why, of course, I'll just use the snowflakes for steps!"

This she did, and the snowflakes made excellent steps, indeed. Then she began to run. Up and up into the gray sky she went. Each time she put one foot down, a snowflake held fast beneath it. She even had time to glance down at the little snow-covered toy world beneath her. Gradually it all blended into gray-blue shadows. High above her, Nancy could see Star's airy form floating ever upward. By running even faster up the magic steps, she was able to overtake the fairy.

"Why are there so many snowflakes all at once?—and all different, too!" Nancy exclaimed to Star.

"You'll see when we reach the Palace," replied Star, somewhat mysteriously, as they ascended higher and higher into the world of flying snow.

Soon Nancy, satisfied for the moment, heard a frosty humming sound something like the faint whirring of fairy wings. The snow flew faster about Nancy and Star, making a strange humming of its own. Suddenly the two emerged above the storm clouds. For a moment Nancy was blinded by the intense blueness of the sky, made deeper by the pure air above the earth. In front of them loomed a dazzling ice palace. It gleamed like glass as the brilliant sunbeams glanced off its chiseled walls.

"Oh!" cried Nancy in awe, "it's so bright that it hurts to look!"

"Here," answered Star, "I'll help your eyes get accustomed to the light."

She then laid two snowflakes on Nancy's closed eyelids. The snowflakes melted immediately, and when Nancy opened her eyes the glare of the ice did not blind her at all. As the two neared the palace, Nancy saw that the crystal portals were delicately carved, and the arched windows were paned with thin sheets of ice. While they walked up the huge flight of spacious steps that entered the palace, the busy humming grew louder and sweeter. When they reached the top step at last, Nancy stopped breathlessly. In front of them stretched a magnificent, lofty room, thinly walled with ice. The sun shone through the angles of the walls, giving the effect of many prisms. Myriads of rainbows spattered themselves on the floor and ceiling. Hundreds of icy spinning wheels were humming away merrily, turned by the flying hands of the Frost Fairies. These lovely little people were clad in stiff, frosty material, and their wings were thin panes of ice veined with rainbows. The most dazzling of these Frost Fairies now approached Nancy and Star.

"The Frost Queen," whispered Star softly to Nancy.

"Welcome, my dear Star!" cried the Frost Queen in a tinkly crystal voice. "So this is Nancy! I have been expecting you."

Before Nancy could reply, the fairy continued, "I must show you our snowflake factory. Come!"

As she led them down to the other end of the workroom, Nancy gazed sidewise at the beautiful Queen. Her frosty white hair fell softly to her shoulders, and was held back by a brilliant diamond crown that shot off fiery white sparks whenever she moved. She was clad in a long, misty robe, and her skin was so transparent that it seemed almost bluish. Nancy thought that the Frost Queen's eyes were so sparkling and blue that stars must have melted in them.

Nancy's thoughts were interrupted by a little poke from Star, so she quickly turned her attention to what the Queen was saying.

"My fairies spin thread from the mists that they gather in the meadows before sunrise," she was telling them. "Then they each crochet their own original snowflake patterns and add their work to our storeroom."

Thereupon the Queen led Nancy and Star to a great ice-hewn door which she threw open wide. The storeroom was heaped to the lofty ceiling with countless piles of snowflakes. Nancy gazed at the stacks of lovely patterns and then looked out of a nearby window. The storm had ceased, and far, far below was a tiny white world glistening in the sun. Nancy began to wish that she were back down there, for beautiful as the Frost Land was, there was something awesome and remote about that Crystal Kingdom. Even the twinkly blue fairies had a hint of stiffness and aloofness about them.

As if she had guessed Nancy's thoughts, Star graciously bade the Frost Queen farewell, saying, "We are deeply sorry that we must leave your enchanting land so soon, but time is getting short."

The Frost Queen did not allow the two to leave before presenting each with a starry, frosty scarf. Nancy was glad to start to her own world once more. She and Star each spread out their scarves, and, seated comfortably on them, floated slowly down to earth. The faint humming of the magic spinners lulled Nancy to sleep, and she was only conscious of a sudden warm rush of air.

When she opened her eyes she found that she was back in her own home once more. Her first thought was of the scarf. It must have melted on the way down. But, lo! There beside her on the window seat lay a tiny lace handkerchief in the shape of a snowflake!

Chapter 9

"Oh," exclaimed Nancy crossly, looking out of the window at the leaden skies, "isn't this snow ever going to stop? It's been winter for *so* long! I don't think there'll be any spring at all this year."

Aunt Lucy looked up from her sewing and agreed, "It does get tiresome after a while, doesn't it!"

"If only I had something to *do*," Nancy went on petulantly. "I can't go outside in this weather and I'm so tired of reading . . ."

"Have you done your lessons for today?" Aunt Lucy asked.

"Yes," said Nancy with a sigh.

"Now let's see," Aunt Lucy pondered. "You haven't played with your clothespin dolls for a long time, have you?"

Nancy brightened up, as her Aunt continued, "I could give you some pretty scraps of cloth for dresses and suits . . ."

"I'll run upstairs and get my box," Nancy interrupted eagerly. In a few moments the girl was back with a carved wooden box from which she removed a handful of clothespins—not ordinary clothespins, to be sure. There was a whole royal family of them—a king and queen and two lovely princesses. They had jolly faces, painted by Aunt Lucy, and bits of yarn glued on for hair. Pipe cleaners served very well for arms.

After her aunt had unearthed a wealth of laces, ribbons and gay remnants of silk, Nancy set to work. She spent the afternoon fashioning crowns out of gilt paper and outfitting the family in regal costumes.

At last, when she had finished, she lined the clothespins up against the little box and admired her work. The king looked quite imposing in his white suit with the purple velvet mantle, and the queen was becomingly arrayed in turquoise satin, bordered by lace. Princess Geraldine wore a trailing robe of flowered yellow muslin, while Princess Annabel was clad in dark blue silk.

All that evening the little girl amused herself by holding an imaginary conversation with the clothespin family, and it was with reluctance that she put them back in their box for the night. There were a few pieces of material left. Nancy's favorite was a large square of dainty pink organdy, embroidered with white daisies. Aunt Lucy had remarked that it came from one of her old evening dresses long, long ago.

Nancy was sound asleep when the strange sound began. As it grew louder, she awoke with a start.

Clump, clump . . . clump, clump . . . nearer and nearer.

"It sounds as if someone's walking across the floor in wooden shoes," she thought, sitting upright and looking around.

Her eyes widened. There was no moon, since the night was cloudy, but by a soft light from across the room, Nancy saw four tall figures approaching her bed. They moved from side to side with an odd rolling motion, and Nancy noticed a peculiar stiffness about their limbs. Suddenly she exclaimed, "Why, you're my clothespin dolls!"

"Such impudence, indeed!" cried a shrill staccato voice indignantly. "*Clothespin* dolls! Indeed!"

"The Queen," thought Nancy.

"That's better," said the voice in evident satisfaction.

"Oh dear," thought Nancy, "they can hear me think!"

"Of course we can," the king piped up in a woodeny tone. "We're the royal family, you know!"

"I suppose you're right," Nancy agreed meekly, wondering if that had anything to do with the matter.

"We've come," Annabel interposed sweetly, "to invite you to our evening festival."

"But . . ." began Nancy.

"Do come on," said Geraldine impatiently. "The music's started already."

And so it had. As Nancy pattered over the floor, following that strange group, she heard faint elfin strains emerging from . . . the carved wooden box! During the night the box had undergone an amazing transformation. Windows and doors had opened up on the walls, and the container itself had swelled to great size.

"Everything must have grown," mused Nancy, "for I'm sure I haven't gotten little. Or have I?"

"The royal palace," announced the king proudly, indicating that Nancy was to precede them through the main entrance. The girl hung back.

"But I can't go in with my *night*gown on," she said.

"Gracious! That's easily remedied," sniffed the queen. Whereupon she stamped three times on the floor.

Clump, clump, clump.

Nancy gasped.

In the twinkling of an eye, her nightgown turned into a green, gauzy dress, banded with gold about the hem, and a pair of gilded wooden shoes adorned her feet. Then Annabel advanced with a crown and placed it on Nancy's dark curls.

"There," she said. "Now you're ready."

As they filed into the palace, Nancy gazed about curiously.

They had come into a high-ceilinged hall, filled with a crowd of clothespin people who stood stiffly at attention, like puppets suspended by invisible strings. As the royal party arrived, there was a loud clumping of feet that was evidently intended for applause, and then the music started up again with a brisk waltz. Couples began to dance down the hall, and when a young prince asked Nancy to be his partner, she accepted.

The prince rocked back and forth in the peculiar way everyone else was dancing, but Nancy's shoes somehow kept her in step. As the two progressed across the room, the girl noticed that the walls were draped with pink curtains, starred with white daisies. Why, she thought, it's just like the material from Aunt Lucy's dress!

"I beg your pardon," said the prince, "but our decorations come from a faraway country, and are of the best quality."

Nancy controlled an impulse to laugh. The man tried so hard to appear dignified and important, but his shrill, squeaky voice served only to make him sound ridiculous.

"Why does everyone look so solemn?" Nancy queried.

"That is because this is a great occasion," the prince replied. "It is not often that we have a costume ball, you know."

"Costume ball?" Nancy repeated.

"Yes," he explained patiently. "Only royalty may be present, and at the end of the evening a prize is given for the most beautiful gown."

Nancy danced with several other princes and a considerable quantity of dukes and lords after that. As a matter of fact, the dancing went on for so long that Nancy began to wonder what she could do to relieve the boredom. Luckily the music ceased at that moment, and three judges came forward.

"Ahem," one cleared his throat pompously.

"We are proud to award the prize for the loveliest costume . . ." said the second.

"To Princess . . . Geraldine," finished the third.

Geraldine smirked and curtsied as gracefully as she was able and stepped up to receive the prize. It was a shiny gold cup.

"This goblet has been shaped by the cleverest of our goldsmiths," one of the judges announced to the gathering. While the crowd "clumped" their applause, Nancy thought, "It *should* be the best gown. After all, I made it."

The noise died down suddenly, and a horrified silence took its place.

"What have I done," thought Nancy wildly as the whole roomful of royalty turned, with much swishing of skirts and craning of necks, and stared at her.

Then the shouting began.

"Done, done! She doesn't know what she has done!"

"A common dressmaker," they shrieked in unison.

"Deceiving us! Indeed!" cried the queen, advancing toward her majestically.

"Oh, dear, you never should have said . . ." whispered the distressed Annabel by her side.

"But I only thought . . ." Nancy began desperately, as the mob started to surround her with measured tread.

"Seize her crown . . ." someone shouted shrilly.

"Impostor!" screamed another.

"Never mind," encouraged Annabel, "I'll save you."

And she commenced to stamp.

Clump! The shouting increased to a deafening roar. Nancy shut her eyes.

Clump! She was back in her nightgown.

Clump! The voices ceased. Slowly she opened her eyes.

She was in her bed, and the morning sunlight shone in through the blinds. A loose shutter was banging somewhere against the house. Clump, it went. Clump, clump.

"Oh," Nancy breathed in relief. "Annabel was so nice. I thought I'd never get away from those horrid people."

She lay still for a while and reviewed the happenings of that night. "I wonder why everyone got so cross all of a sudden," she mused. "Probably because I wasn't royalty," she decided at last.

Then, overcome by curiosity, she tiptoed somewhat timidly to the place where the palace had been. It had dwindled to the accustomed size once more, and there was no evidence of doors or windows. Could she have dreamed about the dance?

Cautiously Nancy removed the box lid and peered inside.

Why! The dolls were so small and lifeless that she laughed. Imagine ever being afraid of harmless clothespins that were no bigger than her finger! "But they *were* big as me last night," she remembered.

Yet . . . Geraldine had never worn that smug smile before. The girl looked around the box carefully. All the things were just where she had left them before going to bed. All the things, that is, except her little gold thimble which she could not find, no matter how hard she searched.

What was that gleaming in Geraldine's hand? Nancy lifted the little princess up and examined her more closely. Then she sat back, even more confused. The gleam came from a tiny gold cup that had "1st Prize" engraved on it in minute letters.

'About a year ago I was babysitting . . .'

Ms fragment,[*] *c.*1948–50, Smith College

About a year ago I was babysitting for a neighbor. It was already well into the evening, and the house was filled with silence. The spasmodic "drip, drip" of a kitchen faucet was loud on the quiet air, and a floorboard creaked occasionally in one of the upstairs rooms.

I paused a moment and put down the magazine I was reading.

The air was still and waiting. Unaccountably I felt as though I was suspended, motionless in time. I don't know how long I sat staring pensively at nothing, but after a while I began to feel a vague uneasiness. It would do no harm to go up and have a look at the children.

Silently I crossed the living room and tiptoed noiselessly up the thickly carpeted staircase. Once outside the boys' room I paused at the doorway. By the dim

---

[*] Manuscript with holograph corrections and additions by SP. Written on Connecticut General Life Insurance Company (Schenectady, NY) letterhead.

light from the hallway I could see the two sleeping forms. There was something defenseless about the two little fellows lying limp and relaxed, deep in slumber. Something made me bend over the youngest and touch his cheek lightly. He stirred briefly and turned his face toward his moist hand, curled on the pillow.

It was then that I heard the sound. It came from Libby's room. Libby was only two and her mother had told me that she might wake up in the middle of the night. The sound ceased, and then began again. It was a low, plaintive cry. I crossed the hall to the little girl's room. The moon shone through the frosty window, and I could see Libby surveying me gravely from her bed. Her hair was long on the pillow and her eyes were strange in the darkness. They were big and wet with tears.

"Libby, baby, what's wrong," I said bending over her. Her breath came in hard uneven gusts.

"I want . . . my . . . mama," she managed and burst into uncontrollable sobs. I picked up the child who was shaking and gulping tears. "Shhh, shhh," I murmured.

"Mummy's not home," I tried to reason, "shh, you'll wake the boys."

"Mammaa . . ." she choked.

I tried bribery. "Libby, want some nice candy?"

"Noo." The sobs turned into a lonely wail.

"Libby, stop this minute." I attempted to sound firm, but it was no use. How frail her little body seemed as I rocked it in my arms. Tears fell hot and wet on my hand.

Suddenly there was nothing in the world that mattered except this child weeping forlornly, bitterly in my arms. There was only Libby, defenseless against the night. There was only Libby, who must be comforted.

"Libby," I began in a low tone, "want me to tell you a story?" The convulsive weeping continued. I began, "Once upon a time there lived a little princess with long yellow hair . . ."

I talked on and on. Gradually the sobs diminished, and the story was punctuated only by an occasional sniffle. Soon even the sniffles ceased, and the little girl breathed evenly, exhausted by her emotion. When she was sleeping soundly I laid her back in bed. Was she dreaming? I could not tell . . . A child's mind is such a secret place, one cannot intrude into their dreams . . . or into their sorrow. One can only begin "Once upon a time . . ." and wait until the young return to you from the land of their imaginations.

As I went from the room, I cast a last look at Libby. The moonlight made elfin sparkles on her long yellow hair.

'A few armchairs and a table ...'

Ms fragment, *c.*1948–50, Sotheby's[*]

A few armchairs and a table set with a tray of steaming food were placed before the fire, which burned merrily on the hearth. A soft bed occupied the opposite side of the room, and beside it was a bookcase on which were arranged a radio and a bed lamp. A great mahogany desk stood in front of the windows on the left side of the room. Large windows were set into three of the four walls, and although the blinds were not drawn, the light afforded by them did not amount to anything, since they were wet and blurred by the sheets of rain beating against them from outside.

The low roar of the sea pounding against the cliffs, the rumble of the thunderstorm overhead, and the spatter of the rain against the windows. My first thought was somewhat unusual for someone who eats as little as I—

"Why I'm practically starved," I exclaimed to myself, in delight. There were three doors leading to my room, all of them were closed. One, of course, led down that rickety old flight of stairs to the first floor. I tried the middle door. It opened easily, revealing the gleaming white tiles of a neat bathroom. I "washed up," making only little headway on the dust that I had collected on my walk over. Then,

'The music wailed out from the radio ...'

Ms fragment, *c.*1948–50, Smith College

The music wailed out from the radio by her bed. The trumpets screamed at her exultantly, wrapping her in a hot, dripping cocoon of sound.

---

[*] Included as part of a lot in a Sotheby's auction of an archive of SP's papers on 2 December 2014 by Sotheby's. The lot did not sell and later portions of the archive appeared in piecemeal fashion via Bonhams.

She sat cross-legged on the green blanket, staring down at the dinner plate in front of her, not eating. The greasy smell of liver sickened her. She listened. In spite of the blaring veneer of jazz, she could still hear the horrible silence downstairs in the dining room. After she had suddenly burst into angry tears and run upstairs to eat alone.

The words echoed over in her head. She heard her petulant "Let me alone, let me alone." She saw the naked hurt on her brother's face; her mother's fork stopped halfway to her mouth; her grandmother's forced smile. And now, at last, she was away from them. She sat there like a discouraged little Buddha, her light brown hair falling over one eye, her muscles slack, her lower lip stuck out, pouting. "I hate them, I hate them," she muttered, her cheeks burning, her hands slippery and cold with sweat. Already it was seven o'clock. One hour more to wait. She watched the second hand of the plump alarm clock on her bureau. Hypnotized, she heard the faint winding sound. Round and round and round.

She tried to rouse herself out of the anesthetic numbness which made her sit there, frozen. But the room was small. The air crushed her, pushing at her from all sides. She felt as if she had swallowed a raw egg whole. She hardly heard the music now, she was accustomed to the barb-wire edge of the melody ripping at her inside, tearing at the lining of her stomach. A big vague lump of something rose in her throat. She saw the day pass before her with chilling clarity, like a colored film.

It started in the afternoon while she was waiting for David to call. This was like no other Saturday in her life, for a week ago David had written to ask for a movie date when he came home from school

Story Ideas

Ms, after June 1949, Smith College

Star Island—Girl's Diary of a week there—Interlude in Boy-Crazy teenage world.

The Bike Ride—Emotional girl goes for a bike ride with Boy she has known—deep friends—he tells her about other girl—she realizes she loves him, but it would never work out . . . cries . . . The afternoon is almost raining—They picnic on a high hill . . . hair straight with damp . . . Bike home in rain.

The Breakwater—4 kids cross . . . agonies of one girl's watery knees, slippery seaweed . . . hatred of 3 careless companions . . . relief at getting back.

The Pink Comb—Hypnotic revulsion of girl toward boy she loves . . . his perpetually food scummed teeth . . . his dirty pink comb

None But the Lonely Heart—I-story of Don Mackay—meets art student on the bus—nice to him—has him worshipping her—he has pale face, stringy hair—knows no one in town—when people fall at her feet she has the irresistible temptation to walk over them—insults him—hurts him to make him leave her alone. She imagines him as a starving artist in a garret—turns out that he used to want to be a veterinarian—

Evening at the Hoftizers—Glittering tension between members of family—tall, heavy, red-faced *father*—in shorts—yelling blustering tyrant of house—*pale wife*—quiet with coronet of braids—*Gamma*—the in-law—pink & plump & powdered gray hair & shawl—plays solitaire. *Marie*—bony, sorrowful spotted hound dog . . . *Jim* lumbering hulk—good-natured about 20. *Henriette*—tall, bony wife of Jim's brother—once good-looking—skin loose—pale white face, stringy short hair—sloppy print dress. Picture of her on the mantel. "I'm just the in-law around here, don't mind me."

Party Girl—Teenage intrigue—dates dance, play jazz—get drunk. Girls flirt with other boys—boys try to get girls away from old dates—pledge true love—all lies—self-centered. "I had a wonderful time." Told about shallow, egotistical girl who suddenly sees how horrible & nightmarish the whole thing is—sees ex-boyfriend there with another girl—saying same things he once said to her—only she meant what she said to him. Cries upstairs in the bathroom, but her hostess comforts her—telling her that the only thing to do is play the role—flirt with other boys she'll get used to it—they all do.—She still has to make the rounds—wait till she's used everyone up.

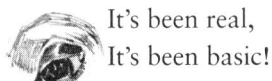

It's been real,
It's been basic!

Irene

Ms fragment, *c.*1949–50, Smith College

Dark—tall—husky—high color—Irish maid about 18—cheerful—sings at work—always funny story to tell—delightful to work with—After 1st week $15 is missing from man of the house's wallet—later found in baby's chair—the lady of the house misses her extra pairs of stockings, her small change, her bathroom mat—she can say nothing to accuse Irene because there is no concrete evidence—Irene takes baby out to park supposedly—really to her own house—later the mother wheels baby in the park and a little girl runs up to the child, calling her by name—so she is Irene's sister and mother finds out that she has played indoors all the while—About a year later Irene's mother comes to Lady o. H. and says she'd better fire Irene. Irene's no good. All the rest of her children are decent, but Irene's no good. L. of H. says that Irene is really a delightful person to work with, but Irene's mother says she'll be sorry if she keeps her. It turns out that Irene has been going around with a policeman, says her mother, and she acts as if bewitched. The girl isn't married, but she's going to have a baby. The L. of H.'s charge account was missing, and a few items were charged to her, but Irene comes in a few days later, saying she'd have to leave work—she's been married some time now, and she just saw her doctor and he said she's going to have a baby—baby is born 2 months later and Irene sends an announcement hinting that she hopes for a gift for the child. Her sister Mary came to work in her place, but she somehow never had the sparkling attraction of her sister Irene.

Sally

Ms fragment,[*] *c.*1949–50, Smith College

She was tall, arrogant and proud. One saw her often down at the tennis courts, tanned, with cruel black eyes and firm, slim legs. With her hair in two thin, dark braids, one might fancy that she was Indian squaw. There was a sharp beauty in her haughty features—her scornful eyes and her disdainful down curving mouth. She wore always a pair of faded blue dungarees, a loose khaki shirt, and a silk print bandana to tie her hair down.

    She had always gotten what she wanted, and she always would. Her voice was harsh sometimes, when harshness served her, but she could drop it to a low huskiness that softened her features amazingly. She had a ruthless assurance, and girls were pliable against her. They were soft, fluttering creatures in ruffled print dresses, while she remained like a reed of steel. Graceful, slender, but hard, unyielding, and unconquerable.

---

[*] Written on verso of Boston University, College of Practical Arts and Letters, 27 Garrison Street, Boston 16, Massachusetts letterhead with a typed date of 3 January 1949 on it.

The Garden Party

Ms fragment,* *c.*1949–50, Smith College

Betsy sat still for a minute, watching the pink sherbet slump and start to trickle down slowly between the pile of cherries and pineapple and peaches all sliced up together on her plate. What a funny way to start dinner, she thought. Ice cream or fruit cups.

Everyone else at the long, linen-covered table was talking and laughing. China tinkled against silver, and the sunlight made its way through the dark green leaves, weaving a lacy pattern of light on the grass. A fountain sparkled out from the mouth of a quaint stone dolphin and fell back upon itself into a quiet pool. Everywhere the lawn stretched away in genteel, cultured slopes of cool, clipped green.

Not like at home, Betsy thought, spooning up pieces of banana, pear, and apple all at once. At home there were sweet peas growing helter-skelter by the sway-backed fence, and there were daisies where Daddy forgot to mow the lawn. She looked at Herbert beside her, busy with his ice cream, and she wanted to talk to him, but was afraid people would turn and stare.

Mother was at the other end of the table talking with Aunt Helene. Aunt Helene was famous for her garden parties. She looked like Cinderella, Betsy decided, admiringly. She was pink and white and gold, like apple blossoms. Betsy had seen such white skin and golden hair only in her picture books. She half-closed her eyes, and Aunt Helene dimmed and shimmered in the sunlight. The white organdy dress fluttered at her shoulder, a hint of elfin wings. Was she . . . was she magic?

An Evening at the Hoftizers

Ms fragment,† *c.*1949–50, Smith College

John and I had spent the early part of the evening driving around the beach wagon and visiting friends of his. He'd saved Jim Hoftizer till the last. Jim was his favorite.

---

* The following notes for the story appear on the last page of the fragment: 'Betsy—twelve—imaginative—pigtailed. Herbert—her little 8-year-old brother blond. Mother & Father. Aunt Helene and Uncle Jon. Mary Lou—a spoiled darling of eight. B & H are exposed to the luxuries of their aunt's home & her spoiled daughter and find that for all the pose and the magic, their relatives are very human, and in some respects, not so fortunate as themselves.'
† Manuscript with holograph corrections and additions by SP. According to a list of dates SP

"You'll laugh when you meet Jim's old man," he grinned. "He says anything that enters his head. When Jim introduced Mr. Hoftizer to his new girl she said, 'I'm very glad to meet you,' and he growled, 'Why the hell should you glad any how?' He's like that."

I felt a tingle of anticipation and uncertainty. Jim himself was unusual enough—a huge husky blond, 6' 5", a sophomore at Harvard with a knack for remembering a suitable joke for any remark you could make. After looking at Jim for a while even the Statue of Liberty would seem a bit dwarfish.

As we crunched up the gravel driveway, the small pebbles tinkling on the side of the car, I caught a confused glimpse of people gathered in the kitchen through the lighted square of the window. There was an unidentified number of faces peering out at us. "Go home, go home!" somebody shouted. I felt suddenly uneasy and clutched John's arm. "Let's not go in. They're busy. Let's go back." But Jim had already opened the door and was lumbering toward us with all the ease of an overgrown elephant.

"Hi," he said laconically. "Come on in if you can stand the atmosphere."

I followed John up the steps and into the brilliantly lighted kitchen with a vague fear throbbing in the pit of my stomach. After the dark outside, the light glancing off the blinding white enamel stabbed sharp flashing arrows at my eyes. I squinted and looked around past the icebox and the sink with the faucets dripping, dripping.

'The New Zealand spinach was good that morning . . .'

Ts and Ms fragment,* summer 1950, Smith College

The New Zealand spinach was good that morning; it was the first picking, and the leaves were large and full. At ten o'clock the sun was high up, pale and distant in a thin blue sky.

Julie picked fast, squatting down, pulling her bushel basket after her, and not talking. Already most of the younger girls were behind her, chattering and

---

went on with various boys and contained with her 1949 diary, she visited the Hoftyzer family in Wellesley, Massachusetts, on 27 August 1949 with 'Paul', possibly Paul Hezlett. The list is held in an envelope with other loose items by the Lilly Library.

* The first three plus pages of story are typewritten, the rest is handwritten by SP. A separate page stored with this fragment includes three drawings by SP of a woman in a halter top, a seated man working with his hands over a basket, and a leg from the knee to the foot.

teasing with the boys in the adjoining rows. But Julie picked the tops of the spinach in clean, quick handfuls, bunching them in solid tiers.

She was the best girl picker in the crew, even better than some of the boys. She packed the top layer tightly and tested the weight, lifting the basket with both hands. It was about right. Slinging the basket up on one hip, she walked barefoot down to the end of the field where Andy was loading the truck.

Andy was tall, lean and blonde, with cold blue eyes and an arrogant way of looking down his nose from under his blue visor cap. He weighed her basket on the scale.

"Twenty pounds. On the dot," he said. He put a cover over the top and heaved it up on the truck. She was trying to pull another basket from the pile when he came over and disengaged it with a single gesture. Their hands touched briefly. Something about his haughty attitude made her sarcastic.

"Do you do that for all the girls?" she asked dryly.

"Only when they're like you," he responded with equal acidity.

Julie turned and walked back to her place. The spinach leaves were cool and wet against her legs. She squatted down again, a slender bronzed figure in her starched cotton shirt with the big red and white checks, her rolled-up dungarees. The sun had bleached her long hair honey-blonde across the top; her eyes were dark, the color of maple syrup. Her long, agile fingers reached among the leaves, making them into little green rosettes, making a green wreath of them on the bottom of the basket, starting another tier. The other girls tossed the spinach in by handfuls, pushing it down. It really didn't matter how you did it, but Julie liked her system best. It was so neat, so rapid once you were accustomed to it.

Mary, the crew boss, came toward her, smiling, pencil and paper in hand.

"That your seventh, Julie?" she asked, nodding at the basket, already half full.

Julie grinned up from her picking. "Uh-huh, that's it."

Mary put down another mark by Julie's name in the little black book and went on to the next row. Julie looked at Mary's retreating back. Mary was twenty. She was not pretty if you analyzed her carefully; her teeth were a bit too prominent, her nose a bit too long, but she was small, with a neat figure. Her short hair shone blue-black in the sun. She had what people called personality.

Nelda, the little girl with blonde braids, paused by Julie breathlessly. Her basket was loosely packed.

"Is that heavy enough, Julie?" she asked anxiously. "It's only my third." The slightly built girl walked slowly to the truck, dragging the bushel behind her with the weary air of someone who knows it won't meet the twenty pound quota.

Julie smiled to herself as she noticed the two girls in back of her. They were so young, so homely. She had been like that when she was in Junior High.

"What scares you most in the Carnival besides the rollercoaster?"

"Oh, I don't know. Lois and I screamed on the Ferris wheel last night. You could hear us from here to Dover."

On the other side of Julie, Carol Ann had come up, a doll of a girl, with a Dutch cut, a tip-tilted nose and twinkling green eyes. She had won baby contests when she was little, the girls said, and she was all talk, all laughter, her adorable nose crinkling up in delight. She chattered easily to Julie, satisfied by Julie's occasional appreciative laugh.

"Did I ever tell you about the time we were on our Scout overnight? I had to sleep on the floor because I laughed too much, and Ginny let the blankets down over me, but in the middle of the night it got cold and she pulled them up and started singing, 'I Can't Give You Anything But Love, Baby.'"

Julie smiled and picked faster. She thought Carol Ann was too tediously cute. Carol Ann, unconcerned, went rattling on to the girl coming up beside her. Soon Julie had left them both behind. Once she glanced back. They were resting, sitting propped up against their baskets amidst the spinach and munching green apples someone had brought from the orchard.[*]

Julie had put the top on her seventh basket before she allowed herself to look at him. She hadn't singled him out from the other boys on the farm until he had been in her crew on beans a few days before. The sight of him now was enough to make the blood quicken in her veins, electric and tingling like bubbly ginger ale. Somewhere inside her there was an acute and wistful anguish, sharp to the point of actual physical pain. She had never yet spoken to him, nor he to her, and she felt unaccountably that he was hers.

Mary had taken a basket of her own now, and she was picking near him. Julie watched in a chill of envy and Mary looked up at him, smiled in her open, friendly way and said something to make him laugh.

"Mary's boss," she thought. "She can get away with talking to all the fellows. She's got one of her own."

Julie picked on with blind venom. Her basket was done. "Seven for me, Mary," she called out gaily on her way to the truck, her voice taut with jealousy.

[*] The typewritten portion ends here and is continued in SP's hand.

He had looked up. She walked with careful grace, hoping he was watching her as she laughed up at the imperturbable Andy, tossed her hair back with a careless gesture, and started back with another empty basket.

Mary came over to list Julie's number. She knelt down confidentially beside her.

"Lynch is awfully nice, *I* think," she said with her pleasant candid smile. "He's just about the nicest boy up here, and very good-looking. Don't you think so?"

Was there a hint of patronizing in Mary's tone? Did she know how Julie felt?

"Ah, he's all right," Julie drawled indifferently.

Julie looked at Lynch out of the corner of her eye as she picked.

He knelt on one knee, bending the other up. She remembered a picture in her history book of Sir Walter Raleigh being knighted. Lynch's back was bare, tan, shining with sweat. His coal black hair was combed in a crest, his thin lips closed tightly over a cigarette. He picked rhythmically, methodically, and he was two baskets ahead of her!

As the sun swam higher, like an iridescent air bubble rising through a sea of blue, the younger boys and girls stopped picking, and gathered around the truck, fooling, laughing, and drinking often out of the tin pail covered with yellow paper to keep the dirt out. The water would be warm, now, thought Julie. The ice would have melted.

Lynch was near her, finishing a basket. She met his gaze.

"How many?" she asked.

"Ten." He grinned at her as he shouldered the bushel and strolled down to the truck. The spinach piece around her was good. He came back.

"So you're going to Smith," he said, at last, with a disarming, crooked smile.

"How did you know?" she was surprised.

"How do you think?"

"I don't know."

"David told me."

Oh, David. He was the good-looking boy who drove the old Chevy truck, and flirted with all the girls. Mary must have told him.

"I might have known," she retorted with a toss of her head. "David keeps up on all the barnyard gossip."

"You won't be working here next year."

"Why?"

His voice was sarcastic, "Not a Smith girl. Not here."

"Why, why . . ." she was indignant. "I will too. I like it, being out in the sun. I've got to work my way through college somehow."

That reached him.

'The Skaters'

Ts fragment,* c. January–May 1952, Lilly Library and Emory University

any of them know? We are a pampered race, Alison thought, staring out of the window again at the blank walls of the station. She thought back to the crowds in New York, of all the people hurrying along the streets doing late Christmas shopping, of the great avenues of lighted stores, the colored panoramas in the windows, with the lights blinking, and the great tree in Rockefeller Center with all the brilliant white lights winking in the raw December wind. Breathless, she had walked down the streets, the cold air like ice water against her mouth, her breath hanging in chill suspended vapor, trailing behind her. There was the glitter of tinsel and frost, and the clear sound of bells above the auto horns. It was a great jubilant carnival, and she had felt the laughter bubbling through her, and the little gasps of excitement as she paused and stopped at the store windows caught and held momentarily by the shine of jewelry and glass, the gleam of red and gold satins, and the warm promise of furs and rich wools. On every side the shops beckoned, wedges of honey-colored light, inviting against the dark and the cold. Her hands, in their brown gloves, were raw from cold, and her eyes were filled with tears from the wind. Her reflection in the windows showed a transparent creature, brown hair blown back from her face, eyes twin points of light, a shade only, pausing amid the ceaseless flow of other shadows, ghostly and without identity, moving on without rest.

The people were delightful, really, Alison decided. They were all so peculiar, so extremely amusing. That little woman there, bundled up like a plum

---

* Title assigned. Lilly typescript is three pages, heavily revised with holograph corrections and additions by SP. On verso is a draft of SP's essay on 'The Equilibrists' by John Crowe Ransom. The Emory typescript has holograph corrections and additions by SP, as well as instructor comments, with pages numbered by SP 6-4, 6-5 and 6-6, making it consistent with the stories she produced in 1951–2 for English 220a/b, Practice in Various Forms of Writing with Evelyn Page. The prefix of '6' here possibly indicates it is the sixth assignment; the second digit is the page number. SP observed ice skaters at Rockefeller Center in December 1951 on her first visit to New York City with Marcia Brown. On this trip she also dated Constantine Sidamon-Eristoff.

pudding, why she could have come from a toy shop for she walked so queerly, as if wound up with a key. And that pale, thin little man. His face had a decidedly yellow cast. He might very well, yes, quite conceivably, have emerged just recently from a cupboard. It was all so exciting, so laughable, with the city just dark, and thousands of people, all crowding and hurrying. And all the noise and flashing lights. The whole performance (for of course it was a performance), was for the benefit of Alison. None other.

The skaters at the Center, though, were the best, by far the best of all. Alison could hardly keep from laughing outright. All the while the great Christmas tree was blinking and shining above they swooped, literally swooped in the most delicious fashion imaginable, gliding in wide curves, with simply breathless leaps and bounds, across the ice.

Truly, it was an amazing cast, hand-picked no doubt, for there could hardly have been a better, a more varied group. The boy, the tall young one in the red woolen sweater, with what pride, what skill, he swerved and leaped, and how boldly he turned in a shower, a twinkling spray, of ice chips. Did he see the girl passing him? Hardly, for he was preoccupied, infinitely concerned with whirling around on one spot, faster and faster, until the colors of his scarf blurred like those of a spinning top.

But the girl, what a lovely, fragile thing she was! All in white, too, with pale yellow hair shining under her little fur cap. Perhaps she was a ballet dancer, for she turned in such flowerlike, such delicate, spirals, leaning, balancing, gliding. But cool. Yes, cool and self-complete. A snowflake, a veritable snowflake.

And then Alison did laugh. She could not help herself, for there, tumbling out onto the ice, tipping, almost sprawling, came the two dearest little boys. They were twins, by the looks of it, for both had red hair, such red hair, and the same jackets, shiny leather, the kind that would smell, oh, the way the beginning of school smelt, of apples, and varnish, and pencils newly sharpened. It was a game of tag, but one could hardly tell which twin was it, for they were exactly alike, one plunging out ahead, and then the other in such a merry chase that it was quite impossible to keep track of the winner. They did manage to keep out from under foot, though, and the rest of the performers hardly seemed to see them, and skating about quite unruffled, if not completely unaware of the unruly pair.

Look there! Almost crying out, Alison leaned forward. There, they had nearly skated between the feet of that woman in purple. But no, she regained her balance and went on twirling. What a fat woman she was, in that terrible purple suit. And her legs. Why, one would think she would be quite ashamed out there in front of all the people, for her legs were so thick and clumsy in their dark brown stockings. They looked quite like ugly, if not misshapen, brown sausages. Alison felt almost sorry for the fat woman, for she seemed so determined to keep on twirling there, all by herself. It was regrettable. And such a tasteless shade of purple, too. Someone should really speak to her about it. One of her friends, perhaps, should warn her (quite nicely, of course), about wearing that shade of purple. In public, particularly.

Now, suddenly, Alison felt a shiver of pleasure. A little drama, quite unobtrusive, but nonetheless intriguing, was going on by the gateway. One of the guards (Alison had hardly noticed that they wore skates too), resplendent in a green uniform, gleaming with a touch, just the right accent, of[*]

And his arm, barely touching her waist, guided her ever so tenderly, gently.

Alison felt a sob rise inexplicably in her breast. For the music, a Strauss waltz, was so lovely, so wistful. It reminded one of something half forgotten, long ago. One could hardly help weeping. Indeed, her eyes were quite full of tears for something, she could not remember just what, but it had been, she was sure, infinitely poignant. Like the pale ghost of a moon rising above deserted buildings, or the indescribable fragrance of broken pine boughs, acutely haunting. Oh, it was altogether unbearable to stand so, the music coming (with what pathos), simply lilting, out of the core, the frozen heart, really, of the bitter air.

The countess (for she was undoubtedly a countess, nobility of some sort) seemed to understand, and she nodded in time to the music, her head tilting now to one side, now to the other, her teeth, small and milky, revealed in an enchanting smile. The general (the military bearing proclaimed it) leaned down toward her with what intense delight, what eagerness, listening for the laughter like the bells, the sweet, almost melancholy bells that rang out across the city.

One, two, three . . . *one*, two, three . . . Slowly, and with a strange sadness, a regret, somehow, of times past, times more fortunate, no doubt, the elderly couple dipped and twirled. The gallantry, the bravery of those two!

The frozen arena, lit by a hundred arc lights, became a mirrored castle hall, and the royal couple danced on and on to the sound of violins (the fiddlers concealed, cleverly, in some alcove or other). Would the music never stop?

It was then that the chill came. Alison felt a sudden coldness, as of ice, begin within her and extend slowly, inexorably, until she was quite numb all over.

[*] The Lilly typescript ends here.

And all because she chanced to think, just to wonder, about what happened when the music stopped.

Of course the music must stop at some time or other. Indeed, the skaters must all go home sooner or later. At any moment, now, they would begin to leave, to go home for dinner. Worse still, there was no doubt some sort of work waiting, daily, for each one.

Even the delicate girl in white would cease twirling, spiraling, revolving on her one pointed silver toe. She might be, for all one could tell, a secretary of some sort, or possibly a clerk in a store. A drab creature, no doubt, without the short white skating costume and the fur cap that crowned her yellow hair. And who could tell, as she trudged in stumpy high heeled shoes to work, that inside she was still circling, white-clad, a princess, with feet darting here, there, like skimming birds.

The little boys, too, no doubt, were let out just for tonight, for a holiday treat, by some indulgent mother or nurse. How sad, how extremely sad, to think of them sitting day after day at a desk in school, side by side, frowning over sums, or scrawling smudgy letter exercises. Now they were free, adorably free, like spaniel puppies, tumbling and pummeling, their shouts lost in the music that rose and swelled.

Alison sighed deeply. The countess, she thought. The countess would go gliding away at any moment now, curtseying goodbye to the general. He would stand at the gate, watching her leave, with his cap in his hand, half saluting, brushing away a stray dust mote from his eye, a mote that might well have been a tear. For when would they meet again? The countess, taking off her skates, would be transformed at once into somebody's aunt, or, even more appalling, into somebody's grandmother. A nondescript elderly woman that one would hardly notice in a crowd.

Alison felt a sudden urge to run away. She could not stand there a minute longer, not with the danger, the fear, that at any moment the music would stop, that the skaters would slow their freewheeling glides to a walk, a stiff, almost mechanical walk.

One, two, three . . . *one*, two, three . . . the magical strains still throbbed in her veins. Surely, now, surely she was going to cry. The tree melted suddenly, and all the lights ran together in one great blur that sent out darting sparks, vertical and horizontal sparks that quivered, poised, and spilled. Big warm drops streamed down her cheeks, and one splashed on her mittened hand. Alison watched it sink into the wool, leaving a dark wet spot. Her face burned where the dry wind blew upon her tears.

She turned away, then, leaving the great tree winking and sparkling behind her, leaving the music that still came from somewhere, she couldn't tell where. She would take the bus home, so she could climb the little narrow stairs to the top deck and watch the store windows from her special seat, the one at the very front, directly over the driver, where the view, she knew from experience, was by far the best.

My dear, hush a minute and look, do look at that skinny[*]

The bus came[†]

My Studio Romance

Ts,[‡] 27–8 March 1952, Lilly Library

and that he had a bachelor apartment, probably full of all sorts of modern art, on Mason Street, where a lot of the profs lived.

There were ten girls in our oil painting class, and we had our own little studio, with a north light and easels and all. I never forgot the first day that second semester when Mr. Cramer walked in. He was late, and all the girls had been clustered around, making wild guesses as to what he would be like. The door swung open, then, and everybody went very quiet all of a sudden.

He was a tall man, with two dark wings of hair on either side of his well-formed forehead. He had deep, enigmatic green eyes that surveyed our little group with a careful swift scrutiny. I felt suddenly very strange in the pit of my stomach. With an odd excitement I waited for the sound of his voice. When he spoke it was low and dry, with a cynical note of humor in it.

He started talking to us, then, about our next project, leaning back against the wall, his pipe clenched between his teeth so that his voice came out slow and deliberately. Somehow, I don't know exactly why, I got the feeling that he was laughing inside at the whole lot of us. I felt right then that he knew about the flutter and the whispered exclamations that would rise the minute he walked out of the room.

"Gosh, isn't he divine!" Betsy hissed in my ear the minute he had gone. And

---

[*] SP added, by hand, a note to 'put at end' this new paragraph.

[†] SP added by hand this with the instruction to 'skip to next page . . .'

[‡] Typescript pages 3, 4 and 14, with significant holograph and typewritten corrections and additions by SP. A draft review of the *Collected Poems of Dylan Thomas* on verso. According to SP's calendar, she worked on this story during her spring vacation. Submitted to *True Story*.

right then and there something perverse and obstinate inside me froze hard. I was determined not to have Mr. Cramer laugh inside at me the way he did at all the other girls. I was going to be very casual, very cool. Nobody would see what I thought of him, not even Betsy.

"Oh, I don't know," I told Betsy in an absent-minded tone of voice, stepping back to check the charcoal composition I had sketched out on the canvas. "I mean I really don't think he's anything special."

"He can't be more than thirty years old," Betsy was saying dreamily. "Gosh, but he's handsome. And so cosmopolitan." She drifted back to her canvas half-heartedly with a resigned sigh as she saw I was too busy to listen to her rapturous observations.

It was amazing how much extra time everyone spent in the studio that week. Mr. Cramer would wander in and out, the pungent aroma of pipe tobacco preceding him and lingering pleasantly after he had gone. The other girls would make up excuses and problems just to talk to him. But I kept my resolution and remained quiet. It paid off, too.

One afternoon, when most of the college was out watching a baseball game between Riverside and its rival college, Glendale, I went up to finish my project. Bill had asked me to go to the game with him, but I said I needed to finish the assignment. I wanted to work without the chatter of the rest of the girls for a while.

I was involved in scraping off a part of the canvas that I wanted to retouch when I heard the door behind me squeak open. I went tense inside for some reason. The odor of pipe tobacco was wafted to my nostrils. I didn't turn around.*

As if propelled by a diabolic mechanism somewhere inside me I stood up and walked toward him. The canvas was rich, deep-toned abstract, with orange and blue-green color glowing out from a dark background, suggesting buildings, faces, lights. I leaned close to look where he was pointing at the paint that stood up in little whorls from the canvas, catching the light. He bent forward too, his head just touching mine.

"You see," he said, pointing, "Here, here . . . and here." I stared, unseeing, feeling only the great warmth of his nearness overcome me, hypnotizing me into inaction.

"Yes," I barely whispered, "yes, I see."

---

* Typescript page 4 ends here.

He put his hand on my shoulder, then, the way he did so often to the girls in class when he came up behind them to look at their paintings. The heat of his fingers burned through my cotton blouse. Was it my imagination, or did his grip on my shoulder tighten?

"You see, Miss Evans?" he repeated, turning me so that I faced him and not letting go of my shoulder. "You see now, perhaps, what I meant by my former remark?" He was looking continually, intently, into my eyes as if trying to read my expression.

"I . . . I don't know . . ." I blushed, stammered, swaying toward him, slightly, as if magnetically drawn by his steady gaze. I could not look away. His eyes were deep bottomless wells of green, I was drowning in them, drowning.

His voice sounded as if it were coming from very far off. "I will repeat," he said, very low, smiling at what he was revealed in my eyes. "You are," he said huskily, slowly pulling me against him, "an extremely provoking girl."

Somehow I was in his arms, then, and his hands were smoothing my hair, traveling caressingly down my back, pressing my body up against his. His lips came casually across my face, teasing my cheeks, seeking my mouth. And then he

'Sassoon was coming . . .'

Ts,* undated *c.* December 1955–March 1956, British Library and Emory University

Sassoon was coming. Sheila folded the crisp pale blue airmail letter covered with his spidery erratic scrawl and, from where she sat curled up on her haircloth sofa by the west gable window, stared out at the English vista of orange-tiled rooftops, chimney pots, and a diminishing perspective of small, fenced-in kitchen gardens which multiplied the few neat rows of cabbage and the several scraggly, scavenging chickens next door to infinity in her mind, like a mirror trick. Already, at teatime, the December evening had shut in and the mists were creeping up from the Cambridge fens, blurring the landscape with veil after veil of grey gauze, until the houses and bare trees seemed to float unreal as a

---

* Three typescript pages with holograph and typewritten additions and corrections by SP. Page number 1 held by British Library with Ted Hughes writing on verso. Pages 2 and 3 held by Emory with Ted Hughes's 'The Harvesting' on verso.

theatrical scrim in the distance. The low hanging sky was the colour of rats' fur.

Directly outside her window, the great plane tree stood stripped for winter, the mottlings of its leprous green-and-yellow bark reminding her of a composition by Hans Arp, titled, perhaps, 'Navels and Clouds'. Below, in the cottage yard, large black rooks lurched over the gravel walks and stabbed at the damp earth with questing beaks. Sheila never liked the way these ungainly birds always halted, teetering on the barbed-wire fences flanking the college grounds, to watch her as she passed. She read in the cold cocked circle of each rook's eye an unpleasant, almost obscene, intelligence. They seemed to be sizing her up, calculating the worth of her very entrails, and, for some secret reason, finding her wanting.[*]

She gave a convulsive shiver. A chill, insidious draught was seeping in from the window frame, and already her fingers were quite numb. There was no getting away from the cold; it penetrated everywhere. The New Zealand butter in her tea cupboard was rigid and well-preserved as the day she bought it last week; the malt bread and macaroons stayed fresh as if stored in a deep freeze. Once, inadvertently standing barefoot on her green rug, Sheila had felt a glacial exaltation of dampness which for a moment made her wonder if there was a bog of ice water underneath her instead of floorboards. Even the wool dress she chose each day from her wardrobe, on the opposite side of the room from the gas fire, brought in its folds an aura of polar regions.

Taking baths, though, was her most stoic gesture. The unheated garret bathroom was on the northern side of the house and the hot water was invariably tepid. Sheila had been horrified that first October morning after her arrival, when she rose pale and dripping from the large, claw-footed tub, to see clouds of white steam emanating from her shivering body, prickly with gooseflesh, while her breath hung in little puffs in the frosty air, like Indian smoke signals.

When she complained, half-jokingly, to the archaeology student from London who lived across the hall that getting into bed at night was like slipping between frozen shroud sheets, the girl suggested that Sheila buy a hot water bottle.

'But I thought you only used those when you were sick,' Sheila said, a bit lamely.

The girl had laughed in that motherly, almost patronisingly, British way which always made Sheila feel naïve and slightly uncouth, rather like an American cowgirl blundering into a labyrinth of Royal Doulton china. 'But I say, how do you think we live through the winter?' the archaeology student had said a trifle more kindly, as if condescending to admit a fictitious common weakness.

---

[*] British Library's typescript page 1 ends here.

Sheila was not really sure she *would* live through the winter. Driven at last to defensive tactics by the inexorable cold and wet, clouded greyness outside her window pane, she started to stock her room full of colour, with all the acquisitive foresight of a squirrel in autumn. Heroically she accepted the threadbare green rug and faded green-and-white flowered curtains and the sallow indefinite colour of the painted walls, but she fought back with rough-textured yellow cushions for the sofa and a large, earthenware vase full of yellow chrysanthemums whose sunburst of petals made her think of Van Gogh's vigorously brush-stroked planets. She extravagantly purchased a thick brown-and-yellow squared travel rug to cover her cot (the colour of chestnuts and sunlight, she thought) and had a reproduction Braque still-life framed to hang above her bed, a pleasant curving composition in rich russets, fawns, and avocado greens with rounded yellow fruit shapes.

Using the liberal expense allowance from her government grant, she went on a book-buying binge every few days at Heffers on Petty Cury. As her shelves filled with more brightly jacketed books than she could possibly read in a year, she became almost hysterical, and began to arrange the books meticulously according to colour and size, as if she were creating a Mondrian abacus of colour on the shelves, and everything depended on achieving a kind of absolute Platonic balance.

Taking a hint from the display counters of Heffers, she carefully chose five books with the most artistic covers and braced them, facing outward, at strategic intervals in her bookcase. She picked the New Classics edition of Rimbaud's *A Season in Hell* because of the whimsical red, purple and white forms; the sloe-eyed greenish damsel on Epstein's *Autobiography*; the sprightly sketch of a fairy-tale princess and a group of mice, fish and birds[*] on[†]

covetous love for things: vase, chestnuts, colored books. acquisitive.

glut: surrounded by books and music: unable to read or play organ:

paralysis: lives like spider on creative spurts of men.

tea: ritual: beginning with bread and butter: progressing to sweets.

juxtapose: fetish of neatness and disciplined order of the diffuse and unruly color of the world: sheila fighting elements of sassoon in self: reaction against the chaos and complexity of creation:

---

[*] SP's Rimbaud held by Smith College. Her Epstein held by Indiana University. The final book described is probably *Märchen der Brüder Grimm* (München, 1937). SP's copy held by Emory University.

[†] The following notes, transcribed exactly as they appear, accompany this Emory typescript.

neatness of nature: moon, cold, distant: refined patterns of stars.

"I have been cold ever since I came here": dwindling to frigid perfection.

Sassoon: careless, gay: never spelled "Whitstead" right, generous.

Crisis: both have shared passion: diverged in opposite directions since: can't recreate that world again. "Make the world come alive for me again," she begs. "find me where the sun's kitchen is, and the blue grotto. I feel so pale, like English dough, sodden and heavy."

statue of little bronze boy in formal Newnham gardens.

The Matisse Chapel

Ts Fragment,[*] 2 February 1956, Lilly Library

Sally kept the Lambretta motorbike in second gear all the way up the hilly zigzag road to Vence, feeling Richard's hands at her waist, lightly touching now, and relaxed. She had persuaded him to let her learn to drive by having a tantrum earlier that morning on the Promenade des Anglais in Nice. ('But it's so *straight* here,' she'd protested, 'so *safe*!' as they passed the elaborate cream-colored façade of the Hotel Ruhl, with the Avenue of violently green palms stretching ahead of them beside the blue blaze of the Baie des Anges.) Now, victorious, Sally sang happily off-key above the whirring motor. In the shadow of the hills, the air was frigid, dark with pine trees, but coming out into the sunlight, it was warm enough for Sally to feel comfortable, if slightly spartan, in her soiled white turtle-neck sweater and tapered grey flannel slacks.

'Oh, *God*!' She exclaimed over her shoulder to Richard every time they

---

[*] Four typescript pages are extant. Pages numbered 1 and 23 are struck through by SP as there are notes on the verso from Cambridge courses. Page 1 has a list of names, some with characteristics: 'Colin', '–donald (proud chief)', 'Guy', '–Maurice (dark)', '–Neil (dark-champion)', 'Philip', 'Pierre' and 'Stuart'. A second page numbered 1 and a page numbered 2 contain numerous holograph corrections and additions by SP. Handwritten at the top of one page is: 'Theme: simple love & mercy – forgives all – light permeates daily dark mystic transcendence, fear.' SP sent the story to the *New Yorker* on 3 February 1956; it was rejected by 21 February 1956. Richard Sassoon wrote a story based on this excursion to Nice and Vence, France: 'In the year of Love and unto Death, the fourth – an Elegy on the Muse', *Northwest Review* (Winter 1962): 103–23. See Andrew Wilson, *Mad Girl's Love Song: Sylvia Plath and Life Before Ted* (London: Simon and Schuster, 2013).

made a sharp turn and a fresh vista of exquisitely small hills and antique pink-walled towns opened up before them. It was Sally's first foreign country (England really didn't count because they spoke the same language), and she had never before in her provincial Bostonian life seen palm trees (except tame ones in hotel lobbies) or frivolous pastel houses or fields of crimson carnations thriving in midwinter. 'Oh, God!' she tossed back now, 'are those *really olive trees?*' With gnarled trunks and blanched sprays of silver-grey leaves, silver-green, the trees clung to a steeply terraced slope. At the left of the road stood a patched, peeling gypsy wagon, next to a heap of rusty metal tyre rims, cans and broke bicycle spokes. Smoke twined out of a small pipe-chimney. 'Do people really *live* there!' Sally yelled above the whirring motor, with a kind of reckless joy. Everything was possible in France, even olive trees, even gypsies.

Richard was happy, too, Sally felt. He had relaxed after her first few jerky stops and starts when she had taken over the Lambretta near the Nice airport, and ever since they'd arrived on the Riviera from Paris at the beginning of the week, he'd been wanting to go to Vence to see the Matisse Chapel. Looking at a map of the Côte d'Azur in their hotel room, they had decided to take a trial trip on the rented Lambretta to Juan-les-Pins, and then an all-day tour through Monaco to the Italian frontier, so Sally could cross the boundary and get her passport stamped, just for fun, they were *so* close. Almost at the same moment, they had seen the circle marking Vence on the map, a mere twenty-five kilometres away, and exclaimed together: 'Matisse!'

Last Christmas, when Sally was still at Smith and Richard was rampaging through his last year at Yale, insulting his professors, writing blasphemous poetry in French and living with Sally in New York on weekends, he had given her the December 1951 issue of *Illustration*, inscribed in his spidery scrawl '*Un petit soupçon de voyage continental.*' In this splendid, glossy magazine, Sally had promptly fallen in love with the pictures of the Matisse chapel.

Every time she plunged into a jagged black mood, bogging down on her senior English thesis ('A Study of the Double Personality in Dostoevsky's Novels'), or becoming impatient with the long winter wait until her Fulbright applications to England were decided, she would turn to the bright yellow page on the two scalloped blue leaves which began the section on the Matisse Chapel, and solace herself with the serenely coloured light of Mediterranean blue, palm-green and sun-yellow that shafted from the leafily patterned stained-glass windows.[*]

◆

---

[*] Typescript page 2 ends here.

740

on which she stood: adoring the oranges, the chickens, the woman in the green print dress.

'You have no love in you,' Richard repeated, as they were forced into a run down a steep little slope covered with wild grass and weeds. 'My parents, my sister, anyone would have wanted me to see the chapel, even if they couldn't. They would have loved me enough to want me to see it and tell them about it even if *they* couldn't see it.'

The cruel clarity of Sally's rational mind flashed back. 'And you,' she retorted, descending, stumbling, 'you are so selfish that you went to see it without me. You knew that *reporting* about it wouldn't mean anything. You wouldn't even tell the Mother Superior: "No, I will not see it without my girl." You didn't even have the courage for that.'

'Remember, I got you in,' Richard said.

'They let *you* in because you looked miserable,' Sally said. 'And they let *me* in because I was crying. Simply because I was crying.'

The radiance of the day was going. It was getting colder, approaching four o'clock, and the sky was thickening from blue to grey, curding over with clouds. Animosity rankled between them. Stubbornly, Sally made the decisive gesture and withdrew her hand from Richard's arm.

'Can't you *see*,' she said hopelessly, wondering if anything could save them now, after they had turned their backs on the coloured chapel and fallen to squabbling again, 'can't you see

Side-Hall Girl

Ts Fragment,* 16 February 1956, University of Victoria

shove your feet into the dirty white terrycloth slippers and pull your beachcoat around you. The blisters at your heels are thickening under the transparent ooze. They say after a while you don't notice your feet any more.

Six-thirty. You can hear the alarms starting to go off in the boys' dorm across the way, one after the other, high and low, long and short, like so many

---

* Typescript page 2; Ted Hughes's 'Chronicle of Fallgrief', a variant title for 'Dully Gumption's Addendum' on verso. The initial idea for the story, based on her experience working in the Belmont Hotel, West Harwich, Massachusetts, in June and early July 1952, dates to 21 June 1952. See *The Letters of Sylvia Plath, Volume 1*: 456. However, SP's calendar indicates she did not type the story until 16 February 1956.

bells going crazy. You get up and go into the john where half the time the toilets don't work anyway, just run all day, and the water from the washbowls is green and tastes like oil.

Mary, the old war-horse, is bending over one of the bowls, coughing and spitting, clearing her throat out. Her cigarette is smouldering on the edge of the stone basin. It is that way always in the morning, she has to have a cigarette first thing while she washes up.

'Hello,' you say, wetting your facecloth with cold water and rubbing it across your shut eyes.

'Hello,' she says in her cracked voice, and her skin, without the caking orange make-up she wears, is sallow and faded, hanging in little pockets under her eyes.

Back in the room, Polly is already half into her uniform, bending over and squinting into the greenish mirror that hangs too low above the bureau. She is straightening her cap.

'I'm damned if I'm going to change my collar and cuffs today,' she says. 'I just reversed them. What do they think, I'm going to spend all my time washing and ironing?'

You laugh and sit down on the edge of the bed to put on

The Black Bull

Ts fragment,[*] *c*.2 August 1956, Emory

as the usher led them down to the first row. 'I don't see how we managed on those cheap tickets: practically right in the ring.'

'I only hope the bulls don't have the same illusion,' Marcia said sarcastically.

The tiers opposite seemed alive with hovering butterflies as the women rapidly fanned themselves. The arena clock read six-fifteen. Marcia, still shaken by her encounter with the beggar, sipped her lemonade and stared at the rusty red-coloured earth of the stadium.

'Wonder if that's bull blood,' Tom said.

---

[*] Typescript pages 9, 11 and 12; Ted Hughes's 'How My Blood Went – It Came First' and 'Last Lines' on versos. According to SP's calendar, she finished typing 'The Black Bull' on 2 August 1956. Story based on seeing a bullfight in Madrid, Spain, 8 July 1956. SP submitted 'The Black Bull', 'That Widow Mangada' and 'Afternoon in Hardcastle Crags' to *Mademoiselle* on 17 September 1956.

In the middle of the ring, someone concealed inside a large green pasteboard bottle advertising brandy kept walking about on two shuffling feet. 'It must be terribly hot under that thing,' Marcia commiserated.

Below her, in the sheltered ring edging the arena, Marcia saw a man whetting the tip of a sword. A gilt-clad matador was practising flicks of his pink-and-yellow cape at an imaginary bull. It was like glimpsing the set-props and waiting actors backstage before a play.

'Tell me,' she asked Tom impulsively, 'just what will the fight be like?' Vaguely, Marcia visualised a daring exhibition of skill by the matador, dancing about and waving his scarlet cape before the raging bull and then, just on the brink of death, stabbing the bull cleanly to the heart.

'Well, it's really an exciting ceremony,' Tom replied, searching for the right words. 'Sort of symbolising man's victory over brute force. Winning out over the powers of darkness, you might say.'

'I've heard some people get sick at bullfights, they're so bloody,' Marcia said tentatively.

'Oh, the first bull's always the hardest,' Tom tossed off with a casual wave of his hand. 'It's a cinch after you get used to it.'[*]

and charged at the man. The fighter ran, ducking to safety behind the guard gate just as the bull banged its horns against the wood. The crowd roared again.

'I wish I knew what they were yelling at,' Marcia said. 'The bull or the man.'

The fighter at the next entry stepped forward and flagged the bull in to him. But then, instead of running off as the previous man had done, he made the bull do a turn or two before he retreated to safety. The crowd murmured its approval.

'Not bad,' Tom observed. 'That last turn had the bull almost grazing his thigh.'

'I don't see how you can tell how close the bull comes,' Marcia said. 'Those dashes all look the same to me.' She was soon bored by the repeated advances of the men with pink capes and kept her eyes on the bull, admiring the force packed into its powerfully built body and the way its horns measured and levelled before it charged. Several more sallies by the men with capes brought the bull almost completely around the ring.

'But where's the chief matador?' Marcia asked, finally. 'They're just taunting the bull and nothing happens.'

---

[*] This is the end of typescript page 9.

'Can't you see how differently each of those fellows handles the bull?' Tom said patronisingly. 'Some just run off when it comes at them. Others hold their ground and manoeuvre its turns really well.'

Marcia shrugged. 'I still think the bull could whip them all single-handed, if they didn't always run and hide behind the guard rails.'

As she spoke, a young boy, elaborately dressed, stalked into the area. He made the bull do a few turns with his cape, which he flaunted more daringly than the others. On the last turn, he held the cape in back of him, so the colour showed on either side of his slender body.

'But how does he know which side the bull will charge at?' Marcia asked, awed in spite of herself.

'Just watch,' Tom said, absorbed.

The bull charged the man head on. As if in a mirror trick, the bull ran through the red cloak, its horns meeting empty air. There was scattered applause.

'There's a real expert for you!' Tom exclaimed admiringly, joining in the clapping.

As the applause died, Marcia noticed that a new procession was entering the ring. The two fat, yellow-costumed men in sombreros, each on a blindfolded horse with its sides skirted about by an armour of heavy straw matting, rode in carrying long, spiked poles. They took up stations on opposite sides of the ring. Each was surrounded by several of the young boys with switches.

'Who are they?' Marcia asked, curious.

'The picadors,' Tom told her, leaning forward in anticipation.

Marcia stared with growing mistrust at their crude, waiting figures. The bullfighters, one by one, were bringing the bull in little short rushes toward the nearest picador. When the bull was close enough to notice the horse, the fighters folded up their capes and the boys whipped the blindfolded horse forward toward the bull with their switches. The bull, attracted by this new motion, ran at the horse to plunge its horns harmlessly into the straw matting.

As the bull came on, the corpulent picador held his spiked pole braced low so that it rammed deep into the bull's charging shoulder. Enraged by the pain of the pick, the bull dug its horns again and again into the straw matting. Terrified, the horse tried to shy back, but the boys went on switching it, keeping its protected side squarely up to the bull. After a few minutes, the picador hauled his pike back. From a large hole in the bull's

Remember the Stick Man

Ts fragment,* August–September 1956, Emory

The maid had brought in another round of beer, and Walt was pouring it out into the glasses. Carmen lay dozing, eyes shut, in her buggy, her face blank and peaceful as an egg. 'Quiet little angel,' Walt said. 'Look, I've got some photos of her I took just after she got home from the hospital.' He handed Janet a stack of black-and-white snapshots.

Sitting down, sipping her beer, Janet was beginning to examine the conventional mother-and-baby shots of Bettina posed holding Carmen this way and that, when Mardie stalked in from the balcony porch. He rummaged in the sideboard drawer and pulled out some more snapshots, came over to stand at Janet's side, and took the snapshots of Carmen out of her hand. Then, with a strange, almost diffident air, he showed her a picture of himself dressed in Sunday best, posed stiffly in somebody's front doorway.

'Mardie, in his new suit,' he informed her.

Bettina giggled. 'We had that suit made here by a tailor just like a little man's, pockets and all, except for the size.'

Mardie pulled out another snapshot, showing himself smiling, crouched naked in a rubber swimming pool. He seemed pleased with this shot. 'Mardie, laughing,' he said. There were other shots, taken at Christmas, of Mardie in a bed, with toys; of Mardie sitting under the Christmas tree in his bathrobe; of Mardie eating turkey in a bib. There was even one of Mardie in a bad temper, his face screwed up like a walnut.

'And what's Mardie doing *here*?' Janet asked with a slight touch of malice.

Mardie was silent for a minute. 'Mardie's crying,' he said at last, shoving the picture to the bottom of the stack and again bringing out the snapshot of himself in his Sunday suit.

Walt leaned over to look. 'Oh, she's already seen that,' he said. Walt took the

---

* Typescript page 11; Ted Hughes's 'The Harvesting' on verso. On 11 August, SP wrote in her calendar, 'bright clear day – long wasted morning talk with landlord – typed long Fulbright letter – lunch & good love met Swiss wife Sylvia gates – revealing evening – ward – crippled painter husband – brat Mardie – queer baby Carmen – maid Cecelia – walk in hills – rabbit dinner – Villa joyosa – Outdoor movies & fireworks – cognac'. Carmen and Mardie feature in 'Remember the Stick Man' which SP drafted from 12 August to 19 September 1956. She submitted it to the *New Yorker* on 12 October 1956.

pile of pictures from Mardie and stowed them away in the sideboard drawer. Mardie stood, glowering at his father.

'Come sit on Janet's lap,' Janet said sweetly, adopting Mardie's use of the third person. 'Do you know any stories?' she

Afternoon in Hardcastle Crags

Ts fragment,* 7–12 September 1956, Emory University and University of Victoria

stomach, cheeks burning, she let her loose brown hair tangle with the grass. Over her duffle coat and wool slacks crawled the lean, black flies; around her face quivered in a gauze of transparent wings. She brought her hand down hard on the knee of her slacks and wiped off the yellow guts of two dead flies on the grass. Little round rabbit droppings pebbled the hummocks. Olwyn put her ear to the earth. She heard no footsteps, only the drumming racket of her own heartbeat.

Cold, she resolved, I shall be cold as he. She lay in the grass, not daring to get up for fear Gerald would spot her and spoil her perfect fury of self-pity. Daylong he sat tousled in his mother's parlour in his old RAF sweater, writing poems about water drops and martyred bishops and playing his battered, cracked Beethoven records over and over. Beethoven's death mask hung waxen and eerie in their bedroom. She had married a genius.

Olwyn saw him famous and suave in a tuxedo, roaring sestinas in a royal godly voice over the BBC, in a dither of actresses, ballet dancers and Italian countesses with a literary flair, while she skulked about choking on cheese rinds like a tear-blind mouse.

Oh, she would make him sorry this last time. She heard the police demanding sternly: 'Gerald, what have you done with your wife?' 'Why,' Gerald said, gnawing absent-minded on a slice of buttered malt bread, 'she lost herself on the moor one day about a week ago. Careless girl.' Perhaps, Olwyn thought, she would only stay out overnight. She tried to remember the direction back to Gerald's mother's house.

In her mind's eye she turned detective, Sherlock Holmesing a path back up the

---

* Typescript page 5; Ted Hughes's 'The Calm' on verso; held by Emory. Typescript page 6; Ted Hughes's 'The Calm' on verso; held by University of Victoria. According to SP's calendar, she began 'Afternoon in Hardcastle Crags' on 7 September 1956 noting it was a 'secret story, slight & subversive'.

gravel road, past the tearoom at the waterfall and over the stepping stones in the peat-brown river. Through a wild raspberry patch, then, and by the grey stone house where she played with the[*] ginger kitten: where Gerald stalked on to lean against a stone wall, wringing rooks necks with his glare while she lingered. A toothless old man had stumped out of the house, his wall-eye staring sideways, astonished, as if an evil demon stood smoking at his shoulder. 'The cat's yours if you want it,' the old man said. 'Yours or the river's.' Olwyn furrowed the purring orange fur with her fingers and looked with love into the sleepy yellow sphinx-eyes. Gerald had promised her a kitten when they got to his house, just a small tottering kitten with a silly beard of warm milk on its chin. 'Well, I don't like kittens,' Gerald's mother said. 'With their messes on the carpet and their claws in the chairs.' Olwyn dropped the ginger kitten quickly on its four cushioned feet and ran to catch up with Gerald. She did not tell him what the man had said.

Before the stone house, they'd trekked down through a wet black wood where she'd almost fallen into a stream when she leapt for a tree branch to swing across. Usually Gerald never stopped to help her, but went striding on. 'I like the way you don't cry to be carried over the rough places,' he told her once. This time, though, he had turned back and run to where she hung kicking on the branch, over the foaming water, trying for enough momentum to fling herself to the opposite bank. She just managed to make it before he came up to her and walked on haughty without a word, rubbing the damp, rotted bark from her fingers like bloodstains.

And before the wood, cow fields, with knee-high grass, and slow cows cruising, revolving their jaws. Yes, she knew the way back fine, even if she always let Gerald lead.

That night she'd been planning to make steak tartare for their supper. Gerald still liked steak tartare the way they'd had it in Paris, even if his mother widened shocked eyes and exclaimed: 'Raw meat! Raw egg! Gerald, you'll get worms!'

The Invisible Man

Ts,[†] October 1956, Emory University and Smith College

from an early age, seemed destined to follow in his father's illustrious footsteps. Undoubtedly, Oswald McQuail ranked among Fortune's favourites. In

---

[*] Typescript page 5 ends here.
[†] Typescript pages 2–8; Ted Hughes's 'The Harvesting' on verso; held by Emory. Typescript

secret, he liked to consider his very success responsible for his invisibility to himself – a kind of minor, modest atonement for his conspicuous good luck at everything he undertook to achieve.

Oswald's youthful career, up to the day he became invisible, was that of any sturdy, well-rounded fellow with more than the usual capacity for being liked by teachers, classmates, summer employers, and, of course, the various young ladies of his acquaintance. Upon receiving a local scholarship to a leading Eastern men's college, Oswald gravitated rapidly into the right circles. He was invited to join one of the best fraternities, excelled in athletics, and managed creditably in all his subjects. Quite simply, Oswald McQuail was one of those frank, friendly, versatile boys who don't have an enemy in the world.

In the spring of his junior year at college, Oswald got pinned to Marilyn Cameron (whom he eventually married), then attending a neighbouring women's college and as popular and prosperous in her own orbit as Oswald was in his. The scholarship committee had just voted to increase his grant; there was little doubt of his being elected president of his fraternity; and, already, his uncle's law firm was taking genuine interest in his progress. It was at this very period, the apex, one might say, of Oswald's college career, that he became invisible.

The first symptoms of his invisibility occurred one morning in early April while Oswald was shaving himself. He noticed, as he lifted his razor, that he could see the apple-green tiles of the bathroom wall showing faintly through his hand and as much of his arm as emerged from the sleeve of his plaid wool dressing gown. Understandably shocked, Oswald stared at his hand, and then into the mirror, which gave back his ruddy, rather handsome face, under a lather of shaving soap, with every semblance of its ordinary solidity. In stubborn disbelief, Oswald held his hand up to the mirror; through the transparent fibre of that very hand, he saw its mirror-image, perfectly intact.

Oswald hoped, at the outset, that something might be wrong with his eyes – some bizarre astigmatism, perhaps, which cause him to see a double image: his own body and, simultaneously, the section of the scene it should have blocked out by its existence in space. Complaining of severe headache,

---

page 15, on verso a draft page of SP's 'Berck-Plage'; held by Smith College. According to SP's calendar she worked on 'The Invisible Man' from 8–10 October 1956, and revised it from 16–19 October 1956. SP sent 'The Invisible Man', 'The Wishing Box' and 'All the Dead Dears' to the *New Yorker* on 30 October 1956. See *The Letters of Sylvia Plath, Volume 1*, 1292.

he made an appointment for an eye examination at the college infirmary that same morning.

'Twenty-twenty!' the white-coated nurse informed Oswald cheerfully, after running him through the routine tests and peering into his pupils with a small flashlight apparatus. 'Couldn't be more normal. Try reading in a better light, and,' she shook her finger playfully at him, 'don't burn too much of that midnight oil.'

Oswald left the doctor's office, perplexed. He decided to walk along the river beyond the crew house to mull over this untoward new development. As Oswald crossed the main campus, several of his friends, passing by, greeted him casually. Nobody gaped, pointed, or screamed. From this evidence, Oswald deduced that his vanishing was apparent to no one but himself; he felt the least bit relieved: he had no intentions, at such a productive, auspicious time in his life, of being forcibly removed from normal human society. Obviously, he realised now, his private problem was not one to be put to psychiatrists, strangers, or intimate friends – no, not even to Marilyn.

About him, on every side, spring waxed prolific: pink dogwood flowering in front of the fraternity houses, multitudes of yellow daffodils dipping their frilled heads behind the college observatory, robins and sparrows trilling, from tree and hedge, their pure panegyrics to the gentle, burgeoning season. In the midst of this universal rejoicing, however, Oswald felt fear, for the first time in his twenty-one years, take its cold, slick stronghold in the pit of his stomach.

He was wearing scuffed loafers, a pair of argyles Marilyn had knitted him for Christmas, grey flannel pants, and a white sports shirt with the sleeves rolled up. Now, through his hands and arms, as they swung with the rhythm of his stride, Oswald could see, in meticulous detail, the green glass-blades and purple crocuses bordering the path, blurred only slightly by the gauze-like stuff of his flesh which, even as he stared, went melting away before his eyes like some fairy gossamer in the sunlight. Hurriedly, Oswald rolled down his shirtsleeves. Under the protective white linen, his arms bulked real enough; there were, however, no hands to be seen. Yet, Oswald told himself emphatically, he *felt* exactly the same. If he shut his eyes (he stopped in a secluded wooded area to try this), and clasped his hands together or touched his toes, he would have sworn that his physical substance had altered not a whit.

Brooding on the riverbank, beside a still, dark pool out of the main current, Oswald leaned over suddenly, as if trying to catch his image off guard, and stared into the depths. His customary reflection leaned up out of the pool to meet him, reduced, to be sure, to a darkish monochrome by the murky water, but unmistakably, line for line, his own face. Idly, Oswald stirred the water with a twig; his image wavered, broke apart into agitated fragments, and then, as the water calmed, returned to its original unity.

If it was true that neither people nor the hard-hearted natural laws of reflection (whatever *those* were) registered his invisibility, Oswald's only concern was developing a constructive attitude toward the vexing lack he discerned in himself. With luck, he might even outgrow his peculiar physical flaw like some adolescent allergy. In pragmatic fashion, Oswald ultimately resolved to make a few cautious tests in private, to tell no one of his malady, and to go about campus exactly as was his wont. His plan of action fixed, he cut his afternoon class in Contract and Tort and shut himself up until dinner in his fraternity rooms.

Alone, Oswald stood a good while before his bedroom mirror wherein he could see himself reflected from the waist up. In that tranquil looking-glass world, at least, all seemed in order, his visibility irrefutable. Indeed, while fully dressed, except for the mortifying absence of his hands and the inability to look down at his nose or up at his unruly forelock of brown hair (fortunately, for his own peace of mind, Oswald felt merely a vague, wistful sense of the void surrounding his eyes, rather than any harrowing total awareness of his head's disappearance), Oswald found himself able to cope with his new state quite philosophically.

He strolled about his room, concentrating, as he never had before, on picking up his reflection everywhere he turned: in the mirror, in the silver tennis trophy cup on the mantel, in the waxed mahogany top of the coffee table, in the gold band of his signet ring: all of these shiny surfaces gave back his image, now with a warped nose, now life-size, now Lilliputian. Each reflecting object exposed its own editorialised version of Oswald McQuail.

At dinner, Oswald gazed with new interest into the eyes of his fraternity brothers; in each pair of eyes he sought twin Oswalds to confirm the material existence of the flesh and blood he could feel but not see. (Incidentally, it was this same direct, intense meeting-of-the-eyes which, later a fixed habit, inspired Oswald's friends and business associates with confidence and admiration; he was considered a fine, solid fellow.)

That night, Oswald had a movie date with Marilyn. When he called for her at her dormitory, she smiled at him, blithe and fond as ever. Just as they were leaving, while yet in the dimly lit hallway, Marilyn asked Oswald for a cigarette. As she bent over his cupped hands to ignite the cigarette from his lighter, she accused, teasingly: 'Your hands are shaking! Have you seen a ghost or something?'

Oswald managed a slight, inscrutable smile. 'Perhaps,' he said noncommittally, 'I have.' Although he *felt* the silver lighter firm in his hands, it rather shook him to watch it flaming independently on the air a few inches from his empty coat-cuffs like some tiny glittering firedrake. Checking his miniature reflection in the side of the lighter before he slipped it back into his pocket, he wondered if it were the silver surface which gave his face that odd pallor.

In the weeks immediately following his discovery of his invisibility, Oswald McQuail fought a brief battle with fear and, thanks to his easy-going, adjustable temperament, emerged the victor. The worst experience by far was undressing alone at night: to take off shirt, pants, shoes and socks, and thus, gradually, limb by limb, betray the nothingness of his own body, was, at first, an irksome ordeal. However, he found that by undressing before the mirror and focusing his gaze upon that hale, heartening image of himself going about its business in the glass, his qualms lessened appreciably. With the light once out, he relaxed, snug and safe as a hibernating bear, in the tangible certainty of his own flesh and blood.

A gregarious chap, Oswald had never kept to himself much; under this new strain, he sought company more than ever before. And it *was* a strain, until Oswald grew accustomed to looking *away* from his own body all the time and seeking its presence in the reflecting surfaces about him. His shadow gave him a minor comfort, but it generally presented either a ridiculously squat or an overly elongated parody of his true silhouette. Almost without his being aware of it, Oswald began keeping this or that friend at his side during meals, in classes, and on the sports field. He felt most secure when in company and managed, with skill, to avoid more than momentary solitude. He could, with increasing facility, lose himself in the conversation and activity of those around him. Oswald was, all his acquaintances agreed, an entertaining, lively asset at any gathering.

By the end of the spring term, Oswald had become expert at reading his own image in other people's eyes. Some eyes offered only a blurred, foggy reproduction, like a badly focused camera snapshot. Some approached the mirror in accuracy. None, gratifyingly enough, were unflattering. It was in Marilyn's clear azure eyes, however, that Oswald discerned his favourite image. He liked Marilyn to keep her eyes open while he kissed her. Then, in that sweet space of physical contact, he would feast on the sight of his miniature in each of those lovely orbs. Perfectly realised, as if suspended in twin globed crystals, his features glowed with an almost celestial radiance. It was after one of these kisses that Oswald asked Marilyn to marry him as soon as he finished law school.

The married life of Oswald and Marilyn McQuail was singularly without blemish. They entertained a good deal and made a striking, sought-after couple at all affairs of social importance. Even in their middle years they were still, as close friends observed, very much in love. Who had not seen those frequent, deep, tender looks exchanged between them whenever they were, momentarily, left alone together in a lull between dances, dinner courses, bridge games, concert pieces, and the like? Their apartment, like their marriage, displayed impeccable harmony: everything simply sparkled and shone. As Marilyn explained to her women friends, Oswald, occasionally feeling hemmed in by city life, liked the 'illusion of space,' hence the numerous mirrors hung, cleverly, in every room, offering tricky extensions of perspective into duplicate, nonexistent rooms.

Oswald's personable young son Michael, while embodying all his father's virtues, seemed gifted, in addition, with an artistic sensitivity of the highest order. Although perhaps more meditative, more reserved in company, than his father, Michael was, Oswald's friends and relatives agreed, what is known in common parlance as a 'chip off the old block.' He was immediately well-liked (without any effort on his own part) by all who encountered him.

Although Oswald McQuail was certainly a devoted family man, he nonetheless enjoyed stag drinking bouts with his many male friends. Usually he met with one or another of them in some plush, gleaming bar where he could glimpse, from time to time, through a jewelled barricade of liquor bottles, the mirror reflection of his attractive, regular features and his strong, capable hands gripping highball glass and cigarette (Marilyn proudly called them 'surgeon's hands'). After turning away from this mirror, his animated gaze would hold, with almost hypnotic intensity, the eyes of his drinking companion; his conversation would scintillate: his assurance grow dynamic.

When the time came for Michael to choose a university, Oswald, having with some difficulty refrained from trying to influence the boy's decision, was pleased to hear his son select his own alma mater. Michael had developed, by now, into a tall, lean, well-coordinated, ruddy-cheeked chap – still rather too much given to daydreaming and a bit on the introspective side (he had won the annual prize for a sonnet sequence in his senior year at prep school), but eminently all-round, nevertheless. It was with a keen sense of pride and love that Oswald took the occasion of a fishing trip in early September to give Michael some man-to-man advice about the trials and temptations of a college career. Oswald stressed the importance of cultivating staunch friends (it's college friends that are friends for life), avoiding serious emotional entanglements with girls of his own set (marriage can be a clog to a brilliant career if it's not the right girl; better to blow off steam in the city, over a weekend, with girls who can take care of themselves and won't cause trouble), and participating fully in all facets of college life (those brightest, sweetest, fleetest years; sentimentality aside, the old songs don't lie). As for Michael's career after college, Oswald cherished a secret hope that the boy would go out for law and, eventually, join Oswald's own firm. It came as rather a surprise to hear that Michael planned to major in English literature.[*]

that he should have done? He rubbed his hand across his aching eyes. For the first time in his life, Oswald McQuail acknowledged himself beaten, utterly vanquished, at a game that was, in some strange, secret way, more intricate, more difficult than he had ever imagined it. He was very tired.

With chastened steps, Oswald McQuail paced back to the hotel, his one concern, now, for Marilyn. It was late, late in the evening; he prayed it was not too late. The years ahead loomed like black juggernauts. Marilyn would stand by him; with Marilyn at his side, he would work out some salvation. If only he had shared the absurd truth with her from those first days; but in those days, his choice had seemed so right, so simple. A judgement, he thought, had been visited on him, after all this time; and on his decision made that long gone spring afternoon.

Oswald entered the hotel unnoticed. Getting off the self-service elevator at the proper floor, he walked down the long, empty corridor to the room he shared with Marilyn. He turned the key in the lock. Then, opening the door to the bedroom, Oswald went in and closed it softly behind him.

Marilyn was breathing evenly, relaxed in the first real sleep she'd taken since they'd received the news of Michael's death. Oswald bent over his wife's pale, tear-ravaged face (still pure, still lovely, he marvelled) and kissed her gently on the lips. Marilyn opened her blue eyes, looking directly at him. But then, instead of responding to the penitent tenderness of his embrace, she recoiled, staring blankly at him, through him, beyond him, and, drawing the bedclothes up about her body like a shield, began, as if it were some perilous phantom standing there, to scream for help.

---

[*] Typescript page 8 ends here.

Venus in the Seventh

Ts,[*] February–July 1957, Smith College, Emory University and University of Victoria

Sky darkening, black shapes looming, speckled with lights. And the fierce, progressive chittering train wheels. A day. A night. Then another train. Jess held herself in. They slowed, the train chuffing. Munich.

I shut up for a change. Followed Winthrop, with his blank tall forehead guileless as an unborn baby's. Up and down stone platforms, corridors lined with glittering shop windows: books, splayed pink and green orchids. The crinkled sheen of cellophane. I kept from sniffing or making sarcastic remarks. It was lucky he found a window where the girl spoke English. Stood back and let them go to it; they changed a few banknotes in the process.

'Well?' that was sweetly said.

'There's a hotel just out front, across the trolley tracks.'

I followed again. I'd have a room, a warm room. All the mechanics of life. Like hot water. I'd shut myself up: consider myself lucky to be warm for one night. Conserve it for the trip to Rome. Synthetic heat energy, until I worshipped the sun-god. Whatever it was in that fierce hot circle in the sky that browned my skin and melted my twitchings out.

We stood a second on the stone steps of the entry. The scene was very ugly. Back-halves of hotels across a wide street, shining with trolley tracks. A wet snow fell, straight down, sludge underfoot. My shoe soles would dissolve in five minutes of trudging in that wet. Across the street, shops.

Winthrop pointed to a green neon sign high above the black rooves. 'That's it. Let's go.'

I stepped, finicky, around brown puddles, caked with sleet. Cars nipped in and out. It didn't do to be proud crossing streets. I took Winthrop's arm and

---

[*] Typescript page 25 has textual changes to a later draft of *The Bell Jar* on verso, held by Smith College; typescript pages 35, 42–3, 64, 65, 68–73, 76 and 79 have Ted Hughes's 'In those first days when a newborn baby', 'July Evening', 'Mountains', 'The Road to Easington' and 'The Wound' on versos, held by Emory University; and typescript page 62 has Ted Hughes's 'New Moon in January' on verso, held by University of Victoria. Throughout her archive, SP's typescripts are double-spaced; however, 'Venus in the Seventh' and the next fragment, 'Hill of Leopards', are single-spaced. SP revised Gerald's forename to Ian. Both names are kept here so that the reader will observe the shift. See Appendix 8 in SP's journals for the original of 'How to win friends and influence people'.

put him between me and the coming wall of traffic. Under the grisly unnatural light, the shiny metal cars were driven by green lepers. With black eye-holes.

Past a couple of frilly candy shops showing off their gigantic chocolate Easter eggs, with purple rosettes of ribbon, and yellow fluffy chicks. Around the corner in the wet cool air. I let the snow mess itself in my hair, which got longer and straighter, considerably, since I'd come out of the station. I'd have smeared my face with mud if it would have disconcerted Winthrop. He had turned dogged now. Which got my ire up. Dogged and nobly silent.

The hotel manager dug up two rooms on the same floor. Very expensive in my book. But that was the advantage of being with a guy you despised. Something compensated. Always.

I could see the manager looking down his dented nose at my grubby raincoat. It was all smudged where I'd sat on the walls along the Seine and a kind of blue splotch had come off on the front where I'd carried one of those cheap carbon paper pads on the hottest day. He shoved us quickly toward the elevator, as if he wanted to get us out of the lobby before any of the proper guests came by.

We got out high up. A long corridor, shining like the alleys of a hospital or a monumental ship. It was frighteningly clean. Really ghastly clean. Everything that shone, shone enough to knock your eyes out, and smelled like wax. That nose-curling stench of polish and breath of hot, disinfected water. The girl in a black dress and white apron was podgy, with thick cow ankles. Rice-pudding face, raisin eyes.

'Your room,' she pronounced in perfect English.

'Danke schöne,' I said, wondering why I didn't give up trying.[*]

In the main station room, a flock of wiry, small blue-uniformed men poised, waiting. Jess braced herself: those beady gimlet-eyes, adding us up for what we're worth. To the last cent. Gesturing, gibbering, the little men surrounded them. Each had the name of a hotel embroidered in his cap, and stuck on a round or square or triangular plaque to this buttonhole.

What dolts we must look to them, Jess thought. Three large ninny Gullivers among the predatory pragmatic Lilliputians.

'Don't bother with them.' She took Winthrop's arm, forcing back an urge to start laying about her, right and left. The men hadn't touched her, but she felt their dark, knotted hands plucking at her coat, clustering like swarms of locusts on her skin. 'Let's get out. We know the name of the hotel.'

---

[*] Typescript page 25 ends here.

'They'll take you to a place miles up the river,' the boy from Miami observed wisely. His eyes, slightly protruding, gave him the air of a young owl. 'Let's get the boat.'

The three of them, ignoring the clamouring men, walked on, through the open doorway, down the granite steps to the pier.

'It's just like in that movie,' the boy observed, with pleased wonder. 'That movie where she . . . you know, Katharine Hepburn, goes off at the end, and the Italian guy comes running after her with a gardenia.'

'Maybe they shot it here,' Jess said crisply. The air from the water blew her hair back damp and fresh. She sensed her edges withering, like that ungiven gardenia. Why was she so dry, so unutterably dry.

Winthrop bought tickets for the boat at the pier. Evidently the ticket seller spoke English, for he said: 'Another boat's coming along in five minutes.'

'Did you ask him where the Patria Tre Rosa was?' Jess noticed, all at once, a small, sallow man at her elbow.

'I know,' he said, in stilted English. 'I take you there.'

Jess drew back.

'All right,' Winthrop told the man, overriding his disdain. 'After all, he knows,' he said to Jess in an undertone.

Jess kept quiet. Let the boys go to it. She'd play out on her leash. It wasn't her problem. She looked across the river to the houses opposite, their steps descending into the water. The station clock said quarter past two. Hardly anyone was about. Water-streets, lights quivering, houses anchored in green mud. What about the basements? How to keep the houses from wearing away, grain by grain. Wearing away and suddenly dissolving into the sea?

If you looked at the world from that angle, the whole underpropping mechanism was a mystery. A mystery and a miracle, like the loaves and fishes.

'Here it comes.' Winthrop pointed. With a slosh and putt-putt, the boat-bus approached, slowed up to the dock, and a deck hand cast a rope around a post, fastening it.

Jess crossed the plank, letting the boys follow, and went up to sit in front. Winthrop followed her.

'How do you like it?'

'Wonderful. All this water. Let's,' she pleaded, 'go gondoling tomorrow.'

'Sure thing,' he said, glad to give her something, at least, which she wanted. 'We'll go gondoling and climb the clock tower in St Mark's Square . . .'*

---

* Typescript page 35 ends here.

She had seen him from the time she was sixteen, each time there was a new man. No, it would take two years at least, of slow, cautious investigation, face to face, to know who he was for sure. To begin, with the utmost caution, assuming nothing, and then, bit by bit, discovering that yes, this was he. And he would be all things to her: as in the stories. Somewhere, in her mind's eye, where a little film ran continually, playing on the past (rewriting the dialogue) and forecasting the future (dreams), she rose, smiling, transfigured. What love did: it transfigured. She knew that all right. From all the small transient transfigurations she had been through already.

What I need: a banging, blasting, ferocious love. But it hurts, one voice said. So what, said the other: better bleed. You need it. Break the magic circle: stop being the Girl Who's Never Been Hurt. Get hurt and be glad of it. Take love on your terms even though he'll never love you but will use you and lunge on through you to the next one.

He. There was one. She saw the small Rousseau postcard floating before her in the dark: the black, indistinct figure of the beast-man with the pipe. The luminous moon eyes of the still tigers and the still owls through the flat bladed grasses. The Snake Charmer. She would return full circle to that. But she did not know how to hope for it. Not yet.

Lying there, her feet on the lukewarm lump of the hot water bottle, she revolved the day. Had they climbed to the top of the pretty blue and white and gilt clock tower? They must have. Her knees had gone watery, the way they always did, on spidery metal stairs she could see through. She had become childish and helpless, making Winthrop go down before her, so she could hold his shoulder and look at his solid back, not down through the million crevices of the spiral stair where, down and down, she could see the hands of people on the bannisters, descending. It was always going down that made her sick. What from, that? Irrational: the fear on steep London escalators: she'd always loved scaring herself as a little girl, pretending her foot might get caught where the stairs slid under the floor, and drag her into the machinery. Or that she could slip through a crevice in an open staircase, and fall below, to smash on the pavement. And now, ten, fifteen years later, without thinking of it, her knees went wobbly, her palms slick with sweat, and her muscles froze.

'I can't go down,' she'd told Winthrop, as they stood on the top of the tower, looking out over the domes of St Mark's and past the brick campanile to the water. The roof tiles of the village shone hot, orange in the sun.

'Of course you can. Here, let me take a picture of you. For your mother.'

Pretending, among the other tourists up there, leaning on the railing, sitting on the cement steps, and taking pictures of each other, to be perfectly unafraid, she stood up against two metal bell-ringers with their raised batons.

Winthrop stepped back, sighted into his camera. 'Cheese.'

She grinned, briefly, and he clicked it into the camera. For Mother. Her happy girl. The chance of a lifetime. And she feels dead as a walking corpse.

Down the stairs, slowly, then. Holding Winthrop's steady shoulder. The blind leading the blind. She kept quiet, praying her bones would not lock. She felt on the brink of that: freezing and going hysterical. Carry me. But she kept quiet, knocking down her own fear, until they stood on the ground.

'Thanks,' she gave Winthrop's arm a brief hug, 'for putting up with me.'

And what did she remember? The hushed interior of St Mark's, under the big hung dome, with the dusty shafts of light, the inlaid floor of coloured tiles, each piece at a slightly different cant. The gold mosaics, the heavenly turquoise colours. They floated, vague and impressionistic, in her head. The curse of imprecision. About all she remembered: moving points of colour and light. Nothing steady, nothing whole. The platitudes flocked, like clattering pigeons, coo-cooing accusations: the worst of the lot was: lose yourself in order to find yourself. Was her self lost? Or was she terribly and finally herself and this deadness the prize? The clock struck; bong, bong. She did not hear it strike again until seven.

The woman in the seat in front of Jess on the train to Rome did not like the blind up. The sun got in her eyes. Jess wanted to see the country. After much jerking – the blind belonged to them both – they settled on a level that shaded the woman's eyes and let Jess, by slouching slightly, see the fruit trees and farm yards. Winthrop sat a few seats up: the train was crowded, and only single seats had been left.

Bless the sun. It was getting hotter and hotter. Travelling to the heart of things. If anything could burn out the black rot in her, the sun could. I shall just sit in Rome, Jess thought, on those Spanish Steps, and lift my face shut-eyed into the sun from the time it rises till the time it sets.

It is almost over.

She felt a run of relief. It is almost over: this is the last train I am on with Winthrop. The last hotel. The last town. I shall never in my life see him again, and he knows it. I shall end them all. One by one. No more letters. No more friendly visits. I hate them all, and they are all dead to me. Perhaps, there might be a letter from Gerald at the American Express. Please, she begged, crossing her fingers, let him ask me to come back. I don't care what he thinks. I just want to see him. To see if I can be the next one. I can be. I'm that strong. I can blast his other girls to hell and back. And I will.

The recklessness grew on her with the strengthening sun. She felt, if she could get tan, quite brown again, she would be strong enough to go back to London. The newness of Gerald caught at her. She knew nothing much. But he was hard, and cruel. And if she could take it without whimpering or spinning sticky nets, just take it for what it was, then she might take life, after a fashion. Instead of tying strings, sogging about in endless analysis. Just feel, stride along with him, until he bashed her head in and went off with the next. No illusions. Therefore: everything as good as it could be. Give everything, though. Keep nothing safe, nothing secret for bad weather.

She pulled half a loaf of crusty white bread out of her bag: she had stuffed it with tuna and mayonnaise before they left, and she began tearing off hunks of the sandwich with her teeth. Something would turn up. To shock her alive. And, in the meantime, the tuna tasted damn good. All by itself*

He, too, as he swung her suitcase after her into the cab, seemed buoyant, more confident than he had been during their whole trip: perhaps she'd hung around his neck the whole time, beaked and feathered, like an albatross.

'Will we get to the terminal in time?' Anxious, as always, at the departure, because of the mechanical inhuman timetables, with their way, was it malevolent? of frustrating human plans. Inexorable trains, buses, planes.

'Of course. We've got over an hour for lunch, too.'

'Let's get my luggage checked and all, first. I have a vision of us just finishing dessert, and the bus sliding out to the airport, without me. The way it does in nightmares.'

'Don't worry.'

Jess sat back, with a sigh. He would manage this. Let him. How pleasant it was, knowing they would never see each other again: and there was this hour, perhaps two, for ceremony and kindness, as there never had been time while she still depended on him, and he, in a fashion, on her, during their trip. She had not known, at the very beginning, whether she could love him again: if he had changed. And he, long after she had stopped dreaming, had still hoped. Feeling this, she had turned wry, even cruel, to cut him down. Now he knew, and they both were free.

---

* Typescript page 43 ends here.

The air terminal at the hotel expected her. She was on the list. Again, she had that split second of fear: of the one omission, the one mistake: the desk clerk looking through his lists once, twice, and then, with a blank shrug: 'I'm sorry, but we don't seem to have you down here: not a spare place.'

They left her suitcase, and went out again into the clear, brilliant morning. 'The Blue Grotto,' Jess pointed at a blue, cave-like entrance directly across the street. 'Do let's eat there. We never did rent a car and drive to Capri.' There was so much, so much, and she flying away within the hour.

The interior of the Blue Grotto disappointed them: somehow, in spite of the elaborate display of fruit and seafood in baskets, the tidy square tables and plaster yellow walls reminding Jess of the colour of Newnham custard, looked very dull and rather British.

Fish soup, noodles, veal and wine sauce, ice cream and a big bottle of wine: they ordered everything, and ate as if it were their last meal on earth.

'Ah,' Winthrop sighed, pushing his chair back from the table, 'I don't think I can move.'

Jess glanced at him, thinking, in spite of herself, how he would grow stocky around the waist, tall as he was: stocky and plodding. More plodding, in spite of the skiing, the tennis, the swimming. Ah, she brightened, she was saving herself. For what she didn't know, but from this security she was turning now for ever: this attractive, smothering chance at security. The money he had coming, the careful conservative plans to travel, perhaps, to Europe every seven years, the ten-year plan to work at one little college, one little place, and work up and up to a position of authority. Buttressed always by a small, tidy private income. Pouf! She blew the crumbs of bread off the tablecloth in a little prickling white cloud, and sat back, laughing, in a kind of relief, like a naughty child.

'You'll be making games up till you're fifty,' Winthrop said, half scornful, half wistful. 'Driving the car on the wrong side of the street so you can splash through the biggest puddles.'[*]

'There's your plane,' Winthrop said, as she came back to him, her face lit, already, with her vision of London and Gerald. Tonight, inevitably, she would walk into the apartment on Rugby Street, inevitably, as the clock ticked.

People were crowding to the glass doorway, barred by a rope. The whole side of the airport was glassed, giving out onto the flat runways and the great turning steel-hatched silver planes, shiny and small as toys in the distance.

---

[*] Typescript page 62 ends here.

'Oh, I must get a window seat!'

Jess shouldered into the crowd, and then the hostess put the rope down, and they were all walking, trotting, rather, each one trying, politely but firmly, to get to the plane first. Waving to Winthrop, Jess raced forward, clutching her pocketbook, her overnight case. The sun shone on everything, shrinking the planes, the coloured flags and uniforms of the officers, to tight, bright Technicolor moving pictures. The vivid air of unreality about it all: the sky blue, the wind light, whipping the windsock full of air.

Jess climbed up the gangway stairs: third. 'Which is the best seat for a view?' she whispered to the pretty stewardess.

The stewardess smiled. 'Oh, anywhere there,' she pointed toward the front of the cabin, 'so long as it's not over the wing.'

Jess walked down the aisle, slowly, trying not to get dizzy, but to choose her seat, firmly and rightly, so she wouldn't spend the rest of the trip wishing she could change. How did she know which side the big mountains would show on? The people, in a long line down the aisle now, pushed her to choice. With a sigh, she took a window toward the front, where she could see over the wing, and began settling into the comfortable chair. A secret excitement flared in her veins, the way it always did when she was travelling from one place to another, without a companion: on the plane, she might be anybody. It was a little like drowning, or the way they claimed it was to drown: you left the husk of one self with the people you left: each person: David, Vida, Ben, Winthrop, even the gigolo, the taxi driver and the Vatican watchman: all would have different husks of her, left in their heads, like the laid out mummies at the museum: a presence, dead to the moment, but yet participating, now and then, in a terrible, living way in their days and nights. All her husks: and she, she cherished the frail shell of her father, her living brother: the men she had once loved, and left. She remembered them, with various gratitude and tenderness: at the pitch of her love for them. While they, was it weaker? denied whatever love there had been because it didn't last: you never really loved us, they said. No use, her swearing that she did. Why, she thought, they're worse than I ever was: trying to pickle the moment in brine, like an egg in water glass. Only I wasn't going to be an egg in water glass for them: to keep tidy and safe in a barrel. The image stopped her, and she played around with it, illogically: she was a golden goose, or the quick of her was, laying eggs day after day: eggs of her selves. Which broke, opened, letting out parti-coloured chickens on the world. Everybody wanted a different colour chicken, to keep with an Easter ribbon around its neck. Nobody wanted the whole goose, with its disturbing potential for laying innumerable and startlingly different eggs. Enough.

A woman, elegant, in perfumed furs, was sitting down beside her. Jess, full of her thoughts, her broth of excitement, could not look at the woman, or be social, pleasant. She stared out the window. A sudden shudder began, vibrating through her armchair, and her fibres. Were they going? Somebody must be winding up the propellers, or whatever they did.

The airport looked small and glittering and very modern. With its triangular coloured flags blowing, and its glass and chrome fittings. Somebody was waving: Winthrop, up on the observation platform. He seemed too big for the airport, too tall to fit inside. He was shading his eyes from the sun, camera strung around his neck, green tie whipping out horizontal in the wind. Full of brimming tenderness, Jess waved. This is what it was: her life: waving, waving goodbye to the selves she was and the people those selves knew, and loved. Her love of Winthrop, which once had bulked monumental in her days (how she had waited for his casual telephone calls, his letters, thick with puns, and puns she first thought were puns, but afterwards, discovered were simply misspellings). She brimmed with tears, a surge of sentiment, clear, poignant, for the passing away of these people, these places: would it always be so? Would there be no one to keep time with her: keep pace? Always the unevenness of growing up (and she never wanted to stop growing up: there was no *summum bonum* for her, where she could sit, complete and philosophically smug, and contemplate her own perfection: the process was everything: the going and the coming).

Winthrop, with his blowing tie, his hand lifted in a kind of salute, was sliding backward, faster and faster, out of her window frame, the glittering airport under him as he stood out there on the observation roof. She waved and waved, leaning to the windowpane, to see him as long as she might. And then they were rolling down the runway.

A labyrinth of white-painted lines, lights, red signs. The plane rolled, turning, and paused, shuddering gently like some whirring dragonfly. The drumming motors turned faster, faster, growing shrill, to a pitch. Such a pitch. Jess held her ears, feeling the shudder through her whole body. If it could always be like this: wound up to the pitch, shuddering with that intense sound: geared up: what was the word?

And then: release. They were running now, free, down the runway, and, without feeling any change, she saw the shadow of the plane drop to the left, behind, and come away clear, a small dark patch, following their flight into the air as they left the earth, a spot moving on the ground to link them to the world. The plane climbed, and she tried to see Rome, the Tiber, to recognise the Spanish Steps. But they were flying, engines drumming steadily now, over a strange country. A country she had never seen before: its streets little lines with black specks moving on them, its buildings and palaces flat two-dimensional outlines. How lovely the waters were: she could see the deepening blues and greens in little ponds, or were they lakes, the way the sea levels were painted on maps: going from light to dark and darker blue.

The stewardess touched her shoulder. 'Lunch?'

Had she been dreaming? Yes. And she was still hungry. Eager to eat lunch in the air. Perhaps she would store some of it in her pockets, to bring to Gerald: a potlatch offering.*

The clouds continued, thick, grey. Over the Channel (they announced it) the rain began, streaming in thin ripply washes back down the windowpane. The plane dipped, began to descend; the world tilted, righted itself. Tilted again.

And the world came up at them: grey, swimming wet, with drab streets and houses brown and black: muck and water.

With bent head, Jess ran from the plane to the airport shelter, mud splashing her calves. The soles of her ballerinas felt uncomfortably soft and clammy: she prayed to keep them whole, at least for one more day. Dully, as if come back from another life, another planet, she followed the right lines through the right gates.

'American? Student? On one of those grants.' The garrulous man at his little desk stamped her passport. 'Better get this renewed over the summer if you're staying.'

The bus to London waited at the kerb. Jess felt the trip in the plane, knitting her to the others, fade away. Strangers were boarding the bus. She climbed aboard, and took a seat next to the window near the back, staring out at the rivulets of muddy water running in the gutter, and the slick blackened stone fronts of the ugly row of semi-detached houses. This is what she had run from: rain, pallid skies, cold, and the colourless ugliness of dirty brick and stone, black cars all like a procession of funeral hearses, and the frigid silence of people, stiffly islanded in themselves on buses, underground, and trains. And now, herself, packed full of sun, colour and flowers, wine, all that she meant when she stretched her arm, gesturing widely: 'You *know*.' And she sat, warm in herself, somehow put back together by this return, like Humpty Dumpty:

---

* Typescript page 65 ends here.

all the king's men didn't do it: but some strange principle of growth, knitting the cracked pieces. A united front: she would meet Ian with that. And giggled.

An attractive, thin, blonde young man was boarding the bus, with a suitcase and peculiar long tin cylinder. He looked quite charming, in a forest-green hat: older, sun-bitten. Eyes lowered, but very much aware of him, Jess willed him to sit beside her. Why had she not noticed him on the plane? Balancing his suitcase and that shiny metal cylinder, he pushed down the aisle, not looking at her. He stowed his luggage on the rack over her head. And came to sit down beside her. Still not looking.

Jess kept her face turned to the window. It was very warm on the bus, but comfortably. Outside, the rain began to flash and quiver with light: twilight, and the street lamps and neons were coming on. Shimmers of red, green, yellow, all winking. Like coloured dragon eyes. That black city coiled on itself, winking and flashing its great eyes. She would reach out, out, and hug it. It was hers. She owned it now.

'Mind if I smoke?'

A lean face, with tawn green eyes. Mischievous.

'Of course not.' Jess gathered herself in a smile. She felt radiant, unbelievably confident. Ian, and Rugby Street suspended in her head: a grail. The only one. 'I like the smell of cigarette smoke.'

'You're American?' He had a good grin.

'Yes.' They can always tell. 'But you . . . not British. Not . . . Australian?'

'South African.'

'They always fool me.' Had he chosen to sit down beside her? There were a lot of other empty seats. But there was an aloofness about him: a reserve.

'Do you work in London?' he asked, blowing, neatly, a blue smoke ring which quavered on the air, dissolving.

So that was it. 'No. I'm at Cambridge.' She waited.

His face lit: 'Really? I graduated from there: three years ago. Jesus.'

'Jesus!' Jess laughed. 'I can't help thinking it's so queer if you stop to think of it: the Varsity headlines: King's beats Jesus. Are you back for a visit?'

'Just flew up from Durban. On business.'

The bus driver climbed up into his seat. The doors wheezed shut. Jess glowed; if she touched the chair in front of her, it would send out a light like radium in the dark. How miraculously easy it was to be happy with a strange, attractive man when she knew he didn't mean anything and would never have to mean anything to her. When Ian waited. She wanted to go to Ian right away, but now she still had two hours before she'd said she would arrive. And she needed badly to freshen up. Now he thinks I'm intelligent, or wealthy. Or both.

'It's good to be back in London,' Jess observed, as the bus swerved out on a black drive along the Thames. 'Good grey wet London. Bonging deep and eternal, like Big Ben.'

'I'm awfully happy they sent me up here. Cambridge: you're lucky to be there still. There's never another time in life like University. It's true, what they say. You're never really carefree again. What times we had!'

Tough, Jess thought. One of the sporting ones: who never actually grows up afterwards. Who gets his kicks with the old school-tie boys drinking and remembering how it was. But what did that mean to her? She wasn't, after all, going to marry him. She giggled.

His eyebrows quirked up. 'Happy. You fairly light up the bus.'

'I can't help it. I'm glad to be home, and I never thought I would be. I just wanted sun, and colour. And I've had it. Now it's lovely to have everything grey and wet. A million shades of grey.'

'But red lights too.'

'And green.'

Neons reflected in the Thames.

'Listen,' he said, and she knew what was coming. 'I'm just having dinner alone by myself tonight. Will you come?' Simple as that. 'I'm staying at the South Africa Sports Club . . .'

She didn't register. Evidently that was supposed to impress. 'I don't know any of these London establishments,' she apologised.

'Oh, it's a posh place. Students get cut rates . . . the only reason I'm there. It used to be just for men, but now there's a ladies' room. By another entrance though. You could wash up and all, and we'd go off. I know a super restaurant. Where you can get rare steak.'

'Rare!' Jess laughed. 'You must know how I've missed it. Except in Europe, of course, where I have it ground raw, just to make up for Newnham leather.'

'Then you'll come?'

'Ye-es. But I have to . . . meet a friend in a couple of hours. I'd love to come, but you won't mind if I have to rush off the minute we've had dessert?'

'Not a bit.' He was, really, quite fine.

They taxied along the Thames. Black velvet. The honeycomb lights of the Royal Festival Hall. And the blatant red sign blinking 'OXO' over the water. What was it Gary had said, with his droll wistfulness: somehow, I feel they should remove that Oxo sign: it rather ruins my vision of the Thames.

The taxi pulled up in front of one of those large, imposing buildings of dirty stone which contained, as Jess came to realise, elegance, wealth, and people bizarre and stiff as caricatures of themselves: ugly women with huge jewel-encrusted bosoms and red-faced men with waxed sand-coloured moustaches.

'Oh,' Jess exclaimed, as the South African helped her out, 'your name! In case they accost me, demanding my entrance card.'

'Michael. Michael Butcher. And you?'

'Jess Greenwood.'

'Delighted.' Michael bowed mock-heroically over her hand. His humour caught her. If that was all there was, fine. It was all she needed right now.

The ladies' room was elegant. Someone had, it seemed, noticed the mud on her calves, and left a neat scrubbing brush on each of the glittering white tile bowls. Mirrors everywhere, at all angles. Jess could see herself back view, side view, from the knees down.

'Pretty shabby,' she said out loud. No one else seemed to be in the room. Humming to herself, she ran a bowlful of steaming water, and, ready to jump to attention the moment the door began to open, she took off her sodden red ballerinas and, standing on one leg, put her right foot into the bowl and began to scrub it down. The water felt deliciously hot. She scrubbed the other foot. The water had suddenly become black. The ballet shoes, with their cardboard linings wet, sticking to her foot sole, looked uninviting. Inspired, she tore off a piece of brown paper from the hand-towel machine and ripped it to fit her shoes: one for each. Pro tem soles. Then she ran another bowl of water, and scrubbed her face. Gradually, warmth stole over her. How heavenly it was to begin to be clean. She hadn't had a bath since Germany. She put her pageboy up, rolling it in three handkerchiefs, so the steam wouldn't straighten it. Then, after she finished washing, she let down her hair and combed it into an even, shoulder-length pageboy, and stuck a gold metal hairband on it to hold it back. Her multi-faceted reflection grinned back at her, slightly gilded with tan from that day in the Roman Forum. Narcissus, she accused. But it was another girl in the mirror: how gay she looked. And what for? Because a strange man made her beautiful. Because she had left the nadir, and after having nothing, could have nothing less than something when she took her steps away from the black, vacant centre. No, that wasn't right. You could walk for ever away from the hole in your head, and meet your reflection, with the ghostly damned expression, in every glass of brandy, store window and chrome railing. This was different. She was going to live inwardly now. She sat down in a chair, and took out her diary, scribbling rules to herself: rules for her being with Ian. Very stern. Directives. And, she knew, remembering the way she had written rules to help her out of that last pit, three years back, they did it. Beginning in a new direction was hell: you felt so gauche, a baby, compared to the extreme you'd got to in the old ways.

'Programme,' she wrote across the head of her ruled notebook page. 'How to win friends and influence people.' Oh, tongue in cheek.

'One: Don't Drink Too Much: remember misfortunes with Iko after St John's party, with Hamish on two dates, St Botolph's party and that last London night. Stay sober.

'Two: Be Chaste: don't throw self at people (e.g. David, Mallory, Hamish, Gavin, and Tony). In spite of rumour and the fat boy, let no one verify this term the flaws of last.

'Three: Be Friendly And More Subdued: if necessary, try smog of "mystery woman": quiet, nice, slightly bewildered at coloured scandals. Refuse ease of Sally Bowles act.

'Four: Don't blab too much: listen more: sympathise and "understand" people.

'Five: Keep Troubles To Self.

'Six: Work On Inner Life: to enrich. Concentrate on work for philosophy. Do French daily. Writing: Poems & more poems.

'Seven: Don't Criticise Anybody To Anybody: misquoting at Cambridge is like a telephone game: the more slurs the better. Bear mean gossip and snubbing and pass beyond it. Be nice and positive to all.

'Eight: Don't date either Gary Or Hamish: be nice but not too enthusiastic to Keith, et al.

'Nine: WRITE.

'Ten.' She pondered. She needed a tenth point. 'Ten: BE STOIC.'

And, she packed the notebook away, that was that. Self-contained, shining, she pushed open the swinging door. Michael stood, urbane, chivalric, in the lobby.

'You look quite magnificent,' he remarked as he helped her into her raincoat as if it were mink. And that was the way she wore it. Defiant: the emperor's new clothes: you think it's a filthy dirty mackintosh? Mud in your eye.

They got out of the taxi near the Marble Arch, and crossed the street.

'It's some little alley down here. I only hope I remember.'

'Oh!' Jess gave a slight skip. They were passing a lighted hotel lobby, and a flower-stand was in the far corner of the room, spilling over with long-stemmed roses, carnations, gardenias. 'I must get a flower! A red rose!'

'Perfect!' Before she could explain, Michael had ushered her into the shop. 'Pick your rose!'

He and the shop lady smiled, while she carefully surveyed the face of every red rose in the tall vase. 'This one!' It was not quite fully open, just unfolding from the exquisite conical bud, in a roundabout of flared red petals.

'It's yours.'

Jess held the rose carefully, in the middle of the long stem, as Michael deftly steered her by her elbow down a crooked street. It had stopped raining. They opened the door of a pub, and Michael stood in the entrance a minute, glancing about him. The barmaid and two customers turned to stare at them.

'Do they still serve meals upstairs?' Michael asked the girl.

'Naw. New management now, sir. Pub only.'

'Well, we'll have a drink. I know. We'll go to this other place. Right nearby. But a drink first.'

'I think I'd like a brandy. No, cider. Half.'

'To you.' He lifted his Guinness.

'And you.' The cider tasted sharp and cool. 'I hate to hurry, but if we're going to eat . . .'

Jess cut into her steak and watched the red juice run out and mix itself with the mushrooms. A bottle of red wine. Michael asked for the date: and so what? Simply, she didn't know or give a damn about dates, kerosene would taste the same to her as vintage champagne. Yet the waiter knew and Michael knew, and she was cared for.

Both of them laughed a good deal, over the meal, talking about Cambridge, and toasting each other with the wine. Somewhere, back in herself, Jess heard a small chuckle: here you sit, not six hours out of Rome, with a completely strange and charming man whom you didn't know existed before today: who serves for a wash, a rose, a dinner with wine. And is perfectly happy to do just that, with no strings attached.

Somewhere, a clock struck. Jess froze, her glass to her lips, listening.

'My God! It can't be nine! I'm already an hour late!'

'You *must* go?'

'Yes. I must get a taxi this minute.'

'Can't I take you wherever it is?'

'No!' If he saw that slum street, with the condemned houses. 'I have to go myself.'

Michael shrugged handsomely. 'Ah, all right then. I'll go flag a taxi for you.'

The blood began to beat in her ears again, and that high, singing sound rang in her temples. What was it? This ungodly tension. She felt she could stride in seven-league steps over the city to Ian. Would he wait? Her heart caught. She was so late, he might think she decided not to come. Sickened, she stood up. The waiter brought her coat. She counted: rose, pocketbook, suitcase.

Michael came back. 'Taxi's at the door. I nipped one just going by.'

This was the way it worked: smooth, oiled: everything righter than could be hoped. Everything fusing together. No more lying in lonely bedrooms with no phone calls, no men, no money, and waiting for the first beck in her direction to take her out of the tailspin. She climbed into the cab, giving her hand to Michael through the window.

'It's been lovely . . .'

'Hey! Your address. If I come up to Cambridge . . .'

'Write me: Newnham. I'll get it.'

'Righto. Good luck!'

'And you!' The taxi pulled out into the street, and she left him, waving at the kerb. Cinderella Greenwood: well, that was dinner. 'Rugby Street,' she told the driver. 'You know where that is?'

'Lamb's Conduit way?'

'Yes.' She could hardly breathe. This was it: if life could be like this, and not fray out into daily routines, the daily coffee (bitter), the daily egg (hard-boiled), the daily smiles (tepid). Blazing, with fever, Jess leaned her head out the open window, letting the wet wind blow her hair back. She would look wild, but what did she care. The recklessness came banging up in her: stronger and fiercer than she had ever known it.

The driver seemed to be going at ten miles an hour.

'Can't you hurry?' Jess begged. 'I'm really in a desperate hurry.' She lay back in the seat, half-fainting, feeling the car move under her. Every time it stopped for a light, she heard her blood banging, banging out the seconds. The street existed. He existed. And she had spoken the address out. She could leave the rest to the driver.

The taxi passed the sign 'Lamb's Conduit Street.' Jess sat up. 'There. No, there!' The driver turned. She paid him, fumbled for a shilling change, and he put out her suitcase on the pavement, and drove off. Dead quiet. Not a soul.

Jess rang the bell: once, twice, three rings. The door seemed to sway, and the house, and the street lamps quivered. She gripped the railing hard, hearing, in a dizzy spin, the sound of someone running downstairs: one flight, two flights, three. What if he wasn't in: had moved in with some other girl? The door opened.

'Hello,' she said shakily.

'Hello.' Ian hulked there, in his black sweater, with the collar up, unshaven.

He stepped back to let her in. 'Well. How was it?' And his voice. Un-British. Refugee Pole rather, mixed with something of Dylan Thomas: rich and mellow-noted: half sung.

'It's Friday the Thirteenth.' She let him pick up her suitcase, and started ahead of him up the rickety stair. Dirty milk bottles crowded the windowsill on the first landing, and the bowl which supplied cold water for the whole apartment was clogged with potato peelings and carrot stubs. She climbed past the first flat, and paused at the second. 'Here?'

'I'll just put your case in. I've been up at Jim's. Come on up.'

She waited. Hating Jim, whoever he was. She just wanted Ian: very simply. She could swim in him: that incredible violent presence of his: leashed. Too much man for this island. The only man on it. He didn't think: he was.

Ian put his hand on her arm, steering her up the stairs, and his fingers burned through her raincoat and sweater: nothing warm, or gentle and conscious. Just firm, hard, and searing. Without pretence, or kindness.

Dazzled, her vision blurred, she walked into Jim's room. 'Oh! It's magnificent. Did you do it?'

The room was painted like the sides of an ABC block: gaudy and startling. One wall pale lavender, one dark purple, one crimson and one pink. A large oil painting of orange twisted girders on a stormy ocean beach dominated the whole room.

Jim grinned, and came to shake her hand. 'Yes.'

'Jim's a commercial artist,' Ian said, sitting her down on the couch, his hands on her shoulders. 'I'm not having you perching on the edge of things again. This girl, she can't sit. Just sit.'

Jess flushed with happiness: he remembered. And he called her Jess, not Judy. She would make her name for him. But downstairs. She wanted to be downstairs with him.

'Wine?' Jim poured her a tumblerful. 'Hope it doesn't taste like toothpaste. But we broke all the glasses last night.'

'That painting,' Jess said, squinting at it, and knowing that if she gulped down the wine the way she was gulping it the girders would reach out and strangle her. 'It's demonic.'[*]

From where that fruitfulness? She felt full, brimming with a clear syrup of peace. If they knew, those others. But they didn't know: they toyed with their

---

[*] Typescript page 73 ends here.

heads. When it came to acting, to taking, and giving her her full self, they failed, grossly.

'I know.' His eyes were grave, reflecting, solemn, that other world from which he had come. 'I was having this beautiful dream.'

'Tell me.'

'A white leopard was standing over this blue stream, its hind legs on one bank, and its forelegs on the other. And a little train of bright red ants was crossing the stream over the leopard, up its tail and along its back and down its nose. To the other side . . .'

'How lovely!' Jess cried in envy.

'Oh, there was lots more. But I forget.'

'But do you always dream like that? What else do you dream?'

'About foxes. And pike. So many different things. They occur, and recur,' he paused, and she waited, hung there, for him to continue. 'There was this fox. I was sitting in a kitchen, with my father and two older brothers . . .'

'Do you really have two?'

'No. Just one. And this fox, all badly burned, its fur scorched black, came running through the kitchen. I got up and went after it. And it led me through a green wood.'

'Oh,' Jess sighed. So that was where he was. 'I dream such black dreams now. Nightmares, all dark and sultry with the air yellow as sulphur. I used to dream the loveliest things when I was little. Complete stories. I learned this trick where I used to think about what I wanted to dream of about half an hour before I went to sleep, and then go on thinking of other things. To cover it up. And I dreamed exactly what I wanted.'

Ian smiled into her shoulder. He kissed her, thoughtfully, on the throat. 'You have the most incredible skin. That's what I remembered, more than anything. All smooth and silvery, like a fish.'

'A fish!'

'A mermaid, then. It's what I meant. If you hadn't come back, I would have come to Cambridge to find you again. To make up for that last time . . .'

Jess shivered, holding herself up against him, their toes touching. 'Oh,' she laughed ruefully. 'It was terrible, that. I went to Paris all scarred. Black and blue . . .'

'But you liked it?'

'Yes.'

'I was furious with myself. I don't know what happened to me . . .'

'It wasn't right, somehow, then. I felt it. You didn't even know my name, really.' She couldn't help coming back to that, finishing it off.

'I do now, though.' He paused. 'That morning. I'll never forget it. When I came out into the streets, the air was all blue, like blue water, and the buildings were covered, just thick, with thrushes. Everything clear and blue. Not a sound. The air isn't like that in London at any other time.'

'Thrushes. I don't even know what they look like. How do you know all about birds, and animals and fishes?'*

'But . . . I can't,' she said, nonplussed, her head all at once empty as a wind tunnel. 'What shall I say?'

'Say one of your own poems.'

She thought. A bad sonnet leapt into her head. It was to him, and he would know it. But she felt shameless. 'It's called "Conversation Among the Ruins",' she told the machine. 'After the De Chirico postcard on my door.'

And she said it through, slowly, emphatically, letting her voice go with the knot and pause and tilt of the words.

'What ceremony of words can patch the havoc?' she finished.

Ian was laughing. 'Fine,' he switched the machine off.

'I forgot to announce the dedication,' Jess said dryly, with humour, 'but it's obvious.'

'You love one-syllabled words, don't you? Squab, patch, crack. Violent.'

'Yes. I guess I do. I hate 'ation' words. They're so abstract. I like words to sound what they say: bang crash. Not mince along in sing-song iambic pentameters. But . . .' she pulled herself up. 'Now you read.'

'All right. But first something not mine. Mad Tom's.'

'Whose?'

'You know: From the hag and hungry goblin?'

'No-o.'

'And you take English! And write poems!'

'I've never read anything, though. Nothing but what I've liked: Chaucer, Shakespeare, Hopkins, Yeats, Joyce, Thomas. That's about it. It's ridiculous, but they never made me read anything but what I thought I wanted to. And so I never had a proper education. I just read the people whose poems I wanted to imitate.'

---

* Typescript page 76 ends here.

'Probably just as well,' he thumbed through a sheaf of papers and pulled out one. Switching the machine on, he began:

'From the hag and hungry goblin
That into rags would rend ye,
The spirit that stands by the naked man
In the Book of Moons defend ye, . . .'

Jess sat still. The mice in the walls listened, and the London pigeons stopped coo-rooing, stock-still on their pink feet. The way he took words, rounded, pitched them. It was holy. I will learn this by heart, she told herself, sunk deep in a quiet, part of her vibrating to the sound of his voice. I will learn it, and hear his voice every time, reading it.

And she really thought she would. That she would never be able, in the blurring days after he left her, to forget the sound of his voice, and every syllable. She watched the flesh of her bare arms go stippled with gooseflesh . . .

'With a burning spear and a horse of air,
To the wilderness I wander . . .'

If there were one poem, to say always, that would be it.
'God,' she said simply, when he was done. 'I want that. Copy it out for me.'
'You like it?' he seemed to test her. Finding her with him. And she sensed this.
'What is it, but this building of words. Breaking them up, and putting them back together. Something the king's men can't do. But this poem: it's an altar to spill blood at.'

Hill of Leopards

Ts fragment,[*] *c.*25 February 1957, Emory University

The dial of her small travel clock, with its pale gilt and luminous hands, said three minutes to ten. It wasn't fair.
'You'll have to go,' she told Ian. 'Curfew for men's at ten, you know.'

---

[*] Typescript page 87 with holograph corrections by SP. 'Hill of Leopards' appears to continue 'Venus in the Seventh'. See *The Letters of Sylvia Plath, Volume 2*: 129.

He looked up at her, as if for the first time realising her presence: 'Come out with me. You can be out till midnight.'

She hung, for a moment, tempted to prolong it: their being together. After all, how did she know how long it would be? But she disciplined herself: feeling, almost intuitively, that she should not be so weak, clinging as long as he would let her cling.

'No,' she said firmly. 'I'm terribly tired and I must get my things put away and go to bed. Tomorrow?'

'Yes. After breakfast. I'll come over.'

'But,' she wondered at his ease. 'Where will you stay? Where will you eat breakfast?' She felt sick at being away from him. As if that Judy, with her pale, freckled face waited somewhere in Cambridge, with a daffodil-yellow wallpapered bedroom and a frying pan full of eggs and bacon for him. What was trust?

'With Luke. He's got a room near the fish and chip shop. Valerie's up from London, staying with him.'

'Is she his mistress, then?'

'Well, yes. Off and on. Luke liked her at first, but now she can't bear to be without him, and he's bored. He's after this ballet dancer who gives classes in Cambridge, and can't think how to get rid of Valerie without hurting her. They've asked us to lunch, whenever we want to come.'

Jess drew a quick breath. She felt explosive. And very much on the side of Valerie, even though she probably was now in a position parallel to that of the more fortunate ballet dancer. So that was part of it: never let him know she couldn't bear to be away from him. The courage of it astounded her: she had always spilled over, completely, frankly, to all her men. But, it was true, they came around very easily and quickly to being devoted to her, and there was no question of devotion from Ian. I am his mistress, she thought. And damn proud of it. And will be, until he takes another. But then. Then. Her mind blacked itself. She could not go on. She knew that now: there would be no other. And she was not exactly the type to become a frigid old-maid schoolteacher, although that was what her exacting conscience would impose: no, her blood would beat through and betray her in the hollowest, most desperate promiscuities.

'I'll go downstairs with you,' Jess said, handing him his black jacket. And then: 'My god! What have you in the pockets?' She could hardly lift the jacket, it was so heavy, and the pockets bulged bulkily.

Ian grinned. 'My horoscope books. I brought them. What's your birthday?'

She told him. 'You know, it's strange. But without knowing it, I always asked people their birthdates, almost before asking their names. And I've never given a thought to horoscopes.'

'You're Scorpio,' Ian told her. 'I'm Leo. Two very violent signs. I've never known a Scorpio who hasn't had something drastic break up their lives, and make its scar somewhere.'

'My cheek,' Jess pointed to her brown scar. 'That's it. But can you really tell people's characters? It's so deterministic.'

'Not really. You just know what you have to work with. I've cast about two thousand, and it's amazing how you get to recognise the types: just by looking at people in the street, I can tell birth months.'

Operation Valentine

Ts fragment,* July–August 1957, Emory University

to be around you. Which means around me, too. Which brings them into Mother's range. And in Mother's opinion, as you should know by now, every day is Valentine's Day."

"Valentine, schmalentine," I blithered. To cover my double-take. "*I* don't have anything to do with choosing your boyfriends, do I? They're just . . . well, they're just *there*. Which I can't exactly help . . ."

"You *can* help it, though." Mrs. Thornton-Smythe wasn't the only lady of the house with a one-track mind.

"Help what?"

"Who's *there*."

"Oh?" One five-star general in the family was enough, I told myself grimly. More than enough. "And just how . . ."

"Ask Gary Craig to come. You can do that. He likes you."

Through Sassy's matter-of-fact words I detected a slight, deep-down quiver. Gary was the exceedingly lean, exceedingly red-headed young tennis instructor at the Ocean Spray Inn, working his way through the first year of the pre-med

---

* Typescript pages 7, 8, 10, 12 and 13; with typed and holograph corrections by SP. Ted Hughes, *Bardo Thodol* on verso. See SP's journals for 18 July to 9 August 1957. SP mailed 'Operation Valentine' and 'The Laundromat Affair' to *Ladies' Home Journal* on 5 August 1957. SP later submitted 'Operation Valentine', 'The Christmas Heart' and 'The Launderette <Laundromat> Affair' to *Woman's Own* on 24 October 1960.

course at State U. But, future or no future, his name did not, at present, adorn Mrs. Thornton-Smythe's private social register.

"You," I queried dubiously, "happen to know the guy?"

"He's only," Sassy didn't falter, "coached me for a couple of tennis lessons." But her eyes gave her away: they went softer than skies in April. An unmistakable symptom—and, in Sassy's case, unprecedented as the 'Frisco quake.

But why, I groaned inwardly, couldn't Sassy's first, fine careless rapture light on some guy in Mrs. Thornton-Smythe's camp? I hung fire, torn between duty and a disastrous sentiment I could only describe as sympathy. Complete sympathy. Something very new and vulnerable in Sassy's expression made me stick my neck out.

"Okay," I said, seeing more complications ahead than tentacles on an octopus, "okay, I'll go ask him." I reaped a harvest in Sassy's grateful look.

Mrs. Thornton-Smythe had, after all, left the details up to me.

I located Gary Craig smashing tennis balls against the backboard in the empty courts, practicing his cuts. He didn't notice me till I'd come up as close to his elbow as I felt consistent with both safety and secrecy.

"Well," his grin flashed whiter than his T-shirt. "The lovely lady-in-waiting. What can I do for you?"

"Busy?"

"No customers for an hour." He leaned engagingly on his tennis racket. "And you?"

"Very busy." I didn't mince matters. "You know Sassy Thornton-Smythe?"

"Sassy? The kid with the yellow hair and the mean backhand? Sure I know her. She giving you any trouble?"

Kid, I thought, my heart sinking. But I hadn't studied political intrigue at State U. for nothing. "Trouble?" I took a deep breath and plunged. "Plenty!" Policy. I figured at this[*]

bright blue bay for an answer. "Why," Sassy didn't let me down, "there she is! Just coming up from a swim."

Mrs. Thornton-Smythe's gaze swerved in time to see her daughter emerging from the sea. With a young man *not* on her guest list.

"And exactly who," she breathed, "is *that*?"

"That," I said, summoning the sangfroid of a desperado, "is . . ."

"Mother," Sassy took the job off my hands, "I'd like you to meet Gary Craig."

---

[*] Typescript page 8 ends here.

Mrs. Thornton-Smythe paused, waiting, obviously, for some sort of clue before clinching her judgment. Sassy gave into her, free for nothing.

"Gary's the tennis instructor at the club, Mother."

"Well! How nice, dear." The tone dripped polite but frosty dismissal. "Is he the swimming instructor, too?"

"No, Mrs. Thornton-Smythe," Gary said, with a pleasant smile. "But your daughter's a fine swimmer. I can tell that without being a professional. If you'll excuse me now, I have a lesson coming up . . ." A quick, deft nod, and he was striding off with all the natural grace of the young Hercules.

That was a week ago. Practically historic. Since then, I have been, to use the appropriate idiom of combat, caught in the crossfire. Between Mrs. Thornton-Smythe's discovery that I had invited Gary Craig to the barbecue and Sassy's swearing me to[*]

snapping shut. With me inside it. I could always try open rebellion, or, more discreetly, incur an immediate case of double pneumonia. But at this point, neither method of escape looked particularly inviting.

"Just see," I scolded Sassy in the kitchen that afternoon while scooping out watermelon balls for a fruit cup viciously as if they were human heads, "what you've bamboozled me into! If Bill got one glimpse of me side by side in a sailboat with that raving, red-headed . . ."

"You," Sassy informed me, "won't be side by side with Gary. I will. What's more, you'll knock Rick out cold, if necessary, and tread water behind the boat until . . ."

"Until your mother hires a motor launch and roars out to check up. And fire me and . . ."

Sassy silenced me with a look. "I need just this one more time with Gary," she said. "To prove something. Please, Litsa."

I knew, without any blueprint, what Sassy meant. Gary liked her, all right. But he still thought of her as a kid. A spoiled rich kid. Now Sassy could hardly pretend she wasn't rich, but she could prove she wasn't spoiled. Or, for that matter, a kid. And before coming straight out and opposing her mother's choice in men once and for all, she needed one vital thing to back her up: Gary.

"I promise," I said, "I won't get pneumonia. But there's another little item bothering me."

"Which is?"

---

[*] Typescript page 10 ends here.

"Which is, I happened to suggest to Gary in the course of events that Rick was a wolf your mother didn't approve of. Now when he sees your mother arranging for you to go off for the day in Rick's sailboat . . ."

"He'll either think you're crazy," Sassy said in dulcet tones, "or that Mother's changed her mind. Or even," she finished pointedly, "that you like Rick too much to leave him in my clutches."

"If I didn't have the deepest faith in you, Sassy," I retorted in accents of wounded nobility, "I would at this moment be courting a case of double pneumonia. Instead of allowing my character to be slandered by . . ."

"You," Sassy said firmly, "look fine. Perfectly fine. Just stay that way, will you?"

And so, on this crucial morning, I was fine. For Sassy's sake. After all, in two more days I was packing up for the summer and heading back to State U. and William Quincy Marshall. For that trifling time, at least, I could afford to be a philanthropist.

This I kept telling myself as I stood in the kitchen after breakfast mixing the fruit punch. Mrs. Thornton-Smythe had ordered some cold roast duckling from a special duck farm, and what with pink-and-white frosted cupcakes and a large carton of Waldorf salad, the picnic already resembled a Hollywood outing: very posh, down to the last decorative olive on the deviled eggs.

Hoisting sail from Rick's mooring in Pleasant Bay, we started out, a motley crew: Sassy in a sleek white bathing suit which set off

The Laundromat Affair

Ts,[*] *c.* August 1957, Emory University

Let me tell you, you can't get away from love. I should know. As if it isn't bad enough to have my sister Meg turn all silly and pink-faced whenever she gets a letter from her boyfriend Barry who is now serving his time in the navy, I have to find hearts and flowers dogging my steps day in, day out. At the launderette,

---

[*] Typescript pages 1, 3, 4, 5, 7 and 9; with holograph corrections and additions by SP. Ted Hughes, *Bardo Thodol* on verso. Typed at top right: 'Sylvia Plath / 337 Elm Street / Apt. 3 rear / Northampton, Mass.' Typed pseudonym Sibyl Hughes under title; SP began the story from January to March 1957 and revised it in July and August 1957. SP submitted 'Operation Valentine', 'The Christmas Heart' and 'The Launderette <Laundromat> Affair' to *Woman's Own* on 24 October 1960.

even. One of the few places left in the world where a girl could concentrate, too. Really think about important problems. Such as how to wham a cut over the tennis net at Jimmy Sullivan so he wouldn't know what hit him. Or what's the best way to practice holding your breath so you can stay underwater longer than anybody at the beach, even that so-called underwater champion breather, Jimmy Sullivan. The truth is: I actually started looking forward to Saturday mornings when Mom sends me down to the launderette with a sack of dishtowels, diapers, and pillowcases because it is the one place I know that is really peaceful.

Peaceful! you say. And what's peaceful about a launderette in the middle of Saturday morning rush? Well, if you had a[*]

"Proteus," I continue, since Mrs. Decker is still standing there in front of me, hands on her hips and a peculiar expression on her face, "was an old sea-god. Turned from one shape to another quick as a flash, the minute you laid hands on him . . ."

I would have gone on enlightening Mrs. Decker if the glass door hadn't swung open just then, letting a blast of cold March wind sweep through the launderette. A tall fellow came in.

"Some people!" Mrs. Decker mutters in that menacing tone of voice she has, like Cassandra, or somebody. And she hustles off to tend to this fellow. He is waiting patiently holding a bundle of laundry tied up in a big towel with rumpled shirtsleeves trailing out, gray as mouse tails.

Now the laundromat regulars are mainly women. Housewives with children. Or office girls. I guess I'm the youngest female customer in the place. But as I tell my sister Meg when she gets on her high horse about idiotic younger sisters and so forth, age doesn't necessarily mean wisdom. Anyway, the only man you ever see in the laundromat is now and then somebody's henpecked husband. Well, this fellow is different. Very different.

In the first place, he is young-looking. With a really nice face. Not the sort of face my sister Meg would look at twice—she likes the slick movie-hero type, all wavy hair and classic profile. This fellow has character. I can tell character a mile off. He also has kind of a stubborn expression, as if it would take a powerful strong argument to convince him of anything he didn't want to be convinced of. His hair's a queer sandy yellow color, like mustard, and he's wearing an old brown tweed jacket with leather patches at the elbows.

---

[*] Typescript page 1 ends here.

While Mrs. Decker leads him up to machine number six, right next to mine, he is looking around the place with eyes you would call preoccupied. Although Mrs. Decker is holding forth in a gentle tone about how the machine works, he doesn't even seem to be listening, but just nods vaguely now and then. I pretend I'm deep in my book, but all the time I keep a steady eye on him over my glasses.

Mrs. Decker flounces off then to help wheezy red-faced Mrs. Christie fold up her sheets, and I eventually turn my attention to the window of machine number seven. It's like looking through the porthole of a ship, with the water sloshing the clothes around inside. Every color of the rainbow—pink dots, yellow checks, green stripes. Better than watching TV—you can make up your own pictures.

I am staring hard at a white flag of truce waving over a battlefield when suddenly it comes to me that it isn't a white flag of truce at all, but Meg's second best nylon slip, and this fellow is still standing at the next machine making no progress whatsoever getting his laundry going. The shirts and socks are stuffed in all right, and the door shut, only he is turning the handle in the wrong direction. Mrs. Decker is busy with her back to us, filling up more little blue and white cups with soap powder at the desk. So it's plain to see nobody is going to inform this poor fellow about how the handle works.

At least that's what I think at first. But I am so absorbed, hypnotized, you might say, watching him turn and turn the handle, that I don't see the girl coming up until she is right at the machine.

"Look," she says sweetly, "you are getting nowhere. This is how you do it."

And the girl not only starts the drum whirring, but waits a couple of minutes until the first red light flashes on and pours soap from the white celluloid cup in through the vent.

"Now," the girl says, in a soft, husky voice, "you just wait a while and when the red light flashes on again, you put in the other cup of soap." She is the very competent type.

"Thank you," the fellow says, rather standoffish. "I think I can manage quite well now. By myself."

The girl just smiles and shrugs her shoulders and goes back to her seat a couple of chairs down from me, next to the door, where she picks up a sock she is knitting. I practically drop my book then and there.

And what is so unusual about this little exchange of conversation, you ask me. Well, how often do you see a fellow with character enough to give a mere pretty girl the brush-off? I say pretty. My sister Meg acts as if she was a movie star or somebody, spending hours in front of the mirror trying on silver eyeshadow and things like that. Let me tell you, she couldn't*

The fellow doesn't raise an eyebrow. "I see." He gives the problem his full consideration. "If I remember correctly, the essay you're talking about claims that women are basically inferior to men . . ."

"And childish!" I interrupt. "And conceited!"

"Fit only," he continues, "for cooking and child-raising."

"Concerning women," I say in contempt, "this philosopher is an out-and-out nincompoop."

"Maybe," the fellow suggests kindly, "he just never met the right sort of woman."

At this crucial point the second red light flashes on machine number six.

"There it goes." I point.

Whereupon the fellow jumps up and pours the soap out of the blue celluloid cup into the machine.

"Women are just as good as men," I continue as he sits down again. "Maybe better. Except the silly, fluttery type. You want to know my theory on the subject?"

He is at this moment troubled by a sudden cough, but in a second he is nodding.

"Well," I tell him, "most people don't realize women got emancipated only about a hundred years ago. Men have had all these centuries to get ahead of them in writing philosophy and such. Most of it propaganda against women. But just you wait. Women will be up front in no time, beating men at their own game." I stop to catch my breath. I am all at once tempted to share my secret ambition with such a rare broad-minded person. "Well, Mister . . ."†

"Excuse me," I say, taking out my of my jacket pocket the little leather-covered diary I carry around when I jot down my observations on human nature. "Miss-oh . . ."

"G-y-n-i-s-t," Harry spells obligingly. "Woman-hater."

On this very interesting note I have to break off our discussion because machine number seven is buzzing out its last rounds loud as a dive-bomber. I wheel my little white barrow of clean laundry over to wait my turn at the drier where Mrs. Cartwright, our next-door neighbor, is pulling out her kitchen

---

* Typescript page 5 ends here.
† Typescript page 7 ends here.

tablecloth, red roses bigger than cabbages splashed all across it. A woman with absolutely no taste.

"And how's the little genius today," she says to me with a large dose of sarcasm. She's never forgiven me for beating her prissy buck-toothed Clarissa last winter at the annual school spelling match.

"Progressing," I reply coolly. "Progressing."

"Huh!" snorts Mrs. Cartwright. "You and the H-bomb!" Whereupon she minces off as if she were the Queen of Siberia.

In no time the clothes are practically dry and I am ready to go home for lunch.

"Goodbye, Harry," I say.

Harry looks up from his book. "See you next Saturday," he grins, and goes back to the book.

And then I do a stupid thing. Lugging that big white laundry bag in front of me I can't see exactly where I'm stepping, so I trip. But I catch myself just in time, and there I am, practically sitting on Blue Girl's lap.

Mrs. McFague and the Corn Vase Girl

Ts fragment,[*] c. August 1957–January 1958, Emory University

And from that day of the quake—red-lit, shuddering, portentous, even, as the creation of a new heaven and earth—Mrs. McFague's memory meandered up to the present like some circuitous but prodigiously lucent river. She could number each sunk object, each living and dead denizen of that stream, describing with meticulous affection the pewter tea-urn her grandmother carried over to America with her on the ship from Ireland; or the occasion when, crossing the continent alone at the age of eight, name and destination written on a slip of paper pinned to her dress, she'd tripped and skinned her knee on a railroad tie at Mount Talma Pass (Rockies) or the time Teddy Roosevelt (illuminated now, in Mrs. McFague's mind, with a gilt plate behind his head, like a figure in Bible pictures) hoisted her onto his shoulder at the cornerstone ceremonies of the Pilgrim Memorial Monument in Provincetown back in the summer of 1907.

---

[*] Typescript pages 3, 4, 5 and 10 with holograph corrections and revisions by SP. Ted Hughes's 'Gog' and 'What Have the Roots Touched' on verso. SP writes about this story in her journals on 21 August 1957, 20 January 1958, and in an undated entry (Appendix 11 in her published journals).

Tookie imagined this scrupulously detailed sequence of people and events playing itself out, over and over, on the dark screen behind Mrs. McFague's hooded eyelids, with a silent soundtrack, while Mrs. McFague went about her daily chores. The soundtrack, however, became audible the moment Mrs. McFague withdrew from the bright, broad sunlight of the present to reminisce, descending, fathom by fathom, into her dusky welter of recollections and moving, like some stout, but elegiac, merlady, among the foundered bones of her own past.

At first Tookie had accepted Mrs. McFague's tales graciously, as colorful furbelows adorning their otherwise utilitarian relationship. But already, only three and a half weeks into July, Mrs. McFague, no doubt unawares, had begun telling her stories two or, now and then, even, three times. Unable to halt these repetitions with a deft, if cutting, "Oh, you've mentioned that before, I think," Tookie found it more and more taxing to sit a hostage listener in the front seat of Mrs. McFague's dented black '47 Plymouth as they jolted convulsively in third gear up the hilly miles to shop in town. Her heart shrank within her when, about a week back, Mrs. McFague jerked the car to a standstill in front of the Zwillingers' cottage after a lengthy shopping excursion and launched, once again, into the account of her marriage to Mr. McFague. "Maybe you don't know this," she used her familiar, confiding preface, "but Mr. McFague is my second husband."

Tookie, sensing the fudge-ripple ice cream melting a hole through her brown paper grocery bag in the stuffy backseat of the car, and the milk curdling to an unpalatable yogurt, felt she knew only too well. Mrs. McFague's first husband had one day dropped dead of a mysterious ailment. Mysterious mainly because Mrs. McFague did not deign to describe it—a truly inconsistent omission, if tallied with her fond, verbal diagrams of doctor's visits and sundry ether-doused sagas at the Hyannis hospital. But, regaled by Mr. McFague's penchant for catching rabid rashes of poison ivy while on the prowl for beach plums, not to mention Mrs. McFague's own grievously blue-patched veins and queer seizures of grippe, Tookie hardly missed a play by play rending of the first husband's deathbed scene. If he had literally "dropped," as Mrs. McFague stressed with a certain relish, he had found, perhaps, no leisure for any deathbed scene at all. However that might be, Mrs. McFague never availed herself of any opportunities for closet-drama on his account. After a résumé of her second marriage ceremony, and her own well-placed, tart words from the stair landing to a few gossip-mongers in the crowd at the reception who had, it appeared,[*]

◆

---

[*] Typescript page 5 ends here.

"She sounds to be nothing but a spoiled brat." Tookie entertained a brief, passing preview of her own unborn children, three or four of them, stationed about the kitchen, immaculate, polite, in their high chairs, asking in chastened tones for second helpings. "I wouldn't let my children talk like that," she added virtuously.

"Me either," Mrs. McFague shook her head. "Why, I used to make my Paula the best little girl in the world simply by having her sit and watch other people eat chocolate pudding. It's no good to deprive kids of what they don't miss, like by sending them to their room when they love to be up in their room, and the one thing Paula missed was chocolate pudding. Oh, she'd get wisecracking off and on, and once, when I'd just finished saying, 'No more chocolate pudding for you next time round, lady,' she came back at me quick as lightning. 'Why Mother,' she says, 'you don't have any chocolate pudding in the icebox.' Well, I didn't contradict her, but I sailed straight out into the kitchen and stirred up a whole bowlful of chocolate pudding. You should have seen her face when I brought it in for dessert that night. 'Please, can I be excused from the table,' she said. 'Not on your life,' I said. And Leroy and I ate every morsel of that pudding up right under her nose. Let me tell you, she went around meek as milk for a couple of weeks after that."

"It's the only way," Tookie said. "It's the only way to manage them." But she wasn't quite sure if she approved of Mrs. McFague's sturdy methods of discipline. Judging from her tales of Paula's slovenly married life, Paula hadn't benefitted greatly by her upbringing.

Runaway

Ts,[*] c. July 1958, Emory University

beat and pound of the hooves on the hard road. Sam was trying to kill her. She felt him, stubborn, faster and faster, under her, and saw the crossroads approaching ahead, with the slowly moving two-decker red buses, the black cars. Sam wouldn't stop. He'd run straight into a bus, and splatter them all. He was running down the middle of the road now, not in the bridle-path. They

---

[*] Typescript pages 8 and 10 with holograph corrections and additions by SP. Ted Hughes's 'The Harvesting' typed on verso. Date supplied from SP's journals, see entry for 17 July 1958. SP wrote about the event that inspired this story in December 1955 letters to family and friends and, as well, in her poem 'Whiteness I Remember'. Page 10 concludes the story.

were passing stopped cars, Mavis glimpsed white faces behind windshields turned up at them, behind raised arms, white undersides of hands and arms. The traffic at the crossroads seemed to be slowing down. Buses pulled to the side of the road. She had lost the sound of Cherry Velvet's echoing hooves. She would be wrenched off under the hooves, under the wheels, so easily. She felt her skull opening like a cracked nutshell on the pavement, the red meat spilling. Which self would she be? The hanger-on, the faller-off?

If Sam would keep straight, she too could keep on like this, with this minimum of grip. Her cheek bounced up and down against the bony back of Sam's neck, her whole body felt beaten, bruising black and blue, but she hung on. Sam swerved right at the crossroads, and she clenched, not to be sideswiped, dragged under his hooves hanging from the useless right stirrup. Boys shouted from a footpath, but she could hear no words, neither advice nor warning. The pitching pound of the horse's body, and the force of the pavement felt through the horse's body, threw Mavis into singleness, into a great peace. Her thoughts fused with her hold on the horse, distracted by nothing, centered in the one need to stay firm where she was. The fraying ends of her early fears knit up into a knot of resoluteness. But then as if he had at last exhausted his repertoire, Sam slowed. He began to walk at the roadside. He stopped to crop a bunch of long grass. Mavis loosened her hands, slipping off his back gently, landing in*

Sam turned right to enter the white stable doors, with the white horse's head painted on them in a black circle. A sturdy, docile head, like Sam's. Sam grayed, palpably, as he clopped onto the paving and stood, waiting for Mavis to dismount, his patience the dogged patience of the long-sufferer, the meek, who have not yet inherited the earth and are growing dubious about the value of meekness.

The square red-faced girl came out of a stall with a deadpan face. "Did you have a nice ride, miss?"

"Lovely," Mavis said, swinging herself down to the pavement. She extricated her foot from the stirrup, which had slipped up on her ankle and caught it. "Perfectly lovely."

"Sam's a good horse," the girl said sturdily, patting his flank with a certain awkwardness. "Safe as they come. You ask for him next time."

"I will," Mavis said. "You may be sure of that."

---

* Typescript page 8 ends here.

DAR Park

Ts fragment,* 2 August 1958, Emory University

Maria Wardle, self-conscious in her rather too small bathing suit for the first time that season, although it was already early August, hoped her thighs didn't bulge out ungracefully from under the tight elasticized pants as she spread the gray canvas on the small sand strip bordering the lake.

"We'll wait for Mummy," Maria said, to the thin blonde girl in faded watermelon-red swimming trunks. "We'll wait for Mummy, Alice, and then we'll go in the water."

Obediently, the girl sat down on the canvas, her skin smooth and downless, still pale after the long summer. Aware of her gold wedding ring, loose, almost heavy, on her finger, Maria realized again that her hands must have been growing bony, extremely slender, since the day she married. She arranged the green, red, and white striped beach towels in a neat little heap, like gaudily colored pillows, across the top of the canvas, looking around her at the other people on the beach in quick little side glances, as if half afraid to meet anybody's eyes. As always, she hoped there would be no one at the beach that she knew. It was so complicated, meeting people one knew, out of context, in a strange context. There were the recognitions, the introductions, the inevitable feeling that the people you introduced already knew one another far better than you knew either of them, that you really should not have come, interloper among old acquaintances. Now, Maria knew, tugging her swimsuit lower over her thighs, seating herself on the canvas beside Alice, the family to the right of them, the crowd of youths behind them, all the people on the beach in fact, would think she was Alice's mother.

"Mummy will be along in a minute." Maria let her voice come clear and loud, so no one would doubt for a minute that she had no children at all of her own.

Alice turned to her, with her mother Vicky's thin features, pale, scant blonde hair, cut short with a vestige of natural curl, blue eyes, more water-color than blue, and narrow lips, the faintest pink, as if her features, her whole

---

* Two unpaginated typescript pages with holograph corrections and additions by SP. Ted Hughes's 'Theology' on verso. The title probably refers to the Daughters of the American Revolution (DAR) State Forest, which is in Goshen, Massachusetts, near Northampton.

complexion, were sketched in by a timid artist in pastels, fearful of any boldness or luxuriance in line and color.

"Will you swim with me, Mrs. Wardle?"

"Yes, yes." Maria tried to sound casual.

That plump, freckled woman in the gray knitted suit a few blankets down kept staring in her direction; the woman had too-bright red hair, obviously dyed. She seemed uncomfortably familiar. She might be the wife of a theater instructor. Or one of the women at the laundromat. Maria squinted into the sun across the lake beyond the area of water enclosed by white-painted floats where the children splashed, to the calm, mirror-surface reflecting the opposite shore of pines and scrub oak. Footsteps approached, crunching on the gravely sand. Maria looked up, grateful.

"Vicky. Are you going in?"

"In a minute."

Vicky set down the wicker basket she was carrying, and unloosed her hand from Richard's. Richard had a birth injury. He found it hard to speak clearly, almost as if he were afflicted with a harelip. He was a tan, stockily built boy of about five, with brown hair cropped in a close wiffle.

"Will you tie this?" He held up an aqua rubber goggle to Maria.

"Let's see." Maria tried to figure out how the rubber straps fastened at the back of Richard's head. "You hold it on the way it should go." Clumsily, Maria began to lace the right hand rubber strap under the buckle of the left hand strap.

"No, it's loose," Richard said.

"Here, Vicky," Maria begged, inadequate, her hands heavy with a lax, almost paralytic fluid of nervousness. "You do it."

Maria watched as Vicky's short, square hands worked with the fastening. Vicky wasn't beautiful, or even pretty, with her tight, straight lips, her skimpy dun hair and unbecoming glasses, but she was capable, magnificently practical. She could run up couch-covers, pleated curtains. She could cook spectacular pilafs and French casseroles with those difficult ingredients, all different troublesome kinds of meat. But then, she'd taken a cooking course at the

Two Fat Girls on Beacon Hill

Ts fragment,* *c.* September 1958–June 1959, Emory University and British Library

She wore the tacitly accepted uniform of young marriageable girls on a Sunday stroll along the river: gray, or khaki-colored Bermuda shorts that straddled her great thighs like burlap stretched over a horse's rump. A jacket, presumably the boy's athletic jacket, in shiny pumpkin-orange and black stripes, draped her great breasts, ensconced as they must have been in bra-compartments the size of pressure cookers. As she passed, clinging to his arm, her blonde bleached hair like artificial rye-sprigs in the sun, her face makeup apparent as makeup on the face of a corpse, she caught our stares. Instead of persisting, heroically, even majestically, through the beams of our eyes, as she had in the twilight of the brick-cobbled hill, she broke off some sweet saying in mid-utterance, gripped the boy's arm convulsively, and tittered, like some fond mistress overheard in a spoken intimacy by some rabble in the street. Her discretion seemed aimed at us more than the boy, who looked no more than eighteen, tall, and rather gormless: she told us, by her break-off, that she had secret words to say, valuable confidences to divulge, important enough to withhold from us, rude starers as we were. At home, in her flat on the hill, she must by now have become resigned to her hugeness; she must eat cream puffs, fried potatoes, chocolate candies, ruining her complexion, bursting out of her dresses, priding herself in a body of rolls, dimples, creases, lumps and humps whereon a man can fall, like an insect into a candle flame, and be consumed in some last expending of his heat. She will endure, though her titters grow more tawdry, her warpaint more difficult to maintain.†

This fat girl sat on the Embankment on a tattered army blanket. She didn't care. She didn't give a damn. She had books, and a beer can, a cigarette, and an old straw visor cap. She was not florid fat, but grub-pale fat. One had the sense of looking at her through several layers of water: her contours were undefined, variable, wavery. A good pal. She too, looked wise with her fat. But not obscene; ribald, rather. A fat woman must have some modicum of philosophy to survive in a world where Renoir is out of favor. When we came

---

* Typescript page 2, Ted Hughes's 'Theology' on verso, held by Emory. Typescript page 3 held by British Library.
† Typescript page 2 ends here.

to the bank, she was sitting in a humped heap, sheltered from the wan, warm September sun under her wickerwork visor, with a long point, like the top of a bird-beak. A ginger-angled pale man with crimped black hair and that pallor on which freckles stand out like ink-blots, sat on her blanket, talking *sotto voce*. A friend or a pick-up. Well, I'll leave you to your reading, he said, as we came up. The girl seemed pleased with herself, pleased by herself. She lay on her fat stomach and read one book of two she had with her. I saw the word Spain on the cover. This minimized her. Was she planning to travel to Spain, learning Spanish, or simply regaling herself with a flowery travelogue among adobes and bullfights. She sipped from her beer can with a boyish air. She wore one of those teacher-sexless white blouses, drab Bermuda shorts, and had a spotty jacket in pale-blue and white stripes that gave the impressions of being gray. Her legs were pale and sausagey, her eyes pale and slippery behind glasses with nondescript rims. She had let her hair go: a dull brown, cut short, uneven, as if cut by a roommate, and unevenly curled, mannish in appearance. She caught us looking at her, and seemed to be smiling to herself. When she got up to go, she pulled on long gray dirty socks & shook her blanket, full of worn rents, cheerfully, as if showing off with a certain insouciance.

A Prospect of Cornucopia

Ts,[*] 25–8 September 1959, Emory

bags under us. Neither of us slept, or spoke. I think now it must have been the electricity in the air got us so nerved-up. Through the netting of the window at the back and the netting set in the zipped door, we could see blue flickers of heat lightning. No thunder, no rain, nothing to ease the air. Just the blue flashes coming and coming, and the black-armed shapes of those cactus coming and going with them.

After a bit, the thumping started. Thump. Thump-thump. Uneven, not too far distant. Somebody's throwing rocks, was my first guess. Some mad rancher trying to scare us off. I'd have been all right if Leroy hadn't said, "What's that?"

---

[*] Typescript pages 3, 4, 5, 6, 7, 8, 9, 10, 12 and 16 with holograph annotations by SP. Ted Hughes's 'On Westminster Bridge', 'July Evening' and 'Beech Tree' on versos. SP submitted 'A Prospect of Cornucopia', 'Johnny Panic and the Bible of Dreams' and 'The Fifty-Ninth Bear' to the *Atlantic Monthly* on 28 September 1959. They were rejected by 20 May 1960. SP and Ted Hughes visited Cornucopia, Wisconsin, in July 1959.

Leroy never asks me what's that, he always tells me what it is, and if it isn't good, he'll tell me something else. If he doesn't know what's that, I'm in no state to figure it out.

"Mightn't it be wild horses?" I tried to reason in a calm style. But the minute I said that, I had a vision of these horses rearing and coming at us, and the tent canvas ripping through like Japanese paper under their hooves.

"Maybe it's the cactus fruit," Leroy said, "dropping to the ground. Those little purple prickly pears, like."

Well, then I began to hear a queer grinding noise not an inch from my ear. The tent on my side started to luff. A coyote's at the pegs, teething like a baby, I thought. There's presences leaning in around this tent, that's plain. I saw Leroy white and gone as marble in the blue light. I touched him, I couldn't help myself, to feel was he still warm.

"Sleep now," he said, "Sleep easy now."

"Leroy," I whispered, thinking: those out there have ears. "Leroy, I'm going to the car, you come with me. This tent's falling in for sure."

It was, too. The canvas was bellying in and sucking out so you'd think some big animal was breathing on it, and the center pole had a mean tilt. I could hear the steel pegs working in the ground like pestles. No sound of a wind, but the ribbon ties stitched along the edge of the door were streaming out horizontal.

"Maybe it's a tornado wind," I said. "They had a tornado in Texas the other week. Trouble is, we never read a paper, never hear a radio, how are we supposed to know when it's a tornado?"

Leroy took one look at the center pole and stirred himself. The tent folded in on itself like a sick flower. By the time we got all our gear packed up and the pegs collected a thin, hot rain was plastering the dust against the windshield. We drove straight through Phoenix in the pitch dark, over a detour where the only signs you could see said DANGER, and ended up at our first motel. I don't think we'd have run off like that if we'd been staying on somebody's land with a clear okay. Strangers though they be, you feel protected then, watched over.

A good time to ask is when you've bought beer or a bite to eat somewhere. Waitresses and pub owners in small towns are just about the best people to ask: they know what's going on all over. One night we were sitting in a truck stop café in the middle of Montana, eating great wedges of homemade boysenberry pie with a crust beyond belief, light and flaky as angels' feathers, nothing like those gluey mass-produced bakery pies you get other places, and washing the pie down with cups of scalding coffee, when we figured it was too dark to ask a private person for a tent spot, even though there were several farms about. Nobody likes to open the door to strangers after sundown, it's a fact. So we leaned over the counter and asked the waitress if she knew of a place. "Well," she said, "there's a churchyard right next to my house down the road a ways. They're saving up for a new lawn next spring, so after that's put in you couldn't camp there, but you could camp there tonight, if you want. Nobody'll mind." We found the church easily enough, a neat white clapboard building with a water pump and an outdoor john, all the conveniences. In the yard on the other side, a couple of children were playing with sparklers left over from the Fourth. You could see their faces in the circle of the orange flares, and the brilliant little motes of light jumping off the sticks they held, but they never even glanced up when Leroy started pounding in the pegs. The cocks woke us about four, it was a Sunday, and we set off well before the people started arriving for early service. The one thing I really regretted was not being around when the café opened up. I never came across a piecrust like that again in nine thousand miles. If I'd taken the name of the lady who baked it, I'd have sent her a postcard to tell her so.

Another time, in another town, so small it wasn't on the state map, and seeing no other soul about, we asked a numb-looking, wall-eyed man mowing a lawn. It took him a while to catch on to what we wanted, and for a time we wondered if we were asking the village idiot, because his mouth hung open in a moist, vacant way. But then he told us to try the schoolyard. "Nobody'll know if you live there two, three days," he said. Behind the two-story brick school, set off a ways from the scant cluster of houses and bars that made up the town, we found another pump. We cooked supper in a grove of aspens opening onto a field of yellow wheat. It must have rained there a lot, recently; the ground was soggy and black with wet, and at sundown the mosquitoes came out in force, but we had a fine sleep. We woke to hear about a million birds singing on every bush and tree, and the wheat glistened in the early light like pure gold.

From the east coast to the west and east again we moved, food and bedding on our backs, always, or nearly always, taking our one-night stands at the edge of a web of streets and lights and secure, lawn-linked homes. We were meaning to sleep out on the Salt Lake Desert once, but come dusk the whiteness of the salt flats grew strange, radiant as phosphor, floating above ground like a nimbus of will o' the wisps in some endless graveyard. So we headed on to a gas-and-food station in the middle of nothing: Oasis, Nevada. The garage man gave us leave to sleep behind the great storage tanks. It was a fair night; we didn't bother to put up the tent. I woke to find the moon full and blue overhead, and the blunt, white face of a Hereford looking at me from a few yards off. Then, after a long, broody pause, he moved from the unfenced nowhere he came from into the nowhere beyond with a couple of other stragglers in his herd, and I dropped back to sleep, easy at the heart as if the Herefords knew we'd asked, and honored the sanction we lay down under.

Even the two nights we slept on a beach fifteen miles north of San Francisco, in a wrack of mottled red jellyfish, shark eggs and barbed, bulbed devil's-tail seaweed, we fared better than among the cactus, if only because the gentle, henpecked owner of the local beer parlor advised us to leave our car behind his place and try the dunes just up from the last shore house.

The stop I recollect above all, though, is a place we hadn't planned on going to, hadn't even known existed until we came to it, a good fifty miles off our route. I supposed there must be towns like Cornucopia scattered throughout America—small, tidy, rich in dairy herds and orchards, streams and lakes brimming with fish—regular milk-and-honey dream towns. We already had a definite stop marked out ahead of us the day we were to discover Cornucopia, a campground at Iron River. For some reason, we weren't too eager to get there. Perhaps it was the name Iron River itself, dark and stern as it sounded. Then, too, all morning we had been following the shoreline of Lake Superior and couldn't get enough of it; Iron River lay inland.

We were boiling potatoes in a roadside picnic area overlooking green hills that blurred, row on row, to a sheer, watery blue in the distance, when the trash collector paused to pass a few words with us. He was a prosperous-looking, stout bellied fellow, and spoke of travelers he had met at those very picnic tables—a family of nine going to try their luck in Alaska, people from all over, heading to the four corners of the continent in search of this or that. When we remarked on the handsomeness of his own countryside, he suggested we skirt a peninsula a few miles ahead if we really wanted to see something fine; became so insistent, so eager, there was nothing for it but to bring out our map and let him indicate the route with a broad thumb. We found ourselves interested, in spite of a certain skepticism—what could such a fellow know of our wishes?—and pressed him to describe the peninsula, to make it worth the hundred-mile detour. He spoke of lake views, agreeable towns, assured us we would find a place to camp with no trouble. "It's wild there." How did he mean, wild? "Oh, lonely—long bare stretches."

We wavered, and were wavering still when we came to the fork where a road turned to the right at the root of the peninsula. Then we had no trouble, but swung off the main highway and followed the blue curve of the lake. Driving northward, no longer squinting into the westering sun, which bleached the color out of the landscape, we felt the shades and tints around us freshen. To the left, neat yellow and green fields webbed the farmhouses; to the right, the land sloped down to the lakeshore, with glimpses, through groves of pine and birch, of landing docks, the masts of small boats. Although it was midsummer, the height of the tourist season, the place had a secret, islanded air. We began, in play talk, to buy up this property and that; to plant kitchen gardens, keep cows and chickens, and a little fishing boat. Still, we did not stop.

For many miles, as we rounded the end of the peninsula, climbing in second gear up the steep, winding roads, and coasting down the hills, we saw no one. Yet the countryside was lush, green with leafy shrubs and pleasant woodlands. Then we came to a town-sign off by itself: Cornucopia. The thought of a white, petunia-bordered post office with Cornucopia written over the door decided us to try asking there. The name of the place alone promised fruits, flowers, all good things. We drove up over another hill and were met by a view of the lake—clear and pale as glass, which we had lost for a while, started to gather momentum, to roll down into Cornucopia. Then we noticed the Coffees' place.

The sun-silvered gray house sat back from the road, ringed by a wide apron of hayfields and orchard and backed by a rise covered with dense, blue-green pines. The headland in which it stood overlooked all Cornucopia: the deep, still green harbor, the fishing shacks, the small shingled houses painted in pink and yellow pastels. The apple orchard shelved steeply away to a rocky beach which formed one tip of the bay's crescent. "That's the place!" I said, spelling out the sign: A. COFFEE, CABINS, FISHING TRIPS, BAIT AND TACKLE lettered on unvarnished boards at the end of the dirt driveway that lost itself in the hay meadow on the way to the house. But we were already drifting past, down the hill into town. How many times we had done just that: drifted by a stand of iced melons, or a clean-looking farm with piglets and puffball chickens dotted over the yard, hankering to stop, but carried on by the tranced motion of the car, promising ourselves: the next place like that, and never finding a next place, only something different, something not so good, nothing at all.

At the bottom of the hill a large paved parking lot opened out, giving access to the beach and several picnic tables facing over the lake. Nobody was there. We pulled in, climbed out of the car and stretched, looking up at the house nested above us and figuring our chances. At the edge of the parking lot a great stone drinking fountain made amiable music, like a brook over pebbles, the water welling up iced and clear. We took turns stepping up and sinking our mouths into the water, and I don't guess we ever came on water so sweet and cold and prodigal again, bubbling without stop from some hidden spring, filling the basin and steaming over the granite rim, losing itself in the sand. Next to the fountain, an historical marker told about some old Indian chief turned into a fox by a tribe of foxes right there on the site of Cornucopia itself.

After a while we decided we'd better try our luck before the sun got any lower. If they had cabins, maybe they wouldn't mind making a dollar or so out of our putting up a tent overnight. We liked the look of the place so much we'd offer to pay something for it, the way we'd have to at a regular campground. So we left the car at the edge of the lake, by the drinking fountain, and climbed back up the hill road. In all the time we'd been there, not a single solitary car had come up or down that road. Hay stalks pricked around our ankles as we approached the house.

Before we had a minute to see where it came from, a sharp-nosed black dog flew out at us, barking loud as he could, his mouth thorny with yellow teeth. We yanked the bell pull on the[*]

When she came back, she had a girl of about eleven with her, skinny and blue-eyed, with bright blonde hair bunched in curls all around her head, her nose white under a thick layer of zinc ointment, and her whole face pink, freckled and peeling. In her arms she was cradling four or five baby ducks. We went to sit with the two of them on a couple of blue-painted benches in an arbor of grape leaves. A mammoth black kitchen range stood between arbor and orchard, half-foundered in the uncut grass. "I cook Sunday dinners out here," Ellen said. "We eat out all the time, when it's nice."

One by one, Josie began showing us things, not saying much at first, but bringing out the old white hen that took the ducklings under her wing and scratched up seeds for them, and a smoke-blue cat called Twilight. By this time the black dog was wagging his whole body at our feet, leaping up every now and then to lick our hands in friendship and contrition. The Coffees had a kitchen garden with tomatoes and beans trained up on sticks, and Josie took us over to see the painted driftwood she and Ellen had set up among the vegetables and ragged marigolds and geraniums: horses' heads, antlered reindeer, a tousled bull—waterworn roots and branches cast up on the beach and given shoe button eyes, red tongues and glossy coats. Josie skittered here and there. From the ice chest in the pump shed she dug up a three pound pike she had caught a week back, a grinning monument, frozen to last as a marvel for visiting cousins all the long summer. On the front porch she kept an aquarium,

---

[*] Typescript page 10 ends here.

air siphoned into it in tiny silver balloons that rose and popped on the surface, the glass tank crammed with scrawny orange and zebra-striped fish she'd sent[*]

and we paused on the other side to pick handfuls of the little, round red wild strawberries growing there, sweet and sun-warm, close to the ground. The Coffees had built the cabins themselves in the cool blue shade of the pines at the cliff edge, looking clear across Cornucopia Bay. Inside, the rooms were papered in holly and pine-bough patterns, floored and roofed with varnished pine boards. Curtains of red-dyed burlap glowed at the windows. They didn't advertise the cabins, Ellen said, and summers, one or two of Art's fishing people would stay there, and a bear hunter, maybe, in winter. Apart from these, nobody knew the cabins existed; so nobody came. Back east, we told her, she'd be getting a hundred dollars a week for cabins like that in the big season. Ellen only smiled; she seemed pleased enough with them, tenants or not.

Then Leroy and I drove with Josie to her fishing place. Leroy had unearthed some fat, pink worms in the garden near the tin pail where the ducklings bobbed and paddled like celluloid toys in a tub and brought them along in an empty V8 can. Josie carried one of her father's spoons, a bent piece of metal, coppery-bright on one side, enameled black with white spots on the other, and a great eye red as a garnet staring out of it. She'd caught good fish on that, she said; it was a lucky thing.

Where the two-rut dirt lane ended in sand, at a point of the bay just opposite the Coffees' house, we parked the car and lugged out our gear. Indian file, we followed Josie through a scrub-growth of blueberry bushes loaded with green and red and purpling berries, out onto a broad spit of clean, fawn-colored sand.

The Mummy

Ts,[†] 4 October 1959, Emory

and went into the house.

As I climbed the stairs my ears burned. I seemed to hear the rustling and

---

[*] Typescript page 12 ends here.
[†] Typescript page 14 with holograph annotations by SP. Ted Hughes's 'Attempts to find a poem for final line "Into the dark gulf of litigation"' on verso. According to her journals, SP worked on 'The Mummy' from 29 September to 3 October 1959, when she submitted it to *New World Writing*. SP received a rejection on 7 November 1959.

APPENDIX I: STORY FRAGMENTS | 795

hasty settling of distant silks. Eyes shut, Mummy lay in the faint glow of the cerise-shaded night lamp, "Did you speak, did you call me?" "No," she said, rousing. "No I did not call." I was reassured, disarmed.

But then, deftly, lightly, as if removing a thorn she saw rankling in my heart, she had my story from me. The kiss, the tremor I felt, the first clear little wave of passion. I could not speak fully enough. The words, tentative, then more assured, tumbled from my lips and into her waiting lap. Oh, she scolded, she teased, she made me feel what a small way I had come. She lingered over a playful tutelage in minor arts, lures which would advance me still more surely on that cherub-circuited sea, among those fabled, delectable islands of Eros toward which I so tardily embarked. When I had undressed, dry, overheated, my mouth a desert, my body an emptied pitcher, she took me in her arms and kissed me.

By some deft thievery she had it all: the kiss, the paltriness of the kiss, the ridiculous secret. She enclosed me, revolved me in the light of her superior knowledge until I showed flimsy as a moth circling the dazzling flare of a lantern.

'Alison'

Ts (photocopy) fragment,* undated, *c.*1960–2, Smith College

the rooftop. There were hundreds of stars caught in the trees, she could see them twinkle and sparkle out as the wind blew.

Magic, the trees said, magic out under the copper beech tree. A hundred smoke-white gulls locked up in the trunk of the beech tree. A hundred singing birds. A hundred silver balls of moonlight.

On the beach there was no one, no one. She could sing, she could call out, no one would hear. She would turn into a mermaid and live for ever at the bottom of the sea in a jade palace set about with shells.

Alison undid her raincoat and let it fall in a little mound upon the sand where it made a dark heap that might have been a rock, a stone.

The sea was big, enormous. It went around the whole world. But she had come to swim in it. She thought of all the people in the town asleep in their warm beds, snug, blind against the night, and oh, suddenly she wanted to be

---

* Title assigned. Typescript pages 10 and 11 with holograph corrections and additions by SP. Drafts of SP's 'Sheep in Fog' on versos, suggesting it is a later story, from *c.*1960–2. The original worksheets for 'Sheep in Fog' sold via Bonhams on 8 May 2013.

a very little girl again. To have somebody tuck her in at night, to cradle her against the colossal dark.

A voice mocked her. 'Why did you come, silly girl? You are frightened.' The small voice gave a clear bright laugh.

No, she would not turn away, not now. A swim, that was all, and then back to bed. Walking erect, she advanced into the first small waves that foamed and sucked soft about her ankles. It was black, so black.

'Oh,' she thought, walking out, out, until the water reached her waist, 'I shall never come back, never.' Somewhere, hidden in the cold, secret depths there was something waiting for her, watching in the fullness of the time for her to come.

'Alison, Alison . . .' Someone, someone was calling her out there, far off, from a boat, from the low hanging stars.

She cast herself into the black water. It was an act of faith. She might sink, she might be dragged down to the very bottom of the sea. But the water bore her up, light as a shaft of driftwood. Floating dreamily on her back she could feel her legs and arms dissolving, melting quite away.

What a foolish cage her body was! All crowded, woven into so small a space, and now, in the water, it was spreading out, diffusing through the huge ocean, out, out. In her new freedom she began to swim, a languid mermaid, her hair streaming wet and heavy along her thin, bare shoulders, twined with seaweed, with rare, rare shells.

'I'm coming,' she whispered to someone, to herself. 'Where are you? Oh, where?'

But there was no answer. It was quite still, now, and the moonlight struck heavy, silver, on the water. Alongshore, the pine trees were black iron spikes against the sky.

The night seemed to fall back, withdrawing from her, dark and silent. A star glared at her. The moon sprouted like a puffball in the heavens. If she lay on her back, she could kick the moon. She could split it open with a kick, and the ashes inside would come falling gently down, on her eyes, on her mouth, in a grey coverlet.

At the bottom of the sea a lobster was laughing at her. She could feel the water shake and bubble, tickling her arm. Foolish Alison, silly girl. She should be in bed where she belonged, asleep, her eyes shut tightly, tightly. Let the moon sail by spilling white flour, let the stars fall among the tree leaves. It had nothing to do with her. Nothing at all.

She began to swim toward shore. Somewhere on the sand there was her raincoat, like a rock, a stone. She found it, drew it on over her

Appendix II

Teenagers Can Shape the Future[*]

Ts, 27 December 1954, Lilly Library

This is the story of a teenage girl who passes through the temptations of the material world, grows aware of her own idealism and power to help others, and discovers the City of God. The story is told in the manner of a symbolic allegory, much like some of the parables in the Bible, and it draws upon the images of religion and literature to express its message.

Marcia Ventura represents the young people of today. Her train trip symbolizes the journey of many young people through life, bored, won over by the pleasures of creature comforts, and unaware of the energy that is in them which, if used according to the principles of Christ, may bring about the City of God in the future.

Marcia, however, achieves a victory. Her traveling companion, the energetic woman who symbolizes the creative forces of the earth as manifestations of the love of God for man, helps Marcia realize that she can free herself from bondage to mere physical ease and find her true identity in the service of God. At the end, Marcia reaches the promised city, planning to dedicate her life to educating others to follow in her path, which is the path of all true Christians.

The Christian symbols which appear in the story are intended to be subtle suggestions of the ever-presence of Bible figures in modern life. The quarreling brothers present-day prototypes of Cain and Abel, for example. The mother and child and the scarecrow in the field show how unheeded and degraded the symbols of faith and holiness can become in the modern world if not seen with Christian insight and reverence. The solution which Marcia finds is a reassertion of the positive, creative force in all young people, which can shape a new and better world in face of great odds. It is a force which may truly bring about the peaceful kingdom of God on this earth.

---

[*] Introduction to 'Marcia Ventura and the Ninth Kingdom' for the Christopher Awards.

Bibliography of Published Prose

1940s

'Hike to Lovell River', *Weetamoe Megaphone* (18 July 1943): 1.
'Girl Scout News: Troop 5 Valentine Party', *The Townsman* (10 March 1944): 4.
'Seventh-grade Girls', *The Phillipian* (November 1944): 16.
'Assembly Lineup: January 30', *The Phillipian* (February 1946): 12.
'Spring Song', *The Phillipian* (April 1946): 13.
'The Pond in Spring', *The Phillipian* (June 1946): 26.
'Cove Unit Report' (*c.*25 July 1946): 1.
'Junior High Briefs', *The Townsman* (17 October 1946): 4.
'Club Doings: Book Lovers and Recreational Reading Club', *The Phillipian* (November 1946): 14.
'A Morning in the Agora', *The Phillipian* (February 1947): 5.
'Club Doings: Book Lovers', *The Phillipian* (February 1947): 18.
'Victory', *The Phillipian* (April 1947): 6.
'Introducin'', *The Bradford* (30 October 1947): 3.
'Miss Palmer's Treasures' [book review], *The Bradford* (6 February 1948): 3.
'The Atomic Threat', *The Bradford* (26 April 1948): 1.
'Who Are They???', *The Bradford* (4 February 1949): 2.
'High School Highlights', *The Townsman* (15 September 1949): 3.
'When I'm a Parent', *Seventeen* (November 1949): 77.

1950s

1950
'*Bradford* Editors Attend Boston Tea Party!!', SP's High School Scrapbook (*c.* January–February 1950): 63.
'Youth's Plea for World Peace', *Christian Science Monitor* (16 March 1950): 19.
'And Summer Will Not Come Again', *Seventeen* (August 1950): 191, 275–6.
'Rewards of a New England Summer', *Christian Science Monitor* (12 September 1950): 15.

1951
'Den of Lions', *Seventeen* (May 1951): 127, 144–5.
'In Retrospect: A Plea for Moderation', *Princeton Tiger* (5 May 1951): 14–15.
'As a Babysitter Sees It' [part I], *Christian Science Monitor* (6 November 1951): 19.
'As a Babysitter Sees It' [part II], *Christian Science Monitor* (7 November 1951): 21.
'Says Capitalism May Save Asia', *Daily Hampshire Gazette* (16 November 1951): 10.

'Can Benefit by the Writing of the Satirists', *Daily Hampshire Gazette* (21 November 1951): 3.
'Smith Girls to Take Exams in Civil Service', *Daily Hampshire Gazette* (5 December 1951): 3.
'"True Health" Lecture Topic at the College', *Daily Hampshire Gazette* (14 December 1951): 7.

1952
'Says Music Can Illustrate Cultural Life of a Nation', *Daily Hampshire Gazette* (17 January 1952): 8.
'Universal Faith Has the Answer, Dr. Niebuhr Says', *Springfield Union* (5 February 1952): 21.
'"Crisis" Is Topic of Dr. Niebuhr in Northampton', *Springfield Union* (6 February 1952): 21.
'Smith Students Have Service of Koffee Klatch', *Daily Hampshire Gazette* (20 February 1952): 3.
'Dr. A. Gesell Gives Lecture for Day School PTA', *Daily Hampshire Gazette* (3 March 1952): 16.
'"Heresy Hunts" Menace Liberty; Struik Claims', *Springfield Union* (4 March 1952): 2.
'Rev. Mr. Roberts Will Be Vespers Speaker', *Daily Hampshire Gazette* (7 March 1952): 6.
'Life University Second Program Slated Sunday', *Springfield Union* (7 March 1952): 30.
'Misery of Man Is Due to His Defects', *Daily Hampshire Gazette* (11 March 1952): 5.
'Marxism Seeks to Replace God, Lecturer Says', *Springfield Union* (13 March 1952): 30.
'Smith Hears Frost in Muse and Views', *Springfield Union* (10 April 1952): 31.
'Frost Presents Poetry Readings', *Daily Hampshire Gazette* (11 April 1952): 12.
'Smith College', *Daily Hampshire Gazette* (18 April 1952): 13.
'Ogden Nash's Rhyming Knack Makes Up for His Talent Lack', *Springfield Union* (1 May 1952): 30.
'Ogden Nash Is Speaker', *Daily Hampshire Gazette* (2 May 1952): 6.
'Smith Library Displaying "Fanny Fern Collection"', *Daily Hampshire Gazette* (5 May 1952): 8.
'TV or Not TV', *Campus Cat* (Commencement 1952): 1.
'Be Mine—For Now', *Campus Cat* (Commencement 1952): 3.
'15 Area Girls to Graduate from Smith College June 9', *Daily Hampshire Gazette* (27 May 1952): 9.
'Sunday at the Mintons", *Mademoiselle* (August 1952): 255, 371–8.
'Sunday at the Mintons", *Smith Review* (Fall 1952): 3–9.
'The Perfect Setup', *Seventeen* (October 1952): 76, 100, 102–4.
'Smith Freshman Given Welcome', *Springfield Daily News* (29 September 1952): 22.
'Freshman at Smith Will Meet Local Ministers', *Daily Hampshire Gazette* (1 October 1952): 9.
'Freshman to Greet Pastors of Churches', *Springfield Daily News* (1 October 1952): 32.
'Smith Events', *Daily Hampshire Gazette* (2 October 1952): 15.
'Succoth Service', *Springfield Daily News* (2 October 1952): 32.
'Can Rent Reproductions', *Daily Hampshire Gazette* (2 October 1952): 15.
'Faith Groups Open Center', *Springfield Daily News* (6 October 1952): 26.

'Central Spot for Religion Groups at Smith', *Daily Hampshire Gazette* (7 October 1952): 16.
'Smith Outing Club Will Bike To Hatfield', *Springfield Daily News* (15 October 1952): 32.
'Lectures Arranged by Hillel Foundation', *Springfield Daily News* (17 October 1952): 32.
'Varied Religions and Cultural Program Planned For Smith College Students', *Daily Hampshire Gazette* (17 October 1952): 6.
'First Recital at Smith College is Sunday at 8:30', *Daily Hampshire Gazette* (24 October 1952): 15.
'First Recital Sunday', *Springfield Daily News* (24 October 1952): 30.
'Smith College Holds Clinic', *Daily Hampshire Gazette* (24 October 1952): 17.
'Sports Clinic at Smith', *Springfield Daily News* (24 October 1952): 30.
'Cheers, Jeers Promised for Smith Game', *Daily Hampshire Gazette* (27 October 1952): 8.
'Smith Girls Will Get Chance to Jeer Faculty', *Springfield Daily News* (27 October 1952): 30.
'Week-End Dance', *Daily Hampshire Gazette* (7 November 1952): 5.
'Hillel Group Plans First Social Function', *Springfield Daily News* (7 November 1952): 32.
'Smith Provides Writing Clinic', *Springfield Sunday Republican* (9 November 1952): 10D.
'Mrs. L. Diem of Cologne Visiting Smith', *Daily Hampshire Gazette* (11 November 1952): 5.
'More Than 100 Varieties of Chrysanthemums Will Be Seen at Lyman Plant House', *Daily Hampshire Gazette* (11 November 1952): 6.
'Chrysanthemums are on Display at Smith', *Springfield Daily News* (11 November 1952): 9.
'Newly Revised Edition of "Smith Review" Has Articles by Students', *Daily Hampshire Gazette* (12 December 1952): 7.
'College Group Will Debate on February 11', *Daily Hampshire Gazette* (13 December 1952): 7.
'Student's Prize Story Featured in Review', *Springfield Daily News* (12 December 1952): 32.

1953
'Initiation', *Seventeen* (January 1953): 65, 92–4.
'Drive for Hymnals at Smith College', *Daily Hampshire Gazette* (13 March 1953): 8.
'Passover Will Be Marked Monday at Smith College', *Daily Hampshire Gazette* (21 March 1953): 4.
'Smith College Seder', *Springfield Daily News* (21 March 1953): 7.
'Fencing Techniques to be Demonstrated', *Springfield Daily News* (21 March 1953): 7.
'Shale that is 400,000,000 Years Old at Smith Lab', *Daily Hampshire Gazette* (14 April 1953): 12.
'John Mason Brown Lectures on Writer's Responsibility', *Daily Hampshire Gazette* (15 April 1953): 18.
'Literary Speakers Mark Symposium at Smith College', *Daily Hampshire Gazette* (24 April 1953): 1, 12.
'Laughton Holds Audience Spellbound with Readings', *Daily Hampshire Gazette* (6 May 1953): 3.
'Smith Christians Group Points to Achievements', *Daily Hampshire Gazette* (14 May 1953): 23.

'Smith College Field Events', *Daily Hampshire Gazette* (15 May 1953): 1, 12.
'Float Night at College', *Springfield Daily News* (15 May 1953): 9.
'Smith College Play Delights 'Hamp Audience', *Springfield Union* (15 May 1953): 31.
'Austrian-Born Junior Enlists in Women's Marine Corps, "Can't wait to get there"', *Daily Hampshire Gazette* (16 May 1953): 2.
'Many Area Students Are Among the 464 Who Will Get Smith Degrees on June 8', *Daily Hampshire Gazette* (20 May 1953): 8.
'Mlle's Last Word on College '53', 'Elizabeth Bowen and Sylvia' and 'Poets on Campus', *Mademoiselle* (August 1953): 235, 282, 290–1.
'Smith Review Revived', *Smith Alumnae Quarterly* (Fall 1953): 26.

1954
'14 Colleges to Take Part in Poetry Reading Festival', *Daily Hampshire Gazette* (6 May 1954): 9.
'In the Mountains', *Smith Review* (Fall 1954): 2–5.
'The Neilson Professor', *Smith Alumnae Quarterly* (Fall 1954): 12.

1955
'Superman and Paula Brown's New Snowsuit', *Smith Review* (Spring 1955): 19–21.

1956
'Leaves from a Cambridge Notebook' [part I], *Christian Science Monitor* (5 March 1956): 17.
'Leaves from a Cambridge Notebook' [part II], *Christian Science Monitor* (6 March 1956): 15.
'Fulbright Scholar Sylvia Plath Describes Her Impressions As . . . An American in Paris', *Varsity* (21 April 1956): 6–7.
'Smith College in Retrospect', *Varsity* (12 May 1956): 6–7.
'Cambridge Letter', *Isis* (16 May 1956): 9.
'Sylvia Plath Tours the Stores and Forecasts May Week Fashions', *Varsity* (26 May 1956): 1, 6, 7.
'B. and K. at the Claridge', *Smith Alumnae Quarterly* (Fall 1956): 16–17.
'The Day Mr. Prescott Died', *Granta* (20 October 1956): 20–3.
'Sketchbook of a Spanish Summer' [part I], *Christian Science Monitor* (5 November 1956): 15.
'Sketchbook of a Spanish Summer' [part II], *Christian Science Monitor* (6 November 1956): 19.

1957
'The Wishing Box', *Granta* (26 January 1957): 3–5.
'All the Dead Dears' and a 'Review of *The Stones of Troy* by C. A. Trypanis', *Gemini* (Summer 1957): 53–9, 98–103.

1958
'Beach Plum Season on Cape Cod', *Christian Science Monitor* (14 August 1958): 17.
'Cambridge Vistas', *Institute of International Education News Bulletin* (December 1958): 22, 24–8.

1959
'Kitchen of the Fig Tree', *Christian Science Monitor* (5 May 1959): 8.
'A Kitchen With a Fig Tree', *Buckingham Post* (29 May 1959): 7.
'A Walk to Withens', *Christian Science Monitor* (6 June 1959): 12.
'Mosaics—an Afternoon of Discovery', *Christian Science Monitor* (12 October 1959): 15.
'Explorations Lead to Interesting Discoveries', *Christian Science Monitor* (19 October 1959): 17.

1960s

1960
'The Daughters of Blossom Street', *London Magazine* (May 1960): 34–48.
'The Fifteen-Dollar Eagle', *Sewanee Review* (Autumn 1960): 603–18.

1961
'The Fifty-Ninth Bear', *London Magazine* (February 1961): 11–20.
'The Perfect Place', *My Weekly* (28 October 1961): 3–7, 31.
'General Jodpur's Conversion', *New Statesman* (11 November 1961): 696, 698.
'Introduction', *American Poetry Now* (*Critical Quarterly* Poetry Supplement, No. 2. 1961): 2.

1962
'Context', *London Magazine* (February 1962): 45–6.
'Pair of Queens', *New Statesman* (27 April 1962): 602–3.
'Oblongs', *New Statesman* (18 May 1962): 724.
'Oregonian Original', *New Statesman* (9 November 1962): 660.
'Suffering Angel', *New Statesman* (7 December 1962): 828–9.

1963
The Bell Jar (London: Heinemann, 1963).
'America! America!' *Punch* (3 April 1963): 482–4.
'Ocean 1212-W', *The Listener* (29 August 1963): 312–13.

1964–9
The Bell Jar (London: Contemporary Fiction, 1964).
'The Wishing Box', *Granta* 75 (15 February 1964): 4–6.
'The Wishing Box', *Atlantic Monthly* (October 1964): 86–9.
The Bell Jar (London: Faber & Faber, 1966).
'Johnny Panic and the Bible of Dreams', *Atlantic Monthly* (September 1968): 54–60.

1970s

The Bell Jar (New York: Harper & Row, 1971).

'What I found out about Buddy Willard' [extract from *The Bell Jar*], *McCall's* (April 1971): 86, 125–9.

[Extract from *The Bell Jar*], *Cosmopolitan* (September 1971): 188–191.

'The Mothers' Union' ['Mothers'], *McCall's* (October 1972): 81, 126, 128, 130, 142.

'The Day Mr. Prescott Died', *Spare Rib* (June 1973): 36–8.

'Day of Success', *Bananas* (1975): 11–13.

'The Novelist and the Poet' ['A Comparison'], *The Listener* (7 July 1977): 26.

'Superman and Paula Brown's New Snowsuit', *Harper's and Queen* (October 1977): 222, 224, 227–8.

Johnny Panic and the Bible of Dreams (London: Faber & Faber, 1977).

'Among the Bumblebees', *Bananas* (Autumn 1978): 14–15.

Johnny Panic and the Bible of Dreams (New York: Harper & Row, 1979).

1980s

A Day in June (Ely: Embers Handpress, 1981).

The Green Rock (Ely: Embers Handpress, 1982).

1990s

The It-Doesn't-Matter Suit (London: Faber & Faber, 1996).

The It-Doesn't-Matter Suit (New York: St Martin's Press, 1996).

2000s

Collected Children's Stories (London: Faber & Faber, 2001).

'A Comparison', *Brick* (Winter 2006): 140–1.

'Sylvia Plath on *Contemporary American Poetry*', *The Spoken Word: Sylvia Plath* (London: British Library, 2010): Track 23.

The It-Doesn't-Matter Suit and Other Stories (London: Faber & Faber, 2014).

'Mary Ventura and the Ninth Kingdom' [short-story extract], *The Guardian* (29 December 2018): 33–5.

'Mary Ventura and the Ninth Kingdom' [short-story extract], *Wall Street Journal* (29 December 2018): C3.

Mary Ventura and the Ninth Kingdom (London: Faber & Faber, 2019).

Mary Ventura and the Ninth Kingdom (New York: HarperCollins, 2019).

'Mary Ventura and the Ninth Kingdom', *Hudson Review* (Spring 2019): 13–28.

Permissions

Part I
Walter B. Gibson, *The Shadow* (excerpt), Condé Nast Archive © Condé Nast.
Excerpt from 'The Hollow Man' and 'East Coker' by T. S. Eliot, in *The Collected Poems 1909–1962*. Reprinted by permission of Faber and Faber Ltd.

Part II
'Youth's Plea for World Peace' reproduced by permission of Perry Norton.
'In Retrospect: A Plea for Moderation' reproduced by permission of the Estate of Marcia Brown Stern.
'In a Station of the Metro' by Ezra Pound, from *Personae*, copyright © 1926 by Ezra Pound. Reprinted by permission of New Directions Publishing Corp.
Excerpts from *Under Milk Wood*: US: copyright © 1952 by Dylan Thomas. Reprinted by permission of New Directions Publishing Corp. UK: © 1952 The Dylan Thomas Trust. Reprinted by permission of David Higham Associates Limited.
Excerpt from *The Confidential Clerk*, by T. S. Eliot, in *The Complete Poems and Plays of T. S. Eliot*. Reprinted by permission of Faber and Faber Ltd.

Part IV
Excerpt from Wanda Gág, *The Funny Thing* (University of Minnesota Press, 2003). Copyright 1929 by Coward-McCann, Inc. Copyright renewed 1957 by Robert Janssen.
Excerpt from 'There Is' by Louis Simpson, in *The Owner of the House: New Collected Poems 1940–2001*. Copyright © 1959, 2003 by Louis Simpson. Reprinted with the permission of The Permissions Company, LLC on behalf of BOA Editions, Ltd, boaeditions.org. All rights reserved.
'Sunday in Glastonbury' by Robert Bly. Copyright © 1962 by Robert Bly. Reprinted by permission of Georges Borchardt, Inc., on behalf of the Estate of Robert Bly.
Excerpt from 'After Greece' from *Collected Poems* by James Merrill, © 2001 by the Literary Estate of James Merrill at Washington University. Used by permission of Alfred A. Knopf, an imprint of the Knopf Doubleday Publishing Group, a division of Penguin Random House LLC. All rights reserved.
'Miners' by James Wright from *Collected Poems* © 1971. Published by Wesleyan University Press. Used by permission.
Excerpt from 'Small Woman on Swallow Street' by W. S. Merwin. Copyright © 2000 by W. S. Merwin, currently collected in *The First Four Books of Poems*, used by permission of The Wylie Agency LLC.
'Flower Herding Pictures on Mount Monadnock' from *Collected Poems* by Galway Kinnell. Copyright © 2017 by The Literary Estate of Galway Kinnell, LLC. Used by permission of HarperCollins Publishers.

Every effort has been made to contact or trace the copyright holders.

Index of Titles

'About a year ago I was babysitting . . .' 719
Above the Oxbow 399
Afternoon in Hardcastle Crags 746
'Alison' 796
All the Dead Dears 306
All-Round Image, The 605
Among the Bumblebees 191
Among the Shadow Throngs 58
And Summer Will Not Come Again 75
Articles for *Vogue*'s Prix de Paris Competition 532
Arts in America, The: 1954: Collage by a Collegian 545
As a Babysitter Sees It 508
Assembly Lineup: January 30 490
Atomic Threat, The 495
Attic View, The 27
Aunt Rennie and the Elves 4
Austrian-Born Junior Enlists in Women's Marine Corps, 'Can't wait to get there' 667
B. and K. at the Claridge 568
Be Mine—For Now 520
Beach Plum Season on Cape Cod 586
Black Bull, The 742
Bookland Carpet, The 5
Bradford Editors Attend Boston Tea Party!! 499
Brink, The 48
Cambridge Letter 573
Cambridge Vistas 559
Can Benefit by the Writing of the Satirists 626
Can Rent Reproductions 645
Change-About in Mrs. Cherry's Kitchen 329
Cheers, Jeers Promised for Smith Game 650
Christmas Heart, The 274
Club Doings: Book Lovers 494
Club Doings: Book Lovers and Recreational Reading Club 494
College Group Will Debate on February 11 656
Comparison, A 603
'Context' 601
Cove Unit Report 490

'Crisis' Is Topic of Dr. Niebuhr in Northampton 630
DAR Park 786
Dark River, The 63
Daughters of Blossom Street, The 404
Day in June, A 79
Day Mr. Prescott Died, The 245
Day of Success 446
Den of Lions 98
Dialogue 166
Dr. A. Gesell Gives Lecture for Day School PTA 632
Drive For Hymnals at Smith College 657
East Wind 66
English Bike, The 94
Evening at the Hoftizers, An 725
Explorations Lead to Interesting Discoveries 599
Faith Groups Open Center 646
Fencing Techniques to be Demonstrated 658
'few armchairs and a table . . ., A' 721
15 Area Girls to Graduate from Smith College June 9 642
Fifteen-Dollar Eagle, The 370
Fifty-ninth Bear, The 426
First Date 88
First Recital at Smith College Is Sunday at 8:30 649
14 Colleges to Take Part in Poetry Reading Festival 672
Freshmen at Smith Will Meet Local Ministers 645
From the Memoirs of a Babysitter 20
Frost Presents Poetry Readings 637
Fulbright Scholar Sylvia Plath Describes Her Impressions As . . . An American in Paris 563
Garden Party, The 725
General Jodpur's Conversion 685
Girl Scout News: Troop 5 Valentine Party 489
Gramercy Park 43
Green Rock, The 82
Heat 46
'Heresy Hunts' Menace Liberty; Struik Claims 633
High School Highlights 498
Hike to Lovell River 489
Hill of Leopards 773
Home Is Where the Heart Is 234
I Lied for Love 197
Ideal Summer, The 521
In Retrospect: A Plea for Moderation 505
In This Field We Wander Through 51
Initiation 158

International Flavor, The 502
Introducin' 495
Introduction (*American Poetry Now*) 601
Invisible Man, The 747
Irene 723
Island, The: A Radio Play 38
It-Doesn't-Matter Suit, The 419
John Mason Brown Lectures on Writer's Responsibility 660
Johnny Panic and the Bible of Dreams 356
Junior High Briefs 492
Kitchen of the Fig Tree 588
Landscape of Childhood 616
Latvian, The 128
Laughton Holds Audience Spellbound with Readings 662
Laundromat Affair, The 778
Life University Second Program Slated Sunday 634
Literary Speakers Mark Symposium at Smith College 661
Lucky Stone, The 436
Many Area Students Are Among the 464 Who Will Get Smith Degrees on June 8 670
Marie 146
Marxism Seeks to Replace God, Lecturer Says 636
Mary Jane's Passport 17
Mary Ventura 119
Mary Ventura and the Ninth Kingdom 178
Matisse Chapel, The 739
May Morning, A 14
Miraculous End of Miss Minton, The 22
Misery of Man Is Due to His Defects 635
Miss Palmer's Treasures 677
MLLE's Last Word on College 530
More Than a Hundred Varieties Of Chrysanthemums Will Be Seen at Lyman Plant House 653
Morning in the Agora, A 19
Mosaics—An Afternoon of Discovery 598
Mothers 477
Mrs. L. Diem of Cologne Visiting Smith 654
Mrs. McFague and the Corn Vase Girl 782
Mummy, The 795
Mummy's Tomb, The 7
'music wailed out from the radio . . ., The' 721
My Studio Romance 734
Neilson Professor, The 530
New Day, The 150
New Girl, The 90

'New Zealand spinach was good that morning . . ., The' 726
Newly Revised Edition of *Smith Review* Has Articles by Students 655
Oblongs 688
Ogden Nash Is Speaker 640
Ogden Nash's Rhyming Knack Makes Up for His Talent Lack 639
On the Penthouse Roof 10
Operation Valentine 775
Oregonian Original 690
Pair of Queens 687
Passover Will Be Marked Monday at Smith College 657
Perfect Setup, The 113
Place: A Bedroom, Saturday Night, in June 70
Place: A City Street Corner, in the Rain 72
Place: Inside a Bus on a Rainy Night 74
Platinum Summer 258
Poets on Campus 528
Pond in Spring, The 6
Poppy Day at Cambridge 580
Prospect of Cornucopia, A 789
Remember the Stick Man 745
Rev. Mr. Roberts Will Be Vespers Speaker 634
Review of *The Stones of Troy* by C. A. Trypanis 677
Rewards of a New England Summer 504
Room in the World 105
Runaway 784
Sally 724
Sarah 31
'Sassoon was coming . . .' 736
Says Capitalism May Save Asia 625
Says Music Can Illustrate Cultural Life of a Nation 620
Seventh-grade Girls 490
Shadow, The 382
Shadow Girl 457
Shale that Is 400 Million Years Old at Smith Lab 659
Side-Hall Girl 741
'Skaters, The' 730
Sketchbook of a Spanish Summer 577
Smith Christian Group Points to Achievements 663
Smith College 638
Smith College Field Events Saturday Afternoon, Night 665
Smith College Holds Clinic 650
Smith College in Retrospect 566
Smith College Play Delights 'Hamp Audience 666
Smith Events 646

Smith Freshman Given Welcome 644
Smith Girls to Take Exams in Civil Service 626
Smith Hears Frost in Muse and Views 637
Smith Library Displaying 'Fanny Fern Collection' 641
Smith Outing Club Will Bike to Hatfield 647
Smith Provides Writing Clinic 652
Smith Review Revived 525
Smith Students Have Service of Koffee Klatch 631
Smoky Blue Piano, The 318
Snow Blitz 608
Social Life Without Sororities: A Profile of Smith College 540
Somebody and We 515
Spring Song 6
Stardust 703
Stone Boy with Dolphin 335
Story Ideas 722
Suburban Nocturne 511
Suffering Angel 693
Sunday at the Mintons' 137
Superman and Paula Brown's New Snowsuit 228
Sweetie Pie and the Gutter Men 389
Sylvia Plath on *Contemporary American Poetry* 696
Sylvia Plath Tours the Stores and Forecasts May Week Fashions 575
Tea With Olive Higgins Prouty 554
Teenagers Can Shape the Future 798
That Widow Mangada 289
'Though Dynasties Pass' 133
Thrilling Journeys of a Penny, The 23
Tomorrow Begins Today 240
Tongues of Stone 252
Trixie and the Balloon 3
'True Health' Lecture Topic at the College 627
TV or Not TV 519
Two Fat Girls on Beacon Hill 788
Universal Faith Has the Answer, Dr. Niebuhr Says 629
Varied Religious and Cultural Program Planned for Smith College Students 648
Venus in the Seventh 754
Victory 15
Visitor, The 34
Walk to Withens, A 591
Watch My Line! 103
Watching the Water-Voles 595
We Hitch Our Wagons: Elizabeth Bowen and Sylvia 527
Week-End Dance 651

When I'm a Parent 498
Who Are They??? 497
Winter and Magic 3
Winter's Tale, A 466
Wishing Box, The 312
Youth's Plea for World Peace 500